More praise for Penny Vincenzi:

'Packed with passion, pain, pace and palaver... it's high-class, well-structured ... with enough juicy sub-plots and interesting minor characters to keep you gripped through many a chilly evening ... Fans are in for a feast' Val Hennessy, *Daily Mail*

'Deliciously readable. Penny Vincenzi's novels are rollicking contemporary fantasies' *Mail on Sunday*

'The literary equivalent of a huge box of beautiful hand-made chocolate truffles – a total indulgence' *Ideal Home*

'It should sell in lorry-loads – these pleasures may be wicked, but they won't rot your teeth or make you fat' Kate Saunders, *Sunday Times*

'Penny Vincenzi has delivered an unputdownable family saga' *The Lady*

'This is another of Penny Vincenzi's unputdownable blockbusters – with a rattling good plot and a feisty heroine' *Woman and Home*

'Like an illicit lover, I have been sloping off all week to snatch another hour's pleasure with *Almost a Crime*, Penny Vincenzi's terrific new novel' Jilly Cooper

'A rampantly riveting read ... This one's the business' *She*

Sheer Abandon

Penny Vincenzi

headline

First published in 2005
by HEADLINE BOOK PUBLISHING

First published in paperback in 2005
by HEADLINE BOOK PUBLISHING

10 9 8 7 6 5 4 3 2 1

ISBN 0 7553 2083 2 (B format paperback)
ISBN 0 7553 2852 3 (A format paperback)

Typeset in New Caledonia by Avon DataSet Ltd,
Bidford-on-Avon, Warwickshire

Printed and bound in Great Britain by
Clays Ltd, St Ives plc

Headline's policy is to use papers that are natural, renewable and
recyclable products and made from wood grown in sustainable
forests. The logging and manufacturing processes are expected to
conform to the environmental regulations of the country of origin.

HEADLINE BOOK PUBLISHING
A division of Hodder Headline
338 Euston Road
London NW1 3BH

www.headline.co.uk
www.hodderheadline.com

For Polly, Sophie, Emily and Claudia:
for every possible kind of help and support
in a very long year.

Acknowledgements

I have been bothering even more people than usual in my quest for background information for *Sheer Abandon*; writing this long thank you makes me realise what a large landscape the book covers.

Beginning at the beginning, a big thank you to Kate de la Grense, Hayley Carson and Nicola Hartley, with whom such a happy evening was spent reliving their travels; to my daughter Sophie, who travelled at the same time as my heroines and spent hours painstakingly defining the differences; and to my youngest daughter Claudia, who accompanied me on a whistle-stop tour of Bangkok and the islands, reliving her own experiences.

And thank you to Simon Cornish for some crucial technological advice; to Bridget Bunnell who gave me some insight into life in a corporate law firm, and to Clodagh Hartley and my daughter Emily, who both brought me smartly up to date from my own rather distant days in tabloid newspapers. I also owe a big debt to Emily for a piece of plot-shaping, without which I would probably now be on Chapter 101 and still no end in sight.

On the political front, so much gratitude to Julia Langdon, Nigel Nelson, Matthew Parris, Carol Sarler, Maggie Pullen, Fraser Kemp MP, Barbara Follett MP and Michael Fabricant MP – who asks me to add that politics is not really such a dirty game as everyone thinks or as it is made out to be in fiction. They all gave me so much of their time and knowledge and the book would be much poorer without them. And thanks to Gyles Brandreth (whose book *Breaking the Code* was also invaluable, as well as great fun – like him!), and to the inestimable Sue Stapely who once again managed to be a positive fountainhead of information. A big vote of thanks to Penny and Tony Rossi, Louise Vivian and Ursula Lloyd, who were my medical dictionaries, and to Roger Freeman, my psychiatric adviser (speaking professionally, of course).

I talked to many people who had been abandoned, or adopted, or had given their own babies up; I would like to thank them all for giving so very generously of their time and experience, so much of it extremely moving. I could not possibly have written the book without them.

I am very, very grateful to all those wonderful people at Hodder Headline who are publishing *Sheer Abandon*: Tim Hely Hutchinson who welcomed me so warmly into the Headline fold in the first place, and to Martin Neild for being so marvellously appreciative of everything, not least the manuscript! Kerr MacRae, Peter Newsom and their respective sales teams, David Grogan, of Head Design, and Louise Rothwell, Production Controller, who between them made the book look so fantastic, and Kate Burke who so patiently went on adding to the mountain of nuts and bolts. And thank you to Kati Nicholl, who carved the book into shape, Georgina Moore who made sure everyone knew about it, and of course Rosie de Courcy, who edited it as she always does with such patience, charm and skill. I sometimes think she is a magician, so brilliantly does she conjure things out of a manuscript that I hardly knew were there.

Huge thanks to Clare Alexander, my brilliantly supportive new agent, and, in memoriam, Desmond Elliott, who looked after me and my books for so long and is now, I feel sure, brokering astounding deals at the great publishing lunch in the sky. Desmond, I miss you still; we all do.

And finally my husband Paul, so unfailingly supportive and encouraging, so swift to respond to my wails of despair and so unselfishly ready to share in my (rather rarer) whoops of delight.

As always, in retrospect, it looks like a lot of fun. And I think it really was.

Prologue

August 1986

People didn't have babies on aeroplanes. They just didn't.

Well – well, actually they did. And then it was all over the newspapers.

'Gallant aircrew deliver bouncing boy,' it said, or words to that effect, and then went on to describe the mother of the bouncing boy in some detail. Her name, where she lived, how she had come to be in the situation in the first place. Usually with a photograph of her with the bouncing boy and the gallant crew.

So – *that* wasn't an option.

She couldn't have a baby on an aeroplane.

Ignore the pain. Not nearly bad enough, anyway. Probably indigestion. Of course: indigestion. Cramped up here, with her vast stomach compressed into what must be the smallest space in the history of aviation for what? – seven hours now. Yes, definitely indigestion . . .

Didn't completely solve the situation though. She was still having a baby. Any day – any hour, even. And would be having it in England now instead of safely – safely? – in Bangkok.

That had been the plan.

But the days had gone by and become a week, and then two, and the date, the wonderfully safe date of her flight, three weeks after the birth, had got nearer and nearer. She'd tried to change it; but she had an Apex seat; she'd lose the whole fare, they explained, very nicely. Have to buy a new ticket.

She couldn't. She absolutely couldn't. She had no money left, and she'd carefully shed the few friends she'd made over the past few months, so there was no danger of them noticing.

Noticing that she wasn't just overweight but that she had, under the Thai fishermen's trousers and huge shirts she wore, a stomach the size of a very large pumpkin.

(The people at the check-in hadn't noticed either, thank God; had looked at her, standing there, hot and tired and sweaty, and seen simply a very overweight girl in loose and grubby clothing.)

So there was no one to borrow from; no one to help. The few hundred she had left were needed for rent. As it turned out, an extra three weeks' rent. She'd tried all the things she'd heard were supposed to help. Had swallowed a bottle-full of castor oil, eaten some strong curry, gone for long walks up and down the hot crowded streets, feeling sometimes a twinge, a throb, and hurried back, desperate to have it over, only to relapse into her static, whale-like stupor.

And now she had – indigestion. God! No. Not indigestion. This was no indigestion. This searing, tugging, violent pain. Invading her, pushing at the very walls of the pumpkin. She bit her lip, clenched her fists, her nails digging into her palms. If this was the beginning, what would the end be like?

The boy sitting next to her, as grubby and tired as she, whose friendliness she'd rejected coldly as they settled into their seats, frowned as she moved about, trying to escape the pain, her bulk invading his space.

'Sorry,' she said. And then it faded again, the pain, disappeared back where it had come from, somewhere in the centre of the pumpkin. She lay back, wiped a tissue across her damp forehead.

Not indigestion. And three hours to go.

'You OK?' The boy was looking at her, concern mixed with distaste.

'Yes. Fine. Thanks.'

He turned away.

They had landed; everyone was standing up, pulling their luggage down from the lockers. The moment had coincided with a very violent pain. She sat in her seat, bent double, breathing heavily. She was getting the measure of them now; they started, gathered momentum, tore at you and then departed again. Leaving you at once feebly grateful and dreadfully fearful of their return.

Well – she hadn't had it on the plane.

For the rest of her life, when she read of people describing bad experiences of childbirth, of inadequate pain relief, of briskly bracing midwives, of the sense of isolation and fear, she thought they should have tried it her way. Alone, in a space little bigger than a cupboard, the only pain relief distraction therapy (she counted the tiles on the walls, more and more as the time went by), her only companion a fly buzzing relentlessly (she worried about the fly, the dirt and disease it might be carrying, looked at it thankfully as it suddenly dropped, exhausted, on its back and expired). And then there were some brushes and mops and some clean towels – thank God for those towels, how could she ever have thought one pack of cotton wool would be enough? Her isolation was absolute, her only midwife herself and her precious book, propped against the wall as she lay on the floor, studying its explicitly sanitised diagrams desperately, heaving her child into the world. How could she be doing this, so afraid of pain she couldn't have a filling without a local anaesthetic, so clumsy she could never fasten her own Brownie tie?

But she did.

She managed because she had to. There was nothing else for it.

And when it was all over, and she had cleaned herself up as best she could, and the room too, and wrapped the baby, the tiny, wailing baby, into the clean sheet and blanket she had packed in her rucksack (along with the sharp, sharp scissors and ball of string and large bottle of water which was the nearest she could get to sterilising anything), she sat on the floor, slumped against the wall, feeling nothing, not even relief, looking at the baby, quiet now, but breathing with astonishing efficiency, its small face peaceful, its eyes closed.

It was over. She had become a mother; and in a very short while she would be one no longer, she could walk away, herself again, free, unencumbered, undisgraced.

She could just forget the whole thing. Completely.

It was over.

Wonderfully, neatly, absolutely over . . .

The Year Before

August 1985

They sat there in the departure lounge, on two separate benches, consulting the same departure board: three girls, strangers to one another, the faded jeans, the long hair, the beaded friendship bracelets, the sneakers, the small rucksacks (vastly bigger ones already checked in) all marking them out as backpackers, and about-to-be-undergraduates. With school and parents shaken off, a few hundred pounds in their new bank accounts, round-the-world tickets in their wallets, they were moving off; to travel a route that would take in one or all of a clearly defined set of destinations: Australia, New Zealand, Thailand, Nepal and the Himalayas, and even the States.

They were very excited, slightly nervous, above all impatient for the journey to begin; constantly exchanging looks, half smiles with one another, moving slowly physically closer as more and more people filled the lounge and the space surrounding them.

It was the announcement that brought them finally together: the announcement that their flight to Bangkok had been delayed for three hours. Their eyes met, eyebrows raised, and they all stood up, picking up their bags, moving towards one another, smiling, annoyed at so early an interruption to their journey, and yet welcoming it as an excuse to meet and to talk.

'Coffee?' said one and 'Great,' said the other two, and they walked slowly towards the cafeteria, already over-full, tables filled with dirty cups, cigarette stubs swimming in spilt coffee, harassed staff wiping grubby surfaces with grubbier cloths.

'Here's a table,' said one of the three. 'I'll keep it – leave the bags,' and she settled at the table, pulling out a pack of Rothmans and studying her new friends as they queued at the service counter. One of them was tall and very slim with a cloud of wild blonde hair, the other shorter and distinctly plump, with her hair pulled back into a plait. The blonde kept looking over her shoulder slightly anxiously.

'We hope it's coffee,' said the plait, as she set the tray down on the corner of the table, 'but we're not sure. It's hot and wet, anyway. Sugar?'

'No thanks. Here, let's clear this muck onto the tray. I'm Martha,' she added, smiling quickly at each of them, pushing back a long mane of loose brown hair, 'Martha Hartley . . .'

'I'm Clio,' said the plait. 'Clio Scott. Spelt with an i. Clio that is.'

'Jocasta,' said the blonde, 'Jocasta Forbes.'

'That's quite a name. Jocasta, I mean.'

'I know. My parents were punishing me for not being a boy.'

'I think it's rather a good name,' said Clio.

'Well, it's all right,' said Jocasta, 'if you don't mind a rather strong association with incest.'

'Did they get the boy in the end?' asked Martha curiously.

'Less than a year later. Only time he's ever arrived anywhere without a long wait. He should be here now and look at him. Or rather don't, since he's not,' she added.

'He's going travelling with you?'

'Yup. Well, we're starting out together. It made our parents less nervous.'

She smiled at them, pushed back her hair. 'Anyway, what about you two? Martha – any story behind your name?'

'My mother said she always identified with Martha rather than Mary, in the Bible you know? She was the one who did all the work while Mary just sat at Jesus' feet doing nothing. My poor mother works terribly hard.'

'It's a nice name anyway,' said Jocasta. She had looked rather blank at the biblical link. 'Clio, what about you?'

'My parents met at Oxford, reading classics. There was a muse and a nymph called Clio. It comes from the Greek word Kleos, which means glory. And my sisters are called Ariadne and Artemis,' she added. 'You did ask!'

'I did. And are you going to follow in their footsteps, read classics?'

'Absolutely not. I'm doing medicine at UCH.'

'I was born there,' said Martha, 'we all were. My sister sixteen years ago today, actually.'

'Who's all?'

'My sister and my baby brother. Only he's not really a baby any more, he's ten. But that's how we all think of him.'

'I have a similar problem,' said Clio, 'only it's me. The baby, I mean. Anyway, what about you two, what are you going to do?'

'I'm going to read law at Bristol,' said Martha.

'Same as my brother,' said Jocasta.

'Is he going to Bristol?'

'No, back to school, to do Oxford entrance. He's horribly clever. He got four A levels, all As, and a year early of course.' She sighed. 'And before you ask, I only got three.'

The eyes of the other two met momentarily, then Martha said: 'And what are you going to do?'

'English. At Durham. I want to be a journalist, a reporter. Tracking down stories, uncovering scandals, that sort of thing.'

'How exciting.'

'Well – I hope so. I'm told I'll spend my first five years at least covering village fetes.'

'Josh, you made it. Amazing. Only an hour late. Lucky they held the plane for you.' Jocasta seemed suddenly less at ease. 'Here, come and join us. This is Martha and this is Clio. And this is my brother Josh.'

And Martha and Clio saw a boy who looked so like Jocasta it was almost shocking. The same wild blond hair, the same dark blue eyes, the same just slightly crooked smile.

'Hi,' he said, holding out a thin hand. 'Nice to meet you.'

'Hi,' said Martha, 'nice to meet you too.'

'You're incredibly alike,' said Clio, 'you could be – '

'We know, we know. Twins. Everyone says so. But we're not. Josh, why are you so late?'

'I lost my passport.'

'Josh – you're so hopeless. And fancy only looking for it this morning.'

'I know, I know. Sorry.'

'Was Mum OK, saying goodbye to you? He's her baby,' she added to the others, 'can't bear to let him out of her sight.'

'She was fine. How was your dinner with Dad?'

'It never took place. He didn't get back till twelve. And this morning he had to rush off to a meeting in Paris, so he couldn't see me off either. What a surprise.'

'So how did you get here?'

'Oh, he put me in a cab.' Her expression was hard; her tone didn't quite match it.

'Our parents are divorced,' Josh explained. 'Usually we live with our mother but my dad wanted – '

'*Said* he wanted,' said Jocasta, 'to spend yesterday evening with me. Anyway, very boring, let's change the subject. I'm going to the loo.'

She walked away rather quickly.

There was a silence. Josh offered a pack of cigarettes, and Martha and Clio each took one. Josh's arrival had brought a tension into the group that was a little uncomfortable. Time to withdraw, at least until the flight . . .

Their seats were far apart, but they managed to spend some of the flight together, standing in the aisles, chatting, swapping magazines, comparing routes and plans. From Bangkok, Josh wanted to go up country; Martha was spending a short time in Bangkok before going on to Sydney, where she was meeting a school friend. She planned to stay a few weeks there, 'working in bars and stuff' before moving up to Ayers Rock and then the rain forest and the Great Barrier Reef. 'After that I don't know, but I want to finish in New York, maybe visit California on the way.'

Clio was island-hopping for a few weeks and then travelling on to Singapore, where a distant cousin of her father's would put her up. 'Just for a couple of weeks. He's got a son who they seem to think might want to travel with me. Apparently I'm sure to like him.'

'What, because he's eighteen too?' said Martha.

'Of course. I'm sure he'll be gross. After that, Australia, probably, but I do want to get to Nepal. I wouldn't do that on my own though; I'm relying on meeting someone.'

Jocasta didn't know what she was going to do. 'Go wherever fate takes me. Start with the islands, definitely. I don't want to go north with Josh, and he wants to get rid of me as soon as he can.'

'Why don't you come to Koh Samui with me?' said Clio. 'You're sure to make friends with someone down there you can travel on with.'

'Yes,' said Martha. 'My best friend's sister, who went last year, said you keep meeting people from your own town, your own school, practically your own family.'

'God, I hope not,' said Jocasta. 'Family, I mean. I've got quite enough of mine with me.'

She looked across the aisle at Josh, who was engrossed in his book, occasionally pushing his wild hair out of his eyes.

'I certainly won't,' said Martha. 'My entire family see a day-trip to France as a huge adventure.'

'I don't want to meet any of mine either,' said Clio. 'This is my first chance to do something on my own without my sisters.'

'Don't you like them?'

'I suppose so. But they're both older than me, both very beautiful and successful and they treat me like I was eight, not eighteen.'

'So – did you have trouble persuading your parents to let you come? As you're the youngest?'

'Well, my mother died when I was tiny. My sisters persuaded my father. Although they all made it very clear they thought I'd be home by Christmas, tail between my legs.'

Her round little face was at once harder and infinitely sad; then she smiled quickly. 'Anyway, I got away.'

'My parents couldn't wait to get rid of me,' said Martha.
'Why?'

'They just find it all so exciting. They lead a rather – well, a very narrow life.'

'In what way?' said Jocasta curiously.

'Well, my father's a vicar. So we have to live in conditions of unbelievable respectability. Nothing remotely racy. And in a spotlight of sorts. A small one, but it's still a spotlight. The whole parish watching.'

'I'm really surprised,' said Clio, 'in this day and age.'

8

''Fraid this day and age hasn't really reached St Andrews, Binsmow. It's in a total time warp.'

'Where is it?'

'Deepest Suffolk. When I tell you I went to the cinema on a Sunday with some friends last year and at least a dozen people got to hear about it and complained to my father, you'll get some idea of what I'm talking about.'

They digested this in silence. Then, 'And what about your mum?'

'She's just a perfect vicar's wife. Runs the WI and stuff. But she loves it. She's absolutely thrilled I'm going away, even though she's a bit worried.'

'How on earth did they get you, these terribly conventional people?' asked Jocasta, laughing. 'Where did you go to school? One of those wacky places?'

'Oh – just a grammar school,' said Martha quickly. 'That's the other thing about being a vicar's family. There isn't a lot of money, to put it mildly. What about you two?'

'Sherborne,' said Jocasta, 'and boarding prep before that.'

'Day school,' said Clio, 'Oxford High. I always longed to go to boarding school.'

'It isn't all fun, I can tell you,' said Jocasta. 'Loneliest place in the world if you're homesick, which I was.'

'I expect you were, at – what were you, eight?' asked Martha.

'Yes. My mother was busy having a nervous breakdown – my father had left her by then and my mother didn't want a stroppy child about the place. Josh stayed at home a bit longer. Of course. But I got used to it. You can get used to anything, can't you? In the end?'

She stared out of the window, clearly discouraging any further probing into her family life. The others looked at one another and started discussing an article in *Cosmopolitan* about how to have it all: career, love, children . . .

'I wouldn't want to,' said Martha. 'Have it all, I mean. Well, certainly not children. My career, that'll be quite enough for me.'

A disembodied voice asked them to return to their seats.

They spent three days together in Bangkok, three extraordinary days in which they bonded absolutely, adjusting to the soup-like heat, the polluted air, the uniquely invasive smell – 'I'd call it a mix of rotting vegetables, traffic fumes and poo,' said Clio cheerfully – staying in the same bleak guest house on the Khao San Road. It was an incredible and wonderful culture shock – hot, noisy, heaving with people, alight with Technicolor flashing signs, lined with massage and tattoo parlours and stalls selling everything from T-shirts to fake Rolexes and illicit cds. Every other building was a guest house, and all along the street neon-lit cafes showed endless videos.

The girls all kept diaries, writing them earnestly each night, and evolved a plan to meet in a year's time to read of one another's adventures.

Jocasta inevitably took hers particularly seriously. Reading it many years later, even while wincing at a rather mannered style, she was transported back to those early days, as they moved around the filthy, teeming, fascinating city. She felt the heat again, the nervousness, and along with it, the sense of total intrigue.

She tasted again the food, sold from stalls on the street, tiny chickens, 'the size of a ten pence piece', stuck four in a row on sticks, to be eaten bones and all, kebabs, even cockroaches and locusts, deep-fried in woks; she stared out again at the waterfalls of warm rain hitting the streets vertically, which, in five minutes, would have them ankle-deep in water – 'Bangkok has the opposite of drainage' – shuddered again at the shanty town ghettoes by the river, and smiled at the incredible near-standstill of traffic which filled the vast streets all day long, the overflowing buses, the tuk tuks, motorised three-wheel taxis, hurtling through the traffic, and the motor scooters transporting families of five, or occasionally glamorous young couples, snogging happily as they sat in the midst of the fumes.

They went to Pat Pong, the red-light district, and watched the lady-boys plying their trade – 'you can tell they're men – they're much better turned out than the women' – to the post office to write to their parents and tell them where they were, checked the *poste restante* desk where a horde of backpackers queued to pick up letters from home, messages from friends arranging meetings; they water-taxied through the stinking canals, shocked at the poverty of the hovels where the river people lived, wondered at the gilded and bejewelled palace and temples, and visited the shopping centre, packed with Gucci and Chanel – 'this is mostly for rich men's mistresses apparently, and you can get real tea, not the endless Lipton's, wonderful!'

What none of them wrote about – with that year-off meeting in mind – was the other girls, or even Josh, but they learned a great deal about each other very quickly in those three days. That Jocasta had fought a life-long battle with Josh to gain her father's affection and attention; that Clio had grown up miserably envious of her older sisters' beauty and brilliance; that Martha's jokey complaints about her strait-laced family masked a fierce defensiveness of them; and that Josh, easily charming, brilliant Josh, was both arrogant and lazy. They learnt that Jocasta for all her wild beauty lacked self-confidence; that Clio felt herself acutely dull; that Martha longed above all things for money.

'I do plan to be really rich,' she said one night as they sat in one of the endless bars, drinking one cocktail after another, daring one another to eat the deep-fried bugs. 'And I mean *really* rich.'

And when they parted, Clio and Jocasta on their way down to Koh Samui, Josh for his trip north and Martha for a couple more days in Bangkok while deciding exactly what to do, they felt they had been friends for years.

'We'll ring each other when we get back,' said Jocasta, giving Martha a last hug, 'but if one of us doesn't, we'll track her down somehow. There'll be no escape.'

But they knew there would be no need for tracking down; it would be a race to the phone. They would want to see one another again more than anything in the world.

Part One

Chapter 1

She always felt exactly the same. It surprised her. Relieved. Excited. And a bit ashamed. Walking away, knowing she'd done it, resisting the temptation to look back, carefully subdued – she could still remember old Bob at the news agency telling her one of the prime qualities for a good reporter was acting ability. Of course, the shame was pretty rare, but if it was a real tragedy, then it did lurk about, the feeling that she was a parasite, making capital out of someone else's unhappiness.

This had been a horror to do; a baby in its pushchair, hit by a stolen car; the driver hadn't stopped, had been caught by the police fifty miles away. The baby was in intensive care and it was touch and go whether he would live; the parents had been angry as well as grief-stricken, sitting clutching each other's hands on the bench just outside the hospital door.

'He'll get what – three years?' the young father had said, lighting his ninth cigarette of the interview – Jocasta always counted things like that, it helped add colour – 'and then get on with his life. Our little chap's only had eight months and he could be gone forever. It makes me sick. I tell you, they should lock them up forever for this sort of thing, lock them up and throw away the key – '

She could see her headline then: and hated herself for seeing it.

While she was in the middle of writing her story, she got an e-mail from the office: could she do a quick piece on Pauline Prescott's hair (a hot topic ever since her husband had made it his excuse for taking the car out to drive a hundred yards); they would send a picture down the line to her. Jocasta, wrenching her mind off the desperately injured baby, wondered if any other job in the world imposed such extraordinarily diverse stress at such short notice. She filed that copy via her mobile and had just returned to the baby when her phone rang.

'Is that you, Miss – '

'Jocasta, yes,' she said, recognising the voice of the baby's father. 'Yes, Dave, it's me. Any news . . . ?'

'Yes,' he said. 'Yes, he's going to be all right, he's going to pull through, we just saw him, he actually managed a smile!'

'Dave, I'm so glad, so very glad,' said Jocasta, hugely relieved, not only that the baby was going to live, but that she was so touched by it, looking at her screen through a blur of tears.

Not a granite-hearted reporter yet, then.

She filed the story, and checked her e-mails; there was an assortment of junk, one from her brother telling her their mother was missing her and to phone her, a couple from friends – and one that made her smile.

Hello, Heavenly Creature. Meet me at the House when you're back. Nick.

She mailed Nick back, telling him she'd be there by nine then, rather reluctantly, dialled her mother's number. And flicking through her diary, knowing her mother would want to make some arrangement for the week, realised it was exactly fifteen years to the day since she had set off for Thailand, in search of adventure. She always remembered it. Well, of course she would. Always. She wondered if the other two did. And what they might be doing. They'd never had their promised reunion. She thought that every year as well, how they had promised one another – and never kept the promise. Probably just as well though. Given everything that had happened . . .

Nick Marshall was the political editor on the *Sketch*, Jocasta's paper; he worked not in the glossy building on Canary Wharf but in one of the shabby offices above the press galleries at the House of Commons. 'More like what newsrooms used to be,' one of the old-timers had told Jocasta. And indeed many journalists, who remembered Fleet Street when it had been a genuine, rather than a notional, location for newspapers, envied the political writers for working at the heart of things, rather than in shining towers a long cab ride away.

It always seemed to Jocasta that political and newspaper life were extraordinarily similar; both being male-orientated, run on gossip and booze (there was no time in the day or night when it was not possible to get a drink at the House of Commons) and with a culture of great and genuine camaraderie between rivals as well as colleagues. She loved them both.

Nick met her in Central Lobby and took her down to Annie's Bar in the bowels of the House, the preserve of MPs, Lobby correspondents and sketch writers. He ushered her towards a small group in the middle.

'What do you want, sweetie?'

'Double chardy.'

'OK. Bad day?'

'No – good, really. But I'm tired. You?'

'Fine. Anyone else want anything?'

The group said 'same again' as one man; Jocasta grinned round at them.

'Hi, guys. So what's new here? Any hot stories?'

'Pretty lukewarm,' said Euan Gregory, sketch writer on the *Sunday News*. 'Labour lead shrinking, Blair losing touch, shades of Maggie, too much spin – you name it, we've heard it before. Isn't that right, Nick?'

''Fraid so. Here you are, sweetie . . .' He bent to kiss her. 'Pleased to see me?'

'Of course.' And she was, she was.

'Good thing somebody loves him,' said Gregory. 'Campbell was giving him the evil eye earlier.'

'Really, Nick? Do you know why?'

'I expect because of what I said on LBC at lunchtime today.'

'Which was? I wish I'd heard you.'

'It was about this new row about spin. I said how Campbell reads everyone's stories on their computers and comments on what they say – that it's like having your homework marked. Oh for the good old days, eh, Bertie, when you wrote stories on pieces of paper and they were for your eyes only.'

'Absolutely. Mind you, you had to phone them in to the copytakers in those days and people might overhear you. But it was so much better. You should hear dear old Bernard Ingham on the subject.'

'I like hearing Bernard Ingham on any subject,' said Nick with a grin. 'In fact, I must buy him lunch. You always get the best quotes from the old guys. Come on, Jocasta, drink up. I'm going to take you out to dinner.'

'My God. What have I done to deserve this?'

'Nothing. I'm hungry and I can see nothing interesting's going to happen here.'

'You're such a gentleman, you know that?' said Jocasta, draining her glass.

In fact Nick *was* a gentleman; nobody was quite sure what he was doing in the world of the tabloid press. His father was a very rich farmer and Nick had got a double first in classics at Oxford. He had rather old-fashioned manners – at any rate with the older generation – and was much mocked for standing up when a grown up, as he put it, came into the room. But he had developed an early passion for politics and after an initial foray into the real thing had decided he could move into the corridors of power faster via the political pages of a newspaper. He was a brilliant investigative journalist, and came up with scoop after scoop, the most famous, if least important, of which was the revelation that a very prominent Tory minister bought all his socks and underpants at charity shops.

It had been love at first sight, Jocasta always said, for her. Nick had walked into the newsroom of the *Sketch* on her very first day there, fresh from a news agency in the West Country, and she had gone literally weak at the knees. Told he was the political editor, she had assumed, joyfully, that she would see him every day; the discovery that he only came in for the occasional editor's conference, or one-to-one meetings with Chris Pollock, the editor, was a serious blow. As was the news that he had a girlfriend on every paper. She wasn't surprised; he was (as well as extremely tall: about 6' 4") very good-looking in an untidy sort of way, with shaggy brown hair, large mournful brown eyes set deep beneath equally shaggy brows, a long and very straight nose, and what she could only describe rather helplessly as a completely sexy mouth. He was very thin and slightly ungainly with very large hands and feet, altogether a bit like an overgrown schoolboy; he was hopeless at all games, but he was a very fine runner and had already done the New York as well as the London marathon, and could be seen early every morning, no matter how drunk he had been the night before, loping round Hampstead Heath where he lived.

It was not entirely true that he had a girlfriend on every paper, but women adored him. His secret was that he adored them back; he found them intriguing, entertaining and treated them, certainly initially, with a rather old-world courtesy. When Jocasta Forbes arrived on the *Sketch* he actually miraculously had no one permanent in his life.

She had pursued him fervently and shamelessly for several months; she would feel she was really making progress, having flirted manically through evening after evening and been told how absolutely gorgeous he thought she was, only to hear nothing from him for weeks until some newspaper happening brought them together again. She had been in despair until one night, about a year previously, when they had both got extremely drunk at the *Spectator* party, and she had decided a proactive approach was the only one that was going to get her anywhere and started to kiss him with great determination. Unwilling, this time, to leave anything to chance, she then suggested they went back to her place. Nick declared himself hooked.

'I've admired you for so long, you have absolutely no idea.'

'No,' she said crossly, 'I haven't. I've made it very clear I admired you though.'

'I know, but I thought you were just being kind. I thought a girl who looked like you was bound to have a dozen boyfriends.'

'Oh for God's sake,' said Jocasta, and got into bed beside him and their relationship had been finally – and very happily – sealed.

Although certainly not signed. And it troubled Jocasta. She stayed at his flat sometimes, and he at hers (in which case it was Clapham Common he loped across), but they were very much an item, recognising that the next step would be moving in together. Nick said repeatedly that there was absolutely no hurry for this: 'We both work horrendous hours, and we're perfectly happy, why change things?'

19

Jocasta could see several reasons for changing things, the strongest being that they had been together for well over a year and if they were so happy, then that was a very good reason indeed to change things. There was also the fact that she was thirty-three, which meant that next birthday she would be thirty-four and everyone knew that thirty-five was the age when being single stopped being a statement of independence and started being a worry. She loved Nick, and she was fairly sure he loved her, although he seldom said so, and usually then with that preface so hated by women, 'of course'. And she felt, with increasing intensity, that the time had come for some proper commitment. At the moment, it seemed no nearer; and it was beginning to worry her. Quite a lot.

'Where are you taking me then?' she said, as they walked into the long corridor.

'Covent Garden,' he said. 'Mon Plaisir. I don't want to see anyone in the business tonight.'

This was unusual; one of the downsides of having a romantic evening with Nick was that he was so in love with his job and so deeply fond of everyone he worked with that she often thought if he ever did get around to proposing to her, and was down on his knees and he saw Trevor Kavanagh from the *Sun* or Eben Black of the *Sunday Times* across the room, he would call them over to join them.

She suddenly realised she hadn't even combed her hair since she had left the hospital. 'Hang on a minute,' she said, 'I need the loo. I'll meet you in Central Lobby.'

But as she reached the vast space at the heart of the House of Commons minutes later, she saw Nick deep in conversation with someone she didn't recognise; he waved her on.

'Sorry,' he said, coming up to her rather breathless, 'we'll have to go up to my office for a bit.'

'Oh, Nick, why? I'm starving.'

'Sorry. That was a rather spectacular little leak.'

'About?'

'Blunkett's latest idea for dealing with asylum seekers.'

'And why did they have to give it to you?' she said, sighing.

'Well, the *Mail* made them really angry last week, running some nasty piece about Cherie, and the *Sun* had that bit of dirt about Mandelson, so they get to annoy both of them by giving it to me. Come on, sweetie, I swear I won't be long.'

'So,' he said as they were finally settled at Mon Plaisir. 'Tell me about your day. You do look tired, Mrs Cook.'

'I *am* tired, Mr Butler.'

They had once gone to a fancy dress party as the cook and the butler and used the names occasionally in their e-mails (the more indiscreet ones), whenever a code was necessary.

'But it was OK. One tragedy, one trivia – Mrs Prescott's hair. I do get so tired of doing those stories.'

'But you're so good at it.'

'I know that, Nick,' she said and indeed she was good at it; she could get into anyone's house, however many other journalists were on the doorstep, make her way into anyone's life, it was all part of her golden charm and, to a degree, she knew, the way she looked. If it was a choice between talking to a male reporter in a sharp suit or an absurdly young-looking girl with long blonde hair and wide blue eyes, whose face melted with sympathy for you and whose voice was touched with feeling as she told you this was the worst part of her job and she absolutely hated having to ask you to talk to her, but if you could bear it, she would make it as easy as possible – then it was not a very difficult decision. Jocasta got more by-lines on human-interest stories, and what were known in the trade as tragedies – and also those about celebrities caught with their trousers literally down – than almost anyone in Fleet Street. But she was weary of it; she longed to be a feature writer, or a foreign correspondent, or even a political editor.

No editor, however, would give her that sort of chance; she was too valuable at what she did. In the predominantly male culture that was newspapers, a dizzy-looking blonde with amazing legs had her place and that was getting the sort of stories other reporters couldn't. Of course she was extremely well rewarded for what she did, she had a very generous expense account and most of the time she was happy. But as in her relationship with Nick she was aware that she wanted more.

'So – anything happen to you today? Apart from your scoop?'

21

'I had lunch with Janet Frean.'

'Should I be jealous?'

'Absolutely not. Very nice, I'm sure, but a Wonderwoman-type, politician, five children, famously pro-European, sacked from the shadow cabinet is not for me. Actually, I don't exactly like her, but she's an incredible force to reckon with.'

'So?'

'So, she's pretty sick of what's going on in the party. They're all feeling depressed. Saying that Hague is just not PM material, that he was a terrible mistake, that the party has got everything wrong. That they'll never get in again, that Blair can walk on water, however often it looks like he'll drown, however much the polls say he's got to do better.'

'So?'

'So – there's talk of some of them doing something about it.'

'Like what?'

'Well, like making a break for it. Backed by a few right-minded people within the party. People who are prepared to stand up and be counted, say this just isn't any good, we know we can do better, come and join us.'

'And do these people exist?'

'Apparently. Chad Lawrence, for a start.'

'Really? Well, I'd vote for him. Most gorgeous man in Westminster. According to *Cosmo* anyway.'

'Which won't do him any harm – women voters by the dozen. And he may be an arrogant bugger, but he's got a lot of energy and a mind like a rattrap. And then they have a couple more quite senior and high-profile people in the party on side. Most notably Jack Kirkland.'

Jack Kirkland had risen from extraordinarily unpromising beginnings – and indeed unlikely for a Tory – from a South London working-class family, to a position as Minister for Education in the Tory party; his journey from grammar school to an Oxford first was extremely well charted in the media as a whole and the *Daily Mail* in particular.

'So – where is this leading, Nick?'

'A new party. A party just left of centre, but still recognisably Tory, headed up by a pretty charismatic lot, which will appeal to both disillusioned Blair and Tory voters. Saying – and it's screamingly obvious isn't it – this lot's not delivering, the others can't, we will. Or something like that.'

'But – that's what every politician since time began has said.'

'I know. But there's a growing disaffection with Blair, with what he isn't achieving. Ditto Hague. There are a lot of instinctive Tory voters out there, longing for change and a sort of pious hope that things might get better. If they could look at someone new and strong and say yes, that's more like it, I could go for that, Kirkland and his merry men could do rather well.'

'And – what does this Frean superwoman want you to do?'

'Get the Ed. on side. Get the paper to support them. When the time comes. I think maybe he would. He's a Tory at heart and the whole thing will appeal to his romantic nature.'

'Romantic! Chris Pollock!'

'Jocasta, he's terribly romantic. Not in your women's fiction sense, but David and Goliath, triumph of the underdog, that sort of thing. And our readers are precisely the sorts of people Frean is talking about.'

'Oh – OK. And when and how might it start?'

'They've got to get some funds together and more people on side. There'll be a lot of plotting – which'll be fun. I would say by conference time it'll all be boiling up nicely.'

His large brown eyes were brilliant as he looked at her; she smiled.

'Is this another exclusive?'

'At the moment. Obviously they chose the finest political editor of the lot.'

'Yes, I suppose so.' She looked at him. 'Maybe,' she said thoughtfully, 'maybe this could give me my big break. Be my first proper story. You never know.'

'Jocasta, I adore you, but this is not a human-interest story.'

'It might be. I bet Chad Lawrence has an intriguing private life for a start. Anyway, I'm not wasting my breath convincing you. I've got champagne to drink. Cheers. Here's to the dawn of New Toryism. Or whatever.'

'And its attendant human interest.'

She looked at him and took a deep breath.

'Nick,' she said.

'Yes?'

'Nick, there's something I really want to discuss with you. Speaking of human interest . . .'

But he dodged the issue, as he always did, told her he was tired and he just wanted to take her home and curl up with her and think how lucky he was. Feebly, she gave in.

Martha looked out of her office window and saw the first streaks of dawn in the sky. She had worked all night. Of course it was July, and dawn came pretty early: it was only – she glanced at the three-faced clock on her desk, showing London, New York and Singapore time – only just after four. It seemed much harder in the winter, when the nights were long and the streetlights were still on at seven-thirty in the morning. People always said how exhausting it must be, which irritated her. She enjoyed the all-night sessions, found them exciting; and perversely she never felt remotely tired. Adrenalin boosted her all through the following day, she seemed to become high on her own nervous energy, only collapsing as she closed her front door on the day and the deal, poured herself a drink, and sank into the hottest bath she could bear – often to fall asleep and wake an hour later to find it cooling rapidly. People warned her it was dangerous, that she could drown in it, or have a heart attack, but Martha pooh poohed this. It was what she did, she said, how she ran her life, it suited her, and as in so many other tenets of hers – like only eating once a day, or never taking more than one week's holiday at a time – it had always worked very well. Martha was extremely sure that what she did was right.

Although just recently she'd been having just a few doubts . . .

Anyway, she had finished now; she had only to get the document typed, complete with its final changes, ready for sign-off. She rang the night secretary; got no answer, and rang again. She'd obviously gone walkabout. They were always doing that, gossiping in each other's offices. Very annoying. Well, it would have to go to the word processing centre. She took it down, told them to call her when it was done and decided to get her head down for an hour and a half in the overnight room and then go to the gym and come back to the office. With the clients coming

24

in and the deal closing at noon, it was terribly important nothing went wrong now. It was one of the biggest acquisitions she had worked on – one financial services company taking over another, made more complex by the world-wide offices of both and a very quixotic CEO in the client company. And the whole thing had begun as a management buyout that had gone wrong in the other company, and the acquisition was salt in the wound of the main protagonist; he had been dragging his feet, looking for a white knight until the eleventh hour, and raising objections to almost every clause in the contract.

But – they had done it. Sayers Wesley, one of the biggest, sleekest operations in London, had fought a mighty battle on behalf of their client, and won. And Martha Hartley, at thirty-three one of the youngest partners, had been in control of that battle.

She was happy: very happy indeed. She always felt the same at this point, her muscles aching as if the battle had been a physical one, and light-headed with relief. She had sent her assistant home to get a few hours' sleep and the poor exhausted trainee as well; she worked best on her own in these last-lap hours, undistracted, her head absolutely clear.

What was more, she had earned a great deal of money for Sayers Wesley, which would be reflected in her salary in due course. Her £300,000 salary. Her dream of becoming rich had certainly come true.

Her father had asked her, quite mildly, the last time she had gone home, what she did with her earnings; she had appeared, to her irritation, in a list of the up and coming women in the City, the new nearly millionaires it had said, and her family had been shocked by the amount she earned. She didn't tell them it had been underestimated by about twenty thousand.

'Spend it,' she had said.

'All of it?'

'Well – I've invested some of course. In shares and so on.' Why was she feeling so defensive, what was she supposed to have done wrong? 'And bought that time-share in Verbier. Which you could also call an investment – I let it if I don't go there.' Which she hadn't for the past two years, she had been too busy. 'My flat was quite expensive –' she hoped he wouldn't ask how expensive – 'and that must be worth at least twice

25

what I paid for it. And I give a lot to charity,' she said, suddenly nettled. 'Really a lot. And I'm ready and waiting to help you and Mum buy your retirement bungalow.'

This was a sore point with her parents. One of the things about being clergy was that you never owned a house, you lived in church accommodation, never had that huge investment most people did nowadays, to cash in on at the end of their lives. Pride had so far kept the Hartleys from accepting money from their children, but it was beginning to appear inevitable – and painful. Martha knew that and was as discreet as she could be about it; but there was no very satisfactory way of saying 'Look, Mum and Dad, take thirty thousand, you need it more than I do.'

She had the money in a high interest-bearing account; had saved it without too much difficulty over the past five years. It almost frightened her to think she could do that.

But most of her life was appallingly self-indulgent, and she knew it. Her apartment was dazzling, in one of the most sought-after high-rise buildings in Docklands, with huge sheet glass windows and coolly pale wood floors, furnished from Conran and Purves and Purves; she owned a soft-top Mercedes SLK, which she used only at weekends; she had a walk-in wardrobe that was an exercise in fashion name-dropping, Armani, Gucci, Ralph Lauren, Donna Karan, and a stack of shoes from Tod and Jimmy Choo and Manolo Blahnik filed in their boxes in the fashionably approved manner, with polaroids stuck on the outside for instant recognition; and she worked on average fourteen hours every day, often over the weekend, had a very limited social life, hardly ever went to the theatre or concerts because she so often had to cancel.

'And what about a boyfriend?' Her sister, married now for seven years with three children. 'I suppose you just go out with people in your own line of work.'

'Yes, that's right,' Martha had said briefly, and it was true; she had had two rather tidy relationships with solicitors on a similar level to her, and one heartbreaker of an affair with a third, an American who had just happened to be married and failed to acquaint her with the fact until it was too late and she was helplessly in love with him. Martha had ended the relationship immediately, but it hurt her horribly, and a year later she was only just able to consider going out with anybody at all.

She wasn't lonely exactly, she worked too hard for that, and she had a few good friends, working women like herself with whom she had dinner occasionally, and a couple of gay men she was immensely fond of, who were invaluable escorts for formal functions. And if an empty Sunday stretched before her, she simply went to the office and worked. But somewhere within her was a deep dark place which she tried to deny, which drew her down into it during her often sleepless nights, usually at the news that yet another friend was settling into a permanent relationship; a place filled with fears: of a life that was not merely independent and successful but solitary and comfortless, where no one would share her triumphs or ease her failures, where fulfilment could only be measured in material things and she would look back with remorse on a life of absolute selfishness.

But (she would tell herself in the morning, having escaped from the dark place), being single was perfectly suited to her, not only to her ferocious ambition; nobody messed up her schedule or interfered with her routine, no untidied clothes or unwashed cups or unfolded newspapers destroyed the perfection of her apartment. Apart from anything else, it meant her life was completely under her control.

She walked back into her office at six, having studied herself in the mirror as she left the overnight room; she certainly didn't look tired. She actually looked as if she had had a good night's sleep.

Martha was not a beautiful girl, and certainly not pretty; she was what the French call *jolie laide*. Her face was small and oval-shaped, her skin creamy, her eyes dark and brilliant, but her nose was just a little too large for her face, a patrician nose, and she hated it and from time to time she considered having surgery, only to reject it again on the grounds that time could not be spared. Her mouth also displeased her, too big again, she felt, for her face, although her teeth were perfect and very pretty. And as for her hair . . . A lovely gleaming brown certainly, but very straight and fine and requiring endless (and extremely expensive) care simply to produce the easy swinging bob that looked as if it could be washed and left to dry on its own.

And yet people always thought her gorgeous: glossy, perfectly dressed, and wand-slim. Her appearance was the result, like everything else in her life, of a great deal of hard work.

There was a weary-looking Asian woman plugging in a vacuum cleaner in her office.

'Lina, good morning. How are you?'

Martha knew her quite well; she was always there at six, her weariness hardly surprising, since this was the first of three jobs that she did each day.

'I'm sorry, Miss Hartley. Shall I come back later?'

'No, no, you carry on. How are you?'

'Oh, I'm pretty well. A little tired.'

'I'm sure you are, Lina. How are the family?'

'Oh – not too bad. But Jasmin is giving me trouble.'

'Jasmin?'

Martha had seen pictures of Jasmin, a beautiful thirteen year old, adored by both her parents.

'Yes. Well, it's the school, really. It's a bad school. Like most schools these days, seems to me. She was doing so well, in her last school, working so hard, getting such good marks in her SATs.'

'And now?'

'Now she's bored. Not learning anything. She says the teachers are rubbish, can't keep any discipline. And if she tries to work, she gets teased, told she's a – boff. You know what a boff is, Miss Hartley?'

Martha shook her head.

'A boffin, someone who studies all the time. So already she's slipping. And you know they said at her last school she was university material. It's breaking my heart, Miss Hartley, it really is.'

'Lina, that's terrible.' Martha meant it; it was the sort of waste she hated. 'Can't you get her into another school?'

'All the neighbourhood schools are bad. I'm thinking of taking another job, in the evening at the supermarket. So I can pay for her to go to a private school.'

'Lina, you can't. You'll be exhausted.'

Lina's eyes met hers, and she smiled.

'You're a fine one to talk about exhaustion, Miss Hartley. Working all the nights.'

'I know – but I don't go home and care for a family.'

'Well, the way I see it, no point caring for them if they're all going to end up on the social.'

'I'm sure Jasmin would never – '

'Half the teenagers on the estate are unemployed. No qualifications, nothing. Only way out of it is education. And Jasmin isn't going to get it if she stays where she is. I've got to get her out of it. And if it means me working harder, I'll work harder.'

'Oh, Lina!' God, this sort of thing made Martha angry. How dare this ghastly system write off children as they did, denying them their most basic right, while swearing via their absurd league tables that standards were rising. She'd read only the other day that a large number of children were arriving in secondary schools still unable to read. She thought of her own wonderful academic education at her grammar school; that should still be available to children like Jasmin, bright children from poor backgrounds, who deserved to have their potential properly fulfilled. Why should people like Lina have to work themselves literally to death to provide what their children should have by right? But there were only a very few grammar schools left and she had heard only the other day some Education Minister pledging to see them all closed by the next Parliament; going as they did, he said, against the comprehensive ideal. Some ideal . . .

'I'm sure she'll cope,' she said rather helplessly to Lina. 'Bright children always do. She'll make her way somehow.'

'Miss Hartley, you're wrong. You don't know what it's like there. And no child wants to be the odd one out. If all Jasmin's friends turn against her because she's trying to do her schoolwork, what's she going to do?'

'I – don't know.' She wondered suddenly, wildly, if she should offer to help pay Jasmin's school fees – but what about all the other Jasmins, the other bright, wasted children: she couldn't help them all. And it wasn't just education; her father was always telling her of elderly parishioners waiting two years for hip replacements and lying frightened and neglected in dirty wards run by hopelessly overworked nursing staff. But – what could she do? What could anyone do?

She dismissed, swiftly and ruthlessly, the thought of what she might actually do. Or at least try to do.

She checked her diary, just to make quite sure that there were no outstanding personal matters to attend to, no birthday cards to be posted that day – she always kept a stack ready in her desk – and no pressing phone calls to make. But it was all under control. She had sent her sister some flowers: she always did remember her birthday. It was the day they had all met at Heathrow, and set off on their travels. And she had said how determined she was to be successful and rich. She wondered if the other two had done as well as she had. And if she would ever see any of them again. It seemed extremely unlikely. And it would certainly be much better not to.

Clio wondered if she was brave enough to do it. To tell him what she had done, tell him why. He wouldn't be pleased. Not in the least. So – oh, Clio, come on, pull yourself together. You may be about to get married, but you're still an individual. Go on, pick up the phone and tell him, or at least tell him you want to talk to him. This is your fiancé you're confronting, not some medical board . . .

'Hello? Josie? It's Clio Scott. Yes, hello. Could I speak to Mr Graves, please? What? Oh, is he? Oh, all right. Must have been a very long list. Well – could he ring me, please? When he's through. No, I'm at home. Thanks, Josie. Bye.'

Damn. No getting it over quickly then. Still time to change her mind. But –

Her phone rang sharply, made her jump. Surely Jeremy hadn't finished already.

'Clio Scott? Hi. Mark Salter here. Just wanted to say how very pleased we are that you're joining us. I'm sure you'll enjoy it and we can certainly use you. When are you actually joining us? Good, good. Sooner the better. I believe you've had the nerve to ask for time off for your honeymoon. Bloody cheek. Well, look forward to seeing you then. Bye, Clio.'

She'd liked Mark Salter. He was a senior partner in the practice and one of the reasons she'd wanted the job so much. That, and the proximity to home. Or rather what would be home. That was one of the things she could tell Jeremy. That one of the things she had based her decision on had been that the job was so near Guildford. He should like that. Surely . . .

'I don't understand.' They were sitting at an outside table in Covent Garden in the early evening sunshine; his face – his slightly severe face – was as much puzzled as angry. If you'd asked for an actor to play a surgeon, Clio often thought, he would have looked like Jeremy, tall, very straight-backed, with brown wavy hair and grey eyes in a perfectly sculpted face. 'I really don't. We agreed – or so I thought – that you'd only work part-time. So that you could support me as much as possible. And get the house done, of course.'

'Yes, I do know, Jeremy.' She waved the hovering waiter away. 'And I know I should have consulted you before I accepted. But – initially – it was a part-time job. But there were two, one full-time. And they just rang up and offered me that, and said they had to know right away, as there were others – '

'I'm sure they'd have waited until you'd discussed it with me.'

'Yes, of course. But – ' Inspiration hit her. Slightly dishonest inspiration. 'I did ring you, Josie must have told you. But you were in theatre. And I had to – to make the decision. I can't understand why you mind so much. You know I've done the GP course, we agreed it would be ideal – '

'That has nothing to do with whether you're working part- or full-time. And if you really can't understand it, then I would say we're in trouble. Serious trouble.'

Clio had a moment of panic; blind, gut emptying panic. She picked up her glass of wine and took a large gulp.

'Jeremy! Don't say that. Please.'

'Well, I have said it. And I mean it.'

'Well, it's ridiculous of you.' She had rallied now. 'I'm not going on the streets. I'm going to be a GP. Pretty near the house we'll be living in. We need the money, you know we do – '

'Clio, being a GP is a pretty full-time job. And then you'll be on call, often at night, at weekends – '

'You work very full-time,' she said, meeting his eyes stormily. 'What am I supposed to do while you're operating six days a week? Polish the non-existent furniture? I'm a trained doctor, Jeremy. I love what I do. It's a wonderful opportunity for me. Please be happy for me.'

'The fact that I work so hard is all the more reason for you to be there when I am at home,' he said. 'It's not easy, my work. It's physically and mentally very hard. I'm trying to make my way in the world. I need support, and the absolute certainty that I'm going to get it. I don't want to arrive home exhausted, and find you equally so, or not there at all. That's not what we agreed, and you know it.'

'Look,' she said, playing for time, knowing that actually she was – to a degree anyway – in the wrong. 'I'm sorry if – if I should have consulted you more. But – I do find it hard to imagine I won't be at home when you are. Ever. And – I got an estimate for the work on the roof today. You know, having it all re-slated. Ten grand, Jeremy. Just for the roof. I don't think even doing your private list on Saturday mornings is going to make that sort of money, do you? Not at the moment. When you're a senior consultant, of course.'

'And until then I have to do without your support? I see.'

'Oh, Jeremy, stop being so ridiculous.' Clio was losing her temper fast; that was good, it was the only way she ever found the courage to face him down. 'You're twisting everything. Of course I support you. My hours will be very proscribed and I won't be travelling for hours to get to work. And the money I earn can go on the house, make it all happen sooner.'

'I'm beginning to think we should never have bought that house,' he said, staring moodily into his drink. 'If it's going to be that much of a burden to us.'

'Jeremy, we knew how much of a burden it was going to be. But we agreed it was worth it.'

As they had; after falling in love with it, a beautiful early Victorian farmhouse, in a pretty village just outside Godalming. It had been going for a song, as Jeremy had said, and as he always added, it was going to cost them a grand opera to make it habitable. Neglected for several decades, with every sort of rot and damp, it was nevertheless their dream house.

'We can live here all our lives,' Clio had said, looking up at the rotten, damp-stained ceiling, on which sunlight nevertheless still danced.

'And that room next to the kitchen will be absolutely superb for parties,' said Jeremy.

'And as for the garden,' said Clio, running out through the rotten back door and into the overgrown jungly mess that seemed to run back for miles, and was overlooked only by a herd of cows in the meadow beyond, 'it's just wonderful. All those trees. I do so love trees.'

So they had offered the absurdly low asking price – and then hit reality as the work estimates began coming in. Which was one of the reasons she had been so extremely tempted by the full-time job. One of them . . .

Jeremy and Clio had met when she was a houseman at UCH and he a senior registrar; she could never quite believe that she had managed to attract someone as handsome and as charismatic as he was. (She was later to discover that he recognised in her – probably subconsciously – a certain willingness to be told what to do, and a rather disproportionate respect for intellect and success.)

She had fallen helplessly in love with him and the hurt when he made it very clear to her that it would be many years before he could consider any sort of proper commitment had been profound. Desperately humiliated, she had fallen into a relationship with one of her fellow housemen; he was funny and fun, and was very fond of her, as she was of him, but after two years of almost living together, as Clio put it, she arrived unexpectedly at his flat late one night to find him in bed with someone else.

Horribly hurt and disillusioned, she set herself against men altogether for a while, and did a series of hugely demanding hospital jobs, finally settling on geriatrics and a consultancy at the Royal Bayswater Hospital.

'It may sound depressing, but actually it's not; they're so much more courteous than most patients and so grateful when you can do something to help,' she said whenever people expressed surprise at this most unglamorous of choices.

It was at a medical conference on geriatrics that she met Jeremy again; he was a consultant at the Duke of Kent Hospital in Guildford and lecturing on orthopaedic surgery in the elderly, and they were placed next to one another at dinner.

'So – are you married?' he asked, after half an hour of careful chit-chat; and, 'No,' she said, 'absolutely not, what about you?'

'Absolutely not either. I never found anyone who came anywhere close to you.'

Recognising this as the smooth chat-up line that it was, Clio still found it impossible not to be charmed by it; she was in bed with him twenty-four hours later.

A year later they were engaged; now they were a few weeks from being married. And she was generally very happy, but at times filled with a lurking unease. As she was now.

'Look,' she said, resting her hand gently on his, 'look, I'm really, really sorry. I never thought it would matter to you so much.' (Liar, Clio, liar; it was an unexpected talent of hers, lying.) 'Let me do the job for six months. If it's still really bothering you after that I'll leave. I promise. How's that?'

He was silent for a moment, clearly still genuinely hurt.

'I just don't understand why you want to do it,' he said finally, 'you could have such an easy life, do a couple of geriatric clinics at the local hospital, or even a family planning clinic – '

'I hate gynae,' said Clio quickly, 'as you very well know. And I don't want an easy life. Let me give it a go, Jeremy. I promise it won't interfere with your job. Promise!'

'All right,' he said finally, 'but I really don't expect to like the arrangement. Now can we please order? I'm desperately hungry. I've done three hips and four knees this afternoon. One of them really complicated – '

'Tell me about them,' she said, summoning the waiter back. There was no swifter way to ease Jeremy back into a good mood than listening to him intently while he talked about his work.

'Well,' he said, sitting back in his chair, having ordered a large fillet steak and a bottle of claret, and clucked as always over her grilled sole, telling her she starved herself, 'the first one, the first hip that is, was very moth-eaten, so I had to – '

Clio sat back and tried to concentrate on what he was saying; a couple had settled down at the next table, both obviously backpackers, sun-bleached and skinny . . . just as they had all been. She hadn't been skinny, of course: not at first anyway. But later . . . She often found herself thinking of the three of them at this point in the year, when London was filled with backpackers, about what the other two might be doing and how well they might get along together now. Probably not well at all; and even more probably they would never find out.

Chapter 2

'She would have let me go! I know she would. My *real* mother. She'd want me to have a good time, not keep me locked up at home like some kind of nun. I just wish she knew how you try and spoil everything for me. And I'm going anyway, you can't stop me.'

Helen looked at the flushed, furious face, at the hatred in the dark eyes and felt sick. This was the only thing she found almost unbearable, when Kate used the fact that she wasn't really her mother against her. She knew it was only her age; she had been warned about it by social workers, by the people from Adoption Support, and from the adoption agency, all those years ago, that there was bound to be trouble sometime and it would probably come when Kate hit adolescence. 'They have to have something to kick against,' Jan had said, 'and she'll have that ready to hand. She'll idealise her birth mother, turn her into everything you're not. Just try not to let it get to you. She won't mean it.'

Not let it get to her? How could you not, when this was someone you loved so much, lashing out at you, wanting to hurt you, turning from you? Someone you'd cared for all her life – unlike her birth mother! – someone you'd sat up feeding what seemed like all night, nursed through endless childhood ailments, someone you'd comforted, petted, soothed, someone you'd wept over, rejoiced with, been proud of. Someone you'd loved so much . . .

Helen felt the searing sense of injustice in her throat. The urge to say something childish, like, 'I hate you too,' or even, 'Your real mother hasn't shown much interest in you so far', was violent. But, 'Don't be silly, Kate,' she said smoothly, 'I don't keep you locked up and I don't want to spoil everything for you. You know that. I just think you're too young to go to the Clothes Show on your own, that's all.'

'I'm not going on my own,' said Kate, 'I'm going with Sarah. And I *am* going. I know why you don't want me to go, you don't like Sarah. You never have. You'd like me to be going round with someone like Rachel, some stupid boff who likes classical music and speaks what you call properly and wears what looks like her mother's clothes. Don't deny it, you know it's true. And don't bother calling me for supper because I'm going up to my room and I don't want any. All right?'

'Fine,' said Helen, 'absolutely fine.'

Adoption Support would have been proud of her, she thought. It wasn't a lot of comfort.

Later, after supper, when Kate had appeared to make a piece of toast with the maximum amount of noise and mess and gone back to her room, all without a word, Helen had asked Jim if perhaps they were being rather too restrictive.

'She is fourteen and a lot of her friends are going.'

'Well, she's not,' said Jim, picking up the paper, leaving Helen to clear away. 'She's too young and that's that. Maybe next year, tell her. That'll calm her down. Thanks for a nice supper.'

Helen started to unload the dishwasher, and think – as she always did on such occasions – about Kate's mother. She supposed she would have let Kate go to the Clothes Show. She would have been that sort of person. Liberal. Fun. And, of course, totally irresponsible . . .

She probably wouldn't have got landed with the washing up either.

Much, much later, after she had gone to bed, she heard Kate crying. She waited for a while, hoping it would stop. It didn't.

She eased herself out of bed, very carefully, so that Jim wouldn't wake, and went quietly along the corridor. She knocked on the door.

'Can I come in?'

There was a pause; that was a good sign. If Kate shouted 'no' at her, a conversation was out of the question. Helen waited. Finally: 'Come in.'

She was lying face down, her tangle of blonde hair spread on the pillow. She didn't move.

'Sweetheart, please don't cry. Want a drink? Some cocoa or something?'

'No thanks.'

The thanks were a good sign too.

'Well – want a chat then?'

Another silence; then, 'Don't care, really.'

That meant she did.

Helen sat down on the bed, very carefully.

'I'm sorry, sweetheart. About the Clothes Show. Dad and I did talk about it again.'

'And?' Kate's voice was hopeful.

'I'm sorry. Next year, maybe.'

'The others won't even want to go next year. They'll be doing something else. Mum – I'm fourteen. Not four. There'll be loads of people there my age. God, Dad is such a dinosaur!'

'Not really,' said Helen, struggling to be loyal. 'We both feel the same. I'm sorry. Look, how would you like it if we went shopping tomorrow? Spent Granny's birthday money?'

'What, and bought some nice white socks or something? No thanks.'

There was a silence. Then Kate said, 'Mum . . .'

'Yes?'

'I don't really hate you.'

'I know you don't, sweetheart. I didn't think you did.'

'Good. I just feel so – so angry sometimes.'

'Most people of your age do,' said Helen, 'it's part of growing up.'

'No. I don't mean that. Of course I get angry with you. You're so – ' her lips twitched – 'so *annoying*.'

'Thanks.'

'That's OK. But I mean – angry with her. With my – my mother. I mean – if I knew why she did it, it might help. How could she have done that? How could she? I might have died, I might – '

'Lovely, I'm sure she made sure someone had found you. Before she – she – went away.'

There was a long silence; then Kate said: 'I want to know about her so much. So, so much.'

'Of course you do.'

'She must have had her reasons, mustn't she?'

'Of course she must. Very good ones.'

'I mean her life must have been very difficult.'

'Very difficult. Impossible.'

'I mean, it must hurt to have a baby. So – to do that all by yourself, not tell anyone – she must have been very brave.'

'Very brave.'

'I wonder sometimes how I'm like her. In what ways. But I don't think I'm that brave. I mean, I wouldn't have a filling without an injection for instance. Having a baby must hurt much more than that.'

'Yes, I think I would say it does. But Kate, you don't know what you can do till you have to.'

'I s'pose so. And then I think, what else do I know about her? Hardly anything. Except that she was terribly irresponsible. Is that what worries you about me? Does it make you extra fussy, do you think I'm going to go off and sleep around and get pregnant? I suppose it does.'

'Kate, of course it doesn't. Don't be ridiculous. We would never think that.'

'Well, why are you so old-fashioned and strict then?'

'We just want to take care of you, that's all. It's –'

'I know, I know, it's a wicked world out there, crazed drug dealers and white slave traffickers on every corner. Especially at the Clothes Show.'

'Kate –'

But then Helen looked at her and saw she was half smiling.

'It's all right, Mum. You can't help being senile.'

'No, I can't. Sorry. You all right now?'

'Sort of. Yes. Thanks for coming in.'

Helen had reached the door, when Kate said: 'Mum. What would you think about me trying to find her?'

'Your birth mother?'

'Mmmm . . .'

'Absolutely fine, sweetheart. Of course, if that's what you want.'

'It is. Yeah.'

'Right then, of course you must.' She hesitated, then: 'If there's any way I can help –'

'No, it's OK.' The small face had closed up again. 'I'd rather do it on my own, thanks.'

Thank God for the darkness, Helen thought, closing the door quickly; otherwise Kate would have seen her crying.

Sometimes, she thought, as she drank the sweet black coffee she always turned to in times of crisis, sometimes she wished she'd ignored all the conventional wisdom and not told Kate the truth. Not, of course, that she was her natural mother; but that her own mother had died and she had adopted her because of that. It would have been so much easier for a child to cope with. How could a small person of seven – which was the age Kate had been when she had actually framed the question, 'What happened to my other mummy?' – possibly digest the news that her other mummy, her real mummy, had abandoned her in a cleaning cupboard at Heathrow airport, leaving her without even a nappy on, wrapped in a blanket, and not so much as a note? Helen had dressed it up, of course, had said she was all tucked up in a blanket, nice and warm and snug, and that her birth mother had made quite, quite sure she had been safely discovered before going away. At the time Kate had appeared to accept it, had listened very intently and then skipped off to play in the garden with her sister. Later she had come in and said, 'I've decided I probably am a princess.'

'You are *my* princess,' Jim had said, having been warned that the dreaded conversation had finally taken place, and Kate had smiled at him radiantly and said: 'Well, you can be my prince. I'd like to marry you anyway.'

Life had been so simple then.

But of course you couldn't lie to them because as they grew older more and more questions would be asked. If the birth mother had died, where was her family, where were Kate's grandparents, surely they'd want to know her, and her father for that matter? And did she have any brothers and sisters, and – no, it would have been impossible to sustain as an explanation. The truth had to be told.

They had several friends with adopted children, made through all the counselling and support groups. Adoption was a fact of Kate's life; indeed when she was very small she had asked everybody if they were adopted. Told that she was special, that she had been chosen by her parents, rather than just been born to them, like her sister Juliet (arriving to her parents' enormous surprise and pleasure just two years after they had adopted Kate), she had for a while been entirely happy about it, had never seemed to give it a great deal of thought; until one terrible day when she had come home from school, aged nine, crying and saying that one of the girls had been teasing her about being adopted.

'She said if my other mum had loved me she wouldn't have left me.'

'Now, Kate, that isn't true,' said Helen, panic rising in her as she recognised the beginning of the real problems that faced them all. 'I've told you, she wanted a happier home for you than she could give you, she wanted you to go to people who could care for you properly. She couldn't – I've explained that to you lots of times.'

Kate had appeared to accept that at the time, but as she grew older and sharper and the truth became balder and uglier, it troubled her more and more. She stopped talking about her other mother, as she called her, pretended to any new friends that Helen and Jim were her real parents, and then a little later, constructed elaborate lies about a mother who had died in childbirth and entrusted her to Helen, her oldest and dearest friend.

Which was fine until other friends, who knew what had really happened, had revealed it. And so in the end, there was no more pretending. And she had to learn to live with the ugly truth.

The coffee on its own wasn't working; Helen poured herself a glass of wine, and hoped that Jim wouldn't come down and accuse her of being an alcoholic like her mother. It wouldn't be a serious accusation and Jilly Bradford, Helen's mother, was very far from being an alcoholic. But she did like her gin and tonic and indeed her red wine and Jim, who felt, with some justification, that Jilly thought he wasn't good enough for her daughter, used the fact as a small ongoing revenge.

'Your mother's coming to lunch,' he would say, 'better stock up on the gin.' Or 'Come on, Jilly, I know you. Mug of Horlicks isn't your idea of a nightcap.'

Jilly didn't mind in the least; she saw it as proof of Jim's commonness as she put it, that he thought women shouldn't drink, and she took some pride anyway in her strong head. But Helen hated it.

Her mother had been very supportive as Kate grew increasingly difficult; having said that she had feared it would happen all along, ever since Helen had told her they were adopting a foundling (as they were still called), she then also told her that she wouldn't say it again. Which she didn't and moreover proceeded to do all she could to help. This mostly consisted of slipping Kate ten-pound notes, taking her on shopping expeditions, 'Of course I know what she'll like, Helen, I'm in the fashion business, aren't I?' and treating her to expensive lunches at smart restaurants. Jim disapproved of the whole relationship, but as Helen pointed out, her mother was a safety valve, someone Kate could talk to if she felt she needed it.

'Why can't she talk to us, for God's sake?'

'Jim, I sometimes despair of you. The whole point is there are things she can't talk to us about. Things she thinks will upset us, things she won't want to tell us. Better my mother, who she sees as someone rather raffish and naughty, than that dreadful Sarah.'

Jim didn't argue. Helen knew there was another reason he didn't like her mother; she favoured Kate over Juliet. Which was on the face of it illogical, since Juliet was Helen's own child; but she was also Jim's, and had many of Jim's characteristics. She was a very sweet child, and extremely clever and musically gifted, but she was quiet and shy, with none of Kate's quicksilver charm, and she found Jilly rather daunting.

It had been one of the most glorious days in Helen's life – her wedding day and that of Juliet's birth being the others – when Mrs Forster from the adoption agency had telephoned to say that there was a baby who they might like to consider adopting. 'She's a foundling,' Mrs Forster had said, 'so there could be no question of her ever going back to her birth family.'

Helen had actually been reading about the baby in the papers; she had made front-page news, as such babies always did; and there had been photographs of her being held by a phalanx of nurses at the South Middlesex Hospital, her small face almost invisible within the folds of blanket.

'Baby Bianca,' the caption had said. 'So called by the nurses because she was found in a cleaning cupboard at Heathrow airport (Bianca is Italian for white), now five days old.' It went on to say that the social services were hoping to contact her mother who might be in need of medical attention and appealed for anyone who had noticed anything untoward at Terminal Three at Heathrow airport, on the night of 16 August, to contact their nearest police station.

How could anyone do that? Helen had said to Jim, and when Baby Bianca was finally handed to her by the foster mother, Helen felt that, to a degree, she already knew her.

Helen had been very nervous, driving to meet Bianca for the first time; what if she didn't feel anything for her? What if the baby started screaming the minute she saw her, sensing her complete inexperience and incompetence? What if she just proved to be totally unmaternal? But it was love at first sight; Bianca (shortly to become Kate) opened large blue eyes (shortly to become deep, dark brown) and stared up at her, waving one tiny, frond-like fist, making little pouting shapes with her small mouth, and Helen knew, quite simply, that she wanted to spend the rest of her life with her.

This had not been one of the happiest days of her life though; she poured herself a second glass of wine and tried to face the reality of that small, dependent creature who had become in some strange way as surely her own flesh and blood as her natural daughter, seeking out the woman who had actually given birth to her and perceiving her as her mother.

Whoever that woman was, Helen thought, and whatever she was like, she would undoubtedly want to kill her.

Chapter 3

'Jocasta! Attempted suicide. Village near Hay Tor, Dartmoor. Go!'

God, this was terrible, this foot and mouth epidemic, she thought, turning her car onto the A303. Every day there were more cases, hundreds of them; the shocked face of Nick Brown, the Agriculture Minister, appeared every day on the television, usually followed by shots of Tony Blair looking carefully ill at ease; they both spoke (also every day) the same platitudes, the fact that it was being contained, the outbreaks were being carefully monitored, if everyone obeyed the strict regulations laid down by the government it would shortly be under control. It hardly seemed like that. Farmers were in despair, their farms under siege, the dreadful pall of smoke drifting from the funeral pyres of cattle, large tracts of the countryside silent, the fields empty of livestock. The royal parks, Richmond and Hampton Court, were shut, and even the Peak District and the Yorkshire Dales were closed to walkers; the land itself seemed dark and despairing.

Jocasta had done a few stories already, but none as desperate as this – although Nick had said half the farmers in the country would be found hanged in their barns if the government didn't do something soon. There were terrible stories of bungled shootings of animals by the police, of huge heaps of unburied cattle in once lovely meadows, of a dreadful stench drifting across a five-mile radius of each one.

'They should get the army in at least,' Nick also said, 'do the job properly. What do these idiots think they're doing, messing about with volunteers?'

Jocasta felt half afraid of what she might find at Watersmeet Farm on the southern edge of Dartmoor.

It was after two when she reached the farm. The gates were barred, disinfectant buckets and beds of straw on either side of them. There were at least half a dozen reporters standing around, and as many photographers, and several police cars as well. She jumped out and went up to one of the reporters she recognised.

'Hi, Phil. What's happening?'

'Not much. The chap's all right, apparently. But the wife's desperate. Whole herd slaughtered yesterday, over there, behind the farmhouse. It's horrible. Poor people. Children in there, too. Anyway, you won't get in, Jocasta. Not even you. *Daily News* has just got very short shrift. Offered money as usual.'

'Are they still here?'

'No, they've gone.'

'Well, I'm going to try my luck,' said Jocasta.

'If you crack this one, Jocasta, I'll eat my notebook.'

Two hours later she called and told him to start munching.

She had gone to the village shop, where she had spent an enormous amount of money on things she didn't want and listened sympathetically to the woman talking about the misery the entire area was enduring, how her own trade had dropped by half, how the whole of the countryside seemed to be dying along with the cattle. Jocasta expressed Nick's view that they should get the army in, do the job properly, and said that her paper thought the same. 'We feel that if we can show how people like you are being betrayed, perhaps it would help others. I'd so love to talk to the poor farmer's wife.'

'Well, I don't know as she'd talk to you, but I could ask her sister what she thinks. She lives next door to me. Angela Goss her name is.'

'Do you think she'd mind? I'd only want a very short time with her.'

Angela Goss said she'd see her, but only for a minute. 'And don't think I can get you into the farm, because I can't.'

'Of course not,' said Jocasta.

What Angela Goss did arrange was for Jocasta to speak to her sister on the phone.

❖   ❖   ❖

It had been the noise at first, she said, the endless firing of the rifles and the cattle bellowing. They had tried not to listen, had put loud music on, but they couldn't help it. And then the silence, it had been awful, that dead, heavy silence, and watching the ewes leading their lambs, some only a couple of days old, into the meadow to be slaughtered.

'They say there's no sentiment in farming, but Geoff was crying, same as me. Course they promised they'd dig trenches, but they didn't have the equipment, so they're piled up there, these beautiful animals in a great horrible heap, starting to smell, it's criminal, it really is.'

Her husband had been very quiet the day of the slaughter, she said, hardly speaking; it was the following morning quite early that she'd realised he was missing. 'I found him in the cowshed; he'd driven his car in, and put the hosepipe through the window; I got him out, just in time. But what for, I'm wondering? What's he got now? Just this ghost of a place. And what's it done to the children, all of it, I'd like to know? What a memory to carry through their lives. I – I must go now,' she said, her voice breaking, 'you'll have to excuse me. But you'll tell them, won't you, your paper, what it's really like, the loss of a future. It's like some terrible bad dream. Only we're not going to wake up.'

Jocasta filed her story and then drove back to London, wondering how many of the farms she passed were living in the same nightmare.

'I can't tell you how awful it was,' she said to Nick on the phone. 'It's a kind of living death they're all in. Poor, poor people. They feel so let down and so ignored.'

'You sound tired, sweetie.'

'I *am* tired,' said Jocasta irritably. 'I've just driven three hundred miles. I feel about a hundred years old.'

'Poor old thing. Would you like me to tuck you up in bed with some hot milk?'

'Well, you can tuck me up in bed with yourself. That'd be nice. But I'm going into the office. Chris wants to see me. Not sure why.'

'Good luck. I'll see you later. I'll be at the House. If I'm not in Annie's, I'll be up in the press dining room.'

Chris Pollock, the editor of the *Sketch*, was young for the job – only forty-one – and was famously easy-going until he wasn't, as one of the reporters had told Jocasta on her first day. He would remain calm and patient in the face of quite considerable crises, leaving his staff to work without too much interference from him – until they either made a mistake, or missed a strong story that another newspaper, most notably the *Mail*, had got. Upon which he became incandescent with rage and the unfortunate reporter – or section editor – was first bawled out and then left to stew for several days before being summoned again, either to be fired or told they were to be given another chance. This was an inescapable process and there was absolutely no knowing which way it would go.

He had his philosophy of the paper – 'soft news with a hard centre' – and expected all the journalists to know what he meant. What it did mean was the human stuff on the front page, 'and I don't mean bloody soaps, I mean people-slanted stories,' an adherence to the paper's politics – 'right with a dash of left, just like New Labour' – and fairly hefty, well-written, slugs of news on pages three, four, five and six. The *Sketch* was also very strong on its female coverage and ran ongoing campaigns about things like health, childcare and education.

As Jocasta went in, Chris was sitting with his back to the window, the lights of London spread out beneath him; he smiled at her. He was an attractive man; short and heavily built, with brilliant blue eyes and close-cropped dark hair, and he had an energy that was like a physical blow. He had a great deal of success with women.

He indicated the chair opposite his desk. That was worrying; it was his bawling-out chair.

But, 'Drink, darling?'

'Oh – yes please.'

'This is a great story.' He thumped a page on his desk. 'Brilliant. You did very, very well. See what we've done with it.'

Jocasta looked; it was a whole page, and there was the photograph Angela Goss had given her of Geoff Hocking and over it a headline that read, 'They killed his cattle. He tried to

47

kill himself,' and underneath as a caption, 'The idle farmer on the silent farm.'

'That's great,' she said. 'I'm so pleased you kept that in. About the silent farm.'

'It's a good quote. Anyone else get in?'

'Don't think so.'

'Good girl. Anyway, nice big display for you.'

'Yes. Thanks, Chris.'

He sat in silence for a moment, looking at her; then he said, 'This is the front page, you know. Did you realise that?'

Jocasta, already overwrought and upset, burst into tears.

'The front page!' she said to Nick. She had found him in the press dining room and had dragged him out onto the corridor. 'I got the front page.' And she was actually jumping up and down. 'Isn't that great? Isn't that fantastic?'

'Fucking fantastic,' he said and gave her a hug. 'You're a genius. How on earth did you do it? I've been watching the news, it looked impenetrable.'

'Let's just say I boldly went where none had gone before.'

'Very boldly. Clever girl.'

'Actually,' she said, 'I have to tell you it wasn't all that difficult. Come on, you can buy me some champagne. I can't believe it! My very own, very first front page.'

Her phone rang endlessly next day. Everyone had seen the story, wanted to congratulate her. Her mother called, Josh called, and even Beatrice, her rather daunting barrister sister-in-law.

'I think it's thrilling,' she said, her clear-cut voice warmer than usual. 'And it's such a very good piece of reporting. I'm extremely impressed. Those poor, wretched people. Well done, Jocasta. Very, very well done.'

'Thank you,' said Jocasta. 'And thank you for calling.'

'My dear girl, anyone would call. It's a great achievement.'

But not anyone would call. The one she had been waiting for, longing for, did not come. Her father as always had chosen to ignore her. And it hurt: dreadfully.

The doorbell ringing endlessly broke into her heavy first sleep; she had had a very long and tedious evening and hadn't filed the story she'd been on until midnight. Nick was working late and going home to Hampstead and she had been looking forward to a long, uninterrupted sleep. She stumbled down the stairs, shouting curses at Nick – he forgot his keys at least once a week – and opened the door to a dishevelled and wretched-looking Josh.

'Can I come in?' he said 'Beatrice has turned me out.'

It was a wonder she hadn't done it before, Jocasta thought, sitting him down on her sofa, going into the kitchen to make him some coffee. He had had his first affair a year into their marriage, and six months after the birth of their second child, he had done it again. A year after that he had had what he swore was a one-night stand with his secretary; Beatrice had said then that the next time would be the last. Now she had discovered an affair that had been going on for five months with an English girl working for the Forbes Parisian office and, true to her word, had literally locked him out of the house.

'I'm such a fool,' Josh kept saying, 'such a bloody fucking idiot,' and 'Yes you are,' Jocasta said, looking at him as he sat there, tousled head in his hands, tears dripping rather unromantically onto his trousers. At thirty-three he still had some vestiges of the beautiful boy he had been, with his blond hair, his high forehead, his rather full, curvy mouth. He was distinctly overweight now and his colour was too high, but he was very attractive, and he had a slightly helpless, self-deprecating charm which made women want to take care of him. He was always late, very untidy, and endlessly good-natured; everyone loved Josh. He wasn't exactly witty, but he was a very funny raconteur, he lit up a room or a dinner table, and had that most priceless social gift of making others feel amusing too.

Jocasta had always thought that Beatrice, less naturally charming and attractive than he, must find it very trying, but her attitude towards Josh was one of slightly amused indulgence, and she tolerated much of his bad behaviour with immense good nature.

Beatrice was not beautiful, but there were things about her that were; her eyes, large, dark and warm (distracting from a heavy nose and jaw), her hair, long, thick and glossy, and her legs, longer even than Jocasta's and as slender. She was, at the time she and Josh met, already making an awesome reputation for herself as a criminal barrister; Josh was drifting through life, ostensibly being groomed to take over the family company. He had given up law even before leaving university, and had read philosophy instead. He had then spent a year auditioning for various drama schools, all of which rejected him, and, finding himself unemployed and unable to finance his fairly expensive lifestyle, had finally gone to his father expressing a rather unlikely and sudden interest in the Forbes business.

Peter Forbes had not greeted this news with the enthusiasm Josh had hoped for, but he said he'd give him a taste of it and see how he liked it. The taste was not too sweet; on the first day Josh was not given the plush room he expected in the London office, but a lesson in driving a fork-lift truck in the factory at Slough. After a month, he progressed to the assembly line and thence to the sales office, where he learnt to use the company computer. He had perversely quite enjoyed the factory period, but this was mind-numbing; he stopped trying, kept calling in sick and taking longer and longer lunch-hours around the pubs of Slough. His father sent for him and told him if he didn't pull himself together he'd be fired; Josh told him that would be a happy release.

That had been the day of the dinner party at which he'd met Beatrice.

Less than a year later they were married; people who didn't know them very well could never quite understand their relationship, why it worked; the simple fact was that they needed one another. Josh needed order and direction; and Beatrice, who had been born ordered and self-motivated, needed the emotional and social support of a husband who also had plenty of money, criminal litigation being the least financially rewarding branch of the law.

She was hugely attracted to Josh, she found him surprisingly interesting, and he was potentially very rich. Josh had discovered that Beatrice was a great deal less confident than she seemed, that she had a sexual appetite which was quite surprising, given her rather stern personality, and also that she was the first person he had met for a long time who seemed to think he had any real potential for anything.

'I think you could do wonderful things with that firm,' she said (by the Monday evening she had looked it up on the Internet and assessed its potential), and sent him back to his father to apologise and to ask for his job back; a month after that, when he was working genuinely hard, she invited Peter Forbes to dinner with her and Josh. They impressed one another equally.

'I can see he's difficult and incredibly authoritarian,' she said to Josh afterwards, 'but he's got so much drive and energy. And I love the way he talks about the company, as if it was someone he's in love with.'

'It is,' said Josh gloomily.

Peter Forbes in his turn found Beatrice's intellect, her clear ambition and her rather intense manner engaging; he told her she was exactly what Josh needed and said he hoped he would be seeing a great deal more of her in the future. Beatrice told him she hoped so too.

Six months later Josh was appointed deputy sales manager for the south of England, and given the longed-for London office, and Beatrice told him she thought they should get married. Josh panicked, and said maybe one day, but what was the rush, things seemed fine to him as they were, and Beatrice said not really, as she was pregnant.

'As if,' Jocasta had said to her mother, who deeply disliked Beatrice, 'a girl like her would get pregnant by accident. I bet she decides exactly when she ovulates as well as everything else. God, he's an idiot.'

But Josh surprised everyone – including Beatrice – by acknowledging his responsibilities and agreeing that they should marry. And they had a small but beautifully organised wedding at Beatrice's home in Wiltshire, and a honeymoon in Tuscany. Peter Forbes was as delighted as his ex-wife was not.

Beatrice had worked until she was eight months pregnant and returned to her chambers two weeks after the birth of Harriet – known as Harry; two years to the day after Harry's birth, Charlotte – inevitably named Charlie – was born.

That had been two years ago; Josh was now deputy managing director of Forbes Furniture, and working just hard enough to keep both Beatrice and his father satisfied, and Beatrice had switched from criminal to family law, as being more compatible with family life and running their large Clapham house and hectic social life with apparent ease. The fact remained that domestic abuse cases were funded by legal aid and therefore still not especially lucrative; Josh paid most of the bills.

Jocasta wanted to dislike Beatrice, but she never managed it; she was, for all her bossy manner and workaholism, surprisingly kind and genuinely interested in Jocasta's life and career. Nick adored her, he said she was the sexiest sort – 'I bet she puts on a gym slip and sets about old Josh with the cane' – and was charmed by the way she always read his column, and discussed whatever story she had most recently read with great seriousness, as indeed she did Jocasta's. There was absolutely no doubt in anyone's mind, both within and outside the family, that Beatrice was the perfect wife for Josh.

'Why did I do it, Jocasta?' he moaned now, between sips of coffee. 'Why am I such an idiot?'

'No idea,' said Jocasta, 'but I have to say, it's Beatrice I feel sorry for. I'd have slung you out the last time. And you realise Dad will be on her side, don't you? He won't let her starve.'

'Don't think I haven't thought of that, either,' said Josh. 'I don't hold a single card, do I? What can I do?'

'You can't actually do anything. Except wait for a while. And keep telling her how sorry you are. You've got one wonderful thing in your favour. And it just might be enough.'

'Jesus, I hope so. I'd do anything, anything at all, if I thought there was a chance she'd forgive me.'

'I suspect she's heard that before.'

'Yes, all right. Don't kick a man when he's down. So – what is this one wonderful thing?'

'I think,' said Jocasta, and her voice was slightly sad, 'that she loves you.'

Martha raised her lips to the silver chalice and took a sip of wine, struggling to concentrate on the moment, on the fact that she was taking the holy sacrament. She never could, of course. Not completely; she had moved so far from her father's church, her parents' faith, she only went to church when she was staying for the weekend in Binsmow. It pleased them, and it charmed the parishioners; the fact that she felt an absolute hypocrite was immaterial. And in a way she enjoyed it, savouring the peace, the reassurance that nothing had changed.

She stood up now, walked slowly back to her seat, her head carefully bowed, taking in nonetheless the fact that the church was three-quarters empty and apart from a few – a very few – teenagers, she was the only person there who could be called young. How could her father do this week after week, year after year? How could his own faith withstand what seemed to Martha the humiliation of knowing that his life's work was for the large part rejected by the community? She had asked him once, and he had said she didn't understand, St Andrews was still the centre of the parish, it didn't matter that the congregation was so small, they turned to him when they needed him, when illness or death or marriage or the christening of a new baby required his services, and that was enough for him.

'But, Dad, don't you want to tell them they should have done a bit more for the church before expecting it to do things for them?'

'Oh, no,' he said and his eyes were amused. 'What good would that do? Alienate them, and fail them in their hours of need? Martha, I believe in what I'm doing and I've never regretted it. And it enables me to do some good. Quite a lot of good, even. I like that. Not many professions allow it.'

'I suppose you mean mine doesn't,' she said irritably.

'I didn't. I wouldn't dream of drawing such a comparison.'

'Good.'

But she knew he would.

She had come down this weekend very much from a sense of duty; her sister had called her to say that her parents were a bit low.

'Mum's arthritis is bad, and Dad gets so upset because he can't help. I try to cheer them up but they see me all the time, I'm not a treat like you are. You haven't been for months, Martha.'

'Well, I'm sorry,' she said. 'I've been – '

'Yes, I know how busy you've been.' Her sister's voice was sharp. 'I've been quite busy too, actually, trying to cope with work and the children. Even Michael gets down more than you do.'

'Yes, all right,' Martha said. She was tempted to say it was easy for Michael, their brother, who was in his first year of teaching, and had a great deal of spare time, but she didn't. In any case, Anne was right, she didn't come down much.

'I promise I'll come very soon,' she said finally. 'I really do promise.'

'Good,' said Anne and rang off.

Martha wished she could like Anne more. But she was so – so sanctimonious, so much too good to be true. She was married to a very hard-working, poorly paid social worker, and they had three children, no help in the house, only one car and Anne did a job as a Special Needs Assistant at one of the local schools to make ends come a little nearer to meeting. On top of that she did a lot of voluntary work and even helped her father in the parish, now that their mother was finding it difficult to cope. To Martha it looked like the life from hell; especially being married to Bob the Social Worker, as she thought of him, rather like Bob the Builder. Martha actually felt Anne would be better off with Bob the Builder; at least he would be some practical use around the house. Bob Gunning added acute unhandiness to his other shortcomings, and all the DIY jobs were done by poor Anne. There really did seem to be very little joy in her life.

Martha could see how excessively irritating her own gilded existence must seem to her sister, not just the apparently limitless money, with only herself to spend it on, the flashy car, the expensive clothes, but the way she did find so little time to visit, to help their parents – other than financially, which in any case they would only accept under extreme pressure. And although she had come down this weekend, it would be the only one for some time, she knew; the General Election was looming and that always resulted in a lot of work, as the money markets became jittery and the big corporations swung into action to accommodate any changes.

Not that they would be very remarkable; Blair continued to sit high in the polls, smiling purposefully, making empty promises. He would get in again; there was no doubt about it.

'Things are pretty bad around here,' her father said.

'In what way?' She took his arm as they walked back.

'The countryside has been dreadfully hit by the foot and mouth business. There's an air of depression over everything.'

'Really?' said Martha. She had read about the foot and mouth tragedy of course, but sheltered as she was in her glass tower in Docklands, it had somehow lacked reality.

'Yes. Poor old Fred Barrett whose family's had a farm just outside Binsmow for five generations has struggled on until now, but this has finished him. He's selling up. Not that anyone will buy the farm. And then I've got God knows how many parishioners waiting to go into hospital. Poor old Mrs Dudley, waiting eighteen months now for a hip replacement, in real pain, and still they tell her another six months. It's criminal, it really is.'

'Everything's a mess,' said Martha, thinking of Lina and her daughter Jasmin, 'absolutely everything.'

She walked into her mother's bedroom; Grace was lying in bed, looking pale.

'Hello, dear. I'm sorry I'm not seeing to breakfast. I slept so badly; the pain wakes me, you see, and then I get back to sleep around six and don't hear the alarm.'

'Oh Mum, I'm so sorry. Can I get you anything, tea, coffee . . . ?'

'I'd love a cup of tea. I'll be down in a minute.'

'No, I'll bring it up,' said Martha, 'spoil you a bit. Is the pain very bad?'

'Sometimes,' said Grace, 'not always. You know. Grumbles away.'

'What does the doctor say?'

'Oh, he's referred me to a consultant, but there's a year's waiting list at least. In the old days, when we still had the local hospital, it would have been much quicker. But it's gone, of course. Dr Ferguson gives me painkillers, which help, but they make me feel sick.'

'Mum – '

'Yes, dear?'

'Mum, won't you let me pay for the orthopaedic consultant at least? You could see him so much more quickly. This week probably.'

'No, Martha. We don't believe in private medicine. Or jumping the queue – it's immoral.'

'You might not believe in it,' said Martha briskly, 'but it would stop you being in pain. Wouldn't that be worth it?'

'Martha, we can't be beholden to you. It's not right.'

'But why not? I was beholden to you for all those years. And – suppose it had been me? When I was a little girl. In pain, not able to see a doctor for over a year. Wouldn't you have thought anything was worth it, to help me? Wouldn't you have set your principles aside?'

'Possibly,' said Grace with a feeble smile. 'I suppose . . .'

'Good,' said Martha, seeing victory. 'It's no more than you deserve. I'd much rather spend some of that disgraceful salary on you than on some new Manolos.'

'What are they, dear?'

'Shoes.'

'Oh, I see. Some new style, is it?'

'Something like that,' said Martha.

After lunch her sister called. Could Martha do her a favour?

'My next-door neighbour – she's a widow – ' she would be, Martha thought – 'needs help. Her son's car's broken down and he needs a lift back up to London. I said I was sure you wouldn't mind taking him.'

Martha felt disproportionately outraged. She did mind: very much. She had been longing for the peaceful drive back to London, with her stereo playing, catching up on phone calls, having the time to think . . . And of course *not* to think. She didn't want some spotty lad sitting beside her for three or four hours, requiring her to make conversation.

'Couldn't he get the train?'

'He could, but he can't afford it. Martha, it's not much to ask, surely. He's quite sweet, I've met him.'

'Yes, but – ' Martha stopped.

'Oh forget it,' said Anne and her voice was really angry. 'I'll tell him he'll have to hitch a lift. You just get on back to your smart life in London.'

Martha promptly felt terrible. What kind of a cow was she turning into? Anne was right, it wasn't a lot to ask. She just didn't want to do it . . .

'No,' she said quickly, 'all right. But he'll have to fit in with me time-wise and I'll drop him at an Underground station, all right? I can't spend half the night driving round London.'

'You're so extremely kind,' said Anne. 'I'll tell him then. What time exactly would suit you, Martha? Fit in best with your very heavy timetable?'

'I'm leaving at about four,' said Martha, refusing to rise to this.

'Could you make the huge detour to pick him up? It would take at least fifteen minutes.'

'I'll pick him up,' said Martha.

Anne came out of her house as Martha drew up; her sniff as she looked at the Mercedes was almost audible.

'So good of you to do this,' she said. 'He's all ready. We've been chatting, haven't we, Ed?'

'Yes. Hey, cool car. It's very kind of you, Miss—'

'Hartley,' said Martha. She had been fiddling with the dashboard, not looking at him; she took in only the voice, the classless young London voice, and sighed. It was going to be a terribly long drive.

Then she got out, took off the sunglasses she had been wearing – and found herself staring at one of the most beautiful young men she had ever seen.

He was quite tall, over six foot, with rather messy short blond hair, and astonishingly deep blue eyes; he was tanned, with a few very carefully scattered freckles on a perfectly straight nose, and his grin, which was wide, revealed absolutely perfect white teeth. He was wearing long baggy shorts, a style she hated, trainers without socks and a rather crumpled white shirt; he looked like an advertisement for Ralph Lauren. Martha felt less resentful suddenly.

'Mum's at church, but she said I was to thank you from her,' he said. 'Shall I put my bags on the back seat?'

'Yes, do,' said Martha. 'Well, Anne, sorry not to have seen more of you. Next time, perhaps.'

'Perhaps,' said Anne. Her tone was still chilly.

'This really is very kind of you,' said Ed again as they pulled down the road. 'I do appreciate it.'

'That's all right,' said Martha. 'What happened to your car?'

'It just died,' he said. 'It was just an old banger. Present from Mum for my twenty-first. She said I shouldn't take it on long journeys. Looks like she was right.'

'So – what will you do?'

'Goodness knows.' He looked round the car. 'This is really cool. Convertible, yeah?'

'Yes.'

'I don't suppose you use this much in London.'

'Not during the week, no,' said Martha. 'Not much use for a car where I live.'

'Which is?'

'Docklands.'

'Cool.'

'Quite cool, I suppose,' she said, hoping she didn't sound like some pathetic older woman acting young.

'And – you're a lawyer?' he said. 'Is that right? Do you get all dressed up in a white wig?'

'No,' she said, smiling against her will, 'I'm not a barrister. I'm a solicitor.'

'Oh, right. So you do people's divorces, help them buy their houses . . .'

'No, I work for a big City firm. Sayers Wesley.'

'Oh, I get you. You work all night, see big deals through, that sort of thing.'

'That sort of thing.' She glanced at him; he had put a baseball cap on back to front, another thing she hated; impossibly, it suited him.

'And earn a fortune? Yeah?'

'I don't know how you would define a fortune,' she said coolly.

'Sorry. I didn't mean to sound rude. I just get interested in people.' He turned to smile at her, an astonishing, beautiful smile.

'So I see. Well, what do you do?'

'I'm just temping at the moment,' he said, 'doing IT stuff. It's pretty boring. But I'm going away in a couple of months. It's paying for that.'

'Where are you going?'

'Oh – Thailand, Oz, all that stuff. Did you do that sort of thing?'

'Yes I did. It was great fun.'

'Yeah, hope so. I should have done it before uni, really.'

'How old are you, Ed?'

'Twenty-two.'

'And – what did you read?' she asked. 'At university?'

'Oh – English. My dad wanted me to read classics because he did. But I couldn't face it.'

'I'm not surprised,' she said and was reminded suddenly and sharply of Clio, pretty plump little Clio, saying almost exactly the same thing, all those years ago. Clio who had wanted to be a doctor, who – enough of that, Martha. Don't go back there.

'I kind of wish I had,' he said, 'it would have made him so happy. Now that he's died, it seems something I should have done for him.'

'Yes,' she said, 'yes, I can see that. But you're wrong, you know. You have to do what's right for you.'

'Yeah,' he said, 'that's what I think, really. But just sometimes . . .'

'Of course. I'm sorry about your dad. What – what was it?'

'Cancer. He was only fifty-four. It was awful. He kept putting off going to the doctor and then there was a long waiting list to see someone, and – well, the whole thing was a mess really.'

'It must have been very hard for you. How long ago was this?'

'Three years,' he said. 'I was at uni and it was really hard for my mum. Your dad was really good to her. She said he really helped her get through. He's all right, your dad. Your sister's pretty nice too.'

'I'm glad you think so,' said Martha.

He turned to look at her consideringly.

'She's not too much like you, though,' he added, and then blushed. 'Sorry. You'll be putting me out on the road next.'

'If you'd told me I was like her, I might,' said Martha, smiling.

'Yeah, well you're not. Of course, she must be much older than you.'

'Actually,' said Martha, 'she's two years younger.'

'You're kidding!'

'I'm not.'

A silence, then, 'That is just so not possible,' he said.

'Ed,' said Martha, 'you just made my weekend. Tell me, where did you go to uni?'

'Bristol.'

'Oh really? That's where I went.'

'Yeah?' He turned to smile at her again, then said, 'I bet you were in Wills Hall.'

'I was,' she said. 'How did you know?'

'All the posh people lived there. It was a public school ghetto. When I was at Bristol anyway.'

'I'm not posh,' she said indignantly, 'and I certainly didn't go to public school. I went to Binsmow Grammar School. When it *was* a grammar school.'

'I went there,' he said, 'but it was a complete dump by then.'

He must be very bright, she thought, to have got into Bristol from a bad comprehensive. And it was bad; her father was on the board of governors and often talked despairingly of it.

They reached Whitechapel about eight-thirty. 'This'll do fine for me,' he said, 'I can get the tube.'

'OK. I'll just pull over there.'

'It's been really nice,' he said, 'thanks. I've enjoyed it. Talking to you and so on.'

'Weren't you expecting to?'

'Well – not really, to tell you the truth. I thought you'd be – it would be – '

'What?' she said laughing.

'A bit of an ordeal. Actually.'

'Well, I'm glad it wasn't.'

'No, it absolutely wasn't.' He got out, shut the door, then opened it again. He looked at her rather awkwardly. 'I don't suppose,' he said, 'you'd like to come for a drink one night?'

'Well,' said Martha, feeling suddenly very uncool indeed, almost flustered, angry with herself for it, 'well, yes, that would be – nice. I'm afraid I – well, I'm afraid I work very late quite often.'

'Oh, OK,' he said. 'Well, it was just an idea.'

He looked mildly dejected and very awkward.

'No, I didn't mean I couldn't,' she said quickly. 'I'd – well I'd like that. But I'm a bit hard to get hold of. That's all.'

'I'll try and manage it,' he said and smiled at her. 'Cheers. Thanks again.'

'Cheers, Ed. It was my pleasure.'

'And mine.'

He shut the door and loped off, pulling a Walkman out of his rucksack; she felt quite sure she would never see him again. Especially if he was going travelling.

And started thinking, as she had not allowed herself to do in church, of those first heady days, the ones when it was still all right . . .

She had decided to go down to the islands after all. After two more days, Bangkok had become claustrophobic, and everyone she met talked about the islands, the beauty of them. What was she doing, missing so important a part of the grand tour?

She travelled down to Koh Samui alone by train overnight. The train had cabins, sleeping six, with small lights; it felt rather colonial, a bit like an economy version of the Orient Express. A uniformed attendant made up the beds and urged them into bed almost as soon as the train left the station. Martha had already eaten – a smiling Thai had taken her order as the train stood at the station and cooked her a delicious meal on the platform – and she lay down obediently and fell almost at once asleep, waking at some time in the middle of the night at Surat Thani where she was transferred by bus to the ferry and a four-hour journey by sea to Koh Samui.

She had made friends on the boat with another girl called Fran who'd been told the best beach was Big Buddha and, for want of any further information, they took the taxi bus there: and felt the world had entirely changed.

Martha never forgot not just her first sight of the long tree-lined sweep of beach, but her first feel of it, the soft white sand, the warm air, incredibly sweet after the gritty stench of Bangkok, the tenderly warm, blue-green water. She and Fran found a hut, rather grandly referred to as a bungalow, for 200 baht a night and thought they would never want to leave it. It had a shower, a veranda and three beds. Time slowed; they drifted through it.

After a few days, with no sense of surprise at all, she found Clio staying a few huts along; it was easy to find people, you just asked around the beach and the bars and if they were there, you found them. Jocasta had already moved on, had gone north. 'But she said she'd be back,' said Clio vaguely. The life encouraged vagueness; it was timeless, aimless, and wonderfully irresponsible.

Where you lived was defined by the name of your beach: people didn't say, 'Where are you staying?' but, 'What beach are you on?' It was immensely beautiful; after the filth and squalor of Bangkok it did seem literally like paradise, the absolutely clear water, the palms waving above it, the endless white sand. Big Buddha sat at the end of the beach, at the top of a huge flight of ornate steps, painted a slightly tatty gold; his stern eyes followed you everywhere.

It was the rainy season, but still extremely warm; it was actually more comfortable in the softly warm sea when the rain fell. They spent a lot of time in it. And because it was the rainy season also, there were the most wonderful sunsets, orange and red and black, hugely dramatic; everyone just sat and watched them as if they were an entertainment, rather like going to the cinema. Only the sunsets were nicer, Martha said . . .

They spent a lot of time sitting on their veranda, hour after hour, talking and talking as the day turned to dusk and then to dark, not just to each other but to anyone else who happened along. The ease with which relationships were formed fascinated Martha, growing up as she had in the strict society of Binsmow. One of the things she most liked was the way everyone was accepted, just as they were, part of this one great, easy tribe. Nothing else mattered, there was no snobbery of any kind; you didn't have to have lots of money, or the right clothes. You were just a backpacker, nothing more or less than that.

On the third day she and Clio hired a motor scooter and drove inland down the bumpy rough tracks; they found some deep pools, with great waterfalls dropping down into them, and swam lazily for hours, discussing how they felt already changed, into different people; easier, more confident, happier people. Martha grew fonder and fonder of Clio; she was so sweet, so eager to please, so good-natured. And so lacking in self-confidence: it was strange, Martha thought, she was so pretty. OK, a bit overweight, but from the way she went on, you'd have thought she was a size 20. Those sisters of hers obviously had a lot to answer for.

There were downsides: Martha's stomach, always delicate,

was almost permanently painful and she suffered from diarrhoea endlessly.

And, 'My periods seem to have gone up the spout,' she said to Clio one morning. 'One started in Bangkok, then stopped after two days, and then I got one again yesterday, and now that seems to be over.' Clio, in her capacity as medical adviser, had been reassuring, said it would be the complete change of food, climate, routine. Martha had tried not to worry about it, and after a few more weeks succeeded. It was all part of this unfamiliar new person she had become, relaxed, easy, untroubled by anything very much. And very, very happy. She found herself waking up every morning, thinking, What can I do today? and knew she could do it, whatever it was.

She felt she had conquered the world.

Lucky, lucky Ed, with all that ahead of him.

Chapter 4

Dreadful sobs came from the room: dreadful sobs telling of dreadful grief. It was the third time Helen had heard them over the past few months; she waited a while hoping they would ease.

The first two had been the result of Kate's so-far fruitless search for her birth mother. She had told Helen what she intended to do the first time, and Helen had listened, her heart sinking at the inadequacy of the plans, not daring to criticise or even make suggestions. She had merely smiled at her brightly, hugged her goodbye as she set off; and waited, sick with anxiety, for her return.

It had come a very few hours later; the front door had opened, slammed shut, there were running footsteps up the stairs, her door shut – and the sobs began.

She had waited fifteen minutes, then followed her up the stairs and knocked on her door.

'Kate, love, can I come in?'

'Yes, all right.'

She was lying on her bed, swollen-eyed, resentful, angry with Helen.

'Why didn't you tell me?'

'Tell you what?'

'That no one would still be at the hospital? People who were there when I was found. Why didn't you tell me?'

'I didn't know. How could I?' Helen tried to be patient. She sat down on Kate's bed and tried to smooth her hair, but Kate shied away from her.

'Look,' said Helen, 'why don't you tell me what happened?'

She had gone to the hospital, the South Middlesex, to Outpatients (not having any idea where else you could go for help); they had looked at her, she said, as if she was mad.

'I mean, is it such a lot to ask? I only wanted to know who'd been on the baby unit in 1986. They just said had I got a letter from anyone? As if I was going in to have an operation or something. I said no, and they said they really couldn't help, I'd have to write in, so that my request could be guided through the proper channels. I mean, please! Anyway, then I followed the signs that said Maternity Unit. It was on the third floor and when I got there, there was this sort of waiting room full of these hideous pregnant women and more of these stupid women on the reception desk. They said there wouldn't be anyone still working there and I said how did they know? And they said because no one had been there more than seven years. So then I said what about the cleaners or something? And they said the cleaning was all done by outside agencies now and then it had been done by staff. So I said what was the name of the agency and they said they had no idea. I saw one of them look at the other and raise her eyebrows and I just walked out. And then just as I was walking down one of those endless corridors I saw a sign that said Administration Offices so I went in there.'

'And?'

'And there was only one nerdy man in there and he said nobody was available on Saturdays, and I said oh, really, what about him, and he said he'd just come in for half an hour. I said that didn't make any difference, I just wanted the names of some people who'd been working there fifteen years ago, and he said that was classified information and couldn't just be handed out to anyone. He said if I wrote in, they might consider my request. And that was that.'

'Well,' said Helen carefully, 'why don't you write in?'

'Mum, they're complete morons. They don't know anything. And they don't want to help.'

'Did you tell any of them why you wanted to know?'

'Of course not. I'm not going round looking like some sad thing looking for her mother. Having everyone sorry for me.'

'Kate, my love,' said Helen, 'I think you're going to have to.

Otherwise your reasons could be very dubious indeed. Just think for a minute.'

Kate stared at her; then she said: 'No, Mum, I can't. I'm not going to do that. I'll do this in my own way. I know what I'm doing.'

'Good,' said Helen.

She did nothing for several months; then she had gone to Heathrow and made for the information desk; how could she make contact with one of the cleaners?

'Do you have a name?' said the overdone blonde, pausing briefly from her interminable computer tapping.

'No.'

She sighed. 'Well then, dear, how can we help you?'

'You must have a list of people.'

'Even if we did, if you don't have a name, what good would a list do? Is this a complaint or something?'

'No,' said Kate, 'no, it's not.'

'So what is it?'

'I – I can't tell you.'

'In that case,' she said, returning to her tapping, 'I really don't think I can help. You could write in to HR if you like.'

'What's HR?'

'Human Resources. Now if you'll excuse me – there are people waiting. Yes, sir – '

And she indicated to Kate to move so that she could talk to the man behind her.

Kate felt the same despairing panic as last time. She went over to one of the cafes and bought a Coke and sat looking around her at all the cleaners and porters. Some of them were quite old. They must have been there for at least fifteen years. And they must all know each other. Bound to. She finished her Coke, and went up to a middle-aged Asian woman wiping the tables; she asked her how long she had worked there.

'Too long, my dear, much too long.' She smiled, a sweet tired smile.

'Fifteen years?'

'Oh, no.'

'Do you know anyone who has?'

'I could ask around for you, I suppose. Why do you want to know, my dear?'

'I can't tell you that. Sorry. But it's nothing – unpleasant.'

'I'll see what I can do – '

Kate sat for a long time, watching her; she asked several of her fellow workers, she saw some of them smiling, some of them raising their eyebrows like the nurses, all of them shaking their heads. Finally an officious-looking man came up to the Asian woman and asked her something; she stopped smiling and pointed in Kate's direction. He walked over to her.

'Excuse me, miss. Is there a problem?'

'No problem,' said Kate, 'I'm just looking for someone.'

'And who would that be?'

'Someone who was working here fifteen years ago.'

'And why would you want such a person?'

'I'm afraid I can't tell you.'

'In that case, I'm afraid I must ask you to stop wasting my staff's time. If you have a request, you must make it through the proper channels. Write in to the HR department. But they won't help you if you don't have a very satisfactory reason.'

She caught the tube back to Ealing and spent the afternoon in her room.

That day she wouldn't even allow Helen in.

And now, today, more sobs. Helen braced herself, knocked at the door. She couldn't leave it; and besides she thought she knew what the sobs were about. Tomorrow was Kate's birthday; how it had upset her for the past few years.

'Kate? Darling, can I help?'

'No. Thanks,' she added, after a pause.

'Not even to listen?'

'I said no.'

'Fine. Well – '

The phone rang; gratefully, Helen went to answer it.

'That was Granny,' she said, walking back into Kate's room. 'She wants to take us all out tomorrow night. To celebrate your birthday. Isn't that nice?'

'Where to? McDonald's?'

'Kate, don't be rude, dear.'

67

'Sor – ry . . .' The word was dragged out, in an exaggerated pretence at politeness.

'To Joe Allen's. In Covent Garden. She says it's great fun.'

'Joe Allen's?' She struggled to stay disinterested, gave up. 'Well done, Gran. She's so cool.'

'I'm glad you think so. Now – you sure there's nothing you want to talk about?'

'Mum! I said no!' But she smiled at Helen, gave her a quick hug. 'I'm OK. Honestly.'

Relieved, Helen went downstairs to tell Jim about Jilly's offer; he wasn't at all pleased as she had expected, said he didn't think they should go.

'We always celebrate birthdays at home. It's a family tradition. And you've already made her cake. What are you supposed to do with that?'

'Have it before we go. Or when we get back. Jim, I think it's important that we go. And it's very generous of my mother. Can I please ring her back and say yes?'

Silence. Then: 'I suppose so,' he said grudgingly.

'Good. Thank you.'

She went to phone Jilly, to say they'd all love to come. Heavens, life was difficult. And of course, the evening itself wouldn't be exactly easy, either; the tension between her mother and Jim always there. However hard they both struggled to hide it. But – for Kate it would be worth it. Like so many things . . .

Jilly had pretended right from the beginning and to absolutely everyone that she liked Jim enormously. In fact she found him boring, self-righteous and – yes, she admitted to herself – just a bit common. He even looked rather common, with his brown, rather neat hair and his slightly round face, and early middle-aged spread. The sort of person Helen would never have married, if things had been different. Different from Jilly being so cruelly widowed, when Helen was only three, and being left not only lonely but very hard up. With admirable courage and determination, she had exchanged her smart Kensington Mews house (of disappointing value, due to its short lease) for a rather modest Edwardian villa in Guildford. Taken a shorthand typing course and spent the next ten years working as a part-time secretary.

She could have married again; had had several offers. But Mike Bradford had genuinely been the love of her life, and she hated the idea of anyone becoming Helen's stepfather. Helen was her life's work; she was not having it thrown away on some mediocre man. Only – Helen had thrown herself away on precisely that. Very mediocre. It was dreadfully depressing. Of course Jim was extremely clever, you didn't get to be deputy head of a comprehensive school at the age of thirty-eight if you weren't. But even so – a teacher! For Helen! And living in a miserable little house in Ealing. And – Jim. Why Jim? Why not James, such a fine name? She had thought that, hearing it spoken for the first time at the wedding. I, James Richard, take thee, Helen Frances . . .

In fact, altogether – why Jim?

Jim because Helen loved him. Very much. She found him gentle and caring, and he gave her self-confidence, not only because he found her extremely attractive and said so ('I always dreamt of a tall girl with dark hair and blue eyes, I never thought I'd get one') but because he found her interesting and said so frequently.

Jim was a wonderful father too; so supportive over the adoption business – lots of men weren't – and terribly involved with every aspect of the girls' upbringing; being rather old-fashioned he hadn't actually felt it was his job to get up in the night or change nappies, but he discussed everything with her, giving it all the seriousness and attention to detail that he did to everything else in his life. Potty training, play-school, discipline. And he was so proud of them both: Kate as well as Juliet. Everyone wondered, Helen knew, if they felt differently about Juliet, being their own child rather than someone else's, but they both said, with absolute truth, that they didn't. They were both their children and they loved them: it was as simple as that.

By the time Kate and Juliet had arrived, Jilly was no longer a secretary; a job in the personnel department of Allders of Croydon had led to a friendship with one of the fashion buyers, who was about to open a shop of her own in Guildford; taking a tremendous chance, Caroline Norton offered her a job as deputy manageress.

'I know you don't know anything about clothes in theory,' she said, 'but anyone can see that you know all about them in practice. Please come.'

Jilly did: and Caroline B (the B was a pretty compliment to Jilly) opened in Guildford in 1984. It was a great success with the ladies of Guildford, offering real clothes for real women, as it said on the window; elegantly simple coats and dresses, stylishly soft tweed suits, and for evening, suits with wide trousers, so kindly flattering to plump, not-so-young legs. And Jilly and Caroline offered not only elegant clothes; they offered a personal service. If a dress didn't become a client, they told her so, albeit with charm and tact; if she wanted an outfit for a particular occasion, they wouldn't rest until they had found one for her. In 1990 a local tycoon had offered to back them in a franchise operation and there were now five Caroline Bs, all immensely successful, all run with the same careful philosophy of personal service. The nearest to London was in Wimbledon; as Caroline said, they would be lost in Town.

Helen knew she loved her mother, and she was very proud of her. She knew how Jilly had struggled to bring her up successfully, but ever since she had even begun to grow up Helen had known she was something of a disappointment (too quiet, too shy, not ambitious enough). And not nearly successful enough with men. In her late teenage years, she had suffered agonies of embarrassment as her mother had organised little supper parties so that she could meet the eligible sons of her friends; and had watched Jilly's irritation as she failed to attract any of them. That was why it had been so wonderful to meet Jim. Who was nothing to do with her mother, or her mother's friends, who didn't have to be charmed or flirted with, who was just – well, just right. Calm, kind, interested in her.

Helen had never even considered going back to work (she had been a secretary); one of the many things Jim and she absolutely agreed on was that mothers should be at home to look after their children, even as they grew older.

Just the same, financially life was a struggle. There was very little money for luxuries and, as the girls grew more expensive,

Kate particularly, wanting what Jim called Label Clothes, and sound systems and mobile phones, it became more of a problem. Kate had been arguing for months now to be allowed to do a Saturday job; 'Sarah works at the hairdresser, she really likes it and they pay good money, I just don't see why not.' Both Jim and Helen saw very clearly why not.

Jilly helped as much as she could, passing clothes on to Helen for nothing which she swore the shop couldn't sell and which Helen was too grateful for to argue about. There was nothing else Jim would accept – apart from the occasional treat – and there had been an appalling row when Jilly had offered to help pay for school fees.

'In the first place I wouldn't take the money, and in the second, there's no question of the girls going to private schools.'

Kate was at the local comprehensive; it was a very good school and she was extremely happy there. But there had been a considerable problem when Juliet had won a music scholarship at the local independent school. The head of her primary school had suggested she try for it and that she had a really good chance of getting in; Jim said that his principles and indeed his own situation would make her taking the place impossible. Helen, unusually firm, said it was a wonderful chance for Juliet and she wasn't having her deprived of it, 'Simply because it goes against the comprehensive ideal. Sorry, Jim, but it's either Gunnersbury High School, or me. If she gets this place she's going and that's that.'

He was shocked into agreement.

When they got to the restaurant, Jilly was already at the table, with a huge box at her side. It proved to be a beautiful soft leather biker jacket; Kate was enraptured with it and insisted on wearing it throughout the meal. 'Isn't it gorgeous?' she kept saying, stroking it and getting up to do a twirl. 'Isn't it great?' Each time followed by a hug and kiss for her grandmother, and a demand that they all agreed how cool she was. Jim was painfully furious that Jilly should have given her something so expensive; Helen knew why: it made their own gift – a new mobile – seem very puny by contrast.

The girls enjoyed the meal, rather noisily spotting celebrities

– Zoë Ball was there, and so was Geri Halliwell and a star from *EastEnders* who Helen had never heard of, and when the waiter arrived with a cake and candles, and led the singing of Happy Birthday, Kate's dark eyes filled rather unexpectedly with tears. 'This is just so cool,' she kept saying. 'So cool . . .'

Jim managed to join in the singing, but said, as soon as the cake had been cut and handed round, that it was a bit of a waste of the cake Helen had baked at home.

'Dad,' said Kate plaintively, 'don't piss on my bonfire.'

'Kate, don't talk like that,' said Helen quite sharply, and Jilly told her not to be silly, that Kate was over-excited.

'Now let's all calm down, shall we, and enjoy our cake. Juliet dear, eat up.'

'It's gorgeous,' said Juliet politely and then defusing the situation nicely, 'Hey, Kate, isn't that Dr Fox?'

'Speaking of doctors,' said Jilly, 'I – '

'Gran!' said Kate. 'Foxy's not a real doctor! He's a DJ. I thought you'd have known that.'

'Take no notice, Mummy,' said Helen. 'Go on.'

'What? Oh, yes. I have a very nice new GP. Charming girl, just arrived at the practice. I liked her enormously. So much nicer than that old bore Gunter.'

'Good,' said Helen politely. 'You're all right, are you, Mummy?'

'Of course I'm all right,' said Jilly, almost indignantly.

'Just a social call, was it?' said Jim, his voice edgy. 'As she was so charming.'

'Yes,' said Jilly firmly, 'yes, it was. Now girls, finish up your cake. I'd like a coffee. Helen, what about you?'

'Oh – no thank you. I won't be able to sleep.'

'Do you know,' said Kate half dreamily, looking across the restaurant at a waiter bearing an ice bucket, 'I've never even tasted champagne.'

'Well, you must now,' said Jilly. 'I'll order us some.'

She knew exactly what she was doing, Helen thought; Jim's last words had annoyed her and she knew she could annoy him back. She had raised her hand to call the waiter; Helen gently put it down again.

'Mummy, please don't. It's such an extravagance, and the girls have already eaten so much rich food. They'll be sick.'

'We will not,' said Kate. 'Will we, Jools?'

'No,' said Juliet slightly nervously.

'Right. Well – '

'Jilly, no,' said Jim. His voice was heavy, his dark eyes hard. 'If you don't mind.'

'Dad – '

'Oh, never mind, Kate,' said Jilly quickly. 'I tell you what, next time you come for the weekend, I'll get some in. How's that? Shall we set a date now?'

'All right,' said Kate sulkily, 'but it would be more fun now.'

Helen felt a wave of rage against her mother. Deliberately setting out to annoy Jim. And what about Juliet, when did she get her chance to have a glamorous champagne-fuelled weekend with her grandmother?

'Perhaps Juliet could come some time. For a weekend,' she said, aware even as she spoke how crass it sounded, and how embarrassed Juliet was.

'Of course!' said Jilly. 'That would be great fun. We'll arrange it very soon. Now, has everyone had enough, and shall I get the bill?'

'Quite enough, thank you,' said Jim.

Helen suddenly wanted to burst into tears.

Kate's birthday always made her emotional, just as it did Kate. She thought of Kate's mother, giving birth to her all alone, with no one to help her; she thought of the new-born Kate and the physical danger she had undoubtedly been in; and then she thought of her being abandoned, left cold and alone, in all her dreadful vulnerability, as her mother walked so determinedly away.

How could any woman do that? How? And where was she now, and on this day of all days, how much was she thinking about that tiny vulnerable baby she had so callously and ruthlessly abandoned?

A lot, Helen, hoped; and she also hoped it hurt.

Chapter 5

It hurt. It really hurt. It was like a physical pain sometimes.

And it was so unfair. That he should belittle her and what she did. He was supposed to love her, for God's sake. He was always telling her he did. And that he needed her.

Sometimes, just sometimes, she actually thought of confronting him, telling him she couldn't stand it, that this wasn't marriage as she understood it. But she lacked the courage, that was the awful truth. And besides, he was too clever for her: he always won any argument. He should have been a barrister, Clio thought savagely, pressing the buzzer for her next patient, not a surgeon, he –

'Oh, Clio. Just before I send Mrs Cudden in, Jeremy's been on the phone.'

Again? The last call had only been half an hour ago. This was just not fair.

'Jeremy! But it's only – I mean he should still be in theatre.'

'Apparently he's at home. Do you want to call him quickly?'

'Um . . .' She thought fast. If she didn't he'd be angry; if she did he'd still be angry because she couldn't talk to him properly.

'No, it's fine. Mrs Cudden's been waiting ages. If he rings again, tell him – tell him I've been called out.'

'OK.'

She loved Jeremy, of course she did, and she was happy being married to him: most of the time anyway. She also – rather perversely she knew, given her professional achievements and ambitions – enjoyed running the house. She found the mechanics of housekeeping rather soothing, a contrast to her chaotic life at the practice. She liked keeping the house clean and tidy, now that the endless building work had been finished; liked keeping the fridge and food cupboards well-stocked, adored cooking, enjoyed arranging flowers, and putting clean linen on the beds.

Her friends teased her about it, telling her she was just a little woman at heart, an anachronism in an age where women were fleeing from such tasks, and claiming them as symbols of male tyranny. Clio didn't see any of it like that. She saw it as the means to the end of a calm, pleasing environment, where she and Jeremy could recover from the stress of their difficult professional lives, and entertain their friends. And she had loved dressing the house up with curtains and carpets and lamps and pictures, and slowly filling the rooms with furniture she and Jeremy chose on long, exhaustive trips to sale rooms and antique shops.

Of course he was arrogant and demanding; he was a surgeon. Clio had spent her working life around surgeons, she knew the culture of adoration and near-reverence in which they worked, knew how they expected perfection and absolute respect in theatre and brought that attitude home with them. Jeremy did see his place at the top of the heap: at home as well as at work. She simply didn't mind. In the first place, he *was* top of the heap and, in the second, she had grown up with her fiercely supercilious father, with his huge intellect and distant manner, and it was something she simply accepted as the norm.

Her sisters, her beautiful and brilliant sisters, both now with doctorates, Artemis in classics at Oxford, Ariadne in chemistry at Cambridge, had always treated her as some kind of rather simple handmaiden, and indeed still did, on the rare occasions when they met. To be looking after someone who actually loved her and appreciated her was a genuine delight.

And she did love her job. Absolutely loved it. Yes, it was stressful, of course, giving patients enough time, fretting over the waiting lists, recognising the lifestyle problems that caused so much illness. But there was the great joy of getting to know her patients, being involved in their lives, knowing which ones to be brisk with, which to give extra time to. It was all so pleasingly different from hospital work where you saw people a very few times out of nowhere and then were parted from them, probably never to see them again. It was so good to become if not exactly a friend, then certainly an ongoing part of their lives, a comfort, a reassurance. Most of them were so brave and so grateful for whatever small thing she could do for them; Clio found the whole thing extremely rewarding.

What she had never realised before, when working in hospital clinics, was the extent to which the buck stopped with the GP. You were the end of the line, the contact with the patients. They relied on you. Especially the old people. She had one couple, the Morrises, of whom she was particularly fond; both in their late eighties, they were still managing to look after themselves at home together, an immaculately clean, ordered home. But they needed to take tablets and the dosage was quite complicated. If they didn't take their tablets, they became confused, and went on a hideously swift downward spiral – and their one daughter living forty or so miles away either couldn't or wouldn't help.

Twice now Clio had received calls from the social services who reported uneaten meals on wheels and had gone round to find old Mrs Morris in her nightdress, sitting in the garden, and her husband wandering about the house trying to find the kettle. Clio had located it in the utility room, inside the washing machine. 'Another day and God knows what would have happened to them,' she said to Mark Salter, 'but I got their medication into them, persuaded Dorothy back into the house, and called back later. They were already much more cheerful, tucking into their tea, watching *Home and Away*. Anyway, I remembered those samples of tablet dispensers a rep left and filled two of them with the right dosage for a week. I can just keep doing that.'

'You're very good, Clio,' said Mark. 'That really is over and above the call of duty.'

'Mark, think of the alternative. They'd be in a home inside a month.'

'It's ridiculous,' he said wearily. 'The carer who goes in the morning to help them get dressed could perfectly well give them the tablets, but she's not allowed to. Bloody regulations. God, when I think of the old days, when my father ran his practice!'

'I know,' said Clio soothingly. 'But things have changed.

Nothing we can do about it, Mark. And the Morrises are on my way in – it's not a problem.'

But – Jeremy was a problem. It wasn't so much that he constantly, albeit gently, belittled her work. It was that he assumed it could be pushed aside on demand. If he had an early night and she was still working, he would arrive at the surgery and send a message through that he was there and would like to take her out to dinner or the cinema, and then sit in reception, asking the receptionist loudly as each of her patients went in if that was the last one. He made an appalling fuss when she had to do her weekends on call (only one in five); and he had a genuine and complete disinterest in her patients and their problems, while expecting her to show an immense interest in his.

Things had got so bad that she had recently asked Mark Salter if she could cut her days down to four; recognising the problem, he had agreed. She was an excellent GP; the patients loved her, especially the elderly ones, and she had the rare talent of being able to give enough time to each one to make them feel cared for, without running too terribly late on her list.

'You're too valuable to lose,' he said, smiling at her. 'If you can manage to do four days, I think we can accommodate that.'

It had satisfied Jeremy for a while; and she actually enjoyed having the extra day in the house, but now his agitation – she could only call it that – was building up again.

There was another problem too, or at any rate a worry: one which only she knew about and which was increasing by the day. Or rather the month.

She was just packing up her things when Margaret the receptionist rang through again.

'Sorry, Clio, but I've got Mrs Bradford on the phone. She says she wants a quick word. Is that all right?'

'Of course.'

She rather liked the glamorous Mrs Bradford, with her sleek blonde hair and her stylish clothes; she had come in a few weeks earlier to ask her for some sleeping pills.

'Now please don't tell me I can manage with a hot drink and some gentle exercise before bed because I can't.'

'I should,' Clio said, 'and it would be better for you, but we'll take it as read, shall we?'

'Do let's,' said Jilly Bradford, smiling at her.

Clio had scribbled the prescription and then said impulsively: 'I do love your jacket.'

'Oh, how kind. Well it came from my – our shop. Do you know it? Caroline B in the High Street. The jacket's MaxMara, we carry a lot of his stuff. Although this is last season's, of course.'

'It's just that I love dogtooth,' said Clio, 'and I've been looking for something to wear to a conference in October.'

'Well, when the next collection comes in, I'll give you a call. I'll be delighted to help you pick something out. It saves so much time, I always think. Which we working women don't have.'

'That would be wonderful, thank you,' said Clio, and promptly forgot about it.

'Mrs Bradford?' she said now. 'What can I do for you?'

'I'm just calling as promised,' Jilly Bradford's rather dated upper-crust voice came down the phone, 'to tell you the new MaxMara collection has arrived. With some very nice jackets. Would you like me to put a couple by for you? I would imagine you're a ten.'

'I wish I was,' said Clio. 'I'm a good twelve.'

'Well, his sizes are on the generous side. I'm sure you'd be a ten. When would you like to come?'

'Saturday afternoon?'

'Wonderful. I shall look forward to seeing you. I won't take any more of your time now. Goodbye, Dr Scott.'

'Goodbye, Mrs Bradford. And thank you.'

Jeremy was in a foul mood when she got home: he was watching the Channel 4 news and eating bread and cheese.

'Oh darling, you shouldn't fill up on that. I've got some lovely trout for our supper.'

'I couldn't wait. I've been here for hours.'

'Why? I thought you had a full list.'

'Just try telling the hospital managers that. Them and their bloody targets. You know as well as I do what happens. Three hips this morning and then a tricky spine fusion this afternoon. Well, that wouldn't do, would it? Only four operations in one day. Do three more hips, they said, and postpone the fusion. And then there was a shortage of nurses in theatre this afternoon, so I only got one done anyway. God, this system! I'd like to get that Milburn creature by the scruff of his neck and march him round a few half-empty wards, and then sit him in Casualty for a day or two. Bloody interference. You know which department has just had its budget upped again? Day Surgery. And you know why? It provides a nice lot of ticks on the target sheet.'

'Darling,' said Clio soothingly, 'I know it's outrageous, but there's nothing we can do about it, is there? Now, why don't you come and chat to me, while I do the supper?'

'I thought we might go away this weekend,' he said, pouring her a glass of wine. 'What do you think?'

'It sounds lovely. Yes.'

'You're not on call, or anything ridiculous?'

With an effort she ignored the 'ridiculous'.

'No. No, it's fine. Jane Harding, the other junior partner, she's doing it, because next weekend – when I *am* on,' she said bravely, thinking it wise to remind him, 'her brother is coming over from the States and – '

'I thought it might be fun to go to Paris,' he said, interrupting her. 'Would you like that?'

'Oh, Jeremy, yes. Yes, I would. Lovely idea.'

'Good. I'll get a couple of cheap flights.'

Clio breathed a sigh of relief and asked him to tell her about the difficult hip operation.

She was doing her home visits when it happened. She had knocked on the door and was wondering rather irritably why a woman who was so worried about her vomiting, feverish child that she had been in tears on the phone should be so long answering her knock. She had actually seen her watching television through the window as she walked down the path. She knocked again.

The woman came to the door; she was white-faced and clearly shocked.

'Oh, Doctor. Yes. Hello. Have you heard the news?'

'What news?'

'A plane has just flown into one of the Twin Towers in New

York. Right into it. Blown up. It's so awful. It's like watching a disaster movie. Yes, please do come in, Chris is in the front room watching it with me.'

And Clio, trying to concentrate on the feverish child, while watching at the same time what was to become the most famous piece of news footage in history, shocked and terrified by what she saw, the savage explosions and great mass of dark smoke bursting into the brilliant blue New York morning, suddenly heard Jane Harding's voice talking about her brother. 'He works in the World Trade Center, very high-powered . . .'

'Oh God,' she said. 'Oh God, poor Jane.'

'Jeremy, shut up! It's only one night. I can join you on Saturday morning. I'll get a cheap flight; I hardly think they're going to be hard to come by. I can't believe we're having this conversation. Suppose it was your brother? If you have that much imagination, which it rather seems you don't.'

As always, when confronted by her rare anger, he pulled back. 'Sorry. Yes. Of course you're right. We'll both go on Saturday. I'm sorry. Of course you must do it.'

Jane Harding's brother had been killed. Or they assumed he had been killed. Later, everyone recognised that as the worst thing, not knowing. Just because he hadn't managed to phone, because they hadn't got through to him at the office on his mobile, or to his apartment, it didn't actually mean he was dead. He might be buried in the rubble. They were getting people out alive all the time. Or he might have been rescued and be in hospital somewhere, unconscious, not able to contact his family. Or horribly injured and – it went on and on.

'Mum wants to go over there,' Jane said the next day, her voice thick with tears on the phone, 'but Dad says it's too dangerous. I don't know what to do. It's so terrible for them. Well, for all of us. They were jumping out of the building, Clio, thirty, forty floors up, anything to escape. Suppose Johnny did that? Or maybe he was trying to get out, down the stairs. We keep on and on phoning his apartment, but there's no reply. And his mobile's dead. There's a help line, but – anyway, I can't leave my parents, they're just distraught. I'm sorry, Clio. Sorry about your weekend.'

'Don't be ridiculous,' said Clio, 'as if it matters in the very least.'

They had shared out the weekend between them; Mark was doing Saturday, and Graham Keir, the senior partner, Sunday.

'But we can't find anyone to do Friday,' said Mark. 'Sorry, Clio.'

'Mark, don't say sorry. Of course I'll do it. Don't even think about it. Jeremy won't mind.'

It had shocked her how much he had minded: until she tore into him.

The whole country was in shock. It was all anyone talked about. The pictures, the famous pictures, of the Towers being hit, exploding, collapsing; the people phoning their loved ones from the Towers to say goodbye, people standing for days at the site, waiting, praying for news, for the recovery of more bodies. There was terror in those first days; everyone afraid, asking where next? Flights were cancelled by the thousand; Clio was grateful that Jeremy wanted to postpone their trip, and told Mark she would do Saturday as well.

'Jeremy's doing some private patients on Saturday now. I might as well.'

There were very few people in surgery, few call-outs. It was as if people didn't like to complain about trifling illnesses, when there was so much grief in the world.

Jeremy called to say he wouldn't be back until teatime: at midday Clio found herself with nothing to do. Nothing to do and no husband. It was a dizzy prospect; she had already shopped, cooked ahead for a lunch party on Sunday, and done the flowers; she would take some time for herself and have a look round the Guildford shops. And then she remembered Jilly Bradford's phone call.

Now that would be fun.

She arrived at the shop about two; it was very quiet, like the rest of the town. Nobody was in shopping mood; Clio felt suddenly guilty.

Jilly smiled at her and said how delighted she was to see her. 'Such a dreadful business, this. I nearly didn't open today, and then I thought that was letting them win. The terrorists, I mean.

Now, I've got your jackets here, and some tops I thought you might like. Shall I put you in one of the changing rooms and you can play around? And would you like a coffee?'

'That would be lovely, yes. Thank you.'

What a charming woman she was; no wonder the shop did so well. And such an advertisement for her own good taste; dressed today in a simple black shift, with black tights and black low-heeled pumps; and she was so slim. Clio promptly felt plump and messy.

The jackets were both extremely nice; after a very brief struggle, she said she would take them both. 'And that black top is lovely too, the plain one.'

'Right. Well, look, I've got your number, and in future I'll call you whenever I get anything in I think would be you. If that's all right, of course.'

'Yes, fine,' said Clio. 'I usually never think about clothes until I need them.'

And then glancing at herself in the mirror, back in her own things, sensible tweed skirt, striped shirt and sleeveless puffa jacket, thought that it showed.

'Well, that's what we're here for,' said Jilly, smiling at her, 'to think of them for you. We are much more than just a shop, you know.'

'Yes, I can see that. Here's my card and – '

The door burst open and a girl burst in: a rather beautiful young girl, with a mass of wild fair hair, large dark eyes and extraordinarily long legs in what were clearly carefully torn and faded jeans.

'Hi, Granny. Sorry I'm early. I couldn't stand Dad going on about terrorists any longer. He seems to think some are about to strike our street. Oh, sorry!' she said, seeing Clio standing by the till.

'It's all right, darling. I'm not terribly busy. Dr Scott, this is my granddaughter, Kate Tarrant. Kate, this is Dr Scott.'

'Hi!' said the girl. She looked at Clio, smiled briefly, then disappeared into the back of the shop.

'Kate comes to spend the weekend with me sometimes,' said Jilly, giving Clio her credit card back. 'We get on rather well.'

'I can see that. Does she live in Guildford?'

'No, my daughter and her husband live in Ealing.'

Something struck Clio as awkward, just slightly awry, about that statement; she couldn't think what it was.

'Well, thank you again,' she said, 'and I hope I won't see you in the surgery. If you see what I mean.'

'Of course. I don't think you will – I'm a tough old bird.'

'Gran . . .' The girl had appeared again; she flashed another brief, brilliant smile at Clio. 'I think I'll go and get some sandwiches. I'm starving. And you haven't got any Coke in the fridge.'

'Sorry, darling. Yes, you go and get me some as well. Sandwiches, not Coke. Here's some money.'

'Thanks.' She was gone.

'What a pretty girl,' said Clio. 'She looks like you.'

'How charming of you to say so,' said Jilly. 'But as a matter of fact – '

The door pinged: another customer. Clio smiled and picked up her bags.

'I'll leave you in peace – thank you again.'

Outside in the street she stood for a moment, looking up and down the street for the girl. There had been something about her. Something slightly – well, slightly familiar. She couldn't imagine what.

People often asked Martha if there had been one single thing that had done it; persuaded her to change her entire life, risk everything she had worked so hard for, and yes, she would say, there had; it had been walking into the mixed-sex ward of St Philip's Hospital where Lina lay, dying quietly and uncomplainingly of inoperable cancer of the liver, deeply distressed because she had wet her bed (having requested a bedpan literally hours earlier) and slowly just fading away, against a background of what could only be described as squalor.

Martha had done her best, of course; she had found a nurse and demanded that the bed be changed, and when the nurse had said she had no time, had walked into the small room marked 'supplies' and found some clean sheets, helped Lina into a chair and started changing the bed herself. A nurse told her she couldn't do that and Martha had said she *was* doing it, clearly nobody else was going to, and that was all there was to it; Staff Nurse had then been summoned and she said what did Martha think she was doing? Martha told her and added, perfectly politely, that she would have thought they would be grateful for some help; adding (with truth) that she was prepared to clean the lavatory as well, that it was truly disgusting and must be spreading infection.

At which point the woman had sighed and said she knew that, and that she had been trying to find the time all day to do it.

'Surely,' Martha said, 'surely the cleaners should be doing it, not you?'

'Oh they're not allowed by their union to touch soiled dressings or human waste. There are special people to do that, but they haven't come today yet. I – ' Then someone called from across the ward to say that a patient's drip had come out, and the nurse had to leave; Martha sat stroking Lina's hand gently and looking over it at the old man sitting on the next bed, his penis hanging out of his pyjamas, while a young couple, presumably relatives of some kind, sat in chairs on either side of it, eating burgers and arguing about what film they were going to see when they left. The picture had stayed with Martha; nothing could erase it.

She was only thankful that her own mother's surgery (a fusion in her lumbar spine) had already been accomplished privately. But that didn't help Lina – or all the other Linas.

That had been June; in August, Lina's friend told her, mopping her streaming eyes, wiping them on the duster she was using on Martha's desk, that Lina had died.

'They said it was the cancer, Miss Hartley,' she said, 'but I think it was that her heart just broke. She felt her family had been failed, and she couldn't bear it.'

And Martha, crying too, remembering Lina's sweet, gentle face, her heroic struggle to care for her family, wondered if there was anything, anything at all, she could do to make things better, not for Lina, it was too late for that now, but for all the other people who were being failed by a country that seemed to have entirely lost its way.

She was upset all day, performing badly in meetings; later

that afternoon, when her friend Richard Ashcombe called her to cancel a visit to the cinema, even that seemed a major blow. 'I'm sorry, Martha; I'd completely forgotten I'm supposed to be having supper with my cousin. I can't let him down.'

'Of course you can't.'

Absurdly, she could hear her own voice shaky, tearful once again at this latest blow.

'Martha, are you all right?'

'Yes. Yes, of course, I'm fine. Honestly. Bit of a bad day, that's all.'

'I'm sorry. But I really do have to go. Of course – ' he said slowly and she could hear him thinking. 'Of course you could come too, if you liked. We don't have all that much in common. In fact conversation's sometimes quite sticky. I know he'd like you and he's a politician, so you can share all your thoughts with him.'

'What thoughts?'

'Oh you know, country going to the dogs, everybody being let down.'

'Do I go on about it that much?'

'Well – quite a lot. But he won't have heard it, will he? And I can just get drunk and not listen. Go on, Martha, you'd be doing me a favour.'

'We-ell.' It was an intriguing thought. 'It might be fun. If you really don't think he'd mind?'

'Of course he wouldn't mind. He'd love it. I'm meeting him at the House of Commons. We're having a drink there. You'd like that, wouldn't you?'

'I'd love it. If you really think he won't mind. Thank you, Richard. But call him first and ask him, won't you? What's your cousin's name?'

'Marcus Denning.'

'What – the Arts Minister?' said Martha.

'Well – shadow *junior* Arts Minister . . . I'll call you when I'm leaving.'

'Thanks, Richard.'

She was very familiar with Denning's name; she loved opera, and was a Friend of both the Royal Opera House and the ENO. Denning had attended several galas in his official capacity and was famous for having a genuine desire to popularise opera. It would be interesting to meet him.

They were late arriving at the House of Commons; the traffic was so bad they paid the taxi off and walked the last quarter mile; as they put their coats and briefcases on the security conveyor belt she spotted Denning, clearly impatient, looking at his watch. Martha stepped through the security arch and the alarm promptly went off (as always); she subjected herself to a search (as always her jewellery was to blame), and then, extremely embarrassed, reached Denning before Richard, who had been asked to unpack the entire contents of his briefcase.

'I'm so sorry to do this to you,' she said, 'first crashing your evening and then being late. Richard did warn you, didn't he?' she added, seeing his slightly bewildered expression. 'That he was going to bring me along?'

'He didn't, no. But what a pleasant surprise.' He held out his hand. 'And you are?'

'Martha Hartley. Richard and I work together.'

'Ah. Another lawyer?'

'Yes, there are a lot of us, I'm afraid.'

'Well, I'm sure we need you.' He looked younger close up; she would have put him at only mid-forties, less daunting when unsurrounded by the dignitaries of the Opera House, and dressed in a shabby suit rather than a dinner jacket. 'Ah, Richard, good to see you. They're not carting you off to the Tower then? No lethal weapons in your briefcase?'

He grinned at Richard and Martha liked him.

'Not this time. Sorry to keep you waiting.'

'That's perfectly all right. Shall we go through? I thought we'd go to the Pugin Room. The Strangers' Bar is packed. Lot of excitement over the Lords Reform.'

'I've never really been here before,' said Martha, 'only very briefly anyway. I was rushed in and out in about five minutes.'

'Oh really? Well, we can do a little tour if it would amuse you.'

'Oh, please, no,' said Richard, 'not the tour. I'm starving.'

'Well, just a mini one. You know what this is – ' he waved his arm above his head, 'Central Lobby. Chamber's through there. Lovely, isn't it, this place?'

'It's glorious,' said Martha, gazing up at the great domed roof, the stained-glass windows, the huge heraldic beasts carved in stone high above her head, aware of the rich, echoing quality of the sound. You could hear history in that sound, she thought.

They set off on their tour; expecting solemnity, Martha was charmed by its acutely sociable nature.

'Now down there,' Marcus said, steering her out of the lobby, ' – oh, hello, Hugh. Nice to see you.'

'Marcus! What did you think of all that?'

'Not a lot, if you want to know. Did you speak to Duggie afterwards?'

'Yes. I'm off up there in a minute. You?'

'No. Taking this charming lady to dinner and this is my cousin, who's playing gooseberry. Come along, Martha,' he said, steering her to the right. 'Now, before we leave, one of the Pugin tiles on the floor is the wrong way round, can you spot it? Evening, Henry. You off? Wise man . . . Just come and look at these busts, Martha, they might amuse you; see that one of Alec Douglas Home? They say he lost the '64 election because he wore half-moon glasses – as you see he doesn't have them on there. Right, we're back in the Commons here. You can tell when you've changed, because of the carpets: Lords red, Commons green. The Lords have a more classy sound to summon them to Divisions as well, we have a bell, and they have a tinkle. Now look, Martha, that's the library. A lot of people have died having sex there.'

'Really?' she said laughing.

'Well – so it's said. And you're not allowed to die anywhere here, as you probably know. They get you off the premises somehow. Now, in here, this is the Pugin Room. He's blamed for most of the decor and all that fancy wallpaper.'

They turned left, walked into a room that was so dazzling, she literally blinked. With its glorious view of the river, the walls and ceiling covered in gilt Pugin wallpaper, and a vast chandelier hovering over the centre, it was rather like the reception area of an exceptionally grand hotel, chairs and sofas arranged in groups, and what looked like elderly retainers carrying drinks on silver trays. Marcus steered them towards a table; someone stood up.

'Marcus, hello. What did you think about all that?'

'Absolute drivel. Are we really expected to appreciate it?'

'I think we are. Can I get you a drink?'

'No, no, we're not staying long. I'm buying these young people dinner.' He sat down, waved across the room at someone else. 'Evening! Nice to see you.'

'This is like going for a walk in my parents' village,' said Martha laughing.

'Oh this whole place is a village. Something like two thousand people work here. It has everything, a florist, post boxes, a ladies' hairdresser. And you can get a drink here twenty-four hours a day, if you know where to look. That's not too much like a village, I suppose. Or maybe it is. And it runs on gossip. What would you like?'

'White wine spritzer, please.' She felt oddly at home and smiled. 'I like it here. I really do!'

They ate at Patrick's, a below-ground restaurant just along the Embankment, actually called Pomegranates. 'We all like it here,' said Marcus, as they settled at their table. 'It's fairly near the House and its other main benefit to political life is that it's just next to Dolphin Square. An awful lot of MPs live there. Used to be that mistresses were kept there – but we all have to be squeaky clean these days.'

'Hardly squeaky,' said Richard. 'A few words like Hinduja and Ecclestone come to mind.'

'Oh, I know, I know. Different sorts of scandals, that's all. A lot less attractive, I have to say. Anyway, it's a pretty depressing business to be in at the moment. Turnout at the last election was the lowest yet. I read the other day that politicians come even lower in the public estimation than journalists. Now that *is* an indictment.'

'But you can't be surprised,' said Martha. 'Everyone feels let down, disillusioned. It's not just your party, of course, it's all of them. And at the moment there's no opposition to speak of. So of course people won't vote. Why should they?'

'What a clever girl you are. You're right. And brilliant political talents are being dreadfully wasted. It really interests you, does it?'

'Oh, yes.'

'Well, you should do something – hello, Janet. Good to see

88

you. Can I introduce my cousin Richard Ashcombe, and his friend, Martha Hartley?'

Martha looked up at Janet Frean and as always when confronted by an absolutely familiar face belonging to a complete stranger felt as if she must know her. It was a nice face, not beautiful by any means, but attractive, with strong features; her hair, which was auburn, was carved into a bob. She was tall and very thin, with good legs and beautiful, slender hands; she smiled at Martha.

'Martha has some very interesting views,' said Marcus, 'you should hear them.'

'I'd love to, but I can't at the moment. I'm waiting for – ah, here he is. Evening, Nick. You know Marcus Denning, of course.'

'Sure. Evening, Marcus.' An extremely tall, rather untidy-looking young man paused by their table, smiled rather vaguely at Martha and Richard, then said: 'Janet, I hate to sound rude, but I've only got half an hour. Then I must be back in the House. Mr Mandelson is giving me a fragment of his precious time. Is Chad here?'

'No, but he will be in five minutes. He just called me. Will you excuse us?' she said to Marcus. 'And I'd love to hear your views some time, Miss Hartley. I really would.'

Martha smiled at her, embarrassed.

'You really don't have to be polite. I'm sure my views are absolutely bog-standard.'

'I doubt it,' Janet Frean said, smiling at her. 'You don't look as if anything about you is bog-standard. What do you do? You're not in this game, are you?'

'No, she's a lawyer,' said Marcus, 'partner at Sayers Wesley. Very high-powered. Anyway, enjoy your meal.'

'Thanks. Oh, here's Chad now. Nick, come on, let's go to our table.'

'I met him once,' said Martha, staring at Chad Lawrence. 'I'm sure he wouldn't remember me, though.'

'I'm quite sure he would. Want to go over? I'll re-introduce you.'

'No, no,' said Martha, 'he looks awfully busy. And who was the Nick person?'

'Nick Marshall. Very, very brilliant young man. Political editor of the *Sketch*. I don't suppose you ever read it.'

'Not often, no. I always read the *Sun* and the *Mail* and that has to do for the tabloids.'

'Well, you should take a look at it – it's very good. Now, are we ready to order?'

Next morning, Martha bought the *Sketch* on her way to work. Marcus was right; it was extremely good. Less predictable than the *Mail*, more serious than the *Sun*, but still lively and intelligent. There was an article by Nicholas Marshall, which she read with huge interest.

Headed 'Is the Party Over?' – she liked that – it was a sober assessment of the Tories and where they were in the polls.

'Despite the fact that there is much that is rotten in the state of Millbank, the Tories seem incapable of making any capital out of it. Is it really possible that, within the confines of the party, there is no one able to fight for it? One of the biggest of the Tory big beasts, now in the Lords, told me last night that if only Janet Frean (sacked from the shadow cabinet eight months ago for her over-vigorous pro-European stance) or Chad Lawrence (similarly treated as a result of his refusal to toe the party line on asylum seekers) were brought back into the front line, the opposition could rediscover some of its muscle. Which has gone very flabby.

'Wanted: a Rambo (or Rambette) for the Tory party. Before it dies on its feet.'

Martha didn't know quite enough about the political press to recognise the article for what it was: not just a piece of political comment, but part of a painstakingly planned piece of propaganda for Lawrence and Frean and whatever it was they might be trying to do, but she did feel a rush of excitement at having met what were clearly key people in an unfolding drama. An excitement which, she realised, the law had failed to deliver to her for some time now.

Just the same, if anyone had told her that less than a year later she would be the prospective parliamentary candidate for Binsmow, she would have assumed they were stark raving mad.

Chapter 6

'What a pair of tossers,' said Kate, peering over her father's shoulder at the newspaper. 'Who are they?'

'Kate, that's not a nice word.'

'Sorry, Dad. Who are they?'

'That one is Kenneth Clarke. And that one is Iain Duncan Smith.'

'So. Who are they?'

'Oh dear. Don't they teach you anything at that school of yours? Iain Duncan Smith has just become leader of the Tory party.'

'Why should they teach us that at school?' she said, genuinely puzzled. 'What have they got to do with us?'

'Well, quite a lot in theory,' said Jim, 'although it's really rather unlikely. I hope so, anyway.'

'Me too. I don't want anything to do with people who look like that. Why've they got those flowers round their necks, anyway?'

'Well, that was taken a few weeks ago, at some Asian gathering. I suppose they felt they would appeal to the community there.'

'Yeah, right. Is it all right for me to go to London on Saturday?'

'It depends where you're going.'

'Oh . . .' Kate's voice was vague. 'You know. Around. Covent Garden, that sort of thing. I'll be back before dark. Don't worry. And I won't talk to any strange drug peddlers. Or join up with any terrorists.'

'Who are you going with?'

'God! What is this? I'm only going shopping. I'm going with Sarah and Bernie and a few others. Look. I'm *fifteen*. I had no idea we were still living in the dark ages . . .'

91

'Kate – '

'I'm going anyway. And now I'm going to school. Is that all right? Or do you want to escort me there? Put me on reins or something?'

'Kate,' said Helen, 'you haven't had any breakfast – '

'I don't want any breakfast. I feel sick. See you. Juliet, you ready? Or are you having a second bowl of fibre, like the good little girl you are?'

'No, I'm ready,' said Juliet, pushing back her chair, following Kate out into the hall. She had actually wanted a piece of toast, but she didn't want to be left alone with her parents after Kate had gone. Kate would accuse her of taking their side against her.

They walked down the street together, Juliet frantically checking what was in her satchel as they went.

'God, they are just so ridiculous,' said Kate. 'I mean, I don't know anyone who has to ask permission to go out shopping. Do you?'

'Well – no,' said Juliet, 'but it's not just shopping, is it? Not to Dad.'

'What does that mean? You think I'm going to meet up with some boys and start smoking spliffs or something?'

'Of course not. Don't be stupid. I suppose he thinks you're going to hang around the streets as he puts it, and meet people he doesn't know – '

'Thank God!'

'And – well, get in with a bad lot. Oh, Kate, don't look at me like that, I'm only telling you what he thinks. I think it's stupid too, of course I do.'

Kate sighed. Then she said, 'It's all because of my mother, I suppose. He's afraid I'm going to turn out really badly like her. Get pregnant, end up on the streets.'

'I – I suppose that might have something to do with it,' said Juliet reluctantly, and then: 'It really is stupid, because he doesn't know she ended up on the streets. She might be some terribly successful person by now. He just doesn't know.'

'Nor do I. None of us do.' Kate's voice was heavy suddenly. 'God, I wish I did. I wish I knew something about her. Just something. What she looked like – '

'Well, you do know that,' said Juliet, struggling to ease her mood. 'A bit. I mean, she's probably tall and slim and blonde, with curly hair like yours – '

'Not necessarily. Your hair isn't like Mum's, you've got brown hair.'

'Mouse, you mean,' said Juliet.

'Well, it was you who said it. You're not a bit like her altogether, much more like Dad; you've got brown eyes and his sort of pale skin. I might be the same, I might be like my dad; my mother might be a tiny round little person, with grey hair in a bun.'

She was silent for a moment, then: 'It's about the worst thing, you know. Not having the faintest idea what's she's like. I mean, sometimes I look at people on the bus, for instance, and I think that woman sits like I do, with her legs crossed quite high up, maybe she's my mum. I have absolutely no idea and no way of finding out. It's like being – oh, I don't know. Like I just didn't come from anywhere. Like I just fell to earth and Mum and Dad picked me up.'

'Like Superman,' said Juliet and giggled. 'Sorry, Kate. I don't think it's funny. I think it's horrid for you. I don't know what I'd do. Are you still looking for her?'

'Of course. But I'm just giving it a rest for a while.'

Her voice was suspiciously vague; Juliet knew that tone. It meant Kate was doing anything but giving it a rest.

'Well,' she said, 'if you want me to help in any way . . .'

'Thanks,' said Kate, 'but no thanks. Look, there are your poncey friends. I'm off. See you tonight, Jools.'

It had been Sarah who had had the idea. She'd really thought about the problem, and come up with something sensible. That was the whole thing about Sarah, Kate thought. She was a real friend, always there for you, not the slag some people thought. She was clever, too. If Sarah had a dad, and her mum was a bit more – well, supportive, and she hadn't got four younger brothers and sisters and the TV wasn't on all the time from breakfast, she'd do well at school. But she only wanted to leave and start working full-time at the hairdresser where she was a Saturday girl. 'Make some money, so I can get away from them all. Find some rich bloke and have a good time. That's what I want.'

Anyway, it had been Sarah's idea to advertise in the paper.

'They all have these – what do you call them, yeah, personal ads. Why don't you try that?'

'What would I say?' Kate's voice was doubtful.

'Something like "If you abandoned a baby at Heathrow airport in August 1986 get in touch with me, your daughter."'

'What? And give my mobile number?'

'No! They have these box numbers; people write in. You might get some nuts calling up otherwise. You have to be careful, Kate. Lot of funny people out there.'

She'd composed her ad very carefully; 'Please help,' it said. 'I'm looking for my mother. She left me at Heathrow airport in August 1986, and I really want to find her.'

The next decision was which paper. Her mother might live anywhere from Land's End to John O'Groats, so it would have to be one of the nationals. Her parents took the *Guardian*, and might see it; none of the papers she liked seemed to have such columns. So it was *The Times* or the *Telegraph*. She had bought a copy of each and studied them; she couldn't imagine that anyone who had been her mother and done what she had would read papers like them, but – of course she didn't know that.

Her mother might be young; well, not so young now, about thirty-something, or she might be much older. She might be married and she might not, she might be married to Kate's father and she might be married to someone else; she might have other children. That hurt more than anything, the thought that other children were with her mother, being loved and looked after by her and going shopping with her and being cooked nice food by her, knowing she was their mother, knowing where they belonged, but having no idea at all that they had a sister who could claim a place in their family, who had every right to it, more than them, actually, since she had been there first.

She had never forgotten the moment when she had first seen her birth certificate. She was ten, just beginning to find that it all really mattered, and she had stood there, staring at it, reading the words 'Mother: unknown, Father: unknown', feeling more alone than she could ever imagine, alone and absolutely up-rooted, torn out of the ground, somehow, and flung down like a weed. Even in the morning she had woken up with a pain in her heart that she could actually feel, physically. And all she had wanted, ever since, was just to know. Know who her mother was, and why she had done what she had.

Sarah's idea hadn't worked. She had called *The Times* and given them the wording – it had been so hard that, hearing her voice saying: 'Please help, I'm looking for my mother', but it seemed to be going all right, and then the woman had said did she know their terms? Eleven pounds a line, plus VAT. Which came to nearly sixty pounds. Sixty! It might as well be six hundred.

Shaking, Kate rang off. Sixty quid! How was she going to get that? If only she had a Saturday job, like Sarah. Then she could earn it. She felt her eyes suddenly blurring. Whichever way she went, her path was blocked. There seemed some conspiracy to keep her from ever finding her mother.

They were sitting in a history lesson, when Sarah suddenly turned round, her face radiant.

'Kate!' she hissed.

'What?'

'What about the web?'

'The what?'

'You know, the web. The Internet. Thought of looking there?'

'Sarah!' Mrs Robson's steely voice rapped out. 'Would you please stop having your private conversation with Kate. Unless it's relevant to the First World War, of course, in which case, please share it with the class.'

'Yeah,' said Sarah, her face assuming its well-known expression of wall-eyed insolence. 'Yeah, it is, miss.'

'Very well.'

'What were the blokes like in the army then? I mean, were they fit or what?'

The class collapsed in giggles; Mrs Robson gave Sarah a look of intense dislike.

'I don't think this is a subject for mirth, Sarah. The blokes in the army, as you call them, the soldiers, average age twenty –'

'Whoah!' said Sarah loudly. 'Cool!' More giggles.

'Average age twenty-one, many of them under-age even,

knowing that being sent out to the front was the equivalent of a death sentence. And it was, for a million of them. A million young men, that is. I doubt if they considered being fit as you call it, as a very high priority. Now, if you would be kind enough to keep your pathetic comments to yourself, the rest of the class can gave its attention to more important matters in hand.'

The class was rather surprisingly silenced by this; and Kate digested what Sarah had said.

It was actually a good idea. She would go to the library – again – after school and see what the web had to offer.

She typed in Missing Persons and waited; a long, long list of organisations came up on the screen. 'People Found', 'Missing Persons throughout the world', 'Find Anyone'.

Sarah was a genius. Why hadn't she thought of this before? She went for 'Find Anyone'.

'Lost persons for $7.95 instantly', it said.

Her heart started to thud. $7.95 for your mother. Not bad.

Half an hour later, she left the library, filled with rage. At herself, this time. She'd been really, really dumb, of course: again. Whatever had made her think she was going to find anything this way? It was the old problem: she didn't know enough even to start. Every site said things like, 'All you need is a first and last name', or, 'If you only have a name to go on, click here for more options'. One organisation told her that if she searched by name only, she would get too many matches. Too many! How about one?

'Good luck,' it said, 'and enjoy your reunion with that special someone.'

If only. She went home, angrier than ever.

After a while, she stopped being angry and felt the old misery and loneliness descend on her instead. It was all very well, her parents telling her how much they loved her, and Juliet saying she did, too; the fact remained that her mother, the person who had given birth to her, had thrown her aside, as casually as if she was a skirt she didn't like, just walked away from her and never came back. Not even to check she was all right.

Of course she did at least know she'd been found; she would have read the papers. And maybe that was enough for her. She didn't want to know if her daughter was well, or happy, or who was looking after her, or what she was like as she began to get a bit older. She had just – wiped her out. The more Kate thought about it, the worse she felt: that the person who should love her most in the world, who should care about her the most, had absolutely no interest in her at all. It was a horrible, hideous thought. It made her feel worthless. If your own mother couldn't be bothered with you, for God's sake, why should anyone else?

Of course, her mother might be going round too, looking at girls of about fifteen or sixteen wondering if they were her daughter. The baby she had tried to throw away. She wouldn't know where to start, either. Only at least she could try the adoption agencies; she could try the missing persons lines and website herself. It wouldn't be nearly so difficult for her, they wouldn't keep telling her she wasn't legally of an age to make such enquiries, or demanding impossible sums of money to advertise for her in the paper. She could do it easily if she wanted to.

The simple fact was that she didn't. She just didn't want to know. Bitch! Horrible, hideous, selfish cow. One thing Kate was quite certain of. If she did ever find her mother now, she would hate her. Absolutely hate her. And make very sure she knew it, too.

Chapter 7

Just as (or so some say) the real action in the House of Commons is not found in the debating chamber but in the committee rooms, corridors and tea rooms, the real business at the party political conferences is conducted not in the conference hall and on the platform but in the bars or at the myriad fringe meetings that take place all day. Rather thinly disguised as discussion groups, sponsored by high-profile but not disinterested associations, the movers and shakers of the parties and those keen to lobby them move from hotel to hotel, hall to hall, from breakfast time until quite late at night, airing and sharing their views with both the press and any interested members of the constituency parties.

Thus a large supermarket chain will sponsor a meeting on community needs and corporate social values, while fairly unsubtly promoting its own case for expansion, or a pharmaceutical chain will field a speaker to debate the state of the NHS, while arguing that there should be an easing of restrictions on sponsored medical research. To the rage of the party organisers, the fringe meetings often attract many more column inches in the press than the dull speeches from the podium.

There is also a lot of sex; the adrenalin-charged atmosphere, the power and intrigue on display and the heady freedom from day to day restraints is, as Nick Marshall once wrote, more powerful than an ocean full of oysters. Many a worthy afternoon speech is missed for a little apolitical activity in a hotel room. Indeed, it is said that if you can remember too much about any party conference, you have missed the best of it.

That autumn at the Tory party conference in Bournemouth, where Iain Duncan Smith made his first lacklustre speech, and a poll by YouGov showed that only 3 per cent of the electorate had recognised many of the party's so-called new stars, a very large and glitzy fringe meeting had been held. On the penultimate evening, funded by Gideon Keeble, the billionaire retailer, it had addressed the question of the nanny state and its sinister and growing power over the family. Speakers had included the charismatic and much televised Lord Collins, professor in child psychiatry at Cambridge, TV agony aunt Victoria Raynsford – and Janet Frean, who, as well as being a prominent Tory MP, had the relevant distinction of having five children. Chad Lawrence had also attended and spoken passionately at the debate that followed. The meeting had been packed with the party faithful and it had scooped up most of the next day's best headlines. IDS was said to be furious.

'And people have been congratulating Janet ever since,' Nick had said to Jocasta over breakfast. 'It would appear she has Keeble on side. Very influential man, is our Gideon. Influential and rich. Exactly what's needed.'

'For the new party?'

'Indeed.'

There had been another important fringe meeting earlier in the week, sponsored by the AngloWelsh bank, on the economic divide in the country. Jack Kirkland, shadow Treasury spokesman, spoke passionately of his own desperately poor background, his heroic 'blood and guts struggle', not just to escape from it, 'but to soar above it', and of the need for what he called a 'heartfelt investment in the people – not just another injection of cash but the careful, cohesive distribution of it'. It was an attack on the government, of course, but on the Tories as well, and on their hopelessly uninspired economic policy.

He earned a great many column inches for that: rightly so, Nick said.

'He is a truly brilliant speaker; takes hold of people's hearts. Strangely, though, he comes across as very unemotional when you meet him. Anyway, that speech will be remembered, and for a long time. He'll make a marvellous spokesman for the new party.'

'It's going to happen, is it?'

'Think so. It's all looking very exciting.'

Jocasta, who was nursing an appalling hangover, found it hard to care.

Nick grinned at her. 'You do look – tired. Now look, I've got to go. What are you going to do?'

'I'm going back to bed.' She kissed Nick rather feebly goodbye and sat sipping coffee and flicking through the pile of newspapers he had left behind. She felt terribly sick; maybe she should get back upstairs.

As she got into the lift, a girl stepped out; she was wearing an almost non-existent dress, some very smudged make-up, and her conference pass round her neck. She had obviously had a very good night.

Jocasta was very glad she'd come. Dreadful as it had been seeing Duncan Smith at his first conference, it had been quite an experience. She had been amazed by his lack of ideas, of charisma, by his amateurish performance – conferences were above all performances – even by the layers of thick make-up on his bald pate. (Matthew Parris had said in *The Times* that he and Hague had looked like two contestants in a Cow and Gate baby competition.) Was this really the very best the Tories could do? It was pathetic. The man in front of her had actually gone to sleep.

She found Nick at lunchtime at a café near the press office; it had been, he said, a morning of dazzling dullness.

'You should have stayed with me,' she said, picking at a rather tired salad sandwich.

'If only I could have done. I must say, my mind strayed towards you repeatedly while they all wittered on. Now look, I've just got to file one last piece and I'll come and find you when I'm done.'

'What? Nick, I've been waiting for you all day!'

'Look, sweetie, I told you not to stay today. I told you it would be boring. You enjoyed the party last night. Until you flaked out on the floor, that is.'

'I did not flake out on the floor! I tripped on my new heels. Can't I come to the press room with you?'

'You can, but you won't find anyone to talk to. Everyone's

either doing their wrap-up jobs, or watching the final session and singing "Land of Hope and Glory".'

Jocasta shuddered.

'I'll come.'

She followed him into the press room, with its rows of desks equipped not only with computers and phones, but TV screens giving constant access to what was going on in the conference hall. She fetched a carton of coffee. God, it was disgusting; it tasted as if they had used the same grains over and over again since Sunday. Nick was already gazing intently at the screen, absolutely lost to her. Jocasta sighed. He was treating her like the little woman, told not to bother her pretty head with difficult stuff like politics. When by his own admission she'd given him at least two ideas for pieces this week. She decided to go for a walk.

She wandered round the near-desolate area leading into the main conference hall, where the stands were already being demolished. She had been amazed by those stands the first time she had gone to a party conference – it was a bit like going to the Ideal Home Exhibition, she had said to Nick, people like the NSPCC and the Countryside Alliance and Scope and BUPA and of course the various newspapers and bookstalls and Internet services: most of them were there to sponsor fringe meetings, some just to gain credence by their presence, or (in the case of the Countryside Alliance) to pick up some important new members. Everyone looked tired.

God, she felt terrible; the *Sketch* had given a party the night before and she'd got incredibly drunk and ended up dancing simultaneously with a reporter from the *Sun*, a cameraman from Channel 4 and someone from the *Today* programme. She'd hoped Nick might see her and be jealous, but every time she looked for him he was huddled with a lot of dreary-looking men. Well, they looked dreary from where she was; when she'd finally fallen – or rather tripped – over, one of them had come over with Nick to help her up and sit her down at the table. He had been, she seemed to remember, quite tasty, in a middle-aged sort of way; he asked her if she was all right and then smiled at her and moved away to another group. God, how embarrassing. She really must stop drinking so much. She –

'Feeling better today?'

The voice – and the smile – swam rather hazily into her consciousness. It was Chad Lawrence. Who'd made a rather good speech, just before Duncan Smith. Why on earth hadn't they elected him as leader? At least he was photogenic.

'Yes. Yes, thank you. I'm fine,' she said briskly.

'Good. That was a nasty purler you took. I was afraid you might be a bit bruised this morning.'

She looked at him helplessly. 'Was it you who – who helped me up?'

'No, that was Gideon Keeble.'

'What, as in Gideon Keeble, the Billionaire Retailing Tycoon?'

'Absolutely.'

'Oh dear.'

'You thanked him very charmingly. And kissed him tenderly as well.'

'God!' This was getting worse. 'It was just – just my heels, they were so high.'

'Of course. Very pretty though. The shoes, I mean. Did you enjoy the party? Otherwise, I mean?'

'Yes, I did. Did you?'

'Oh – yes. I suppose so. Been to a few too many this week. I'll be glad to get home.'

'Me too. Not my favourite place in the world, this. Although . . .' Her voice tailed off.

Across the lobby was the horribly familiar figure of Gideon Keeble followed by a hotel lackey pushing a luggage trolley: at least four suitcases, a Gladstone bag, a flight bag and a suit carrier, all (apart from the Gladstone which was old and leathery) predictably Louis Vuitton. How absurd! Did anyone need that much luggage for four days?

She was about to make a run for it, to say she had to go to the loo, when Chad hailed him.

'Gideon, hello! You off? I was hoping I'd catch you. You'll remember our young friend of last night. She was just telling me how enormously grateful she was for your help on the dance floor last night, when her heel broke.'

Jocasta looked distractedly up at Gideon Keeble. How could she possibly not have recognised him last night? God, she must have been drunk. He was very tall, about six foot five, and powerfully built, without being in the least fat. He was tanned and looked enormously well, as if he spent a lot of time outdoors, and he had an energy that was almost infectious; he wasn't exactly good-looking, but he had very large and brilliant blue eyes, and his dark curly hair was exactly the length Jocasta liked, a little longer than was fashionable, and just flecked with grey.

'Yes. Yes, I was,' she said helplessly, 'very grateful. Thank you.'

'It was entirely my pleasure.' He had an accent just tinged with Irish and he smiled at her, a brilliant, warm smile. 'Is the shoe too sick to be cured?'

'Oh – no, I don't think so. I hope not.'

'Where on earth are you going with all that luggage, Gideon, you old poseur?' asked Chad.

'To the States for a week or two. There's a tempting little morsel over there I've got my eye on. I'll call you when I get back.'

'Fine. Look forward to it. Bye.'

'Goodbye. And goodbye to you, Jocasta. May I say I enjoy your articles very much.'

'You've read them?'

'Of course. I regard it as my business to read everything I can. I especially enjoyed your piece last week about that girl in the Bournemouth hotel. The one who said the only people who'd ever properly thanked her for what she'd done for them, in five years of conferences, had been Maggie and the Prescotts. That sounds a bit like a TV programme, doesn't it? Maggie and the Prescotts – someone should commission it. No, it was excellent. Your piece, I mean.'

'Thank you,' she said, smiling at him. She got a warmth and excitement that was almost sexual when people admired her work. 'From you that's really praise.'

'Deserved. You're a clever girl,' he added. 'And what a lucky man Nicholas is. I was telling him only last night, he should make an honest woman of you.'

The dark blue eyes sparkled at her. He was flirting with her. How morale boosting was that? And he really was *very* attractive.

'I wish,' she said, laughing. But her heart squeezed suddenly. She wondered what Nick might have said. Whether she could possibly ask . . . No, she couldn't. Anyway, she could guess.

'I think he prefers me dishonest,' she said, trying to sound amused.

'Then he's a fool. Girls like you don't come along too often. With both brains and beauty. Oh, I can see my driver looking extremely constipated over there. I'd better go. Farewell to you both.'

'He's very nice,' said Jocasta, looking after him. She felt slightly weak-kneed.

'Oh, don't be deceived,' said Chad Lawrence. 'That charm is hugely dangerous. And his temper is legendary. Now, let me buy you a coffee or a drink.'

Jocasta was miserable and irritable when they finally got to London: Nick had spent the entire journey in a huddle with a couple of other *Sketch* writers, getting steadily drunk. She had thought she would be able to sleep her hangover off, but she couldn't; just sat there through the endless uncomfortable journey, with her eyes closed.

'Well,' Nick said as they got off the train, 'it seems they've made their minds up. Full steam ahead.'

'Ahead where?' she said confusedly.

'The new party. They've got some funding now – Keeble has pledged a million or two, and Jackie Bragg's coming up with an obscene amount. You met her once, didn't you?'

'Oh yes,' she said. 'Very clever girl, Jackie.'

Jackie Bragg had just floated her hugely successful brainchild on the Stock Exchange. Hair's to You sent a fleet of highly trained hair stylists to visit offices at any point during the day to blow-dry the tresses of female (and male) executives too busy to leave their desks. Five years ago she had been a brand manager in a small manufacturing company, with a boss who had complained that she never had time to go to the hairdresser; she was now well up the *Sunday Times* Rich List with a second project (the same but different, she was often quoted as saying) planned.

'Indeed. And both are good commercial names – essential when they go on the charm offensive. The new party, that is.'

'I would have thought they'd have a name by now,' said Jocasta.

'Well, they haven't. Can't hack that. If *you* can, they'll probably reward you with a damehood when they come to power. Oh, and did I tell you? The Ed is persuaded it's a good idea. Chad's invited him up for a shooting weekend – you know how he loves all that country gentleman stuff even while he says they should all be strung up – and of course he and Keeble are old muckers. And – '

'Nick, this is all very fascinating, but I'm terribly tired. I think I'll just go straight home to Clapham,' she said, expecting him to argue, or at least to say he would come with her; but he gave her a swift kiss on her cheek and said: 'OK, sweetie, you do look done for. Call me tomorrow.'

Jocasta stared at him.

'Nick!'

'What?'

'Nick, I can't believe you just said that.'

'Said what?'

'What you just did.'

He looked at her.

'Sorry, you've lost me. I thought you said you wanted to go back to Clapham.'

'I did. I thought you might want to come with me. Oh, it doesn't matter.'

She felt like crying; crying or hitting him.

'Jocasta – '

'Nick, I trekked all the way up to Blackpool to be with you.'

'That's not true,' he said easily. 'You had to cover the party.'

'Anyone could have done it. I wangled it specially – Chris wasn't that keen. But that's not the point.'

'Yes, it is. Jocasta, I'm sorry if I've upset you, but I really – '

'Oh, just shut up, will you?' She wasn't sure why she was feeling quite so hostile; she just was.

He stared at her. 'OK. I will. Bye.'

And he walked away from her, his tall body melting into the crowd, his mobile held to his ear.

Something had to be settled, they couldn't go on like this. It had happened just one too many times, his behaving as if she was just some casual girlfriend he was moderately fond of, who should be incredibly grateful if he suggested they went home together. She felt used, disregarded, undervalued. She kept hearing Gideon Keeble's words: 'He should make an honest woman of you.' Probably, she thought, misery making her emotionally reckless, probably the entire conference, the whole newspaper industry, had been watching them, thinking exactly the same. It was a humiliating thought.

Anyway, she didn't want to be made a completely honest woman. Not with a wedding ring. Not quite yet anyway. But Nick could at least make a start: commit to her, suggest they moved in together.

She drifted off to sleep at about four, and got through the day somehow, expecting him to call any moment; he did, at about five thirty. 'I'll be very late. Sorry. Big debate on security.'

'That's absolutely fine by me,' said Jocasta and put the phone down.

She spent a long and miserable evening, and another wretched night, waking on Saturday with her mind made up. She went for a walk, deliberately leaving her mobile behind. When she got back mid-morning, he had called and left a message on her answering machine.

'Hi. It's me. Do you want to see me? I'd like to see you.'

She called his mobile; it was on message.

'Yes,' she said. 'We need to talk.'

He arrived with a bottle of red wine and some flowers that clearly came from a garage, and bent to kiss her rather cautiously.

'Hi.' He handed her the flowers. 'For you.'

'Thank you. Would you like some coffee?'

'That'd be great.' He watched her as she made the coffee in silence; then: 'Jocasta, what is this all about?'

'Me, Nick. That's what it's about.'

'I can see that. Do I come into it at all?'

'That's up to you. Look, would you like to tell me just exactly where you think we're going?'

'Well – forwards. I thought.'

'And – together?'

'Well, obviously.'

'So – what exactly does that mean?'

'It means I love you – '

'You do?'

'Jocasta, you know I do.'

'I don't,' she said, 'actually. I know you enjoy my company, I know you like having me around, I think I know you like sleeping with me. But I certainly don't know you love me. What have you ever done to make me know that? Nick, we've been together for about two and a half years and you still treat me like some quite new girlfriend. We've never even been on holiday together.'

'Well,' he said equably, 'I hate the sun. You hate the countryside. What would be the point?'

'Nick, it isn't about holidays. It's about life. You know. Planning a future together. Being together all the time, not just when it's convenient. Saying, yes, Jocasta, I do want to be with you. Properly.'

'I'd rather be with you improperly,' he said, coming over to her, trying to kiss her.

'Don't try and charm me out of this, please, Nick. I've had enough of it. I want you to say or do something that . . . that – I want you to make a commitment to me,' she said. 'I want you to say – ' She stopped.

'Say what?'

'You're enjoying this, aren't you?' she said, her voice rising with her misery. 'Enjoying seeing me squirm, enjoying making me say things that – that – '

'Jocasta,' he said and his voice was gentle suddenly, 'I'm not enjoying it at all. It's making me feel very miserable seeing you so unhappy. But if you want me down on one knee, asking you to become Mrs Marshall, I really can't do that. Not yet. I just don't feel ready for it.'

'No,' she said, dully, 'no, that's pretty obvious.'

'And if I did do that, propose, just to make you happy – well I don't think it would do much good to either of us.'

'But, Nick, you're thirty-five. When are you going to feel ready for it?'

'I don't know,' he said. 'The idea simply fills me with terror. Maybe because so many of my friends have got married and then unmarried again, with enormous unhappiness. I don't feel settled enough, I don't feel well off enough, I don't feel – '

'Grown-up enough?' she said, her voice heavy with irony.

'Well – yes, yes that's about it. Actually. I don't. I'm sorry.'

Jocasta suddenly felt very tired. They were no further along than – well, than the last time they had had this conversation. Further back if anything.

'Jocasta,' he said gently. He put his hand on her arm. 'Jocasta, I'm sorry. I wish – '

She interrupted him in a haze of rage and despair.

'Oh just shut the fuck up, will you? Stop saying you're sorry when I know you're not!' She was crying now, out of control, hurting dreadfully. 'Go away, why don't you? Just go away and – '

'But – but what for?' His voice was genuinely bemused. 'What would be the point of that? We love being together. And I really do love you, Jocasta. It's very unfortunate for you that I'm an immature commitment-phobe. But I am maturing. There has to be hope. And meanwhile, why can't we go on as we are? Or – is there someone else? Is that what you're trying to tell me?'

'Of course not,' she said, sniffing, reaching for the handkerchief he was holding out to her. 'I wish there was.' She managed a half smile.

'Well, I don't. And there's certainly no one else for me. Never could be. Not after you.' He reached out tentatively, stroked her cheek. 'Please, Jocasta, give me just a little more time. I'll try very hard to do some growing up. I do want to, I promise.'

'Well – ' She hesitated. He leant forward and started to kiss her; tenderly at first, then harder, his mouth working on hers. Against her will, against all common sense, something stirred deep, deep within her, something dark and soft and treacherous. He pushed his hand under her T-shirt, began encircling one of her nipples with his thumb. She shivered in anticipation, then pulled back from him; his eyes on hers were very bright, very tender.

'I meant it,' he said, 'I do love you. I'm sorry if I don't make it plain enough. Now – shall we go and lie down and recover?'

But all through the sex which followed, lovely and healing as

108

it was, Nick gentle and tender, waiting for her a long, long time as she softened, sweetened under him, coaxing her body skilfully in the way he knew best, into a mounting, brightening pleasure; even as she felt her climax gather and grow and then spread out into starry, piercing release, she felt still wary, still hurt; and as she lay beside him, his hand tangling in her hair, his eyes smiling into hers, she knew that however much he said he loved her, it was not enough. And that once again she seemed to love someone more than he loved her.

Chapter 8

Clio sat staring at Jeremy; she felt terribly frightened. Really throw-up, shit-in-the-pants frightened.

He stared at her, his face cold and distasteful. When he was in this mood, his face became mean, his eyes narrow, his lips tight. She hated it. At this very moment she hated him.

It had all begun – rather absurdly – with the Morrises. They had been found in the middle of the town, wearing their night clothes. Mrs Morris had failed to take her pills, woke up hungry, walked down to Waitrose and was found tucking sweets and crisps into her dressing-gown pocket; Mr Morris had, meanwhile, gone to look for her, also in his dressing-gown, and was apprehended, as the police called it, driving in the wrong direction down a one-way street, frantic with worry. The social services had been called and the pronouncement had been made that the Morrises were not coping and would have to go into a home.

'But they can't,' Clio said to Mark Salter, almost in tears. 'They're fine if they take their pills. I should have popped in every day, then they'd be all right.'

'Clio, stop it,' said Mark. 'The Morrises are not your personal responsibility. I can't think of anyone who'd have done what you have.'

'It's not enough though, is it?' said Clio. 'The poor old souls are going to end up in some hideous place, removed from everything familiar, and they'll absolutely gallop downhill.'

'Dear Clio, calm down. You don't know that.'

'I know it,' said Clio, 'and I'm very upset. This whole system stinks. Where are they?'

'At home. The daughter's with them apparently.'

'Better not visit, then. I'd want to ram her mother's pills down her fat throat.'

'Clio, Clio.' He twinkled at her. 'That's not a nice thing to say.'

'She's not a nice woman.'

Just as she was leaving, her phone rang; it was a friend of hers, Anna Richardson, another geriatrician, from the Royal Bayswater Hospital where Clio had been working before moving to Guildford.

'Hi, Clio, how's it going?'

'Oh – fine, thank you. Lovely to hear from you, Anna. I'm sorry I haven't called.'

'It's OK. Neither of us has that sort of time. How's Jeremy?'

'Oh – you know. Still Jeremy. That's why I haven't called. How's Alan?'

'Still Alan. Are we feeble or what?'

'We're feeble. How're things there?'

'Good. Still enjoying general practice?'

'Loving it. It's more – personal. You feel more in control.'

Anna laughed. 'You certainly can't say that of hospital life. Look, I've rung to say goodbye for a bit. Alan's been offered a job in the States. In Washington. Huge salary hike, loads of perks. So, obviously we're going.'

'That's fantastic.'

'I s'pose so. I'd rather stay here. But – you know. No choice really. I mean, who's got the real career? Anyway, I've decided to put mine on hold, have a baby or two.'

'Really?' Clio tried to keep her voice casual; this was the third friend who had made this particular announcement in the past month. It made her feel panicky.

'Yes. You're not?'

'Oh – gosh no. Not yet.'

'Well, look, Clio, there was one other thing. Old Beaky's retiring in a year or so.'

'Bless him.'

Donald Bryan, whose vast nose had given him his nickname, was the senior geriatrician at the Royal Bayswater and their boss. He had been much loved.

'Yes. So if you wanted to get back into the swing of things, they'll be looking for at least one person to replace me and if they promote from within to Beaky's job, two. And – well, your name did come up.'

'Golly.' Clio sat staring out of the window; it was a grey miserable day, and suddenly it looked quite different. Brighter. More interesting. Of course there was no question of her taking what she thought of as a proper job again, and certainly not one in London, but still – it was wonderful to know that she should be considered sufficiently good at what she did to be at least a possible contender for a moderately senior position. 'So – who mentioned me?'

'Well, Beaky himself. And a couple of other people. If you're interested, Clio, I would say you only had to lift the phone and they'd ask you to apply. Anyway, I thought you'd want to know. Even if only for a bit of an ego boost.'

'Yes. I do. Bless you!'

After Anna had rung off, Clio sat at her desk, doodling on a piece of paper, and feeling, briefly, like a different person. Not a rather unsatisfactory wife, not the family dunce, not a junior member of a general practice, but someone clever, someone sought after, someone doing well in her chosen profession. Just for a very little while she felt sleeker, more successful, oddly confident. And she would tell Jeremy; he'd be pleased for her at least. She was sure about that.

She combed her hair, smiled at herself in the mirror and set off for home, thinking how foolish she was. And how happy.

She dropped in on the Morrises on her way home; they were both subdued and frightened and their daughter hustled her out again as fast as she could.

'They can't cope,' she said, 'and it's no use turning a blind eye any longer. They need to be in a home for their own sake. Now I'm sorry, but I have to get them to bed. They're very tired and being quite difficult.'

She spoke of them as if they were naughty children. Clio left with a heavy heart.

She was late home: Jeremy's face was like thunder. 'I thought you were going to be early tonight. We were supposed to be going to the cinema.'

She had forgotten. 'Jeremy, I'm really sorry. But I had a big surgery and then the Morrises, you remember, the poor old couple who – '

'Clio, I've told you before, I really can't be expected to remember details of all your patients.'

'Of course not. But – sorry,' she said again. 'Is it really too late? It's only seven – '

'Much too late,' he said. 'Can we eat soon, or shall I make a sandwich?'

'Could we go out? I hadn't planned on cooking, because of the cinema.'

'I thought you'd forgotten about the cinema?'

'Only briefly. Could we go out?'

He hesitated, then said: 'Yes, all right.'

They went to the local Italian; he cheered up after a bit, telling her about a tricky knee operation he had performed that afternoon which had gone well.

'Oh, and I forgot to tell you. I've been asked to do another session at the Princess Diana.'

'Jeremy, that's marvellous. I'm proud of you.' She meant it; she really was.

He smiled at her. 'Thank you. More wine?'

It seemed a good moment to tell him her news. Not that it was news, of course. Just a bit of gossip really. She waited until he had filled the glasses, then said:

'Anna rang me today. You remember, Anna Richardson? She and her husband are moving to Washington.'

'Oh yes?'

There was a silence; clearly he wasn't finding the conversation very interesting.

'Anna told me something quite – nice,' she said. 'She said there were a couple of jobs going at the Bayswater. In geriatrics.'

Suddenly she had his attention. 'And?'

'And – my name had come up, she said. Isn't that nice?'

'Your name had come up? For a job in London?'

'Yes. Well, not exactly for one, but – '

'And you call that nice?'

'Well – yes. Yes, I do.'

He stared at her; his eyes almost black.

'Are you quite mad? Are you seriously considering a job in London?'

'No. Of course I'm not. I was just pleased they'd thought of me. I thought you would be too. Obviously I was wrong.'

'You are. *Very* wrong. I find the whole idea absurd.'

'Absurd? Why?'

'Well, that you should be thinking about your career at all.'

'Why shouldn't I think about my career? It's important to me. Terribly important. I've trained for it, worked hard for it. Can't you see that I want to do well?'

'Not really,' he said. 'And I hope you mean it when you say you have no intention of taking a job in London.'

'Of course I mean it. I just was pleased I hadn't been forgotten and that while I was there they valued me. It was nice to hear.'

'Right. And what exactly do you mean by wanting to do well? I thought we had agreed that any work you did was temporary and a means to an end. I hope you won't be working at all soon. As you very well know. Now, shall we order a pudding, or shall I get the bill?'

'Get the bill.'

She was silent all the way home: hurt beyond anything. And thinking this wasn't a marriage at all: or not the kind she had looked for.

She woke up the next day feeling dreadfully depressed. Apart from the row the night before, she was tired, and worried about the Morrises, who were being 'assessed'. It was practice conference day, when they all met in the lunch-hour to discuss patients and any problems, and it was a rather depressing meeting that day. Mark had a case even more heart-breaking than the Morrises, a young woman in her thirties with severe cerebral palsy. Her parents were elderly and could cope with her no longer; she had to be moved into a home, and the only suitable one locally was full of old people.

'She'll just sit there, rotting. With carers, the parents might have managed. But – '

They all knew about the 'but'. The bureaucracy that surrounded the carers was appalling, police vetting, a mass of paperwork, time pressures – it just wasn't worth it, for £4.50 an hour. Few people were prepared to do it.

As Clio left the room, Mark asked her if she was all right. She managed a smile and an assurance that she was, then shut herself in the loo and had a good cry.

At four o'clock, just as she was settling down to some paperwork, Jeremy phoned.

'Clio, I'm sorry. I'm going to be very late. Simmonds wants to have a meeting with me and suggested we have a meal afterwards. No idea when I'll be back. Don't wait up for me.'

Angry, useless thoughts shot into her head: why was he allowed to work late, without warning, when she was not?

Margaret came in. 'I've put all the stuff about the Morrises in this file, as you asked me. You look all-in, Clio.'

'I feel it.'

'I'm off to the pictures tonight with a couple of girlfriends. Any chance of your coming? It'd cheer you up.'

In a flurry of what she knew was rather short-lived courage, she said: 'I'd love to. Jeremy's out, so – '

'So – good,' said Margaret.

They saw *Notting Hill* which was wonderfully distracting, and then went for a curry. It was really fun. Clio felt much better about everything. Even Jeremy. She ought to do this more, fuss over him and his attitude to her less. He meant no harm, he was just a bit old-fashioned. She just had to keep a sense of proportion, that was all. She'd just have to be a bit firmer with him.

As she turned into the drive, she tensed: Jeremy's Audi was there and the house was a blaze of light. He always did that if she was home after him, went roaring round the house looking in every room, even the attic bedrooms, just to make the point.

She swallowed hard, went in.

'Hi.'

He appeared from the kitchen, scowling.

'Where the hell have you been?'

'I've been – well, I've been at the cinema.'

'The cinema? Who with, for God's sake? And why couldn't you have left a note? I've been worried sick.'

'You could have called me,' she said, 'on my mobile. And I

haven't been home, I stayed in the surgery working until I went out – '

'And you went to the cinema?'

'Yes. Why shouldn't I?' She faced him, angry suddenly. 'You were out with your cronies. Anyway, what happened, why are you home so early?'

'Simmonds cancelled dinner. I foolishly thought you'd be pleased to see me, that we could have a nice evening together. But, as usual, you weren't here. I just don't understand you going out, when there is so much to see to here. Incidentally, that wretched cleaner didn't come again, the breakfast things were still sitting on the sink.'

Something snapped in Clio.

'Just stop it, Jeremy! Stop it. I'm not here just to run the house, and do what you tell me. You constantly diminish my job, you have no real interest in what I do, what I'm about.'

He was silent for a moment; then he said: 'Clio, I've had enough of this, quite enough. I want you to stop working.'

'Jeremy – '

'No, Clio, I mean it. I want you to give up your job. You say we need the money, but it seems to bring in precious little to me, once you've paid the cleaner and so on, and bought expensive clothes that you tell me you need. And I shall be getting more from my private work. So – tell Salter tomorrow, please.'

Clio fought to stay calm. 'Jeremy, please! You're talking nonsense. And besides, what on earth would I do all day, it's not as if – '

She stopped; she had walked into a trap. He slammed it shut; she felt the steel bite into her as harshly as if it was physical.

'As if what? As if you had a baby? I was coming to that, Clio. I really think the time has come. You're not getting any younger, you're thirty-five – '

'Thirty-four,' she said automatically.

'Thirty-five next birthday. You of all people should know the risks involved in leaving it too late. And I would like to have a child well before I'm forty. Which doesn't leave much time. About two years, in fact.'

'But, Jeremy – '

116

'Yes? What are you about to tell me? That you don't want one?'

'No,' she said quietly, 'no, I do. I'd love to have a child. But – '

'But what? Is there something you haven't told me, Clio? Something I ought to know?'

'No. No, of course not.'

But there was. And he was going to have to know sooner or later. It was incredibly wrong of her not to have told him before. She stood there, staring at him, willing up the courage to say it; and failed totally.

'I agree,' she said, quietly. 'Yes. Yes, we should. Let's – let's try to have a baby. Before it's too late.'

Chapter 9

What was she doing, even thinking about it? For God's sake, was she completely mad? How had this even begun to happen, let alone managed to sweep her along on this huge, breaking wave that had left her fighting for breath, absolutely terrified – and yet desperately, wildly excited?

Actually, of course, Martha knew very well. It was a congruence of everything that mattered to her: her own ambition; an infinitesimal but dangerous boredom with the law; a sense of emptiness in her personal life; and the sheer irresistible force of four very powerful people all telling her they needed her. Just the same, it still seemed a very scary thing for her to do, to consider actually moving into politics, herself.

It had begun – well, when and where had it actually begun? In that hospital ward with poor Lina dying? In the House of Commons that night, when she had found the atmosphere so beguiling? Or when Paul Quenell the senior partner had asked if she would like to become part of his team working on a new client of his, the Centre Forward Party – 'It's a new political party, might interest you, breakaway from the Right –'

'Ah,' she had said, 'Chad Lawrence, Janet Frean, that lot,' and he had been so impressed by her knowledge of them that it had given her an almost physical excitement to be so carelessly close to the corridors of power. That had been a very big factor.

She had gone to the House of Commons several times to meet them, had grown familiar with its complex geography, had listened to debates from the public gallery, had slowly begun to understand how it worked. She had got to know Chad and Janet Frean rather well, even Jack Kirkland a little. Kirkland fascinated her, his passionate idealism, his scowling intensity, his gift for oratory, and the way, just occasionally, he would suddenly and visibly relax, start listening rather than just talking, and even laughing, when something amused him: a great bear-like infectious laugh. They were so hard to resist, these people, possessed of a quality she could only rather feebly call charisma, that made you want to impress and please them. And then when you did, you felt absolutely fantastic, clever and starry and – God, it was all so schoolgirly!

It was all madness, total madness, and she knew it, with her life already so over-stretched, her time so limited, her commitment to her work so necessarily intense. It helped that the party was officially a client, but she found herself proof-reading their policy documents, suggesting likely supporters and attending schmoozy lunches or dinners, or even – occasionally – drafting press releases on their behalf. It was partly vanity, she knew, vanity and excitement that she, Martha Hartley, had become someone in at the centre – or near the centre – of something so important, so high profile, in however modest a capacity.

But there was a serious side to it too, of course, in that she believed in them; she felt she was involved in something that could actually help the likes of Lina and her family, trapped in a cycle of deprivation. It was the kind of thing that she thought she could be proud of – and that her parents could be proud of too.

And there was also the fact that she seemed to have tumbled into her natural habitat. She loved the way politics was a world of its own, loved the villagey atmosphere of the House, the way everyone knew everyone else, the way people could be screaming at one another across the Chamber one minute and sharing a bottle of claret the next; she loved the way it ran on gossip and inside knowledge and deals and what she had once described to Marcus as a live game of chess.

They had, from time to time, suggested she thought about going into it at the sharp end herself. 'You're a natural, I'd say,' said Chad, looking at her one evening on his return from a

119

protracted and fruitless struggle with a local constituency. 'We should parachute you in somewhere. You'd love it, I know you would.'

'Don't be ridiculous,' she had said, laughing. 'I don't know anything about it.'

'Rubbish. It's not rocket science. Common sense and energy are the main ingredients. And being moderately articulate, I suppose. All of which you are. You should think about it.'

And, 'You really might like to think about joining us, Martha,' Jack Kirkland had said another time, his burning dark eyes on hers. 'You'd be very good. We need new candidates desperately. Find yourself a constituency and we'll back you.'

She had joked that she hardly had time to find her own office, never mind a parliamentary constituency.

'No, no, you are not to make a joke of it. I'm entirely serious.'

How could she not respond to that? To one of the most famous politicians of his day, telling her he would like her to join his party?

It was all extraordinarily exciting.

She was sitting at her desk one morning in late January, when her phone rang.

'Martha Hartley.'

'Hi,' said a voice, 'this is Ed Forrest. I don't suppose you remember me. You gave me a lift up to London, one night last year.'

She did remember, of course: beautiful, charming Ed.

'Ed,' she said, 'how lovely to hear from you. I thought you were in Thailand or something.'

'I was. But I'm back now. And I thought I should call you. Fix a date. I said I'd buy you a drink. I felt bad, never doing it, but I kind of ran out of time. Sorry.'

'Ed, it's quite all right. I haven't been harbouring a grudge against you all this time.'

'I didn't think you had,' he said. 'You don't seem that sort of person. And anyway, I'd really like to see you again.'

'Well, that's a lovely idea,' she said, hesitating. But – what was the harm? What on earth was the harm? 'It – it would be nice,' she said. 'Only it will have to be – let's see – the end of the week. Like Friday.'

Maybe he'd be busy. They always were busy on Fridays, people his age. It was the beginning of the weekend, it was for getting drunk, making a noise, planning the rest of the weekend.

'Friday'd be cool,' he said. 'Where should we go, do you think? Smiths? Or do you go there all the time?'

'Why should I?'

'I'm told lots of you City types do.'

'Well, this one doesn't. Anyway, I like it there.'

Now, how stupid was that, she thought, putting the phone down. When she could hardly find the time even to breathe? Yes, she should cancel it. Or postpone it anyway.

He was sitting at a table just inside the door, in the dim light and raucous noise of Smiths, and she felt a shock of pleasure just looking at him; she had forgotten how absurdly beautiful he was. He was very tanned, and his blond hair, shorter even than she remembered, was bleached with the sun and he was wearing a suit, a dark navy suit, with a pale blue open-necked shirt. The smile, the wonderful, heart-lurching smile, was as she remembered, and the intensely blue eyes, and ridiculously long blond eyelashes.

He stood up, came forward to greet her.

'Hi. You look great.'

'Thanks.'

She wished she had worn something less severe than her black suit – although the white Donna Karan top she had changed into was quite sexy. 'Sorry I'm late,' she said, feeling suddenly foolish.

'That's OK. I thought you probably would be, doing lots of high-powered things.'

'Well, I wasn't,' she said and laughed. 'I was waiting for a cab and discovering my phone was very low. Which is why I didn't call you.'

'It's cool. It's good to see you. You look great. What do you want to drink?'

'Oh – ' She hesitated. 'White wine?'

'What do you like? Chardy?'

'Um – yes, that'd be nice.' Actually, she hated Chardonnay.

He loped off and came back with two glasses and a bottle of Sauvignon.

'What happened to the Chardonnay?'

'I could tell you didn't like it. So I took a flier on the Sauvignon. Am I right?'

'Absolutely right,' she said.

She felt suddenly almost scared. How on earth did he read her so well? Already?

Three quarters of an hour later the bottle was empty; and to her infinite surprise she had told Ed about what he called 'your life-changing changes'. His response had been predictably low-key and approving – and she heard herself agreeing, as the noise and smoke level in Smiths rose, to have a meal with him.

'But I mustn't be long,' she said. 'I've got a lot of work to do.'

'What, tonight? Why?'

'Well – because it's got to be done. Sorry, Ed. I really do have to be home by around ten.'

'Well, you must take time to eat,' he said. 'If you don't, you'll get ill and you won't be able to work. Anyway, we've still got lots of ground to cover.'

'I know,' she said, suddenly remorseful that they had hardly discussed him, apart from his travelling experiences. 'I want to know about your plans.'

'Well, I'll tell you while we eat. Come on, where shall we go?'

Martha considered his probable disposable income, and that he might not let her contribute.

'There's a very nice Thai place just down the road,' she said, 'called the Bricklayers' Arms.'

'Doesn't sound very Thai.'

'I know. But trust me.'

'OK. I'll just go and pay for the wine.'

'Can I – '

'Of course not,' he said, and his blue eyes were genuinely shocked. She smiled at him.

'Thank you,' she said. 'It was the nicest Sauvignon I've had for a long time.'

'That's good,' he said. 'I really wanted you to like it.'

✼ ✼ ✼

He had been for several interviews, since he got back: 'And today, just today I got a second interview somewhere, and I think I got the job.'

'Ed, that's great! Where?'

'With an independent television company; I want to be a researcher. And funnily enough,' he said, nibbling on a rice cracker, 'the first programme I'd be working on is about politics. So knowing a politician myself would be a big help.'

'Ed,' she said laughing, 'no way am I a politician.'

'No, but I bet you will be,' he said. 'More wine?'

It was almost midnight when they left the restaurant.

'It's been such fun,' she said. 'Thank you. Let me know about the job. And if you get it, I could certainly arrange for you to meet some MPs.'

'You could? I'll tell them that.'

He got the job; Chad Lawrence agreed to see him, and arrange a tour of the House for him. 'But there's a price tag on this, Martha. You've got to join us.'

'Oh, Chad, shut up.'

'I won't. Why should I help you get yourself a toy boy for nothing?'

She did the tour with him, then said she would buy him dinner. 'I owe you one.'

They went to Shepherds, where she felt like an old hand, pointing out various politicians to him, telling him morsels of gossip. Almost against her will, she heard herself agreeing to see him again.

'I'll see if they'll let you come into the office,' he said. 'They've been interviewing young people about politics – that would interest you, wouldn't it? You could see some of the tapes.'

The filmed interviews were rather depressing; she began to see why people like Chad were so keen to have her on board. The general attitude was of total disaffection with politics; at least three-quarters of them said they distrusted politicians totally, that they had no idea what young people's lives were like or what they cared about; most of them also said that they couldn't see any point in voting anyway, since whatever the election pledges were, they were never kept. Clearly there was much work to be done persuading them otherwise.

She spent a couple of hours there, talking to Ed's colleagues, and liked them very much, a young, aggressive, feisty lot. She was intrigued by the creative mind, the way it said 'Let's try' and 'Why not?' rather than 'That's not possible' and 'We'd have to find a precedent'. She enjoyed the way they grabbed ideas out of the air and pushed them around, rather than looking at the facts and lining them neatly into shape; Ed had let her see some of the tapes of his political interviews and she was fascinated – if a little shocked – by the way they were put together, taking remarks out of context, editing out what they didn't like.

'That's really rather dishonest,' she said, laughing, as they watched the rough tape of the first interview, and then the neatly clipped result. 'Because that girl, the rather earnest one, said she found it hard to trust any politician, but she quite liked Tony Blair, and she really admired Cherie, found a lot of the New Labour ideas interesting, and she'd like to know more about them even though she probably wouldn't vote for anybody. Out of all that, she's left saying she doesn't trust politicians and she wouldn't vote for anybody.'

'Well, that's what she meant,' said the producer, 'the rest was just padding. But let's go for a drink, shall we? Then you can give us some more of your views. Maybe we should interview you,' he added thoughtfully.

'Me! I thought this film was about young people.'

'Well, you are quite young,' he said. 'For an MP, anyway.'

'I'm not an MP,' she said firmly. 'I'm simply involved with this new party.'

'We could say you were an MP, a new one.'

'No, you couldn't,' she said.

'Well, let's go for a drink anyway.'

That was when she began to feel bad. She stood in a Wardour Street bar with Ed's arm round her shoulders – she liked that, it was the first time he had touched her apart from some very brief goodbye kisses – chatting to them, and they were joined by a few more of his friends, all in the same business, and they thought it was odd, the relationship: she could see that. In their early- to mid-twenties, most of them, how could they relate to a woman who must seem to them already nearly middle-aged? And it wasn't just her age that set her apart. They were just starting out on their careers, many of them not sure what they wanted ultimately to do, some of them still working for nothing, as runners, just hoping to get proper jobs: how could they talk satisfactorily to a woman so successful she was one of the highest earners in the country? Which they seemed to know she was. Clearly Ed had been talking about her.

She hadn't felt really bad until the cameraman left and one of them said, 'Nice old buffer, isn't he?' and she had thought that actually she was probably nearer to the old buffer in age than she was to Ed and his friends. And although it didn't matter, it had made her feel vulnerable and uncertain; and she had realised, too, that this was going to happen over and over again, if she continued to see Ed.

'Are you all right?' Ed's face was concerned as he looked at Martha. They were in the Pizza Express in Covent Garden; it seemed to her to be full of twenty year olds.

'Yes. Yes, of course. Just a bit tired.'

'Well, that's a first,' he said cheerfully. 'You're never tired. You told me you didn't believe in being tired – '

'Well, that was very arrogant of me. And I can't quite believe I said it.'

'You did. On our first date. I was well impressed. Have you decided what you want to eat?'

'Yes. The pollo. With no dressing.'

'Frites?'

'Oh, no thank you!'

'No need to sound quite so horrified,' he said. 'I'm offering you a few slivers of fried potato, not a plate of cow with foot and mouth.'

'Sorry.' She smiled quickly. 'I just don't – don't like chips.'

'Like you don't like cream or chocolate or pastry? Or salad dressing?'

'Well, yes. Actually.'

'Not because you're on some rigid eating programme?'

It wasn't a good evening; she was edgy, not at her best. Conversation flagged. At about ten thirty, she said she must go. 'I have so much to do tomorrow. It's been great, Ed, honestly.'

'No it hasn't,' he said. 'It's been crap. Anyway, I'll find you a cab.'

'No need, I'll call one.'

'You're very self-sufficient, aren't you?' he said, his voice rather flat. 'And very in control –'

'Yes, I suppose I am. I've had to be.'

'It's a pity,' he said. 'You should let go a bit.'

'I don't think so,' she said.

'Fine. Well, go on then.'

'Go on what?'

'Getting the cab.'

'Yes, all right.'

He looked baffled, dejected. More than anything she wanted to explain, to say it was nothing to do with him, her disquiet; but the only solution was to end the whole thing, here and now. There was no future in it, in their relationship, it was a piece of absurd fantasy, vanity on her part.

'Ed,' she said, and he looked at her, his blue eyes very wary. 'Ed, I really think –'

'It's OK,' he said. 'I understand. I'm not what you want, am I? I don't suit you. I shouldn't have tried, even. So – best leave it. Pity. It could have been great. Well, for me anyway . . .'

And what, she thought afterwards, what if she had just nodded, kissed him briefly on the cheek and left? As she knew very clearly would be – sensible. Only she looked at him, staring down at the table, everything about him dejected, and she felt a terrible need to tell him that the fault was not his.

'I would say it was the other way round, actually. Surely you can see that. You don't need some bossy, older woman, with a complicated life –'

'Oh, for fuck's sake,' he said, and there was real anger in his voice, 'stop presenting yourself as some dried-up old school-marm. When you're beautiful and clever and sexy –'

'Sexy? Oh, Ed, I don't think so,' she said, managing to smile.

'Well, you think wrong. Anyway, you're hardly the one to judge, are you? That's my job.'

She sat there staring at him, feeling suddenly very confused and . . . something else as well, a lick of desire, brief but horribly, dangerously strong, and it must have showed because he suddenly smiled, a slow, almost triumphant smile, and said: 'Come on. Let's go and get into an ordinary cab, one I can pay for, and I'll take you home.' They sat in the back of a black cab, and all the way from Soho to Docklands he kissed her, slowly, gently, at first, then harder, with a skill that she would not have expected, and she felt herself whirling into a confusion of hunger and pleasure and fear and a pure, flying excitement. And when the cab finally stopped, she wanted to ask him into her flat more than anything, and she might even have done so, so badly did she want him, but he said: 'I'll call you tomorrow. OK?' and she nodded, feebly, and said nothing.

As he paid off the cab, he turned to her and smiled, his beautiful, heart-wrenching smile, and said: 'You're totally gorgeous, Martha. Totally. Bye now.'

And he was gone, loping down the street, not looking back, exactly as he had done the night she met him, that long year ago.

And so it began: she felt sometimes, not of her own volition, as if he had worked some sleight of hand while she wasn't looking. It was so ridiculous, such a totally unsuitable liaison, between this beautiful man, little more than a boy, and herself, a lot more than a girl; she didn't have time and she didn't want to get involved. But – she went on and on wanting to see him. And seeing him. It was just that he made her feel so happy.

She felt uncertain a lot of the time with him. It was part of his charm. Or rather the charm of what he did to her. She was used to being absolutely certain; of who she was, what she wanted, where she was going, what she was going to do. Ed questioned all of it.

'Why?' he would say. 'Why work on a Sunday, for God's sake?'

'Because there's so much to do.'

'Can't it wait?'

'No, it can't. The client wants it first thing.'

'And he'll leave, will he, go to some other poncey firm, if he gets it second thing?'

'No, of course not.'

'Well, then. Don't go to work. Come out with me instead. We'll have fun.'

Or, 'Why? Why don't you eat more?'

'Because I don't want to get fat.'

'Martha, you're so not fat. So not anywhere near it. Anyway, why does it matter?'

'Because I like being thin.'

'But you'd still be thin, you've got a long way to go. Would you die, or something, if you went up a size?'

'No, of course not.'

'Well, then. Have some frites. They're really good.'

That had been the night she had first gone to bed with him; determined to resist, she had allowed him to argue himself into her bed.

'I just don't think it's a good idea.'

'Why not?'

'Because – well, because this isn't a very sensible relationship.'

'Relationships shouldn't be sensible. They should be good. Anyway, why isn't it sensible?'

'Well – because – oh, Ed you know. You're twenty-three, I'm – '

'You're beautiful and interesting and I want to have sex with you. What's me being twenty-three got to do with it?'

'I – don't know.'

'Well, then. Let's go.'

As she lay in bed and watched him undressing, looked at his beautiful boy's body, she felt a stab of terror. Suppose she was a disappointment? Almost certainly he had only known young, young girls. Suppose, in spite of all her care and attention, her body was beginning to look less good. Suppose – she felt taut, tense with fear, almost told him to go away, to leave her to herself.

But, 'You are so beautiful,' he said, sliding in beside her, pulling back the cover, studying her, 'you are just so, so beautiful . . .'

And gently, slowly, very tenderly, he was somehow all over her, everywhere, kissing her breasts, stroking her stomach, moulding her buttocks. Then he was in her, infinitely gentle, desperately slow, and then, then she wanted him terribly, and she was going to meet him, rising, falling, pushing, thrusting herself on him, and the great tangled waves of need grew higher and higher, and she thought she would never get there, reach the crest. She was struggling, fighting, desperate: and then she was there and she rode it, shouting with joy, and on and on she went, for what seemed a long, long time, swooping and flying, and then slowly and almost reluctantly she let it go, released it, and fell down slowly and sweetly into peace.

Afterwards, lying beside him, her body finally relaxed, fractured with pleasure, more than she could ever remember, smiling at him, half surprised at herself, half delighted, she wondered how she could ever have thought it might not be a good idea.

But it did frighten her: a lot. She was frightened of giving too much of herself away, of losing her iron control on her life, of ceasing to function in her own, ordered, Martha-like way. Yes, she would think, as she lay restless and anxious in the small hours, she'd enjoy it for just a few weeks and then end it; before she made a fool of herself, before her life was too disrupted. He must see it couldn't go on forever, that he really needed someone much nearer to his own age. As she did.

But she wouldn't do it just yet. She was too happy.

It was absurd, how well they got on. How easily they talked, how much they managed to enjoy the same things, how seldom it seemed to matter that she was ten years older than he was. She even shared her smaller insecurities with him; she had never done that before.

'I hate my nose. It's too big. Too much.'

'It's a fine nose.'

'It isn't.'

'Rubbish. You can smell with it, can't you? It lets the bogeys out.'

'My boobs are so pathetic.'

'They are not pathetic.'

'They are. They're so small.'

'They're not too small to kiss. They give your bra something to do.'

The sex became more wonderful as she became less afraid; he was all the things she might have expected, inventive, tireless, sensuous, but others that she had not: tender, careful, infinitely patient. He would spend a long time arousing her, kissing, talking, easing her into excitement; she told him how lovely that was, how much she appreciated it.

'What about all your other lovers?' he said, grinning. 'Didn't they do that for you?'

'Ed, I haven't had many other lovers,' she said truthfully and then regretted it. She tried not to do that: to talk about anything personal. Apart from him, apart from them.

'Why not?'

'I – just haven't. Didn't want to. Didn't – '

'Have time?'

'Well – obviously,' she said, laughing, glad to be able to turn it into a joke.

'Did you – love anyone? Ever?'

'Once, yes, I did.'

'And . . . ?'

'And it ended.'

'Why?'

'He was married,' she said quickly, 'and I don't want to talk about it.'

'OK.' He always respected that if she spelt it out.

Martha was happier than she could ever remember.

And knowing that it couldn't last made it sweeter still.

For just three weeks, she felt very, very happy.

And then it was Valentine's Day.

It started out quite well, for a man who told her he wasn't romantic; a posy of red roses the night before, some sex at midnight – 'I was hoping I could make you come as the clock struck, but I think I failed – let's see – yes, it's 12.13, damn' – and he rang her just before her six o'clock alarm call, to say Happy Valentine's Day – 'that was the hardest part, waking up before you'.

They were going out to dinner at the Pont de la Tour – her

treat, she said – and had agreed to meet at eight, but at seven-thirty he called and said he'd been held up doing some important editing and would she come down to Soho instead. Slightly irritated – while reminding herself this was what she did to him all the time – she cancelled the table and got a cab to a Thai restaurant in Old Compton Street, which he said would remind them both of their travels. He wasn't there when she arrived, but a table had been booked and there was a bottle of white wine on ice beside it; she sat down, ordered some water instead and waited. For twenty minutes she waited, and there was no phone call, no sign of him; she was about to walk out when one of the boys who worked with him came in, breathless, and said Ed would be just another ten minutes, his phone had died, he was really sorry and could she please hang on? Martha thanked him for coming, but after fifteen minutes, she couldn't stand it any longer, got up and stalked round to Wardour Street to the building where he worked; she pushed the entryphone bell, and announced herself.

'Come on up,' said a voice and she went up the rather scruffy stairs and into the minuscule space that called itself reception.

There was nobody there; she had just started walking along the corridor when she heard a voice coming out of one of the offices. And heard her name.

'She was in a right state, Ms Martha was.' It was the boy who had come round to the restaurant. 'Don't rate his chances much tonight. She practically smacked my hand just now. Not pleased.'

'Yeah? Maybe that's how their relationship works – maybe she dresses up in leather and whips him.'

'Nah. Anyway, it's not a relationship, not really. How could it be? I reckon, now he's won his bet, it'll be all over in next to no time . . .'

Martha took a deep breath, walked on and pushed open the door of the editing room. Ed sat staring at a screen, scrolling images backwards and forwards.

'Fuck off,' he said without looking round. 'Can't you see I'm busy?'

'Yes,' she said, 'actually. I can. And I won't be interrupting you any longer, Ed, not tonight, not ever. I'm so glad I helped you win your bet. Now why don't you fuck off yourself.'

And she walked out of the building, got into a taxi and went back to her apartment. And refused to answer any of the twenty-two calls he made before he gave up and, she imagined, shrugged his shoulders, and went out to have fun with some people his own age.

Chapter 10

'Now, shall we get a Chinese? Mum's left me some money.'

'You're so lucky, Sarah,' said Kate wistfully. 'No one nagging at you all the time to do your homework and tidy your room, or turn your music down. And you can eat whenever you like. We have to sit down every night, all four of us round the table, and make polite conversation, it's gross. Dad calls it communicating. God! He doesn't know what the word means.'

'Yeah, well, it's all right here in some ways,' said Sarah. 'Sometimes it's not so good. Like I have to look after the little ones a lot. Mum's never here, not in the evenings.'

'Where does she go?'

'Oh – out. After she's finished at the pub. Drinking. Clubbing.'

'Clubbing! At her age?'

'I know. It's pathetic. And then she stays over at Jerry's place quite often.'

'What, the guy with the motor bike?'

'Yeah, he's her boyfriend. Didn't you realise?'

'Not really.' Kate digested this in silence. 'Do you think they – they –'

'Yeah, course,' said Sarah. 'What else do you think they do?'

'I don't know . . .' said Kate. She looked at Sarah in silence for a moment, then: 'You haven't yet, have you?'

'Course not! I'm thinking of it, though.'

'With Darren?'

'Yeah – he's so fit.'

'But – but what's the point? Really?'

'The point is I want to,' said Sarah. 'At least, I think so. I mean, half the class has. I'm beginning to feel like an alien. Aren't you?'

'No,' said Kate firmly. 'I'm not.'

'Not even if you finally landed Nat Tucker?'

'No way!'

Nat Tucker had been in the year above them and the object of a great many girls' desire; he was tall, dark and although only moderately good-looking and at times even slightly spotty, he was extremely sexy. He had left school and was working as an apprentice at his father's garage and had consequently acquired a car which he drove round the neighbourhood, stereo at full volume, one arm dangling out of the window, nonchalantly holding a cigarette. He had twice told Kate he was going to take her out; so far nothing had happened.

'S'pose you got pregnant with Darren. Then what'd you do?'

'I wouldn't,' said Sarah. 'I'd make him wear something.' She looked at Kate. 'It's because of your mum, isn't it? Your *real* mum? You're afraid of the same thing happening to you.'

'Course not,' said Kate. 'I'm just not that stupid. Now listen, I've got a new idea.'

She had seen an ad in the local paper. 'Private Detective Agency', it had said, 'Company Searches, Matrimonial, Missing Persons Etc. Discreet and Confidential'. And then the magic words, 'No Find, No Fee'.

Well, it was worth a try. And if she did find her mother, then she could pay the bill. Bitch. It would be the least she could do. Shaking slightly, she had called the agency; a bright and breezy woman answered the phone.

'Yes?'

'I – want to speak to someone about finding someone. Please.'

'Ye-es. Can you tell me a little more? Is this a relative?'

'Yes. Yes, it is. I want to – want to find – my – ' She stopped. God, this was always so hard. 'My mother,' she said firmly.

'I see.' The voice was reassuringly calm. 'Well, we'll do our very best. But before we can go any further, I shall have to take a few details.'

'I – I don't have a name. Of any kind. So – '

'Well, that does make it more difficult – but not impossible. We have solved similar cases.'

It was raining; a grey and wretched day. To Kate it suddenly seemed filled with sunshine.

'Could you give us any idea of location, where she might be?'

A few clouds gathered. 'No. None at all, I'm afraid.'

'Well – do you have a starting point? Like where you were born? And when?'

'Oh yes.' This was easy. Gloriously easy. 'I was born at Heathrow airport. On August the fifteenth, 1986.'

A long silence; then: 'Actually at the airport?'

'Well – yes. And then she – well, I – that is, I was found – a bit later that day.'

'I think,' said the voice, 'you really should come in and see us. We obviously need to discuss this very carefully.'

Sarah offered to go with her, but Kate thought she should go alone. 'It looks more – more grown up.'

She went after school next day. The offices were over a jewellery shop: quite flashy, not seedy as Kate had expected, and Mr Graham was not the sad old man she had expected either. He was dapper, quite good-looking, well-spoken. He was fairly old, she thought, although not as old as her parents, probably about forty. He gave her a horrible cup of coffee and told her to tell him what she wanted.

After about five minutes he held up his hand. 'Now look, dear. We could just possibly find her, find your mother – '

'You could? Oh my God!'

He said all sorts of encouraging things: that they knew where she was born, the hospital she was taken to, that trails could be picked up long after they'd seemed to go cold. It was like some wonderful fairy story. And then came the bad bit: that they couldn't possibly do it for no fee. That it was going to be a long haul, a big investment of their time. He'd want at least £300 on account.

She felt sick: the tantalisingly bright vision, of her mother delivered to her, fading slowly.

'Look,' said Richard Graham, who was not an unkind man. 'Look, you speak to your mum and dad. The ones who adopted you. See if they can help. And then tell them to come back to me.'

135

There was no way her parents would part with £300. Not for this. They would tell her it was all very dodgy, warn her it could run into much more money, and that someone like the National Organisation for the Counselling of Adoptees and Parents (NORCAP) would help her for nothing, when she was eighteen.

When she was eighteen. More than two years away. And even then they'd say all the usual things, like did she really want to, and was it a good idea, and what about counselling first? And they were very hard up at the moment, anyway. They kept saying so. She felt totally miserable; it was as if she had been told her mother was just round the corner and that, if she hurried, she would find her there. Only someone had anchored her to the street, so she couldn't hurry. It wasn't fair! It just wasn't fair!

And then – she stood stock still, right in the middle of the pavement, felt herself getting quite hot – her grandmother could afford £300. There was no doubt about that. And she'd be more sympathetic, less fussy too. She might even go and see Mr Graham with her. She'd think it was exciting, a bit of an adventure.

The more Kate thought about it, the better an idea it seemed. She was due to go and stay with Granny next weekend; she would ask her then. Maybe, just maybe, she really was getting a little bit nearer.

When Martha left the office late on Wednesday evening, it was raining. Dismal, cold, wind-driven rain. God, she hated February. She walked down the steps towards her waiting cab and then noticed that a couple of people in front of her were pointing at something just out of sight and laughing. As she reached the bottom step she saw why; a six-foot-high bright yellow chicken was walking towards her. Very elaborate, it was, with a proper chicken body, a long, rather ostrich-like neck, and sturdy legs above its splayed chicken feet. It had started to skip now, and it was holding an envelope in its beak. Even in her cold, wet misery she had to smile, then giggle, it was so absurd. And then:

'Miss Martha Hartley?' it said. Its voice was high, drag-style high, and very American. 'Letter for you. Special delivery.'

It was a huge yellow plastic envelope bearing the words,

'Chicken Post: We Beat the Pigeons to it', with a large bunch of yellow feathers fixed where a stamp might be.

'I'm sorry,' said Martha, trying very hard to look severe. 'I don't really want anything.'

'You want this, believe me,' the chicken said, dropping the letter at her feet and skipping off down the road away from her. 'Good news in there, I can tell you,' it called over its shoulder, with a flap of its wings.

Martha picked it up, looked rather awkwardly at the people around her and got into her cab.

'You get all sorts round here, don't you?' said the driver.

Afterwards, she couldn't believe that she hadn't thought it might be from Ed. If she had, she would have dropped it down the nearest drain. As it was, she opened the envelope, found another inside and then another inside that, and hadn't even opened the final bright yellow envelope by the time she reached her apartment; she was changing by then, running her bath.

She started reading the chicken's letter and recognised Ed's appalling writing.

'Stop!' it said. 'Don't throw it away. Read this. Please, please, please read it.' Martha, wearing nothing but a pair of silk knickers, her heart thumping uncomfortably hard, read it.

'OK,' it said, 'you were a bet. Getting you into bed was a bet. But before I knew you, before our first date. I can produce witnesses. Colin is strung up by his balls, waiting for your call. Hopefully you're still reading.

I just want to tell you a few things.

1. You're fantastic.

2. I feel like a complete load of shit.

3. I wouldn't have hurt you for anything.

4. I miss you.

5. It's totally horrible without you.

6. I think you're quite right never to eat more than once a day.

7. Nobody should ever go away for more than a week at a time.

8. Everybody should work at least twelve hours a day and on Sundays.

9. Nobody should have sex when they've got a meeting in the morning.
10. Your nose is not too big.
11. Your boobs are not too small.
12. I want you back.

Ed. X

Her doorbell rang.

'Who is it?'

'It's me. The chicken. Can I come up?'

And reluctantly smiling she pressed the entryphone.

'It was Mum's idea,' he said, as they sat on her sofa, his arm round her; she was still stiff, edgy, ready to be hurt.

'Your mother's? Ed, you didn't tell her?'

'Course not. Well, not that it was you. But that I'd upset someone, couldn't get her to talk to me even. She said Dad could always get round her, however angry she was with him, if he made her laugh. She said once she'd laughed, she'd had it, because she'd let go a bit. I'd been out there hours, waiting in my car. Got a lot of funny looks. But driving there was the worst. Every time I stopped at traffic lights, people started pointing at me and laughing. And then I wanted to pee and I couldn't. Just had to hang on. Once you'd gone, I ripped the whole kit off, rushed into a doorway. I was afraid of peeing on your feet,' he added, 'ruining your Jacky Choos.'

'Jimmy Choos,' she said automatically.

'Sorry. It's a good thing I've got you back, correcting my mistakes.'

At which, Martha burst into tears.

'Don't you see?' she said, wiping her eyes. 'That was why it hurt so much. It was exactly what I was afraid of, that first night I met your friends, here was me, crusty old battleaxe, bossing you about, telling you what to do, laying down the law, and you, you – '

'Me what?' he said tenderly. 'Me, the complete idiot. I don't know nothing from nothing . . .'

'You just don't get it, do you? That's the whole point. That's how I make you feel. And I hate it. I hate myself being that person.'

'Look,' he said, 'I'll be the judge of how I feel and whether I like it. OK, you're a bossy old bag. I don't mind – I find it rather sexy, actually. I specially like it when you stop being bossy. When – ' he looked at her thoughtfully ' – when we're in bed. You're very different in bed, you know, Martha. You get all – biddable. You want to please me. It's sweet. Very, very sweet.'

'Oh,' she said.

'And you know something else? Here you are, this hyper-controlling, brilliantly clever woman, running the world, knowing more than I ever will, and the whole of the British legal system cowering before you . . . And you know how I feel?'

'No.'

'I feel really proud. Proud you want to be with me. Proud you want me. It's gorgeous.'

Martha felt her eyes fill with tears. She sat digesting all this for a long time in silence. Then she smiled at him.

'So – am I forgiven?' he said.

'Yes. You are. Totally. Thank you.'

'It's OK. I'll leave now. Leave you in peace.'

'Oh,' she said. She felt rather surprised; and discomfited.

'I think it would be best,' he said. 'Really.'

'No,' she said, 'no, it wouldn't. I'd like you to stay.' She wasn't used to asking for anything from him. It was difficult. 'Please, Ed, please stay – I don't want you to go away again.'

'You'll be telling me you need me next,' he said, and very slowly and gently started to undo her bathrobe. 'Now,' he said, minutes later, 'what are those incredibly voluptuous things I see there? Between your neck and your waist. Can they be breasts? And please may I kiss them?'

Chapter 11

The Centre Forward party had actually been launched: at the Connaught Rooms, the same location that the SDP had used a little less than twenty years previously. There was no hidden agenda in this; it was simply central, large enough, famous enough and splendid enough. The KFL trio – as they came swiftly to be known – who had made it happen, and who had equal billing – 'until we're elected' – were Jack Kirkland, Janet Frean and Chad Lawrence.

They boasted twenty-one backbenchers, most of whose constituencies had agreed to let them stand under their new colours until the next election. Chad Lawrence's constituency was one of the few to force a by-election and he had won easily.

Their timing was perfect: with their slogan of 'People First, Politics Second', they had swept a rather tacky board and for a moment in history, at least, had everything going their way. Their timing was not just careful – after the budget in April and with a little time at least to prepare for the local elections in May – but lucky. In-fighting and despair had swept the Tory party, and fresh horror stories about hospitals, schools and crime had beset New Labour.

And the Queen Mother's funeral had sparked a wave of patriotism; people were in the mood for something uplifting and new. In a new political party, Kirkland said, they just might feel they had got it.

Nobody could have asked for more publicity. From the first interview (the 8.10 slot on the *Today* programme with a sceptical but agreeable John Humphrys talking to Jack Kirkland) to the last (*Newsnight*, with an equally sceptical and less agreeable Paxman talking to Chad Lawrence) a visitor from Mars might have assumed absolutely nothing else was happening in the country that day. Every notable programme featured the launch: Breakfast TV, *Woman's Hour* and *Richard and Judy* all interviewed Janet Frean; *The World at One*, Sky, Channel 4 and *PM* had Kirkland. Every newspaper gave them the front page; many of the stories had included the results of a YouGov poll showing that 30 per cent of disaffected Tories would vote today for a new party, 25 per cent of New Labour voters, and a massive 40 per cent of those who hadn't voted at all in the last election.

Three newspapers had come down heavily on their side, the *Sketch*, the *Independent* and the *News*; others were more sceptical, but still welcomed what everyone was calling a fresh breeze in politics. The name was a huge success and the sketch writers had a field day, comparing the first press conference variously to a photocall for the World Cup and to the line up of the runners in the Grand National.

There was much purplish prose about months of plotting in smart houses in Pimlico, dark corridors and underground committee rooms in Portcullis House; it all sounded rather easy and far removed from the reality, the all-night sessions in various flats and restaurants, the endless patient planning, the ongoing struggle to persuade people away from a Tory party they had served all their lives, and to get them on side, the heroic battles to enthuse the constituency party workers.

There had been some very nasty stories planted about the three of them and there were also a great many unfounded rumours about who was leaving which party for the new one, the wildest being that Gordon Brown was to join them, and the most likely that Michael Portillo would. Neither did. Both Tony Blair and IDS said – through clearly gritted teeth – that this was what democracy was all about, while regretting (on IDS's part) the disloyalty that had spawned it, and on Tony Blair's, a reminder that the SDP had had an equally triumphant birth and a funeral seven years later.

All the main protagonists, Lawrence, Frean and Kirkland, were on the front pages and many of the inside ones as well.

All had attractive families, wheeled out, smiling dutifully, for photo-opportunities; Gideon Keeble said that he was proud to be involved and so did Jackie Bragg, who said that she knew a good idea when she saw it, and she was proud to be part of this one. There was an interview with Keeble in the T2 section of *The Times*, complete with a photograph of him in front of his Irish mansion, flanked by two Irish setters, and a quote that what you needed, in both politics and the press, was above all courage; and one with Bragg in the *Mail*, which plugged her company Hair's to You rather heavily (a condition laid down by her, in return for a photo-shoot in her house) but in which she said that for something to succeed in today's world, it had above all to be sexy, and the Centre Forward party was certainly that. The City had analysed the fortunes of Keeble, Bragg and other big backers, and the extent to which they had been prepared to put their money where their mouths were; there was much talk also of anonymous donors.

Wherever the money had come from, it had come: to the tune of twenty million. Quite a large percentage of this had come from private individuals, over fifty thousand of them, who had pledged sums ranging from twenty-five pounds to a thousand on their credit cards. Chad Lawrence said repeatedly in interviews that this said more about the popularity of their cause than anything. It was observed by more than one commentator that this was a team which included people outside the world of politics, who were businesslike and successful in their own lives and had a better than average chance of actually getting things done. Many of the people tasked with setting up the party on their own patch were still doing the day job, and came with no personal experience in politics; this was a big factor in the fresh thinking. And this group, of course, included Martha Hartley.

On Friday 19 April, a very big party was thrown in Centre Forward House, a new building in Admiralty Row. This was partly a thank you to all the workers, partly a further PR initiative. Apart from the politicians and the backers, a handful of City men and as many celebrities as the combined address books and e-mail directories of the core team could muster were invited, together with every journalist from the world of print and radio and television. The food was good, the wine excellent, and the atmosphere heady. If you hadn't been invited and were an obvious contender, you hot-footed it out of Town.

Jocasta Forbes was there; she would have been there anyway, brought by her boyfriend, but her editor (who was also present) had briefed her to write a big piece about it for the gossip column the next day. 'And find a few unusual people. I don't want to read about Hugh Grant or the Frosts, God help me.'

Several people had remarked that Jocasta was looking less dazzling lately; she had lost weight and had a weariness about her. But her stories were better than ever; that day alone she had had two, one about a woman who was suing her credit card company – 'If people can sue the tobacco people, why not, they shouldn't make it so easy for us to borrow,' – and another about a scientist who had successfully cloned his own cat and was offering his services to the owners of elderly moggies on the Internet.

She did look dazzling that night, however, dressed in a very short black leather skirt and jacket and a sequinned top which showed most of her bosom and quite a lot of her tummy. She arrived with Nick, but promptly left his side and, inside an hour, had quotes from such disparate guests as Will Young, the public-school-educated sensation from *Pop Idol*, the Duchess of Carmarthen, resplendent in diamonds, who said it was the first political gathering she had been to since the war, and Alan Titchmarsh, charmingly self-deprecating as always, who said he had always wanted to do a patio garden on the terrace at the House of Commons and could Jocasta help him with a contact there.

After that she relaxed, drained a glass of champagne and then took another and began to wander round the room; Nick was doing his political groupie number with Janet Frean, and Chris Pollock was locked in a fierce argument with Carol Sarler of the *Daily Express*.

'Well, if it isn't my favourite reporter. How very, very lovely you look this evening. I've been hoping against hope that you'd be here.'

It was Gideon Keeble, smiling down at her; looking wonderful as always, holding a bottle of champagne in his hand.

'Hello, Mr Keeble,' she said rather uncertainly, allowing him to fill her glass. 'There are waiters to do that, you know.'

'I do know, but this is such an excellent way of extricating myself from boring people and involving myself with interesting and beautiful ones, such as yourself. And please don't call me Mr Keeble; it makes me feel most dreadfully old. Gideon, please. And where is your charming boyfriend?'

'God knows,' said Jocasta, 'but wherever he is, he's talking. And not in the least concerned with me.'

She didn't mean to sound edgy, but she did; Gideon Keeble's eyes met hers.

'What a foolish young man he is. I hope he's heeded my advice now, and put a ring on your finger.'

'Not quite,' said Jocasta determinedly smiling, 'but if he had, one thing is quite certain, I wouldn't like it. His taste in jewellery is execrable.'

'Well, that is a serious shortcoming in a young man. I pride myself on my own. Jewellery is like perfume – it should complement the wearer's style.'

'And what would you think my style was?'

'Well, now, let me see.' His brilliant blue eyes were on her, half serious, half not. 'I think you are a diamond girl. Glittering and brilliant. But – not big diamonds. Nothing vulgar. Small, intense ones. With white gold.'

'It sounds wonderful,' said Jocasta, 'but Nick isn't in the diamond league. Sadly.'

'I wasn't thinking of Nick,' he said. 'I was thinking of you. I would like to settle some diamonds on you here –' he touched one ear gently – 'and a few more – let me see – yes, there.' And he picked up her hand and settled it in the valley of her breasts. It was an oddly erotic gesture, far more so than if he had touched her himself.

There was a silence; then she said, briskly careless, 'Well, that would be lovely. Very lovely. Now – perhaps you could tell me about a few more of the people who are here. And going to be here. I am half on duty, you see.'

'What a shame. I was hoping to spend quite a time with you.'

'You can, if you like. Just take me round and introduce me to a few importantly famous people. Or famously important, whichever you prefer.'

'Very well. Do you know Dick Aoki, chair of the Jap-Manhat bank, as it is rather disrespectfully known?'

'No. What on earth has he got to do with a new British political party?'

'Nothing. Yet. Come along, I'll introduce you.'

She liked Aoki; half Japanese, half American, he was amusing and self-deprecating.

'I'm buying a house in Wiltshire,' he said. 'Do you think the English country house set will accept me?'

'Of course,' she said. 'If you spent enough money entertaining them. They're all tarts really, that lot.'

'Oh really? An interesting view. I fear they might not. But it is a very beautiful house and if I am forced to live there in total isolation, I will not mind. You've seen Gideon's house in Cork, I presume.'

'No,' she said, 'no, I haven't.'

'What a dreadful shame. Gideon, you should take her there. They would suit each other.'

Gideon looked at her consideringly.

'You're right. I would never have thought of it. Very well, Jocasta, you shall come as soon as I can arrange it. Would you like that? You must bring Nick, of course, I am not looking to compromise you.'

'I'd love to come,' she said. She smiled at him and he smiled back, holding her eyes for just slightly too long. Why wasn't Nick around, noticing this?

'Now let me find you some more copy. Ah, there's a nice story over there . . .' He introduced her to an American film star who looked like a blond Richard Gere, who 'happened to be in Town', an Irish racehorse owner, en route to Dubai and what he described as acquisition-bound, and several English bankers.

'Now, who next?' he said, his eyes scanning the room.

'Gideon, there's no need for any more,' she said, laughing. 'You've done brilliantly.'

'Good. I'm delighted to hear it. Now, what are you and Nick doing after the party? I'm taking a few people out to dinner, would you like to join us?'

She certainly would, she thought happily. Without Nick if she could possibly arrange it.

Martha Hartley arrived at the party very late. She had been delayed by a call from Ed, checking on the arrangements for the weekend. He had been upset that she hadn't been able to take him to the party: so upset that she had thought at first he was putting it on.

'I bet you'd be able to take one of those important old guys you know,' he said. 'I bet it's only because it's me. I'm not quite up to its standard.'

'Ed, that is so not true. Invitations are like gold dust. I couldn't take you if you were – well, Prince William.'

'Now, why do I find that hard to believe?' he said.

She sighed. 'Sorry, bad example. But some of the partners are dying to come and can't, honestly.'

There was a silence; then, 'OK,' he said. But he clearly wasn't convinced. Matters weren't improved by her being unable to see him for over a week; she genuinely was too busy. He had become very cross and even sulky about it. Sulking was one of the few things he did that reminded her how young he was.

Only the promise of a whole weekend spent in his company had mollified him.

'And you'd better not shave so much as five minutes off it.'

She promised she wouldn't.

Her main concern at that moment, however, was whether she was dressed appropriately. She had chosen a black crepe Armani trouser suit, very simple, lent a certain pizzazz by the addition of some very over-the-top diamanté drop earrings. Her brown hair in its sleek swinging bob was caught back on one side by a matching clip, and her new Jimmy Choos – perilously high, with diamanté ankle straps – made her feel sexy and daring.

When she arrived, the room was so thick with people that movement seemed impossible. There must have been at least three hundred people. She spotted Marcus and went over to him.

'Hi, Marcus. Sorry I'm late.'

'I'd say it doesn't matter, but it does.'

'Oh, God, why?' She had a vision of being asked to say a few words, talk to a journalist, check a legal document.

He smiled, his plump, twinkly smile.

'Because you look so lovely. The room looks about a hundred per cent better for your arrival. Now, do you see anyone you know –'

'It's hard. Oh, yes – Jackie Bragg. I'll go and talk to her.'

Jackie Bragg was in high spirits: 'I just met a guy from Japan who thought I should open Hair's in Tokyo.'

'I agree with him. Absolutely.'

'Good. Hurry up and get on side and we'll plan it together.'

Martha laughed. 'Jackie, you'll do much better without me. Lawyers tend to put the brakes on rather than the accelerator. You wouldn't have started Hair's to You yet if I'd been on your board.'

'Well – maybe. You know, Martha, you really should think of having your hair shorter. It would suit you. And a bit of colour . . .'

'Jackie! One of the three a.m. girls wants to interview you about life in the fast lane. OK? I know how much experience of that you've got.' It was Chad. 'Oh, hello, Martha. Glad you made it. You look stunning, you really do. I'll be back in a minute. Jackie, follow me.'

She didn't expect him back; she started wandering round the room, surprised by how few people she knew. Jack Kirkland waved at her, but he was deeply embroiled in conversation with Greg Dyke, and a couple of people from the ad agency said hello and moved swiftly on; she was trying to look busy, sipping her glass of champagne, when she heard a familiar voice.

'Martha. Hi. Nice to see you. You look great.'

It was Nick Marshall; she had met him a couple of times now, but had never talked to him for more than a minute or so; like her, he was terminally in a hurry. But she had always liked what she saw, the long lean body, the interested, interesting face.

'This has been quite a day,' she said. 'You guys have all done a very good job for us. *Them*,' she corrected herself hastily.

'Martha, my lovely girl, hello.' Gideon Keeble gave her a giant hug. 'My God, you look wonderful. This room is full of beauty. We poor lowly males can only look and wonder at you.'

147

'Gideon, you do talk nonsense – but it's very nice nonsense. Thank you.'

'Gideon.' It was Marcus, puffing slightly, pink in the face from champagne and the heat. 'Quentin Letts from the *Mail* wants a chat. Would you mind?'

'I would not. Martha, my darling, I'll see you later. And Marcus, you stay here and look after this beautiful creature.'

'I will,' said Marcus. 'Bit of bad news just now, I'm afraid. We've lost one of our most fervent supporters, out in the wilds of Suffolk, heart attack, poor chap. He'll need to retire.'

'Oh,' she said, 'you mean Norman Brampton.'

'Yes, that's right. How do you know about him?'

'My parents live in his constituency. He practically dandled me on his knee. My father, I'm sure I've told you, is the vicar there, knows him very well.'

'I see.' There was a long silence, while he stared at her.

'Marcus, whatever is it? Have I got spinach between my teeth or something?'

'No, no. I was just – thinking about something. Now look, would you mind if I asked you to chat to a couple of constituency workers? They're a bit lost here, and I don't want them feeling we don't care about them.'

'Of course I don't mind,' she said.

She was saved from too long a stint by Chad who took her arm and drew her away.

'I wonder – could we have a word afterwards?'

'Could it be now? I've got to leave early, I'm afraid.'

'What on earth for?'

'Oh – let's just say a bit of arm-twisting. Client business. I'm sorry, Chad, but it's terribly important.'

'You never stop, do you? You ought to get a different job, one that allows you a bit of leisure.'

'What, like politics, you mean?' she said laughing. 'Yeah, right. And spend my evenings shouting in the chamber instead.'

'Not every evening. Martha, I'm serious. We would so much like to have you on board. We really want you to take on a constituency. Think about it.'

'I *have* thought about it. In fact I've finished thinking about it. Sorry. Look, I have really got to go. Back to the day job. Or rather night.'

She reached up to give him a kiss; and over his shoulder, she saw the room as if she had only just arrived, saw the people in it as if she had never seen them before, powerful, brilliant people, all involved in something important, really important, something she already felt a little a part of; and she felt something shift in her head. And he sensed it; brilliant tactician that he was, and he moved in on her.

'Well, look, could we talk in the morning? Meet maybe for brunch?'

'Yes, maybe,' she said, slowly, 'but I've got a lunch appointment.'

'Client business?'

'No,' she said, 'personal.'

She was meeting Ed, persuaded by him tonight.

He gave her a quick kiss. 'Wonderful. Joe Allen's at eleven, then?'

'Fine.'

He left her; she chose not to see Marcus waving at her across the room, because she could afford no more delay.

She had no idea, no idea at all that he had wanted to introduce her to Nick Marshall's girlfriend, who was a journalist on the *Sketch*. Or that the girlfriend had been at the party at all: or indeed that Jocasta Forbes was moving, albeit on the outer edges, in the same orbit as herself.

Jeremy was working late, the night of the launch. Clio sat watching the TV news, trying to distract herself, watching them all being interviewed endlessly. She envied the woman, what was her name? Frean. Janet Frean. Her husband hadn't told *her* to stop working when she had a baby. She had five, for God's sake. Even Clio felt that was going a bit far. Her children couldn't get a lot of mothering that way. But at least she had children.

Clio was depressed; she was dreading leaving the practice, and her patients. The Morrises were now in a home, despite all her efforts, and she suspected the staff of overdoing the sedatives. They were subdued and silent when she visited them, not the bright, eccentric pair she had first met. Mark Salter's patient, Josie Griggs, the girl with cerebral palsy, was in the same home. It hurt Clio even to look at her. She was in the day room, staring hopelessly at the television. She was the youngest person in the home by forty years. It was hideous.

The interview with Janet Frean ended and Clio got up to make herself a cup of tea. A new wave of depression hit her; her period had started that morning and the cramps were unusually bad. Jeremy didn't know yet. God, this was a nightmare; she had to tell him, absolutely had to. But – how could she? Now? When every month, every period, made it worse. Worse and more impossible. Why, in the name of God, hadn't she done it before?

But – no use going down that road, Clio. You didn't. And somehow, now, it really was too late. She just had to hope: hope and pray. At least nobody, nobody at all could possibly know about it. Except of course for that gynaecologist. All the gynaecologists.

Thank God for medical ethics.

Kate Tarrant was completely unaware of the new party. If she had been asked at gunpoint what had been in the papers most days she could not have told you. But she had particularly exciting things to think about that day. Like the weekend ahead of her, which she was spending with her grandmother and which she really believed this time could lead her to her mother.

Jocasta went to dinner with Gideon Keeble. At Langans. Not alone of course. With about a dozen other people. Only they hadn't included Nick. And she had been sitting next to Gideon.

Chad was there, and so was Mrs Chad. She'd never met her before, just seen her in lots of gossip columns. Abigail Lawrence. Tall, dark, beautiful, very cool, very composed.

Marcus was there, and his wife, a lovely warm, bubbly woman, who obviously adored him. She'd had an engrossing conversation with her about universities – their eldest child was doing her application forms – and after that they were friends for life. Jack Kirkland stayed only for a drink. He looked exhausted.

'Is there a Mrs Kirkland?' she asked Gideon, and he said: 'No longer, sadly. Brilliant woman, they met at Cambridge. She said she couldn't compete with his mistress . . .'

'His mistress?'

'Yes. Well, there have been two. First the Tory party, and now the Centre Forward.'

Jackie Bragg was there, with her new husband, much older than she was. He was her financial adviser.

'He liked the company so much he married it,' said Gideon, laughing, 'and now he treats it rather like a train set.'

'And what about you, Gideon,' she said. 'Do you have many expensive toys to play with?'

'Oh, a great many,' he said smiling at her, deliberately obtuse. 'I have my cars – '

He had a fleet of vintage racing cars which he put on show once a year for charity and which he occasionally drove at Irish rallies.

'I'd love to see them,' she said, and meant it. 'I love old cars. My grandfather had a wonderful collection, but my father sold them all. Terrible thing to do.'

'Not for me,' said Gideon. 'I bought a couple of them.'

'Really? I had no idea. Which ones?'

'The Phantom Rolls. And the Allard. That was a wonderful auction. I never could understand how your father could have let them go. They have souls, those cars.'

'Yes, well, my father doesn't care about anything, except money,' said Jocasta, 'and he wouldn't recognise a soul if he tripped over it in the street. Sorry. We're not very good friends, my father and I.'

'No, so I gathered.'

'Who from?' she said curiously.

'Oh – a few people who've been talking about you.'

'And why should anyone have been talking to you about me?'

'I invited them to,' he said, and her head and her heart lurched in unison.

'Why?' she asked.

'I find you extremely interesting. As well as beautiful. I wanted to know more about you. Now tell me, is it true, has your brother really left his clever wife?'

'Not exactly. She threw him out. Rather sensibly. And says she's going to divorce him.'

'Why was that so sensible?'

'Because he got caught playing away just once too often. I'd rather not talk about it, if you don't mind.'

'Of course. I'm sorry. Now come along, you're not eating. I'm sure your mother told you to finish everything on your plate.'

'My mother certainly didn't. We ate most of our meals in the nursery. But my nanny did. And you – were you trained to eat up?'

'I grew up in a rather crowded environment in Dublin. There were nine of us, and we ate in two shifts. It certainly taught me to eat quickly. And to finish everything on my plate. Which was not always quite enough.'

He sounded not remotely bitter, or as if he was playing on her sympathy; quite cheerful in fact. He smiled at her again.

'Now, I am neglecting the charming lady on my left. But I shall come back to you later. Eat your greens.'

It had gone on like that, a series of brief, seductive conversations, and gradually the table thinned out; and finally there was only herself, the Lawrences and the Dennings. And Gideon. They relaxed into chat, gossip, swapping anecdotes about the party; Gideon said several times what a shame Nick wasn't with them, wouldn't she like to call him again. She said untruthfully that she had, when she went to the ladies.

'Perhaps he ran away with Martha,' said Marcus, laughing. 'They disappeared at about the same time.'

'Martha? Martha who?'

'Martha Hartley. Lovely girl. Lawyer. She's been doing a bit for us. And her firm has acted for us.'

'Martha Hartley is working for the Centre Forward party?' said Jocasta. 'How extraordinary. Nick never mentioned it.'

'Why, do you know her?'

'I met her once. Long ago. When we were just kids. How on earth did she get mixed up with you lot?'

'Her firm acts for us,' said Marcus. 'Charming girl. Very bright. And very attractive, too.'

'And is she – you know, married or anything?'

'I haven't heard anything of it. Since she, like all those lawyers, works round the clock, at least seven days a week, I think I would be rather sorry for him.'

152

'Oh Marcus, that is such an old-fashioned attitude,' said Jocasta. 'Slippers by the hearth and nicely ironed shirts are history. You're showing your age, big time.'

'Then I think I should show my own by agreeing with Marcus,' said Gideon, his eyes smiling at her. 'And when you are sitting next to an old man like me, you should be careful what you say.'

She turned and looked at him.

'You're special,' she said. 'I couldn't think of you as any age. Not young, not old. Just – just you.'

'Well,' he said, 'I'm glad to hear that. And very prettily put, if I may say so. Now, does anyone want another brandy or shall I ask for the bill?'

He drove her home; he said he couldn't possibly entrust her to a taxi.

His car, brought to the front of Langans by the doorman, was glorious; a pre-war Mercedes in gleaming black, with spoked wheels and a running board. She had expected a driver, but there was none; Gideon said he didn't like being driven, he preferred to remain in control. 'And besides, I wouldn't trust this car to many people.'

She climbed in, looked round her.

'This is gorgeous.'

'Thank you. Now, where do we go?'

'Clapham, please.'

God, this was amazing. Alone with him, in this incredible car. And when they got there, then what? Did she ask him in? Did he want her to ask him in? Was this a huge pass, or just a kind man giving her a lift?

He chatted easily all the way; asking her about the *Sketch*, what she thought of it, how she got on with Pollock, her personal ambitions, whether she thought they would be fulfilled.

They finally reached her street and she realised they hadn't talked about him at all and said so.

'Oh,' he said, 'I would much rather talk about you.'

'But I must seem so self-centred.'

'Oh, now that is nonsense. I encouraged you.'

'Well – thank you. And for the lift. And for dinner, of course. I – ' She hesitated. No, she'd ask him. What harm could it do? 'Would – would you like to come in for – for a nightcap?'

'Oh, now that would be very dangerous, don't you think?' he said and his face was very serious. 'I would think that not very sensible at all. You are far too beautiful and far too beguiling to be in a room alone with me, Jocasta. Unless, of course, a few things were different. In which case I would like it beyond anything. Obviously.'

'I – suppose so,' she said. 'Yes. But – ' She stopped, looking at him rather helplessly. What could she say, that wouldn't appear brazen, or duplicitous, or any number of other unattractive things?

'Anyway, it's late and you are very tired.' He leant forward, kissed her very gently on the mouth. 'Now off you go. Sleep well. And tell young Nick that I think he is the luckiest young man in Christendom. Good night. Sweet dreams.'

She watched him drive down the street in the absurdly beautiful car and wished, passionately, that she had still been in it with him.

Next morning she felt terrible; not only hungover, but terribly guilty. She should at least have told Nick. Have called him. He would certainly have called her. Probably lots of times. She made herself some weak tea, then propped herself up on her pillows and forced herself to listen to her messages.

'Jocasta! Hello sweet pea, where are you? I'm in the press room. I'll wait till I hear from you.'

OK. That was one.

'Mrs Cook, hi. I'm going down to Shepherds. Chris has booked a big table. Come and join us.'

Two.

'Jocasta, where the hell are you? It's eleven o'clock and I'm at Shepherds. Ring me.'

Three.

'Jocasta, ring me. Please. I don't know where you are, but I'm worried about you.'

Four.

'Jocasta, it's almost one. I'm going home to Hampstead. I heard you'd gone off with Gideon and some other people. Thanks for letting me know. Perhaps you'd call me in the morning.'

Now that had been wrong. To let him worry about her. She should have called him.

Tentatively, almost nervously she dialled his number: mercifully it was on message.

'Hi, Nick, it's me. I'm fine, sorry about last night. I got caught up in Gideon's party and he said he'd left a message for you. They obviously didn't deliver it. Sorry you were worried. I was fine. Speak later.'

That might – just might – do it. He might believe that. And if he didn't – tough. Two people could play at non-commitment.

Still, this morning her mind, sobered and uncertain, was exercised with three things. Whether she had just been foolishly flattered by Gideon the night before, or had he had something more serious in mind? How cross Nick was going to be with her and how much it mattered? And – rather more mildly – what Martha Hartley might be like now, what she was doing, and whether it would be worth seeking her out for their very long-postponed reunion.

'No,' Martha kept saying. 'No, no, no.'

'But why not?'

'Well – I couldn't possibly do it. That's the main reason. And I don't have time. That's another main reason.'

She sat looking at them; when she arrived at Joe Allen's, Marcus was there as well. That was a shock.

'Being an MP doesn't take that much time,' said Chad, 'especially if you're not in government. Which we just possibly may not be.'

'Oh, Chad, please! I work six days a week as it is. I was working until the small hours this morning.'

'Oh, all right. Well, maybe you could cut it down to five. Or work locally instead.'

'I don't want to work locally instead. I love what I do.'

'Do you? Do you really?' said Marcus. 'You told me the other day you were falling out of love with it.'

'I know. But I didn't mean it.'

She felt as if she was falling into a deep, deep hole. She felt panicked, terrified.

'Look, Martha, you would almost definitely be selected,' said Chad. 'You're a dream candidate. Local girl, well-known family, young, dynamic . . .'

155

'Female,' said Marcus.

'Well spotted.'

'And – is this what's known as parachuting in?'

'It is. But us being a new party and squeaky clean, it would not be good to appear to be doing anything so manipulative. We would stress that you were only one of a field – a very level playing field. Only of course it wouldn't be.'

Chad smiled at her again. 'How does it all sound?'

'I keep telling you, not what I want. Anyway, I don't understand, Norman Brampton's a Tory.'

'A disillusioned one. He'd already signed up to the new policies, and persuaded a goodly quotient of his constituency committee to do the same. Of course there are at least an equal number of old die-hards, who are staying with the Tories. They'll be looking at prospective candidates too, of course. But you're off to a flying start. And they don't want to risk a by-election. There's a very brisk young New Labour candidate down there – '

'Oh, God, Dick Stephens.'

'You know him?'

'Not personally. My mother and her friends would like to send him to Siberia. He's very cocky, apparently, and very keen on things like new housing. Anti-hunting, of course, and totally out of sympathy with the farming community. When he came to a parish do, he upset all the stalwarts by calling them by their Christian names, without being invited.'

She felt, rather than saw, Chad and Marcus exchange glances.

'Martha,' said Chad, 'wouldn't you like to be an MP?'

'Well – maybe one day. Not now. I've got no political background – '

'You have now. And she did six months on the Citizens' Advice Bureau you know, Chad,' said Marcus.

'Oh God,' said Chad, 'you really are made in heaven. *Please*, Martha. At least think about it. I know you'd do it well. And I know you'd love it.'

She was silent: thinking. Thinking properly, for the first time, of what it would mean. Could mean.

A new life. A new purpose to it. A chance to do something, to make a difference. A stab at real achievement, a grasp at real power, real success. She had seen enough of politicians now to know she possibly did have what it took.

Chad Lawrence saw her hesitation, saw her thinking and said, quite quietly: 'We're being unfair. Rushing you, pushing you. Think about it, for a day or two. If you're even half-minded, give me a call, and I'll sound Norman Brampton out.'

'And then what?'

'Well, then you can slap in your CV and he would "advise", in quotes, the party members to adopt you. And with your particular presentational skills, I think you'd walk it. Martha, you're in with a flying chance. It's God-given.'

'Do you really think God has any interest in politics?' said Martha with a feeble smile.

'Of course He has,' said Marcus briskly. 'Immense. And just think, you'd have Him on your side, your dad being the vicar and all. Anyway, Chad's right. We shouldn't be rushing you like this. You go home and think about it. And take your time.'

'Yes,' said Chad, 'any time before Monday morning would do.'

Ed was waiting at the table for her, sitting outside in the April sunshine; as always her heart lurched.

He had a bottle of white wine in an ice bucket by the table, and a plate of nibbles.

'Sorry I'm late,' she said, kissing him briefly.

'That's all right. Wine?'

'Just a small one.'

'How was the party?'

'Oh – great. I didn't stay for long. Had to get back for a meeting.'

'No! Not a meeting!'

He seemed slightly subdued, less good-natured than usual.

'Are you all right?' she said, taking his hand.

'Yes I'm fine, thanks. Do you want to eat?'

'Oh – no thank you. I've just had brunch.'

'Oh really. With . . . ?'

'Marcus Denning and Chad Lawrence. I'll tell you why later. Bit of a – a dilemma.'

He didn't ask what it was about; she was surprised.

157

'Well, I'd like to eat,' he said, slightly truculent.

'Of course. You go ahead. I'll just watch.'

'You know it's really fun, eating on your own,' he said suddenly, 'being watched. It makes everything taste much nicer.'

'Ed, I'm sorry. But I couldn't eat any more.'

'No, of course not. You must have had – God, what? A croissant? With some honey on it. No, probably not honey. Just the croissant and some black coffee on the side. I asked you for lunch, Martha. I haven't seen you for ten days.'

'I'm sorry,' she said, realising he was genuinely upset. 'Let's share a big Caesar salad. I'd like that.'

'Whatever you want.'

'Ed, what's the matter?'

'I told you, nothing. I – nothing.'

He ordered the salad and a big bowl of frites; she picked at them carefully. He seemed happier after a while.

'So – what have you been doing?' she asked.

'Not a lot. Going to work, getting pissed in the pub, you know, that sort of thing. How was the party?'

'Oh, pretty exciting. Everybody was there, Ed, Jeremy Paxman, both the Dimblebys, Greg Dyke – you'd have enjoyed it.'

'Pity I couldn't have come, then,' he said.

'Yes, it was,' she said, realising suddenly she was being tactless. 'Although I wasn't there long. Had to leave and persuade some whiz-kid tax lawyer to join our team. And then go back to see Paul Quenell –'

'What would we all do without you, Martha?' he said, and his tone was almost hostile. She stared at him. Something passed between them, something that hadn't been there before. Irritation, resentment, and impatience: real life, she thought. Maybe the honeymoon was over. She felt a flash of panic.

'Come on,' she said, covering his hand with hers, 'please tell me what the matter is.'

'Oh – it's nothing,' he said after a bit and smiled at her and suddenly he was Ed again, the Ed she knew and loved. 'Sorry. Got out of bed the wrong side. Tell me about your dilemma. Then maybe we could go for a movie.'

'Wonderful. Yes, well, it is all a bit peculiar. I really would like to know what you think.'

He was surprisingly interested in the idea. He couldn't see why she thought it was so ridiculous.

'Yeah,' he said, 'why not? You've been talking about it long enough. Sort of. And you'd be good at it. And it would mean you could actually do something about the things you're always going on about.'

'Like what?'

'Well, like your friend. The one you were so upset about, the one who died in hospital. And lots of politicians are lawyers, aren't they? Tony and Ken Clarke and Michael Howard – see, I've been mugging up on all these guys.'

Of course, it was true. There were endless ex-barristers and QCs in Parliament. She supposed it was because speaking in public came so naturally to them; that and the huge confidence that they all seemed to have imbibed with their mother's milk. That she certainly didn't have: the only confidence within Martha Hartley had come from a sense of achievement at her own success, the order and sense of purpose she had brought to her own life. Which she would lose if she started again . . .

'I couldn't do it,' she said finally. 'I really couldn't. And it would mean leaving Wesley's. Come on, let's go to the movies.'

'Right. And then can we go to bed afterwards?'

'Oh, I should think so,' she said, leaning forward, giving him a kiss.

'Perhaps you should get yourself checked out,' said Jeremy.

'What do you mean?' She was surprised to hear her voice sounding so normal: calm and almost surprised.

'I mean checked out. Gynaecologically.'

'What on earth for? More salad?'

'No thanks. You know what for. Three months and you're not pregnant. Maybe there's something wrong.'

'Jeremy, three months is nothing. And I was on the pill, don't forget. I think it would be surprising if I was pregnant.'

'Yes. Yes, I suppose so. Well – we'll give it a bit longer.'

'Anyway, it's fun trying,' she said and managed to smile at him. 'Now, shall we go for a walk? I feel I need some exercise.'

'OK. Good idea. We could go up on the Hog's Back.'

They walked along in silence for a while; then she said: 'You know, I'd like to get a puppy.'

'A puppy? What on earth for?'

'Oh – I've always liked dogs. And it would be company for me when I leave the practice.'

'I'm not too keen on dogs,' he said. His tone was dismissive.

'I wasn't actually thinking of you. I said it would be company for me.'

'Don't start that. Implying you're going to be lonely and bored. That you're dreading giving up your job.'

'Well, I am,' she said, reasonably. 'And I don't think it's necessary, but I've agreed to do it, to make you happy, and I don't see why I shouldn't have – '

'I think you should be happy to be spending more time at home, our home, not always rushing in exhausted.'

'I am not always rushing in exhausted.'

'Besides, you're more likely to get pregnant if you're less tired, if you're calmer – '

'Jeremy, that is absolute crap. The world is full of frantically busy, exhausted women getting pregnant. Anyway, I don't want to talk about it. It's so unimportant.'

'What? That you're failing to get pregnant?'

'Oh, Jeremy! For God's sake can we please stop this? *Please*. Otherwise I'd like to go straight home.'

'Oh all right,' he said. 'What would you like to talk about instead? The weather?'

'No,' she said, 'our holiday. I want to go to the Scottish Highlands. I've never been. What would you think about that?'

'Well, I'm not sure,' said Jilly. She looked at Kate and smiled gently. 'I can see this is terribly tempting, darling. I can see how much you want to find your mother.'

'I don't even exactly want to,' said Kate. 'I know I'll hate her.'

'Why are you so sure about that?'

'Granny! She has to be horrible. Doing what she did. But I just feel I've got to. Until I do I can't settle. I feel I don't know – well . . .'

'Who you are?'

'No. Who I might become. I mean Sarah, my friend – you

can see she's turning into her mum. And Juliet's turning into *our* mum, she's, like, so nice and hard-working and – and annoying. Sorry, I know Mum's your daughter, but she *is* annoying. Well, isn't she?'

'Just occasionally,' said Jilly carefully.

'So what am I going to turn into? Someone awful and – and irresponsible? Like my birth mother, who didn't care, just left me in a cupboard?'

'Kate, she must have been absolutely desperate. It's hard to imagine what she went through. What she's still going through. I'm sure she thinks about you every day.'

'Yeah? So why doesn't she come and find me? That wouldn't be very difficult.'

Jilly was silent; then she said: 'Well, I tell you what, Kate. I might go and see this man. On my own. I don't mind how angry your parents are with me, but I don't want them feeling I'm driving a wedge between you and them. All right? Now, what film are we going to see?'

'So – you think I should do it?' Martha said.

'Yeah, I do. Want some of this one? Very spicy, be careful.'

They were sitting at her small dining table, looking over the lights of London, eating a Thai meal that she had had delivered.

'Ed! Is that it?'

'I'd say so, yes.'

'But – we've hardly discussed it.'

'God,' he said, pushing his plate aside, folding his hands neatly in an exaggerated pantomime, fixing his eyes on hers, 'so sorry. Right. From the top. Let's go through it again. There's nothing to discuss, Martha. I think it's a good idea. OK?'

'Oh,' she said. She felt rather confused. She had wanted a full-blown, careful dissection of the whole thing, the risks, the advantages, her ability to cope with it. 'Well, if that's really what you think . . .'

'Of course it's what I think! I'm finding it a tiny bit tedious, to tell you the truth.'

'I'm sorry,' she said, slightly indignant. 'What would you like to talk about instead? You?'

'Well, it might make a change,' he said.

She stared at him. 'That's not fair!'

'It's perfectly fair. I hadn't seen you for almost a fortnight, and how long before we got onto you? Roughly sixty seconds. Telling me about the fucking party, about how wonderful it had been, about how you had to leave early to go back to a meeting and then suddenly remembering me and asking me politely what I'd been doing. And then back to you again, and what did I think about this thing with Chad or whatever his name is, should you do it, on and on. Somehow, you know, I don't think you ever will. You'd have to make time for it. Spare it some of your precious energy, interrupt your sacred routine. You should try thinking about something other than yourself for a bit, Martha. It might even be interesting for you.'

She felt as if he had hit her.

'I mean, look at us, eating this – this fucking neat and tidy meal, with the telly turned off because you don't like eating when it's on, even though I do, and you picking at it like some kind of dainty vulture. It's all so fucking *ordered*. I tell you, Martha, if you'd started stuffing your face and talking with your mouth full, I just might still be sitting and debating your future. I do have a life, you know,' he said. 'I do have my own problems.'

'Like – what?' she said. She felt quite shocked; she had never seen him like this.

'Oh – doesn't matter.'

'No, tell me.'

'Look, Martha,' he said, 'I might have wanted to talk about it earlier. I don't now. I'm not in the mood. OK? Now for God's sake eat something. And actually, I think I'd better go. I've got work to do tomorrow. You're not the only one, you know, with extra hours to put in.'

He stood up, picked up his jacket from the sofa, bent and kissed her briefly. 'Cheers. See you in a bit.'

The door slammed. He was gone. And Martha was left, staring out of the window, not sure how she felt, just slowly and very carefully, rather as if she had still been eating her Thai meal, carefully and painstakingly picking over what he had said, putting it into neat rows and piles and trying to digest it.

* * *

'Right. Here we are . . .' Jilly pulled up in front of her house; it was raining. 'Now you bring the food, darling, and I'll go ahead and open the door. Only be careful, because the path gets very slippery.'

Kate watched her walking up the path in her high heels. She had heard that accidents seemed to put things in slow motion and had never believed it; but she watched her grandmother turn to check she was following safely, then very, very slowly and gracefully, turn almost in a pirouette and skid sideways, her skirt floating up and then down again, settling round her in a sort of blanket as she fell, equally slowly, down onto the ground. And lie there, absolutely still.

Jocasta switched her mobile off and smiled at Josh.

'Sorry about that.'

She wasn't quite sure what she felt. Guilty? A bit. Worried? She supposed so. And – what else? Well, you know what else, Jocasta? You're excited. Very, very excited.

She was having supper with Josh: a rather subdued Josh, because it was his birthday and she had felt she couldn't leave him all alone. Nick had refused to come; he'd been furious when she finally spoke to him about her disappearance the night before.

'It'd have been nice if you'd tried a bit harder to contact me. I was actually worried about you, Jocasta.'

She'd told him she couldn't count the number of times he hadn't contacted her under similar circumstances, and he'd said OK, fair enough and let's not go down that road, but he really couldn't face supper with Josh.

'But he's so lonely, Nick.'

'I expect he is. Stupid bugger. Would that be his third birthday? Or maybe even his fourth?'

'Well – I know. But I can't help feeling sorry for him. Living all alone in that beastly flat – '

'What – that little hovel in Chelsea, you mean?'

'Oh Nick, shut up. Don't you have any human feelings?'

'Yes, for Beatrice. Anyway, I've just got an exclusive interview with IDS, comments on the new party and the future of his own as he sees it. The Sunday paper wants it first thing in the morning.'

'Fine. Absolutely fine. Don't you worry about me.'

'I'll call you in the morning.'

'And what were you thinking we might do tomorrow? Read your piece? Read everyone else's? And then read yours again, and say how much better it is than theirs?'

'Oh, Jocasta, don't be childish. I'll call you in the morning. I'm having lunch with David Owen, but apart from that I'm free.'

'Wow,' she said, 'that does sound marvellous – Sunday evening, *maybe*, after you've finished that piece. Don't bother, Nick!' She rang off, knowing she had to an extent picked a quarrel with him, and knowing very well why. Picking quarrels was one of her talents. So Nick said.

That was when she started wondering how she felt.

And now she was really wondering. It had been Gideon Keeble on her mobile. Would she and Nick like to come to lunch with him the next day?

'Nick isn't free,' she said, her head already fizzing with excitement. 'So –'

'So –' he said and there was a long silence. 'So what about you? If you'd like to risk a boring Sunday with an old man, you're very welcome. It's up to you.'

'I'd love it,' she said. 'Thank you.'

'Excellent. How do you feel about the Waterside Inn?'

'I feel very, very warmly about it,' she said. It was good that: far less compromising. Not that she cared about being compromised. Not in the least.

'Good. I'll pick you up at – what? Eleven-thirty?'

'Great. I'll be ready. Bye, Gideon.'

Actually, she felt guilty, she realised, as she pushed calamari round her plate: very guilty indeed . . .

'I must ask you to switch your phone off at once.'

The voice rapped across the waiting room: a bored, harsh voice.

'But I want to call my mum. That's my gran in there . . .' She indicated the cubicle where Jilly lay. 'My mum needs to know.'

'Well, you must use the public call box. Mobiles interfere with hospital equipment. You can see the notice there.'

'So where do I find a public call box?'

'There's one in the main hospital entrance.'

'Yeah, and it's not working. I've tried it. Any other suggestions?'

Everyone was looking at her now: a packed Casualty department. White-faced young families, with babies, small children crying, one vomiting constantly into a plastic sandwich box, a drunk with a bleeding head, several more drunks lolling against the wall, a pitifully young Asian girl, visibly pregnant, holding her husband's hand, at least three elderly couples, a couple of middle-aged men, one with his foot roughly bandaged: a sad wave of misery and pain and anxiety washed up on a hostile shore, waiting with painful patience, occasionally going up to the desk to ask how much longer it would be, only to be sent back again to sit down and wait some more. They all welcomed the diversion of the small drama.

'There's no need to be rude,' said the woman behind the desk.

'I wasn't being rude. I was asking for another suggestion. Since that one was totally unhelpful.'

Misery and anxiety was making Kate feel worse by the minute; she had expected comfort, attention, a swift resolution of her grandmother's troubles, had thought to see her safely tucked up in a warm hospital bed, her pain dealt with efficiently and fast. Instead she had been lying on a trolley in a cubicle for almost two hours, ever since the ambulance which had come after forty long minutes had delivered them here, waiting to be taken to X-ray, with no discernible improvement in her condition whatsoever. A doctor had examined her, said it might be a broken hip or a fractured pelvis; he could do nothing until she had been X-rayed.

She was still in her rain-soaked clothes, despite a nurse having promised three times to get her something warmer, shivering violently. Kate had offered to take her to X-ray herself, since no porter was forthcoming; they had looked at her as if she had suggested she should do a strip in the middle of Casualty.

'A porter has to do it, she can't be moved off that bed.'

'I could push it.'

'I expect you could,' said a nurse, pulling the curtains round her grandmother, 'but you don't know where to go.'

'You could tell me,' said Kate.

'I could,' she said wearily. 'But I still couldn't let you do it. I'm sorry. The porter shouldn't be long.'

She looked exhausted; she seemed at least kinder than the others, said she would go and find Jilly another blanket.

She hadn't.

Jilly was finally X-rayed at 1 a.m.; her pelvis was fractured, but her hip wasn't broken.

'So there's no need to operate,' said the doctor, summoned back to her cubicle. 'The pelvis will heal itself, given time. Now then, I think as she has possible concussion, and in view of her age, we'll get her up into a ward, settle her down for the night, sort out some pain relief.'

'She's terribly cold,' said Kate, 'she keeps shivering.'

'That's shock,' he said. The nurse, standing beside him, nodded sagely. The minute a doctor appeared, there seemed to be plenty of nurses; the rest of the time there were none to be seen. They'd even managed to get her out of her wet clothes.

The doctor patted Jilly's blanket condescendingly. 'Poor old soul. What name is it – oh yes, Jillian. Soon have you nicely tucked up, Jillian.'

'My name,' said Jilly, and her voice was steadier suddenly, 'is Mrs Bradford. That is how I wish to be addressed.'

The doctor and the nurse exchanged glances.

When Helen and Jim arrived it was two in the morning; Kate had finally gone outside and called them, after the doctor had been.

'Where is she?' said Helen. 'Is she in bed?'

'No,' said Kate, 'she's on a trolley. They're totally useless. She was freezing to death until I made them get a blanket. She's had nothing, except for the cup of tea I got her. No painkillers, nothing. Stupid tossers!' she added loudly.

'Kate, dear, don't talk like that,' said Helen. 'Er – do you think I could go and see my mother?' she asked the woman behind the desk rather tentatively.

'Of course you can,' said Kate. 'Don't ask anything, they only know how to say no.'

An old woman with no teeth cackled loudly.

'She's a right one, isn't she?' she said to Helen. 'She's put 'em all to rights round here. More guts than all the rest of us put together. You should be proud of her.'

Helen smiled rather nervously and followed Kate to Jilly's cubicle.

Kate woke up with a start; her head was in her mother's lap. She was asleep, too, her head on Jim's shoulder. Daylight was coming in through the dingy net curtains. Kate looked at her watch; it was half past six.

She sat up, walked over to the cubicle; please, please let her be gone.

She wasn't; she was still there, wide awake, feverish.

'Kate! Oh, how nice to see you. I thought you'd all gone.'

'Of course we haven't gone. Oh Gran, I'm so sorry. How is it now?'

'Painful,' said Jilly, 'terribly painful. Could you ask again for painkillers? I can't stand it much longer. And Kate, darling, could you get me another cup of tea? Or even a glass of water?'

By ten o'clock, still no bed had been found. Kate slumped in Casualty, biting her nails. This was unbelievable. She was exhausted: how on earth did her grandmother feel? She walked round the room, her arms folded, trying not to scream. Her mother was standing anxiously by the cubicle; her father had gone for what he called a little walk. He hated hospitals.

Someone had left a newspaper behind; she picked it up idly. It was the *Sketch*. There was a big article on the inside page, about an old lady who'd been on a hospital trolley without food or water for twelve hours and had died. It was a disgrace, the *Sketch* said, that such things happened in a country that had pioneered the National Health Service; the old woman's daughter was saying she would sue the hospital, the doctor, and the NHS.

At least they had some guts, Kate thought; they didn't just sit around saying yes doctor, no doctor, three bags full doctor.

God, this was awful. What could she do? Who would help?

And then she remembered her grandmother's nice doctor.

The one who'd come into the shop that day. Surely she would be able to do something.

She went into the cubicle; Jilly was dozing restlessly.

'Granny?'

'Yes?' She woke up at once.

'Granny, what's the name of your doctor? The lady who came into the shop that day?'

'Oh – Dr Scott. Yes. Nice girl.'

'Do you have her number? I thought I'd ring her. See if she can help.'

'It's in my address book. In my bag.' Her voice was slightly slurred. 'But darling, she won't come on a Sunday. And what could she do?'

Kate shrugged. 'Dunno. But it's worth a try.'

She went outside and rang the surgery number. A robot answered.

'The surgery is closed. You have a choice. If it is a real emergency, you should go to the Casualty department at the Duke of Kent Hospital. If it is a minor problem, call the NHS Direct helpline. Or stay on the line to be connected to our duty doctor who can advise you further.'

Kate stayed on the line. Please, please God, let it be her. Let it be Dr Scott.

Chapter 12

Somewhere in the long wakeful hours (however could they be called small?) she had made the decision. She called Chad early, and said she would do it. Well, begin to do it. Go along with them, just a little way at first, see what happened, try and judge whether it was even possible. Take a week's leave – once the big presentation was over – and really give it her best shot.

Chad had been very surprised; delighted, excited even, but still surprised.

'All I'm saying,' she warned him, 'is that I'll go down there with you. Talk to the constituency people, to Norman Brampton. All right?'

'All right. Martha, that's fantastic. I know we can make it work. Absolutely know it.'

'You don't,' she said. 'But at least this way you'll know if you can't.'

'I'll arrange to go down there with you – when? Next Saturday? That'd be best.'

'Saturday would be fine,' she said. She sounded odd. She could hear it herself.

'Well, that's marvellous. I'll call Marcus.'

Marcus was pleased and extremely surprised also.

'Wonder what persuaded her?'

'God knows. Let's just be thankful. And put some arrangements in place before she changes her mind.'

Chad had invited Jack Kirkland and Janet Frean for a working lunch at his London flat, to discuss policy. The next day, Chad said, they would – hopefully – stop being front-page celebrities and become working politicians again instead. The electorate was a bit tired of celebrities; it wanted the country in the hands of sensible, grown-up people.

The immediate challenge was persuading as many MPs as possible to join them; a list of possibles, probables and no-hopers had been drawn up. They compared them, adjusted their ratings, and allocated themselves a handful each, starting with the probables. There was also the need to establish local councillors where humanly possible. A handful were in place, but with only a little over two weeks to the May elections there was a serious limit to what more could be achieved.

It was going to be tough: but a few gains would grab all the headlines and put them on a roll. The more success they had, the better the publicity; the better the publicity, the greater the chance of success. At the same time, they were embarking on a heavy programme of public round-the-country speeches. Kirkland would be taking on the home counties and London, Janet the midlands, Chad the north, 'but then on Saturday I'll come down south, head for East Anglia, starting with Binsmow in Suffolk, with our lovely young putative candidate and see what I can do there. Best I go personally, for several reasons, not least that I've had several conversations with Norman Brampton already.'

'Which lovely young putative candidate?' asked Kirkland. His voice was slightly edgy.

'Martha Hartley.'

'Good Lord!' He had wagered Chad that Martha would say no.

'Yes, indeed. So you owe me a hundred pounds, I think.'

'It's extraordinary. Maybe she really is out of love with the law,' said Kirkland.

'Maybe. Maybe she really does think she'll enjoy it,' said Chad.

'Maybe she's just a bit star-struck,' said Janet. 'It's hard to imagine the slog of the thing until you've done it.'

They agreed it was probably a combination of all those things.

Clio arrived just after two. 'I'm sorry I've been so long,' she said rushing into Casualty. 'I was on endless calls this morning. It's Kate, isn't it?'

'Yes,' said Kate. She looked exhausted, Clio thought. Her wild hair was straggling round her white, tear-stained face, her eyes were dark and heavy, and she also looked rather grubby.

'How is your grandmother? And where is she?'

'In something called HDU,' said Kate and burst into tears.

'Oh no. Look, I'll go and find out – oh, hello. You must be Kate's mother.'

'That's right. It's very good of you to come, Dr Scott.' Helen looked and sounded very tired. 'We need some help. My mother's just been rushed off to HDU and then we had a bit of an upset. Kate started shouting at a nurse.'

'I wouldn't worry,' said Clio, 'they're quite used to it. But why is she in HDU?'

'Something about a clot. She was having pains in her legs, said she didn't like to complain and then suddenly had quite bad chest pains. Oh dear. It's all such a nightmare.'

'I'll go and see what I can find out,' said Clio patting her hand. 'Try not to worry too much.'

Some insistent questioning of the duty doctor revealed that not only did Jilly have a deep vein thrombosis – arguably caused by the long period on the trolley – but it had moved upwards and part of it had lodged in her pulmonary artery. Clio returned to Helen and Kate and broke the news as gently as she could.

'I know it's terribly worrying for you. But she's getting the best possible care now. She's on intravenous heparin which is a wonderful drug, and the doctor will keep you informed – he's promised to come down as soon as he knows any more. I'm afraid they wouldn't let me see her, but she's basically fit, and she should be fine. She's such a – such a splendid woman,' she added, flailing around rather wildly for things to say, cheerful, positive things. 'So smart and attractive. I love her shop.'

When Clio left, Kate was talking to some young man who'd walked into Casualty who obviously wasn't a patient. Maybe he'd come to collect someone. He was clearly very taken with Kate; not surprisingly. She was very attractive: even with her dirty face. But who did she remind her of? Who, who?

Clio thought of herself at sixteen, tubby, plain, anxious, pushed about by her sisters, totally devoid of self-confidence. She could never have done what Kate had done, battled with bureaucracy, questioned authority. She could hardly do it now, for God's sake; she couldn't even stand up to her own husband.

'You remind me of my mother,' said Gideon Keeble. 'She was the great love of my life,' he added, smiling, 'although I don't suppose you would quite regard that as a compliment. But you would have loved her. And she would have loved you.'

'When – when did she die?'

'Five and a half years ago. She did very well, she was nearly ninety.'

'Ninety!'

That was quite old. Too old, she felt, to be Gideon's mother. He read her thoughts.

'I was her last but one child. She was almost forty when I was born. Let me put you out of your misery. I'm fifty-one. Not quite Methuselah.'

'I told you, Gideon, you seem absolutely ageless to me.'

'Well – I should be thankful for that.'

It was true; sitting there, smiling, in the sunshine, his blue eyes boring into hers, he was no age at all, just a powerfully attractive man.

'And – how am I like your mother?'

'Oh – well now, she was clever. And tough.'

'How do you know I'm either of those things?'

'You couldn't do the job you do if you weren't. And then you're both charming. And loving.'

'And how do you know I'm loving?'

'I – sense it,' he said, and it was one of the most erotic things that had ever been said to her.

'Now,' he added, 'what would you like to talk about?'

'You,' she said. 'Please. Tell me about you.'

She knew a lot of it, of course: the rise from a childhood spent in considerable poverty to a fortune that was now counted in billions rather than millions, from a first job as a messenger and a second as a salesman for a small Dublin menswear store, to the ownership of a worldwide retail organisation. There had been titanic struggles for the control of other companies, famous bidding wars, even more famous deals. He owned fashion chains in Europe, America and Australia; and large furniture warehouses, operating largely in out-of-town shopping centres. He also had a chain of small exclusive stores selling what he called couture for the home. He had recently branched into hotels, 'boutique hotels, you'll have heard of them no doubt', foodie shops, and delis cashing in on the fashion for what he called smart food, and a worldwide chain of coffee shops. A great deal of his wealth inevitably came from real estate, shop frontage on some of the world's most famous streets.

Along the way were casualties, namely three marriages, and – on one famous occasion – almost himself. A massive heart attack, five years earlier, had left him half dead, but absolutely opposed to doing what he was told and taking life more quietly.

'What would I do with a quiet life? I would get very noisy indeed, noisy and troublesome.'

He worked as hard as ever now, he said, but with the important difference that he took care of himself. 'I don't smoke, hardly drink. I swim two miles a day, which is excessively boring, but I do it.'

'Wherever do you do that?' she said.

'Oh, well now, in my house in London I have one of those very clever little pools that sets up a current against you and each length measures about half a mile; in the country I have a bigger one, rather vulgar but none the worse for that, and in Ireland, unless the weather is absolutely frightful, I swim in my lake.'

'Oh my God,' said Jocasta.

'Yes, I do call on Him quite often as I plunge in. But it is truly wonderful once you get going. I shall make you sample it.'

'Then I shan't come!'

'In which case, I promise not to make you sample it. Anyway, for all those reasons I am now as fit as the proverbial flea. A rather large one, it has to be said. Look, shall we forget about the food, since you are so clearly not enjoying it, and take their very splendid boat trip instead? And after that I am afraid I shall have to start heading back to London. I have to catch a plane to Australia very early in the morning and I have a great deal of work to do first.'

* * *

173

She arrived home feeling drunk: not with wine, of which she had had very little, but with him. He had hardly touched her, except to kiss her as he picked her up and again as they parted, to hand her into the boat and to help her into her jacket; but she felt disturbed by him nonetheless. Much of it, she knew very well, was the dizzy pleasure of being with someone so famous and powerful, of him finding her desirable and interesting. It made her feel soothed and comforted, made Nick's rejection just a little less painful.

'It has been very lovely,' he said, smiling at her across the considerable width of the car. 'I don't know when I enjoyed a day so much. Would you like to do it again? Well, perhaps not an absolute repetition, but – well, I'm sure we can find something similar.'

'Yes,' she said, reckless with the excitement of it, 'I would love that. I really would.'

'Then speak to Nick,' he said, 'and when you have done that, let me know.'

'Dr Scott? It's Kate.'

'Oh – hi, Kate.' She looked across the room at Jeremy; he was deep in the motoring section of the *Sunday Telegraph*. 'Any news?'

'Not really. The clot thing's quite serious. She's really ill and they won't let me see her. They said Mum could, but not me. What's going on, do you think?'

'I don't know, Kate. But I expect she's been sedated, and they think too many visitors are a bad idea. When she's better, you'll be able to, I'm sure.'

'OK.' She sounded child-like, near to tears.

'Look,' Clio looked at Jeremy again; he was waving at her, tapping his watch, 'look, I've got to go now, I'm so sorry. Let me know how she's doing. And if you're really still worried, I'll try and come back, get some more news. All right?'

'Yeah, OK. Thanks. Bye.'

There was a click as she hung up. She had failed her, Clio thought, she should have offered to go back anyway: only there really was nothing she could do. And what on earth would she say to Jeremy?

In fact, she didn't have to say anything to Jeremy for quite a while; he was called in to the Duke of Kent's Hospital himself to operate on one of his private patients who had fallen and broken her hip. Clio prayed that no one would mention her presence there a few hours earlier because she hadn't told him . . .

'So – how was lunch with the billionaire retailer?' Nick's voice was light, teasing; it annoyed her.

'Fine,' she said, slightly coolly.

'Where did you go?'

'The Waterside Inn.'

'Well, get you. Wish I were a billionaire retailer. I'd like to have taken you there.'

'You could have done. Actually.'

'Jocasta, don't be difficult. I'm trying to make amends.'

'Sorry. How was David Owen?'

'He was charming. Very helpful. Now, I'd like to come and see you. If that's all right.'

'Well . . .' Did she really want to see him? She felt unsettled by her day. If he came round, they'd have another row. She knew it. Nick would be full of political gossip and professional chitchat. She wanted more of Gideon Keeble, flattering her, telling her how beguiling she was . . .

'Well, the thing is,' she said, playing for time, 'I – '

Her mobile leapt into life: she looked at it, wondering if it was Gideon, if it could possibly be Gideon, wondering what she could say to Nick if it was.

It wasn't Gideon. It was the news editor at the *Sketch*.

'Hold on, Nick,' she said, 'it's the news desk, sorry.'

'Jocasta? Trolley tragedy. Duke of Kent Hospital, Guildford. Agency bloke already there, with photographer. Quick as you can.'

Derek Bateson felt rather pleased with himself. He had only been working as a stringer for the North Surrey News Agency for three months and this was his third big story. Of course this one didn't compete with the one in January where someone had been on a trolley for three days, covered in blood; but it wasn't bad, given that this old lady was so ill.

'Derek Bateson? Hi!' A slightly breathless voice sounded behind him.

Derek turned; an amazing-looking girl was smiling at him, holding out her hand. She was very tall, and she had all this blonde hair, and legs that seemed to start at her shoulders, and the most brilliant blue eyes.

'I'm Jocasta,' she said, 'from the *Sketch*. So tell me what's happened.'

'Well, this woman, Jilly Bradford, slipped last night, broke her pelvis, the usual after that, long wait for ambulance, the granddaughter was with her, then all night on a trolley, nothing happening, apart from an X-ray, then around lunchtime her leg got really painful, and she's got a pulmonary embolism. She's in Intensive Care and apparently it's touch-and-go.'

'Poor lady! And – relatives? Any here?'

'Her daughter. Nice sort of woman, very quiet, and the grand-daughter – now she's a livewire. She tore them all off a strip earlier, for not doing anything, and she's been trouble all night according to some old biddy who's been here nearly as long.'

'Well done her. So – who can I talk to?'

'I'd say start with her but her mum's taken her off to her grandma's house for a shower and that. They're not allowed to see the old lady for a bit.'

'Well, she'll be back soon I expect. What about the duty doctor?'

'He's over there. But it's not the one who was on last night.'

'I'll have a word with him. Thanks, Derek. Is your photo-grapher around? Just in case we need him.'

'In the pub. But we can get him any time.'

'Great.'

God, she was gorgeous. Maybe she'd like a drink later on.

'So – where exactly is Mrs Bradford now?'

'In HDU.' The doctor looked at Jocasta coldly. He was very thin, with huge bony hands and a long bony nose, and a crop of spots on his chin. She wondered how old he was; probably younger than her. Like policemen, doctors were getting younger.

'I imagine you won't suggest interviewing her there,' he said. This was clearly intended as cutting irony.

'I'd love to.' She smiled at him. 'But I can see that's not at all practical. Maybe a little later on.'

'I can assure you that you won't be seeing her at any point, later or sooner.'

'Well, that will be up to her, won't it? Who was on duty last night?'

'I don't have to answer that question.'

'No, of course you don't. Well, thank you so much, you've been terribly helpful.'

She looked around: a very young girl was tidying up a bed in one of the cubicles. She looked much more promising. Jocasta waited until the doctor had disappeared into another cubicle and drawn the curtain, then went over to the nurse.

She was very forthcoming. Yes, Mrs Bradford had been brought in at about nine. 'Poor lady. With her granddaughter. She was in awful pain, soaked through from the rain. She was seen quite quickly by a doctor. And then sent down to X-ray. I mean, it wasn't as if she was ignored or anything.'

'Of course not. It must be so difficult, especially on a Saturday night. Lot of drunks and so on, I expect.'

'Yes. And drugs and that. And we get a lot of abuse, you know, and we really are doing our best.'

'I'm sure. And no thanks either, I don't suppose. Now, after she'd been seen, what happened?'

'I don't really know. I was very, very busy. We had a couple of overdoses, that's always a nightmare. A girl having a miscarriage, which was awful. Everyone was completely over-stretched. I went off duty at breakfast-time. But apparently, the granddaughter phoned Mrs Bradford's GP and she came to see if she could help. That set the cat among the pigeons – they don't like that, and you can see why.'

'Of course. But it was nice of her to come. Do you know her name?'

'Who, the GP? I don't, sorry. But she went down to X-ray, they might just know.'

'Well thank you – ' She peered at the nurse's badge. 'Thank you, Sue. You've been really kind.'

Jocasta had learnt long ago that you could walk about unquestioned in a great many places where you had no business to be, providing you proceeded fast and confidently, smiling at anyone you passed, and were carrying a file of papers. She took off her jacket, filched a brown file from a trolley (first emptying it of the papers inside in case they were, literally, life and death), tucked the *Sunday Times* inside it and followed the signs to X-ray.

The X-ray department looked like a scene from a documentary on the plight of the NHS. Dingy, dimly lit, with two depressed fish swimming round a tank, and a pile of broken toys on the floor, and year-old magazines on a low table, it housed several people staring listlessly in front of them.

Jocasta went over to the desk.

'Hi. I wonder if you can help me. There was a Mrs Bradford here last night; she'd fractured her pelvis. Her GP was with her, and I need the GP's name.'

The woman looked terminally bored, leafed through some papers. 'Who's it for, Admin?'

'Yes, that's right.'

'Mrs Jillian Bradford – GP's down here as Dr Scott.'

'And do you have the number?'

'Only the group practice number. It's Guildford.' She looked at Jocasta. 'I thought you were from Admin. They've got all the practice numbers up there.'

'I know, but they're closed. I'm just doing a bit of overtime, catching up on records.'

'Oh, right. Well – it's Guildford 78640.' She looked at Jocasta again. 'You're not the press, are you?'

'I wish. Might be a bit more excitement in my life.'

'Only we've all just been told not to speak to the press. Order from on high. And it was to do with this Mrs Bradford.'

'Really? Wonder why.'

'Some cock-up, apparently. She was left too long, got a clot on her leg – we had her down again for a venography this morning.'

'Did you see her yourself?'

'Couldn't say – it's all a blur, this point in the day. One patient is just like another . . .'

Derek Bateson was still in Casualty when she got back.

'Has the granddaughter come back?'

'Not yet. I've got her mobile number, though. Do you want that?'

'Oh – yes, please!'

Stupid twit. Why couldn't he have told her that, saved her all that nonsense in X-ray. Except she had got a useful quote out of it.

'Hello. Who is this?'

It was a young, wary voice.

'Oh, hello. I presume that's Kate. My name is Jocasta Forbes from the *Sketch* newspaper. I'm so sorry about your grandmother – '

'Is there any news about her?'

'Not yet. I really want to talk to her GP, the one who came today. Derek who you've been talking to, said you might have the number.'

'Yeah, I do. But – what, Mum, for God's sake? It's just someone from the newspaper, she – ' A pause, then she said, clearly cross: 'My mum wants to talk to you.'

A pleasant, worried voice came on the phone.

'Hello. Look, if you don't mind, I think we don't want to get involved with the press. Sorry.'

'That's all right. I can imagine you must feel dreadful, I'm so sorry about your mother.'

'Yes, well, it has been a dreadful day. We're just on our way back there now.'

'I see. Well – I don't want to upset you any further. The only thing is – '

'I'm sorry,' said Helen. 'I really rather would not talk about it.'

Clio was trying to concentrate on a programme about wildlife when the phone rang.

'Hello?'

'Hello. Is that Dr Scott?'

'Ye-es.'

'Hi. Dr Scott, I'm so sorry to bother you at home. My name is Jocasta Forbes. I write for the *Sketch* – '

It was at moments like this, Clio thought, that the earth really moved: moments of shock, of strangeness, even of fear, rocking you dizzily about.

'Did you say Jocasta?' she said finally, hearing her own voice shaky, odd. 'Jocasta Forbes?'

'I did, yes. Why?'

'Oh my God!' said Clio and she had to sit down suddenly. 'I can't believe it. Jocasta Forbes. So you made it, you did what you said!'

'I'm really sorry, but – have we met or something?'

'Jocasta, it's Clio. Clio Scott. Well, Clio Graves, actually. Thailand, eighteen years ago. How amazing. How absolutely amazing!'

'Clio! Oh, my God. How are you? How extraordinary – '

'Totally extraordinary. All those clichés about small worlds are so true. God, it's so weird. But why are you calling me now? And how did you get my number?'

'I'm doing a story about one of your patients. Mrs Bradford.'

'A story! Why is it a story?'

'Well, as I understand it, she was on a trolley for a long time and now she's quite ill. In the HDU. Tabloids like these stories. I've been at the hospital, but her granddaughter – '

'Kate Tarrant?'

'Yes. Haven't met her yet, but she gave me your number. She sounds like quite a girl. Anyway, that's not very important. Oh, Clio, I'd so love to see you! Why on earth didn't we do what we agreed and meet when we all got home again all those years ago? Could I come round, do you think?'

'Um – hold on a minute, Jocasta, could you? My husband's just come in.'

'Your husband! How very grown up of you. Look, ring me back in five minutes. Number's – got a pencil? Right – '

Jeremy came in, tired and irritable. 'Chaos there, some woman's got a pulmonary embolism, supposed to have been left on a trolley, press involved, dreadful nonsense.'

'And – how is she?'

'God, Clio, I don't know. Can we have that soup now?'

'Yes. Yes, of course. It's on the stove. Only – well, Jeremy, I'm terribly sorry, but I've got to go out again. The child with meningitis this morning – the mother's still very worried. So – '

'Dear God, I'll be glad when all this nonsense is over. All right. Don't be long, will you? This has been a dreadful Sunday.'

'Of course. I mean of course not. But I might – might be a bit of a while. Sorry.'

'What's this rubbish?' He was pouring himself a scotch, staring at the television, already engrossed in a programme.

Clio left the house quietly, drove down the lane, stopped and phoned Jocasta.

'Hi. It's me. Look – I don't want to come to the hospital. Medical conventions and all that. Could we meet at the pub just down the road from the hospital? It's called the Dog and Fox. Saloon bar.'

'Sure. Can't wait.'

Clio saw Jocasta immediately as she hurried into the pub. She was sitting at a table by the window, smoking, reading something; she had a bottle of wine and two glasses in front of her. She looked up, saw her, and smiled, then stood up, pushed her mane of hair back and came towards her; and in that moment Clio knew exactly who it was that Kate Tarrant had reminded her of.

'There's not a lot more news, I'm afraid.' Staff Nurse Campbell smiled with officious patience at Helen and Kate. 'Your mother is still in HDU – the High Dependency Unit – receiving the very best, most technologically advanced care available, on a virtually one-to-one basis. Believe me, she is in the very best place.'

'It might be the best place now,' said Kate. 'But if you'd looked after her properly in the beginning, she wouldn't need all that, would she? If she hadn't been lying in the gutter for hours and then on that trolley all night and half today she wouldn't have to be given all that crap.'

'Kate! I'm sorry,' Helen said apologetically to Nurse Campbell, 'she's very upset.'

'I daresay.' The look Nurse Campbell gave Kate would have terrified even a slightly frailer spirit. 'Well, I think the best thing would be for you to go home and come back in the morning. Your mother isn't really aware of very much at the moment and if she was . . . If she was, I don't think this young lady's attitude would help. She needs peace and quiet, not aggravation.'

'Oh and she's had that, has she?' asked Kate. 'I don't

remember much peace and quiet down in that cruddy Casualty all last night, people throwing up and shouting and shitting themselves in that filthy toilet!'

'Kate, please! Be quiet! I do apologise,' said Helen.

'Oh don't worry, Mrs Tarrant. We get used to hysteria, I do assure you. Now I really would advise you very strongly to go home.'

'Is there nowhere we could wait here?' asked Helen humbly. 'We live quite a way away, you see.'

'There is a relatives' room,' said Nurse Campbell reluctantly. 'On the ground floor. But it's not very comfortable.'

'I wonder how we knew that,' said Kate. 'Come on, Mum, let's go.'

Helen followed Kate down the corridor, too weary and anxious to reprimand her further.

'I could sit here forever,' said Jocasta stubbing out her cigarette. 'We haven't even started on our travels, have we? Just tell me one thing – did you stick to your plan? End up where you thought and so on?'

'No, I didn't. Not really. I often wonder what Martha's doing.'

'I heard something about her the other day. Right out of the blue. She's in politics, I was told. Well, on the edge. In with this new party, apparently. I was going to try and track her down as well. Oh, dear, I must go.'

'What – what exactly are you going to – to write?' asked Clio.

'Oh – you know. Lots of sob stuff. And shock-horror, NHS fails again. Yet another old lady left on a trolley.'

'Jocasta, she's hardly an old lady,' said Clio. 'She's a rather glamorous sixty.'

'She is? God, I wish I could meet her. Do you think I could?'

'Absolutely not, if she's in the HDU.'

'Have you met the daughter?'

'Yes. She's very nice indeed. The granddaughter . . .' She hesitated; she was still – absurdly she knew, for what reason for it could there possibly be? – slightly bothered by the resemblance between Kate and Jocasta. 'She's a tough little nut.'

'Yes, so I gathered. Maybe I could find her at least.'

'Maybe. Yes, it would be interesting for you.' She would be

interested herself. Would Jocasta see the likeness between them? Probably not. There were after all only so many variations that could be worked on two eyes, a nose and a mouth. The tumble of a billion genes was bound to yield some duplication . . .

Her stomach lurched. She looked at Jocasta, said hesitantly, 'Jocasta, I know it's your job and everything, but, well, do you think it's going to do any good? Writing this story, putting the names of these nice people all over the paper?'

'Oh Clio!' Jocasta shook her head sorrowfully. 'I'm not about doing good. I'm about doing a good job. It's what I'm paid for. I'm sorry. I hope it's not going to strike our friendship down at the first hurdle, but I really, really do have to write it.'

'Yes. Yes, I see.' She couldn't really. 'But it will make things much worse for poor Mrs Bradford – the hospital will hate it, I can tell you that. And – well, my husband would absolutely kill me if his name got into it. Or mine.'

'Why should his name get into it?'

'Well, he's one of the consultants there. Quite an important one.'

'OK. So why should he kill you? It won't be your fault.'

'He'd think it was. If he knew I knew you . . .'

'Well he won't, don't fret about that. I won't use either of your names. They don't really improve the story and it's the system we're on about, not the people. Now look, where might I find a white coat? You'd be amazed how far I've got in the past with one on. Practically into the operating theatre.'

'Jocasta, that's so terrible.'

'Not at all. You haven't got one, have you?'

'No, I have not,' said Clio untruthfully.

'Doesn't matter, I'll find the hospital laundry. I've done that a few times. Now look, call me in a day or two. Here's my card, phone number, e-mail address and everything. And I should warn you, the other rats will be down tomorrow.'

'What other rats?'

'The other papers.'

'Oh God, Jocasta, do you have to – '

'Yes, I do. Sorry.' She leant forward and kissed Clio. 'I'm so, so glad I found you. Don't worry about the story. Tomorrow's fish-and-chip wrapping, you know.' She always said that; it was doubly untrue, now that fish and chips were wrapped in hygienic white paper, and every story was available to be read afresh on the Internet at the press of a button or two. But it still comforted people.

Helen was dozing fitfully in the shabby discomfort of the visitors' room, and Kate was reading old copies of *Hello!* when a doctor walked in.

She didn't look much like a doctor, apart from her white coat. She was very young and pretty, and she smiled at Kate and put her fingers on her lips.

'Kate?' she whispered.

'Yes. What is it, is Gran –?'

Jocasta jerked her head towards the door; Kate got up gingerly and followed her out into the corridor.

'As far as I know your gran's just about the same. But I'm not actually a doctor. I'm Jocasta from the *Sketch*. We talked earlier.' She smiled at Kate; she looked exhausted, poor little thing; it must have been a terrible ordeal for her. 'How're you doing?'

'Pretty worried; they just won't tell us anything and I want to see Granny and they won't let me.'

'Well – we'll go up there in a minute, shall we? See what we can find out. I don't know how far Dr Jocasta will get, but we might make first base. Are you hungry? I've got some crisps outside.'

'Oh yes please. I'm starving. How did you get this far? They said the outside doors were all locked now.'

'Casualty's always open. I just walked in.'

She was great, Kate thought, wolfing down the crisps gratefully minutes later; really, really great. She liked her a lot.

Chapter 13

She could hear the shock in their voices. Of all the things she had done that they found difficult to understand, this clearly topped the list.

'But, dear,' her mother said, 'of course we would be very pleased. And proud. But – why? I thought you loved your job.'

'I do. I do love it. And in any case, I wouldn't be thinking of leaving it until I get selected. Which I almost certainly won't. But, well just lately I've found it a bit less satisfying. And I'm intrigued by this as a – challenge.' She needed a challenge. She needed something. If she couldn't have Ed.

'But you don't know anything about politics.'

'Well – I didn't. But I've been working for this party, doing bits of legal work and so on, for a while. And I like what I see of it. Well, some of it anyway. Honestly, I'm almost as surprised as you are that they've asked me. And I'm as sure as I'm sitting here that I won't even be short-listed. Let alone adopted as the local party candidate. So it's all a bit of a farce, really. But I've said I'll give it a go.'

Only because of what Ed had said, really. Only because of the expression on his face when he left, which had looked like dislike . . .

After she had rung off, she decided to allow herself another, proper cry. It seemed to help with the pain: briefly.

'Oh, what fun! This is doing me much more good than all that awful stuff they keep pumping into me. There! How do I look?'

'Mummy, I'm not sure about this,' said Helen.

She sounded as exhausted as she looked; Jilly, on the other

hand, was rosy and brilliant-eyed, lying back on her pillows, fluffing up her hair and contemplating herself in her small mirror. Anyone studying them would have thought it was Helen and not her mother who had almost died four days earlier.

'Not sure about what, darling?'

'You seeing this girl again. She's caused so much trouble – '

'Not for me she hasn't,' said Jilly briskly. 'If it hadn't been for her, I would never have seen you the other night. Or Kate. And then being able to tell her exactly how ghastly it was, and reading about it the next day – or was it the next, I'm rather confused now . . .'

'It was yesterday, that bit of the story,' said Helen.

'Oh, yes. Well, it did feel like revenge, of a sort. On all those stupid people in Casualty, and that dreadful Staff Nurse up here. All so pleased with themselves, so unconcerned about everyone's suffering. And then it's splendid that they've put me in this nice little room, isn't it? So thoughtful.'

Helen was silent; her mother had been put in a side ward at the express instructions of one of the senior consultants, Mr Graves, under whose care she was, who had been incandescent with rage at the story in the *Sketch* on the Monday morning and the descent of at least a dozen other journalists and photographers on what he called his hospital. It had been a mistake that, leading as it had to a seventy-two-point headline in the *Sun* reading, 'They're our hospitals, actually, Mr Graves.'

Jocasta had visited a rather frail but animated Jilly in her room at about noon on Monday; the rest of the press had been kept out, but as the new best friend of Jilly Bradford's granddaughter, there had been no such control over her, and in any case, with her unruly hair tucked neatly under a baseball cap, nobody recognised her as the young woman masquerading as a doctor who had caused such trouble the night before, walking into HDU to check on Mrs Bradford's progress and, having ascertained it was satisfactory, telling the agency nurse in charge that she thought seeing her daughter and granddaughter for a minute or two would do her good.

A real doctor had arrived very shortly afterwards, Jocasta had been thrown out, and the nurse had been most severely reprimanded, but had defended herself, saying that she could hardly be expected to know every houseman walking about the hospital, and adding that if this was the National Health in England, she couldn't wait to get back to her own hospital in South Africa.

This had been reported back to Jocasta who had passed it on to her readers, along with the quote from a girl in the X-ray department that one patient seemed much like another, and another from a nurse in Casualty, that it was impossible to look after people properly, so understaffed were they, and it simply wasn't right.

'How much longer are we going to have to put up with this sort of thing?' her emotive article had ended. 'In a health service that used to be the envy of the world? How many more patients are going to die, how many more old ladies are to be left alone and frightened, and in the case of Jilly Bradford, soaked to the skin after lying in the rain for hours waiting for an ambulance? And then denied such basic comforts as a warm bed and a cup of tea? How much longer do we all have to wait before someone takes the NHS in hand?'

Apart from finding herself described as an old lady, Jilly was entranced by the article and her starring role in it.

'I'm sorry about that,' Jocasta said to Kate, who reported it, giggling. 'But we'll get a nice picture of her in a day or so when she's looking a bit better, and show everyone that she isn't really an old lady at all.'

Clio had crept out early on the Monday morning to buy the *Sketch*, had sat in her car reading it, her heart in her mouth, absolutely horrified by almost every word. Jocasta had kept her promise, there was no mention of her by name, or even by reference, as Mrs Bradford's GP, but the opprobrium she had heaped on the hospital, the out-of-context quotes from various departments – it all made her feel very sick.

She had managed somehow to chat normally over breakfast with Jeremy, saw him off to the hospital with a sigh of huge relief, and got ready for work herself; maybe that would be the end of it. But it wasn't; two copies of the *Sketch* were being fought over in the surgery, and the receptionist wanted to know if the paper had approached her.

'Why should they, for goodness' sake?' asked Clio.

'Well, you *are* Mrs Bradford's GP – and I bet they get onto your husband. He's the consultant orthopod there.'

'Well,' she said, reluctantly, 'I suppose so. But – '

'Clio,' said Mark Salter, 'if there's a follow-up on this, someone's bound to want to talk to Jeremy. I'm surprised the girl who wrote this piece didn't try herself.'

'She obviously didn't think it was very important,' said Clio coolly; blissfully unaware that at that very moment, a reporter from the *Daily Express* and another from the *Sun* were standing in front of Jeremy, demanding a quote, even as he ordered them out of Outpatients. That was when he had made the unfortunate remark about it being *his* hospital.

An hour later the papers caught up with her; there were several phone calls, followed by a visit from three reporters and two photographers, who sat in the surgery reception for hours: did she, as Mrs Bradford's GP, have anything to say about the conditions at the Duke of Kent Hospital, and how had it been possible for such an old lady to be treated, or rather not treated, in such a way? While she was stalling helplessly, feeling like a rat in a trap, Jocasta phoned; angry with her as she was, Clio accepted her advice to give them a quote.

She cobbled something together about the Health Service struggling under enormous pressure and everyone doing their utmost to cope, and that she greatly regretted what had happened to Mrs Bradford, 'But the GP's role is quite separate from that of the hospital's and I cannot possibly comment on what happened to her while she was not in my direct care.'

She sent this out via Margaret, neatly typed on her computer, refusing to see anyone personally. Her quote was sufficiently dull to persuade the reporters they were wasting their time and to send them back to the much greater excitement of the hospital.

Both her sisters phoned, intrigued by the fracas and the way in which Jeremy had been vilified. Ariadne, who loathed him, was clearly hugely amused. Several friends in the medical profession called to sympathise.

All the papers covered the story on Tuesday; the *Sketch* was still winning the race by a head, with a brief personal interview given by Mrs Bradford 'in a frail whisper' to Jocasta Forbes, relating all that she had endured, and paying tribute to her granddaughter, Kate, who had gone into battle so manfully for her, and, indeed, to Miss Forbes herself who had managed to help her daughter to visit her in the HDU when she felt desperate for reassurance and personal contact.

'I would say it was at that moment that I began to turn the corner.'

The reporters were all desperate to get a shot of Kate, who had become very much the heroine of the hour, and she was desperate to be allowed to talk to them, but Helen refused point blank. Jocasta, her sympathies torn between the two of them, managed to smuggle them out of the hospital that evening, by a back door; but her car was spotted and a rather blurry picture of Kate, sitting in the back seat and smiling at them delightedly, appeared in a great many papers next day.

But by Wednesday it was all dying down, apart from a paragraph in Lynda Lee-Potter's column in the *Daily Mail*, blaming the whole affair on the demise of the matron and the fact that nurses were no longer trained on the wards.

'Right, now this is for tomorrow's paper,' said Jocasta. 'I promise you that after this I'll be leaving you in peace.'

'Oh, please don't,' said Kate, 'I'll really miss you. It's been great.'

'Hardly great,' said Helen slightly coldly. She found Kate's adoration of Jocasta irritating and misplaced; as far as she could see, Jocasta had caused them a great deal of trouble. Of course she had managed to smuggle her in to see her mother that night; and Jilly, once she was out of danger, had hugely enjoyed herself. Her pelvis was still painful, but she was displaying, as always, her robust constitution, had recovered from the surgery very fast and was eating well and even demanding wine with her meals.

'I'm afraid only the private patients get that, darlin',' said the large Jamaican lady who brought her food round, 'and you're not one of them, even if you are in this very nice room.'

She was to be allowed out at the weekend, but not to her own home; she was going – with extreme reluctance – to stay with Helen for a week or two. Kate was thrilled.

'We can have a great time. I'll be chief nurse, and bring you all the champagne you want, and I'll get you loads of videos and stuff.'

'Oh Kate,' said Jilly, patting her arm, smiling at her affectionately, 'what would I have done without you? Died, I should think. Now, Jocasta dear, I've done my best with my hair and Kate's fetched me this pretty bed jacket – will that do?'

'It's gorgeous,' said Jocasta and indeed it was, palest pink, edged with swansdown.

Kate looked at Jocasta and smiled. 'You don't think I could be in one of the pictures, do you?'

'Well – '

'Kate!' said Helen. 'That's out of the question.'

'Why? Gran just said I'd saved her life. I don't see why I shouldn't. It would be so great. I might even be discovered by some model agency.'

This was her current ambition: to be a supermodel. She had confided it to Jocasta, who had actually thought she could be very successful, but hadn't said so. She knew too much about the dark drug-fuelled world of some of the fashion industry, and wouldn't have encouraged Kate into it for the world.

'I really don't see why she shouldn't be in the photographs,' said Jilly. 'She saved my life, it's perfectly true. I'd like it very much. Jocasta, what do you think?'

'I think it would be lovely,' said Jocasta carefully. It would give the pictures a much greater interest for the readers, this beautiful child, who had fought so hard for her grandmother.

'Mum! Please!'

'I do think it would be very nice to have Kate in the picture, Mrs Tarrant,' said Jocasta, suddenly firm. 'She's so much part of the story. So – let's just get on with it, shall we?' There were certain times when you could bulldoze people into what you wanted, when their resistance suddenly lowered. She had felt Helen's go then. 'I'll get the photographer in straight away. Kate, go and comb your hair. You don't want to meet the press looking less than your best.'

Kate giggled.

The photographer set up his camera. 'This'll make a great shot,' he said to Jocasta, while Jilly fussed over her hair for the umpteenth time and Kate settled on the bed beside her, putting her arm round her grandmother's shoulder. 'Probably get the front page.'

'Hope so. But get on with it – the mother's not happy, and I don't want to upset her.'

'The kid's gorgeous. And you know something? She looks a bit like you.'

'God, I wish,' said Jocasta.

'Those should be lovely,' said Jocasta, smiling at them when he had gone. 'You both looked very glamorous.'

'Well, thank you,' said Jilly. 'I doubt it, rather. It's when one is unwell that the years show.'

'I promise – they don't show on you. And Kate's wrinkles didn't look too bad either. You both looked great. She really does look a lot like you.'

'Well, it would be nice to think so,' said Jilly, 'but unfortunately that's quite impossible.'

'Really? Why?'

'Well, you see – '

'Mummy,' said Helen, and her voice was very cold, 'not now.'

Kate was staring at her mother; then she looked at Jocasta and smiled at her quickly.

'I'll come and see you off.'

'Fine,' said Jocasta. 'Well, goodbye, Mrs Bradford, I'm so glad you're recovering so well.'

'Thank you, my dear. And thank you for all your help. I'm sure you've helped a great many other people, indirectly. And if ever you're in Guildford, come and find my shop. Caroline B, in the High Street.'

Kate was going to miss Jocasta; she really liked her so much. She wasn't scared of anyone, just went for it and got what she wanted.

'Will you just be writing about Granny?' she asked. 'To go with that picture?'

'Oh no,' said Jocasta, 'we need to remind them of the whole story. Four days, which is what it will be, between this picture

191

and the last, is a very long time in newspapers. So I'll certainly be mentioning you and all you did.'

'Great! Thanks for persuading Mum. Um – could you do one more thing? Put my whole name in. There are so many Kates, it's really boring.'

'OK,' said Jocasta smiling. 'What is your whole name?'

'Kate Bianca Tarrant.'

'That's a pretty name. Bianca, I mean.'

'Yeah. When I'm older I'm thinking I might call myself that. Your job must be so fun,' said Kate wistfully. 'Maybe I could be a reporter, instead of a model.'

'Well, it is fun. And you do get to meet a whole lot of people you never would normally. And hear some incredible things. But there's a lot of dogsbody work, as there is in everything. I actually think,' she said looking at Kate consideringly, 'you'd be rather good at it.'

'Cool! Well that's what I'll do, then. Could you get me a job?' Jocasta laughed.

'Not at the moment. You're a bit young. And these days, they want you to have a degree.'

'Degree! No thanks. I can hardly face A levels.'

'Well, it's up to you. Tell you what, we do sometimes take on people for work experience. Maybe this summer holidays, if you wanted, I could get you a week. Not necessarily with me. Maybe even in the fashion department.'

'Oh wow, yeah! That'd be great. Don't forget, will you?'

'I don't suppose you'll let me,' said Jocasta. 'Here, take my card. All my numbers and my e-mail address. Is that any good to you?'

'Yeah, Dad's got a computer. Thanks, Jocasta. I'm going to miss you.'

'Me too.'

'Sorry about Mum, just then. I don't know what's the matter with her. Honestly, she's so weird – usually she tells everyone. It was because I'm adopted.'

'Oh, are you?' said Jocasta. She didn't appear surprised, Kate noticed, just politely interested.

'Yeah.'

'You all seem very close anyway.'

'I s'pose we are, really. To be honest, I get on with Gran best. She's such fun. My dad's all right, but even stricter than my mum, and then I've got a little sister who's just Little Miss Perfect, all clever and hard-working, with a scholarship to some posh school for her music.'

'Is she adopted too?'

'No, she's theirs. She was born after they adopted me.'

'And – how do you feel about being adopted?' said Jocasta. 'Sorry, do you hate talking about it?'

'Course not. It's cool.'

'And – do you know anything about your – your birth mother? Would you like to meet her one day?'

'No,' said Kate firmly, 'I mean, what would be the point? After what she did to me.'

'And – what exactly did she do to you? Did you hand you over when you were a baby, or – sorry,' she said again, 'is this upsetting you?'

'Course not,' said Kate. 'Yes, that's right. Well, I was still a baby anyway.'

She was beginning to wish she hadn't embarked on this. She certainly wasn't about to tell Jocasta, cool, clever, successful Jocasta, all the shameful, painful facts, about being abandoned like a piece of rubbish in a cleaning cupboard. 'She was a – a student,' she improvised wildly, 'from – from Ireland. She was a Catholic, so she couldn't possibly have had an abortion. But she loved me and she wanted to know I was in a good home. In fact, she wouldn't let me go to the first people who wanted me, she waited till my mum and dad turned up and she was really satisfied they'd look after me properly. All right?'

She felt aggressive now, and angry, as if Jocasta had dragged the information out of her in the first place. She turned away, looked across the car park. Suddenly she felt an arm round her shoulders.

'Kate. It's OK. Calm down. I didn't think anything bad about your mother at all. Not for a moment. She must have been very special to have you. And very brave to have let go of you for your own sake. Very brave indeed. Now look, it's been really fun getting to know you. Don't forget about the work experience, will you? Just give me a call when you feel you're ready. Or even if you just want to go out to lunch or something. I hate to think I'm never going to see you again, I really do.'

She probably didn't mean it, Kate thought, watching the black Golf zoom out of the car park; and they'd probably never meet again. Why should they, after all?

'Jocasta, you all right?'

It was Chris Pollock; he had called her in to congratulate her on the story.

'Yes. Yes, I'm fine. Thank you.'

'You seem a bit – distracted.'

'Oh – I'm a bit tired, I guess.'

'Reporters aren't allowed to get tired. I've got a real beauty for you this afternoon. Some poor cow's just had a baby in Holloway, while shackled to the delivery bed. Her mum's just phoned, wants to talk to us. Right up your street. She lives in Dalston – news desk have the address. Now, are you really OK? I don't want this story messed up.'

'You're such a gentleman, Chris. Don't worry. It won't be.'

She did feel tired: terribly tired. And depressed. Nick hadn't called. And she had missed him. In spite of his refusal to do what she asked, to commit himself to her, in spite of the heady excitement – fading now – of the lunch with Gideon.

So much about him was right for her: he understood her, knew her completely, admired what she did. But in one way he failed her. One huge way. He might tell her he loved her, but what he did made her doubt it. And there was nothing, nothing at all, she could do about it. It made her very sad.

Dalston 1 mile, said a sign. Forget Nick. She had more important things to think about.

She got home very late that night; Nick was waiting for her at her house.

'I wanted to see you,' he said, giving her a kiss. 'Am I forgiven?'

In that moment, in her weariness, she was only pleased to see him: everything else was wiped out. 'You're forgiven,' she said, going into his arms.

'I'm really working hard on myself – '

'Nick, let's not even talk about it. I'm just glad you're here.'

'Well, that's nice. That's very nice. I'm glad I'm here too. And you don't have any retailing billionaires hidden anywhere?'

So he had noticed. Had even – possibly – minded.

'Not one.'

'I'm pleased to hear it. He's just a tad too attractive, to my way of thinking.'

'Is he?' she asked, her eyes very wide. 'I hadn't really noticed. He's just – '

'I know. An ordinary old billionaire. You look all in, sweet pea.'

'I feel it. I've had an awful day. Well, not awful. But upsetting.'

'What, steely old Jocasta, aka Lois Lane, upset? Must have been childbirth. Here, have a glass of wine. I've left you just about enough.'

'It was. You're right. I'm so phobic about it, Nick. It's so pathetic.'

'Not really,' he said, handing her the glass, 'not after what you went through.'

'Yes, it is. I should have got over it years ago.'

'A trauma's a trauma, honeybunch. My godmother never got over being blooded on the hunting field, still practically throws up at the sight of a fox, even rifling through her Kensington dustbin. I've told you.'

'I know. But . . . well, anyway, this poor woman, she had a baby in prison. She was actually in chains, Nick, while she was having it. And it was an awful birth, went on for hours and hours and in the end they had to – well, I won't go into detail. But her mother did. I've got it all on tape. She was screaming and screaming for help. And the baby practically died. I just didn't know how to sit there, how to go on listening. I actually had to ask to go to her bathroom and I was sick. And then I had to write it and something was wrong with my e-mail connection, so I had to phone it in.'

'Poor baby. *You*, I mean.'

'I could never ever go through it, Nick. Not in a million years. I just couldn't. Even with all the anaesthesia anyone could offer me. I'd just start remembering and – oh God!' She started to cry, helplessly, like a child. 'Sorry, I'm so sorry . . .'

'Look at you,' he said, giving her a kiss, taking her in his arms. 'Look at the state of you. You silly moo. No one's going to ask you to go through it. Come on, drink that all down. And then I'm going to take you out to dinner. All right?'

'All right,' said Jocasta. 'But first of all I'm going to pull that tape out of its cassette and shred it. And don't let me even near the paper in the morning, to read the story. OK?'

'OK. I love you. And I'm sorry again, about – well everything.'

She stared at him. He so seldom said he was sorry. It was even rarer than his telling her he loved her. Her day and its traumas promptly faded into near-nothingness.

'I love you too,' she said. 'And I'm sorry too. Let's not go out to dinner.'

'Let's not.'

It had come without warning. Friday, the fateful Friday, had been the most beautiful day, windy and sun-dappled; although it was her last day at the practice, Clio felt oddly happy. It might not be so bad. She did after all enjoy being at home. And it would give her a chance to – well, see if she could sort things out, she'd have some time. All might not be lost. And Jeremy would be better tempered and happier. Which would help a lot. She did still love him. She did. She knew she did.

At lunchtime, on a whim, she called him. She had had her farewell drinks at the surgery the night before – Mark was away on the Friday on a course and he had wanted to be there.

'We'll miss you so much, Clio,' he had said, handing over a big scented candle and a box of chocolates. 'And this comes with all our love. You've been the most marvellous member of the team, and we're as fortunate as your patients. God knows how we're going to replace you. Well, we're not. As you know. Series of locums, right up till the end of June. Still, no doubt the practice loss will be your gain. And Jeremy's, of course.'

Clio, eyes filled with tears, said she wasn't sure that either of those statements were correct, and said how much she would miss them too. In the end it had all been quite jolly; but she had felt very tearful again at bedtime (which she managed to conceal from Jeremy) and fate had managed to send her not one but three of her very worst patients that morning. It would be quite nice to be rid of them, at least. And then in the afternoon, she was on call, and was planning to drop in on the Morrises and Josie Higgs at the Hollies, to make sure they were doing as well as they could possibly be; so there would be no painful last departure from the practice.

Jeremy agreed to lunch: 'It would be good to get out for an hour or so. One o'clock all right with you?'

'Of course. Order me a chilli jacket if you get there first.'

'Fine. Look forward to it. Thanks.'

She drove towards the pub singing. She could do a lot of this sort of thing in the future, make him happier. And that in turn would make her happier.

Clio got to the pub first; Jeremy walked in at about one fifteen, looking harassed. She waved at him.

'I've got you a drink. Virgin Mary!'

'Thanks. But I'll have to just have a sandwich – they've added to my list.'

'Oh no. Poor you. OK, I'll go and change the order.'

'I'll come with you. I want more ice in this.'

It was the unofficial hospital local. Several people recognised them, said hello. Clio noticed that a couple of them looked at Jeremy rather oddly. She supposed it must have been the article; they hadn't been out since. She prayed no one would mention it and wished fervently she hadn't suggested this, of all pubs.

Jeremy went off to the gents; Clio returned to their table. A large woman had perched herself at the corner of it, on a stool she had dragged over from the other side of the bar.

'You don't mind, do you? There's nowhere else to sit.'

'Well – not really,' said Clio, knowing that Jeremy would be furious, 'but – '

He came back, glared at the woman.

'This is our table. Sorry.'

'Well, I'm sorry too, but there's nowhere else and I wasn't aware tables in pubs could be exclusively booked,' she said, and then stared at him rather intently. 'I don't know you, do I?'

'Absolutely not,' said Jeremy. He turned his glare on Clio. 'You should have kept the table. Can't we find another?'

The woman sighed and got out a crumpled paperback.

'Please don't worry,' she said, with heavy irony. 'I won't disturb you.'

Maurice Trent, the landlord, appeared with their food.

'Here we are then. Sorry to have kept you. Nice to see you both. What a to-do this week, eh? Paparazzi all over the place, load of rubbish all of it. That girl you were talking to on Sunday, Dr Scott, she was one of them, wasn't she? Nice, she seemed, not the sort you'd expect on a paper like that.'

Clio had often read of bowels turning to water and had scoffed at it; she knew suddenly exactly what it meant.

'What girl was that?' said Jeremy, his expression ice-hard.

'Oh – just one of the reporters,' said Maurice. 'First one down, I think. Yes, all right, all right,' he called to the barmaid who was gesticulating at him. 'Coming. You can't get the help these days, I tell you that. Enjoy your meal.'

Jeremy sat and stared at Clio, who felt violently sick.

'You were talking to one of the reporters? On Sunday? And you didn't mention it?'

'No. I mean yes. Well, not because she was a reporter. Honestly, Jeremy, I promise you. She – she just turned up out of the blue. I mean, she *is* a reporter, but we – we went travelling together years ago, when we were both eighteen. I hadn't seen her since. I – '

'And she just turned up, on your doorstep, at precisely the right moment. How very convenient for her.'

'Yes, well she rang me because I was Mrs Bradford's GP, and then she recognised my name, you know how these things happen, what a small world it is – '

'No I don't. Actually. And this was Sunday?'

'Yes,' she said, very quietly.

'As far as I can remember, you sneaked out of the house, under the pretence of making some house calls. And actually came to meet her here, and – '

'Jeremy, please be quiet. Everyone's looking.'

He turned round; it was true, half the bar was staring at them. He stood up.

'We can discuss this later. Perhaps you'd be kind enough to settle the bill.'

'Yes. Of course. But Jeremy – '

He was gone. The fat woman looked up from her paperback. 'I've just realised why he looks familiar,' she said. 'He's the one in the *Sun*, isn't he? The one who said – '

Clio half ran to the bar, flung a twenty-pound note at the bemused Maurice Trent and went out into the car park. Jeremy's car had gone.

'Martha?'

'Yes. Yes, it is. Hi, Ed.'

She had literally dreamt of this, imagined it so often over the past few days, while the phone so determinedly rang, delivering unwelcome other people to her, bleeped her endlessly with text messages from other equally unwelcome other people, while e-mails leapt relentlessly onto her screen from nobody she wished to hear from: so that now, when it was really him, she wasn't really surprised at all. Just – terrified.

Her voice didn't sound terrified; it sounded its brisk, orderly self.

'I – I'm sorry about the other night,' he said. 'I said some pretty bad things.'

'Justified, most of them, I'd say.'

Less orderly, the voice, then. Shaky, out of breath.

'Even if they were – I shouldn't have said them.'

'Well, they did some good,' she said, 'or maybe they did. I've – ' No, she mustn't say that. Start talking about herself, her career. 'I've done a lot of thinking,' she said.

'Oh. Well – I didn't want to leave it like that. That's all. I wanted us to stay – stay friends at least.'

'Of course.' God, this hurt worse than she could have believed.

'Yes. So – sorry.'

'Ed, it's OK.' She struggled to sound light-hearted. 'I forgive you.'

A long silence, then: 'Great,' he said, 'I'm glad. Maybe – '

'Yes?' Don't sound hopeful, Martha, for God's sake.

'Maybe we could have a drink one night.'

'Yes. Let's. Call me. Or I'll call you.'

'Fine. Right, well – well, cheers. See you later.'

If only, if only those words could have had their real meaning: if only she *could* see him later, see him smile, feel his lips brush her hair, take his hand, kiss him, hold him, lie down with him, have him . . .

'Bye Ed,' she said. Very cool, very controlled again. Martha, again, in fact. Only Martha had never hurt like this before. Well, not quite like this.

Thank God, thank God, she was so busy. How could she have coped with this misery if she wasn't?

Jocasta was walking into a bar when her phone rang.

'Is that Jocasta? This is Jilly. Jilly Bradford.'

'Oh – hi, Mrs Bradford. How are you? Nice to hear from you.'

'I'm very much better, thank you. Bored to death, of course. They won't let me out of here until I can manage the stairs, and even then I can't go home, I've got to stay with my daughter. Of course I'm very fond of them all, but I want to be in my own home. Anyway, I just wanted to thank you for putting that very nice photograph in the paper. It was very flattering, but it will certainly disabuse everyone of the notion that I'm some senile old woman – '

'Yes, it will. I'm glad you liked it.'

'I did. Kate bought about six copies. She's the heroine of the hour at school, of course. Very indignant that your name wasn't on it, though.'

Jocasta laughed. 'That often happens in a follow-up like this one. She's so great, your granddaughter. I think she'll do very well in life.'

'I think so, too. I hope so, anyway. She deserves to.'

There is a sensation that every good reporter knows: a kind of creeping excitement, a thud of recognition at something forming itself just out of reach, something worth pursuing: Jocasta felt it then.

'She was telling me all about being adopted,' she said.

'Was she? She obviously sensed a kindred spirit. She doesn't normally like talking about it.'

'Oh really? No, she was very open with me, brought the subject up herself, in fact.'

'Extraordinary story, isn't it?'

'Well, not that extraordinary. Except that these days most girls don't give their babies up; they keep them and raise them on their own.'

'I didn't mean that. I meant her being found in that way, at the airport. Didn't she tell you that bit?'

'Well – well, not in any detail, no.' Careful, Jocasta, careful . . .

'Oh, I see. But she told you the rest?'

'Well – yes, she – '

'It's so hard for her. She feels it very keenly, poor little thing. Being just abandoned like that.'

'Yes, it must be – hard.'

Her phone bleeped warningly. Shit. If it ran out of power now, she'd scream.

'Terribly hard. She wants to find her, of course, but I think – '

Another bleep.

'Mrs Bradford, I'm going to have to ring you back. My phone's dying on me. If you – '

'Oh, my dear, no need. I just wanted to say thank you. Come and see me when I get home to Guildford; I'll tell Kate to organise it. Or we could have a jolly lunch in Town. That would probably suit you better. Goodbye and – '

The phone died; Jocasta wanted to throw it on the ground and jump up and down on it. It was her own fault, of course, totally her own fault; she'd known it was low; she should have done it that evening before she left, but – well.

Now what did she do? She could hardly ring Jilly back, on a public hospital phone, and say, 'Now, about Kate and her adoption, do go on . . .'

The moment had been lost. And it was totally and absolutely her own fault.

Jeremy came in at about eight, the taut fury, which she had grown to dread, set on his face. She smiled awkwardly, said: 'Jeremy, hello. You must be hungry. I've got some very nice jugged hare if you'd – '

'Please don't try that,' he said.

'Try what?'

'Pretending everything's normal. It simply makes it worse.'

201

'Jeremy, I wish you'd let me explain. I didn't say anything about the hospital or Mrs Bradford to Jocasta – '

'Jocasta?'

'Yes. The reporter.'

'I thought you met her in the pub.'

'I did. But only to talk about old times.'

'Which you couldn't have done in the house? You had to sneak off without explaining she was an old friend?'

'Well – yes. I thought you'd be suspicious, that you wouldn't believe me. I knew you wouldn't listen, that you wouldn't let me go.' She was beginning to feel angry herself.

'I wouldn't let you go! Is that how you see me? As some kind of tyrant? I find that immensely insulting.'

'Well, it isn't meant to be. I'm just trying to explain how it happened, why I did what I did.'

'And then you sat with her in the pub, this reporter friend of yours, and didn't even discuss the wretched Bradford woman? You expect me to believe that?'

'Yes! In fact I actually asked her not to write the story and certainly not to implicate you or me in it.'

'And that was very successful, wasn't it?'

'Actually, yes. If you read the piece you'll see she made no mention of either of us. I could get it if you like – '

'You actually expect me to read that drivel?'

'Oh shut up,' said Clio wearily, surprising herself.

He was clearly surprised too; she so seldom went on the offensive.

'I just can't get over your deceiving me like that,' he said, changing tack. 'It was so unnecessary.'

'Well, maybe if you weren't such a bully, if you didn't treat me like some kind of inferior – '

'That's a filthy thing to say!'

'But it's true. You *do* bully me. You don't respect what I do, you've made me give up a job I absolutely love, you're dismissive of almost everything I say, you're always in a bad temper – well, not always,' she added, anxious, even in her rage and misery, to be accurate, 'but very often. You won't allow me to do anything on my own, you blame me for everything that goes wrong in our lives, even the simplest thing, like someone sitting at our table in

202

the pub – can you wonder I didn't ask you if I could invite an old friend round for a chat? I think it's time you took a proper look at yourself, Jeremy, I really do.'

He said nothing, just stood staring at her in silence for several moments; then he turned and went upstairs to their room. She followed him; he had pulled out a suitcase and was putting things in it.

'What are you doing?' she asked. She was frightened now.

'I'm packing. I would have thought that was perfectly evident.'

'To go – where?'

'I'm not sure. But there clearly is no room for me here. I have nothing to contribute to our marriage. So I think it's better I go.'

'Jeremy, don't be stupid. Please!' She could hear the panic in her voice.

'I see nothing stupid in it. You're obviously much better on your own. Doing your job, which clearly means much more to you than I do. It made me feel quite ill listening to you last night, telling me how sorry everyone was, how they hadn't replaced you yet, how much they were going to miss you. My God, how are the sick folk of Guildford going to get on without you, Clio? Could you move, please, I want to get at my shirts.'

'Fuck your shirts,' she said in a quiet voice, 'and fuck you. And how dare you diminish my work like that?'

'You never even consulted me over taking that job in the first place,' he said. 'I had something altogether different in mind, not a part-time wife, obsessed with her career. I had hoped we would have had children by now, but I've been denied those as well. I wonder if you're trying to cheat me there, as well. I wouldn't put anything past you, Clio.'

'You bastard!' she said, tears smarting at the back of her eyes, a lurch of dreadful pain somewhere deep inside her. 'You absolute bastard. How dare you, how dare you say that!' Then suddenly everything shifted, and she felt very strong, and she looked at him, in all his arrogant self-pity and cruelty, and knew she couldn't stand another day, another hour of him. 'Don't bother packing any more, Jeremy, I'm going myself. I don't want to spend another night in this house, where we could have been so happy and where you have managed to make us so miserable.

I want to get out of it, and out of this marriage. It's a travesty. I hate it.'

And without taking any more than her bag and her car keys, she walked out of the house and got into her car and drove away from him and their brief, disastrous marriage.

Chapter 14

She had tried to shrug it off; to tell herself it wasn't that important, but she knew it was. An abandoned baby was a fantastically exciting story. Especially an abandoned baby who had grown up into the most beautiful girl, beautiful enough, indeed, to be a supermodel; a troublesome, beautiful girl, who wanted to find the woman who had abandoned her.

It was an absolutely wonderful story. It made her feel quite sick, so wonderful was it.

Only – and this was where the occasional struggle Jocasta had with herself began – this could really hurt Kate: damage her dreadfully. The mother might not turn up at all and break Kate's heart. Or she might be absolutely wonderful, claim Kate and break the Tarrants' hearts. Or she might be an absolute horror: how much better for everyone if Jocasta forgot about it, let them all be. She knew all too well the demons released from Pandora's box by tabloid newspapers, by any newspaper, indeed; she saw it all the time.

Jocasta thought suddenly of Clio and how she was coping with the aftermath of the story; Clio and her dreadful, arrogant husband. How did a sweet, clever girl like her come to be married to such a creature? She hoped she hadn't caused any trouble between them. She might call her and see if she was all right. And then – Kate? She could talk to her direct; make the excuse of the work experience in the summer. She could get her to talk, she knew she could. Especially now she knew the sort of things she should ask her. And then not take it any further, if it seemed really, really wrong. Yes, that's what she could do; she told herself that, very firmly, while knowing it was almost certainly a lie.

But she had to get the story; she just had to.

Martha was listening to her own voice when her mobile rang, listening to herself making her presentation on her tape recorder, making notes of minor adjustments and at the same time carefully sorting through the contents of her briefcase. Chad again, she thought, it could only be him. And decided not to answer it. She was extremely tired of his endless phone calls. Working with him had become a lot less attractive this week. There was something of the old woman about him, very much at odds with his brusque manner and svelte appearance.

She had finished her notes and was sitting on her bed, leafing through the political pages in the papers, when her landline rang. Bloody man, she thought, walking through into the living room, this was not what she needed.

'Chad,' she said, snatching it up, 'please – ' But: 'Martha, dear, it's Mum. Your father and I just wanted to wish you well for tomorrow.'

'Thanks, Mum,' said Martha, 'that's very sweet of you.'

'I know you'll do well, dear. Everyone is so excited about it, about your going into politics. Anyway good luck, and mind you get a good night's sleep.'

'I will. I'm in bed now as a matter of fact. Thank you for calling.'

She put the phone down and realised the message light was blinking. Someone had called before and she hadn't noticed. Also Chad, no doubt. Well, she'd better check. Bloody bore he was. She'd have to say something if –

'Martha, hi. This is Ed. I – I hoped we could talk. I'll try your mobile.'

'Oh my God!' she said aloud, and went back to bed, dialled his number, shaking violently; it was answered at once.

'Hi.'

'Hi, Ed. It's me. Sorry, I didn't realise you'd rung.'

'That's OK.'

'Um – what can I do for you?'

'I – ' There was a long silence, then 'I just wanted to wish you luck. For tomorrow.'

206

'Ed, who on earth told you?'

'Mum. She called this evening, said did I know you were going to be the new MP for Binsmow.'

Martha started to laugh.

'Oh God,' she said, 'mothers!'

'Yeah, well. You should have told me.'

'Why?'

'Well – because of what I said. It was obviously unjust. I'm sorry, Martha. Sorry I said all those things. I was totally out of order. I can see that now.' There was a silence, then he said, 'I've missed you so much. I thought I could do without you – but I can't.'

'Ed,' said Martha. 'I *am* self-obsessed. I *am* a control freak. But I'm trying very hard not to be. If you hadn't said – what you did, I'd have said no to Chad. Now then – I've got an important meeting tomorrow. I've got an early start – '

'Yeah, OK,' he said, 'sorry. I just wanted to – '

'But even so, why don't you come round? We can discuss my presentation. Among other things.'

Well, she thought, switching off her mobile, at least she'd be in bed early.

She drove down the M11 on Saturday morning, feeling extremely nervous. She had woken at six, leaving Ed fast asleep, gone to the gym and then suddenly realised a Mercedes convertible wasn't exactly a tactful vehicle to arrive in. She wished she'd thought of it earlier. She would just have to dump the Merc in the car park of the Coach and Horses and use Chad's car instead.

She ran over her ten-minute presentation speech again and again and rehearsed answers to imagined questions. Certain rather insistent images and memories kept disturbing her concentration; she tried to ignore them. Even Ed telling her it was the best sex he had ever had; and falling asleep hearing him say – no, she would allow herself to replay this one at least, she thought, smiling foolishly at the memory.

'I really, really love you,' he had said. 'I know I do. I wasn't sure before.' That had been the best. She would pick it all over and enjoy it properly later.

She felt fantastic: energetic, alive, and smoothly, sleekly happy. She was wearing a pair of leather trousers and an extremely expensive Joseph sweater for the journey, but on a hanger in the car was more modest stuff, a navy suit from Hobbs, and a pale pink top with a slash neckline; she wore a little make-up, no nail polish, and her shoes and bag were from LK Bennett, rather than the more exclusive shelves of Gucci. She changed at the service station about ten miles before Binsmow.

When she got to the Coach and Horses, Chad was already there, drinking orange juice; he stood up and gave her a kiss.

'Like the outfit. Very good. You look straight out of central casting for a prospective near-Tory candidate. Want anything?'

'Not to eat; maybe a tonic water. I feel terribly nervous.'

'That's good. You'll perform better. Very valuable things, nerves. Get the adrenalin pumping.'

'Oh, Chad. And when did you last feel nervous?'

'Oh – day before yesterday,' he said, surprising her. 'I often think I'm going to throw up whenever I have to speak in the House.'

'Oh,' she said, and felt strangely comforted.

'I hope you had a good night last night.'

'Very, very good,' she said, and felt herself flush as a particularly vivid memory hit her; surely a prospective candidate should not, a few hours before her presentation, be lying over her beautiful young lover, head flung back, body arched, invaded with sweet sweeping pleasure, and calling out with the raw, joyful noise of sex? But: 'Yes, it was excellent.'

'Good. Now any points you'd like to run through?'

'Well – I don't think so. I've mugged up on the town and everything and I just had a look at a proposed by-pass site. It would do dreadful things, Chad. I'm sure I could get very worked up about that.'

'Well, be careful,' he said, 'you mustn't assume that they'll see it in quite the same way. A lot of these schemes may cut through hallowed woods and so on, but they relieve noise and pollution in residential areas. One of the committee members may well live on a street that is shaken to its foundations by articulated lorries a dozen times a day. Just feel your way. Now do you want to run through your presentation with me?'

'I think I'd better,' she said and handed him her notes.

A jolly red-faced young man called Colin Black, dressed in a tweed suit and extremely well-shined shoes, arrived; he would be her agent, advise her on local matters, help at election time. He had been a Tory agent, become disillusioned and 'Come out to bat for you lot,' he said, grinning his rosy grin. He turned out to be a rather well-heeled farmer with a background in student politics. Martha liked him.

'Sorry we couldn't have met before,' he said. 'All been a bit of a rush. Look, they're all ready for you, looking forward to meeting you. They're mustard-keen on the party, even though they only represent about a third of the old committee. They've seen the three others already. Only one of them should cause you any concern. Young chap. Teacher. The other's a woman, very good, very sound, but a bit of a wild card. Comes from the north.' Clearly, coming from the north was tantamount to coming from Sodom and Gomorrah. 'Anyway, nothing more for me to say except good luck. Chad will have briefed you on the form, no doubt.'

Martha said he had, but added tactfully that she'd be grateful for any further advice. 'Best I can give you is have as few notes as possible; speak from the heart. They can see through anything else.'

'I won't have any notes,' said Martha. 'It's all in my head.'

'Jolly good. Well, best go. Good luck.'

On the way her phone bleeped: it was Ed. 'Good luck. I love you xxx.'

They arrived at two-thirty at a large building in the old Market Square, where Martha had gone with her mother every Saturday morning to buy fresh fruit and vegetables, and went upstairs to a large room, where a rather tired-looking middle-aged woman was pulling chairs into a semi-circle; Chad offered to help her. She was clearly dazzled by his presence; when Martha offered to help as well, she seemed rather disdainful and said she could get the small table out for her notes if she liked.

'That one over there. I hope it's big enough for you. There's nothing else.'

Martha said it was fine.

The room filled up quite quickly with an equal number of men and women. They were mostly middle-aged, friendly in a rather distant way, smiled at her briefly and then carried on talking to one another. Only one very imposing woman even talked to Chad. They were clearly both being put in their place.

At three o'clock exactly, the imposing woman, who proved to be the chairman, clapped her hands and said would everyone take their places; they all sat down in a semi-circle, with Martha placed at her small table in the middle. She felt rather like the boy in the 'When did you last see your father?' painting. Chad indicated to her to sit down, then stood beside her, smiled his brilliant smile and made a brief speech, thanking them for giving the party a chance, at least, outlined their general policy, and said he was confident that, with the backing of people like the residents of Binsmow, they could radically cut Tony Blair's majority at the next election. They continued to sit looking stony-faced.

And then it was Martha's turn. She started fairly confidently, she played the local card, threw in a couple of childhood reminiscences – the market shopping, the grammar school and picnicking in the meadows on the edge of the town – hoping for some kind of reaction she could build on. She got none. They just sat and listened to her, fairly expressionless; they didn't smile, nor did they frown. She had decided to be honest, no point pretending a life-long passion for politics – simply said that she had felt her interest in the subject growing over the past year, along with her association with the Centre Forward party. She said she had done some citizens' advice work in Binsmow itself, and had some practical experience of people's problems and how to solve them. She referred to Lina and her distress over the sink estates and poor schools that she and others like her had to endure; and said that had been the turning point that had led her into politics.

'Barbara Follett, whom I met once, told me that, in her experience, it was always some personal experience which led women into politics, whereas for men it was much more likely to be a matter of personal ambition. I want to do something that can make a difference, improve people's lives in however small a way.' She had expected some reaction to that, at least; there was none. She began to panic, but managed to stick to her script, said how much she liked the Centre Forward philosophy – People before Politics – and then expressed a little of her own; that a revived sense of community would help so many problems in society, and promised to run a fortnightly free legal advice service if she was selected.

Still no reaction: increasing panic. What on earth was she doing here? The toughest argument in court was easier than this. Well, no way back now. Just keep going, Martha.

Somehow she got to the end of her speech: 'I would dearly love to work for the people of Binsmow and to give back something of what they gave me.'

When she had finished and sat down, there was a silence in the room; it was unnerving. She hadn't expected applause, but she had hoped for some reaction, some questions. Everyone looked down at the pads of paper on which they were scribbling notes.

I was a disaster, she thought miserably, and looked at Chad; he winked at her.

'Right,' he said, 'well, I think you know a little about Martha and her – and *our* philosophies – now. Would you like to ask her some questions, find out some more?'

It got a bit better after that; the chairman, whose name was Geraldine Curtis, smiled at him graciously.

'I certainly would. May I begin by thanking you for a very interesting presentation? I am sure we all enjoyed it. Now – you are very young, Miss Hartley, and inexperienced. I wonder what makes you think you could take this constituency on?'

She was ready for that; Chad had coached her.

'I wonder it, too,' she said, and smiled; for the first time she got a smile back. 'Of course I'm young. That has its drawbacks of course; I lack experience and political skills. But it has its advantages. I have a great deal of energy. I am very, very willing to learn; indeed I am longing to do so. I don't have any preconceptions. I have a questioning mind. And being a lawyer, a very clear one. But I do worry that you may think I am arrogant, that I expect it all to be easy. I can only say I don't. But maybe it's a measure of my potential that people like Chad Lawrence and Jack Kirkland, and the wonderful Janet Frean, of course, are all backing me. I do want to learn and to learn fast: and I think that I can.'

Mrs Curtis smiled again.

'Well, that was honest, at least. Does anyone else have a question?'

There were several. Would she move down to Binsmow? Did she, as a single, and clearly well-off, young woman, really understand the financial pressures and problems faced by families? If she did marry and had a family, would she see herself continuing as an MP? What had drawn her to the Centre Forward party, what had she against the traditional Tories? (Careful on this one, Chad had said, there are sure to be at least a couple of doubters on the committee who will be opposed to you on principle: don't knock the others, just say you feel instinctively, as a young, ambitious person that this is the party for you.) What were her views on primary education? How would she go about recreating the sense of community she spoke so emotively of? What did she think about the by-pass? At this point, Geraldine Curtis clearly felt the questions were becoming too specific and she rose rather majestically and clapped her hands.

'I think that will do for now. I wonder if we could have tea, Betty, and then we can talk to Miss Hartley more informally? I would personally love to hear about her childhood in Binsmow and her education at the grammar school.'

Betty, the downtrodden placer of chairs, disappeared into the back of the hall followed by a couple more members; they came back with a trolley laden with cups of tea, and plates of biscuits. Martha decided that this was the one time in her life when calories wouldn't count, except in her favour, and ate several. They were all very soggy. She stood there, smiling endlessly, answering questions, charming the men with ease and the women, particularly the younger ones, with more difficulty, expressing huge interest in housing schemes, playgroups, the possibility of a local radio station, youth clubs, and realised, with a sudden thud of excitement, that everything Chad had said was true, that it really wasn't rocket science and that she could – if they gave her the chance – probably do it. And she realised she wanted that chance – very, very badly.

The worst thing, Clio thought, was the feeling she had nowhere to go. That she was, temporarily in any case, homeless. After some thought, she had driven herself to a motel on the edge of the town and booked herself in for the night. Settling herself into the anonymity of her small beige cell, she had felt it was extraordinarily suited to her situation, a place with no past and no future, only the present. To her great surprise, she slept for a few hours, and woke at six, with a sense of dreadful panic and loneliness.

Now what?

She realised that she had very few close friends. Actually, she had *no* close friends. Not any more. Couples, yes, halves of couples, even, but only on a rather superficial level. Jeremy had most effectively driven a wedge between her and her previous girlfriends; expressing first hurt and later irritation if she wanted to spend time with them rather than with him. And she had never had a soul-baring kind of friendship with anyone; she supposed it was all to do with her rather emotionally starved childhood, her sense of failure, her comparison with herself and her brilliant sisters. She could certainly never go to them for help; her major ambition, from the day she left to go travelling on that fateful August day, had been to show them that she could manage on her own. She would starve to death before admitting she had failed. Her father, too, would never be a source of comfort or strength to her; he had always made it clear that she was a worry to him, more demanding and distracting than her sisters, and clearly destined to be less successful. She was simply an anxiety that he didn't want.

What she couldn't understand was that she didn't feel more unhappy. Scared, yes; lonely, yes; and desperately worried, yes. But not actually unhappy. She supposed that would come; she was still anaesthetised by shock.

She got into her car and drove – for some reason – along the A3 towards London. It seemed as good a route as any. She felt a need for coffee and turned her car into a Little Chef; the coffee was good and she suddenly wanted some toast as well. She was biting into the second slice when her mobile rang.

Jeremy? Worrying about her, wondering where she was?

'Clio? Hi, it's Jocasta. I just wondered how you were, hoped that story hadn't done you too much damage.'

'Oh,' said Clio lightly, and was astonished to find she could be honest, indeed wanted to be. 'Not really. I've left my husband, as a result, don't have a home any more, that sort of thing. But don't worry about it, Jocasta, not your fault.'

'Oh my God! You *are* joking, aren't you?'

'No, actually. I'm in a Little Chef on the A3 with no home, and nowhere to go, and only the clothes I'm standing up in. Oh, and no job, either.'

'My God! Oh, Clio, I'm so, so sorry. And how inadequate is that? Jesus. What happened, was it really my fault?'

'Oh no, not really,' said Clio with a sigh. 'I mean, you might have been the catalyst – well, the story might, but it was all there, really.'

'What was all there?'

'I don't want to talk about it, Jocasta. Sorry.'

And then her calm and her bravado suddenly left her and she started to cry, huge heavy sobs; the three other people in the Little Chef all stared at her. She cut Jocasta off and fled to the ladies', where she shut herself in one of the stalls, and sat on the loo, her head buried in her arms, weeping endlessly.

Every so often, her phone rang; she ignored it. After about half an hour, she couldn't cry any longer; she felt strangely calm. She washed her face, combed her hair and walked as nonchalantly as she could manage back to the restaurant, where she paid her bill and then went out to the car.

'She was marvellous. Really marvellous.' Chad smiled at Grace Hartley; they were, inevitably, in the vicarage drawing room, using the best china, with enough cakes on the tiered wooden cake stand to feed the entire Centre Forward party. 'Thank you so much, Mrs Hartley, that lemon cake looks wonderful. Go on, Martha, have a piece.'

'Martha never eats anything,' said Grace with a sigh, 'and certainly not cakes.'

'She was tucking into the committee's biscuits. Weren't you, Martha?'

'Well, I thought I should.'

'And so you should eat your mother's lemon cake. Go on.'

Martha held her plate out resignedly; she could see politics could make her fat.

Chad was saying how well she'd done, even better than he'd hoped, that they wouldn't know for a while, probably not for a week, 'Just to show us at Westminster who's really in charge.'

His phone rang and they all jumped. He went out of the room, closing the door. It was obviously someone from the committee: so swift a decision must mean bad news, Martha thought miserably. It felt very bad. She had failed at something really important. Something she really wanted. And very publicly. Everyone would be so disappointed in her. She was even more disappointed in herself. It was going to take a long time to –

The door opened; Chad was smiling. 'Well,' he said, 'very, very good news. That was Norman Brampton. It's unofficial but – Martha, they want you! Geraldine Curtis called him. They were very impressed indeed. They accept your inexperience, but they feel you'll appeal to young people, which is so important to us. And there's the local card, of course, which you played so well.'

'Oh my God!' said Martha. She felt extraordinary. In that moment she could have flown. She felt completely inviolate. She hadn't failed. Hadn't made a fool of herself. She'd done it. She had succeeded. She . . .

'Oh, that's so wonderful, darling,' said Grace. 'Well done. Let me give you a kiss.'

'Marvellous,' said Peter Hartley. 'What a clever girl you are. It's absolutely wonderful. We're so proud of you, Martha. And how lovely it will be to have you down here – '

'Now, you must keep this under your collective hats,' said Chad. 'Norman really shouldn't have told me. But he was quite certain – you've definitely done it!'

She went back to the pub with Chad to collect her car and realised that it was practically out of petrol; she'd fill it up on her way back to her parents', maybe even go for a little drive. She needed to unwind.

There was something wrong with one of the pumps; it required a lot of jiggling about to get the petrol running and then it suddenly spurted out. Damn! That wouldn't do her suit any good. And she was going to be wearing it a lot, it seemed. She finished filling the car, paid for the petrol and then went to the lavatory to wash her hands.

It was predictably filthy, paper towels littered the floor, together with some fag ends, there was an oily rag in the washbasin and a tabloid newspaper balanced on top of the hand dryer. As she switched the dryer on, the paper slithered onto the floor. Martha, deciding it was in its rightful place, was about to unlock the door to leave, when her mobile rang; as she fumbled for it in her bag, one of the neat leather gloves that she had brought to complete her new persona fell down onto the floor.

She swore, checked her mobile – it was Ed, wanting to know how she had got on – and bent down to pick up the glove. And there it was: the photograph. A very ordinary photograph, really, taking up about a quarter of the page; it showed a middle-aged woman, apparently in a hospital bed, and a young girl. The woman was dressed in a bed jacket and some rather incongruously large pearl earrings. The girl, who had a great deal of curly fair hair, was wearing a denim jacket and several studs in one of her ears. She had one arm round the woman's shoulders, and was smiling radiantly at the camera.

'What Katy Did', said the caption.

And Martha, crouching there on the floor, strangely compelled to read on, discovered precisely what Katy had done, which was care for her 'beloved grandmother', as she became desperately ill, after spending twenty hours in Casualty on a hospital trolley.

'But there was a very happy ending. Mrs Jilly Bradford is now recovering fast and has nothing but praise for her granddaughter's courage, as she battled with NHS staff to secure attention and treatment for her. Fifteen-year-old Kate Bianca – as she likes to be known – has ambitions to be a model. Why not a career in hospital management, Kate?'

Martha leant over the filthy lavatory bowl and was violently sick.

Chapter 15

'Of course I won't tell anyone. Of course. My dear, if you knew how many confidences I have kept over the years, you wouldn't even ask. But look – do you have anywhere to go?'

'Oh – yes.' Clio wasn't going to tell Barbara Salter, so orderly, so nice, that she had nothing of the sort, no refuge of any kind; it was too humiliating. 'Yes, I'm on my way to friends in London now. But – well – thank you so much for listening to me.'

'I'm only sorry I couldn't do more. Now, I'll get Mark to call you as soon as he gets in. On your mobile, yes? Try not to worry, my dear. These things so often blow over. It's all part of the fun and games of being married.'

'Yes, well maybe – '

As if Barbara and Mark could possibly have had arguments over anything more serious than his tea being too strong. Everyone at the surgery hated making it for him. But: 'Yes,' she said again, trying to sound more cheerful, 'yes, I expect it is.'

She had been very surprised to find herself calling Mark; it was just that out of the panic and loneliness that had taken her over, she had suddenly realised that her work, her job, was the one stable thing that she could cling to and find comfort in. And yes, she had left the practice, but they had no replacement for her, only a locum for a couple of weeks and then another one, and neither had really pleased Mark at all. So maybe – just maybe – he would allow her back.

She had spent the second night in another anonymous motel-style place by the river in Battersea. When she got up to her room, she found herself with a breathtaking view of the river, and when she opened the window, she could hear tugs hooting and sea gulls crying, and it was like stepping into another country. She had happened upon it completely by chance, driving listlessly into London, but it had seemed a happy accident. She wondered if Jeremy would ever phone her and see if she was all right; after a while, she got into bed and then lay awake fearful and tearful. In the morning she phoned Jeremy, simply to say she was all right. There was no answer except the answering machine. 'It's me, Clio,' she said, and then stopped, for what could she say? 'I hope you're not worried', or, 'I'm fine, don't try and find me'? He was so clearly not worried, had no intention of trying to find her . . . She fell foolishly silent and then just said: 'I'm fine,' and rang off.

She put the phone down and felt the tears welling again. It was at this point that her mobile rang and she answered it without checking: it was Jocasta. Yet again.

Nick was not entirely pleased that a long-lost friend of Jocasta's youth who had just left her husband was about to descend on their Sunday morning peace.

'I thought we were going up to Camden Lock.'

'She can come too.'

'What, blubbing all the way? Hasn't she got other friends?'

'I don't know. Nick, she's spent two nights in motels – '

'I know, I know. I just think there's something odd about a woman who has nowhere to go except to motels and to someone she last met sixteen years earlier.'

'Seventeen. Well, you can think what you like. I'm sure she has, she just doesn't want to start getting into long explanations.'

Clio stood on the doorstep, looking up at Jocasta's pretty little house and trying to pluck up the courage to ring the bell. What on earth was she doing here, at the worst hour of her life, paying a call on someone who was virtually a stranger? It made her feel more pathetic than ever. It was just that at that precise moment, in her acute loneliness, Jocasta had called. And had been so kind, so friendly, so genuinely concerned, it suddenly seemed quite a good idea.

She was just considering running away, when the door opened

and a very tall, very thin man dressed in running gear appeared, smiled at her and said: 'You must be Clio. Go along in. I'm going for a run, so you and Jocasta can enjoy some girly talk. I'm Nick,' he added, holding out a bony hand. 'Nick Marshall. Friend of Jocasta's. See you later.'

Clio smiled up at him. 'Thank you,' she said, and then worried that it might sound rude, to be thanking someone for going away from their own house. Or their girlfriend's house.

'Cheers then.' He was gone, a long, loping figure; and then: 'Clio, come on in,' said Jocasta's voice and she was not only in the house, but held in Jocasta's arms, and she was crying again, and Jocasta was stroking her hair, and talking meaningless, soothing nonsense and then leading her into a warm, chaotic kitchen where she sat her down and placed a large mug of coffee in front of her and Clio stared at her and thought, as she had thought so long ago, what an amazingly nice person she was, and wished she hadn't let her go.

Chad would have been proud of her next day, Martha thought, half impressed, half ashamed of herself; after her feverish, fretful night, she got up early, took Bella the elderly labrador for a walk (knowing she would meet other dog walkers she might be able to talk to about her political plans) and then attended family communion and the coffee-and-biscuits get-together in the vestry afterwards: saying that yes, it was true, she was hoping to be adopted as the local candidate for the Centre Forward party, that she did indeed have the support of Norman Brampton, adding that she would be around all week, apart from Monday, that if anyone wanted to talk to her about it further, she would be at the vicarage: saying that the new party represented all the best of the old Toryism, but with some fresh and very good ideas as well, and that if anything would get Tony Blair out, the Centre Forward party had the best chance and that she actually had some leaflets about it if they were interested. After that, she went to see Norman Brampton who was sitting down, clearly bored while his wife fussed around him.

'Give anything to be in your shoes,' he said, 'going mad here. Anyway, I'm delighted with what's happened – you'd certainly have been my choice and you've obviously impressed them no end. And what's Jack Kirkland like? I always admired him, but he keeps one at arm's length rather, doesn't he?'

'He's a bit of an enigma, actually,' said Martha. 'He seems so forbidding and stern, but in fact he's extremely kind and thoughtful. He's wonderful in the chamber – '

'I see you've picked up all the jargon,' he said, smiling at her. 'Well done. Now, how about another coffee, while we discuss the next year or so?'

And so the day went on; Martha went home and managed to eat quite a lot of the lunch her mother had cooked – she must have put on pounds this weekend – and helped her clear away, against a backdrop of Binsmow gossip. Then she took her for a drive out to the meadows and walked slowly along the tow path with Bella and then home again, where she helped her father sort out some flyers for a concert at the church in early June. And all the time doing what she had done all her life, suppressing the fear, denying the memory, struggling to control the uncontrollable.

She had sat for a long time the evening before, in a lay-by, staring at the photograph, reading and re-reading the caption, calming herself by sheer willpower. Of course she was being absurd. Hysterical. The country was filled with thousands – millions – of fifteen-year-old girls. Several hundred of them undoubtedly called Bianca. It wasn't that unusual a name now. Anyway, this one, the one with the beloved grandmother (would you be that close to an adoptive grandmother? – surely not) wasn't called Bianca, she was called Kate. Bianca was just a middle name, an afterthought. And – what if she did have that hair? Millions of them had that hair, that long, wild hair. Blonde hair. Probably carefully lightened by the newspaper, to make her look more glamorous. And she was only fifteen. No – nearly sixteen. They would have said that if she was. In fact, Kate Bianca would have said she was *six*teen. All girls of that age wanted to be thought older than they were. No, the whole thing was ridiculous.

And she put the paper in a rubbish bin, very carefully and deliberately, and texted Ed – she didn't dare speak to him just yet – then drove slowly home where she sat and watched television with her mother, while her father wrote his sermon.

First *Blind Date*, then *Casualty* and then a murder mystery, an endless stream of mind-numbing rubbish. Only it didn't numb her mind quite enough; when she went up to bed it was still throbbing feverishly.

There was a text from Ed. 'All hail to the new PM,' it said. 'Love you. Ed xx.' It made her feel suddenly, wonderfully better.

But not for long . . .

She stood at the window, staring out at the starry sky, wishing the night away. It would be better in the morning; everything was always better in the morning. And how often had she told herself that, almost sixteen years ago?

'I cannot believe this is still going on. Haven't people got anything better to think about?'

'What's still going on, dear?'

'Look for yourself. Half a page nearly. What's this garbage doing here anyway?'

Jim passed a crumpled copy of the *News on Sunday* across the supper table to Helen.

'Is the NHS right off its trolley?' it said right across one of the inside pages.

'That's clever,' said Kate, craning her neck to read it. And then as her father frowned at her, 'Sorry, Dad. It's Sarah's. She brought it round because there was a story about Robbie in it.'

'Robbie who?'

'Dad! Get with the programme. Robbie Williams.'

'Oh, I rather like him,' said Jilly. 'Though I preferred him when he was in Take That. We always loved them, didn't we, Kate?'

'Yes, we did,' said Kate. She shot an expression of triumph at her father.

'Well, anyway, Jim, why shouldn't people read about him if they want to?' said Jilly.

'Gran, it's not about him. It's about *you*!'

'Me! Oh, how exciting. Is there a picture?'

'There is no picture,' said Jim heavily.

'Well, I'd still like to read it. Helen, after you, dear – thank you. Good heavens! Listen to this, Kate – "In the week that has followed the latest hospital scandal, and a neglected elderly patient . . ." – I do wish they'd stop calling me elderly; I thought the picture in the *Sketch* would have stopped that – where was I, oh, yes, ". . . Mrs Jillian Bradford, nearly died on a hospital trolley as a result of negligence, questions are still being asked. Tony Blair will face a roasting in Prime Minister's question time on Wednesday and a poll commissioned by this newspaper shows that 57 per cent of voters now think the NHS is in a worse state than it was when New Labour came to power in 1997. What is to be done about it? If anything? Or will Mrs Bradford and others continue to lose their lives, as Tony Blair continues to play his guitar, while the NHS burns?" '

'What does that mean?' asked Kate.

'It refers to Nero,' said Juliet. 'You know, fiddling while Rome burnt.'

'Well obviously, Miss Smartarse, I don't know,' said Kate. 'It must be so wonderful to be you!'

'Kate,' said Helen, 'Juliet was simply answering your question. Now apologise. Please.'

'Sorry,' said Kate in the flat, automatic tone she always used when asked to apologise.

'It's not very clever to display ignorance, you know,' said Jim. 'You've had a perfectly good education and that is a basic piece of knowledge.'

'Oh for God's sake!' said Kate. 'I'm going upstairs.'

'You are not. It's your turn to clear away.'

'Oh, for f – OK, OK, don't say any more.'

She got up, started packing the dishwasher very noisily, cramming two plates into the space designed for one, pulling bowls away from people before they were empty.

'Kate, stop that at once,' said Jim sharply.

'You told me to clear away. Make your bloody mind up.'

'Kate! How dare you speak to me like that! Go to your room.'

'It'll be a pleasure. And then Little Miss Mealy Mouth can do it all nicely and you can sit and admire her – '

'Kate, you are not to speak of your sister like that.'

'I'll speak about her how I like. Anyway, she's not my sister, thank God. Not really.'

'Kate!'

'I think I'll just go into the other room,' said Jilly, 'watch *Monarch of the Glen*, it's so marvellous – '

'She's upset again,' said Helen, when she and Jim were finally on their own. Kate had apologised to Juliet and stormed upstairs, and Juliet had been comforted and was doing her piano practice. 'I don't know why. I mean, I do know it's about her mother, but quite why at this point I – '

'I'm getting very tired of that as an excuse,' said Jim. 'She can't be allowed to behave exactly how she chooses, simply because she's had some trauma in her life. We've all had our troubles – '

'Jim, I don't think anything you've had to endure could compare with what Kate has been through.' Jilly's voice came from the doorway. 'I'm sorry to interfere – and I agree she was very naughty and rude this evening – but knowing she was abandoned by a mother who apparently had no interest in whether she lived or died is a dreadful, dreadful thing.'

'Mummy, please don't – ' said Helen, but it was too late. Jim had stormed out of the kitchen and into the sitting room, and the sweet tinkling of Susan Hampshire's voice had been replaced by the harsh tones of Taggart.

'Now are you sure you're going to be all right?' Jocasta looked at Clio thoughtfully.

'Of course. I'll go to these friends in Guildford, and they'll put me up for a few days. While I sort myself out.'

'You've spoken to them, have you?'

'Of course.'

It was not a complete lie; Mark Salter had called her and in his sweet, tactful way had said there was no need for explanations, Barbara had told him all he needed to know, and that nothing would make him happier than to have her back in the practice, but that he would have to honour his fortnight's commitment to the first locum. 'I'm only sorry the circumstances are so unhappy for you.'

She had had that conversation in Jocasta's bedroom, having explained it was rather delicate; Jocasta had clearly assumed it was Jeremy, and had made a second jug of coffee. Nick had returned by then and was smiling dutifully at her; Clio had suddenly felt appalling, a burden on a lot of perfectly nice people who were trying to have a normal, peaceful Sunday.

'I must go,' she said. 'Honestly, I can't take up any more of your time.'

'Of course you mustn't go,' said Jocasta, 'you're staying right there. We're not doing anything, are we, Nick?' and, 'No,' he had said, after the most momentary of pauses, 'no, nothing. In fact I've got to get back to my place and write a piece for tomorrow's paper – Chris called while I was out running.'

'Well, there you are,' said Jocasta. 'Think how lonely and lost I'd be without you, Clio. It happens all the time, you know, I get abandoned just like that.'

Clio excused herself and went to the lavatory, so that they could communicate in peace; when she came back, Nick was in the shower.

'I'm sure you think he made that up,' said Jocasta, grinning at her, 'but he didn't. It's the local elections in a couple of weeks and Nick just got a quote from IDS about it. So – that's his Sunday gone. Or most of it.'

'What a complicated life you two must lead,' said Clio. 'It all sounds terribly intriguing.'

'Well – some is. Anyway, we can have a nice day together.'

Clio was feeling too lonely and too dispirited to protest any further.

She tried not to tell her too much; it seemed absurdly disloyal to discuss a marriage – albeit a failed one – with someone who was not a close friend, but Jocasta was dangerously easy to talk to. She sat in silence most of the time, only speaking when a silence became just too long, and then only in the most minimal terms – 'And then?' or 'So you?' – before waiting quietly.

Clio tried to ignore the prompts, but as the silences grew, it became very difficult, and later, eased into greater intimacy by a great deal of wine, she told Jocasta this. She laughed.

'It's one of the first things you learn, the pressure of the silence. Carol Sarler, she is the *Daily Express* columnist, you know, unutterably brilliant, she told me that she once sat for nearly two minutes in complete silence waiting for one of her interviewees to answer one of her more difficult questions.

And he did. In the end, everyone does. Or walks out. But I try not to practise it in my personal life. Sorry, Clio.'

'It's all right,' said Clio, 'I'm sure it's done me good. In a way it's better than some mutual friend who'll feel they're taking sides.'

'Hope so. It does sound like you've done the right thing. Maybe a bit rash actually walking out, but – '

'Jocasta, if I hadn't walked out, he'd have talked me round. He's a brilliant tactician. You've no idea how often I've gone into arguments knowing I'm right, absolutely knowing it, and ended up sobbing and asking him to forgive me.'

Jocasta said nothing.

'So – I'm glad, really. But it's been very drastic. I wouldn't like to relive this weekend.'

'How many times has he called you?'

A very long silence; then Clio said, not looking up at her, 'He hasn't. Not once.'

'Clio,' said Jocasta, refilling her glass yet again, 'you have done absolutely the right thing. I know I shouldn't say that, but it has to be true. And – at least you haven't had any children.'

'No,' said Clio. And burst into tears again.

This time she resisted the silence.

'I think you should stay here tonight,' Jocasta said.

'Jocasta, I can't. And what would Nick say?'

Jocasta stared at her.

'I don't give a shit what Nick says. This is my house, my life. It's nothing to do with Nick.'

'Yes, but – '

'Look,' said Jocasta, 'one, he won't come back; he's at his place, and two, if he does, that's absolutely fine. This is not the 1950s. And we haven't even started on Martha yet.'

'Martha! Have you seen her?'

'Not exactly, but our paths may cross. She wants to be an MP, according to Nick. He's met her. Says she's rather important and successful.'

'Well, she did seem very ambitious, even then. Funny thing, ambition, isn't it? It seems to be in people's genes. How about you, are your ambition genes powerful?'

'Pretty powerful. Yours?'

'More than I thought,' said Clio slowly. 'I mean, when I first married Jeremy, I thought I'd want to give it all up, but I didn't at all. I really minded leaving my job at the hospital – '

'What did you do?'

'I was a junior consultant. In geriatrics. I know it sounds rather dreary, but it isn't, it's fascinating and lovely and very rewarding. And then I really enjoyed general practice. I was so miserable the day I left. It wasn't just because it coincided with the end of my marriage.'

'So – now what?'

'Well – for the time being I can go back.'

'And long-term?'

'I don't know. Funnily enough, just a few weeks ago I heard from a colleague that there are a couple of new jobs in my department. And they wanted me to apply. Of course it was out of the question, Jeremy was furious at the very idea – '

There was a silence while Jocasta clearly struggled not to comment on Jeremy and his behaviour; then she said: 'But now – why not?'

'I don't think I've got the stomach for it, just at the moment. I'm feeling a bit fragile, to put it mildly.'

'Of course you are. But you won't always. And it could be just what you need. New challenge, all that. It might not be the best thing, going back to Guildford, where Jeremy is. Look, why don't you call those people and tell them you're not coming tonight? We've got too much to talk about, and – Clio!' – she had obviously read her face. 'You weren't going there anyway, were you?'

'Not – exactly,' said Clio, 'no. But – '

'Right. You're staying. Another bottle of wine, I think. I wish you smoked, Clio – you make me feel so corrupt.'

She fetched a bottle of wine, opened it, and poured Clio a glass. 'Cheers. Again. It's lovely to see you. Even under such unhappy circumstances. Now – ' There was a loud ring at the door.

'Shit,' said Jocasta. 'Excuse me a minute – '

Clio took a large slug of wine, not really wanting to see anyone either, half listening to Jocasta greeting someone, then speaking rather quietly (obviously telling whoever it was she had an awkward visitor) and then finally walking in and saying, 'Clio, look who's turned up – Josh!'

And there he was, standing in front of her, not greatly changed, much as she remembered him indeed, only there was rather more of him, all blond hair and blue eyes and wide, white-teethed grin, the cause – albeit indirect – of so many of her troubles. And now what did she do?

Chapter 16

'Hi, Martha! Blast from the past. Don't you dare say you don't remember me!' For the second time in forty-eight hours Martha felt time jerk to a standstill. She knew that voice so well; that musical, slightly low-pitched voice. The last time she had heard it, it had been calling her name across the crowded station in Bangkok. She felt the heat again, the suffocating humid heat, and she could hear the noise, that strange, unmistakable blend of foreign babble, slurring Anglo-American and the relentless pumping of pop music; and she felt her panic again, saw herself hurrying away, pretending she hadn't heard or seen Jocasta, slipping into a tiny narrow street and taking refuge in the chaos of the stalls.

'Martha? It is you, isn't it? Chad Lawrence gave me your number. It's Jocasta. Jocasta Forbes.'

'No, of course not. I mean, of course I remember you. It's very good to hear from you.' She could hear her own voice, astonishingly normal, pleasant, friendly, but no more.

'I'd love to see you, Martha. You know, this weekend, it's really weird, I've been with Clio.'

'Clio Scott?' This was getting worse by the minute.

'Yes. Bit of a long story how, big coincidence, I won't bore you with it. Anyway, Chad tells me you're joining them.'

'Well – only thinking of it.'

'Really? I heard prospective candidate for your hometown.'

'No! Not yet anyway. I'm only a little way along the road. I'm sure it won't happen. Look, it's a bit difficult to talk just now.'

'Exactly why I'm calling. To try and fix a meeting. Chad called me because he said he thought I might write an article about you for the paper.'

God. Dear God. What might she ask, what?

'In the paper?'

'Yes. The *Sketch*, I write for it. I thought Chad had told you.'

Pull yourself together, Martha, she must think you're a complete idiot.

'So – what about it? It would really raise your profile, you know.'

'I'm not sure I want it raised,' she said, and her voice now was really cool.

There was a silence, and then Jocasta said, her own voice changed: 'Well, if you're going into politics you'd better get used to the idea. You can't run with a low one, I'll tell you that. Anyway, here's my mobile number. Give me a call if you want to meet. When you want to do the piece.'

'The piece?'

'The article.'

'Oh. Oh, yes. Well – honestly, Jocasta, I don't think so. Sorry.'

'Fine. Absolutely fine. Bye now.'

'Goodbye, Jocasta. And thanks for calling.'

'Silly bitch,' said Jocasta aloud as she put the phone down.

'I – wondered what your plans were.'

Jeremy's voice was as she had never heard it; almost diffident, just short of nervous. Clio was standing looking at the shampoo range in Boots; she was so surprised she practically dropped the basket.

'Well – I'm not absolutely sure, to be honest.'

'Where – where are you living?'

'In a flat in Guildford. Or I'm about to be. At the end of the week. I just signed the agreement this morning. Meanwhile I'm staying with the Salters.'

'The Salters! You've told them about – about what's happened?'

'That I've left you? Well, yes. I had to really. But look, Jeremy, I'm in Boots – not the place to have a conversation like this. If you really want to talk to me, we'd better meet.' She felt rather cool and in control.

'Yes. I think we should. Would you like to come to the house?'

'I'd rather not. A pub?'

'Of course. What about the one at Thursley? About six?'

'What, tonight? No, I can't do tonight. Sorry.'

She could, of course, but . . .

'Oh. Well, tomorrow, then? Maybe nearer seven, I've got a long list.'

Clio switched off her mobile and went to join the queue at the checkout; her mood of confidence and pleasure had been very short-lived. Still – it had been a beginning.

'Do you have a Boots card?' said the girl.

'Oh – no. No, I don't.'

'Pity.' She was very friendly. 'You've got an awful lot of stuff here. You going on holiday or something?'

'No,' said Clio, 'just re-stocking.'

Re-stocking her life. It was a rather good phrase, she thought. Her spirits see-sawed up again.

'Jocasta, hi. I just wanted to say thanks for last night.'

'That's OK. Any time you need a square meal. But Josh, you've got to get your life sorted out.'

'I know, I know. It's not a lot of fun without Beatrice, and I'm missing those children horribly.'

'I expect you are. Still –' Her voice softened. 'I don't suppose she means it about divorce. She's just trying to teach you a lesson.'

''Fraid not. She's seen a solicitor.'

'Oh God, Josh, I'm so sorry. You didn't say that last night.'

'Well – I didn't want to, in front of Clio.'

'She's so sweet, isn't she? I really, really like her. But she seemed a bit – awkward with you, I thought. Josh, is there something I should know? About you and her? You didn't – well, sleep with her, did you? While we were all travelling?'

'Of course I didn't!' He sounded so genuinely indignant that Jocasta believed him.

'Sorry. She just seemed a bit thrown. I wondered, that's all.'

'Well – you can stop wondering. I didn't sleep with her.'

'Sure?'

'Jocasta, nothing happened between Clio and me. OK?'

230

Martha was trying to do some work when the phone rang again. It was Chad.

'Martha, what do you think you're playing at?' he said, his voice clipped and harsh.

'What do you mean?'

'Turning down what would have been a very big article in the *Sketch*? Are you mad? It could have won you hundreds, possibly even thousands of votes. I would advise you very strongly to see Jocasta Forbes. It's the opportunity of a political lifetime. Well, at your stage, anyway.'

'Yes, but – '

'Martha, just do it. She's not going to say anything unpleasant about you. Even if she does, it won't do you any harm. It's exposure. But why should she? It's such a charming story, all of it. Binsmow childhood, going travelling together, and then your dizzy rise in the law, the cleaner dying, converting you to politics . . . It's so good it sounds as if we made it up. If you get selected, you are to call Jocasta immediately. And eat a little humble pie when you do so – she was quite sniffy about it all.'

Martha was silent.

'Look,' he said, as if he were talking to a young child, 'look, Martha, either you do this thing, or you don't. Politics is a high-profile profession. I thought you'd have realised that by now.'

'I'm beginning to,' she said, 'and actually, Chad – '

Maybe she could get out of this, even now.

'Hold on a minute,' he said, 'my other line's going.'

She sat waiting; why had she got into this, why hadn't she thought about it properly? She was such a fool, such an absolute fool . . .

'Yes, what was that?'

'I – well, I was just wondering if – if . . .' Go on, Martha, say it, get it over, it's only a sentence, a few words, then you'll be safe again.

'Martha, what is it? I'm very busy.'

'If I could change my mind.'

There was a long silence; when he spoke, his voice was absolutely incredulous.

'Change your mind? What, stand down again?'

231

'Well – yes.'

'Martha, what the *fuck* is the matter with you?' She was shocked; she had never heard him swear.

'Nothing. I've just been thinking and – '

'You've been thinking! A little late, I have to say. Don't you realise the amount of effort that's been put into this for you? That Jack Kirkland's written to the constituency himself? That I've given up a lot of time for you? That Norman Brampton has been working his tail off, making phone calls, probably incurring another heart attack? That the constituency workers have been persuaded against considerable doubt not only to back us, but you as our representative? Do you realise what courage that actually requires on their part? How dare you start playing games with us all, like some silly tart! I'm beginning to think we've made an appalling mistake.'

She was silent; wondering if she dared push on, wondering which fear was greater.

'Look,' he said, 'I've got to go. You'd better pull yourself together, Martha, and pretty damn quick. Make your mind up, one way or another.'

'Chad – '

But he had gone.

A little later her phone rang yet again. It was Janet Frean.

'Hello, Martha. I just called to congratulate you. You really have done awfully well. It's hard enough when you've spent years in the business. I should know.'

'Thank you, Janet. Look – '

'We really need you, you know. People like you. You're going to be the backbone of the party. I really mean it. And we so need women, and especially young successful women like you. Now, I gather you're feeling a bit wobbly. It's completely natural – anyone would. I remember going into mega panic mode more than once. It's pretty terrifying. But – you'll feel better again soon. Honestly.'

'Janet, I – '

'Look, if I could make a suggestion, what about a media course? They're so worthwhile, they teach you presentation, how to deal with both radio and television, how to get your points across, even what to wear. I'll give you the name and number of the one I did. And don't let Chad bully you. Any worries, come to me with them. All right?'

As if, Janet, as if.

And then there was an e-mail. From Jack Kirkland.

'Hello, Martha. Just to say congratulations. Very well done. I knew you could do it. All we need is about a hundred more of you. Don't fail us now. We need you. Jack.'

'Oh God,' said Martha, and buried her head in her hands.

And then Chad called again.

'Darling, I'm sorry I bawled you out. It's natural you should be nervous. Absolutely natural. But you're doing so well. And we're all behind you. All right?'

'Yes, Chad.'

'Good girl. And call Jocasta back, will you? Soon as you can.'

God, thought Martha wearily, he's got a hide like a whole herd of rhinos.

'Yes, Chad,' she said again.

'Oh, and Janet called me, said she'd suggested a media course for you. Excellent idea, should have thought of it myself. I'll get HO to book it for you. It'll help you a lot. Right, well I'll leave you to make that call.'

'Yes, Chad.'

She seemed to be stuck with it; she couldn't fight this lot.

And when she got back to her flat that night, her father had written to her; she recognised his beautiful handwriting. She stood there, reading, tears in her eyes.

'. . . People keep coming up to us, saying how much they hope you'll be selected, and how proud of you we must be. Which we are, my darling, so very proud. And we're being extremely discreet, of course. We both send you very much love. See you in a day or two.'

How could she turn her back on that, tell them she wasn't going to do it after all?

And after all, she thought, her panic receding again, why should she? She had this great new opportunity; she had wanted it so much. She couldn't throw it away. Not now.

Millions of girls, millions of girls . . .

✵ ✵ ✵

Jack Kirkland smiled at Janet across his desk, gestured to her to sit down.

'Thanks for sparing the time. I just wanted to run something past you.'

'Oh yes?'

'We seem to have got young Martha back on the rails. I really wouldn't want to lose her. It's not so much herself that's valuable to us – God knows how she'll turn out – it's what she represents, youth, a corner in the professional business world, a –'

'Jack, I'm sorry, but if you just want to talk about Martha Hartley, I have to be in a committee room in ten minutes –'

'No, no, of course not. Sorry, Janet. No, I think we've got Eliot Griers on board.'

'Oh, really?' Eliot Griers was the Conservative member for Surrey North; he was deceptively soft spoken, savage in debate, and had been promised a position in the shadow cabinet by Iain Duncan Smith, which had never materialised.

'Yes. He's confident he can talk his constituency party round. Enough of it anyway. How would you feel about that? Personally I'd be delighted. High profile, very clever, he's more of what we need.'

'Well – obviously, I'd be extremely pleased. He's very clever. No doubt about that. Surprised though. Last time I spoke to him, he went on and on about how courageous we were, seemed in no mind to join us.'

'That was before he didn't get his shadow cabinet post. He's very bitter about that. Of course he'd want a seat on the top table, so to speak. He'd be coming in very much at our level. A spokesman for the party in a big way. We'd make a big song and dance about him.'

There was an almost unnoticeable pause. Then: 'So – why are you asking me?'

'Well, he'd be very visible. I wouldn't want you to feel in any way sidelined.'

Janet stood up, pushed her chair back rather vehemently. Her eyes looked dark and almost angry.

'Jack, I would hope I'm above such things. What I care about, above all, is the party and its success. I am not in this thing for personal gain. Women mostly aren't, you know. They have other concerns.'

'So you always say, all of you. I'd personally beg leave to doubt it. I've always regarded you as pretty ambitious, Janet.'

'Well, of course I'm ambitious. But if you think I'm looking for the top job in any party, you'd be wrong. I do have another life, you know. I'm not married to Westminster.'

This was a slightly cheap jibe; given Kirkland's failed marriage. He flushed.

'Good,' he said. 'Well, as long as you don't have a problem with Griers. I was only clearing the deck, so to speak.'

'Yes, and I appreciate it. Sorry, Jack. No, Griers would be nothing but good news.' She hesitated, then said, 'His marriage is all right now, is it?'

'Oh, that stuff years ago? Gossip, Janet, nothing more. I've spoken to Caroline, lovely girl, she's right behind him in every way. And like you, he's got a very attractive family, always a help.'

'Well, he seems just about perfect then,' said Janet. 'Thanks, Jack. I really appreciate your . . . thoughtfulness. But I'd be more than happy to have Eliot Griers on board.'

Several people serving on the Joint Committee on Human Rights with Janet Frean that day remarked that she didn't seem in the best of tempers.

'You're a star,' Ed said, 'an absolute star. I'm so proud of you.'

She'd been afraid of seeing him after the weekend, afraid he might sense there was something wrong, something worrying her. He read her so well.

'Ed, don't. I've got such a long way to go. I may never get elected at all, I – '

'I know all that,' he said, 'I'm just proud of you for having a go.'

'I wouldn't have without you,' she said. 'I'd still be dithering.'

'Nah. You'd have done it anyway. I know you.' He smiled at her, raised his glass. 'Or I'm beginning to. To the Right Hon Martha. Long may she reign.'

It was a perfect May evening; the light brilliant, the air cool and clear, drenched with a recent shower. They were sitting on Martha's balcony, drinking some champagne Ed had brought round.

'Are you all right?' he said suddenly. 'You seem a bit edgy.'

'Oh – oh, I'm all right. I was a bit – worried about something.'

'Not any longer?'

'I don't seem to be, no,' she said, half surprised.

'Well, that's being with me. Cure for any amount of worry, I am. Give us a kiss. And – now look at that, will you? Rainbow.'

And indeed there was, glancing down from a newly black sky onto the shimmering buildings across the river.

'Well, that should do it, even if I don't. Melt your troubles away like sherbet lemons or whatever it is.'

'Lemon drops. Oh Ed – how did I ever manage without you?'

'I have absolutely no idea,' he said complacently. 'Now you know what I was just thinking?'

'No.'

'I've never been to bed with a politician. Could you put it in your manifesto, do you think? Sex for the masses?'

'Certainly not,' she said, 'just the chosen few.'

'Well, here's the first of the few. All ready and waiting.'

And as she took the hand he held out and followed him inside, laughing, she thought that he would never agree to her giving up politics again, either.

Clio looked at Jeremy as he put a white wine spritzer down in front of her; he was pale and seemed very tired. He smiled at her almost nervously and said: 'Well, how are you?'

'I'm – fine. Considering.'

'Good. Is it all right at the Salters'? What did you tell them? About us?'

She looked at him; he was sweating slightly. She was surprised. Why should he care so much? She supposed it was all part of his arrogance, not wishing to appear in any way less than perfect.

'I told them we'd separated. I had to. Why else should I need somewhere to stay? And my job back.'

'Your job back?'

'Well, yes. I have to live, Jeremy. I'm not the sort to demand huge alimony payments. And anyway, I love my job. There seems no reason to give it up now.'

'You decided that? Without consulting me?'

'Why should I consult you? You made it perfectly clear our marriage was over. I don't see what it has to do with you.'

'I was – upset,' he said. 'And I – I'd like you to reconsider. Well, both of us to reconsider.'

'What do you mean?'

'That we should – should try again.' She stared at him; this was the last thing she had expected. 'Clio, I was very hasty. I said a lot of harsh things and I really don't want to live without you. I don't want our marriage to end.'

She was silent.

'So – '

'Jeremy, on what basis? I mean, do I still have to give up my job?'

'No,' he said quietly, after a long pause, 'no, you don't. That was . . . unreasonable of me.'

She stared at him. She felt very odd.

'Clio,' he said, 'I can't face life without you. I came to see very quickly that I . . . well, I do still love you. I want you back. I really do.' He waited, as she stared at him. 'What do you say?'

'I – I'm not sure,' she said. 'I mean it was a bit of a shock, all that. But – you mean I can go on working and everything?'

'Yes, you can.'

It was tempting. So very tempting. The thought of living alone, of making her own way again might be attractive in theory, but in practice it was scary. She was used to being married, to be living with someone, considering them. And he had made several huge concessions. She had never heard him apologise before. To anyone. Clearly he had missed her considerably. Even allowing for the fact he would have found it so hard to admit to his colleagues and their mutual friends that their marriage was a failure, this was pretty astonishing stuff.

'Well,' she said again, 'as long as I could work . . .'

'You can work, Clio. I promise.'

He stopped and looked at her.

'Yes?'

'Of course I would hope it wouldn't be for long. That we should be having children pretty soon. I mean, that is a given, as far as I'm concerned. And you too, I'm sure.'

Clio knew the moment had come, that she couldn't go on any

longer, deceiving him, when he had made such huge concessions to her.

'Jeremy,' she said, 'Jeremy, I'm afraid that isn't going to happen. Or almost certainly isn't going to happen.'

He stared at her, his face absolutely puzzled.

'What?'

Clio took a deep breath.

'I've got something to tell you, Jeremy, something I should have told you a long time ago. Should we talk here, or would you like to go back to the house?'

'Let's talk here,' he said. His face was expressionless.

Clio moved to sit beside him. She took his hand and, feeling sorry for him, as she had never thought to be again, her voice surprisingly steady, she began to tell him.

Chapter 17

She hadn't seen Ed for almost a week. He'd been filming out of London and she'd missed him horribly. He'd called her a couple of times, but rather briefly, saying he was frantic. It had been unnerving – she felt eighteen again. Had he gone off her? Had he found someone younger, or prettier, someone with curly hair and a small nose? Probably. She had missed him dreadfully. She wanted to see him, talk to him, be with him, have him. She really, really wanted to have him . . . Maybe she never would again, maybe that had been the last time . . .

Her phone rang.

'I just wondered if you could give me a lift to Suffolk this weekend, Miss Hartley. I ought to visit my mum and my car's completely fucked up.'

'I hope you don't use that sort of language in front of your mother.'

'Of course I don't. Also, I have this girlfriend down there I really want to see. She's the most fantastic lay and I've been missing her a lot.'

'Well, I'll have to look at my diary. Let's see . . . Yes, I think I could just about fit you in. What? Don't be coarse. Now I do warn you, Ed, I'm horribly busy. I've got to see the Centre Forward people, I've got to do an interview with the local paper and Norman Brampton has asked my parents and me to supper on Saturday evening. I'm sorry – '

'That's OK. I could come along, say I was your secretary. Hold your microphone while you address your adoring public.'

'Yes, that's a really good idea.'

'Or I could gatecrash the wild evening at the Bramptons'.

239

That sounds really cool. We might even be able to sneak upstairs after the dessert.'

'Yes, that's an excellent notion too.'

'Or – how about we leave early on Friday and spend the night at some luxury hotel off the M11? We could have dinner on the way.'

'Now that really is clever. You're on.'

'That's my girl. You're really living dangerously these days, aren't you?'

If only he knew how dangerously. Or rather, if only he never would.

Tension, trauma, the delight of finally being with Ed again, had made her over-excited; she came swiftly, heard herself shouting as she did so, as the bolts of pleasure shot into her, bright, dazzling, ferocious. Later, it was softer, sweeter, and very slow; and after that, she lay curled against him, her arm across him, and told him how happy he made her.

She woke to find him shaking her, saying: 'There, there, it's OK, shush, shush. You had a bad dream,' he said, as she stared at him. 'You were crying, talking in your sleep – '

'Talking? What did I say?' she asked sharply, terrified.

'Oh, just a lot of nonsense. Nothing that made any kind of sense.'

'Yes, but what?'

'Just a lot of words,' he said, folding her into his arms again, 'rubbishy words. Go back to sleep.'

But she was too afraid for that; and lay awake until dawn, watching him and wondering whatever he would do or say to her, if he knew.

She felt much better in the morning. She bought a pile of papers and they sat reading them over breakfast, Martha drinking orange juice and coffee, Ed eating what the place called a Full English. He kept offering her bits of it, feeding her mushrooms and tiny slivers of bacon on his fork.

'I'll have you overweight in no time,' he said, and then, grinning: 'Tell you what you did say last night. When you were asleep.'

Terror hit her: 'What?' she said. 'What did I say?'

'You said, "Treacle tart",' he said, 'and then you said, "Chips, please". Pretty incriminating stuff, wouldn't you say?'

'Oh shut up,' said Martha, and threw a bread roll at him.

They parted at the Coach and Horses, where she was meeting Colin Black; he said he'd call her at her parents' house in the morning.

'We could go for a walk. If your busy schedule allows it.'

'It might. Does your mum know I'm here?'

'Course. I told her you were giving me a lift up.'

Clio sat on her new beanbag in her new sitting room and stared at her new television. She couldn't, at this precise moment, quite think why she had got it; it was only Jeremy who had watched TV, but when she had bought the stereo, the young man had said they had special offers on televisions and she had suddenly thought that, actually, she would be on her own rather a lot and she wouldn't be getting Jeremy's supper or catching up on paperwork, or returning phone calls, which were all the things she did while he watched it, because she'd have time to do that whenever she wanted, and maybe she'd even be rather bored sometimes, and a television might actually be rather a good idea.

She looked up at the bare windows and at the blinds still in their Habitat bags, then she wandered into the kitchen, put on her new kettle and made herself a cup of coffee in one of her new mugs and wondered however she was going to survive her new life.

He had taken it quite well, really. He had listened to her quietly and politely and at the end they had agreed that really the only thing was to part.

He wanted a chance at least of having children, and clearly, with Clio, it was very unlikely. And she was (equally clearly) not really quite the person he had thought; and although the deception had initially been very minimal, almost non-existent indeed, it had grown so disproportionately fast, and in the end had become so tragically huge, that he could not contemplate trying to cope with it.

Chlamydia. It was rather a pretty word. It could almost be a girl's name. It certainly didn't sound like the name of an ugly, loathsome disease. A disease that appeared to have rendered her totally infertile.

Of course she still didn't know if it had. There was still hope. But the two last gynaecologists had both expressed grave doubts. Her fallopian tubes appeared completely blocked. And it was her own fault, absolutely her own fault. She had slept with several men she had hardly known, and had contracted, in blithe ignorance, this awful, symptomless, unsuspected thing that had come back to haunt her when it was – probably – far too late to do anything about. One of the things she most longed for, motherhood, was to be denied her: all as a result of some foolish, irresponsible behaviour when she was eighteen years old.

It was on the trip to the island, that it started. The dreadful need to know that men – any man – could want her, find her sexually attractive.

She hadn't somehow expected sex to matter so much. She had just thought it would be a wonderful trip, meeting lots of people, seeing fantastic places; it hadn't struck her that of course, with hundreds, thousands of young people wandering untrammelled by any kind of discipline all over the world, pleasure of every kind must include sex in a big way. No one had thought to say, 'Now look, Clio, everyone will be having sex all around you, all the time.' Or even tell her that she was very unlikely to return a virgin. Why should they? She had grown up in this extraordinarily uncommunicative family, repressed by her father, suppressed by her sisters, made to feel less pretty, less clever, less interesting than she actually was. She had gone to an all-girls' school, and had never developed much of a social life, largely because she was shy and overweight and, when she did go to parties, would find herself bypassed for the other sorts of girls, the skinny, confident ones who knew exactly how to exploit their own attractions. After a few miserable experiences of standing in corners, talking to other dull girls, it became easier just to say she wouldn't go. Of course her sisters had made even that worse, had commented on her weight and the fact that she didn't seem to go out much, and told her she should learn to deal with her shyness, not give in to it.

'It's a form of arrogance,' Artemis had said once, 'thinking everyone's going to be looking at you,' and Ariadne had said yes, quite right and why should they, for heaven's sake?

'Just forget about yourself for once, Clio, think of other people instead.'

That had been bad enough; it was worse when they tried to be kind and help her with her hair and make-up and suggest diets; none of their advice ever did any good. She had had one boyfriend in her last term at school; she hadn't even liked him, but he was someone to go to the cinema with, and take to the end of term dance. He had kissed her a couple of times, which she had found revolting, but nothing worse than that; the best thing he had done for her was tell her she was pretty, and she had liked his best friend a lot, which had goaded her into dieting, so that by the time she actually set off on her travels she had lost about a stone and although comparing herself with the other two she felt she was the size of a house – she took a size fourteen and they clearly took tens – she knew she did look much better. Almost pretty in fact.

And because the Thai food was the opposite of fattening, she had lost another half stone by the end of the second week on Koh Samui. She caught sight of herself in a cracked mirror in someone's hut one morning and thought she was almost not fat any more; her hair had gone lighter with the sun, and she was brown and – well, she began to feel just a little bit self-confident, less apologetic about her appearance, at least.

Although that was a long way from being sexy.

It was only when she went to Koh Pha Ngan, for one of the full moon parties that everyone had told her were so wonderful, that she had felt hopelessly, helplessly virginal. She had watched them in the darkness, against the background of the throbbing music, all the wonderful skinny brown bodies, enjoying each other, and although she had started talking to a very sweet boy, who was obviously also a virgin, and they had kissed a bit, nothing else had happened and he had fallen asleep on the sand, after smoking a lot of dope. Clio was still at the stage of refusing dope – there were all sorts of scary warnings that the Thai police were at the parties under cover, offering spliffs and then arresting people who took them, but she had gone on drinking rather a lot. And in the end she had felt so wretched and sick that she had gone back to the hut and lain on her bed all alone, wondering if she might go on to Sydney much sooner than she had planned.

And had gone back rather miserably to the relative homeliness of Koh Samui.

And then something wonderful happened. The next morning, as she drank some very nasty coffee on the veranda of the hut, Josh suddenly appeared. Gorgeous, sexy, charming Josh.

He had been up in the far north. It was amazing he said, he'd done a three-day trip walking through the jungle – 'It was uphill mostly, miles and miles, eight hours a day, and incredibly hot and humid, I was practically hallucinating about a shower and my bed –' He had done a four-hour boat trip to an elephant village, where they stayed for several days. 'But it was getting a bit like hard work, so I decided to come down here.'

Clio offered him some of the disgusting coffee and they sat on the beach and he went on talking about his trip.

'They're really poor up there; they live in these little huts, off the ground, with animals living underneath them. They wear proper tribal gear, with wonderful headdresses and then Snoopy T-shirts underneath that the tourists have given them. You'd have loved it, Clio.'

She knew why he said that and it hurt: because he saw her as a swot, not the sort of sexy girl who pulled a different bloke every night. But she managed to smile, and say it sounded wonderful.

'It is,' he said with a grin. 'You feel you're in another century as well as another place. There's no contraception, of course, so there are absolutely loads of children. The poverty's dreadful and quite little girls are sent south and sold into prostitution. Very sad.'

He said he'd been a great novelty there, being blond, and that the whole village had been summoned to stare at him. 'And they sat and stroked my arms, because I'm so hairy.'

'I'd love to go,' she said, and then, because it would give her an excuse to leave the beach, she said she was thinking of moving on and she might make her way up there.

'Oh, but you mustn't go on your own,' he said. 'It's much more dangerous up there, you must go with a guide, pay for your food and accommodation in advance. You do that in Bangkok, it's quite easy. Now, you in touch with the others?'

'No. Jocasta left weeks ago to go north – I'm surprised you didn't bump into each other – and Martha left about a fortnight ago. To go to Phuket, I think.'

'So you're on your own?'

'Well – no, not really. I'm staying here with two other girls and a bloke.'

'Do you know anywhere I could sleep?'

'In my bungalow,' she said and then thought he might think she was trying to pull him and flushed. 'The thing is, there are four of us, and one is moving on today. We could go and ask the guy who runs the place.'

'Cool. Well, if you don't mind. I'm going to check a few things out.'

He came back quite quickly; she was sitting chatting to a couple of the little Thai boys who swept the beach and put out the loungers, enjoying their sweet friendliness, their pride in earning some money for their families.

'Hi. Well, apparently Ang Thong is a must. The maritime park; you done that yet?'

'No, I haven't.'

'Well, come too, why don't you? It's a day trip; boat goes from Na Thon, at eight-thirty.' He had looked at her rather consideringly with his amazing blue eyes and suddenly grinned and said: 'You look great, Clio. Being here obviously suits you.'

Clio didn't eat anything for the rest of the day, in case her flattening stomach re-developed a bulge.

She felt distinctly nervous but hugely excited next day, joining Josh and half a dozen friends he'd made the night before; it was a stunning morning, clear and blue, as they moved out of the harbour towards the archipelago of Ang Thong. The boat served the usual disgusting coffee and some rather nice cakes for breakfast and, after a bit, Josh and most of his new friends fell asleep, stretched out on the hard benches in the sun. Clio stayed carefully under the tarpaulin; she burnt easily, in spite of her dark hair.

After about half an hour, Josh woke up, saw her sitting alone and patted the bench next to him. 'Here,' he said. 'Come and sit with me.'

245

And she had, her head swimming with excitement, sat down next to him and he'd grinned at her and put his arm round her and passed her his beer to share. He liked her! Josh Forbes, the gorgeous, *gorgeous* Josh liked her. Fancied her. She could feel it. And somehow it didn't matter when another girl arrived and sat the other side of him and he put his other arm round her, because for the first time in her life she felt good about herself, and she knew that really he liked her best.

The boat had reached the mass of islands now, was making its way between them, some of them quite large and lush, others little more than huge rocks, carved into incredible shapes by the sea. They saw dolphins playing, and above them clouds of seabirds crying in the wind; and nearer to shore gazed down at rainbow-coloured fish through the incredibly clear water above the coral reef. It was an extraordinary journey.

They anchored finally off the biggest of the islands, and transferred to a longtail boat to take them in to shore. They jumped out into water knee-deep and, even by Thai standards, warm – 'Too hot to swim in,' Clio said to Josh – and the boat's captain pointed them in the direction of the island's greatest challenge, a steep 500-metre climb in a hollow behind the beach.

'Very, very hard,' he said. 'Not danger, but hard.'

'Right,' Josh said, 'I'm off. Who's coming with me?'

Clio was: and to her slight disappointment, all the others too.

It was an incredibly tough climb; through hard scrub and awkward boulders, up and up, sheltered to an extent from the sun, but not the heat, by the trees. They began light-heartedly, larking about, became tired and hot and increasingly silent. Two of the girls gave up, started slithering down, laughing again, telling them they were mad. Clio, directly behind Josh now, less fit than they were, knew she would rather die than give in.

As she struggled on, feeling her own salty sweat stinging her eyes, her muscles straining, everything hurting, dying seemed quite likely.

But – she made it, emerged from the darkness of the trees into brilliant blue light and up the last few metres to the summit; and then stood there, weariness set aside. It was as if she was flying above the islands, spread below and beyond her, jagged shapes, rimmed with white sand, carved out of the blue, mystically beautiful. Even Josh seemed moved by it, stood there, gazing at it in silence; and then smiled at her rather slowly without speaking. Clio wished she wasn't quite so drenched in sweat.

She had expected the descent to be easy, but it wasn't, and she was tired, dreadfully tired. As she neared the bottom, she began to feel dizzy and sick, the sun seemed horribly dazzling and she found it hard to find footholds; twice she slipped. Josh was ahead, and she was thankful; she didn't want him thinking she was pathetic.

There was a stretch of grass at the bottom of the steps; Clio just reached it, collapsed onto it, under a palm tree, her legs completely without strength. She sat, her head buried in her arms, feeling faint and dreadfully thirsty; she knew she had to get back to the boat within a few minutes, everyone else had gone, but she literally couldn't walk. Nor did she care.

'You OK?' It was Josh's voice, clearly anxious.

'Yes, I'm fine. Thanks.'

'You don't look it. You look awful. Quite green.'

'I'm OK.' She struggled to stand up and couldn't.

'Clio, you're not. You're dehydrated. Stay there, I'll get some stuff for you.'

He was back in minutes, carrying not only water, but crisps ('You need salt') and cola ('You need sugar'), and stood over her while she consumed them. Their captain waved to them to hurry; Josh shouted that he had to wait, gesturing to Clio lying on the ground; everyone stared. She could imagine them getting impatient, scornful of her, and worst of all, amused.

Gradually she felt her strength return and managed to stagger to the boat, leaning on Josh's arm, and felt self-conscious, sitting in the longboat, smiling feebly at people.

'Right,' said Josh, handing her up the ladder into the other boat, 'there you go. OK now?'

'Yes, I'm fine,' she said. 'Thank you. Sorry.'

'Don't be silly. You did well.'

He grinned at her.

She had expected him to leave her then, but he sat by her while they ate the lunch, and the others came over to them and chatted, asked her if she was all right. She felt wonderful; she

247

could have laughed for joy, sitting there, with Josh at her side looking after her, sharing his bottle of beer.

They stopped again later, on a much smaller island called Mae Koh, where another wonder awaited them – 'And another climb, great!' said Josh – but this one was easy, leading through a narrow gorge and suddenly arriving at an extraordinary green-blue lake, far, far below, entirely circled by cliffs, and filled with fresh seawater by way of an underground tunnel. It had a magical quality. Clio half expected some exotic sea creature to rise from it in greeting, and said so; two of the girls looked at her and then each other and raised their eyebrows; she felt incredibly foolish, until Josh said, 'Or even a mermaid,' and again she felt fantastically happy.

They snorkelled and then sat on the beach in the sun; one of the girls passed round a spliff and this time Clio took it – it was obviously so boring not to, and she inhaled, felt an easy warmth, a heady spinning of her senses. The girl wandered off down the beach, her small, perfect bottom moving very gently from side to side.

'She's nice,' said Clio, looking enviously at the bottom.

'She's OK,' Josh said, beginning to roll another spliff, 'not as nice as you,' and gave her a kiss on the top of her head. They smoked together for a few minutes, Clio feeling increasingly wonderful. And then he said that she was burning: 'Why don't we move round there, into that sort of cave thing, you'll be sheltered there.'

That had done it, really. She had known this was it, now, here, at last: a man wanted her and she wanted him. She was suddenly sexy and confident and they were away from the others at his instigation, so surely he felt the same too. She turned to him and pulled his head down to hers and kissed him on the mouth. She could feel him first hesitate, and then respond; he was a very, very good kisser, she thought confusedly, a lot better than anyone who had ever kissed her before.

She found she was experiencing a lot of strange things, strange sensations; there seemed to be some link between her mouth and a place deep within her, a dark, sweetly soft place, that seemed to move every time he kissed her, and her heart was

248

racing. She felt warm and relaxed and excited all at the same time, and she could feel a longing, that was exactly like hunger – or was it thirst? Somehow the two fused together – to have Josh there, meeting the place – and she turned on her back and tried to pull him onto her.

'Hey, now,' he said, very gently. 'Careful, Clio.'

But she was beyond being careful, beyond sense, beyond caution or anything, she just wanted him; she could feel his penis stiffening against her, and he was kissing her again, but very gently, and she tried desperately with her free hand, the one that was not holding his head onto hers, to pull off her bikini pants.

She thought he would go on kissing her, but he had stopped. Maybe he was going to take his own shorts off; she lay back, breathing heavily, looking at him, then pulling his head down again, pushing her tongue into his mouth, wondering how to find his penis, urge it into her, and all the time this fierce, strange, violent sensation: but then, suddenly, it was different. He was resisting her, pulling his head back slightly; and then he said: 'Clio, not now, not just now. Calm down.' And then he stopped, and gave her a half-smile, and even through the booze and the dope and her own ignorance, she knew. He didn't want her – not now, not ever. She was being rejected, turned away as she always was, as she always had been, she felt fat again, naive, uncool; and looking over his shoulder she saw the girl, the other girl watching them from the other side of the rocks, a half-amused look on her face. Hot with shame and misery, she turned away from Josh, pulled up her pants, and ran fast, as fast as she could, down to the sea and into it, careless of the coral hurting her feet, and if she had had the courage she would have walked on and on until she could be seen no more, but it was no good, she couldn't do that, and finally, she turned and looked for him on the beach, but he had gone and was walking towards the long queue forming to get back to the boat.

They were on their way back; Josh was standing with a group of friends at the bows of the boat; he saw her looking at him, waved awkwardly, and then turned away, staring out to sea. A girl joined him, put her arm round his waist, pushed her hand into the pocket of his trunks, and it hurt Clio physically to see them, it was like a twisting wound in her stomach. The journey back seemed endless.

And then that night, as they all sat on the beach, Clio desperate for an excuse to go inside, to bed, still watching the group miserably, expelled from it by her own foolishness, it happened. A boy – quite a nice-looking boy – asked if he could join her, offered her some drink, and after a little while, started to kiss her and then to stroke her breasts, and then to push his hands down into her pants, probing into her pubic hair and then further still; and after only a very little time, she was leading him into their hut, giggling deliberately loud, making sure that Josh was watching. And already a little of her humiliation and sense of worthlessness had gone.

It was not a good experience; the boy was inside her swiftly, far too swiftly, and it hurt dreadfully, but she felt healed and restored and less humiliated, all at the same time, and she hoped against all hope that Josh might realise someone did want her, and assume that he had been alone on the beach and on the boat, and even in the whole of Thailand, in being foolish enough to reject her.

Over the next few months, she slept with a great many boys, some of them extremely good-looking and sexy, some of them less so; sometimes she enjoyed it and sometimes she didn't. The important thing seemed to be that she could persuade them to want her. She had become, she supposed, that much-despised creature, a slag, and she also supposed she should despise herself, but she didn't; she felt very little about herself at all. She was simply running, running away from the plump, dull, innocent person she had been and was so afraid of; and every time she had sex with someone, that person was further away from her.

A new Clio came home, the old one left behind in the sun and the islands or perhaps in the hill villages of the north, or even the glittering ostentation of Singapore: a slim, even thin Clio, with sun-streaked hair and a deep, deep tan, a Clio who could attract men quite easily, but who was still anxious, still eager to please, still very far from sexually confident.

And the new Clio did not know, had not even considered, that she might carry a legacy from those dangerously careless days that would damage her for the rest of her life.

'I wondered – I wondered if we could meet.' It was Kate's unmistakable little voice, rather shakier than usual. Clearly she was nervous. 'Have lunch or something, like you said.'

'Of course.' Jocasta smiled into the phone. 'It would be lovely. When did you have in mind?'

'Well, Saturdays are best. Because of school.'

'I can't do today. Next week? Where would you like to go?'

'Oh, I don't mind really.'

'Shall we say the Bluebird? In the King's Road? It's really fun there, specially on Saturday.'

'Well – I'm not sure. Is it very expensive?'

Jocasta's heart turned over. What a baby Kate was. How could she be even thinking about –? Well, she wasn't. Of course she wasn't.

'Kate, this is on me. I suggested it, didn't I? Do you know where it is? Right down the end, near World's End.'

'I think so, yes. I'll find it anyway.'

'Good girl. Half past one?'

'Cool.'

'Oh, Kate – '

Jocasta, don't. Don't do it . . .

'Yeah, what?'

'When – when's your birthday?'

'August the fifteenth. Why do you want to know?'

'Oh, I was just thinking about your work experience, you know. OK. See you on Saturday. How's your gran?'

'She's fine, thanks. Bye, Jocasta.'

'Bye, Kate.'

Jocasta put down the phone, and sat staring at it for quite a long time; then very, very slowly, as if someone was physically holding her back, she called up the *Sketch* archive site on her computer and typed in 15 August 1986.

Chapter 18

Carla Giannini was one of the great tabloid fashion editors. She understood precisely what fashion meant to tabloid readers: not so much silhouettes and hem lengths and fabric and cut, but sex. She ignored the collections and the couture designers; using upmarket photographers she had them shoot sharp trouser suits and dresses from Zara, Top Shop and Oasis, shoes from Office, jeans and knitwear from Gap, on young, long-legged, bosomy models, who preened themselves on her pages, saucer-eyed and sexy.

Carla was herself a beauty, dark-eyed and slightly heavy-featured, in the style of the young Sophia Loren, the child of an English aristocrat mother and an Italian car mechanic father. It was, against all odds, a very happy marriage, lived against the background of industrial Milan; but at seventeen, Carla had left home and moved to London and a new life – she hoped – as a model. She established herself quite quickly as an underwear model which she hated; but she made enough money to do an evening course and became a much sought-after make-up artist. She didn't like that much either, but she made a lot of very good contacts in the business and from there managed to move into what she realised she really wanted to do: fashion journalism. After a few years establishing herself on women's magazines, she finally found her true home – newspapers. Chris Pollock installed her in her office at the *Sketch* on her thirty-ninth birthday.

Carla had her own office, just off the newsroom, and Jocasta's desk was nearest to it; they were not exactly friends, but they fed each other cigarettes and quite often compared their extraordinarily different problems at the end of the day in the nearest wine bar, and occasionally Carla invited Jocasta to go with her to health farms like Ragdale Hall and Champneys, whose press agents invited journalists for the weekend, in the hope that they would write about them, or better still, use them in photographs.

Carla's major problem was finding girls to photograph; she liked real girls, not quite off the street, but singers, actresses, designers, anyone with more of a story to them than their statistics and their model books. She used friends, daughters of friends, her boyfriends' sisters, even her own sisters; she had tried to persuade Jocasta to model for her, with a complete lack of success; Jocasta said she was too old for it and that it was so much the sort of thing she hated. 'And I don't think Chris would like it.'

'Of course he would,' said Carla briskly. 'You know how he loves the whole personality thing. You have such a great look, Jocasta, and for God's sake, Elle is pushing forty, Naomi's no spring chicken and look at Jerry Hall!'

'Well, I know,' said Jocasta, 'but the big difference between them and me is they all really care about how they look and know how to make the most of themselves. I don't. I mean, I can't even remember when I last wore any make-up, apart from on my eyes.'

'Yes, and that's a story in itself,' said Carla and sighed. 'Well, I'll just keep nagging on.'

She felt all her birthdays had come at once, therefore, when she was walking past the Bluebird Cafe at lunchtime one Saturday and saw Jocasta sitting at a table, talking earnestly to one of the most beautiful young girls she had seen for a very long time.

Anna Richardson called Clio again.

'We're off tomorrow. Look, do think about applying for that job at the Bayswater. They asked me if I'd mentioned it. They really want you.'

Clio said she would think about it. Hard. And poured herself a glass of wine to celebrate. At least somebody wanted her. And not just any old place, but one of the best teaching hospitals in London. It made her feel quite different. Happier. Sleeker. Less of a disaster.

After drinking another glass of wine, she sat down at the table and starting drafting a letter.

Martha had told Paul Quenell about her new life. She felt she must. He had been surprisingly sympathetic and very interested; and far from saying she must resign, that her work for Wesley's was sure to suffer, he told her that as long as it only encroached on her life at weekends, then it was fine by him.

'Although I suppose if you get elected, you'll be leaving.'

'Well – yes. But I won't be elected, I'm sure.'

'I certainly hope not,' said Paul, and then he smiled at her. 'I wonder if I could sue them for enticement?'

He was a tall, stylish man, very slim, with thick grey curly hair and a rather ascetic face; his smile, which rarely came, was a rather minimal affair. He was forty-five years old, divorced without children; that was the sum total of what anybody knew about his personal life.

'I – don't think so,' said Martha very seriously.

'What a waste,' he said. 'If you go, I mean. But I'm full of admiration for you. Well done. I thought of going into politics myself once, you know.'

'Really? Why didn't you?'

'Mostly because I couldn't face the very considerable loss of income. Anyway – ' He walked over to the fridge set into one of the tall cupboards that lined his walls. 'I think your success thus far should be celebrated. Champagne?' She was so astonished by the whole encounter that she could hardly swallow the glass of extraordinarily good Krug that he poured for her.

'No,' said Jocasta. 'No, no, no, Carla. You can't. You are not even to try to, OK?'

'But Jocasta, why not? She's *gorgeous*. Beautiful. Please. I'll take you to Babington House for the weekend. I'll buy you dinner at Daphne's. I'll let you borrow my Chanel jacket . . .'

'No,' said Jocasta.

'But I'm not going to sell her into white slavery, for God's sake. I'm just going to put some clothes on her and take some pictures. Who is she, anyway?'

'I'm not going to tell you. She's just a girl I've met.'

'She seemed rather young to be a friend.'

'Don't be so rude,' said Jocasta.

'Well, darling, it's you who's always going on about your wrinkles. Actually, she looked a bit like you – she could have been your younger sister.'

'Yeah, right,' said Jocasta: and then, 'Funny, Sim said that as well. Oh shit.' She stared at Carla and prayed she hadn't taken in what she had said. Her prayers were not answered.

'Sim? Sim Jenkins the staff photographer? Jocasta, has this girl got anything to do with that story about the old woman on the hospital trolley? She's not the granddaughter, is she?'

'No,' said Jocasta firmly.

'I'm sure she is.' Carla's vast brown eyes were amused.

'Yes, all right, she is. But her parents are very protective of her, they didn't want her even in that shot, and anyway, she's not sixteen yet.'

'Why are they so against it?'

'I suppose they mistrust newspapers. Quite right too. He's a teacher and she's a full-time mum, they're real innocents abroad. So you are not to do anything, Carla. Absolutely not to. We're talking important things like people's lives here. Not just some cruddy fashion pages.'

'I don't do cruddy pages,' said Carla with dignity.

'Anyway, I must go,' said Jocasta, standing up, pulling her tape recorder out of her drawer. 'I've got to go and interview this girl – woman – I used to know. Well, I didn't know her really; I travelled with her for a few days when we were eighteen.'

She was feeling edgy, nervous; she told herself it was because this interview was important, but she knew it was nothing of the sort. Gideon Keeble had phoned her that morning, asked her if she would like to take him up on his invitation to stay with him in Ireland.

'I'm here for a few days and my doctor has told me to rest.'

'Gideon, you're not ill, are you?'

'No, no, just a little tired. Now I'm not compromising you, of course. It's the pair of you I'm after, you and your lovely boyfriend.'

'You sound much more Irish than usual,' she said laughing. 'Is that how you talk when you're over there?'

'Maybe. What do you say? Could you consider it, even? Just a few days, around this weekend.'

Jocasta considered it. The very idea of spending any time at all in Ireland, under the same roof as Gideon Keeble, excited her. He was an extremely rich and powerful man; that he wanted to spend time with her – and Nick of course – was amazingly flattering. And she did find Gideon horribly attractive. It wasn't just the aura that all powerful men trail around with them – when he looked at her, with those amazing blue eyes of his, she just wanted to get into bed with him. At once. Without further ado. And she was sure he recognised it.

God, she wanted to go, wanted to say yes. But – Nick was away. For the weekend. So – what did she do? And more importantly, what did she say?

'Nick's away for the weekend,' she said. Leaving it up to him.

'Then,' he said, and she could feel him refusing to do it for her, 'then, Jocasta, it is entirely up to you. But – I would love to see you.'

And knowing with absolute certainty that if she went, she would never see Nick again, and summoning up every shred of willpower (weakened considerably by the image of Gideon, the sound of his voice) she said, very quickly and before she could change her mind, that she thought it would be better not.

'A pity,' he said, 'but you know, I have to tell you, Jocasta, that I am encouraged by your refusal.'

'Why?' she said laughing.

'Well – if you had said you would come, I would have assumed you saw me as a nice old gentleman who would not disturb your relationship or trouble you in any way. And I think we both suspect that is not the case. Goodbye, Jocasta. Thank you for considering it.'

She put the phone down and had to take several deep breaths before she could even stand up.

'I told her. I told her everything. And she's going to see what she can do. She was great.'

'Told you.'

It had been Sarah's idea: for Kate to talk to Jocasta, tell her everything, get her to write about it, so that her mother could get in touch with her. Since the detective agency idea had never got off the ground.

'And do your mum and dad know?'

Kate look discomfited.

'No. Jocasta did say I should talk to them some more. She said she wouldn't like to do anything until she was sure they were happy.'

'Oh I wouldn't take any notice of that,' said Sarah. 'She's a journalist and they'll do anything for a good story. Honestly, Kate, if she wants to write about you, she will. She won't wait for you to ask your mum.'

'I – think she will,' said Kate. Her heart was beating a little faster than usual.

'Kate, she won't. Anyway, what's it matter? I thought that's why you told her in the first place.'

'Yes, well it was. But – well in the end, I think I would want to talk to Mum about it. It would be awful not to. She'd be really upset. Jocasta said that as well,' she added.

'But, Kate, that's the whole point, isn't it? Your mum would never agree.'

'She might,' said Kate. She was beginning to wish she had never had the conversation with Jocasta. 'Anyway,' she said, slightly aggressively, to Sarah, 'she said she wouldn't do anything in a hurry.'

'I thought you were in a hurry?'

'Oh for God's sake!' Kate was getting irritable. 'Look, it's up to Jocasta, OK? Not my parents.'

'That's what I just said. Course it is. Crikey, Kate! Do you realise, you might even find out who your real father is, as well?'

'Yes,' said Kate, 'I thought of that. How he must be a complete arsehole.'

'Most men are,' said Sarah knowledgeably.

'Hi.' Kate, waiting for her bus, looked up from her *Heat* magazine. Nat Tucker stood in front of her. He had had his black hair cut very short and he was wearing baggy combats and a white sleeveless T-shirt. He looked fantastic. Why did it have to be today, here, with her in her school uniform? Thank God she'd taken her tie off.

'Hi,' she said, pulling her headphones out of her ears.

'You all right?' he said.

'Yeah. Yeah, cool thanks.'

'Still at school?'

'Yeah. Doing my exams, aren't I?'

'S'pose so. Want a lift home?'

'Oh – ' She swallowed hard, simply to delay her answer, not sound too eager. 'Well – maybe. Yeah. Thanks.'

'Car's round here.' He jerked his elbow in the direction of a side road, started walking. Kate followed him. This was amazing. A-mazing.

'You've got a new car,' she said, looking at it admiringly.

'Yeah. It's a Citroën. Citroën Sax Bomb.'

'Great,' said Kate carefully.

'My dad got it into the workshop, let me do it up. Like the spoiler?'

'Course.'

'I lowered the suspension seventy mill all round, looks better, don't it?'

'Yeah.'

'It'll be lower when I've finished with it. It does hundred and eleven,' he said, with an attempt at nonchalance. 'I upgraded the ignition and that. And the sound's great.'

'So – your dad let you have it for nothing?'

'No,' he said indignantly, 'I have to work for him, don't I? Well, get in. Here, give us your bag.'

He threw her school bag into the boot, and got in beside her, switched on the stereo. The street was filled with the thumping, punching rhythms of So Solid Crew. He started the engine, pulled away with a loud screech, dangerously close to the kerb. A middle-aged woman jumped back, scowling at him, shouted something; he grinned widely at Kate.

'Can't see for looking, can they, those grannies. So – what you going to do next? After the exams I mean?'

'Oh – don't know. Go to college I suppose.'

'What?' His voice was incredulous. 'You get out of school and go straight back in again?'

'Yes. Well, I want to do A levels.'

'Yeah? What for?'

'Well – to go to uni?'

'What for?' he said, clearly genuinely puzzled. 'I haven't got any GCSEs even, and I got a good job, plenty of dosh.'

'Yeah, but Nat, I can't go and work for my dad like you. I want to work for a newspaper or a magazine, something like that.'

'What, as a model or something?'

'No. A writer. Why should I be a model?' she said, stretching out her legs, surreptitiously easing her skirt a little higher.

'Well – you've got the looks and that. Make a lot of money that way, you could.'

Kate was silent; this was beyond her wildest dreams.

'Where d'you want to go?' he asked.

'Oh – Franklin Avenue, please.'

'How's Sarah?' he said.

'She's OK.'

He nodded. That's why he wanted to talk to me, she thought, he wants to know about Sarah. Sarah was more his type, dark, small, loud. Kate tried to be as lippy with boys as Sarah was, but she never could quite manage it.

'She still at school?'

'Yeah. Then she's going to go fulltime at the salon. The one where she's a Saturday girl.'

'What, she's going to be a hairdresser?' he asked and his face was incredulous, as if Kate had said Sarah was planning on entering a convent. 'How sad is that?'

'What's sad about hairdressing?' said Kate defensively. 'She likes it.'

'It's a sad job,' he said, 'running around old women all day, asking them if what they've done is all right, would they like a magazine to read, all that crap. My mum's one and I used to go and see her after school when I was younger. Awful job.'

'Well, Sarah likes it. She gets good tips.'

'Yeah?' He didn't seem very interested in Sarah any more. Kate's heart lifted; maybe he'd just been making polite conversation. Not that it was really his style.

'Well, here we are,' he said, turning into her road, pulling up with a screech of brakes. He left the stereo running; she could see her grandmother looking out of the window. God. Suppose she came out, asked to be introduced to him.

'I must go,' she said. 'Thanks for the lift.'

'Want to come out Saturday?' he asked. He was looking at her legs as she swung them sideways out of the car.

'With you?' she said. And then realised how stupid she must sound.

'Yeah. Clubbing over Brixton.'

Kate felt herself starting to blush with excitement. This was unbelievable. Nat Tucker was asking her out.

'Well – ' She managed to wait a moment, then said: 'Yeah, thanks.' Her voice sounded astonishingly level.

'I'll pick you up. Nine-ish. OK?'

'Yeah. OK.'

The effort of keeping her face expressionless, her voice level and disinterested, was so immense she found it hard to breathe. She was halfway up the path when he called her.

'Don't you want yer bag?'

'Oh. Oh yeah. Thanks.'

He got out of the car, pulled it out of the boot, slung it over the gate.

'Cheers. See you later.'

Kate was incapable of further speech.

'Martha? Hi, I'm Jocasta.'

'I think I'd have known that,' said Martha. She smiled, a charming, courteous smile. 'You look just the same. Do come in.'

'I'm afraid I don't look just the same.' Jocasta walked into the apartment. It was quite simply stunning. A mass of ash-blond wood flooring, white walls, huge windows, and a minimal amount of black and chrome furniture. 'This is gorgeous,' she said.

'Thank you. I like it. And it's near to my work.'

Martha was gorgeous too: in a cool, careful way. Slim, very slim, wearing dark grey trousers, and a cream silk shirt; her skin was creamy too, and almost make-up-less, with just some eye shadow and mascara and a beige-brown lipstick. Her hair, brown, straight, shining hair, streaked with ash, was cut into a neat, sleek bob.

'Which is where?' Jocasta asked. 'Your work, I mean?'

'Oh – just over there.' Martha waved rather vaguely down at the world below her.

'Yes, but what's it called, what do you exactly do?'

'I'm a partner with a City law firm. At the moment.' She ignored the request for the name.

'Oh, OK. Fun?'

'Not exactly fun. I like it though. Can I offer you a coffee or something?'

'Yes, that'd be great.'

'Fine. Just excuse me a moment. Make yourself at home. Do you need a table or anything to write on?'

'No, thanks, it's fine.'

She disappeared. Snooty cow, thought Jocasta; and thought of that other Martha, slightly nervous, eager to be friends, mildly defensive about her background. She had been so polite, so eager to please; what had changed her so much? Clio had hardly changed at all.

And she had been fun. Undoubtedly fun. The very first night in Bangkok, they'd all huddled together in one bed, the three of them, screaming at the cockroaches that had appeared when they put the light on, and then she'd pulled a bottle of wine from her bag and they'd shared it, drinking from the bottle, giggling and shaking at the same time.

'Right. Here we are.' She appeared again, with a dark wooden tray, set with white cups, a cafetiere, milk jug, a bowl of brown and white sugar lumps. Jocasta almost expected her to put a bill down on the table in front of her.

'Thanks. So – cheers.' She raised her coffee cup. 'It's good to see you.'

'And you.'

She was very still, Jocasta noticed, still and totally self-controlled. She was also, clearly, very nervous. It seemed strange, when she was so patently self-confident. Well, that was what interviews were all about. Finding out.

'Tell me,' she said, 'what's your brother doing? Is he a barrister?'

'God no,' said Jocasta, 'much too much like hard work. He works for the family company. He's married – just about. Got two little girls.' She smiled at Martha. 'So – you went to Bristol Uni, did you?'

'Yes, I did.'

'And – did you like it?'

'Yes, very much.'

'What degree did you get?'

'A first. In law. Look – is this part of the interview? Because I did say –'

'Martha,' said Jocasta as patiently as she could, 'I'm just playing catch-up. I'll tell you all about me if you like. And Clio.'

Martha visibly seized on this.

'How is Clio?'

'Not very happy,' said Jocasta. 'She's getting divorced. She's doing very well at her job, though.'

'That's so sad. About her divorce I mean. Have you met the husband?'

'No. He sounds like an arsehole.' She smiled expansively at Martha. 'He's a surgeon. Arrogant. Totally up himself. She's better off without him. Mind you, I did upset him.'

'I thought you hadn't met him?'

'I didn't. But I wrote about his hospital. Long story. Anyway, he didn't like it.'

'I don't suppose he did,' said Martha. She picked up her cup of black coffee. Her hand was shaking slightly, Jocasta noticed. Her small, beautifully manicured hand.

'But she's just the same, dear little Clio – remember how we started calling her that, on the second day in Bangkok?'

'No, I don't think I do,' said Martha.

She was clearly going to block any attempt at reminiscence.

'Anyway, did you do what you said, do Oz, and end up in New York?'

'You have an amazing memory,' said Martha, and there was a silence. Then she said: 'Oz, certainly. I didn't see much of the States. Look, Jocasta, I don't want to be rude, but I don't have an awful lot of time. So maybe we should start.'

'Of course. Fine. Well, look, let's start with a few basic facts –'

'Like what?'

'Oh, you know, your age, what you do, how you got drawn into politics, all that stuff. Then we can do some details. It's a very good story, I think.'

She watched her very slowly relaxing, growing in confidence as she took control, presented what was obviously a very carefully rehearsed story. And it was a good one, from a spin point of view: the death of the office cleaner, her longing to do something to help, to change things, her growing involvement with Centre Forward, her returning to her roots.

Jocasta listened politely, asking questions about Centre Forward, about the number of MPs they had, how many they hoped to field for the general election; went on to some incredibly boring stuff about the election process. And then began to move, very stealthily, in. What she had so far wasn't going to make her the next Lynda Lee-Potter.

'You're obviously doing awfully well at your firm,' she said. 'Won't you miss it?'

'Well yes, but I think it'll be worth it if I can make a difference, even quite a small one.'

'I meant the trappings?'

'I'm sorry?'

'Well, this flat obviously didn't come cheap. And you clearly like nice clothes – I know a pair of Jimmy Choos when I see them. And a Gucci bag, come to that.'

'Jocasta, I don't think this is relevant.' She was looking edgy again, fiddling with one of her earrings.

'Of course it is. You must care an awful lot to give it all up. I think that's great.'

'Well – ' she relaxed a little – 'well, as I told you, it'd be nice to be able to make a difference. And Gucci bags don't exactly melt, do they? I just won't be able to have the latest models any more. If I get in, that is.'

'You'll be doing a lot of driving up and down to Suffolk, won't you?'

'Quite a bit. Every weekend.'

'What car do you drive?'

'I – does that matter?'

'Not really. I just wondered if you'd have to change that too? Chad said it was a Mercedes convertible, is that right?'

'Well – yes. I really don't know if I'll be changing it. Maybe.'

'And – what about your personal life?'

'My what?' She had flushed scarlet. 'Jocasta – '

'You'll be moving down to Binsmow. I just thought if there's a man in your life, he might not like that. It's a pretty radical step. Or does he live down there?'

'No. I mean, I don't have a man in my life. Not – not an important one. Just a few good friends.'

'That's lucky. Or maybe it isn't.'

'I'm sorry, I don't know what you mean – '

'I mean, it may be lucky for your political plans, but wouldn't you like to have someone?'

'I really don't want to comment on that.'

'Oh, OK. Well – from what you've seen of it, is politics really very sexy?'

'I don't quite know what you mean . . .'

'Oh, Martha, come on, all that power, all those secrets, husbands living away from home, nubile secretaries and researchers at every corner. I find it very sexy, and I'm only on the edges of it!'

'Perhaps that's why,' said Martha coolly. 'I can only tell you I have no personal experience of that kind of thing.'

Jocasta gave up. 'I remember you being rather shy. When we first met. So – how different are you today from the young Martha? The one I went travelling with?'

'Jocasta,' said Martha, 'I don't want to go into all that.'

'But – why not? I really don't understand. It's such a sweet story. Three little girls from school, meeting by chance, setting off round the world, and then meeting up again all these years later, all of us quite successful – no, it's too good not to use, Martha.'

'I don't want it used.'

'Honestly, I'm sorry, but there's no reason not to. It's not unsavoury or anything, it just makes you sound more colourful and interesting. It must surely be one of the things that have made you who you are. I mean, it was a pretty defining experience for me. Wasn't it for you?'

'Not really. No, I wouldn't say it was.'

She was growing agitated now.

'Look – I said right at the beginning I didn't want this to be a personal article.'

'Did you do a lot of drugs or something?' said Jocasta. She

was growing curious now. 'Because naturally I wouldn't mention anything like that.'

'Of course I didn't do a lot of drugs!'

'Well, I did,' Jocasta said cheerfully. 'And I got ill as well. Horribly ill. Dengue fever. You never had anything like that? Never had to go to one of their hospitals?'

'No. I – I didn't stay long in Thailand at all, I went off to Sydney.'

'When was that?'

'What?'

'I said when did you go to Sydney? Don't look so scared, I just wondered. I was there in the January.'

'I'm really not very sure. It's so long ago. Jocasta – '

'And then did you go up to Cairns? And the rain forest?'

'Yes, for a bit. It was wonderful.'

'And you really didn't feel that year changed you much? It didn't affect what you might now call your political philosophy?'

'No,' said Martha firmly, 'no, it didn't. I'm afraid I really do have to go in a minute, Jocasta – '

'So – what is your political philosophy? Could you encapsulate it for me?'

She was caught unawares by this sudden return to safe ground.

'Well, yes. It's that people, all people, ought to be given a chance. Lots of chances. Good education, decent health care, reasonable living conditions. No one should be written off, abandoned to – to his or her fate.'

'That's really nice,' said Jocasta, smiling at her sweetly. 'I like that. Thank you. Thank you so much, Martha, you've been great. I can do a nice piece about this and I'm sure Chad will be very pleased.'

'Can I – can I see the piece? Before it's published?'

'I'm sorry, we can't do that. The editor doesn't allow it.'

'Why not?'

'Well – just think about it. If everyone we wrote about every day had to read their copy, and maybe change it, then it had to be re-jigged and shown to them again, we'd never get the paper to bed at all.'

'I would have thought this was slightly different,' said Martha, her voice very crisp now. 'It's not a news story, it doesn't have to be rushed to – to bed as you call it.'

'You're wrong there, I'm afraid. This is scheduled for the Saturday magazine section, and that goes to press tomorrow. Sorry.'

'Jocasta, I really would like to read it,' said Martha and there was an underlying anxiety in her voice. 'You could e-mail it to me and I'd e-mail it right back.'

'Honestly. It would be more than my job was worth. You can ask Nick, if you don't believe me.'

'I think it's rather different in his case. He's writing about politicians, news stories – '

'Well, you're a politician. Surely. And this is a news story. You've only just been elected – '

'Selected,' said Martha. 'You see, it's so important to get these things right. Please, Jocasta – '

Why was she so worried? It was odd. Jocasta raked back over the interview; she hadn't said anything that could be remotely misconstrued. She'd been minimal with most of her information. In fact, it was going to be a pretty dull piece. She actually felt rather worried about it.

'I can only tell you,' she said, 'that you have absolutely nothing to worry about. You've been the soul of discretion, Martha – you're going to come out of this squeaky clean.'

'I don't know why you should say that,' she said and there was a spot of high colour on her cheeks now. 'Why on earth shouldn't I come out squeaky clean, as you put it? Are you implying – ' She stopped, visibly took a deep breath. 'I hope you're not going to imply the reverse.'

'Of course I'm not! Calm down.'

'I'm perfectly calm. Sorry. It's just that you – well, this is a new game for me.'

'Of course. But – '

Martha's mobile rang; she answered it at once.

'Hi,' she said, her face immobile. 'Yes, I know, but I've been very busy. What? No, I'm looking forward to it. Yes, about eight. I can't talk now. I'll see you later. Sorry, Jocasta,' she said.

'That's OK. Martha, when did you get back?'

'When did I get back? Where from?'

266

'From travelling,' said Jocasta patiently. 'I just wondered if you did anything between getting back and going to uni.'

'Of course not,' said Martha and she suddenly sounded almost angry. 'How could I have? There was no time.'

'But –'

'Excuse me,' she said suddenly, 'I've just remembered something.' She stood up and walked, very quickly, out of the room – and that was what did it for Jocasta. Turned over the memory: one that she had long ago decided was not a memory at all, but a mistake, a case of totally mistaken identity, made as she was pushed and jostled in a swarming, stinking street. She sat and turned it over, that memory, reviving it, breathing life into it and waiting for Martha to return.

She was quite a long time; Jocasta heard the loo flush, and then a tap running. When Martha came back in, she had renewed her lipstick, and clearly re-sprayed her perfume.

'Sorry about that,' she said. 'I just remembered I had to check an e-mail.'

'That's all right,' said Jocasta. 'Well, I must go. And I promise you faithfully the article will be nothing but positive about you. You and the party.'

'Thank you. Right. Well, I'll have to trust you.'

'Yes, you will. Now, what we must have is a nice picture of you. Chad gave me the one that was on your leaflet, but it looked a bit dire to me. Would you mind if we took one? It really wouldn't take a minute to do – our chaps are really quick. Someone could come to your office even –'

'Absolutely not. I have back-to-back meetings for the next two days.'

'Oh, all right,' said Jocasta with a sigh, 'we'll use the one Chad gave me. Well, bye, Martha. And we must have a threesome one evening, you and me and Clio. Such a shame we all lost touch. We've missed so much out of each other's lives. Still – we've found each other now.' She walked to the door, picked up her jacket, and smiled at Martha.

'Please don't worry about the piece.'

She saw her relax. 'I won't,' she said, and smiled back. For the first time she looked more friendly, less aggressive. Jocasta took a deep breath. This was the moment.

'I just remembered something,' she said. 'Off the record – don't look so scared. You didn't go back to Bangkok, did you? That year? In – let me see – yes, in late June?'

The smile went completely. Martha looked – what did she look? Angry? Frightened? No, worse than that, terrified. Trapped. As she had looked that day. And then angry.

'Go back? Of course not. I told you, I went to the States – I went home from there – '

'I must have been mistaken then,' said Jocasta, her voice at its sweetest. 'I thought it was unlikely. But I thought I saw you there. I went back that way, you see. It was outside the station, Bangkok station. I called your name. Quite loudly, but whoever it was just walked away, disappeared.'

'Well, I expect she did,' said Martha. 'If her name wasn't Martha.'

Of course it had been Martha. She knew in that moment as certainly as she knew anything. And Martha knew she knew.

So – why was she lying about it?

Chapter 19

Kate couldn't ever remember being so angry. How could they do this to her, how dare they? The most important thing in her whole life and they were wrecking it for her.

'I just don't believe this,' she kept saying, 'I just don't believe you're doing this to me.'

'We're not doing anything to you, Kate,' Helen said, 'except trying to look after you.'

'Oh right. So you do that by not letting me go out for a few hours with my friends?'

'Kate, we're not talking about your going out for a few hours with your friends,' said Jim. 'You've just told us you're going to a club in one of the most crime-ridden neighbourhoods in London with some layabout – '

'Jim,' said Helen warningly. But it was too late.

'He is not a layabout!' shouted Kate. 'He works for a living. You know? Earns money, does a job. That sort of thing. And what do you know about Brixton?'

'It's very – very rough,' said Helen.

'What you mean is it's got a lot of black people there. You don't know any more about it than that. You're racist, as well as everything else.'

'Kate!'

'The whole point about clubs in Brixton is they're cool. Sarah's been there lots of times. Dad, what do you think's going to happen to me, for God's sake? That I'll take some ecstasy and die? That I'll be beaten up? End up on the streets? I'm going with Nat. He'll look after me.'

'No,' said Jim. 'You are not going with anybody, and that's my last word.'

Kate glared at him; then she said: 'I cannot believe you are so pathetically ignorant,' and left the room. Very shortly the familiar thud of her music filled the house.

Jim looked at Helen.

'You do agree with me, don't you?' he said.

'Of course. Of course I do. It's a terrible place, soaring crime rate – and she's still a child. Oh – hello, Mummy.'

'What was that all about?'

'Kate wants to go clubbing in Brixton,' said Helen reluctantly. She knew what her mother's reaction would be.

'Oh really? And you won't let her, I suppose?'

'Of course not.'

Jilly sighed, put down the silver-topped cane she had taken to using, rather than a walking stick, and sat down.

'My mother forbade me to go to a club called the Blue Angel. It was considered very racy in its day – there was a wonderful black pianist there called Hutch who was supposed to have had an affair, apparently, with the Duchess of Kent – anyway, I went there about a year later and of course it was really quite all right, and I had a wonderful time. All that happened was that I decided my mother was rather foolish and lost some of my respect for her.'

'Mummy, I don't think clubs in Brixton quite compare with the Blue Angel. It's you who's being foolish.'

'These things are all relative. Anyway, who does she want to go with?'

'Some dreadful boy who's going to drive her there in his car.'

'Not the one who brought her home from school the other day?' said Jilly. 'He's frightfully good-looking. I can see why she wants to go out with him. I'd go myself if I could. Maybe that would be the answer,' she added, 'I could chaperone her. It would be fun!'

'Oh, Mummy, really!' said Helen wearily.

Her mother was going home in a few days' time and she couldn't help looking forward to it.

Jilly heard Kate come downstairs when everyone else had gone to bed. She heaved herself out of her bed in the dining room

270

and went into the kitchen; Kate was making a cup of tea.

'Hello, darling. Make one for me, would you? I'm sorry about your date with your young man.'

Kate turned a swollen face to her. 'Oh Gran,' she said, 'what am I going to tell him? That's the worst thing, thinking of something that doesn't sound totally sad.'

'Maybe I can help,' said Jilly. 'I've always been very good at lies.'

They came up with the best they could manage: that Jilly was going home that weekend and Helen had insisted Kate went too, to look after her. Kate rang Nat and struggled with this, but she could tell he wasn't impressed.

'Can't you tell them you won't? That you're coming out with me?'

'Not really,' said Kate sadly.

'OK. Fine. See you around.'

His phone went dead. Kate went upstairs and cried.

She was walking down the street with Bernie next day, when there was a screaming of brakes and thumping of music; it was Nat in his Sax Bomb.

'Hi,' he said.

'Hi.'

'You want to come out Sat'dy, then, Bern?'

'I might. Where you going?'

'Brixton.'

'Yeah. OK. Cool.'

'Cheers. See you later.'

He ignored Kate. The effort of looking disinterested was so great, she felt it as a physical pain. Especially when Bernie got out her mobile and rang about a dozen people and told them. How was she ever going to live this down? Everybody, absolutely everybody, would think she was so sad.

It was the Tories, the right-wing Tories, who really hated the new party; Blair was quite kindly disposed towards them. From his point of view they had done him a favour, and weakened the opposition. Chad Lawrence was the first to feel the vitriol one day shortly after the launch, when he went into the members' smoking room, that enclave of Tory MPs, and found himself

271

totally shunned: backs were turned, newspapers raised in front of faces, and icy silence greeted his attempts to pass the time of day. Indeed one venerable member said he would like to remind him that he was no longer a Tory: 'More than that, you are a traitor. We cannot forbid you this place, but we can refuse you any kind of a welcome here.' Chad went downstairs to the Pugin Room, surprised at his own distress.

Janet Frean was in the Pugin Room having tea; Chad asked if he could join her.

'Just got the bum's rush up in the members' smoking room. More or less told I wasn't a gentleman.'

'Good God,' said Janet. 'So – is it pistols at dawn?'

'Of course.' He smiled at her. And thought how nice she was, although her persona, that of pleasant, sympathetic wife and mother and committed campaigner on behalf of the elderly and the dispossessed, disguised the fact that she could have put Machiavelli firmly in the shade.

Chad ordered a double whisky. 'It's not easy, is it? Sometimes –' he looked at her '– sometimes, do you feel it too? Right deep down at the bottom of your soul?'

'Of course I do.'

The three of them were performing a very tricky act on the Westminster stage that summer – Nicholas Marshall in the *Sketch* had compared it to the dance of the little swans, supporting first one party, now the other, while struggling to create a voice of their own. They were still too small to make any important impression on the national consciousness, or to come anywhere near to forming a credible opposition, and when they were not at Westminster, they were travelling the length and breadth of the land, urging, coercing, tempting people onto their side.

'In my darkest hours,' Janet said now, 'I think of the SDP. They got off to the same wonderful, high-profile start and then still lost it all.' She reached for his glass, took a sip of his whisky. 'But then dawn breaks and I think how defeatist and foolish I am.'

'You're neither,' said Chad. 'I think of you as our Boadicea, riding across Westminster Bridge. It'll be good to have Griers on board, won't it? He's a marvellous, heavyweight addition.'

272

'Yes . . .'

There was something in her voice that made him look at her intently.

'You don't like him?'

'Of course I like him. He's charming. Not sure how heavyweight, that's the only thing. Oh, I know he's marvellous in debate and all that. But a couple of people have said he's not quite so good when it comes to rolling up his sleeves and doing some work. I'm being unfair, I'm sure.'

'Hope so. The only thing that would worry me is his tendency to drop his trousers. Great ladies' man. Or used to be. We've got a sleaze-free platform to keep clean.'

'I mentioned that to Jack. Got ticked off for paying attention to gossip. Anyway, I'm sure he'll be a great addition to the team.'

'I hope so.'

'He will. Courage, Chad. Cometh the hour, cometh the man.'

'Or woman. I know. Of course. You're right.'

Chris Pollock came storming across the newsroom and threw Jocasta's copy onto her desk.

'What the fuck do you think this is? If it's your idea of a profile, Jocasta, you'd better go and find another paper to put it in. I'm not printing this crap. It's dull, it's uninformative, it's got no life – '

'Bit like the subject,' said Jocasta under her breath.

'What's that?'

'Nothing. No. I'm sorry, Chris. I didn't think much of it myself. To be honest.'

'Well, what the fuck did you turn it in for then? And this picture. I mean, give me strength! I'm not running this unless you can get more out of her, or give it a decent angle. Preferably both. Anyway, I can't waste any more time on it now, I've got to fill the fucking space somehow. Jesus wept!'

He walked off, shouting across the room at the picture desk as he went; Carla came out of her office.

'What was that about?'

Jocasta told her; Carla looked at her thoughtfully.

'Show me the picture.'

'Here. She's about a thousand times better looking than that. Great figure too.'

'Well, darling, we're looking at the answer, aren't we? She can be my fashion feature next week. It's a great story. We can dress her for her new life. Then your copy won't matter.'

'Thanks,' said Jocasta.

'No, honestly, darling, it's a great idea. Let me talk to Chris, then you can ring the bitch.'

'I don't know that she'll agree,' said Jocasta.

'Of course she will. It's what she wants, from everything you've told me about her. Publicity without pain.'

Carla was right. It was exactly what Martha wanted. It was safer, less intrusive. And it would give her a chance, maybe, to see the copy. Jocasta sounded nervous, anxious even for her to agree. That would give her a lever too. 'Yes, I think that would be all right. I'd quite like that, I think, as long as it could be done at the end of the day.'

'Oh, Martha, I'm sure it could.' Jocasta's voice was light with relief.

'Especially if it meant I could maybe see the copy. I mean clearly, there's time now.'

'Well – yes. Yes, I'm sure you could. See my draft anyway. Right. Well, I'll tell Carla and she'll probably contact you direct. She's called Carla Giannini – she's really nice. Thank you so, so much, Martha.'

'That's my pleasure,' said Martha.

'And then he said – ' Jocasta paused, refilled her glass for the third time in twenty minutes – 'then he said I'd better find another paper to put the story in. I mean, it wasn't *that* bad. I can't believe it. My big chance and I've bloody well blown it. It's not fair, it really isn't. Well, is it? Nick?'

'Well, I don't think you can say it's not fair. The thing is, sweetie, you turned in a bad piece. By your own admission.'

'It wasn't bad,' said Jocasta. 'It just wasn't great.'

'And that's no good. You write a big piece, it has to be great. Simple as that.'

'Thanks,' said Jocasta, glaring at him. 'I thought I might get a bit of comfort and – and reassurance from you, not a lecture on journalistic standards. You're supposed to be on my side, or so I thought – '

'I *am* on your side. That's not the same thing as trying to discuss the situation properly.'

'Oh really? You could have fooled me. I've been waiting around for days to see you, and you were away for the weekend with your bloody mother – again. Two weekends in a row you've been up there.'

'For two good reasons. Rupert's birthday and then Mummy and Pa's anniversary. Anyway, you were invited. And actually, I found it quite difficult, explaining why you couldn't come for a second time.'

So this was what she got for turning down a weekend with Gideon Keeble, resisting the temptation of a lifetime.

'Oh, well, I'm so sorry, Nick. Sorry I make your life difficult. It's just that sitting around in a freezing dining room, while everyone talks about the hunt ball and who's going salmon fishing, isn't quite my idea of fun.'

'Jocasta, you're being very unpleasant. It's not like you.'

'I feel unpleasant. You're not being very nice either, saying I shouldn't file lousy pieces.'

'I said nothing of the sort. Don't be so absurd.'

'Oh for God's sake,' said Jocasta, 'why don't you just go away? Back to mummy, maybe? I'm sure you'd rather!'

'Jocasta, please – ' He smiled at her. 'You're being so ridiculous. Come here, let me give you a hug.'

'I don't want a hug,' she said, and to her horror, she started to cry. 'I want you to support me properly. I want you to be there for me, when I need you – '

'I *am* there for you.'

'Nick, you so are not! You just go on and on your own sweet way, doing exactly what you please, working all the hours of the day and night, seeing your friends, going home to mummy, and just coming round here when you feel in need of a fuck!'

'That's a filthy thing to say!'

'It's true. And I'm sick of it. If you really cared about me, you'd have made some sort of commitment by now – '

'Oh, so that's what this is all about. The fact I haven't gone down on one knee and put a ring on your finger.'

'No. Not entirely. But – '

'Jocasta, I've told you over and over again. I'm sorry. I would if I could. But I don't feel – '

'You don't feel ready. And when do you think you might? When you're forty? Fifty? I'm absolutely sick of the whole thing, Nick, I really am. I feel so – so unimportant to you – '

'Well, I'm sorry to hear that,' he said, standing up, picking up his car keys.

'Where are you going?'

'I'm going home. I'm not going to listen to any more of this.'

'Good!'

And he walked out, not slamming the door, as she would have done, but shutting it very slowly and carefully behind him; Jocasta picked up a heavy glass ashtray and hurled it at the door. It gouged out a chunk of wood before falling onto the tiled floor and shattering. She was standing there, staring at it, when her mobile rang. She looked to see who it was: Chris Pollock. Now what had she done?

'Jocasta? I want you on a plane to Dublin. Tonight if you can manage it. Gideon Keeble's daughter's run away from school with a rock star. You know Keeble. Don't come back till you've got the full story, OK? I don't want a repetition of that fuck-up with Martha Whatshername.'

'There won't be,' said Jocasta.

It was one of the longest days she could ever remember. And the most miserable. Almost worse than when they'd first said she couldn't go.

It never stopped all day: Bernie going on and on about what a great time she'd had with Nat, how he'd driven her to Brixton in the Sax Bomb, how he'd looked so fit in his combats and vest, how he could really, really dance and how they'd been there till five in the morning and then – at this point the story was repeated in a whisper into various ears, amidst wild shrieks and giggles. Even Sarah couldn't resist it, although she tried for a while for Kate's sake. 'Sorry,' she said to Kate afterwards; Kate shrugged and said she couldn't care less, and Bernie was welcome to him as far as she was concerned. By the time she got home she was beside herself with rage and resentment; even her grandmother's tactful questioning infuriated her.

'They all had a great time, Gran, and I didn't, OK?'

She went up to her room, turned on the radio and lay down on her bed. It was so unfair. So totally, totally unfair. Everything was shit. He'd never ask her out again, not now. She was branded as a poor sad creature still under the thumb of her parents. She hated everyone. She hated her parents, she hated Juliet, even now earnestly practising her violin, she even nearly hated her grandmother, fussing about, talking in her posh voice, pretending she understood, telling her about some crap place she hadn't been allowed to visit when she was what she called a girl.

Nobody was on her side, even Sarah was deserting her now, and she was no nearer finding her mother. Even Jocasta seemed to have forgotten about her, it was two weeks since they'd had lunch and she hadn't heard a word . . .

Suddenly angry with Jocasta as well, she decided to ring her. She shouldn't have agreed to see her if she wasn't going to help. She dialled Jocasta's mobile. It seemed to be switched off. Funny, she'd told Kate it was her most precious possession, that she couldn't do her job without it; maybe it was out of range. Or – maybe she was at the paper. She could try there.

Endless ringing; on and on it went without being answered. Obviously she was away on a story. Bloody typical, Kate thought, just her luck. She was just going to ring off, when a voice said: 'Hello, Jocasta's phone.'

'Oh, hi,' said Kate, nervous suddenly. 'Is – is she there?'

'No, I'm sorry. She's away for a few days.' It was a nice voice, slightly foreign, quite deep.

'Oh. OK. Well – sorry to bother you.'

'Can I take a message?'

'Um – no. No, it's OK. I'll ring again. Could you tell her Kate rang.'

'Kate? Is that Kate Moss?'

'I wish,' said Kate.

'Sorry. You sound a bit like her. Well, like her when she was younger anyway. So, Kate who?'

'Kate Tarrant.'

There was a brief but quite noticeable silence, then the voice said: 'The girl with the granny? At the hospital?'

'Yeah.'

'How is your grandmother now?'

'Oh – she's fine, thanks.'

'Good. Yes, I think I saw you the other day, having lunch with Jocasta at the Bluebird. Would that have been you? Long blonde hair?'

'Yes, that's me,' said Kate.

Then the voice said: 'You know, I wanted to meet you. I told Jocasta I thought you could perhaps be in one of my fashion features. My name is Carla Giannini, I'm the fashion editor of the *Sketch*.'

'You did?' Kate's heart began to pound. 'Do you really think that?'

'Well, I think you might photograph very well. I couldn't say, until I've done a few test shots. But I think it's more than possible. You should come in and see me one day. It would be nice to meet you, anyway, such a brave young girl, taking on the NHS single-handed!' She laughed, a throaty, husky laugh. Kate felt dizzy.

'Do you mean that? That I should come and see you?'

'Of course. Look, think about it and give me a ring. Maybe tomorrow? I'll give you my direct line.'

'Yeah. Yeah, that'd be great. Thanks.'

Wow. WOW! Cool, or what? God. That would change Nat's mind about her being sad. A model. In the newspapers. Wow. Oh – my – God.

Kate went downstairs singing.

'Hi, Mum. Want a cup of tea?'

Carla put the phone down and smiled into it. Good. Very good. She had no doubt Kate would be in to see her. Jocasta wouldn't like it, but that was too bad. She had no claim on Kate. And Carla had pages to fill.

She'd actually quite enjoyed doing the shoot with Martha Hartley. She hadn't been nearly as bad as Jocasta had made out.

A bit – reserved. But she was a lawyer. And she was certainly very attractive, and she wore the clothes – a suit, a jacket and an evening dress all from Zara – very well. Jocasta not being there had obviously helped; far from being bothered by her absence, Carla had been relieved. It was always easier with these shoots if she could have the subject to herself. As she would have Kate, with luck. Jocasta had called to say she was going to be away for at least two more days.

Half an hour later, as Carla had known she would, Kate called her. Would it be all right if she came in after school the next day – 'I could be there about five, five-thirty.'

Carla said that would be perfectly all right and put in a call to Marc Jones, a rather sexy young photographer she had used for the first time the week before, to ask him to come in to do some test shots of Kate.

Jocasta stood at the gates of Gideon Keeble's glorious house, and waited, along with roughly two dozen other reporters, a large clutch of photographers, cameramen and the policeman who was on duty. She had been waiting for some time now, about twelve hours; it was the first crucial thing you learnt as a reporter (or a photographer) to do. Nobody exactly enjoyed it, but nobody minded either; there was great camaraderie, time passed, people shared cigarettes and chocolate and swapped reminiscences and such scraps of news as they possessed. Generosity was, in fact, the name of the game, unless someone actually managed to get a huge scoop or an exclusive. That was not expected to be shared.

Dungarven House was on the top of a hill; every so often, someone would go up to the locked gates and peer through them, which was fairly fruitless, since the drive curved away to the right of the two lodges, and there was nothing to be seen except a tall beech hedge and, to the left of it, a thick wood. Gideon Keeble was certainly inside; he had been driven in the night before, looking very grim, and the gates had not been opened since. A local reporter had assured them there was no other vehicle access to the estate and an enterprising reporter, unwilling to accept his word, had skirted the entire area by bicycle, and reported only several small gates in the twelve-foot wall that surrounded it, which were locked with huge padlocks, with nothing more than rough tracks leading up to them. The southernmost tip of the estate was bounded by the famous lake, which was impassable from the other side, except by boat; Dungarven House was almost a fortress.

Of course Mr Keeble might have sailed across the lake, but had he done so, he would have a long walk to any road. Their radios told them hourly that Fionnuala Keeble, the beautiful fifteen-year-old daughter of retailing billionaire Gideon Keeble, had run away from her convent school with rock musician Zebedee and had still not been found; police were watching ports and airports but there had been no sightings of her, so it was presumed she must still be in the country. Her mother, now Lady Carlingford, was on her way back from Barbados where she lived and was not available for comment. It was generally agreed that if Fionnuala was found, she would be returned to her father at Dungarven House.

Jocasta spent quite a few of those twelve hours trying to get hold of Gideon's private number; but the charming, easy, hospitable Gideon Keeble, who had called her direct on her mobile, had done so from a number which told her politely now that Mr Keeble was not available and to try later; there was no facility even to leave a message. The same applied to all his office numbers. His e-mail address was equally elusive; the one everyone had was at his London office and although she had sent what she thought was an irresistible appeal, it had yielded nothing. Well, she didn't blame him. She'd felt pretty shitty even asking.

She returned every so often to her hire car, which was parked a quarter of a mile or so down the lane, to check her e-mails, and as darkness fell on the Cork countryside, and the shadows of the great trees surrounding Dungarven House deepened, could only try to imagine what fear and anger Gideon Keeble must be experiencing over the disappearance of his beloved only daughter.

She looked at her screen as she typed her thoughts and sighed. That wasn't going to redeem her in Chris Pollock's eyes. Give me a break, she said, looking up at the half-moon just rising now in the soft dusk sky, please, please give me a break.

She pulled a second sweater on; it was getting very chilly. Most of them had agreed that they would give things until ten and then go and book into the pub. Jocasta was unwilling to do that. With the run of bad luck she seemed to be having, Fionnuala and Zebedee would arrive naked, astride a white horse, the minute she'd left the gates. She had already decided to sleep in her car.

God, she wanted to pee. She'd have to go and find a bush – again. She shouldn't have drunk all that coffee. She struck out to the right of the lane, and made her way across the rough moorland into a small hollow; it was safer down here, away from the good-naturedly ribald comments from the others.

She stood up gingerly, pulling up her trousers; she really was getting terribly cold. Maybe she should go for another walk, get her circulation going. If she walked down the lane she wasn't going to miss a car. She set out briskly; and after about ten minutes she saw a tiny pin-prick of light coming towards her. It was fairly steady, not the up and down movement of a walker's torch. And certainly not a car. There was complete silence. So what – oh, of course! It was a bicycle. Someone was cycling up the hill. A farm worker perhaps, working on the estate. But – why should he be coming up at this hour? She waited, almost holding her breath, and the light suddenly swerved off the lane and disappeared. Or rather went off to the right. Its rear light bounced up and down now, but proceeded quite steadily; it must be a track of sorts. Jocasta decided to follow. It was probably a wild goose chase, but – And then there was a muffled cry and a curse and the light went out.

Jocasta walked cautiously over to the dark heap that the bike and its rider had become.

'Hello?' she said. 'You all right?'

There was silence.

'I said hello. Anyone there?'

Nothing.

She was right up to the heap now; it took shape; it was a boy of about fifteen, sitting on the ground, rubbing his ankle. He had a canvas bag beside him.

'Are you all right?' she said again.

'Sure I'm all right.'

The accent was strong.

'Good. I thought you might have hurt yourself. Bit of a bad place to fall off your bike.'

He tried to stand up and winced.

'Fock,' he said. 'Focking Mary and Joseph.'

'You've hurt yourself. Want me to look?'

He shook his head.

'Funny night for a bike ride,' she said.

No reply.

'You on your way up to the big house?'

'I am not. Making my way home.'

'Which is where?'

'Down there.' He pointed down into the darkness.

'Strange, you seemed to be going in the opposite direction,' she said. 'Anyway, you won't get home in that state. Would you like me to drive you?'

'No thanks.' He stared at her. 'You one of those reporters?'

'Yup.'

He hesitated. Then, 'You won't write about me, will you?' he said.

'I might,' said Jocasta coolly. 'Depends.'

'On what?'

'Let me have a look at your ankle.'

He scowled at her, then pushed his foot towards her.

She felt it gingerly, then very gently and slowly moved it. It didn't seem to be broken.

'I think it's just a bad sprain. You got a torch?'

'Only on the bike.'

'OK. Let's just – ' She pulled the light off the bike, shone it on his ankle. It was already swelling. 'Are you sure you wouldn't like me to take you home?'

'No, I'll be fine. It's downhill to the village all the way, I can just sit on the bike.'

'Pity.' She looked at him consideringly. 'Quite a good night for poaching, isn't it? Not much of a moon, just enough light.'

'I am not going poachin'!'

'Oh really? Well, you certainly aren't any longer,' said Jocasta. 'I think you'd better let me take you home. And I swear I won't tell anyone, anyone at all.'

'You won't?' His eyes in the half-light shone wide with fear. 'Me mother would take a belt to me.'

'Quite right, too. And your father, I daresay.'

'Me father has passed on. There's just me and me mother. And the little ones.'

'How many little ones?'

'Five. I'm the eldest.'

'I see. So – the odd trout or hare must be a big help. Now look – I'll just drop you at your house, no one will know. I swear.'

He looked down at his ankle. 'OK,' he said finally. And then, reluctantly, 'Thanks.'

'That's OK. One thing in return. How do you get into the grounds? You must know a way?'

'I don't.'

'Of course you do,' said Jocasta briskly, 'don't be silly.'

There was a long silence; then the boy said: 'Follow this track right up to the wall. Follow round to your right. Few hundred yards along, there's a big tree. One of the branches hangs over the wall.'

'Bit of a drop, isn't it?' said Jocasta thoughtfully. 'That wall's twelve, maybe fifteen feet high. And then how do you get out again?'

'I'm not telling you any more,' he said. 'I thought you just wanted to get in.'

She thought for a moment. It was quite true; she would find her own way out somehow.

'Right,' she said standing up, holding out her hand to pull him up, 'let's get going.'

Twenty minutes later, she was back. She parked her car quite a lot further down the hill. She didn't want any of the others getting on her trail. She pulled the torch out of the car, slung her rucksack onto her back and then shut the car door very quietly. She pulled up the hood of her sweatshirt and started walking up the lane again, on the grass verge, looking out for the track. She'd better not get on the wrong one. Getting lost was all she needed.

Right. Here was the wall. To the right, he had said, a few hundred yards . . . Tree, tree, where was the bloody tree?

There! Right there, just in a curve of the wall. Not too bad to climb, either, until she was level with the top of the wall, standing on a very strong branch with a helpfully placed parallel one to hold onto.

Then it got worse. She could step onto the wall quite easily; but she then had to get down on the other side. And it was a good twelve-foot jump: onto grass to be sure, but nonetheless it looked like a long way down.

And there was absolutely no sign of the house; she had no real idea of the direction she should walk in. A mental calculation told her about ten o'clock from where she landed, but that was pure guesswork.

Shit, shit. She should have bought a map of some kind. And suppose Keeble had dogs roaming the ground, or even an armed guard as it was rumoured the Barclay twins did?

'Oh for fuck's sake,' she said aloud; unhitched her rucksack, threw it down, and then, wondering in the slow motion of fear if this would be the last thing she ever did, jumped after it.

Chapter 20

Kate called Sarah.

'I've got to go somewhere tomorrow. After school. I don't want to tell my mum. Will you say I'm with you, if she calls?'

'Course. Where are you going?'

'I'll tell you about it when I get back, OK?'

'Cool. See you later.'

'See you later,' said Kate.

Right. She'd made it. She hadn't broken her leg, there were no dogs savaging her, or guards standing over her with rifles. She hadn't even lost her rucksack. She was safely inside the grounds of Dungarven House and all she had to do now was find the house. She hitched her rucksack onto her back, and following her hunch, set out in what she thought was the right direction.

The moon had come out again now, and together with the light from her torch she could see quite easily. She came out of the thicket and looked around her – no sign of a house. Never mind. She'd find it. She'd done brilliantly so far. Chris Pollock would be proud of her. As for Nick – she hadn't given Nick a thought, she realised, for hours. Good!

Suddenly she heard a dog barking. So he did have guard dogs. But the sound didn't move. It stayed. Which could only mean that it was either tied up somewhere, or was inside the house. She would follow the sound.

She wondered as she walked, slowly and carefully, keeping her torch shining low on the ground, what Fionnuala was like. She had looked her up in the cuttings: her mother, Aisling, Gideon's second wife, had married Michael Carlingford a couple of years ago and spent half her time in Barbados, half in London. The divorce had been unpleasant and noisy and Fionnuala had obviously been shipped off to boarding school, so as to be the least possible bother to her parents. Jocasta knew what *that* felt like. If she had had the chance to run off with a rock star, she would have done so, just to cause them the maximum trouble and embarrassment.

One of the few pieces of information available on Fionnuala was that she was a fine rider, and expensive horseflesh had been placed at her disposal almost from the moment she had been able to sit up. She rode in the occasional one-day event, and hunted from time to time, and those were the only occasions that yielded any photographs. Rather unsatisfactory ones for the gossip columns, of a rather rigid, unsmiling little face under her riding hat.

On the two occasions she had talked to him at any length, Gideon Keeble had not mentioned her; indeed, she would not have known he had a child. Another similarity between herself and Fionnuala.

The barking was getting louder; she was walking up a slight incline now into a group of trees – and through them she could see a light. Several lights, in fact. And as she stepped out of the trees, yes, there it was. A large house: but not a huge one. She stayed close to the trees, worked her way towards the back of it: and as she did so, saw a great incline falling down again from the house itself, and below that a shimmer of light. The lake. Moonlight reflected in the lake.

Jocasta looked up at the sky, clear as it never was in the city, studded with a myriad stars, and she would have stood there for a long time, just drinking it in, had not the dog started barking again and, using the sound as a guide, she began to walk towards the house.

'You sound absolutely terrible, love.'

'I feel absolutely terrible. I don't think I can stand it much longer.'

It was so unlike Helen to complain that there was a silence; everyone stopped what they were doing and stared at her.

Helen did feel appalling. She had had bronchitis after

Christmas, just as she did every year, but it appeared to have reignited; over the past few weeks, she had coughed repeatedly, night after night, went short of sleep, had a constant headache.

'Have you been taking your antibiotics?' asked Jim severely.

'Yes. Of course. He might as well have told me to eat sugar lumps.'

'Might have been better, love. You're skin and bone. It's all this worry, I'm sure. Your mother, the publicity, all that. It's been a big strain on you. I'm sure you'll feel better soon.'

'Dad!' said Juliet. 'Is that the best you can do? Poor Mum. You ought to – well, what about taking her away for a few days? See she has a bit of sunshine.'

'Juliet,' said Jim, 'you sound like your sister. Where do you suggest I take her, the south of France or something?'

'Well – yes. Why not? It'd be lovely down there now.'

'I daresay it would. And my name's Midas. Do you realise what it would cost just to get down there?'

'Forty-five pounds each,' said Juliet firmly. 'Look, it says so here in the newspaper. EasyJet to Nice. Forty-five pounds.'

'Catch me on one of those things,' said Jim, 'tied together with bits of string.'

'Oh Dad, honestly. Charlotte Smith's parents did it last week, and they're a) not rich and b) not exactly reckless.'

'It does sound a lovely idea, Jim,' said Helen. 'And a bit of sun would be so nice.'

They all stared at her; she so seldom asked for anything for herself.

'And it's half term next week,' said Juliet. 'Go on, Dad, give poor Mum a break.'

'And who's going to look after you two?'

'We could go to Gran. We both could, as it's half term.'

'Yes, or I could go to Charlotte,' said Juliet. 'Oh go on, Dad. Live dangerously.'

Helen giggled, which triggered a spasm of coughing.

Jim looked at her, then at Juliet. Then he said: 'Well – I'll look into it. Give me that paper. I might look on the web as well.'

Janet was walking across Central Lobby, carrying her coat and her laptop, when she heard her name called.

'Janet! Hi. How are you? I've been trying to catch you for days.' It was Eliot Griers; he smiled his sweetly boyish smile at her. 'Have you got time for a drink?'

'I'm sorry, Eliot, I haven't. I'm having one of my early nights. It's only half-past eight.'

'Well – never mind. I'll see you tomorrow, won't I? At Jack's welcome drinks? Thank you for your e-mail by the way. I'm so looking forward to working with you all.'

'Great. Yes, it'll be marvellous to have you on board. Bit of a struggle at the moment, as you can imagine.'

'Of course. But very exciting. Anyway, Janet, I wondered if I could ask you a favour?'

'You could ask,' she said, smiling at him slightly coolly. It seemed a bit early to be asking favours.

'I've got a constituent – nice girl – who's a human rights lawyer. I mentioned you were on the all-party committee and she said she'd absolutely love to meet you. I wondered if you could bear to spare her half an hour.'

'Of course,' she said. 'Call my diary secretary tomorrow and fix it.'

'That's marvellous. I told her I'd give her a tour as well. Always bait for constituents. Can't do too much of all that sort of thing at the moment, can we? And she really is very bright, won't waste your time.'

She would be very pretty, too, Janet was quite sure about that.

Jocasta found herself at the back of the house; it was beautiful, very beautiful indeed, classic Georgian, with wonderful tall windows also reflecting the moonlight, and a terrace, running its full length. Jocasta walked towards the terrace, wondering for the first time what on earth she was going to do next. Did she knock on the door, tell the elderly retainer who would surely answer it that she had come to see Mr Keeble? Did she try to get into the house – she remembered Gideon himself telling her doors in rural Ireland were never locked – or did she stand peering through the windows, rather like Peter Pan, observing the household as it went about its business?

She suddenly felt almost embarrassed. She walked quietly

along the terrace, looking into a series of rooms, a drawing room dimly lit, what appeared to be a library, in semi-darkness, the walls lined with books; then a couple more rooms in total darkness and then – then what was obviously a study. The light in there was quite bright. Very traditional, it was book-lined again, two leather chairs either side of a fireplace and a huge wooden desk – housing incongruously a large computer, a laptop, a fax machine, several telephones. And as she watched, Gideon Keeble came into the room, talking into a mobile; he sat down at the desk, and suddenly switched it off and sat staring at it as if he had never seen anything like it before. Then he put it down, very slowly and gently, on the desk, and then, almost as if he was rehearsing for a play, he folded his arms on the desk and buried his great head in them.

Jocasta watched him, paralysed, feeling like the worst kind of voyeur, probing into an intensely private grief. How could she have done this, how could she have broken into this self-contained world where Gideon felt himself safe? Better to return to London with no story, a failure, than confront him with her crass curiosity, her crude questioning.

She was actually contemplating stealing away, when a door further along the terrace opened and an Irish setter puppy, about six months old, bounded up to her, leapt up and licked her face, as if she was a long-lost member of its own family. It was followed by an older dog, its mother, she guessed, barking too, almost sternly, and after that she heard a woman's voice calling their names, 'Sheba! Pebble! Will you come along back in, at once, and stop that noise!'

The noise ceased briefly as the puppy continued to greet her ecstatically, and then started again; then after a moment or two, as she patted and stroked and tried to hush the dogs, she saw Gideon stand up, and walk to the door, clearly calling someone, and then he disappeared. As she stood petrified, both dogs now barking loudly and relentlessly, he came out through the side door. He was carrying a flashlight, which he shone around the lawns and then along the terrace in a great wide beam; she stood there, frozen like a rabbit in the headlights of a car, braced for abuse, for fury, for outrage, watching him walking towards her, very slowly. But as he reached her, he said, in tones of absolute good nature, as if she had just wandered into a restaurant or an airport lounge or some other very public place where he happened to be, 'Why, Jocasta – what a pleasant surprise. You decided to come after all.'

'And you found her – where?'

'In a restaurant.'

'Jesus. I can't believe nobody got there first.'

It was late in the evening; Marc Jones had just returned with the test shots of Kate. Carla was waiting for him with a bottle of wine.

'I know. It was just lucky,' she said modestly. 'So, how are the shots?'

'Sensational.'

He flung a sheet of black and white contacts down on the desk; Carla pulled a magnifier out of her desk and bent over them. They were remarkable. Despite having been in the studio herself when they were taken, she saw something else now, something that had not been apparently there, the strange alchemy between subject and lens that occasionally takes place, an extra dimension, almost another person indeed. A stroppy, nervous schoolgirl had walked into the studio; and there in front of them now was a gangly, wild-haired beauty, with an absolute knowledge of her own sexuality and how to confront the camera with it.

'Very, very lovely. Got any colour?'

'Yeah, I'll put them on the light box. They're great, too. It's the dark eyes and the fair hair. When are you going to use her?'

'Next week, probably. I'll go and see Chris in a minute, see what he thinks.'

'And – who's going to do the snaps?'

'Marc, really. Who do you think? David Bailey?'

'Great.' He grinned. 'Just give me a date. What's the fashion story?'

'I thought we'd let Kate choose her own. I'll take her to Top Shop, Miss Selfridge, Kookai, and let her loose. That street fashion thing is a story in itself.'

'Fine. When do you want to do it?'

'Soon as possible. I'll let you know. I'll have to speak to the parents, of course. She's not sixteen yet. But it should be OK. I can't think why not.'

'Would you let your daughter loose in the fashion business?'

'I don't have a daughter,' said Carla briefly.

She went to see Chris Pollock with Kate's pictures.

Kate was still high on her session in the studio, being flirted with by Marc Jones – God he'd fancied himself – and chatted up – that was the only word for it – by Carla Giannini. She'd really liked her, she was so warm and funny and appreciative of her rather crappy efforts. At least, Kate felt they must be crappy; although she had somehow known what to do in front of the camera, known how to move a bit between shots, especially as the session went on, and she had felt increasingly confident, had started pushing her hair about and moving her hips a bit, pulling off her denim jacket and letting it dangle off her fingers. Carla had told her she really was a natural.

It all seemed a bit of a dream now, back at home, standing in the kitchen, pouring herself a Coke, waiting to be told it was time she went to bed, asked if she had done all her homework. If only they knew! They'd be so amazed, shocked even, tell her what a dangerous world she was getting into. Only her grandmother would appreciate the excitement and importance of it all. It would be quite fun to tell her, actually.

Jim had managed to book a week in a three-star hotel near Nice; Helen was torn between excitement and guilt and worry at leaving Kate at such an important time in her life.

'If you fail these exams, you won't get a second chance, you know. You need good grades for Richmond, and – '

'Honestly, Mum, I'll revise. I swear. Even if Gran lets me off, Juliet won't, she'll probably call the hotel and tell you if I stop for more than five minutes.'

'I won't!' said Juliet indignantly. 'Anyway, I'm doing that music course, don't forget. You can bunk off as much as you like.'

Martha pounded the running machine, sweat pouring off her; her legs throbbed, her lungs felt close to explosion. She was exhausted; she had another five minutes to go of this; she'd never last. Only – of course she would. Because that's what she had decided, that's what she had set herself. It was as simple as that.

She could do so much with that will. The demons that had attacked her in all their horror as she knelt in that filthy lavatory, vomiting into the disgusting bowl, that had hung, obscenely threatening, above her bed, during the long night that followed, had left her again, banished almost entirely. Almost.

She had finished. Target achieved. She stepped off the running machine, staggered to the shower. Now she could go back to her apartment, have a herbal tea, sort out her clothes for the morning, listen to some music and do some background reading for a meeting. She'd told Ed she couldn't see him. Not tonight. Tomorrow they had a date though. It was their four-month anniversary. Four months since they'd first gone out. Four months of being astonishingly happy.

Happiness was not an entirely familiar condition to Martha. She knew about achievement, about meeting her own standards, she knew about success. She knew about pleasure, about the joys of having the home, the car, the clothes she wanted. But happiness: happiness was something else. Happiness was unexpected and uncontrollable; happiness was sweet and swift and induced by the simplest things, a phone call, a silly joke, an appreciation for something small, but important. Happiness was an entirely new set of values.

Ed had taught her all that as he had led her into love. She did love him; she knew that. She had resisted it for a long time, that knowledge. She was frightened of love. It scared her. She hadn't yet told Ed she loved him. It was risking too much, giving too much away.

Her first tentative courtship of her own constituency was proving as satisfying to her as she had hoped. Local politics might well be dull, but it was also a genuine opportunity to help the underdog, and to give people a voice. Her first legal advice clinic, held at her father's parish hall, had been a revelation; the terrible impotence of ordinary people when confronted by even the smallest threat to their lives – new noisy neighbours, a cowboy builder, an over-large bill sent in error – shocked her.

Accustomed to working for the rich and powerful, to dealing with vast meaningless sums of money, she felt a surge of power herself as she promised to write to the electricity company for one old lady about her charges, terrified, as she put it, of upsetting them.

But it was above all – and this was what she found most exciting – a fight for hearts and minds. She was battling not only for them, but also for herself, to persuade them to give her power, power to help them more.

The article she had been so fearful of had become a bland fashion feature, with the copy – over which she had had final approval – little more than an extended caption, gratifyingly generous about her political career and pleasingly flattering about the Centre Forward party. Chad would be very pleased. She had liked the pictures too. Martha was not vain; her appearance was simply one of her assets, one that she used and worked hard to improve, but no more than that. Nonetheless, the publication across a double-page spread in a national newspaper of three extremely flattering photographs of herself, wearing very nice clothes extremely well, was quite a pleasing prospect.

Clio had decided to write to her family; she had after all left her husband, ended her marriage, there was a certain obligation to inform them, though she had very little expectation of hearing from any of them.

She was quite surprised, therefore, to hear Artemis's cool clipped tones on her answerphone on Thursday evening: 'Clio. We should talk. Give me a call.'

No expression of sympathy or even interest; just, 'We should talk.' And why should that hurt? When it was more than she had expected.

Artemis was briskly sympathetic about the divorce: she asked if Clio was all right and said that all men were fools, clearly assuming that there was someone else and Jeremy had walked out on her without warning. 'No,' said Clio, 'actually, no. I told you, it was just a basic incompatibility.'

'Hardly worth ending a marriage for, in my opinion,' said Artemis. 'Lucien and I could be said to be fairly incompatible, but we've worked out a *modus operandi*, over the years. Of course we have the children to think of, so it's rather different. I'm surprised you haven't had a child by now, Clio; it was certainly something Jeremy was hoping for in the very near future, I do know that. He told me at your wedding.'

'Yes, well, I haven't,' said Clio, wondering how anything could hurt quite so much.

'Well, it's too late now. What a pity. I must say I rather liked Jeremy. You're all right, are you, living on your own?'

'Actually,' said Clio firmly, 'I rather like it.'

'Oh really? Well, I suppose it's just as well. Anyway, I told Father I'd call you – he was a little worried. I said I was sure you'd be quite all right – you're so self-sufficient. Ariadne said she'd write. Do let us know if there's anything we can do, won't you?'

Ariadne did write: a supposedly consoling letter, saying she had never liked Jeremy – which irritated Clio profoundly – and telling her she should come to stay whenever she wanted.

'Only not in term time, of course.'

And that was the end of the matter for all three of them. No wonder she felt so alone, Clio thought bitterly. But she had written to Beaky, who had expressed great delight at her interest in the job and invited her to lunch with him.

'Happy anniversary. I got you a present.'

'Oh, Ed. We said we wouldn't.'

'Yeah, I know. But don't feel bad about not getting me anything. It's really stupid.'

'Well, actually,' she said, 'I did. And it's pretty stupid too.'

'Go on then. You first. Open it.'

It was a book called *Tantric Yoga for Beginners*.

'I hope you're not suggesting I try this,' she said, giggling.

'Absolutely I am. There's a chapter on sex. It says you can keep going for six hours. How about that?'

'Sounds a bit tiring. What's wrong with what we're doing now?'

'Nothing. It's great. I just liked this idea even better. That'd have her late for meetings, I thought.'

'Yes. Well – I promise to read it. Now open yours.'

'Hey,' he said smiling, 'that's really cute. I love it.' It was a framed picture of the two of them, sheets pulled up to their chins, sitting up in Martha's bed; she had used the remote setting on her camera to take it. 'I remember that night,' he added.

'Of course you don't.'

'Of course I do. You know why? It was a big first. You didn't hang your clothes up neatly before you got into bed. Just left them on the floor.'

'You're making it up,' said Martha, laughing.

'I'm not. How could I forget that? I thought: She's more bothered about having sex with me than hanging up her Armani jacket. I must be some stud.'

'You are . . .'

They were having the long-postponed dinner at the Pont de la Tour.

'It should have unhappy memories, I know,' she had said, 'but I thought I should lay the ghost. And it's so near my flat and it's lovely, OK?'

'OK.'

After dinner they walked along Butler's Wharf holding hands. He had been slightly quiet for the last half hour; she asked him if anything was the matter.

'Not – exactly.'

'Well, how about inexactly?'

'I didn't want to tell you tonight.'

Her heart felt as if something was squeezing it – very hard.

'But, well – I've been offered a new job.'

'Ed, that's great. What's wrong with that?'

'Not a lot. More money, much the same sort of thing, bit more responsibility.'

'Well – take it.'

'I – that is – well, it's in Edinburgh. Working for the Beeb.'

'Edinburgh!'

'Yes. Very buzzy city Edinburgh, these days. They even have a Harvey Nichols, my spies tell me. So – what do you think?'

'Well,' she said briskly bright, 'I think of course you must take it.'

'You do?'

'Of course. Why ever shouldn't you?' She wouldn't mind; it

would be fine. She could see him – quite often. Not very often. But – enough.

'Well, I can think of one very good reason.'

'What's that?'

'It's called Martha.'

'Ed, you can't give up a really good opportunity for me. Anyway, we could still see each other.' When, though? Not evenings. Not many weekends, either. Given her work in Binsmow. Building up now. Her Saturday surgeries. So – she'd only see him – very occasionally.

'Well – I could. I thought I would. Actually. Give it up. But if you really think so. I mean, it would be great.'

'Right, well that's settled then. Of course you must take it. We can have wonderful weekends, now and again, and you . . . you . . .' Her voice tailed off.

'I what?'

'You'll do so well, Ed. It's such a thing, working for the Beeb. You'd be set up for life.'

'Yes. Good. Thanks, Martha. You're so – so grown up.' He smiled at her, just a bit too brightly.

'I should be. At my age. Let's go back now, shall we? I'm getting cold.' She'd feel better about it later; when she got used to the idea. She was the last person to cling onto someone, the first to know how important taking opportunities was.

Bloody Pont de la Tour. It was jinxed for them.

'That was great,' he said sleepily. 'Night, Martha.'

'Night, Ed.'

It hadn't been: not great. It was as if it had all been slightly out of focus. Nothing sharp enough.

The pleasure dulled – just a bit.

She lay there, thinking about him being in Edinburgh, how far away it was, how with the best will in the world, they would drift apart, the sweet, dizzy closeness lost.

She got up and wandered into the sitting room, stood at the window, staring at the lights, thinking how far away he would seem, how lonely she would be. She felt a stab of pure misery, sat down, huddled in her bathrobe, fighting it down. Well – she would get over it. She'd been perfectly all right before she met him. Absolutely all right. She just wasn't a dependent sort of person. She had a horror of it.

And it was difficult, conducting a love affair with her life as it was; she was aware that she was fighting for time, pushing back boundaries. Mostly at the expense of sleep. She'd get a bit more of that, at least. But –

Damn, now she was going to cry. Shit. Ed mustn't hear her, mustn't know. He was obviously so keen to go, to take the job . . .

She got up, went to the loo and sat on the seat, wiping her eyes and blowing her nose. That was better – she could do this, for God's sake.

The door opened; Ed came in.

'Sorry,' he said. 'Just wanted a pee.'

'That's OK,' she said, 'I'm just – leaving.'

'You OK?' he said.

'Yes, I'm fine. Of course.'

He switched the light on, looked at her.

'Martha, you're crying. What is it?'

'I don't want you to go,' she said, and her voice was hopeless with misery. She felt appalled at herself, that she could give so much of herself away. 'I'm sorry, I'm so sorry, Ed. I'll be all right in the morning.'

'You don't want me to go?' he said, and his voice was very quiet, very gentle.

'No. Well, obviously not, I mean I've got used to us being together, so it's a bit of a shock, but I'll be all right. Sorry, Ed, sorry . . .'

'You're actually saying you don't want me to go?'

'Yes. Yes, I am. I know it's wrong, but – '

'It's not wrong,' he said. 'It's terribly, terribly right. God Almighty, Martha, I've spent the last four months trying to tell myself that you really do care about me and now I know you do. Of course I won't go, you silly moo. I don't want to leave you, either. I want to stay here with you. Even in spite of your gigantic nose. And your pathetic tits. I wanted you to tell me not to go. More than anything I can ever remember.'

'Oh, Ed.' She looked up at him and suddenly it was an explosion in her head, and she had to say it, had to tell him.

'I – well, the thing is, I – I – '

'Come on. Spit it out. You what?'

'I love you,' she said, and her voice was almost desperate with both anxiety and the effort of saying it.

'You do? Say it again.'

'I love you,' she said, and he bent down and gave her a kiss and then started to laugh.

'This is one hell of a place for a love scene,' he said. 'I love you, too. And now, if you could just shift your very well-toned little arse, I'd like to have my pee.'

'I'm so sorry,' said Jocasta, 'so terribly sorry.'

She was sitting in what Gideon called the playroom; it was a rather grown-up playroom, with two huge sofas, a large television, a music system with two tall speakers, and three stacks of CDs, a low table covered with what catalogues call executive toys, the walls lined with books. There was a huge fire burning in the stone fireplace, the lights were low and soothing. A large painting hung on one wall, of a beautiful blonde woman in a black low-cut evening dress, the second Mrs Keeble. Fionnuala's mother.

'And what are you sorry for,' Gideon said, 'exactly?'

He smiled at her; a rather formal smile that didn't reach his eyes.

'I'm sorry about being here. I feel so – so awful.'

'Oh, that's perfectly all right,' he said. 'You are doing your job and I have to admire your initiative. You must tell me where you made your break-in, though. I didn't realise it was so easy.'

'It wasn't easy!' said Jocasta, mildly indignant. 'It was very difficult. I had to climb a huge tree and then jump down that massive wall – '

'Now, I hope you are not looking for sympathy,' he said. 'That would really seem a little unreasonable of you.'

'No, of course not,' she said. 'Sorry, Gideon. Again.'

'Don't keep saying you are sorry,' he said. She found his expression hard to read: it was not his usual benign smile, but neither was it at all hostile; it was simply rather detached. 'But I don't know how much I can offer you in the way of a story. We are all very quiet here. As you see.'

'Yes, of course. Well – don't worry about it,' she said and then thought how absurd she must sound. 'I'm so sorry about your daughter, Gideon. About Fionnuala. You must be terribly upset.'

'I'm not in the least upset,' he said. 'It takes more than a naughty daughter to have any effect on me.'

She was reminded, once again, of her own father; he would have dismissed the whole thing thus, as a naughty, childish prank, no more, not a desperate cry for help, not concerned for the danger of the situation. She began to like him less.

'You – haven't heard from her?'

'Now, would I be telling you if I had?' He smiled again, the same polite, detached smile.

'No. No, of course not.'

This was a nightmare; what was she going to do?

He sat, drumming his fingers gently on the arm of the sofa, apparently relaxed.

'You're all right, are you?' she said. 'I mean, you said you hadn't been well.'

'I think I said the doctors said I needed a rest. Which I am not getting at the moment, of course. Now it might be an idea,' he added, 'if you gave me your mobile. I'm sorry if I appear discourteous, but I really would prefer you not filing any stories just at the moment.'

Jocasta flushed. 'Of course,' she said. There seemed little else that she could say. She pulled her mobile from her rucksack and handed it to him.

'Thank you. Now, I think if you will excuse me, Jocasta, I have work to do. Do let Mrs Mitchell know if you want coffee. You know where she is, just along the corridor.'

'Yes, of course,' she said, 'thank you.'

Should she make a run for it? For the front gates, climb over, forget her scoop? Anything would be better than this.

And then she heard it: first the distant whirring, then the increased beating of helicopter blades, cutting through the silence.

Gideon stood up, white suddenly, his face very drawn. He looked out of the window onto the lawn behind the house; Jocasta stood up too, and in the sudden brilliant light that flooded the area, watched the helicopter land, saw the pilot jump down, and then shortly after, a slight figure wearing trousers and some kind of large jacket follow him and run under the spinning blades towards the house. It must be Fionnuala. Must be. Returned to her father.

Gideon didn't move; just stood there, staring out. As the figure reached the terrace, she stood still herself, looking up at the house, and then began walking swiftly towards the side door. Not Fionnuala, but her mother, Aisling. Mrs Mitchell appeared on the terrace, and walked towards her; they stood together for a moment or two, then walked back towards the house. Finally Jocasta couldn't bear it any longer.

'Aren't you – aren't you going to go and meet her?' she said; and Gideon gave a great sigh, almost visibly shook himself and then walked silently and very slowly out of the room.

For want of anything else to do, Jocasta stayed exactly where she was, shamefully aware that she was writing the most important article of her life, inside her head.

Chapter 21

'Dressed for success', it said, right across the centre spread. 'Is Martha Hartley the future face of politics?'

And then under the headline, several extremely nice photographs of the future face. And figure.

She did look absolutely wonderful, Clio thought.

Sleek and self-assured: and sounded it too. Talking about her new career, her view on politics, her life in general, in absolutely clear, concise terms. Clio tried to remember those qualities in the rather nervy girl she had last seen on Koh Samui and completely failed. How did anyone change that much? She certainly hadn't, and neither had Jocasta, not really. Obviously Martha's life had been very confidence-building. Well lucky her.

There was a lot of stuff about the Centre Forward party too, about how it was the party of the future, for young professional people like herself, while still adhering to all the true Tory values. Very neatly and succinctly expressed.

Clio looked to see who had written the words beside the photographs; she expected to see Jocasta's name, but it was someone called Carla Giannini, the fashion editor. She wondered what had happened. Maybe she should call Jocasta. It would be good to talk to her anyway; but Jocasta's phone seemed to be switched off.

Martha and Ed had studied the article in bed that morning. Martha had been quite pleased with the pictures but furious about the mention of her car and her salary: 'What right does the bitch have to put that in? I told her there was to be nothing personal. It wasn't in the final copy I read. God, it's outrageous. I've a good mind to call the editor and complain!'

Ed leant forward and took her face between his hands.

'Martha,' he said, between kisses, 'you look utterly, utterly gorgeous, almost as gorgeous as you do without any clothes on. Now, if they had shown that, you might have something to complain about. You're successful, for fuck's sake. What's wrong with that?'

'A lot,' said Martha. 'People won't like this, Ed, they'll think I have no idea what ordinary life is like, they'll be suspicious of me, and they'll – '

'Oh just shut up,' he said, pulling the paper away from her, pushing her back on the pillows, bending to kiss her on the stomach, the thighs, his tongue lingering tantalisingly on her pubic hair, probing it. 'Anyway, I've got a complaint about it, too. You haven't even mentioned your amazing stud of a boyfriend. Why not? Why does the Merc get bigger billing than I do?'

She stared at him, thinking he was serious, started to say: 'But Ed – ' and then saw his grin, smiled reluctantly herself.

'Now look,' he said, sitting up again, 'I know you've got to go to Binsmow today, and I know you've got to leave quite soon. Two questions: can I come too? And can we have a fuck before you go?'

'You certainly can't come too,' said Martha firmly. 'Your mother might start to put two and two together. This is serious stuff; I've got a school fayre and two church concerts to go to, as well as my surgery. I can't be distracted by you. And no, we can't have a fuck before I go – I'm late already. I seem to remember plenty of that in the last four or five hours. And it was lovely, thank you very much.'

'Well, I don't know,' he said. 'There's still time for me to accept that job in Edinburgh, you know . . .'

'Ed,' said Martha, very serious suddenly, 'if you really want it, then you must take it. We'll get by.'

'I don't. I don't want us getting by. I'm still reeling at the Rt Hon Hartley admitting to needing me . . .'

It had been a very big admission she had made to him, she thought, stepping into the shower. It frightened her in a way. What price control, now? She hoped it would be all right.

Kate had been looking at the pictures of Martha on and off all day. If her pictures were anything like as good as that, it would be awesome. She'd have the last laugh then, all right. And it would be this space; Carla had said when she called that she'd like her to be in the Saturday paper.

'Next Saturday, if possible. Are there any days you could get away from school early? Say by lunchtime.'

'Any day,' Kate had said. 'It's half term.'

'Wonderful! Then how about Tuesday? And we could go out on Monday and pick out some things you like for the pictures. I thought I'd let you choose your own. Oh, and Kate, do bring one of your parents along with you to the session – I wouldn't want them worried in any way about all this.'

'They're away,' said Kate, 'for a week.'

'Oh, I see,' said Carla, thinking that there must indeed be a God. 'Well, is there anyone else, an elder sister, perhaps?'

'I could bring my gran,' said Kate. 'She's looking after my sister and me next week. She's got a clothes shop and she's really cool. She'd love to come.'

'Fine. Well, tell her to call me if she has any queries.'

Kate hadn't spoken to Jilly yet; she'd been waiting for the right moment. Maybe this evening – that would be a good time. Juliet was playing in some crap concert and they didn't have to go, thank God. It would be the perfect time to tell Jilly all about it and show her the paper and everything, so she could see how important it all was. God, it was exciting!

Janet Frean read the piece about Martha Hartley; she didn't normally take the *Sketch* but a very excited Jack Kirkland had faxed her a copy of the spread.

He called her half an hour later.

'Didn't she do well? Got all the points across. Very professional, I thought. Considering it's her first exposure to the press.'

'Indeed,' said Janet. 'And yes, she does look extremely nice. Pity she talked about her personal dresser: could alienate a few people. But she'll learn. And it's only a detail.'

'What's so great about her,' said Jack, 'is that she's young and successful herself. Out in the real world. Not much of that in politics today. I think she's a real find.'

'Indeed,' said Janet. 'Jack, you must excuse me, I've got a line of people waiting for their breakfast here.'

Bob Frean, who was actually serving up the family breakfast, wondered what the loud crash was that emanated downstairs from her study and sent Lucy, the fourteen year old, to find out. Lucy came back grinning.

'She's fine,' she said. 'In one of her strops, that's all. Threw a paperweight right across the room. She says she doesn't want any breakfast.'

'Fine by me,' said Bob.

Nick read the piece about Martha Hartley with only mild interest. He had liked her when he'd met her; he thought she came across as less engaging in this piece. He was still slightly baffled as to how Jocasta had had such trouble getting a story out of her – there was obviously more to them and their relationship than Jocasta was telling. The most likely explanation was that they'd been fighting over some man, Jocasta had won and Martha had never forgiven her. Or something like that. Well, if push came to shove, most men would choose Jocasta, he thought miserably. He was missing her terribly.

He knew she'd been sent to Ireland, on the Keeble story, but she seemed to have disappeared into thin air. He'd asked Chris Pollock if he'd heard from her, and he said he hadn't since she'd filed her copy two days earlier.

'Bloody useless it was too. I don't know what's the matter with the girl. She seems to have completely lost it. If you do speak to her, Nick, tell her she's in danger of finding herself without a job, if she doesn't file soon.'

Nick was sure Jocasta hadn't lost it, that she had found someone, somewhere, who knew something and was even now probably writing her story, beating the opposition with some extraordinary exclusive. He knew Chris felt the same, that there was no real question of Jocasta losing her job. One of Chris's strengths as an editor was the trust he placed in his writers and reporters, his willingness to support them.

* * *

'Darling, it's terribly exciting!' Jilly looked at Kate's flushed face, looked down at the newspaper with the pictures of Martha again. 'And I can see it would be lovely for you, but – well, I really don't know what your parents would say. I think maybe you should wait until they get back – '

'Oh no!' said Kate, who knew very well what her parents would say. 'Granny, it can't wait. She said herself it was really important we did it this week, that otherwise it wouldn't be for ages, and anyway, then I'll be doing my exams so God – I mean goodness knows when it could be. They'd probably forget about me altogether. Oh, please, Granny, please say yes! It's such a brilliant chance for me. And honestly this woman's so nice, and she wants you to come with me. She says to call her with any questions you've got.'

'Oh, well, that's a little different,' said Jilly. 'She's obviously a nice, responsible woman. Yes, I'll ring her on Monday, Kate, and have a chat with her.'

'You could ring her today,' said Kate. 'She gave me her mobile number, said any time. She needs to know as soon as possible, so she can make the arrangements with the photographer and all that.'

'But it's Saturday, Kate, surely she won't want to be bothered with work – '

'Gran, please. *Please*. She can always say she'll ring you back.'

'Oh, very well,' said Jilly, 'but only if you go upstairs immediately afterwards and do at least two hours' revision. And then I'll test you on it. And don't call me Gran – you know I don't like it.'

'Sorry, Granny. And of course I'll work now. Of *course*,' said Kate earnestly.

Carla Giannini did seem to be an extremely nice woman: clearly interested in and concerned for Kate and her future.

'I really think she has the making of a model,' she said. 'If you like, I'll send over the test shots we did of her. Apart from her figure, which is wonderful – so rare you get the height with the narrow build – she has an absolutely unique quality, quite vulnerable and quite self-confident at the same time. And she has a real flair for wearing the clothes. And Mrs Bradford – '

305

'Oh, do please call me Jilly.'

'Thank you. You're obviously a very young grandmother. Well, I know what you look like, of course, from that photograph in the paper with Kate.'

'Oh that was very unflattering, I'm afraid,' said Jilly.

'Nonsense. You looked great. Anyway, what I was going to say, Jilly, is that the *Sketch* is a very respectable paper. I'll send you a few back copies of my pages, together with the photographs of Kate,' said Carla.

'That would be kind. But is there really that much hurry? My daughter and her husband are away, as you know, and I would really like to get their permission for this. It's rather a big decision for me to take and – '

'I can see that of course,' said Carla, instantly sympathetic, 'but next Saturday really would be ideal. I have girls booked for the next three or four weeks, so it would mean going forward a long way. When, as I understand it, she'll be doing her exams. I don't want to interfere with those in any way, of course . . .'

'That's very understanding of you.' Jilly liked her more and more.

'So I would have a problem if I had to pull Kate out now. Would it be possible for you to e-mail your daughter, or speak to her on the phone?'

'I might be able to speak to her, yes.'

'Wonderful. But . . .' Carla hesitated. 'I will need to know almost at once. I'm afraid Kate did lead me to understand that it would be all right.'

'Yes, she shouldn't have, of course, naughty girl,' said Jilly. 'But – '

'I know. Of course I understand. It's so exciting for her, such a big opportunity – she's certainly not going to want to risk her parents saying no. But I really can't see why they should – I mean, I would absolutely insist on your being at the session, and if there's anything you're unhappy about, you have only to say – '

'Yes, and I'll explain all that to my daughter,' said Jilly, 'but . . .' It seemed so dreadful to risk depriving Kate of what was clearly an extraordinary opportunity. 'Look, I'll try and get hold of my daughter in the morning, or even this evening. And I'll ring you

306

straight back. I mean, I have no reservations at all, I know what your business is like – '

'Yes, Kate told me you had a shop. Which designers do you buy?'

'Oh – the usuals. Nicole Farhi, Gerard Darel, MaxMara, of course – I'm limited by my clientele, naturally. The Guildford housewife isn't exactly a trendsetter.'

'Of course not. How clever of you to know her so well. And those are all wonderful names. It's obviously a very good shop. If I possibly can I'll mention it in the article.'

'What, by name?' said Jilly. She thought of how much she'd been worrying abut the shop in her absence, and the difference even a sixteenth-page ad in the Guildford paper made.

'Of course. Otherwise what would be the point? And it all makes for more interesting copy. In fact, it's a very nice line, her inheriting your fashion sense, as she clearly does.'

'Yes, possibly,' said Jilly. This was not the moment to elaborate on Kate's origins. 'Carla, that would be simply marvellous. Thank you so much. Now I'll get back to you as soon as I can.'

'Thank you, Jilly. It really does have to be tomorrow at the latest, I'm afraid. It's such a marvellous thing for a fashion editor to discover a model, you know. So thrilling. And I have a really strong feeling about Kate.'

Carla smiled into the phone as she put it down. It would be all right. Nothing like a bit of time pressure to make people anxious, make them agree to what you wanted. And she had to get this settled before Jocasta returned. She was so oddly defensive about Kate . . .

Chris Pollock was becoming seriously anxious about Jocasta. It really was very unlike her, this silence. He hoped nothing had happened to her. He was beginning to worry more about that than the loss of the Keeble story. Where the fuck was she? And why hadn't she been in touch? Not even a text message from her since Friday night and now it was Sunday morning.

He rang Nick's number; a rather slurry voice answered.

'Nick Marshall . . .'

'Nick. It's Chris. Any news from Jocasta?'

'Nope. Not a dicky bird.'

'Shit. Where *is* the bloody girl, Nick?'

'I don't know. I wish I did. Mind you, I'm hardly going to be the first to know. We had a bust up last week.'

'Oh really? Nothing serious, I hope.'

'Chris, who knows what's serious to a woman? I certainly don't. I could ask Josh. Her brother. They're pretty close. In a funny way.'

'What's he like, Old Forbes's son and heir? I've never really met him.'

'Oh, bit of a waste of space between you and me. Anyway, yes, I'll give him a call.'

'Thanks, Nick. And call me back, yeah?'

Josh was clearly very distracted when Nick rang.

'Got the kids here, Nick. Bit hectic. Just going to take them out to lunch, and – oh God, hang on, Nick, one of them's just spilt her drink all over the other.'

A lot of wailing and shouting came down the line, with Josh distractedly saying things like, 'No, Harry, don't do that,' and, 'Come on, Charlie, stop crying,' and, 'Now play nicely together just for a minute, while Daddy talks on the phone.'

'Sorry, Josh. Bad moment,' Nick said when Josh came back on. 'I just wondered if you'd heard from Jocasta over the past couple of days?'

'Jocasta? No. Nothing. Why, where's she supposed to be?'

'Well, she's supposed to be in Ireland, doing a story. But there's been no news from her at all.'

'Oh, I shouldn't worry,' said Josh, 'she's pretty good at looking after herself. Look, Nick, I've got to go. If I do hear anything I'll let you know, OK?'

'OK,' said Nick, and put the phone down. Where was the bloody girl? Just where was she? And what the hell was she doing?

Jilly didn't sleep well. She should never have even half agreed to this business with Kate. Not without checking with Helen. She had led Carla to assume it was more or less a certainty. And she knew what Helen would say. That she had left her in charge of the girls, and had trusted her to see they were all right, and that agreeing to Kate being photographed by a national newspaper was not within those terms of reference.

But – what harm could it possibly do? The child would look absolutely beautiful and it really was a wonderful opportunity for her; she had studied with great care the pictures that Carla had sent over by messenger, and Kate did look glorious. Clearly, if she wanted to, she could become a professional model. And this was the kind of opportunity that didn't come along more than once in a lifetime. Just the same . . .

'Oh dear,' she said aloud.

'Is anything the matter, Granny?'

It was Juliet.

'Oh – no, darling. Not really. I was just – just thinking about something. About Kate, as a matter of fact.'

'About Kate? What's she done now? Hey, what are these?' She picked up the pictures of Kate. 'God, she looks amazing. Who did them?'

'A professional photographer on a newspaper,' said Jilly. 'They are very good, aren't they?'

'Fantastic!' said Juliet. 'Are they going to publish them? How exciting. I wish she'd told me.'

'She hasn't told anyone,' said Jilly, 'not even your parents. And no, they're not going to publish these, but they want to do some more, as a fashion feature for next week's paper. But I'm not sure about it.'

'Why ever not?' said Juliet. 'It'd be lovely for her. Specially at the moment, when she's so gutted over Nat and everything.'

'And – what do you think your parents would say?'

'Probably try and stop her – they're parents, aren't they? But I'm sure once they were published, they'd just be proud. And it would be too late anyway. Oh, hi, Kate, I've just seen these pictures. They're amazing – and Granny says they want to use some more in the paper next week. How exciting!'

'Yeah, well – '

'You must do it, Kate. Granny says you're worried about Mum and Dad, what they'd say, but like I was saying to Granny, if you did it, and the first they knew you were in the paper, they'd just be proud of you, I'm sure. I mean, you could ask them first, I

309

suppose,' she added, 'but they'd only say no. And then the chance'd be gone. Or could you do it later?'

'No,' said Kate quickly. 'It's this week or never, Carla says.'

'Who's Carla?'

'The fashion editor. She's really nice, isn't she, Granny?'

'Oh charming,' said Jilly, 'and she insists I come to the photographic session.'

'Well, it *must* be totally respectable. Not even Dad could complain about that. Oh, just do it, Kate! Honestly, what harm could it do?'

'Absolutely none,' said Jilly. 'Good advice, Juliet. Thank you. But of course I must tell them.'

She called the hotel; a sullen French voice told her, with an almost audible shrug, that Mr and Mrs Tarrant were out and that she could leave a message if she liked. Jilly left a message and spent the rest of the day assuring herself that if the sensible and extremely mature Juliet thought it was all right, then it probably was.

Helen phoned that evening: they were having a wonderful time, the hotel was nice, the weather was beautiful, and Jim was taking her out to dinner at some very pretty restaurant down the road.

'I just lay by the pool all afternoon, and felt so relaxed. And do you know, I'm coughing less already.'

'I'm so glad, darling. You didn't get my message?'

'No,' said Helen, 'they're not too good about things like that here. Is anything wrong?'

'No, no,' said Jilly hastily. 'Of course not. No, I just – well, I'm so glad, darling. That's wonderful. And you mustn't worry about us, we're fine, and Kate is working really hard.'

'I'm not worrying, Mummy, not in the least. I feel marvellous. I'm pleased about Kate, though. Now, they're both being nice to you, are they?'

'Absolutely sweet. Helen, there's just – '

'Oh, dear, Jim's making faces, says we'll lose our table. Thank you once more. I'll ring again in a day or two.'

'Yes, but – '

'Mummy, I must go. Sorry. Love to the girls.'

Well, thought Jilly, she'd done her best. It wasn't her fault if

Helen didn't have time to discuss things with her.

She called Carla Giananni and told her she hadn't been able to ask her daughter about Kate. 'But I do feel quite happy about it myself.'

'Good. I'm so delighted. Now, would you like to come shopping with us tomorrow, picking out the clothes for Kate to wear? You would obviously be a great asset. And you could make sure they were all quite – suitable.'

'Oh – I don't think so,' said Jilly. 'I still get rather tired. And you'll have more fun without me.'

'I'm not so sure about that. Well – till Tuesday, then.'

Chris Pollock was in his office late that Sunday night when the call came.

'Hi, Chris. It's me, Jocasta.'

'Jocasta, where the fuck have you been? And what do you think you're playing at? And where's the fucking story?'

'I've been here. In Ireland. In Gideon's house.'

'In Gideon Keeble's house? My God, Jocasta, that must be some story. You've been there all this time?'

'Yes. And I'm really sorry, Chris, but there isn't going to be a story. Not from me anyway. Well, you can say she's safely home again, but that's all. And the other thing is, Chris, and I'm truly sorry about this too, but I'm afraid I'm going to give in my notice.'

She had been quite frightened, that first evening. Sitting there, trapped in the vast house, living out this extraordinary adventure, with no idea what she should do; just waiting, waiting for time to pass: it had been much more scary than any other job she could remember.

She had drunk a cup of tea that Mrs Mitchell had brought her and wolfed down the biscuits that had accompanied it on the tray, had begun to study the books that lined the walls – wonderful, wonderful books, some of them, first editions of Dickens, or Trollope, or Defoe, beautifully illustrated volumes of things like *The Arabian Nights* and Grimm's *Fairy Tales*, and Kate Greenaway, the pages tipped, rather than bound in, all the poets, complete sets of encyclopaedias, of catalogues of art sales, books about vintage cars, books about racing, books about paintings. And interspersed with them, in glorious carelessness of their value, paperbacks by the hundred; he liked all the popular stuff, she saw, Grisham and Patricia Cornwell and Stephen King and Maeve Binchy – well, he would of course, she was Irish – and Jilly Cooper. She picked the latest Grisham off the shelves and set it down on the arm of the sofa, then moved on to the stack of CDs on the other side. Very catholic, his musical taste as well: ranging from church choral music, through Mozart, and Mahler, into jazz, swing, and thus to the present, to Bruce Springsteen, Bob Dylan and 'My God, Leonard Cohen,' she said aloud.

'And what is so surprising about that?' she heard Gideon's voice asking her and she swung round and smiled at him and said: 'I absolutely love him. He's so – so wonderfully dismal. Not many people do. We're in a very small minority, you and I.'

'Sondheim?' he asked.

'Adore him.'

'Opera?'

'Don't get it.'

'Bob Marley?'

'Of course.'

'Well,' he said, 'we are clearly made for one another. Musically, if in no other way.'

She looked at him nervously. He wasn't smiling.

'Now, I have come to see if you would like a bed for the night. We have a few to spare.'

'Well – I am tired. But – what's the alternative?'

'There isn't one,' he said. 'I'm not going to let you out yet. I'm sorry.'

'It's all right. I can see you can't.'

She accepted with absolute equanimity his low opinion of her. She had broken into his house, in order to steal something of infinite importance and delicacy, his relationship with his runaway daughter, and she had no right to feel even remotely indignant.

'Very well, then. And in the morning, we can perhaps agree on some strategy. But not yet. Things are too – too delicate. Too difficult. I will tell Mrs Mitchell to show you to your room. Good night, Jocasta. I hope you sleep well. And – I hope you will forgive me – I have disconnected the landlines. So there would be no point your trying to make any calls.'

'Fine,' she said.

The room was on the second floor, high-ceilinged, shuttered, and very cold, with an exquisite fireplace (devoid of a fire), and a surprisingly high, hard bed. The bathroom was next door: even colder, with an enormous bath and a throne-like loo. Mrs Mitchell, who clearly thought Jocasta a trollop, ushered her in, asked her if there was anything she might be wanting and left again very swiftly. Jocasta undressed with great speed, fell into bed and went straight to sleep.

She awoke, literally shivering; it was six o'clock. She got out of bed, folded back the shutters and realised why: the windows were wide open. Expecting a wonderful view, she could see only thick, grey mist; and it was raining. She shut the windows, pulled her clothes on – she wasn't risking that ice box of a bathroom and, good reporter that she was, she had things like clean knickers and a toothbrush in her rucksack – and went stealthily along the corridor, down the stairs, and managed to find her way to the kitchen. No one was about, not even the dogs.

The kitchen was vast: and warmer than the rest of the house, thanks to an extremely elderly-looking cream Aga. The floor was slate, the walls whitewashed and there were the inevitable shutters at the window. It looked a little like a photograph in *Interiors*, except that it was devoid of the bunches of dried flowers, pots of herbs, copper pans, and Shaker-style furniture that would have given it page-appeal. It was devoid of anything, in fact, apart from a very large scrubbed table and three chairs, one of which was broken. Jocasta thought of the leather sofas and complex music systems in the playroom and the study, the fine furniture she had glimpsed through what was obviously the drawing-room door, as Mrs Mitchell led her upstairs, and felt almost sorry for her. Almost.

She filled the vast kettle that sat on the Aga, managed to find a slightly chipped mug, took some milk out of the 1950s-style fridge, and went to the back door. She looked along the terrace; it was so drenched in mist she couldn't even see the end of it, and the rain was growing heavier. Well, this was no moment for exploring, trying to find a tradesman's entrance – or exit – or even a path round the grounds. She went back inside, walked back along the corridor, into the playroom. That, too, was cold. And it was May! God, this was going to make a good story. No wonder Aisling Keeble had searched for lovers in warmer climates!

There was a phone ringing, quite persistently. Did that mean he had reconnected the landline? Now that was worth investigating. At least she could make a quick call to Chris. She went out of the playroom, followed the sound down the corridor; she had passed three doors before she reached it: of course! This was his study. She looked up and down the corridor, then slipped inside the room and closed the door. Odd; surely he had an extension by his bed? Would he really not be hearing it? She waited for four more rings, and then picked it up, waited. Silence.

'Hello,' she said cautiously, and then: 'Mr Keeble's residence.'

'Who's that?' The voice was young, light, cautious. Fionnuala? Could be. 'Mummy? It's Fionnuala.'

Fionnuala. Jocasta Forbes, this really is the scoop of your career.

'No. Shall I get her for you?'

'Who is that?'

'A friend of – of your father's. Or shall I get him?'

'No thanks.' A voice, Gideon's voice, cut in, saying 'Hello? Hello?' and then the phone went dead.

She stood there, still holding the receiver, feeling oddly frightened. She was just putting the phone down, wondering why she wasn't doing it more quickly, when the door opened and Gideon came in, wearing nothing but a white towelling robe; he was barefoot, his hair wild, his face white, his eyes black with fury.

'What the hell are you doing in here?' he demanded, and for a moment she thought he was going to hit her. 'How dare you? Get out. Just get the fuck out. Now!'

It was the first time she had ever seen him other than relaxed, easy, charming; it was an alarming transformation. So this was the famous temper. She stood her ground.

'I *was* going. I wish I could go further. Unfortunately I seem to be a prisoner here.'

'And what do you expect? Breaking into my home, prying into my most personal life? What do you think you're doing?'

'As you said last night,' said Jocasta, calm now, astonished at the extent of it, 'I'm doing my job. Which does consist, unfortunately, of prying into people's most personal lives. I'm sorry, Gideon, very sorry, and I'm actually not enjoying it. Any of it.'

'I had thought better of you,' he said, and his tone was full of deep contempt.

'Oh really? And why should that be? I seem to remember your congratulating me on some of my stories when we met at the Tory conference last autumn. What's changed, Gideon? I'd really like to know.'

He stared at her for a moment, and then said, still icily hostile: 'So, who was that?'

'It was your daughter.'

'And what did she say?'

'Not a lot. She asked who I was. I said I was a friend of yours. I offered to fetch you.'

'And?'

'And she said . . .' she hesitated, 'she said, "no thanks". And rang off. Sorry, Gideon.'

His face changed; just for a moment, she caught him off guard, saw that she had hurt him, saw how much. Then, 'Well, thank you for that, Jocasta. Depriving me of a chance to speak to my daughter.'

'Gideon, I didn't deprive you. She didn't want to. Don't shoot the messenger.'

'And what in the name of sweet fuck were you doing answering my phone?'

'It was ringing,' she said. 'No one else was. I assumed you and your wife must have left again.'

'I was in the shower. My wife – or more accurately my ex-wife – was no doubt on her own telephone. Speaking to her very unpleasant husband. Anyway, Fionnuala has been found, by the police. At Belfast airport. Mr Zebedee is in police custody, although as Fionnuala is swearing he hasn't touched her, I doubt if he will remain there for long. So very soon you can go and write your wonderful story. What a lot of colourful detail it will have. Now just get out of here, will you. Right out.'

'Yes, all right.'

She turned just as she reached the door, to look at him. He was slumped at his desk, staring at the phone; she saw him dash his hand across his eyes. 'Gideon,' she said, very tentatively.

'I said get out,' he said, and half rose towards her, his expression intensely angry.

She stood her ground. 'I am so, so sorry,' she said again.

'For what?' he said and sat down heavily again. 'Just what are you sorry for? Breaking into my house? Planning to trade on my good nature? Which, as you are discovering, is rather less good than you thought. I'm afraid I find your remorse rather hard to believe in, Jocasta.'

'I expect you do. But I'm also – so sorry for you.'

'Well, you have a strange way of showing that,' he said. 'I thought you were a friend, at the very least.'

'I thought so too. I never will be now, will I?'

'Absolutely you will not. No doubt Mr Pollock said to you, "You know him. You can get into his house. You can make him talk." Or words to that effect. Am I right?'

'Yes. You are, I'm afraid.'

'And you thought, no doubt, something along the lines of, Well, yes, I can. He fancies me. I can get him to talk. Didn't you?'

'Yes, Gideon, I suppose I did. And I'm very, very ashamed of myself.'

'It's such a pity,' he said. 'I liked you so much, Jocasta. And, yes, I did fancy you. Who wouldn't? I was even foolish enough to think – well, yes, that was very foolish.'

'No,' she said quietly, knowing what he meant. 'It wasn't foolish. It wasn't foolish at all.'

Just for a second his expression softened, then: 'Well, I hardly think that makes your behaviour seem any better. Rather worse, in fact.'

She was silent.

'It really hurts, you know. To think you were willing to trade on my admiration, purely in order to advance your career, to take on

316

a situation so painful to me, and so intimate, simply to have a few more cuttings on file.'

She remained silent.

'Oh, this is ridiculous,' he said suddenly. 'I have no real interest in explaining to you just why I am so angry. If you can't see it for yourself, then what would be the point?'

'Of course I can see it,' she said. 'Of course I'm ashamed of myself. I feel absolutely . . . wretched.'

'Well, I suppose that is something,' he said and gave a look of such withering dislike she felt sick. 'Now I really would rather you left me alone. I have a great deal to do.'

He turned away from her, and she saw him shake his head quickly, as if he were trying to rid himself of her and thoughts of her.

Jocasta looked at him, and was reminded of countless similar incidents, when her father had ordered her from his presence, had made it plain he wanted none of her, and she felt, quite suddenly, a rush of courage, and knew what she should say to him.

'Gideon – there are other things I'm sorry about.'

'And they are?'

'Fionnuala,' she said quietly. 'I feel very, very sorry about her. And for her.'

'And what do you know about it? What right do you have to feel sorry for her? I really think you should stop this, Jocasta. I am in no mood for ignorant comment.'

'It's not so ignorant,' she said. 'I know something of what Fionnuala feels. Well, not exactly, of course. But I know how it is to be her.'

'I don't think you do,' he said. But his face had changed; he was clearly ready to listen.

'Of course I do. I also have a father who is rich and high profile. Who I hardly ever saw. Who seemed to have no interest in me. Except when I did bad things, of course.'

'Be careful, Jocasta,' he said, 'be very careful.'

'I can't, Gideon, if being careful means not telling you what seems to me so obvious. What might help. My father was empire-building, making money, moving round the world. There wasn't any room for me. Little girls don't belong on business trips. God, how many times was I told that!'

'I'm sorry you had such an unhappy childhood, Jocasta. You must write about it some day.'

'Oh shut up!' she said and, horrified, found herself on the edge of tears. 'Look, don't you see, you have a daughter who doesn't know you. Who probably thinks you don't care about her. Who has no happy memories of you, except maybe the occasional week here and there, who feels your business is much more important to you than she is. Can't you see how much that hurts? Can't you see it makes her want to do anything – anything at all – to make you take notice of her?'

'Oh please,' he said. 'Spare me the pop psychology.'

'The thing about pop psychology is that it has quite a lot of truth in it. And common sense.'

'Well,' he said, 'at least I acknowledge my daughter. Your father seems to deny your very existence.'

He was trying to hurt her now: and succeeding. She was silent, struggling again not to cry.

'You'll be telling me next he abused you. That seems to be a prerequisite for most successful young people of today. Perhaps you could work that into this piece, Jocasta. Make it even more moving and dramatic.'

'You bastard!' she said and then the tears did come, strong, choking tears, and the memories with them, crashing in on her, horrible, miserable memories. She turned and ran out of the room, found the playroom, rushed in, slamming the door, sat on the sofa, her arms folded across her stomach, bending over them as if in physical pain, sobbing helplessly.

She heard the door open, turned and saw him standing there, just staring at her, with an expression on his face that was somehow close to fear.

'I'm sorry,' he said. 'I shouldn't have said that. Please forgive me.'

She said nothing, continued to sob; he sat down beside her, put his arm round her shoulders, tentatively. She shook it off.

'Did he? Is that what he did?'

'No,' she said, shaking her head. 'Of course not. Well – not sexually. I never quite know what abuse is,' she added with a watery smile. 'I mean, does it have to be sexual? Or even physical? It's such a hazy area. Ironic, isn't it, and me a tabloid journalist.'

'It is indeed. I would personally define it as something permanently damaging. Which I am clearly guilty of. In your court at any rate.'

'I don't think you are,' she said slowly. 'My father was cruel, terribly cruel, and I know you're not. I'm not comparing the two of you, just our situations, Fionnuala's and mine.'

'Well, I think I deserve a few lashes. I have clearly made what is known here as a complete dog's dick of fatherhood.'

In spite of herself, she giggled.

'That's better. Do you want to talk about your father? It might help. It might even help me. You never know.'

'You don't want to hear about my relationship with my father.'

'I have nothing else to do at the moment. And it might be relevant. As you say.'

'He just – bullied me,' she said, 'right from the beginning. Not physically, he never hit me once, but he mocked me, put me down, even when I was quite tiny, he diminished me. He humiliated me in front of people, said "Oh, it's kinder to ignore her, she's only got half a brain," when they tried to talk to me, and then laughed and said it was only a joke. And there was endless comparison with Josh, even when I rode better, did everything physical better. "Why can't you be more like your brother?" he'd say. God, that'll be engraved on my heart. And then he made a big thing of planning treats and then cancelling them at the very last minute, and holidays, and ignoring my birthday, things like that. I tried and tried to please him but it never worked. I can never remember him saying anything kind to me, or even smiling at me. Then, when I was about seven, I changed, started standing up to him, arguing with him, and that made it worse, made him terribly angry. Josh never did that, he just went along with it all.'

'And you've no idea why he disliked you?'

'Some drunken old uncle of ours told Josh our mother had trapped him into marrying her, got pregnant on purpose. He certainly hated her. Which is probably why he hated me, if the story's true. I've often thought he'd just planned to have the son, and then leave her, and I was a daughter and he was stuck with

319

her, waiting for the boy. The minute Josh was born, almost, he left her.'

'He could have got the son from someone else, surely?'

'Yes, I know but – oh, he's just a bit mad, I think.' She sighed and then, wiping her nose with the back of her hand, said: 'Do you have a hanky?'

'Of course,' he said, and rummaged in the pocket of his bathrobe. 'Here, and in fact, here is another.'

'Thank you.'

She took one, blew her nose on it, then looked at him and managed a weak smile.

'I'm sorry,' she said. 'I never in a million years meant you were like my father.'

'Well, that is a relief,' he said, 'considering how much you dislike him. Now, would you like a good strong cup of tea? With a lot of sugar. My mother's remedy for everything.'

'No. No, thank you.' She was silent, then: 'I was just thinking earlier, how you once said I reminded you of your mother. And that you would never say that now.'

'On the contrary. She, too, was very brave. Like a little lion. She is the only other person who has dared to tell me those things.'

'What things?'

'About how I treated Fionnuala. She said I neglected her, tried to win her over with material things, all that stuff – '

'Really?'

'Really. Of course I ignored her. As one does with one's mother. But yes, I did say you were like her. I remember saying it. And I meant it. It was true.'

'Oh,' she said, and wondered how much of the conversation he actually remembered, the qualities he had attributed to her.

'Well,' she said, with a sigh, 'I still have behaved horribly badly. I should never have come. And I certainly shouldn't have said all those things to you. It was nothing to do with me.'

'I daresay it was good for me,' he said. 'One of the things about being an important person . . .' he smiled at her, to show that this much, at least, was intended as a joke, 'is that very few people are brave enough to tell you the facts of life. The real ones, that is. And you live in a rather comfortable little bubble, thinking how clever you are and how right about everything. So – you've possibly done me a great service, Miss Jocasta Forbes. And Fionnuala, too. Now I must go, if you will forgive me. Aisling is going down to collect her and bring her back here. So that we can speak to her together, with a capital S, find out what's actually happened. And then, I suppose, Aisling will take her back to that horrible island she lives on. The half term is nearly over, and she's leaving that school anyway, in a few weeks.'

'Does Fionnuala think Barbados horrible?'

'I really don't know. I think she has quite a nice time there. She's learning to play polo – Aisling is friendly with the Kidds.'

'I see. Well – you'd better go. You can't arrive at a police station dressed like that.'

'Oh I'm not going,' he said, 'she has made it very plain she doesn't want me there. She hates me; she told me that last night and would no doubt have done again this morning, had you not intercepted her. She'll probably spit in my face if I turn up.'

'Gideon!' said Jocasta. 'You haven't taken in a word of what we've said, your mother and I. Go, for God's sake. If she spits in your face, at least while she's doing it she'll know you could be bothered to come.'

He was silent for a while, staring out at the mist. Then: 'I don't know if I should,' he said.

'Oh get a grip,' said Jocasta, and she was smiling at him now. 'Go on. Go and get your clothes on.'

He came back in ten minutes; he was wearing one of his perfectly cut tweed suits, under a long Barbour. He looked very stylish: a caricature of a country gentleman. 'I've shaved as well,' he said, 'the better to receive the spittle.'

'Good. I promise you it'll be worth it. Is she really coming back here?'

'Oh yes.'

'Good. Then I might meet her.'

'Jocasta, you must go. I can't detain you any longer. People will be worried about you. And you have a story to write. I'll tell Mrs Mitchell to take you, when she goes down to the village. I'm sure your car will still be there.' He bent down, kissed her briefly on the top of her head. Then, 'Go a little easy on me,' he said. 'If you can.'

It was late afternoon when they came back. Jocasta was watching from her bedroom window. The clouds were finally breaking up and a washed-out sun was gleaming through them. The landscape eased into colour, the black and grey of the trees and mist turning slowly green again. The drenched grass gave way a little as the helicopter landed; Gideon got out, then Aisling, and then he turned and reached up his hand to the top of the steps. A girl got out: slight, dark-haired, dressed in jeans and a leather jacket. That was all Jocasta could see: except the way she shook her father's hand off and then stalked ahead of him towards the house, after her mother. She was hunched into her clothes, hands in her pockets.

Two hours passed; there was the sound of shouting, first from the ground floor, then outside on the terrace; mostly indistinguishable words, occasionally the predictable phrases, slung out like stones, 'What do you expect?' 'After all we've done,' 'How could you be so stupid?' 'You've ruined my life!' 'I hate you both.'

Then slamming doors, pounding footsteps, up the stairs and along the corridor. And then more slamming doors. Gideon walked out, across the drenched grass, his head bent, down out of sight towards the lake. A solitary, wretched figure. Jocasta observed it all, phrases drifting into her head; it was a perfect story, with every possible element in it: not merely love, lust, lawlessness, but riches, power, beauty – and wilful youth. Even, should she care to mention it, her own incarceration.

And then she saw them, walking back across the lawn, Aisling and Fionnuala and Gideon following behind them; the helicopter blades began to spin, and the two of them ran under the wind, climbed into it. Slowly it lifted, tilting dangerously, then began to climb. All that could be seen was a small white circle in the window, a face, Fionnuala's face, looking down. Gideon waved, and: please, please, Jocasta thought, wave back, please; but the circle did not move and there was no sign of any response. He turned again, and walked back, towards the house, looking as if he was the last person left in the world.

Jocasta turned also, and for the first time since early that morning, left her room.

He was in the study, as she had known he would be, staring at his laptop screen, his huge hands moving with odd deftness over the keyboard. She tapped on the door.

'Not now, Mrs Mitchell,' he said.

'It's not Mrs Mitchell. It's me.'

He swung round; his face ashen with strain, his eyes red-rimmed.

'Why haven't you gone?' he asked, and his voice was expressionless.

'Oh – Mrs Mitchell didn't want to take me.'

'Well, she should have done. I'll call her now.'

'Do you have to? Can't I stay a bit longer?'

'I'd rather you didn't. I'm sorry, Jocasta, but I'm terribly tired and – '

'How did it go?'

'What?'

'I said how did it go?'

'Not well,' he said, 'not well at all . . . But I really don't want to discuss it, I'm afraid. You must have quite enough for your piece. Especially if you've been here all day.' He looked at her and said, 'Are you sure Mrs Mitchell refused to take you? That you haven't just stayed here, gathering material all this time? Because – '

'Gathering material for what, Gideon?' she said, and carefully made her voice child-like and innocent.

'Your story,' he said, 'that's what. Your bloody, undoubtedly brilliant, story. Are you happy with it now, Jocasta? I expect you are.'

'Oh, very happy,' she said, 'and it is undoubtedly brilliant.'

'Well, good. Perhaps it will even win you an award. I hope you're not going to ask if you can file it from here. There are limits, you know, even to my good nature.'

'Of course,' she said, 'I realise that. And there are limits to even my ruthlessness. Actually.'

'Well, good for you,' he said, and half rose. 'I'll go and find Mrs Mitchell.'

'Yes, thank you. But – well, actually, Gideon – '

'Yes?'

'It isn't ready to be filed. It hasn't actually been written. Except in my head.'

'Well, you'd better get on with it,' he said, 'or it'll be late. And all those exclusives will be wasted.'

'I'm not going to write it. I'm not going to file it. There is no story, as far as I'm concerned. OK?'

'What?' he said, staring at her, sitting down heavily again. 'What did you say?'

'I didn't realise you were that decrepit,' she said, smiling at him, moving slowly across the room towards him. 'I didn't realise your hearing was faulty. I said . . .' and she was quite near him now, 'I said, can you hear me all right now, Gideon, there is no story. Not from me, anyway.'

'I don't understand.'

'Then your brain must be failing as well. And your animal instincts, come to that. I can't do that to you, Gideon, I just can't. I care about you too much. It's perfectly simple. Now you'd better get that – ' she gestured towards his ringing phone – 'it might be important. I'll leave you in peace. I'll be in the playroom. If you want me.'

A few minutes later he came in; he sat down beside her, and studied her as if he had never seen her before. Then he reached out his hand and pushed back her hair, leant forward and kissed her, very gently on the cheek.

'Thank you,' he said.

'That's all right. Honestly.'

'It's more than all right, Jocasta. Much, much more than all right. I can imagine what that cost you.'

'Not as much as you might think.'

'Oh really? I'm surprised.'

'Well – you don't know me very well, do you?' she said. 'Not yet, anyway. Who was that on the phone?'

'It was – it was Fionnuala.'

'Oh really? And what did she say?'

'She said – do you really want to know?'

'Of course I do.'

'Well, it wasn't much. She just said – ' and he had clearly been playing and replaying it over and over in his head and there was a slight shake in his voice – 'she just said, "Hi Dad. Thanks for coming today."'

'That sounds quite a lot to me,' said Jocasta. 'Not easy for her, that. Now, I wonder if I could go for a walk? I've been shut indoors all day. And . . .'

'I would say that was absolutely your own fault,' he said, and he kissed her then, very softly, on the mouth, leant back and smiled at her. 'And I wonder if you would allow me to join you? I think we have rather a lot to talk about . . .'

'I do, too,' said Jocasta.

Chapter 22

Nick was walking along the Burma Road, as the Westminster press corridor was known ('Because everyone ends up there,' he had explained to a breathlessly interested Jocasta what seemed a lifetime ago), when his phone rang. He looked at the number; it was her. She had finally deigned to contact him, then. He had heard, of course, from Pollock, a white-faced, raging Pollock, who clearly felt some of the blame must be due to him, Nick, as the person closest to her, that she had not only failed to deliver what would have been the most brilliant piece, but that she was leaving the paper.

'As from now. And she'd better not show so much as an inch of her arse in this place ever again. It's so unlike her, so unprofessional. I suppose you know what it's all about?'

'Of course I don't,' said Nick. 'I don't know anything at all. I've been trying to contact her, but her phone's been switched off.'

'Yeah? What's the silly bitch up to over there, then?'

'I honestly don't know,' said Nick, 'and I'm trying not to even consider the possibilities.'

'Do you think she's with Keeble?'

'I – suppose it might be a possibility,' said Nick, and just saying the words was like drawing teeth.

And thought that, actually, it might be something to do with him, for if he had asked her to marry him, even at some fairly distant date, she would be filing a story right now, and Gideon Keeble would have not even earned a second of her consideration. But, even in his misery, he thought still that he couldn't have done it.

And now here she was, on his mobile, several days after disappearing, several days of not caring for his anxiety, his concern.

'Yes?' he said shortly.

'Nick? Did – Chris tell you?'

'He did. I have to say I'd have expected to be your first port of call, Jocasta.'

'Sorry, Nick, but – I had to tell Chris about the story. And then – well, I wanted to think.'

'What about?'

'Well, about what I was going to say to you.'

'And it didn't even occur to you that I might have been worried out of my mind? So – what are you going to say? What are your plans? Perhaps you'd be good enough to share them with me.'

'Well – I'm going to stay here for a few more days.'

'So am I to infer you're there with Gideon Keeble? I mean actually *with* him? In his –' He stopped. He couldn't bring himself to say the word 'bed', it hurt too much. 'In his house?'

'Well – yes. I am. Obviously.'

'Obviously? I don't understand quite why it's obvious.'

'Well – I couldn't do the story because of – of Gideon.'

'But the story was *about* Gideon. You might just have realised that. Before you left even.'

'Yes, I did. But I didn't care then.'

'What, so in forty-eight hours from not caring about him at all, you cared so much that you've thrown your entire career away?'

'Well – it's a bit more complicated than that,' she said. 'It wasn't just about Gideon. I did realise what harm I could do to them all. By writing the story.'

'Oh, please!' he said. 'You've developed a social conscience – is that what you're saying?'

'Sort of, yes, only it was about Gideon as well. That was what made me realise. I suppose.'

'How touching!'

She was silent. Then: 'Sorry, Nick. I'm very sorry.'

'Jocasta, how can you turn your back on – on us? How can

327

you throw away a long and very happy relationship just like that? On a whim.'

'It wasn't just on a whim. It absolutely wasn't.'

'Oh really? So you'd been planning it for some time, had you?'

'I suppose so. In a way. Without realising it.'

'Oh, for fuck's sake! I've never heard such drivel.'

'It's not drivel!' she said. 'And if you thought for just a little while, you'd realise why it happened.'

'Dare I assume this has something to do with my refusing to trail down the altar after you?'

'Actually,' she said, 'I'd be trailing after you. You obviously haven't been to many weddings, Nick. But yes, just something. In a way.'

'How fucking pathetic,' he said, and cut her off.

Not even a rather juicy little leak over Clare Short's reaction to the brewing Iraq crisis, and Tony Blair's part in it, could ease his misery.

Jocasta went to find Gideon. It was a glorious day, blue and green and golden, the kind Ireland did best. She lifted her head to the sun and it felt warm and welcoming. She found Gideon walking towards the stables.

'Hi,' she said, and tucked her hand into his back pocket.

'Hello, my darling. Did you do it?'

'Yes, I did.'

'And? You've been crying.'

'Yes, well, I feel bad and sad. It was – I mean, it's been a long time, Nick and me. It's hard to – to just end it. Even though I knew it was over before – well before – you. But I'm fine. I know I did the right thing. And it made me realise how much I actually do love you.'

'Well, I'm very happy about that. And I love you, very, very badly.'

'You can't love someone badly, Gideon.'

'I can. As in, "I want that very badly".'

'Oh, all right. I love you very badly too. And want you very badly.'

'That's nice to know.'

So – how exactly had it come to this? So quickly and with such astonishing ease? It had been like a film, moving the story forward in a series of short sequences, all intercut, with no dialogue, just wonderful emotive music; there had been the walk down to the lake, the two of them together, walking apart at first and then gradually moving closer together, until his arm was round her shoulders, hers round his waist; there had been the kiss, tender, not passionate, actually by the lake; there had been dinner, served by Mrs Mitchell in the very grand dining room; there had been his taking her hand and leading her upstairs, only to bid her goodnight on the second-floor landing, very properly; there had been her lying awake, staring into the darkness (and she supposed further intercutting of a shot of him also lying awake); and then her padding along the corridor, in search of him, opening several doors, the moonlight shafting most obligingly through the vast window at the top of the stairs; and then hearing someone behind her on the landing and turning in panic to see him smiling at her; and of course the sex scene, wonderfully passionate (the music rising to a crescendo here); and then finally, before the film returned to proper time and words and all that sort of thing, them lying in bed together, smiling at one another, with the sun streaming in the window.

It was all just slightly over the top, glorious setting, dashing hero, marvellous trappings – horses, servants, the incredible cars, he had actually allowed her to drive the Bugatti – but extremely wonderful just the same.

'I keep thinking I'm going to wake up,' she said to Gideon, 'find it's all a dream.'

'Well, you're not,' he said, 'this is real life. Although I should have tried to seduce you much earlier.'

'You did try. I think,' said Jocasta. 'But in a horribly gentlemanly way. Always including Nick in your invitations. I mean, really! No wonder progress was slow.'

'Well, I'm a patient fellow. I saw you, dancing in that ridiculous way at the conference, Jocasta, and I wanted you. And I knew that sooner or later I'd have to have you. It was as simple as that. I've been just waiting for the opportunity. My only fear was that

Nicholas would have made an honest woman of you in the meantime.'

'He was never going to,' said Jocasta, 'and until yesterday, I thought it mattered. Now I know it doesn't. Not in the very, very least.'

And it didn't.

'Fionnuala wants a new horse,' he said, as they walked back into the house. 'A polo pony, actually.'

'How do you know?'

'She texted me.'

'Well, that's good. That she's texting you. What did it say? Or would you rather I didn't see it?'

'Of course not. Here you are.'

He passed her his phone; she looked at it.

'Hi Dad. Having fun here. Wd like polo pony for birthday. Any chance? Fionnuala xxx.'

'It's nice she's keeping in touch,' said Jocasta carefully.

'Isn't it? I can't think when she last put kisses after her name.'

'I think,' she said, 'you shouldn't just say yes.'

'Oh really? And why not, my little relationship guru?'

'Because you'd just be buying her toys again. Why don't you say you'd like to go and see her, look at some ponies with her?'

'I am not,' he said firmly, 'going to that filthy place, forced to be courteous to that slimy poof, Carlingford.'

'All right. Tell her to come to Ireland, that you'll buy her one here. That you want to be part of the choice.'

'She wouldn't come.'

'Try her. Go on. Text her back. Here, I'll do it, you're so hopeless at it. I expect it's your age.' She smiled at him, reached up to kiss him. 'What shall I say?'

'You're the expert. But I'm not sure this is a good idea.'

'Yes, it is.'

She began punching out letters, her face very serious. She held it out to him.

'Here. How's this? "Nice idea, but I'd like to choose it with you. What about you come here? Dad xxx." '

'OK,' he said, after a moment or two. 'Send it.'

Five minutes later a message came back.

'No point. No polo ponies in Ireland. They're all here. F.'

'See,' he said, 'no kisses even. I told you.'

'Oh shut up,' said Jocasta. 'You can't give up that easily.'

She wrote another message, handed it to him. 'OK?'

He looked at it. 'No, it is not OK. I told you – oh, all right. See what she says.'

She smiled, re-read her message; 'I cd come there? xxx', and sent it.

It was half an hour later, as an increasingly bad-tempered Gideon stalked ahead of Jocasta down to the lake and sat scowling at the brilliant water, that a text message reached his phone.

'Cool. When? Fionnuala xxx.'

'See?' said Jocasta. 'What did I tell you?'

'Yes, all right,' he said, smiling at her reluctantly. 'Clever clogs. I hope you realise what this means? I'll have to actually go to the bloody place.'

'I promise you,' said Jocasta, 'I promise you it will be worth it.'

She was in love with him. Wasn't she? Desperately, terribly in love with him. Of course she was. She felt extraordinarily happy. All the time. She just couldn't believe it. And he was in love with her. He kept saying so. Telling her that he couldn't remember ever being so happy, that he couldn't believe that anyone so young and so beautiful could be bothered with him, 'Old and difficult and scratchy as I am.'

'You are not old,' she said. 'You may be difficult, but I haven't seen it yet. And I've seen a lot scratchier. So – here I am, youngish – and beautiful – maybe – and amazingly happy to be with you. OK?'

'Very OK,' he said.

He was absurdly romantic; she would wake in the morning to find him missing and he would come in, smiling, with a great bunch of wild flowers he had just picked. He chartered a small plane for the day and flew her over the Mountains of Mourne, simply because she said she had always wanted to see them. They went riding by moonlight, they drank champagne on a boat on the lake, he named one of his thoroughbred foals after her. 'Until you arrived, she was the most beautiful female to come to this place all year.'

She felt her own past was completely left behind her; she had only the clothes from her rucksack, and her phone, nothing else. It was as if she had been set down and told her life was to start all over again. It was all too good to be true, exactly what her romantic soul craved. Just the two of them, for just a little while, cocooned from the world, feasting on pleasure; looking back, she saw that it was their honeymoon.

And then there was the sex.

The sex was – well, it was good. It was very good. Obviously. She was enjoying it a lot.

'Well, I think that's enough.' Carla smiled at Kate.

They had had a wonderful morning, combing Top Shop and then just in case it looked as if they'd paid for the publicity, to Oasis and River Island as well. The last two had been a bit of a rush, as Kate had promised Jilly she'd be home by soon after lunch to get on with her revision; but Carla knew they had enough. Kate had chosen almost everything herself; it always showed, Carla thought, the eye for clothes, not so much in the actual outfits as the accessories. Belts, scarves, tights, sunglasses: the choice had been unerring, some things which Carla wouldn't even have considered herself, but looked wonderful on.

'I think so, too,' said Kate. 'I'm so excited. What time do you want us?'

'As early as possible. I've ordered a cab and I've booked someone from Nicky Clarke to do your hair, and a lovely girl to do the make-up, which I promise won't be much. Now – let's get you onto your tube. I don't want your grandmother worried. She's terrific, Kate. You're very lucky.'

'I know,' said Kate. 'She always seems younger than my mum.'

'You look a bit like her too. Same colouring.'

'Pure coincidence,' said Kate.

'Why?'

'I'm adopted,' said Kate. 'Look, I'd better go. Thanks, Carla. It's been great. Bye!'

Carla looked after her thoughtfully as she disappeared down the escalator, a whirl of blonde hair and long, long legs. Adopted? That was interesting. Another dimension to the story, perhaps. She must find out more about that tomorrow.

'The girl with tunnel vision', the article was sub-headed. And went on to describe how Martha had been driven all her life – 'no serious boyfriends while she was at school, in case they distracted her, working at least a twelve-hour day, and even now, still only one week's holiday at a time . . .'

Jack Kirkland had organised it: the woman's editor was a friend, had said they'd seen the one in the *Sketch* and were looking for a woman in politics to interview. Martha had said why not Janet and he'd said Janet was interviewed out; they wanted someone new, someone younger.

'Well, don't tell Janet that,' she'd said.

'Why not? Anyway, I already did.'

'Jack! Just think how she'd feel.'

'Too late,' he'd said. 'But she didn't seem to mind. She agreed, more or less, said she was sick of doing them.'

Anyway, she hadn't been so scared this time; she'd felt in control of the whole thing. And it read well. She was learning: fast.

She binned the paper, resolving to buy another later. She was out for a run; it was just six, a perfect May morning. Pounding over Tower Bridge, taking in the glorious view down-river, the wonderful tapestry of old and new buildings carved against the sky, glorying in having the city almost to herself, she thought she had never felt quite so happy. She had taken all these risks with her life, stepped outside her own closely defined comfort zone, breathed in the heady air – and found herself still safe. It was – well, it was hard to believe. She should have trusted herself earlier, she thought; she'd missed a lot. She'd even done something which had astonished her, and been to an audition for *Question Time*. The publicity department had been over the moon when she was invited; had said people struggled for years to get on the programme. And she'd actually quite enjoyed it; challenging though it had been, sitting round a table in a dining room in Lime Grove, with the producer and some other potential guests. It wasn't as if she'd had to say a word about herself, she had simply had to talk politics, prove her views were strong enough and that she was sufficiently articulate. She'd felt she'd done quite well, but it had been weeks since then, so probably she hadn't.

Anyway, she was altogether feeling rather bullish. She'd be going on holiday with Ed soon, as he so wanted her to.

'What harm would it do?' he said. 'We'd have fun. Heard about fun, Martha? It's what other people have. You ought to investigate it. Just a week, I promise I won't ask for more. Go on: be really, really reckless.'

So far she'd said no; but this morning, standing here, astride her life and its success, she could just about imagine – well, maybe more than imagine . . .

'Well, that's about it,' said Marc Jones. 'You were great, Kate.'

'You really were,' said Carla. 'Fantastic. Those last shots, when you started dancing – well, I'll want to put them on the front page.'

'Oh please do!' said Kate. She was flushed, flying, triumphant. For the first time in her life she felt properly confident. Someone in charge of her life, someone who mattered; not someone of no consequence, with no proper footing in the world, no proper roots.

'Well, I doubt we'll get that. But you'll certainly be a double page spread – hopefully the centre of the paper. Aren't you proud of her, Jilly?'

'I'm terribly proud of her,' said Jilly. 'I thought she was marvellous. She looked as if she'd been doing it for years.'

She did feel very happy about it; entirely justified in her decision. She had seen something happen to Kate that morning, just as Kate had felt it herself; she had shaken off some of her insecurities, her doubts about herself, become someone new. If Helen was upset, she would tell her all that, tell her what it had meant to Kate. A lot more than simply being photographed in the paper. In a funny way, Kate had found herself. Her own self. It was lovely to see.

Carla was taking them all out for tea: lunch had been a sandwich.

'I thought we'd go to the Ritz,' she said. 'I've booked a table.'

'The Ritz!' said Jilly. 'I haven't had tea at the Ritz since I was a girl.'

'I'm sure it hasn't changed,' said Carla, smiling. 'I don't suppose even the waiters have changed.'

'Still tea in the Palm Court?'

'Still tea in the Palm Court. We can have a champagne tea, if you like.'

'Oh I don't think we should do that,' said Jilly.

'Granny! I think we should. We've got a lot to celebrate. Haven't we, Marc? You'll come, won't you?'

She was flirting with him, Jilly thought; how sweet.

'Fraid I can't,' said Marc regretfully. 'Got to go back and get this lot processed. But another time, Kate. Another session. I'm sure there'll be one.'

'Are you really?'

'Absolutely. The other Kate will be looking to her laurels soon, you mark my words.'

'Oh, wow!' said Kate.

They did have the champagne tea. Sitting amongst the excesses of the Palm Court, with its crystal chandeliers and huge palms, painted murals and wonderfully old-fashioned pianist. Champagne, and a pile of tiny sandwiches, scones with cream, very fancy iced cakes, meringues and éclairs, and a pot of fragrant Earl Grey.

Jilly was struggling weakly to refuse a second glass when Carla got her notebook out.

'You may as well, Jilly, I've got to ask a lot of boring stuff now. Like Kate's age, where she goes to school, what she's interested in and what she wants to do. Anything really, that you might think would give her a bit of colour, as we call it in the trade.'

'Well, my full name is Kate Bianca Tarrant,' said Kate. 'Make sure you put the Bianca in, won't you? Kate's such a dull name.'

'Of course. We could reverse them if you like – Bianca Kate sounds better than the other way round.'

'OK, cool.' She seemed pleased.

'Why Bianca? It's quite unusual. Did it mean something special to your mother?'

'Oh – no, not really. I think – she just liked it,' said Kate. She sounded guarded suddenly. 'Anyway, my birthday's August the fifteenth.'

'And you'll be sixteen?'

'Yeah. Then I can do what I like!' She grinned happily.

'And what would that be?'

'Oh – no doubt about that. Be a model. Now I know how great it is.'

'Fine. And – what other interests do you have? Hobbies?'

'Don't have many. Clothes. Clubbing,' said Kate vaguely. 'My sister's the one. She got a music scholarship, and she plays the piano and the violin and belongs to two orchestras.'

'Yes, she's very talented,' said Jilly fondly. 'We're extremely proud of Juliet.'

'Is she adopted too?' asked Carla.

Jilly looked at her sharply. 'I didn't know you knew that.'

'Oh yes, Kate told me about it yesterday, didn't you, Kate?'

'Yes, yes, I did. Juliet's not adopted, no.'

'Right. Well, you obviously get on.'

'Quite,' said Kate. 'She makes me look a bit hopeless.'

'No she doesn't, darling,' said Jilly, patting her knee. 'You're just very different.'

'Hardly surprising,' said Carla, 'since you're not real sisters. Kate – do you know who your real mother is? Are you in touch with her?'

'No,' said Kate shortly.

'Would you like to be?'

'No, I wouldn't. And it's *birth* mother, not *real* mother,' she added, rather severely. 'My real mum and my real dad – that's what they are to me – they're the ones who brought me up, they're the ones I care about.'

'Of course,' said Carla soothingly, 'and I'm sure they know that.'

'Of course they do,' said Jilly. She could see that Kate was getting upset. 'They're a very happy family.'

'I'm sure. So – any boyfriends, Kate?'

'No. No one serious, anyway.'

'And – what sort of boys do you like?'

'Oh . . .' A picture of Nat swam into Kate's head. 'Cool ones, obviously. Tall. Dark. With really cool clothes.'

'And what do cool boys wear?'

'Well – combats. Really good boots. Sleeveless T-shirts. Leather jackets. And they drive cool cars.'

'And what's a cool car. To you? A Porsche?'

'No!' Kate's expression was a mixture of pity and disdain.

'That's an old bloke's car. No, maybe an Escort, or a Citroën, that's been, like, souped-up, something with a spoiler, that sort of thing.'

'Sounds great,' said Carla. 'And tell me which clubs you go to.'

'Oh, all over the place,' said Kate airily. 'The Ministry of Sound, The Shed in Brixton.'

'They have a wonderful time these days,' said Jilly, relieved that the conversation had turned away from Kate's adoption. 'Of course we did, too. In our own way. I used to come dancing here, you know.'

Kate sighed and said she'd like to go to the loo.

'It's over there,' said Carla, 'just down those steps to the right.'

'Cool. See you in a bit. I might clean some of this muck off my face.'

'Kate seems a little defensive about her adoption,' said Carla casually, after several minutes of how Jilly and her husband had been two of the earliest members of Annabel's.

'Yes, well it's not surprising, especially under her particular circumstances.'

'What – particular circumstances?'

'Oh, she – ' Jilly stopped, took a large sip of champagne. 'Carla, this is not for publication, is it?'

'Of course not. It's got nothing to do with the article.'

'No. Well, she has absolutely no idea who her mother is. None of us do.'

'Oh, really? I thought these days it was all very open, that they can go in search of their birth mothers.'

'Yes, that's right. And normally, of course, they can, but because she was just left like that – oh, Kate darling, there you are. We really should go. I'm worrying about Juliet.'

'I've got a car waiting,' said Carla. 'It'll take you home. Look, I've got all I could possibly need. I'll send some of the pictures over tomorrow, and I could have a couple mounted for your parents, Kate, if you like. As a coming home present.'

'That'd be cool,' said Kate. 'Thanks.'

Jilly said that she didn't know what Kate would do if the word cool hadn't been invented, drained her glass of champagne, and followed Carla, slightly unsteadily, out to the front of the Ritz.

What a wonderful day it had been: she felt sure it would prove a huge turning point in Kate's life.

'Good God,' said Chad, 'who's that with Eliot? Looks like old Sven's girlfriend, Nancy del something or other.'

'Olio,' said Janet. 'Yes, she does. Is she his human rights lawyer, do you think?'

'Doesn't look like one. Now that's very sexist of me, isn't it?'

'Very,' said Janet severely. Her mobile rang. She started buttering a scone and talking into it at the same time.

'Yes,' she said, 'yes. I would like to hear your poem, very much. What? No, read it to me now. And then – well, tell Daddy he's not to. Tell him I said so. And – yes, I'm listening.' There was a silence; then she said: 'Lovely. Really lovely. I specially like the bit about turning off the sunshine. Clever girl. Yes, I'll be home for bathtime. Promise. Love you. Bye, now.

'Sorry about that,' she said, switching her phone off, holding out her hand. 'The trials of working motherhood. Well, maybe not trials. You must be Miss Harrington. It's very nice to meet you. Eliot's talked about you a lot. What would you like? Tea?'

Her phone rang again. 'Sorry,' she said to them, and then, 'Hi, Bob, what is it? Yes, it's tonight. Here. Sorry, can't talk now. See you later. Bye . . . Now, Miss Harrington, I'm sorry I haven't got long – as you just heard, I have a hot date in a bathroom, but I'd love to have a quick chat. Eliot tells me you do a lot of work with Amnesty International . . .'

She was an old pro, Chad thought, watching her, apparently being charming and helpful, actually being nothing of the sort, just fobbing Suzanne Harrington off. 'Look, I'm working on an all-party committee right now, looking at all this. If you let me have details, chapter and verse of the kind of problems you come across, it would really help. And as soon as you can. And – '

'Eliot!' It was Jack Kirkland, calling him from the doorway.

He got up. 'Excuse me a moment. Won't be long.'

'So – Eliot's clearly working hard in your constituency, Miss Harrington?' said Chad. 'That's good.'

'Yes, everyone thinks very highly of him. Well, in my profession, anyway.'

'And of course, he's a very sweet man,' Janet said, her voice dripping honey. Chad looked at her, amused.

'Yes, he's been terribly kind to me. He even put some blinds up for me, in my new flat, totally beyond the bounds of duty, but I'm on my own and –'

'Well, I'm delighted to hear it,' said Janet. 'He does like to help the weaker sex, which is how I'm afraid he regards us. Ah, here he is back now. I might make this my exit. Sorry but it's back to bathtime for me tonight. Now, about the Division tomorrow, Chad, could you just . . .'

They moved out of earshot; Eliot smiled at Suzanne quickly.

'Sorry that was so brief. But she is terribly busy.'

'No, no, she was marvellous. Now what about this tour you've promised me? Is it true there's a chapel in the bowels of the House? I'd love to see that.'

'Indeed, it's called St Mary's Undercroft – known as The Crypt. Absolutely beautiful, like an illustration from a child's Bible, all gold and stained glass.'

'Could we go there?'

'Of course. It's underneath Westminster Hall. We'll start there . . . Oh, hello, John, old man,' he said, as they passed the adjacent table. 'How are you?'

It was the same Old Tory who had attacked Chad in the Smoking Room; he glared at Eliot and said nothing.

'This is Suzanne Harrington, a constituent of mine,' said Eliot, unfazed. 'Just taking her off on the tour. She wants to see The Crypt.'

The reply was a newspaper, raised to cover the Old Tory face.

Janet was halfway out of the building when she realised she had forgotten her phone. Damn. Maybe she'd left it in the Pugin Room. She hurried back there; it seemed to have disappeared.

She peered over the newspaper, wondering if Eliot might be behind it. An irate pair of eyes met hers.

'If you're looking for Griers, he's not here. Taken some totty to The Crypt. Disgraceful behaviour.'

Janet construed rightly that he was referring to Eliot leaving the Tories, rather than taking someone down to The Crypt, and was leaving again when Chad appeared, holding her phone.

'This what you're looking for?'

'Oh, yes. Thanks, Chad. See you tomorrow.'

Carla was in the office, looking enraptured at the pictures of Kate that Marc had brought in; the girl seemed to leap off the page, alive, carelessly confident, quite, quite beautiful.

Now, what was she going to write about Kate? Just an extended caption? Or a bit more? She wasn't really particularly interesting. Just one of a million other fifteen year olds. Best to concentrate on that. 'An extraordinary ordinary girl,' she wrote, 'who could be working in a branch of Top Shop, or – '

No, it wasn't good enough. It just wasn't. She'd read that so many times in other fashion editors' pages. It was a cliché. And she wanted to capture in words as well as the pictures the quality of Kate, to make her special, her toughness, her prickliness. All because of the adoption, she supposed. Well, they obviously wouldn't want that written about. And there was nothing special about that really, either. If they'd known who the mother was, it might be different.

Her door burst open; Johnny Hadley, the diary editor, came in, looking flustered.

'Carla. Hi. Look, do me a favour, would you? I'm frantic, got to check a couple of things for the lawyers. I'm running a nice story on Sophie Wessex. A few months ago, Jocasta interviewed some woman in the powder room at the Dorchester Hotel, or wherever it was, when there was all that trouble about the bogus sheik, remember? She said how sweet Sophie was, how she always had a kind word for everyone. It never ran, so could you have a rummage in her desk, see if you can find it. It would just make a nice bit of background. God, who's that? Lovely pair of boobs. And talking about Jocasta, she looks a bit like her, wouldn't you say? Or am I imagining it?'

'No,' said Carla, glancing down at the pictures of Kate, 'I've said it myself. She's my latest discovery. Yes, all right, Johnny, I'll bring the piece in if I can find it.'

She went out to Jocasta's desk and pulled out the top drawer; nothing in that but a stack of old tapes, some rather dubious-looking lipsticks and a packet of Tampax. The next one looked more promising: cuttings from the paper, printouts of e-mails, a few drafts of articles. Nothing about Sophie Wessex. The third drawer was total chaos: a mass of papers, notes, typed copy, more printed e-mails. Bloody hell. She'd just have a quick rummage and then say she couldn't find it. It was –

'Oh my God!' said Carla. She sat down suddenly, at Jocasta's desk, and began to read a set of pages. Feverishly, not once, but two, three times. And then picked them up, took them into her office and shut the door and read them again.

It was *exactly* what she had been looking for. Only it wasn't an article about the chatelaine of the toilets at the Dorchester. It was something quite, quite different. A printout from the *Sketch* archives, and another from the *Mail* and yet another from the *Sun*, about a baby, abandoned at Heathrow airport. On 15 August, almost sixteen years ago. Whom the nurses who cared for her had named Bianca. And whose mother had apparently never been found.

Part Two

Chapter 23

It was a bit like when President Kennedy was shot, the older people concerned said. And like when Princess Diana had been killed, said the younger ones. You knew exactly what you were doing when you heard about it: or rather read it. And you knew you would never forget the moment as long as you lived.

'Oh, no,' whispered Helen, 'oh, no, please no,' as she read the story, read it again, and again, and then sitting there, white-faced under her new tan, concentrating on the pictures of Kate, the extraordinary pictures of Kate, as if by ignoring the words enough, she could will them away.

Jim, literally speechless with rage, was pacing up and down the kitchen, pausing occasionally to bang his fist on the back door; and Jilly, the one most responsible for the horror, sat in the dining room, too shocked even to think, confronted by the very worst of all the scenarios she had imagined since Carla's phone call, twenty-four hours earlier.

When Gideon found Jocasta, she was sitting on the grass by the lake, still and stunned, holding the paper close to her, wondering how such a thing could possibly have happened, and cursing Carla with a venom which surprised even her.

Clio, doing a Saturday morning surgery, was shown the article by the receptionist, excited at the rebirth of the story about one of their patients. 'It mentions Mrs Bradford and her shop by name,' she said excitedly. Clio sat in her room, reading and re-reading it, wondering how much Kate had contributed to the

345

story herself, and hoping against hope it had been nothing to do with Jocasta. And wondering how Kate's mother, her real mother, must be feeling when she saw it, as she surely would.

Nat Tucker read it as he sat in his mother's kitchen, ignoring his father's exhortations to shift his bloody arse and get on down to the garage, and wondering not only if he should call Kate or just go round and see her, but how he could never have realised how totally gorgeous she was, and enjoying the very clear description of himself and his car. And, with a sensitivity that would have surprised most of his mates, and the whole of his family, thinking that it couldn't be that great, having the fact you'd been abandoned in a cleaning cupboard splashed all over some cruddy newspaper.

Carla, who had seen the pages the night before at proof stage and felt extremely satisfied with herself, was having a little trouble confronting the reality. Of course she had only been doing her job; of course Jilly, clearly shocked and even frightened, had confirmed (Carla having put her phone onto 'record', when she spoke to her, as instructed by the lawyers) that yes, it was correct and abandoned baby Bianca was indeed Kate; and of course nothing had changed and Kate still clearly had a dazzling future as a model. But somehow, seeing her there in the paper, in all her young vulnerability, with her small sad history spelt out in fourteen point, for the almost two million readers of the *Sketch* to be entertained by as they ate their breakfasts, Carla didn't feel quite so pleased with herself.

Martha saw the story trailed on the front page of the *Sketch* while she was out on her early run: 'The abandoned baby: now tipped as the latest face in fashion. Meet Bianca Kate, modelling for the first time in the *Sketch* today.' She read the story, put the paper, folded neatly, into a rubbish bin, ran back to her apartment, showered and dressed in one of her constituency suits, and drove down to Binsmow. She arrived, as promised, at the vicarage at eleven-thirty, did a brief legal surgery, and met Geraldine Curtis at one-thirty at a school Summer Fayre. That evening she and her parents attended a charity concert in Binsmow Town Hall, where she bought five books of raffle tickets and won a rather grubby-looking bottle of bubble bath. She left Binsmow early next morning, after going to early communion and then breakfasting with her mother, who was engrossed in the story of Bianca Kate, the abandoned baby, which had found its way into the *Sunday Times* as well as the *Mail on Sunday*. She agreed it was the most dreadful thing to abandon a baby and that she couldn't imagine anyone doing such a thing, then drove back to London and her apartment, where she spent the day working and dealing with personal admin. In the evening she went to the gym, where she did a spinning class and swam thirty lengths of the pool.

Ed Forrest, who had left four messages on her landline, several more on her mobile and a couple of text messages as well, asking her to call him to discuss, among other things, a trip to Venice he had organised, was first hurt, then annoyed and finally seriously anxious, when she failed to answer any of them.

And Kate, her golden, dazzling day turned dark and ugly, sat in her bedroom, the door firmly locked, crying endlessly and silently, and feeling more wretched and ashamed than she could have believed possible.

'Can I persuade you to talk about this?' said Gideon.

'I suppose so,' she said, turning a face, swollen with crying, to him. 'It's something horrible, Gideon, something I – well, something I was implicated in . . .'

'But you weren't there,' he said when she had finished. 'It's not your story. It's nothing to do with you.'

'Gideon, it is, it is. Oh God, I have to go to London. Go and see Kate. I really have to.'

'All right, my darling one. If you have to. Maybe I should come with you. I'm worried about you, you look dreadful.'

'No,' she said, leaning forward to kiss him, resting her head briefly on his shoulder. 'No, I've got to do this by myself.'

'All right. If that's how it is.'

'It is. Oh, Gideon, it's such a horrible thing to happen. To a little girl.'

'What, being abandoned at an airport? It is indeed. But she has a lovely family now, from the sound of it – and maybe she told Carla herself. Maybe it wasn't your fault at all, nothing to do with you.'

'I asked Carla that when I rang her,' said Jocasta, starting to cry again, 'and she said Kate didn't tell her anything. Well, only that she was adopted. She got it all – she said – from the archives.'

'She could well have done.'

'Yes, but I had a lot about Kate in my desk; I think she found that. And she certainly didn't warn the poor little thing what she was going to do. She admitted that. Bitch! It's so cruel, so dreadfully cruel.'

She blew her nose, managed a wobbly smile. Gideon looked at her, then back at the newspaper.

Then, 'I suppose,' he said quite quietly, 'no one has mentioned any resemblance between you and this girl?'

Jocasta started to laugh: a loud, almost hysterical laugh.

'Yes,' she said, 'actually they have.'

Clio decided she should ring Jilly Bradford. She had liked her so much and she could imagine how dreadful she must be feeling. There were no quotes from her, or indeed from any of the family. Including Kate.

She got a recorded message in Jilly's slightly dated, upper-class accent. She left the message, saying how sorry she was, and then pressed her buzzer for the next patient. What an awful mess. Poor little Kate. Poor, poor little thing. God, these newspapers had a lot to answer for. Surely, surely Jocasta couldn't have done this. But it was her paper.

Back in her flat, feeling half ashamed, she decided to call her. Her mobile was on message. Clio left her number, asked her to call, and was still wondering if she could actually be bothered to make herself anything more than a sandwich, when Jocasta rang.

'Hi, Clio. It's Jocasta. How are you?'

'Fine. I just saw the article about Kate and – '

'It was nothing to do with me, Clio. Honestly. Well, only in the most indirect way and – well, actually I've left the *Sketch*.'

'You've left? Why?'

'Oh – bit of a long story. Look, I'm in Ireland at the moment, about to fly to London. I'm going to try and see Kate, because I do feel responsible. In a way.'

'Jocasta, you're talking in riddles.'

'I know. Sorry. Look, if I haven't been beaten up by the Tarrants, could we meet this evening? I could come to you, if you like. It'd be good to talk it through with someone who knows Kate. Would you mind?'

'Of course not. Don't be silly. Just call me.'

'Is that Mrs Tarrant?'

'Yes?'

It was a soft voice with a slightly north country accent.

'Mrs Tarrant, you don't know me, but I think I could be Bianca's mother. You see, I left a baby at the airport seventeen years ago . . .'

Helen thought she might be sick.

'Sixteen years,' she said sharply.

'What? Oh I'm sorry, I thought it said seventeen.'

Helen slammed the phone down and burst into tears; and greatly against her will, feeling every word threatening to choke her, she called Carla Giannini.

Carla had called first thing: bright and confident. Weren't the pictures lovely, didn't Kate look great, they must all be so proud of her. Helen had been so shocked she had mumbled something totally inane.

'Would Kate like to speak to me, I wonder?'

'No,' said Helen in the same quiet, numb voice, 'no, I'm sure she wouldn't.'

'Well, later, perhaps. Tell her I've had several offers for her already.'

'What sort of offers?'

'Modelling agencies. Of course, that is all entirely up to you.'

'I'm so glad something is,' Helen said icily. She was beginning to regain her confidence.

Carla ignored this. 'There is one thing, Mrs Tarrant – one thing I should warn you about. You could get calls. From women claiming to be Kate's mother. We've had a couple already. Now, I would advise you to let us handle these for you. Put any calls on to us. It's – '

'I don't want you to handle anything for us,' said Helen, and she could hear the loathing in her voice, the rage and the misery. 'You've done enough damage – please leave us alone.'

And she put the phone down, very carefully. What was she going to do? How were they going to get through this? How?

After two more phone calls from women, she realised, very reluctantly, that they couldn't do it alone.

Carla was brisk and efficient: 'Just redirect them all to us.'

'And suppose – suppose one of them was genuine?' The words hurt her to speak them. 'How would we know?'

'Well, we would ask for proof of some kind.'

'What sort of proof?' said Helen, desperately.

'Well – is there anything at all that you know, about the way Kate was abandoned, that wasn't in the story? Like the time it was, or what she was wearing.'

'I don't think so,' said Helen bitterly. 'Every wretched detail is there.'

'Well, try and think of something. And call me back.'

So far, Helen couldn't.

She went and opened the dining-room door without knocking, looked at Jilly with cold dislike.

'I think I'd like to take you home. Jim and I both feel we need to be on our own with the girls.'

'Of course,' said Jilly humbly. 'But no need to take me, I'll get a cab. There – there haven't been any calls for me, have there?'

'I've stopped answering the phone, we've had so many. Jim's going out to buy an answering machine.'

'Oh dear, how dreadful. Who from?'

'Oh, other reporters mostly. From other papers. Do we have anything to add, could they interview Kate, that sort of thing.'

She didn't tell her about the women, the would-be mothers; she couldn't bear it.

'Helen, I must just say once more how sorry I am. But I really didn't tell this woman anything, she had all the information already – '

'Mummy, for what must be the tenth time, if you hadn't agreed to let Kate do those wretched photographs, none of it would have happened. How could you, without asking us, when you were supposed to be responsible for her?'

'I – ' Jilly stopped. She had no defence, she knew.

350

'Mummy, it really wasn't just Granny's fault.' Juliet had appeared, her face pale. 'I told her to go ahead. I said it would be so great for Kate and – '

'Juliet, you are fourteen years old,' said Helen wearily, 'I hardly think it was very sensible of your grandmother to rely on your opinion.'

'But – '

'Juliet, darling, it's nice of you to stand up for me, but your mother's quite right. I should never have agreed. Could I just say goodbye to Kate?'

'If you have to.'

Helen was disproportionately pleased when Kate refused to let her into her room.

Half an hour later, when Jilly had departed, there was a ring at the door. Helen answered it. It was Nat Tucker. The Sax Bomb stood at the gate, its engine still running, its sound system at apparently full volume.

'Oh,' she said. 'Nat. Hello.'

'Mornin',' he said. 'Kate in?'

'Er – she is,' said Helen, 'but I'm afraid she's not very well.'

'Oh, right. Just tell her I came then. And that I saw her photos in the paper.'

'Fine. Yes. Of course.'

'Nice, aren't they?' he said. 'She looks great. Well, see you later.'

And he ambled down the path, pulling a packet of cigarettes out of the pocket of his extremely low-slung trousers. Helen and Juliet, who had heard his voice, stood staring after him.

'How sweet,' said Juliet, 'how really, really sweet. Wait till I tell Kate.'

Helen caught her arm.

'Juliet, you are not to tell Kate.'

Juliet stared at her.

'Why on earth not?'

'Because I can't face any more upsets this morning.'

'Mum! That's horrible. Why should there be an upset? He's the one person in the whole world, probably, who can make Kate feel better just now.'

'Don't be so ridiculous,' said Helen.

'It's true! She only did it to make him notice her. She'll be so pleased he came round. And don't you realise, half of what's making her so upset is thinking everyone'll know what happened to her, that her mother just – well, just threw her away, as she sees it, and she feels it's like a public humiliation. If Nat Tucker doesn't care about it, she'll be so much happier – '

'Juliet, Nat Tucker is not the sort of boy I want Kate getting mixed up with,' said Helen.

'You sound like Granny,' said Juliet, in a tone of complete contempt. 'Actually, worse. At least she thinks Nat's good-looking. Anyway, he was nice enough to come round, so I'm going up to tell Kate and you can't stop me.'

Kate was wondering how she could ever leave her room again: face a world that knew what had happened to her, that must be either despising her or feeling sorry for her or even laughing at her, when Juliet called through her door with the news that Nat had actually come to the house, had wanted to see her, had said she looked great: it was like – well, she didn't know what it was like. Like being given a present. No, better than that. Like the dentist's drill stopping. She opened the door, let Juliet in, and sat on the bed, staring at her, as if she had never seen her before.

'Did he really? Come here?'

'He really did. He's so sweet, Kate. Honestly. It can't have been easy for him. He obviously does like you a lot. Why don't you call him?'

'Yes. Yes, I might. Later. When I feel a bit better. God, I can't believe that. I really, really can't.'

'Well, he did.' Juliet studied her. 'Better not ask him round yet, though. You look awful – your eyes look about half the size. And your face is all swollen and blotchy.'

'Yes, all right, all right,' said Kate irritably. 'God, Jools, think of that. He actually came. Came here. That is so cool. Tell me again exactly what he said. Exactly . . .'

Helen recognised Jocasta; she was looking nervously from behind the curtains in the front room at the slowly growing crowd at the gate. She turned to Jim.

'It's Jocasta. You know, Jocasta Forbes – '

'Well, I'll tell her to bugger off,' he said. Helen had never heard him use a stronger profanity than bloody.

'Jim!'

'Well,' he said, his tone infinitely weary, 'she was where it all began. No doubt she told that other woman all about Kate. I don't want her here; I don't want her anywhere near us. And if we let her in, those other vultures will follow her. Or try to. God, here's another, looks like a photographer. Jesus, Helen, what are we going to do?'

'I think we should let Jocasta in,' said Helen bravely. 'My mother said it was nothing to do with her.'

'Helen, I am not having that woman in my house,' said Jim. 'I won't allow it. It's as simple as that.'

'It's not your house,' said Helen, emboldened by the desperate situation. 'It's *ours*. And I think she might be able to help.'

He said nothing, just sat in his chair, biting his fist.

Helen walked over to the door, shouted through it: 'What do you want, Jocasta?'

'I want to talk to you. And to Kate. I want to try and explain. That it wasn't me. I want to tell Kate that. I think it might just help. Please, Mrs Tarrant. *Please.*'

'All right,' said Helen, 'I'll open the door. I don't know if Kate'll want to see you though.'

'Thanks. Thank you so much.'

'It was totally awful,' Jocasta said to Clio later, over a glass of wine. She had arrived on Clio's doorstep, pale and very shaken. 'None of them believed me. Kate refused even to see me. She just said she thought she could trust me. That she thought I was her friend. Shouting through her door at me. Oh God, Clio, what an awful, awful mess. What have I done?'

'Nothing – I thought,' said Clio.

'Well – I did do one thing,' said Jocasta, lighting a cigarette. 'Sorry about this, Clio. I really need it.'

'That's OK. What did you do?'

'I looked Kate up in the archives. I was – well, I was intrigued. Her grandmother told me she'd been abandoned, and Kate had told me when her birthday was. I – I printed the story off. It was in all the papers at the time. About Baby Bianca being found.'

353

'And – then what?'

'Well, and then Kate told me all about it herself. She obviously finds it really, really hard to cope with, but she thought if I wrote about it, her mother might come and find her. I certainly wasn't going to do anything without her parents' permission, but I put all the printouts in a file in my drawer. I shouldn't have. If I'd thought for five minutes, I'd have shredded them or something. But – well, I didn't know I was going to leave. I didn't know that cow Carla was going to go through my desk.'

'Is that what she did?'

'She must have done. She says she didn't, but I don't believe her. God, I feel so sick. Oh, Clio, what am I going to do?'

'I don't know,' said Clio, 'but I'm sure Kate will calm down. She's obviously terribly shocked. I just spoke to her grandmother. She was very subdued . . . It turned out she'd agreed to the fashion session, while the Tarrants were away. Apparently this Carla woman had called her to confirm the story. Anyway, she said it was all her fault. She said Kate had been shouting at her, telling her she hated her. Clearly,' she added, refilling Jocasta's glass, 'you aren't entirely to blame.'

Jocasta's mobile rang. 'Hi,' she said. 'Oh, hello, Gideon. How absolutely lovely to hear your voice. No, everything's not all right. It's ghastly. It didn't do any good. Look, I'll call you later. I'm with a friend. An old friend.' She smiled at Clio. 'Yes, you would like her. A lot. She's really, really normal. We went travelling together. With that bitch Martha I told you about. What? Oh, Gideon! Well, I know I did but – oh, all right. I might stay in London, till you get back. I don't think I can cope with Mrs Mitchell on my own. Yes, I will. I promise. I love you too.'

'Who was that?' Clio asked.

'Gideon Keeble. He's Irish and quite famous – owns dozens of shopping malls all over the world and God knows what else. Several houses. He's had umpteen wives and he's got a nightmare teenage daughter, who he's just off to see in Barbados, that's why he rang, to buy her some polo ponies.'

'*Some?*' said Clio, incredulously.

'Yes. One is nothing like enough, apparently. Anyway, he's older than me and a complete workaholic and it's all completely unsuitable. And I am totally, totally in love with him. I've left Nick, given up my job, given up my whole life here. Just to be with Gideon.'

'God,' said Clio, 'he must be very special.'

'He is. I can't imagine how I could have ever thought I was happy until now. I feel – oh I don't know. As if my real life has only just begun. It's so strange.'

Sasha Berkeley was the deputy diary editor of the *News on Sunday*, the sister paper to the *Daily News*. She was new to the job, had moved from one of the tabloids only a few weeks ago; she was pretty, sassy and very tough, and she was dragging the *News* diary into the twenty-first century.

'Politicians are the new really hot news,' she said to her editor. 'It would be much more exciting if Tony Blair started playing away, than David Beckham, for instance. Think about it.'

The editor agreed that politicians did have a good hold on the public perception at the moment – however unpopular they were. 'And certainly if they're caught with their pants down. Like dear old Paddy.'

Sasha was rather intrigued, therefore, when Euan Gregory, the *News*' political sketch writer, called with a story that she might like. Eliot Griers, one of the founders of the new Centre Forward party, with its absolute commitment against sleaze of any kind, had been seen entering The Crypt at the House of Commons a couple of nights earlier, accompanied by a very attractive girl, and that it had been some time before they emerged again. 'Apparently the temperature was rising down there quite nicely.'

'You mean they were snogging?'

'You're so crude, Sasha. I would prefer something like, "in one another's arms".'

'But not actually shagging?'

'Of course not!'

'Goodness,' said Sasha, 'thanks, Euan. Are you quite sure it was Eliot Griers?'

'Apparently, yes. Impeccable source.'

'And that the lady with him wasn't Mrs Griers?'

'Mrs Griers is blonde. This girl was dark. Very pretty. Don't have a name though.'

'Marvellous. Thanks, Euan.'

Eliot was enjoying a club sandwich from room service, washed down by an ice-cold beer, and working on his speech for the next evening, when the phone rang. He sighed. Caroline, probably.

It wasn't Caroline. It was Sasha Berkeley. Just wondering if he would like to comment on a story about him and a woman who had been seen entering the chapel underneath the House of Commons the previous Tuesday evening. And had even been observed to be 'Well, as I understand it, in very close contact indeed.'

The club sandwich was never finished.

Clio woke up to hear sobbing coming from the sitting room, where Jocasta was sleeping on her futon; she went in to see her.

'Jocasta! What is it? Is it just Kate? Because – '

'No,' said Jocasta, wiping her eyes. 'A bad dream and then – '

'Do you often have such bad dreams?'

'Yes – quite often.'

'What? What about? Go on, Jocasta, it sounds bad. Trust me, I'm a doctor,' she added with a grin. Jocasta smiled reluctantly back at her. 'Anyway, there's nothing to be ashamed of in having bad dreams.'

'All right. I will tell you. It's pathetic really. Nick's the only other person who knows. He was always great,' she added, slightly reluctantly.

'What are they about, your dreams?' Clio asked.

'About – ' she took a deep breath – 'about childbirth.'

'Childbirth!' Clio looked at her sharply. 'Why childbirth, Jocasta, for heaven's sake?'

'I suppose,' said Jocasta, 'it's just all this business with Kate. It's brought it back.'

Chapter 24

Nick was grazing through the Sunday papers, his mind half on Jocasta and how much he missed her, while still able to admire his own leading article. It was far better, he thought immodestly, than any of the other tabloids, based on the Martin Sixsmith resignation and the on-going struggle of the government to misrepresent the truth. Of course the political leaders in tabloids were not really written for the public; they were designed to impress other journalists and editors, and particularly the politicians. They were a bid for stories, really. If one of them thought you were going to be sympathetic to a point of view, was considering giving you a major story, then a leader might tip the balance. This one could lead to something, if he was lucky. He turned to the *News on Sunday*, flicking over the pages, in search of the political stuff – and then he saw it, in the diary.

'God,' he said aloud. 'Jesus,' and, 'Stupid bloody idiot,' and then, 'This won't do their cause any good.'

He pulled out his mobile and scrolled through it, looking for Eliot's number. He called him; not too surprisingly, it was on message.

Caroline Griers was squeezing oranges for breakfast when Eliot called.

'Hello, Eliot. How are you?'

'Oh – fine. Yes. You?'

'Absolutely fine. Any chance of you getting home some time this evening? You said you might.'

'Well – actually, Caroline, I'll be home much sooner than this evening. Probably before lunch.'

357

'Oh – all right.' Her voice was as cool, and pleasant as always. 'I'll put some extra potatoes on for you.'

'Great. Well, see you then.'

'Yes. Goodbye, Eliot.'

Eliot switched off his phone, sweating slightly. Well, she hadn't seen it yet. But of course someone would call her – or maybe they wouldn't call her. Maybe they'd just call other people, friends: telling them that there was an item about Eliot Griers in the paper; a gossipy item, concerning him and another woman. It would spread very fast. Very fast. There was no hope of any alternative. God, he was a fool. An absolute bloody fool. And now, of all times, when one of the major tenets of the Centre Forward party was its pledge against any kind of immorality. Only this hadn't been like that. In the past, yes, but not this time. He'd just been trying to comfort her. Over her divorce, which she said had upset her so terribly; being in The Crypt, she said, had brought it all back. He had thought he'd heard the door, but when he'd checked there'd been no one there.

His denial looked pathetic; he and Chad had worked it over and over the night before, it was the best they could do. That she was a constituent, who had come in for a meeting with Janet Frean, and he had volunteered to give her a tour of the House. Yeah right, as his daughters would say. Very convincing.

It had been rotten luck, of course: how many people went to The Crypt in the course of a day? Or even a week. And then, someone who wanted to get him. But – who? Who hated him that much? That old Tory bugger? Or one of the complacent, feminist Blair Babes, who all seemed to feel men were only in Parliament for one thing: a bit of crumpet? Or even that policeman on duty? No, they were all pure gold, they never talked.

Well – there was only one thing to do. Bluff it out.

Helen was laying the breakfast table; she wasn't sure why. No one would come down. Kate was still more or less locked in her room and since the altercation with her mother over Nat, Juliet refused to communicate with her, had eaten supper in Kate's room, and even slept in there. She had become, in Kate's hour of need, her best, her most loyal friend, the only person Kate would talk to. So – some good had come out of it, Helen thought wearily.

Jim certainly wouldn't want breakfast; he was still raging, so angry and upset, that he had been up half the night with dreadful indigestion, pacing up and down, snapping at Helen if she even tried to say anything. He was asleep now: a fitful, noisy sleep, but at least asleep.

At any rate, the reporters had gone. Jocasta had said they would. 'It's not a big enough story to keep them all night. They'll just rehash what's on the files.'

Jocasta had asked about cranks, too; clearly it was a standard hazard. She seemed relieved that Carla was doing something to help.

'And – have you had many calls?'

'About five now,' said Helen. 'I've told them all to ring the paper. But I'm so afraid that – well – '

She stopped. 'I can imagine,' said Jocasta gently. 'That one of them might be the real mother.'

'Yes. The Giannini woman said to try and think of something that could be a sort of test question. To put to them. And there is just one thing. She wasn't wearing a nappy. That wasn't ever – ever detailed.'

'That would do,' said Jocasta. In fact it would do wonderfully well. No one would expect a baby to be left without a nappy on. 'Tell Carla. Better still, I'll do it for you. Right now. And I do think you should change your telephone number, Mrs Tarrant, go ex-directory. Otherwise you – well, let's say an answering machine just isn't what you want.'

Very shortly after that she left.

Suddenly, Helen heard pounding on the stairs; she looked into the hall. Kate was disappearing through the front door, her hair flying behind her; she was wearing jeans, an extremely skimpy top and her highest heeled boots.

'Kate!' she shouted, running to open it again. 'Kate, where are you – '

But all that was left of Kate was a roar of exhaust and a screech of tyres; the Sax Bomb was just disappearing round the corner.

'Sorry, Mum.' It was Juliet, looking slightly shame-faced. 'She won't be long. She says she wants to talk to him. He rang again this morning. We couldn't tell you, because we knew you wouldn't let her go. She'll be back for lunch: promise. Shall I get that?' she said as the phone started to ring.

'No,' said Helen sharply. 'Let the machine pick it up. And –' as another female voice spoke, 'don't listen to it, Juliet. Please.'

But it was too late.

Jack Kirkland was raging. He had called Eliot, bawled him out. It was like having some ferocious father, thought Eliot, standing with the phone held away from his ear.

'What the hell do you think you're doing? At a time when we can't afford anything like this, anything at all when you've only just joined the party, I can't believe it!'

'Jack, I was only showing the bloody woman round. She's a constituent, for God's sake. She'd come to see Janet. Ask her, if you don't believe me.'

'So you take her down into The Crypt. On your own. What the hell for?'

'It's a fascinating place,' said Eliot, as firmly as he could.

'Oh, for Christ's sake,' said Kirkland, 'I wasn't born yesterday. God knows what harm this will do us. It may not be very serious in itself; in fact, I'm very inclined to believe you. But we simply can't have the faintest whisper of scandal. Not at the moment. They'll all swoop, you must realise that. Have you talked to Caroline yet?'

'No. On my way home now.'

'Let's hope she'll be her usual marvellous self.'

'I'm sure she will.'

'Speak to Martin. See if he can suggest anything.'

Martin Farrow was Centre Forward's publicity director; shrewd and confident. Eliot loathed him.

'Is that really necessary?'

'It's really necessary,' said Kirkland and put the phone down.

Eliot feared Martin would suggest a photo opportunity. Known in the trade now as a 'swinging gate', after the infamous picture of David Mellor and his family, in the wake of his affair with the actress Antonia de Sancha. Swinging Gates were vomit-inducing shots of the wronged wife cuddling up to her wronging

360

spouse, preferably surrounded by several children and a couple of labradors. Unfortunately he had all those things. Well, he wasn't going to do it. He just wasn't. Farrow would have to do better than that. But it was hard to think what.

Janet Frean was cooking lunch for her large family, when Jack Kirkland rang.

'Hello, Jack, how are you?'

'Not particularly good. Have you seen the *News*?'

'No. I try not to look at any of the papers on Sunday.'

'Well, there's an ugly little item about Eliot, saying that he was seen in the House of Commons crypt with an attractive lady, who was not his lovely blonde wife. And a rather feeble explanation from Eliot himself. Bloody vultures, I could kill them.'

Janet stood there, listening to him, and reflecting that no man could possibly stir gravy, hold a toddler and concentrate on an important conversation, all at the same time.

'So – what do you think?' said Jack.

'What?' She was chasing a stubborn lump of flour round the gravy tin. 'Oh, Jack, I don't know. I can't believe that of Eliot. Well – not any more. We all know about his past, but now – '

'Anyway, it's true, is it: he did bring this woman in to see you?'

'Yes, he did. I thought she was very nice. Very bright, she's a lawyer – '

'Yes, yes, so Eliot told me.'

'I liked her. And Eliot obviously did. Oh, sorry, shouldn't have said that. I just mean he liked her.'

'Is she pretty?'

'Very . . .'

'Eliot says she's divorced?'

'Oh, is she? Well, that won't help. Anyway that explains it: apparently he'd helped her put up some blinds. I thought that was very sweet of him.'

'Did you?' said Kirkland grimly. 'I'd have another word for it. Was anyone else around?'

'Well no, it was pretty quiet. Jack, he was just showing her round out of a sense of duty.'

'You just said he obviously liked her.'

'Did I? Sorry. Milly, don't do that – look, Jack, I have to go. I really don't think I can add to this discussion. And I've got a little bit of quality time with my family at last, and I want to make the most of it. I'm off on another leg of the Centre Forward charm offensive tomorrow. Don't worry about all this – it'll blow over.'

'Thank God I've got one morally sound member of my party!' said Kirkland, and rang off.

Kate returned, looking flushed and almost cheerful, at one o'clock. Juliet rushed her up to her room.

'Kate! There are people – women ringing – saying they're your mother. Can you believe that?'

'How do you know?'

'I heard one. On the answering machine. Mum's telling them all to ring the *Sketch*. They're dealing with them.'

'Dealing with them?' Kate shouted. 'What do you mean, dealing with them?'

'Getting rid of them, I s'pose.'

Kate stared at her. 'But Juliet, one of them might actually be my mother! How can they do that? How can they fucking do that?'

'Shush!' said Juliet.

Clio felt completely bewildered, almost shocked, by Jocasta's behaviour.

She had sent her off for a walk on the Hog's Back; she was on call that Sunday morning, but that evening they were going up to London together, to stay in Jocasta's house in Clapham.

The next day was important for Clio; she was having lunch with dear old Beaky, Professor Bryan. She had told Mark – hating to deceive him, when he'd been so kind – that she had to see her solicitor about the divorce. Which was true, she had arranged that too. She didn't have very high hopes of the job at the Bayswater, but she was determined to try. General practice in a country town was fine, if you had a life outside it; she didn't and she already felt the loneliness beginning to bite.

But as she drove from house to house, on her rounds, it was Jocasta, not her patients, claiming her concentration.

For someone of eighteen, like the blithely irresponsible

Jocasta she had first met, to turn her back on real life and run away with a rich man, yes, perhaps. But at thirty-five, with a flourishing career and a long-term relationship under her belt – oh, please! It seemed to Clio – only just beginning to recover from her own marriage break-up – that Jocasta was standing near a very large drain and pouring every treasure she possessed down it.

Gideon Keeble might be very charismatic and charming, in the way of extremely rich men; Jocasta might have been growing weary of waiting for Nick to put a ring on her finger, and the life of a tabloid reporter might be losing some of its charm. But did she really think she was going to find happiness in a way of life so totally unfamiliar to her?

Clio did realise, of course, that it was much harder for her to understand, not having met Keeble; he veered in her imagination between being a self-indulgent over-grown child who had to have everything he wanted, and a kind of evil enchanter, who had bewitched Jocasta and swept her away to his castle.

Well, sooner or later, providing the affair lasted – and Clio found herself devoutly hoping it wouldn't – she would meet Gideon Keeble, and then it might be easier for her to understand. She might even like him. But it did seem rather unlikely.

Jocasta still felt terribly guilty. She didn't seem to have done much for Kate, but then, who could? Kate's refusal to see her had hurt dreadfully; she obviously blamed her. God, it was a relief to be out of all that. All that potential for damage to people's lives. And Clio, so sensible and calm and kind. It had been so comforting, talking to her last night, confronting what had happened, all those years ago. She'd told Nick about it, but all the time running away from the memories. With Clio she had relived them; and it had been healing, in a way.

It was the screaming she would never forget; that raw, dreadful screaming. On and on it went, in rhythmic waves, through the night and half the next day. Every time she heard screaming now, she was back there, back in that room, with the stifling heat and noise of the fans . . .

Koh Pha Ngan had been filling up for days. Jocasta and several others had arrived on the island over a week before, had managed to get a decent hut on Hat Rin Sunrise, the party beach, basic, but at least clean and with a toilet; as the days went by, and boatloads of people went on and on arriving at the port, floors in people's outbuildings and even tarpaulins slung across a yard were being rented as sleeping space. On the day of the full moon party itself, apparently, boats would come into the bay, fleets of them, organised from Koh Samui, and anchor there overnight. The beach itself was packed, people sleeping there as well.

The evenings building up to the party were magical; little low tables were brought out by the bars onto the sand where they had been sitting all day, set with candles, and they would lounge there in the warm darkness far into the night, drinking beer or the disgusting rice wine, or a hooch peculiar to the islands, of cheap whisky and Coke. 'Get drunk on that,' one girl warned them happily 'and you'll have no idea what you've been doing in the morning.' And there they would stay, talking, talking, the only interruption coming from the hundreds of stray dogs on the island, in search of food, and trips into the bars for more drink.

The rave was an incredible experience; Jocasta stood at the heart of it, at about two in the morning, as yet another DJ took over, committing it to memory, while the massive crowds of people danced on the sand and in the water, glowing with luminous body paint, and all along the beach, the Thai boys, some as young as seven or eight, juggled with fire rings, huge hoops of fire you could roly-poly through, if you were drunk enough. Jocasta decided she wasn't – quite.

She met, in the darkness that night, what seemed like hundreds of people she knew, and then lost them again. Everyone was smoking dope, and drinking, but the real high, for Jocasta, was the sensation of being at one with a great tribe which she had joined, simply by virtue of being there. She felt completely in love with each and every one of them.

All night and half the following day it went on. By that evening, things had returned almost to normal and the extra boats had left the bay; Jocasta felt tired and vaguely out of sorts;

she and a girl called Jan, who she had befriended on a reggae boat trip, decided to go to bed early. She woke in the night to hear Jan moving round, in search of water.

'I've got a filthy headache,' she said, 'and it's not a hangover, it's worse than that. And I feel shivery too. Sort of clammy.'

As daylight came, she was complaining of pains in her legs and arms; and the shivering was worse. Jocasta told her to stay in bed, and offered to sponge her down. She was surprised when Jan accepted; she was usually a very self-contained girl, educated at Wycombe Abbey, with a place to read history at Cambridge.

As she sat there, offering Jan water, a little worried by her condition, she realised she had a very nasty headache herself.

Right through until the early evening it went on, the brilliant hot day outside a totally unsuitable backdrop to their wretchedness. Jocasta realised she was developing whatever Jan had, but roughly four hours behind her – the aching limbs, the shivering, the fever. It was awful, just watching her, seeing what lay ahead. A mounting fever, violent pain in the joints, vomiting, hallucinations; before she started hallucinating herself, Jocasta staggered out into the path by the huts and called someone over.

'Please try and get help,' she said. 'We're dying in here.'

He assumed it was a bad trip; fetched his mate. They managed to persuade him otherwise.

'Hang on. We'll see what we can do.'

They came back with a young Thai boy, who looked at them, sighed and shook his head sorrowfully.

'Dengue fever,' he said. 'You must go to clinic. I will help you.'

He fetched his father and a truck; together they managed to lift Jan – now more or less unconscious – into the back of it. Jocasta managed to crawl in beside her.

The noise, the heat struck Jocasta like a blow; she whined in pain, turned her head away from the light. The truck was started; the noise bored through her head.

And so it began, a nightmare journey across the island, on half-made-up roads much of the way, labouring up steep hills, trundling down again, the violent twists and turns, throwing them about in a bone-shaking agony. The sun beat down on them and it was very hot still, the road dusty, the noise awful. If there was a hell, Jocasta thought, this would be it. The pain in her limbs was frightful, and she vomited continually.

Dusk was falling as they pulled in to the hospital and nurses helped carry them in; they couldn't walk. They were placed on stretcher beds in Outpatients; it was all surprisingly modern, reassuring, a familiar, clean proper hospital. With a green lawn outside and a large sign proclaiming the word Hospital in English. Perhaps the worst was over, Jocasta thought, closing her eyes gratefully, as uniformed nurses in white plimsolls came and went, bringing her water, taking her temperature, talking cheerfully to one another in Thai.

Finally, the doctor came; he went off duty at four in the afternoon, the nurses explained in halting English, and only came back for emergencies. They assumed the emergency must be them, but it wasn't.

He confirmed the boy's diagnosis: dengue fever. 'From mosquito. You have been inland, to the jungle?'

Jocasta remembered the reggae boat trip and swinging joyfully on ropes across a lake. She managed to nod feebly.

'You must stay here. You will be better later on. We will give you something for the pain.'

They were put in a ward with six beds; it was very hot, in spite of the whirling fan.

In a corner, behind screens, an old woman was dying, surrounded by weeping relatives. And in the bed next to Jocasta was a girl who was having a baby.

All night she screamed; tore at her hair, at her own skin, at the sheet her mother had knotted to the bed head for her to hold onto. And she prayed to die.

Jocasta followed her agony: the rise and fall of her contractions, their increasing frequency, their growing strength. Her mother was sponging her down, making soothing noises, trying to make her sip something. As it grew light, she got worse, screaming endlessly, biting and kicking like a terrified horse, whenever a nurse or a doctor tried to examine her.

The mother spoke a little English; Jocasta, feeling slightly better, compelled to become involved, asked if there was nothing anyone could do.

'No, no, baby not come yet,' she said, with a sweet, patient smile.

At last, the nurse came back with a doctor and, together with her mother, they managed to get the girl's desperately heaving body onto a stretcher.

As she was taken out of the room, the girl looked back at Jocasta; she looked like an old woman, her hair drenched with sweat, her face contorted, and in her great dark eyes, Jocasta saw agony and absolute terror. In some strange way she felt she was absorbing both.

The doctor spoke quickly to the mother; she nodded and started to follow them.

'What?' Jocasta said to her. 'What now?'

'Baby breech,' she said. 'Baby stuck.'

Jocasta called out to the nurse: 'Can't you help her?'

'We do help,' she said. 'Forceps now.'

Jocasta turned her head and buried it in her hard pillow, but she could hear her still, for over an hour, the dreadful, raw animal screaming: and then a sudden awful silence.

And then the mother appeared, weeping, to pick up her own belongings. She looked at Jocasta, and struggled to smile.

'Baby dead,' she said.

'Oh no,' said Jocasta. It seemed dreadful to think, after all that suffering, that the cause of it was dead. She began to cry, her own weak state making it all seem worse.

'I'm so sorry. And your daughter?'

'Oh we hope,' said the woman and managed the light Thai giggle, 'but – not so good.'

Later she came back. 'She dead too,' she said almost brightly. 'Lose too much blood.'

Those words had never left Jocasta.

Chapter 25

All she had to do was keep completely calm. Nothing could happen, if she did that. No one could possibly think she had the slightest connection with this rather sensational story in the tabloid press. There was no connection. None at all. The only person who might think there was anything disturbing her was Ed, because he had been so close to her. But he couldn't be any more. He would have to be out of her life. And then she would be safe. As long as she kept calm. Perfectly calm.

And not even look at the tabloids for the next few days. And certainly not at any pictures of that girl.

Kate had called Jocasta as she waited for Clio; she sounded very shaky.

She said she was sorry she'd been so rude to Jocasta and that she totally believed that Jocasta had had nothing to do with the story.

'I was just upset. It was all such a – a shock.'

'Of course it was. I was so sorry for you. The pictures were lovely,' she added carefully.

'Yeah, well. Pity about the rest. But it's not so bad, I s'pose. I don't have to go to school at the moment, because I'm on study leave, so I can avoid the really cowy girls. But I need your help really badly, Jocasta. All these women keep ringing up, saying they're my mother, about a dozen of them now, and I'm so scared one of them really is my mother, after all this, and I'm going to miss her. I just don't know what to do.'

'Well, I'm sure the paper will be keeping names and so on.'

'Yes, but I need to – to know,' said Kate desperately. 'I can't lose her now. And what about the model agencies, what should I do about that? Mum is so totally no use, and Dad's gone completely ballistic, and Juliet said we should ask you. Could you help, do you think? Please, Jocasta, please.'

Jocasta was so touched by this plea that she was half inclined to rush straight over to Ealing and the Tarrants, but she called Gideon and he had wiser counsel.

'You can't do it, Jocasta, don't be insane. You're too involved and the responsibility is just too much. And very dangerous. Now listen, I have the very man for you.'

'Gideon's such an angel. You can't imagine,' Jocasta said to Clio. 'He's so kind and so concerned for me. I'm so lucky. Just wait till you meet him, Clio, you really will love him, I promise.'

'I'm sure I will,' said Clio carefully.

'Meanwhile, you're going to meet a friend of his. Who's going to sort Kate out. Gideon's going to get him to call me. His name's Fergus Trehearn.'

Fergus Trehearn was Ireland's answer to Max Clifford, Jocasta explained to a rather bemused Clio, 'Only he operates from here now. Not quite so successfully. But – well, anyway . . . You must know about Max Clifford,' she added, seeing Clio's puzzled face. Clio said humbly that she didn't and when she had heard what Max Clifford did – 'He sort of manipulates everybody including the press – ' she said she was surprised that anyone should want to.

'Oh, Fergus is a complete sweetheart, apparently,' said Jocasta, 'and Kate certainly needs him. She – they just can't cope with it all. Fergus will take the whole thing on, sorting all these women out, getting Kate the best contract with a model agency, deal with offers from other papers and magazines for her story – '

'She won't want anything like that, will she?' said Clio.

'Not at the moment, no. But the thing is, you see, as far as the media is concerned, Kate will be Abandoned Baby Bianca for the rest of her life. Any story about her will refer to it and maybe one day, who knows, she might want to tell her story. And if her mother turns up – well. That could be huge. Anyway, she needs her interests protected. Fergus will draw up contracts, all that sort of thing. Stop unscrupulous people taking advantage of her. And her parents. Anyway, I said Fergus should come to my house. You don't mind, do you?'

'Of course not,' said Clio bravely.

The last thing she wanted was to have to meet some flashy gold-medallion man and sit and listen to him talking about manipulating the press.

But it was not a medallion man who sat in Jocasta's untidy sitting room, listening carefully to her as she talked; it was someone charming and courteous and extremely well dressed, in a linen suit. He was in his early forties, tall, slim, and extremely good-looking, with close-cropped grey hair, and very dark brown eyes. He was Irish, garrulous, and funny and she found it hard not to like him. Jocasta introduced her as her brilliant friend who was a consultant physician and he appeared duly impressed, even as she protested and said she was nothing of the sort.

His manner, as he listened, was concerned, and sweetly interested. It completely belied the ruthless opportunism that drove him. No one would have thought that this Fergus Trehearn, gently sympathetic over the dreadful wickedness of Carla Giannini, hardly able indeed to believe the depths of her treachery, was the same one who had conducted a telephone auction between two major newspapers, for the story of a beautiful refugee girl from Bosnia who had become a call girl (under cover of a chambermaid's job at a West End hotel) and then staged a roasting by a posse of drunken footballers; or who had negotiated a hefty media deal for a young couple arrested for, and duly acquitted of, having sex on the hard shoulder of the M25.

'He will be perfect for Kate,' Jocasta said to Clio happily, after he had gone, 'absolutely perfect, keep all the sharks at bay and make her lots of money. And what's more I know he'll be able to persuade the Tarrants. Isn't he a sweetheart?'

Jocasta called the Tarrants, explained what Fergus did and begged them to see him. Helen, exhausted and still deeply distressed, finally agreed. Jim said he would personally throw him out of the house, but Helen was learning to ignore such threats. They had to get through this somehow and it sounded as if Fergus Trehearn might be able to help. An appointment was fixed for six on Monday evening.

'I know it's a little late,' he said apologetically to Helen, 'but that's the earliest I can manage. Do you have any of those inky vultures at your gate now?'

Helen, who had thought she would never smile again, recognised this as a description of the press and actually laughed.

'They've gone,' she said, 'but we're still getting so many calls.'

'I'll take them all off you,' he said, 'if you'll let me. I'll see you at six, Mrs Tarrant, and your husband too, of course. And after we have talked, then, if you're happy with me, I'll meet your beautiful daughter.'

'He'd deal with the press,' said Helen to Jim, 'and the women. And Kate. With all these offers we keep getting.'

'And what's that going to cost us?' said Jim. 'Don't tell me he's doing it out of the goodness of his heart.'

'I'll ask Jocasta,' said Helen uncertainly. She hadn't thought of this.

'Oh, that's a really good idea,' said Jim, his voice heavily sarcastic. 'They're probably hand in glove. You can see him if you like, Helen, but I won't. And don't expect a penny out of me for him, either.'

Helen sighed and went out of the room to telephone Jocasta.

Jocasta was very reassuring about the money.

'He won't want any, unless Kate starts to do well as a model,' she said, 'then he'll probably act as her agent and take a percentage. They work on a sort of no win, no fee basis, like all the lawyers are doing now.'

Had Helen been even slightly worldlier she might have found this a little suspicious; she was not to know that Gideon Keeble had already agreed to pay Fergus's bill, until something was resolved with Kate.

'And if it isn't, I'll still do it,' Gideon said to Jocasta. 'It's a very small price to pay, my darling, for you to be sounding happier.'

'Gideon, I don't know how to thank you,' said Jocasta.

'Oh, I'll show you,' he said, 'when I get back from Barbados.'

* * *

371

'Look,' said Martha, 'I'm sorry. I've said at least three times now. I can't go away to Venice. Not at the moment. I don't know why you can't accept that.'

It had taken her all day to bring herself to make this call; and every word that she said hurt more than the last. She kept seeing him, sitting there, confused, bewildered by the change in her, and she didn't quite know how to bear it. But it had to be done.

Suppose he'd read about it, asked her about it even, said he couldn't imagine anyone doing such a thing. Or said how dreadful, how awful the mother must be.

No, it was very clear. The need for control was back. And to be in control, you had to be independent, answerable to no one. Ed loved her. And she loved him. And love was powerful, when it came to secrets. Huge, dangerous secrets. It saw them, it found them out.

She took another deep breath.

'So – I can't go to Venice. Is that all right?'

'Of course it's not all right! Two days ago you said you could.' Ed's voice was very quiet. 'What's changed?'

'Nothing's changed, Ed. I can't go just now, please understand that. I'm sorry.'

'Yeah, so sorry you couldn't even be arsed to call me all weekend, didn't return my calls. Why not, Martha, would you just tell me that?'

'There just wasn't an opportunity . . .'

'Oh, right. All weekend. Not a single five-minute – what do you call it? Oh, yes, window, not a five-minute window to pick up your fucking phone and say hi, Ed, sorry I can't talk now, I'll ring later. Is that right?'

'Yes,' she said and her voice was so cool, so steady, it amazed her, 'yes that's right.'

'Oh, for fuck's sake,' he said suddenly, 'I've had enough of this. Don't you care that I was worried out of my skull? Don't you?' His voice was less angry, was cracked with pain.

'Yes, of course I care, Ed, but as I told you, I – '

'You're made of fucking stone,' he said, 'you know that?'

She was silent for a moment; then she said: 'Ed, I really don't like being abused like this. If you can't cope with my life and the way I am, then we would do far better to end this whole thing.'

'What whole thing?'

'Our relationship, of course.'

'Relationship!' he said. 'You call what we have a relationship? Right now, I'd call it a load of bullshit, Martha, total fucking bullshit. You tell me what to do and say and think, where to be and when, and I just tag along behind you, licking your arse. Well, you can find someone else to lick it, because I'm finding it extremely tedious all of a sudden. OK?'

And he slammed the phone down.

Martha sat for a long time, completely still, just staring at it. Wanting more than anything to pick it up again, fighting the instinct to say she was sorry, she hadn't meant it, and she loved him, wanted to see him.

But she couldn't. It was too dangerous.

By the end of the weekend, Kate was feeling better. She couldn't help it. Yes, it had been awful, the shock; yes, she felt hideously ashamed still, that everyone knew what had happened to her, that everyone must be pointing her out, saying that's the girl whose mother just threw her away, and she still felt as if she was walking down the road with all her clothes off, totally naked and exposed; and yes, it was horrible to have trusted someone like Carla and then found yourself just totally let down. It was appalling to think that one of those women who had phoned up might be her birth mother, and that she was having to wait quietly when the most tumultuous discovery in her life might be within reach. She wanted to rush into the offices of the *Sketch*, and just demand to see the list, see the women, organise the DNA testing. But it was also quite nice, she had to admit, to have not just the *Sketch* but papers like the *Sunday Times* describing you with words like beautiful and dazzling, and to see your pictures in them, as well.

And to have model agencies ringing up, asking you to go and see them, and even magazines, asking if they could come and interview you – that was pretty cool.

And then there was Nat. It had almost been worth it all, to have Nat calling her twice a day and taking her out in the Sax Bomb and saying what about going to the Fridge this Saturday. She'd said that would be cool, that she'd most definitely come;

she'd worry about her parents and what they might say when the time came. The thing they didn't understand – that nobody seemed to understand – was what a nice person Nat was. The first thing he'd said when she'd got in the car was, 'You all right?' and, 'Yes,' she'd said, yes, she was fine, thank you. And he'd said, 'I meant about the story in the paper, like, about your mum,' and it had completely wiped her out, that he'd understood how she might be feeling, had actually thought about it. He'd obviously read the article properly, because he'd said, with that grin of his, that he'd liked the way she'd talked about his clothes and his car.

Then he leant forward and started to kiss her; he was a very, very good kisser. Nice and slow and careful, his tongue moving round, sort of stroking hers. Kate hadn't experienced good kissing before and it was wonderful. They were parked on the edge of a park, under some trees; it was terribly romantic.

'You going to do more of this modelling, then?' he said, when he had finally finished, and lit a cigarette.

'Course,' she said.

'Cool. I wouldn't mind coming along, if they ever wanted a bloke,' he added.

Kate said she didn't know how it worked, but she could ask, if the occasion arose.

'Yeah, right,' he said, and drove her home in silence. Or as close to silence as the Red Hot Chilli Peppers, at top volume, would permit.

'So – are you looking forward to your lunch with your professor tomorrow?' Jocasta asked.

'Half. And half dreading it. I keep thinking he's asked me to lunch to soften the blow, to say there's no point my applying for the job.'

'I really don't think people spend money giving you bad news,' said Jocasta. 'Polite little notes, more like it. No, he wants to encourage you. Goodness, Clio, a consultant. I shall be proud to know you.'

'I'll be pretty proud to know me, too. If I am one again.'

The only place she felt pleased with herself was at work. It was odd: she felt somehow in charge when she was working; it was like going downhill on a bicycle, after struggling up the other side, not easy exactly, but exhilarating, everything running smoothly and to order. She sighed; Jocasta looked at her.

'You'll be fine,' she said, 'I know you will. Let's go for a drink. Just a few quiet ones.'

They went out to one of the pubs on the common, sat outside in the gathering dusk. A sliver of moon was rising gently into the turquoise sky, the sun a vast display of crimson, hugging the horizon.

'It's like a child showing off,' said Jocasta. 'Look at it, saying let me stay, let me stay. Do you remember those sunsets in Thailand, Clio, so unbelievably dramatic, especially when it had been raining? I must take Gideon to Thailand, he'd love it.'

Like everyone in love, she managed to bring every discussion round to the subject of the beloved.

'I can't wait for you to meet him. You'll really love him. He's so – so exciting. And so interested in absolutely everything. I mean, he'd be talking about your work right now, getting really involved.'

'Really?'

'Yes, he really would.'

'Don't you ever miss Nick?' asked Clio curiously. 'He seemed so lovely to me.'

'He *was* lovely. Just not lovely enough. And the way I love Gideon is quite unlike anything I felt before. For anybody. It's so – so violent, Clio. It's just – taken me over. I just feel I'm where I ought to be, when I'm with him. It's as simple as that. I didn't feel like that with Nick. I thought I did, but I didn't.'

'But you had so much in common with Nick and you cared so much about your work. What are you going to do, Jocasta, just stop working altogether, be with Gideon wherever he is?'

'Yes, probably,' said Jocasta vaguely, 'I haven't even thought about it.'

'Martha, are you all right?'

Paul Quenell's voice seemed to be coming from far away. It was a long time since Martha had felt like this: swimmy-headed, clammy and as if she was going to be sick. Probably not since she had been at St Andrews for early communion, and having terrible period pains. She sat down abruptly.

'Yes,' she said, 'yes, I'm fine. Thank you. Just a bit – a bit – sorry, Paul.'

What was it doing here, on his desk, the *Sunday Times*, open at the article about – about – Was he going to show it to her, ask if she knew anything about it?

'Jane,' he called through the open door, 'bring a glass of water in, would you?' And then, gently stern, 'You've been working too hard.'

'Well, yes, maybe just a bit.'

'It's all this extra-curricular stuff,' he said, and smiled his swift apology of a smile, 'you shouldn't do it, you know.'

'Maybe not.'

'Thanks, Jane. Just put it down there. You can take this now . . .' He folded the paper, held it out to his long-suffering secretary. 'I've seen all I needed.' All he needed? Why should he need anything? What did it have to do with him? She felt hot, violently sick again.

'Jane spotted this piece about the new senior partner at Kindersleys.' Paul sat down at his desk again. 'Hannah Roberts, one of these superwomen, five children at least. Come across her?'

'Once or twice,' she said, and relief flooded her, cool, soothing relief.

'Anyway, I'm going to stop the extra-curricular stuff for a day or two. I'm sending you on a little trip. Not a long one, a week at the most. But you should be able to grab a couple of days of rest out of it.'

'A trip? Where?'

It was actually the last thing she wanted; she only felt safe doing completely familiar things, in completely familiar places. Even going to a new restaurant the day before had been unsettling.

'Sydney.'

'Sydney!'

It couldn't have been worse. That was where – when –

She hauled herself back to the present. 'Why?'

'You don't look as pleased as I hoped. It's such a wonderful place. You've been there, I presume?'

'No! Well – ' She mustn't start lying. That could become very dangerous. 'Well, only for about two days. Long ago. On my way somewhere else.'

'Oh I see. Well, you'll love it. It's on Mackenzie business, of course.'

'Of course.' She was regaining her cool now, back in control, Mackenzie was a world-wide property chain – 'intergalactic' as Paul had once said. 'They've got some massive new takeover in their sights on the waterfront over there, they need advice.'

'Can't the Sydney office manage?'

'Of course. But Donald wants someone from London. He likes to see us earning our fees, as you know.'

Martha smiled. 'I do indeed.' Donald Mackenzie was famous for querying every invoice.

'He asked for me, then when I said it was out of the question, he specified you. I'll get Jane to book your flight and hotel.'

On her way back to her own office, she felt dizzy again; she managed to make the ladies and sat on a loo seat for a long time, her head between her knees.

Just keep calm, Martha; just keep calm . . .

'None of those women had left names.' Fergus Trehearn smiled at Kate. 'And of course, no numbers or addresses.'

'Oh,' she said. She wasn't sure how she felt: disappointed, she supposed.

'The thing is,' he said gently, 'it's a criminal offence, abandoning a baby. So they're not going to be terribly upfront about themselves. Although they may not have understood that. But each and every one of them failed the nappy test. Most of them said it had been a disposable nappy, a few had apparently put a towelling one on you . . .'

'Yes, I see.' She felt dreadfully bleak. It somehow underlined her poor, destitute, baby self, not just that she had had no nappy on, but that this fact was being used in this horrible mechanical way to catch her would-be mother out. All her would-be mothers.

'I'm sorry,' he said, 'this must be so difficult for you. But I think I can assure you that you haven't missed your real mother. Whoever she is, she hasn't declared herself.'

'What about the first few? Before we thought about the nappy thing? One of them might have been her.'

'Kate, if that is true, she will call again. She's not going to give up at the first hurdle.'

'She might. It might have taken all her courage to make that one call, and then when – when – ' She fought back the tears.

'Well, that is a possibility, of course,' said Fergus gently. 'But I think a remote one. And Kate, it is still possible that you will hear. Very possible. People behave strangely under pressure. Any sort of pressure. And I'm no psychiatrist, but I would imagine that if you've kept something like this to yourself for sixteen years, it could be pretty difficult suddenly to acknowledge it. It might seem better to wait until the fuss has begun to die down. And then again, I suppose, she might not have seen the article immediately.'

'Not very likely,' said Kate. 'It's been in most of the papers. And mentioned on the radio as well.'

'Indeed. Now that is a relevant observation – *Woman's Hour* are very eager to do something about it, to talk to you, Helen, and to Kate – '

'No,' said Helen sharply.

'Why not?' said Kate. 'Just why exactly not?'

'Because I don't want this thing prolonged,' said Helen wearily. 'You've been upset enough, Kate, and – '

'So it's over, is it?' said Kate. 'I hadn't realised that. What do you mean, Mum, for God's sake? You don't want it prolonged! How ridiculous is that? What about me? Yeah, I've been upset. But if anything good comes out of it at all, it'll be finding my mother. And I think the radio would be good. I could say what I wanted, not what the paper said I had. Like I really want to see her still.'

'It's a very nice programme, Helen,' said Fergus. 'Jenni Murray is a superb interviewer – she's very gentle with her interviewees, and very sensitive about her material. If Kate still hopes to find her mother, then it could be a good way forward. There's something very honest about radio. As Kate says, they can't distort your words. She could make a direct appeal to her mother. It could be very emotive. But – Kate, if your mum doesn't like the idea, then it would be wrong for you, too.'

He moved into safer territory: both the *Sun* and the *Mirror* wanted interviews, but he thought not. 'You'll just get more of the sensationalism, and I think you've had enough of that,' and several model agencies wanted to see her, three of them really good ones.

'And –' Helen hesitated, fearing another outburst from Kate, 'are we sure about – about the modelling?'

'Mum! What do you mean, are we sure? It's something I can do, make lots of money, be successful, all that sort of thing!'

'But Kate, what about your exams?'

'Oh God! Mum, I'll do my exams. Of course I will.'

'And college?'

'Well – maybe. I'll see. Point is – '

'The point is,' said Fergus, sweetly reasonable, 'she can do her modelling in the holidays. Work round her college terms. A lot of girls do that.'

'Do they?' Helen looked slightly less distraught.

'Fergus,' said Kate suddenly, 'will you be my agent? Do I have to go to one of these other places?'

'Well – I don't know . . .' Fergus's voice was heavily cautious. No one would have suspected that this was what he had been hoping for, ever since Gideon Keeble had contacted him, the long-term reward from this project: this and a good publishing deal for the whole story, when the mother turned up. As he was sure she would. It was a fantastic story; it could be a big money spinner. And the more famous Kate was, the bigger it would be. For the time being, that must be his goal. He smiled modestly. 'I'm not familiar with the fashion scene, you know, and – '

'Couldn't you find out? It would be so much nicer. Wouldn't it, Mum? We trust you, I feel like we've known you forever.'

'I have to tell you, I think you might do better with a conventional agency – although there are precedents, of course. Twiggy – you've heard of Twiggy I expect . . . ?'

'Yeah, course. She was in a magazine the other day; she's really old now, isn't she? But she still looks OK.'

'Well, anyway, she wasn't with a standard agency. Her boyfriend managed her very successfully, and he was a hair-dresser.'

'There you are. Oh, Fergus, please, I'd like it so much and so would Mum, wouldn't you?'

'But there would be one important condition, Kate,' said Fergus, and his voice was quite stern. 'You must do your very best in your exams. They're very important. Very important indeed. You could regret throwing away your chances. Things change, and not every girl who is spotted by a fashion editor makes it big time. I would be very unhappy if you started doing any modelling at all, until those are over. What would you say to that?'

'I'd say cool,' said Kate with a shrug. 'As long as they don't all forget about me.'

'Don't worry about that,' said Fergus. 'I won't let them forget about you, Kate, not for a single moment. Now, you and your mum have your little conversation and let me know what you decide about *Woman's Hour*.'

Clio felt very tired when she got home: not sure if she was happy or not. The lunch with Beaky had been wonderful; he had told her how much she had been missed and how he hoped very much that she would apply for the consultant's job.

'I've got a very good team there,' he said. 'Keen, clever, mostly young. I can hardly bear to think of leaving it. You'd fit in jolly well, Clio. We've got a couple of research projects going, we're doing some trials with a new Alzheimer drug and we've got a wonderful new psychiatric chap.'

'It does sound wonderful,' she said wistfully, 'but – do you really think I'm up to it?'

'Clio! Is this really the brightest new consultant in the department for years talking? You do put yourself down, dear girl, and you really mustn't do it. I wouldn't have invited you to apply, if I didn't think you were absolutely up to it, as you put it. As far as I can see, you're the perfect candidate. You're familiar with the hospital and the workings of the department, you did very well when you were here, everyone liked you – and from what you tell me, you've done a lot of geriatric work while you've been in general practice. And I'm sure you can slot back into the rotation system, no one's going to object on procedural grounds.'

'Good,' said Clio. 'I was worrying about that a bit.'

'No need.' He patted her hand. 'Not enough people going into geriatrics. We need you.'

'How are you coping with all the targets and tables and so on these days?' she said. 'We're protected from that in general practice, to a degree at least. They're clearly getting worse every year.'

'Oh, we manage all right. Now one thing you must do – I'd very strongly advise it anyway – is visit a couple of the outlying hospitals, see what's going on there. Before your interview board, that is.'

She smiled at him. 'You seem very sure I'll get an interview.'

'Of course you will.'

She left him, promising to apply, and made her way to the solicitor's office.

She had been warned it would be wretched: it was. It was one thing to agree, however sadly, that your marriage was over; it was quite another to find yourself in an adversarial situation, picking over the balance sheet of that marriage. She had agreed that she wouldn't contest the divorce and had expected a certain generosity in return; but Jeremy was even querying her right to a share of the house, claiming she had walked out on a marriage that she had entered into under false pretences.

'Don't worry, Mrs Graves, they all start like this.' Her solicitor, a very nice sympathetic woman, smiled at her encouragingly. 'He'll come down.' She passed Clio a tissue from the box on the desk between them. 'It's horrid. I know.'

'I put so much work into that house,' said Clio, blowing her nose. 'Sorry about this.'

'It's all right. I never remember having a preliminary consultation over divorce when the tissues weren't needed. And of course you worked hard on the house.'

'And I paid for a lot of the work on it,' said Clio.

'I know. Don't worry. We'll get you everything that's due to you . . .'

'I missed you,' said Gideon. 'Very much.'

They were lying in bed; he had returned from Barbados, leaving an extremely contented Fionnuala behind him, the owner of three superb polo ponies.

'She was very pleased,' he said, 'and most affectionate. It was all very sweet.'

'I expect it was,' said Jocasta and hoped her voice didn't sound barbed.

It was very early in the morning; they were in his London house, in Kensington Palace Gardens. It had slightly shocked Jocasta, that house: shocked and almost intimidated her. It could only be described as a mansion, a five-year-old Palladian-style mansion, complete with a ballroom, several vast reception rooms, a staff flat, and ten bedrooms. It was a very strong statement, about its owner, about the sort of money he had and the sort of taste. Excessive, in all cases: did a man with almost no family really need ten bedrooms?

'I missed you too,' she said. 'Terribly.'

'I'm pleased to hear it. I would have liked to think you were terribly unhappy. Oh God – ' he pushed the sheet back, sat up and studied her, 'you are the most beautiful thing. I can't imagine what you're doing with an old man like me.'

'I love you,' she said, 'old as you are. Believe it or not. I just love you. I can't imagine how I got through even a week of my life without you, never mind thirty-five years. It seems most peculiar.'

'I was thinking, while you were away,' he said, bending down and kissing first one breast, then the other, 'thinking how you told me you loved me, and thinking how much I loved you, and that neither of us really knew the other at all.'

'I thought that, too. But I feel I do. I feel I've known you always. I feel I know everything about you. How ridiculous is that?'

'Very ridiculous. And very dangerous. You may have discovered some of my virtues. My vices are mercifully a closed book to you.'

'Oh, I don't know. I know you're quite ruthless. I know you have a terrible temper. I know you can be stubborn – '

'That's quite enough. I don't like this game.'

'We can talk about my vices, if you like, if that'll make you feel better.'

'And what are they? I thought you had none.'

'OK. I'm impatient. Self-centred. Cowardly. I dread pain. I'm terribly easily bored. And then I'm vain – '

'With good reason.'

'Thank you. And generally rather silly.'

'Silliness is not a vice. I rather encourage it in myself. Let's do virtues now. You're clever. Imaginative. Tender-hearted. Beautiful . . .'

'That's not a virtue. That's a bit of luck. Let's do yours. You're generous and generous-hearted. Kind. Thoughtful. And – I like the way you care about everything so much.'

It was true: he sought the highest standards in everything; he said that was what life was for, to find the best. From the houses he lived in, to the clothes he wore, from the food he ate and the wine he drank, to the way he travelled and the people he employed, everything must meet not just his approval, but his high approval.

'Otherwise what is the point?' he would say.

'Anyway, the States next week. Looking forward to it?'

'Of course. So much. I plan to shop for England. And Ireland.'

'That's my girl.'

Martha got out of the cab, went into her building, pressed the lift button. She felt just a little better: her life almost whole again. She had had a very good meeting with Paul, she was on top of her work, her assistant and her trainee were well briefed for the following week, and the night before she had actually managed to sleep with only one sleeping pill.

No journalist had rung her; and after – what – three days, it didn't seem likely that they would.

The only thing was – of course – how much she was still hurting over Ed. It was awful; it was like the pain of a burn, searing, shocking, beyond the reach of any analgesic. It woke her up, that pain; disturbed her as she worked, dug into her consciousness at the most unexpected times.

But it would pass: of course it would. It had to. There was no alternative. And he seemed to have accepted it; there had been no phone calls, no appearances in reception, no e-mails. Just – nothing.

She was leaving her apartment at five-thirty in the morning, so that she could go to the gym; with twenty-one hours on the plane ahead of her, she would need that. She was actually looking

383

forward to the trip now that she had it all properly under control.

And going away now seemed, suddenly and surprisingly, what she needed.

She poured herself a glass of mineral water and carried it into her bedroom, to finish her packing. She had just pulled fourteen pairs of pants (two for each day) out of a drawer when the doorbell rang. That would be the papers Paul had promised to have sent round that night, extra background information on Mackenzie's, so that she could study them in bed.

She went to her door, pushed the buzzer.

'Yes?'

But it wasn't papers; it was Ed.

'You can't stay,' she said, staring at him, as he stood in her hallway, thinking with complete irrelevance that he looked absolutely wonderful, wearing an open-necked white shirt and jeans, like someone in a film. 'I'm packing, I've got a plane to catch.'

'I don't care if you've got a fucking rocket to catch,' he said, 'I want to know what's going on. Something's happened, Martha, hasn't it? I don't care what it is, I don't care if you're in love with someone else, I don't care if you're terminally ill – well that's bollocks, of course I care, but I've just got to know. I can't stand it. You've got to tell me.'

'Nothing's happened,' she said, fists clenched, meeting his eyes with considerable courage, for what might he read there? 'Nothing's happened at all. I'm just – just terribly busy. I'm going to Sydney tomorrow.'

'Sydney? How long for?'

'Just a week. We have a client there. A very important client,' she added firmly.

'Martha, for fuck's sake, what is it? What's happened to you? You've got to tell me, I'm not going away until you do.'

'Nothing's happened,' she said, and she was quite frightened now, he looked so desperate.

'Martha,' he said very quietly, 'I love you. I know you really rather well. I know every inch of you. Literally. I know how you are when you're happy and when you're upset and when you're stressed and when you want sex, and I know when you want to talk and when you want to be quiet and when you're feeling rotten and tired and mean. And I know something's happened to you – I *know* it. This is not about you being busy. It's about you being scared. What are you scared of, Martha? You've got to tell me. What have you done? Nothing you did could shock me, or upset me, unless it was falling in love with someone else. I'd have to get over that, but at least I'd know. Is that it, is there somebody else?'

'No,' she said, very quietly, 'there's no one else.'

'So – what is it?'

She was silent.

'Martha, look at me. Tell me what's fucking happened.'

And just for a moment she wanted to tell him. Just to get it over, just to know that someone else knew, it wasn't locked away, struggling to escape, this awful, dreadful shocking thing, that she had denied for so long, managed to contain, this fearful obscene monster. Just to be able to say to someone what should I do, where can I go, where shall I start? Instead of crushing it, endlessly, pulping it to –

But she couldn't.

'Nothing's happened,' she said finally and then, 'You must excuse me, I don't feel very well.'

And she rushed into her bathroom, slammed the door, and was violently sick, over and over again, and then sat on the lavatory, shivering and shaking, awful pain driving through her stomach, wondering how she could ever go out of the room again.

She heard him knocking on the door, very gently, calling through it; and she made a supreme effort, washed her face and cleaned her teeth and walked out, facing him, trying to smile into his concern.

'Sorry,' she said. 'I'm so sorry.'

And that was when he had said it: the worst thing he could possibly have said.

'Martha, you're not pregnant, are you?'

She started to laugh; weak hysterical laughter that turned, in time, to tears, shaking her head from side to side, avoiding his eyes. He helped her into the sitting room, sat her down on the sofa, sat watching her as she wept and wailed and keened, like some wild, primitive woman; and then finally as she quietened, he came to sit next to her and put his arms round her, drew her head onto his shoulder. She sat there, briefly sweetly at peace, where she wanted to be, and she picked up his hand and intertwined it with her own, then raised it to her lips and kissed it.

'Thank you,' she said, 'thank you so much. I'm sorry.'

'Oh, Martha,' he said, kissing her hand in return, 'I wish you could trust me. Whatever it is you've done, I would understand and I would forgive you. And I shall find out, you know. I'll find out somehow. I won't leave you alone until I do, and I won't leave you alone, even then. I think you need me.'

'No,' she said, summoning up all her will, releasing his hand, moving slightly from him, 'no, I don't. I don't need you, Ed. And you certainly don't need me.'

'That's where you're wrong,' he said, 'I do need you. We need each other. I'm going now. But when you get back – when is that, next weekend?'

She nodded feebly.

'I'll be here for you. Don't think I won't; don't think I'll give up. I love you too much. Now go to bed and get some sleep, for God's sake. Shall I stay? In here, I mean?' he added, with a faint touch of a smile.

'No,' she said, 'of course not. You must go. But – thank you for the offer. You're very kind, Ed. Very kind indeed.'

'No,' he said, 'not kind at all. I keep telling you. I love you.'

And then he was gone.

She was awake all night. She had set her alarm for five, but she watched the hours, the quarter hours; she felt appalling fear, her heart pounding, her stomach churning. She was sick again: more than once. She had never felt so alone: not even in that dreadful tiled room, in appalling pain, pushing her baby out in abject terror, looking at it.

No, Martha, don't think about that, that of all things, never, ever that. Don't think about that face, that puckered anguished face, so peaceful when you left it, fast asleep. Don't remember, don't, don't.

When the alarm went off, finally, she was sitting on her bed, her head in her arms, trying not to remember.

It was the first time her own will had failed her. She couldn't stand, couldn't walk, even across the room. She shook, in every part of her body, shook violently. She was first hot, then cold. Her head ached, she could hardly see. She lay down on the bed, pulled the sheet over her, closed her eyes. She would stay there, just for an hour. She didn't have to go to the gym, she could get into the office at seven. Or even eight. Eight would be fine, everything was done.

But at seven and at eight, she was still helpless, her body uselessly disobedient; it would not stand or sit, it would not even turn in bed. She managed to put an arm out to put the radio on, heard John Humphrys' wonderful, reassuring voice, like a comforting presence in the room; and then fell suddenly asleep, drifting in and out of dreams, horrible stifling dreams, about obscene creatures behind half-open doors and hiding and falling and darkness and blood. And then woke, finally, to the sound of her daughter's voice.

Chapter 26

Well, at least it was over. She had got through it somehow. It was true what everyone had said, Jenni Murray made them feel wonderfully relaxed and at home, so much so that she had almost forgotten there were millions of people out there, listening to them. Kate, of course, had been fine, chatting easily away, wonderfully composed. Where did that come from, Helen wondered wearily, lying back in the car the BBC had kindly provided, that self-confidence, that ability to deal with unfamiliar situations, and then thought, how absurd a question: from one of her parents, obviously.

One of the worst things, she felt, was that she had become relegated to some kind of second-division, no longer properly Kate's mother, no longer in charge of her life. Kate no longer seemed her child, seemed not a child at all, indeed, but a newly created being, making her own decisions, constructing her own future.

Tomorrow she was going out with Nat Tucker to a club in Brixton; she had said, perfectly politely but very firmly, that he had asked her and she would like to go. Given everything that was happening to her, it seemed a little absurd to try to stop her. They had compromised on a 2 a.m. latest return; she had hoped Nat would object to that, and the thing would be cancelled, but he had apparently said it was cool. Cool. Helen often thought she would scream if she heard that word once more.

She had to admit she had been wrong about Nat; his manners were on the primitive side, but he always said hello to her when she answered the door, and asked her how she was doing, and ground out his cigarette butt on the path before coming into the house. And he was very sweet with Kate.

He came round most days, but not until after tea; he seemed to have a great respect for Kate's academic future.

'I know she's got her exams to do,' he'd say, as Helen apologised for her non-appearance.

The fact that Kate was more likely to be applying a sixth coat of mascara, than rehearsing her French verbs, never seemed to occur to him.

A very nice researcher had come round and told them more or less how the interview on *Woman's Hour* would go: 'Just a few questions on the early days, Helen, how you came to adopt Kate, and then how the story came out. How you're both feeling about it now. And how Kate sees her future, and what she feels about the woman who left her that day.'

Which was how Martha came to hear her daughter's voice, for the first time. And to learn that she would like to meet her, 'Very, very much.'

That Friday morning, lying listlessly in bed, trying to summon up the strength to get up and go to work – when had she last missed what was already most of a morning? She really couldn't remember – she had woken to hear a light, pretty voice, saying: 'I would like to meet my birth mother, yes, of course I would.' And then, 'Yes, very, very much.'

'And – how do you think you might feel?' Jenni Murray sounded gently intrigued.

'Well – I don't know. Confused, I s'pose. And – maybe angry. And really interested in what she was like. What sort of person she was.'

'And – what would you say to her? Have you thought about that?'

'I'd ask her why she did it. That's the main thing I want to know.'

'Of course. Well, Kate, Helen, you've been great. Thank you so much for talking to us. And I hope you do hear from your birth mother, if that's what you want.'

'It is,' said Kate very simply. 'It really is.'

Martha found that far more moving and disturbing than seeing her photograph in the newspapers.

Beatrice also heard *Woman's Hour* that morning for the first time for years: and also from a bed that never saw her after 7 a.m. even on Sundays. Thank God, just thank God, she wasn't meant to be in court. But she was supposed to be in Chambers; they had clearly taken a rather dim view of her phone call, with the news that she was ill. She wasn't exactly ill: she had an appalling migraine, such as only hit her when life threatened to completely defeat her. It didn't often defeat her, but the night before, her nanny had given in her notice and although she had said that she would, of course, work her three months out, Beatrice had found the news almost unbearable.

Nothing can distress the working mother more, however brilliant, successful and efficient she may be, than the loss of her nanny. On the strength of those hugely expensive, neatly dressed shoulders rests most of the superstructure of her life. Beatrice, deprived of even this comfort and support, felt totally bereft and the very thought of the process of interviewing made her feel hysterical. She had several very important cases coming up, not to mention Charlie and Harry's joint birthday party, and even a holiday of her own, which she badly needed and which would now have to be sacrificed. She paid Christine extremely well, she had her own flat at the top of the house, she had full use of a car, and the girls were well past the most demanding age. But that, actually, had been the reason for Christine's resignation; she liked looking after babies, she said, and much as she loved Charlie and Harry, they became more independent every day.

As Beatrice tossed and turned miserably in her bed, her mobile rang. Checking it, she saw it was her mother. She decided to tell her her problems; her mother was rather brusquely unsympathetic.

'Darling, you've got three months. Surely that's enough. It's not as if they were babies.'

'It isn't just that,' Beatrice said. 'It's having no support of any kind at home, with Josh gone.'

'Now you know how I feel about that. You turned him out. It was your decision.'

'Mother! He was having an affair.'

'Beatrice, none of Josh's little flings have been what I would call an affair. They were more or less one-night stands. They meant nothing. I sympathise with you, of course. But there was no emotion involved; Josh adores you, you know he does.'

'He's got a funny way of showing it,' said Beatrice bitterly.

'Beatrice, he's a man. It's as simple as that. They can't resist sex, if it's offered them. It's beyond them, any of them. And there are far worse things, to my mind, than that. Josh is a very good husband, in a lot of ways. He's wonderful with the children; he pays all the bills, including the nanny, when many men would have seen that as your responsibility. He's very good-natured. And he's always very nice to me,' she added.

'Yes, I know he is. I don't think that's absolutely relevant.'

Her mother ignored this. 'Does he want to come back?'

'I – think so,' said Beatrice. Thinking of Josh's endless pleas to be forgiven, his protestations of remorse, his complaints of loneliness.

'I think you should consider it,' said her mother, 'I really do. I'm thinking of you, darling, not Josh. You need a husband. It's not as if he knocks you about, or anything. And do you really think it's going to be of benefit to those girls, growing up without their father? Think about it, Beatrice. You're being very stubborn, cutting off your nose to spite your face. Always have been. Now I must go . . .'

Beatrice spent the next hour considering what her mother had said. And deciding that, to an extent at least, she was right. She did need a husband. Quite badly.

Somehow Martha managed to get up and shower.

It was one o'clock; her flight was at seven-thirty. She called a cab, asked him to come up and get her bags. She wasn't sure she could manage even wheeling them to the lift. Finishing her packing had been hard enough.

She began to feel better as soon as the car pulled away from the building; it was as if she had left at least some of her traumatised self behind in it.

By the time she was in the plane, she felt almost human. She settled into her seat, smiled gratefully at the hostess, took a glass of orange juice.

'And here's the menu, Miss Hartley.'

'I won't want dinner,' said Martha. 'I'm awfully tired. What time do we get to Singapore?'

'Oh – local time, three p.m. Are you disembarking, or going through?'

'Going straight through,' said Martha.

She settled back, and almost as if watching a movie, allowed thoughts of sweeter, happier things to drift through her head; of Ed and how much he clearly loved her, and of her daughter with the lovely face and the pretty voice, who had said she wanted to meet her, and for the first time, the very first time, wondered if it might, after all, be something she would enjoy, rather than endure. She felt changed about Kate: she was no longer something dark and dreadful, to be denied at all costs, rather the reverse, indeed, a source of possible happiness and even pride. Even if they could never meet, never know one another; even if she could never explain and Kate never understand. She had been found, that dreadful day, cared for and had grown up safely, into someone clearly confident and happy, and, for that, Martha felt deeply grateful.

There was nothing she could do about either of them, Kate and Ed, and neither of them could be allowed into her life; but for a brief time, they at least moved into an easier place for her.

After a while, she took a sleeping pill and slept for over four hours. And dreamt; not frightening, dark dreams, but oddly sweet ones, of sunlit beaches and calm blue sea. And after that, instead of working as she always did, she watched one of the appalling movies which are apparently only shown on long plane journeys, and woke up feeling refreshed and almost happy in Singapore.

Helen looked rather nervously at Nat. She had asked him to Sunday lunch; Kate had been rushing off to meet him again, straight after breakfast, and Helen couldn't bear it. Kate was clearly delighted, had thrown her arms round her and kissed her.

'You're ace, Mum!'

'He might not want to come,' said Helen hopefully, looking

after Jim, who had gone into the garden and slammed the back door.

'He'll come,' said Kate. 'Just don't try and make him talk about politics or the news, Mum, yeah? He's a bit shy.'

And now here was Jim, stopping mid-carve, saying that these politicians were all the same, totally immoral, and he wouldn't vote for any of them.

'That Mrs Thatcher, she was all right,' said Nat. The entire family stared at him; it was as if he had declared his intention to take up ballet.

'Mrs Thatcher?' said Kate incredulously. 'I thought she was a real old bag.'

'No way. She had the right ideas, my dad says, sorted the unions out and that. He says they needed their heads examined, kicking her out. She wouldn't have let all these people in, neither.'

'What people?' said Juliet.

'These foreigners. Refugees and that. Taking over all our houses and hospitals and stuff. And Alton Towers,' he added as if this was the final felony, putting a large forkful of Yorkshire pudding into his mouth.

'Alton Towers?' Helen and Kate spoke in unison.

'Yeah. They sent a whole load of them there free last week. Said in the paper.'

'Good gracious,' said Helen. 'I had no idea.'

'She was good on the radio, wasn't she?' said Nat after a long, chewy silence, pointing his fork at Kate. 'I thought her mum might come on the programme, that she'd be, like, listening.'

'It wasn't – wasn't a phone-in,' said Helen gently.

There was a long silence; then: 'Yeah? What's the point in that, then?'

Kate stared at him; then she said: 'That's a really good idea, Nat. I might ask Fergus about it.'

Martha stepped out of the rather English luxury of the Observatory Hotel and into the Sydney sunshine. It was absolutely beautiful: a cool but brilliant day. She smiled up at the blue sky, and asked the doorman to get her a cab.

She was going to the Rocks, to do some shopping, wander round Darling Harbour, go back for an early dinner and then prepare for tomorrow's meetings. How absurd that she had been worried about being here. About the ghosts. This lovely place was so far removed from the other Sydney, the Sydney where worry had turned to fear and fear to panic. This Sydney was smooth and luxurious and busy and beautiful. She looked down at this Sydney, at the legendary view, the white wings of the opera house carved into the blue sky, the flying sails of the yachts in the harbour, the great bridge arched over it all, and the ranks of dazzling new buildings, gleaming in the sun: and turned her back absolutely and resolutely on the other, the scruffy room, the endless smell of frying food, the relentless heat. It had been another Martha who had lived there, too, an uncertain, frightened, lonely Martha; the one standing here now, in her linen trousers, her silk sweater, with a dozen appointments in her diary, three people waiting to buy her dinner, she had nothing to do with that one, she was no more. Nobody knew about her; she was safe from her, she had escaped.

'Where would you like to go then, on this beautiful day?'

The cab driver was friendly, good-natured, anxious to help; and of course she wanted to go down to the harbour, to buy T-shirts at Ken Done, and then to sit in the sun on the quay, drink lattes and maybe take a waterbus across the harbour, then back to the hotel to wait to be picked up for dinner, down on the Rocks. She did not even consider visiting the northern beaches of Collaroy and Mona Vale and Avalon, that was back, not forward, and forward was where she had to go, the only place indeed and –

'Do you have plenty of time?' she said.

'As much as you want,' he said with a dazzling smile – Australian teeth were as good as American ones, she thought irrelevantly.

'Could – could we go up to Avalon, please?' she said.

She got off the bus on the Barrenjoey Road, blinking in the fierce brilliance of the sun: it was unusually hot for the time of year, everyone said. She had seen the beaches, all along the road from Sydney, stuck sweatily to her seat, longing to be in the cool of the water. The two boys she was with were surf-struck, boasting of the waves they would catch, the boards they would ride; Martha listened to them, smiling to herself, wondering just how their English-school swimming would survive the reality of waves and rips.

They had been directed to Avalon by a boy they met at the airport, who was doing the trip the other way round; 'It's the only real surfers' hostel near Sydney, really great place.'

And so they had heaved their rucksacks onto the bus and sat there for over two hours, as it lurched through the suburbs of the city and out again the other side, riding the high bridges, gazing awestruck at the dazzling harbour below them, out through the smart suburbs of Northern Sydney, of Mosman and Clontarf, and then along the endless, charmless highway, studded with car salerooms and cheap restaurants – and surf shops, always surf shops.

She stood on the dizzily high cliffs of Avalon, looking down to the beach; and there it was, not just the sight but the sound of the sea, roaring and rolling in, and the smell of it too, fresh, salty, and altogether beautiful. She stood there for a long time, watching the surfies riding the waves, huge, rolling breakers, deceptively small from her viewpoint; and then she hoisted her rucksack on again, and walked down the steep hill and into Avalon, thinking how inappropriate was its name, so importantly a part of the English myth of Camelot, this infinitely Australian place.

Avalon was built on a crossroads, little more than a village really, and the Avalon Beach Hostel was just along one of the roads forming the cross. It was quite large, sleeping ninety-six, and the first one of its kind in the Sydney area, the warden told her. 'It's based on the ones up at Cape Tribulation, a real surfies' place.'

Martha looked up at it rather nervously as she walked through the big gates and across the paved courtyard; she was easily intimidated in those days, and the sun-bleached boys sitting on the long veranda overlooking the courtyard, some lolling back with long brown legs propped on the rail, others leaning over it chatting and smoking, looked as settled as if it were home. Which it was to many of them; they stayed here for weeks, months even.

She booked in, was given a room: or rather one sixth of a room, a hard bunk fixed to the wall by ropes, and a locker. It was very primitive, the floor simply painted concrete, but it was clean and the girls' bathroom, equally spartan and clean, was just opposite her door.

'Stove's here,' said the warden, who seemed about the same age as she was, leading her into the large room behind the veranda, half filled with long tables and benches, the walls covered with surfing posters. 'And here's the fridges; just bag one of the empty compartments, put your name on it, and it's yours till you leave. Everyone eats in here.'

Martha smiled rather nervously at the boys on the veranda; they grinned back, asked her where she'd come from, where she was going. She felt very happy suddenly; she would like it here.

She did: it was absolutely wonderful. She loved Avalon, the villagey atmosphere, the small shops, and the French restaurant, with its red and white checked cloths, where they very occasionally ate. There was a bookshop called Bookoccino, the Gourmet Deli, where they couldn't afford to shop (but an excellent Woolworths supermarket where they could), and astonishingly, a cinema, which was apparently owned by someone who had a mid-day TV show. Whoever he was, he took the cultural life of Avalon seriously and showed foreign films on Sundays. Not that going to the cinema was a priority: it was January and very, very hot.

She made two good friends there, a boy called Stuart, inevitably named Stewpot, and a girl called Dinah. Dinah came from Yorkshire, and her father was also a vicar: 'The worst thing, isn't it,' said Dinah, passing Martha the joint she was smoking, 'is being so poor and having to be posh. And the whole bloody parish watching you, of course. Can you imagine if you got pregnant or something, what on earth they'd do?'

Martha shuddered, then laughed and passed the joint back.

The three of them became a very tight little unit; Stewpot had tried surfing and had a bad fright, caught in a rip, and was content to swim with the girls in the safety of the rock pools, the natural swimming pools filled every day by the sea. Together they roamed the lovely white beaches, went up to Palm Beach, to the exclusive, tree-lined shore of Whale Beach, and to Newport and Mona Vale and Bilgola. At night they sat on the beach at Avalon and smoked and talked with all the others;

cooked on the beach barbecues, swam in the black and silver sea. Martha preferred this life to the self-indulgence of student Thailand; she liked the colder sea, the comparative order of the hostel, the more familiar food. She loved the Australians too, so easily friendly, upbeat, absolutely lacking in pretension; looking across from this golden place at the dark, rainy English winter, she even considered, briefly, staying herself.

She told Dinah, as they sat on the beach one night in the warm darkness; she was horrified.

'Martha, you couldn't. It's so – so unsubtle. And the men are such chauvinists.'

'They may be chauvinists, but they're very kind,' said Martha. 'I'd rather have them any day than some stuffy public school wally, thank you very much.'

'Plenty of those in your prospective profession,' said Dinah. 'Are you sure you've chosen the right career?'

'Oh yes,' said Martha. Without knowing why, she had an absolute certainty that the law would suit her. 'But you're right. Especially the barristers.'

'Which you're not going to be?'

'No, I'm not. Can't afford it for a start, you need very rich parents for that. You can be years waiting to earn any money. And no thanks, no more beer. I feel a bit queasy. Don't know why. I did last night, as well.'

Dinah laughed. 'Don't tell me the nightmare's come true, you've got a baby to take home to the vicarage.'

'Of course not,' said Martha, almost crossly; and then – although she was not remotely worried, she told herself – when she got back to the hostel, she got out her diary. Her periods had been chaotic ever since she had arrived in Thailand. But no, it was all right, she'd had one in Singapore – very light, but nonetheless, a period; and that had been well after Koh Tao. And since then: no sex.

At the beginning of February, Stuart and his harem (as the other boys called them) set off for the north. They got a bus from Sydney, all the way up to Ayers Rock: two and a half days of jolting along the long, endlessly straight roads. It was only moderately uncomfortable; the bus was air-conditioned and it stopped every four hours or so. The worst thing was the boredom; the unchanging scenery for most of the way, the red earth, the flat scrub, the unvarying speed.

The bus was full of backpackers; they made friends, swapped chewing gum, cigarettes and the sweets Dinah had christened anaesthetics. They stopped at Alice Springs for the night, and then in the morning caught another bus to Ayers Rock; together they gazed in awe at it, at the great looming cliché, watched it turn purple at sunset, climbed it in the cold desert dawn, stood together, holding hands on the summit, faces raised to the sun, and felt – in spite of all the other tourists – alone in the world, while the desert stretched away from them, absolute emptiness in every direction.

When they got down, Martha felt odd; she sat down for a while in the shade, and then was extremely sick; and was then repeatedly sick again on the bus, as they travelled endlessly on up north to Cape Tribulation.

'Martha,' said Dinah gently, as she wiped her friend's sweaty forehead by the side of the bus – it had stopped for her – 'Martha, you don't have anything to tell me, do you?'

Martha said irritably that no, she hadn't; a distant crawling fear had begun to trouble her. But once they arrived at Cape Tribulation, she stopped being sick – and she started her period.

'You see,' she said, waving a Tampax triumphantly at Dinah, on her way to the loo, 'it's perfectly all right.'

Two days later it was over; but that was surely fine?

They stayed at Cape Tribulation, where the rain forest so famously meets the sea, for a month; they made friends with someone who had a boat and he took them out to the reef several times; they snorkelled and explored the underworld there, the hills and valleys of coral, the sweetly smiling, brilliantly coloured fish, the friendly baby sharks, who swam up to them to investigate them. Martha was entranced by the silence and calm beneath the water, and the gentle slowing of time; she longed to try diving, but couldn't afford it.

She and Dinah got work in one of the beach bars, and made enough money to get back to Sydney by train. It was March by then; the temperature was cooling just a little. The harem broke up; Dinah was going on to California and Stuart was planning to go to New Zealand. Martha planned to fly to New York. But they stayed a few days in Avalon, together first, rediscovering the place, feeling they had come home.

The second evening was quite cool: 'I'm going to put on some trousers,' said Martha, and delved into her locker to find them, unworn for months. And they wouldn't go on. They weren't just a bit tight; they simply wouldn't go on.

She told herself it was all the food she'd been eating up at Cape Tribulation and the beer; it was a well-established fact of travelling that you lost weight in Thailand and piled it on again in Oz, but this was different, her arms were still stick-thin, and, forcing herself, with a supreme effort of will, to look sideways at herself in the small bathroom mirror – she had to stand on the loo to do it – she could see a distinct doming of her flat stomach. She felt sick again: but differently, the sickness of panic. And then told herself that she was just being hysterical, that she had had two periods, after all. Just the same, she went into the Avalon chemist, bought a pregnancy testing kit, locked herself in the bathroom the next morning to use it. An unmistakably distinct blue ring told her she was pregnant.

Terrified, she gathered all her courage together and went to the Avalon doctor.

He was young, with brilliant blue eyes; brisk, cheerful, very Australian.

'Those tests in the chemists aren't always reliable,' he said and she could have kissed him. 'But let me have a look at you and then we'll know what we're talking about.'

He was quite a long time, gently palpating on her stomach, feeling her breasts, doing an internal. A nurse stood watching, her face expressionless.

'All righty, Martha,' he said finally, 'you get your clothes on. And then we'll have that talk.'

He told her she was about five months' pregnant. 'But I can't be,' she said, her mind flying back in hot, black panic to Koh Tao, five months earlier. 'I've had periods, one just about a month ago.'

'Can still happen. Was it quite light?'

'Well – quite.'

'How long did it last?'

'About – about two days.'

'Martha – I'm sorry, that's quite common. Have you had any nausea?'

'A – bit. But not every day, just – well, for a few days. I can't be pregnant, I really can't.'

'Are you telling me you haven't done anything to get pregnant?' he said, his blue eyes twinkling at her.

She managed to smile.

'Well – I have. But only – only once.'

Twice actually, she thought, thinking of the next morning, and the immeasurably increased pleasure of it.

'It only takes once. I'm sorry, Martha. There really is no doubt. When was this one time?'

'At the end of October.'

'I'm afraid that exactly adds up. Exactly.'

He was kindness itself; did she want to go home to England, was there anyone with her who could help?

'I'll have to have a termination,' she said immediately, ignoring his questions. 'It's the only thing.'

'Martha, I'm very sorry,' he said, and his voice was gentle and almost hesitant, 'it's much too late for that.'

Chapter 27

The wheeling and dealing that goes on between politicians and the press, their mutual dependence, their ruthless pragmatism towards each other, is one of the most crucial ingredients in political life.

'We don't have any power without the politicians,' Nicholas Marshall had explained to more than one fascinated dinner party, 'but we have a hell of a lot of influence over political events. And they're frightened of that influence. Mostly because they don't know where it's going to come from next.'

He often said nobody outside the business would believe his life; the mysterious phone calls with anonymous tip-offs, the invitations to meet politicians in the bars of London pubs (most notably the Red Lion halfway down Whitehall, opposite 10 Downing Street, a favourite haunt of the Gordon Brown mob), the offers of leaked documents, the waylaying in the busy corners and corridors of the House of Commons to have a piece of gossip of extraordinary sensitivity whispered in his ear. Or the exclusive stories from high-ranking cabinet ministers and senior civil servants, either in return for his on-going loyalty to their party's cause, or to buy his temporary silence over something that might have caused them embarrassment.

The phone call he got quite early that Monday morning, as he ran across Hampstead Heath, didn't actually seem particularly intriguing. Theodore Buchanan (Tory MP for South Cirencester, known to his friends as Teddy) invited him to lunch at the Ritz and told him he might have quite a nice little story for him. Nick knew Teddy Buchanan quite well, a nice old buffer, traditional Tory, who had a soft spot for Nick because he was a country boy, and understood about things like foxhunting and its importance to the life of the countryside.

Nick was at the Ritz, in the absurdly over-dressed restaurant, ten minutes early; he sat there alternately studying the menu and the clientele, who seemed to be getting older and older. The food was as fussily got up as the restaurant itself: everything encased in something else, rich pastry, truffles, double cream, nothing simple at all. He ordered himself a gin and tonic, which seemed in keeping with the place, and reflected rather sadly that nothing seemed much fun at the moment. God, he missed Jocasta. She had left a dark and silent void in his life and he couldn't imagine how he was ever going to get over her.

The thought of commitment, of marriage even, no longer seemed so terrifying; indeed a life of ongoing bachelorhood seemed a great deal worse. He wondered how long her affair with bloody Keeble would last, and if she'd get over it and come back to him.

He sipped his gin and tonic, and sat back in his chair, trying to distract himself by watching a very pretty girl who had just come in: tall, slim, with long dark hair and wonderful legs; she was wearing what even Nick could recognise as Chanel. Rich then. No, rich daddy, that was more like it; he had come to join her, had kissed her, sat down opposite her. Or – rich sugar daddy, more like it still. How could they do it, these lovely things, sleep with these old men? He had heard it referred to by a girl on the paper as antiquing, it was extraordinary; and then realised that Jocasta had done exactly that. Shit! Why had he let her go, why, why? He was thirty-six, more than old enough to settle down; silly bugger that he was, running around like some pathetic adolescent.

A dazzling smile came at him from across the room, a slim, elegant figure crossed towards him, shook him by the hand; it was Fergus Trehearn.

'Hello, Nick. What a wonderful surprise. What are you doing here?'

Nick liked Fergus. He had met him six months ago when he had been handling some sixteen year old who had been propositioned by a Tory MP. Of course he was as ruthless and devious as all the others, but he was a lot more pleasant to be with.

'Hi, Fergus. Waiting for my lunch date.'

'A beautiful young girl, no doubt?'

'A rather portly middle-aged politician.'

'Well, that's a terrible shame. I'm doing a little better than that. As you will see. She'll be here any minute. With her mother, let me add, before you get any unpleasant ideas. You'll have heard about Baby Bianca, no doubt? The abandoned baby, found at Heathrow.'

'I certainly have,' said Nick. 'Jocasta had some dealings with her. You're not handling her, are you?'

'I am indeed. And I'm doing a very good job for her as well. We're no nearer finding her mother, but we have fashion editors slavering over her and newspapers trying to sign her up.'

'And you're buying her lunch at the Ritz?'

'It was her choice. We've just been in to see the fashion editor of *Style*, and this is her treat, in return for promising to get on with studying for her GCSEs for the next six weeks or so. Then I hope she'll be back in the public eye with a vengeance. She's a sweetie – ah, here they are now. Do you want to meet her?'

'I certainly wouldn't mind,' said Nick, staring transfixed at Kate who had just walked into the restaurant. She was stunning; actually rather more striking than the girl with the sugar daddy. A wonderful mixture of tenderly gawky youth and innocence, and a slightly self-conscious sexiness. She was wearing a black trouser suit with a white vest top, very high-heeled boots and her hair, her long blonde curly hair, was pulled back in a pony tail.

Fergus walked over to them, kissed both Kate and her mother and led them over to Nick.

'Nicholas Marshall, Kate and Helen Tarrant. My dates for lunch. Nick, aren't I the lucky man?'

Nick stood up briefly, shook both their hands, managed to mumble something at Kate and then, as Fergus led them off again to a table on the other side of the room, sat down again rather heavily. He felt slightly shaken, but not by Kate's beauty, or Helen's nervousness: it was the fact that Kate did bear a considerable resemblance to Jocasta.

Teddy Buchanan arrived at almost half past one, full of apologies. He had been held up in a committee meeting.

'So sorry, Nicholas. Have you ordered? No? That a G & T? I'll join you. Splendid idea. Let's order straightaway, shall we, and we can get on with the matter in hand.'

'Fine,' said Nick, but it was only as Teddy settled to his main course – steak topped with truffles in filo pastry – that he suddenly put down his knife and fork, picked up his glass of claret and said, 'Well, you'll be wondering why I've brought you here, Nick.'

Nick said yes, he was, but that he was greatly enjoying himself anyway. 'Excellent,' said Buchanan. 'Well, I've got a very good little story for you . . .'

He leant forward, started speaking very quietly in Nick's ear. After a few minutes, Nick forgot all about Kate Tarrant, and the girl in Chanel with the sugar daddy, and even Jocasta. It was a very, very good little story indeed.

'Chad, hi. This is Nick Marshall.'

'Hello, Nick. How are things?'

'Oh – pretty good. Yes.'

'How's the lovely Jocasta?'

'I don't know,' said Nick shortly.

'Oh, right. Well, what can I do for you?'

'Meet me?' said Nick.

'Sure. Where?'

'Wherever it suits you. Red Lion?'

'Sounds good. Going to tell me what it's about?' Chad's slightly clipped voice was very confident: obviously he had no skeletons in his cupboard, Nick thought. Not that he was aware of anyway.

Chad's face was expressionless as he looked at Nick. 'Would you mind telling me who fed you this fascinating piece of information?' he said.

'Now, Chad, you know I can't do that. Not possibly.'

'And – are you planning to use it?'

'Well, it's a very good story,' said Nick.

'Yes, and that's exactly what it is. A story. Load of bollocks.'

'Good. Fine. Well, you won't mind my checking it out, then?'

'Of course I bloody well mind! Poking into my affairs –'

'Chad,' said Nick almost sorrowfully, 'that's my job.'

Chad glared at him. 'I thought your paper was supposed to support our party,' he said.

'Of course. We do. But not against this sort of thing. Look, I've done you the service of warning you. I could have just published and been damned. I'll speak to you soon, Chad. Sorry about all this.'

He put his beer down, only half finished, and walked out of the Red Lion; when he looked back Chad was staring into his own glass, his expression murderous.

Chad and Jonny Farquarson had been at Eton together; had been good friends. They had gone to each other's weddings; each was godfather to one of the other's children. After that, for several years they drifted apart; Chad fighting his way up the political ladder, Jonny running the family business, an engineering firm called Farjon, hugely successful since the turn of the twentieth century. When Chad was promoted to the shadow cabinet by William Hague, Jonny called him, invited him to lunch at the Reform. They chatted; Jonny said things were pretty bloody splendid with Farjon.

'Good,' said Chad. 'I know some of you boys have had a hard time, now it's getting so much cheaper to buy from overseas.'

'Well, that's true,' said Jonny, calling the waiter over for another brandy, 'but we seem to be coping. Profits not quite so big, of course, but still fairly impressive.'

'Good,' said Chad. He refused the brandy, said he had a big debate that evening, told Jonny how glad he was to hear he was prospering and they parted for another five years.

Jonny called Chad when the Centre Forward party was formed: could he help in any way?

'That means with money. At the moment.'

'Might be a possibility. I'll have a think.'

And thus it was that Jonny Farquarson had supplied Chad Lawrence with a million pounds to fund the Centre Forward Think Tank.

Jesus, why hadn't he checked this out: why? Because he'd been so bloody busy, that was why; every moment at that time precious. And he'd known Jonny so long, trusted him absolutely. There was no way he'd have deceived him in any way.

Just the same, trawling through the *Financial Times* website, sweating heavily, feeling increasingly sick, Chad discovered that Farjon had indeed gone bankrupt eighteen months previously, just as Nick Marshall had said.

So how the fuck had Jonny managed to donate a million pounds to the Centre Forward party?

'You what!' said Chad. 'Jesus, how could you do this to me? Jonny, I can't believe you could be so stupid.'

'Come on, Chad. Hardly stupid.' The bluff Etonian voice was almost plaintive. 'I supplied your party with a million pounds. You seemed pretty bloody pleased at the time.'

'Well, I was. Of course. I just didn't know that Farjon was now a company operating out of Hong Kong. Backed by Chinese money. I mean, you could have mentioned it.'

'Well, I'm sorry, Chad. You didn't ask. Maybe you should have. It matters, does it?'

'Of course it bloody well matters! It's illegal for an overseas company to fund an English political party.'

'You don't say!'

The voice was suddenly rather knowing; Chad realised, in a stomach-lurching moment, that he had been set up.

Clio had applied for the job at the Royal Bayswater. It had taken a lot of courage; she knew how devastated she was going to feel if she didn't get it. Her confidence was at an all-time low, and almost every day delivered yet another misery-producing request or phone call or letter from either her solicitor or Jeremy's.

Just the same, she knew herself very well; and she knew that staying in the backwater that was the Guildford practice was going to prove ever more dispiriting. She did love it; but it wasn't what she needed any more. She needed challenge, new people, and new problems. And she really wanted to get back to London.

She still hadn't said anything to Mark, but she was taking Beaky's advice and visiting the other hospitals in the Bayswater group, had taken a few days of leave to do it. Apart from it being politically astute and impressing the board, it would get her back into hospital procedure and give her some insight into the

Bayswater philosophy. The first hospital she was going to visit was in Highbury; they had promised her a day in Outpatients; 'And if you can get here by eight, we've a management meeting, that might be interesting for you.'

The thought of getting to Highbury from Guildford by eight in the morning made her quail.

'Borrow my house,' Jocasta had said promptly when she heard. 'Honestly, it would enjoy the company and I'd love to think I'd helped you get your job. People next door have the key.'

Clio arrived in the early evening, when the pavements outside the cafes and bars of Clapham and Battersea were filling up with pretty, noisy young people; within ten minutes she felt at home. The house was so pretty, every room dizzily crammed with books and pictures and ephemera of every type; Jocasta collected a range of things, advertising memorabilia, silk shawls which were strewn as throws across every imaginable surface, and 1930s books of school stories by people like Angela Brazil. There were also several collages, made up with snapshots from Jocasta's childhood, mostly pictures of her and Josh with their mother, a rather severe-looking woman – and only one with their father, taken at what was presumably Jocasta's eighteenth. That was Jocasta of the year they had met, skinny, very brown, in a strapless black dress with her hair up. Ronald Forbes was what people described as a fine-looking man, tall and blond, very like Jocasta – or Josh – wearing a dinner jacket, standing close to Jocasta, but not touching her, and not smiling either. It was not in a collage, that picture, but mounted in a silver frame; whatever she said, he clearly mattered to her – very, very much. Partly the basis for her relationship with Gideon, Clio thought: she had a father complex.

There were other collages, of her schooldays and her travels and even, rather touchingly, of her life with Nick, a dizzy display, taken in bars and restaurants, at parties and out with friends. Poor Nick: Clio, who had liked what little she had seen of him, felt very sad for him. She felt increasingly doubtful about Jocasta's new relationship.

She had brought a few things for her supper with her and had just uncorked a bottle of wine, when the phone rang.

'Is that Jocasta?'

'No, it's not, I'm afraid. Who's calling?'

'Is that Clio? What a wonderful surprise to hear your voice.'

It was Fergus Trehearn.

'Yes. I mean, is it?' God, she must sound ridiculous. 'Jocasta lent me her house for a day or so. I've got to be in London and –'

'This is Fergus Trehearn.'

'I know. I mean, I recognised your voice.'

'Well, it's very nice that it made such an impression on you. My voice, that is. Now it's ridiculous to be calling her there, I know, but she told me she pops in from time to time and I can't raise her anywhere else. Her mobile is switched off. How are you, Clio?'

'Very well, thank you. Fergus, if you want Jocasta, she's in New York. With Gideon. They're staying at the Carlyle.'

'Ah, yes. It's one of Gideon's favourites. I'll call her there. It's not urgent, just something about Kate.'

'Fine. Well, I hope you get hold of her.'

'I will. And I hope your business goes well. Some terribly high-powered medical conference, I expect?'

'No, not exactly,' said Clio. 'I'm – visiting a hospital. I'm applying for a job at my old hospital and this place I'm going to is affiliated to it.'

'Applying for a job? As a hospital doctor?'

'Well – yes. A consultant. A consultant geriatrician. Which is what I was before.'

Why was she telling him all this?

'Geriatrics – that's the care of the elderly, isn't it?'

'It is indeed.'

'What a wonderful job, what marvellous work to be doing. It breaks my heart to think of old people being neglected, uncared for. When they've done so much for us. And I wouldn't mind betting they're a little more courteous than your younger patients might be.'

'That's exactly right,' said Clio, smiling, surprised at his insight. 'Anyway, I'm sorry, I'm keeping you . . .'

'Not at all. I would love to continue the conversation. But – yes, I should call Jocasta. More's the pity. Goodbye, Clio, it's been extremely nice talking to you.'

'Goodbye, Fergus.'

She wished she could dislike him, because she so totally disapproved of what he did. But she couldn't. He had the same effect on her, she reflected, putting the phone down, as drinking a glass of very good red wine. Soothed. Pleased. The opposite of irritable.

On an impulse, and prompted by a picture on the wall of the three of them at Heathrow in a backpacking collage, she decided to try and raise Martha Hartley. It was only half-past six, and since she had said in her interviews that she frequently worked till midnight, she might just catch her. She called Sayers Wesley and was put through to a girl with a coolly clipped accent, who told her that Miss Hartley was away, but that she would pass on the message then.

'But I should warn you, she will be extremely busy for a few days at least. I can't promise anything.'

Clio put the phone down feeling ruffled. Snooty bitch. She probably only passed on the messages she thought sufficiently important. For some reason she thought of Martha, all those years ago, talking about her very different life then as a vicar's daughter, the conditions of what she described as 'unbelievable respectability', in which she had grown up 'in a spotlight of sorts. The whole parish watching.'

Well, the parish would be watching her now; it was also her constituency. Binsmow in Suffolk. Now there was a way of tracking her down. She said in the article she went there every weekend, on constituency business. And her parents were bound to be nice people.

Clio suddenly felt rather excited; she would call them. See if they knew when Martha would be back; they would definitely pass the message on. She was intrigued now by Martha, the totally changed Martha. She had become a challenge. She dialled directory enquiries. 'Binsmow, Suffolk,' she said. 'The name is Hartley. It's a vicarage.'

Nick Marshall was walking over Westminster Bridge next morning when his phone went; it was Theodore Buchanan.

'Hello, young Nicholas. Nice piece yesterday. Well done.'

'That's OK,' said Nick. He had run an item about rural

unemployment, quoting several MPs on the devastating effect a hunting ban would have on employment in the area. It was a neat payment for Buchanan's story about Chad Lawrence.

'I just thought you'd like to know,' Buchanan was saying, 'I'm going to raise the other matter as a point of order this evening. I've given advance warning to the Speaker's Office. It'll be pretty late, probably about nine, because there's a lot of stuff about the Lords Reform. Now, this is what I'm going to say . . .'

Later that day, Nick wrote his story and filed it – after re-checking with Buchanan that he was indeed making his point of order. He had run so many of these exclusive stories and they never failed to worry, as well as excite him. The great fear being, with the story set and ready to run, that something would prevent that statement (with its consequent parliamentary privilege) from being made.

'So that the newspaper isn't actually reporting what an MP has said at all, but making an actionable statement of its own,' he had explained once to Jocasta, 'and therefore laying itself open to the laws of libel.'

Theodore Buchanan reassured him once again that there was absolutely no question but that the point of order would be made, 'In roughly two hours from now, I'd say.'

Chapter 28

Sometimes they made her feel terribly hunted, her e-mails; they pursued her wherever she went. This morning she was checking them from her suite at the Observatory. Quite a long list, as usual. Mostly administrative matters: could she attend this meeting, agree to that memo, was she available for a session with Paul Quenell on the internal affairs of her department the following Wednesday; and then there was a list of people who had called. She skimmed through them: mostly from outside the firm concerning committees and charitable boards she had agreed to sit on, functions she was invited to attend; could she call the management people of her apartment building about the entrance space; and then a name that made her heart lurch: Clio Scott. Would Martha call her about a meeting, as soon as she could?

Martha sat staring at the screen, feeling her mind fracture; Mackenzie, Paul Quenell, Sayers Wesley, Jack Kirkland, Centre Forward were in one part of it, a smoothly controlled, well-conducted place; and Clio was in quite another. What did she want? Why had she suddenly called? What could she possibly want with her, what might she know, what could she do?

Stop it, Martha, stop it; you're panicking. It's panic that's dangerous. The only thing that's dangerous. Calm is everything, calm and control: that's what keeps you safe. Everything was perfectly all right. Maybe Clio wanted to arrange a reunion for the three of them. Jocasta had mentioned something of the sort. Yes, that was actually quite likely. Quite likely.

A sliver of cool was parting the hot panic, sending it away. There was no need to see Clio, talk to her even. She could

411

simply tell her PA to say that she was too busy and she'd call her when her diary was a little less full. That was what she always said to unwelcome invitations and it always worked. Then she never called them; and usually they never called her back.

So – it was fine. Clio could be banished again, there was no need to admit her any further into her life. She would be disposed of neatly: and that would be that.

And now she would go to the gym for half an hour; before she had to set out for Wesley's offices and another tedious, but infinitely controllable meeting with Donald Mackenzie.

At one point she had been afraid she would have to stay on, but they seemed to be nearly there now; and she would fly back on Friday night, and be in London for the one really important event in her political diary, a meeting with Janet Frean on Sunday, along with several other party members, to discuss a standing committee Janet had been invited to serve on, in connection with benefit fraud. She had specifically wanted Martha, she said, as she felt her experiences with the CAB and, more recently, her legal surgeries might be relevant. Martha felt really excited at the prospect, at politics coming properly alive.

She was amazed how much better she felt out here; the trip out to Avalon had, against all odds, done her good. She had looked at the other Martha and wondered at what she had survived and how well, had left her there, sitting on the beach, dressed in tattered Bermuda shorts and baggy T-shirt, staring panicked out to sea, and taken her successful, accomplished self back to Sydney Harbour. Avalon had changed along with her, she thought, had become chic and successful, full of smart pavement cafes, and expensive boutiques; she had even found the time to sit at one of the tables and have a skinny latte and watch the world going by, a world of chic young people and perfectly dressed young families. Only the surfers had not changed: they wandered along on bare feet, carrying their boards, sun-bleached and deep-down brown, and talking, talking endlessly, on their way to ride the waves. Such a lovely lifestyle it had been. Such a lovely lifestyle it clearly still was.

'Clean sheet party and the Chinese Laundry . . .

'Chad Lawrence, the charismatic MP whose blond good

412

looks and public school charm made him a favourite with the old Tory party, has behaved with uncharacteristic carelessness over the funding of his new party's Think Tank. So claimed Theodore Buchanan, in a point of order in the House this evening.

'He asked the House if it was in order "for the Centre Forward party to be receiving funds from a source within the Chinese People's Republic? Is it not the case that British political parties – in this House – are forbidden from receiving finance from foreign interests? Mr Speaker, should not the Committee of Standards and Privileges investigate this disgrace as a matter of urgency?"

'At which point Mr Buchanan sat down amidst a great deal of booing and cheering.

'When an old school (Eton, where else?) chum, Jonathan Farquarson, offered the new party a million pounds for party funding last autumn, Lawrence (Ullswater North) failed to check that Mr Farquarson's engineering company, Farjon, was entirely UK based; after a bankruptcy two years ago, it was acquired by a Chinese company operating from the north of Hong Kong. Not only is it against the law for a British political party to receive finance from foreign interests, it is quite possible that Mr Lawrence could find himself under pressure to secure favourable import tariffs for the company. Once tipped as a future Tory Prime Minister, he was one of the founding members of the Centre Forward party, the left-of-centre breakaway group from the Tories.

'The party pledged to be squeaky clean, devoid of sleaze and cronyism; unfortunately for Mr Lawrence, he has found himself in the middle of a row involving both.

'It is unfortunate for the new party's reputation that only two weeks ago, Eliot Griers, another prominent member of the new party (along with Janet Frean, the only senior female MP to join the party to date), was in the news in the already infamous Clinch in The Crypt case, involving Mr Griers and a young woman lawyer in his constituency.

'Jack Kirkland, sitting with Chad Lawrence on the opposition benches, rose to say that the matter was receiving his full attention and meanwhile he would continue to have every confidence in his Honourable Friend, the member for Ullswater North.

'Nobody was remotely deceived.'

'What I want to know,' said Jack Kirkland, passing a glass of wine to Janet Frean, who had offered him her company that evening, 'is who on earth can have tipped Buchanan off. He's not the sharpest knife in the drawer – someone must have helped him. God, what a mess. In just six weeks. Fallen from our shiny pedestal, right down into the murky squalor, along with the rest of them. I suppose it was naive of me to think our little band was unique. Above all this sort of thing.'

'Not really. I thought so, too. It's very sad.'

'Not sad, Janet, *bloody* stupid. Feckless.' He sighed. 'I honestly think we may not recover from this, you know.'

'Oh don't be ridiculous, Jack,' she said, and her strong-jawed, rather handsome face was full of sympathy. 'Of course we can. Tomorrow it'll be someone else, something quite different. How about a new Mandelson scandal? I'd put quite a lot of money on that.'

He managed a smile.

'You could be right. Well, thank God for you. You're not going to do anything dreadful to me, are you, Janet? You're not going to be found snogging in the press gallery with someone or handing out houses for votes, like Mrs Porter?'

She laughed. 'Bob wouldn't like the former too much and I don't have the means for the latter. Sometimes I think I should have stuck to my original profession, the law, and made some money. But no, don't worry, Jack, I won't let you down. Promise.'

He looked at her very seriously.

'I know you won't. I trust you totally. I've always thought women were a far better bet for politics. Less power-crazed, more genuinely idealistic. I'd forgotten you were a lawyer. Like the blessed Margaret. And young Martha, of course.'

'Indeed.'

There was an edge to her voice he didn't notice.

'Now there's a clever girl. I think she's absolutely splendid.'

'I agree. Although she seriously lacks experience.'

'She'll gain it fast.'

'Well, let's hope so. I've invited her to a meeting with several others, to talk about this new select committee I've been asked to serve on.'

'Good for you. Involve her as much as you can, Janet. I really think it could be worth it. I see her as our future. In an odd way.'

'Very odd,' said Janet, and this time he did notice her tone, 'considering she's had about two months' experience.'

'Janet, Janet,' he said, patting her hand, 'you're not feeling jealous, are you? She may be the future; you're our present. Incidentally, I heard a rumour that IDS is going to make Theresa May chairman of the Tory party.'

'What? I don't believe it!'

'Oh, I think it's very possibly true. One of his cleverer moves, I'd say. Putting a woman into that job. Just think, Janet, it might have been you.'

'Indeed,' said Janet briefly.

He stared at her. 'You wouldn't have wanted that, surely? With that lot?'

'Of course not,' she said.

Shortly after that, she made her excuses and left; when she reached home she poured herself a very large whisky and went up to her study. Bob Frean found her pacing up and down the room, fists clenched, raging silently; rather wearily, he asked her what the matter was.

'Just go back to bed and leave me alone,' she said. 'I don't want to discuss it.'

He reflected that very few people would have recognised the calm, brilliant, superwoman in that near-frenzied creature.

He was never quite sure how much he disliked her. Or even if he disliked her at all any more, simply felt nothing for her. He had fallen in love with her at university, a brilliant girl, not beautiful but very attractive, reading law, had been flattered by her interest in him and even more so by her desire first to move in with him and then to marry him. It took a time for him to realise this had been largely inspired by his money – he was the beneficiary of a large trust fund – but by then it was much too late. He suited her beautifully, both financially and practically, as support for her ambition to become the second woman Prime Minister: he paid the bills – including those for her political expenses – babysat endlessly, oversaw the children's upbringing, smiled at her side at functions and interviews.

But as she rose in the political firmament, she became increasingly dismissive of him, ignoring him whenever possible, eating alone, saying she had papers to read, work to do, walking away from him when he tried to talk to her. That was when he began to dislike her.

The only place she appeared to welcome him was in the bedroom – she was sexually voracious, too voracious, indeed, for him. It took a while for him to realise that his role there was as much for the begetting of their children, as satisfying her physically. It suited her career; her large family was a most useful tool in her self-publicity, a kind of shorthand for her image – Janet Frean, the mother of five, Janet Frean the superwoman, Janet Frean who showed women they could indeed have it all.

Her career was of prime importance to her, and everything was sacrificed on its altar; primarily Bob, of course, but her children, her friends, her health, her own sanity, it seemed. He had become aware early in their relationship of the fanatical side of her nature, her ruthless destruction of anything in her path, her capacity to drive herself beyond exhaustion.

At first he admired it, then became wary of it and finally anxious about it, recognising it as something almost manic, a psychological flaw. He looked at her sometimes, white and exhausted, after late-night sessions at the House, saw her drained face, her taut neck muscles, her white knuckles as she chatted easily on the phone, to constituents, to party workers. Her control was awesome. He often wondered when she would crack; it was only a matter of time. But he knew there was nothing he or anyone could do about it, and she should go to hell in her own way.

It was Wednesday evening; Clio was packing her things and leaving Jocasta's house: rather regretfully. She had loved the whole of the three days. The morning at the Highbury Hospital had been fascinating, and she had sat in on all the interviews. There were several very sad cases, reminiscent of the Morrises; she had shared her frustrations with the consultant over the problems of getting medication safely organised for the elderly, and the frustrations with the red tape binding up the carers. She had told him how she had taken to visiting her patients personally, with their carefully allotted doses in containers, and he had been impressed.

'You really care about them, your patients, don't you?'

'I do. That's the thing about general practice that I like best, you get really involved, can make a difference.'

He had given her the address of one of the care homes they visited, and she had gone there, too. It was much better run than the Laurels; the patients were bright and busy, were allowed their own bits of garden, and had the run of the kitchen in the afternoons, when they could bake cakes for their visitors.

She called the consultant at Highbury and thanked him for organising it.

'That's all right, Clio. Good luck with it. I'll hope to be working with you – you'd almost certainly have a clinic here if you get the job.'

She had also spent a day in the psychiatric unit of a small hospital in Harrow and was given access to research material on various trials that were being conducted there.

'Dementia and its affiliated horrors are still some of the biggest problems in geriatrics,' the consultant told her, 'even with all these new drugs. It leads to such dreadful social problems, of course, and isolation from society.'

It had all been fascinating – and stimulating. She realised she did desperately want this job.

She had done some shopping while she was in London, had bought herself a new suit and shoes for the interview, if she got it; she decided to try them on and was buttoning the jacket when she heard a key in the front door. Jocasta? Couldn't be. Not Nick, please not Nick, she'd be so embarrassed.

'Hello?' she called down rather nervously; and 'Who's that then?' came a voice up the stairs.

It was Josh.

'Who called?' said Martha. 'Who did you say?'

She had rung her parents to make sure they were all right and that they hadn't been too bothered by constituents the weekend before, and her mother had told her a Clio Scott had rung.

'She was very nice,' she said, 'apparently you went travelling with her.'

How dare she? How dare she? Worming her way into her most private life, ringing up her parents, for God's sake. What did she want, that she was pursuing her like this, like a stalker almost? It was outrageous, she had no right.

'She only wanted you to ring her, dear,' her mother had said half apologetically, clearly surprised by Martha's reaction. 'She said it would be wonderful to see you. I don't know why you're so upset. I thought she sounded very nice. We had a little chat about your travelling days.'

'You what?' Martha felt hot suddenly, hot and shaky. 'What on earth were you doing, discussing that with her? What's it got to do with her? Or you, come to that?'

'Martha, dear, are you all right? You don't sound yourself. I suppose it's the journey. You must be exhausted.'

'I'm perfectly all right,' said Martha, 'I just don't like people pestering me. Give me her number, please Mum, and I'll tell her to stop. It's too bad. What? No, of course I won't be rude to her. Why should I be? Yes, I'll be home next Friday. I'll call you before then.'

Clio was making Josh a cup of coffee when her mobile rang.

He had come, he said, clearly deeply embarrassed, to try and find a belt he had lost. 'I stayed here recently and I thought it might be here. It was a birthday present from Beatrice – that's my wife – and she keeps asking where it is. I was just passing, sorry if it's an inconvenient moment.'

Clio said it wasn't inconvenient at all, that Jocasta had very kindly lent her the house for a couple of days.

'She's been such a good friend to me. I don't know what I'd have done without her.'

'Is she with this Keeble fellow?'

'Yes.'

'Odd that,' he said. 'I mean, he's jolly nice, of course, but Nick was so – so right for her. And giving up her job. The last thing I'd have expected.'

'Well, I'm sure she knows what she's doing,' said Clio carefully. 'Now, do you take sugar?'

That was when her phone rang.

'Phew,' she said, switching it off a few minutes later. 'I just got what we used to call a bollocking.'

'Oh yes? Who from?'

'From Martha Hartley. Remember Martha?'

'I do,' he said, after a moment's pause, 'of course.' Then he looked at her slightly awkwardly. 'Er – Clio . . .'

'Josh, don't say a single word. That was another lifetime. It's really nice we've met again now.'

'Happy days, weren't they?' he said, with a grin, taking a sip of coffee.

'So happy. Wonderful kick-off to grown-up life.'

'Anyway, what on earth was Martha on about?'

'I've been trying to contact her. Just because – well, just because I thought it might be fun. Anyway, I rang her PA and I rang her parents, and it seems I shouldn't have. She said I had no right to be contacting them, could I please not worry them again, and that she was far too busy to meet me at the moment. And then rang off.'

'Blimey. Obviously a complete nutcase. Well, her loss, Clio, not yours.'

He was a charmer, she thought: still. Impossible to dislike.

Beatrice reflected, as she got ready for her dinner, that her mother had been absolutely right. Life seemed so much better already. What would she have done this evening, for instance, with the nanny going off for interviews? Got some strange babysitter in, which would have upset the children? They were so happy with Josh: he was absurdly indulgent with them, but he also was a very good father, attentive, loving and really very hands-on. He had been from the beginning, ready to share nappy-changing and mopping up, as well as the fun things.

The atmosphere in the house had definitely lifted since he came home, officially on a trial basis – for both of them, she had added, she didn't want to sound too domineering. And he was so desperate to please her, to show her how happy he was to be back; it was very sweet. Of course he was a bit of a philanderer – but her mother was also right about that, it wasn't everything. Or so she was teaching herself to think. He was also wonderfully generous, while being surprisingly organised financially; he was very good-tempered, and extremely kind. And admired her and was actually proud of her success. So – the balance sheet could be said to show a large credit in his favour at the moment.

She heard him coming in, in good time as he had promised. He ran up the stairs, came into their room, gave her a kiss.

'Hi. Your resident babysitter reporting. You look gorgeous.'

Beatrice knew she didn't, she wasn't the gorgeous type. But it was nice to hear, nonetheless. She returned the kiss.

'Thank you,' she said, then stood back and studied him. He was still so good-looking. She still fancied him – actually. Which was lucky. They hadn't had sex yet, not since his return. She hadn't been able to face it. Quite.

Suddenly it seemed possible. More than possible. A nice idea even.

'Josh,' she said, as he walked towards the door, 'Josh, try not to go to sleep before I get home. I'd – I'd like to tell you about the evening.'

His eyes met hers; he smiled. He knew exactly what she meant.

'I won't be asleep,' he said.

'Clio? Clio, it's me, Jocasta. How are you?'

'I'm fine. Back at work. Had a lovely time at your house. How's New York?'

'New York's wonderful. Really wonderful. Clio, I've got some news. Big news. We're married. Me and Gideon.'

'Married! But – '

'Don't but. We just did it. Went down to Vegas, actually. Anyway, I'm Mrs Gideon Keeble now. How cool is that?'

'Very cool.'

'Well! Don't you have anything else to say – like congratulations or something?'

Clio felt a pang of remorse. What must Jocasta think, ringing her with such momentous news, clearly expecting her to be delirious with joy for her, and the best she could manage was 'very cool'.

'Of course I do. Of course. I'm absolutely so happy for you. Both of you. It's wonderful, really, really wonderful. Give my love to Gideon, won't you? Tell him he's a lucky man.'

'I will. Anyway, we'll be home in a week, and we're going to give the most ginormous party. In Gideon's London house, probably. Haven't quite got a date yet, but pretty soon. Keep everything clear, won't you?'

'Of course I will,' said Clio. 'And – and congratulations again.'

Mrs Gideon Keeble. How insane was that? As Jocasta might have said.

Jocasta would actually have said it was reckless, daft even, if she'd read about it in the papers: someone of thirty-five, someone independent and ambitious, marrying a millionaire – well, a billionaire, actually – of fifty-one, who had three ex-wives and a difficult daughter. She'd have said it must be for his money, that she couldn't possibly fancy him, that the sex must be rubbish.

Well, it certainly wasn't for his money; she knew she would have married him anyway. Although she did rather like the glamour it had brought her, the first-class travel, what she called the ten-star hotels, the limitless amount of clothes she could buy, the beautiful cars, the knowledge that whatever she wanted she could have. And she was, she knew, rather besotted with Gideon's power. It all gave him another dimension, made him intriguing and exciting. In every way.

She did fancy him: a lot. He was very fanciable. Amazingly so, for someone of his age. The sex was – well, it was fine. Not specially, incredibly interesting, but maybe older men didn't do interesting. Anyway, she'd had plenty of interesting sex with Nick. It just didn't matter. It wasn't important. It was good and she really, really enjoyed it. They both did.

And she certainly didn't miss her job; she found Gideon much more interesting and rewarding, and being his wife much less demeaning and demoralising than door-stepping unhappy people.

She wasn't sure what she was going to do all day, but there were lots of possibilities. She wanted to buy a house that wasn't his, but theirs. She wanted to see a lot of the world. She wanted to entertain all the immensely interesting and famous (and not famous at all, come to that, but still interesting) people that he seemed to know. She wanted to talk to him forever.

When she met him at Heathrow after he got back from Barbados, he was smiling so much his face seemed fractured in two, and the first thing he said to her was, 'You're a magician!'

Hardly right, of course; her advice had been pretty standard agony aunt stuff – with a bit of personal experience thrown in – but apparently after a sticky start Fionnuala and he had talked more in five days than they had since she was ten.

Obviously the three polo ponies had pleased Fionnuala more than a bit, but she had actually asked him if there was anything he'd like to do on his last day and they'd gone up to Crane Beach, where the surf came in and the water was green, and swum and sunbathed all day and had a fish and fries lunch at the Crane Hotel on the top of the cliffs. She'd told him what she really wanted to do was be a doctor, and Gideon had nearly cried with pleasure.

Jocasta hadn't met Fionnuala yet, of course, and it would obviously be sticky when she did; but she'd worry about that when it happened.

So here she was, sated with happiness, with two days of shopping to do, and then home to England. And their wedding party.

She was still slightly reeling from the fact that she was married. It had rather seemed to happen, in retrospect at least, as she told Clio, 'by accident. I mean, there we were in Vegas, wandering about after lunch one day, having the most lovely time, and I suddenly thought, This is like a honeymoon, and I said so to Gideon, and – well, I don't know, we just decided to do it. We did the classic Vegas thing, walked into a register office, and asked two people off the street to be our witnesses. And I came out Mrs Gideon Keeble. Just like that. It was terribly exciting. And Gideon really wanted it. He's a Catholic, you know, and – '

'Jocasta,' said Clio, laughing, 'I don't think a register office in Vegas would quite satisfy the Catholic Church.'

'Wouldn't it? No, probably not. But it was a statement of commitment. A wonderful one. I'm so, so happy, you can't think.'

She had been half shocked, half amused by Gideon's confession of his Catholicism.

'Gideon, you don't really believe all that stuff, do you?'

'I don't exactly know,' he said, serious for a moment. 'It's pretty deep-seated, you know, when you've imbibed it with your mother's milk. Are you telling me you don't have a God of any kind?'

'No way.'

'So – your life is your own, is it? Entirely down to you?'

'Not any longer,' she said, suddenly serious. 'It's yours now instead.'

'Oh dear,' he said, and the intense blue eyes suddenly filled with tears. 'Oh dear, Jocasta, you mustn't say things like that. It's a bit too much for an old man.'

'There is just one thing,' she said. 'You don't – don't want me to have babies, do you? Because I can't, you know. I've told you why.'

'Jocasta, the last thing I want is any more babies. To have to share you. That's a promise.'

'That's all right then,' she said.

'I don't like all this sleaze in the Centre Forward party,' he said, now, slightly grimly. 'It's depressing. I've told Jack I'll pay off Farjon, though. He seemed grateful.'

'I should think he was. A million pounds!'

'It's only money. But I've also told him he's got to get them under control. They're throwing away everything they've achieved.'

'It's odd, isn't it? I mean, they all seemed so – so suitable. So totally one hundred and one per cent sleaze-less.'

'Few people are,' said Gideon, 'and certainly not in that business. It breeds trouble. It's the power. The fact that most of them look like bank clerks, taken one by one, doesn't alter the fact that together they can push the entire country around. They think, in no time at all, that they can walk on water. And then they get careless. It's as simple as that.'

The date of the party was set for 22 June; Jocasta had re-thought the thing and decided on the Berkshire house as the setting.

'It'll be a midsummer night's dream,' she said joyfully. 'How lovely! Maybe we should theme it, tell everyone to come as fairies.'

Gideon said she could do whatever she liked, but there was no way he was going as Oberon.

'I don't have the legs for it.'

'I think you have lovely legs,' said Jocasta.

'You have a biased view. Thank God.'

The guest list currently stood at three hundred and rising; Jocasta kept remembering people she wanted to ask. People she had been at school with, at university with, had worked with. She had invited the entire staff of the *Sketch*, including Nick. She had agonised over that; she knew he wouldn't want to come, but she could hardly exclude him from an invitation.

She rang him up, said how she'd love him to be there and why; he was short with her, thanked her, said he was going home to the country that weekend, but that he hoped she would be very happy. For the first time since she had married Gideon, Jocasta felt actually miserable; she thought of all the years with Nick, the fun they had had, how close they had been, and how much she hated hurting him. She put the phone down and cried for quite a long time.

The formal invitations to the Keeblefest, as Gideon persisted in calling it, went out in the last week of May. It was a little tight, but Jocasta said everyone would want to come so much they'd cancel almost anything except their own wedding.

Cruxbury Manor was the perfect setting, a piece of Georgian perfection, standing just slightly above the grounds, said to have been designed by Capability Brown.

'Which I don't believe,' Gideon said. 'If that man had really designed half the gardens ascribed to him, he would have had to work seven days a week for a hundred years. And he was less than sixty when he died.'

She had hired a party planner, Angie Cassell, a silvery stick-thin blonde, and in a few days she had caterers, menus, marquees, bands and DJs lined up. She also persuaded an extremely camp designer called MM, who refused to reveal his full name, to consider her theme. He dressed in white, did a lot of hand kissing and had an accent that would have vied with

Scarlett O'Hara's. He advised against the midsummer night's dream: 'It's just a little too overdone,' he said, making Jocasta feel rather small. 'I think we should go for Gatsby. The costumes are sooooo flattering. You don't want your guests cringing at their pictures in *Tatler*.'

Jazz bands, bootlegger bars, speakeasy-style dining tents, and gun-toting gangsters in spats and trilbies roaming the grounds sounded fun, and it was true: white suits and beaded Charleston dresses were infinitely more flattering than floating chiffon.

'And what about an on-going ten-minute crash course in the Charleston,' said Jocasta, 'from a professional, so people aren't afraid of trying?' Angie said she thought that would be the hugest fun, and MM clasped his hands together and cried, 'Perfect!'

Clio's first emotion on getting her invitation was panic. All those glittering people, all knowing each other, all those wonderful costumes: and she was a terrible dancer. And who should she take with her? It was hardly something you could go to alone. Could she be ill? Maybe that would be the best thing. She could accept and then phone on the morning with a stomach bug. Yes, that was a really good idea.

She wrote a formal acceptance, feeling quite pleased with herself; Jocasta called the next day, saying she wanted Clio to come the night before.

'I know it'll be difficult for you to get here and someone'll need to hold my hand through the day. What are you going to wear?'

Clio said, trying to sound delighted, that she thought she would hire something.

'Well, look, I've got a sweet girl making me something. Would you like her to do one for you?'

'Won't that be awfully expensive?' said Clio, while thinking that it would be one huge anxiety out of the way,

'No way,' said Jocasta airily. 'This is fake stuff, cheap as anything. She's doing one for Beatrice as well, so it can all go on the same bill and we can sort it out later.'

Clio tried very hard to believe her.

Chad Lawrence was going: of course. The entire Centre Forward party – or at least its major players – had been invited.

He wasn't exactly looking forward to it; he seemed to have survived the Farjon scandal by way of an apology to the House for his lack of care, and assurance that the money had already been repaid. But he was aware that his glossily successful image had been badly dulled. It had been his first serious bit of wrong-footing, and he didn't like it. And his constituency party had not been impressed.

Jack Kirkland, who hated parties, called Martha Hartley to see if she would like to go with him. His irritation when she said she couldn't go, that she was away that weekend, was profound.

'Martha,' he said, 'you are *not* away that weekend. You are going to the party. Gideon Keeble has just given us another million pounds, to bale us out of the Farjon debacle. This is a three-line whip. *You* are going. We are *all* going. Now do you want to come with me, or would you like to bring someone else?'

Martha, sounding rather shaken, said she would very much like to go with him.

Bob Frean was dreading the party. He could cope with Janet's political career, her ferocious ambition, and her absences from home – just. What he objected to was being dragged into it. He did it – occasionally – when he had to. But this was different; this was social. The kind of thing he most loathed.

She was in a dangerous mood at the moment; half-excited, half-withdrawn. It was one he knew well and dreaded. And she had developed one of her obsessions against someone. There was always someone; usually some rival in the party. It was generally another woman; she had hated that extremely nice woman, Amanda Platell, who had masterminded publicity for Hague's last campaign, and Theresa May, because of her shoe obsession. Just now it was this new girl, Martha Hartley, who was getting so much attention from everyone. She could hardly bring herself to utter her name.

Fergus Trehearn was euphoric at being invited. It was exactly the sort of occasion he loved best: glamorous, fun, high profile, and crawling with media. He would have a wonderful night. He also adored dancing, loved dressing up and was never happier than watching pretty women partying.

Fionnuala Keeble, with wisdom beyond her years, refused

the invitation. She did it by way of a text message to her father, which made him smile.

A large Irish contingent was expected, many of them Gideon's relatives.

'It'll be great for them to meet you at last,' said Gideon, smiling at Jocasta. She smiled back and thought how sweet that his accent always intensified when he was even talking about Ireland.

Josh was longing for the party; he and Beatrice had agreed that, for the time being, they would stay at home, working things out, spending weekends almost entirely with the children, and refusing all but work-based invitations. Of course it was worth it, but the thought of a night of social excitement was extremely welcome. And Beatrice had thrown herself into it, suggested they went as Scott and Zelda Fitzgerald, and had even hired a (fake) Bugatti for them to arrive in. He'd have fun: only of course he'd be very sensible and careful. The two were not incompatible after all.

Ronald Forbes, after carefully considering the invitation to his only daughter's wedding party, sent a note accepting, telling her he hoped she and Gideon would be very happy and enclosing a very large cheque by way of a wedding present. He knew it was a meaningless gesture: as meaningless, indeed, as his acceptance, which he had absolutely no intention of honouring. Nevertheless Jocasta was disproportionately pleased.

'I never thought he'd come, I really never did.'

'Well, there you are,' said Gideon, giving her a kiss.

Several days after the mass of invitations had been sent out, Jocasta had the idea.

'I'm going to ask Kate Tarrant,' she said to Gideon.

'What on earth for?'

'Because she'd love it. It would be the hugest treat for her. And it would sort of make up for all the trouble I've caused her. I'll tell her to bring her boyfriend, obviously, and maybe a couple of friends. Actually, I'll ask her parents as well, I think; that'll reassure them. Oh, and her grandmother.'

'Her grandmother! Jocasta, what on earth are you doing

inviting grandmothers to your parties? Unless it's to make me feel young.'

'Gideon, I swear you could fancy Kate's grandmother. She's really, really glamorous. You'll probably spend most of the night dancing with her.'

'I doubt it. And what about Carla? Do you really think they should come face to face?'

'Carla's not coming. She's staying with her mother in Milan. Honestly, Gideon, it'd be fun. And I'd love you to meet Kate. Do you really think it's a bad idea?'

'I think it's a terrible idea,' said Gideon.

'But why? What harm could it do?'

'Quite a lot, I'd say,' said Gideon. 'But I can see you're going to do it anyway. Just don't blame me if the boyfriend's sick all over the speakeasy.'

'If that's the worst thing you can think of,' said Jocasta, 'it isn't very serious.'

Chapter 29

Janet Frean had got Martha a ticket to hear Chad speak.

'On Thursday afternoon. About foxhunting. It's an important subject to us, because the rural vote is up for grabs. You really ought to be here, if you can possibly get away. Why don't you come and hear him, then we'll go out after that?'

'Oh – OK.' She was flattered. 'I'd like that. Thank you.'

She liked Janet very much: she was so supportive and always friendly, and an evening at her house in the company of a lot of other MPs, not talking about politics at all, had really made her feel much nearer to belonging.

She managed to get away for the debate, slipped into the public gallery, and sat there, enjoying the unfailing sense of excitement that sitting in the chamber gave her, remembering what had ensnared her in the first place.

Chad spoke witheringly of the 'Islington Government' and its lack of grasp of what foxhunting meant to the rural communities; said how many jobs would be lost, and how his party and his party alone seemed to understand that. There was a lot of shouting and booing, 'Take all your toffs over to China, teach *them* about hunting!' shouted some wit. Chad seemed unmoved. 'They'd probably enjoy it, they haven't heard of class envy over there,' he shouted back.

There was a lot more; afterwards they met him in the Strangers' Bar for a drink.

'I don't know how you can bear it,' said Martha. 'All that abuse. I know I never could.'

'My darling, you could and you will,' said Chad. He was high on adrenalin. 'It's rather fun, once you get going. I'm afraid we'll never win this one, though. No hope. The pressure to come in behind Tony will be incredible.'

'I don't really understand all that,' said Martha. 'How does it work?'

'Bargaining. The whips go round, the night before a big division, wheeling and dealing. They know everyone personally; they know what they all want. You give us your vote, they say, and we'll see your bill gets a third reading. You give us your vote and you'll get funding for your by-pass; you give us your vote, tell your old lady the knighthood's on its way. It's shameless.'

'That's terrible,' said Martha.

'That's politics. Oh – hi, Jack. Were you in the chamber just now?'

'No,' said Kirkland. He looked grim. 'I was at HQ. Hideous results from that focus group research are in. We've lost about ten per cent of our potential vote. Just over the last two months. I don't need to tell you why.' He glared at Chad. 'Mercifully, it was something I commissioned privately. We come in a good fourth, even after IDS. I'd hoped to publish it, if it was good news. As it is, I'm keeping it quiet. It's a rolling disaster, this sort of thing. People see you sinking, wonder what was so wonderful about you in the first place, switch back to something safer.'

'Oh God,' said Janet, 'that's appalling. I'm so sorry, Jack. I suppose saying it's mid-term won't help?'

'Of course not. We should be in our heyday still. Shiny new. We look old and sleazy already. Bloody shame. And it's so hard on the party workers, this sort of thing. It sends morale right down, makes their job twice as difficult.'

'Could I see the research? Maybe it isn't as bad as you think.'

'Janet, it's appalling. But – yes, if you like. Keep it confidential, for Christ's sake. You'd better take a look as well, Chad. See what you've done. God, it's depressing.'

'I think it'll be all right,' said Janet to Martha later. They were eating in Shepherds in Marsham Street. 'We've just had a run of bad luck, that's all. People's memories are very short. A bit more idiocy from IDS, another gaffe from Mandy and we'll be up there again, flying high, promising the world to the voters. A good conference – not that we can afford one – and we'll be back.'

'I was reading about the SDP,' said Martha. 'They had their first conference on a train. Took the party to the voters. I thought that was brilliant.'

Janet looked at her thoughtfully. Then she said: 'Yes, but we can't copy them. People would say that we had no original ideas.'

'Oh, I see,' said Martha humbly.

'Sorry. Didn't mean to crush you. I worry about you, you know. You've got a lot on your plate. Your job, which is terribly demanding, and your constituency duties every weekend. I would imagine those surgeries you do are a lot of work. And no one to confide in, to talk to. Or have you?'

'Well – not in the way you mean,' said Martha carefully.

'I know about pressure. And it's very, very tough, especially for a woman. This place is hard for us. It's such a male club. So – any problems you do have, that you need a sympathetic ear for, you know you can always bring them to me. I've been round the block a few times. And you'll find you do need a confidante – someone who knows what the pressures are.'

'Well – thank you,' said Martha, slightly awkwardly.

'Don't thank me. It's lovely to have an ally, a female ally. Potentially, anyway. We have to stick together.'

First thing the next morning, Janet went to Jack's office to see the research. It was very depressing. She saw what he meant.

'I feel we've squandered everything. Bloody Chad.'

'It's not all his fault,' she said.

'Oh really? Who else would you blame?'

'Eliot,' she said and then laughed. 'Sorry, Jack. Not funny.'

'Not in the least. No, it's the pair of them, you're right. God. What are we going to do?'

'Just keep trucking,' she said. 'Now look: I've been thinking. We ought to have a conference.'

'I know that. But we can't afford one.'

'Not the standard kind, no. But – remember what the old SDP did?'

'Of course. The train.'

'It was a brilliant idea, a PR coup in itself. I really think we might do something similar.'

431

'It was brilliant,' he said, 'but Janet, there are enough jibes about copying them already.'

'I realise that. But we could make a virtue of it. Come out with our hands up, saying yes, we know it's not our idea, but we're big enough to say so. It would be affordable, it would be brilliant publicity, and it is exactly what we could afford. Think about it, anyway.'

'I will,' he said slowly.

'Or we could adapt it. Call it a road show, keep the train idea, but get off it at all the major cities, link up with all the local people there, press, constituency workers and so on. Only that's not so different from the election battle buses. And you know, Jack, we all remember these things, but the punters don't. I bet not one in a hundred knows that's what the SDP did.'

'I'll think about it. Thank you. And this research – it never happened.'

'It never did.'

He smiled at her rather wearily. 'At least I can trust you, Janet.'

'You can indeed,' she said.

Jocasta was waiting at Heathrow for Gideon to arrive back from Washington. He had been there for a week, and she had missed him horribly. She had wanted to go with him, but with the party two days off now, with marquees and fountains and flowers and table plans to attend to, even she could see it wasn't possible.

Her father had sent a fax that day, telling her that after all he was unable to come to the party. She had been horribly hurt: it had surprised her how much.

'I should have known better by now,' she wailed on the phone to Josh. He tried, helplessly, to comfort her, saying he knew how busy their father was, how he knew he had been looking forward to the party. She was not in the least comforted.

'He went to your wedding,' she said bitterly. 'I don't think he'd even bother going to my funeral.'

'With a bit of luck,' said Josh, 'he won't be around.'

'I bet he will.'

She had been at the airport half an hour already and the plane wasn't due for another fifteen minutes. This must be love, she thought smiling to herself, being at arrivals for an hour longer than you needed to be.

Nicholas Marshall would often walk from Hampstead at least as far as St John's Wood before getting on the tube. Or get off the tube at Baker Street and walk the rest of the way to the House. It was the best way to see London, and you saw things that you'd never see from a taxi even, let alone the tube. Like – that Friday – walking down towards Carlos Place from Grosvenor Square, at about three o'clock, when he saw Janet Frean coming out of the Connaught and getting into one taxi, and shortly after her, Michael Fitzroy, Tory MP for West Birmingham, getting into another. Well. Who'd have thought that? She was a dark horse. All that stuff about the importance of the family and her superwoman image, and she was having it away with someone in an expensive hotel at lunchtime. Not quite as straightforward as she seemed then. He might tease her about it, if he got really bored. He felt bored quite a lot these days. Bored and lonely.

Nick was right that Janet was a dark horse, but wrong about the manner of it. As for Michael Fitzroy, as soon as he got back to the House, he called the political editor of the *Daily News* and told him he had an interesting story; when could they meet? It was about the Centre Forward party and some research.

Nothing had happened, no reporter had arrived on her doorstep, no accusing voice had come on the phone, no angry, accusing child had come into her life. It was going to be all right: she allowed herself to think that now. It had all died down, as she had told herself it would. Everything was safely and neatly parcelled up again; the past in the past, the present in the present.

But there was one thing straddling the two: and that was Ed.

He simply wouldn't go away. He called her and texted her endlessly. He had been in reception at Wesley her first day back. He was patient, reasonable, not aggressive, not difficult; he said he wasn't into stalking her, or pestering her, he just wanted to know she was all right.

A pattern had developed; he would call her every other day

or so on her mobile and as many times at home; he sounded surprisingly cheerful, absolutely calm, asking how she was. And she would tell him she was fine, that there was nothing wrong, that he had to forget about her, and he would say it was impossible, until he knew why he should. He would ask her what she was doing, and she would reply that she was working, or going to Binsmow, and after a few more pleasantries, he would tell her he would call her again soon and hang up. It was all very agreeable really: only it hurt more than she would have believed.

She missed him: horribly.

But – she was surviving. Everything did seem perfectly all right. And a blank, bland sexless life seemed a small price to pay for that.

'I'm fine, Ed,' she said, picking up the phone now, slightly reluctantly, 'really fine. Thank you.'

'Good. And are you going to this bash tonight?'

'What bash?' she said carefully.

'The big party that guy Gideon Keeble and his girlfriend are giving. To celebrate their wedding. I read about it in the *Mail*, about how you have to have a security number to give the guy at the gate, so you can get in.'

'No,' she said firmly. 'Why should I be going to that?'

'It said the whole of the Centre Forward party was going. I assume that includes you.'

'No, Ed, it doesn't.'

'I don't believe you,' he said. 'I shall call tomorrow and see how you enjoyed it.'

She knew whatever she said, he would.

'Bye, Ed,' she said firmly.

'What do you think then?'

Kate walked into the sitting room, where Nat was waiting for her. She was wearing an extremely short silver sequinned shift dress, almost backless, with a silver chiffon sash round the dropped waist. Her long legs were encased in white tights, and her shoes were silver also, high heeled with a bar across the instep. Her hair was in a long, loose plait, draped across her right shoulder; she wore a silver band on her forehead, dangly, glittery earrings and a slave bangle in the shape of a snake, coiled round her upper arm. Her huge dark eyes were heavily made up, with long, overtly fake eyelashes, and her mouth was a slash of red against her white skin. She carried a vast white fur stole, draped over one arm. There was a silence. Then he said:

'You look pretty – pretty cool.'

'Nat! I've been three hours getting like this. You have to do better than that.'

'Oh, OK then. You look great.'

'That's better. You don't look so bad yourself.'

'This OK, is it?' he said anxiously. 'I don't look like a tosser?'

'Not a bit. Did you have that suit before?'

'Course not. I bought it, didn't I? What'd I want with a dinner suit?' She considered his life and saw that he might not.

'Well, it suits you. You look really – really sexy.'

'Yeah?' He studied himself closely in the small oval mirror over the fireplace. 'So where'd you get that dress, Kate, it's well nice.'

'A fancy dress place Fergus took me to.'

'Oh yeah?'

Nat scowled; he wasn't keen on Fergus, he thought Kate took too much notice of him.

'What about your hair, I suppose Fergus did that an' all?'

'Don't be silly, Nat. He's not a hairdresser. No, Gran did it.'

'Yeah? She's all right, your gran. She still coming?'

'Of course. She's coming in the other car with Mum and Dad and some old bloke she calls her date. She's really excited. Mum and Dad aren't exactly looking forward to it,' she added. 'Dad's really miserable.'

'He'll be all right,' said Nat confidently. 'He can stick with me.'

It was a tribute to Fergus's powers of persuasion that Kate was going at all, let alone her parents. They had been completely horrified when the invitations arrived, one for Kate and partner, one for Mr and Mrs James Tarrant. Jim had told Helen to put theirs in the bin where it belonged, that Kate would go over his dead body and wild horses wouldn't drag him there.

'Well, you'll have to die then,' said Kate calmly, 'because I'm going. I'm not missing this, not for anything.'

435

'No harm can possibly come to her,' Fergus told them, earnestly. 'This will be a grown-up party; in fact she'll probably be bored in no time. But it will be wonderful for her to go, and a lovely reward for working so hard at her exams. And isn't that great, Jocasta inviting you, too? You'll have a wonderful night, I promise you. She told me she was asking Kate's grandmother as well: I think that's a very nice touch.'

'Oh God,' said Jim.

Finally, because Kate was so determined to go, they all went. She couldn't go alone, with Nat and Sarah and Bernie, Helen thought, and it was asking too much of Fergus to look after her. There was no way Jim would entrust her to Jilly – 'She'd be selling her into the white slave trade before the end of the night,' he said.

As time went by, Helen was actually beginning to look forward to the party, just a little. It sounded so glamorous; Fergus had helped her with hiring her costume, a very nice silver shift dress, and her mother had suggested she had her hair pulled back into a loose chignon, wear long glittery earrings and carry a long cigarette holder. After all, as she said to Jim, no one would expect anything of them, they wouldn't have to talk to anyone frightening, except of course Jocasta's new husband, who was, after all, their own generation. And he must be a very respectable person; Kate had told her that he and Jocasta were going to the concert and fireworks at the Palace for the Queen's Golden Jubilee. That had clinched it, really, for Helen. They could just sit there and eat some food, which she was sure would be very nice, and watch. It would be like going to the cinema.

Jilly was beside herself with excitement, trying on and rejecting dress after dress, discussing her hairstyle endlessly with Laura at Hair and Now in Guildford, over old copies of *Vogue*, practising the Charleston in her sitting room. The invitation had said – of course – 'Mrs Jillian Bradford and partner' and she had agonised over who to take; finally settling on Martin Bruce, who had been best man at her own wedding and was a recent widower.

Sarah and Bernie and two of the more reliable boys they went round with, all invited by Kate, had pretended to be cool about it at first, but as the days went by and the column inches

436

about the party grew, they gave up and became very excited. The rumour that Westlife were going to do a spot really pushed them over the top. OK, they were a bit naff, but still they were – well, they were Westlife, for God's sake. There. In the flesh. To dance to. It wasn't exactly bad.

'Right,' said Nat, as the doorbell rang, 'that'll be our car then. S'pose we'd better go.'

He was interestingly composed; nothing really fazed him. His attitude to life was very attractive, Helen thought: she had become quite fond of him over the past few weeks. He was cheerful, good-natured and, in a rather idiosyncratic way, very nicely mannered; he was also touchingly thoughtful and clearly devoted to Kate. Helen hoped she wasn't being naive in her confidence that they weren't sleeping together.

Clio was still wrestling with her hair when the first cars started coming up the drive. She had a wild desire to run away; Jocasta would never miss her now – she was standing on the steps of the house in a state of high excitement, greeting, kissing, laughing, hugging. She had done her duty after all, Clio thought; calming her all day and just occasionally wandering round the grounds, marvelling at what imagination, combined with money, could accomplish. Jay Gatsby would have been very satisfied with this.

A massive marquee stood just to the rear of the house, with lanterns strung across the trees above it; there was a jazz band on a platform on one side, and a white grand piano, complete with pianist in white tie and tails, on the other. A fountain, made of outsize champagne glasses, played on the terrace; and beside that stood Gideon's pride and joy, a black and silver twenties Chevrolet; a photographer was on hand for any guests who might wish to pose in it. Several cocktail bars, complete with barmen, were dotted about the grounds; a flashing sign on a gleaming black-and-silver deco-style structure said 'Casino', and next to it, something that declared itself to be a cinema.

Girls in long white crepe dresses wandered languidly about with borzois on leads ('Actually not Gatsby at all, more thirties, but never mind,' Jocasta said to Clio), men in Al Capone suits and slouch hats carried trays of drinks, and gangsters' molls, with too much make-up and floozies' curls, offered cigarettes and lighters. After dinner, and before the dancing, there was to be a treasure hunt, a great twenties craze.

It was a perfect evening, warm, but not hot, the sky starry, a half moon hanging obligingly in it.

And of course she had met Gideon. And of course she had been totally charmed by him. She could see so easily how Jocasta would have fallen in love with him, how it had all happened. Warm, easy, tactile – and extremely attractive, not only good-looking, in his untidy Irish way, but with that crackling energy, and capacity for intent concentration on whoever he was talking to. Clio felt she could have fallen in love with him herself. For a person as romantic, emotionally hungry as Jocasta: well, he had obviously been irresistible.

Just the same, she thought, observing him over the twenty-four hours, watching as he appeared from time to time, then vanished again, completely uninvolved in the party, in what was going on, while striding about the house, mobile clamped to his ear, jabbing at his Palm Pilot, summoned frequently by the PA he had installed at the house for the day, to deal with some crisis or other, to take calls, sign faxes, read e-mails, was this really the husband Jocasta needed?

When the first few months were over would she just become part of his empire, another dazzling acquisition to be displayed and admired, but no longer the absolute object of his attention? Clio feared for Jocasta.

And now the party was about to come to life; the guests, all the brilliant, famous, distinguished guests would appear, and Clio felt as close to terrified as she could ever remember. The dressmaker had done her proud, made her a pale blue chiffon dress, ankle-length with a drifting skirt, set off with long ropes of pearls; and her hair lent itself perfectly to the period, curved obediently into Marcel-like waves, held back from her face with a pair of diamanté clips.

But her spirit didn't quite match it. She sprayed herself lavishly with scent, touched up her already brilliant red mouth – and then sank back on her bed, feeling dreadful. Whoever could she talk to, who on earth would she know? God. What a nightmare. She couldn't do this, she really couldn't.

And then she had the idea. She could leave now. She would just quietly slip away: no one would miss her. Least of all Jocasta. It was perfectly brilliant. Why hadn't she thought of it before? She could call for a cab once she reached the lane that led to the house; it would be easy.

She smiled at herself in the mirror with positive pleasure. Deciding to stay in her costume – she might meet Jocasta on the stairs or something if she changed – she picked up her bag and the fox stole she had hired and cautiously opened her door. The corridor was deserted; she was nearly at the bottom of the stairs, when she heard her name.

'Clio, hello! How lovely to see you.'

It was Fergus, smiling up at her, wonderfully handsome in white tie and tails; he came up to her, caught her hand and kissed it.

'You look marvellous. A real twenties femme fatale! What a lucky man I am, to have caught you on your own.'

She smiled at him rather feebly, wondering what she might do next.

'Would you like to take a turn round the grounds with me? Once everyone arrives, we won't be able to see for looking.'

'Well – I – ' This was hugely tempting; Fergus was the opposite of demanding company, so easy and charming and funny. She might begin to feel part of the evening with him, even enjoy it a bit, and then when he found someone better, which he surely would, she could slip away.

'Or,' he said, 'do you have a beau waiting for you to come down and join him? I expect you do.'

'Fergus, I don't have any beau anywhere,' she said laughing, 'and I'd love to take a turn with you. I've been sitting up there in my room, feeling quite scared.'

'You ridiculous woman,' he said, 'what have you to be scared of? It's going to be fun, just you see if it isn't. And did you know we're on the same table for dinner? With old Johnny Hadley, diary writer on the *Sketch*. He's the best fun in the world and has so many scurrilous stories. We'll all have a wonderful time together. Come along, my darling, and let's take a tour. Now, did you get that hospital job you were after?'

'Good heavens,' said Jilly, 'isn't this absolutely out of this world? Just look at those lights – oh, thank you so much,' she said graciously to the driver. 'Martin, dear, take my stole for a moment, would you – and that fountain over there, how absolutely marvellous – oh, now there is Jocasta. My God, what a dress!'

Jocasta stood on the steps of the house, with Gideon, wearing a dress that was a faithful copy of a Chanel, vintage 1924. It was ankle-length chiffon, in palest grey, with a layered petal-like hem, the fabric printed in a spiders' web pattern in a darker grey. When she raised her arms, wings unfolded from the dress in the same floating fabric, falling from her fingers; she looked like a dancer, the star of some exotic revue – a shining, glittering star.

'Jilly, how perfectly wonderful to see you! You look younger than ever. I want you to meet my husband, Gideon Keeble, I've told him so much about you. Helen and Jim, it's so nice of you to come, and where is the lovely Kate? Kate, darling, come and give me a kiss. My God, you look wonderful, and who is this desperately handsome man you've got with you?'

'Nat Tucker,' said Nat, holding out his hand. 'Pleased to meet you. Nice place you've got here,' he added, 'very nice indeed.'

'We like it,' said Jocasta, 'thank you. I'll catch up with you all later, just a bit busy at the moment – go through there and you'll all be looked after.'

'She's very nice-looking,' said Nat, the first to take a glass of champagne, leading the way through the arch of flowers that led across the side of the house and down to the wonderland below.

'Isn't she? And nice too,' said Kate, following his example, sipping at her glass, aware that a great many people were staring at her. 'Oh my God, Sarah, look, a cocktail bar and there's another; this is going to be really cool! Let's explore.'

'Kate . . .' called Helen feebly, as the six of them disappeared into the lantern-lit twilight. But she was gone.

'I think we should do exactly the same,' said Jilly. 'Just look over there, it's – my goodness, a casino, and – I don't believe it, there's even a cinema! Do let's see what's on.'

* * *

'Well, he's certainly pushed the boat out for her, hasn't he?' said Josh. He and Beatrice were settling themselves at their table for dinner: the family table, with Gideon and Jocasta, their two young half brothers and their girlfriends and Jocasta's godmother and her husband, substituting for Ronald Forbes. Jocasta had changed the table plan through a blur of tears.

The marquee slowly filled, the buzz of conversation rising and falling as people moved to their tables, greeting people on the way; it was almost half an hour before everyone was seated.

'And soul food!' said Fergus to Clio. 'What a brilliant idea. Don't look like that, you'll love it. And if you don't, there's an alternative. Of course.'

'They really have thought of everything, haven't they?' said Jack Kirkland to Martha. She smiled.

'Indeed. It's been quite wonderful.'

So far it really had been fine; Jack had been a marvellous escort, courteous and attentive, introducing her to anyone who would listen as one of Centre Forward's brightest stars. Janet Frean, rather surprisingly dressed in tie and tails herself, her auburn hair slicked back – 'Well, I don't like dresses' – had been warm and friendly.

A rather subdued Chad told her she would greatly improve the standard of looks in the House when she got there. Eliot Griers, more subdued still, told her it was nice to see her, and asked her how she was getting on; Caroline Griers was effusively friendly. Actually sitting next to her was Chris Pollock, the editor of the *Sketch*, whom she had liked enormously when she met him at the Centre Forward launch. Chad was on her other side; she asked him where his daughters were.

'Oh, there's a younger contingent down there,' he said gesturing vaguely towards the other side of the marquee. 'They're having a wonderful time. Too many cocktails, I'm afraid, but it's that sort of night, isn't it?'

Martha agreed and noticed that, like her, he was hardly drinking. She would have liked a little more champagne, but she knew she couldn't afford to. She still felt the need to be very watchful.

Towards the end of the meal, Gideon stood up. He smiled round the vast space, raised his hands for silence, picked up a microphone.

'He looks marvellous, doesn't he?' whispered Beatrice to Josh. 'He really is wonderfully handsome.'

Gideon had refused to dress up; he said people his age and size had no business to be embarrassing everyone. His only concession to the theme was a wing collar on his dress shirt.

'No speeches, I've promised Jocasta. Except for two things: thank you all for coming. It's been a wonderful night – so far. I'm told it is yet extremely young. Not being quite that myself, I am hoping I can last a little longer.

'And I just wanted to tell you all, our friends, our very good friends, how much I love Jocasta and how happy she has made me.' He reached down and took her hand; a chiffon wing spread itself across the space between them. 'I don't know what I've done to deserve her, but I only hope I can make her as happy in return.'

Jocasta promptly started to cry; Gideon leant over and wiped her tears tenderly away with his fingers.

'She's like that,' he said, 'terribly predictable.'

A roar of laughter went up. As it died again, he said, 'Next on the programme is the treasure hunt; each table has a list of clues. First back here wins. I shall be waiting patiently. Good luck.'

One of the half brothers' girlfriends, a giggly blonde with wonderful legs and a very impressive cleavage, reached for the list and said: 'Shall I read it and pass it on?'

'No,' said Josh, who was sitting next to her, close enough to feel her warmth and smell her musky perfume, 'read it aloud. We'll all listen very attentively.'

He leant over her, studying the list, along with her cleavage; Beatrice watched him from the other side of the table: he was very drunk already. Still, he'd been so extremely good lately; maybe she could allow him just one night off.

'I'm going to go and visit the Tarrants at their table,' whispered Fergus in Clio's ear. 'But I will be back, I promise. Don't go off treasure hunting without me.'

'I won't,' she said laughing and then turned back to Johnny Hadley who was telling her yet another scurrilous story about Charles and Camilla. He could hardly believe his luck in finding a pretty woman who had never heard any of his sort of well-worn gossip before, and instead of mocking him, as the media girls did, Clio's eyes got bigger with every story.

She found it hard now to believe she hadn't wanted to come to this party. She had had a wonderful time; Fergus, she discovered, was not just charming and amusing himself, he made you feel the same. For almost the first time in her life Clio was experiencing the dizzy experience of making someone else laugh. And although he did disappear from time to time, at the sighting of some new high-profile celebrity, he kept coming back to her.

She just wished he did something else for a living – and then wondered why on earth it mattered to her.

'Martha – isn't it?'

'Yes. Yes, it is. Hello, Josh.'

'Hello. Wonderful to see you.'

'And you.'

'Who'd have thought we should all be reunited at a bash like this?'

'Who indeed?'

'What are you doing these days? Law, isn't it?'

'Law, yes. And a foray into politics. And you?'

'Oh – working for the old family firm. Are you – married or anything?'

'No, nothing. You?'

'Oh, I'm married. Yes. Very much so. Two children as well. Girls. Dear little things.'

'And is your wife here?'

'Oh – yes. Somewhere. Well – what a long time ago that seems, doesn't it?'

'It does indeed. Another lifetime altogether . . . Well, I must be getting back to my table. Nice to see you, Josh.'

'Nice to see you too. Very nice dress,' he added.

'Thank you.'

Well, that had been all right. She'd got through that. No awkward questions. He still looked pretty good, a bit heavier, maybe, and possibly a bit less hair, but you could still just about see the golden boy there.

Yes, it had been fine. She needn't have worried about that.

'Who was your smooth friend?' It was Bob Frean's voice; Janet had proved a rather enthusiastic treasure seeker and been missing for ages.

'Oh – Jocasta's brother, Josh,' she said carefully.

'I didn't know you knew them that well.'

'Oh – I don't really. Not any more. I met them when we were young.'

She was beginning to feel a bit panicky; she took a deep breath, smiled at him feebly.

'Do you want to go over to the casino? Or have a dance, even?'

'I'd love to go to the casino,' she said. She had learnt, when she was feeling like this, that the trick was to keep moving.

'Come on, then.'

He took her hand, pulled her out of her chair. 'Want to take a drink with you?'

'No, no, I'm fine. Are you sure Janet won't be wondering where you are?'

'It'll make a change if she does,' he said and smiled just the briefest moment too late. Ah, Martha thought, not quite the perfect partnership then.

They walked slowly away from the table: she felt better already.

'Clio! There you are, my darling. I've been looking for you everywhere. Come along, the nightclub awaits.'

She had been walking back from the ladies, had seen him talking to Jocasta rather intently. Probably she'd told him to keep an eye on her that evening, she thought, suddenly less sure of herself.

'Fergus, I'm sure you've got lots of mingling to do,' she said, trying to sound cool.

'I haven't. Let's go and dance.'

'You really don't have to, you know.'

'Now look,' he said, sitting down on the grass, pulling her down beside him, 'look, Clio, you have to get over this ridiculous inferiority complex of yours. You are a very attractive, very sexy woman. And a very nice and interesting one. Anyone would be pleased to dance with you, to talk to you. I watched Johnny Hadley drooling over you at dinner. Now come along, I saw you in the Charleston school. You were the star pupil at the time. Which is more than I could say for myself. Maybe you can give me a hint or two.'

'Well – '

'Oh, stop dithering,' he said, 'or I really will go and find someone to mingle with. But I don't want to. How do I get that into your extremely beautiful, but it seems rather thick, little head?'

He stood up, held out his hand; Clio took it and followed him meekly to the nightclub.

'Oh, this is so cool.'

Kate was over-excited, drunk not only with champagne and cocktails, but with the noise, the music, the awareness that a great many people were looking at her, admiring her, pointing her out. 'You enjoying it, Nat?'

'Yeah. Pity about the music.'

'Well, it's an old people's party, isn't it? What do you expect? It's still fun, come and dance. Bernie, you coming?'

'No, not for the moment. Cal's not feeling so well.'

'Where is he?'

Bernie indicated the bushes.

'I said I'd go with him, hold his head and that, but he said to leave him alone. Oh, here he is now. You all right, Cal?'

'Yeah, fine.' He was greenish white; he sat down unsteadily. 'Wouldn't mind some water. Well – maybe in a minute.' And he disappeared back towards the bushes.

'Well, my ex-star reporter, how is married life treating you? Is it really better than the *Sketch*?'

Chris Pollock had invited Jocasta to dance; they were walking towards the disco.

'It's wonderful,' said Jocasta. 'Truly.'

'You don't miss it at all?'

'Not at all. Honestly.'

445

'Well, I suppose I should be happy for you. But we certainly miss you. Conference is not the same without your often daft suggestions. The newsroom is not the same without your legs – '

'Chris! That is so chauvinist.'

'Sorry. I was born that way. And the paper is not the same without your by-line and the stories beneath it.'

'Really?'

She stopped suddenly, looked at him; and for a moment she knew she did miss it, and how much, missed the excitement, the pursuit of stories, the absurd panics, missed the easy chat of the morning conference, moving, with the relentless rhythm of a newspaper's day, into the tension of the evening one. Missed the gossip, the absurd rumours, missed the rivalry, missed the fun.

'Well – maybe just a bit,' she said finally.

'Thought so. Young Nick misses you. That's for sure. He's a man with a broken heart.'

'Well,' said Jocasta, 'if he hadn't been such a commitment-phobe, maybe it needn't have been broken.'

'Are you telling me,' he said, his eyes dancing with malice, 'you married Gideon on the rebound?'

'No, I am not. Of course I'm not. Don't put words into my mouth.'

'Sorry, darling. Only teasing. I know love when I see it.'

'You? Oh, please!'

'Of course. Nothing more sentimental than a newspaper editor. You should know that.'

'Martha! It is you, isn't it? How lovely!' A girl was standing in front of her; a small, slender girl, holding the hand of a rather handsome man with close-cropped grey hair. 'I'm Clio. I hoped I'd find you.'

She would never have recognised her: tubby, shy Clio, transformed into this pretty, sparkly woman with diamonds in her hair. She managed to smile.

'Yes, yes, it's me. Hello, Clio. I – I thought you might be here. This is Bob Frean. Bob – Clio Scott. We – knew each other when we were younger.'

'We went travelling together,' said Clio, smiling. 'In what is now known as a gap year. I've been so impressed with everything

I've read about you, Martha. Especially the political bit. Are you in politics, Bob?'

'Thankfully not. But my wife is.' He looked rather uncertainly at Fergus.

'Oh, I'm sorry,' said Clio, 'this is Fergus Trehearn.'

'Hi,' said Fergus. 'Isn't this a fantastic party? And doesn't Jocasta look wonderful?'

'She certainly does.'

There was a silence; then Clio said: 'So – where are you off to? The cinema? The disco?'

'The casino,' said Bob Frean. 'I'm no dancer, I'm afraid.'

'Well, it's worth looking in at the disco,' said Clio, 'honestly. Just put your head in. We're going that way, we're off to the cinema next, they're showing *The Jazz Singer*.'

'How marvellous,' said Bob Frean. 'I don't think I can resist that. Martha, fancy a movie?'

'No,' said Martha hastily. Here was her escape: she could disappear, call a cab, tell Jack Kirkland she wasn't well, she'd surely done enough for the wretched party for one evening, she could get out safely, before –

'Clio dear! You look marvellous. And Fergus, how nice!'

A glamorous woman was hurrying towards them.

'My goodness, Mrs Bradford,' Clio said, 'how lovely to see you, that dress is – '

'Would you just excuse me a moment?' said Fergus. 'I see Helen on her own over there.'

'How sweet of you, Fergus,' said Jilly. 'What a party, Clio! My dear, I didn't think they did them like this any more. So generous of Jocasta to invite us all. But I'm sorry, I'm interrupting your conversation – '

'No, no, it's fine,' said Clio. 'Mrs Bradford, this is Martha Hartley, an old friend of mine and Jocasta's – Martha, this is Mrs Bradford – '

'Oh, Jilly, please. How do you do, Martha? I was just dragging Martin off to look in the disco, the children are all having a ball in there – such fun to watch.'

'I said the same,' said Clio. 'Come on.'

'Do you mind, Martha?' said Bob. 'It sounds like fun.'

'Of course not.'

They stood just inside the disco, taking it in, the strobe lighting, the gyrating bodies; the music was very loud, very strong. Martha suddenly felt dizzy; she put out her hand to steady herself on one of the tables.

Bob Frean noticed. 'Do you want to sit down?'

'No, no, I'm just a bit hot. Maybe I should go back outside –'

She did feel very dizzy; she sat down abruptly.

And then it happened.

'Gran! Come and dance. Come on, I'll show you.'

'Darling, no. I couldn't possibly –'

'Oh, hi, Dr Scott. I didn't know you were here. Isn't this cool, isn't it great? Are you enjoying yourself?'

'I certainly am.'

She must get outside. She must.

She was tall, this girl in a silver dress, tall with long, long legs and wild fair hair. She looked like – she looked just like . . .

It wasn't possible. Of course it wasn't possible. Why, how could it be? Just a girl, they all looked the same, exactly the same. Sit quietly, Martha, sit still, don't stare – they all look the same . . .

'Oh, here's Fergus. You'll come and dance with me, won't you, Fergus? I'm having such a good time. Come on –' She twined her hand in his, pulled him onto the dance floor, walking backwards, laughing. She heard him say: 'Kate, Kate!'

Kate. Kate.

'We should go,' she said to Bob.

But another girl had come over now; another young one, very, very young. She seized Bob's hand, and Martin's too, pulled them after her. They were all laughing, the men clearly flattered, old men invited to dance by beautiful young girls.

'What fun!' the Bradford woman kept saying. 'What fun.'

The room spun, the music seemed to roar; it was hot, poundingly hot, she was going to faint, it was all blurry now, blurry and far away.

She managed somehow to stand up. 'Sorry. Must get outside.'

Away from her. Away from having to look at her.

'You look awful, Martha.' Clio's face was concerned. 'Here, sit down, put your head between your knees. Jilly, could you find some water?'

She was just beginning to feel a little better, standing again, trying to get outside when: 'Gran, come on. *Please*. Your boyfriend's doing awfully well. A real cool dude.'

'Just a minute, dear. We're going outside for a moment.'

'No need for you to come,' said Martha. 'I feel better now. Honestly.'

'You look better,' said Clio, 'much better. Let's go outside, into the air.'

She took Martha's arm, began to usher her out.

'Darling, get another glass of water, would you?' said Jilly to Kate. 'Miss Hartley isn't feeling very well.'

'Yeah, sure,' said the girl. She grabbed a glass, followed them outside.

'Thank you, darling. Here you are, Martha, dear, drink this. Just little sips. That's right. Deep breaths.'

'You really do look better, Martha,' said Clio. 'Less green. Good. It really was awfully hot in there.'

'Oh dreadful,' said Jilly Bradford. 'Of course you don't notice it,' she added to the girl with the flying hair. The girl called Kate. Sitting so near she could touch her. 'Martha, have a little more water. That's right. I don't think you've been introduced to my granddaughter, have you? This is Kate, Kate Bianca Tarrant as she likes to be called these days. Kate, darling, this is – Oh my God. Clio, she's fainted!'

Chapter 30

How on earth had this happened? She was in bed in a room in Jocasta's house, with no chance of getting home. Unless she walked. Which she couldn't. What could she do, how could she escape?

It had been all right at first, after she had fainted; Bob had helped her back to the table, and she had persuaded them all that she was fine, that she could just leave in her car, it was here already, waiting for her; she was simply exhausted, had been working too hard, and it had been terribly hot in the disco. It was too early for anyone to leave, it would break up the party, and she was fine. Really fine.

She sat calmly arguing her case, her teeth chattering, despite the heat. She knew what it was: shock. It was hard to conceal. She saw Janet Frean watching her carefully, her dark eyes thoughtful; after a while, she stood up and said: 'Martha, we're going to take you home. There's no way you're going to go off on your own. Come along, I'll bring your things – unless you want to stay a little longer and recover?'

'No,' she said, 'no, I don't want to stay.'

She kept her eyes fixed on Janet's face; she was afraid that if she allowed herself to look around her, she might see – see the girl again. She couldn't allow that. She really couldn't.

Somehow she managed to stand up; her legs obeyed her to that extent. What they wouldn't do, it seemed, was walk; and then she suddenly found she couldn't breathe properly either, she was struggling for breath. And then she felt suddenly quite desperately ill; she had pains in her chest, and she could feel her heart thudding so hard, and beating so violently that she could hardly bear it. She was having a heart attack, she thought, she was going to die, and her last thought was that it was not entirely a bad thing, if she died now, no one would ever know.

She started trembling violently, shuddering in every part of her, and heard someone saying 'Get that other girl, the doctor, for God's sake!'

She came back to herself, very slowly; she was sitting on a chair, and someone, she didn't know who, was holding a paper bag over her face.

'Try to breathe steadily,' said a voice, a female voice, vaguely familiar. 'You're fine, I'm pretty sure you're just having a panic attack. That's better. Good. Go on, deep breaths.'

Martha had heard of people having panic attacks; she rather disapproved of them, dismissed them as hysterical.

She tried to push the paper bag away. 'Just leave it a tiny bit longer. It'll help,' said the voice again and she realised who it was: Clio, Clio who had been looking after her earlier.

'You're fine, Martha, you really are. Feel a bit better?'

Her voice was calm, her smile, as Martha looked at her, very kind. She was nice, Martha thought, she shouldn't have been so rude to her. She'd have to apologise; when she felt better.

'Yes, thank you. I do. A bit.'

Clio said, 'Fergus, if you could help her into the house, she can lie down, get some rest. That's what she needs.'

Into the house, she couldn't go into this house, Jocasta's house. It was dangerous, much too dangerous.

'Please,' she said in a feeble whisper, 'please, I'm fine, I'd just like to go home.'

'Not a good idea,' said Clio, 'not yet, anyway. Now, this very kind gentleman is going to carry you – '

'Well you're certainly not heavy,' said an Irish voice, picking her up gently. 'What do you live on, air? Or do you allow yourself a little bit of water with it?' He smiled at her, clearly anxious to make her feel better, and he carried her easily up through the gardens into the house, then Fergus and Clio were helping her to a couch in some large room and Clio said: 'I'll just get you some water and a blanket, just stay there and don't worry about anything.'

451

'I should go,' said Martha, 'some people have very kindly offered to take me home, they'll be waiting.'

'They're not waiting, I told them you'd be staying the night,' said Clio firmly.

'I can't stay the night,' said Martha. 'It's out of the question. Please, Clio, do let me go home.'

'You're honestly not up to it,' said Clio, 'and you can't be alone.'

'Why not?' asked Martha.

'Because it might happen again. Now look, Martha, calm down, you can go home in the morning – I'll take you myself, if necessary. But right now, you've got to stay put and rest. Jocasta's organising a room for you, she won't be long.'

God. Jocasta as well; both of them, in the same house. She felt as if she was held in some terrible trap.

'Hi, Martha.' It was Jocasta, smiling down at her, in a way she really didn't deserve. Why did they both have to be so nice? 'I've got a bedroom for you. Fergus is going to take you up there and – '

'Please,' said Martha for the last desperate time, 'please let me go home. You've been so kind but I'm all right now and – '

'You can't go home,' said Jocasta. 'Dr Scott says so. Now I have some guests to attend to, but I'll see you later. Or in the morning. Just try and rest. The room's on the second floor, sorry.'

'It's me you should be saying sorry to,' said Fergus.

'Oh nonsense, the exercise'll do you good. Anyway, she can't weigh more than about three stone. Sleep well, Martha.'

She gave in, allowed herself to be carried upstairs by Fergus and helped into bed by Clio. And now she felt more alone and more frightened than she had ever been in her life.

Everything had changed suddenly, she realised. That was the most frightening thing of all. She couldn't deny it all any longer. The child she had left behind was no longer Baby Bianca, totally anonymous, forever a baby; she had become Kate, a beautiful sixteen-year-old girl. She had been in the same room as her, breathed the same air, seen her, watched her, almost touched her; she had become reality.

She sat up, bolt upright, feeling the panic coming back, the breathlessness, the sweating.

'God,' she said aloud, 'God, what do I do?'

And then the door opened and Janet Frean came in.

Martha was so pleased to see her, a friendly, reassuring person, that she burst into tears. Janet sat down on the bed, held her like a child and told her to cry as much as she liked. Which Martha did, and for quite a long time: helpless, uncontrollable tears; and Janet just sat there, in complete silence, except for the occasional soothing, hushing noise, until finally Martha stopped crying and lay back on her pillows.

'I'm so sorry,' she said, 'so terribly sorry.'

'Martha,' said Janet, smiling at her gently, 'Martha, stop apologising. Please. You've done nothing wrong.'

Shocked into speech suddenly, she said: 'Oh, but I have. That's the whole point, Janet. You don't understand.'

'Do you want to talk about it? This wrong thing you say you've done? Which I'm sure you haven't.'

This denial, of what Martha knew to be true, made her agitated again; she started to shiver, to feel the breathlessness coming on.

'Janet, I have, I have! I've done something terrible, I – oh God!'

'Well – all right,' said Janet calmly, 'you've done something terrible. Why don't you tell me about it? Nothing seems as bad once you've shared it with someone, it's a fact. And I would say I'm totally unshockable – having five children and spending a great deal of my life at Westminster has done that for me, at least. Try me. Try talking about it. Please, I can't bear to see you like this. Tell me what it is.'

And suddenly, she did. She had to. She couldn't fight it all any longer.

She knew she shouldn't, shouldn't admit to it, to this extraordinary, dreadful shocking thing that she had kept locked away inside her head for all those years; but suddenly the deniable had become undeniable, and she lay weak and wretched on her pillows in the dim room, with the noise of the party in the distance, the party where her daughter danced the night away, and told Janet what she had done.

Part Three

Chapter 31

'She was weird,' said Kate, sinking back in the limo, 'really weird. Didn't you think she was weird, Nat?'

'Don't know,' he said, 'didn't really talk to her. I was looking after poor old Cal. He was in a bad way.'

'Is he all right now?'

'He's asleep,' said Bernie's voice behind them.

'He looks fine to me,' said Sarah, examining Cal's apparently lifeless form. 'What a tosser. He must have missed half the party.'

'So, who was weird?' asked Kevin.

'That woman,' said Kate. 'The one who fainted.'

'Yeah, she took one look at you and fainted,' said Bernie, giggling. 'Honest, she was all right up till then, as I said to the doctor woman. What was her name?'

'Clio,' said Kate. 'She's my gran's doctor.'

'What? Who fainted?' Kevin sounded irritable. 'You're talking bloody riddles.'

'We're not. You're not concentrating. A friend of Jocasta's did,' said Kate. 'Well, she was her friend when they were young. She was in the paper the week before me, she's in politics and law and she knew Clio as well – that's the doctor, for those of you with learning difficulties.'

Bernie giggled.

'Now *she* was nice,' said Nat approvingly. 'Anyway, it was a good bash. And what about them snappers, Kate, calling your name as we left. You're a celeb now, whether you like it or not.'

He sounded rather complacent, as if the credit was largely his. Rather than Fergus, who had quietly tipped a couple of

457

papers off about Baby Bianca's attendance at the bash of the year.

'I thought I might be in some of the pictures an' all,' he added hopefully.

Jack Kirkland was deep in conversation with Gideon Keeble when Janet rejoined them.

'You've been a while,' he said. 'Is she all right?'

'She's fine. Asleep. Goodness knows what it was all about, poor little thing.'

'I don't think I would describe Martha in quite those terms,' said Gideon lightly. 'Tough little cookie, if you ask me.'

'I think I'd agree with Gideon,' said Jack Kirkland. 'She is quite tough. Law at the level she practises it is no easy option. And to manage to fit in the politics as well – pretty remarkable.'

'That's the whole point about women, Jack, they can do a whole lot of things at the same time,' said Janet. 'We all can.'

'Like bring up five children and run a political party, you mean?' said Gideon.

'Well – I don't exactly run it, do I? Just turn up at the House now and then.'

'Oh Janet, come on, you could run it if I wasn't there. Maybe you should,' said Kirkland.

'Oh yes? What about Eliot and Chad?'

'As far as I'm concerned, you're a better contender than either of them,' said Jack. 'After what's happened.'

'Well – happily for me, you *are* still there,' said Janet. 'Nothing I'd hate more. Honestly.'

Gideon Keeble, who had not risen from the slums of Dublin without an ability to sniff out a lie at very long distance, looked at them both with interest. Jack clearly believed her; and more importantly, Janet knew he did.

'Well, that's all right then,' he said and went to find Jocasta.

On her way to bed, Clio looked in on Martha. She was fast asleep.

Poor Martha. Something quite traumatic must have happened to her, to give her a panic attack as severe as that one.

❈   ❈   ❈

'Oh, look at this picture of Kate!' Clio passed the *People* across the table. 'Naughty girl, leaning out of the stretch window, waving at the cameras. I thought the whole idea was to keep well inside those things. Doesn't she look sweet? And the boy looks rather handsome too.'

'He *is* rather handsome,' said Jocasta. 'And he's a poppet. Who else did they get? God, the nights I've spent with the paps, outside rich people's gates. And now they're my gates and I'm inside.'

'Is that right?' said Gideon. 'I think they're mine as well, those gates. Actually.'

'Sorry, Gideon. I'm confused. Still half drunk, I think. God, I loved it. I want to give another. Oh look, here's Jamie Oliver and Jules. I hope he liked the food. And Jonathan Ross, I still can't believe he came, and the gaggle of It Girls, in their gangster car. It was so sweet, everyone going to so much trouble.'

It was half past ten. Gideon had already swum and had been making coffee for hours; people were drifting down to the kitchen, including several of Gideon's brothers and sisters. Jocasta embraced them all fondly; she had long since given up trying to work out which of them was which. Beatrice, considerably the worse for wear, huddled behind the newspapers. Josh, most unfairly full of beans, had already been for one walk and was suggesting another.

'There's a whole crowd of people down there still in the tent, Gideon. They appear not to have gone to bed.'

'Quite possibly not. It'll be the Dublin lot still exchanging the craic. They're tireless once they get going. I must go down and offer them some coffee.'

'I think I should check on Martha,' said Clio. 'I'm surprised she's not down.'

She came back in five minutes. 'Down and out,' she said. 'She's gone. Is that strange behaviour, or what?'

'Very strange,' said Jocasta, staring at her. 'How did she get away, anyway?'

'She said she got a cab. She's left a note,' said Clio holding it out. 'It's very polite, so sorry to have put us to so much bother, thanking us for all our kindness, but she had to get home.'

'She is the strangest girl,' said Jocasta. 'I think she didn't like it that we'd all seen her out of control. I never met anyone quite so tight-arsed in my entire life.'

Martha had spent the entire day in a desperate effort to calm down. She felt terrible: her pulse was racing, her heart pounding. She tried to tell herself she was being absurd, that there was nothing wrong; she was in no danger of any kind. But she was. She had committed an act of unbelievable folly: she had done what she had never even considered doing. Obviously it would be perfectly all right: obviously. Janet Frean was the kindest, most dependable woman, and, more important, absolutely discreet. There was no way she was a gossip, no way she would talk to anyone about what Martha had told her. Of course she wouldn't. She just – wouldn't. And anyway, why should she? What would be the point?

It went on all day, round and round Martha's aching head, in desperate convoluted circles, until she felt she might actually go mad. For the first time since – well, since that day – she was no longer in control, was at someone else's mercy.

The phone rang. It was Ed.

'Hi, it's me. Just rang to see if you enjoyed the party. I saw the pictures. Why none of you? I'll call again – '

Without thinking clearly what she was doing, desperate just to have someone to talk to, to take herself out of the prison in her head, she picked up the phone.

'Hi, Ed, it's me.'

'Hi. You all right?'

'Yes, yes, I'm fine. Thank you.'

'Good. Well it's just the usual call. Making sure you're OK. You wouldn't like to come for a drink or anything, I suppose?'

'No,' she said quickly, 'no, Ed, I wouldn't. Thank you. Not – not today anyway.'

'Tomorrow then?' His voice was hopeful. Something else she shouldn't have said, then.

'No. No, not tomorrow,' she said quickly. 'I meant not – not at all.'

'Martha – you sound weird. Are you all right?'

'Yes. Yes, I'm fine. Thank you.'

'You don't sound fine.'

'Well, I am. Absolutely. Yes.'

'OK.' She could almost hear the shrug. 'I'll call again. Tomorrow probably.'

Well, that hadn't helped. Maybe it was Ed she should have told. At least she knew he loved her, wished her well. Why did she tell Janet, whom she didn't know at all? Not really. Who might even now – oh God! Of course she wasn't. Of course –

The phone rang again. She snatched it up.

'Ed, please – '

But it wasn't Ed. It was Janet. 'Hello, Martha, only me. Wondering how you were.'

Her voice was warm, friendly, gentle. Martha felt better at once. How ridiculous she'd been, thinking that this kind, caring woman would do her any harm.

'Hello, Janet,' she said, and she could hear the relief in her own voice. 'How kind of you. I'm fine, really. Much, much better. And thank you again for last night, you were wonderful.'

'My dearest girl, it was nothing, I was just a shoulder to cry on, that's all.'

'No! You – you saved my sanity, I think.'

Damn. Shouldn't have said that. Sounds a bit – desperate.

'You seem pretty sane to me. Listen – I thought – '

'Janet,' said Martha, 'Janet, you – you wouldn't tell anyone, would you?'

'Martha! Martha, of course I wouldn't tell anyone. What kind of person do you think me, for heaven's sake?'

God, she'd offended her. Now what might she do?

'No, of course not. I mean – I didn't mean anything like that. It's just that – '

'Martha . . .' the voice was soothing now, soothing and infinitely kind, 'Martha, listen to me. You needed to talk. You couldn't have kept that to yourself forever. Even if – if she hadn't been there, at the party. It's an intolerable burden – God knows how you've coped all these years. You're clearly making yourself ill. And I'd like to think talking to me helped – just a little.'

'It did, Janet, it really did.'

Liar, Martha, it didn't help, it's frightened you horribly.

'And of course you're anxious about it. About me talking. I can understand that, I really can. But I won't. Ever. It would be unthinkable. I feel deeply honoured that you confided in me. Showed me that kind of trust. And I won't betray it. I swear to you, Martha. So please stop worrying. Please.'

'Thank you, Janet, so much. I won't worry any more.'

She wouldn't. She really, really wouldn't.

Clio got home to a letter from the Royal Bayswater. Would she be able to attend an interview board on Wednesday, 3 July, for a post of consultant geriatrician?

She felt flooded with happiness and triumph. OK, she hadn't got the job, she'd just got a shot at it. That was a lot. To her at this moment that was a huge lot.

She'd had a very good few days, she thought happily, sitting back on her sofa, what with the party, and this and – and Fergus. Did he like her? Really like her? And, more to the point, did she want him to?

Nothing could change what he did, the sort of person he was: and even if she came to understand his work, to see it as less – disreputable – could their lives blend in any way?

Oh, for God's sake, Clio, what are you thinking about? Your lives blend? You've met the man precisely twice, talked to him a few times more. He's amusing, he's attractive, he's a man you enjoyed a party with: leave it at that.

She did want to tell someone though, about her interview. That was one of the worst things about being on your own, she had discovered: day to day was all right, even bad days could be coped with, but happiness, however small, needed to be shared.

She decided to call Jocasta; her phone was switched off.

She couldn't tell Mark, or anyone at the practice, about her interview, and she was just beginning to feel her bright pleasure tarnish slightly, when, as if by magic, perfectly on cue, Fergus called.

'I just wanted to thank you for your company last night. And to make sure you were safely home.'

Clio told him she was indeed safely home: and that she had been called for an interview for the consultant's job.

'I wonder why I'm not surprised,' he said, and she could hear him smiling.

*　*　*

462

Jocasta had invited Kate to lunch the Monday after the party; Gideon was in his London office and she travelled up with him. She was sitting at a table at the Bluebird when Kate got there.

'Hi! You look nice.'

'Thanks.'

'Seen anyone today? About your modelling?'

'No, not till Friday now. Then it's this cosmetic company, Smith, and I think I'm getting a spot. I told Fergus and he said they'd be able to see past it.'

'He's absolutely right,' said Jocasta, 'of course they will. He's still looking after you all right, is he?'

'Yeah. Really well. He's cool. Mum really likes him. I think she fancies him, actually.'

'Goodness! Now what do you want to eat? And then tell me if you enjoyed the party and if your mum and dad did. And your very handsome boyfriend.'

Kate said it had been a really cool party and that Nat had really enjoyed it.

'He's lovely, your Nat,' said Jocasta, 'I really like him.'

'He's all right,' said Kate, and then looked at Jocasta and smiled, quite nervously for her. 'I worry a bit he hasn't got any ambition, though. I mean, he's nineteen and he's not really getting anywhere, just quite happy to go on working for his dad's garage.'

Jocasta said, carefully, that she thought Nat had plenty of time and that Kate shouldn't worry. 'Anyway, if his dad's got a garage and Nat took it over one day, that'd be great, wouldn't it? Always money in cars.'

'I s'pose so. But he lets his dad think for him – he doesn't have his own ideas. Whatever we're talking about, he tells us what his dad says. It's seriously annoying sometimes.'

'I'm sure it is. Men are annoying,' she added. 'They can't help it. But Kate, how are you feeling about everything now? About your mother and so on? A bit better?'

'I don't know. I mean even after all this, she could still be anyone, she could be Madonna, and she could be the woman who cleans the toilets down at the park. It's horrible. Really horrible, not knowing, always wondering . . .'

Her voice shook; she picked up Jocasta's glass and took a large gulp of wine. 'Sorry.'

'Sweetie, don't be sorry. I'm really sorry. Oh, dear. You're no nearer, are you?'

'No nearer,' said Kate. She was obviously extremely upset.

'Oh, no!' Chad's voice was quiet, shocked. 'God Almighty, I don't believe it. How, in God's name, did that get out?'

'What?' Abigail got up, walked round the table, and leant over him, reading over his shoulder. 'What is it? Oh, yes. I see. Oh dear . . .'

'How the fuck did it happen?' he asked. 'I mean, nobody had seen it except just the few of us. *Nobody*. And the research company, obviously. But they wouldn't. They just wouldn't!'

'Wouldn't what?'

'Leak it.'

'Does it have to be a deliberate leak?' said Abigail.

'Absolutely deliberate. But who?' The phone rang. 'Jesus. Get that, Abi, would you?'

She picked it up. 'Abigail Lawrence – oh. Oh, yes, Jack, he's here. What? Yes, I'm afraid he has . . .'

And against a background of Chad, quietly reasonable at first, then his voice rising in indignation – 'No, I did not! Of course I didn't. Not to anyone. For fuck's sake, Jack – ' she read the story on the front page of the *News*.

'Centre Forward's Losing Streak continues,' writes Martin Buckley, Political Editor. 'Left of centre breakaway political party, Centre Forward, which made its debut only a few months ago, is enduring serious teething troubles. Launched on a platform of sleazeless and crony-free politics, it has been dogged by scandals. High-profile ex-Tory MP, Eliot Griers, was involved in the so-called Clinch in The Crypt scandal, when he was discovered in St Mary's Undercroft, the chapel in the bowels of the House of Commons, with a divorced woman. A few weeks ago, Chad Lawrence, charismatic MP for Ullswater North (voted the sexiest man in Westminster last year by *Cosmopolitan* magazine), was discovered to have founded the new party's Think Tank with money from a Chinese-owned company, based in Hong Kong.

'Despite its flying start in the polls, the party is beginning to flag, as the scandals bite. A Focus Group Research, commissioned by the putative party leader, Jack Kirkland, showed a ten per cent loss of potential followers. Originally Centre Forward captured the public imagination, but it seems now that the electorate's cynicism with the entire political system in this country is extending to the new party.

'Unless Centre Forward achieve a big breakthrough in the next few weeks, it could be destined to find its place as the shortest-lived political party in history. Which, given the considerable talent within its ranks, would be a tragedy of some magnitude.'

Martha Hartley, reading the report in the *News* with a sinking heart, could not but reflect that a further – and shocking – scandal within those talented ranks could actually prove fatal.

Nick Marshall was waiting in the press dining room at the House of Commons for a rather dreary example of a Blair's Babe when he saw Martin Buckley leaving alone.

'Hi. Nice story today. Intriguing.'

'Thanks.'

'I'm rather sad about it. I'd have put money on them at least continuing to nip at the others' heels.'

'Yes?'

'Yes. A casual observer might imagine someone was out to do them down.'

'He wouldn't need to be a genius, your casual observer. The list of suspects would be very long.'

'I know. Well, here's my lunch date. See you around.'

The Babe looked after Buckley. 'That was an interesting story about Centre Forward this morning, wasn't it? Of course I'm not surprised, it was all much too good to be true.'

'Indeed. I agree.'

'I like Martin. He's always very fair to both sides.'

'I think that's not quite accurate. He's much more often on your side, if you ask me.'

'Well – not necessarily. I saw him on Monday, lunching with Michael Fitzroy.'

'Oh really?' said Nick. 'Well, maybe I'm wrong.'

Interesting. Michael Fitzroy, having lunch with Buckley.

Michael Fitzroy having lunch with Janet Frean. Didn't necessarily mean anything, of course. But – interesting. Very interesting. Maybe a little chat with Teddy Buchanan might be even more so . . .

'Martha! What do you think?'

'Oh – I'm sorry, Paul.'

She met his eyes across the conference table. They were sharp with irritation. This was the second time today she'd lost concentration.

'Maybe you'd like a bit more time.'

Her. Martha Hartley. Needing more time: not delivering absolutely on the minute. This was serious.

'No, of course not. I'm so sorry. No, I don't think there'd be a tax advantage in holding back. We need to push things forward, surely. It's a time-sensitive merger; they need it settled before the Christmas deadline. There's more money in that, ultimately, than any tax savings.'

'And what about changing distribution channels, how much is that going to cost them?'

Shit! Shit! She'd meant to send her trainee into the data room that morning to check on everything; and forgotten. What was the matter with her? What? As if she didn't know.

She took a deep breath. 'I'm sorry, Paul. Very sorry. I haven't checked that yet. Maybe I do need a little more time. Perhaps – tomorrow morning?' If she had to spend the night in the data room herself, she would.

He sighed. 'Yes, all right.' He looked at her rather searchingly, and then said: 'Martha, I agreed to help you in your political ambitions because I felt sure that, short term, you'd be able to cope. Please don't let me down. Or I might have to revise my thoughts on the whole thing. See you in the morning, then?'

'In the morning, Paul, yes. Seven-thirty.'

If only it was her political ambitions that were absorbing her time and concentration. If only.

'Clio, this is Fergus. Again.'

'Oh – hello, Fergus.'

Damn, she sounded breathless, nervous. Not cool and in control.

'I wondered if you were free on Saturday evening. For dinner.'

'Dinner would be lovely. Thank you!'

She put the phone down and tried to compose herself before her next patient came in. She looked in the mirror; she was slightly flushed. Now come on, Clio, this won't do. Fergus is just looking for a pleasant evening. Probably his regular girlfriend is away or something. Calm down. You've got to start taking things in your stride. It's just a dinner date, not a proposal of marriage. Be cool.

She pressed her buzzer. 'Send my next dinner date in, would you, Margaret?'

'I'm sorry, Clio?' said Margaret and she could hear her smiling. 'What did you say?'

'I must fly.' Gideon leant over to Jocasta and kissed the top of her head. She was burrowed into the pillows of the vast bed in their room at Cruxbury and still half asleep. 'See you in forty-eight hours.'

'Forty-eight!' She stared up at him, blinking her way into consciousness. 'I thought you said it was just one night.'

'It was. It's just become two. I'm relieved in a way – I was thinking of staying over anyway.'

'You were?'

'Yes. I was. I was actually contemplating being away from you for two nights and not one. I must be getting bored with you.'

'Gideon, that's not funny!'

'I'm sorry.'

'You know I'd have come, if it had been more than a night. I said so.'

'Did you? I'm sorry, I'd forgotten.'

'Well, I think that's a bit important, just to forget. Of course I'd have come. I don't like you going away.'

'Well, darling, you can come, if you want to.'

'I can't now. There's no point anyway, you obviously don't care if I come or not.'

'Jocasta, that's ridiculous,' he said, smiling at her. 'You're putting words into my mouth. Of course I care.'

'Then how can you forget to tell me you're staying away another night?'

He became visibly less patient.

'Jocasta, this is absurd. Look, I'm very, very late, do you want to come or not? Because if you do, you have about five minutes to pack.'

'No, I don't want to come. Thank you.' She turned away from him, feeling absurdly near to tears. What was happening to her? To the independent Jocasta Forbes. How had she begun to be this dependent, clinging creature, crying because her husband was going away for two days? It was pathetic.

'Jocasta – '

'Gideon, it's fine. Just go. I'll see you in a couple of days.'

'I thought I'd come back to London. Can you be there?'

'I'm – not sure,' she said.

'Do you have business down here?'

The dark blue eyes were snapping with irritation now.

'I – might have.'

'Oh Jocasta, you're being so childish. I'm off – ' His mobile rang. 'Hello? How are you, darling? No, of course not, never too busy for you.' His voice had changed. Totally. It must be Fionnuala. She lay, with her eyes closed, pretending she wasn't listening. Listening to every inflection, every syllable.

'Yes, as a matter of fact, I will. I'm going to LA, and then across to Miami. So it couldn't be better. I could easily pop down there for twenty-four hours. Tell Mum to call me. What? I'm leaving Cruxbury now, catching the midday flight. Bye, my love.' He looked at Jocasta, smiled at her, his irritation totally gone.

'That was Fionnuala.'

'I sort of worked that out.'

'She wants me to have a look at another pony for her.'

'Another! Gideon, you've just bought her three.'

'I know, but this one is special, apparently. Anyway, sorry darling, that means another day, I'm afraid. So I'll be back in London on Friday. Please be there for me. We can spend the weekend in London; you'd like that, wouldn't you?'

'Yes, it'd be really exciting,' said Jocasta, struggling to sound ironic.

'Good.' Clearly the irony had failed. 'Think of some things you'd like to see, places to go, and get Marissa to book them. Love you.'

'Bye,' said Jocasta and burrowed back into her pillows.

As soon as he'd gone, she felt terrible. How could she behave like that? Like a spoilt child. And she hadn't even said goodbye properly, hadn't told him she loved him. Suppose his plane crashed, suppose – she seized her mobile, tried to dial him. It was on message. Suppose he'd done that on purpose, suppose he was so angry with her he didn't want to speak to her. She tried again, left a message, 'Sorry I didn't say goodbye properly. Love you too. Call me when you get this.'

She got up, stared out at the garden. It was a beautiful day. So – what was she supposed to do? Walk? Do a little light weeding? Swim in the pool? Alone? All day? Shit, this was pathetic. There was so much she wanted to do. What had she been telling Clio so stoutly? Find a new house for a start. A house for them. For her and Gideon. Well, she could do that. She'd call up all the estate agents in – in where? They had houses in the best places in England already. Why buy another? Wales? Not many nice houses. Scotland? So cold. All right then, France. She hated the French. Italy? That might be nice. That might be very nice. Or the States? California? What about somewhere like Virginia? That would be great. She'd never been there, but she'd heard it was fantastic. Horse country. Fionnuala would like that. Did she want to buy a house where Fionnuala was always coming to stay? Probably not.

'Oh shit!' said Jocasta aloud. People never thought of this, people who weren't rich. She certainly never had. When you could have everything, nothing was right, nothing was good enough. Not just houses, but clothes. If you could buy a Chanel jacket, and then a Gucci leather coat and then a Valentino evening dress, where was the fun? Shopping was about choices, about decisions, what suited you best, not about having whatever your eye lighted on.

Well, maybe she should do something completely different. Find some new challenge. Like – well – yes, like learn to fly. That would be really great. She'd always wanted to do that. Always. That'd be something to get excited about, get the adrenalin pumping. That was the main problem: she wasn't making adrenalin. Or rather her life wasn't.

And Gideon's life, of course, was; it was all about work and pressure and deadlines and moving on to the next thing. God, she was going to seem pretty boring to him, pretty soon. An empty-headed wife, who had to get all her kicks out of stupid hobbies, like learning to fly, or tagged along after him on business trips. Where all there was to do was shop some more and have more stupid hobbies. And the business trips were a big part of his life; Gideon's world was lived largely out of his Vuitton suitcases.

Jocasta felt her heart literally lurch. Had she, after all, been completely sensible, giving up her job? Should she have hung on for a bit? Until – well until what? Until she had a family, people would say. That would inevitably be what they would say. But she wasn't going to have a family. She absolutely wasn't.

Oh God. She'd been all through all these options and Gideon had only been gone for twenty-five minutes. She had another three whole days to get through. What was she going to do? What?

The old adage about marrying in haste and repenting at leisure drifted into her head; she drove it out again with sheer willpower: but all day, as she swam in the pool and then packed up her things and left Cruxbury, and made her way to London and settled herself into the vast house in Kensington Palace Gardens that was Gideon's, not hers, it kept returning to her. And the thought that she had allowed it into her consciousness so early in her marriage. She had been Mrs Gideon Keeble for just over a month and she was already not entirely happy about it. What kind of person was she, for God's sake? What kind of stupid, reckless, ungrateful, unloving person?

By five o'clock that afternoon – by now in possession of a Chanel jacket, and with the first of a dozen flying lessons booked for the next day, and a silver BMW Z3 on order – she was still depressed. Depressed and almost frightened.

Chapter 32

'Martha, we have to talk.' Janet's voice was very brisk, very cool.

Don't panic, Martha, don't.

'What – what about? Anything important?'

'Depends on your viewpoint, I'd say. I thought you might be able to meet me after work today.'

'I'm sorry, Janet, I'm going to be terribly late tonight. Tomorrow might be possible.'

'Look.' Janet sounded almost impatient now. 'Look, I'm busy too, you know. But we've got to do this thing and – '

'Janet, what thing? I'm afraid I don't understand – '

'Oh God. Hasn't Chad called you?'

Chad? Had she told Chad? 'No. But I've been in a meeting all morning. He couldn't have.'

'Oh, I see. Well, he's arranged for what he calls the female force to be interviewed. By some girl from *The Times* for Saturday's paper. He thinks we can save the party.'

'Save what party?'

Relief had made her stupid.

'Martha dear, you'll have to do better than that,' said Janet, her voice slightly kinder.

The female force consisted of Janet, Martha, and Mary Norton, one of very few defectors from the Labour party to Centre Forward. Fortyish, sensible, articulate, with a strong northern accent. She was very good with the media and a frequent guest on both *Any Questions* and *Question Time*. Martha had only met her once and found her even more awe-inspiring than Janet Frean.

'Jack thinks we'll make a good team.'

'You and Mary will,' said Martha carefully.

'Yes, but Jack sees you as the future,' said Janet. She sounded very cool. 'And of course,' she added, quite brightly, 'you are much the best-looking of the three of us.'

That was all right then; she was to be cast as the group's bit of fluff. Fine. She would normally have resisted that, but under the circumstances, it was less frightening.

'Your skin is just so, like, totally perfect.' The make-up artist smiled at Kate. He was black, with white-blond hair, and rather red lips. She smiled back, rather nervously. Crew, as he was inexplicably called, was hard to talk to; he was from New York, for a start, so that cut out any conversations about shops or clubs, and when Kate admired his shirt, he said he bought all his clothes from what he called thrift shops.

He worked exclusively for Smith Cosmetics, so she couldn't ask him what other jobs he did, what famous people he'd made up; and anyway, whenever she tried to talk, he held up his hand and said: 'Don't talk for, like, just a tiny moment,' and the tiny moment seemed to mean the entire duration of the session.

Every so often the door would open and two women would come in; they were, it had been explained to her, the creative director and the advertising director of Smith and neither of them had talked to her at all, beyond saying: 'Hi, Kate, we're just totally thrilled to have you on board,' when she was first introduced to them. Since then, they would stand and study her, each time, as if she was a shop window model, not a girl at all, narrowing their eyes at her reflection in the mirror, and then leaving again, talking very quietly and occasionally saying, 'Difficult forehead,' or, 'The hair's too full,' and telling Crew to try wider eyes. Or fresher skin tone. Or bigger lips. Mostly he just nodded and said he was like totally willing to try, but when they said bigger lips, he shook his head and said, without collagen there was like, no way.

'So I think we should either postpone and go for the collagen, or use what we have, and like make the story less is more.'

After an hour of this, Kate was convinced they had decided they had made a mistake even to be doing test shots, and was all

472

ready to be told to go home – and thinking she actually would like that.

The photographer hadn't even appeared yet, but the way everyone talked about him, he was obviously very big and important in the company; it was, 'Oh, Rufus would never consider sleeves' and, 'Rufus never does curly', as what she might wear, or how her hair might be done, was discussed. She imagined some huge man with a booming voice and a suit, but when Rufus appeared, he was tiny, about five foot six, dressed in white trousers and a beige T-shirt. His voice was very quiet and in fact everyone had trouble hearing what he said, which irritated him; but he smiled at Kate in the mirror and said hi, he was Rufus Corelli and then turned her to face him, pushed back her hair and studied her for what seemed like forever and then said: 'She's sixteen, for fuck's sake. You have to take most of that shit off.'

Kate expected the women to argue, and Crew to have a tantrum, but they all meekly nodded and Crew said: 'But her skin will have to rest, it's like, so over-absorbing already,' and he cleaned her make-up right off and told her to sit very quietly in the reception area of the studio, where it was, like, fresher air.

It was two o'clock before they did the first test shots; and that was fraught as well, because Rufus said he wanted the studio cleared. 'I want no one here, except the model,' he said, as if she didn't have a name. She was a bit scared of being alone with him, but he actually became much nicer and said she still had too much make-up on, didn't these people understand what young looked like, and offered her a stick of his chewing gum and asked her where she got her jeans.

'The thing is,' he whispered, 'the thing is, I'm so tiny, I can wear girls' clothes, it's such a help.'

Kate wasn't sure in what way that could be a help, and thought her jeans would be much too long for him anyway, but again she didn't like to say so and told him they were Paper Denim & Cloth from Harvey Nichols. They were actually her only extravagance from her *Sketch* money, but he wasn't to know that.

'Right,' he whispered, pulling a Polaroid out of his camera and tucking it under his arm, 'what we're going to do is nothing like those obscene roughs. Jed, did you see those roughs, aren't they completely obscene?'

Jed, his assistant, had come in when everyone else had left the studio; he was about twice as tall as Rufus, but no wider and he also spoke very quietly.

'Completely obscene,' he said.

'Now, Kate, this is nice,' Rufus said, studying the Polaroid, 'but you're trying too hard. I want you to think about nothing at all. Certainly not this – this rubbish. Just empty your head. What I don't want is sexy. Or mannered. Just – be. Be you. Before any of this happened to you.' She nodded. It was quite difficult, thinking of nothing at all. After three more tries, she was getting upset; and then Rufus suddenly rushed out of the studio and disappeared.

He was complaining she was no good, he wanted another model, she thought; but he was back with a pile of magazines, *Seventeen* and *Glamour* and *Company*.

He gave her one. 'Right. Read it. Really read it, find something you're interested in, OK?'

She nodded; opened *Glamour*, which was her favourite, and flicked through it. And found an article on how you'd know if you were in love. She was always wondering if she was in love with Nat. She rather thought she wasn't.

'I've got something.'

'Good. Now sit there, on that stool, where you were before, that's right, and read it. Really read it.'

It was easier than she'd expected She was just into the second question, wondering if what she felt when Nat kissed her was exciting, very exciting or totally off the scale, when Rufus said, 'Kate!'

She looked up, not sure what he might want. The camera flashed.

'OK,' he said. 'Carry on.'

After three more, he came over to her, with some Polaroids. 'There,' he said, 'how's that?'

Kate looked; she could have been her own younger sister; almost no make-up visible, her hair just tumbled over one shoulder. She looked slightly surprised, sweetly confused, her dark eyes wide and questioning, her pale lips just parted.

'It's glorious,' said Rufus. 'Can you do that over and over again, do you think?'

'Oh yes,' said Kate, more confident now she knew what he wanted, 'yes, I'm sure I can.'

Next day, Smith made their offer: a three-year contract for Kate to be the face for their new young range, Smith's Club, for a million dollars a year. The terms of the contract would include a publicity tour in both the States and the UK, as well as public appearances at Ascot and Smith's Lawn polo and various film premieres: and a free hand for Smiths with press briefings. Fergus told them he would have to discuss it with Kate and her parents and that he would get back to them after the weekend.

He spent the next twenty-four hours wondering how best to present the news to the Tarrants, in order to ensure their agreement, while thinking what he could do with twenty per cent of three million dollars. And just occasionally considering what the whole thing might do to a vulnerable child of not quite sixteen, with a sad and difficult history: then telling himself that was absolutely no concern of his, that his job was to do his best for her. And securing three million dollars was a pretty good start.

Nick was in the Members' lobby on Thursday morning, only half listening to a story he had already heard too often, about how Gordon Brown was about to demand the leadership before the next election or resign, when he saw Teddy Buchanan moving on his self-important way towards the chamber.

Nick waylaid him, and invited him to dinner the following Monday; at the Stafford Hotel, not only a great purveyor of the sort of food and wine Teddy most loved, but far more discreet than the Connaught or the Savoy. Teddy accepted with alacrity.

Jack Kirkland was on the phone before seven on Saturday morning. 'Know it's a bit early, but wanted to catch you. I know you go off to Suffolk early. Have you seen *The Times*?'

'Yes, I have.'

'I'm extremely pleased,' he said, 'extremely. It really puts over a new message. Makes us human, sensible, aware of real life. You've all, in your different ways, done a wonderful job.

Well done, Martha. I know you don't like this publicity business, but you're going to have to get used to it. You're a natural.'

'Oh – not really,' she said. 'But I'm glad if I've helped. Um – have you spoken to Janet yet?'

'No, Bob said she was sleeping in. Bit unlike her: she's more of a Martha, up with the lark, getting on with all her lives. Have you?'

'No. No, she wouldn't – didn't want to speak to me, either.'

'Well, she deserves a bit of a rest. So do you. You mustn't do too much, Martha, but I know what these surgeries mean to you – and your constituents. Very valuable. Very clever idea.'

The girl from *The Times* had said that: and put it in her article. It was a very nice article, Martha thought, glancing at it again. Only – it did rather flatter her.

'The Headmistress, the Prefect and the New Girl' had been the headline: Janet, of course, being the headmistress, was described as one of the leaders of the new party, 'passionate about the need to nurture it, educate it, and improve its health both physically and morally'. It all sounded a bit – well, nannyish. And Janet looked nannyish in the photograph, wearing her 'uniform', her hair rather severely combed back. And then Mary Norton, talking about women's role in politics, the need to expand their power base, for positive discrimination, about women as a force within the trade unions, how she would aim for double the number of creches in the workplace, paternity leave, increased maternity leave. She sounded very feminist, very left wing: Martha was surprised Jack was so pleased about her contribution. Mary, with her curly, styleless greying hair, her twin set, her obviously make-up-less face, appeared very formidable. And then there was Martha: Martha gazing into the camera, all wide brown eyes and sleek, streaky hair, in a slash-necked T-shirt and a sharply cut jacket, saying she cared most for the little people, male or female, mentioning Lina and the horror of her mixed ward, her own grammar school, wrecked by the 'comprehensive ideal', talking about her legal surgeries in the town where she had grown up, and about how she viewed politics from 'my new girl point of view'.

She came across as charming, thoughtful and modest; she looked lovely. The writer had singled her out as 'Perhaps the most human of the three, the one still living in the real world, the one most aware of what she wants from politics and with the charisma to win her seat, and put her ideas into practice. Jack Kirkland, Centre Forward's party leader, is certainly right behind her: he says she represents the future of the party.'

That was what had worried her most: from the first moment she had read it, late the night before on Waterloo station, worried her through a restless night. To be so singled out, so favoured, was worrying her even more now, after Janet had refused to take her calls.

Because if she were Janet, she wouldn't have liked being cast as the older statesman, wouldn't have liked the nannyish implications – or the unflattering photographs. In spite of protesting that she didn't care what she looked like, Janet did: she cared quite a lot. She had her bob cut at Nicky Clarke and blow-dried twice a week, and her uniform suits were all from places like Jaeger and MaxMara. Mary Norton really didn't care. She had true political integrity, and was absorbed in her ideals. The simple fact was that Janet came over as the least charismatic of the three of them: and charisma was the bottom line in politics. It was what kept Tony Blair so resolutely in place.

Martha tried Janet's number once more, left a second message on her phone – Bob was obviously weary of playing private secretary – checked her e-mails once more in case Janet had written. Nothing from her.

'Martha my dear, forgive me for not getting back to you before. I've had a beast of a morning. Wasn't that a wonderful piece? I thought she got us all to an absolute T. I was very pleased, especially with the way she got almost all my points across. And I know Jack was. Lovely picture of you. Not so hot of Mary and me – but that's not the point, is it? Thank you so much for making the time.'

Martha was driving down the M11 and she felt the car could have taken off and flown, Chitty Chitty Bang Bang-style. She really should stop worrying about Janet; it was a waste of her precious energy. And there really did seem to be no need.

❄ ❄ ❄

Clio looked at Fergus across the table, and wondered if she should tell him she didn't have to catch the last train home, that she was once again borrowing Jocasta's house in Clapham.

But it might look a bit – forward. Like an invitation. And he was expecting her to go, had twice said, very sweetly, they must keep an eye on the clock – and added that he didn't like the idea of her being on public transport, late on a Saturday night, didn't she worry about it? Clio had said she never did, she had spent most of her youth and much of her adult life on late trains and the last one was particularly safe, always packed with people. And her car was at the station. All of which was true.

But she was having such a lovely time; they were in Mon Plaisir, in Covent Garden, and its warm, golden charm, its wonderful food, its pretty young waiters had relaxed her totally. She had been horribly nervous – of course. She had no idea what you wore to a London restaurant these days – studying the fashion magazines all week, it seemed to her shorts, high boots and a sou-wester would have been just as appropriate as a little black dress. What had happened to clothes? Why didn't she know about them? As Fergus so clearly would.

She had gone down to Caroline B to buy herself something, but Jilly Bradford hadn't been there and she didn't trust the taste of the rather aggressively middle-aged woman who was standing in for her and who had none of her taste and chic. She bought some tops, all of which she thought would go with a black crepe suit she called her Doubt Suit (when in doubt, wear it) but somehow none of them did. At six o'clock, when she should have been in the bath, she was frantically ironing a cream silk shirt, which was five years old. Fergus told her she looked lovely and she tried to believe him. He was, of course, looking wonderful in a cream linen suit and black silk shirt, which made her feel more dowdy than ever.

But she stopped worrying about her clothes after about three minutes. Fergus had been absolutely sweet all evening, attentive, flattering, and amusing – why did he like her, why? – making her laugh, making her make him laugh – how did he do that? – asking her opinion very seriously on whether he should buy a flat he was considering in Putney.

'Don't ask me,' she said, laughing, 'I don't know anything about London property. Of course, if I get this job, I'll have to.'

'Ah,' he said, smiling at her, 'but you have huge common sense, and I can't afford this flat, not really, not at the moment, anyway.'

'Then don't buy it.'

'I knew you'd say that,' he said.

'So why ask me?'

'Well, I thought I could talk you round and convince myself at the same time. It is absolutely beautiful, right on the river, and with a little roof garden – well, more of a balcony really, you'd love it, Clio.'

She had pondered the relevance of this briefly, and decided, rather sadly, that it was a figure of speech.

He then moved on to all the shows in the West End: what had she seen, what would she like to see?

'*My Fair Lady*,' she said promptly, and then realised how hopelessly suburban she must sound and blushed.

But, 'Me too,' he said, 'so shall we go together? I would also love to see *Les Mis*,' he went on. 'See how up to date I am?'

Clio had been afraid he had just been being kind again, humouring her, and said she'd like it too, nonetheless.

'And *Chicago*.'

'Then we have a busy time ahead of us,' he said, and glanced at his watch. Now he was bored, she thought, checking on how much longer the evening had to be; but 'It's getting late,' he said. And that was when he said he didn't like the idea of her being on the train.

So – should she say it, or not? That she didn't have to catch the train at all; but how, exactly? What did she say? She sighed, without meaning to; then, as he looked at her, said: 'I must go to the loo. Excuse me.'

She was a while, tidying up her face, spraying herself with perfume, studying herself in her middle-aged suit; when she came out, she saw there was a girl at the table, sitting in her place, a beautiful girl, with a perfectly carved die-straight bob, wearing a silk wraparound dress. She was sitting sideways on the chair and Clio could see her perfect legs and the high heels of her silver sandals; she glanced down at her own black court

479

shoes and wanted to run away. Probably he had told this girl to come and meet him there. 'This woman I'm having dinner with has to leave at eleven,' he would have said, 'get back to the suburbs, we can go on somewhere then.'

She took a deep breath, went over to the table.

'Clio! Clio, this is Joy. Joy Mattingly. She and I are old workmates, aren't we, darling?'

'We certainly are,' she said, smiling at him, and then up at Clio. 'The fun we've had, Fergus, eh?' Her voice was rather deep, with just a touch of an Irish accent; she picked a sugar lump out of the bowl, dipped it in Fergus's coffee and licked at it slowly. Clio watched her, transfixed.

'Well, I must go,' Joy said, standing up slowly; she was incredibly tall. 'See you around, Fergus darling. Have fun.'

He stood up as she left, and kissed her, and then sat down again, gesturing at Clio's chair.

'Sorry.'

'No, no,' she said, 'don't be silly. But I must go, Fergus, it's late and – '

'And you'll miss your train,' he said, and his voice was very flat. 'Of course. I'll see you to a cab. Are you sure you'll be all right?'

'Of course I will,' she said.

'Right,' said Fergus, and she saw him blow a kiss at Joy across the restaurant and felt more miserable than ever, 'let's find you a cab.'

And when one pulled up almost instantly, he said quite briskly: 'Right, well, safe journey, Clio, I've so enjoyed it. We must do it again some time.'

He hurried back into the restaurant. Clio sat staring at the crowded streets, at all the happy couples in it, holding hands, laughing, their arms round one another, and found it quite hard not to cry.

Inside the restaurant, a depressed Fergus was telling a patently bored Joy Mattingly that he feared Clio, so brilliantly clever, so obviously successful in her career, found him frivolous and rather uninteresting.

'I don't usually admire clever women, but she is something quite, quite different,' he said, ordering them both a large brandy. 'It's the combination of brains and beauty; it's a very rare thing. Well, it's clearly not to be. I had my hopes, but – '

He sighed and drained the glass and then refused Joy's invitation to join her and her party at Annabel's. She stared at him; she had known Fergus for many years and she had never yet known him turn down an opportunity to network.

He must be in love.

Chapter 33

'No, young man, I can't tell you that. Honour among thieves and so on.'

Teddy Buchanan's face was flushed as he drained his second glass of port. God, this had been a lot of money for nothing, Nick thought.

'Teddy, I only want a name.'

'Only a name! You boys never give away your sources, do you? Don't start asking us to do it for you.'

Unless it suits you, thought Nick, unless you want to land someone in it, or start a new plot, or fuel an old fire. Then you tell us anything.

'No,' he said, 'no, of course not.'

'Still – it's been a jolly good dinner. Thank you. So look – I think I'd have a word with Griers, if I were you. Good chap, Griers. Great loss to the party. Anyway, he was the first victim of all this fun and games, wasn't he? I'd get a bit more detail from him, if I were you.'

'The place was almost deserted,' said Eliot. He was looking particularly Hamlet-like, Nick thought, pale and slightly anguished. And he'd lost weight. 'Everyone had gone home early; it was one of those nights.'

'So – did anyone know you were showing that woman round?'

'Well – yes. Chad did. But he left, very soon. Oh, and Janet. But she was going home early. No one else was around. As I say, it was deserted.'

'I see,' said Nick. 'So – all the more noticeable if anyone did spot you.'

'But nobody did, I could swear. The odd cop – but they just don't, do they?'

'No,' said Nick, 'they don't. And you say Janet had gone?'

'She certainly had.'

'You sure?'

'Nick, of course I'm sure. Anyway, you're surely not saying Janet ratted on us? Her own party? That's absurd.'

'Yes, of course it is,' said Nick.

'We couldn't possibly agree to that,' said Helen. She was flushed and on the verge of tears. 'Not possibly. Could we, Jim?'

'No, we couldn't. She's too young and too vulnerable. And we don't want any more publicity for her of that sort.'

Fergus had expected them to be upset. In a way, he was impressed. Not many people would turn down three million dollars. In a way he even agreed with them. But . . .

'Helen, Jim, this is a lot of money,' he said gently.

'We know that,' said Helen. 'It's part of what we don't like.'

'Yes, but think about it. Please. Just for a moment. Any dreams you might have had for Kate, this could buy. Any travelling, university education, all that sort of thing. And what are you going to tell her?'

'Well – can't we say they didn't want her?'

'Not really. Think about it. Look – ' He hesitated. 'What do you think she'd say later in life, if she found out you'd turned this down without consulting her? She'd be very angry. Rightly so, many would say.'

'Yes, but we have to think what's best for her now,' said Helen. 'She's very vulnerable. She's a child, Fergus, not an adult . . .'

After he had gone, Helen and Jim studied the pictures of Kate in silence.

'This is very, very difficult,' said Helen.

'I know it is,' said Jim.

'Martha? Martha Hartley?'

'Yes?'

It was Martin Farrow, head of publicity at Centre Forward House. They needed to talk to her urgently; a request had come through for her to appear on *Question Time* that week, Clare

Short had pulled out at the last minute and they'd like Martha.

'They say you acquitted yourself extremely well at the lunch at the studios. They said you were very articulate and opinionated. They want you, Martha.'

'Oh, God.' Why hadn't she just sat there like a pudding, not saying anything? She felt absolutely terrified. 'They should have Janet Frean,' she said. 'Obviously. Please, please tell them to ask her.'

Farrow said, slightly awkwardly: 'We did suggest her, of course. But they said they'd rather have you. They said you were a new face, and they've already got two political heavies. They'd seen the piece in *The Times* on Saturday, and we sent some tapes of you on local radio and your show-reel and – it's you they want.'

'Well, I can't do it,' said Martha flatly. 'I'm frantically busy here, and anyway, I don't want to. And I couldn't, I'd be useless.'

'Martha, I keep telling you; they think you'll be marvellous. They know you'll be marvellous, they've heard you talk!'

'That's quite different. I wasn't nervous then. And what would Janet say?'

That was the worst thing: too hideous to contemplate. How Janet must be feeling: turned down for *Question Time*, the most desirable slot on television for a politician, in favour of her. Not Janet Frean, experienced, brilliant professional, but Martha Hartley, inexperienced amateur. She'd want to kill her. She'd want to – oh, God, what might she want to do? What might she do?

'I can't do it,' she said. 'Sorry.'

'Martha, this is Jack. What is this nonsense about not doing *Question Time*? Of course you must do it. It's the chance of a lifetime.'

'Jack, I couldn't.'

'Martha, this is Chad. Look, I hear you just turned down *Question Time*. You can't. You really can't. Most people would give their eyeteeth for it. You'd be marvellous. You've got to do it.'

'Chad, I can't!'

484

'Martha, this is Mary Norton. You've got to do *Question Time*.
Got to. No excuses. No excuses at all.'

'Mary, I'm not going to.'

'Martha, this is Nick Marshall of the *Sketch* – we've met a few
times. Listen, I just heard you've turned down *Question Time*.
Can I have a quote from you on that?'

'Martha, this is Paul Quenell. I've heard on the grapevine that
you've been invited onto *Question Time*. I am *extremely*
impressed. What? Of course you must do it. I shall be very
proud indeed. Especially if you can give Wesley a plug.'

'Paul, I really don't think I can.'

'Martha? My dear, this is Geraldine Curtis. I just heard the
marvellous news about *Question Time*. Of course you're going
to do it. What? Well, why on earth not? We're all absolutely
thrilled down here, it will do wonders for us.'

'Martha? This is Mum. Is it true you're going to be on *Question
Time*? No? I thought it couldn't be. What a pity, dear.'

The only person in the world who didn't seem to want to talk to
her was Janet. She had called her at least five times. It was
hardly surprising. What was she going to do?

'Martha, dear, this is Janet. I hear they've asked you to do
Question Time. I think that's marvellous. Of course you must do
it. As long as you really think you can cope. It is very frightening.
No one knows that better than I – I've done it a few times. Oh,
but I'm sure you can. Once you get going, it's absolutely fine.
What? No, of course I don't mind. I'm relieved it's not me, as a
matter of fact. I'll so enjoy watching you. Now, if you want any
tips, we could have a little session, maybe the night before,
something like that.'

She didn't mind! She didn't mind! It was all right. God, she
was so nice. So generous. Well, in that case – just maybe.

'Is this Kate? Kate Tarrant?'

'Yes, it is.'

'Oh hi, Kate, this is Jed. Mr Corelli's assistant.'

'Oh, hi.'

'He wants to know where you got your jeans. He made a note and then forgot.'

'Harvey Nichols,' said Kate.

'Harvey Nichols! Well, that is just wonderful. We'll go there tomorrow. Did you like the pictures?'

'I haven't seen them yet.'

'Oh, I sent a few over to your agent.'

'Yeah? Well, I haven't seen him today. I've been out shopping.'

'Oh, OK. Well, I heard they were *very* pleased. The Smith people. You must be *so* excited.'

She ended the call and immediately called Fergus.

Kate was in upset mode: flushed, brilliant-eyed, hands clenched.

'Thanks for telling me!'

'Telling you what, Kate?'

'You know. About the contract. Fergus said he'd discussed it with you, that I should ask you about it.'

'Yes, that's right.'

'So – when was that?'

'Yesterday, dear.'

'And you didn't think to talk to me about it?'

'Well, we were waiting for the right moment.'

'Well,' said Kate, 'here it is.'

'Your father's not here.'

'I don't care.'

'Well, I do,' said Helen, struggling to sound firm. 'This is an important matter and I don't want to discuss it without your father.'

Kate walked out of the house, slamming the door so hard the windows drummed in response.

The waiter eased a salmon steak onto the plate, poured the juices from the pan over it, all with great care, and then leaning over Nick in order to place the vegetables carefully on the table, said very quietly, 'Mr Marshall, there's something in your jacket pocket.'

486

'Thanks. Thanks very much.'

Nick was lunching in the press dining room with one of the boys from the Foreign Office; he excused himself as soon as he decently could and walked slowly out of the dining room. His jacket was hanging on a coat-rack. He picked it up casually, went into the gents, and sat down in one of the stalls. This was not the first time this had happened: it was a classic way of imparting information discreetly. But it was always exciting – he felt as if he was in a mini-series or something.

There was a note folded neatly in the inside pocket of the jacket, marked Confidential.

'I'd love to have a chat with you sometime,' it said, 'about Centre Forward and its future. I've got some stuff you'd find really interesting. Maybe you could call me on my mobile.'

It was signed Janet Frean.

Clio often thought that if she had been a more truthful person, then the whole of her life might have turned out differently.

If she had told Mark what she was really doing the day of her interview board, instead of creating an entirely fictional visit to an orthodontist, which necessitated her leaving the practice at lunchtime, then – well, everything really would have been very different. She would have taken the whole day off to prepare for her interview and gone up to London in the morning, so as to be sure to have plenty of time. But – she felt it was tempting fate to tell Mark what she was doing; the interview was late enough to enable her to do her morning surgery and still have time to go home, change into her new suit, and catch a train at around two. All she had to get cover for were her home visits; very few at the moment.

With that in mind, she wore a shirt that was – well, not exactly shabby, but certainly not stylish or even particularly crisp-looking, and a skirt that had also seen better days. And her oldest, most comfortable shoes. Her surgery had over-run, not finished until ten to one, but that was still fine. She could be home by one, and then –

'Clio? It's The Laurels.' Margaret sounded diffident. 'The matron says it's important. It's about the Morrises.'

'Put her through,' she said.

487

Mrs Morris had died that morning, the matron said. 'It was quite peaceful. And Mr Morris was with her.'

'Oh, that's so sad . . .' Clio's eyes filled with tears. Dear, sweet Mrs Morris, with her sparkly, pale blue eyes and her bright brave smile. Mrs Morris, baking cakes every day for the husband she loved so much – even if she sometimes didn't put the oven on. Mrs Morris, so fastidious about her husband's appearance and her own – occasionally popping an apron or a headscarf on him, rather than herself, but everything always immaculately clean and ironed. Dear, sweet Mrs Morris.

'I'm so sorry,' she said, 'so very sorry. How is Mr Morris?'

'That's why I'm phoning,' said the matron. 'He's terribly upset. And asking for you. I wondered if . . .'

'I can't,' said Clio. 'I have to go to London and – '

Ten minutes later she arrived at the Laurels.

Mr Morris was sitting with Mrs Morris, holding her hand. She had been prettily dressed in a clean nightdress and her face wore the neatly peaceful smile of death. Clio pulled up a chair and sat down next to him, took his other hand. He looked at her and said, tears rolling down his face: 'She's gone, Dr Scott. Gone without me.'

'I know,' she said gently, 'I know. I'm so sorry.'

'She promised she wouldn't. She promised she'd wait for me. What am I going to do without her?' he said, and a drop fell off the end of his fine old nose. Clio reached out and wiped it gently with a tissue.

'We've been married sixty-two years – I can't manage without her, I really can't. Who's going to talk to me, who's going to listen to me now? "No one else would listen to you, Trevor," she used to say, "you talk too much." '

'Did she?'

'She did.' He managed a feeble smile. 'But she talked a lot, too. We both did, all our lives. No need, really, in the end – we knew what the other was going to say, but we went on just the same. "Not that old story again," I'd say and she'd say, "If it was interesting the first time, it'll be interesting now." What am I going to do without her, what?'

'Were you with her?' asked Clio, wiping his tears again.

'Yes. They were very kind; they let me stay all the time. Since six this morning I've been here. Except – just after, you know . . .'

'I know. Well, I'm glad. That you were together then.'

'Yes. We were. It was very peaceful. She just drifted away from me. Last thing she said was, "Sorry, Trevor." That would have been for not waiting for me. And then a little smile and she was gone.' He turned and looked at her. 'Do you believe in the next life, Dr Scott? A lot of people don't any more.'

'I do indeed,' said Clio, and in that moment, she was as convinced as she was of anything that Mrs Morris was up somewhere in a sweet blue heaven, bright and smiling, waiting for her Trevor, with a nicely ironed shirt and a freshly baked cake.

'And you think I'll see her again?'

'Of course you will. Of course.'

'I'm so glad you think that. Sometimes . . .' He turned to look at her, and managed a weak, watery smile, '. . . sometimes I have wondered. Thank you for coming, Dr Scott. Thank you so much.'

It was two o'clock. She screeched down the drive, only just missing the butcher's van coming up it. She hoped it had been worth it. It *had* been worth it. She was glad she'd done it. Whatever the cost.

Now what did she do? If she went straight to the station, she might still catch the two-thirty. Which meant she would be able to get there, compose herself and her thoughts and present herself just about in time; while wearing her oldest shirt and skirt, and her kicked-out driving shoes. On the other hand, she could appear, neat, smart – and late.

Clio thought about the people who would probably be sitting on the board and their concerns and decided they would not be focused on her Paul Costelloe jacket and her Jigsaw trousers. She headed for the station.

'Holy fucking shit,' said Eliot Griers.

Chad Lawrence looked at him; not many people had heard Eliot swear. Most of the time his language would not have offended a cloisterful of nuns on their way to matins.

'Thought that might get you going,' he said.

'It is amazing. Why didn't you tell me before, you useless fucker?'

'Eliot!' But he was smiling. 'I'm really, really sorry. I had truly forgotten. You know how things get into the grubby corners of your mind and just – seem to stay there. I've been turning that evening over and over, trying to remember anything relevant, and it came to me last night. She definitely came back; she'd left her mobile behind. You'd gone off with your bit of crumpet – '

'She was *not* a bit of crumpet.'

'No, all right, your heartbroken widow, or divorcee or whatever she was. So she could – just conceivably – have seen you. It's possible. And she did just also happen to see the research figures, you know.'

Clio caught the two-thirty – just. She sank into the corner of the compartment, trying to get her breath back, rummaged in her bag for a comb. No comb. Lucky she had a small one in her make-up bag, she could – 'Shit,' she said aloud. No make-up bag either.

This was grim. Sat-out skirts were one thing; smudged mascara from crying and a seriously shiny nose were another. Well, maybe she could get something from Boots on Waterloo station. No, she wouldn't have time. Oh God . . .

Now then. The journey from Waterloo to Bayswater was not easy. Cab? Dodgy, and she didn't have that much cash on her. She could go to the cash machine, but there was always a long queue at Waterloo. The tube then: Lancaster Gate was the nearest and only involved one change – one change, yes, and a lot of underground corridors – but then she could get a cab from there. If there was one. The Royal Bayswater was tucked into a difficult little triangle, bordered by Sussex Gardens and the Edgware Road, a truly hideous place to get to. Oh, God. Would it be worth phoning? Saying she might be a few minutes late? Not yet. No point giving herself a black mark before she had to.

She switched on her phone, carefully silenced for poor Mr Morris; it bleeped. A text message from Fergus, saying, 'Good luck with the interview. Hope you're wearing the wedding party dress.' What a treasure he was. Maybe he hadn't found her so dull, maybe . . . She texted back.

'Thanks vv much. I wish. Wearing oldest clothes. Look terrible. Clio.'

He texted back at once. 'Why?'

'V long story. Might not make it.'

It was passing the time at least. Was this train going slowly? No, it must be her imagination. It was a fast train. A fast train going slowly. Shit!

'We apologise to customers for any delay. Due to a signal failure at Waterloo, this train will terminate at Vauxhall. Customers are advised . . .'

Customers!

'We are not bloody customers!' she shouted at a hapless ticket inspector who was working through the carriage. 'We're passengers. People who want to get somewhere. On your trains. You know?'

He shrugged. 'Don't blame me, love,' he said and walked on.

Shit shit shit! She just wasn't meant to get this job. She wasn't. She might as well –

Her mobile rang.

'Clio? It's Fergus. Is anything wrong?'

Jocasta was rather earnestly preparing for Gideon's return that weekend; she felt like a Stepford wife. She had filled the house with flowers, arranged them herself – and then felt a mixture of foolishness and rage when the housekeeper said, infinitely polite, 'I always do the flowers on Fridays, Mrs Keeble. If you'd rather I didn't . . .'

'I would rather you didn't, yes,' said Jocasta briskly. 'I love doing flowers.'

She had arranged to have her hair trimmed and the highlights done and she had bought herself a new nightie from Agent Provocateur. She'd probably only have it on for a few minutes, but it was still very pretty. Well, pretty wasn't quite the word. Sexy. All black satin and cream lace, and not much of either. Gideon would like it. He was a bit old-fashioned when it came to underwear. He was a bit old-fashioned altogether.

She had also booked some tickets for a Mozart concert at the Wigmore Hall, which she knew he would enjoy much more than she would, and then a table at the Caprice for dinner.

She felt delighted with herself; this would please him, would show him she was a mature woman, a suitable wife for him, not an immature selfish brat. Like that bloody daughter of his.

She looked at her watch and sighed: only halfway through Wednesday afternoon. What should she do now? A bit more shopping, perhaps? No, she'd go for a run in the park. It was wonderful to be so near to the park, just be able to walk across the road and into the green of Kensington Gardens, not the scratchy, cigarette-scarred grass of Clapham Common. Nick hated running on Clapham Common.

She suddenly had a vision of Nick taking off on a run from her house on a Sunday morning, his long lean body moving smoothly and steadily down the street, his brown hair flopping, waving to her without turning round. And then her going back into the house and making some coffee, frantically trying to defrost the orange juice she had left too long in the freezer and tidying up the piles of newspapers that covered the bed. They very often had sex on Sunday mornings, lovely slow, lazy sex; how he could run after it she could never understand.

Stop it, Jocasta! That was all very well, and it was terrific fun and the sex was fantastic, but he didn't love you. Well, not enough. Gideon does. Which is wonderful.

She wondered how Clio was getting on; it was her interview today. She was sure she'd get her job. She had been very disappointed in Clio's relationship with Fergus; it seemed to be fizzling out. Their careers were such worlds apart, but there was something about them that was exactly right; they were like two wiggly pieces of jigsaw that suddenly fitted together. Maybe it wasn't too late. Maybe she could organise a dinner party or something, make sure they kept in touch.

Fergus had said he would meet Clio at Vauxhall: 'I can cut across London, easily. Across Vauxhall Bridge, up Park Lane, you'll be there in a trice. Don't worry.'

She had protested, said he must have other things to do, like work, but, 'Nonsense,' he said. 'I'm as free as air this afternoon. Had a hot date with the VAT inspector, but she came this morning instead. Anything else I can do for you?'

'Well . . .' She hesitated; it seemed an awful lot to ask. 'Well, actually, Fergus, if you could just – '

He must like her; he must.

They pulled in to Vauxhall station at 3.35 and he was waiting for her outside the station, grinning, holding a Boots bag. 'And in the back there is a jacket. I think it should fit you. It's not bad, quite nice in fact. A girl I fell out with left it behind, it's Jigsaw, size twelve.'

'Oh, Fergus!' said Clio, and careless of whether she might be embarrassing him or not, she gave him a kiss. 'You are an angel.'

'Not quite, and that certainly wasn't her view, but – come along now, into the car, you can do your face as we go.'

He had even brought some tissues.

At five to four they were at the bottom of the car park that was called Park Lane.

'Clio, hello!' It was Beaky's secretary. 'Are you in the building?'

'No,' wailed Clio, 'I'm at the bottom of Park Lane. Stuck! They're not running late or anything, are they?'

''Fraid not. Dr Smartarse – I didn't say that – your only real rival is in there now. Due to come out any minute. God, Clio, shall I warn them?'

'I think you'd better,' said Clio.

At quarter past four they were approaching Sussex Gardens; the traffic was still crawling.

'I think you'd be quicker legging it from here,' said Fergus. 'I'll park and come and find you. Good luck. I'll be waiting.'

She wrenched the door open and started running. At least there was one benefit in her old shoes. As she reached the doors of the Royal Bayswater, she realised she had left her notes in the car.

Fergus was trying to reverse his car into a space too small for it, and on double yellow lines, when he caught sight of the notes for the presentation part of her interview on the back seat; the hard stuff about why she wanted the job, about funding, how she saw the geriatrics department fitting in with the rest of the hospital administration and the internal politics. She had been studying them, trying to keep calm as they drove. They obviously mattered. But she was five minutes ahead of him now. At least. And the hospital was still a way away.

Clio stood in reception, trying to impress upon the woman,

who had no knowledge of any interview board, the urgency of her case. 'Just call Professor Bryan's secretary,' she said. 'She'll know where I should be.'

God. If only she had her notes. If only. She felt so confused, so brain-dead.

'Clio! Come along. They're giving you till half past, I made them some more tea.'

It was Beaky's secretary; she must send her some flowers.

'Clio!'

It was Fergus, waving something at her. Her notes.

'Oh my God,' she said, 'how did you manage that?'

'I once got a medal for running, the only prize I ever won at school,' he said. 'I'll wait here. Good luck. That jacket suits you,' he added. 'Looks much nicer on you than on her.'

'Your boyfriend?' asked Beaky's secretary. 'What a sweetie.'

They all looked at her very coldly when she went into the room. Even Beaky. There were five of them: some familiar, some not. The Chief Executive of the hospital, an outside assessor, the Clinical Director, one of the other consultants – and Beaky.

'I'm so, so sorry,' she said, sinking onto the chair they indicated. 'I can explain if you like . . .'

'Not now,' said the administrator. 'I think we have been delayed enough. If we could just begin . . .'

Astonishingly, once she started, she felt coolly together, all her facts and theories marshalled, her experience summoned, made to seem clearly relevant. She answered all their questions smoothly and easily, expressed her view that as much a part of geriatrics as medicine was the social side, the importance of enabling elderly people to continue in the community by way of careful monitoring, drug therapy and support from the social services. She had done some research of her own on late-onset diabetes and on stroke management, was absolutely up to date on treatment, both in the UK and the States; she could see that impressed them. She discussed her days in the outlying hospitals, said how impressed she had been with the care home in Highbury and its policy of patient independence. And finally, expressed her personal view of the frustration of the carers, prevented from giving out drugs by red tape and meaningless regulations.

'I know this is more politics than medicine,' she said, 'but it is so important. I firmly believe we would see smaller clinics here, fewer beds needed, less pressure on the homes if we could only overcome it.'

And then heard, to her horror, her own voice shake as she said it, felt her eyes stab with tears, thinking with fierce regret that the Morrises might still be safely at home together, had she only been able to ensure that they had got their medication at the right time and in the right doses every day.

'I'm sorry,' she said, seeing them look at her oddly, 'I've had a bit of an upsetting day with a patient. It's why I was late.'

'Perhaps, Dr Scott,' said Beaky gently, clearly seeing his opportunity to push her forward, 'you would now like to tell us about it.'

She waited outside with the three other candidates. The one who was clearly Dr Smartarse sat drumming his fingers on his leg, looking at his watch. The other two read their newspapers and weren't very friendly either. She supposed she had held them all up.

Finally she spoke into the tension.

'I'm so sorry I was so late,' she said, 'but you see – '

The door opened; there was an interminable silence; then: 'Dr Scott, could you come back in, please.'

She was never sure afterwards when it had gone wrong: when the hugs and kisses outside the hospital, the sense of warm euphoria and sweetly shared triumph ended, and the chill began. He had even bought her some flowers. 'I knew you'd earn them,' and insisted on driving into Covent Garden – 'perfect place to celebrate'.

She thought of Saturday's dinner there and hoped he was right.

Fergus had ordered a bottle of champagne.

'Here's to you, Consultant Scott.' Fergus raised his glass to her. 'I'm very proud indeed to know you.'

'Thank you. A whole bottle! Fergus! Your eyes are bigger than your stomach. As my nanny used to say.'

'Your nanny! How very grand,' he said. 'Where I come from your nanny is your gran.'

'Fergus. I only had a nanny because I didn't have a mother,' said Clio. She could feel herself blushing. Had that been it? She had certainly felt awkward suddenly, less happy.

'You had no mother?'

'No. She died when I was a baby.'

'That's terribly sad.'

'Not really. I know that sounds dreadful, but I never knew her, I didn't know any different. Anyway, that's not what I want to talk about. Oh, Fergus! I'd never have done it without you. Never. I just don't know how to thank you.'

'You don't have to,' he said, 'I feel rewarded enough that you got it. You were a long time,' he added. 'I was beginning to wonder if you'd popped out the back way.'

'Fergus! Of course not. There's a lot to discuss at these boards, you know, it's not just like a simple interview – ' She stopped, fearing she sounded condescending.

'I daresay. The only interview I ever attended was for the position of filing clerk. It lasted about two and a half minutes. Since then, I've just wheedled my way into places.'

'I'm afraid wheedling isn't a recognised interview technique for doctors,' she said. Damn. She'd done it again She smiled at him, still afraid it sounded schoolmistressy.

'Yes, well, our worlds are obviously pretty far apart,' he said. And this time he didn't smile back.

She had begun to feel panicky. It couldn't all go wrong today. Not now. Not after all he'd done.

'You were so kind, Fergus,' she said again. 'So, so kind.'

'Now let's not OD on the praise,' he said. 'It was just what any friend would do.'

A friend. Any friend. That was how he saw her. He had just been helping a friend.

'And what are you doing this evening?' he said.

'Oh – just getting back.'

'But – you have to?'

'Oh yes,' she said quickly. She didn't want him to feel he had to amuse her, go on helping her to celebrate. She'd imposed on him enough.

'Right. Well, I must get back to the office too.'

'You certainly must. I've robbed you of hours of useful occupation.'

'Debatable I'd say. That it was useful.'

'What? Your occupation? Don't be silly.'

'It's not exactly a useful occupation, is it? Not like being a doctor.' He sounded edgy, almost defensive. 'But anyway, it was a pleasure helping you. It really was.'

A long silence; then: 'Can I give you a lift to Waterloo?'

'Oh – no. Honestly. That would be too kind. I'll just make my own way, get a cab probably. I'd much rather actually.'

'Right,' he said, 'fine.' His voice had become cool, distant.

It was all going wrong. Horribly wrong. She looked round the bar; it was full of pretty girls, with long brown bare legs and low-cut tops. She felt appallingly out of place – again – in her shabby skirt and kicked out shoes. And her – oh, God, flesh-coloured tights. And the jacket he had lent her was a bit tight. That girl, whoever she was, had obviously been really skinny. She had to get out of here.

'Well, I'll just go and get a cab. I don't think I could walk another inch.' She stood up. 'Thank you again for the champagne, Fergus. And for everything.'

'There's a lot of champagne left,' he said indicating it.

'Oh – I'm sure you'll manage.' God. Now he'd think she meant he was an alcoholic.

'You couldn't stay for another glass?' he said.

She should have said yes then, she knew she should; he must be thinking she'd just been using him all afternoon and now she wanted to get away; but she could just feel everything she said going from bad to worse.

'No, no, I couldn't. I'd love to, but – I really must get back. Back to – to The Laurels – you know, the nursing home. I said I would.'

'OK, fine. I can see that is really important. Well – I'll see you to your cab.'

'There's no need.'

'I know that,' he said and his voice was even slightly impatient. 'But I will, just the same. I have been properly brought up, you know. Even if I didn't have a nanny.'

'Fergus, that's – that's silly.'

'I'm a pretty silly fellow. Come on.'

Where had it all gone, she thought, all that happiness, all that triumph, all that closeness? She thought of him buying her mascara and lipstick in Boots, pounding up Sussex Gardens, desperate to give her her notes. How had she managed to wreck that, and so quickly? God, she was a disaster. It was hopeless. Completely hopeless.

'Here's a cab,' he said.

'Thanks. Thanks for everything, Fergus. I do hope – ' What did she hope? Nothing that wouldn't sound boring. Or as if she was forcing herself on him. 'I do hope you get everything done.'

Now, how crass was that?

'I will,' he said.

She got into the cab, leant forward. 'Waterloo,' she said and turned to say goodbye: only he had wrenched the door open, was climbing in beside her.

'That'll be extra,' said the cabbie, pressing his meter.

'That's fine,' said Fergus.

'Fergus, what – '

'I want to talk to you,' he said. 'Get to the bottom of this – this personality change you go through. It keeps happening. One minute you're you, all warm and chatty, and the next all buttoned up, holding me at arm's length. What is it, what do I do?'

'It's not you,' she said quickly. 'Really it isn't, it's me.'

'What do you mean, you?'

'I can't explain,' she said wretchedly, and she felt, to her horror, the tears well up and she fished in her bag for a tissue and blew her nose.

'Hay fever,' she said by way of explanation.

'I don't see any hay,' he said, taking the tissue away from her and wiping her eyes tenderly. 'Come along, Clio, tell me what's wrong, please. Otherwise – ' he looked out of the window, they were on Waterloo Bridge now – 'I shall throw myself into the river.'

Clio giggled in spite of herself, and then sniffed rather unromantically.

'I can't tell you – ' she said.

'Rubbish,' he said, and started to try to open the door.

'Mind out, guv, it's locked,' said the driver.

'Clio! Come on!'

'Well – oh dear!' The tears were flowing fast now. 'It's just that – that –'

'That what? Are you in love with someone else?'

'No, no, it's nothing like that – it's just that I'm so – so dull. And middle-aged and – and –'

'What are you talking about?' he said, looking genuinely mystified.

'I'm dull, not exciting. Serious. Not like the people you know. Not like Joy the other night. I don't know why you wanted to have dinner with me, Fergus, I suppose you were just being kind like today, and you were so kind, but –'

'Which entrance?' said the driver.

'Oh – Eurostar will do,' said Fergus. 'Clio, I wanted to have dinner with you because I love your company – I adore your company. You're so interesting and thoughtful –'

'Oh yes,' she said, 'very exciting that makes me sound. Interesting and thoughtful . . .'

'It is to me, you silly bitch,' he said.

She stared at him. 'What did you say?'

'I said you were exciting, to me. I find you very exciting. And today I was so proud of you and –'

'Yes, but what else?'

'I said you were a silly bitch. OK? I'm sorry.'

'Seven quid,' said the driver.

Fergus fumbled in his wallet, pulled out a tenner, thrust it at him.

'That's all right, keep it.'

'Fergus, that's terrible,' said Clio, shocked by this piece of wanton extravagance. 'You can't just give him three pounds –'

'I can. Of course I can. Come on. OUT!'

She got out: meekly followed him into the Eurostar building, and then up the escalator. At the top he turned and faced her.

'Look,' he said, 'I don't know how I can convince you that I like being with you. That I find you terribly attractive. You're driving me mad. What do you want, woman? A signed declaration? Here –' he pulled a sheet of paper out of the small Filofax he kept in his pocket, 'here you are. I, Fergus Trehearn,

499

find you, Clio Scott – don't know what your married name is, but if I could get hold of your husband I'd punch the living daylights out of him, for doing what he has to you, I find you incredibly exciting and interesting and desirable and I would like to remove all your clothing right here.' He tore the paper off, handed it to her. 'There. Will that do? Now then, we'd better go and find your bloody train.'

Clio stood very still and stared, first at him, then at the piece of paper; then she said: 'Fergus, I don't want to get the bloody train. And I don't have to. I want to stay with you. And I want you to remove all my clothing. As soon as possible. Only not just here, maybe.'

'Well, where then?' he said, speaking very slowly. He raised his hand, tilted her face up to his.

Clio felt a lurch in what she could only describe as her guts. A strong, probing lurch. It led to part of her anatomy that had been dormant for quite a long time. It wasn't dormant now. It appeared to be on the rampage.

'I believe you've got a flat,' she said very quietly. 'And could you just say that once again?'

'What?'

'You know, about me being a silly bitch?'

'But why?'

'Well, because it proves you weren't just being polite. It's about the biggest compliment I ever had.'

'I can do a lot better than that,' he said, 'you silly bitch.' And he started to kiss her.

Chapter 34

'I don't know what I think. Not really. It's well confusing.'

'That's why I asked you,' said Kate, her voice exasperated. 'I want to be less confused.'

'Yeah, I know, but you can't think something to order. I'm not like my dad. You've only got to say something to my dad, like – well, like police, or posh, and he's off.'

'What does he think about being posh, then?' said Kate curiously.

'Not being posh, Posh. Like Posh Spice.'

'Oh, right. What does he think about her?'

'He says she's addled Beckham's brain, dressing him up in skirts and that. That's why we lost the World Cup, he says, all her fault. I agree with him,' he added.

Nat usually did agree with his father.

'Yes, but Nat, that's things he already knows about. What do you think he'd have to say about this contract and me? Just for instance.'

'Well, I don't know. I could ask him.'

'No, don't,' said Kate hastily. She sighed. 'So – suppose I was *your* daughter. What would you do?'

Nat considered this carefully. Then, 'I would worry about it. I mean you're not sixteen yet. You'd only spend it on clothes and that, wouldn't you?'

'No,' said Kate, 'course not. I'd invest it.'

'Yeah, but what in? You wouldn't know. Anyway, it's not the money, is it?'

'Isn't it?'

'Kate, you know that. What it's really about is the publicity and that, isn't it? I mean, you don't want all that stuff in the papers again, do you?'

'Well, no. I don't. But – '

'Kate, you don't. And you heard what Fergus said. It's not going to go away.'

'It won't go away, whatever I do,' said Kate rather sadly. 'And what am I supposed to do, stay in my bedroom for the rest of my life? Not do anything interesting?'

'Course not. But you don't have to do something like modelling, do you? I mean you're clever, and you've done your exams. You could be a teacher, or something.'

'Nat, I've got a lot more exams to do before I could be a teacher!'

'Yeah? My dad says they're a waste of space, teachers, don't teach kids nothing these days.'

'Well,' said Kate, 'I don't think I want to be something that your dad considers a waste of space.'

She was getting bored with this conversation. 'Let's go for a drive.'

'Tell you something else,' he said, 'there's no rush. Keep 'em waiting, tell Fergus that and all.'

'That's a very good point,' she said.

She reached across to kiss him; she was almost as tall as he was, in her high heels. 'Thanks, Nat. What would I do without you?'

'Walk everywhere,' he said, and grinned. 'Kate, I wish you could find your mum, then you wouldn't mind all the crap, would you?'

'I s'pose I wouldn't,' she said, 'not so much anyway. But I don't think I'm going to. Not now.'

'You don't know that,' he said. 'You never know what's round the corner.'

'And who says that, your dad?' she asked, teasing him.

'No,' he said, very seriously, 'my mum. Mind you, she needs to think that, married to my dad. But matter of fact, it's true.'

Martha woke up on Thursday and thought that whatever else happened, this was the last morning *Question Time* would be hanging over her, like some vast brooding predator. Tomorrow it would be over; she might have made a complete fool of herself, she might have been taken off the air, but at least she wouldn't be dreading it any more.

God, she was scared. She wondered if anyone had ever actually thrown up on camera. That would be an interesting first.

She got up, put on her running things, clipped her tiny radio to her shorts and set off for Tower Bridge, while listening to John Humphrys on the row over Tony Blair and the Queen Mother's funeral, which was still going on. And the on-going Hinduja business. And the equally on-going debate on ID cards. And Cherie and her remarks about the suicide bombers. And who might be Archbishop of Canterbury. And why it still mattered. The trouble was, as Janet had told her, you could think you were right on top of the news, and then the hot topic that night could be something you knew next-to-nothing about. That hadn't helped to make her feel more confident.

She was going to the hairdresser on her way into the office. She had been told that the studio hairdresser was pretty useless. 'They just comb it,' Janet had said. 'Take a hair styler with you and loads of hairspray.'

She had been great: coaching her, giving her practice questions, telling her the one cardinal sin was to look at the camera, advising her on her jacket – 'not blue, not patterned' – and to try to eat something beforehand, 'or your stomach will rumble and your mike will pick it up. It's a nightmare.'

Martha felt she was in some nightmare already: how much worse could it get?

For some reason, the other nightmare, the really hideous one, seemed to have receded. She supposed there just wasn't room for it. It would be back, but she was grateful for the respite.

Janet had asked Nick to meet her for an early supper at the Savoy.

'Not the Grill. The Savoy Upstairs. It's very quiet there and we can talk as much as we like. Then I can be back in time to watch *Question Time*. You know Martha Hartley's on tonight?'

Nick said he did. And that he was planning to watch it too.

'She's very bright. I've met her once or twice. She went

503

travelling with Jocasta, way back in the eighties, did you know that?'

Janet said yes, she did.

It was a very long morning. Martha had a difficult client meeting booked, which she had expected to distract her, but it was cancelled at the last minute; she worked on a presentation document and prepared a report, but it wasn't the all-consuming stuff she needed.

She had to leave at two; the BBC was sending a car for her. She sat watching the clock as it crawled the last half hour; this must be like waiting for the executioner, she thought. She had a fat bundle of briefing material, sent over from Jack Kirkland's office, which she knew more or less by heart, and she had the day's papers to read in the car.

She kept going to the loo, and checking and re-checking the holdall she had brought, containing her precious hair styler, and three different tops (to go with either of the suits she was taking for final approval, one bright red, which she loved, but feared might be a bit much on camera, and one grey and white Prince of Wales check, which she also loved, but feared might count as the busy pattern Janet had advised her against).

At five to two the phone rang; she let her voice mail pick it up. It was Ed.

'Hi, Martha. I just discovered you're on telly tonight. Mum told me. Cool. Good luck. And – '

Suddenly she wanted to speak to him. Terribly.

She grabbed the phone. 'Hi, Ed. I'm here. Just leaving now.'

'Yeah? How do you feel?'

'Terrible. Absolutely terrible. So frightened, you can't imagine!'

'Is this the cucumber-cool Miss Martha Hartley, prospective parliamentary candidate for Binsmow? Martha, don't be scared, you'll be fine. Just keep your hands over your nose, dreadful if people spotted that.'

'Oh, don't! And I won't be fine, I know I won't.'

'Would you like me to come?'

'What? To Birmingham?'

'Is that where it is? Cool, I love Brum, they have some great clubs there, we could go out afterwards.'

504

'Ed, I'll be in no state to go clubbing.'

'OK, we'll just sit in the green room and watch the re-runs. Do you have anything planned for afterwards?'

'Suicide,' she said.

'Terrible waste. Look – I mean it; I will come if you want me to. I'd love to.'

She was silent for a moment, then, 'I'd absolutely love it,' she said simply. 'It would make all the difference. But God knows if you'll be able to get in.'

'I'll think of something. If I can't get in, I'll wait in reception and watch you on the monitor.'

'Oh, Ed.' Her eyes filled with tears. God, she'd missed him. And God alone knew what she was doing, letting him back into her life. It was hugely dangerous, she was over-emotional, frightened, she might say or do anything. It was also exceedingly selfish. But – she'd worry about that afterwards.

All the way up, she read the papers again. All of them. She also yet again read the stuff from Centre Forward House. And looked increasingly anxiously at her two suits and wished she'd brought a third.

'Goodness,' said Clio, 'Martha's on *Question Time* tonight. You remember Martha, don't you, Fergus?'

'Could I ever forget her? I bore her in my arms up to her bedroom, and laid her on the bed, lucky man that I am. She's very pretty.'

'Mmm . . .' said Clio.

'Not as pretty as you, though, I don't want any neuroses starting up. And I'm sure her breasts aren't nearly as nice.'

He had a bit of a thing about her breasts; he said they were the prettiest he had ever seen.

'They're like you,' he said, gazing at them tenderly, as she sat bolt upright in his bed the night before, still slightly shocked by the turn of events. 'Sweet and charming.'

'Fergus, how can breasts be charming?' she asked, laughing, suddenly relaxed.

'Yours demonstrate it beautifully. Can I kiss them?'

'Of course.'

He bent his head and kissed them, slowly and contemplatively, one at a time; her last distinct memory was of his tongue circling her nipples, teasing, caressing, infinitely gentle. And after that it became a blur, a joyful, greedy, melting, astonishing blur. And after that, peace, silence, stillness. And then: 'You silly bitch,' he said. 'You gorgeous, lovely, silly bitch. Think of all the time we've wasted.'

'Well, we can make up for it now,' said Clio.

'I think the red . . .' The floor manager considered Martha's suits. 'It suits you and it looks very zingy. Good. Now if you'd like to get changed, dinner will start in about half an hour. There are some really nice people coming, local dignitaries as well as your fellow panellists, and you can chat away and keep up to date with the news at the same time.'

'Oh – great,' said Martha.

She went into the dining room at about seven; it appeared full. A large table, laid as if for a formal dinner party, was in the centre of the room, with a group of people at one end, at least three with faces she found terrifyingly recognisable. She was introduced to them, given the glass of water she had requested, and left to sink or swim. Two of the Faces smiled at her kindly, asked her how she felt, assured her it would all be fine, and then returned to their previous conversations. She longed to run away. She went to the lavatory and guiltily switched on her mobile. There was nothing from Ed. It was almost seven o'clock.

Ed was sitting in one of the biggest traffic jams he had ever seen. His mobile had inexplicably run out of juice; and he was desperate for a pee. Otherwise everything was fine.

'What will you have to drink?' asked Nick. He smiled encouragingly at Janet Frean; she appeared to be in a rather tense mood.

'Oh – just some Perrier, I think.'

'Fine. Me too. It's nice up here, I've often wondered about it, but never actually got any further.'

'Very few people have,' said Janet. 'It's very good for a discreet rendezvous, for that very reason.'

'Indeed. Well, Janet, how are things at Centre Forward House? You've had a bit of bad luck lately.'

'I know. It's been very unfortunate. After all our hard work, people being so courageous and backing us, people in the field that is. Very dispiriting. It does make you wonder, just sometimes, if the game's worth the candle.'

Nick looked at her. He often found himself on the receiving end of such reflections – politicians tended to use journalists not just to disperse information stories, or berate them when they didn't write exactly what they were told, but rather surprisingly to share their self-doubt with them, use them as a sort of personal confessional.

'Well – I hope you're not giving up,' he said.

'Heavens, no!' She suddenly became herself again, brisk, incisive. 'Not after all this. I'd be pretty annoyed with whoever spilt the beans over the poll figures if I came across him – or her – but the others were just plain bad luck, stories waiting to be stumbled over.'

'Well – yes,' said Nick carefully. He wondered what she'd say if he told her he'd seen her with Michael Fitzroy that lunchtime.

'Martha, can you come to make-up now, please?'

She followed the make-up girl meekly; this had to be better than discussing the progress of the various planning committees in Birmingham while trying (mindful of Janet's dictum) to swallow some rather tough chicken – where would politics be without chicken, she wondered rather wildly – and follow Sky News on the television in the corner nearest to her.

She wondered what on earth the point of this dinner was: all any of them wanted was to watch the news and see what topics were developing. She felt terribly sick; her stomach was churning, and her mouth was increasingly dry. How on earth was she going to talk coherently for the cameras?

'Lovely colour, your suit,' said the girl chattily, 'I always think red's so cheerful. Your skin's lovely,' she added, 'really young-looking.'

'Well,' said Martha, 'it is quite. Young I mean. But thank you anyway.'

Maybe the town planners were better than this, after all.

She checked her mobile: there was still nothing from Ed.

'Oh wow!' said Jocasta. 'Gideon, guess what –'

'What, darling? You couldn't tie this for me, could you?'

'Course. I always had to do it for Nick.'

He was off to a dinner: an all-male dinner, he told her, regretfully; there was no way she could come.

'That's all right. The Little Woman will be waiting for you when you get home.'

She was really working very hard on being a good wife.

'In bed, I hope, wearing nothing but your perfume, Marilyn-style?'

'Not that nightie?'

'I prefer nothing.'

'Well – depends how late you are . . . There you are.' She considered him, his large powerful body in the perfectly tailored dinner jacket, his tanned face, his brilliant blue eyes, and smiled. 'I could really fancy you in that get-up, you know. I mean *really* fancy you. Come here . . .'

She reached up to him, kissed him very hard on the mouth. 'Why don't you take it all off again, and come to bed with me instead?'

'Darling, I can't. I'm so sorry.'

'Oh well. Actually, I just discovered Martha's on *Question Time* tonight. Martha Hartley, you know – I want to watch her.'

'Oh, really? Well, I would think she'd be very good; she's very articulate and composed . . . Darling, I must go. Sorry. Enjoy your programme.'

'Yes, I will, thanks. Love you.'

'I love you, too.' He disappeared; then she heard his footsteps coming back. He opened the door and looked at her. 'Never leave me, will you?' His expression was very serious, very intense. 'Never.'

'I never will,' she said. 'I promise.'

Nick was beginning to feel frustrated. So far he'd been listening to Janet Frean for an hour and a half and he'd got nothing from her but a lot of rather dull policy statements and a bit of banging on about her personal hobby horses, like NHS reforms.

508

'We have to get rid of the managers,' she was saying now, slightly pink-faced – she had begun to drink during the main course and had actually had rather a lot. Nick was surprised. Usually, in his experience, she was virtually teetotal.

'I tell you, Nick, those managers are a far bigger obstacle to NHS efficiency than lack of funds. And Centre Forward's policy of less interference would extend above all to that sort of thing.'

'Yes,' said Nick. 'Absolutely.'

'Bob trained as a paediatrician,' she said after a pause, 'as you probably know.'

'I do. Why did he leave it, go into industry?'

'Because of the system,' said Janet, 'and there must be hundreds, probably thousands, like him who couldn't stand it any longer. Of course it's not quite industry, Nick, it's pharmaceutical research.'

'Yeah, well . . .'

'Could you excuse me for a moment?' she said 'I just need to find the loo.'

'Of course.'

Nick was looking out of the window when she got back; he had just spotted Jerry Hall, looking ravishing, moving across the courtyard with her languid walk.

'Look at her,' he said to Janet. 'Isn't she marvellous?'

And then he looked at Janet; her demeanour appeared to have totally changed, she looked purposeful, brisk, almost excited.

'Anyway,' she said, sitting down again, picking up her glass, 'anyway, Nick, that's enough of the politics. How would you like a bit of gossip?'

'I'd love it. Political gossip?'

'Well – you could say that. It concerns a politician. An up and coming one. It's quite a story . . .'

'Kate, you up there?'

It was Juliet's voice.

'Yeah, in my room.'

Juliet came in; she was carrying her violin case. 'You ought to watch *Question Time* tonight. That woman's on, Martha Hartley, the one who was in the paper the week before you, in the fashion feature. It'd be interesting, wouldn't it, watching someone you knew?'

'Well, I don't exactly know her.'

'I thought you said she was at the party.'

'She was, but I never spoke to her. She was in the disco and then Gran looked after her when she fainted. I really didn't like her; she was well up herself. But yeah, let's watch it.'

'I will if I can. But I've got a lot of practice to do first.'

'Juliet,' said Kate, 'you are just so much too good to be true.'

'Oh, come on,' said Ed to the girl in reception. 'I only want to say good luck.'

'I'm sorry; it's more than my job's worth. No one's allowed in without a pass.'

'Well, you could give me a pass.'

'No, I couldn't. I really can't do that,' she said, 'but I will get a message to her. If you write her a note, I'll take it to her. OK?'

'Well, it'd be better than nothing,' said Ed, and then, seeing her face, 'I mean, it'd be great. Really, really cool. Thank you.'

He had just started to write when he heard his name.

'Ed! What are you doing here?'

It was someone he'd been at uni with. Judging from his uniform – T-shirt, jeans, clipboard and headset – he was clearly some kind of technician.

Ed explained his problem and the guy grinned.

'Tell you what I can do,' he said. 'I'll get a bigger sheet of paper.'

They were in position now, sitting at the table. Martha was at the end, two away from David Dimbleby, next to a rotund Tory. He was being very nice to her; so was Dimbleby, they were all trying to put her at her ease, but she felt dreadfully sick. But there was no escape and there was still nothing from Ed. What had happened to him, for God's sake? Probably decided not to come after all: well, she deserved it.

'Right, we're going to put a dummy question to each of you, to get the sound levels,' said the floor manager. 'Martha, you first. How do you rate your chances tonight?'

'On a scale of one to ten, zero,' she said, and everyone

laughed; she felt briefly better. And then much worse again.

What happened if she just couldn't think of anything to say at all? Some completely wild card might come up. The researchers were moving about amongst the audience now, getting questions, deciding which ones to take; these were written down, but that was only for Dimbleby's benefit – and he kept the paper covered, so that the people on either side of him couldn't get a preview. The first the panel knew was literally when the questions were put, and it was, she had been warned (again by Janet), often hard to hear.

She took deep breaths, trying to calm her heaving stomach.

And then she heard one of the cameramen calling her name, very quietly.

'Martha. Over here.'

She looked at him, at Camera Two or whatever it was: he was grinning at her, and gesturing just below the camera. There was a large hand-lettered sign there.

'Hi, Martha. Go for it! Ed xxx.'

She laughed aloud – and suddenly everything seemed much better.

'Nick! Why on earth are you ringing me at this time of night? I'm in bed. What? No, alone. He's out. No, of course you can't, I'd be in the divorce courts – what? WHAT? My God, Nick. Yes, of course. Come at once. I'll let you in. Sure, bye.'

Clio was in the kitchen when her mobile rang; Fergus had demanded a cup of cocoa before they went to bed. Who on earth would ring at this time of night?

'Hello? Jocasta! No, I'm making cocoa. Oh, shut up. We don't all live on champagne and – no, I'm listening. What? WHAT? My God, Jocasta. My God!'

An hour later, she and Fergus had arrived at Kensington Palace Gardens; Gideon was still out.

'I'm glad you're here, actually,' Jocasta said, hugging them both. 'Me being alone in the house with Nick is just a tad compromising. Cocoa? Or something even more exciting? Just look at the two of you, I think it's so wonderful!'

'Cocoa will do fine,' said Fergus, smiling at her, 'and we think it's wonderful too. And it's all because of you.'

'Aw, shucks,' said Jocasta. 'Now come on, Nick's in the drawing room. I'll go and get the cocoa.'

She came in with a tray; she looked absurdly out of place in the vast room, Clio thought, with its heavy brocade curtains, its embossed wallpaper, its chandeliers, its Antique (with a capital A) furniture, dressed in nothing but an oversize T-shirt, padding across the (no doubt priceless) Indian carpet in her bare feet. It somehow seemed to sum up the whole marriage; she didn't belong here, it didn't suit her. But then – Gideon did, she told herself firmly. He suited her perfectly. And she suited him. That was what mattered . . .

'Well, all I can say, Nick,' said Jocasta, putting the tray down, 'is that Martha was very lucky Janet chose to tell *you*. Not someone from the *Sun*. Or the *Mirror*. It'd be in tomorrow's paper, no messing. I s'pose it's because we – I mean the *Sketch* – had the exclusive on the Baby Bianca story. What did you say to her, anyway? I suppose you've got it on tape?'

'Yes. In my pocket, right here.' He patted it. 'I must make a duplicate before something happens. I just thanked her for giving me the story, said I wasn't sure what would happen next and legged it as fast as I could. I was terrified she'd change her mind, ask for the tape back. Not that it would have made any difference, but she's obviously a bit deranged.'

'Is she?' asked Clio. 'Why do you say that?'

'It's a very odd thing to do. If she wanted to discredit that party of hers, she's going the right way about it – it would just about finish it off, all the scandals it's had lately. Incidentally, I'm pretty bloody sure she was behind the leak about the polls. I saw her in what you might call a compromising situation. Yet she talks about the party as if it was another child she adores. I don't understand it. Anyway, what do we do next? What do I, in particular, do next? Chris would have my balls if he knew I was sitting on this. And she could be talking to the *Sun* right now. I could have just been a rehearsal. God, what a mess.'

'We have to tell Martha,' said Jocasta, 'absolutely have to.'

'So – what do we do?' asked Nick. 'Ring her, say oh hi, Martha, nice performance, and we know you're Baby Bianca's mother.'

'And there's another thing,' said Jocasta. 'Who's going to tell Kate?'

'Well, Martha must,' said Clio, 'of course. My God. No wonder the poor girl fainted.'

'What poor girl?' said Jocasta. 'Martha? You're not saying you're sorry for her, I hope?'

'Of course I'm sorry for her. Just think what she's been going through for the last sixteen years. I think it's one of the saddest stories I ever heard.'

'Me too,' said Fergus.

Jocasta looked at him thoughtfully.

'This relationship with Clio is turning you soft, Fergus Trehearn. Now come on, who's going to make this call?'

Martha was half asleep in the car, her head on Ed's shoulder, when her mobile rang.

'Oh, let's just ignore it,' she said sleepily. 'It won't be anyone I want to speak to. Probably Jack, having yet another orgasm.'

Kirkland had already rung twice, the first time to congratulate her in general terms, the second to say how brilliantly he felt she had put the party philosophy over. Chad, Eliot, Geraldine Curtis and her parents had also all called.

'Yeah, OK. Speaking of orgasms, I hope you're going to be a bit more alert than this when we get home.'

Martha turned to him, pulled his face down to hers, and kissed him with great thoroughness.

'That's on account. A sort of down payment. I feel very, very alert in the relevant department.'

They had discussed staying in Birmingham, but Ed said he had to be in London first thing, and 'So what do you think I'm doing?' said Martha indignantly. 'Sleeping in?'

'Only thing is – my car overheated all the way up. Hate to drive it down now.'

'We can both go in the Beeb car. We can drive up and get yours on Saturday. Oh, no, I'll be in Binsmow. Well, Sunday, then. No, I've got a garden party. Sunday night, maybe? No – '

'How about dawn on Wednesday week?'

'You're on.'

'You were fantastic, you know. Really, really good.'

'I wouldn't have been,' she said, 'without your lovely message.

513

Oh, Ed, what on earth was I thinking of, keeping you away from me all this time?'

'If you can't answer that,' said Ed, 'there's no hope for any of us. When are you going to tell me the reason?'

'I'm not.'

They reached Canary Wharf just before two.

'I'm sorry,' she said, as they walked in the door, 'I just absolutely have to have a shower. I was sweating like a pig under those lights.'

'The cool Ms Hartley sweating? I don't believe it. All right. Tell you what, I'll join you. How would that be?'

'Heavenly,' said Martha.

They stood together in the thudding water; Ed began to kiss her, slowly, almost lazily. Martha began to soar; soar into a sweet dark place, pierced with brilliance and promise. Why had she denied herself this for so long, how could she have borne it? Ed's hands were on her buttocks, holding her against him; she could feel him hard and very strong, and her own response to him, liquid and longing. He lifted her slightly, so that she was on him. 'I love you,' he was saying through the kissing, through the water, and almost before she was ready, it came; she felt herself suddenly, swiftly, gather and tauten and then release in an explosion she could almost see, it was so bright and strong.

'I love you too,' she said, smiling, leaning gently now against him. 'I love you so, so much.'

'Good,' he said, 'you've come to your senses. Now let's go to bed.'

He wrapped her tenderly in a towel and half carried her to the bed. And unwrapped the towel again, and lay, looking at her, at her face, ravished with weariness and sex, at her body, her neat, tough little body, her mound, perfectly waxed. 'There's just one thing wrong with you, Martha Hartley,' he said, wiping her face on the sleeve of his bathrobe.

'Only one?'

'Only one. Your pubes. I know you like minimal, but there's a time and place for everything – and right there and as soon as possible, I'd personally like more of a bush. Will you grow it for me? Prove that you love me?'

'I will,' she said. 'If that's all it takes.'

At that moment the landline went, and the answering machine cut in.

'At last,' said Jocasta, 'she said she only just got back. She obviously had someone with her.'

Fergus had left. It was agreed that he should, that this was best handled by the three of them. Gideon had come home, and gone straight up to bed. If he was curious at the presence of his wife's ex-lover and her best friend in his house, he didn't show it.

'Enjoy your party,' was all he said.

'I'm sorry, Gideon, I'll explain everything in the morning.'

'Fine. Good night all of you.'

He left with a wave, and his oddly sweet smile.

'I want to come,' said Ed.

'No, Ed, you can't. I'm sorry. It's too – complicated. But I will be back, I swear, and I'll tell you everything then.'

'All right.' He sighed. 'But I don't like you driving. You're exhausted, you're upset – '

'I'll be all right. Promise.'

'Suppose I drive you over, wait outside?'

'No, Ed. I might be hours.'

'I've waited weeks for you already,' he said. 'What's a few more hours? Please, Martha.'

She looked at him. 'All right. If you really want to.'

'I really want to. And I don't mind how long you are.'

Jocasta opened the door; she had put on some jeans under her oversized T-shirt and looked about seventeen. She smiled at Martha.

'Hi. Come in. Is that – ' She peered out at the car. 'Is that someone with you?'

'Yes, but he's waiting outside,' said Martha, 'I don't want him with us while we talk.'

'Oh – OK.'

She led the way into the drawing room; Clio had made a jug of coffee.

'Hi, Martha. How are you? You were so good tonight.'

'Thanks. First and last time, I guess.'

515

She managed a smile: a cool, slightly sad little smile.

'Well – who knows. Now – how do you want to play this? Coffee?'

'Yes, please. Black no sugar.'

'I'm sorry about this, Martha,' said Nick, holding out his hand rather formally.

She took it. 'Not your fault.'

They all sat down again.

'Look,' Martha said suddenly, 'this is a bit – hard for me. I don't really want to talk to all of you at once.'

'That's fine,' said Jocasta. 'We're only all here because – well, because Nick knew I'd be able to get hold of you. And it was obviously urgent. God knows who else she might have told.'

'It's not in the other papers,' said Clio quickly. 'We went to Waterloo and got them, so we've got a few hours at least. Days hopefully.'

'But – it's got to happen, I suppose? Got to come out?'

She sounded vulnerable at last.

'I – would say so, yes. I'm so sorry.'

'No, no, it's very nice of you to try to help, I haven't exactly been very friendly to you.'

'Well – we know why now,' said Jocasta.

'Anyway,' said Clio, 'we felt that – perhaps – you might find it easiest to talk to me. I'm a doctor, after all. Hippocratic oath and all that.'

'Actually,' said Martha, 'you were right. I think I would like to start with you, Clio. If you others don't mind.'

'Of course not,' said Jocasta. 'We'll be in the kitchen if you want us.'

'I cannot believe I've been so stupid,' said Martha suddenly, 'telling that bloody woman. I mean – why her?'

'It was at the party, wasn't it?' said Clio. 'You were obviously very distressed. Ill, actually, I'd say. And you had just been confronted by it all. Literally.'

'I suppose so. But – oh God. Oh God, oh God . . .'

She dropped her head into her hands and began to cry. Clio went over and sat next to her, put her arm round her.

'I'm so, so sorry,' Clio said. 'Really, I couldn't be sorrier.

I can't imagine how you must be feeling. But – we do all want to help. We're so totally on your side.'

'I know,' said Martha, pulling a handkerchief out of her pocket. 'And I do appreciate it. I'm sorry. Sorry I wasn't more friendly, Clio, so sorry.'

'Don't be ridiculous. Look – why don't you try telling me about it? When you're ready. There's no hurry.'

And Martha sat there with Clio, in the quiet drawing room, already growing light in the midsummer dawn, and started.

Because she had done it just a few weeks earlier, it was easier than it might have been, but she still had to force every word out of herself, the painful, difficult words. It was a bit like giving birth again, she thought, giving birth to Kate, and she couldn't believe she was releasing them: the words she had kept inside her head, buried deep in her consciousness for sixteen years. Telling of the dreadful days, weeks in Bangkok, in the awful, airless room, the terrible boredom, passing the time by walking, walking miles and miles round the hot, dirty, stinking city, and reading, reading – 'I got some of the cheap travellers' used paperbacks.'

'So, how long were you there?'

'Oh – about two and a half months.'

'That's a very long time in Bangkok.'

'It was indeed. It was horrendous at first; I thought I'd go mad. But actually, it got better. I worked myself into a routine, just took one day at a time. I went to the markets a lot, I stayed downtown, on the left bank of the river, there's a kind of ghetto of guest houses, really cheap. Anyway, I found a room there, without windows – you can imagine how cheap they are – and ate off those street stalls. I tried to eat properly, I realised that mattered, but I must have been spending about a pound a day altogether, and I just waited, waited for the baby to be born. I – well, I sort of hoped I could have it there, by myself.'

'By yourself! You thought you could have a baby all by yourself?'

'Well, yes. I mean, people do. I kept thinking about a girl I'd read about in the paper once, who had a baby in her bedroom while her parents watched television downstairs, they had no idea, and then she took it out and left it on a park bench and went back to the house and went to bed. I thought if she could do that, then so could I.

'I'd bought a medical book in Australia, so I knew exactly what to expect. I knew all about cutting the cord and everything. I bought some really big, sharp scissors and some strong string – '

'Martha, this is a terrible story! God, how brave you must be. And you must have felt so terrible, so alone.'

'I did, yes. But I had to manage. There was a lovely old Thai woman I made friends with; she was so kind and she used to give me massages and rub my back and everything. In return I taught her English. I thought she'd help me if – well, things went wrong. And of course, there was no way she could ask awkward questions.'

'But – what did you plan to do with the baby, Martha? Afterwards? What did you think would happen to it? In a place like Bangkok?'

Martha met her eyes with great difficulty.

'I – I decided to take it to a hospital. I investigated them all – you'd have thought I was going to have it there – and finally decided on the Bangkok Christian Hospital. I thought I could leave it there, by the main door, and it would be found by someone, and be really well looked after. And then probably adopted by someone European. I'm sorry, Clio, I can see you think it's appalling of me, but you have to understand how desperate I was. It – it wasn't really a baby to me. It was something dreadful that I'd done, that I had to – to put behind me. Literally. I had to have it, and then – leave it behind. So I could go home, and everything would be all right again and I'd be safe.'

'Yes. Yes, I see.'

'And the baby just wouldn't come. After all those weeks, it wouldn't come. I tried everything, I took castor oil and walked miles and jumped off the bed, and sat in a hot bath, and the old woman gave me an enema, and lots of herbs and stuff, but it wouldn't come and I had to get home. I was completely out of money, completely. I could never have got another ticket, the cheap flights were all booked anyway for weeks ahead. So I thought, Well, I can't stay here forever, I'll just have to go and

518

sort something out when I get back. Maybe go to a hospital somewhere in the north of England – I just wasn't thinking logically at all. And then – well, it started on the plane. I crawled off it, and headed for a lavatory, and saw this room on the way in marked Staff Only. It had cleaning stuff in it, and a sink, and just room for me to lie down – and I had her there. I just did. It was – well, quite awful. But I didn't have any choice. If anyone had known, I'd have been taken off to hospital and I'd have had to give my name, my parents would have been told . . .'

'Martha, couldn't you possibly have told your parents?' Her voice was very gentle. 'Had the baby adopted after that, fine, but at least told them, got some help?'

'No. I couldn't. Well, I can see now, that just possibly I could have done, but then – Clio, you don't know what Binsmow's like. You can't sneeze without everyone knowing. And discussing where you got the germs from. I was the vicar's daughter and I'd done the most awful thing a girl could do. I'd have brought disgrace on them . . .'

'You're talking like a Victorian nóvel,' said Clio, and smiled for the first time. 'Bringing disgrace on them? Martha, for God's sake, this was the 1980s.'

'But I would have done. The whole parish respected my father so, he would never, ever have recovered. I honestly believe that he'd have had to move away, he could never have lived it down. I was the star of the family, you see, they were so proud of me, getting into Bristol, getting straight As in my A levels, doing law, all his parishioners were so impressed, how could I have failed them, said sorry, I'm not what you thought, I'm not your darling innocent daughter, I've done something terrible, I've had a baby, and I did think of it like that, as something terrible I'd done –'

'So – how did you feel? When you left her?'

'Well, I rested for a bit, and – and cleaned myself up, and then I thought, Well, that's it, it's over, I've done it, and I held her for a little while and then wrapped her up very carefully in a sheet and a blanket I'd bought for her in Bangkok, and laid her in a sort of trolley basket thing with towels in it. And then I went and sat on a bench just opposite, and waited until someone found her. I was very worried because I'd somehow not thought to get her any nappies; I thought she'd pee on the blankets. After all that, and I was worried about a bit of pee. Anyway, someone did find her, some Asian woman cleaner, and she came out calling for help and there was a lot of fuss, of course, and people coming and going and then a policewoman just took her away.'

'Didn't you feel – upset?'

'Honestly? No. Not then. Just – relief. I thought, She's safe now, and it's over, and that's all I felt. I'm sure you must think I'm dreadful, but I didn't feel sad, or any of the things you might expect. Later on, yes, but not then.'

'I don't think you're dreadful,' Clio said. 'I'm just so sad for you. And full of admiration, that you could be so brave.'

'I told you, I had to be. And then I just thought, Now I can go home. Only of course, I couldn't, not straight away, I didn't dare, my parents might have noticed something. I wasn't feeling very well. I was – was bleeding quite a lot. So I went into the ladies, and had a shower – that was so nice – and then I lay down on some seats upstairs, and slept for ages. I felt quite happy, actually. I knew the baby was safe, and that was all that mattered. She wasn't my worry any more. And that was when it began: I just knew I had to put her out of my head. I've read lots of articles since, about women who have given up their babies at birth and even do what I did. And they go into denial, complete denial. They don't allow it into their lives any more, they block it out, it's just something that happened, that they've put right away from them. That's what I did.'

'Yes, I see. I have heard that, actually. So – when did you go home?'

'After a couple of days – well, four, actually. When – when I seemed to be all right. I went to a YWCA hostel in Hayes; I had just enough money, and I slept a lot and looked after myself as best I could . . .'

'Didn't you get milk?' asked Clio very gently.

'Yes, I did.' Tears welled up again. 'I wasn't expecting that. It was awful. That did make me cry. I kept looking at it, I didn't know what it was at first, and thinking, This was meant for her. It was horrible. And quite painful. I bought some pad things at Boots and stuffed them in my bra. After a few days it dried up.'

520

'And – and your parents didn't suspect anything?'

'Why should they? I'd put on some weight, of course, but plenty of people do when they're travelling. I'd bought lots of kaftan things, and those fishermen's trousers, so I wore them. I was all right. I was very tired, but that was to be expected.'

'And what about letters, didn't they want some kind of address all that time?'

'Yes, and I gave them the *poste restante* in Bangkok. Told them I was doing some more travelling in Thailand. I told them I ran out of money, so I couldn't go to America. And I'd done enough to satisfy them. Singapore, Australia, Thailand – it sounds a lot to people who've never left England. Quite enough to fill a year.

'Anyway, I knew I'd done the right thing. And every day I felt safer. I got a sort of high just from doing it, getting away with it. And I knew she was all right, because I read the papers.'

'Did you keep the papers?'

She hesitated, then: 'No, I didn't. I know that sounds awful, but it was all part of her not being anything to do with me. I couldn't let myself think about her, because then I'd acknowledge her.'

'Yes, I see,' said Clio carefully. 'And – how did you cope? Didn't you feel unhappy at all?'

'Well, in a way, yes. But I just buried it and buried it. And got on with my life. Worked terribly hard, did well. It all helped. And developed into the terrible control freak you see before you. But all alone, in private, I'd remember her quite suddenly, remember what she looked like, remember holding her, specially on her birthday – that's always hard – but even that somehow wasn't real. It was like something that had happened to someone else, not me. But over the years, if anything upset me, it would – sometimes, not always – come back to her. I would start crying and go back to that time. I did cry a lot at the beginning. I felt very – strange. Very confused. Funnily enough, she never got any older than about one. Not in my head. She stayed tiny, I never grew her up.'

'Didn't you long to tell someone?'

'No, I was terrified of telling someone. I was terrified of getting that close to anyone. I had very few friends, always. Men were a bit safer. It wasn't the sort of thing you'd tell a man.'

'I suppose. Oh, Martha. What a story.'

'It is quite, isn't it? And then all these extraordinary coincidences that have brought us together. That was such a terrible day – I was out running and there she was in the paper, Abandoned Baby Bianca. I did go a bit – strange then.'

'And now?'

'Now I don't know,' she said. 'I really don't know what now. I mean, it's the end of my life as I know it.'

'Martha, no it isn't!'

'Yes, it is. Look at me, a highly paid lawyer. It's a criminal offence, you know. Abandoning a baby. You can get ten years in jail for it. And – worse than that, I'm a prospective parliamentary candidate. For Binsmow, for God's sake. Where my father's the vicar. You have to sign something saying there's nothing in your past that would cause your party any difficulty or embarrassment, you know.'

'Yes,' Clio said quietly, 'yes, I can see you're right. Martha – the father – did he ever have any idea?'

'No,' she said quickly, 'absolutely none. I couldn't possibly have told him. Not possibly.'

'Because?'

'I don't want to go on with this,' she said. 'Sorry.'

'All right. But – what about Kate, Martha? She's going to have to know.'

'I know. I know. How on earth is that going to be done? Who's going to tell her?'

'Well – I thought – you should,' said Clio, very gently. 'You're the only person who can make her understand.'

Martha stared at her. 'I really don't think I can do that,' she said.

Chapter 35

'Poor you. Poor, poor you.'

Ed's voice was very gentle. Taking courage from it, Martha forced herself to look at his face. It was tender, concerned, there was no judgement, no shock, even; it was as if she had told him someone dear to her had died. She supposed, in a way, that was right: the cool, efficient, hypersuccessful Martha had died; and in her place was someone flawed and very frightened, someone who had done something so shocking and shameful that she had kept it hidden for sixteen years.

'You're going to have to tell me what to do, Ed,' she said. 'For the first time I have no idea. No idea at all.'

'I'll try,' he said. 'I'll try very hard. I'd like to meet your friends, talk to them.'

'Of course. They're being so good to me. I really don't deserve it, I was vile to them.'

'I tell you what's the first thing you should do,' he said.

'What?'

'You should stop crucifying yourself. You haven't committed a crime.'

'Ed, that's exactly what I've done. I told you. A crime with a ten-year prison sentence.'

'Yes, OK, I hear what you say. But it isn't really a crime, not morally. You knew she was all right, you saw her safely taken away, you knew she was being cared for by people who knew what they were doing. After that, you just got on with your life. Calling it a crime is just a technicality.'

'Ed! I think you're a bit prejudiced. How do you think the press are going to present this?'

'Fuck the press.'

'No, you can't say that. They're going to call me a harridan, a monster, a ruthless bitch. That's what people will take in. What kind of woman abandons her child and never goes near it again? Someone kind and caring? I don't think so.'

'I think you should go and see her,' he said.

'Kate? I can't, Ed. Maybe when she knows, maybe when she's got used to the idea, but – '

'No, not her. The woman. Janet whatever-her-name is. Find out what she might do next, if your friend doesn't run the story. He must be a great guy,' he added. 'Most hacks'd have it out on the street by now.'

'He is. He's a sweetheart. I always liked him.'

'A sweetheart, eh? Not sure I like that.'

'Oh, Ed. No one's as much of a sweetheart as you.'

She looked at him and smiled tenderly; he was clearly shocked. He was only twenty-three, with very little experience of life. How could he be expected to cope with all this? Then she thought of herself at twenty-three, a first in law under her belt, working as a trainee solicitor in one of London's finest firms, all after coming through almost unbelievable trauma: they were obviously two of a kind, she and Ed.

'I love you,' she said simply. 'I really, really love you . . .'

'Good God,' said Gideon, 'the poor, poor child. That is a terrible story, Jocasta.'

'I know. Isn't it? Doing what she did, all alone . . .' She shuddered. 'I'd rather have died. Well, I probably would have died of terror.'

'No you wouldn't,' he said. 'You'd have done it because you had to. You're a lot braver than you think you are, you know. Now then, let's think what's best to be done for Martha. I have to say, it's a very nasty situation. Very nasty indeed.'

'I know. I keep thinking of all the people she ought to tell. Before they hear anyway, in tabloid speak.'

'Young Nicholas wouldn't do tabloid speak.'

'No, of course not. But the others'll pick it up and run with it. I can see it now. "The ruthless career woman who abandoned her baby", or, "Baby Bianca's Heartless Mother". I mean, it doesn't help that Kate's so bloody famous. It's a gift as a story, you must admit.'

'Oh, I admit it. Pollock will murder Nick if he finds out. Now, this is only idle curiosity, but has anyone asked Martha if the father knows?'

'No. I don't suppose she has the faintest idea where he is.'

'Or even who?'

'Oh, I think she'd know who, Gideon. Martha isn't a sleeper around.'

'You didn't think she'd abandon a child until today, did you? You of all people, Jocasta, know how unpredictable people are.'

'I know. But – I bet she knows. I'd put quite a lot of money on it.'

'None of mine, please. Now, I have a fancy she should go and confront Mrs Frean. If she can find the courage.'

Jocasta's mobile went; she looked at it.

'Hi, Martha, how are you doing? What? That's interesting. Gideon said the same. Hold on a minute . . .' She looked at Gideon. 'Ed, Martha's boyfriend, says the same thing.'

'Then he must be a very bright fellow. A man after my own heart. I wonder if he'd go with her?'

'I'm sure he would. Martha, would Ed go with you?'

'He says he will.'

'OK,' said Jocasta. 'Go for it.'

'Martha dear, hello. How lovely to hear from you. I meant to call you last night, you were marvellous. Absolutely marvellous. Congratulations.'

Martha was not as surprised by this as she might have been. She was beginning to get Janet Frean's measure.

'Thank you, Janet. I wondered if – if I could come and see you.'

'Well – when did you have in mind? I'm very busy today and then, of course, it's the weekend – Monday maybe?'

'But it's awfully urgent.'

'Really? Well, it'll have to wait, I'm afraid. I'm so sorry.'

'But Janet, I – that is – don't you know what it's about?'

'I have no idea. But I really can't see you this weekend. There's no question of it. I won't even be here. I'm sorry.'

Martha looked at Ed.

'Now what do we do?'

Janet Frean put down the phone and went in search of her husband; he was sitting out in the garden, reading the *Daily Telegraph* and drinking a very large mug of coffee.

'Bob – I did tell you, didn't I, that I had to be out of town on Saturday night?'

'I don't know. Anyway, it doesn't matter; we haven't got anything on. Party business, I presume?'

'Of course. Charm offensive has to continue but – you can cope with the children, can you? It's Kirsty's weekend off.'

'I usually do,' he said dryly.

Martha had broken one of her own unbreakable laws and called in sick. She actually spoke to Paul Quenell, who was so excited by her performance on *Question Time* that she felt he would have given her the whole week off, had she asked.

'Of course, Martha. You must be exhausted. Splendid they mentioned Wesley by name. Well done. You're a clever girl. Enjoy the weekend, see you on Monday.'

Martha put the phone down, wondering if she would ever see him again. Once, she supposed, when she resigned.

She felt oddly calm. It was ten in the morning; Ed was asleep, having called in sick himself. She had a shower, then wandered round her flat tidying it, flicking through magazines, organising her laundry and staring out of the window. Mostly, she stared out of the window. And thought about Kate and what on earth she could say to her and how.

Clio had also called in sick; she had slept for a few hours, but at ten o'clock she was in the kitchen, hoping to find Jocasta.

Gideon was there, in a towelling robe; he smiled at her.

'Hello, my darling girl. Excuse my rather informal attire; I've been having my swim. You should try my mechanical pool, it's very clever. Tedious, but clever. How are you? Tired, I expect.'

'Not too bad,' said Clio. 'Is Jocasta about?'

'I'm here.' Jocasta came into the kitchen; she looked rather pale.

'Jocasta, I've been thinking,' said Clio. 'If Martha agrees, I think you should tell Kate. First off, that is. I mean, she doesn't know Martha; it'd be the most awful shock. And she's so fond of you. You won't mind how she reacts, whereas Martha might. She's probably going to be very stroppy, very hurt.'

'I rather agree with that,' said Gideon. 'Jocasta, what do you think?'

'I think so, too, I'm afraid. The only other thing would be for me to tell her mother and for her to tell Kate.'

'It would come better from you,' said Clio. 'Apart from anything else, you know Martha. But probably her mother should be there. And her father. I don't think they'll help, but they'd be outraged if you told her first.'

'God,' said Jocasta, 'I don't like this!'

Nick was walking through Central Lobby when he saw Janet Frean.

'Look,' she said, 'our conversation last night – you haven't run the story today, I see.'

'No, I needed to do some more research on it.'

'Well – don't leave it too long. I'd hate to see it wasted and I'm sure the *Sun* would love it.'

'I'm sure they would.'

'So – when do you think you might run it?'

'Janet, I don't know. Obviously there's a degree of urgency. But I must talk to Martha – and Chris Pollock is the final arbiter.'

'Yes. Well, keep in touch.'

'Sure.'

'Kate darling, this is Jocasta.'

'Hi, Jocasta – how are you?'

'Good, thanks, Kate. Look, I wondered – what are you doing today?'

'Nothing, really. Going shopping with Bernie. Seeing Nat later. Why?'

'I – thought I might come and see you.'

'Cool. But you don't want to come to Ealing. It's not exactly hopping. Why don't I come into Town, see you?'

'Well – the thing is, Kate, I'd quite like your mum and dad to be there.'

'What? Oh, I get it. It's about my contract, yeah? Is Fergus coming?'

'Oh, I think so,' said Jocasta. 'Yes. Look, I – we'll be over in about an hour. Is that OK?'

'Well – Dad won't be here.'

'Is your mum there now?'

'Yeah. Do you want to speak to her?'

'Yes, please.'

'Fine. See you later.'

Never had that irritating phrase had so much menace in it.

Helen felt physically sick. After all these years, the worst was going to happen: Kate's mother was going to become reality, no longer a distant, shadowy figure who could be warded off, talked away, but a person, a dreadfully dangerous person, who could come and claim her daughter. Not literally of course: but emotionally. The mystery that had hurt Kate so badly for so many years was about to be solved. She would know what her mother looked like, sounded like, she could talk to her, ask her questions, find out why she had done what she had done. This woman would walk in and take her rightful place in Kate's life and she and Jim would be relegated to theirs – second best, understudies, caretakers.

How could she bear it, if Kate wanted to live with her? If Kate fell in love with her, declared her everything she had ever wanted. She had often thought that the most dreadful grief possible would be the death of a child; this seemed to her to have echoes of that.

Jocasta had given her no details: only said she knew who Kate's mother was, and that she wanted Helen and Jim to be there when she told her. She was such a nice girl, Jocasta, Helen thought: how badly they had misjudged her.

Jim was on his way home, had said he would be there within the hour; Jocasta said she would wait until he was there, before arriving herself.

'Otherwise Kate will start pestering me. I won't be far away, just ring me on my mobile.'

'You're not – not bringing – you know – *her* – with you?' Helen had said, her voice shaky, and no, Jocasta had said, there would be plenty of time for that, when they had got used to the idea and were ready to meet her, 'Although I don't think Kate will want to wait for long.'

Helen was sure she wouldn't . . .

'Why are they taking so long?' said Martha. She was white-faced, her eyes haunted. 'What are they doing?'

'Martha,' said Ed, 'try not to be so ridiculous. I'd say Jocasta has only been there half an hour and it's not a conversation she can have quickly. Two more hours and I'd say you could start to worry. Right now, I think we should go for a walk.'

'A walk!'

'Yes, a walk. You know, one leg after the other, move along the street, that sort of thing. You can take your mobile, you won't miss anything. Come on. Let's go.'

Helen went to the corner shop and bought some biscuits. They could have them with the coffee, she thought. As she came out, she saw Kate coming towards her; she was walking very quickly and she waved as she saw Helen. Maybe Jocasta was there already, Helen thought, maybe she had brought Her, maybe Jocasta had already introduced them, and she was coming to tell Helen about her, about this wonderful person who had come at last into her life

But: 'Hi, Mum. Would you mind if I got Nat round? Thing is, he's quite interested in this contract, he made some really good points about it.'

'Well – ' Did she mind? Did she? Probably not. Nat had been part of the family for the past few weeks, and she was very fond of him – he was oddly gentle and thoughtful, might even help ease the emotional tension.

'No, I wouldn't mind,' she said.

'Cool. Thanks. You all right, Mum? You look a bit tense.'

'No, I'm fine.'

Kate put her arm through Helen's.

'Mum, I'm sorry I got in such a strop about the contract. Very sorry. Nat said I shouldn't have, he said you were only trying to do your best for me, and of course he's right. He's often right. He's quite clever really, you know, under all that rubbish he talks about his dad and so on . . . Mum, you're crying, whatever is it?'

'Nothing,' said Helen, smiling at her through her tears, 'nothing at all. And it doesn't matter about you being in a strop, we understood. Oh, look, there's your father now. Go on in and put the kettle on, Kate, there's a good girl.'

She watched her striding up the path on her long bare legs, her wild hair falling down her back, pushing the buttons on her mobile to summon Nat: and thought that this was the last time, the very last time, Kate would be properly hers . . .

'So – why didn't she come herself?' asked Kate. She was white and very shocked, sitting close to her mother, with Nat on her other side, holding her hand.

'I – we – '

'Who's we?'

'Me, and Clio and Martha herself, we all felt it best if I told you,' said Jocasta. 'You know me, you can yell your head off at me and I won't mind. And your mum and dad know me too. It just seemed more sensible.'

Kate nodded.

'So – does she want to see me?'

'Kate, of course she does,' said Jocasta, hoping devoutly this was true. 'But she wants you to get used to the idea. I mean, she's a complete stranger to you, isn't she?'

'Yeah . . . Yeah, she is.' She sat in silence for a moment, then: 'What's she like, Jocasta? I mean, what sort of person is she?'

'Well, I don't really know her either. When we were all your age, well, a bit older, we went travelling together, and I suppose we spent a week altogether in each other's company. Fast forward sixteen years and I've met her about twice since. Very briefly.'

'But – do you like her?'

'Well – yes. I think so.'

'And – she's never told anyone at all?'

'No one at all. Except this madwoman, and that was at the party.'

'But – had she seen about me in the paper?'

'Well – yes.'

'So why the fuck didn't she come and see me then?' She was angry now, two spots of colour high on her cheeks.

'Kate, there's no need to swear,' said Jim.

'Yes there is! She's a cow, a stupid, fucking cow. I hate her! I hate her already. I didn't like her at the party, I thought she was right up her own arse, and now I like her a whole lot less. Seems to me the only reason she's come clean now is because she's got to. Because she's scared it'll all be in the papers. Not because she gives a toss about me, not because she wants to see me. Cow!' She pulled her hand free of Nat's, folded her arms across her chest. 'Well, you can tell her I don't want to see her. Ever. You can tell her she's a stupid bitch, and I hate her.'

'Kate,' said Nat gently, his face troubled, 'Kate, you can't hate someone you don't know.'

'I don't need to know her. I hate her! I hate what she did to me – God, why did it have to be her?' She started to cry. Nat put his arm round her; she shook it off.

'I'm sorry, Kate,' said Jocasta quietly, 'so sorry. Look – why don't I go now, give you all a chance to talk about it. You've got my number, if you change your mind, Kate, decide you want to talk to Martha. It might make you feel differently, you know.'

'I don't want to talk to her. I never will. Cow. Fucking cow. God!'

She stood up, started pacing up and down the room; they all sat silent, watching her, not knowing what to do. Finally Nat stood up, took her hand.

'Come on, Kate,' he said, 'let's go for a bit of a drive. OK with you, Mrs Tarrant? I think it'll calm her down.'

Helen nodded; and they watched him lead her out of the room, smiling at her encouragingly, saying, 'That's right, come on, it'll be all right,' as if she were a small child being led into school for the first time, or to the dentist.

Finally she said: 'That boy is an absolute treasure.'

'He is indeed,' said Jocasta. 'Are you all right, Helen?'

'Yes, I'm fine, thank you. Absolutely fine.'

'One thing,' said Ed, as they walked along the street, 'does the – the – well, does he know?'

'No,' said Martha. 'No, he has no idea.'

'Did he then?'

'No. I never told him – anything.'

'But you know who he was?'

'Ed – '

'Look,' he said, and for the first time there was irritation, something raw in his attitude, 'look, I've been OK so far. Like totally on your side. I think I have a right to ask a few questions, don't you?'

'Of course you do. But – I can't answer that one. I'm sorry.'

'What, you don't know who it was?'

'I do know who it was. Yes. But I don't intend to talk about – about him. Ever.'

There was a long silence; then: 'Seems to me it means you don't trust me. Unless you're still in love with him, that is.'

'I am not still in love with him. I never was in love with him. It was just – just something that happened. By the time I knew I was pregnant, I had no idea where he was.'

'But now you do?'

She was silent.

'You do! For Christ's sake, Martha, don't you think you should tell him? Don't you think she'll want to know?'

'Who?'

'Who? The girl. Kate. Your daughter. God! This is beginning to get to me, Martha. Don't you think the poor little cow has a right to know who her dad is?'

'I – don't know,' she said. 'Does she?'

'For fuck's sake,' he said. 'Look, I need to be on my own for a bit. Suddenly I can't cope with this. I'll see you later. I'll call you, OK?'

'OK.'

She watched him go, her eyes blurred with tears.

And wishing she could tell him.

She had been half asleep on the boat, coming back from Koh Tao to Koh Samui. She had gone there for a couple of days, having been told it was the most beautiful of all the islands, that she must see it. She had been told that about most of them, but had been half-inclined this time to agree; a white-rimmed jewel in the dazzling sea, electricity which only ran in the evenings, and huts so basic they made the ones on Samui seem quite luxurious. The girl she had gone over with had stayed to do some scuba diving; Martha's money didn't extend to that, and ravishing as the island was, it didn't take hold of her heart as Koh Samui had.

The boat seemed unusually rickety, even by Thai standards – very basic, with no toilet on board. She slung her rucksack onto the huge pile with all the others, found a quiet corner and settled down with her book. She had found it on the second-hand shelf, at the dock at Mae Hat, the first half of the *Hitchhiker's Guide to the Galaxy*; it was the custom to rip books in two, to save rucksack space, and leave behind what you'd read. It could sometimes be months before you could find the second half.

The trip was quite long, over three hours, and a wind had come up. Martha, who was a good sailor, had drifted off to sleep, lulled by the rise and fall of the boat; she woke once to see her rucksack tumble onto the mailbags on the lower deck. She reached over and tried to haul it back up, but she couldn't reach it, and went back to her corner. They were about thirty minutes from the jetty at Hat Bophut, when she heard his voice.

'Hi, Martha! I only just realised it was you. Your hair's different.'

She struggled to sit up, slightly dazed, and saw him, smiling down at her.

'Hi! Oh, the braids? Yes, I had it done on the beach. Were you on Koh Tao?'

She wasn't remotely surprised to see him; that was the whole thing about travelling. People came into your life, you became involved with them, and then you parted, to meet up with them again months later, in an entirely different place.

'Yeah. Been diving. You?'

'No, just snorkelling. Being a poor relation. Lovely though.'

'Isn't it? And – where now?'

'Oh, back to Big Buddha for a few days and then I've got a vague arrangement with some girl to move over to Phuket.'

'It's lovely there. And Krabi. And green sea, rather than blue. You been north yet?'

'Yes, it was amazing.'

'Isn't it? Can I sit here?'

She nodded; he smiled, slung his rucksack down on top of Martha's and the mail pile, and offered her a cigarette. Martha shook her head.

'So, where are you going now?'

'Oh – up to Bangkok for a few days. Girl I knew quite well was in a scooter accident on Koh Pha Ngan, pretty badly hurt, she was taken up there. Here, Martha, can you smell burning?'

'Only your cigarette.'

'No, it's not that. I'm sure I – Christ! Look, look at that smoke!'

She looked; there was a thick grey cloud pouring out of the engine room. Nobody seemed terribly concerned; the guy who was driving the boat smiled determinedly and there was a complete absence of anyone else who might have been considered crew. The smoke grew thicker.

'Shit!' he said. 'I don't like this. Jesus, I'm right too, bloody flames now!'

Martha was suddenly very, very frightened. These boats, old and battered, usually had one lifebelt, at the most.

She looked towards land, at the comforting white curve of the beach, and the stern towering figure of Big Buddha, and felt better. They were surely near enough to swim to shore if necessary. She said so.

'No way, Martha – that's at least a mile and this is shark territory. Shit, shit, shit!'

Everyone was beginning to panic now, pointing at the flames, shouting at the captain, who was continuing to steer his boat doggedly towards the land, grinning determinedly.

'What do we do?' asked someone.

'Jump!' said someone else.

'No, it's much too far,' said another.

'Sharks!' said someone else, voice trembling.

The fire was quite obviously out of control now.

One girl started to scream, and then another. An old Thai woman started muttering what was obviously a prayer.

And then . . .

'Dunkirk,' said Martha pointing. 'Look!'

A small armada of longtail boats, their deafening diesel

534

engines at full throttle, was setting out from the shore. One pilot per boat with two small boys perched at the stern of each.

They must have noticed the fire, Martha thought, almost as soon as it began, and simply set off. No official rescue could have been better.

One after another the longtails pulled up alongside the burning boat and people scrambled over the side and down into them. The flames were increasing all the time and there was still a slight swell; some people were clearly terrified, screaming and crying, but the boatmen remained not only calm but cheerful, urging and coaxing them along.

The backpackers left the boat last; being inherently courteous (and English, she said) Martha, hiding her terror, was in the very last one; her last desperate thought as she slithered down the ladder, that she should somehow rescue her rucksack. Only it was at the other end of the boat, near the flames.

As the longtails made in convoy for Bophut, the captain and a boy were struggling to rescue some of the luggage, while the flames began to consume the boat in earnest. Martha gazed at them trustingly; they would surely get her rucksack, they surely, surely would. And then, knowing that even just five minutes later they would have been in very, very real danger, found herself crying.

They stood on the shore watching as the ship went up like a fireball. Martha felt sick; she had stopped crying but she was shivering violently, even in the hot sun.

'Hey,' he said, coming over to her, putting his arm round her shoulders, 'you're cold. Here, have my sweater.'

He put it round her.

'I think I'm a bit shocked,' she said. 'I mean, if it had happened even half an hour earlier we'd be dead. We couldn't have swum it, and there were definitely sharks out there.'

'I know. But it didn't happen half an hour earlier, and we're not dead. Think of it as an adventure. At last, something worth writing home about. On second thoughts, perhaps not. Hey now, here's baggage reclaim. And Martha – who are the lucky ones? I see both our rucksacks, nobody else's. And you know why? They came in on the mailcoach. Look!'

It was true; four mail sacks and two rucksacks had been

brought safely in to land. The rest of the luggage was clearly at the bottom of the sea.

Everyone was dreadfully shaken. The tourists left in taxis, the backpackers all went into the cafe by the jetty that doubled as a ticket office, bought Coke, swapped cigarettes, fretted over their rucksacks. For many of them it was extremely serious; your rucksack was your life, your home, you never left it without padlocking every pocket separately. Most of them did have their day packs, the small bum bags containing such vital things as tickets, passports and money, but a few had lost everything. Several girls were hysterical.

Martha looked at them and felt upset herself: 'What can we do to help?' and, 'Nothing,' he said, 'really nothing. How could we? They'll be all right. They'll go into town, go to the *poste restante* and cable home, and there are phones there too, and then they'll try the tourist police, who'll probably find them huts to stay in free of charge for a day or two until things begin to get sorted out, and they'll all sit on Big Buddha beach, smoking grass and telling everyone who comes along how exciting it was and what heroes they are.'

'You're so cynical,' she said laughing.

'I know.'

'I feel so guilty. It seems so unfair.'

'Not unfair. But we were lucky. Right. What shall we do?'

'I don't know,' she said, and suddenly started to feel rather bad again, shivery and miserable. 'It's all a bit . . . horrid. Isn't it?'

'Mmm. You look a bit green, actually.'

'I feel green,' she said. 'Oh, God – excuse me!'

And she bolted into the toilet and was very sick.

'Poor old you,' he said when she emerged. 'Here, I've got some water for you. Have a sip, that's right. Look – tell you what. I just happen to have rather a lot of money on me – my dad cabled me some extra. Why don't we treat ourselves to a night in a hotel? To be honest, I don't feel exactly great myself.'

And indeed he didn't look it; he was suddenly pale under his tan and sweating.

'Sounds lovely. But I don't have any money. You'll have to go on your own.'

'I don't want to go on my own. I want you to come with me. I might have nightmares. Don't look at me like that – two rooms, no hidden agenda, honest. There's a really cool luxury beach resort near Chaweng, Coral Winds. And let's get a cab, none of your bus rubbish.'

Martha still felt terrible; she knew he was rich – it was patent from various things he had said – and their shared adventure had indeed made her feel as if he was an old and extremely close friend, or even a relative. She suddenly had a sense of total unreality.

'It sounds wonderful,' she said. 'Thank you.'

There is something about being in a very expensive hotel that is the opposite of character forming. There is a strong sense, born at the reception desk, that the servility and cosseting on offer are an absolute right, to be maintained at all times, and from which the most momentary lapse is an outrage.

Martha, who had been brought up to regard frugality as the ultimate virtue and arrogance as the ultimate vice, found herself settled by the flower- and fern-fringed pool at the Coral Winds Hotel, a mere sixty minutes or so after unpacking her rucksack (while picking her way through the bowl filled with peaches and grapes supplied to her room by the management and sending down her crumpled and grubby shorts and T-shirts to the hotel express laundry), waving at the pool boy and asking, just very slightly irritably, if her second cocktail was on its way.

Having received a profuse apology, along with the cocktail, she sipped it briefly and then stood up, walked to the edge of the pool and dived neatly in, swam a length or two and then walked languidly back to her place and lay down again, aware that she was being watched appreciatively by most of the men sitting around the pool. The fact that they were mostly middle-aged and for the most part accompanied by young Thai girls – or boys – increased her pleasure; it felt rather good to be the only Western girl there and to have a novelty value.

'Hi,' he said, appearing from inside the hotel. 'You OK now?'

'Absolutely OK,' she said, 'thank you.'

'Excellent. Me too. What's that you're drinking?'

'A Bellini.' She spoke as if she drank them quite often; she had only ordered it because it was at the top of the menu. It was extremely nice.

'Ah, one of my favourites. I'll join you. I thought we'd have lunch here. They do a very good club sandwich, I'm told. Would that suit you?'

'Perfectly,' she said, 'but – ' conscience cutting briefly in – 'couldn't we just go to the beach or something?'

'No, I really don't want to move. It's awfully hot. We can eat there tonight.'

'Fine,' said Martha, 'my treat.'

'Oh – OK.'

Lunch was brought and they ate it in a companionable silence, watching one of the men taking endless photographs of his Thai boyfriend.

That evening they wandered along the beach in the soft darkness; every hundred yards or so was a restaurant, candlelit tables set on the sand, a stall of fresh fish laid out on ice and a barbecue alight to cook it. They sat down, ordered barracuda, and while they waited for it, drank iced beer and watched the water lapping on the shore.

'This is the life,' she said. 'What a lovely day it's turned out to be. I feel quite, quite different.'

'You seem quite different,' he said, 'different from how I remember you.'

'Oh really? Well, I'm just the same.' Really she wasn't; she had become, just for the duration of the fairy tale, careless and confident, another sort of girl altogether, no longer Cinderella but the princess, and – until the clock struck and they left in the morning – so she would remain.

After dinner they walked slowly back to the hotel; there was a jazz singer in the bar, and they sat and listened to her, while drinking more cocktails. 'Honestly,' said Martha, 'I've drunk more today than I have in the last three months.'

'It suits you,' he said. 'Have another, have a Bellini, that's what you've become, a Bellini girl. I've enjoyed the transformation.'

'Thank you.'

'No, no, it's been huge fun altogether. Thank you! It's been a very nice interlude. And tomorrow I fly up to Bangkok – so come on, one more drink and then I think we should go to bed.'

That was what had done it, that one more drink. One more Bellini. She had become tipsy, silly, more and more confident.

So that, when they were walking to their rooms, and he leant forward and kissed her very gently, saying, 'It's been really fun,' she responded rather more enthusiastically than she had intended. She sensed his slight shock, then his pleasure; and then he took her hand and led her along the wooden, palm-fringed walkways towards their bungalows and said: 'Tell you what, shall we have yet another last drink? I've got half a bottle of champagne in my mini bar and I'm sure you have too, so why don't we enjoy them together?'

Which they did; and then, somehow, it seemed really rather a good idea to sit down on the bed and let him kiss her again; and after that, it was just the shortest step to continue being one of those carelessly confident girls who took sex, along with all the other pleasures, not especially seriously.

'You're absolutely gorgeous,' he said, 'really absolutely. I had no idea, I had no idea at all . . .' And it was so wonderful to be told that, and by someone so beautiful himself. She really wasn't about to become boring, buttoned-up Martha again, until she absolutely had to.

Her last thought, as she lay down and watched him pulling off his clothes, was one of gratitude to a boy who had relieved her of her virginity in the north, in the elephant village near Chiang Mai. That might not have been a beautiful experience, but it meant she could really enjoy this one. Well, concentrate on enjoying it, anyway. As she did. Very much. And even more the following morning, just before dawn, and before he left for the airport in one of the hotel limos, and she became Cinderella again. It had been fun while it lasted: and so very unlike her. But now it was over. Completely and absolutely over. She had no illusions whatsoever about that.

Chapter 36

They had had another row.

Gideon had had a call from a chain of food stores he owned in the southern States; there was a crisis over redundancies, the unions were getting heavy and he said he really needed to go to Seattle the next day, and sort it out.

'Is that OK?' he had said, putting down the phone. 'I'm sorry, my darling. You can come too, obviously, and then we'll go down to San Francisco for a couple of days if you like. I'm sure I can fit it in.'

She hesitated, then said: 'I can't. I really feel I must be around London for the next few days. Kate's rather depending on me at the moment. She keeps calling. And I'm the link with Martha; I feel I can't let her down. Especially if the story comes out.'

'I'm really worried about her,' Helen had said when she'd called on the Friday evening. 'She's very withdrawn, just stays in her room, won't even talk to Nat. I think, really, she ought to meet this – this woman, but she says she doesn't want to, ever, that she hates her. She's not going to get over it that way, is she?'

'No,' said Jocasta. 'Oh, dear. I'll give her a call, Helen; see if I can persuade her. Even if she never sees her again, she's got to confront her. However painful for everyone.'

But Kate wouldn't. 'She's a stupid cow. Sorry, Jocasta, but I don't see the point.'

'OK. But if you change your mind, let me know. I'll come with you. If that would help.'

'It wouldn't help, because I'm not going,' said Kate. 'But I might just call for a chat. I'm so glad you're around, Jocasta. It's difficult to talk to Mum about it.'

So – how could she go running off to Seattle?

'Quite easily I should say,' said Gideon now. 'I think you're getting this thing a bit out of proportion, Jocasta. She's not your child, she's not your responsibility – '

'But I feel she is. I'm so involved with her, Gideon, you don't understand.'

'No,' he said, 'it seems I don't. We've only been married a few weeks and I'm beginning to feel marginalised. Already.'

'Well, you're a fine one to talk,' she said. 'Since we got married we've hardly been together. You're always away, I'm always alone.'

'Don't be absurd. There is absolutely no reason for you not to come with me, whenever you want. Clearly you don't. Or not enough.'

'That's crap!'

'It's not crap. It's true. My life is hugely complex, you know that, you knew it when we got married, I have commitments all over the world.'

'Yes, and they're the ones that count, aren't they? Yours. Mine are of no importance whatsoever, it seems – '

'You're being childish,' he said. It was already one of his favourite taunts.

Jocasta went out of the room and slammed the door.

Later they made up, magnificently, in bed.

But it still meant being alone. For at least a week.

She decided to call up some of her old friends, see if she could spend some time with them. They were all delighted to hear from her, and she fixed up a Saturday lunch in Clapham, and a couple of her girlfriends asked her to go clubbing that evening. But – somehow that didn't feel right any more, married to Gideon. How could you get drunk and dance the night away in some club, being eyed up by blokes – even if you had not the slightest intention of having anything to do with any of them – if you were a married woman and your husband was thousands of miles away, alone in some hotel room? You couldn't. Better to be alone. Anyway, there was this other wretched business. Maybe she could talk to Clio about that.

But Clio was unavailable; she and Fergus were going to Paris for the weekend.

'Isn't that romantic? He booked it for me as a surprise. Of course I could cancel it but – '

'Clio!' said Jocasta, 'Of course you can't cancel it. Don't be ridiculous. Enjoy.'

She drove herself back to Kensington Palace Gardens, after her lunch on Saturday, feeling depressed. Even lunch had been not entirely satisfactory; already a gap was opening between herself and her friends. She was not of their world any more, no longer a career girl about town with a fun boyfriend, but a rich woman with a middle-aged husband.

Jocasta knew whose company she would have preferred herself.

She was just parking, when her mobile rang.

'Jocasta, hi, it's Nick. Are you busy?'

'I'm going to go and ask her. Will you come with me?'

Nat looked at her; her face was very set.

'Yeah, if you want. Course I will. Give her a ring. See if she's in. You got her number, haven't you?'

'Yes.' She put out her hand, grabbed his. 'Right. Here goes.'

Martha had been about to leave for Suffolk when her mobile rang. She knew she had to do it: tell her parents. She couldn't risk it any longer. Just because the story hadn't been in the paper today, or yesterday, it didn't mean it wouldn't be tomorrow. Nick was being wonderful, but there were other papers, and Janet wasn't going to wait forever.

She felt very bad. Ed had not come back. He had called, saying he needed time to think, that he did love her, but he really needed to know more. 'It's not fair, otherwise. You're asking me to take too much on trust. This is pretty basic stuff, Martha.'

'But Ed – '

'No, it isn't but. I've backed you every inch of the way; I think I've a right to know who this bloke was. I'm the person who loves you, but I can't hack it. Give me a bell if anything changes. I'm not going anywhere. But I do need a bit of help over this one.'

So she had phoned her parents, said she was coming up, that she needed to talk to them.

'Well, that'll be lovely, dear,' Grace had said. 'We weren't expecting you this weekend. When will you be here?'

'Oh – quite late, around nine or ten.'

'Lovely.'

No, it won't be lovely, Martha thought, it will be dreadful. But there seemed absolutely no alternative. It had to be done. Too many people knew already, quite apart from the press. There was no knowing what Kate might do, for instance.

And then she rang.

'This is Kate Tarrant. I'd like to come and see you. In about an hour. I presume you'll be there?'

'Yes,' said Martha rather weakly, 'yes, I'll be here.' And rang her parents and told them she'd be much later, to go to bed and she'd see them in the morning. It would be far better anyway: better than telling them late at night.

'I've just had another call from Frean,' Nick said. 'She says she's going to give the story to the *Sun*, if I haven't run it by Monday. Honestly, Jocasta, this is a nightmare.'

'Did you speak to her?'

'No, my phone was on message.'

'God, what a filthy mess. But I'm sure there must be something clever we could do. If we thought hard enough. Look – what are you doing now?'

'Nothing. Fretting.'

'Well, why don't you come round and we'll have a brainstorming session. I'll order a takeaway – '

'What, give staff a night off? Very democratic of you. Where's Gideon?'

'He's away,' she said.

'Then I don't think I should come round.'

She knew he was right; and the thud of disappointment she felt proved it. It was completely impossible to have had the kind of relationship she had had with Nick – absolutely close, very sexy, and for the most part extremely happy – and suddenly just be friends. And the fact that he was being so good about Martha was testimony to his extraordinary niceness.

But – she didn't actually love him any more. Did she? No, of course she didn't. She maybe never had. She'd loved his company and their life together; but was that love? What she felt for Gideon was overwhelming and extraordinarily intense. Yes, he was spoilt, he could be difficult, he could be filthy-tempered, and he liked his own way, but he was, above all things, generous-hearted, thoughtful, and immensely, tenderly loving. And he loved her as she loved him: absolutely, with no reservations of any kind.

He was worth being lonely for. And she mustn't let it happen again; he was right. It really was up to her. Once this wretched business with Martha and Kate was settled, she'd never let him go away without her again.

'Hi,' said Kate. She was dressed in jeans and a T-shirt that showed a great deal of her flat stomach. Her hair was tied back, and she wore no make-up. She was a lot taller than Martha. Martha tried to feel something, but couldn't: except discomfort.

'This is Nat Tucker,' said Kate. 'He's a friend of mine.'

'Hello, Nat,' said Martha. 'Do come in, both of you. What can I offer you, a drink or something?'

'Nothing, thanks,' said Kate. She walked in, looked round. Nat followed her.

There was a long, frozen silence; Nat broke it.

'Very nice,' he said. 'Very nice indeed. Good view.'

'Thank you,' said Martha. 'Would you – would you like to sit down?'

Nat dropped onto one of the low black leather sofas; Kate stayed on her feet, turned to face Martha.

'I want to know who my father is,' she said. 'That's all. Nothing else.'

Martha had not really been expecting this; not at this stage.

'I'm – sorry?' she said.

'I said I want to know who my father is. Unlike you, he might actually want to meet me.'

'I'm afraid I can't tell you that.'

'No? Why not? Don't you know?' The dark eyes were very hard. 'Was it, like, a one-night stand?'

She's bound to be angry, Martha thought, bound to be hostile.

'I – just can't tell you,' she said.

'Yeah? Are you still in touch with him, then?'

'No. I'm not. But he has no idea. And I don't think it's right to – to tell him now. After all these years.'

'Oh, you don't think it's right? I see. You think it was right to leave me though, do you? Just left, along with a bit of cleaning fluid.'

'Kate – '

'And you thought it was right not to come and see me, when it was in the paper and everything, and you could have done it so easily. That was fine, was it? Funny idea of right and wrong you've got! You left me there, a newborn baby, all alone, I could have died – '

'I waited,' said Martha, 'I waited until I knew you'd been found, that you were all right – '

'Oh, you did? Well, that was really good of you. I s'pose you thought that was that, did you?'

'I – '

'You never thought how I might feel, later on. Knowing my mother, my own mother, just wasn't interested in me. What do you think that's like? To be so not wanted. So not important. Don't you think that must be totally horrible? Anyway, luckily for me, I've had a real mother, a proper mother. *She* cared about me. She still does. I reckon I'd have been better off with her, anyway. I don't know what kind of mother you think you'd have been, but I can tell you, you'd have been shit!'

'Kate,' said Nat mildly, from the depths of the sofa.

'She'd have been shit,' said Kate looking at him briefly, then turning back to Martha. 'So I should be thanking you, really. For getting out of my life. Anyway, I don't want to carry on with this, it's totally pointless. But I do want to know who my father was. So if you'll just give me his name, I'll leave you in peace. Which is what you've wanted all along, obviously. Sorry to have had to disturb it.'

'Kate, I'm really sorry, but I'm not going to do that. I can't.'

She looked at her steadily, trying to equate this girl, this beautiful grown-up creature, with the tiny baby she had left behind, trying to make sense of it all, to believe that she had carried her around in her body all those endless months, actually given birth to her, pushed her out of her body. She couldn't.

'I'm sorry,' said Kate, 'but you've got to. Don't you think you owe me anything?'

'Of course I do. But – not that.'

'You cow.' Kate walked over to her; for a moment, Martha thought she was going to hit her. 'You stupid cow.'

Nat stood up.

'Kate, there's no need for this. It isn't helping. If she won't tell you, she won't tell you. She's got her reasons, I'm sure.'

'Yeah, like she had them for abandoning me. Well, it won't do. I want to meet my father. He might be a bit more satisfactory. Stupid cow,' she added.

'Kate!' said Nat again. 'I'm sorry,' he said, addressing Martha, 'she's not usually so rude.'

For some reason this amused Martha: so much so that she smiled, almost giggled. She supposed it was a relief from the tension.

Kate walked over to her and slapped her hard across the face.

'Don't you laugh at him,' she said, 'he's worth a million of you.'

'Kate, I wasn't laughing at him,' said Martha, shocked. She put her hand up and touched her face. 'I was laughing at – well – it doesn't matter.'

'Like I don't,' said Kate. 'Like I don't to you. Not at all. Like I never have. Just something to get rid of, I was, wasn't I? Why didn't you have an abortion? Tell me that. Why didn't you just flush me down the toilet, that would've been much better, wouldn't it?'

And she started to cry, great noisy sobs, that got louder and louder, rose to a scream; Nat tried to calm her, but it was hopeless. She went on and on, beating her clenched fists helplessly against her sides; and then collapsed onto the sofa, her head buried in her arms, her hair showering over them.

Martha looked at her, and suddenly felt something: felt something for Kate for the very first time. Felt a stir, a stab of sorrow, to see her like this, in such grief, in such pain. It touched her, that pain, and it was like none that she had ever felt before, it was deeper, sharper, more dreadful. She wondered if it was some sort of maternal feeling for Kate, belatedly felt; it was certainly feeling for her, of a kind, and in some strange way, a relief.

She sat down beside her, put an arm rather tentatively round her shoulders; Kate shook it off viciously.

'Don't! Get off me.'

But that feeling, that stab of feeling, had given Martha courage. 'Could you just listen to me, just for a little while?' she said.

'What, and you try to explain? No thanks.'

But she had at least looked at her, while sniffing and wiping her eyes on the back of her hand; it was a contact of sorts. Martha went to fetch her some tissues; she took them without a word.

'I think we'd best go,' Kate said to Nat, 'there's no point staying here.'

'Don't you think it might be an idea, Kate, to listen to what she's got to say?'

'No,' said Kate briefly, 'I don't. Only thing I want to hear from her is my dad's name. Come on, Nat, let's go.'

She walked over to the door; she had trouble with the lock. Martha followed her, undid it for her.

'I'm – so sorry,' she said, meeting her eyes. 'I know it doesn't mean anything to you, but I am, truly sorry. I wish you'd let me talk to you.'

'You could have done that months ago,' said Kate. 'It's too late now.'

And she and Nat were gone.

Janet Frean was getting very impatient. The story was going to lose impetus if it wasn't run soon. The child would be less famous; Martha's temporarily high profile would drop. It was ridiculous. Why weren't they doing it? It was a brilliant story; Nick was a brilliant journalist. The timing – her timing – had been perfect. She had tossed a gift into their laps. She was going to be very angry if it didn't appear. Had Nick gone soft suddenly? Surely not.

She looked at her watch; she had to leave in an hour. She was speaking at a dinner in Bournemouth, a medical conference, and she couldn't be late. She called Nick: no reply. She left a message and went to change. Half an hour later he still hadn't contacted her. She really needed to speak to him, find out what he thought he was doing.

While she was packing her overnight bag, she decided to e-mail him. She could tantalise him with a few more details, make it spicier still – she hadn't said, for instance, that Martha knew who the father was and she could imply she had told her. That would be intriguing. That would at least make him get in touch. There'd be something very wrong if it didn't.

She went into her study, switched on her laptop. There were several e-mails for her, one from Kirkland, telling her to be sure to spell out their policy on health that evening, that their line on it was their trump card at the moment. As if she needed to be told. It was a medical conference, for Christ's sake. God Almighty, what did he think she was?

She scrolled through her address book, found Nick's name and started to write.

'She's sent me an e-mail,' said Nick to Jocasta. 'She really is not going to wait much longer. Hold on, I'll read it to you – she says she doesn't want the story wasted, now – oh yes, "Please don't leave it too long. I don't want to have to give it to someone else. Incidentally, I have a bit more to tell you – details of the family tree – let me know if you want it." '

'What do you think that means? Who the father is? Shit, I'd so love to know.'

'God knows. And then she says not to delay too long, and then, that if I haven't done it by Monday, she's going to the *Sun*.'

'Bloody hell! Bloody, bloody hell, Nick. What are you going to say?'

'God knows. *I* certainly don't . . .'

'Mum! I feel sick.'

Janet looked doubtfully at Arthur. He was her second youngest, and his digestion was delicate. He did look very green. She glanced at the clock: she really should have gone.

'Where's Dad?'

'In his study. On the phone. He told me to find you.'

'Well, let's get you downstairs, maybe some TV would help – oh, Arthur!'

Everything Arthur did, he did thoroughly. Including vomiting. Janet's trouser suit was clearly no longer fit for public viewing. By the time she had got Bob off the phone, Arthur cleaned up, and changed her suit, she was extremely late.

She was driving herself; she grabbed her briefcase and her overnight bag, ran to the car and started it. And realised she had forgotten her handheld. A nifty little device, which could send and receive e-mails: and act as a mobile. Pretty crucial this evening.

She ran back into the house; Bob was in the hall.

'Thought you'd gone.'

'I had, but I'd forgotten my BlackBerry.'

'What on earth do you want that for?'

'It's got some notes for my speech on it.'

He knew that was a lie; he'd already seen the whole speech, neatly printed, lying on her desk. He went back into the house and to Arthur, who was now very cheerfully watching some old *Starsky and Hutch* videos and demanding ice cream.

Martha hadn't realised how tired she was until she was on the A12. Driving out through the endless suburbs of East London at least offered some variety, required the occasional gear change. Confronted by the endless sheet of road ahead of her, she felt her brain begin to glaze over.

Maybe she should stop, stay at a motel, and drive on in the morning. She could call her parents and tell them what she was doing, so they wouldn't worry. She dialled their number. God, what had everyone done before there were car phones? The answerphone cut in. She knew what that meant, that they were watching television. *Casualty*, probably. They never heard the phone from the sitting room. Damn. And they very seldom checked the answer machine until the morning. Well, she could keep trying, but she left a message anyway, saying she might find a B&B and come on in the morning.

She felt her eyes getting sore: another symptom of tiredness. She rubbed them, started playing the number games she always used at these times to keep her awake. Counting backwards in threes, counting upwards in sevens, doubling numbers – it helped for a bit. Maybe she could get there.

She felt terrible. Really terrible. The encounter with Kate had shaken her horribly. For some reason, she hadn't expected quite so much hostility. Naive really. She probed her feelings for Kate, as if they were an aching tooth. The main thing seemed to be a total lack of them. That was in itself disturbing. Surely she should have felt something, some sort of recognition of their relationship. She was her mother, for God's sake. Not love, of course, that was the stuff of fairy tales, but concern, sympathy, sadness that she had missed so much of her. It wasn't there. Only one thing was there and that was guilt. In spades.

She hadn't even liked her; she had seemed a hard little thing. And distinctly lacking in charm. But then – as situations went, it had hardly been one to bring the best out in her. The boy had been rather sweet, she'd thought; she'd liked him much more.

She was obviously completely lacking in any kind of maternal instinct. Probably if she'd had any, she couldn't have abandoned Kate in the first place. Clearly, she was exactly as Kate saw her, tough, uncaring, totally self-centred. It wasn't a very happy thought. She supposed the guilt was something in her favour: she'd never felt it over Kate before. Mostly because she hadn't allowed herself to. Guilt would have meant an acknowledgement of what she'd done: there could be no question of it.

She tried the vicarage again: still no reply. Well, maybe she could make it. She'd have a coffee at a Little Chef and carry on. It would be much nicer to get there, get to her own bed.

Nick had finally replied to Janet's e-mail.

'Janet: Doing my best, lot of ends to tie up. Please bear with me. Re family tree, what do you mean exactly? Nick.'

Janet was not impressed.

Martha was back on the road; she felt quite wide-awake now. She began to try to frame her conversation with her parents, wondering how to lead into it. How could you possibly break such news gently? Maybe she should show them the cuttings about Kate, the story that Carla Giannini had written? And then say – well – what? 'I'm actually her mother. It was me that abandoned her in the cleaning cupboard.' That would really be easy for them, wouldn't it?

Well, what about the early cuttings? Would that be better? 'This is what I actually did when I got back from travelling. I was too afraid to tell you.' How would that make them feel?

Or, 'You've got another granddaughter. She's called Kate and she's sixteen.'

'Fuck,' said Martha aloud.

And this was only the beginning. There was Paul Quenell to inform, and Jack Kirkland. Her friends. What friends? They seemed very few in number suddenly. But they all had to be told and within the next few days, possibly the next few hours, if Janet went to another paper.

From janet @hotwest.com to nick@*Sketch*westminster.com
'There can't be that many loose ends. And what do you think family tree means? Use your common sense. Might speak to Chris myself; he could push it forward. Terrible waste, Nick, if he won't run it. He would have done last Friday I'm sure, with our subject hot off the TV. Maybe you could let me have a draft? Janet.'

Shit. Now what did he do? Suppose she did talk to Pollock? Nick began to panic. Better call him himself, warn him. But then he'd want to know what it was about. Shit.

From nick@*Sketch*westminster.com to janet@hotwest.com
'Janet: What??!! You know we never show drafts. Talk to Chris if you want to, but he's entertaining heavily this weekend, never welcomes interruptions.'

This was true; he was. He always was, he took his Saturday nights very seriously. He and the current Mrs Pollock, a television executive, gave famously large and starry dinner parties, followed by even larger brunches the following day. Only the kind of headline that took over the whole of the front page was allowed to interrupt them; and however much they all cared about Baby

Bianca, she didn't justify seventy-two point. So – quite a clever move there.

'I'm really doing my best. Obviously family tree interesting. Speak maybe tomorrow. Nick.'

Please God that would keep her quiet.

But:
From janet@hotwest.com to nick@*Sketch*westminster.com
   'OK. Let's speak. I'll call tomorrow lunchtime, check on progress. Maybe you could confirm this is OK.'

This was getting very, very difficult. Maybe he was going to have to run the story after all. To save Martha and Kate from something much worse.

Martha knew it was crazy, but she rang Ed. She felt so lonely, so besieged by fate; losing him now when she had found him again, albeit so briefly, was almost unbearable. She was beginning to wonder why she was being protective of – of him. She certainly didn't owe him anything. But – she did. It was ripples in the pond – the wider they went, the worse it got, the more people were hurt. 'Hi, Ed, it's me. Just wondered how you were. Give me a call if you can, I'm in the car.'

   It was horribly reminiscent of his endless, caring calls to her; he must have known, like her, that there was little chance of a response: or the response he wanted, anyway. It was a measure of how low she was feeling that she was prepared to put herself at such risk. Martha Hartley didn't do risk.

   She was getting sleepy again: very sleepy. She was going to have to stop. Only there were fewer motels out here, and it was too late to go off the road, find a B&B. She put a Stones CD on and turned the volume right up. That often helped.

   Then the phone went. Ed's name came up on the screen. Her heart lurched.

   'Hi, Ed.'
   'Hi. Where are you?'
   'About an hour from Binsmow.'

'Yeah?' The voice was polite, no more. 'Going to see your parents?'

'Yes. And to – well, to tell them.'

'Yeah?'

This was awful. She had only heard his voice this hard once before and that had been the night of their terrible row, when he had gone for her, told her how cold and controlling she was. She threw caution not just to the winds, but into outer space.

'I'm scared, Ed. So scared.'

'Of what?'

'Of hurting them. That's the main thing, you know. That's how it all began.'

'Yeah. Well, I'm sure you'll manage.'

'Ed –'

'Yes, Martha?'

'I'm missing you.'

This was unbelievable: that she was talking to him like this, throwing herself on him.

'Well, I miss you too. But like I said, there are limits. I can't cope with all this shit, you know? About the father.'

'I know, but –'

'Are you going to tell me or not?'

'No, Ed, I'm not. Not yet anyway. I wish you could under-stand –'

'Sorry, but I can't, not at the moment. You never change, do you, really? You just call me in when you need me, focused entirely on yourself, you're still doing it.'

'I'm not!'

'Martha, you are. You should listen to yourself. On and on, round and round like a bloody cracked record. Saying how you don't want to hurt your parents, that was how it all began. Assuming I've got time for you, that I'll just drop everything, to listen to you. Well, I can't. I'm busy right now; I'm in the editing suite. Just give it a rest. OK? I'll call you in a day or two.'

She managed to say goodbye, and then started to cry, the tears blurring her eyes. She had to stop. Together with her tiredness, it was a fatal combination. She pulled across to the inside lane, meaning to pull over onto the hard shoulder. She missed the fact that a slip road was coming onto the A12 from her left; a large lorry, being driven only a little too fast, was coming down it, its driver momentarily distracted, himself, by a call from his girlfriend. He pulled out to try to avoid her, hit her anyway, and skidded right across the width of the road, taking the Mercedes with him.

Chapter 37

'Martha's very late,' said Grace, switching off Michael Parkinson and moving into her bedtime ritual of cushion plumping, cat ejecting and newspaper collection. 'I hope she's all right.'

'I'm sure she is,' said Peter. 'I'll just go and switch off my computer, read through that sermon again, and see if she's called.'

He came back, smiling. 'She's probably going to stop on the way. She was very tired, she said, so she might book into a motel and be here for breakfast.'

'Well, I'm glad she's so sensible. And we're too tired ourselves to talk to her now. You go up, dear, and I'll make the tea.'

Because the accident had taken place on a curve in the road, it was hard to see it coming. Two more cars had piled into the wreckage before a man, driving slowly and carefully enough to spot it in time, stopped to turn on his hazard lights and phone the police. Then he pulled his fire extinguisher out of his own car and ran across to the mass blocking the road. He felt more than a little frightened.

The cars at the rear were not too seriously affected; their bonnets were crushed, and in one case, the front wheels were totally buckled, and the horn of the other appeared to be jammed on, but the drivers of both were conscious and had had the presence of mind to switch off their engines. The driver of the less damaged car was bleeding from a gash in his head, but otherwise appeared completely unhurt. He climbed rather unsteadily out of his car and he said he had no passengers.

'Just getting home. Only five miles to go. Shocking mess. You got a phone, mate?'

555

'I've called the police if that's what you mean. Or do you want to phone home?'

'Yeah, please. God, that lorry's in a bad way.'

'It does seem to be. What about this car, next to you?'

There was the sound of a child crying; they ran over to it, peered in. A baby of about one was yelling lustily in its car seat; a young couple, presumably its parents, were rather dazedly trying to turn round and pacify it. Neither of them appeared hurt either, although the girl was crying.

'Just shock,' said the father. He appeared quite shocked himself; he kept rubbing his eyes and blowing on his hands, but making no attempt to get out.

The two men got the little family out, and helped them to the side of the road. By now a couple of other cars had arrived and were parked just short of the crash, all with their hazard lights flashing.

'Best – best have a look in the lorry,' said the man with the cut head. He mopped it with his handkerchief; it had almost stopped bleeding. 'Christ, I've been lucky. Thanks for that.' He held out his hand. 'Derek Jones.'

'Peter Morrison. Didn't do anything.' He walked rather nervously round the great hulk of the lorry; the cab was half on its side, the engine still running. Peter Morrison handed his fire extinguisher to Derek Jones and said: 'Cover me, there's a good chap. First sign of trouble use this. I'll just get the engine switched off.'

It meant climbing up the steps, hauling open the door, leaning in and switching off the ignition.

He was, as he said on his return to his new friend, shitting himself pretty bloody hard. But it had been done.

'Anyone in there?'

'Yeah, driver. On his own. Unconscious. Breathing, though. Don't want to move him. Might do more harm than good.'

'Right. Well, we'd better look at the other car, I suppose. Blimey. It's a fucking Mercedes. Bet he was drunk.'

They looked almost dispassionately at the car. It seemed impossible that anyone could be in it and live. It was jammed beneath one of the lorry's wheels, its roof entirely crushed, its windscreen smashed in.

'Poor bleeder,' said Derek Jones. 'Must have copped it.'

'Yeah. What do we do?'

'Don't know, mate.'

And then through the darkness, just before the blessed wailing of the police sirens, came the unmistakable sound of a mobile phone ringing from inside the car.

'Fuck,' said Ed. She must have reached the vicarage, switched off her phone. Well, there was no way he could call her there, at this time of night. He'd do it first thing in the morning. That was one of the great things about Martha, you couldn't ring her too early; she was always awake by six, even on Sundays. Well, sometimes on Sunday it was half-past.

He switched his phone off; he felt bad. He'd been much too hard on her. He hadn't meant to give her such an earful. She hadn't deserved it. She was very upset and he should have been more . . . supportive. Trouble was, he was really rather tired of being supportive, and she absolutely didn't seem to realise that, or be in the least grateful for what he did.

Still – these were rather exceptional circumstances. She'd had the sort of forty-eight hours that would have destroyed most people entirely. And in some ways he supposed he should admire her for not telling him who the father was. She obviously wanted to protect him. She must have been very fond of him, to be so bothered, though. That was what had been bugging him. Which was pretty childish really, since it had been sixteen years ago.

Funny sort of bloke, if that had been the case, though, that she hadn't been able to tell him at the time. Well, it was a funny thing, travelling: it did weird things, all those relationships, starting and ending without a backward or a forward glance. She probably didn't know where to contact him; it must have been dead difficult in those days, before there were mobiles. Oh, well. He'd call her in the morning, say he was sorry, try and make it up to her. He went back to his editing.

The police were fucking marvellous, Peter and Derek agreed. Calm, organised, setting up a road block in no time, so there was no danger of anyone else piling in – although they reckoned they'd done a pretty good job of that themselves with their hazard lights. Got the ambulance to the front, using the hard shoulder, and started with the poor bugger in the lorry.

He was probably going to be OK, actually, the ambulance men said. He was clearly concussed, but he was breathing, and his pulse was steady; which probably precluded any serious internal injury. Every so often he came to and groaned. They were trying to get him out, but it was difficult; they had to cut out the steering wheel before they could free him. Both his arms were probably broken, they said, and some ribs, but his legs looked OK.

'Bloody lucky,' one of them said. 'Going to have a bit of a headache tomorrow, but it could be much worse.'

Derek asked what the chances were for the other bloke, the one in the Mercedes, and they said God alone knew, they couldn't do anything till the lifting equipment arrived, but it was a miracle it hadn't exploded with the impact.

'Part of this cab's lying on top of him, that's the trouble. He might be all right, might not. Can't say – ah, here they come. We'll find out pretty soon now.'

'You know,' said Clio, 'I can't stop thinking about Martha.'

'Well, that's very fine,' said Fergus, 'and I admire your Christian spirit, but I can't help feeling it's me you should be thinking about. To the exclusion of anything else. I've brought you here to tell you how much I care about you, and what do you do but tell me you're thinking about your best friend. Or whatever she is.'

'Not my best friend,' said Clio, 'I hardly know her. But I keep thinking what an awful situation she's in, and no one there for her, to hold her hand . . .'

'I thought she had a beautiful young man to hold her hand?'

'Well, she does, and my God he is beautiful, but it's not the same, is it? Not quite.'

'Not quite the same as what? A woman? I'm not sure I like that too much, either.'

'Oh, Fergus!' She punched him gently on the arm. 'Look, it's only eleven-thirty in England. She's bound to be awake, she never sleeps, and she'll be worrying and – all alone.'

'And suppose she's not all alone, suppose she has the beautiful young man in bed with her, then what?'

'Well then, she won't pick up the phone. Let's just call her, Fergus, tell her we're thinking about her. Come on.'

'All right. Here's my phone. You can use it, on condition we go straight back to the hotel and get on with what we were doing at lunchtime.'

'It's a deal,' said Clio, leaning over the table to kiss him. She called the landline: Martha's cool tones told her that she was busy right now, but that she would call her back.

'Don't worry, Martha. Hopefully that means there's someone with you. Or you're asleep. This is Clio. Fergus and I were just thinking about you, hoping you're OK. We both send our love. Over and out. Now, Fergus, I'll just try her mobile – oh dear, horrible noise. Listen.'

Fergus listened. 'It's out of range, or out of order, or something. I think we've done all we can. Now – how about the rest of the arrangement?'

'Can't wait. We can ring her again in the morning, can't we?'

'For God's sake stop talking about Martha Hartley,' said Fergus, 'and get your delicious little arse out of here. She's fine. I'm absolutely certain of it.'

'Well, she's alive,' said the paramedic, 'losing quite a lot of blood, and her chest is crushed, but she's breathing. Blood pressure's very low. Can't say more till we get her to hospital. Scuse me, mate.'

Derek looked at Peter. 'Fucking hell. What a waste. A girl. Owning a car like that.'

'Is that the Reverend Peter Hartley? I'm sorry to ring you in the middle of the night, sir. This is the police. I'm afraid there's been an accident . . .'

He put the phone down and looked at his wife. Her eyes were wide with fear. He didn't need to tell her.

'Is she alive?' she said. 'And where is she?'

'She's alive. But in intensive care. In Bury St Edmunds Hospital.'

'Well – let's go,' she said, climbing out of bed, very calm, reaching for the clothes she had laid out for the morning, as she always did. 'Quickly, Peter. She needs us.'

As he pulled on his own clothes (adding his clerical collar; it could be very useful, he had discovered) Peter Hartley started to pray silently. He could pray while he did anything: drove the car, did the supermarket shop, weeded the garden, tidied his study. He didn't stop until they reached the hospital. And then prayed briefly that they were not too late.

Janet Frean couldn't sleep. She never could, after she had made a successful speech. She felt wired up, reliving the evening, the applause, the sense that she had the whole room with her – a lot of people, over three hundred, you couldn't beat a medical conference – and she really had felt she had convinced them of the rightness of the Centre Forward policy. They had clapped for what had seemed a long time, and then come to her table, an endless flow of medics, all telling her they hadn't heard so much sense talked for a long time. A lot of them had promised to vote for Centre Forward, to switch from their present parties.

'At last,' said one rather arrogant surgeon – well, were any surgeons not arrogant? – 'a politician who seems to understand our profession, doesn't seem hell-bent on undermining it. Jolly good. Well done.'

She saved that up to tell Jack next day; it was all grist for her mill.

There had been a disco after that, for the younger contingent, and the older ones were settling down to some hard drinking. A lot of wives had slipped upstairs; Janet decided to follow their example.

In her room, she kicked off her shoes, and looked at her handheld. Now – what from Nick Marshall? There had better be something. Something very tangible. Otherwise she wasn't going to wait even till Monday.

The worst thing, they had been told, were her abdominal injuries: her spleen was ruptured.

'Which has resulted in considerable blood loss,' the hollow-eyed houseman told them. 'We're giving her transfusions, obviously, but we're going to have to remove the spleen. She also has several fractured ribs, and her left arm is broken. But those are not serious.'

'And the spleen is?'

'I'm afraid so. That and the subsequent blood loss. But she has no head injuries, for which we can all be grateful. She was lucky to escape them. She was lucky to escape with her life.'

'Can we – see her?'

He hesitated. 'You can. But it might be distressing for you.'

'Why?' said Grace, her voice tremulous. 'Is she – disfigured?'

'No, no. Well, not permanently. She's cut and bruised about the face and head, obviously. But she's got drips up and God knows what else, and these bleeping machines we use.' He smiled at them rather wearily. 'But you'll have watched *Casualty*, I expect; no surprises for you there.'

'No,' said Grace, 'we were watching it tonight, as a matter of fact, it was about a car crash – ' And then realised not only how absurd she must sound, but that it had been *Casualty* which had prevented them from hearing the phone that evening, and speaking to Martha. The words 'for the last time' tried to surface in her shocked brain; she managed to suppress them.

'And she's absolutely unconscious. Probably will be for many hours.'

'Yes, well, we'd still like to see her, if we may.'

'Fine. Nurse, take Mr and Mrs Hartley up to ITU, would you?'

Helen couldn't sleep either. This was not an unusual state of affairs; indeed, since the first story about Kate had hit the front pages, it had become more or less the norm. It was particularly bad at the moment.

At five she eased herself from beside the snoring Jim, and went downstairs to make a cup of tea. It was already light, and very warm. She opened the kitchen door and stepped out onto the patio, and sat there amidst the birdsong, trying to think what she should do. She felt she had to do something. Make some gesture. Kate's rage and hostility towards Martha Hartley were increasing almost by the hour: and they were bad for her.

She had waited, in a state of great agitation, for Kate and Nat to return from their visit to Martha; Kate was white and tear-stained and went straight up to her room. Nat sat and told them what had happened.

'She was very upset,' he said, 'very upset indeed. Not too nice to the woman.'

'Oh dear,' said Helen. She had the inconsequential thought that Martha would think she'd made a bad job of bringing Kate up, never taught her any manners.

'But I think she understood. Miss Hartley, that is. She was quite patient with her.'

I expect she was, Helen thought, she's never had to deal with her before this.

'She seems a very nice sort of person,' said Nat, accepting the beer Jim had handed him. 'Cheers. Very nicely spoken and that. Course she would be, doing that job. And lovely place she's got,' he added. 'Lot of money, I'd say.'

'Yes, I'm sure she has,' said Jim. 'She hasn't had to spend any of it raising a family, has she?'

He was nearly as angry with Martha as Kate was; Helen felt she was alone in a desire to be at least a little conciliatory.

'That's true,' said Nat, 'and anyway, lawyers, they're all well rich, aren't they? My dad says they're just parasites, what with the – what you call it, the compensation culture and all. He says we'll soon be suing our own parents for not doing well enough for us.'

'I'd say your dad was right there,' said Jim.

'Yeah, well. I don't think Kate'll be suing you,' said Nat. 'I'm always telling her how lucky she is.'

'Oh Nat,' said Helen, 'thank you.'

'But I tell you what,' he said, putting down his beer, pulling out his cigarettes, 'she's getting well upset over all this. I think it's making her ill. She won't eat even. I tried to get her to come for a curry, but she wouldn't.'

'Oh dear . . .' said Helen.

So – how were they to help Kate? she wondered now. She obviously wasn't going to fall into Martha's arms with cries of 'Mother' – and, even in her anxiety, Helen was forced to admit that the hostility was easier to bear than that particular alternative – but it would be much better for Kate if she could accept her, think in more positive terms about her, try to understand why she had done what she had done. Otherwise she was going to be angry and bitter for the rest of her life. Maybe, just maybe – and even the thought was quite difficult to cope with – she should go to see her herself, see if they couldn't find some way together of explaining to Kate, making everything less difficult for her.

The more she thought about it, the better an idea it seemed. It would be horribly difficult and she would need to summon all her courage, but she could. For Kate. She could do anything for Kate. Anything in the world.

She would ring Martha in the morning and try to fix an appointment. She just hoped Martha would agree.

It was eight o'clock. Martha had survived the hours of surgery, but she was very ill. Her blood pressure had dropped alarmingly with the blood loss, and the surgeon had told the Hartleys that at one stage he had been really quite worried. He was still in his thirties, the caricature of a surgeon, confident, arrogantly tactless. But he was kind, as well; he came striding down the corridor from theatre to where they sat in silence, holding hands, Grace frozen with fear, Peter continuing to pray, and said immediately, reluctant to give them one minute more terror than was necessary:

'Well, so far, so good. I tell you, if she wasn't so fit she wouldn't have made it. She's an example to us all. Not an ounce of spare fat on her, heart like an ox. Jolly good.'

Grace thought of all the times she had tried to make Martha eat more and felt ashamed.

'So – is she all right now?'

'Well – can't quite say that for sure. Sorry, but I don't want to mislead you. She really has lost so much blood, and her pulse is very erratic. There's always a fear of secondary infections in these cases. But we're pumping her with blood and antibiotics and all sorts of other stuff, and of course she's had no head injuries. Very lucky escape. It could have been so much worse. Terrible crash, as far as I can make out. Amazing no one was killed.'

'She hadn't been drinking, or anything,' said Grace. She was anxious that he should know. 'She'd been working all day, and she was just driving down to – to see us, have a bit of peace and quiet. Oh, dear – '

She started to cry. The surgeon patted her shoulder.

'No, no, there was no alcohol in her blood. Don't worry about that. But you know, tiredness is as big a cause of road accidents as alcohol. Anyway, she's been lucky – so far. I should go home, get some rest if I were you.'

Grace wondered if he had any children and decided not; if he had, he'd never have suggested anything so absurd. And Peter thought of the hours of prayer he had sent up for Martha, and knew that it had not just been luck that had seen her through.

'We'll stay,' they said, simultaneously.

'Fine. Well, it's up to you. Coffee machine down the corridor. Try not to worry.'

And he was gone, with another dazzling smile.

Peter called his curate at seven, told him he'd have to take the communion service – 'And the rest actually, I'll be here all day.'

The curate said that would be the least he could do and that of course he would include prayers for Martha at every service.

Which was how Ed's mother Mrs Forrest, who had gone to early communion, rather than evensong as she usually did, learnt about the accident. She was very upset.

Grace was dozing, her head against Peter's shoulder, when a nurse came running past her. She stared rather sleepily after her. And then felt a clutch of fear at her heart. She had read a great many of the Sue Barton books when she was a girl; Sue Barton who rose from being a student nurse to Sister with rather dizzy speed. Sue Barton was told on her first day on the wards that a nurse only ran for three reasons: flood, fire and haemorrhage. There was clearly no flood or fire. Therefore . . .

Nick was rather half-heartedly beginning to put together the draft of a piece about Martha and Kate, when Janet called him.

'Hi, Nick, I wondered how you were doing?'

'Fine. Yes. Just working on it now.'

'Well, you would say that, wouldn't you?'

'Janet, it's true. I swear.'

'And – have you talked to Chris?'

'For God's sake, it's eleven on Sunday morning! The Pollock brunch party will be just warming up. It would be more than my job was worth. And you wouldn't want that right now, would you?'

'Oh, I don't know. The *Sun* might be a bit quicker off the mark than you. Anyway – we'll speak later. I'm still in Bournemouth.'

'What are you doing in Bournemouth?'

'I made a speech here last night. At a medical conference. I'm doing a bit of work before I leave for the bedlam I call home.' She was clearly trying to be funny. 'So if you'd like to e-mail me any thoughts you've got . . .'

'Sure.'

She was like a fucking ferret, Nick thought.

Martha was back in surgery; there was some unexplained internal bleeding, they told the Hartleys, and her blood pressure had dropped again. For the time being, they couldn't tell them any more.

Ed was eating his usual Sunday morning breakfast – a doughnut and a coffee in Starbucks – when his mother rang.

'Edward? Are you busy, dear?'

'No. Not at all. You OK, Mum?' She sounded a bit funny. He thought hard: he'd been down two weekends ago; she couldn't be trying to hint that he should be there, surely? It would be totally out of character, anyway.

'I'm fine. I've just been to church.'

'Oh yeah? How was the Rev?'

'He wasn't there, dear. That's why I'm ringing. Andrew took the service.'

'Yeah? Cool.' He took a large bite of doughnut. Hardly worth a phone call – she'd obviously not got enough to do.

'Yes. Poor Mr Hartley was at the hospital.'

'The hospital? What's wrong with him?'

'Nothing, dear. But I thought you'd want to know. It's their daughter, the lawyer. Martha, you know.' The doughnut was turning to something very unpleasant in Ed's mouth; he spat what was left of it out into his napkin, took a swig of coffee.

'What's happened to her?'

'She's been in a terrible accident. A car crash. She's still alive at the moment. But it's very serious, apparently. Anyway, I wanted to tell you, because I knew you'd met her. She drove you up to Town once, didn't she, one Sunday night? Very kind, that was. They're such a lovely family.'

'Yeah, I know that. Can you – can you tell me a bit more, Mum?'

'Well, not a lot, dear. She had a collision with a big lorry. Last night. Her car was under it, apparently. There were several cars involved. She's had surgery and she's in a critical condition, Andrew was saying. Poor girl. After all she's trying to do for Binsmow as well, with her legal sessions – '

'Surgeries,' said Ed automatically.

'What, dear?'

'Surgeries, they're called surgeries. What hospital is she in, Mum, do you know?'

'Bury. She's in intensive care. You sound quite upset, dear. Did you ever see more of her?'

'A bit,' said Ed, and put the phone down.

A bit. Quite a bit. All of her, in fact. All of her lovely, skinny, sexy body, all of her tough, awkward, fierce mind; he knew every mood of her, knew her loving, knew her laughing, knew her angry, knew her – very occasionally – calm. Usually when they had had sex.

And now she was lying in intensive care, her body crushed and broken, dangerously, critically ill. Her car under a lorry: last night. After he had spoken to her, after he had been so cruel to her. She had rung him for help and he had refused it. It could all have been his fault.

Ed suddenly felt terribly sick.

'I'm sorry, you can't see her now.' The Sister in ITU sounded rather dismissive. 'There would be no point. She's very ill, she's completely unconscious.'

'I realise that. But I'm her father.'

'I'm afraid that doesn't make any difference.'

'I'm also a priest,' he said, very gently, 'and I would like to be with her while I pray for her.'

She looked at him, looked at his face, looked at his clerical collar and hesitated and he could see that he had won. There was only one authority higher even than the consultant in hospital life: and that was God. God was permitted to be with the most desperate cases, the most dreadful situations, borne by His earthly representatives; and God, she had seen for herself, from time to time, had wrought what appeared to be miracles. The doctors would have none of it, of course, said it was coincidence, but Sister knew otherwise. There were too many such coincidences for that to be true.

She hesitated, and then said, looking rather nervously up and down the corridor, 'All right. Just for a few minutes.'

And Peter Hartley took God in with him to see his daughter.

'Is that Jocasta Forbes?'

Now, who was that? The voice was vaguely familiar. Jocasta, surfacing from a very deep sleep, said: 'Yes. Well, Jocasta Keeble, if you're being pedantic.'

'Jocasta, this is Ed. Ed Forrest. Martha's friend.'

Of course. The gorgeous boy. Nothing had surprised them all more than Martha's choice of boyfriend. They'd expected some smooth, buttoned-up lawyer, and had met instead this easy, beautiful creature who seemed far too young for her. Who clearly adored her.

'Oh, hi, Ed. What can I do for you?'

'I don't know,' he said, 'but I thought you ought to know, Martha's had a terrible accident. A car crash, she – she's in intensive care. I don't know much more than that . . .'

'Oh Ed, no! I'm so sorry.'

'I'm going up there right away,' he said, 'to see her. But I thought you should tell Nick – sorry, I can't remember his name, but the journalist – '

'Yes, yes, of course.'

'So he can tell that woman. Get her off our backs, I mean. She won't do anything now, will she?'

'I – shouldn't think so,' said Jocasta quickly. 'God, how awful. Where is she? Which hospital?'

'Bury St Edmunds. So – quite a way. I must go.'

'Of course. Ed, give her our love. I'm sure she'll be fine. And don't worry about Janet Frean. We'll deal with her. I'll call Nick right away.'

'Thanks.'

* * *

The *Sun*'s stringer in Colchester had got the story about Martha. He called the news desk.

Chad Lawrence had one of the best-known mobile numbers in Westminster: he was also one of the best-known faces.

At midday a reporter from the *Sun* called.

'I expect you've heard about Martha Hartley, Mr Lawrence.'

'No,' said Chad shortly, 'I haven't.'

'No? Well, she's in hospital. Critical condition. Terrible car crash. We're doing a paragraph for tomorrow's paper, wondered if you had a quote you could give me about her.'

'That's appalling,' said Chad and he was indeed very shocked. 'I had no idea, no. Is she all right?'

'Like I said, she's critical. Not well at all, from the sound of it.'

'God!'

'So – could you give me a quote? I know she's one of the new stars of your party.'

'No, I couldn't,' said Chad and put the phone down.

He called Jack Kirkland.

'Martha's had a car crash. A bad one. She's in intensive care, as far as I can make out. I thought you ought to know.'

'Good God, how dreadful. How did you find out?'

'I had a call from a bloke on the *Sun*. He wanted a quote about her. I said I wouldn't give him one.'

'Why on earth not?'

'Well – I don't know. It just didn't seem very appropriate.'

'Nonsense. It's very appropriate. Do you have a name?'

'No.'

'I'll call them myself.'

Funny bugger, Chad thought, putting down the phone. He felt genuinely upset. He was very fond of Martha.

Jack Kirkland spoke fulsomely and at some length about Martha; about her brilliance, her promise, how she was the future of the new party; the reporter, who was only planning a paragraph, grew impatient.

'Thanks very much, Mr Kirkland,' he said, cutting into a pause.

'That's my pleasure. Oh, and perhaps you should talk to Janet

568

Frean. She's the female face of our leadership. She's been very good to Martha, helped her along, and taken a motherly interest in her. You should speak to her. I'll get her to call you.'

'That's terrible,' said Clio, 'I'm so, so sorry. We tried to call her last night, couldn't get an answer. We know why now. Oh, God. Can we send flowers or something?'

'I don't think she's quite up to flowers,' said Jocasta soberly.

She would have liked to talk to Gideon; he was very fond of Martha. She looked at her watch: no. He'd be fast asleep; it was about four in the morning in Seattle. She felt very lonely, and very upset. She decided to call Nick back.

'Bob, hello. This is Jack Kirkland. Sorry to intrude on your Sunday morning.'

'That's fine, Jack,' said Bob Frean. 'I'm on nanny duty. Nice to talk to a human being. What? Oh, good God. How appalling. Poor Martha. Is she on the danger list? God, how dreadful. Yes, of course I'll tell her as soon as she gets here. She shouldn't be long.'

'Janet? This is Nick Marshall.'

'Oh yes?'

'Janet, Martha's had an accident. A car crash. She's very seriously hurt. I imagine this changes everything, for the time being.'

'Of course. How dreadful. Yes, we'll speak later.'

Janet drove on, feeling thoughtful. Actually, it would make the whole story more brilliant still. Give it an added edge. A poignancy even. She could see it now. Yes. It would work very well. As long as Martha lived, of course. Which she would, obviously. Nick was exaggerating the seriousness of the accident to buy himself more time. She really didn't see him doing the story now.

At this rate, Ed thought, his tyres screaming between lanes on the A12, he'd be joining Martha in intensive care. Which wasn't going to help either of them. He tried to calm down; but all he could think of, all that was in his head, running and re-running, was his conversation with Martha, his last words to her: 'Just give it a rest.

569

OK?' What sort of man said that to the woman he was supposed to love? A pretty bloody rotten one.

'Bastard,' he kept saying aloud to himself, 'you bastard.'

Helen called Jocasta's number; she was very apologetic, this being Sunday morning, probably Jocasta and her new husband were busy, giving a grand lunch party or something. But – there was no time like the present.

'Helen, it's fine. Honestly. But – '

Helen interrupted her.

'I won't keep you a minute. I just wanted Martha Hartley's phone number. I thought it might help Kate if I went to see her, tried to – '

'Helen, I'm afraid you can't go and see her. Well, not at the moment, anyway, although I think it's a lovely idea. She's in hospital. She's had an accident, she's been very badly hurt.'

'Oh,' said Helen. 'Oh dear.'

'She's in intensive care.'

'So – is it very bad?'

'Very bad, I'm afraid,' said Jocasta.

Helen put the phone down, wondering how Kate would react to this: and decided that until they knew a little more, she wouldn't tell her.

'I thought we might ask Jocasta over for lunch,' said Beatrice. 'She's all on her own, and it'd be nice to see her.'

'Good idea,' said Josh. He was heavily involved with Jeremy Clarkson, as he always was on Sunday morning.

Beatrice came back into the room a few minutes later, looking shaken.

'She can't come. She's with Nick.'

'Nick? What on earth's she doing with him?'

'I'm not sure,' said Beatrice, 'helping him with a story, I expect.'

'What, with Gideon away? Bit odd, I'd have thought.'

Beatrice gave him a look that meant he was no arbiter of any kind of behaviour and said: 'Anyway, apparently that girl Martha Hartley's in hospital. You know, the one who was ill at the party, who rushed off in the morning – '

'Yes, yes. Why is she in hospital?'

'She's had an accident. A car accident. She's in intensive care. Unconscious. Poor thing.'

'God. How dreadful.'

'Yes, isn't it? I mean, I didn't actually meet her, but you knew her, didn't you?'

'Well – hardly. Haven't seen her for seventeen years. But we had a little chat at the party. How ghastly. Is Jocasta going to keep us informed?'

'I expect so. Anyway, she was very upset. I was quite surprised how much; she said after the party she really hardly knew her.'

'Yes, well, it's always a shock when something like this happens to someone you know,' said Josh. 'I feel a bit shaken myself, to tell you the truth.'

'You do look a bit pale,' said Beatrice briskly. 'Why don't you take the children to the park for an hour or so, while I do lunch? Bit of fresh air will do you good.'

Jocasta was also surprised to find how upset she was.

'It's not as if we were friends,' she said to Nick. 'I hadn't seen her for nearly seventeen years, and she was pretty vile when I went to interview her. But she has had a basinful, poor girl. It was probably worrying so much that caused it, she wasn't concentrating.'

'Probably.'

'Ed was so upset. Distraught. He obviously really loves her. It's a weird relationship, though, isn't it?'

'I don't see why.'

'Well, he's so much younger than her, for a start. And what can they possibly have in common?'

'You're a fair bit younger than Gideon,' said Nick, 'and what do you two have in common, after all?' His tone was quite hostile; Jocasta stared at him.

They had met for coffee at Starbucks in Hampstead; Nick was writing a quick piece about Peter Hain and Europe, he said. 'Well, I'm not doing anything,' Jocasta said, 'so I'll come up to you.'

She wasn't sure why she wanted to be with him; she told herself it was because of their joint involvement in this extraordinary drama. Talking to anyone out of its loop would have felt irrelevant that morning. They sat in the sunshine, drinking lattes. It was like the old days, Jocasta thought, the old Sundays: and then crushed the thought firmly.

'I'm still worried about Janet,' said Nick, 'I just don't trust her.'

'Nick! No one's going to rat on someone when they're lying in intensive care. They just aren't.'

'I'm not sure. Anyway, I don't know that I spelt out how bad Martha was to the bloody woman. I might just ring her again.'

But the usual enraging voice told them that the number they were calling had been switched off and suggested they left a message, adding brightly, 'or why not send a text?'

Nick threw his own mobile across the table.

'Bloody woman. Bloody, bloody woman. What is she up to now?'

'God,' said Ed.

He knew he couldn't risk it, the petrol gauge had been running on empty for miles; he would have to stop at the next garage.

He pulled in and could smell the burning rubber of his own tyres as he got out of the car. He put twenty litres in, decided that would get him there and ran into the pay station.

'Fifteen quid, mate.'

Ed fumbled for his credit cards.

'Shit,' he said, and then again, 'shit.'

'Left your cards at home?'

The expression on the man's face was not attractive.

'Yes, I have, Look – I'll leave you my watch. I won't be long.'

'Yeah? If you could see the pile of watches I've got here, mate, you'd wonder why I didn't open a shop. Funny thing, their owners never come back. Never pay for the fuel either. I'll have to call the police, I'm afraid.'

'But my girlfriend's in intensive care, I've got to get there!'

The man shook his head. 'We get a lot of them and all. Now if you just wait over there, while I make the call . . .'

'Oh, bloody hell. You can't do this to me!'

' 'Fraid I can.'

Ed stood staring at him, frozen to the spot. Then he said: 'Can I go and look in the car again. I might find some cash.'

'Only if you leave your keys.'

'Yes, OK.'

He threw them at the guy, walked out to the car, feverishly started searching it again. Nothing. Not in the glove compartment, not on the back seat, not in the boot, not in the door pockets . . .

And then – 'Shit,' he said. 'Fuck me.'

Falling out of his *A to Z* was a twenty-pound note. What was that doing there, how did it get there? And then he remembered. It was Martha; she'd tried to pay for some petrol, months ago, but he wouldn't let her and she'd stuffed the £20 into the *A to Z*. She'd even written 'Love from Martha', in her neat writing in the corner. It was – well, it was –

'It's a bloody miracle,' he said, staring at it, and rushed up to the man who was tidying a row of cigarettes behind him.

'Give me my keys, please,' he said. 'Quickly.'

'Oh. Right. Well – don't you want any change?'

But Ed was gone.

When Janet got back to the house, it was unnaturally quiet. The only child present was Lucy, her fourteen year old.

'Hi, Mum. Go well last night?'

'Yes, fine. Everything OK here?'

'Yes, I think so. We weren't expecting you yet. Dad's taken the littles to the corner shop, said to tell you, if you did get back, that he wanted to talk to you. Oh, and Jack Kirkland rang. Wants you to ring him.'

'OK, I will. Any other messages?'

'Don't think so. Anyway, I'm watching *EastEnders*, see you later.'

'Fine.'

A major earthquake in the next street would not keep Lucy from *EastEnders*.

Janet went up to her study, rang Jack.

'Oh, hello, Janet. You heard about Martha?'

'Yes. Very sad. Is there any more news?'

'No. I just wanted to make sure Bob had told you about the *Sun*.'

'The *Sun*? No.'

Surely they couldn't have got a hint of the story already?

'Yes, they want you to ring them with a quote. About Martha. I've already given them one, but I thought it would be nice if you did, too. As a fellow woman politician. Do ring this chap, he's waiting to hear from you. His name's – '

Janet scribbled down the name, her head whirling. If ever there was a piece of serendipity, it was here.

Martha was not very well, Sister told Peter and Grace. Her blood pressure was falling again, she had bleeped the doctor. Yes, if they wanted to see her for a moment . . .

'Dear God,' whispered Grace.

Ed had arrived at the hospital. He screeched to a halt in the only space he could see, which stated clearly that it was reserved for medical staff only, and rushed into the building.

'I've come to see one of the patients,' he said to the woman on reception, 'Martha Hartley.'

'Hartley, Hartley – let me see . . .'

An officious-looking man came up behind him.

'That your car, sir? The old Golf?'

He put the emphasis on the word old.

'Yes,' said Ed, without looking at him. The woman was clicking keys endlessly on her computer.

'Going to have to ask you to move it, sir, I'm afraid. That's a consultant's space.'

'Yes, well, he's not here, is he?'

'She's on the second floor, Ward F. But you won't be able to see her.'

'I've got to!'

'Well, I'm afraid you can't.'

'Can I go up there?'

'There's no point.'

'I really must ask you to move your car, sir. If Mr – '

The door to reception opened sharply: 'Who's parked in my space, Evans?'

'I'm sorry, Mr Thompson, sir. This gentleman – '

'Look, I'm in a terrible hurry. I've got a seriously ill patient in surgery and I can't waste time with bloody cars. Get it moved, will you? Here are my keys.'

'Yes, Mr Thompson. Right away.' He turned to Ed, put his hand on his shoulder.

'Now, sir, would you please move your car? At once. As you can see, you're disrupting serious medical procedures – '

'Oh fuck the cars!' said Ed. He threw the keys at him. 'Move it yourself. Sorry,' he added, seeing the man's face, 'but my girlfriend's desperately ill, I have to get to her.'

'You won't be able to,' said the woman again. But Ed was gone.

'Is that the news desk? Yes? This is Janet Frean, I think you're expecting my call. It's about Martha Hartley, the girl in the car crash – yes, I'll wait.'

Ward F was very quiet; even hospitals seemed to respond to the mood of Sunday mornings. Ed ran along the corridor, desperately trying to find anyone, anyone at all.

He saw a door marked ITU. He tried to open it, but it was locked; there was a bank of numbers on the door. Bloody combination lock. Shit. He hammered on the door.

An irritable face appeared.

'I think my girlfriend's in there. Martha Hartley?'

'If she is, you certainly can't see her. This is ITU. No visitors.'

'Oh, God. Please, PLEASE!'

'I'm sorry, no. Please wait outside, and someone will help you in a minute.'

'But – Oh, Mr Hartley. How are you? I mean, how is she? I mean – '

Peter Hartley's face was ravaged with grief.

'She's not very well, Ed,' he said simply. He showed no sign of surprise at seeing him there. 'Couldn't you let this young man in, Sister? Just for a moment? It can't make any difference now . . .'

Bob Frean stood in the doorway of Janet's study. His face was very cold, very blank.

'Janet – '

She raised her finger to her lips, put her hand over the receiver.

'Sorry, talking to the *Sun*. Won't be long – '

Bob walked forward and put his hand on the receiver.

'Bob! What are you doing, you've cut me off!'

'Good,' he said, 'that was what I intended. And before you ring them back, I have just one thing to say to you, Janet. If you tell the *Sun* anything at all unpleasant about Martha Hartley, I shall tell them a great many unpleasant things about you. Starting with your rather odd relationship with Michael Fitzroy.' He smiled at her, quite politely. And then turned and walked out again: Janet sat staring at the telephone, listening to his footsteps going along the corridor.

Martha was on the bed, her eyes closed; she looked perfectly peaceful, her face slightly swollen and bruised, but no worse. Tubes seemed to be coming out of every part of her; drips hung above her on both sides of the bed, one delivering blood, the others, he supposed, drugs of some sort. A bank of monitors to her right blinked various incomprehensible messages: the one comfort he could find was that there was no dreadful straight line on any of them: the line so familiar to viewers of hospital soap operas, signalling, as it did, the end of a story.

But this was not a soap opera and this was not a story line. And the person on the bed was not an actor, but Martha, his Martha, who he loved more than he had ever even realised. And who it seemed he was about to lose.

He looked, panic-stricken, at the Hartleys; Grace was very calm, sitting by the bed, her eyes fixed on Martha's face, Peter was holding one of her hands.

Ed moved round the bed, and very carefully picked up the other hand. She had very small hands, she was quite small altogether, he thought; it was rather as if he was realising this properly for the first time. The hand felt quite warm. Well, that had to mean something good.

'Can I – am I allowed to speak to her?' he said, very quietly, remembering, from his own father's death, that hearing was the last sense to go.

'Yes, of course,' said Grace.

She sat there watching him now, as he bent down, totally unselfconscious, and said very gently, very quietly, 'Martha, it's me. Ed. I'm here now. I'm here with you.'

If this was *Casualty*, Grace thought, Martha's eyelids would flicker, she'd move her head, she'd squeeze his hand. But it isn't, it's real life and none of those things will happen. Real life isn't like *Casualty*; real life is much harsher, much crueller than that.

And Peter thought, if she recovers now, it would be a miracle. And struggle as he might, in that moment he didn't believe in miracles.

Ed was still talking: in the same gentle voice.

'Martha, I'm so sorry. What I said last night. So sorry.'

Still real life. Still no miracles.

'I don't care about Kate. I don't care about any of it. I love you, Martha. Very, very much. I really, really love you.'

And then it happened, against every possible expectation, and Grace and Peter watched, awed, as Martha's eyelids did indeed flicker and she turned her head, just very slightly. No more than a hair's breadth but enough to be seen, in Ed's direction, and a glancing shadow of a smile touched her face; and two great tears, Ed's tears, fell on the hand that had – almost imperceptibly – squeezed his.

It was only a small miracle: but in some ways it was enough.

Afterwards, real life came swiftly in again: and the line on the monitor grew straight and Martha's story was written gently out of the script. But Ed, who had both worked and experienced the miracle, felt, as he bade her farewell, just a little comforted.

And thought later, as he sat outside the room, numb with shock, while Martha's parents said their own goodbyes to her, that it had actually been the second miracle that day.

Chapter 38

'I don't know why I feel so upset,' Jocasta said. She was sitting in Nick's flat in Hampstead, weeping; his arms were round her, and he was tenderly stroking her hair. 'It's not as if I'd been close to her, or anything. I suppose it was Kate; she came with Kate, in a way. Oh dear. Nick, it's so sad.'

'It is sad,' he said, 'dreadfully sad. I can't believe it, not any of it.'

'But at least Ed got there. That's something. He was so distraught, Nick, I can't tell you. He said he was going to stay with his mum tonight, in Binsmow, and he'd see us tomorrow. He said – ' She swallowed hard, sniffed loudly, 'he said he thought they'd like us to be at the funeral. He said we'd done so much for her. I wish.'

'Well, we tried,' said Nick. 'We did our best. I think Janet must be feeling pretty bad.'

'I bloody well hope so,' said Jocasta.

'That's dreadful,' said Helen, 'I'm shocked. I mean, I never even met her, but obviously – well, she's part of us now, after all. It's a very odd feeling. Kate's in a very strange state.'

'I expect she is,' said Jocasta, 'poor little thing.'

'I feel awful,' said Kate. 'Really bad. Just think, my mother, all my life I've been looking for her, and then I find her and all I ever said to her was horrible things. God, Nat, I really am a right cow!'

'No, you're not,' he said. 'You weren't to know. And you don't owe her nothing, don't forget. It's not like she was your real mum.'

'Nat!' said Kate. 'She *was* my real mum. That's the whole point, don't be stupid.'

'No, she wasn't. She didn't, like, look after you, did she, didn't bring you up? I'd say your mum, downstairs, she's your real mum. Think how you'd feel if it was her.'

'Oh, don't!' said Kate. 'I'd rather die myself.'

'Well, there you are.'

'I know, but – she – Martha – must have died thinking I hated her. That's not very good, is it?'

'Well – no. But – '

'And then, just think, finally I found her, finally I could've got to know her, and now I've lost her again forever. It's not fair, Nat, it really, really isn't fair!'

Nat left shortly after that. Kate was crying again and he was beginning to feel he'd had enough. But before he went, he looked in on Helen, who was in the kitchen, rather feebly peeling potatoes, and told her that Kate had just said that, if it had been Helen who'd been killed, she'd prefer to be dead herself. He thought she'd like to hear that, but he was wrong. Helen burst into tears.

Nat's dad had often told him women were a complete mystery and it was a waste of time and energy to even try to understand them. Nat decided he agreed with him.

'Oh, it's so, so sad,' said Clio. Her eyes were red with weeping; like Jocasta she couldn't quite work out why she was so upset. Fergus told her it was because she was so tender-hearted, but she knew it was more than that. In a few short weeks Martha had wound her way into their lives, just as insistently as if they had had the annual meetings they had promised one another all those years ago. She kept thinking of Martha as she had last seen her on the beach in Thailand, brown, smiling, her hair sun-streaked, no longer touchy and inhibited, but happily easy, and thought of the dreadful ending to that happiness, the long, long days in the hot, filthy city, waiting and waiting in dread for her baby to be born, and then of what must have been the nightmare of that birth, all alone, with nothing and no one to help her through the pain. And then she thought of her making her new life, her perfectly accomplished and successful new life, and all the time with her dreadful secret, and she thought that Martha was, without doubt, not only the bravest person she had ever met, but the bravest that she was ever likely to meet.

Beatrice had called Jocasta for news of Martha; she expected to be told she was better, or at least holding her own. She went to tell Josh, and he had been clearly upset as well; it was just that it was a shock, they agreed, as they sat drinking larger than usual gin and tonics before dinner that night. Of course neither of them had known her at all well, they said, in fact Beatrice had scarcely met her, it was just the thought of that lovely, brilliant girl, with so much promise and so much life before her, being no more, her light put out forever, all by a moment's lack of attention.

They agreed that there was no reason for them to go to the funeral, but that they would send some flowers.

Jack Kirkland called Janet Frean.

'It's about Martha. Dreadful thing. She's died.'

There was an endless silence: then: 'Died!' The word shot from her, very loud.

'Yes. I'm afraid so.'

'But I thought – Jack, are you sure?'

'I'm very sure. Nick Marshall just rang me.'

'Nick Marshall! What's it got to do with him?'

Her tone was very harsh.

'Oh, she and Jocasta were friendly, as you know. They went travelling together when they were girls. Anyway, she died. Around lunchtime today. Janet – are you all right?'

The line went suddenly dead; puzzled, he rang off, waited for her to ring him back and then called Eliot Griers and Chad Lawrence.

Half an hour later, he rang again. Bob Frean answered the phone.

'Oh, hello, Bob. I was talking to Janet about half an hour ago, and we were cut off. Could I speak to her?'

'I'm afraid not.' Bob sounded awkward. 'She's – lying down. Not very well.'

'Oh, I'm sorry. She does too much. I thought she sounded rather odd when I told her about Martha. She was very fond of her, of course.'

'Indeed.'

'It was about the funeral. Obviously we should all go. It's at her father's church in Suffolk; he's taking the service, poor man. Next Monday. Chad and Eliot and a great many others will be there. I know Janet will want to come.'

'Yes, of course. Well – I'll tell her. I'd like to come myself, if that would be all right. I was very fond of Martha.'

'Perfectly all right, yes. Well, give Janet my best.'

Bob went into the bedroom he and Janet occasionally shared. Most of the time he slept in another room, on the next floor. She was lying on the bed, staring up at the ceiling, ashen-faced, very still. She looked almost lifeless herself.

'That was Kirkland.'

She said nothing.

'It was about the funeral. Martha's funeral.' Silence still.

'It's next Monday. Jack said they were all going and naturally would expect you. I said we'd both go.'

'I can't go,' she said, her voice as expressionless as her face.

'Janet,' he said, 'you're going.'

Martha had not been unlike her in some ways, he thought. She had that same capacity for self-control. The same near-fanaticism in pursuit of her own success. But she was a much nicer person. Janet was not a nice person.

He had had no clear idea what she was going to tell Nicholas Marshall or the *Sun* about Martha; but he knew something was going on, by the simple device of reading her e-mails, latterly on her BlackBerry. He had been doing that on and off for a while. Thus Bob learnt about a great many tedious things – select committees she was asked to serve on, local planning laws she had pledged to fight, NHS reforms, the Lords reform, European regulations, important Divisions – and a few more interesting ones. Such as this latest, concerning Martha. It astonished him that she had never realised he might do so: perhaps she did, and her contempt for him was such that she never thought he would do anything with the knowledge.

'How did you know?' she said that morning, lying on her bed, white-faced and hollow-eyed.

'Oh, Janet,' he said in his courteous voice, 'you really think I'm very stupid, don't you? I've been reading your e-mails, of course.'

'But – you couldn't have. The most recent ones hadn't even been opened.'

'Well, I'm afraid they had. That latest little gadget of yours, the BlackBerry, I've had a lot of fun and games with it. You'd be surprised what you can do with a password and a bit of know-how. Not nice, what you had planned for Martha. Well, I'll leave you to rest, shall I?'

As he went back to the garden, he thought sadly that although he might have saved Martha from Janet, it was of little use to her now.

Gideon Keeble found himself very moist-eyed when Jocasta told him the news. 'Silly old fool that I am,' he said to her, 'but she was a lovely thing, and so charming and clever. What a waste, what a dreadful waste.'

Jocasta agreed.

'The funeral's next Monday, Gideon, will you be able to come? Will you be back? I'd so love it if you would.'

'Of course I'll come. If that's what her parents want.'

'I think the more people who come, the better. Nothing worse than a small funeral. And they've invited me, through Ed, who seems to be doing a lot of the organising, and if I'm there, I want you to be.'

'I'll be there.'

'Thank you. I love you, Gideon.'

'I love you too, Jocasta. Where are you, incidentally? I've been calling the house.'

'I'm at Nick's,' she said, without thinking.

Before Ed went home to Binsmow, he drove back up the A12 to the petrol station where he had filled his car earlier in the day. The same man was on duty.

'Hi,' said Ed heavily, 'remember me?'

The attendant looked uneasy.

'Yeah.'

'I wondered if you could very kindly give me that £20 note back. Here's another.'

He had found his wallet with his cards; it had been on the floor of the car, under his seat. Had he been calmer, he'd have found it.

'You want the same note back? You'll be lucky.'

'Yes, I realise that, but I'd like you to try. It – was signed. By my girlfriend.'

'Oh yeah? The one that was in intensive care? S'pose she's OK now, is she?'

'No,' said Ed, very quietly, 'she isn't. She died.'

He hadn't often seen a jaw drop; he saw it now. And a red flush rising from the man's neck, up to his forehead.

'Sorry, mate,' he said, 'very sorry.'

'Yes, well, perhaps you'd be kind enough to look through your till. You'll know it, if you see it – I'm sure not many of them are signed.'

The man pulled out the drawer, sorted through the row of notes. After a few minutes he pulled one out, handed it to Ed in silence. Ed walked back to his car, looking at the note, at the writing, the neatly inscribed, 'Love from Martha'.

It wasn't much to have of someone; but it was something. He had very little else: a few shirts, a couple of books – they, too, were signed the same way, nothing effusive, but then she wasn't – hadn't been – effusive – a few CDs. A couple of photographs of the two of them on her balcony and the one in her bed, that he'd framed, all taken with the auto on his camera. And a lot of memories.

The loss of her suddenly hit him, almost physically; he felt breathless, weak, and absolutely alone. He put his head on his arms on the steering wheel and sobbed like a small child.

'I think I'd like to go to the funeral,' said Kate.

Helen stared at her; she was pale, but otherwise composed, not hysterical.

'Kate, love, are you sure?'

'Yes, of course I'm sure. Perfectly sure. Why shouldn't I be?'

'But – you didn't know her,' said Helen, realising the absurdity of this statement, even as she made it,

'Mum! I know that. But I'd like to say goodbye to her. Properly. I – well, I wasn't very nice to her when I met her. I feel bad about it.'

'Oh dear.' Helen sighed. She wasn't at all sure about this. For all sorts of reasons. Not least – 'Kate, what do you think Martha's family will think about it? This is no time for you to be upsetting them.'

'I'm not going to upset them. What do you think I am, some kind of moron?'

'But – won't they wonder who you are?'

'I'll tell them I'm a friend of Jocasta's, that I met Martha through her. I've thought of that.'

'I'll see what your father thinks,' said Helen.

'I don't care what he thinks. It's nothing to do with him – I'm going, OK?'

'Oh dear,' said Helen again. 'Kate, I don't think I can go. Even if you do. It would be very difficult. I don't expect you to understand, but – '

'Oh Mum!' Kate's expression suddenly softened; she put her arms round her mother. 'Of course I understand. You do think I'm a moron, don't you? Of course you don't have to come, it'd be hideous for you. I'll go with Jocasta. She'll take me. And Fergus will be there. I'll be fine. Honestly.'

Jocasta thought it was a good idea for Kate to go to the funeral.

'I can see it sounds a bit strange, but I think it will help her. And of course she can come with me. Us. Gideon will be back. It's kind of final, draws a line for her, as much as anyone.'

'She's really not herself,' said Helen. 'She's very quiet, not going out anywhere. Nat's been banished.'

'The lovely Nat? Poor little Kate. It's all very difficult for her, isn't it? She's lost her all over again. Without learning anything at all.'

'I'm afraid so,' said Helen with a sigh.

'Beatrice . . . I know this might sound a bit odd, but – I think I'd like to go to Martha Hartley's funeral.'

'Really? Why?'

'Oh – hard to explain. I'd just like to. I feel I should. No need for you to come, of course.'

'No, it would be out of the question anyway. Well, I suppose if you want to, Josh. It seems totally out of proportion to me – '

'I know. But – oh I don't know, it's just that she's the first, the very first of our generation to go. I still feel quite shocked. I'd met her, and I'd like to – to acknowledge the fact.'

'Fine. You go. I'm sure Jocasta will be pleased.'

Janet was in a really very odd state: even by her own standards, Bob thought. She had hardly emerged from the bedroom in twenty-four hours; she hadn't left the house on Monday, and had even missed PM's Question Time on Wednesday. She appeared for family meals, but sat rather silently, listening to the racket but taking no part in it and certainly not instigating the political discussions she managed to dredge up, as Lucy had once rather forcibly put it, from almost any topic, including what groups were in the charts (the apoliticism of youth) and what Betsy, the baby, had done at her playgroup that day (the lack of nursery places).

She clearly wasn't sleeping, Bob heard her moving around the house in the middle of the night, when it was quiet, and assumed she was working, but when he went to her study to check, she was never there, and he would find her sitting in the drawing room in total darkness. She refused to talk to him. But as the week wore on, she became increasingly distracted, shouting at the children, snapping at anyone else who crossed her path; the only time she became alive and herself again was when she went off on Friday night to make a speech at a charity dinner in the constituency. Then she appeared, wearing her favourite evening trouser suit, her hair done, her make-up immaculate, sparkling at the driver waiting in the hall for her, and came back, flushed with triumph, saying it had been superb and everyone had congratulated her on what she and the rest of Centre Forward were achieving.

Bob had thought that Saturday might see the more familiar Janet back. But she appeared still more depressed, lying in bed until mid-morning and then setting off in her car for what she called a bit of a drive. She was gone four hours. It was a measure of her dispensability to the family, he thought, that no one even asked where she might have gone. The nanny had taken the younger four to Chessington World of Adventures and Lucy was shopping with her best friend; what price superwoman now?

It was Sunday night; with enormous determination, Peter Hartley had taken two of the three Sunday services, but was now lying down, exhausted. Grace, who had hardly slept at all, was pretending to read the papers, and wondering when, if ever, the wild pain she was experiencing might even begin to ease.

Martha had been brought home; her coffin lay in the church and an enormous number of people had been to pay their respects, some of them spending quite a long time with her, kneeling in prayer. If only she knew, Grace thought, how many there were, how fond people all were of her; and then felt guilty, because Peter would have said, of course, that she would know. His faith appeared unshaken; Grace's was becoming very frail indeed.

She felt daunted at the thought of what was clearly going to be a large funeral the next day, but comforted too; she had always worried that Martha didn't have many friends, but clearly an enormous number had loved and admired her. Her boss, Paul Quenell, had phoned Grace and said he would, of course, be there, and that he was bringing several of Martha's colleagues – including her friend, Richard Ashcombe, who was flying over from New York.

The thought of someone flying from America to attend Martha's funeral impressed Grace almost more than anything.

'I always wondered about Martha and him,' she said to Paul Quenell, 'whether something might – well, come of it. She was always talking about him, they seemed so fond of one another.'

Paul Quenell said, without more than a second's hesitation, that he too had been struck by their close friendship.

'But of course we were wrong, she chose a local boy in the end, Ed Forrest, I don't know if you ever met him?'

'I didn't, but I heard he was absolutely charming.' Paul had not even been aware of Ed's existence until that moment; but he was sure this, too, was what Martha's mother would want to hear.

'And of course she thought so much of you. She was always talking about you. It'll be a pleasure to meet you at last.'

If only, Paul thought, as he said goodbye to her, if only the meeting could be a pleasure, rather than a dreadful tragic duty.

There was a ring at the bell: it was Ed. He was pale and didn't look as if he'd been sleeping much, but he looked fairly cheerful.

'I just popped round to see you. And Martha,' he added. 'And Mum says is there anything more at all that she can do for tomorrow?'

Mrs Forrest had already made ninety-six vol au vents; Grace said she had done enough.

'Are you all right, Ed dear?'

'Well – you know. I'll be glad when it's over. In a way.'

'I know what you mean,' said Grace. 'We've still got her at the moment. We haven't said goodbye, yet.'

She smiled at Ed; if only she'd known that he and Martha had been – well, been in love, she would have been so happy. It had always been her dearest wish that Martha would come home to Binsmow, perhaps work as a solicitor there; her political ambitions had seemed a promising step along that road. And with Ed – so handsome, so charming, such a wonderful son – it would have been too good to be true. As it exactly had been: too good to be true. She looked at him now and her eyes filled with tears; he put his arms round her and they stood there, the two of them, remembering Martha and thinking how much they had both loved her.

Later that evening, Gideon phoned. 'Jocasta, my darling, I'm going to fail you. I can't get there in time for tomorrow.'

She felt disproportionately angry and upset.

'Why? What's happened?'

'Some kind of breakdown in air traffic control. So I can't even charter anything. Darling, I am so, so sorry. I've been trying to get something sorted for hours. I didn't want to ring you until I knew it was hopeless.'

'Yes, well, now you have,' said Jocasta.

'Darling one, don't sound so angry.'

'I *am* angry. If you'd left a day earlier, as you should have done, anyway, to be sure of getting back in time, you'd be here by now.'

'Jocasta, I haven't exactly been on holiday, you know.'

'I do know, and I shouldn't think you ever will be. Oh never mind, doesn't matter. I'll get by without you. Everyone else is coming. Even Josh.'

'Josh? Why on earth should he be going? He didn't know Martha, surely?'

'He did. Briefly. He was with us when we first went travelling. And he met her again at our wedding party. Anyway, he wanted to say goodbye. Pay his respects, he said. Don't worry, Gideon, I'll be fine.'

'Jocasta – ' But she had put the phone down.

Fergus wondered if he could talk to Kate about her contract with Smith before the funeral and decided he couldn't. She was, Helen told him, very worked up about everything. Fergus said of course he understood, but it really couldn't be left much longer.

'They think we're playing games and they're getting impatient,' he had said to Kate earlier in the week.

'Well – let them. I don't really care. Honestly. I've got the magazine work, haven't I?'

Two e-mails from Smith later and he was getting worried. And it wasn't just that Smith would be disenchanted with Kate soon, word would get round that she was awkward, difficult, played games. She wasn't so successful that she could afford to mess people around. These were very early days.

And he had his own agenda, although he tried not to think about it: his commission on the magazine work would be small change compared to the Smith contract. On the other hand – Fergus knew very well what the other hand held: more unwelcome publicity, increasing media pressure on Kate – 'How do you feel about not knowing who your mother is, Kate?' 'Do you think you'll ever know who your father is?' . . . He knew in his heart of hearts she would be better without it. But – what would three million dollars do for her as a start in life? A very great deal. And continued to try to crush the thought of what 20 per cent of it could do for him.

He had tried to discuss his dilemma with Clio, but they had already had a fierce argument about it.

'I don't know how you can even think of putting pressure on her at a time like this. Beastly people can wait.'

Fergus said he was trying not to put pressure on her, but that it wasn't a decision he could take for her, and that Smith, with the best will in the world, could hardly have known Kate was having a difficult time and simply needed to have the whole thing settled.

'It's a commercial matter, Clio, they have deadlines to meet.'

'Then tell them she's having a difficult time, for heaven's sake. I'm sure they'll understand. And if they don't, they don't deserve her anyway.'

It was at such times that Fergus worried about their relationship, so far apart were their attitudes to his career. To Clio it was something distinctly shameful; to him it earned him more than a few crusts in the only way he knew, and for the most part enjoyed.

The whole thing didn't quite add up.

'You two go down together, then,' said Jocasta to Clio, 'and Nick can take Josh – Beatrice isn't coming and it won't be much fun for him driving down alone. I really can't imagine why he's going at all, but it's very sweet of him. And I'll bring Kate. I think it's best she's alone with me, she might be very upset. Just as well Gideon isn't coming, really.'

'Does Josh know about Kate?' Clio asked. 'I mean, who does he think she is?'

'He knows she's Baby Bianca, but he has no idea she's anything to do with Martha. I just told him she met her at the party and wanted to come. He's awfully thick, you know, he never thinks anything much at all.'

'Jocasta,' said Clio, 'that's rubbish! He's terribly clever, he got a first, didn't he, and God knows how many A levels when he was about twelve?'

'Yes, but he's incredibly stupid when it comes to real life,' said Jocasta, 'just misses the point of everything.'

'Oh I see,' said Clio. 'Are you all right, Jocasta?'

'Yes. Course. I'm fine. Why shouldn't I be?'

'I'm not sure. You just don't seem quite yourself.'

'I'm absolutely myself.'

Clio decided to let it rest.

The funeral was to start at two. By just after one, cars began to fill St Andrew's Road. By one-thirty people were standing awkwardly about outside, greeting those they knew, smiling uncertainly at those they didn't. At twenty to two, they moved into the church.

Martha's coffin was standing now in the vicarage porch. The flowers inside the church had been done, as always, by the ladies of the Women's Institute: great fountains of lilies and lisianthus and white roses on the altar and in the huge urns on either side of the nave, vases of roses on each window, and on the side of every pew a simple posy of sweet peas, Martha's favourite flowers, tied with white ribbons.

It was a tremulously perfect English summer day, a blue, blue sky, a few white scudding clouds, the lightest breeze. Grace, who had woken to it before dawn, listened to the birds in their heartlessly joyful chorus and hoped that crying so much then would save her later on. It did not.

St Andrews was not a large church, but it was not a small one, either; by ten to two it was full. The older members of the parish had come in force, all wanting to say goodbye to the little girl they had watched grow up; and Martha's constituents too, wishing to show their gratitude for the help she had given them so freely, albeit for so brief a time. Geraldine Curtis was there, looking stern, Mr Curtis obediently in tow. Colin Black, Martha's political agent, was there, his face sombre.

There were several middle-aged ladies, Martha's teachers at the grammar school – 'Such a brilliant girl,' they kept saying to anyone who would listen, 'the cleverest of a clever year. It was a privilege to teach her.'

And then there were the Other People, as Grace called them to herself, the people from London, carloads of them: a large contingent from Sayers Wesley, many of the younger partners, Martha's contemporaries, and the older ones too, all marshalled in by a stony-faced Paul Quenell. The Centre Forward party had come in force: Jack Kirkland, of course, and Chad Lawrence and Eliot Griers and their wives, Janet Frean, horribly pale and almost haggard-looking, with her husband. Martin Farrow, the publicity director and his team, and then another whole row of party members, other candidates, and the secretaries from Centre Forward House. And a small Asian family, a beautiful teenage girl and an embarrassed-looking boy, and their father, smiling awkwardly: Lina's family, come to show their respects to Martha for what she had tried to do for Lina.

And finally, her friends: Jocasta, with a stricken-looking Kate, Clio, Josh, Fergus, Nick, all filing in together. Ed saw them first, as he walked in behind the coffin, together with Martha's brother and father; they gave him courage as he heard the awful words, in Peter Hartley's beautiful voice, 'I am the resurrection and the life,' and wondered in genuine bewilderment how they could possibly apply to the person he had loved so much, the person who was such an important and lovely part of his life, who was lying in this flower-drenched coffin, with his own small wreath set beside her parents' larger one, a ring of white roses with the words: 'Martha, my love always, Ed' on the card, written in his own untidy, near-illegible hand.

Jocasta had been right, she thought, a full church did make a funeral more bearable. So many people, so determinedly there for Martha. She stood, holding Kate's hand, singing 'Lord of All Hopefulness', and thought how it had to bring some comfort to the Hartleys. Lovely people, both of them – she had hugged Grace and told her what a good friend Martha had always been to her: such things could not be said too often, and watched Peter Hartley now, looking at his flock over his daughter's coffin, and wondered how anyone could be so brave. She smiled encouragingly at Kate; she did not smile back.

The elderly organist, who had played at Martha's christening and confirmation, was pouring his heart into Elgar's Nimrod for her, tears blurring his eyes; Nick, sitting with Clio and Fergus, looked at the two political rows, the only people he properly knew here, apart from Jocasta, and wondered what Martha could have found in them, self-seeking, power-obsessed people, that could have lured her under their spell. What was it about politics that people found so irresistible, and worth sacrificing so much for? To observe, to be entertained by, to pronounce upon it, that was one thing: to be a part of it quite another. And if she had resisted them, then she would, very probably, have been alive today. He tried not to dwell on that; it was too awful.

Richard Ashcombe was standing up now, moving to the lectern; deeply touched to have been asked by Grace and Peter to read St Paul's letter to the Corinthians. He only hoped he would not fail them. He felt desperately upset; the last time he had seen Martha had been at his leaving party, in fact she had made a brief speech; he could see her now, her small face laughing at him, pushing back her hair, holding out his present (a gold champagne bottle stopper, engraved with his name), telling him that the London office would be more sober, and more effective, with him removed, 'although a great deal less fun', and then giving him a kiss. How could she be gone, how was it possible? He reached the end – just.

It was with the words 'the greatest of these is charity' that Ed's heart felt as if it might explode with pain; he gripped the pew in front of him and bowed his head, fighting his tears back; Jocasta, who was sitting behind him, reached forward and placed her hand on one of his shoulders to let him know she was there and wept too. They all loved her, Grace thought, noticing this, how can she have gone and left us alone?

Paula Ballantine, who sang at every funeral in the district and had done for forty years, was giving Martha an Ave Maria all the richer for her voice occasionally losing its certainty: Fergus, who had an Irish love of music, and who had actually hardly met Martha, found himself deeply moved. It was the waste, he thought, looking at the coffin, the waste of a bright and lovely life: albeit filled with hidden darkness, and thought then that she had taken her secrets with her and that no one need know them now. No one who was not deemed fit to know them; he thought how hard her parents would have found it, and wondered if, in fact, they would ever wish to know. It was a very difficult question.

And then, praying for enough strength to do it, Peter Hartley spoke the briefest of eulogies.

'You must forgive me,' he said, 'if I am unable to finish this. But with God's help I will. I want only to say a very few words of farewell to Martha. She was not, in any case, an effusive person, and as most of you know, anything flowery irritated her. Although I think she would have liked this church today. She was a remarkable person, and even allowing for some natural prejudice, strong as well as gentle, kind as well as ambitious, brave as well as tender-hearted. She was a perfectionist, as many of you will also know, and hard at times to live up to. We were always immensely proud of her, and although it was sad to lose her to the big city, and her high-flying career, we could see that was where she belonged. But this year she had come back to Binsmow, and was working for the community in a new way, in her guise as a fledgling politician. Who knows what might have happened to her? Maybe a future second woman prime minister grew up in this parish and in the house next door. We shall never now know. But what we do know is that while she was – ' his voice shook – 'while she was with us, for that too-short a time, she failed no one. Not her family, not her colleagues, not her friends. And we all loved her.

'There could be no better epitaph than that. Thank you all for coming to say goodbye to her. My wife and I thank you from the bottom of our hearts.'

Kate was aware of something strange happening to her, which had begun as they first went into the church, a little melting of the cold around her heart. This mother of hers, this woman who had abandoned her as a baby and pursued her own interests ever since, had begun to change – just a little. That person, had she been as cold and as selfish as she had imagined, could not have earned all this. All these flowers, all these people, all this love. It wasn't possible. There must have been a different Martha, a kind and generous one, who meant a great deal to a great many people – who were those Asian people, for instance? And who was that gorgeous bloke, sitting and crying right in front of them? He was quite young, maybe a brother or something – she must have been not at all as Kate had thought. Better. Not all bad. And her poor mum, she looked really nice, and her dad too – that had been brave, standing up and saying all that. How could they have had a daughter who had done what she did to her? And what would they say, if she said: 'Hi, I'm Kate. I'm your granddaughter, thought I'd just say hello.' The inappropriateness of this, the tension of the occasion, suddenly had a dreadful effect on Kate; she felt an overwhelming desire to giggle. She bit her lip, looked at Jocasta, and at Clio, Martha's friends, her real mother's friends; they were both crying and it sobered her. They were both so nice, so cool: how could they have cared so much about the monster she had created in her head?

God, if only she'd known her, if only she'd been a bit nicer that day.

Bach's Toccata and Fugue in D minor filled the church now from the organ loft; Clio, who had been sitting clutching Fergus's hand, listening and watching and remembering as if in a dream, saw the whole thing almost detachedly, as if she was watching a film, a strange, disconnected series of images. The pallbearers picked up the coffin, turned very, very slowly; she looked at Jocasta, wiping her eyes, and at Kate, her small face frozen with confusion, and thought, for the thousandth time, how absurdly alike they were.

And then the coffin began to move, slowly, so slowly down the nave, the flowers spilling over it, the sunlight streaming so determinedly in – she would always think of Martha in sunshine, Clio thought, only not here, not in this church, but on a sun-drenched white beach. And then she looked at Ed, ashen-pale, his eyes red-rimmed and still full of tears, moving off behind the coffin, and thought she had never seen such pain on so young a face, it was too soon, far too soon – and then Martha's mother she supposed it was, leaning on a young woman's arm, her other daughter obviously – sobbing in a dreadful silence.

She looked at Nick, at dear, sweet, good Nick who had struggled so hard to save Martha from pain, and thought how special he was, and then at Josh, standing next to Jocasta – how strange that he had come, that he had wanted to come. They had all been so surprised, and he looked really upset, white and heavy-eyed. Why, when he had hardly known Martha? God, they were alike, he and Jocasta, like twins, as she had thought when she first saw them, and then it was her turn to leave and she began to move slowly down the aisle, holding Fergus's hand. Outside, it was all confusion; the hearse bearing the family was already gone to the cemetery, and another car behind it, clearly with more relatives; she had become separated from the others now, had become caught up somehow in the political lot. She saw Eliot Griers, and Chad Lawrence, totally subdued, and Jack Kirkland, blowing his nose repeatedly on his handkerchief; and the hideous Janet Frean. God, she had a nerve coming – Clio supposed she should admire her in a way, so much easier to have feigned illness and she did actually look ill, dreadfully ill, her eyes huge and staring in her gaunt, almost grey face, her mouth set rigid – well, good, she deserved to be ill.

This wouldn't do, she must get back to the others, Jocasta might need her, Kate might be very distressed. There they were now, the three of them standing together, Kate between them, they could almost be a family, they all looked alike. Josh and Jocasta could have been the parents, young, young parents, and Kate the child – and then everything really did move into slow motion, and the sound around her was echoey and the sunlight dazzled her and she began to hear things, over and over again, echoing through her head . . . they could be twins . . . Kate looks just like Jocasta . . . why should Josh be coming, I wonder . . . Josh seemed really upset . . . And Fergus said: 'Clio, are you all right, you look a bit faint,' and she said, 'Shush,' quite fiercely and the thoughts and the words kept on and on coming at her, relentlessly, words and memories. Martha telling her she couldn't tell her who the father was, studying the old photographs of them as children, so amazingly alike, she had thought, and someone at the party saying how alike they still were . . . Kate looks so like Jocasta . . . Josh seemed really upset . . . I can't tell you who the father is . . . and then it was there, right there, as it had been all the time, in front of their eyes, and she looked again across at Jocasta and Josh, standing there together, so alike, so fatally, extraordinarily alike, and Kate so like both of them, like both of them, like a family, just like a family: and Clio knew in that moment, in a roar of shock and with an absolute certainty, who Kate's father was.

Chapter 39

He was really nice, Kate thought, Jocasta's brother. Very kind and jolly; she liked him a lot. Jocasta didn't have time to introduce them until after the service – he'd been almost late, arriving with Nick with about five minutes to spare. Jocasta had been furious, spitting tacks at him as he slipped into the pew about three along from them.

It didn't seem that bad to Kate – they got there, and that was all that mattered, but she kept muttering things to Clio like, 'typical', and, 'this is just so Josh'.

Since it turned out it had been Nick's fault, and not even his, really, he'd had a puncture, this seemed pretty unfair; but Kate was beginning to learn that the Jocasta she had for a long time considered perfect did actually have some faults, and one of them was jumping to conclusions – often wrong – and overreacting accordingly.

As they walked out into the sunshine (she'd been feeling pretty odd, upset and a bit happier at the same time), he'd held out his hand to her and said: 'Hi. I'm Josh, Jocasta's little brother. You must be Kate.'

He didn't look that old, he was a bit fatter than Jocasta and very tall, with the same blond hair and the same blue eyes; he was wearing old people's clothes, of course, a suit and so on, but quite a nice one, dark grey. Clothes for funerals were obviously a sort of uniform; her mother had been very worried about what she should wear today and sent her down to Guildford to her grandmother, who had bought her a black shift dress and long jacket in Jigsaw, and some black pumps as well; she'd felt like some old woman, but once she got there she could see Jilly had been right, and she'd have felt a total idiot in the light blue trouser suit she'd wanted.

She'd smiled at Josh and said yes, she was Kate, and he'd said something like it was jolly nice of her to come when she'd hardly met Martha. 'It's a lovely day for it, anyway,' he said, moving into grown-up rubbish, and then asked her how her exams had gone, he'd heard she was doing her GCSEs.

'Oh – fine, thanks,' said Kate, and then Jocasta told her to come over to the house, and that the Hartleys would probably be quite grateful if she wouldn't mind passing plates of food round. It seemed quite odd to Kate that something so emotional and sad should have turned into a sort of party, with people shouting, 'nice to see you', and, 'how are the children?' at each other, but she was glad to have something to do. She'd been a bit worried that people might be wondering what on earth she was doing there and who she was, but mostly they didn't, just smiled vaguely at her and took their vol au vents or whatever, and if they did ask, she simply said she had met Martha through her best friend, which was what Jocasta had told her to say. She still felt totally dazed, and hoped they wouldn't have to stay too long; she was dreading she might have to meet Mr and Mrs Hartley.

The Asian family were standing alone, looking lost; she went over to them with her vol au vents, but they shook their heads.

'And how do you fit into this gathering?' the man said and she made her small speech and asked, because she was genuinely curious, how they had known Miss Hartley, as she called her. Martha felt a bit over-familiar, somehow.

'Oh, she was so extremely good to my wife,' said the man. 'She has died now, but she worked for Miss Hartley, cleaning her office, and she was always so kind, took such an interest in Jasmin here, my daughter, and her studies, found books from her own collection that would help her. And also she visited my wife when she was in hospital, and fought a battle with the authorities for her, tried to get her moved into another ward – she really was the most kind person.'

Kate smiled and moved on with her plates, feeling more confused and upset than ever.

Jocasta appeared at her side and said: 'I think we'll leave in about ten minutes, Kate. I'm sure you won't mind and we're not really needed here. I'd just like to say hello to the Hartleys and then we'll slip off.'

At this point she heard someone saying: 'You must be Kate. I'm Ed, hi!' and she turned round and felt she must be looking at a picture in a magazine or something. It was the gorgeous bloke in the church, he was blond and quite tall, with the most amazing smile, and although he was wearing a suit, it wasn't an old person's suit, it was really cool; very, very dark navy, lined in dark green, with a lighter blue shirt, the colour of his eyes. Kate's knees felt quite weak; she wished to God she wasn't wearing these mumsy clothes.

'Hi,' she said, smiling at him, taking the hand he offered, wondering wildly who he was and how he fitted into the day's proceedings; and then he said, 'It's very nice to meet you, Kate. I'm Martha's – friend. Well, I was. It's lovely of you to come.'

Of course: she remembered now, Jocasta had told her about him, as she had about lots of people on the way down, and of course she knew Martha's boyfriend would be there, but she hadn't expected he'd be like this, more like the one from New York, probably, who'd read the lesson. Not young and looking like something out of a Calvin Klein Eternity ad. How had Martha done that? Got a bloke as fit as this one? He must be at least ten years younger than her. Weird.

It felt a bit weird altogether, talking to him; presumably he must know who she was. Kate felt more and more as if she had walked into some strange film.

'Oh, hi, Ed. Lovely to see you.' It was Jocasta; she kissed him and gave him a hug. 'I see you've met Kate.'

'I have indeed. Thank you for coming, Jocasta, it's really good to have you all here.'

'It's the least we can do,' said Jocasta, 'and I'm just sorry Gideon hasn't made it – he's been held up in Canada. I won't ask you how you're feeling, because it must be perfectly dreadful, but I'm going to call you later in the week, and get you round for supper with Clio and me. Only if you can't face it, just say so, we'll totally understand.'

'I think I'd like that,' he said, 'and thank you, but I'm not sure how next week will be, how I'll be feeling – '

'You can decide an hour before,' said Jocasta, giving him another kiss, 'half an hour if you like, five minutes. Now, if you don't mind, we're going to go. Nick had a puncture on the way down and he's got to get back to work, and we've promised to follow him up to London, make sure another one doesn't go. I've spoken to poor Mrs Hartley – she was completely dazed, obviously didn't have the slightest idea who I was.'

'No, she's in a bit of a state, poor lady. Anyway, I must go. Thank you again. You two could be sisters,' he said suddenly, adding, 'Sorry, Kate. Don't suppose that's exactly a compliment to you.'

'Well, it is to me,' said Jocasta, 'so that's fine. And we're always being told that. Aren't we, Kate? It's only our hair.'

They set off in convoy; Clio said she wasn't feeling too good and was happy to leave. She did look a bit rough, Jocasta thought, exhausted and very pale. Well, it had been a hell of a day. She didn't feel great herself; she wondered when Gideon would be home. She really didn't feel up to the Big Welcome.

As they reached London, Nick drove off with a wave of his hand, and Josh got into their car. Kate moved into the back; she had been asleep and said she had a headache.

'Poor old you. Are you all right?'

'Yes, I'm fine. Just a bit – confused. But I don't want to talk about it. I'm glad I went, though.'

'Have you decided what you're going to do about your contract?' said Jocasta.

'No, I can't. I know everyone thinks I'm stupid when it's so much money, but I sort of agree with Mum. It's too much; in a way, it's scary.'

'What's this?' said Josh.

'She's been offered a fortune to model some make-up range,' said Jocasta.

'What sort of a fortune?'

'Lots of noughts,' said Jocasta briefly, giving him a look.

'So why don't you want to do it, Kate?'

'I'm not even sure I don't want to, but I feel like I'm signing my life away.'

'Take it from me, young Kate,' said Josh, swivelling round to look at her, 'if you're not sure, don't do it. No point doing some job you don't like, just for the money. I should know. I've spent my life doing exactly that. Ask yourself if you'd do it for nothing. Or very little. That's the test.'

Kate was silent for a while, then she said: 'I don't think I would. I mean, it's so boring. Everyone thinks it's so glamorous and it's not. I can't stand all this, where did you get your Botox done, rubbish. And acting like your jeans were a religion.'

'What?' said Josh, laughing.

Kate told him about Rufus and Jed, and their whispering, and Crew as well: 'They're completely insane. Not like lovely Marc, who did the shoot for the *Sketch*,' she added to Jocasta. 'He's really quite normal. Although in that business, abnormal is normal.'

'You ought to be a writer,' said Josh, 'like my sister. You have a great turn of phrase.'

'I did think of it for a while,' said Kate, sounding at least forty-five, 'but I don't think it's for me. I tell you what I would like – I'd like to be a photographer. That seems much more fun to me. You're really doing something then, aren't you? Making something, I mean, not just sitting there.'

'How extraordinary,' said Josh. 'I've often said that's what I'd like to do, given my time over again. Remember all those pictures I brought back from Thailand, Jocasta? Some of them were really quite good; I was looking at them the other day.'

'I don't, actually,' said Jocasta.

'Well, anyway, Kate, I think you've really hit on a good career there. Much better than modelling. Tell you what; I've got a whole drawerful of pretty good cameras I never use. Bit antique, some of them, but they're what the real boys use, none of your automatic nonsense.'

Bought by our father, thought Jocasta tartly, when it was that month's fad.

'I could give you one if you like, get you going,' Josh was saying. 'Give you a couple of lessons, even.'

'Josh,' said Jocasta warningly. She gave him an icy look. She could see he was very taken with Kate. Silly bugger. How Beatrice stood it, she couldn't imagine.

* * *

600

On the way back to London, Janet Frean was repeatedly and violently sick; when she got home, she locked herself in her bedroom and refused to come out. Bob found it hard to care; she'd done what she needed to do, attended the funeral of the woman she must realise she had – possibly – helped to kill and she now had to face her demons. He made her a cup of tea, called to her that it was outside her door and went to see his children.

Clio didn't know what to do. She could be wrong. Josh might never have slept with Martha and it was hardly something you could ask. She had no proof at all. Jocasta always said that the only real similarity between her and Kate was their hair. And how awful if she was wrong: if she accused him of something he was totally innocent of. And even if he weren't, what good would it do now if it came out? It would create dreadful problems in his marriage and he had enough of those. Maybe she should just remain silent. But – she knew, as surely as she knew anything, that she wasn't wrong. There was more to that likeness than hair; it was a smile, a way of standing, and an overall impression. And it all added up. If it had been some bloke Martha had just met travelling, she would have told them. She had said – what had been her exact words? 'I couldn't possibly have told him. Not possibly.'

That fitted too: she couldn't possibly, not then. It would have been too late then, he could have been anywhere and what could he have done? And later – well, Clio could see why not later. The humiliation, the admission of incompetence, running after the glamorous Josh, who wouldn't want her, who would be horrified, saying, 'Do something, I'm about to have your baby.' Or even, 'I've had your baby.' Some girls would do that, wouldn't see it as a humiliation, but as a bringing to book, a demand for justice. Not Martha.

She fell into a feverish sleep, woke to find the car stopped and Fergus smiling down at her.

'Whatever's going on in your pretty little head? You've been muttering all kinds of nonsense.'

'I – had a bad dream,' she said, managing to smile at him. 'Sorry. Can we stop and have a cup of tea? I've got an awful headache.'

* * *

Gideon Keeble arrived home at Kensington Palace Gardens at seven that evening, exhausted and on the edge of extreme bad temper. He had hoped to find Jocasta waiting for him with dinner organised; he found instead an empty house and a note to Mrs Hutching.

'Mrs Hutching, don't worry about dinner, going out. See you in the morning. JFK.'

She was very tickled with her new initials, he thought, momentarily less irritated.

He went into his study, expecting to find a note from Jocasta: there was none. Nor in their bedroom, nor in his dressing room. He called her mobile; it was on message. He checked his own: there were none.

It is virtually impossible for extremely – or even moderately – rich people not to expect to get what they want, whenever they want it. They may imagine themselves reasonable, patient, easy; the fact is that the various people who are dependent upon them work to make their lives so agreeable that they do not have to become unreasonable, or impatient, or difficult. This process is in direct proportion to how rich they are; and Gideon Keeble was extremely rich. As nobody that night was making the slightest effort to make his life agreeable, he lost his temper very thoroughly.

He didn't lose it immediately. He called Mrs Hutching down from her flat and asked, very nicely, for a light supper; he didn't ask her if she knew where Jocasta was, that would have been humiliating. And then he went into his study to do some work and wait for her. She surely wouldn't be long; she surely would call him.

She was a very long time; and she didn't call. And her phone remained on message.

He didn't leave one for her; that too, he felt, was undignified.

At ten o'clock he went, exhausted, to bed; at eleven-thirty he heard a taxi throbbing outside. He heard her come in, heard her pause – while presumably Mrs Hutching told her he was back – heard her running upstairs. She came in; she was flushed, had obviously had more than a glass of wine. She smiled at him uncertainly.

'Hi.'

She bent down, gave him a kiss; he could smell the wine on her breath. It wasn't very attractive.

'Hello, Jocasta. And where have you been?'

He managed to sound playful, good-natured, even; he saw her relax.

'Just – having dinner.'

'With –?'

'With friends.'

'Oh, yes. Which friends? Nicholas Marshall, for one?'

'For one, yes.'

'Any others?'

'Of course others. Gideon, I've had a shitty day, you weren't here, I didn't want to be at home on my own – '

'Which other friends?'

'People from the old days, on the paper. You wouldn't know them. What is this, some kind of inquisition?'

'I think I have a right to know who you've been with.'

'Oh, really? A right? That sounds very old-fashioned to me.'

'It does? I happen to think that as your husband I do have rights. Old-fashioned, yes. Reasonable – again yes. You seem to take a different view of these things.'

'Oh, Gideon, stop it.' She sounded exhausted; she sat down on the bed. The flush had faded now and she looked very tired. 'I've had such an awful day. You can't think how sad it all was, the funeral and everything – '

'I'm sure. I, too, have had an awful day. Trying to get on flights, changing at absurd places like Munich, all to get home sooner to you. And what do I find? An empty house, no note, nothing arranged for me and you out with your previous lover – '

'Gideon, don't. Just don't.'

'Don't what?'

'Don't do that. It's so dangerous.'

'What is?'

'Implying that I'm back with Nick.'

'And that's not dangerous, I suppose? Your being with him? As you were the other day – '

'I – what?'

603

'You were with him on Sunday morning. I asked you where you were and you said you were at his flat.'

'Gideon, for fuck's sake, I wasn't at his flat.'

'Don't swear at me.'

'Well, it's ridiculous. I was dreadfully upset; I needed to be with someone. We went to a coffee place.'

'Oh yes. And you were with him this evening, by your own admission.'

'Yes, I was with him. And about ten other people. At a bar in Soho. Perhaps you'd like me to call them, get witnesses –'

'Oh, get out of here,' he said, suddenly switching off the light, turning away from her. 'Just get out. I'm extremely tired, I need some rest.'

Jocasta got out.

'I just can't cope with this,' she said tearfully to Clio next morning on the phone. 'I'm beginning to think I've made a terrible mistake.'

Clio had a full surgery; she couldn't really give this the attention it deserved. Just the same it seemed too absurd to ignore.

'Jocasta, don't be ridiculous, you've told me so often that you love him, that you never knew what love meant before, that –'

'Yes, and it's true. I do love him. So, so much. But I don't see how I can live with him, be his wife. It's a horrible, awful, pointless life and I hate it.'

'But Jocasta, don't you think that's a bit – childish?'

'Oh, don't you start on that one. It's Gideon's line.'

Clio felt a wave of sympathy for Gideon.

'Look, Jocasta, I can't talk now. I've got patients waiting. I'll call you later. Try to – to calm down. I'm sure you'll feel differently later.'

'I'm perfectly calm!' Jocasta's voice was rising now. 'And I won't feel differently. I wish I'd never told you if you're going to start talking crap like that.'

She slammed the phone down. Almost gratefully, Clio pressed the buzzer for her next patient.

Five minutes later, Jocasta tried to ring her back. The

receptionist said Dr Scott was with a patient and that she'd get her to call back later. Jocasta burst into tears.

Gideon had left for work at seven, without even saying goodbye. She felt dreadfully alone, and shocked with herself at being so unpleasant to Clio of all people. What was happening to her? What was she turning into? Some kind of spoilt bitch, who had too little to do. Like the three other Mrs Keebles, perhaps. God, it was difficult being married. If she'd realised . . .

The phone rang; she snatched it up. Clio. Thank goodness.

'Clio, I'm so –'

But it wasn't Clio, it was Gideon.

'I'm sorry, my darling,' he said, 'I'm so, so sorry. I behaved like a brat.'

'I was just thinking the same,' said Jocasta, a laugh rising through her tears, 'about me, I mean.'

'No, no, you didn't. You'd had a dreadful day and I should have been more understanding. Is there anything I can do to make you love me again?'

'Well –'

'How about lunch?'

'Lunch?' Was that the best he could do?

'Yes. I thought we might go to the Crillon.'

'The Crillon? Gideon, that's in Paris!'

'I do know that.'

'But – it's almost ten o'clock.'

'I know that too. If you can get over to City Airport, I'll meet you there in an hour. Table's booked for one. Please say you'll come.'

'I – might,' said Jocasta.

It was a very good lunch; at the end of it, she leant across the table and kissed him.

'Thank you. That was – gorgeous.'

'Good. So, am I forgiven?'

'Totally. Am I?'

'Nothing to forgive. Now – little walk across the Place de la Concorde? Or a little lie down? You choose.'

'Lying down sounds nicer. But – where?'

'I have a suite booked,' he said. 'If you wouldn't think that too corny.'

'I love corn.' Suddenly she wanted him terribly. She stood up, took his hand. 'Come on, let's go.'

Later, she lay smiling at him, thinking how much she loved him, wondering at the raging anger she had felt only a few hours earlier. How could that happen, how could this simple biological event, this fusion of bodies, heal hurt, soothe anger, restore tenderness?

'Clever old thing, isn't she?' he said. 'Mother Nature.'

'That's just what I was thinking. Sort of.'

'Well, there you are. Like-minded or what? As you would say.' He bent and kissed her breasts, then said, 'So – a new beginning, Mrs Keeble?'

'A new beginning. And I will try to be better.'

'I don't think,' he said, 'that you could be better, in one regard, at least.'

And kissed her again.

At half past eleven that night, an ambulance arrived outside the Frean house. Janet had taken an overdose: whether or not it was too late to save her, nobody could say.

But Bob, pacing up and down the hospital corridor an hour later, as they administered various drugs and antidotes, thought that he really should have foreseen the possibility of it, and felt an appalling remorse. In spite of everything.

Chapter 40

A dreadful rage was building up in Grace. She was angry with everyone: with her husband, who appeared to be coping with the loss of Martha far better than she was, by burying himself in his work; with Anne, who was still alive, while Martha was dead, and who kept telling her she must try to concentrate on the positive things in her life; with her son, who was not only still alive, but also had a new girlfriend, who was a therapist of all things, and kept offering her skills to Grace – who most assuredly didn't want them.

She was also very angry with everyone in the parish who kept on and on asking with infinite kindness how she was, when they could perfectly well see how she was, which was in a dreadful state of misery; with the GP who had called round and suggested she perhaps considered some medication for her insomnia, when the only good which could come of that, as far as Grace could see, was that if she took them all at once, then her misery would be well and truly over. She managed to say that, so the doctor would understand; he patted her hand and told her she was too good and too sensible to even consider such a thing. That made her angry, too.

She was terribly angry with God, for allowing such a thing to happen, and also because He appeared to be withholding from her any of the comfort He was clearly showering down upon her husband.

She was angry, too, with Ed, for not telling them he was in love with Martha, and denying them the happiness it would have brought, however briefly.

And worst of all, she was angry with Martha: that she could

have been so reckless, so stupid, driving when she was tired, driving that ridiculous car which went so much too fast, trying to do so much with her life, spreading herself so much too thin. And for leaving nothing of herself behind, nothing except this awful, bleeding blank.

Every day she got angrier.

'My darling, could we have a little talk?'

Jocasta was lying in bed, watching Gideon while he dressed. This was increasingly a pattern; she had nothing to get up for, so she would wait until he had gone, and then lie in the bath for anything up to an hour, making non-plans, as she thought of them, to fill her day. It was actually quite nice, the watching; she would comment on his clothes, he would consult her on which tie he should wear, and tell her what he was doing for the rest of the day. On a good morning he would suggest what they might do in the evening, or even (occasionally) for lunch; he had been in London now for over a week and said he had at least another two, before a big trip to the States she was to accompany him on. Life was rather more as she had imagined it.

'Goodness, Gideon,' she said, 'when my father said things like that, it meant I was in serious trouble.'

He smiled at her, came over to kiss her.

'Not serious.'

'Unserious trouble?'

'Not trouble at all. But – '

Jocasta was beginning to feel irritated.

'Gideon, do come to the point.'

'Sorry. Are you all right, darling? You look very tired.'

'I'm not tired at all, thank you. I'm fine.'

'You said you had a headache last night.'

'I did. But it's gone now.'

'What d'you think that was? Actually, I had a bit of a headache too, maybe it was that wine, I thought it tasted a bit off.'

He took his health rather seriously; Jocasta tried to tell herself that anyone who'd nearly died of a major heart attack would do. She still found it irritating.

'It might have been,' she said, 'I didn't notice.' She sighed. 'Gideon, what did you want to talk about?'

'I know,' he said, a note of triumph in his voice, 'you're pre-menstrual.'

'Oh Gideon, for God's sake! What is this, the ladies' changing room? I don't get pre-menstrual, I don't have my period, I don't have a headache, and I just want to get on with this conversation. OK?'

'All right. Sorry. Right. It goes like this. I want to give a couple of big dinner parties within the next month. In London. Mostly business, but a few friends. Could you liaise with Sarah, and then get planning with Mrs Hutching on menus and so on. I'll do the guest lists, obviously – '

'I'm sorry?'

'I said I'll do the guest lists.'

'Why?'

'Why? Well, I just told you, these are mostly business affairs. I have to do them.'

'You said a few friends.'

'Yes, I know, but I meant – ' He stopped.

'You meant *your* friends?'

'Well – yes. But I very much hope they will become our friends.'

'What's wrong with mine?'

'Jocasta, please. There's nothing wrong with them, but most of your friends wouldn't fit in with a large, rather serious dinner party with a lot of middle-aged people.'

'And – would I?'

He looked at her rather awkwardly. 'Well, you're different, aren't you? I mean you're my wife.'

'So you're stuck with me at this rather serious dinner party, which I won't fit in with? Thanks!'

'You're being difficult.'

'I am not being difficult. And I would venture to suggest that if you want to have a dinner party, which I won't enjoy, you should have it at a restaurant. Or in your boardroom. Or I'll go out.'

'Oh, for God's sake,' he said, irritable himself, now. 'I think we'd better stop this. If you're not prepared even to organise a dinner party for me – '

'Even? What do you mean even?'

609

'Well, let's say that so far, you haven't exactly troubled yourself with domesticity, have you?'

'And what's that supposed to mean?'

'Mrs Hutching says when she tries to discuss menus, or the flowers, or even general arrangements, where we might be when and so on, you just tell her to go ahead and do what she thinks best.'

'That's not true. I said I liked to do the flowers.'

'Yes, she did say that. But that you appeared to have forgotten lately.'

'Oh, for God's sake! Anyway, what's wrong with her doing it all? She's much better at it than I am.'

'That's hardly the point. I would like *you* to be good at it, to run our lives. In the way you want. Obviously.'

'Gideon, there's no question of running our lives in the way I want. We live your lives. In your houses, with your staff, in your way. I don't come into it at all, except trying to fit in.'

'Well, as far as I can see, very little trying is going on. Actually. Oh, forget it. I'll speak to Mrs Hutching myself.'

'Yes, and give me the dates and I'll make sure to be out.'

He looked at her with intense dislike and slammed the bedroom door without saying another word.

She lay in her long bath, wondering what non-plans she could make for the day, feeling miserable. What was she supposed to be, some kind of secondary housekeeper? She didn't know anything about that sort of thing, menus, guest lists, table linen, not even flowers, not really. It wasn't what she was about.

So – what was she about? She really didn't know any more. She got out of the bath, wrapped herself in her bathrobe and, greatly to her surprise, she started to cry. What was the matter with her? Maybe she was pre-menstrual. She probably was. Yes, that was it. She didn't often get pre-menstrual, but when she did, it was awful. Only she'd been feeling like this for weeks. So it wasn't that. It wasn't at all. It was because she felt so useless. So lost.

She got dressed, went down to the kitchen, made herself some coffee and drank it quickly, before Mrs Hutching could appear and offer her breakfast, ask her if she'd be in for lunch – God, it was awful, not living in your own house – and almost ran out of the front door.

As she stood waiting for a cab, Nick called her. She was so pleased to hear from him, she burst into tears again.

'What on earth's the matter?'

'Oh – nothing. Just me. Sorry. Rewind, yes, Nick, nice to hear from you, how are you?'

'I'm fine,' he said, 'thanks. I rang you because I had a clearout at the weekend and I found a few of your things. Wasn't sure what to do about them.'

'What sort of things?' She felt rather bleak suddenly, seeing his bright white flat, with its tall ceilings, looking over the Heath, where she had spent so much time over the past few years.

'Oh – you know. Jewellery mostly. One of your innumerable watches, a baby G. A gold bracelet, the one your dad gave you – '

'Oh yes.' She remembered that episode: her birthday, her father had cancelled a dinner with her and sent it instead, clearly horribly expensive, she had sat looking at it and crying and Nick had tried to comfort her, and they had ended up in bed.

'And a few bits of rather expensive-looking lingerie – '

She thought he might have wanted to keep that, as a memento. The tears started again.

'Just throw it in the bin, why don't you?' she said and switched off her phone abruptly. It rang again.

'Jocasta, is something wrong? Want to talk? I'm free for lunch.'

'Well . . .' It was so tempting. So terribly tempting. And if Gideon saw her as little better than a glorified housekeeper, then why not? Why the fuck not?

'Yes, all right,' she said finally, 'that'd be lovely.'

Bob Frean called Jack Kirkland.

'Sorry, Jack, you'll have to manage without your female lead for a while.'

'Oh really? Is she not well?'

'I'm afraid she's very unwell indeed,' said Bob. 'She's had a complete breakdown. She's in the Priory.'

'What? I don't believe it. She's so strong, tougher than any of us. What a dreadful thing, Bob, I'm so sorry. What on earth brought that on?'

'Life, I think,' said Bob and put the phone down.

Helen got more worried about Kate every day. She simply wasn't herself. She was quiet, withdrawn, touchy – well, that, at least, was like herself. She didn't want to go out, she said, she didn't want to do anything.

'I just feel – horrible,' she said to her mother. 'I can't explain why. I suppose it's like I said, I had her for a few days and now I've lost her – forever. And I don't know any more about her than I did. Or why she did it, or anything. It's worse than before. At least then I had a chance of finding her.'

Helen said it wasn't really worse than before, surely, and that at least Kate knew who her mother had been, and a bit about her; Kate clearly found this immensely irritating.

'You don't understand,' she said, 'nobody could.'

She had told Fergus she still couldn't decide about Smith and that she might not want to model at all, but do a photography course instead. Jim was investigating this; he felt it was something at least he could do for her. He felt even more helpless than Helen; Kate wouldn't talk to him at all, she was polite and little more.

Nat had also been banished. 'There doesn't seem to be much point seeing him,' she said to Sarah. 'I don't seem to actually love him, and he loves me, so it's just not fair on him.'

Sarah said if that was really the case, could she tell Bernie; Kate said what for and Sarah said Bernie still fancied Nat.

'Well, he doesn't fancy her,' said Kate, 'and no, you can't.'

'You're just a bitch in the manger,' said Sarah. 'You don't want him, but you don't want anyone else having him. Classic!'

'Oh, piss off!' said Kate.

'I just feel – lost,' said Jocasta, stirring her fork round and round her rocket salad. They were in Rumours, in Covent Garden, not usually a stamping ground for retailing billionaires. 'Anyway, I don't care,' she had said, when Nick proposed the venue, 'I don't care if he sees me with you or not.'

Nick was unable to decide whether this meant that she saw him as someone of very little importance, or Gideon as someone worthy of very little consideration; he hoped the latter.

'In what way lost?'

'Oh – I don't know. I feel sort of incompetent. As if I've got some terrific part in a film and the cameras are turning and I don't know my lines. Or what to do, even.'

'You could try to learn them,' he said carefully.

'Nick, I can't. Anyway, I don't want to.'

'Well, those are rather different things. Wouldn't you say?'

'No.'

'Jocasta, they are. You can, perfectly well. Not wanting to is the problem.'

'But I don't know how to be a good wife. I don't know about running houses and giving grand dinner parties and telling staff what to do. It's not me.'

'Well, sweetie – ' the endearment slipped out, 'it's got to be you, don't you think?'

'Why?'

'Jocasta, you've married someone who wants you to do those things. He's a high-maintenance husband, he needs a highly maintaining wife.'

'Well, he's got the wrong one.'

'Jocasta, you've married him, for God's sake!'

He sounded angry; she looked at him. He was angry.

'Look,' he said, 'I don't think this is a very healthy conversation. Do you?'

'Why not?'

'Jocasta, if you don't know why not, you are truly stupid. It isn't healthy and it isn't very kind.'

'Who isn't it kind to?'

'To me, for crying out loud,' he said and there was a note in his voice she had hardly ever heard before. 'Can't you see how hideous it is for me to sit here, listening to you wailing about your marriage and what a mistake it seems to be, when I still – ' he stopped – 'still care about you? Just grow up, Jocasta. For God's sake. Try thinking about someone other than yourself for a few minutes, why don't you?'

He left the table, settled the bill at the front desk and left without another word.

When Gideon got home that evening, an immense bunch of flowers in his arms, Jocasta was sitting in the kitchen with Mrs

Hutching, a sheaf of menus fanned out between them. She got up and went into his arms, kissed him fondly.

'I'm so, so sorry about this morning,' she said.

'Me too. So very, very sorry.'

Mrs Hutching gathered up her menus and hurried upstairs.

Kate kept thinking about the Hartleys. Her grandparents. Of course they didn't know they were her grandparents, but they were. And they had seemed incredibly nice. She felt so sorry for them. It must be awful, knowing your own child had died. She wondered if there was anything she could do, to make them feel better. Certainly not telling them who she was. But she could write a note to them, say she hoped they were feeling a little better, saying how lovely the service had been, and – goodness knows what else.

She consulted her mother; Helen said she thought that was a lovely idea. 'The shortest note would do, I'm sure they'll be very touched.'

'I'll do it then. Would you read it, make sure it's all right?'

When she'd done that, she thought, she must ring Fergus.

'Hi, Fergus, it's Kate.'

'Hello, Kate my darling. How are you?'

He managed to sound a great deal more cheerful than he felt; he'd had a very bad morning; a client he'd thought pretty much in the bag, a footballer accused of roasting, had gone to Max Clifford instead. True, he had that cute little singer who was in dispute with his dad over his earnings, but that wasn't going to pay many bills. Wouldn't even pay the rent for this place, never mind a mortgage for the riverside apartment in Putney. And he was badly out of pocket with Kate; her earnings so far were non-existent and although Gideon had offered to pay the preliminary expenses, Fergus's professional pride wouldn't allow him to take him up on it until he had managed to show something for her.

'I'm fine. But I've made up my mind. I think. I don't want that contract.'

'Right.' Fergus tried to suppress the slug of disappointment. 'Right, I see. Are you sure?'

'Absolutely sure. I know it's a lot of money and everything, but – I just can't cope with the rest of it.'

'Like what, Kate?'

'Oh, you know, the publicity. It'll all start again, just as it's beginning to die down. Asking me about my mother and everything. And now I know – well, I can face it even less. Sorry.'

'That's all right, I understand.'

'Anyway, I don't really like it. In fact I hate it.'

'What, the modelling?'

'Well – yes. The cosmetic stuff anyway. It's so, like, totally boring. And I hate the people, they're just crap. Fashion's better, I could still do that.'

'Yes?' Well, that was something, he supposed. A few hundreds commission, instead of a few hundred thousands, but –

'Yes, I think so. Although not yet.'

'Kate, I'm sorry; you've got your first cover session with *Style* in a couple of weeks. You'll have to do that.'

'I don't think I can. I'm sorry, Fergus, I just feel so down.'

Fergus counted to ten silently. This was a nightmare. Silly, arrogant little thing, imagining she could play games with these people, tossing a three-million-dollar contract down the drain as if it was a used Kleenex, saying she didn't think she could do a cover session for one of the country's leading magazines because she was feeling down. Who did she think she was? Naomi Campbell?

'Kate, my love, you really will have to do that. Everything's booked, they confirmed it this morning, make-up artist, hair, photographer, you can't – '

'Fergus, I told you. I can't. Just leave me alone! They'll have to find someone else. Sorry,' she added rather reluctantly.

He was staring out of the window, trying to pluck up the courage to ring *Style* and tell them, when Clio rang. He felt better at once.

'How are you?'

'Fine,' she said, 'really fine. Just calling about tonight. Is dinner still on?'

'I hope so. God, I hope so. I've got nothing left to look forward to.'

'What's happened?'

'Oh – Kate's being impossible. Totally impossible. She's refusing to sign the contract with the cosmetic people and now she won't even do the cover session with *Style*. It's all booked, it's too bad of her, it really is. Totally unprofessional.'

'Fergus, she's only sixteen. She can't be expected to – '

'At sixteen I'd been hard at work for over a year, learning not to let people down.'

Clio thought about this, as she often did. About Fergus's difficult childhood and the success he had made of his life against considerable odds. It had been a remarkable achievement, however much she might dislike the way in which he had done it.

'I'm sorry,' she said carefully, 'really sorry. Maybe Jocasta could talk to her about it; Kate seems to think the sun shines out of her every orifice. At least make her think really hard about what she's doing.'

'That's a good idea,' he said, his voice brightening. 'Oh, Clio, you're a star. I wish it were dinnertime now. I'm missing you dreadfully.'

'Fergus, it's only two days since we were together.'

'You have a heart of stone. That's forty-eight hours. How early could you meet me?'

'If you came down here, at about six o'clock.'

'I'm on my way.'

She was really totally happy with him, apart from what he did. He was sweet, kind, thoughtful. He was sitting outside the surgery when she came out that evening, with a ready-to-cook meal that he had bought on the way down; she sat watching him as he bustled about her kitchen, thinking how lucky she was to have found him.

She was a bit low herself; Mark had been very upset that she was leaving, and although he had been extremely nice about it, she could see he was annoyed. She could understand it; he had taken her back once after she had given in her notice, and now she was doing it again. She'd have been pretty annoyed herself – but it had taken the edge off the intense pleasure of getting the job. And then she had visited Mr Morris at The Laurels that morning and become very upset in the face of his helpless grief.

Fergus listened to her patiently while she ranted against the matron of The Laurels and her authoritarian approach to her patients, as she insisted on calling them – 'They're not patients, Fergus, they're just old people who need a little help' – and against the daughter, who had been too busy and too callous to find someone who could help them to remain at home. He told her the Morrises had been lucky to have her as a doctor – 'I don't think so, Fergus, I don't think so at all, and anyway, what could I do? Against that bloody system. It's a cumbersome load of crap, and – '

'Hey now,' he said, 'this is no language for a lady.'

She smiled at him through her tears.

'Sorry. But it makes me so angry. And what can I do?'

'I'm not sure. Launch an appeal; try to get a campaign going. Interest some politicians. See if one of those people in the Centre Forward party could help. It's the sort of thing politicians like, a cause that will make them appear noble and altruistic, rather than the self-seeking creatures they really are. I'll help you, if you like, draft something, maybe put out a press release.'

'Oh Fergus . . .' She looked at him very seriously. 'You are a complete mystery to me. I mean, you spend your days helping greedy, badly behaved people manipulate the media – '

'Hey,' he said, 'that's not entirely fair. Would you call Kate greedy and badly behaved?'

'No. Of course not. But she's a little bit unusual, as your clients go, you must admit. Anyway, in spite of all that, you have this heart of pure gold, beating away.'

'Maybe it needs polishing up, my heart of gold,' he said. 'Maybe I just need to be with the right person. I'll have a word with Gideon, see if he can arrange a little chat with someone. Now, would it seem too terribly insensitive of me to ask for another glass of that very delicious wine? And to let me put my arms round you for a moment or two?'

'Terribly,' said Clio, 'but it wasn't very sensitive of you to call me a silly bitch, was it? And look where that got us.'

She longed to tell him about Josh; somehow she couldn't. Maybe, in a day or two. There really was no hurry. And there were enough dramas to be going on with.

* * *

Jocasta was trying very hard now to be a good wife. She was too frightened not to be. She had to make this work, she just had to. It had been a moment of terrible truth, her lunch with Nick. She had seen with horrible clarity how he saw her: spoilt, self-centred, and totally immature. Yes, he had asked her to lunch, but he had been worried about her, thought she was properly unhappy; all she had done was bemoan her fate. Her rather luxurious fate.

And so she had planned the dinner parties, twenty people at each, twenty people she didn't know, and as well as agreeing the menus, had discussed flowers with Mrs Hutching, and even the music with Gideon. He was rather charmed by that idea; he said he didn't usually like background music but that it could be the emblem of the new era – the Jocasta era.

She had also made tentative suggestions about the decor of the house, starting in the kitchen. 'It's so old-fashioned, Gideon, and over the top. Doesn't do for a kitchen these days, I thought something totally minimal – '

'Any other room my darling, but not the kitchen. That's Mrs Hutching's, she hates change.'

She opened her mouth to argue, and then shut it again.

'OK. What about the garden room? I'd love to tack on a conservatory, and have a lovely tiled floor – '

'Sounds wonderful. Just go ahead and do it.'

She was a bit disappointed by his lack of interest and indeed in the fact that she was doing it at all, but she was determined to be mature and spent the next three days poring over *Interiors* and *Elle Decoration*. After that she rather lost interest.

She had also broached with him the subject of a house. 'Ours, not just yours. It would be lovely. I wondered about France, sort of Biarritz way. Or maybe America, the East Coast, Maine, somewhere like that.'

'Darling, I rather think we've got enough houses. But yes, if you think it'll make you happy, see what you can find. '

She called all the estate agents, and began to put together a portfolio to show Gideon. It felt a bit of a solitary task, but some of the houses were lovely, and it would be fun going to see them. The only problem was finding a space in his diary to do it. 'How about a year next January?' she said, exasperated, and he smiled at her.

'Sorry, darling. I did warn you, you've married a workaholic.'

She thought that he hadn't actually, but she didn't say so. She was learning to hold her tongue; it was against her nature and lowered her spirits.

She sat through a couple of dinner parties, too, trying to make conversation with people with whom she had nothing in common; the men had been all right, although clearly regarded her as a complete airhead, a bit of arm candy Gideon had been clever enough to acquire, but the women were horrendous, bored and boring, obsessed with their looks, their houses, their children, their sports coaches and personal trainers, and treated her as if she was some interesting but distinctly inferior species. They had even all gone upstairs without the men for an hour, 'To discuss detox and Botox,' Jocasta said to Clio next day. She thought of the old dinner parties she and Nick had given, easy sprawling affairs, the atmosphere funny and flirty, with everyone getting steadily and happily drunk and sometimes stoned as well. But she managed to tell Gideon she had enjoyed it; she was amazed when he seemed to believe her.

She had rung Nick to apologise for whining at him over lunch that day; he was friendly but brisk with her, said it was fine, and had all her things biked back to her with a perfectly nice but cool note. She felt rejected and miserable for days.

Anyway, she felt she was getting somewhere with learning to be Mrs Keeble. It was bound to take time, to settle into all this; she'd get used to it. Of course she would.

And then it happened.

It had started quite gently: he asked her to go on a business trip with him in a few weeks' time. It wouldn't be the most exciting event in the world, he said, it was a three-day weekend for captains of industry in Munich, but he thought she would manage to enjoy it and he would really benefit from her being there.

Jocasta tried to feel enthusiastic; she smiled and said it sounded very nice and she had never been to Munich and she was sure it would be fun, but she could hear her own voice being rather sure it wouldn't be fun, or even very nice. She wasn't feeling very well, nauseous and headachy, she said to Gideon, anxious he might think she simply didn't want to go on the trip.

619

'Darling, I'm sorry. I hope you're not pregnant.'

He often said that; his flippant disregard for her phobia upset her considerably. Nick had always been infinitely sweet about it: 'I don't understand it,' he had said when she first told him about it, 'but I can see what it does to you. And I'm really sorry.'

'Of course I'm not pregnant, Gideon,' she said.

'You sure?'

'I'm absolutely sure. I couldn't be surer actually, as of about six hours ago. All right?'

'All right. Sorry, darling, I didn't mean to annoy you.'

But he had; and she was already feeling raw and bruised when he said: 'Poor darling. Well, anyway, I think you'll enjoy this trip, there's quite a nice spousal programme, lots of shopping and sightseeing – '

'A what?'

'A spousal programme. Surely you know what that is.'

'Actually, Gideon, I don't. Sorry to appear so simple.'

'What a very sheltered life you've led. It's what wives do while the husbands do business.'

'What, all together? Me and the other wives? A load of old trouts?'

Gideon said they wouldn't all be old trouts, there were bound to be some younger wives for her to make friends with and –

'For young read forty-five,' said Jocasta, 'like at that dinner the other night, with perma tans and discussing their face lifts. Oh, Gideon, don't make me, please!'

'I'm not making you,' he said, his face developing the rigid look that she knew prefaced a loss of temper, 'I'm saying it would be very nice for me, and helpful too.'

She was silent. He sighed, then said: 'This marriage seems to be turning into a bit of a one-way street, Jocasta.'

'And what's that supposed to mean?'

'I mean it only goes the way you want. For God's sake, you don't have to do much – '

'Oh really? Not sort out your meals and your housekeepers and wait quietly until you deign to come home, and – '

'I don't consider that very onerous. Actually. In return for – '

'In return for what, Gideon? Do tell me.'

Her stomach hurt and she was tired; his words touched a raw nerve.

'In return for quite a lot. Like that – ' he indicated a pile of unopened bags in the corner, from Harvey Nichols, Chanel, Gucci – she was getting into her stride now, with the shopping, 'and flying lessons and cars – '

'Oh, so it's a credit and debit arrangement is it, our marriage? I hadn't realised that. Well, let me see, perhaps we should set a price on a few things. How much for two hours, just waiting for you to come home for dinner, a whole morning sorting out your wardrobe – '

'Jocasta, don't be childish!'

'Don't say that to me! It's a disgusting thing to say. Insulting, horrible.'

'This is a disgusting argument.'

'I'm sorry, but you started it. Talking about what I did in return for your fucking money. And talking about fucking, what about sex, Gideon, is there a price on that? How should we set that, how much does a high-class tart earn these days? I'm sure you know.'

'Can we just stop this horrible conversation?' he said, the white line appearing now round his mouth.

'No, I don't think we can. I want to get it sorted out. And little things like trips to Paris for lunch, is that set against my account as well?'

He came over to her, his face heavy with rage; she really thought he was going to hit her. She stood up quickly and knocked over her bag; a bundle of credit card slips fell out. He picked them up, started going through them.

'Don't do that, Gideon, please. They're mine, nothing to do with you.'

'Unfortunately, they almost certainly are. Look at this, thousands of pounds all on a lot of rubbish – '

'Well, I'm so sorry. I'll take it all back tomorrow.'

'And – lunch for two at the Caprice. Pretty pricey, even by their standards. Champagne, eighty pounds. Who did you share that with, Jocasta? Nicholas Marshall?'

'No,' she shouted, 'no, no, no. It was my mother, actually.'

'You took your mother to the Caprice and bought her vintage champagne? I find that very hard to believe.'

'Ask them,' she said, handing him her mobile. 'Go on, check up on me. Do you really think I'd take Nick to the Caprice if I were having an affair with him? What is this, Gideon? You're getting obsessed with this idea, why on earth should I be having an affair with anybody?'

'Let's just say your behaviour doesn't inspire confidence,' he said.

Jocasta went upstairs, and packed a rather minimal bag, containing none of the new clothes she had bought, and then went down again, and into his study.

'I'm leaving,' she said, 'and I'm not coming back. I can't. Not until you apologise.'

Gideon said that as far as he could see, he had absolutely nothing to apologise for, and told her to pull herself together and grow up. For the very first time, Jocasta felt a pang of sympathy for Aisling Carlingford. She went out and called a cab – for how could she take her new car? – and directed it to Clapham.

Chapter 41

She sat in her house, waiting for him to call for three days; he didn't. She couldn't ever remember feeling so lonely. Normally she would have rung friends, but she felt she couldn't. She couldn't face them. She kept thinking of the party, only a few weeks ago, of that excessively lavish display of the new Jocasta and her new life and how everyone would laugh at her, or at best feel sorry for her, and say how stupid and immature she had been, how anyone could see it wouldn't work, and how she had only left Nick in some fit of pique. She simply couldn't bear it.

More than anything, she dreaded Nick hearing about it, Nick who had berated her, told her to grow up, Nick who clearly despised her now. Whatever would he think of this latest demonstration of her childishness, as he would see it, walking out on a three-month-old marriage with cries of how horrid Gideon was to her and how it wasn't fair? For some reason, she minded the thought of that more than anything.

Finally she called Gideon and said she was sorry for her part in their quarrel and asked if they could meet and discuss things. It was agony; she had to have several drinks before she could get up the courage; but she did it. If anything meant she had grown up, she thought, that did.

He was in a meeting, he said, he'd call her back.

'A meeting? Gideon, it's eight o'clock in the evening.'

'I do know that. I said I'll call you back.'

That was all; not the slightest gesture in her direction, not even thank you. She had another two glasses of wine, telling herself his pride was hurt, she must make allowances; it was another hour before he rang her back.

He was going to be very late; he'd like to talk tomorrow. Would the evening be all right? He hoped she was all right.

Jocasta took a hugely deep breath and said yes, it would. 'Fine,' he said, 'let's have dinner. I'll call you.' And then added, 'Thank you for phoning.'

He rang off; and Jocasta, not sure whether to laugh or cry, had her revelation. Seeing things very clearly, as she always did when she was drunk, she suddenly knew what had happened to their marriage. She'd got it wrong. She was trying too hard. She was becoming someone different, not the person Gideon had fallen in love with. It was so obvious she laughed aloud.

The person she was turning into wouldn't have scaled the wall of Dungarven House in order to get into his sanctuary; nor would she have fallen over her own feet, dancing at the conference, nor told him how to treat his own daughter. All she had to do was become that Jocasta again and all would be well. Gideon would fall in love with her all over again. It was easy. And life would be fun again. She would fill the house with her friends, who Gideon did adore, he had told her so, and infiltrate them into his boring dinner parties, where everyone would laugh a lot, and get drunk; she might even tell him she wanted to go back to work.

She had a shower, pulled on her skimpiest top, some jeans and her highest heels and called a taxi to take her to Kensington Palace Gardens.

'It was horrible,' she said to Clio, her voice broken with tears next morning on the phone, 'so horrible. He was so cold and distant and he wouldn't talk to me, told me I was drunk, and he wouldn't even have sex with me. And I'd gone there, ready to try so hard, meet him three-quarters of the way, and I've been so good, Clio, you've no idea, organising his horrible dinner parties, even agreeing to be part of a spousal programme – did you ever hear of anything so absurd in this day and age? – I can't believe that lovely, gentle, kind person was actually such a monster. He's a time warp, Clio, he wants a Stepford wife.'

Clio didn't say that she had been part of several spousal programmes on Jeremy's behalf, nor did she say that if you married someone nearly twenty years older than you were, he

624

was almost certainly in a time warp anyway. She knew it was completely fruitless.

She tried to soothe and comfort Jocasta, told her she'd come and see her if she liked; Jocasta leapt on this and begged her to come to stay the night.

'I will come,' said Clio, 'but only if you promise to discuss it all sensibly.'

'Clio, I tried to do that with Gideon, and look where it got me! I tell you, he's beyond sense. But yes, I promise.'

Clio spent the evening with her, struggling to appear non-partisan, agreeing that yes, Gideon was very unreasonable, but that surely Jocasta could see he was having to make huge adjustments, too?

'He isn't, Clio, that's the whole point. He isn't making any adjustments at all.'

'I think he probably is,' said Clio, 'but maybe you can't see them. Any more than he can see yours. You were so in love with him, Jocasta, it can't have all just – gone.'

'Of course it hasn't! I still adore him, really. That's why I went round there last night, and he was just so – horrible.'

Clio could imagine the scene rather clearly: a tired and exasperated Gideon, confronted by an over-excited and emotional Jocasta, slightly the worse for drink, expecting him to be deeply touched and grateful for her visit. It wouldn't have been an ideal marriage-mending scenario.

'Well, look. I'll call again in the morning. No, I'll call now – it's only ten o'clock. And see what happens then. Then you'll at least know I've tried. And see what I'm up against.' She started to cry.

'Jocasta, don't call now. You've had a lot of wine and it'll be the same thing all over again.'

'You think I'm a lush, don't you?' said Jocasta with a watery smile.

'Of course not. But right now, the state you're in, you're not going to get anywhere at all. Now, let's go to bed.'

Later, when Jocasta was asleep, exhausted by emotion, Clio went outside and called Fergus.

'I'm sorry; I hoped I might be able to get away. It's awful, Fergus, I really think the whole thing is going to come crashing down. They are just so – unsuited, that's the real problem, their lives are completely incompatible. They might love each other, but it isn't enough.'

Fergus said he hoped that it was enough in their case and Clio said she thought they were sublimely suited, compared with Jocasta and Gideon, and that she'd see him the next evening.

In the morning Jocasta called Gideon on all three numbers: the house, his mobile and the office, saying she wanted to talk; an hour later there had been no response. After another hour, during which she raged and ranted, she left another message, saying that if he didn't call, he wouldn't hear from her again – ever. He called then and said how dared she threaten him; she put the phone down. After several hours, he rang again; didn't she think she owed him an apology? She said she'd made several and if he couldn't even acknowledge that, then there could be no future for them of any kind. Gideon said as far as he was concerned, that would be a happy release and that she should just go back to Nick, which was clearly what she wanted.

'I've just been a device, as far as I can see, to make him come to heel. Well, I don't like it, Jocasta. I'm not prepared to put up with it. Please don't call again.'

Jocasta phoned Clio, told her everything that had happened and said that was it, it was over.

'I couldn't have tried harder, Clio, I really couldn't. So – that's it. End of chapter. Thanks for everything and please don't tell anyone but – you can stop trying to help. Sorry.'

Clio still didn't take it terribly seriously; in fact she could hardly believe the absurdity of it; two adults, behaving like very small, extremely spoilt children. Giving up on a marriage after three months! It was ridiculous. It would blow over; they'd still be all right.

Fergus, when she told him, was more doubtful.

'I've seen Gideon through two of his divorces, you know. And once he thinks he's been wronged and he's dug those well-shod heels in, that's it. Trying to budge him is like taking an elbow to the Rock of Gibraltar.'

'Fergus, he hasn't been wronged, as you put it, she's done nothing except – well – except be Jocasta.'

'She's left home. He would see that as being wronged.'

'You mean he thinks she's been unfaithful? Because she hasn't.'

'No, no, not in the traditional sense. I'm sure all this stuff about Nick is just a smokescreen. What he minds is her not accommodating him, one hundred per cent. That's what he expects. It comes with the territory, Clio. Just be thankful that I'm not rich and powerful.'

Clio said she wouldn't mind in the least and said goodbye, feeling very sad. She thought of her struggles to preserve her own marriage: and then thought that it had done her little good and maybe it was better that Jocasta's was ended, anyway. Perhaps it had all been a fantasy, a display of self-indulgent, self-deluding emotion; how could it possibly survive more than a few weeks of real life?

Several days had now passed with Grace hardly eating at all; Peter observed a pattern forming. She would lie in bed until about eleven, then get up and do minimal housework, have a cup of tea while he ate a lunch that he had prepared, take a rest, serve a perfunctory supper, which she would pick at, and then retire to bed again. She hardly spoke to him; she had withdrawn into a solitary, silent world.

And pray for guidance as he might, Peter found himself just beginning to resent it.

'I wish you'd tell me what the matter is,' said Nat. 'I can't help you if you don't.'

He had phoned to ask Kate if she wanted to go out; she had said she thought it better not.

'And I can't tell you what the matter is, because I don't really know myself. Except that it's worse than ever . . .'

'What is?'

'Not knowing about my mum. At least before I'd found her, I could keep hoping.'

'Hoping for what?'

'Well, that she'd be the sort of person I'd like. Which she wasn't.'

627

'You don't know that, though, do you? You only met her once.'

'Yes, and that was a real success, wasn't it? And now she's gone, and I'll never know anything about her, why she did it – anything. No answers, Nat, just more and more questions. I'm sick of it!'

'So you don't even want to go to the cinema. There's that *Matrix* film, you'd like that.'

'No,' said Kate with a sigh, 'I don't think so, Nat. You go. And I've turned that contract down, and all. That's made me feel bad.'

'But you didn't want to do it.'

'I know that. But you think about turning down three million dollars. It's well scary.'

'I'd rather not,' said Nat with a shudder.

Kate went out into the garden; her mother was watering the roses.

'Hi, Mum.'

'Hello, love. You feeling any better?'

'Not really. I don't know what's the matter with me.'

'I do,' said Helen, 'you've had too much to cope with, that's what's the matter. What with – with finding out who your mother was, and then what happened to her, and all this worry about the contract. It's too much for anyone, let alone someone of your age.'

'Yeah, I suppose so. I feel so bad about Nat, too. He's been so good and I just can't be – well, very nice to him. I don't feel sort of – positive about anything.'

'I think that'll get better,' said Helen, 'I really do. I hope so.' She smiled at Kate. 'I miss him. Him and his dad.'

Kate smiled and put her arm round her mother's shoulders. 'Thanks, Mum. You've been great. Don't know what – shit, if that's Nat again, tell him I'm asleep or something! Why's he ringing the landline anyway? He's such a tosser sometimes.'

'Don't swear, dear,' said Helen rather feebly.

Nick was packing; the parliamentary summer recess had begun and he was going home for a couple of weeks to stay with his parents. He did it every year and could never see anything remotely odd about this: his friends went off scuba diving in the Maldives, or sailing off the coast of Ireland or trekking in the Himalayas. But Nick was perfectly content to help on the farm, lounge in the garden, hike across the Somerset hills, go on riding picnics with any small nieces and nephews who might be around, chat with his brothers and sisters and trounce everyone at Monopoly or backgammon after dinner. That was what he enjoyed, he said; why pretend he wanted to do anything else? In his holidaymaking, as in everything else, it was generally agreed, Nicholas Marshall was an absolute one-off.

He pulled down the battered old leather Gladstone bag from the shelf in his bedroom and tipped its contents out on the bed. This was always an interesting moment; he could never be bothered to finish unpacking when he got back from the trips the paper sent him on – usually to follow sundry politicians around the globe – and this evening's yield, following a trip to Washington in the early spring, was no exception. A couple of half-read paperbacks, three American newspapers, several packs of chewing gum – intended for Jocasta, to help her in her bi-annual struggle to give up smoking. A pair of socks – clean, thank God – and some gold cuff-links his father had given him. Thank God for that – he'd thought he'd lost them.

And a tape recorder, still in its box; a present from Jocasta for the trip. 'It's a nice modern one, that old clockwork one of yours is going to die on you one of these days, probably interviewing Bill Clinton,' she'd said. He'd never used it, preferred his old one, tried and true as it was; and although he'd thanked her for it, had never even used it.

It was a very nice one about a quarter of the size of his old one, with tiny tapes; one was labelled, 'Play me.' Curious, he slipped it into the machine and pressed play. Jocasta's voice came out.

'Hello, darling Nick. This is your devoted – well, fairly devoted – girlfriend, wishing you *bon voyage* and *bonne chance* and all that sort of thing. Have fun, but not too much and don't forget the Hershey bars.' (Of course he had.) 'Love you loads and loads and thank you for the best time last night. Lovely dinner, lovely everything; kiss kiss.'

Nick played it again, and then again. Thinking about her,

about how that tape was just like her, sweet and funny and loving. And thinking how much he had loved her. Still loved her. And that he really hadn't been very nice to her, last time they had met. Still less so when he'd sent her stuff back. It was terrible to think of all that love, evaporated into coldness and distance. Forever.

He picked up the phone and rang her.

Jocasta was lying in bed, feeling extremely sorry for herself. She had had a long and lonely weekend, and had sent out for a curry on Saturday evening; it had been the first meal she had eaten for days, and she gorged herself on it, washed it down with an entire bottle of rather rough red wine and finished off with some ice cream, over which she had poured a melted Mars bar, one of her favourite puddings. Whether it was the curry, the gorging, or the wine, she had been extremely ill much of Saturday night and most of Sunday; she was only just beginning to feel better. And still terribly lonely.

Nick's voice was, therefore, even more irresistible than she might have expected.

'Hi,' she said carefully, 'it's lovely to hear from you.'

'Hello, Jocasta. I – just thought I'd phone. Make sure you were all right.'

'I'm fine, yes. Thank you. That's very sweet of you.'

'You sound a bit – tired.'

'I had some bad curry on Saturday night.'

'I'm sorry. I wouldn't have thought curry of any kind would be on the menu for Mrs Gideon Keeble.'

'No, well – obviously it wouldn't normally. But he was – he was out, and I just fancied it. You know.'

'Oh I do. In the old days you'd have had ice cream and melted Mars bar to follow.'

'I did,' she said without thinking.

'Jocasta! The staff must have had the night off.'

'What? Oh – yes. Yes, they did. Um – where are you, Nick?'

'Just packing. To go down to Somerset for a couple of weeks. And I found the tape recorder you gave me. In my bag.'

'Oh – yes. I hoped it'd be useful. Obviously it hasn't, if it's still in your bag.'

'Oh, it has. Of course it has. And – I played the tape you put

630

in for me. Again, I mean. It was very sweet, and I just wanted to thank you.'

She could remember the tape. She had wanted him to have it, to have something of her. She could remember the whole thing, making the tape and sending it to him, because it had been his last trip abroad; just before the whole drama had begun, Centre Forward, Gideon, Kate, Martha. God, it had been a year. Less than a year. It felt like five. Anyway, she'd intended to give the recorder to him, and they'd gone out to dinner but she'd had too much wine, as usual, and got very emotional about him going away. Then they'd gone home and had the most mind-blowing sex, and she'd completely forgotten until next day, when she'd found it in her bag and biked it over to his office. First making her little recording.

'That's OK,' she said, smiling at the memory.

'So – where are you?'

'Oh – at home,' she said without thinking.

'What, at the Big House?'

'Of – of course.'

'And you're really all right?'

'Of course I'm all right, Nick. Why shouldn't I be?'

'Well, last time we met you weren't.'

'I know. But I took your words to heart – it was the best thing anyone ever said to me, and I'm a reformed character, learning to be a good wife and – '

'I'm pleased to have had such an excellent effect on you,' he said. 'And you're happy?'

'Terribly happy,' she said. 'Yes, thank you. Oh – hang on, Nick, there's someone at the door. Won't be a minute.'

Nick sat there waiting; he could hear the roar of traffic in the background, a police siren, hear her saying, 'Yes, that's for me, thank you, do I need to sign, fine, there you are,' heard the door slamming, heard her walking back across the wooden floor – the wooden floor? Roar of traffic? Answering the door herself?

'Jocasta, where are you?'

'I told you – '

'I know what you told me,' he said, 'but I don't recall traffic roaring up and down Kensington Palace Gardens. I would have thought staff would take in parcels. And I seem to remember a

631

lot of carpeting everywhere, and quite a distance from the front door to anywhere.'

There was a silence; then she said: 'I'm in Clapham, Nick. I've just – come to collect a few things.'

'So why lie to me about it?'

'Oh – I don't know. It seemed simpler.'

'Jocasta, what's happened? Please tell me.'

She wouldn't let him come to Clapham; it was too dangerous. She said she'd meet him in Queen Mary's Rose Garden in Regent's Park. It had been a favourite place of theirs, in the early days, halfway between both their houses. She looked at him sitting there on a bench, his long rangy body stretched out in the sunshine, his untidy brown hair flopping into his eyes, and thought how she missed him more every single day, and that even this was not exactly sensible. She sat down beside him; he gave her a kiss.

'That allowed?'

'Of course.' She smiled at him, and told him some of what had happened: very unemotionally.

'I'm really, really not complaining, Nick,' she said carefully, 'I can see a lot of it was – *is* – my fault. Most of it. But it just isn't working – just at the moment. It might still. I hope so.'

It was a lie: of course. She didn't think so at all. She just couldn't let him think it was over, that she was throwing herself at him, expecting to be taken back.

He was very sweet, very unreproachful.

He said if that was the case then he certainly wouldn't want to be the cause of it not working out; he said he would like always to be her friend, her best friend; he said he missed her terribly.

'I miss you too,' she said, brightly, 'so yes, let's be friends. Best friends.'

She stood up, smiled down at him, and had just managed to say, 'Well, I must be getting back then,' when she felt suddenly terribly dizzy and faint; she supposed it was the emotion, the tearing, mixed-up emotion, and also because she hadn't really eaten since she had left Gideon, apart from the thrown-up curry. She swayed visibly and was unable to walk calmly and steadily towards the entrance of the garden, as she had planned, but had to sit down again, her head between her knees.

And after that, it was only a very short – and logical – progress to his car and thence to his flat. He bought some food on the way, good, bland, binding food, he said firmly, eggs and bread and some Vichy water – 'full of minerals'. And then he cooked her an omelette, made her some toast, and – well, somehow after that, there they were, alone, in his flat, and try as she might, she couldn't remain unemotional and said she thought she should go. To which he suddenly said, quite sweetly, that she should never have left him, and that reminded her exactly why she had, and she got angry and told him.

'I loved you,' he said. 'So much.'

'And how was I to know that?'

'I kept telling you.'

'But you didn't show me,' she said. 'You never showed me.'

'Oh, this is ridiculous!' he said. 'I couldn't show you then, not how you wanted. I didn't know – ' He stopped.

'Didn't know what?' she asked, but he wouldn't answer her, just turned away and looked out of the window, and then suddenly it was the old situation starting again, and she couldn't bear it and she said, very wearily, 'I must go.'

'Yes, I think you should. I'll call you a cab. I'm – very sorry, Jocasta. For all of it. I hope it works out for you, I really do.'

'Thank you,' she said.

'Can I kiss you goodbye? Old times' sake?'

'Old times' sake . . .'

He bent to kiss her on the cheek; only somehow she moved and his mouth met hers instead. And – that was that, really.

How she did it, she afterwards never knew; one moment she was feeling frail, dizzy again, wretchedly confused, the next full of a powerful, surging energy and certainty. Nick was there in front of her, and she wanted him, and she had to have him; and he felt it – she saw him feel it – saw him smile, saw him acknowledge it, saw him certain, too.

They were naked before they reached the bedroom; she flung herself back onto the bed, holding out her arms to him, saying his name over and over again, hearing him saying hers, both of them talking fast, feverishly, 'Want you, missed you, love you,' and then his mouth was everywhere on her: her throat, her breasts, her stomach, her thighs, and hers on him, moving over

633

him, frantic for him, a great tangle of desire growing and growing in her, pushing at her. She lowered herself onto him, feeling him, moving on him, round him, melting, softening, sweetening for him, crying out as the sensations grew, sitting on him now, riding him, twisting, turning, journeying through some dark, wonderfully difficult place, reaching for the light at the end of it, feeling herself growing, clenching, climbing, struggling and then yes, yes, that was it, the height, the peak and she was there, shouting, yelling with triumph and then she felt him come too and she came again, in great warm, easy, spreading circles, until finally she fell into a deep, sweet peace.

'Now what?' he said, and his brown eyes, smiling into hers, were very sweet, very tender.

'God knows,' she said, and went suddenly and happily to sleep.

Clio had finally told Fergus about Josh. About Josh and Kate, that was. When she had finished he said: 'Of course. How clever of you. It was all so obvious, wasn't it? Staring in our faces all the time?'

'So obvious. But Fergus, I don't know what to do. I just don't. Whatever I do, I shall upset Josh – '

'I shouldn't worry too much about him, spoilt brat of a man that he is.'

'Fergus, that's not true! He may be spoilt, but he's very sweet really. But think what it would do to poor Beatrice. And their rather strained marriage.'

'Think indeed.'

'But then Kate *needs* to know. I really think it would help her now. She's so – bewildered, still. Martha dying has just made her worse. You said yourself she was very down. So – what do I do? I feel as if I'm holding a time bomb. And Jocasta about to – well, I don't know what she's about to do. She's in the most extraordinary state. Not miserable any more. Excited, almost, but incredibly emotional. Saying one minute she wants a divorce, the next she doesn't, not yet anyway.'

'There's nothing any of us can do about that,' he said, 'and you must just wait with this Josh business. It's been a secret for many years and it will keep a few more weeks. Although I agree, it would probably help Kate. But the moment will arrive. It always does.'

'I hope so,' said Clio miserably. 'I can't stand much more of this.'

Jocasta had said goodbye to Nick and gone home. He had not argued, had not tried to detain her. It was all rather unnerving.

The afternoon in his flat had acquired a dreamlike quality – there were even times when she thought she must have imagined it. Nick was being as evasive, as enraging as ever: if she had been looking for some great expression of commitment, she would have been sadly disappointed.

He simply told her he would always love her, that he would always be there for her, her very best friend as he had said: and then agreed that the best thing for both of them was for him to go home as planned and for her to go back to Gideon.

'Back to the Big House?'

'Of course. I'll send you a postcard,' he said. 'I know how much you like getting postcards.'

'Thank you,' she said.

'And I certainly don't see any need for foolhardy confessions, or anything like that.'

'Of course not,' she said, bravely bright. 'It was just a bit of – of lovely, naughty fun.'

But when she got home to Clapham, digested what had happened, thought over what he had said, she felt a disappointment so crushing she could hardly bear it.

She would have been comforted and totally astonished over the next few days, had she heard him talking endlessly to his favourite brother, telling him how much he still adored Jocasta, loved her more than ever, indeed, but that she had made it very plain she was still hoping to salvage her marriage and it would be dreadfully wrong of him to do anything to scupper that.

'Grace, dear, you must eat.' Peter Hartley looked at yet another untouched breakfast tray. He had had to leave her that morning, to do some parish visits, but he had prepared a tempting breakfast, muesli, yogurt, fruit – all the things she liked – in very small portions.

'I can't eat. It was very nice, but I just don't want it. Please, take it away.'

She pushed it aside fretfully, and lay down again, pulled the covers over her head.

Peter took it away.

Janet Frean wasn't eating very much either, but it was enough, as her doctor reported to Bob that morning. 'She doesn't need a lot of food, and don't worry, we're keeping a careful eye on it.' She was doing very well really, he said; she had had several sessions now with the resident psychiatrist, who had prescribed drug therapy, one-to-one sessions with him or one of the other psychiatrists, and possibly, as she began to feel better, group therapy.

'It often helps, to hear other people describing their own torments,' the psychiatrist said to Bob.

Bob told him he didn't think anyone could have had torments more dreadful and complex than Janet's; the psychiatrist patted him on the arm.

'There you would be very wrong,' he said.

'Has she told you anything yet?'

'A little. I don't have time to discuss it with you now, I'm afraid. But don't worry, she's a far from hopeless case. Believe me. Try not to worry too much.'

They didn't understand, Janet thought, lying back on her pillows after a particularly exhausting attack of rage on her therapist – she probably shouldn't have attacked her physically like that, but she had made Janet so angry, with her soothing rubbish – they absolutely didn't understand.

Nobody could. They all thought it was because of Martha Hartley, her breakdown. It wasn't at all. Of course she was sorry about Martha, and she did feel some degree of guilt; but not to the extent they all thought. Martha's secret would have come out, it was too big, too dangerous; she could not have hoped that the concentric circles she had built so carefully about her life to protect her would remain so; sooner or later another event would have exploded into them, pushing them together, forcing a revelation. And really, what happy ending could there possibly have been for her, once the revelation was out? Her career, her personal life, certainly her political life would have been fatally damaged. It could be argued Janet had done her a favour.

No, the reason she had wanted to end her own life was because everything she had ever worked for, hoped for – and taken such risks for – was now gone from her forever. Irretrievably gone. She could never have it back. And if the Centre Forward party survived, Jack would be its leader, probably with Chad as his chief henchman.

And if it did not, how could she go back to the Tories now? Even if there was another, better leader who would value her properly, Theresa May was the queen bee now; she had the job, or one of the jobs, Janet had longed for. She would always be one of the foot soldiers now, branded disloyal, unreliable, not to be trusted.

She thought about Chad and Eliot Griers, too, and how pathetic they were, in their male arrogance. Both of them thinking they could walk on water, in their different ways. Well, she had outsmarted them for a while, had begun the rot in their careers, diminished them in Kirkland's eyes. But it hadn't been enough; they could override her now, now that she was gone.

As for Kirkland, she had more respect for him; the best she could have hoped for while he was in power was the post of deputy leader. But that would almost have satisfied her. She would have even considered that winning: a uniquely high-profile position. Given that she was a woman. She had got rid of Martha. There was just Mary Norton to deal with now. And that should be quite easy; a few hints about her lesbian friends, and the electorate would start wavering. Then she'd find something else. Well, maybe all was not lost. Maybe. She could still come back. She could. She would . . .

'Mrs Frean is asleep,' her nurse reported to the psychiatrist, ten minutes later, 'the sedative has worked very well. I'll let you know if there's any change.'

Smith Cosmetics had thanked Fergus for his e-mail and said that they were now looking at other young girls. They said in the unlikely event of their not finding anyone else, they might contact him again, should Kate change her mind. They said there might be some leeway on the financial front, but they couldn't possibly give any undertakings on the publicity side of the contract, which he'd told them was what worried Kate most.

'As you must know, the press make their own decisions about what and what not to print.'

It was a very friendly and gracious response, Fergus thought, given all the time and money they had wasted on Kate, a testimony to how much they had wanted her. Still wanted her. It comforted him, just a bit. Things might change.

Fergus was the eternal optimist.

Clio spent Sunday with Jocasta; she found her still in an odd mood, on an emotional see-saw, over-excited one minute, tearful the next. She said she was just trying to work out what to do, that she might go back to work, might do something quite different – when pressed on what, she said vaguely that she'd thought of property, or maybe interior design. Clio had said what a good idea; there was no point arguing with her. She was beyond reason.

She had arrived still hoping she might help to effect a reconciliation, because she did still think that was what Jocasta wanted. She tried reason, humour, appeals to common sense. But it appeared to be a complete impasse. There had been another very ugly row the day before; Gideon had demanded that she meet him to try to have a reasonable discussion about what they were going to do next, and Jocasta had said it wasn't possible to have a reasonable discussion with a person so unreasonable that he was actually unstable; each confrontation was infinitely worse than the last, making that one seem comparatively pleasant, almost an exchange of views.

Right in the middle of telling Clio this, Jocasta burst into tears, and when Clio asked her if there was anything particularly the matter, said there was, but she couldn't talk about it. She was still drinking and smoking far too much, seemed unable to rest, or settle to anything for more than five minutes; all she wanted to do was talk interminably about Gideon and his shortcomings.

In the end, Clio gave up and said she must go home.

'Oh, please don't go,' said Jocasta. She had been talking to someone on the phone, sounding increasingly hostile. 'That was Josh. He's threatening to come round; he thinks he can make me see sense, as he puts it. Such a wonderful arbiter of relationships, such an example to us all.'

Clio sighed.

'Well – I've failed. Maybe he will be able to help.'

'Clio, he won't. And it's not a question of you failing. It's the marriage that's failed.'

'Jocasta, I must go. It's Monday tomorrow and I've got an early surgery. And I do want to see Fergus this evening before I go home.'

'You're so lucky to have such a normal, stable relationship,' said Jocasta wistfully. 'Oh, Clio, don't go! You can't leave me with Josh; he's going to upset me. Stay and go down in the morning, you always say how easy it is. Please, Clio, please.'

Clio hesitated.

'Well – no. No, Jocasta, I really don't think I can.'

'You can, you can't fail me, and you're such an angel, such a good friend.'

Clio wondered what on earth Jocasta would say or do if she knew the real reason for her reluctance to see Josh.

She stayed for his visit: of course. She could never quite work out how Jocasta managed to persuade people to do what she wanted, how she used that intense will of hers, a mixture of charm and absolute determination: she had a hunch that Gideon might have been subjected to the full force of it. Would he really have wanted to get married, after being with Jocasta – what – three weeks, if he hadn't? The fact was, she was absolutely irresistible.

And here Clio was, in Jocasta's sitting room, trying not to look too often at the photographs on the table of Jocasta and Josh as children, while Jocasta sat ordering a takeaway from the local Thai restaurant.

'I haven't eaten all weekend and suddenly I'm hungry. Hope it doesn't make me ill, like the curry did.'

Josh arrived, finally, almost an hour late, so that the Thai was half cold; it wasn't even very nice. Clio sat picking at it miserably, wishing Josh would stop telling Jocasta that she was being immature and unrealistic, wondering what the point of her being there could possibly be.

'The thing is, Jocasta,' he was saying now, 'marriage is almost

impossible, even when you're trying really hard. If you're not –
well, forget it.'

'That's *exactly* what I'm doing,' said Jocasta. 'Or was trying to
do, I mean.'

'But I thought you loved Gideon?'

'I do. Well, anyway, thought I did. But I can't live with him;
he's a monster, leading a monstrous life. I should have seen that
long ago.'

'But he's such a nice man,' said Josh. 'He's kind and generous
and he obviously adores you – that's what you have to concentrate
on, Jocasta, Beatrice always says that.'

'What does Beatrice always say?' said Jocasta, her tone
deceptively mild.

'Well, that in a marriage you tend to just take the good things
for granted, and only notice the bad. That's what finishes most
of them off.'

'What nearly finished yours off,' said Jocasta, 'was your
inability to be faithful to Beatrice. And what saved it was her
incredible facility for forgiveness. Don't ever try and get a job as
a therapist, will you?'

'Oh, piss off!' said Josh. He had gone rather red. 'I'm only
trying to help, I can't bear to see you two making each other so
unhappy.'

'I know and I'm very grateful,' said Jocasta, suddenly
remorseful, 'but honestly, you're not doing any good at all. It's
much better this way. Let's talk about something else. What's in
that bag?'

'Oh – I found my pictures of Thailand. They were in the
bottom of a cupboard, with my cameras. I thought they might
amuse you.'

'Oh, now you're talking,' said Jocasta. 'Let's have a look. Come
on, Clio, let's clear the table.'

He pulled them out: batch after batch, in no kind of order,
shots of the steaming jungle up in the north, shots of elephants,
of monkeys, of the hill villages, the sweet, smiling children; of
the temples and palaces and floating markets and canals in
Bangkok – 'God, I can smell it just looking at them,' said Clio –
of the chaos of the Khao San Road, the lady boys in Pat Pong –
'They obviously fancied you, just look at them vamping it up,'

said Jocasta. The tuk tuks, the longtail boats on the great river: and then the islands, endless shots of sweeping white beaches backed by green, green hills, of waterfalls, of lakes, of palms tipping gracefully into water, of sheer cliffs, of brilliant flowers, of shrines, of Big Buddha – 'Dear old Big Buddha,' said Clio, 'I still think about him sometimes, sitting there, those eyes of his following you everywhere. Golly, this is a trip down memory lane, I feel eighteen again.'

And then there were shots with people in them, some occasions they remembered – 'Look, there we are at the airport,' said Josh, 'all of us, that nice old chap took it, remember?' – frozen in time, smiling, tidy-looking, everything ahead of them. 'Poor Martha,' said Clio, studying her. 'God, if we'd known . . .'

'Best we didn't,' said Jocasta soberly.

And then there was island life, hundreds of people, most of whom they couldn't remember, smiling, always smiling, smoking, drinking, waving, hugging each other; lying on the beaches, sitting in the boats, swinging on ropes over lakes, swimming under waterfalls, elephant riding, snorkelling. There were some frenetically blurred shots of the full moon parties, people dancing, the beach covered in candles, and, 'Here, look at this, remember the reggae boat?' said Josh. 'Yes thanks,' said Jocasta, 'that was how I got dengue fever, from a mosquito on one of those lakes, too stoned to feel it.'

'What on earth are you doing there?' asked Clio, intrigued, looking at a shot of Josh lying on a rug, inhaling from a large pipe.

'Taking opium.'

'Josh! You never told me. What on earth was that like?'

'Absolutely nothing,' he said, laughing. 'I think it was talcum powder.'

'God, it was all fun,' said Jocasta, 'such, such fun. Hey – Josh, what's this, posh hotel, or what? And who's this? Martha? By that amazing pool? And on that terrace? Josh, you never told me about this, whatever happened?'

'God – didn't know that was there,' said Josh, flushing a dark red, and went on rather hurriedly to explain that he'd bumped into Martha leaving Koh Tao, there'd been a fire on the boat and they'd all nearly drowned. 'No, it's true, I'm not making it up.'

They'd both felt pretty rough, and he'd had plenty of money on him, so they'd gone to a hotel near Chaweng, stayed there one night . . .

'Mmm,' said Jocasta, her eyes dancing, 'you dark horse. You pair of dark horses. You never said. When was that? You obviously had lots of fun. Is that why you wanted to come to the funeral?'

'No. Well – sort of. I mean – yes, it was, actually.'

'I think that's very sweet.'

Clio had been literally praying for some bell, however faint, to ring in Jocasta's head. It clearly wasn't going to. She had to do it. And it was now or never: she took a deep breath, and said: 'Josh, when exactly was that? Can you remember?'

'I don't know,' he said. 'Does it matter?'

'Yes. It – could.'

'Why?'

'Well . . .'

'Clio,' said Jocasta, 'what are you on about?'

'I – well, I just thought of something. I was just thinking about – about Martha. That's all.'

'What about her? Except that she was obviously a darker horse than we thought. I mean – with Josh! And never telling us. And – oh my God! You don't think – I mean – Josh – oh my God!'

'What?' he said irritably. 'What's the matter with you both?'

'Just tell us when you and Martha had your little – fling.' Jocasta was speaking very slowly. 'It's terribly important.'

'I'll try. But I don't see –'

'Josh! Think!'

'Well – it was before Christmas, definitely, because I was in Malaysia then. Sometime around October, November, I suppose. You know how meaningless time is out there, weeks feel like months and vice versa.'

'Josh, you've got to do better than that. Sorry . . .'

'I'm trying, for God's sake. Right – well, actually, it must have been October, yes, it definitely was, because I was on my way up to Bangkok, to see my girlfriend, well, not exactly my girlfriend, but we had been pretty involved, and she was in hospital, she'd had a scooter crash on Koh Pha Ngan, and I had my birthday up there, my eighteenth, I do remember that.'

'And on the way you took Martha to a hotel. Josh, Josh, you are – oh God, you're so awful!' said Jocasta.

'Yes, I get the message. I thought you wanted to know when I was there with Martha.'

Jocasta looked at Clio. 'So that's October the twenty-sixth, his birthday. And Kate was born in the middle of August, so it would have had to have been November, wouldn't it?' she said.

'Sorry,' Clio said. 'Kate was nearly three weeks late. Martha told me. That was the whole point, why she was – here when she had her. So the end of October would be just right.'

'What are you two going on about?' asked Josh. 'You really have lost me.'

'Josh,' said Jocasta, filling his glass to the brim, 'drink that. You're going to need it. You really are . . .'

Chapter 42

Josh had hardly slept. He felt he would never sleep again. He had spent the night tossing fretfully on the spare room bed – he had told Beatrice he had indigestion, that he'd keep her awake.

It seemed to him it was impossible to do the right thing. He either had to tell Beatrice, who would be horrified, not to mention terribly hurt, probably finally throw him out – and what on earth would the little girls make of it, suddenly having a big sister? Or he could just not say a word and live with this awful, oppressing piece of knowledge for the rest of his life.

It wasn't as if she was just any old girl either: she was famous. Well, quite famous. What was it Jocasta was always saying? Once something was in the cuttings, it was there forever. It would be like a time bomb, waiting to go off. He supposed this must have been exactly what Martha had felt, and wondered how on earth she had stood it. God, she must have been brave. Brave and tough.

And then there was Kate. Kate his daughter. The vision of her kept rising before him, all night. The girl at the funeral, so lovely, so funny, so clearly clever, discussing her future with him, was his daughter. He had a grown-up daughter. It just didn't seem remotely possible. He thought of Charlie and Harry, still babies really, clambering all over him, pulling his hair, tweaking his nose, giggling, making faces at him, splashing him with their bath water, lying on his lap, sucking their thumbs while he read them stories. They were the sort of daughters he wanted. That he could cope with. Not a dangerously attractive girl of sixteen. He had fancied her himself, he thought, and his blood curdled.

And – how could you start being a father to someone you'd

met for the first time at that age? She was grown up, processed, done. He had had no part of her, she was nothing to do with him; another man had done all that, read to her, bathed her, played with her, chosen her schools, laid down the rules, there was nothing of him in her.

But there was, of course, he thought, sitting up suddenly, there was half of him in her. One night with someone, one pretty good night actually, as far as he could recall, at the age of seventeen, well, nearly eighteen, that's all he'd been, one and a bit years older than Kate herself, carefree, happy, just enjoying life, having fun and – there you were, a father. It was a bad system, that, very dangerous. He had no idea how it could have happened; he'd always been jolly careful, always used french letters, but everyone knew they could fail, spring a leak. That was obviously what had happened.

Why hadn't the bloody girl had a termination? They weren't hard to come by, so why on earth had she hung onto it? Why had she never tried to find him, for that matter? He'd have helped her out, helped her decide what to do, given her money. At this moment, Josh suddenly had a clear vision of himself at seventeen, utterly selfish, totally immature, and thought rather sadly that he could actually see very clearly why she hadn't sought him out. He wouldn't have seemed to her a very good bet.

And anyway, she might not have been sure it was him. She might have been very promiscuous, sleeping with every guy she came across. She'd certainly been pretty keen, hadn't taken much persuasion. But – clearly it had been him. Kate was his. She looked exactly like him. Or to be precise, like Jocasta.

And – what would she want? This new, problematic daughter? Jocasta and Clio had both told him she was very hurt by what had happened to her, that she had been searching for her mother all her life, ever more confused and upset.

'She just wants to know where she belongs,' Clio had said, 'where she came from, if you like. You can see how dreadfully confusing for her it all is. She loves her parents dearly but they can't supply the answers. And Martha's death has been yet another blow; she didn't provide any, either.'

Whatever he decided, they all agreed, Beatrice must be protected.

'She's so bloody marvellous, she'll probably be magnificent,' said Josh gloomily, 'offer Kate a home and –'

'Kate doesn't need a home,' Jocasta said sharply, 'she's very happy where she is. She doesn't lack for love or attention and her adoptive parents are great. She just wants to know how – and why – it all happened. She's got the dearest boyfriend,' she added.

Josh groaned. 'I can't cope with her,' he said, 'let alone her boyfriend.'

When the clock struck four, he went downstairs to make himself a hot toddy.

Peter Hartley had been in church since very early. He had spent a little time on his knees alone, remembering Martha, and quite a lot of time in the vestry tidying up, hanging up the choirboys' cassocks and sweeping the floor; it was only when he found himself sorting out the prayer and hymn books, a job that the verger and his wife always did, and indeed enjoyed doing so, that he realised what he was really doing: postponing his return to the vicarage and to Grace.

He felt very bad; it was only a very few weeks since Martha had died and he missed her and the brilliant light she had shone into his rather drab life, terribly. Nobody knew it was drab, of course, or, rather, that he found it so. His unshakeable faith helped a great deal, and the knowledge that he was doing it all for God; and there were wonderful moments, at weddings and confirmations particularly, but also when he was taking the communion service, or delivered what he felt was a good, rather than an all right sermon, but the fact remained that day to day, his life was filled with thankless and tedious tasks.

His other prop and mainstay was his beloved Grace and being apparently robbed of her, as well as of Martha, was proving almost unbearable. What had begun as bewilderment and moved to reproach was now turning to hostility: based, as far as he could see, on a deep resentment that he was finding comfort from God and she was not.

'It's all right for you,' she had actually said. 'You've got comfort – I haven't got any.'

Meanwhile, she continued not to eat: or rather, as he was beginning to see it, to starve herself.

When he got back to the vicarage, the post had arrived; the usual junk mail and two proper letters, as he thought of them. One from a parishioner, asking if he would sponsor her son on a trans-Siberian cycle ride, and another, written in a very childish hand, from someone called Kate Tarrant.

I just wanted to say that I've been thinking of you both a lot, and I do hope you are beginning to feel a little bit better now. I only met your daughter twice, but she seemed a very nice and interesting person. It was a very good experience to be at the funeral and to learn more about her and all the things she had achieved in her life. With very good wishes, yours sincerely, Kate Tarrant.

Kate Tarrant: now who on earth was she? She'd been at the funeral, she said, but he had no idea who she might have been. Until he saw her helpful PS on the other side of the paper: 'I came with Jocasta Forbes,' she had written, 'one of the girls your daughter went travelling with before she went to university.'

Now, Jocasta he did remember; she had come up to them and talked for quite a while. A beautiful girl, very charming. There had been two other girls with her: one who had also gone travelling with Martha, very nice, a doctor he seemed to recall, one much younger, with long blonde hair: perhaps that had been Kate. Grace might remember. Or young Ed – he had seemed to know that particular crowd. It would give him something to talk to Grace about later, perhaps even lift her from her dreadful lethargy. His busy, bustling Grace: lethargic. It was terribly hard to bear.

He took it up to her.

'Now look, we've had such a nice letter. From one of the young people who came to the funeral. You remember Jocasta, with the blonde hair who went travelling with Martha all those years ago?'

'Not really.'

'Yes you do, dear. She spoke to us for quite a while.'

'Peter, it's all a blur.'

'Well, anyway, there was another girl with her, much younger. Nearer Ed's age, I'd say. It's from her. Kate's her name. Such a sweet little note.'

'Well –' she shrugged, 'well, that's nice. What does she say?'

'I'll leave it here, you can read it for yourself.'

'I've got a terrible headache. I really don't feel up to reading.'

'It's very short. I'll go and get your tea. If you haven't read it when I get back, I'll read it to you.'

He laid the letter on her bed and walked out; when he looked back, she had picked it up and was reaching for her glasses. It was odd, the way these young friends of Martha seemed able to cheer her up. Or at least interest her.

Grace did remember Kate now. Pretty girl. She'd noticed her, because she had that lovely fair hair and then those huge, dark eyes, a bit like Martha's. Her mother was lucky. She still had her daughter. She hadn't seen her wiped out, her brilliantly promising life ended, all through a bit of stupidity. She hadn't got to go on living on a planet that didn't contain her daughter, full of people who didn't matter because they weren't her.

She wished she and Martha had been closer; she'd always had the feeling that Martha was keeping her just slightly at arm's length. Never discussing her boyfriends, her private life, only her career, always her career. She'd probably be alive today without that career. She wouldn't have been driving up from London, far too late and much too fast, in that car. She'd be working safely in Binsmow, where they could keep an eye on her.

Ed had obviously known her very well. She wondered if they'd got engaged or anything like that. Of all the people who kept coming to see her, she actually only enjoyed seeing Ed. She could talk to him about Martha, learn a bit more. She would like to see more of Jocasta, too. And Clio, the pretty dark-haired one, the third of the trio. The travelling trio. She'd liked her, too. Between them, they probably knew more about Martha than she did. Well, it was no use thinking they'd have time to come all this way to see her. They were young, they had their own lives, and they were busy, happy . . .

Grace turned on her side again and started to cry. She felt so alone, alone in her grief. Peter had his God. She had no one.

Jocasta would not have said she was pleased about the drama of Josh and Kate; but it gave her something else to think and worry about, apart from her own worries and misery.

In spite of everything they had said, she had expected to hear something from Nick. If only a note. Or a call on her mobile. Or the promised postcard. Just to check that she was – well, she wasn't sure what he would be checking, but they had shared a fairly amazing experience that afternoon – God, already over a week ago – and a complete silence was a bit unnerving. Maybe now he just saw her as another girl; but that wasn't right, he had said he would always love her. And that he would always be her best friend. Did being your best friend really include having that sort of amazing, stunning sex? Maybe it did. And oh, God, it *had* been amazing. Every so often she just sat very still and concentrated on remembering it; and became hideously excited.

Whatever else it had done for her, that afternoon, it had made her realise she couldn't go back to Gideon. Sex with Gideon was – well, it was dull. It was fine, it could be very good in fact, at worst it was extremely pleasant and – well, obviously bonding – but it was always the same. She felt terrible comparing him with Nick in bed, it made her feel dreadfully disloyal, and even a bit of a trollop, but she couldn't help it.

She had expected thunder and lightning, given his intensity and his experience and his dangerously seductive tongue, and she had got only a sunlit afternoon. A very nice sunlit afternoon, to be sure; but one that just went on and on. In fact – and she would never have believed this possible of herself – she had come to be quite grateful for the nights he just fell asleep, while she sat beside him reading. Or even – on some truly awful occasions – carrying on and on reading until he went to sleep. She had heard girls – usually ones in very long-established relationships – saying things like that and been quite shocked. And very sorry for them. Now she understood.

Sex with Nick had always been good; always, always. Not necessarily extraordinary, but good. Sometimes fun, sometimes more serious, occasionally really quick, now and again very, very long – Sunday sex, as she thought of it – when she came and came and wanted it never to end: but never dull. And they were absolutely honest: that had to be important. If she didn't want it, she said so, and he never minded; if he was too tired, he said so and she understood. They told each other if they didn't like something, or if there was something they thought they might try – which often led to giggling failures and an agreement that the missionary position had a lot to be said for it; she couldn't imagine that sort of honesty with Gideon.

And then they had it in all sorts of places, some more unlikely than others, sitting in the bath, standing up in the hall, on the beach, in the woods, even occasionally, and rather riskily, in Nick's car. The point was it was an integral part of them being together, as much a part of their lives as eating or drinking or working; she could no more imagine a sexless life with Nick, as one without conversation. She could very easily imagine a sexless life with Gideon.

Well, life with him just wasn't going to happen: sexless or otherwise. She had written to him now; telling him that she thought they should get a divorce as soon as possible, that she could see no hope of their ever being able to live together happily, and that prolonging matters was just making them worse. She gave him the name and address of her solicitor, and said she would hope to hear from him very shortly. She supposed she should feel sad, but she didn't; apart from being lonely, her only emotion was still anger.

Maybe she should write to Nick; but saying – what? That she missed him, that she still loved him, that she wanted to see him? No. That was out of the question. He would think she had come back to him on the rebound; or that she was whining again. She had to get his respect back; she had to be strong. If, in the fullness of time, he heard that she had left Gideon, that would be quite different; but he mustn't think it was anything to do with him. That would be emotional blackmail; it wouldn't be fair.

Gideon read her letter and then tore it up and threw it in the waste paper basket. If she thought he was going to make things easy for her, so that she could marry Nick sooner, she was very wrong. He had managed to convince himself that she had left him because she had gone back to Nick. His vanity would not allow him to consider any alternative. A young rival was better than an intrinsic fault in himself.

Beatrice had been absolutely wonderful; Josh had called her from his office at midday, unable to stand it any longer, and asked if they could meet after work for a drink.

'What on earth for, Josh? Why not at home?'

'Because I've got something I want to talk about and I don't want the girls around. Or anyone, come to that.'

They met in the American bar at the Connaught. Beatrice arrived, looking rather pale. She clearly thought Josh was going to tell her he had some new girlfriend.

'Which I suppose, in a way, he had,' she said to Jocasta, brightly.

The news had been so extraordinary and so shocking that she had found it difficult to find an appropriate reaction at all. What exactly did you say, when your husband told you he had just discovered he had a sixteen-year-old daughter? 'How nice,' or 'I can't wait to meet her'? Or, 'How could you?' Or, 'How dare you?' Or, 'Never darken my doors again'?

None of them seemed right. Beatrice sat and looked at him, at this person she really did love, who had hurt her and humiliated her a great deal, who had vowed never to do so again, this charming, good-looking, troublesome person, and found that her overwhelming emotion was sympathy. She waited for this to be replaced by something less noble, like rage, or outrage, or jealousy and it wasn't. Sympathy remained: and she said so.

'For heaven's sake, Josh,' she said quite sternly, 'a lot of seventeen-year-old boys sleep around. That was just incredibly unfortunate.'

'Yes,' he said, 'I suppose it was.'

'And certainly Martha was. Poor Martha.'

'Yes,' he said, 'poor Martha.'

'I can't imagine why she didn't tell you.'

'Nor me.'

'Or her parents.'

'Indeed.'

'I suppose she just felt she couldn't.'

'I suppose.'

'What a sad, sad story.'

'Absolutely. I feel so bad,' he said suddenly then, 'that she had to cope with it all, and I just got away scot-free. It seems so terrible.'

'Yes, well,' said Beatrice, slightly brisker, 'you have a certain talent for getting away scot-free, Josh.'

The sympathy was waning now – just a little. She looked ahead and saw enormous problems. Did they tell Kate? What did they tell Kate? Did they tell the girls? *What* would they tell the girls? How would they understand? Josh and Beatrice had only just begun to broach the subject of babies in mummies' tummies growing from little seeds.

What about the media, did they need to know? And most problematic of all, how did she fit into this new relationship? Not very comfortably. People would talk, laugh even: she would appear foolish, naive, cuckolded all over again. Josh might have been only seventeen at the time of Kate's conception, but the fact remained that, once again, he had been caught with his trousers down. Very far down. People would remember the last time. And the time before that. And would they believe that he had known nothing about it? Probably not.

'I think I need some time on my own,' Beatrice said, 'just for a while. I'll see you at home.'

She went for a walk; it was a perfect evening, golden and warm; the buildings all touched by the late sunlight, the streets, if you caught them at the right angle, did indeed seem paved with gold. She walked through Berkeley Square and into Bond Street, wandered up and down it, looking in the shop windows, in Aspreys, and Chanel and Tiffany and Ralph Lauren, finding them strangely distracting from Josh's clumsy, painful story, and even managed to admire a coat here, a bracelet there.

And then through into Regent Street, where she contemplated, as she always did, the perfection of its architecture, and marvelled that she could do so, crossed it and went beyond, into the seediness of Soho. As she walked among the strip joints and the blaring music and the pimps and the throbbing motor bikes and the shop windows filled with underwear and studded leather and impossibly high-heeled feather-trimmed shoes, all serving as half-distraction, half-background, she saw a girl, no older than Kate, her face horribly childlike, despite its heavy lipstick and its fake eyelashes, hanging around a doorway with a man, dressed in a flashy suit and a lot of gold jewellery, clearly old enough to be her father, clearly her pimp. And she thought what an obscenity that was, and that it should be stopped, somehow, that children should be children, should be safe from adult life and its ugliness. And that thought brought her rather tortuously to Kate, where her emotions somehow settled, shook down into some sort of order, and she discovered, above all, a concern for Kate. Her childhood might have been happy, but it had had its ugly, dark side – a mother who had abandoned her, and a father vanished, no one wanting her, coming to claim her. That was ugly.

Of them all, Kate had had the worst of it and she deserved the best now. She was a child and they were adults; if Josh found the situation distressing and she found it painful and Kate's adoptive parents found it difficult, that was their problem. Kate must come first, and they should all do what was best for her. It was perfectly simple.

She called Josh and said she was coming home.

It was Jocasta's suggestion that she and Josh went together to see Kate.

'I know it seems I keep muscling in on these occasions, but she does know me best. I don't even know that we should tell her, not straight away. I think we should take her out for a drink or something, and just chat and she can get used to Josh – not that anyone ever could – but she obviously liked him a lot the other day, after the funeral, and relax her a bit and then we can decide whether we should even tell her then, or wait till another time altogether. Not another great solemn sit-down, like when we told her about Martha. What do you think, Beatrice?'

Beatrice said she thought that was probably rather a good idea, and hopefully less shocking for Kate.

'God,' said Jocasta, 'you are being stunningly wonderful, Beatrice. I'm totally filled with admiration.'

Beatrice felt she didn't have much option, but she smiled

politely and said she'd go for a little walk while Jocasta called Helen.

'And then, Jocasta, maybe we should talk about you and your problems.'

Jocasta said airily that she didn't really have any problems, that the problem had been the marriage, but now that that was going to be over, she'd be fine and she could get on with the rest of her life.

'I'm really, really all right,' she said. 'Absolutely no need to worry about me.'

Beatrice, looking at her brilliant eyes, her drawn face, hearing the exaggeratedly bright voice, felt that there was actually a considerable need to worry about her.

Helen had taken the news with remarkable calm; so much had happened to her over the past few weeks that she would hardly have been surprised if Jocasta had told her Prince Charles was Kate's father. Or Brad Pitt. Or David Beckham.

It actually seemed a fairly happy option. At least it was someone they had all met and Kate liked.

'I suppose that explains the similarity between you and Kate,' she said to Jocasta.

'Yes, it does.'

She agreed that Jocasta and Josh should tell Kate together.

'It will come much better from you. And he can answer lots of her questions. Including hopefully about – about Martha.'

She still found it difficult to refer to Martha as Kate's mother. She told Jim, who was less pleased.

'Public school, I suppose,' he said irritably. 'Like his sister.'

'Well, yes.'

'Any idea which one?'

'Eton, I think.'

'Well, that's all I need.'

Helen opened her mouth to tell him not to be so silly and shut it again. She knew what this was about: what she had been through a few weeks earlier. When Jim had done his best to comfort her, but not really understood at all. He did now. Fearing rejection, criticism, comparison. Most of all comparison.

She also knew that despite his passionate socialism, his total

654

commitment to the comprehensive ideal, and his hostility to the public school culture, Jim felt threatened by the innate confidence which an expensive education provided. The thought of his beloved Kate being the offspring of an old Etonian made him feel physically ill.

'Did we meet him? At the party?'

'No, I don't think so. But I did see him. Jocasta pointed him out to me.'

'Oh yes. What did he look like?'

'Well – he looked – you know. Tall. Blond. Slightly overweight. He was dancing the Charleston, rather well actually, with some girl.'

'His wife?'

'Oh no, I don't think so. She's a barrister. This girl looked about eighteen.'

'Dear God,' said Jim, 'a lecher. That's all I need.'

'Don't be silly, dear,' said Helen.

'I'm not being silly. What sort of man makes a fool of himself with young girls?'

'Jim, he wasn't making a fool of himself. He was just dancing.'

'I would call that one and the same thing. Well, I don't think that's going to impress Kate at all. She's far too sensible. I don't want him coming here,' he added abruptly.

'Jim! He's bound to come here, if Kate likes him. Be sensible, Jim,' she said gently, 'whatever he's like, and however much or little Kate likes him, you really don't have to worry. She's much too sensible and she knows where she belongs. She knows who her father is and it's not him. Not really.'

'Yes, it is,' he said and walked out of the room.

They took Kate out for a meal: to the Bluebird.

'She loves it there,' Jocasta said. 'It's become our place, hers and mine.'

She had walked in looking stunning, not, for once, in jeans, but a long, bias-cut floral skirt, and a white T under a denim jacket, her hair hanging loose over her shoulders. Heads had turned.

'Oh, God,' said Josh.

Jocasta patted his arm encouragingly. 'It'll be fine.'

'Maybe. But I'm glad I know who she is. If you see what I mean.'

'I do. Good thing Beatrice isn't here.'

They both stood up as Kate reached the table, kissed her.

'This is so nice of you,' she said. 'I've been looking forward to it all day.'

'So have we.'

'I thought I'd bring you those cameras I was talking about,' said Josh, 'show you how they worked, maybe later.'

'Cool.'

She smiled at him. Jocasta had told her that he knew about Martha being her mother: 'But if you don't want to talk about her, that's fine. It's up to you.'

'It's really very kind of you,' she said now, 'to lend them to me.'

'Not at all. Pleasure.'

'They look expensive, I'll take great care of them.'

There was a slightly awkward silence. 'Let's choose,' Jocasta said, 'then we can relax.'

'Glass of wine, young Kate?' said Josh.

'Yes please.' She grinned at him. 'It's really weird, you calling me young Kate. It makes you sound like some elderly uncle. Which you're not.'

'Sorry.'

'No, it's cool.'

Another awkward silence. Jocasta hadn't expected this, had expected Kate would chatter away as she usually did.

'I finally decided about the contract,' she said, into the silence. 'Did Mum tell you? Or Fergus?'

'No, what did you decide?'

'Not to do it. Now I'm really worried it was the wrong decision. I mean, it's just so much money to say no to. Think what it could have done for us all, me and Mum and Dad. And Juliet, of course. She's going to be very expensive with her music.'

'Well, it wouldn't have done anything for you,' said Josh, 'not if you hate it as much as you say. And I'm sure your mum and dad would rather take care of everything, anyway. They wouldn't like being indebted to you. Uncomfortable for them, I'd say.'

'I hadn't thought of that. Yes, of course. If there'd been no question of that money, they'd be finding a way to pay for her somehow, wouldn't they?'

'Of course.'

She smiled at him. 'Thanks for that. I feel better now.'

'And *Style*?' said Jocasta. 'When's that shoot?'

'I told Fergus I couldn't do it.'

'Why? Kate, they'll have everything booked.'

'Yeah, I know. Don't you start. I just don't feel I can do it, I feel so down still.'

'Sweetheart, I'm sorry. What sort of down?'

'Well – you know.' She looked at Josh, clearly uncomfortable at discussing it in front of him. 'The usual. Like I said to you, no further forward really.'

'No?' said Josh. 'But you know who – who your mother was now.'

'Well, yeah. But she's – well, she's gone, hasn't she?'

Jocasta decided this was getting too heavy too soon. She changed the subject.

'I'm thinking of going back to work.'

'Really? Why?'

'I miss it.'

'I thought you would,' said Kate, rather complacently. 'You're much too clever to be sitting around all day, waiting for your husband to come home.'

Josh laughed. 'Beatrice would agree with you. She doesn't wait for me either.'

'No? What does she do?'

'She's a barrister.'

'So she must be pretty clever.'

'She is. Cleverer than me, I can tell you that.'

'I'm sure she's not,' said Kate politely. 'But anyway, Jocasta, that's really cool. I mean, I'm sure Gideon wouldn't have expected you to give it up for long – and it's not as if you've got a baby, or anything.'

'No,' said Jocasta quickly, 'absolutely not!'

'Would you like to have one?'

'Oh – I don't think so, no.'

'What, never?' Kate was looking at Jocasta interestedly. 'Because you'd be a very good mother, I think.'

'Now why do you say that?' asked Josh.

'Well, she's so cool. She wouldn't fuss. And she's so sympathetic, always knows how you feel. And she's fun. My mum's great, but she's a bit – old. She doesn't know what's going on.'

'But if Jocasta did have a baby, she'd be old too, when it was your age,' said Josh. He was so genuinely interested in the conversation, he had almost forgotten why they were there.

'Yeah, I suppose so. But I think Jocasta'd stay young.'

'Well, I'm not going to have a baby and that's that,' said Jocasta.

There was another silence; then: 'Gideon's got a daughter about my age, hasn't he? She must be pretty spoilt.'

'Well – in some ways. In others, far from it. He never sees her, she lives with her mother, when she's not at her boarding school.'

'Were you two spoilt?' Kate asked, looking at them. 'I mean, your dad's pretty rich, isn't he?'

'Not like Gideon is,' said Jocasta, 'and we weren't spoilt, no. Well, I suppose we had everything we wanted. But our parents were divorced and we – *I* – never saw my dad. My dear little brother did, though.'

'Yeah?' said Kate, turning to Josh. 'And do you get on with your dad?'

'Oh – you know. OK.'

'I think that's awful,' said Kate. 'I can't imagine being sent away like that, not seeing your parents every day. I mean, mine are gruesome in some ways, but we're all together and we know what we're all on about at least. My mum has this thing about all of us eating together and I'm just beginning to see the point of it. I didn't when I was younger. What sort of a dad are you?' she asked Josh. 'I mean, you've got kids, would you send them away to school? Probably you would, I s'pose.'

Josh took a very deep breath; if ever the Almighty had delivered a cue, this was it.

'What sort of a dad am I?' he said. 'Well, that's a very interesting question. I try to be a good one. I like to be with my children a lot and I don't want them to be sent away to school. Um – Jocasta, what sort of a dad would you say I was?'

Jocasta had heard the cue, heard the deep breath also.

'Pretty good, I'd say,' she said. 'Really pretty good. Now – Kate, when you've finished that, let's go, shall we? Go for a walk or something?'

She looked at them, clearly puzzled by this swift ending to the meal; she had been looking forward to the pudding.

'OK.'

They called for the bill; Josh paid it in silence. He couldn't remember ever feeling so frightened, not even when he had been left at his prep school for the first time, at the age of seven. He led the way outside.

'I've got my car,' he said, 'let's go down to the river, shall we?'

'Cool car,' said Kate. It was a Saab convertible and he put the hood down. At the river, he parked it, rather recklessly, on a yellow line, on a corner.

'It'll be OK,' he said. 'Come on, let's walk.'

He pulled Kate's arm through his; Jocasta did the same. Kate looked at them both and smiled.

'We look like a family,' she said.

'Funny you should say that,' said Jocasta.

'Why?'

'Well – now Kate, this is going to be a shock.' They were down on the river walk now. 'Let's sit down,' said Jocasta, indicating a seat. 'Come on. Kate, darling, hold my hand. Josh, this is your story. Off you go.'

Kate sat in silence listening, looking up at him intently and occasionally at Jocasta. He stumbled along: it was difficult. He told her that he and Martha had been quite close, had done some travelling together – he and Jocasta had agreed that a one-night stand was not an attractive notion – but that afterwards he had moved on to Australia, and she hadn't been able to get in touch with him.

'No mobiles, you see. All we had were *poste restante* addresses, and nobody knew where anybody was going to be, or when.'

She said nothing.

'And I think, then, she decided to manage on her own,' said Jocasta, 'she was a very independent lady. That much you must have learnt. And as I told you the other day, she felt she couldn't tell her parents.'

'That's so weird,' Kate said, 'I've thought about that so much. About feeling it was worse than just – just leaving your baby, I don't understand it, still.'

'I know,' said Josh, 'it does seem jolly odd. I think you just have to accept it. They might be lovely people, they are lovely people, but Martha obviously felt they wouldn't have been able to stand it, the shame and so on, because he's a vicar.'

'This is so much the sort of thing I wanted to talk to her about,' said Kate sadly. 'Only she would have been able to help me understand, only she could have made sense of it. And why didn't she come forward when the story was in the paper? None of it makes sense to me still. And what did I do, the one time I met her? I just shouted at her and said all I wanted to know was who my father was.'

'And – what did she say?' said Josh.

'She said she couldn't tell me. She said he – *you* – didn't know and she didn't think it was right to tell you after all these years.'

There was a silence; then Kate said: 'I was shouting at her. A lot. I wish I hadn't now. And she said she wished I'd let her try and explain. She said, "Could you just listen to me, for just a little while?" I said no and left in a strop. I wish I had,' she said and started to cry, 'let her try. It might have helped.'

They all sat there for a while, staring at the river, then she said: 'The thing is, though, that whatever she said, it comes down to the same thing: she was ashamed of me. Ashamed of having me. That isn't very nice to know.'

'Well, I'm not,' said Josh and put his arm round her, kissed the top of her head. 'I'm very proud.'

When she got home, Helen and Jim were reading. Helen smiled at her; Jim didn't look up from his paper.

'How was it, dear?'

'It was – fine. Yes. I s'pose Jocasta told you, he's my dad. Her brother Josh.'

'Yes, yes, she did. But we thought they should tell you. How do you feel about that? Oh, dear, what a silly question.'

'No, it's not. When I've got used to the idea, I think I'll be quite pleased. He's nice. I mean really nice. And he came to tell me straight away, the minute he knew. I think that's lovely. Not like her. Still – ' she added, 'I even feel a bit better about her, now.'

'What's he do, then?' said Jim. 'This paragon?'

'Jim,' said Helen warningly.

'He works for his dad. He doesn't like it much. He wishes he'd been a photographer.'

'His dad seems to pay him plenty of money,' said Jim. 'Nice car that.'

'Yes, it's cool.'

'Well, I expect you'll be seeing a lot of him now,' said Jim, 'now you've found him.'

'Quite a lot, I expect, yes. I hope so, anyway.'

She looked at Jim and then went over to him and wriggled onto his knee, put her arms round his neck.

'He is very nice,' she said, 'and he's quite good-looking and I can see he's fun. But you're my dad. You so are still my dad.'

Chapter 43

'And – what happened exactly?' The doctor looked anxious: for a doctor, very anxious.

'She fainted. I heard a thud and rushed upstairs and – there she was. Out cold on the floor. She must have hit her head as she fell.'

'Well, her pulse is rather low, and of course, where she hit her head there's going to be a nasty bruise. But I don't think she's concussed. She's got very – thin,' he added. 'Worryingly so.'

'I know. She's just not eating. It's a nightmare, Douglas. I've tried everything. It's as if she – '

'Doesn't want to go on? Poor Grace. I – just don't know how you're standing it, yourself.' Douglas Cummings was of their generation, had looked after all their children.

'Well,' Peter Hartley sighed, 'I'm not too sure, either. I suppose one just does. But Grace really isn't coping. And she has this obsession that I have my faith to sustain me, which she doesn't. She says she's lost hers. That it's easier for me. And – maybe she's right. I wouldn't say easier is the word, though. A little less dreadful, perhaps. Anyway, that makes her angry. And she's feeling totally bereft. She did adore Martha. Mothers don't have favourites, but – '

'If she did, then for Grace, poor soul, it would have been Martha,' said Dr Cummings. 'Well, she was an exceptional young woman.'

'Indeed she was. I find it so hard to bear, you know, all that brilliance, just lost, nothing to show for her life. The only time Grace cheers up at all is when young Ed comes round. She sees him as a link with Martha. But he's gone back to London, of course, so – oh God – I just don't know what to do for her, how to help her . . .'

'I'm afraid,' said Dr Cummings, 'that time is the only cure. Although we must try to get some nourishment into her. Self-starvation is one of the hardest things to deal with. Whatever the age of the patient,' he added. 'Try to get her to take one of the food supplements. I'll put my thinking cap on, I certainly don't want to hospitalise her. But – '

'Oh, dear God, no. Please don't even think about it!'

'I'm afraid we might have to,' said Dr Cummings.

After he had gone, Peter Hartley went upstairs and looked at Grace. She was asleep now; her face oddly pinched-looking, an ugly bruise forming on her forehead where she had hit her head. She looked very small, almost shrivelled; she was also cold. He fetched another duvet from the spare room and laid that gently over her, then decided to sit with her for a while. She had seemed confused while the doctor was there; he didn't want her to wake alone.

She had always been so full of life. Even when her back had hurt her so much she had struggled on, insisting she was fine, refusing to let it win, as she put it. She had taken too many painkillers, he kept telling her she shouldn't, but she had said it was the lesser of two evils. Nothing had ever got the better of her, until now. She sighed, opened her eyes. He smiled at her.

'Hello, Grace.'

She didn't smile back; she just stared at him, rather blankly, and then turned on her side, away from him.

'Would you like some tea, dear?'

'No thank you,' she said, very politely. 'I don't want anything. Just leave me alone, Peter, please.'

Clio felt irritable; Fergus and she had arranged a little holiday in Italy, towards the end of August, just a long weekend, really, but she had been looking forward to it so much, a proper stretch of time together, just to enjoy one another, away from all the hysteria of Jocasta and Gideon and Josh and Kate. Sometimes she wondered if she shouldn't stay peacefully in Guildford, working as a GP. It might not be exactly the sharp end, but it wasn't one long exhausting drama, either.

She was due to start at the Royal Bayswater on 1 October; plenty of time to work out her notice, put her flat on the market, find somewhere in London to live. And go on a little holiday.

Only, Fergus had called and said he just might not be able to make it.

'Oh Fergus! Why on earth not?'

'I might just have got a very hot new client. Which could run for several weeks.'

'And that takes precedence over our holiday. Great!'

'Clio, I'm sorry, but I have to be practical. I don't have any money in reserve. If I don't work, I don't get paid. I haven't done at all well lately, you know. Kate's let me down – '

'Fergus! I think that's stretching things a bit. She's a little girl. She's been through no end of an upheaval. She needs support, not pressure.'

'Of course. But it is difficult, you know: you arrange things, and we're not talking chicken feed here, this is big money, important assignments, and everything goes hang on the whim of a sixteen year old.'

'Exactly. A sixteen year old. Anyway, who or what is the client?'

'Oh – it's another rent boy story. Been totally screwed in both senses by his manager, he's a singer, and now the bastard's – '

'Fergus, please don't go on. *That's* what's coming between us and Italy?'

'Yes. It's work, Clio, as – '

'Work!'

'Yes, work. I know you despise it, but it earns me my crust and, as I've said before, I don't know any other way. I can't, unfortunately, get a highly paid job as a hospital consultant, and be a pillar of the community, as you can.'

'Oh, for God's sake,' said Clio, 'don't start that!'

And she put the phone down.

Half an hour later, she rang to apologise, but got the answering machine. She decided not to leave a message.

Fergus was in a financial mess. He was seriously out of pocket over Kate. Gideon's promise to pick up the tab until she began to make money for him had not been honoured, and though he knew Gideon had simply forgotten, Fergus didn't feel able to ask him for it. He had, the last time he'd checked, about seven hundred pounds in the company bank account, and a large overdraft on his personal one. He'd have to get an extension to the overdraft, simply to pay the rent. He felt angry with Clio, and bitter at her judgmental attitude towards him and his work; and he was buggered if he was going to run back to her just because she'd snapped her fingers.

She rang him again the next morning. 'I'm sorry,' she said, 'about yesterday.'

'That's all right.'

'Look – if I pay for the holiday would that help?'

Fergus felt a flood of rage towards her.

'No, Clio, it wouldn't. In the first place, I still need to be around, I've got this client now, and in the second, I've no wish to be beholden to you.'

'That's ridiculous! I'd like to pay for you.'

'Well, I wouldn't like it. However kindly it's meant. I'm trying to run a business, Clio. I know you have trouble recognising it as such, and you see it as little better than running a brothel – '

'Of course I don't!'

'Well, that's the message that comes over very loud and clear. You obviously don't realise it. So – let's cool it for a bit, OK?'

'Absolutely OK. I just wanted to relieve you of feeling you had to put any pressure on Kate.'

'That's a filthy thing to say!' he said and rang off.

Jocasta was wandering rather aimlessly round the supermarket, when it hit her. Hit her with the force of a rather large truck. And left her almost physically reeling.

She was feeling very miserable. It was the middle of August and everyone was away; she couldn't have seen any of her old friends if she'd wanted to. She really must make contact with them all in September; she couldn't avoid them forever. Even if it did mean admitting to everyone that her marriage was over.

Even Clio seemed to be avoiding her; she had been rather odd, almost distant, said she wasn't coming to London this weekend, when Jocasta had asked her, and hadn't invited her down to Guildford either.

She had heard nothing from Nick: not even the promised

postcard. Every day she told herself she'd ring him in the morning and every morning she didn't. She mustn't. She wasn't going to appear to be chasing him.

She had heard nothing from Gideon, either, not even from his solicitors; but there had been a picture of him, in the *Evening Standard*, the day before, smiling and looking rather pleased with himself. He looked a lot happier than she was. The caption said he was going on a business trip to the east coast of America. She had thought of the houses she had lined up for him to look at there and just for a moment she felt really sad, instead of angry. She could have gone with him and they could have seen them at the same time, maybe even chosen one; that would have given her something to do.

And then the really dreadful thought came, that perhaps even now it wasn't too late. She had crushed it very hastily, but it had still disturbed her. She must be feeling very, very bad.

Come on, Jocasta, concentrate. Coffee, tea, better get some milk; the last lot had been off. Bread, got that. Toiletries – shampoo, soap, Tampax and – that was when it hit her.

Now, this was absurd. One day, one day late: well, two. Actually, she could remember that last time so clearly, it was the night she had walked out on Gideon, that terrible, terrible Thursday. Two days was nothing. Nothing.

Actually, though, it was, when you were so regular you could literally set the clock by it. Well, that was the pill of course. No need to worry, she was on the pill. You didn't get pregnant on the pill. You just didn't. Unless you forgot to take it. Which she never, ever did, it was too important.

Or – and this was the second ramming by the truck – or you had a stomach upset. Which she had had. A truly terrible one. Throwing up, diarrhoea, the lot, for two days. And hadn't even taken the bloody thing for one day. Actually, two. She decided there was no point, especially as she wasn't having sex.

Only – she had. Hadn't she? Sex with Nick, amazing sex with Nick, a few days after the stomach upset, right bang in the middle of her cycle.

Oh God. Oh – my – God!

Now, calm down, Jocasta. You're one day late. All right, two days late. It's nothing. It happens sometimes. Maybe not to her, but to other people. So it could perfectly well happen to her, as well. That was all it was: she'd missed a period.

Anyway, no need to worry about it. She could do a test. You could do them on the very day your period was due, and it was something like 98 per cent accurate. She'd go to Boots and buy a test, and take it home and it would be negative and then everything would be all right and her period would probably start straight away.

She looked at her watch: five-twenty. If she legged it over to Boots now, or to the chemist in the North End Road, she should be just in time.

When she got to Boots it was shut.

So that meant either one of the late-night chemists: or waiting till tomorrow. It was no contest. There was one in Wandsworth: open until seven, she was sure. But when she got there, that was closed too: from one o'clock every Saturday, it informed her, with an infuriating smugness. She drove home and started frantically leafing through the Yellow Pages.

Kate was getting ready to go out with Nat.

It was extraordinary how much happier she felt, all of a sudden, knowing Josh was her father, knowing he had wanted to tell her, wanted to be her friend. He'd actually said that: 'I don't feel quite like your father, not yet anyway, it seems so – odd. Maybe we could start by being friends.'

Kate had liked that so much; she had never entertained any ideas about falling into her birth parents' arms, she had simply wanted to know who they were and to find out how it had all happened. Of course it wasn't exactly nice to discover you were the result of what amounted to a holiday romance; but they'd been awfully young: only a bit older than she was now.

She could tell from some of the answers Josh had given her about Martha that he really hadn't known her at all well. She'd have preferred it to have been some passionate, forbidden affair. But Josh was so nice, even if he was a bit silly, so she was sure he must have liked Martha quite a lot, it hadn't been just sex. And if he'd known about – about her, he would have helped Martha. She could tell. She'd never know why Martha hadn't told him, she'd never know an awful lot of things; but she was discovering that a great many people had liked Martha, thought a lot of her. Which was nice for her. You didn't want your mother to be a one hundred per cent bitch. You wanted her to be nice. And Ed, that gorgeous Ed, he was so nice too, and he'd really loved Martha. She'd never seen a man cry like that, like he did at the funeral; it had been very upsetting.

Anyway, feeling happier had made her feel she wanted to see Nat again. There seemed some point in it. There seemed a point to quite a lot of things. She thought she might even go and see Fergus, and really talk through the contract with Smith. Maybe it wasn't too late. He'd said something about the door still being open. Three million dollars really was a lot of money to turn down. She'd already told him she'd do the *Style* cover, which had seemed to cheer him up a bit. She was quite looking forward to that, mostly so she could talk to the photographer.

She was just trying to untangle her hair, when Jilly rang.

'Hello, my darling, how are you?'

'I'm fine. Mum told you about Josh? Jocasta's brother?'

'She did indeed. What an extraordinary coincidence. Although not really, when you think about it. Just imagine, Kate, if I hadn't fallen on the step that night, none of this would have happened.'

'Yeah, I know. I was thinking that.'

'And – I hear you like him?'

'I do. I really like him. He doesn't feel like my dad, exactly, but he's good fun and it's lovely talking to him and everything. He can't answer all my questions, but he tries. He's well posh, Granny, you'll love him.'

What had her mother said? Oh, yes, 'Just wait till Granny knows where he went to school, she'll have a heart attack with excitement.'

'There's more to liking someone than their social class,' said Jilly slightly stiffly.

'Course there is,' said Kate.

Jocasta stood in her bathroom, her heart thudding so hard she felt her body could hardly contain it. She had gone to Boots in Piccadilly in the end, because it was always open. Right round the clock. The pregnancy test had cost her £90 so far, because

668

she couldn't find anywhere to park, and so she'd left her car on a yellow line in Jermyn Street with a note on it, thinking she'd only be five minutes, and of course she had been about fifteen, by the time she'd found the wretched things and read all the instructions and decided which one would be best and then queued to pay for it. It had been a long queue. A long, hot queue, composed largely of tourists. There was also a very long queue at the pharmacy end, presumably all the druggies, getting their stuff. Anyway, by the time she got back to her car, it had a ticket. A self-satisfied-looking female warden was just placing it on the windscreen.

'Please,' said Jocasta, 'please! I was only getting something from Boots. Look, I left a note saying so –'

The woman shrugged.

'Doesn't mean you won't get a ticket,' she said.

'But it was an emergency!'

She didn't even reply.

Anyway, she had the test. She would just go home and use it and get the matter settled. Maybe she was getting her period anyway, she felt a bit – achy.

She did the test.

The instructions were very clear; you had to hold the end of the stick thing – it looked a bit like a thermometer – into your pee for five seconds only (this bit was in bold type) and then keep it pointing downwards for one minute. There were two little windows at the other end of the stick. At the end of the one minute, a blue line should appear in the end window and then you could read the result window. A plus meant pregnant, a minus not.

She timed the five-second dip into the pee she'd collected (in a clean dry container as they had said, a large breakfast cup actually) and then dipped what they called the absorbent sampler into it. And then waited. For one minute. In one minute she'd be fine, in one minute a nice neat minus sign would tell her she was not pregnant, and – God! It was there! Unmistakably a minus. She wasn't pregnant. She was fine. For heaven's sake. How ridiculous to think she could have been! How could she? Of course she wasn't. She felt quite dizzy, light-headed with relief. She – the doorbell rang. She stuffed the box into the cupboard under the bathroom sink and went to answer it. It was a young man, asking her to sponsor him on a trek over the Himalayas. Jocasta gave him £25 and then opened a bottle of champagne to celebrate.

'You look rotten.'

'Thanks. I expect it's the heat. You know how much I hate it.'

Gideon was not on a business trip in the States, as he had told the reporter at Heathrow, he was in Barbados.

'Possibly.' Aisling Carlingford shrugged her slender, pale brown shoulders, took a sip of her crushed fruit cocktail. 'You didn't have to come.'

'I know that. I wanted to see Fionnuala.'

'Well, you've seen her now. There she is, swimming up and down. So you can go again, back to the rainy mists of Ireland. She does look lovely, doesn't she?'

'Very lovely.'

Fionnuala saw them admiring her, got out of the pool, dived neatly back in again, and swam the length of it underwater. She surfaced near them and smiled. 'Hello. Dad, you look awfully hot.'

'I feel hot,' said Gideon irritably.

'Well, come and join me.'

'I will in a minute. Can we ride this afternoon?'

'Sorry, got a polo lesson. Mummy'll go with you, won't you, Mummy?'

'I might,' said Aisling, surprising him. 'Late afternoon, when it's cooler.'

'Good. Thanks.'

She looked at him rather more intently. 'So – where's the lovely young wife?'

'I told you. In London. Possibly in Berkshire. Not sure.'

'And why did you leave her behind?'

'Aisling, I was hardly going to bring her here.'

'It's gone wrong, hasn't it?'

Gideon hesitated, then said with great reluctance, 'Yes. It has.'

'You shouldn't have married her. It was a terrible mistake.'

'I think it probably was. She hasn't turned out as I hoped.'

'I meant it was a terrible mistake for her, Gideon. Mistake on your part. Wrong of you, you know?'

'I think that's a little unfair.'

'Is it? Anyone could see, just looking at her, she was completely overwhelmed by you.'

'Aisling, she wasn't some naive child. She was a very sophisticated girl, a successful journalist. Her father is a rich and successful man.'

'Oh come on, Gideon. What did she know of your life? Of what it meant? She's nearly twenty years younger than you for a start. Marriage has come to mean something very different in the last twenty years, for girls like her. There's no way she could be expected to understand her role as your consort. I feel very sorry for her.'

'Sorry for her?'

'Yes. Extremely.'

'This is a ridiculous conversation,' said Gideon.

'Don't start losing your temper. Just think about it for a bit. I suppose you thought you were in love with her.'

'I – was very much in love with her. I still am.'

'Rubbish. You're in love with love, you always have been. You're a romantic old thing, that's why I fell in love with you. And I'm sure it tickled your fancy, having a lovely trophy like that on your arm. "Look what I can still catch," that's what that said. Honestly, Gideon, you ought to be ashamed of yourself. I suppose she was more impressive as a wife than a girlfriend, but still – '

'She was very anxious to marry me,' said Gideon. 'It was all her idea, she practically dragged me into the registry in Vegas.'

'Oh, yes, and you're such a pushover, aren't you? It's so extremely easy to make you do something you don't want! Gideon, honestly, you can't expect me to believe that. It's all horribly plain to me. And then the honeymoon was over and that wonderful party, that sounded fun, I'd have liked to be there, and you got back to work, and she was left alone twiddling her pretty little thumbs. Feeling all the worse for the fact that she'd actually had a career before. Hello, darling.'

'Hi!' Fionnuala came over to them, dripping, flung herself on the sunbed next to her father. 'I'm hungry, Mummy, when's lunch?'

'In an hour. Unless you need it sooner.'

'I do.'

'Then go and sort something out with the kitchen.'

'OK, I will. How's Jocasta, Dad? She sounds so cool.'

'She's fine,' said Gideon with great difficulty.

'Good. See you.'

'So what are you going to do?' said Aisling, when she had gone.

'Oh, I don't know. She wants a divorce.'

'Well, give it to her. I know you find that hard, but what's the point otherwise? You're probably not even properly married, anyway. Think of it as a wedding present for her,' she said, and started laughing at her own joke.

Gideon stood up and dived into the pool, swam a few lengths and then settled at the other end, looking at his ex-wife. His second ex-wife. She was a lovely thing – still. Blonde, reed-slim, but full-breasted, her sleek body and almost unlined face a testimony to the wonders of cosmetic science. He had loved her so much. As much as he had loved Jocasta. Probably more. Aisling was right; he *was* a romantic old fool. And he shouldn't have married Jocasta. Who he still loved – in a way. Enough – just maybe – to set her free again.

After lunch, while Aisling had her siesta, he wrote some e-mails.

Jocasta sat staring at the little blue plus sign. Plus. Not minus, this time, but plus. Plus meant pregnant. It was very simple. She was plus something. Plus a pregnancy. Plus a baby. Plus Nick's baby.

She felt very odd. Very odd indeed. Not entirely as she would have expected. The thing that she had dreaded all her life had happened and she felt shocked and horrified and terrified; but she felt something else, as well. Almost – awed. That it could have happened. That she and Nick could have made a baby. They had made love and made a baby. Something that was partly her and partly Nick. It was an extraordinary thought.

Only – of course it wasn't a baby: it was a cluster of cells. She was – what was she? Three weeks pregnant. Three and a half weeks. Whatever it was, it was pinprick size. A tiny, pinprick size cluster of cells. It was not a baby. And she could get rid of it. Quickly and easily.

She must get rid of it. Obviously.

Quite apart from the fact she could never, ever have a baby – and even the thought of the cluster being inside her made her feel panicky – what on earth would Nick do or say, if he knew? Nick, who still couldn't contemplate any sort of commitment, not even living together, certainly not getting married, how would he react to the news that he was a father? Well, not a father, but going to be a father. It was absolutely unthinkable.

She decided to go and see Clio.

Clio – of course – gave her all the wrong advice.

Like she shouldn't do anything too hasty. Like she should wait a few more days, these tests weren't entirely reliable, whatever they said, it was very early days. Like was she really sure it was Nick's. Like she ought to tell Nick.

'Tell Nick! Clio, are you mad? Of course I can't tell Nick. He'd be horrified, he'd run away, he'd hate it, he'd hate me. No, I must just – just have a termination as soon as possible and – '

'Jocasta, I really think you should tell him. If you're really pregnant and it's really his, you should tell him.'

'But why?'

'Because it's his baby, too. It's wrong not to. It's a terrible thing to do, just deciding to get rid of a baby, without telling its father.'

'Clio, you don't know Nick and I do. He would not want a baby. He doesn't even want *me*. And if you're even contemplating telling him yourself, you'd better just stop right away, at once, you've got to promise me not to, promise, Clio, all right, now, at once, on your life – '

She was crying now; Clio went over to her, put her arms round her.

'Of course I won't tell him. I promise, on my life, I won't.'

'Never, ever?'

'Never ever. Come on, sit down, have a cup of tea.'

'Coffee, please. Nice and strong.'

'Fine.' She went into the kitchen; Jocasta followed her, sat down at the table.

'You might not be, you know. When was your period due?'

'Last Thursday.'

'That's a very short time. It could all be a mistake. You don't feel – funny or anything? Sick, or tired or – '

'Absolutely not,' said Jocasta.

'I should wait a few more days, then do another test. Go and see your doctor, or your gynaecologist, see what he says – '

'She,' said Jocasta.

'She. Various things can affect these tests – I presume you're still taking the pill. Here's your coffee.'

Jocasta took one sip of it, put it down, made a face.

'God, that tastes disgusting. What have you put in it, Clio? It makes me want to heave.'

Clio looked at her very soberly, in silence. Then she said: 'Jocasta, I'm sorry, but I would say that rather clinches it. You definitely are pregnant.'

Sarah Kershaw confirmed Clio's diagnosis.

She had been Jocasta's gynaecologist for years; she was in her early forties, high-powered, sympathetic.

'I'll do a lab test, of course. We can do it now, this afternoon. Think you can pee?'

'God, yes,' said Jocasta, 'I never stop.'

'That's another symptom, I'm afraid. Sorry, Jocasta. We'll do the test, anyway. Now, what do you want to do about it?'

'I want to have a termination. Obviously. And I want to be sterilised at the same time.'

'That's a very drastic decision.'

'Not really. I've been meaning to do it for years. You know I have.'

'I do know. But you're upset, your hormones are in a state of total upheaval – '

'I'm not upset, Mrs Kershaw. Or in a state of upheaval, actually. I feel very calm. That's what I want to do.'

'Well – it's your decision of course. Have you – talked it over carefully with your husband?'

'No. We're getting divorced. So – no point.'

'He might feel differently.'

'What about? The divorce?'

'Obviously I can't tell you that. I meant about the baby.'

Jocasta was silent; there was no way she was going to tell Sarah Kershaw that the baby was not her husband's, that it had been conceived in adultery, one dizzy afternoon.

'Look,' Sarah Kershaw said. 'This is your decision, obviously. Now, you're clearly distressed about your marriage, but has the marriage actually broken down? Irretrievably?'

'Sorry,' said Jocasta, 'I haven't come to discuss my marriage.'

'I know that. But even if you don't realise it, you're not thinking entirely clearly. Perhaps not the best way to be taking extremely important decisions.'

'I'm thinking very clearly. I'm feeling perfectly well. I don't understand all this fuss about pregnancy making you ill. I haven't felt sick once and I've got loads of energy.'

'Well, you're very lucky. I'm happy for you. Even so, believe me, you're not quite yourself. And this is a bigger decision than perhaps you actually realise. Especially the sterilisation.'

'Mrs Kershaw, please. I don't want bloody counselling. I don't need it. I want a termination and I want to be sterilised. What do I have to do?'

'If I was just having the termination,' she told Clio, 'I could have what they called a con-op, first a consultation, then the termination, all on the same day. But as I want to be sterilised, they'll counsel me, as they call it, and then book me in for another day. But there's no problem. I can do it.'

It sounded terrible to Clio. 'What did she say about telling – telling the father? Does he have a right to know?'

She knew he didn't; but she was hoping Jocasta's mind might have been at least alerted to the possibility.

'She said I didn't have to, and he couldn't stop me having the termination. It's totally up to me. The doctors and me. All I need is a legal justification and of course I've got one. Change of life circumstances it's called. So – in about ten days, with luck. Will you come with me?'

'I don't think I can,' said Clio and slammed the phone down.

She found it hard to believe that, even in her manically self-absorbed state, Jocasta could be asking her to go with her to get rid of her baby. Could be so grossly insensitive not to have remembered Clio's grief on the subject of her own infertility. It hurt almost more than she would have believed.

The phone rang again almost at once: she picked it up, feeling remorseful. She had misjudged her, Jocasta had phoned to apologise . . .

'Clio, don't know what happened then. Look, I've heard from Gideon, he wants to see me, discuss things. I'm absolutely petrified, he wants me to go round to the house tomorrow afternoon, can you come up afterwards?'

'No,' said Clio, 'I can't. I do have a life of my own, you know, Jocasta. I can't actually drop everything, just whenever it suits you. Sorry.'

There was a silence: then Jocasta said, her voice absolutely astonished: 'OK, OK. Easy. I thought you'd want to help.'

Clio said she was getting a bit tired of helping, and put the phone down for the second time.

She was a fine friend, Jocasta thought. When she really needed her, where was she? Having a hissy fit in Guildford. Well, too bad. She could manage without her. She could manage without anyone. She was just fine. She was getting her life back. As soon as she'd had this – thing done next week, she would go to see Chris Pollock. She couldn't imagine how she could ever have thought she could give up her job. And her freedom and her independence. She must have been completely mad. Gideon had driven her mad.

She wondered what on earth he was going to say to her tomorrow. She hadn't been making it up when she told Clio she was terrified. But it had been a nice and very friendly e-mail; she really felt she should agree to see him.

Nick was still in Somerset. He had been showing off to the children when they were all out riding one afternoon, and fell off, breaking his radius. An extremely painful four hours later, he was back at the house with his arm in a sling and ordered not to drive, or indeed do anything much, for two or three weeks.

'You are an idiot,' his mother said, 'galloping off like that over the moor. I bet it was a rabbit hole, wasn't it?'

'Yes, I think so,' said Nick humbly. 'Sorry, Mummy.'

'I'll get you some tea. And they gave you some painkillers, I presume.'

'Yes. But it's wearing off already. I couldn't have a whisky, could I?'

'I think that's a terrible idea, on top of painkillers. Go on up to bed, and I'll bring the tea up.'

'Thanks. You couldn't bring my mobile, could you? I must let them know at the office.'

'Of course. Although I really can't think it could matter much if you're not there for a bit. Those dreadful people you write about, they're all away. There was a picture of the Blairs this morning, in Tuscany I think, or was it the Bahamas? I don't know why they can't holiday in this country.'

She brought Nick his mobile with the tea; he checked it to see if there was a message from Jocasta. That was the real reason he wanted it. There wasn't: again. God, he missed her. God, it hurt. Much, much more than his arm.

Jocasta drove up to Kensington Palace Gardens; she had dressed very carefully, in a short black linen shift that was just slightly too large for her. She knew her boobs were slightly bigger than they had been and she was terrified Gideon would notice. Notice and guess.

She knocked on the door tentatively; Mrs Hutching opened it, smiled at her rather awkwardly.

'Hello – Mrs Keeble.'

'Hi,' said Jocasta. She had tried to get Mrs Hutching to call her Jocasta; it had never worked, and now the poor woman was embarrassed, whatever name she used.

'Mr Keeble isn't here yet. He asked me to give you tea in the garden room. He said he wouldn't be long.'

'Lovely. Thank you.'

As she walked through the hall, she glanced at the letter rack; there were two postcards in it. Two sepia-tinted postcards. She pulled one of them out. It was a picture of Exmoor and it was Nick's writing.

'This is for me,' she said. 'Why didn't you send it on?'

'I don't think it is for you, Mrs Keeble. It's addressed to a Mrs Cook. It's certainly this address. I thought perhaps one of the agency cleaners we have in August might claim it – '

'It's OK. It's from a friend of mine. A sort of – joke.'

'Oh, I see. I'm so sorry.'

'It's OK.'

OK! When she had been waiting for this for two and a half very long weeks. Why hadn't she thought of this: of course Nick would have sent it here, he thought she was living here.

Dear Mrs Cook, Thank you so much for a very pleasant afternoon. I enjoyed it enormously. I hope your health has improved and that you are able to get out and about in this lovely summer weather. It is wonderfully beautiful down here; I know you don't admire the countryside, but the moors are amazingly lovely. The air is so very clean and clear; I wish I had been able to persuade you to join me here occasionally in the past. Yrs, with every good wish, James Butler.

The other card was slightly less enigmatic;

Dear Mrs Cook, I am worried that you might not have got my last card and hope you continue in good health. Do let me know. James Butler.

She slipped them into her bag, feeling much happier, and went into the garden room to wait for Gideon – who was actually very nice, friendly and courteous. He said he was sorry things had got so bad between them, that he had never intended it and he saw himself as at least partly to blame. He had been doing a lot of thinking, and if she wanted a divorce, then he would not contest it, however sad he might feel. He was sure they could come to an amicable arrangement over a settlement; she must let him know . . .

At this point, Jocasta could bear it no longer. The old Gideon had come back, kind, gentle, charming; how did it happen, where did the demons come from? Clearly she released them in him; it wasn't a very nice thought.

'I don't want a settlement, Gideon,' she said. 'I don't want anything. Nothing at all. Really. I couldn't possibly take any money from you.'

'Of course you could.'

'I couldn't. Honestly. I really, really don't want anything.'

'Jocasta –'

'No, Gideon, I don't. I feel bad enough already.'

There was a silence, then he said: 'Well, you may change your mind. You look tired – are you all right?'

'I'm absolutely fine,' she said quickly.

How on earth would he react, if he knew she was pregnant? With another man's baby, the ink on their marriage licence hardly dry? Or thought it might be his? It was terrifying. God, she was a disaster!

'Good. I would really like you to have something. So if you change your mind – '

'I won't,' she said, 'I know I won't.'

'Well, at the very least take the clothes,' he said. 'They are clogging up cupboard space and they don't suit me at all.'

She smiled. 'Oh, Gideon. This is so sad. We should just have had an affair.'

'But you didn't want an affair,' he said, 'you wanted a marriage. Come along, Jocasta, admit it.'

'I – admit it,' she said.

'But I encouraged you.'

'Yes, you did. And most of the time, it was great, great fun.'

'I'm so glad you thought so,' he said. 'I enjoyed it, too. Most of it. Now – drink up your tea, and then you must excuse me. I have to go back to the office. And before that I have to pick up some luggage. I'm – '

'Going away tomorrow,' she said and laughed. 'Oh, Gideon. I'm so sorry. I behaved so badly.'

'I behaved badly, also. And I am sorry for it. Well, it was a short marriage but mostly a merry one. Thank you for coming today. I just wanted us to part friends.'

'Friends it is,' she said and went over to his chair, bent to kiss him. 'Goodbye, Gideon.'

'Goodbye, Jocasta. And – I would be hugely grateful if the press didn't hear of this just for a little while.'

'They won't. I promise.'

They wouldn't. The press getting hold of it was the last thing she wanted. Especially one member of the press.

Just the same, Nick had sent a postcard. Two postcards. And had clearly been thinking about her. That was nice.

The minute she got into her car, she called his mobile; it was not Nick who answered.

'Hello. Pattie Marshall. Can I help?'

'Oh – sorry, Mrs Marshall. It's Jocasta here, Jocasta Forbes.'

'Hello, Jocasta.' The voice was very cool; they had never liked one another. 'I expect you're wondering why I'm answering Nicholas's phone. He's broken his right radius – '

'What's that?' Pattie always used medical terms; it had been one of the many things that got up Jocasta's nose.

'It's one of the bones in the forearm.'

'I'm so sorry. Is he all right?'

'Yes, he's fine. He fell off a horse – bit of a shame. It isn't serious, but he's asleep at the moment, and he asked me to switch off his phone and I forgot.'

'I'm so sorry. So, he's staying with you?'

'Yes, of course. I'm certainly not up in London with him.'

'Of course not. Please give him my – my best wishes. Tell him I'm sorry. And thank him for the postcards. When – when will he be back in London?'

'Oh – not for a couple of weeks, I should think. I'll get him to call you.'

'Well, only if he – if he feels like it. Thank you.'

'And are you at home?'

'Yes,' she said, and then quickly, 'tell him I'm at the Big House. He'll know what I mean.'

'Very well.'

When Nick woke up, Pattie Marshall told him that Jocasta had called and sent her best wishes. And that she was staying at the Big House.

'She says you'll know what that means.'

Nick did; it meant she was staying at the Big House – not leaving it. He'd lost her – again.

Chapter 44

This time tomorrow it would be over. Just – over. She wouldn't be pregnant any more. Fantastic. She hadn't really felt pregnant anyway; it had never been real. It had been a non-happening. One missed period and now nearly another. That was all. She'd never felt sick, she'd never felt anything; people made an awful fuss about nothing, as far as she could see. And she certainly hadn't felt emotional. Not in the least. She just wasn't maternal; she didn't have any maternal feelings. She'd have been a terrible mother.

Jocasta looked down at her stomach; it was totally flat. It was impossible to believe there was anything alive in there, certainly not a baby. A child. Hers and Nick's child. Maybe it was all just a fantasy, something she'd imagined. But – she'd done three tests altogether and Sarah Kershaw had done hers; there was no doubt. Nick's baby was in there.

She wondered what on earth Nick would say, if he knew: if he knew she was pregnant. He'd be terrified: absolutely terrified. He'd want to just run away. And what if he knew she'd had a termination without telling him? Well, that was a bit – tricky. He might be cross. He might say he had had a right to know. But he still wouldn't want it. So it was certainly infinitely better he didn't. Much better. He'd never know; the only person who did know was Clio, and she'd never tell. Nick was still down in Somerset: that was lucky. She was sorry he'd broken his arm, or whatever it was, but it was – lucky.

Clio was still being weird; very cold and distant, when she'd called her, not even interested in how Josh was getting on with Kate. She didn't know what the matter with her was. She'd asked Fergus and he'd said he had no idea; he hadn't spoken to her for a bit. He'd sounded quite down, but when she asked him if there was a problem, he said of course not. Obviously there was; they'd had a row or something. It would blow over.

Anyway, she'd be fine tomorrow. They had warned her she might feel very sore, but that it was a relatively minor procedure.

The counselling had been crap. Had she really thought about it? Was she absolutely sure about sterilisation? It was a very big step. Jocasta said she knew that and she had thought about it. It was what she wanted. Definitely.

'I see that you and your husband are separating,' the woman said.

'Yes, that's right.'

'Which is a perfectly acceptable reason for a termination, as far as we're concerned. Mrs Kershaw also says you have what amounts to a phobia about childbirth. Interesting. Where does that come from, do you think?'

'Oh – hideous experience in Thailand,' said Jocasta. 'Not me, a girl I was in hospital with. I really don't want to talk about it.'

'That's fine. Now how is your general health, Miss Forbes? Any problems, anything we should know about?'

They had told her she would be in for the whole day, that she would have a general anaesthetic, because of the sterilisation, that someone should come and collect her, she wouldn't be able to drive herself home. Well, if Clio wouldn't come with her – and she wouldn't – she would go on her own, get a cab home. She'd be fine.

She wondered if Martha had felt like this: that it was just a matter of time and then it would be over. Probably. Only Martha had had to have a baby first. Whenever she thought about that, Jocasta felt physically faint, clammily nauseous. All alone, all alone in that dreadful screaming pain: how had she stood it, how had she coped with the mechanics of it, the reality? At this point she veered her mind away from the whole thing. It was just – unthinkable. She could never have done it. Never. Well: she didn't have to. There would be no baby, so no labour. After tomorrow. Fine. Just fine. Much better.

The phone rang sharply; she picked it up. It was Clio.

'Hi, Jocasta. It's me.'

'Oh – hello,' she said, just a little cool.

'I wanted to talk to you.'

'Oh yes? What about?'

'This baby. I know it's nothing to do with me, but Jocasta, I still think you should tell Nick, it's his baby too. It's wrong not to. I –'

'Clio, I'm not very interested in your opinion on this, and you're right, it isn't anything to do with you. It's me that's pregnant, and it's my body and my decision. Nick's a commitment phobe. He wouldn't even live with me. He will not want a baby.'

'But –'

'Look, what would be the point? Just tell me that? All I'd be doing is upsetting him. And you're upsetting me, come to that. For nothing.'

'Not for nothing, Jocasta, for a baby. And you might – you just might change your mind. At least don't be sterilised yet.'

'Oh for God's sake, Clio. I'm not having it. You know I can't, and anyway, I don't want it, can't have it, and tomorrow I'm just going to – to have the termination, and that'll be it. Over, finished, done and dusted.'

'I wish you wouldn't talk about it like that,' said Clio quietly. 'It's a baby you've got in there, Jocasta, not some sort of parasite.'

'Babies are parasites, as far as I'm concerned. Right from conception.'

'Oh shut up,' said Clio. She suddenly sounded quite hysterical. 'Just shut up, will you?'

'You started this,' said Jocasta, 'so don't tell me to shut up. Perhaps you'd like me to have it, and then you could adopt it. What about that for an idea?'

'It's about the only way I'm going to get a baby,' said Clio, and her voice cracked with hurt, 'adopting one, so –'

There was a dreadful silence; in the middle of it, Jocasta remembered. Remembered what she should never have forgotten for a moment, remembered what would have made the whole thing of telling Clio, saying she was going to have an abortion, savagely cruel. Asking her to go with her when it was done, for God's sake. How had she done that? How had she been so totally, utterly callous to Clio, poor sweet Clio who wanted babies more than anything, but could never have them?

What was the matter with her, how had she turned into this monster? It was Gideon's fault; he'd done it . . .

'Clio,' she said, 'Clio, I'm so, so sorry. I forgot. I'm so totally wrapped up in myself at the moment. God I'm a cow, a foul, hideous cow, Clio, I'm so sorry . . .'

'It's all right,' said Clio and rang off. When Jocasta tried to ring her back, the answering machine was on and her mobile was on message.

She felt so guilty, she felt sick. She actually thought she was going to be sick. How could she have done that, been so brutal, how could she have forgotten? Clio was supposed to be her best friend, and she'd hurt her in that awful, vicious way.

She kept ringing the number, kept saying, 'Please Clio, pick up the phone,' but she wouldn't.

What had she done, dear God, what had she done?

Jocasta rang Fergus; it seemed the next best thing to speaking to Clio.

He was short with her.

'I'm afraid Clio and I aren't really in touch at the moment.'

'Oh Fergus, why on earth not? What's happened? You were made in heaven!'

'Call it a clash of ideologies,' he said, rather stiffly, 'so, not made in heaven at all.'

'I'm so sorry. Are you going to tell me any more?'

'I don't think so.'

'But the thing is, Fergus, I need to contact her. I've done something really, really dreadful and I need to speak to her and she won't speak to me. Won't even pick up the phone. Could you help?'

'I really don't think I could,' he said, and his voice was very sad. 'She won't pick up the phone to me, either. I'm sorry, Jocasta. I'd love to help, but I can't.'

'Oh. Oh, OK. I'll have to think of something else.'

He sounded dreadful; she felt quite anxious about him. 'How are things generally, Fergus, darling? You're wonderfully busy, surely?'

'Oh – you know. Difficult. Not a lot of work coming in, to be honest with you.'

'I'm sorry. And Kate isn't coming to anything, is she? In the financial sense. Not doing the Smith work?'

''Fraid not. No.'

'I hope my soon-to-be-ex-husband paid you for her,' said Jocasta suddenly. 'I do remember him promising to, but he might need chasing on it. Just at the moment.'

'Well – he hasn't, Jocasta, as a matter of fact. Obviously it's slipped his mind, rather more important things on it – ' She could hear his voice, determinedly light, almost amused.

'Oh, Fergus, I'm so sorry. That's unforgivable. I'll ring his PA – '

'I have rung her, of course. I'm sure it'll be through soon.'

'Look,' said Jocasta, 'I'll ring Gideon myself. It's all right; we're back on speaking terms. And I've still got a joint account chequebook. I'll write you a cheque on that, if all else fails.'

'Oh, my darling, I don't think you'd better do that. He might be very cross.'

'He can be as cross as he likes. I don't care. You need your money. You've got bills to pay. And – God – we landed you with Kate. Anyway, I'm sure he's just forgotten. I've probably driven everything out of his head. He does have his faults, but he's certainly not mean. I'll call him right away.'

Gideon said he was very sorry; he'd have a cheque biked round to Fergus within the hour.

It might help both him and Clio a bit, Jocasta thought. At least she'd been able to do something for them.

Peter Hartley was sitting in the kitchen, as close to despair as he had ever been, when Maureen Forrest arrived with a large bunch of dahlias.

'I brought these for Mrs Hartley. I'm sorry I'm so early, but I'm on my way to work. Ed said she didn't seem too good when he came on Saturday.'

'She isn't, I'm afraid. She's – well, she's so frail. And this morning early, she just fainted dead away.'

'Oh, I'm so sorry. Is she all right?'

'I'm afraid she is very down. I can't get her to eat – Dr Cummings says he'll have to hospitalise her soon, if it goes on.'

'I'm so sorry, Mr Hartley. You've got enough to cope with yourself, without this.'

'Oh, I'm all right. It was so nice of Ed to come and see her at the weekend. Somehow he seems to get through to her when no one else can. I suppose because he was so close to Martha. She feels he's a link.'

'Well, I'm glad it helped. Ed's very down himself, of course. Although – it's a dreadful thing to say, but he's young. You and I both know he'll get over it one day. Not completely, of course, and he'll never forget her, but – he'll find someone else. Of course I wouldn't say that to him, he wouldn't believe me, and it sounds rather – ' She stopped.

'Heartless?' he said and smiled.

'Yes. But it's not. He's only twenty-three; what you and Mrs Hartley have lost is so much worse. When John was dying, I kept thinking, At least it's not Ed. Does that sound very bad?'

'Of course not,' said Peter and patted her shoulder. 'Yes, it's the worst loss of all. I – well, I'm afraid I'm finding it almost unbearable. It's the wrong order of things. I can't make sense of it.'

'I'm so sorry. So sorry for you both. Anyway, I'll pop in again in a day or so. And I'll tell Ed what you said. He'll be pleased.'

Jocasta had decided to go and see Clio; it was too important not to. She hadn't got anything else to do, for God's sake.

She was just leaving, when Beatrice rang.

'Jocasta, how are you?'

'I'm fine. You? You amazingly wonderful and selfless woman.'

'Don't know about that. Not too thrilled with Josh.'

'I'm sure you're not. But – it is a long time ago. Sixteen years, or whatever.'

'Yes, I know. But it still hurts, I don't know why. I suppose because – oh I don't know. It just doesn't help me to trust him. Silly, I know. But clearly, this sort of thing is in his genes.'

'Not silly at all. I'd feel exactly the same. But – he has been behaving himself lately, hasn't he?'

'Oh, yes,' said Beatrice quickly, 'he really has.' She managed a laugh. 'I sound like his mother, don't I? Or his big sister.'

'You take a much better view of him than his big sister,' said Jocasta. 'You must love him a lot, Beatrice.'

'I suppose I must. Anyway, it's obviously best for Kate. Josh tells me she's really happy about it.'

'Yes, I think she is. You haven't met her yet?'

'No, she's coming to tea next Sunday. I do want to meet her properly and we thought it would be easier if she came here.'

'I think you'll like her,' said Jocasta, 'she's very sweet. Very bright. Presumably you're not going to tell the girls?'

'Oh – no. Not yet. Now, Jocasta, I've actually rung up to ask you something.'

'Yes?'

'Are you going back to Gideon?'

Jocasta was caught off her guard. 'Of course not. Absolutely not.'

'I see. We've been worrying about you. We'd hoped that things might be better.'

'Well, they are better. We seem to be friends again. Probably because we haven't seen each other for weeks and weeks. But we are getting divorced. And I'm altogether fine, I feel extremely happy, as a matter of fact, happy as a lark, just don't worry about me, please.'

'Good. I'm delighted.'

'Anyway, sweet of you to call. I've got to go now, sorry. Speak soon, you're a total heroine.'

'I wish,' said Beatrice.

Ed was drinking his third coffee of the day and wishing he could feel the slightest interest in what he was doing, when his mother called. She did most mornings; he wasn't sure whether it helped, or not.

'How are you today, dear?'

'Oh – you know. Bit bad, I think.'

'I know,' she said gently. 'It comes and goes, doesn't it? Mostly it comes, especially at the beginning.'

'Yes. Well, you should know, Mum.'

His parents' marriage had been particularly happy; it was, he had told Martha, how he knew about love. 'Proper love. The on and on sort. The you and me sort.'

'I do,' said Maureen softly. 'And I tell you what, Edward. After a while, the memories become happier. They really do.'

'Good,' he said, 'something needs to. Thanks, Mum.'

'I popped in at the vicarage this morning. Poor Mr Hartley's so worried about his wife. She had a fall this morning, and apparently she won't eat, she's just turned her face to the wall. The doctor says he's going to have to put her in hospital, in a day or two.'

'Oh dear. I'm sorry.'

'Anyway the real reason I rang you was that Mr Hartley says the one thing that's cheered Mrs Hartley up lately was your visit. He said he thinks it was you being so close to Martha, it brings her back, in a funny way.'

'That's nice,' said Ed. He wished someone could bring Martha back for him in any way at all. Funny or not.

'Yes, well, take care of yourself, love. I'll ring in a day or two.'

Nick had decided he must get back to London. It was all very well being at home with his parents when he was haring round doing things and enjoying himself, but being marooned there, confined to the house, was rather different. Most of the family had left; he had nothing to do but read, and go for solitary walks.

And think: to a large degree about Jocasta. And what a fool he'd been. An absolute bloody fool. Why hadn't he moved in with her, married her for God's sake, if that's what she wanted? From his lonely perspective now, that looked a pretty attractive proposition. All his three brothers, one of them younger than him, were married, and they seemed perfectly contented. And they had all these children, jolly little things. He often thought he'd like some children. He got on with them terribly well. Of course that wouldn't have been possible with Jocasta, she'd never get over that phobia of hers: maybe that, at least, was consolation for losing her. He might find another girl he could love as much, who was dying to have babies. He might.

He kept conjuring Jocasta up, warm, laughing, happy, talking nonsense – and as she had been that last afternoon, lying in bed, her lovely body naked, her astonishing hair splayed across the pillow, her huge eyes brilliant as she looked at him, holding out her arms to him, telling him she loved him. Yes, she had said that, there had been no doubt about it – wanted him, talking her way through love-making as she so engagingly did: 'That's lovely, so lovely. God it's gorgeous, fantastic . . . here I go now, Nick, I can't bear it . . . go on, go on . . .'

He snapped his mind shut. This was ridiculous. She'd gone back to Keeble, and who could blame her. He had to get on with his life. And he'd start by going back to London. The very next day.

Jocasta reached Clio's flat at six o'clock; it had taken her much longer than usual. She had developed a headache, driving into the sun, and was feeling rather nauseous. She wondered if this was the beginning of the pregnancy sickness. If she was going to start feeling ill, then the – well, what she was going to do tomorrow was even better timing.

She pressed the bell: Clio's voice came through the intercom.

'Hello. Who is it?'

'It's me, Jocasta. Can I come in?'

There was a silence: then, 'Sure.'

She was looking rotten: white and drawn. She had obviously been crying.

'Oh, Clio,' said Jocasta, 'Clio, I'm so sorry. Sorry to have been so beastly, and so insensitive, and sorry about you. Please forgive me. I don't deserve it, but please do.'

Clio managed a smile. 'Of course. I understand.'

'I expect you do,' said Jocasta, 'understand what a brat I am, what an unfeeling, pathetic brat. I need my bottom smacked very hard. Would you like to do it?' she added, with a smile. 'I'm sure it would do me good.'

'I wouldn't dream of it,' said Clio. She managed a weak smile. 'What would the neighbours say?' And then two tears trickled down her face.

'Oh Clio,' said Jocasta. 'Here, let me give you a hug.'

She opened her arms and Clio went into them, and sobbed for a long time.

'It's so unfair,' she said, 'so, so unfair!'

'I know. I know it is. It's dreadful for you. There really is nothing you can do?'

'Apparently not. My tubes are buggered and that's it.'

'Well – you should know. What – what about IVF?'

'It's a possibility of course. Quite a good one – in theory.'

'And in practice?'

'It's a pretty miserable business. Someone's got to love you an

689

awful lot to submit themselves to it. Dodgy, too. I mean it doesn't work all nice and neatly the first time. There are very long waiting lists. And going privately, it's thousands of pounds a time.'

'Couldn't you jump the queue? Being in the business and everything?'

'Of course not!' Clio sounded quite shocked. 'I wouldn't dream of it. Anyway, I don't know why I'm being so pathetic, who's going to give me a baby anyway? In some new relationship? I'm already thirty-five.'

'Fergus?'

'I'm afraid not. That's dead in the water.'

'Clio, are you sure?'

'Quite sure.'

'That's not the impression I got.'

'What do you mean?'

'I rang him just now, see if he could help me get through to you. He said you weren't getting on very well, said something about a clash of ideologies? Anyway, he'd been trying to ring you. He said you wouldn't speak to him. Doesn't sound quite a corpse to me.'

'Maybe not now. But it would never work, Jocasta. In the first place, I can't approve of what he does – '

'Why?'

'Oh, it seems to me the very worst sort of cashing in on other people's misfortunes. I know you see it differently but – '

'Clio, it *is* different. It's helping people through them.'

'What? People like footballers who've been shagging six girls at a time, presenting their cases in the best possible light?'

'But it's not all that. Look at what a lot he's done for Kate, and he hasn't even been paid yet, not a penny, I've just discovered. By my beloved nearly-ex-husband. Well, he has now. I hope.'

'Gideon! What's he got to do with Kate?'

'Oh – he said he'd pay Fergus until Kate could. That was the whole basis for the deal. And the poor guy hasn't had a penny out of him. Anyway – don't you think that was amazingly nice of Fergus? When he'd never met Kate, didn't know the first thing about her?'

'No,' said Clio, 'it was only money.'

'Oh, shut up! Now, come on, what else does the poor bloke

do wrong? Apart from earn a crust the only way he knows?'

'Nothing, really,' said Clio feebly.

Jocasta left quite soon after that: her headache was worse, and she was very tired. They had, by common assent, not discussed her situation; she had made up her mind, she told Clio, and nothing was going to change it.

'I know you think it's wrong of me, but we'll have to agree to differ. At least we're friends again.'

'You – wouldn't like me to come back with you? Be with you tonight?'

'Oh – God, no. I am so not worried about it. Honestly. And it would be awful for you. I'll be fine. I really will. Just totally, totally fine. Bye, Clio darling, and please go on forgiving me. Lots of love. I'll call you in a day or two. And – give Fergus a ring. Go on.'

Nick was on his way to London. He was driving; his mother had been absolutely horrified, but he said his arm was fine out of its sling, he could do most of the driving with his left arm. 'I'm sorry, Mummy, but I've got to get back. So much to do. And I swear I'll go and see my own quack first thing tomorrow. OK?'

Pattie Marshall sighed. 'I can't stop you, I know, but I think it's very foolish. And you'd better not have an accident. The police would throw the book at you.'

Nick promised not to.

Jocasta walked into her house and sank onto her bed. She felt absolutely dreadful. Less sick now, but lonely, frightened, bereft. The thought of what she had to go through in the morning suddenly seemed rather – unpleasant. It wasn't the pain; Sarah Kershaw had assured her it would be minimal. 'You'll just be sore. And bleeding rather a lot, at first. You have arranged for someone to drive you home?'

'Of course,' said Jocasta. 'No problem. Absolutely no problem at all.'

She had booked a cab: both ways.

So what was troubling her about the morning? She wanted to be rid of the – pregnancy. She would never have to worry about another. She wasn't afraid of the procedure. Nick would never know. She'd have her life back after it. She'd be fine.

It was just a bit – sad. Yes, she did feel a bit sad. That was natural. You'd be pretty odd if you didn't feel anything about getting rid of – ending a pregnancy. Actually, she was almost relieved that she did. That she wasn't totally hard-hearted after all. Of course it wasn't a baby: she kept telling herself that. It was a pregnancy, that was the thing to hang onto, a medical condition, which she was dealing with, in a very adult way. The fact that if she didn't deal with it, in something like seven months there'd be a small creature in the world that had been put there by her and Nick didn't merit even thinking about. She wouldn't think about it. There was nothing to think about.

She poured herself a glass of red wine, had a long bath, and grazed through the papers: she was still horribly awake. Maybe she should take a sleeping pill. Maybe not: on top of the red wine, which had made her feel sick. Maybe she should watch TV; that always sent her to sleep, it was like flicking a switch. There was a good movie on, *When Harry Met Sally*. She'd watch that. She always loved it.

Halfway through the orgasm scene, she switched it off. It was annoying her. Really annoying her. As if anyone would sit in a cafe and pretend to have an orgasm, that loudly. Stupid. She poured herself another glass of wine and reflected she'd only faked one herself a couple of times: when she'd been just so tired and all she wanted was to go to sleep. It was amazing how they didn't know. Couldn't tell. She'd certainly never, ever faked with Nick. Their sex had always been amazing. Had made a baby even.

Stop it, Jocasta. It is not a baby. It really is not a baby.

She was still horribly awake, and horribly frightened again. She looked at the clock. Only half past twelve. How was she going to get through the rest of the night? Shit. This was awful.

But it was the last one. The very last one.

Nick woke early. It had been a hell of a drive, but he'd done it, and fallen exhausted into bed in Hampstead, at midnight. But the pain in his arm had woken him up; he struggled into the kitchen, took a couple of the painkillers – they were bloody strong, made him feel quite woozy – and made himself a cup of tea. Maybe he should go for a walk; clear his head. God, he'd be glad when he could run again; at the moment it jarred his arm too much, destroyed the pleasure. Yes, he'd go for a stroll, buy the papers, come back and have breakfast and then head down to Westminster. There was bound to be something going on; and it would be good to get back there. He'd really missed it: funny old place.

He walked down to Heath Street, bought *The Times* and the *Guardian* and the *Daily Mail* – they would put him back in touch with the country between them, his parents only took the *Telegraph* – dropped in at the deli for a couple of croissants and went home.

He was halfway through the second croissant when a feature in the *Mail* caught his eye: Holiday Getaway Gear, it said, and was a piece about what to wear when travelling and how to look as good – or as bad – as the rich and famous. Lots of shots of people leaving airports, over the past few days – Madonna, Nicole Appleton, Kate Moss, Jude Law, Jonathan Ross, Jasper Conran – and Gideon Keeble. Terrifically well-dressed as always – probably better than most of the others, in a linen suit and panama hat. Bastard. All that money, and looks and style as well.

The captions said where they were all going: mostly to the sun. Workaholic Keeble, as they called him, was off to Melbourne, on a business trip. God, he really was a workaholic. No Jocasta in sight; not famous enough, he supposed. Not that Keeble was, really; they must have been scraping the barrel, needed a last person to fill the page. Maybe she hadn't gone: maybe she was still in London, in that absurd mansion. Or down in Wiltshire – was it? Or Berkshire?

He could try. He could ring her; she had phoned and left that message he'd never responded to – well, it had been a bit cool, and unmistakable in its meaning, and he'd been a bit cross, actually, that she'd been so long in acknowledging his postcards. But he could ring, tell her that he was fine, back in London if she needed him – no, that would be wrong, why should she need him – well just back, thank her for calling –

It took him a few minutes to decide actually to do it; then telling himself they had agreed to be friends, and it was what any friend would do, he called her mobile.

It was switched off.

693

Well – best leave it then. Only – maybe he could try the house. Just see if she was there. Why not? No reason, it was much less clandestine, really, than using her mobile. It proved how innocent his call was. Simply – friendly.

He dialled the Big House; a foreign voice answered. A Philippino-sort of a foreign voice.

'Mr Keeble's residence.'

Slightly odd phraseology. Surely it was the Keeble residence now?

'Good morning. Is Mrs Keeble there?'

'Mrs Keeble? No, Mrs Keeble not here.'

'Oh, fine. She's away with Mr Keeble, then? Or in the country.'

'Mrs Keeble not living here now. She – '

There was a sort of scuffle at the end of the line; then Mrs Hutching, he recognised her voice, said, 'Good morning! Can I help you?'

Nick's heart was doing slightly peculiar things.

'Mrs Hutching, isn't it? Good morning. You won't remember me, but I'm a friend of Mrs Keeble's, Nicholas Marshall, I came to the house once or twice. I wanted to speak to her, if she's around.'

'I'm sorry, Mr Marshall, she isn't here. She's away.'

'With Mr Keeble? Or in the country?'

'I'm not absolutely sure. I'm sorry. If you like to leave a message – '

Nick left a message and then put the phone down. He felt slightly dizzy. Must be the pills, of course. But – the first woman, she'd said Jocasta didn't live there any more. Of course she was foreign, and might have meant something different, like she wasn't living there at the moment. But then Mrs Hutching had sounded pretty bloody odd, as well. Actually.

Shit. Had Jocasta actually left Gideon? She couldn't have. She couldn't. She'd have told him. Surely. And if she hadn't told him, the outlook wasn't too good for him anyway.

Nick stood up, walked up and down his small kitchen a couple of times and then rang Clio. She'd know. She'd tell him.

Jocasta had been awake for three hours; the longest three hours she could ever remember. She had just lain there and watched

694

the clock tick the seconds past, longing for it to be later. It took its time. It was still only half past six. She felt altogether dreadful; her headache was worse and she felt terribly sick. If this were indeed pregnancy sickness, thank God this would be the last day of it.

She felt really frightened and really alone. If only, if only she had someone to talk to. To tell her not to worry, that she was doing the right thing, that she'd be fine. Even Clio, telling her she was doing the wrong one, would have been preferable to this. But – there was no one. And three more endless hours stretched ahead of her.

She couldn't stand any of it any longer; she decided to go for a walk.

All Clio could think about when she woke up was Jocasta. How she must be feeling; for all her brave tough words, she knew she was frightened and upset. The more Jocasta talked and protested, the more upset she was. She was talking a lot at the moment.

She would call her; and arrange to go to see her that evening. She'd be feeling awful, even if she weren't upset, sore and tired. And no matter what anyone said, from Clio's experience at any rate, it wasn't true that what most women felt after a termination was relief. They did feel relief, of course: they also felt guilt and misery and regret.

She rang the house: the answering machine was on.

'Only me,' she said. 'I'm just calling to see if you're OK, wish you luck. I thought I'd come and see you this evening. No need to call back, I'll be there about seven. Unless you don't want me. Lots of love.'

She looked at the clock: nearly seven. She might as well stay up now. Get a good start on the day. She had a shower, was just starting to get dressed, when the phone rang. Hopefully Jocasta, having got her message.

But it wasn't Jocasta; it was Nick.

Jocasta was in the middle of Clapham Common when she felt faint. She sank rather dramatically onto her haunches, dropped her head in her arms, taking deep breaths, and tried not to panic. Now what did she do?

'You OK?' A girl, a jogger, had stopped, was bending over her. Jocasta looked up at her, tried to smile and then threw up onto the grass.

'Sorry,' she said, 'so sorry. Yes, I – well, no, I don't feel too good. Have you got a mobile?'

'Sure.' She rummaged in her bum bag, handed her phone to Jocasta. Even making the call was almost beyond her.

Clio felt dreadful. She was the worst liar in the world. She had done her best, had stumbled through her story that she hadn't seen Jocasta for a while, that she didn't know if she was still with Gideon and that she didn't know where she was. It had been totally pathetic. Nick had actually said that. He'd said, quite nicely, 'Clio, that is just so pathetic. Of course you know where she is. Come on. At her house? In Clapham. Look, I can see you're protecting her for some reason. She probably made you swear not to say. So if you don't say anything I'll assume it's Clapham, OK?'

Clio was dutifully silent.

Nick got into his car and set out for Clapham.

'You are just so stupid,' said Beatrice severely, helping Jocasta up the steps of their house and into the sitting room. It had taken her five minutes to get to the common and twenty-five to get back in the building traffic. During which she had had to stop twice for Jocasta to be sick. 'You should have told us before.'

'I couldn't,' said Jocasta wearily, dropping down onto the sofa. 'I just couldn't bear to talk about it. Or think about it. Bit like Martha, I suppose.'

'I think you're a little better off than she was, poor girl. I presume Gideon knows about this?'

'Well – '

'Jocasta! I can't believe this. Of course you must tell him.'

'It isn't Gideon's baby,' said Jocasta.

Nick stood outside Jocasta's house alternately ringing the bell and banging on the door. He was convinced she was in there, hiding, that she knew it was him.

After five minutes he decided to let himself in. Even if she wasn't there, he might get some clue as to where he might find her. Or what had happened.

Thank God he had never given the key back.

She wasn't there: but she had clearly only just left. Her duvet was flung back, there was the usual incredible mess in her bedroom, several used cups piled up by the dishwasher. She always did that, never put them in it. It had driven him mad. Even the radio was on: Chris Tarrant burbling cheerfully away. She would obviously be back any minute.

God, his arm hurt. So, so much. They'd obviously known what they were talking about, telling him to rest it. Bloody agony. And he'd left his pills behind, of course. Jocasta always had plenty of painkillers; she was a bit of an addict. He'd take some of hers, have a cup of tea and wait for her. He put the kettle on, went to the cupboard under the bathroom basin.

It was a shrine to her messiness; two or three Tampax packets, one of them empty, a very exhausted-looking toothbrush, a mass of hair bands, a spilt box of cotton buds, two packs of dental floss, both in use; a half-empty bottle of mouthwash, two rather evil-looking flannels, and – yes – rummaging a little, bravely on, two bottles of painkillers, not particularly strong ones, she usually had more than that, two large tubes of fake tan, several double A batteries, a packet of something that called itself a natural sleep remedy, an enormous bottle of vitamin C tablets and – what was this? God in heaven, what was this? It couldn't be – no, it wasn't – yes it was, it really indubitably, really horribly was, a pregnancy testing kit, and sweet Jesus, another, both used, the instructions for one crumpled up and pushed back into the box, the other still neatly folded, clearly unread.

What was this, what had been going on here, what had she been doing, why hadn't she told him? Absurd, ridiculous, pointless, cretinous questions. And how long ago had this happened, when had she bought these tests, was the baby Gideon's? Must be, that would explain her extraordinary behaviour, avoiding him. It surely, surely couldn't be his – could it? If there was one? And how did he know that, even? What had she done since? He would have put nothing past her, nothing at all. Why hadn't she told him? It must be Gideon's, must be, must be, otherwise she'd have told him surely, surely.

Nick walked out of the bathroom and sat down, his legs having become suddenly weak, totally devoid of substance; and then rang Clio again.

She didn't answer.

'Look, Beatrice, I'm not having it. Nick won't want it. I know he won't. You know what he's like; the last thing in the world he'd want is a child.'

'That's not quite the same thing as not knowing he's got one. In the making, at least.'

'Beatrice, I can't tell him. Believe me, I can't.'

'Well – I do beg to differ. Look – I'd love to stay with you, but I can't, I have to be in court in under an hour. We can discuss it all tonight. Are you going to stay down here, or do you want to go up to bed? Christine'll look after you. She's taking the children to school now, but I'll leave her a note. Josh is away, somewhere up in the midlands.'

'Fine. Thank you so much, Beatrice.'

'That's OK. Now promise me, rest.'

'I promise.'

Good thing Beatrice was going out, thought Jocasta. She felt much better. She had an hour still; she'd have a shower, borrow one of Beatrice's rather severe tracksuits and set off. God, and change the cab arrangement. Better do that first.

Josh was still asleep, when Beatrice rang. He'd had a bit of a night with the sales force, his head was agony.

'Josh, this is Beatrice. Look, I've got something to tell you. You are coming back tonight, aren't you?'

'Of course.'

'Right, well, Jocasta will be there.'

'Jocasta! Why?'

'She's pregnant.'

'Pregnant!'

'Yes. And – wait for it. It's not Gideon's. It's Nick's. And she's clearly planning a termination.'

'Nick's! How terrible. Can't we stop her?'

'I'm not sure. But the point is, he doesn't know. And he really should. She swears he wouldn't want it, but he ought to have a chance to say so himself. He can't stop her legally, of course, but – anyway, do you have his number?'

'I think so. You really think he ought to be told?'

'I really think so.'

'Lord. Poor Jocasta.'

Clio was frantically worried; Jocasta appeared to have gone missing. She had tried her several more times and each time there had been more bleeps on the answering machine and no reply on her mobile.

She actually picked up the phone to call Nick once or twice and then put it down again hastily. He had called her, but she hadn't picked up the phone. God, she was a coward. Or was she just being a good friend, keeping Jocasta's counsel?

She wished she could talk to Fergus about it all. He would know what to do. That was one of the wonderful things about Fergus, he was so sensible. And sympathetic. He was such a Jekyll and Hyde, he had been so sweet about the Morrises, for instance. Stop thinking about Fergus, Clio, concentrate on Jocasta and what's going on.

Her phone rang: she jumped, but it wasn't Nick, it was Josh. Did she have Nick's mobile number? Or even his flat? It was urgent . . .

'Well – '

'Oh, Clio, come on.'

'Do you know where she is?'

'Yes, she's at our house.'

'Oh – thank God. I've been so worried about her. Yes, of course, I'll give you his number. But don't say I gave it you. And you can tell him what you like. Only, I swore I wouldn't – '

'Thanks. You don't happen to know when – if – she might be having a termination, do you?'

'Well – yes. She is. This morning, I'm afraid. And she's going to be sterilised – '

'Jesus! Where?'

'I don't know. She wouldn't tell me. I think she thought I might tell Nick; we'd had a row – '

'Look, call her at our house, Clio, would you? Try to find out where she's going, try to delay her. And I'll ring Nick.'

Jocasta was feeling much better. She could go to the clinic. She'd be fine. She had three quarters of an hour before the cab came. She might just have a bath rather than a shower, it would be more relaxing.

Sitting in the bath with the door shut and Capital Radio on loudly, to distract her, she didn't hear the phone ringing.

'Nick? This is Josh.'

'Josh! Thank God. Maybe you can help. I'm terribly worried about Jocasta, I don't know where she is and – '

'She's at our house.'

'At yours?'

'Yes. Now the thing is – that is – oh God, this might be a bit of a shock, Nick, but she's – well, she's pregnant. Sorry to spring it on you, but . . .'

'I did – think she might be,' said Nick. He was speaking rather slowly. 'I just found some tests. I'm at her place now. But – why are you ringing me?'

'Because it's yours.'

'Mine?' said Nick and he felt as if he was falling through a large silent space, with Josh's voice echoing in the heart of it. 'My baby? Are you absolutely sure?'

'Well – Jocasta is. She told Beatrice.'

'Good God,' said Nick. 'Dear, sweet Jesus.'

'Yes. And she's about to have a termination.' There was a silence. 'Nick? You still there?'

'Yes. Yes, I'm still here.'

'Nick, I'm so sorry. Bloody awful thing to hear out of the blue. But Jocasta's at our house, if you want to stop her.'

'Of course I want to stop her, for God's sake!'

'Well, call her. Got the number? I think you really have to put your skates on, Nick, and – '

But Nick had already cut him off.

'Mr Hartley, hello. This is Ed. Ed Forrest. I just heard from Mum, she said Mrs Hartley might have to go into hospital. I'm so sorry. How is she now?'

'Oh – nice of you to call, Ed. Yes, she isn't very well.

700

Dreadfully low, I'm afraid. Just as you must be. How are you feeling?'

'Oh – not too bad,' said Ed quickly. He didn't like talking about how much he hurt; that was his property, part of Martha and of how much he had loved her, not to be shared.

'Your visit was the one thing which seemed to cheer my wife up. I was so grateful to you, Ed. Oh, and could you thank Kate? Her letter seemed to help, as well. It was so kind of her to write. I've been meaning to write to her, myself, but I've been so busy. I think Grace feels Martha's friends bring her closer, somehow.'

'Yes, well, that's nice. And I will tell Kate, yeah. I'm not sure if I'll be up again this weekend, Mr Hartley, but if I am, I'll certainly come and see her again. Cheers. Take care.'

'It's Grace who needs to take care. But thank you, Ed, so much.' Poor old chap. Poor, poor old chap. He'd tell Kate. She was a nice kid. Pretty too. Bit spiky. Like her mother.

'Miss Forbes, isn't it? Yes. And you're booked in for – yes, a termination this morning? And a sterilisation.'

The nurse smiled at her encouragingly.

'Yes,' said Jocasta, 'that's right.'

'If you'd like to come with me, I'll take you up to your room. We can do your admission; check everything's in order, ask you to sign the consent form, all that sort of thing. You've had nothing, since six o'clock, to eat or drink?'

'No, I haven't.'

'Good. Now I think we'll start with taking your blood pressure.'

'I'm sorry, Mr Marshall, but Jocasta's gone.' The nanny was clearly anxious. 'Yes. She left about – oh, I don't know, about half an hour ago. I'm sorry, I didn't – what? In a cab. Yes. No, it was a mini cab. I have no idea, I'm afraid – oh hang on, he's left a card. I can't stand the way they always do that, can you? Oh, sorry, yes, Clapham Cars, does that ring a bell? Yes? Well, the number's –'

Kate was on her way to see Fergus; she had definitely decided to sign the contract, if Smith hadn't found anyone else. It was only three years, it was such a lot of money, it would set her up for life, as a photographer maybe, or whatever else she decided to do.

It was all very well for Josh to tell her not to, if it bored her: he had plenty of money already. And she could see how it would help her parents, and Juliet for that matter. And now she was feeling so much better about everything, she thought she could handle the publicity.

She knew Fergus would be pleased. And rather better off as a result. So it would benefit everyone, really. After all, it was only three years.

Peter was in the middle of dealing with some correspondence, when Grace called him.

'Could I have some painkillers, Peter, please? My head is dreadful.'

'Of course. I'll bring them up.'

He walked in; she looked terrible.

'Poor old love. Here they are. I'll get a couple out for you – '

The phone started to ring.

'I'll do it, Peter, thank you.'

She tipped out a couple of the tablets, and swallowed them and had just started to replace the cap when something stopped her. She sat looking at the bottle. There were plenty more. She could just take a handful. That should do it: quite quickly. The other way was taking too long and making her feel too bad. Lucky whoever it was had called then. Really lucky . . .

'Would that have been a Miss Forbes?'

'I – would imagine so. Yes.'

'Let me see. She changed the booking, from Haines Road, to Old Town pick-up – yes, here we are. She's booked to Gower Street. That sound right?'

'Yes, definitely.'

'OK. The GG & O Clinic, Gower Street, it was. Just down from UCH. Pick-up this afternoon, time to be confirmed.'

'Thank you,' said Nick, 'thank you so much.'

If she was having this awful thing done this morning it could be any time now. It could be now. He'd better get his skates on. As Josh had said.

'Kate, my darling, come along in. You're looking perfectly gorgeous, as usual. How are you?'

'I'm good, thanks, Fergus. Now who's that – excuse me, sorry – '

It was extraordinary, the way the young responded to their mobiles, Fergus thought, as if every call was crucial, far more crucial than anything else they might be involved in. You saw them, sitting in a group, a large group, and half of them, at any given time, were on their mobiles. Very odd. And they didn't seem to think breaking off whatever conversation they were having was remotely anti-social.

'Sorry. I'll switch it off now. That was Ed. You know Ed? Martha's boyfriend.'

'I do. Rather handsome, as I recall.'

'Handsome or what! Yeah. Anyway, apparently Mrs Hartley, that's Martha's mum, she's really low. And I wrote to them both. I was thinking, you know, that she was my gran really, another gran, and she seemed really lovely, and I felt so sorry for her, and Mr Hartley said my letter had really cheered her up, can't think why, and could Ed let me know. It's a pity we can't tell them, in a way – '

'I do hope you won't,' said Fergus anxiously. 'I don't think that would be a good idea, at all.'

'Fergus! I'm not that stupid. Anyway, I've come to talk about the contract with Smith. I really do think I should sign it. I feel so different now and – '

Nick roared along Knightsbridge and cut up into the park; please God don't let the Horse Guards be going along it. They were. He sat there in agony for a moment or two, then did a U-turn and screeched back, cutting up into the Bayswater Road. The traffic there was fairly solid, too: he shot across it, and took a back route, weaving round the narrow streets and squares, cutting up other motorists (surprised at their outrage, he was only driving as he always did, only faster), nearly killing two dogs, one cat and frightening the life out of a rather grand-looking old lady, stepping out into the road without looking, as grand old ladies tended to. She shook her fist at him, and when last seen in his rear-view mirror, she was pointing out his car to a passer-by. He shot across Baker Street, wove his way along Welbeck Street, and then struck north, his mind wiped clear of everything except the need to get to Gower Street, in time. At one point he found himself confronted by a no-entry sign and a one-way street; it seemed entirely logical to take it on. He was lucky.

In Gower Street, he had to find the clinic, right at the top it had been, the man had said: where was the bloody place: ah, there. No meters of course, only double yellow lines everywhere.

He abandoned the car and faced a traffic warden who asked him what he thought he was doing: 'Saving a life,' he said.

The man had clearly heard this before. 'I'll have to give you a ticket,' he said.

'Great. Fine. I'd really like that. Just go ahead.'

The warden stared at him and then started to write the ticket, shaking his head.

And there it was, a discreet, very freshly painted door: with GG & O Clinic on a brass plate. GG & O – what sort of bloody nonsense was that? He pushed on the bell; the door opened with a self-important burr.

There was a reception desk in the hall, with a vast urn of flowers on it; to the left of the urn was a smiling young woman in a navy suit and a flowered shirt, with a bow at the neck.

'Good morning,' she said. 'How can I help you?'

'By telling me where – where my wife is,' said Nick. He somehow felt they'd be more helpful if he assumed husband status. He sat down breathing heavily. He felt rather odd.

'Would you like to give me her name?'

'Keeble. Jocasta Keeble.'

'And – who is she seeing today?'

'I'm afraid I can't tell you. I don't know.'

The woman started to press the keys on her computer. Enough keys, it seemed to Nick, to be writing a book. Or certainly a very long article. What a bloody waste of time and energy those things were. All she needed was an appointment book and a pencil.

'Keeble, you say, Keeble. No – I don't have anyone of that name this morning.'

Her phone had just rung. 'Gower Gynaecology and Obstetrics. Mr Cartwright? Yes, if you could just wait a moment.' More key-tapping.

'Look,' said Nick, 'this is so urgent, I can't begin to tell you. Please, please tell me where she is.'

'Just a moment, please. So sorry, Mr Cartwright, just putting you through now.'

She smiled at him; a less friendly smile.

'Now: no Keeble today. Definitely.'

'Well – how about Forbes?'

'Forbes, Forbes . . . oh, yes. Yes, here she is. Good. If you'd like to sit down over there, I'll let Mrs Miles know you're here. Do help yourself to tea or coffee.'

'I don't want any coffee and I certainly don't want Mrs Miles. I want my – wife.'

'Mrs Miles is looking after your wife today. Please try to be patient – hello? Susan, it's about a Mrs Forbes. One of Mrs Miles's patients. Her husband is here. Is she in theatre – Ah, yes, I see. Thank you . . .' She sat back in her chair, gave Nick an even more gracious smile.

'I'm so sorry, Mr Keeble. Your wife has already left.'

He could see at once what she had done. She was looking – odd. A mixture of defiant and excited. The paracetamol bottle was placed neatly on the bedside table, with its cap on; she glanced at it. He picked it up. It was empty.

'Oh, Grace, Grace, my darling, you shouldn't have done that, I know why, but – God, let's ring Douglas – dear God – '

Grace started to cry.

Douglas Cummings's advice was succinct.

'Get her into hospital. At once. It's a lethal drug. However she seems, just bring her in. Do you want an ambulance?'

'No,' said Peter wearily, 'it's only five minutes away. I'll drive her.'

He hoped very much it wouldn't be the last thing he did for her.

Nick walked very slowly back to the car. It had been clamped.

He decided he couldn't sort it out yet; he would just leave it.

The one good thing about being clamped was that the car was safe.

He felt rather sick, and terribly tired. Apart from that, nothing: not sad, not angry, just – nothing. His arm hurt. He hailed a cab, directed it to Hampstead. He sat in it, staring out of the window, at the rather depressing upper reaches of Gower Street, looking at people, lucky people, who had normal relationships and happy families.

He tried very hard not to think about Jocasta and even harder not to think about the baby she had just thrown away. He failed. His mind felt as if it would never think of anything else again. Of her, and how much he had loved her – still loved her, so, so much – and how he would have behaved, what he would have wanted, if he had known. And he knew he would have wanted it. Very, very much. Even now, thinking about the baby, a baby that no longer existed, he felt new and totally unfamiliar things. He wasn't quite sure what they were, but there seemed to be pride there, and a fierce protectiveness and a degree of awe at what they had accomplished, Jocasta and he. Yes. No doubt. He would have wanted it: his baby.

It would have been absolutely terrifying: it would have meant not only commitment, absolute commitment, abruptly and forcibly entered into, but a new and entirely different life. There would have been no period of adjustment for the two of them, no time to learn to live together, no time for him to come to terms with his new condition. He would have had to make the leap from single man to husband and father, with scarcely time between to take breath. It would have been very, very difficult. But – it was what he would have wanted.

And as he sat there, astonished at the sadness of it, of what he had lost, they had both lost, he thought it was as well he wasn't going to see her, for he would not be able to answer for what he might do to her; and then he leant forward and tapped on the window and said to the cabbie, 'Could you change that, take me to Clapham, North End Road, instead. Please.'

She would probably be all right, they said, because he'd acted so quickly.

'The trouble with paracetamol is that it doesn't seem to have had any effect and all the time there's appalling liver damage going on,' said the young doctor to Peter. He had come out of the room where Grace lay, to find him, head in hands, weeping quietly. He was very young, the doctor; he normally found patients' grief extremely difficult to deal with, but his father was a clergyman and this sweet man seemed somehow familiar.

'I really think she'll be all right. We've given her a very powerful antidote, washed her stomach out, of course, and she's sleeping now. Try not to worry. She seemed quite peaceful.'

Peter nodded; he was unable to speak.

'Look,' said the doctor, 'I know she's frail and not so young, but she has a huge spirit. I could tell that, just from being with her, and she kept saying she was sorry. Try not to worry,' he said again.

'Yes,' said Peter, wiping his eyes. 'Yes, thank you.'

'Get yourself a cup of tea, I would.'

'Yes, I will.'

Peter watched him as he hurried off in response to another patient, another crisis; he hardly looked old enough to be in charge of a medicine chest, let alone a busy Casualty clinic, very thin, lanky almost, in his white coat, his hair flopping into his eyes.

Suddenly the young man turned and came back to him.

'There was something I forgot to tell you,' he said to Peter. 'Your wife said it had been an accident. She said that about three times. She's obviously regretting it terribly. I think that's good news. The really serious cases are when they don't want to be brought round.'

Peter thanked him. But he knew Grace would actually have loved to go. Go to join Martha.

'Call for you, Clio. I think it's your journalist friend,' said Margaret. 'Shall I put her through?'

'Oh – yes. Please do. How many still waiting?'

'Only Mrs Cudden.'

'Bless her. Tell her I won't be a minute. Tell her I'll drive her home.'

'You sure?'

'Absolutely sure. Jocasta, hello, are you all right?'

'Oh, Clio, Clio – ' Jocasta got no further; huge sobs came down the line.

'Oh, Jocasta, darling, what happened, what is it?'

'It was all so terrible, so awful. I was so frightened and I – oh God. Clio, please come. As soon as you can. Sorry, Clio, so sorry, I'm all right really, I just – '

'Jocasta, you shouldn't be alone. You should have someone with you. Where are you?'

'At home. I'm fine, honestly. I'll be all right.'

'I can be there by about five,' said Clio. 'Is that all right?'

'Yes. Thank you.' She sounded terribly weepy; Clio rang off and buzzed for Mrs Cudden.

Maybe she could get the new young locum to take her afternoon surgery.

'You can see her now, Mr Hartley.' The young nurse smiled at him encouragingly. 'She's had a little sleep. She says she wants to go home, but because of her age and everything, we feel she should stay in for a couple of days. Just so we can keep a check on her liver and so on. We've got a room in Florence, we'll move her up there as soon as we can.'

'Thank you,' said Peter. He wondered rather distractedly how many millions of hospital wards were called Florence, and went in to see Grace.

She was lying on her back, staring up at the ceiling; she was rather yellow-looking.

'Hello, Grace darling.'

She turned her head and looked at him: and dissolved into tears.

'Oh, Peter, I'm so sorry. It was so wrong of me. Please forgive me.'

'Of course I forgive you. I'd forgive you anything. You know that. I love you so much, Grace.'

'I know. And I love you. But – everything seems so hopeless. So dreadfully hopeless. I looked into that bottle and saw the answer.'

'I know, darling, I know.'

'It just hurts so much; I don't know how to bear it. I don't seem to have God, any more, as you do. Not helping me, as He is you. Please forgive me, Peter, please.'

'Grace, He isn't helping me very much, either, at the moment. I can't imagine ever feeling any better.'

'Really?' she said.

'Really. There have even been times when I felt I had lost my faith entirely.'

'Oh, Peter. I didn't realise, I thought – '

'You thought wrongly. But I know He will help. Sooner or later. I just have to hang on. As you must. I can't afford to lose you, as well,' he added with a rather weary smile.

Grace looked at him. It seemed dreadful to feel better, because she knew Peter felt worse. But somehow, it helped. Knowing they were in it together, knowing she wasn't enduring the worst of it all alone. She managed a smile back.

'I'm so sorry,' she said again, and then, 'I must look so awful!'

'You always look beautiful to me.'

'Oh don't,' she said, turning her head away. The endless tears started again.

Peter sighed. She still had a long way to go. But he felt an important marker in the road had been passed. They were at least together again. He could feel it.

'Edward?'

'Yes, Mum.' He could hear his own voice, slightly irritable; he must be careful. But this was getting a bit much: second time today.

'Edward, I've got some rather sad news.'

Not more. He couldn't take it. 'What?'

'Poor Mrs Hartley – '

'What's happened now?'

'She took an overdose, Ed. So sad.'

'Oh no! Is she – '

'No, no, she's going to be all right. But – think how dreadful she must be feeling. Poor soul. She's still in hospital, Dorothy told me, you know, she's my friend from Weight Watchers – '

'Yes, Mum.'

'She's a nurse. Of course she shouldn't have told me, but – I thought you'd like to know.'

'Yes, I'm glad you told me.' He felt sharply depressed; how long and how far were the effects of Martha's death going to spread? 'Yes, I'll send her a card.'

'Could you? And perhaps you could ask that girl – Kate, was it? – to do the same? I found cards, the briefest note, so helpful. Just to know people are thinking of you.'

'Sure. I will.'

He'd ring her later; he couldn't face it now.

'Clio, this is Fergus.'

'Oh – hello!'

'How are you?'

'I'm fine, Fergus, yes, thank you. And you?'

'Also absolutely fine. Clio, I just wanted to tell you something – '

'Look, Fergus, I'm sorry, but I'm terribly busy. I've got to – well, do something, leave Guildford in a couple of hours and see a waiting room full of patients first. Another time – '

Fergus rang off without even saying goodbye.

Nick stood looking at Jocasta's little house for a moment, listening to the taxi drive away. He felt almost frightened to go in, afraid of how he might feel about it and her, of how dangerously it all might have changed. Of how dangerously she had changed, from someone easy and irresponsible and transparent into someone capable of huge deception and terrible arrogance – and great courage. To do what she had done, entirely alone. He almost wanted to go away, to keep her as she had always been; but he knew he had to see her, face her, find out what she had become and why. He raised his finger and pressed the bell; there was quite a long silence. And then he heard her voice.

'Who is it?'

'Nick.'

A moment's pause, he could hear her shock. Then he heard the chain being undone, watched the door open, saw her.

She looked dreadful; she was very white and her eyes were red and swollen with crying. Her hair hung lankly round her face, and she was twisting a handkerchief in both hands. She was wearing one of the most hideous tracksuits he had ever seen. She managed a half-smile.

'Hi!'

'Hello?'

'Do you want to come in?'

'If I may.'

'Of course . . .' She led him into her sitting room; surprisingly tidy, by her standards.

'Would you like a cup of tea?'

'No thanks. How are you feeling?'

'Terrible.'

'Ah.'

There was a long silence; then she said, 'Excuse me,' and rushed out of the room. He heard various unpleasant noises coming from the lavatory; she emerged finally, whiter than ever, stood twisting a tissue in her hands.

'Sorry.'

'The anaesthetic, I suppose,' he said.

She looked at him sharply.

'You know?'

'Yes, I know. I've just come from the clinic.'

'From the – Nick, who told you?'

'I'm quite a good detective,' he said. 'It's part of being a journalist. As you know.'

'Yes, but – '

'Oh, I had a little help.'

'From Clio, I suppose?'

'No. Not from Clio. She wouldn't tell me anything.'

He looked at her and shook his head.

'This is a fine thing that you've done, Jocasta. A very fine thing. Why on God's earth didn't you tell me? Don't you think I had a right to know? About – about a baby that wasn't just yours, but mine as well. Ours. Don't you think I would have wanted to know, to talk about it, to tell you what I felt? How could you decide all on your own what was best, for – for all of us? It was terribly arrogant and it's made me terribly, terribly unhappy.'

'Unhappy?'

'Of course. Jocasta, I love you. I love you so much. How could you think I should have no part in all this?'

'Nick – Nick, you don't mean – you don't mean you'd have wanted me to have a baby?'

'Of course I'd have wanted you to have our baby. I might not have chosen it, just now. But that doesn't mean I'd have

711

wanted you to – to throw it away. Given the choice. Of course I wouldn't.'

'Oh,' she said, 'oh I see. Yes.'

'And I can't begin to think how you could have done that. Without talking to me.'

'No. No, indeed. Well – well, you see, the thing is – '

'The thing is, what? I don't think I can cope with any justifications.'

'You're not going to get any. The thing is, Nick,' she said, slowly and very gently, 'actually, it is rather a fine thing I've done. I think.'

He stared at her. 'What do you mean?'

'I mean I couldn't do it,' she said, 'not in the end. I just couldn't. I got into that room, and I lay there, thinking, really thinking, about what I was doing, what was going to happen, and then after a bit, I just got up and left. So – actually, Nick, I'm still pregnant. What are we going to do about that?'

Chapter 45

Clio looked, with great foreboding, up at Jocasta's windows. She was terrified of what she might find. It wasn't going to be easy. She was actually finding it very hard. Even now. That someone, especially someone she was fond of, could so carelessly – literally – discard a baby, hurt her a lot. But – Jocasta's reasons, however tortuous, had seemed insurmountable to her; and it was Jocasta they had to look after now.

Very tentatively she pressed the bell; after a few minutes, she heard Jocasta's voice.

'Hello? Who is it?'

She sounded remarkably cheerful; she looked remarkably cheerful, as she opened the door. She was very pale, but – yes, unmistakably cheerful. She was recovering very fast, Clio thought, and tried to suppress her irritation.

'Hello, darling Clio. Let me give you a hug. Come in, it's so lovely to see you.'

'I came as soon as I could – '

'I know. You're an angel. Thank you.'

She led the way into the sitting room. Clio followed her. Jocasta seemed perfectly all right. She could have given her patients a bit more attention this afternoon after all.

'Well – how do you feel?' she asked.

'Dreadful. I keep being sick.'

'Oh, Jocasta, I'm sorry. You've been very unlucky. The anaesthetics don't usually do that, these days.'

'Don't they? I wouldn't know.'

'What?'

'I said I wouldn't know. I didn't have one.'

'You what? You mean, they didn't give you anything?'

'Nothing. Nothing at all.'

'Jocasta – '

Clio looked at her; her eyes were sparkling in her white face, she was smiling.

'I didn't have it. I didn't have the termination,' she said. 'I'm still pregnant. I can't think how I'm going to cope with it, but – I am. I just walked out. Told them not to do it, just as they were coming in to get me. They were awfully cross,' she added.

Clio felt as if someone had just given her irrefutable evidence that the earth was flat. She sat there, staring at Jocasta, trying to work out what she felt. Finally she realised: irritation. Major irritation.

'You cow,' she said, 'you absolute cow. Letting me break the speed limit all the way here – I've probably got all my points at once, this afternoon – worrying me, crying like that – oh, Jocasta!'

She started to cry herself.

'Clio, darling, don't, don't, I know it's hard, but – '

'No,' she said, going over to her, giving her a hug, 'it's not hard. Not at all. You getting rid of it was hard. I'm actually really, really happy for you.'

'Oh, good. Because I'm happy for me too. Very happy. I'd be ecstatic, if I could stop being sick. Serves me right for being so snooty about it.'

'Yes, maybe it does. Have you told Nick?'

'Yes. He came round.'

'What did he say?'

'Clio, he was terribly, terribly happy about it. He was actually excited. And until he knew it was all right, he was terribly upset. I can't quite believe it – '

'Jocasta,' said Clio, 'I hate to say this, no, I don't hate to say it, I'm enjoying saying it, but I did tell you so!'

'Where is Nick?' she said, half an hour later, after she had made Jocasta some camomile tea.

'God knows. Yes, I do. He's had to go and sort out his car – it got clamped. He belongs to some weird thing that stays with the car for you, while they come and unclamp it, but it was too late, they'd taken it away, so he had to go and find it. Silly bugger,' she added fondly.

Her mobile rang. 'Hi, Kate. How are you – oh God,' she handed it to Clio, 'I've got to go back to the loo. Sorry.'

Clio made sympathetic faces and said, 'Kate, it's me, Clio.'

'What's the matter with Jocasta?'

'She's – got a tummy bug.'

'Oh no. Poor thing. I'll come round and see her, shall I, bring her some flowers? I've got Nat with me, we're in Clapham, just down the road from her, we've looked it up on the *A to Z*.'

'Kate, I really don't think – '

But she had rung off.

Jocasta was surprisingly pleased by the prospect.

'I'd love to see her. Honestly.'

'And Nat? Are you sure?'

'Well – maybe just for a minute or two. I know why she's coming, she called me yesterday: it's about the Smith contract. She's changed her mind, she's going to do it.'

'Oh yes?' said Clio. She didn't think she wanted to hear about Kate and her contract. Her contract and Fergus.

Thinking about Fergus made her feel suddenly terrible. She was happy for Jocasta, of course, and for Nick, but – here she was, alone again. Very alone. With no prospect of being less so. No doubt that was why Fergus had called her; to tell her what a wonderful contract he had fixed for Kate. He was so bloody insensitive. And self-centred.

Kate came in, looking radiant, holding a large, but rather inelegant bunch of flowers.

'Darling, they're lovely,' said Jocasta.

'I hope so. We got them from the garage. Nat chose them, while I was in the toilet.'

'They're lovely. Thank you, Nat.'

'That's OK. Sorry you're not feeling so good.'

'You know something?' said Jocasta. 'I'm feeling perfectly wonderful!'

'Really?' said Kate. 'Clio said you had a tummy bug.'

'Oh, did she? No, I haven't got a tummy bug. I'm going to have a baby, Kate. What do you think about that?'

Kate stared at her. 'You said you'd never have one.'

'I know. But – these things happen.'

'Yeah, well.' She was quiet for a moment, obviously thinking.

715

Then she said: 'I think that's really cool. Like I said, you'll be a great mother. Don't you think so, Nat?'

'Yes,' he said, his face very solemn, obviously thinking about it. 'Let's hope so, anyway.'

Jocasta smiled at him. 'I'm hoping so, too.'

'Gideon must be pleased.'

'It – isn't Gideon's,' said Jocasta carefully. 'Gideon and I are getting divorced.'

Kate looked very confused. As well she might, Jocasta thought.

'So whose is it then?'

'It's Nick's.'

'Nick, who used to be your boyfriend? Who came to the funeral?'

'The very one.'

'Oh.' She digested this for a bit. 'So – are you going to marry him now?'

'Probably. He's a bit anti actual marriage. But he seems very keen on the baby.'

'Well, that's a good thing, I s'pose . . . I'm sorry about Gideon, though. I really liked him.'

'Oh, Kate, so do I. But it's all right. We should never have got married in the first place. It was a stupid mistake. Mostly on my part. And we're still good friends.'

'Cool.' She was clearly baffled; out of her depth. Jocasta decided she should change the subject. 'Now, tell me all about your contract,' she said. 'Have you actually signed it, and when are you going to start with them?'

'I'm not,' she said. 'I didn't sign it. Fergus told me not to.'

'Fergus told you not to?'

'Yeah. I was all set to, went in to see him for a meeting and he told me not to. He said I just didn't realise what I was letting myself in for, he said it would all start all over again, with the press and that, and – well, he just wouldn't let me. I'm really relieved now,' she added. 'Even in spite of the money, deep down I didn't want to.'

'Yes, well money isn't everything, it is?' said Nat.

'It absolutely isn't. Clio, where are you going? Clio – '

Clio drove as fast as she could to Fergus's office. More speeding tickets, probably. She prayed he'd still be there. This wasn't something that could be settled on the phone. As she reached the North End Road, and his building, she saw him standing at the first-floor window, staring down at the street. He looked terribly unhappy. She parked the car, careless that it was on the zigzag lines next to the crossing, and ran across the road, pressed her finger on the bell.

He was a long time answering it. Supposing he'd seen her, supposing he didn't want to let her in, or see her? She wouldn't blame him; she'd been so vile to him.

Finally he spoke on the intercom. 'Who is it?'

'It's Clio. Please let me in.'

'Oh – OK.' He didn't sound exactly pleased to hear her voice. She took a deep breath, pushed on the door, and ran up the stairs. He was sitting in the minute room that he called his reception area, and looked at her rather coolly.

'Hello.'

'Hello, Fergus. I've come to – to apologise to you.'

'What?'

'Yes. I'm so sorry I said all those things about you being cynical and trading on people's misery and all that. Very sorry.'

'I see.'

'Yes. It was terribly wrong of me, I had no right to say any of them.'

'No.'

This wasn't going very well. Maybe she'd hurt him too much for him to forgive her. Oh, God.

'Fergus, I – Fergus, I really, really want you to know that I – I – well, that I care about you so, so much. I've missed you terribly. I was thinking only today how much I missed you, that I shouldn't have been so stupid and – '

'That's all right,' he said. He was still staring at her, his face expressionless.

This was terrible. She really had obviously upset him, beyond redemption. Well, it served her right. She was a pompous, self-righteous woman; she didn't deserve someone as lovely as Fergus. She should have trusted him, she should have known better. She looked at him again. Still the frozen face.

'Well,' she said finally, her voice trembling, 'well, that's all I came to say. It needed to be said. I thought.'

She turned towards the door. If she could only get out without crying, that'd be something.

'Where are you going now?' he said.

'I don't know. Home, I suppose. Home to Guildford.'

'You are not,' he said, 'you are most definitely not.'

'What?'

'You're staying here with me.'

'Staying here?'

'Yes,' he said, 'staying here. I love you.'

'You love me?' she said.

'Yes. I love you. Love you an awful lot. You silly bitch,' he added.

'Grace, dear, you've got some visitors.' Peter's voice was slightly tentative. 'Can I bring them up?'

'Oh – oh dear. I'm not sure. I'm very tired.'

'We won't stay long, Mrs Hartley.'

'Oh,' she said, and they could all hear the pleasure in her voice. 'Oh, Ed. How nice. Yes, do bring them up, Peter.'

'There's two of us,' said Ed. 'I've brought Kate with me.'

It had been arranged on the spur of the moment; he had called Kate to tell her that Grace was in hospital and she'd said she'd send a card; and then he said he was going up this weekend, after all: one of his mates was having a party, and he'd take it.

'Fine,' she said and then a bit later, she called him back.

'I was thinking,' she said, 'should I come with you? Like, to see her. Just for a little while?'

'It's a long way, Kate, for a little while.' Ed sounded doubtful.

'Doesn't matter. Nat could bring me. He's got some new wheels for his car and he wants to show them off.'

'Yeah. What's he got then?'

'Saxo.'

'What, the bomb?'

He sounded very impressed; they cared more about their cars than anything, Kate thought.

'Yeah.'

'Wow. I couldn't – hitch a ride, could I?'

'Course you could. He loves showing it off.'

'Well – OK then. You'd better ask him.'

'Oh no,' she said, her voice absolutely confident. 'He'll be pleased. Honest. I'll tell him to be,' she added.

'Good. Well, thanks.'

She was a one-off, Ed thought, switching off his phone. Absolutely totally gorgeous and funny and really quite bright. He liked her a lot. Of course, he could never fancy her. Not really. She was Martha's daughter and that made it unthinkable. But he did like her. Somehow, she comforted him. Made him feel just a little less desperate. She wasn't Martha, but – in a funny way she was. Part of her. Literally. There was something about her voice, for instance, a note in it that was Martha. And when she giggled, that was Martha, too. And her eyes, those huge dark eyes, they were Martha's eyes. It ought to hurt and in a way, it did. But in another, it absolutely didn't.

'Well – here she is. Only been home for a couple of days and she gets very tired, but – just a few minutes.'

'Hello, Mrs Hartley,' said Ed. 'How are you?'

'Oh – you know. A little bit better.'

'You remember Kate?'

'Yes, of course I do. It's very good of you to come, dear.'

'It's cool. Here, we brought you these.'

Helen had chosen the flowers and they were beautiful.

'How sweet of you. Peter, go and put them in water, love. It's a long journey you've done,' she said to Kate.

'Oh, not really. My boyfriend brought me. In his car. He's gone shopping for it,' she said hastily, clearly anxious that Grace shouldn't feel she should ask the boyfriend in, as well. 'It needs a new trim, or something.'

'Oh, I see.' She looked at her. 'How old are you, Kate?'

'Sixteen.'

'You're still at school?'

'Yes.'

'And what do you want to do?'

'I think I want to be a photographer. But then again, I might be a lawyer.'

'A lawyer! My goodness. Like Martha.'

'Well, yeah. And Ally McBeal.'

'Who, dear?'

'Ally McBeal. She's a lawyer on TV. You ought to watch it, it's really good.'

'I'll look out for it. And how is Jocasta? That's right, isn't it?'

'Yes, that's right,' said Kate, 'she's fine. She's going to have a baby.'

'A baby! How lovely. I'm so pleased.'

'Yes.' She paused, looked at Ed for a moment, then said: 'She sent you her good wishes and she said – '

'Yes? What did she say?'

'She said if it was a girl,' said Kate, and she smiled, with great sweetness, at Grace, 'she said to tell you that, if it's a girl, she's going to call her Martha.'

Monday's Child

Louise Bagshawe

According to the old rhyme, 'Monday's child is fair of face' – but life isn't always so simple.

Gorgeous goddesses seem to surround script-reader and wannabe movie-maker Anna Brown – from her deranged glamour-queen boss to her perfect, pouting flatmates. For Anna, being less than beautiful is very hard to bear.

In fashion-and-beauty-crazed London, perhaps being talented just isn't enough. Enter Mark Swan, Britain's hottest director. Rugged, reclusive and powerful, he could be Anna's ticket to the top, but how can she ever hope to snag such a bright star?

Fed up of being downbeat and dowdy, Anna decides to chase her dreams and, with a little help from her friends, embarks on a madcap scheme to get just what she's after . . .

'Mouth-wateringly addictive . . . fast-paced and full of characters you'd love to call a friend' *OK!* magazine

'A gripping page-turner' *Heat*

'One of the most charming and lively romances I've read in a decade . . . I couldn't stop reading it, or cheering on the heroine' *Australian Women's Weekly*

0 7553 0425 X

headline

The Linnet Bird

Linda Holeman

'For you, I will write of it all – part truth, part memory, part nightmare – my life, the one that started so long ago, in a place so far from here . . .'

India, 1839: Linny Gow, a respectable young wife and mother, settles down to write her life story. To outside appearances Linny is the perfect Colonial wife: beautiful, gracious, subservient. But appearances can be very deceptive . . .

An unforgettable book, richly descriptive and mesmerising from the start, *The Linnet Bird* is the spellbinding story of the journey of Linny Gow – child prostitute turned social climber turned colonial wife turned adventuress. Frequently disturbing, often moving and always enthralling, it is that rare thing: a once-in-a-lifetime read.

'We use that old cliché "unputdownable" so often that it has little real meaning any more, but I can assure you The Linnet Bird *stands alone, proud and beautiful . . . I turned the final page with deep regret'* Lesley Pearse

0 7553 2463 3

headline

Now you can buy any of these other bestselling books from your bookshop or *direct from the publisher*.

FREE P&P AND UK DELIVERY
(Overseas and Ireland £3.50 per book)

The Wedding Day	Catherine Alliott	£6.99
A Married Man	Catherine Alliott	£6.99
Monday's Child	Louise Bagshawe	£6.99
Cuban Heels	Emily Barr	£6.99
Atlantic Shift	Emily Barr	£6.99
Secrets of a Family Album	Isla Dewar	£6.99
Singing Bird	Roisin McAuley	£5.99
Anyone But Him	Sheila O'Flanagan	£6.99
On Dancing Hill	Sarah Challis	£6.99
The Distance Between Us	Maggie O'Farrell	£6.99
Amazing Grace	Clare Dowling	£6.99
The Woman on the Bus	Pauline McLynn	£7.99
Play it Again?	Julie Highmore	£6.99

TO ORDER SIMPLY CALL THIS NUMBER

01235 400 414

or visit our website: www.madaboutbooks.com

Prices and availability subject to change without notice.

THE COUSINS' WAR

The Lady
of the Rivers

Philippa Gregory

THORNDIKE
WINDSOR
PARAGON

This Large Print edition is published by Thorndike Press, Waterville, Maine USA and by AudioGo Ltd, Bath, England.
Copyright © 2011 by Philippa Gregory Limited.
The moral right of the author has been asserted.
Thorndike Press, a part of Gale, Cengage Learning.

ALL RIGHTS RESERVED

Thorndike Press® Large Print Core.
The text of this Large Print edition is unabridged.
Other aspects of the book may vary from the original edition.
Set in 16 pt. Plantin.

LIBRARY OF CONGRESS CATALOGING-IN-PUBLICATION DATA

Gregory, Philippa.
    The lady of the rivers : the cousins war / by Philippa Gregory.
        p. cm. — (Thorndike Press large print core) (The cousins' war)
    Include bibliographical references
    ISBN-13: 978-1-4104-4206-2 (hardcover)
    ISBN-10: 1-4104-4206-3 (hardcover)
    1. Jacquetta, Duchess of Bedford, 1416?–1472—Fiction. 2. Great Britain—History—Wars of the Roses, 1455–1485—Fiction. 3. Large type books. I. Title.
    PR6057.R386L33 2011b
    823'.914—dc22   2011031130

BRITISH LIBRARY CATALOGUING-IN-PUBLICATION DATA AVAILABLE
Published in the U.S. in 2011 by arrangement with Simon & Schuster, Inc.
Published in the U.K. in 2012 by arrangement with Simon & Schuster UK Limited.
U.K. Hardcover: 978 1 445 87248 3 (Windsor Large Print)
U.K. Softcover: 978 1 445 87249 0 (Paragon Large Print)

Printed and bound in Great Britain by MPG Books Group Limited
1 2 3 4 5 6 7 15 14 13 12 11

For Victoria

JACQUETTA's FAMILY TREE

*Note: Dates of birth of Jacquetta's children
are approximate*

Louis of Luxembourg
1418–1475

(1) Sir John Grey m Elizabeth (Woodville) 1437–1492

Lewis
1438
(died in
infancy)

Anne
b. 1439

Martha
b. 1450

Thomas Grey
Marquis of Dorset

Richard Grey

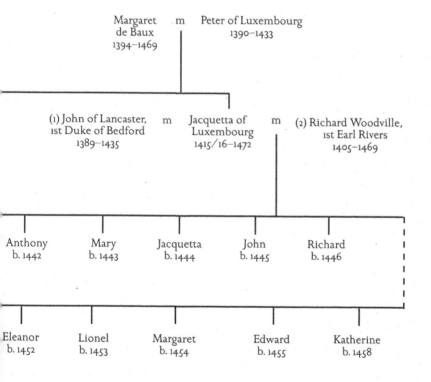

Margaret
de Baux
1394–1469

m

Peter of Luxembourg
1390–1433

(1) John of Lancaster,
1st Duke of Bedford
1389–1435

m

Jacquetta of
Luxembourg
1415/16–1472

m

(2) Richard Woodville,
1st Earl Rivers
1405–1469

Anthony
b. 1442

Mary
b. 1443

Jacquetta
b. 1444

John
b. 1445

Richard
b. 1446

Eleanor
b. 1452

Lionel
b. 1453

Margaret
b. 1454

Edward
b. 1455

Katherine
b. 1458

LANCASTER

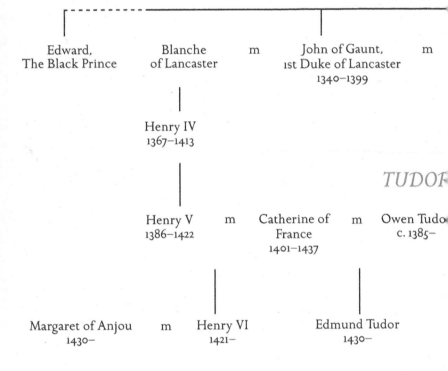

Edward, The Black Prince	Blanche of Lancaster	m	John of Gaunt, 1st Duke of Lancaster 1340–1399	m

Henry IV
1367–1413

TUDOR

Henry V
1386–1422   m   Catherine of France 1401–1437   m   Owen Tudor c. 1385–

Margaret of Anjou   m   Henry VI   Edmund Tudor
1430–   1421–   1430–

THE COUSINS AT WAR

The Houses of York, Lancaster & Tudor,
1452

YORK

therine Swynford   Edmund,   m   Isabelle of Castille
                          Duke of York
                          1341–1402

John Beaufort,   Richard,
Earl of Somerset   Earl of Cambridge
1373–1410   1373–1415

John Beaufort,   Richard,   m   Cecily Neville
Duke of Somerset   Duke of York
1404–1444   1411–

Margaret   Edward IV   George,   Richard,
Beaufort   1442–   Duke of Clarence   Duke of Gloucester
1443–   1449–   1452–

Battles in
The Cousins' War

○ Lancaster victories
◇ York victories

Inverness
Aberdeen
Dunure
Stirling
Glasgow
Edinburgh
Hedgeley Moor 1464
Skye

NORTH SEA

FRANCE

Calais

Ipswich

Losecote Field 1470

St. Albans 1455, 1461

Northampton 1460

Barnet 1471

LONDON

Dover

Hastings

Lewes

Chichester

ENGLISH CHANNEL

Winchester

Hexham 1464

York

Lincoln

Towton 1461

Ferrybridge 1461

Wakefield 1460

Stoke 1487

Blore Heath 1459

Bosworth 1485

Edgecote 1469

Lancaster

Preston

Chester

Shrewsbury

Ludford Bridge 1459

Mortimer's Cross 1461

Tewkesbury 1471

Bristol

Southampton

Dorchester

Exeter

Plymouth

Taunton

Swansea

Cardiff

Caernarfon

Aberystwyth

Fishguard

Isle of Man

IRISH SEA

Penzance

France 1430

ENGLAND

Calais

Rouen   Rheims

Paris

Troyes

Dijon

Chinon   Nevers

French lands

English lands

Burgundian
lands

FRANCE

Bordeaux

CASTLE OF BEAUREVOIR, NEAR ARRAS, FRANCE, SUMMER–WINTER 1430

She sits, this odd trophy of war, as neat as an obedient child, on a small stool in the corner of her cell. At her feet are the remains of her dinner on a pewter platter, laid on the straw. I notice that my uncle has sent good slices of meat, and even the white bread from his own table; but she has eaten little. I find I am staring at her, from her boy's riding boots to the man's bonnet crammed on her brown cropped hair, as if she were some exotic animal, trapped for our amusement, as if someone had sent a lion cub all the way from Ethiopia to entertain the great family of Luxembourg, for us to keep in our collection. A lady behind me crosses herself and whispers: "Is this a witch?"

I don't know. How does one ever know?

"This is ridiculous," my great-aunt says boldly. "Who has ordered the poor girl to be chained? Open the door at once."

There is a confused muttering of men trying to shift the responsibility, and then someone turns the big key in the cell door and my great-aunt stalks in. The girl — she must be about seventeen or eighteen, only a few years older than me — looks up from under her jagged fringe of hair as my great-aunt stands before her, and then slowly she rises to her feet, doffs her cap, and gives an awkward little bow.

"I am the Lady Jehanne, the Demoiselle of Luxembourg," my great-aunt says. "This is the castle of Lord John of Luxembourg." She gestures to my aunt: "This is his wife, the lady of the castle, Jehanne of Bethune, and this is my great-niece Jacquetta."

The girl looks steadily at all of us and gives a nod of her head to each. As she looks at me I feel a little tap-tap for my attention, as palpable as the brush of a fingertip on the nape of my neck, a whisper of magic. I wonder if standing behind her there are indeed two accompanying angels, as she claims, and it is their presence that I sense.

"Can you speak, maid?" my great-aunt asks, when the girl says nothing.

"Oh yes, my lady," the girl replies in the hard accent of the Champagne region. I realize that it is true what they say about her: she is no more than a peasant girl, though she has led an army and crowned a king.

"Will you give me your word not to escape if I have these chains taken off your legs?"

She hesitates, as if she were in any position

14

to choose. "No, I can't."

My great-aunt smiles. "Do you understand the offer of parole? I can release you to live with us here in my nephew's castle, but you have to promise not to run away?"

The girl turns her head, frowning. It is almost as if she is listening for advice, then she shakes her head. "I know this parole. It is when one knight makes a promise to another. They have rules as if they were jousting. I'm not like that. My words are real, not like a troubadour's poem. And this is no game for me."

"Maid: parole is not a game!" Aunt Jehanne interrupts.

The girl looks at her. "Oh, but it is, my lady. The noblemen are not serious about these matters. Not serious like me. They play at war and make up rules. They ride out and lay waste to good people's farms and laugh as the thatched roofs burn. Besides, I cannot make promises. I am promised already."

"To the one who wrongly calls himself the King of France?"

"To the King of Heaven."

My great-aunt pauses for a moment's thought. "I will tell them to take the chains off you and guard you so that you do not escape, and then you can come and sit with us in my rooms. I think what you have done for your country and for your prince has been very great, Joan, though mistaken. And I will

15

not see you here, under my roof, a captive in chains."

"Will you tell your nephew to set me free?"

My great-aunt hesitates. "I cannot order him, but I will do everything I can to send you back to your home. At any event, I won't let him release you to the English."

At the very word the girl shudders and makes the sign of the cross, thumping her head and her chest in the most ridiculous way, as a peasant might cross himself at the name of Old Hob. I have to choke back a laugh. This draws the girl's dark gaze to me.

"They are only mortal men," I explain to her. "The English have no powers beyond that of mortal men. You need not fear them so. You need not cross yourself at their name."

"I don't fear them. I am not such a fool as to fear that they have powers. It's not that. It's that they know that *I* have powers. That's what makes them such a danger. They are mad with fear of me. They fear me so much that they will destroy me the moment I fall into their hands. I am their terror. I am their fear that walks by night."

"While I live, they won't have you," my great-aunt assures her; and at once, unmistakably, Joan looks straight at me, a hard dark gaze as if to see that I too have heard, in this sincere assertion, the ring of an utterly empty promise.

My great-aunt believes that if she can bring Joan into our company, talk with her, cool her religious fervor, perhaps educate her, then the girl will be led, in time, to wear the dress of a young woman, and the fighting youth who was dragged off the white horse at Compiègne will be transformed, like Mass reversed, from strong wine into water, and she will become a young woman who can be seated among waiting women, who will answer to a command and not to the ringing church bells, and will then, perhaps, be overlooked by the English, who are demanding that we surrender the hermaphrodite murderous witch to them. If we have nothing to offer them but a remorseful obedient maid-in-waiting, perhaps they will be satisfied and go on their violent way.

Joan herself is exhausted by recent defeats and by her uneasy sense that the king she has crowned is not worthy of the holy oil, that the enemy she had on the run has recoiled on her, and that the mission given to her by God Himself is falling away from her. Everything that made her the maid before her adoring troop of soldiers has become uncertain. Under my great-aunt's steady kindness she is becoming once more an awkward country girl: nothing special.

Of course, all the maids-in-waiting to my great-aunt want to know about the adventure that is ending in this slow creep of defeat, and as Joan spends her days with us, learning to be a girl and not the maid, they pluck up the courage to ask her.

"How were you so brave?" one demands. "How did you learn to be so brave? In battle, I mean."

Joan smiles at the question. There are four of us, seated on a grass bank beside the moat of the castle, as idle as children. The July sun is beating down, and the pasture lands around the castle are shimmering in the haze of heat; even the bees are lazy, buzzing and then falling silent as if drunk on flowers. We have chosen to sit in the deep shadow of the highest tower; behind us, in the glassy water of the moat, we can hear the occasional bubble of a carp coming to the surface.

Joan is sprawled like a boy, one hand dabbling in the water, her cap over her eyes. In the basket beside me are half-sewn shirts that we are supposed to hem for the poor children of nearby Cambrai. But the maids avoid work of any sort, Joan has no skill, and I have my great-aunt's precious pack of playing cards in my hands and am shuffling and cutting them and idly looking at the pictures.

"I knew I was called by God," Joan said simply. "And that He would protect me, so I had no fear. Not even in the worst of the battles. He warned me that I would be injured but that I would feel no pain, so I knew I could go on fighting. I even warned my men that I would be injured that day. I knew before we went into battle. I just knew."

"Do you really hear voices?" I ask.

"Do you?"

The question is so shocking that the girls whip round to stare at me, and under their joint gaze I find I am blushing as if for something shameful. "No! No!"

"Then what?"

"What do you mean?"

"What do you hear?" she asks, as reasonably as if everyone hears something.

"Well, not voices, exactly," I say.

"What do you hear?"

I glance behind me as if the very fish might rise to eavesdrop. "When someone in my family is going to die, then I hear a noise," I say. "A special noise."

"What sort of noise?" the girl, Elizabeth, asks. "I didn't know this. Could I hear it?"

"You are not of my house," I say irritably. "Of course you wouldn't hear it. You would have to be a descendant of . . . and anyway, you must never speak of this. You shouldn't really be listening. I shouldn't be telling you."

"What sort of noise?" Joan repeats.

"Like singing," I say, and see her nod, as if she too has heard singing.

"They say it is the voice of Melusina, the

19

first lady of the House of Luxembourg," I whisper. "They say she was a water goddess who came out of the river to marry the first duke, but she couldn't be a mortal woman. She comes back to cry for the loss of her children."

"And when have you heard her?"

"The night that my baby sister died. I heard something. And I knew at once that it was Melusina."

"But how did you know it was her?" the other maid whispers, afraid of being excluded from the conversation.

I shrug, and Joan smiles in recognition of truths that cannot be explained. "I just knew," I say. "It was as if I recognized her voice. As if I had always known it."

"That's true. You just know," Joan nods. "But how do you know that it comes from God and not from the Devil?"

I hesitate. Any spiritual questions should be taken to my confessor, or at the very least to my mother or my great-aunt. But the song of Melusina, and the shiver on my spine, and my occasional sight of the unseen — something half lost, sometimes vanishing around a corner, lighter gray in a gray twilight, a dream that is too clear to be forgotten, a glimpse of foresight but never anything that I can describe — these things are too thin for speech. How can I ask about them when I cannot even put them into words? How can I

20

bear to have someone clumsily name them or, even worse, try to explain them? I might as well try to hold the greenish water of the moat in my cupped hands.

"I've never asked," I say. "Because it is hardly anything. Like when you go into a room and it is quiet — but you know, you can just tell, that someone is there. You can't hear them or see them, but you just know. It's little more than that. I never think of it as a gift coming from God or the Devil. It is just nothing."

"My voices come from God," Joan says certainly. "I know it. If it were not true, I should be utterly lost."

"So can you tell fortunes?" Elizabeth asks me childishly.

My fingers close over my cards. "No," I say. "And these don't tell fortunes, they are just for playing. They're just playing cards. I don't tell fortunes. My great-aunt would not allow me to do it, even if I could."

"Oh, do mine!"

"These are just playing cards," I insist. "I'm no soothsayer."

"Oh, draw a card for me and tell me," Elizabeth says. "And for Joan. What's going to become of her? Surely you want to know what's going to happen to Joan?"

"It means nothing," I say to Joan. "And I only brought them so we could play."

"They are beautiful," she says. "They

21

taught me to play at court with cards like these. How bright they are."

I hand them to her. "Take care with them, they're very precious," I say jealously as she spreads them in her calloused hands. "The demoiselle showed them to me when I was a little girl and told me the names of the pictures. She lets me borrow them because I love to play. But I promised her I would take care of them."

Joan passes the pack back to me, and though she is careful, and my hands are ready for them, one of the thick cards tumbles between us and falls facedown, on the grass.

"Oh! Sorry," Joan exclaims, and quickly picks it up.

I can feel a whisper, like a cool breath down my spine. The meadow before me and the cows flicking their tails in the shade of the tree seem far away, as if we two are enclosed in a glass, butterflies in a bowl, in another world. "You had better look at it now," I hear myself say to her.

Joan looks at the brightly painted picture, her eyes widen slightly, and then she shows it to me. "What does this mean?"

It is a painting of a man dressed in a livery of blue, hanging upside down from one extended foot, the other leg crooked easily, his toe pointed and placed against his straight leg as if he were dancing, inverted in the air. His hands are clasped behind his back as if he is bowing, we both see the happy fall of his blue hair as he hangs, upside down, smiling.

"'Le Pendu,'" Elizabeth reads. "How horrid. What does it mean? Oh, surely it doesn't mean . . ." She breaks off.

"It doesn't mean you will be hanged," I say quickly to Joan. "So don't think that. It's just a playing card; it can't mean anything like that."

"But what does it mean?" the other girl demands, though Joan is silent, as if it is not her card, not her fortune that I am refusing to tell.

"His gallows is two growing trees," I say. I am playing for time under Joan's serious brown gaze. "This means spring and renewal and life — not death. And there are two trees; the man is balanced between them. He is the very center of resurrection."

Joan nods.

"They are bowed down to him; he is happy. And look: he is not hanged by his neck to kill him, but tied by his foot," I say. "If he wanted, he could stretch up and untie himself. He could set himself free, if he wanted."

"But he doesn't set himself free," the girl observes. "He is like a tumbler, an acrobat. What does that mean?"

"It means that he is willingly there, willingly waiting, allowing himself to be held by his foot, hanging in the air."

23

"To be a living sacrifice?" Joan says slowly, in the words of the Mass.

"He is not crucified," I point out quickly. It is as if every word I say leads us to another form of death. "This doesn't mean anything."

"No," she says. "These are just playing cards, and we are just playing a game with them. It is a pretty card, the Hanged Man. He looks happy. He looks happy to be upside down in springtime. Shall I teach you a game with counters that we play in Champagne?"

"Yes," I say. I hold out my hand for her card, and she looks at it for a moment before she hands it back to me.

"Honestly, it means nothing," I say again to her.

She smiles at me, her clear, honest smile. "I know well enough what it means," she says.

"Shall we play?" I start to shuffle the cards and one turns over in my hand.

"Now that's a good card," Joan remarks, *"La Roue de Fortune."*

I hold it out to show it to her. "It is the Wheel of Fortune that can throw you up very high, or bring you down very low. Its message is to be indifferent to victory and defeat, as they both come on the turn of the wheel."

"In my country the farmers make a sign for fortune's wheel," Joan remarks. "They draw a circle in the air with their forefinger when something very good or something very bad happens. Someone inherits money, or some-

24

one loses a prize cow, they do this." She points her finger in the air and draws a circle. "And they say something."

"A spell?"

"Not really a spell." She smiles mischievously.

"What then?"

She giggles. "They say *'merde.'*"

I am so shocked that I rock back with laughter.

"What? What?" the younger maid demands.

"Nothing, nothing," I say. Joan is still giggling. "Joan's countrymen say rightly that everything comes to dust, and all that a man can do about it is to learn indifference."

Joan's future hangs in the balance; she is swinging like the Hanged Man. All of my family, my father, Pierre, the Count of St. Pol, my uncle, Louis of Luxembourg, and my favorite uncle, John of Luxembourg, are allied with the English. My father writes from our home at the chateau at St. Pol to his brother John, and commands him, as the head of our family, to hand over Joan to the English. But my great-aunt the demoiselle insists we keep her safe, and my uncle John hesitates.

The English demand his prisoner and, since the English command nearly all of France and their ally the Duke of Burgundy commands most of the rest, what they say usually happens. Their common soldiers went down on their knees on the battlefield to give thanks, and wept with joy when the maid was captured. There is no doubt in their mind that without her the French army, their enemy, will collapse into the frightened rabble that they were before she came to them.

The Duke of Bedford, the English regent who rules the English lands in France, almost all of the north of the country, sends daily letters to my uncle invoking his loyalty to English rule, their long friendship, and promising money. I like to watch for the English messengers who come dressed in the fine livery of the royal duke, on beautiful horses. Everyone says that the duke is a great man and well loved, the greatest man in France, an ill man to cross; but so far, my uncle obeys his aunt, the demoiselle, and does not hand over our prisoner.

My uncle expects the French court to make a bid for her — they owe their very existence to her after all — but they are oddly silent, even after he writes to them and says that he has the maid, and that she is ready to return to the court of her king and serve again in his army. With her leading them, they could ride out against the English and win. Surely they will send a fortune to get her back?

"They don't want her," my great-aunt advises him. They are at their private dining

table; the great dinner for the whole household has taken place in the hall, and the two
of them have sat before my uncle's men,
tasted the dishes and sent them round the
room as a gift to their special favorites. Now
they are comfortable, seated at a little table
before the fire in my great-aunt's private
rooms, her personal servants in attendance. I
am to stand during the serving of dinner with
another lady-in-waiting. It is my job to watch
the servants, summon them forwards as
required, clasp my hands modestly before
me, and hear nothing. Of course, I listen all
the time.

"Joan made a man out of the boy Prince
Charles, he was nothing until she came to
him with her vision, then she made that man
into a king. She taught him to claim his inheritance. She made an army out of his camp
followers, and made that army victorious. If
they had followed her advice as she followed
her voices, they would have driven the English
out of these lands and back to their foggy
islands, and we would be rid of them forever."

My uncle smiles. "Oh, my lady aunt! This
is a war that has gone on for nearly a century.
Do you really think it will end because some
girl from who knows where hears voices? She
could never drive the English away. They
would never have gone; they will never go.
These are their lands by right, by true right
of inheritance, and by conquest too. All they

have to do is to have the courage and the strength to hold them, and John, Duke of Bedford, will see to that." He glances at his wineglass, and I snap my fingers to the groom of the servery to pour him some more red wine. Then I step forwards to hold the glass as the man pours, and then I put it carefully on the table. They are using fine glassware; my uncle is wealthy and my great-aunt never has anything but the very best. "The English king may be little more than a child, but it makes no difference to the safety of his kingdom, for his uncle Bedford is loyal to him here, and his uncle the Duke of Gloucester is loyal to him in England. Bedford has the courage and the allies to hold the English lands here, and I think they will drive the dauphin farther and farther south. They will drive him into the sea. The maid had her season, and it was a remarkable one; but in the end, the English will win the war and hold the lands that are theirs by right, and all of our lords who are sworn against them now will bow the knee and serve them."

"I don't think so," my great-aunt says staunchly. "The English are terrified of her. They say she is unbeatable."

"Not anymore," my uncle observes. "For behold! She is a prisoner, and the cell doors don't burst open. They know she is mortal now. They saw her with an arrow in her thigh outside the walls of Paris, and her own army

28

marched off and left her. The French themselves taught the English that she could be brought down and abandoned."

"But you won't give her to the English," my great-aunt states. "It would be to dishonor us forever, in the eyes of God and the world."

My uncle leans forwards to speak confidentially. "You take it so seriously? You really think she is more than a mountebank? You really think she is something more than a peasant girl spouting nonsense? You know I could find half a dozen such as her?"

"You could find half a dozen who say they are like her," she says. "But not one like her. I think she is a special girl. Truly I do, nephew. I have a very strong sense of this."

He pauses, as if her sense of things, though she is only a woman, is something to be considered. "You have had a vision of her success? A foretelling?"

For a moment she hesitates, then she quickly shakes her head. "Nothing so clear. But nonetheless, I must insist that we protect her."

He pauses, not wanting to contradict her. She is the Demoiselle of Luxembourg, the head of our family. My father will inherit the title when she dies, but she also owns great lands that are all at her own disposition: she can will them to anyone she chooses. My uncle John is her favorite nephew; he has hopes, and he does not want to offend her.

"The French will have to pay a good price for her," he says. "I don't intend to lose money on her. She is worth a king's ransom. They know this."

My great-aunt nods. "I will write to the Dauphin Charles, and he will ransom her," she tells him. "Whatever his advisors say, he will still listen to me, though he is blown about like a leaf by his favorites. But I am his godmother. It is a question of honor. He owes all that he is to the maid."

"Very well. But do it at once. The English are very pressing, and I won't offend the Duke of Bedford. He is a powerful man, and a fair one. He is the best ruler of France that we could hope for. If he were a Frenchman, he would be wholly loved."

My great-aunt laughs. "Yes, but he is not! He's the English regent, and he should go back to his own damp island and his little nephew, the poor king, and make what they can of their own kingdom and leave us to rule France."

"Us?" my uncle queries, as if to ask her if she thinks that our family, who already rule half a dozen earldoms and who count kinship to the Holy Roman emperors, should be French kings as well.

She smiles. "Us," she says blandly.

Next day I walk with Joan to the little chapel in the castle and kneel beside her on the chancel steps. She prays fervently, her head bowed for an hour, and then the priest comes and serves the Mass and Joan takes the holy bread and wine. I wait for her at the back of the church. Joan is the only person I know who takes the bread and wine every day, as if it were her breakfast. My own mother, who is more observant than most, takes communion only once a month. We walk back to my great-aunt's rooms together, the strewing herbs swishing around our feet. Joan laughs at me, as I have to duck my head to get my tall conical headdress through the narrow doorways.

"It is very beautiful," she says. "But I should not like to wear such a thing."

I pause and twirl before her in the bright sunlight from the arrow slit. The colors of my gown are brilliant: a skirt of dark blue and an underskirt of sharper turquoise, the skirts flaring from the high belt tied tight on my rib cage. The high henin headdress sits like a cone on my head and sprouts a veil of pale blue from the peak that drops down my back, concealing and enhancing my fair hair. I spread my arms to show the big triangular sleeves, trimmed with the most beautiful embroidery in gold thread, and I lift the hem to show my scarlet slippers with the upturned toes.

"But you cannot work, or ride a horse, or even run in such a gown," she says.

31

"It's not for riding or working or running," I reply reasonably. "It's for showing off. It is to show the world that I am young and beautiful and ready for marriage. It is to show that my father is so wealthy that I can wear gold thread on my sleeves and silk in my headdress. It shows that I am so nobly born that I can wear velvet and silk, not wool like a poor girl."

"I couldn't bear to be showed off in such a thing."

"You wouldn't be allowed to," I point out disagreeably. "You have to dress for your position in life; you would have to obey the law and wear browns and grays. Did you really think you were important enough to wear ermine? Or do you want your gold surcoat back? They say you were as fine as any knight in battle. You dressed like a nobleman then. They say that you loved your beautiful standard and your polished armor, and a fine gold surcoat over all. They say you were guilty of the sin of vanity."

She flushes. "I had to be seen," she says defensively. "At the front of my army."

"Gold?"

"I had to honor God."

"Well anyway, you wouldn't get a headdress like this if you put on women's clothes," I say. "You would wear something more modest, like the ladies-in-waiting, nothing so high or so awkward, just a neat hood to cover your hair. And you could wear your boots under your gown; you could still walk about. Won't you try wearing a gown, Joan? It would mean that they couldn't accuse you of wearing men's clothes. It is a sign of heresy for a woman to dress as a man. Why not put on a dress, and then they can say nothing against you? Something plain?"

She shakes her head. "I am promised," she says simply. "Promised to God. And when the king calls for me, I must be ready to ride to arms again. I am a soldier-in-waiting, not a lady-in-waiting. I will dress like a soldier. And my king will call for me, any day now."

I glance behind us. A page boy carrying a jug of hot water is in earshot. I wait till he has nodded a bow and gone past us. "Hush," I say quietly. "You shouldn't even call him king."

She laughs, as if she fears nothing. "I took him to his coronation, I stood under my own standard in Reims Cathedral when he was anointed with the oil of Clovis. I saw him presented to his people in his crown. Of course he is King of France: he is crowned and anointed."

"The English slit the tongues of anyone who says that," I remind her. "That's for the first offense. The second time you say it, they brand your forehead so you are scarred for life. The English king, Henry VI, is to be called King of France; the one you call the

French king is to be called the dauphin, never anything but the dauphin."

She laughs with genuine amusement. "He is not even to be called French," she exclaims. "Your great Duke Bedford says that he is to be called Armagnac. But the great Duke Bedford was shaking with fear and running around Rouen for recruits when I came up to the walls of Paris with the French army — yes, I will say it! — the French army to claim our own city for our king, a French king; and we nearly took it, too."

I put my hands over my ears. "I won't hear you, and you shouldn't speak like this. I shall be whipped if I listen to you."

At once she takes my hands; she is penitent. "Ah, Jacquetta, I won't get you into trouble. Look! I will say nothing. But you must see that I have done far worse than use words against the English. I have used arrows and cannon shot and battering rams and guns against them! The English will hardly trouble themselves over the words I have said and the breeches I wear. I have defeated them and shown everyone that they have no right to France. I led an army against them and defeated them over and over again."

"I hope they never get hold of you, and never question you. Not about words, nor arrows, nor cannon."

She goes a little pale at the thought of it. "Please God, I hope so too. Merciful God, I hope so too."

"My great-aunt is writing to the dauphin," I say very low. "They were speaking of it at dinner last night. She will write to the dauphin and invite him to ransom you. And my uncle will release you to the Fr . . . to the Armagnacs."

She bows her head and her lips move in prayer. "My king will send for me," she says trustingly. "Without a doubt he will send for me to come to him, and we can start our battles again."

It grows even hotter in August, and my great-aunt rests on a daybed in her inner room every afternoon, with the light curtains of silk around the bed soaked in lavender water and the closed shutters throwing barred shadows across the stone floor. She likes me to read to her, as she lies with her eyes closed and her hands folded on the high waistline of her dress, as if she were a sculpted effigy of herself in some shaded tomb. She puts aside the big horned headdress that she always wears and lets her long graying hair spread over the cool embroidered pillows. She gives me books from her own library that tell of great romances and troubadours and ladies in tangled forests, and then one afternoon she puts a book in my hand and says, "Read this today."

It is hand-copied in old French, and I

stumble over the words. It is hard to read: the illustrations in the margins are like briars and flowers threading through the letters, and the clerk who copied each word had an ornate style of writing that I find hard to decipher. But slowly the story emerges. It is the story of a knight riding through a dark forest who has lost his way. He hears the sound of water and goes towards it. In a clearing, in the moonlight, he sees a white basin and a splashing fountain, and in the water is a woman of such beauty that her skin is paler than the white marble and her hair is darker than the night skies. He falls in love with her at once, and she with him, and he takes her to the castle and makes her his wife. She has only one condition: that every month he must leave her alone to bathe.

"Do you know this story?" my great-aunt asks me. "Has your father told you of it?"

"I have heard something like it," I say cautiously. My great-aunt is notoriously quick-tempered with my father, and I don't know if I daresay that I think this is the legend of the founding of our house.

"Well, now you are reading the true story," she says. She closes her eyes again. "It is time you knew. Go on."

The young couple are happier than any in the world, and people come from far and wide to visit them. They have children: beautiful girls and strange wild boys.

"Sons," my great-aunt whispers to herself. "If only a woman could have sons by wishing, if only they could be as she wishes."

The wife never loses her beauty though the years go by, and her husband grows more and more curious. One day, he cannot bear the mystery of her secret bathing any longer, and he creeps down to her bathhouse and spies on her.

My great-aunt raises her hand. "Do you know what he sees?" she asks me.

I lift my face from the book, my finger under the illustration of the man peering through the slats of the bathhouse. In the foreground is the woman in the bath, her beautiful hair snaked around her white shoulders. And gleaming in the water . . . her large scaled tail.

"Is she a fish?" I whisper.

"She is a being not of this world," my great-aunt says quietly. "She tried to live like an ordinary woman, but some women cannot live an ordinary life. She tried to walk in the common ways, but some women cannot put their feet to that path. This is a man's world, Jacquetta, and some women cannot march to the beat of a man's drum. Do you understand?"

I don't, of course. I am too young to understand that a man and a woman can love each other so deeply that their hearts beat as if they were one heart, and yet, at the same time, know that they are utterly hopelessly different.

"Anyway, you can read on. It's not long now."

The husband cannot bear to know that his wife is a strange being. She cannot forgive him for spying on her. She leaves him, taking her beautiful daughters, and he lives alone with the sons, heartbroken. But at his death, as at the death of everyone of our house, his wife Melusina, the beautiful woman who was an undine, a water goddess, comes back to him, and he hears her crying around the battlements for the children she has lost, for the husband she still loves, and for the world that has no place for her.

I close the book, and there is such a long silence that I think my great-aunt has fallen asleep.

"Some of the women of our family have the gift of foresight," my great-aunt remarks quietly. "Some of them have inherited powers from Melusina, powers of the other world where she lives. Some of us are her daughters, her heirs."

I hardly dare to breathe, I am so anxious that she should go on speaking to me.

"Jacquetta, do you think you might be one of these women?"

"I might be," I whisper. "I hope so."

"You have to listen," she says softly. "Listen to silence, watch for nothing. And be on your guard. Melusina is a shape-shifter; like quicksilver, she can flow from one thing to another. You may see her anywhere; she is like water. Or you may see only your own reflection in the surface of a stream though you are straining your eyes to see into the green depths for her."

"Will she be my guide?"

"You must be your own guide, but you might hear her when she speaks to you." She pauses. "Fetch my jewel box." She gestures towards the great chest at the foot of her bed. I open the creaking lid and inside, beside the gowns wrapped in powdered silk is a large wooden box. I take it out. Inside is a series of drawers, each one filled with my great-aunt's fortune of jewels. "Look in the smallest drawer," she says.

I find it. Inside is a small black velvet purse. I untie the tasseled threads, open the mouth, and a heavy golden bracelet falls into my hand, laden with about two hundred little charms, each one a different shape. I see a ship, a horse, a star, a spoon, a whip, a hawk, a spur.

"When you want to know something very, very important, you choose two or three of the charms — charms that signify the thing that might be, the choices before you. You tie each one on a string and you put them in a river, the river nearest to your home, the river that you hear at night when everything is silent but the voice of the waters. You leave it until the moon is new. Then you cut all the strings but one, and pull that one out to see your future. The river will give you the answer. The river will tell you what you should do."

I nod. The bracelet is cold and heavy in my hand, each charm a choice, each charm an opportunity, each charm a mistake in waiting.

"And when you want something: go out and whisper it to the river — like a prayer. When you curse somebody: write it on a piece of paper, and put the paper into the river, float it like a little paper boat. The river is your ally, your friend, your lady — do you understand?"

I nod, though I don't understand.

"When you curse somebody . . ." She pauses and sighs as if she is very weary. "Take care with your words, Jacquetta, especially in cursing. Only say the things you mean, make sure you lay your curse on the right man. For be very sure that when you put such words out in the world they can overshoot — like an arrow, a curse can go beyond your target and harm another. A wise woman curses very sparingly."

I shiver, though the room is hot.

"I will teach you more," she promises me. "It is your inheritance, since you are the oldest girl."

"Do boys not know? My brother Louis?"

Her lazy eyes half open, and she smiles at me. "Men command the world that they know," she says. "Everything that men know, they make their own. Everything that they learn, they claim for themselves. They are like the alchemists who look for the laws that govern the world, and then want to own them and keep them secret. Everything they discover, they hug to themselves; they shape knowledge into their own selfish image. What is left to us women but the realms of the unknown?"

"But can women not take a great place in the world? You do, Great-aunt, and Yolande of Aragon is called the Queen of Four Kingdoms. Shall I not command great lands like you and her?"

"You might. But I warn you that a woman who seeks great power and wealth has to pay a great price. Perhaps you will be a great woman like Melusina, or Yolande, or like me; but you will be like all women: uneasy in the world of men. You will do your best — perhaps you will gain some power if you marry well or inherit well — but you will always find the road is hard beneath your feet. In the other world — well, who knows about the other world? Maybe they will hear you, and perhaps you will hear them."

"What will I hear?"

She smiles. "You know. You hear it already."

41

"Voices?" I ask, thinking of Joan.

"Perhaps."

Slowly, the intense heat of the summer starts to fade, and it grows cooler in September. The trees of the great forest that surround the lake start to turn color from tired green to sere yellow, and the swallows swirl around the turrets of the castle every evening, as if to say good-bye for another year. They chase each other round and round in a dizzying train, like a veil being whirled in a dance. The rows on rows of vines grow heavy with fruit, and every day the peasant women go out with their sleeves rolled up over their big forearms and pick and pick the fruit into big wicker baskets, which the men swing onto carts and take back to the press. The smell of fruit and fermenting wine is heavy in the village; everyone has blue-stained hems to their gowns and purple feet, and they say it will be a good year this year, rich and lush. When the ladies-in-waiting and I ride through the village, they call us to taste the new wine, and it is light and sharp and fizzy in our mouths, and they laugh at our puckered faces.

My great-aunt does not sit straight-backed in her chair, overseeing her women and beyond them the castle and my uncle's lands, as she did at the start of the summer. As the sun loses its heat she too seems to be growing pale and cold. She lies down from the middle of the morning to the early evening, and only rises from her bed to walk into the great hall beside my uncle and nod her head at the rumble of greeting, as the men look up at their lord and lady and hammer on the wooden tables with their daggers.

Joan prays for her, by name, in her daily attendance at church, but I, childlike, just accept the new rhythm of my great-aunt's day, and sit with her to read in the afternoon, and wait for her to talk to me about the prayers floated like paper ships on the waters of rivers that were flowing to the sea before I was born. She tells me to spread out the cards of her pack and teaches me the name and the quality of each one.

"And now read them for me," she says one day, and then taps a card with her thin finger. "What is this one?"

I turn it over for her. The dark-hooded shape of Death looks back at us, his face hidden in the shadow of his hood, his scythe over his hunched shoulder.

"Ah well," she says. "So are you here at last, my friend? Jacquetta, you had better ask your uncle to come to see me."

I show him into her room, and he kneels at the side of her bed. She puts her hand on his head as if in blessing. Then she pushes him gently away.

"I cannot bear this weather," she says

43

crossly to my uncle, as if the cooling days are his fault. "How can you bear to live here? It is as cold as England, and the winters last forever. I shall go south; I shall go to Provence."

"Are you sure?" he asks. "I thought you were feeling tired. Should you not rest here?"

She snaps her fingers irritably. "I'm too cold," she says imperiously. "You can order me a guard and I shall have my litter lined with furs. I shall come back in spring."

"Surely you would be more comfortable here?" he suggests.

"I have a fancy to see the Rhône once more," she says. "Besides, I have business to do."

Nobody can ever argue against her — she is the demoiselle — and within days she has her great litter at the door, furs heaped on the bed, a brass hand warmer filled with hot coals, the floor of the litter packed with oven-heated bricks to keep her warm, the household lined up to say farewell.

She gives her hand to Joan, and then she kisses my aunt Jehanne and me. My uncle helps her into the litter, and she clutches his arm with her thin hand. "Keep the maid safe," she says. "Keep her from the English: it is my command."

He ducks his head. "Come back to us soon."

His wife, whose life is easier when the great

44

lady has moved on, steps forwards to tuck her in and kiss her pale cool cheeks. But it is me that the Demoiselle of Luxembourg calls torwards her with one crook of her skinny finger.

"God bless you, Jacquetta," she says to me. "You will remember all that I have taught you. And you will go far." She smiles at me. "Farther than you can imagine."

"But I will see you in spring?"

"I will send you my books," she says. "And my bracelet."

"And you will come to visit my mother and father at St. Pol in the spring?"

Her smile tells me that I will not see her again. "God bless," she repeats, and draws the curtains of her litter against the cold morning air as the cavalcade starts out of the gate.

In November, I am awakened in the darkest of the night, and I sit up in the little bed I share with Elizabeth the maid, and listen. It is as if someone is calling my name in a sweet voice: very high, and very thin. Then I am sure I can hear someone singing. Oddly, the noise is coming from outside our window, though we are high up in the turret of the castle. I pull on my cloak over my nightgown and go to the window and look out through the crack in the wooden shutters. There are no lights showing outside, the fields and the woods around the castle are as black as felted wool; there is nothing but this clear keening noise, not a nightingale but as high and as pure as a nightingale. Not an owl, far too musical and continuous, something like a boy singer in a choir. I turn to the bed and shake Elizabeth awake.

"Can you hear that?"

She does not even wake. "Nothing," she says, half asleep. "Stop it, Jacquetta. I'm asleep."

The stone floor is icy beneath my bare feet. I jump back into bed and put my cold feet in the warm space near Elizabeth. She gives a little bad-tempered grunt and rolls away from me, and then — though I think I will lie in the warm and listen to the voices — I fall asleep.

Six days later they tell me that my great-aunt, Jehanne of Luxembourg, died in her sleep, in the darkest hour of the night, in Avignon, beside the great River Rhône. Then I know whose voice it was I heard, singing around the turrets.

As soon as the English Duke of Bedford learns that Joan has lost her greatest protector, he sends the judge Pierre Cauchon, with a troop of men behind him, to negotiate for her ransom. She is summoned by a Church court on charges of heresy. Enormous sums of money change hands: twenty thousand livres for the man who pulled her off her horse, ten thousand francs to be paid to my uncle with the good wishes of the King of England. My uncle does not listen to his wife, who pleads that Joan shall be left with us. I am too unimportant even to have a voice, and so I have to watch in silence as my uncle makes an agreement that Joan shall be released to the Church for questioning. "I am not handing her over to the English," he says to his wife. "As the demoiselle asked me, and I have not forgotten, I have not handed her over to the English. I have only released her to the Church. This allows her to clear her name of all the charges against her. She will be judged by men of God; if she is innocent they will say so, and she will be released."

She looks at him as blankly as if he were Death himself, and I wonder if he believes this nonsense, or if he thinks that we, being women, are such fools as to think that a church dependent on the English, with bishops appointed by the English, are going to tell their rulers and paymasters that the girl who raised all of France against them is just an ordinary girl, perhaps a little noisy, perhaps a little naughty, and she should be given three Hail Marys and sent back to her farm, to her mother and her father and her cows.

"My lord, who is going to tell Joan?" is all I

47

dare to ask.

"Oh, she knows already," he says over his shoulder as he goes out of the hall, to bid farewell to Pierre Cauchon at the great gate. "I sent a page to tell her to get ready. She is to leave with them now."

As soon as I hear the words I am filled with a sudden terror, a gale of premonition, and I start running, running as if for my own life. I don't even go to the women's apartments, where the page boy will have found Joan to tell her that the English are to have her. I don't run towards her old cell, thinking she has gone there to fetch her little knapsack of things: her wooden spoon, her sharp dagger, the prayer book that my great-aunt gave her. Instead, I race up the winding stair to the first floor above the great hall, and then dash across the gallery, through the tiny doorway where the archway knocks my headdress off, tearing at the pins in my hair, and then I hammer up the circular stone stair, my feet pounding on the steps, my breath coming shorter and shorter, my gown clutched in my hands, so that I can burst out onto the flat roof at the very top of the tower and see Joan, poised like a bird ready to fly, balanced on the wall of the turret. As she hears the door bang open she looks over her shoulder at me and hears me scream: "Joan! No!" and she steps out into the void below her.

The worst thing of all, the very worst thing,

is that she does not leap into nothing, like a frightened deer. I was dreading that she would jump, but she does something far worse than that. She dives. She goes headfirst over the battlement, and as I fling myself to the edge I can see that she goes down like a dancer, an acrobat, her hands clasped behind her, one leg extended like a dancer, the other bent, the toe pointed to her knee, and I see that for that heart-stopping moment as she falls, she is in the pose of *le Pendu,* the Hanged Man, and she is going headfirst to her death with his calm smile on her serene face.

The thud when she hits the ground at the base of the tower is terrible. It echoes in my ears as if it is my own head that has struck the mud. I want to run down to lift her body, Joan, the maid, crumpled like a bag of old clothes; but I cannot move. My knees have given way beneath me; I am clinging to the stone battlements, and they are as cold as my scraped hands. I am not crying for her, though my breath is still coming in gulping sobs; I am frozen with horror, I am felled by horror. Joan was a young woman who tried to walk her own path in the world of men, just as my great-aunt told me. And it led her to this cold tower, this swan dive, this death.

They pick her up lifeless, and for four days she does not move or stir, but then she comes out of her stupor and gets up slowly from her bed, patting herself all over, as if to make sure that she is whole. Amazingly, no bones have been broken in her fall — she has not cracked her skull, nor snapped so much as a finger. It is as if her angels held her up, even when she gave herself into their element. Of course, this will not serve her; they are quick to say that only the Devil could have saved a girl who went headfirst like that from such a tall tower. If she had died, they would have said God's justice had been done. My uncle, a man of dour common sense, says that the ground is so sodden, after weeks of winter rain, and lapped by the moat, that she was in more danger of drowning than being broken; but now he is determined that she shall leave at once. He doesn't want the responsibility of the maid in his house, without the demoiselle to keep everything safe. He sends her first to his house in Arras, the Coeur le Comte, and then we follow, as she is transferred to the English city of Rouen for trial.

We have to attend. A great lord such as my uncle must be there to see justice being done, and his household must stand behind him. My aunt Jehanne takes me to witness the end of the dauphin's holy guide — the pretend prophet of the pretend king. Half of France is trooping to Rouen to see the end of the maid, and we have to be foremost among them.

For someone that they declare is nothing more than a peasant girl run mad, they are taking no chances. She is housed in the Castle Bouvreuil and kept in chains, in a cell with a double-locked door and the window boarded over. They are all in a terror that she will run like a mouse under the door, or fly like a bird through a crack in the window. They ask her to give an undertaking that she will not try to escape and, when she refuses, they chain her to the bed.

"She won't like that," my aunt Jehanne says sorrowfully.

"No."

They are waiting for the Duke of Bedford, and in the very last days of December he marches into the town with his guard dressed in the colors of roses, the bright red and white of England. He is a great man on horseback; he wears armor polished so brightly that you would take it for silver, and beneath his huge helmet his face is grave and stern, his big beak of a nose making him look like a predatory bird: an eagle. He was brother to the great English king Henry V, and he guards the lands that his brother won in France at the great battle of Agincourt. Now the dead king's young son is the new victor of France, and this is his most loyal uncle: seldom out of his armor or out of the saddle, never at peace.

We are all lined up at the great gate of Bouvreuil as he rides in, and his dark gaze rakes us all, looking from one to another as if to sniff out treason. My aunt and I curtsey low, and my uncle John doffs his hat and bows. Our house has been in alliance with the English for years; my other uncle, Louis of Luxembourg, is the duke's chancellor and swears that he is the greatest man ever to rule France.

Heavily, he gets off his horse and stands like a fortress himself, as the men line up to greet him, bowing over his hand, some of them almost going down to their knees. A man comes forwards, and as Bedford acknowledges him with a lordly tip of his head, his glance goes over his vassal's head and sees me. I am staring at him, of course — he is the greatest spectacle on this cold winter day — but now he is looking back at me, and there is a flash in his eyes that I see and cannot recognize. It is something like a sudden hunger, like a fasting man seeing a banquet. I step back. I am neither afraid nor coquettish, but I am only fourteen years of age, and there is something about the power of this man and his energy that I don't want turned in my direction. I slide back a little so I am behind my aunt, and I watch the rest of the greetings masked by her headdress and veil.

A great litter comes up, thick curtains tied tight with gold cord against the cold, and Bedford's wife, the Duchess Anne, is helped out. A small cheer greets her from our men: she is of the House of Burgundy, our liege lords and relations, and we all dip in a little bow to her. She is as plain as all the Burgundy family, poor things, but her smile is merry and kind, and she greets her husband warmly and then stands with her hand comfortably tucked in the crook of his arm and looks about her with a cheerful face. She waves at my aunt and points inside the castle to say that we must come to her later. "We'll go at dinnertime," my aunt says to me in a whisper. "Nobody in the world eats better than the Dukes of Burgundy."

Bedford takes off his helmet and bows to the crowd in general, raises a gauntleted hand to the people who are leaning from upper windows, and balancing on garden walls to see the great man. Then he turns and leads his wife inside, and everyone has a sense that we have seen the cast of players and the opening scene of a traveling show. But whether it is a masque or a party, funeral rites or the baiting of a wild animal that has brought so many of the greatest people in France to Rouen, it is about to begin.

ROUEN, FRANCE, SPRING 1431

And then they bodge it. They harass her with erudite questions, query her replies, double back on her answers, write down things she says in moments of weariness and bring them back to her later, define their terms in the most learned ways and ask her what she means, so that she does not understand the question and tells them simply "pass on" or "spare me that." Once or twice she just says: "I don't know. I am a simple girl with no learning. How would I know?"

My uncle gets an anguished letter from Queen Yolande of Aragon, who says she is certain that the dauphin will ransom Joan, she just needs another three days, another week to persuade him, can we not delay the trial? Can we not ask for a few days' delay? But the Church has the girl wound tight in the web of inquiry, and now they will never let her go.

Everything that highly educated men can do to obscure a simple truth, to make a woman doubt her feelings, to make her own thoughts a muddle, they do to her. They use their learning as a hurdle to herd her one way and then another, and then finally trap her in contradictions of which she can make no sense. Sometimes they accuse her in Latin, and she looks at them, baffled by a language that she has only ever heard spoken in church, in the Mass that she loves. How could these very sounds, these familiar beloved tones, so solemn and musical to her, now be the voice of accusation?

Sometimes they bring scandal against her in the words of her own people, old earthy stories from Domrémy of vanity, of false pride. They say she jilted a man before marriage; they say she ran away from good parents; they say she worked in an alehouse and was free with her favors like any village slut; they say she rode with the soldiers as their doxy; they say she is no maid but a harlot, and that everyone knew it.

It takes Anne, the kindhearted little Duchess of Bedford herself, to assert that Joan is a virgin, and to demand that the men who guard her are forbidden from touching or abusing her. They must be ordered that it is not the work of God to assault her. Then, as soon as this order is given, they say that since she is now so safe, guarded by the word of the duchess, that she has no excuse for wearing men's clothes and that she must dress in a gown, for now they tell her it is a sin, a mortal sin, to wear breeches.

They turn her head; they puzzle her beyond bearing. They are great men of the Church, and Joan is a peasant girl, a devout girl who has always done as the priest ordered until she heard the voices of angels who told her to do more. She cries in the end; she breaks down and cries like a child; she puts on the gown as they order her; and confesses to all the sins that they name to her. I don't know if she even understands the long list. She makes her mark on her confession — she writes her name and then signs a cross beside it as if to deny her signature. She admits that there were no angels and no voices, and that the dauphin is nothing more than the dauphin and not the King of France, that his coronation was a sham and her beautiful armor an offense to God and man, and that she is a girl, a silly girl, who tried to lead grown men as if she could know the way better than they. She says she is a vain fool to think that a girl might lead men, she is a woman worse than Eve for giving advice, an assistant to the Devil himself.

"What?" bellows the Duke of Bedford. We are visiting his wife the duchess, seated in her rooms before a good fire, a lute player twanging away in the corner, small glasses of the best wine on every table, everything elegant and beautiful; but we can hear his deplorable

English bellow through two closed doors.

We hear the doors bang as the Earl of Warwick flings himself out of the duke's apartments to find out what has gone wrong, and in this revealing burst of rage we see — as if we had ever been in any doubt — that these English never wanted the Church to wrestle with the soul of a mistaken girl and restore her to her senses, bring her to confession, penitence, and forgiveness; it has all along been nothing but a witch hunt determined to find a witch, a bonfire looking for a brand, Death waiting for a maiden. The duchess goes to the door, and the servants throw it open before her so we can all hear, disastrously clearly, her husband bellow at Pierre Cauchon the bishop, Cauchon the judge, Cauchon the man, who is there apparently representing — all at the same time — God and justice and the Church, "For the sake of Christ! I don't want her pleading guilty, I don't want her recanting, I don't want her confessed and shriven, I don't bloody well want her imprisoned for life! What safety is there in that for me? I want her as a pile of ashes blowing away in the wind. How much clearer do I have to be? Goddamn! Do I have to burn her myself? You said the Church would do it for me! Do it!"

The duchess steps back rapidly and gestures for the doors to her room to be closed, but we can still hear the regent, swearing and damning his soul at the top of his voice. The duchess shrugs — men will be men, and this is wartime — and my aunt smiles understandingly; the lute player increases his volume as best he can and starts to sing. I go to the window and look out.

In the market square they have a half-built pyre, a strong structure with a big central beam and the wood stacked around it. Joan has confessed and recanted; she has been found guilty of her crimes and sentenced to imprisonment.

But they are not taking the wood away.

My aunt gives me a nod that we are going to leave, and I go to the hall to wait for her as she delays inside the duchess's rooms, saying a few words of farewell. I have my hood pulled up over my head, my hands tucked inside my cape. It is cold for May. I wonder if Joan has blankets in her cell, as the big double doors to the duke's public rooms are thrown open and the duke himself comes quickly out.

I sink down into a curtsey, and I imagine he can barely see me, wrapped in my dark cape in the shadowy doorway. I expect him to brush past, but he pauses. "Jacquetta? Jacquetta St. Pol?"

I sink even lower. "Yes, Your Grace."

He puts a firm hand under my elbow and raises me up. His other hand pushes back my hood and turns my face to the light of the open doorway, his hand under my chin as if I am a child, and he is looking to see if my mouth is clean. His men are waiting for him; there must be a dozen people around us, but he acts as if we are quite alone. He stares at me intently, as if he would read me. I look back at him blankly, I don't know what he wants with me, and my aunt will be angry if I say the wrong thing to this most important man. I give my lip a little nip, and I hear his sudden intake of breath.

"My God, how old are you?"

"I am fifteen this year, Your Grace."

"And here with your father?"

"With my uncle, Your Grace. My father is Pierre, the new Count of Luxembourg."

"The new count?" he asks, staring at my mouth.

"On the death of the Demoiselle of Luxembourg," I mutter. "My father is now Count of Luxembourg. He was her heir."

"Of course, of course."

There seems nothing else to say, but still he is staring at me, still he holds me, one hand on my elbow, the other on the edge of my hood.

"Your Grace?" I whisper, hoping he will come to his senses and let me go.

"Jacquetta?" He whispers my name as if he is speaking to himself.

"May I serve you in some way?" I mean to say "please let me go," but a girl of my age cannot say such a thing to the greatest man in France.

He gives a little choke. "Indeed, I think you may. Jacquetta, you are going to be a beautiful woman, a beautiful young woman."

I glance around. His entourage are waiting for him, hardly moving, pretending not to see, not to listen. Nobody here is going to tell him to let me go, and I cannot do so.

"Do you have a sweetheart? Eh? Someone taken your fancy? Some cheeky little page boy given you a kiss?"

"No, my lord. No, of course not . . ." I am stammering as if I am in the wrong, as if I have done something as stupid and as vulgar as he suggests. He is chuckling as though to indulge me, but the grip on my elbow is hard as if he is angry. I lean back from his grip, from his avid gaze. "My father is very strict," I say feebly. "The honor of my family . . . I have been staying with my uncle John and his wife Jehanne. They would never allow —"

"You don't wish for a husband?" he asks me disbelievingly. "Don't you think of the man who will marry you, when you are in your bed at night? Do you dream of a young husband who will come for you like a troubadour and speak of love?"

I am trembling now; this is a nightmare. His grip is as hard as ever, but his hawkish face comes closer and closer, and now he is whispering in my ear. I begin to think he has gone mad. He looks at me as if he would eat me, and I have a shuddering sense of a world opening up before me that I don't want to know.

"No, no," I whisper. But then, as he does not release me but presses me closer, I have a sudden spurt of anger. I remember in a rush who I am, what I am. "May it please Your Grace, I am a maid," I say, the words tumbling. "A maid of the House of Luxembourg. No man has laid a hand on me; no man would dare. I was in the keeping of the Demoiselle of Luxembourg, a virgin like myself. I am fit to capture a unicorn, and I should not be so questioned . . ."

There is a noise from the duchess's room, and the door behind us suddenly opens, and at once he drops me, like a boy throwing down a stolen pastry. He turns and stretches out both his hands to his plain little wife. "My dear! I was just coming to find you."

Her bright gaze takes me in, my white face, my hood pulled back, and his rosy bonhomie. "Well, here I am," she says dryly. "So you need look no more. And I see you found little Jacquetta St. Pol instead."

I curtsey again, as he glances at me as if seeing me for the first time. "Good day," he says carelessly, and to his wife he says, confidentially: "I must go. They are making a muddle of it. I have to go."

She nods her head to him with an easy

smile, and he turns and goes out, all his men marching after him with a heavy tread. I dread his wife Anne asking me if her husband spoke to me, what he said, what I was doing with him in the darkness of the hall, why he spoke to me of love and troubadours. For I could not answer such questions. I don't know what he was doing; I don't know why he took hold of me. I feel sick, and my knees are trembling to think of his bright eyes on my face and his insinuating whisper. But I know he had no right. And I know that I defended myself, and I know that it is true: I am a virgin so pure that I could capture a unicorn.

But it is worse than this, far worse; she just looks at me steadily, and my sense of outrage slowly drains from me, for she does not ask me what I was doing with her husband; she looks at me as if she knows already. She looks me up and down, as if she knows everything. She gives me a small complicit smile as if she thinks I am some little thief and she has just caught me with my fingers in her purse.

Lord John, the Duke of Bedford, has his way, the great Earl of Warwick has his way, the great men of England have their way. Joan alone, without advisors to keep her safe, changes her mind about her confession, takes off her woman's gown, and puts her boy's clothes back on. She cries out that she was wrong to deny her voices, wrong to plead guilty. She is not a heretic; she is not an idolator; she is not a witch or an hermaphrodite or a monster; she will not confess to such things; she cannot force herself to confess to sins she has never committed. She is a girl guided by the angels to seek the Prince of France and call him to greatness. She has heard angels; they told her to see him crowned as king. This is the truth before God, she proclaims — and so the jaws of England snap shut on her with relish.

From my room in the castle I can see the pyre as they build it even higher. They build a stand for the nobility to watch the spectacle as if it were a joust, and barriers to hold back the thousands who will come to see. Finally, my aunt tells me to put on my best gown and my tall hat and come with her.

"I am ill; I cannot come," I whisper, but for once she is stern. I cannot be excused; I must be there. I must be seen, beside my aunt, beside Anne the Duchess of Bedford. We have to play our part in this scene as witnesses, as women who walk inside the rule of men. I will be there to show how girls should be: virgins who do not hear voices, women who do not think that they know better than men. My aunt and the duchess and I represent women as men would like them to be. Joan is a woman that men cannot tolerate.

We stand in the warm May sunshine as if

we were waiting for the starting trumpet of a joust. The crowd is noisy and cheerful all around us. A very few people are silent; some women hold a crucifix; one or two have their hands on a cross at their necks. But most people are enjoying the day out, cracking nuts and swigging from flasks, a merry outing on a sunny day in May and the cheering spectacle of a public burning at the end of it.

Then the door opens, and the men of the guard march out and push back the crowd who whisper and hiss and boo at the opening inner door, craning their necks to be the first to see her.

She does not look like my friend Joan — that is my first thought when they bring her out of the little sally port of the castle. She is wearing her boy's boots once more, but she is not striding out in her loose-limbed, confident walk. I guess that they have tortured her and perhaps the bones of her feet are broken, her toes crushed on the rack. They half drag her, and she makes little paddling steps, as if she is trying to find her footing on uncertain ground.

She is not wearing her boy's bonnet on her brown cropped hair, for they have shaved her head, and she is as bald as a shamed whore. On her bare cold scalp, stained here and there with dried blood where the razor has nicked her pale skin, they have crammed a tall hat of paper like a bishop's miter, and on it are written her sins, in clumsy block letters for everyone to see: Heretic. Witch. Traitor. She wears a shapeless white robe, knotted with a cheap piece of cord at her waist. It is too long for her, and the hem drags around her stumbling feet. She looks ridiculous, a figure of fun, and the people start to catcall and laugh, and someone throws a handful of mud.

She looks around, as if she is desperate for something; her eyes dart everywhere, and I am terrified that she will see me and know that I have failed to save her, that even now I am doing nothing, and I will do nothing to save her. I am terrified that she will call my name and everyone will know that this broken clown was my friend and that I will be shamed by her. But she is not looking at the faces crowding around her, alight with excitement, she is asking for something. I can see her urgently pleading; and then a soldier, a common English soldier, thrusts a wooden cross into her hands, and she clutches it as they lift her and push her upwards to the bonfire.

They have built it so high it is hard to get her up. Her feet scrabble on the ladder, and her hands cannot grip. But they push her roughly, cheerfully, from behind, hands on her back, her buttocks, her thighs, and then a big soldier goes up the ladder with her and takes a handful of the coarse material of her robe and hauls her up beside him like a sack, turns her round, and puts her back to the stake that runs through the pyre. They throw up a length of chain to him, and he loops it around and around her and then fastens it with a bolt behind. He tugs at it, workmanlike, and tucks the wooden cross in the front of her gown, and in the crowd below a friar pushes to the front and holds up a crucifix. She stares at it unblinkingly, and I know, to my shame, that I am glad she has fixed her eyes on the cross so that she will not look at me, in my best gown and my new velvet cap, among the nobility who are talking and laughing all around me.

The priest walks around the bottom of the pyre reading in Latin, the ritual cursing of the heretic; but I can hardly hear him above the yells of encouragement and the rumble of growing excitement from the crowd. The men with the burning torches come from the castle and walk around the pyre, lighting it all the way round the base, and then laying the torches against the wood. Someone has dampened the wood so that it will burn slowly, to give her the greatest pain, and the smoke billows around her.

I can see her lips moving. She is still looking at the upheld cross, and I see that she is saying "Jesus, Jesus" over and over, and for a moment I think that perhaps there will be a miracle, a storm to drown the fire, a lightning raid from the Armagnac forces. But there is nothing. Just the swirling thick smoke, and her white face, and her lips moving.

The fire is slow to catch; the crowd jeer the soldiers for laying a poor bonfire; my toes are cramped in my best shoes. The great bell starts to ring, slowly and solemnly, and though I can hardly see Joan through the thickening cloud of smoke, I recognize the turn of her head, under the great paper miter, as she listens, and I wonder if she is hearing her angels through the tolling of the bell and what they are saying to her now.

The wood shifts a little, and the flames start to lick. The inside of the pile is drier — they built it weeks ago for her — and now with a crackle and a blaze it is starting to brighten. The light makes the ramshackle buildings of the square jump and loom, the smoke swirls more quickly, the brightness of the fire throws a flickering glow on Joan, and I see her look up, clearly I see her form the word *Jesus,* and then like a child going to sleep her head droops and she is quiet.

Childishly, I think for a moment perhaps she has gone to sleep, perhaps this is the miracle sent by God; then there is a sudden blaze as the long white robe catches fire and a tongue of flame flickers up her back and the paper miter starts to brown and curl. She is still, silent as a little stone angel, and the pyre shifts and the bright sparks fly up.

I grit my teeth, and I find my aunt's hand

clutching mine. "Don't faint," she hisses. "You have to stand up." We stand hand-clasped, our faces quite blank, as if this were not a nightmare that tells me, as clearly as if it were written in letters of fire, what ending a girl may expect if she defies the rules of men and thinks she can make her own destiny. I am here not only to witness what happens to a heretic. I am here to witness what happens to a woman who thinks she knows more than men.

I look through the haze of the fire to our window in the castle, and I see the maid, Elizabeth, looking down. She sees me look up at her, and our eyes meet, blank with horror. Slowly, she stretches out her hand and makes the sign that Joan showed us that day by the moat in the hot sunshine. Elizabeth draws a circle in the air with her forefinger, the sign for the wheel of fortune, which can throw a woman so high in the world that she can command a king, or pull her down to this: a dishonored agonizing death.

CASTLE OF ST. POL, ARTOIS, SPRING 1433

After a few more months with my uncle John, and then a yearlong visit to our Brienne kinsfolk, my mother regards me as sufficiently polished to return home while they plan my marriage, and so I am living at our castle in St. Pol when we hear the news that Anne, Duchess of Bedford, has died and the duke is lost without her. Then a letter comes from my uncle Louis, the duke's chancellor.

"Jacquetta, this concerns you." My mother summons me to her rooms, where I find her seated, my father standing behind her chair. They both look at me sternly, and I make a rapid review of my day's doings. I have not completed the many tasks that I am supposed to do, and I skipped attendance at church this morning. My room is untidy, and I am behind with my sewing, but surely my father would not come to my mother's apartment to reprimand me for this?

"Yes, Lady Mother?"

My mother hesitates, glances up at my

father, and then presses on. "Of course your father and I have been considering a husband for you, and we have been looking at who might be suitable — we hoped that . . . but it does not matter, for you are lucky, we have had a most advantageous offer. In short, your uncle Louis has suggested you as a wife for the Duke of Bedford."

I am so surprised that I say nothing.

"A great honor," my father says shortly. "A great position for you. You will be an English duchess, the first lady after the king's mother in England, the first lady bar none in France. You should go down on your knees and thank God for this opportunity."

"What?"

My mother nods, confirming this. They both stare at me, expecting a response.

"But his wife has only just died," I say weakly.

"Yes indeed, your uncle Louis has done very well for you, to get your name put forwards this early."

"I would have thought he would have wanted to wait a little while."

"Didn't the duke see you at Rouen?" my mother asks. "And then again in Paris?"

"Yes, but he was married," I say foolishly. "He saw me . . ." I remember that dark predatory look, when I was little more than a girl, and my stepping behind my aunt to hide from it. I remember the shadowy hall and the man who whispered in my ear and then went out to order the burning of the Maid. "And the duchess was there. I knew her too. We saw her far more than we saw him."

My father shrugs. "At any rate, he liked the look of you, and your uncle has put your name in his ear, and you are to be his wife."

"He's very old," I say quietly, directing this at my mother.

"Not very. A little over forty," she says.

"And I thought you told me he was ill," I say to my father.

"All the better for you," my mother says. Clearly she means that an elderly husband may be less demanding than a young one, and if he dies then I shall be a dowager duchess at seventeen, which would be the only thing better than being a duchess at seventeen.

"I had not looked for such an honor," I say feebly to them both. "May I be excused? I fear I am not worthy."

"We are of the greatest family in Christendom," my father says grandly. "Kin to the Holy Roman emperor. How would you not be worthy?"

"You cannot be excused," my mother says. "Indeed, you would be a fool to be anything but delighted. Any girl in France and England would give her right hand for such a match." She pauses and clears her throat. "He is the greatest man in France and England after the

King of England. And if the king were to die . . ."

"Which God forbid," my father says hastily.

"God forbid, indeed, but if the king were to die, then the duke would be heir to the throne of England and you would be Queen of England. What d'you think of that?"

"I had not thought of marriage to such a man as the duke."

"Think now then," my father says briskly. "For he is coming here in April, to marry you."

My uncle Louis, who is Bishop of Therouanne as well as the duke's chancellor, is both host and priest at this wedding of his own making. He entertains us in his episcopal palace, and John, Duke of Bedford, rides in with his guard in the English livery of red and white, as I stand at the doorway of the palace in a gown of palest yellow with a veil of tissue of gold floating from my high headdress.

His page runs forwards to hold his horse's head, and another kneels on the ground alongside and then drops to his hands and knees to form a human mounting block. The duke climbs down heavily, from the stirrup onto the man's back, and then steps down to the ground. Nobody remarks on this. The duke is such a great man that his pages take it as an honor for him to stand on them. His squire takes his helmet and his metaled gauntlets, and steps aside.

"My lord." My uncle the bishop greets his master with obvious affection and then bows to kiss his hand. The duke claps him on the back and then turns to my father and my mother. Only when the courtesies with them are complete does he turn to me, and he steps forwards, takes both of my hands, pulls me towards him, and kisses me on the mouth.

His chin is rough with stubble, his breath tainted; it is like being licked by a hound. His face seems very big as it comes down towards me, and very big as he moves away. He does not pause to look at me, or to smile, just that one aggressive kiss, then he turns to my uncle and says: "*Do* you have no wine?" and they laugh for it is a private joke, based on their years of friendship, and my uncle leads the way inside, and my mother and father follow them, and I am left for a moment, looking after the older people, with the squire at my side.

"My lady," he says. He has passed the duke's armor to another, and now he bows to me and doffs his hat. His dark hair is cut straight in a fringe above his brows; his eyes are gray as slate, perhaps blue. He has a funny twist in his smile, as if something is amusing him. He is stunningly handsome, I can hear the ladies-in-waiting behind me give a little murmur. He makes a bow and offers me his arm to take me inside. I put my hand on his and feel the warmth of his hand through the soft leather of his glove. At once, he pulls off the glove so his fingers are holding mine. I feel as if I would like him to take my hand in his, to put his warm palm against mine. I feel I would like him to take hold of my shoulders, to grip me at the waist.

I shake my head to clear my mind of such ridiculous thoughts, and I say, abruptly, like an awkward girl: "I'll go in alone, thank you," and I drop his hand and follow them inside.

The three men are seated, wineglasses in their hands; my mother is in a window embrasure, watching the servants bring little cakes and top up their glasses. I go to her side with her ladies-in-waiting, and my two little sisters who are dressed in their best and trusted to stand with the adults on this most important day. I wish that I was eight years old like Isabelle, and could look at John, Duke of Bedford, and marvel at his greatness and know that he would say nothing to me, that he would not even see me. But I am not a little girl anymore, and as I look across at him, he does see me; he looks at me with a sort of avid curiosity, and this time there is nowhere for me to hide.

My mother comes to my room the night before my wedding. She brings the gown for the next day and lays it carefully in the chest at the foot of my bed. The tall headdress and veil are mounted on a stand, safely out of the way of candles or dust.

My maid is brushing my fair hair before the beaten silver mirror, but as my mother comes in I say, "You can stop now, Margarethe," and she twists the long fall into a loose plait, ties it with a ribbon, and goes from the room.

Mother sits awkwardly on the bed. "I need to speak to you about marriage," she starts. "About what your duties will be as a married woman. I suppose you should know."

I turn on my stool and wait, saying nothing.

"This is a marriage of great advantage to you," she says. "We are of Luxembourg, of course, but to gain the position of an English duchess is a great thing."

I nod. I wonder if she is going to say anything about what happens on the wedding night. I am afraid of the great duke, and I am dreading the thought of spending the night with him. The last wedding I went to they put the couple in bed together, and in the morning they fetched them out with music and singing and laughing. Then the mother went in and brought out the sheets, and they were red with blood. Nobody would tell me what had happened, if there had been some sort of accident. Everyone behaved as if everything was quite wonderful, as if they were pleased at the sight of blood on the linen. Indeed, they were laughing and congratulating the bridegroom. I wonder if my mother is going to explain now.

"But for him, it is not a marriage of advantage," she says. "It may cost him very dear."

"The jointure?" I ask, thinking that it must cost him money to pay me my allowance.

"His allies," she says. "He has been in alliance with the Dukes of Burgundy to fight against the Armagnacs. England could not have fought such a war without their support. His wife was Anne of Burgundy — the present duke was her brother — and she made it her business to keep her brother and her husband in good friendship. Now she has died, there is no one to keep the friendship, no one to help them resolve their disagreements."

"Well, I can't," I say, thinking of the Duke of Burgundy, whom I have seen half a dozen times in my whole life, while certainly he has never noticed me at all.

"You will have to try," my mother says. "It will be your duty, as an English duchess, to hold Burgundy in alliance with England. Your husband will expect you to entertain his allies and to be charming."

"Charming?"

"Yes. But there is a difficulty. Because my lord John of Bedford is marrying you so soon after the death of his wife, the Duke of Burgundy is offended at the insult to his dead sister. He has taken it badly."

"Then why are we marrying so quickly?" I ask. "If it upsets the Duke of Burgundy? Surely we should leave it a year and not displease him? He is our kinsman, as well as the Duke of Bedford's ally. Surely we should not offend him?"

My mother smiles faintly. "It makes you a duchess," she reminds me. "A greater title even than mine."

"I could be a duchess next year." The thought of escaping this marriage, even for a year, fills me with hope. "We could just be betrothed."

"Lord John won't wait," she says flatly. "So don't hope for that. I just want to warn you that he may lose his ally by marrying you. You must do all that you can to retain the friendship of the Duke of Burgundy, and remind them both that you are a kinswoman of Burgundy and his vassal. Speak to the Duke of Burgundy privately and promise him that you remember your kinship to the Burgundians. Do all you can to keep the friendship between the two of them, Jacquetta."

I nod. I really don't know what she thinks I can do, a seventeen-year-old girl, to maintain an alliance of two great men old enough to be my father. But I will have to promise to do my best.

"And the marriage . . ." I begin.

"Yes?"

I take a breath. "What exactly happens?"

She shrugs; she makes a little face as if talk of it is beneath her, or embarrassing, or even worse — too disagreeable for words. "Oh, my dear, you just do your duty. He will tell you what he expects. He will tell you what to do. He won't expect you to know anything; he will prefer to be your instructor."

"Does it hurt?" I ask.

"Yes," she says unhelpfully. "But not for very long. Since he is older and practiced, he should do his best to see that you are not hurt too badly." She hesitates. "But if he does hurt you . . ."

"Yes?"

"Don't complain of it."

The wedding is to be at midday and I start preparing at eight in the morning when my maid brings me bread and meat and small ale to sustain me through the long day. I giggle when I see the tray heaped with food. "I'm not going out hunting, you know."

"No," she says ominously, "you are to be hunted," and the other maids with her all cackle like a pen of hens, and that is the last joke I am going to offer all day.

I sit at the table in a sulk, and eat, while they embroider versions of the theme of my being hunted and caught and enjoying the chase, until my mother comes in, and behind her come two serving men, rolling the great wooden barrel of a bath.

They place it before the fire in my bedroom, line it with linen, and start to pour in jug after jug of hot water. The maids bustle about bringing drying sheets and start to lay out my new undergowns, with much comment about the lace and the ribbons and how fine everything is, and how lucky I am. My mother sees my strained expression and shoos them all from the room except our old nursemaid, who is to scrub my back and wash my hair and add jugs of hot water. I feel like a sacrificial lamb being cleaned and brushed before having its throat cut, and it is not a pleasant thought.

But our nursemaid Mary is cheerful and full of her usual clucking approbation of my beautiful hair and my beautiful skin, and if she had half my looks she would have run away to Paris — as ever — and when I have bathed and she has dried my hair and plaited it, I cannot help but be encouraged by the linen undergown with the new ribbons, and by the new shoes and by the beautiful cloth-of-gold gown, and the headdress. The maids come back in to help me dress, and tie the laces of the gown and straighten my head-dress and pull the veil over my shoulders and finally pronounce me ready for my wedding and as beautiful as a bride should be.

I turn to the great looking glass that my mother has ordered to be carried into my chamber, and my reflection looks back at me. The maids hold it before me and tip it slightly downwards so that I can first see the hem of my gown, embroidered with little red lions rampant, from the standard of our house, and my red leather slippers with the curling toes. Then they hold the mirror straight, and I can see the cloth-of-gold gown gathered at the high waist and the embroidered heavy belt of gold that is slung low over my slim hips. I gesture, and they raise the mirror so I can see the expensive cream lace veiling the low-cut neck of the gown, the gold sleeves falling from my shoulders, with the white linen undergown revealed tantalizingly through the slashings at the shoulders, and then my face. My fair hair is plaited away and tucked under the tall headdress, and my face looks solemnly at me, enhanced by the silvery reflection of the mirror. My gray eyes are wide in this light, my skin clear and pearly; the mirror makes me look like a statue of a beauty, a marble girl. I gaze at myself as if I would know who I am, and for a moment I think I see Melusina, the founder of our house, looking back at me through moonlit water.

"When you are a duchess, you will have a great mirror of your own," my mother says. "Everything fine. And you will have all her old clothes."

"Duchess Anne's clothes?"

"Yes," she says, as if wearing the wardrobe of a recently dead woman should be a great treat for me. "Her sables are the best I have ever seen. Now they will be yours."

"Wonderful," I say politely. "Will I get my own clothes as well?"

She laughs. "You will be the first lady in France, all but the first lady in England. You will be able to have whatever your husband wants to give you. And you will soon learn how to persuade him."

A woman whispers something behind her hand about how a girl like me might persuade a man as old as he with one hand tied behind her back. Someone says, "Better with both hands tied," and a couple of them laugh. I have no idea what they mean.

"He will love you," my mother promises. "He is quite mad for you."

I don't reply. I just look at the young woman in the mirror. The thought of John, Duke of Bedford, running mad for me is not encouraging at all.

The wedding service lasts about an hour. It is all in Latin, so half of the vows are incomprehensible to me, anyway. It is not a private plighting of promises, but more a great announcement as the hall of the bishop's palace fills with strangers come to look at me and celebrate my good fortune. When the vows are done and we walk through the crowd, I am escorted by my new husband, my fingertips resting on his sleeve, there is a roar of approbation and everywhere I look I see smiling avid faces.

We sit at the top table, facing the room. There is a bawl of trumpets from the gallery and the first of dozens of plates of food is marched into the room at shoulder height. The servers come to us at the high table first and put a little from every dish on each golden plate; then the duke points them here and there down the hall so that his favorites may share our dishes. For everyone else, the great bowls of meat come in and the great platters of white bread. It is a huge feast, my uncle Louis has spared no expense to please his patron and to celebrate my rise to the royalty of England.

They bring in wine in great golden jugs, and they pour glass after glass at the high table. The honored guests, those who sit above the great golden bowl of salt, have as much wine as they can drink, as fast as they can drink it. In the hall the men have tankard after tankard of ale, the best ale: wedding ale specially brewed for today, specially sweetened and spicy.

There is a challenger, who rides his horse right into the hall and throws down his gauntlet in my name. His horse curves its heavy muscled neck and eyes the tables and the great circular fireplace in the center of the hall. I have to get up from my place and come round on the raised dais of the high table to give him a golden cup, and then he goes all round the hall at a powerful trot, his rider sitting heavily in the embossed saddle, before cantering out of the double doors. It seems quite ridiculous to me, to ride a horse into dinner, especially such a heavy horse and such a weighty knight. I look up, and I meet the gaze of the young squire who is dangerously near to laughter, as I am. Quickly, we both look away from each other's dancing eyes before I betray myself and giggle.

There are twenty courses of meats, and then ten of fish; then everything is taken away and Rhenish wine is served with a voider course of potted fruit, sugared plums, and sweetmeats. When everyone has tasted all of these, they bring in the final course of marchpane, pastries, sugared fruits, and gingerbread decorated with real gold leaf. In comes the Fool, who juggles and cracks bawdy jokes about youth and age, male and female, and the heat of the wedding bed, which is the fire to forge a new life. He is followed by dancers and players, who perform a masque celebrating the power of England and the beauty of Luxembourg, with a beautiful woman, almost naked but for her long green tail of silk, who symbolizes Melusina. The best of them all is a costumed lion, the emblem of both our countries, who cavorts and dances with strength and grace, and finally comes, panting a little, to the high table and bows his great head to me. His mane is a mass of golden curls smelling of sacking, his face a mask of painted paper, with a smiling honest look. I have a gold chain to put around his neck, and as I stretch towards him and he bows his head to me, I recognize the gleam of blue eyes through the mask and know that my hands are on the shoulders of the handsome squire, and that I am standing close enough to embrace him as I put my chain around his neck.

My mother nods to me that we can leave, and the women and the musicians all rise up and dance in a line round the length of the hall and then make an archway with their hands held high and I walk through it, with all the girls wishing me luck and the women calling blessings down on me. I am preceded by my dancing little sisters who scatter rose petals and little golden keys on the floor where I walk. Everyone escorts me up the great flight of stairs to the best chambers, and they all seem disposed to crowd into the bedroom with me; but my father stops them at the door, and I go in with just my mother and the ladies of her court.

First they unpin my high headdress and lift it carefully away, and then they unpin my hair. My scalp aches as the tightly plaited

84

hair tumbles down, and I rub my face. They untie the laces of my gown at my shoulders to take off the sleeves; then they untie the fastenings at the back and drop it to the floor, and I carefully step out of it. They take it away to shake it and powder it and store it carefully for the next important event when I will wear it as the Duchess of Bedford, and the red lions on the hem will symbolize the house that once was mine. They untie the laces of my undergown and strip me naked; then, while I shiver, they throw my nightgown over my head and put a wrap around my shoulders. They seat me on a stool and bring a bowl of hot scented water, and I soak my cold feet and lean back as one of them brushes my hair while the others pull at the embroidered hem of the gown, tidy the fall of the wrap, and put the room to rights. Finally they pat my feet dry, plait my hair, tie a nightcap on my head, and then they throw open the door.

My uncle Louis comes in, dressed in his bishop's cope and miter, swinging a censer, and he proceeds all round the room, blessing every corner, and wishing me happiness, wealth, and above all fertility in this great match between England and the county of Luxembourg. "Amen," I say, "amen," but it seems that he will never stop, and then, from the hall below, comes a great rumble of male voices and laughter and the blare of trumpets and the banging of drums and they are bringing my bridegroom, the old duke, to my room.

They carry him shoulder high, shouting "Hurrah! Hurrah!" and they set him on his feet just outside my door so that he can walk in and they can all tumble in behind him. Hundreds are left in the rooms outside, craning to see, and shouting for others to move up. The Fool capers in, his bladder in his hand, poking at the bed and declaring that it need be soft, for the duke will make a heavy landing. There is a roar of laughter at this, which spreads out of the room to the chambers beyond and even down to the hall as the jest is repeated. Then the Fool commands the girls to build up the fire to keep the bed warm, and top up the wedding ale for the duke may get a thirst on, and then he may need to get up in the night. "Up in the night!" he says again, and everyone laughs.

The trumpets blast a summons, deafening in the bedroom, and my father says, "Well, we will leave them! God bless, and good night." My mother kisses me on the forehead, and all her ladies and half of the guests kiss me too. Then my mother leads me to the bed and helps me climb into it. I sit there, propped on pillows like a hand-carved poppet. On the other side, the duke is throwing off his dressing gown, and his squire pulls back the sheets and helps his lord into bed.

The squire keeps his eyes down and does not look at me, and I am still, like a stiff little doll, one hand holding the neck of my nightgown tightly under my chin.

We sit bolt upright, side by side, while everyone laughs and cheers and wishes us well, and then my father and my uncle guide and half push the revelers from the room. They close the door on us, and we can still hear them, singing their way down the stairs back to the hall and shouting for more drink to toast the health of the happy couple and wet the head of the baby who will be made, God willing, this very night.

"Are you well, Jacquetta?" the duke asks me as the room grows slowly quiet and the candles burn more steadily, now that the doors are closed.

"I am well, my lord," I say. My heart is beating so loudly that I think he must hear it. More than anything else I am painfully aware that I have no idea what I should do, or what he may ask of me.

"You can go to sleep," he says heavily. "For I am dead drunk. I hope you will be happy, Jacquetta. I will be a kind husband to you. But go to sleep now, for I am drunk as a bishop."

He heaves the bedclothes over his own shoulders and rolls over on his side, as if there was nothing more to say or do, and within moments he is snoring so loudly that I fear they will hear him in the hall below. I lie still, almost afraid to move, and then, as his breathing deepens and slows, and the snores settle to a steady low roar and grunt, I slip from the bed, take a sip of the wedding ale — since after all it is my wedding day — blow out the candles, and then climb back between the warm sheets beside the unfamiliar bulk of a sleeping man.

I think I will never sleep. I can hear the singing from the hall below and then the noise as people spill out into the courtyard outside and shout for torches and servants to show them to their beds for the night. The steady rumble of my husband's snore is like the roar from a bear pit, pointlessly loud and threatening. I think I will never ever sleep with such a great man in my bed, and amid this buzz of thoughts in my head, and my grumbles to myself about this discomfort, and how unfair it is to me, I slide into sleep.

I wake to find my new husband already awake, pulling on his breeches, his white linen shirt open to his broad waist, his fleshy hairy chest and big belly half exposed. I sit up in bed and gather my nightgown around me. "My lord."

"Good morning, wife!" he says with a smile. "Did you sleep well?"

"Yes," I say. "I think you did?"

"Did I snore?" he asks cheerfully.

"A little."

"More than a little, I wager. Was it like a thunderstorm?"

"Well, yes."

He grins. "You will get used to it. Anne used to say it was like living by the sea. You get used to the noise. It is when there is silence that it wakes you."

I blink at the opinions of my predecessor.

He comes around to my side of the bed and sits heavily on my feet. "Ah, excuse me."

I move out of his way, and he sits again. "Jacquetta, I am a good deal older than you. I must tell you, I will not be able to give you a son, nor any child at all. I am sorry for that."

I take a little breath and wait to see what terrible thing he will say next. I had thought he had married me to get an heir. Why else would a man want a young bride? He answers this at once, before it is even spoken.

"Nor shall I take your virginity," he says quietly. "For one thing, I am unmanned, and so I cannot readily do it; for another, I don't want to do it with you."

My hand tightens on the nightgown at my throat. My mother will be appalled when she finds out about this. I am going to be in so much trouble with my father. "My lord, I am very sorry. You don't like me?"

He laughs shortly. "What man could not? You are the most exquisite girl in France, I chose you for your beauty and for your youth

— but for something else too. I have a better task for you than being my bedmate. I could command any girl in France. But you, I trust, are fit to do something more. Do you not know?"

Dumbly, I shake my head.

"The demoiselle said you had a gift," he says quietly.

"My great-aunt?"

"Yes. She told your uncle that you had the gift of your family; she said you have the Sight. And he told me."

I am silent for a moment. "I don't know."

"She said she thought you might have. She said she had spoken with you. Your uncle tells me that you studied with her, that she left you her books, her bracelet with charms for foreseeing. That you can hear singing."

"He told you that?"

"Yes, and I assume that she left her things to you because she thought you would be able to make use of them."

"My lord —"

"This is not a trap, Jacquetta. I am not tricking you into a confession."

You tricked Joan, I think to myself.

"I am working for my king and for my country; we are near to finding, please God, the elixir that brings a cure for death, and makes the philosopher's stone."

"The philosopher's stone?"

"Jacquetta, I think we are very close to finding the way to turn iron into gold. We are very close. And then . . ."

I wait.

"Then I will have enough coin to pay my troops to fight for every town in France. Then the rule of England can spread peace over all our lands. Then my nephew can sit firmly on his throne, and the poor people of England can work for their living without being taxed into poverty. It would be a new world, Jacquetta. We would command it. We would pay for everything with gold that we could make in London. We would not have to dig it in Cornwall nor pan for it in Wales. We would have a country richer than any dream. And I am, I think, perhaps only a few months from finding it."

"And what about me?"

He nods, as I return him to the reality of this wedding-day morning, which is not a real wedding at all. "Oh yes. You. My alchemists, my astrologers tell me that I need someone with your gifts. Someone who can scry, who can look into a mirror or into water and see the truth, the future. They need an assistant with clean hands and a pure heart. It has to be a woman, a young woman who has never taken a life, never stolen, never known lust. When I first met you, they had just told me that they could go no further without a young woman, a virgin, who could see the future. In short, I needed a girl who could capture a unicorn."

"My Lord Duke —"

"You said that. D'you remember? In the hall of the castle at Rouen? You said you were a girl so pure that you could capture a unicorn."

I nod. I did say it. I wish I had not.

"I understand that you are shy. You will be anxious to tell me you cannot do these things. I understand your reserve. But tell me only this. Have you taken a life?"

"No, of course not."

"Have you stolen? Even a little fairing? Even a coin from another's pocket?"

"No."

"Have you lusted for a man?"

"No!" I say emphatically.

"Have you ever foretold the future, in any way at all?"

I hesitate. I think of Joan and the card of *le Pendu,* and the wheel of fortune that bore her down so low. I think of the singing around the turrets on the night that the demoiselle died. "I think so. I cannot be sure. Sometimes things come to me; it is not that I call them."

"Could you capture a unicorn?"

I give a little nervous laugh. "My lord. It is just a saying; it is just a tapestry picture. I wouldn't know what one is supposed to do . . ."

"They say that the only way to capture a

unicorn is for a virgin to go alone into the forest, that no man can set a hand on it, but that it will come to a virgin and lay its beautiful head in her lap."

I shake my head. "I know this is what they say, but I don't know anything about unicorns. My lord, I don't even know if they are real."

"At any rate, as a virgin you are of great value to me, a very precious thing to me. As a virginal daughter of the House of Melusina, as an heiress of her gifts, you are beyond precious. As a young wife you would be a pleasure to me, but nothing more. I have married you to do far, far more than merely lie on your back and please me. Do you understand now?"

"Not really."

"Never mind. What I want is a young woman pure in heart, a virgin, who will do my bidding, who is mine as much as if I had bought a slave from the Turkish galleys. And this is what I have in you. You will learn what I want from you later; you will do what I want. But you won't be hurt or frightened — you have my word."

He gets to his feet and takes his dagger from the sheath at his belt. "Now we have to stain the sheets," he says. "And if anyone asks you, your mother or your father, you tell them that I got on top of you, that it hurt a little, and that you hope we have made a child. Say

93

nothing about the life we are to have. Let them think that you are an ordinary wife and that I have deflowered you."

He takes his dagger and without another word he makes a quick slice against his left wrist, and the blood wells up quickly from the scratch. He lets it come, and then he pulls back the covers of the bed, ignoring me as I tuck my bare feet out of sight, and he holds out his hand and drips a few spots of red blood onto the sheets. I stare at them as the stain spreads, feeling utterly ashamed, thinking that this is my marriage, that starts in my husband's blood, with a lie.

"That'll do," he says. "Your mother will come to see this and believe that I have had you. D'you remember what to tell her?"

"That you got on top of me, that it hurt a little, and that I hope we have made a child," I repeat obediently.

"That I am going to keep you as a virgin is our secret." He is suddenly serious, almost threatening. "Don't forget that. As my wife you will know my secrets, and this is the first, and one of the greatest of them. The alchemy, the foreseeing, your virginity, these are all secrets that you must keep, on your honor, and tell no one. You are of the royal house of England now, which will bring you greatness but also great cost. You have to pay the price as well as enjoy the wealth."

I nod, my eyes on his dark face.

He rises from the bed and takes his dagger to the bottom sheet. Without thinking of the cost, he slices a thin strip of linen. Mutely he holds it out to me, and I tie it around his wrist over the cut. "Pretty maid," he says. "I shall see you at breakfast," and then he pulls on his boots and walks from the room.

PARIS, FRANCE, MAY 1433

We travel with a great entourage as befits the ruler of France, especially a ruler who holds his lands by force. Ahead of us go an armed guard, a vanguard under the command of the blue-eyed squire, to make sure that the way is safe. Then, after a little gap to let the dust settle, come my lord duke and I. I ride behind a burly man-at-arms, seated pillion, my hands on his belt. My lord rides his warhorse beside me, as if for company, but he barely says one word.

"I wish I could ride a horse on my own," I remark.

He glances at me as if he had forgotten I was there at all. "Not today," he says. "It will be hard riding today, and if we meet trouble, we might have to go fast. We can't go at a lady's pace, a girl's pace."

I say nothing, for it is true, I am not much of a rider. Then I try again to make a conversation with him. "And why is it hard riding today, my lord?"

For a moment he is silent, as if considering whether he can be troubled to answer me.

"We're not going to Paris. We're going north to Calais."

"Excuse me, but I thought we were going to Paris. Why are we going to Calais, my lord?"

He sighs as if two questions are too much for a man to bear.

"There was a mutiny at Calais among the garrison, my soldiers, recruited and commanded by me. Bloody fools. I called in on my way to you. Hanged the ringleaders. Now I'm going back to make sure the rest have learned their lesson."

"You hanged men on your way to our wedding?"

He turns his dark gaze on me. "Why not?"

I can't really say why not; it just seems to me rather disagreeable. I make a little face and turn away. He laughs shortly. "Better for you that the garrison should be strong," he says. "Calais is the rock. All of England's lands in northern France are built on our holding Calais."

We ride on in silence. He says almost nothing when we stop to eat at midday, except to ask if I am very tired, and when I say no, he sees that I am fed and then lifts me back to the pillion saddle for the rest of the ride. The squire comes back and sweeps his hat off to me in a low bow and then mutters to my lord in a rapid conference, after which we all fall in and ride on.

It is twilight as we see the great walls of the castle of Calais looming out of the misty sea plain ahead of us. The land all around is intersected with ditches and canals, divided with little gates, each of them swirling with mist. My lord's squire comes riding back when the flag over the top tower of the castle dips in acknowledgment, and the great gates ahead of us swing open. "Soon be home," he says cheerfully to me as he wheels his horse round.

"Not my home," I observe shortly.

"Oh, it will be," he says. "This is one of your greatest castles."

"In the middle of a mutiny?"

He shakes his head. "That's over now. The garrison hadn't been paid for months, and so the soldiers took the wool from the Calais merchants, stole it from their stores. Then the merchants paid to get their goods back; now my lord the duke will repay them." He grins at my puzzled face. "It's nothing. If the soldiers had been paid on time, it would never have happened."

"Then why did my lord execute someone?"

His smile dims. "So that they remember that next time their wages are late, they have to wait on his pleasure."

I glance at my silently listening husband on my other side.

98

"And what happens now?"

We are approaching the walls; the soldiers are mustering into a guard of honor, running down the steep hill from the castle, which sits at the center of the town, guarding the port to the north and the marshy land to the south.

"Now I dismiss the men who stole the goods, dismiss their commander, and appoint a new Captain of Calais," my husband says shortly. He looks across me at the squire. "You."

"I, my lord?"

"Yes."

"I'm honored, but —"

"Are you arguing with me?"

"No, my lord, of course not."

My husband smiles at the silenced young man. "That's good." To me, he says, "This young man, my squire, my friend, Richard Woodville, has fought in almost every campaign here in France and was knighted on the battlefield by the late king, my brother. His father served us too. He's not yet thirty years old, but I know of no one more loyal or trustworthy. He can command this garrison, and while he is here I can be sure that there will be no mutinies, and no complaints, and no pretty thieving. And there will be no arguing about my orders. Is that right, Woodville?"

"Quite right, sir," he says.

And then the three of us go through the

dark echoing doorway and up the cobbled streets, past the hanged mutineers swinging silently on the gallows, through the bowing citizens to the castle of Calais.

"Am I to stay here now?" Woodville asks, as if it is a mere matter of a bed for the night.

"Not yet," my husband says. "I have need of you by me."

We stay only three nights, long enough for my husband to dismiss half of the soldiers of the garrison and send to England for their replacements, long enough to warn their commander that he will be replaced by the squire Sir Richard Woodville, and then we rattle down the cobbled street and out of the gateway and go south down the road to Paris, the squire Woodville at the head of the troop once more, me on the lumbering horse of the man-at-arms, and my husband in grim silence.

It is a two-day ride before we see the Grange Batelière standing over the desolate countryside outside the city. Beyond it are worked fields and little dairy farms that gradually give way to small market gardens that surround the city walls. We enter through the northwest gate, close to the Louvre, and see at once my Paris home, the Hôtel de Bourbon, one of the greatest houses in the city, as befits the ruler of France. It stands beside the king's palace of the Louvre, looking south over the river, like a building in marchpane, all turrets and roofs and towers and balconies. I should have known that it would be a great house, having seen my lord's castle at Rouen; but when we ride up to the great gates, I feel like a princess in a story being taken into a giant's fortress. A fortified wall runs all around, and there is a guard-house at every gate, which reminds me, if I were in any danger of forgetting, that my husband may be the ruler, but not everyone recognizes him as the representative of the God-given king. The one whom many prefer to call the King of France is not far away, at Chinon, eyeing our lands and stirring up trouble. The one whom we call the King of France and England is safe in London, too poor to send my husband the money and troops he needs to keep these faithless lands in subjection, too weak to command his lords to come to fight under our standard.

My lord gives me several days of freedom to find my way around my new home, to discover the former duchess's jewel box, and her dressing room of furs and fine gowns, and then he comes to my room after Matins and says, "Come, Jacquetta, I have work for you today."

I follow him, trotting like a puppy at his heels, as he leads me through the gallery where tapestries of gods look down on us, to a double door at the end, two men-at-arms on either side, and his squire, Woodville, lounging on the windowsill. He jumps up when he sees us and gives me a low bow.

The men-at-arms swing open the doors, and we go inside. I don't know what I am expecting — certainly not this. First there is a room as big as a great hall but looking like a library in a monastery. There are shelves of dark wood, and on them are scrolls and books, locked away behind brass grilles. There are tall tables and high stools so that you can sit up at a desk and unfurl a scroll and read it at your leisure. There are tables made ready for study with pots of ink and sharpened quills and pages of paper ready for taking notes. I have never seen anything like it outside of an abbey, and I look up at my husband with new respect. He has spent a fortune here: each one of these books will have cost as much as the duchess's jewels.

"I have the finest collection of books and manuscripts outside the Church in Europe," he says. "And my own copyists." He gestures to two young men, either side of a stand, one of whom is intoning strange words, reading from a scroll, while the other, painstakingly, writes. "Translating from the Arabic," my husband says. "Arabic to Latin and from there, to French or English. The Moors are the source of great knowledge, of all mathematics, all science. I buy the scrolls, and I have them translated myself. This is how I have put us ahead in the search for knowledge. Because I have tapped the source." He smiles, suddenly pleased with me. "Just as I have with you. I have gone to the very source of the mysteries."

In the center of the room is a great table, painted and sculpted. I exclaim in delight and step closer to examine it. It is enchanting, like a little country, if one could view it from above, flying high over it like an eagle. It is the country of France; I can see the outer wall of the city of Paris, and the Seine flowing through, painted bright blue. I can see the Île de Paris, a little maze of buildings shaped like a boat itself, set in the river. Then I can see how the land is divided: the top half of France is painted white and red in the colors of England, and the bottom half is left blank, and an Armagnac flag shows Charles, the pretend king, in his lands at Chinon. A series of scratches shows where the little flags were stabbed, furiously, rapidly, in the plan marking the triumphant march of Joan of Arc, halfway across France, victorious all the way, and then up to the very walls of Paris, only two years ago.

"The whole of France is ours by right," my husband says, looking jealously at the green lands that lead down to the Mediterranean Sea. "And we will have it. We will have it. I shall win it for God and King Harry."

He leans forwards. "Look, we are advancing," he says, showing me the little flags of

103

St. George for England spreading over the east of France. "And if the Duke of Burgundy will remain true, and a good ally, we can win back our lands in Maine. If the dauphin is fool enough to attack the duke — and I think that he is — and if I can persuade the duke that we both fight at once . . ." He breaks off as he sees I am looking upwards. "Oh, those are my planets," he says, as if he owns the night skies quite as much as he does France.

Suspended from crisscrossing wooden beams is a series of beautiful silver spheres, some of them ringed with silver haloes, some with other tiny balls floating nearby. It is such a pretty sight that I forget all about the map and the flags of campaigns and clasp my hands together. "Oh, how pretty! What is this?"

Woodville, the squire, gives a little choke of laughter.

"It is not for amusement," my husband says dourly. Then he nods at one of the clerks. "Oh well — show the duchess the skies at her birth."

The young man steps forwards. "Excuse me, Your Grace, when were you born?"

I flush. Like almost all girls I don't know the date of my birth: my parents did not trouble to record the day and the time. I only know the year and the season, and I only know the season because my mother had a great desire for asparagus when she was car-

104

rying me and swears that she ate it too green and her bellyache brought on my birth. "Spring 1416," I say. "Perhaps May?"

He pulls out a scroll from the library and spreads it across the tall desk. He looks at it carefully, then reaches out and pulls one of the levers, then another, then another. To my absolute delight the balls, with their haloes, and the little balls spinning, descend from the rafters, and move gently around until they are positioned, swaying slightly, in the places in heaven that they held at the moment of my birth. There is a sweet tinkling noise, and I see that the spheres have tiny silver bells attached to the strings that move them, so they play as they take their places.

"I can predict where the planets will be before I start a battle," my husband says. "I only launch a campaign when they tell me the stars are propitious. But it takes hours to calculate on paper, and it is easy to make a mistake. Here we have built a mechanism as beautiful and as regular as God made when He put the stars in the sky and set them in motion. I have made a machine like the workings of God Himself."

"Can you foretell with them? Can you know what will happen?"

He shakes his head. "Not as I hope that you will do for us. I can tell when the time is ripe, but not the nature of the fruit. I can tell that our star is in the ascendant but not the outcome of a particular battle. And we had no warning at all of the witch of Arc."

The clerk tilts his head sadly. "Satan hid her from us," he says simply. "There was no darkness, there was no comet, there was nothing to show her rising, and nothing marked her death, praise to God."

My husband nods and puts his hand under my arm and leads me away from the table and past the clerk. "My brother was a man of Mars," he says. "Heat and fire, heat and dryness: a man born to fight and win battles. His son is wet and cold, a man young in years but like a child in his heart, damp like a wet baby drinking milk and pissing in his clout. I have to wait for the stars to put some fire into his cause; I have to study for weapons to put into his hand. He is my nephew, and I must guide him. I am his uncle, and he is my king; I have to make him victorious. It is my duty; it is my destiny. You will help me in this too."

Woodville waits for a moment, then, as my lord seems to have fallen into deep thought, he opens the door to the next room, pushes it wide, and stands back so we can go through. I step into the stone-floored room, and my nose prickles at the strange scents. There is a tang like the smell of a forge — hot metal, but also something acidic and sharp. The air is acrid with a smoke that stings my eyes. In the center of the room are four men, dressed in leather aprons, charcoal fires glowing before them in little braziers set into stone benches, vessels of bronze bubbling like sauce pots. Beyond them, through the open door that leads to an inner yard, I can see a lad stripped to the waist working the bellows of a furnace, heating a great chamber like a bread oven. I look across at Woodville. He gives me a reassuring nod as if to say, "Don't be afraid." But the smell of the room is sulfurous, and the furnace outside glows like the entrance to hell. I shrink back, and my husband laughs at my pale face.

"Nothing to fear, I told you there would be nothing to fear. This is where they work on the recipes; this is where they try one elixir and then another. Out there we forge the metals and bring them in to be tested. This is where we are going to make silver, gold, to make life itself."

"It's so hot," I say weakly.

"These are the fires that make water turn to wine," he explains. "That make iron turn to gold, that make earth turn to life. Everything in this world is growing to a state of purity, of perfection. This is where we speed it up; this is where we make the changes to metals and to waters that the world itself does in its deep bowels, over centuries, with heat like hatching an egg into a chicken. We make it hotter; we make it faster. This is where we can test what we know, and see what we learn. This is the heart of my life's work."

Outside in the yard someone pulls a red-hot bar of metal from the coals of the furnace and starts to hammer it flat.

"Just think if I could make gold," he says longingly. "If I could take iron and purify it so that the common traces were burned from it, washed away, so that we had gold coin. I could hire soldiers; I could reinforce defenses; I could feed Paris. If I had my own mint and my own gold mine, I could take all of France for my nephew and keep it forever."

"Is it possible?"

"We know it can be done," he says. "Indeed, it has been done, many, many times, though always in secret. All metal is of the same nature, everything is made of the same thing: 'first matter,' they call it in the books, 'dark matter.' This is the stuff that the world is made of. We have to remake it, make it again. So we take dark matter, and we refine it, and refine it again. We make it transform into its purest and best nature." He pauses, looking at my puzzled face. "You know that they make wine with the juice that comes from grapes?"

I nod.

"Any French peasant can do that. First he takes the grapes, then he crushes them for their juice. He takes a fruit — a solid thing, growing on a vine — and makes it into a liquid. That's alchemy itself, making that change. Then he stores it and lets the life within it change that juice into wine. Another liquid but one with quite different properties from the juice. Now I can go further. I have done another change, right here. I can make an essence from wine that is a hundred times stronger than wine, which burns at the sight of a flame, which cures a man of melancholy and watery humors. It is a liquid, but it is hot and dry. We call it aqua vitae — the water of life. All this I can do already; I can change juice to aqua vitae — the gold is just the next step, gold from iron."

"And what am I to do?" I ask nervously.

"Nothing today," he says. "But perhaps tomorrow, or the next day, they will need you to come and pour some liquid from a flask, or stir a bowl, or sieve some dust. Nothing more than that, you could have done as much in your mother's dairy."

I look at him blankly.

"It is your touch I want," he says. "The pure touch."

One of the men, who has been watching a flask bubble and then overflow through a tube into a cooled dish set in a bath of ice, puts it to one side and comes towards us, wiping his hands on his apron and bowing to my husband.

"The Maid," my husband says, gesturing to me as if I am as much an object as the fluid in the flask or the iron in the furnace. I flinch at being given Joan's name. "As I promised. I have her. Melusina's daughter and a virgin untouched by any man."

I put out my hand in greeting, but the man recoils from me. He laughs at himself and says, smiling to my husband, "I hardly dare to touch her. Indeed, I dare not!"

Instead, he puts his hand behind his back and bows very low and says directly to me, "You are welcome, Lady Bedford. Your presence here has been needed for a long time. We have waited for you. We have hoped that you would come. You will bring a harmony with you; you will bring the power of the moon and water with you, and your touch will make all things pure."

I step awkwardly from one foot to the other and glance at my husband. He is looking at me with a sort of hot approbation. "I found her, and I recognized at once what she could be," he says. "What she could do. I knew that she could be Luna for us. She has water in her veins, and her heart is pure. Who knows what she might not be able to do?"

"Can she scry?" the man asks eagerly.

"She says she has never tried, but she has already foreseen the future," my husband replies. "Shall we try her?"

"In the library." The man leads the way back through the door. My husband snaps his fingers, and the two scholars take themselves off into a side room, as the alchemist and Woodville the squire pull a cloth off the biggest looking glass I have ever seen, framed in a case, completely round, shining silver, like a full moon.

"Close the shutters," my husband says. "And light the candles." He is breathless; I can hear the excitement in his voice, and it makes me fearful. They ring me with candles so that I am encircled in fire, and they put me before the big mirror. It is so bright I can hardly see for the winking, bobbing flames around me.

"You ask her," my husband says to the alchemist. "Before God, I am so excited, I can't speak. But don't tax her overmuch; let's just see if she has a gift."

"Look in the mirror," the man commands me quietly. "Let yourself look in the mirror and let yourself dream. Now, Maid, what can you see?"

I look at the mirror. Surely it is obvious what I can see? Myself, in a velvet gown cut in the very latest fashion with a horned head-dress on my head, my golden hair captured in a thick net on each side of my face, and the most wonderful shoes of blue leather. I have never before seen a mirror that could show me myself, all of me, full size. I lift my gown a little so I can admire my shoes, and the alchemist makes a little dry cough as if to remind me to beware vanity. "What can you see when you look deeply, Duchess?"

Behind me and to the side of me is a dazzle of candles so bright that they drain the color from the gown, even from the blue shoes, even from the shelves and the books behind me that, as I look, grow darker and more misty.

"Look deep into the mirror and say what you can see," the man urges again, his voice low. "Tell us what you can see, Lady Bedford. What can you see?"

The light is overwhelming, too bright to see anything; I cannot even see my own face, dazzled by the hundreds of candles. And then I see her, as clearly as the day when we lazed by the moat, as brightly as when she was alive and laughing, before the moment when she drew the card of *le Pendu* in his suit as blue as my shoes.

"Joan," I say quietly with deep sorrow. "Oh, Joan. The maid."

I struggle to come back to wakefulness through the noise of the alchemist flapping at the candles to put them out. Some must have fallen over when I went down in a faint. Woodville the squire has me in his arms, holding up my head, and my husband is sprinkling cold water in my face.

"What did you see?" my lord demands as soon as my eyelids flutter open.

"I don't know." For some reason, a sudden pang of fear warns me. I don't want to tell him. I don't want to say Joan's name to the man who had her burned alive.

"What did she say?" He glares at the squire and at the alchemist. "As she went down? She said something. I heard something. What did she say?"

"Did she say 'the maid'?" the alchemist asks. "I think she did."

They both look at Woodville.

"She said 'it's made,' " he lies easily.

"What could she mean?" The duke looks at me. "What did you mean? What d'you mean, Jacquetta?"

"Would it be Your Grace's university at Caen?" Woodville asks. "I think she said, 'Caen,' and then she said, 'it's made.' "

"I saw Your Grace's planned university at Caen," I say, taking up the prompt. "Completed. Beautiful. That's what I said: 'It's made.' "

He smiles; he is pleased. "Well, that's a good vision," he says, encouraged. "That's a good glimpse of a safe and happy future. That's good news. And best of all, we see she can do it."

He puts out his arm and helps me to my feet. "So," he says with a triumphant smile to the alchemist, "I will bring her back tomorrow, after Mass, after she has broken her fast. Get a chair for her to sit on next time, and make the room ready for her. We will see what she can tell us. But she can do it, can't she?"

"Without a doubt," agrees the alchemist.

"And I will have everything ready."

He bows and goes back into the inner room, and Woodville picks up the rest of the candles and blows them out, and my lord straightens the mirror. I lean for a moment against an archway between one set of shelves and another, and my husband glances up and sees me.

"Stand there." He gestures me to the center of the arch and watches as I obey him. I stand still, framed in the arch, wondering what he wants now. He is staring at me as if I were a picture or a tapestry myself, as if he sees me as an object, a new thing to be framed or translated or shelved. He narrows his eyes as if considering me as a vista or a statue that he might have bought. "I am so glad that I married you," he says, and there is no affection in his voice at all but the satisfied tone of a man who has added something to his beautiful collection — and that at a good price. "Whatever it costs me, with Burgundy, with whoever, I am so glad that I married you. You are my treasure."

I glance nervously at Richard Woodville, who has heard this speech of acquisition; but he is busy throwing the cloth over the looking glass, and quite deaf.

Every morning my lord escorts me to the library, and they seat me before the mirror and light the candles all around me and ask

114

me to look into the brightness and tell them what I see. I find I go into a sort of daze, not quite asleep but almost dreaming, and sometimes I see extraordinary visions on the swimming silver surface of the mirror. I see a baby in a cradle; I see a ring shaped like a golden crown dangling from a dripping thread; and one morning I turn from the mirror crying out, for I see a battle, and behind it another battle, a long lane of battles and men dying, dying in mist, dying in snow, dying in a churchyard.

"Did you see the standards?" my husband demands as they press a glass of small ale into my hand. "Drink. Did you see the standards? You said nothing clearly. Did you see where the battles were taking place? Could you tell the armies one from another?"

I shake my head.

"Could you see what town? Was it anywhere you recognize? Come and see if you can point out the town on the map. Do you think it is happening right now, or is it a vision from the future that will come?"

He drags me to the table where the little world of France is laid before me, and I look, dazed, at the patchwork of ownership and roll of the hills. "I don't know," I say. "There was a mist and an army forcing their way uphill. There was snow, and it was red with blood. There was a queen with her horse at a forge, and they were putting the horseshoes

115

on backwards."

He looks at me as if he would like to shake some sense out of me. "This is no good to me, girl," he says, his voice very low. "I can get cursed in any Saturday market. I need to know what is going to happen this year. I need to know what is going to happen in France. I need names of towns and the numbers of rebels. I need to know in detail."

Dumbly, I look back at him. His face is suffused with darkness in his frustration with me. "I am saving a kingdom here," he says. "I need more than mist and snow. I did not marry you for you to tell me about queens with their horseshoes on back to front. What next? Mermaids in the bath?"

I shake my head. Truly, I know nothing.

"Jacquetta, I swear, you will be sorry if you defy me," he says with quiet menace. "This is too important for you to play the fool."

"Perhaps we should not overtax her?" Woodville suggests, addressing the bookshelves. "Perhaps every day is too much for her. She is only young and new to the work. Perhaps we should train her up to it, like a little eyas, a young falcon. Perhaps we should release her to ride and walk in the mornings, and only have her scry perhaps once a week?"

"Not if she has a warning!" the duke breaks out. "Not if it is now! She cannot rest if we are in danger. If this battle in mist and this battle in snow is going to be fought this winter in France, we need to know now."

"You know that the dauphin has not the arms or the allies for it to be now." Woodville turns to him. "It cannot be a warning of now, it will be a fearful dream of the future. Her head is filled with fears of war, and we ourselves have frightened her. We have put the visions in her mind. But we need to clear her head; we need to give her some peace so that she can be a clean stream for us. You bought her" — he stumbles and corrects himself — "You found her unspoiled. We must take care not to muddy the waters."

"Once a month!" the alchemist suddenly remarks. "As I said at the start, my lord, she should be speaking when her element is on the rise. On the eve of the new moon. She is a being of the moon and of water; she will see most clearly and speak most clearly when the moon is in the ascendant. She should work on those days, under a rising moon."

"She could come in the evening, by moonlight." My husband thinks aloud. "That might help." He looks critically at me, as I lean back in the chair, my hand on my throbbing forehead. "You're right," he says to Woodville. "We have asked too much of her, too soon. Take her out riding, take her down by the river. And we set off for England next week; we can go by easy stages. She's pale; she needs to rest. Take her out this morning." He smiles at me. "I am not a hard taskmaster,

Jacquetta, though there is much to be done, and I am in a hurry to do it. You can have some time at your leisure. Go to the stables; you will see I have left a surprise for you there."

I am so relieved to be out of the room that I don't remember to say "thank you," and only when the door is closed behind us do I start to be curious.

"What does my lord have for me in the stables?" I ask Woodville as he follows, half a step behind me, down the circular stair from the gallery to the inner courtyard, and as we walk across the cobbles, past the armory to the stable yard. Menservants carrying vegetables to the kitchens and butchers with great haunches of beef slung over their shoulders fall back before me and bow. The milkmaids coming in from the fields with buckets swinging from their yokes drop down in a curtsey so low that their pails clatter on the cobbles. I don't acknowledge them; now I hardly see them. I have been a duchess for only a few weeks, and already I am accustomed to the exaggerated bows that precede me wherever I go, and the reverent murmur of my name as I walk past.

"What would be your greatest wish?" Woodville asks me. He at any rate does not serve me in awestruck silence. He has the confidence born of being at my husband's right

118

hand since he was a boy. His father served the English king Henry V, and then my husband the duke, and now Woodville, raised in the duke's service, is the most trusted and most beloved of all the squires, Commander of Calais, trusted with the keys to France.

"A new litter?" I ask. "One with golden curtains and furs?"

"Perhaps. Would you really want that more than anything else?"

I pause. "Does he have a horse for me? A new horse of my very own?"

He looks thoughtful. "What color horse would you like best?"

"A gray!" I say longingly. "A beautiful dappled gray horse with a mane like white silk, and dark interesting eyes."

"Interesting?" He chokes on his laughter. "Interesting eyes?"

"You know what I mean, eyes that look as if the horse can understand you, as if she is thinking."

He nods. "I do know what you mean, actually."

He gives me his arm to guide me round a cart laden with pikes; we are passing the armory, and the weapons master is counting in a new delivery with a tally stick. Hundreds, thousands of pikes are being unloaded; the campaign season is starting again. No wonder my husband sits me before the scrying mirror every day to ask me where is the best place to mount our attack. We are at war, constantly at war, and none of us has ever lived in a country at peace.

We go through the archway to the stables, and Woodville steps back to see my face as I scan the yard. Each of the horses of the household has a stall facing south, so the mellow stone is warmed through the day. I see my husband's four great warhorses, their heads nodding over the door. I see Woodville's strong horse for jousting and his other horses for hunting and riding messages, and then I see, smaller than any of them, with bright ears that flick one way and another, the perfectly shaped head of a gray horse, so bright in color that she is almost like silver in the sunshine of the yard.

"Is that mine?" I whisper to Woodville. "Is that for me?"

"That is yours," he says almost reverently. "As beautiful and as high bred as her mistress."

"A mare?"

"Of course."

I go towards her, and her ears point to listen to my footsteps and my cooing voice as I come close. Woodville puts a crust of bread into my hand, and I step up to her and take in the dark liquid eyes, the beautifully straight face, the silvery mane of the horse that I described, here before me, as if I had performed magic and wished her into being. I stretch out my hand, and she sniffs, her nostrils wide, and then she lips the treat from my hand. I can smell her warm coat, her oaty breath, the comfortable scent of the barn behind her.

Woodville opens the stable door for me, and without hesitation I step inside. She shifts a little to make room for me and turns her head and sniffs at me, the pockets of my gown, my belt, my trailing sleeves, and then my shoulders, my neck, and my face. And as she sniffs me, I turn to her, as if we are two animals coming together. Then slowly, gently, I reach out my hand and she droops her head for my caress.

Her neck is warm, her coat silky, the skin behind her ears is tender and soft; she allows me gently to pull the mane on her poll, to stroke her face, and then she raises her head and I touch her flared nostrils, the soft delicate skin of her muzzle, her warm muscled lips, and hold, in my cupped hand, the fat curve of her chin.

"Is it love?" Woodville asks quietly from the doorway. "For it looks like love from here."

"It is love," I breathe.

"Your first love," he confirms.

"My only love," I whisper to her.

He laughs like an indulgent brother. "Then you must compose a poem and come and sing to her like a woman troubador, a *trobairitz*. But what is your fair lady's name?"

121

I look thoughtfully at her, as she moves quietly away from me and takes a mouthful of hay. The scent of the meadow comes from the crushed grasses. "Mercury," I say. "I think I'll call her Mercury."

He looks a little oddly at me. "That's not such a good name. The alchemists are always talking of Mercury," he says. "A shape-shifter, a messenger from the gods, one of the three great ingredients of their work. Sometimes Mercury is helpful, sometimes not, a partner to Melusina, the water goddess who also changes her form. A messenger that you have to employ in the absence of any other, but not always reliable."

I shrug my shoulders. "I don't want more alchemy," I insist. "Not in the stable yard as well as everywhere else. I shall call her Merry, but she and I will know her true name."

"I will know too," he says, but I have already turned my back on him to pull out wisps of hay to give to her.

"You don't matter," I observe.

I ride my horse every morning, with an armed escort of ten men ahead of me and ten behind, and Woodville at my side. We go through the streets of Paris, looking away from the beggars starving in the gutters, and we ignore the people who stretch out imploring hands. There is terrible poverty in the city, and the countryside is all but waste; the farmers cannot get their produce to market, and the crops are constantly trampled by one or other of the armies. The men run away from their villages and hide in the forests for fear of being recruited or hanged as traitors, so there is no one but women to work the fields. The price of bread in the city is more than a man can earn, and besides, there is no work but soldiering, and the English are late with their wages again. Woodville gives orders that we must ride at a hand gallop through the streets, not just for fear of beggars but also for fear of disease. My predecessor, the Duchess Anne, died of a fever after visiting the hospital. Now my lord swears that I shall not so much as speak to a poor person, and Woodville rushes me through the streets, and I don't draw breath until we are out of the city gates and going through what once were busy gardens, the fertile tilled land that lies between the city walls and the river. Only then does Woodville order the armed men to halt and dismount and wait for us, while the two of us ride down to the river and take the towpath and listen to the water as if we were a couple riding in a countryside at peace.

We go companionably, side by side, and talk of nothing of any importance. He helps me with my riding. I have never ridden so fine a horse as Merry, and he shows me how to straighten up in the saddle, and gather her up so she curves her neck and stretches out her stride. He shows me how he rides a cavalry charge, bent low over the horse's neck, going ahead of me down the track and thundering back towards us, pulling up at the last moment so Merry sidles and dances on the spot. He teaches me how to jump, getting off his horse to drag little branches of wood across the deserted track, building them higher and higher as my confidence increases. He teaches me the exercises his father taught him in the lanes of England, riding exercises to improve balance and courage: sitting sideways like a girl riding pillion, lying backwards across the horse, with the saddle in the small of my back, while the horse jogs along, sitting up tall and stretching one arm then another up to the sky, crouching down low to touch my stirrups, anything that accustoms the horse to the idea that it must go on steadily and safely, whatever the rider does, whatever happens around it.

"More than once my horse has taken me to safety when I was hurt and didn't have a clue where we were going," Richard says. "And my father held the standard before Henry V of England, and so he rode at a gallop all the time, with only one hand on the reins. You will never ride in battle, but we might run into trouble here or in England, and it is good to know that Merry will carry you through anything."

He dismounts and takes my stirrups and

crosses them out of the way, in front of me. "We'll do a mile at trot, without stirrups. To improve your balance."

"How should we ride into trouble?" I ask as he gets back on his own horse.

He shrugs. "There was a plan to ambush the duke only a few years ago as they came back to Paris, and he and the Duchess Anne had to take to the forest tracks and ride round the enemy camp. And I hear that the roads in England are now as unsafe as those in France. There are robbers and highwaymen on every English road, and near the coast there are pirates who land and take captives and sell them into slavery."

We start off at a walk. I seat myself more firmly in the saddle and Merry's ears go forwards. "Why does the King of England not guard his coasts?"

"He's still a child, and the country is ruled by his other uncle, Humphrey, the Duke of Gloucester. My lord and the Duke of Gloucester are the royal uncles, each regents of France and England, until the king takes his power."

"When will he do that?"

"He should have done it by now, really," Woodville says. "He is twelve years old — a boy still, but old enough to rule with good advisors. And he has been crowned at Notre Dame in Paris, and in England, and he has a Parliament and a council that have promised to obey him. But he is guided by his uncle the Duke of Gloucester, and all of his friends; and then his mind is changed by his other kinsman, Cardinal Beaufort, a very powerful and persuasive man. Between the two of them he is blown about one way to another, and he never sees our lord the Duke of Bedford, who can do no more than write to him and try to keep him to one path. They say that he does the bidding of the person who spoke to him last.

"But anyway, even if he were older, or firmer, there would be no money to pay for defenses from the sea, and the English lords don't make the rule of law run through their lands as they should. Now we shall trot."

He waits for me to squeeze my legs on Merry and she goes forwards into a trot, with me sitting heavily, like a fat cavalry knight, deep in the saddle.

"That's good," he says. "Now go forwards to canter."

"You said trot!"

"You're doing so well," he says with a grin. I urge Merry on, and she goes into her quick-paced canter. I am a little afraid without the stirrups to use as balance, but he is right: I can sit in the saddle and grip with my legs as we go cantering down the towpath until he gives the hand signal to slow, then pull up.

"Why do I have to learn this?" I ask breathlessly as he dismounts again to restore my stirrups.

"In case you lose your stirrups, or one breaks, or if we have to ride away some time, when we can get hold of horses but no saddles. It's good to be prepared for anything. Tomorrow we will practice riding bareback. I shall make you into a horsewoman. Already you could be trusted on a long ride."

He swings back into his own saddle, and we turn the horses' heads for home.

"And why don't the English lords make the rule of law run through the country?" I ask, returning to our conversation. "In France there are two rules of law, two kings. But at least the lords are obedient to the king who rules in their part."

"In England, they each make their own little lordship," he says. "They use the troubled times as a screen to serve themselves, to gain their own land, to make war on their neighbors. When the young king does decide to take his power, he will find he has to challenge the very people who should be his friends and advisors. He will need my lord duke at his side then."

"Will we have to go to England and live there? Will I have to live in England?" I ask anxiously.

"It is home," he says simply. "And even at its worst, one acre of England is worth ten square miles of France."

I look at him blankly. "All you Englishmen

are the same," I tell him. "You all think that you are divinely blessed by God for no better reason than you had the longbow at Agincourt."

He laughs. "We are," he says. "We think rightly. We are divinely blessed. And perhaps when we go to England there will be time for me to show you my home. And perhaps you will agree with me."

I have a little thrill of pleasure, as if something wonderful were going to happen to me. "Where is your home?" I ask.

"Grafton, Northamptonshire," he says, and I can hear the love in his voice. "Probably the most beautiful countryside, in what is the best country in all the world."

We have one more attempt at scrying at the mirror before it is packed up to travel with us as we start on our journey to England. My lord is anxious for me to predict if it is safe for him to leave France. The Armagnac pretender has no money and no army and is badly advised by his court of favorites, but still my lord John is afraid that if he goes to England there will be no one who can hold France against this man who claims he is king. I completely fail in my wifely duty to advise him; I see nothing. They sit me on a chair, and I stare into the bright reflected candlelight until I am dizzy and — far from fainting — am in danger of falling asleep. For two hours my lord stands behind me and shakes my shoulder when he sees my head nod, until the alchemist says quietly, "I don't think it is coming to her today, my lord," and the duke turns and stalks out of the room without a word to me.

The alchemist helps me from the chair, and Woodville blows out the candles and opens the shutters to let the smell of smoke out of the room. The small sickle of a new moon looks in on me, and I dip a curtsey and turn over the coins in my little pocket and make a wish. The alchemist exchanges a look with Woodville as if they have spent all the evening with a peasant girl who curtseys to a new moon and wishes for a lover, but has no learning and has no vision and is a waste of everyone's time.

"Never mind," Woodville says cheerfully, offering me his arm. "We leave for England in the morning, and they won't ask you to do this for another month."

"Are they bringing the mirror with us?" I ask apprehensively.

"The mirror and some of the books, but the vessels and the oven and the forge stay here, of course; they will continue with their work while we are away."

"And do they discover anything?"

He nods. "Oh yes, my lord has refined silver and gold to a purer level than any man has ever done before. He is working on new metals, new combinations for greater strength or greater suppleness. And of course, if he could make the stone itself . . ."

"The stone?"

"They call it the philosopher's stone, that turns metal to gold, water to the elixir vitae, that gives the owner eternal life."

"Is there such a thing?" I ask.

He shrugs. "There have been many reports of it, it is well known in the old manuscripts that he has had translated here. Throughout Christendom and in the East there will be hundreds, perhaps thousands of men working on it right now. But my lord duke is in the vanguard. If he could find it, if you could help him to find it, we could bring peace to France and to England."

The noise of the castle packing up and readying for a great journey wakes me at dawn, and I go to the chapel to hear Matins as the sun is rising. The priest finishes the service and starts to pack up the sacred pictures and the crucifix and the monstrance. We are taking almost everything with us.

In my own rooms my ladies-in-waiting are folding my gowns into great traveling chests and calling the pages to cord them up and the grooms of the household to seal them. The jewel boxes they will carry themselves; my furs will be guarded by the grooms of the household. Nobody knows how long we will stay in England. Woodville becomes very cautious when I ask him. Clearly, my husband is not being adequately supported by his nephew the king, nor financed as he should be by the English Parliament that has to raise taxes for the war in France. The purpose of the trip is to make them see that English coins buy French support, and they must pay. But nobody knows how long it will take to make the English understand that they cannot have an army for free.

I am quite at a loss in all the bustle. I have put my books that the demoiselle left to me for safekeeping with my husband's library, and they will be guarded by the scholars while we are away. I have put her beautiful cards with my jewels for safety. Her gold bracelet with the charms I carry in a purse slung around my neck. I don't want anyone else touching them. I have dressed for the journey and eaten my breakfast, served in my rooms, by maids in a hurry. I wait about; I don't know what to do to be helpful, and I am too important for anyone to give me a task. The head of my ladies-in-waiting commands everything in my rooms, so I just have to wait for everything to be ready for us to leave, and in the meantime there is nothing for me to do but watch the servants and the ladies running from one task to another.

By midday we are ready to leave, though the grooms of the hall, the stable and the armory are all still packing things up. My lord takes my hand and leads me down the stairs and through the great hall, where the servants are lined up to bow and wish us Godspeed on our journey. Then we go out into the stable yard, where I blink at the cavalcade preparing to depart. It is like a small town on the move. There is the armed guard: we are traveling with hundreds of soldiers, some in armor but most in livery, and they are waiting beside their horses, taking a last drink of ale, flirting with the maids. There are nearly fifty wooden wagons waiting in order, the ones carrying the valuables at the head of the line, with a guard at the front and back, the boxes chained to the sides of the wagon, sealed with the great Bedford seal. The grooms of the household will ride with these, and each has responsibility for his own load. We are taking all our clothes, jewels, and personal goods. We are taking all our household linen, cutlery, glassware, knives, spoons, saltcellars, spice pots. The household furniture is being shipped too; my lord's groom of the bedchamber has ordered the careful dismantling of my lord's great bed with its covers, curtains, and tester, and the grooms of my chambers are bringing my bed, my tables, my beautiful Turkey carpets, and there are two whole wagons just for shipping the household tapestries.

The kitchen servants have loaded their essentials onto a line of wagons; we are bringing food as well as hens, ducks, geese, sheep, and a couple of cows that will walk behind the wagons to give us fresh milk every day. The hawks from the mews are loaded on their own specially made carriage, where they can perch, blinded by their hoods; and the leather curtains are already tied down to shelter them so they are not frightened by the noise of the road. My lord's deerhounds will run alongside the procession, his foxhounds whipped in at the rear. The master of horse has all the workhorses harnessed to the wagons, and all the spare riding horses are bridled and in the care of a groom who rides one horse and leads one on either side. And this is only half the procession. The wagons carrying the essential goods to make us comfortable tonight when we stop at Senlis have already gone; they left at dawn. And amid all this noise and chaos Richard Woodville comes smiling up the stairs, bows to my lord and to me, and says, as if hell were not boiling over in the yard, "I think we are ready, my lord, and what they have forgotten, they can always send on."

"My horse?" the duke asks. Woodville snaps his fingers, and a waiting groom brings my lord's great warhorse forwards.

"And my lady is going in her litter?"

"Her Grace said she wanted to ride."

My lord duke turns to me. "It is a long way, Jacquetta; we will go north out of Paris and sleep tonight at Senlis. You will be in the saddle for the whole day."

"I can do that," I say, and I glance at Woodville.

"She's a strong horse; you chose well," he says to my husband. "And the duchess is a good rider; she will be able to keep up. It would probably be more pleasant for her than jolting around in her litter, though I will have it follow behind us, so if she gets tired she can change."

"Very well then," the duke agrees. He smiles at me. "I shall enjoy your company. What d'you call your mare?"

"I call her Merry," I say.

"God send that we are all merry," he says, stepping on the mounting block to haul himself into the saddle. Woodville takes me by the waist and lifts me up into my saddle, and then stands back while my lady-in-waiting bustles forwards and pulls the long skirts of my gown so they fall down either side, hiding my leather riding boots.

"All right?" Woodville asks me quietly, standing close to the horse as he checks the tightness of the girth.

"Yes."

"I'll be just behind you, if you want anything. If you get tired, or need to stop, just raise your hand. I'll be watching. We will ride for a couple of hours and then stop to eat."

My husband stands up in his stirrups. He

bellows, "À Bedford!" and the whole stable yard shouts back, "À Bedford!" They swing the great gates open and my lord leads the way, out through the crowded streets of Paris, where people stare as we go by and cry out for alms or favors, and then through the great north gate, and out into the country towards the narrow seas and England, the unknown shore that I am supposed to call home.

My lord duke and I ride at the head of the procession so we are not troubled with dust, and once we are away from Paris my husband judges that we are safe enough to go before the armed guard so it is just him and me, Woodville and my lady-in-waiting riding out in the sunshine as if for pleasure. The road winds ahead of us, well traveled by English merchants and soldiers going through the English lands from the English capital of Paris to the English castle of Calais. We stop to dine at the edge of the forest of Chantilly, where they have set up pretty tents and have cooked a haunch of venison. I am glad to rest for an hour in the shade of a tree, but I am happy to go on when Woodville orders the guard into the saddle again. When my husband asks me if I would like to complete the journey sitting in my litter drawn by the mules, I tell him no. The afternoon is sunny and warm, and when we enter the green shade of the forest of Chantilly, we put our

135

horses into a canter, and my mare pulls a little and is eager to gallop. My husband laughs and says, "Don't let her run off with you, Jacquetta."

I laugh too as his big horse lengthens its great pace to draw neck and neck with Merry, and we go a little faster, and then suddenly, there is a crashing noise and a tree plunges down, all its branches breaking together like a scream, over the road in front of us, and Merry rears in terror and I hear my husband bellow like a trumpet, "À Bedford! 'Ware ambush!" but I am clinging to the mane and nearly out of the saddle, slipping backwards, as Merry plunges to the side, terrified by the noise, and bolts, madly bolts. I haul myself into the saddle, cling to her neck, and bend low as she dashes among the trees, flinging herself to right and left, fleeing where her own frightened senses prompt her. I cannot steer her — I have dropped the reins — I certainly cannot stop her; I can barely cling on, until finally she slows to a trot, and then a walk, and then blows out and stops.

Shakily, I slip from the saddle and collapse to the ground. My jacket has been torn by low-hanging branches, my bonnet was knocked from my head and is flapping on its cord; my hair is falling down, tangled with twigs. I give a little sob of fear and shock, and Merry turns to one side and nibbles at a shrub, pulling at it nervously, her ears flicking in all directions.

I take hold of her reins so she cannot dash away again, and I look around me. The forest is cool and dark, absolutely silent but for birdsong from high in the upper branches and the buzz of insects. There is no noise of marching men, creaking wagons: nothing. I cannot even tell where I have come from, nor how far I am from the road. Merry's headlong flight seemed to last for a lifetime, but even if they were close at hand, I would not know in which direction. Certainly, she didn't go straight, we twisted and turned through the trees, and there is no path for me to retrace.

"Goddamn," I say quietly to myself like an Englishman. "Merry, we are completely lost."

I know that Woodville will ride out to find me, and perhaps he can follow Merry's little hoofprints. But if the falling tree was an ambush, then perhaps he and my husband are fighting for their lives, and nobody yet has had time to think about me. Even worse, if the fight is going against them, then perhaps they will be captured or killed and there will be no one to search for me at all, and then I am in danger indeed: alone and lost in a hostile country. Either way, I had better save myself if I can.

I know that we were traveling north to Calais, and I can remember enough of the great plan in my husband's library to know that if I can get myself onto the north road again, there will be many villages, churches, and religious houses where I can find hospitality and help. It is a road well traveled, and I am certain to meet a party of English people and my title will command their assistance. But only if I can find the road. I look on the ground around us to see if I can trace Merry's hoofprints and follow them back the way we came, and there is one hoofprint in the mud, and then another, a little gap where the leaves cover the ground, but beyond it, the trail picks up again. I take the reins over her head and hold them in my right hand, and say in a voice I try to make sound confident, "Well, silly girl, we have to find our way home now," and I walk back the way we came with her following behind me, her head bent, as if she is sorry for the trouble she has caused.

We walk for what seems like hours. The tracks give out after a little while, for the floor of the forest is so thick with leaves and twigs that there are no prints to follow. I guess at the way, and we go steadily, but I am more and more afraid that we are wandering lost, perhaps even going round in circles like enchanted knights in a fairy-tale forest. Thinking this, I am hardly surprised when I hear the sound of water and turn towards it, and we come to a little stream and a pool. It is almost a fountain, so round and banked with green moss. I have a moment when I think perhaps Melusina will rise from the magical pool to help me, her daughter; but nothing happens, so I tie Merry to a tree and wash my face and drink the water, and then I bring her to the stream and she drops her white head and sucks up the water quietly, and drinks deep.

The trees have made a little glade around the stream, and a beam of sunlight comes through the thick canopy of leaves. Still holding Merry's reins, I sit down in the sunshine to rest for a few minutes. In a moment, I think, I will get up, and we will put the sun on our left and walk steadily; that will take us north and must take us, surely, to the Paris road where they will, surely, be looking for me. I am so tired, and the sun is so warm, that I lean back against a tree trunk and close my eyes. In minutes I am fast asleep.

The knight left his horse behind with his comrades and followed her tracks on foot through the forest, a burning torch held before him, calling her name, calling her name over and over. The forest was unearthly at night; once he caught a glimpse of bright dark eyes and stepped back with an oath and then saw the pale rump of a deer slide away into the shadows. As the moon came up he thought he would see better without the torch, doused it on the ground in the thick leaf mold, and went on, straining his eyes in the silvery half-light. Bushes and trees loomed up at him, darker in the gloom, and without the yellow torchlight he felt he did not want to shout out loudly for her, but instead walked in silence, looking around him all the time, a fear gripping at his heart that he had failed to teach her how to ride, that he had failed to train the horse, that he had failed to tell her what to do in just these circumstances, that he had failed to predict that such a thing might happen: that he had utterly and comprehensively failed her.

At this thought, so awful to him since he had sworn privately that he would serve and protect her to death, he stopped still and put his hand to a tree trunk to support himself, and bowed his head in shame. She was his lady, he was her knight, and at this, the very first test, he had failed; now she was somewhere lost in the darkness, and he could not find her.

He raised his head, and what he saw made him blink his eyes; what he saw made him rub his eyes, to see without a doubt, without a shadow of a doubt, the glimmering white light of an enchantment, a chimera, and at the heart of it, gleaming, a little white horse, alone in the forest. But as it turned its head and he could see its profile, he saw the silvery horn of a unicorn. The white beast looked at him with its dark gaze, and then slowly walked away, glancing over its shoulder, walking slowly enough for him to follow. Entranced, he stepped quietly behind it, guided by the flickering silvery light, and seeing the little hoofprints that shone in the

dead leaves with a white fire, and then faded as he walked by.

He had a sense that he should not try to catch the unicorn; he remembered that all the legends warned that it would turn on him and attack him if he came too close. Only one being in this world can catch a unicorn, and he had seen the capture in half a dozen tapestries and in a dozen woodcuts in storybooks, since his youngest boyhood.

The little animal turned off the path, and now he could hear the splashing sound of water as they came upon a clearing. He bit his tongue on an exclamation as he saw her, asleep like a nymph, as if she were growing in the wood herself, at the foot of the tree as if she were a bank of flowers, her green velvet dress outspread, her brown bonnet like a pillow under her golden hair, her face as peaceful in sleep as a blossom. He stood waiting, uncertain what he should do, and as he watched, the unicorn went forwards, lay down beside her, and placed its long head with the silver horn gently in the lap of the sleeping maid, just as all the legends had always said that it would.

The sound of a footstep wakes me. I know at once that I am lost in the wood in danger and that I have foolishly slept. I wake in a panic, in darkness, and I jump up, and Merry, who has been sleeping, head bowed beside me, wheels around to stare, ears pricked, as

the two of us see the figure of a man, a dark outline in the shifting twilight. "Who's there?" I say, my hand clenching on my whip. "Beware! I have a sword!"

"It's me: Woodville," the squire says and steps closer so I can see him. He looks pale, as if he is as afraid as me. "Are you all right, my lady?"

"My God, my God, Woodville! I am so pleased to see you!" I run forwards with my hands outstretched, and he falls to his knees, takes my hands, and kisses them passionately.

"My lady," he whispers. "My lady. Thank God I find you safe! Are you unhurt?"

"Yes, yes, I was just resting. I fell asleep; I had been walking for so long, trying to find my way back to the road, but then I was so foolish — I sat down and I fell asleep . . ."

He stumbles to his feet. "It's not far; I have been looking for you all evening, but it's not far."

"Is it late now?"

"No more than eleven. We're all looking for you. The duke is mad with worry. I was trying to follow your tracks . . . but I would never have found you but for . . ."

"And is my lord duke safe? Was it an ambush?"

He shakes his head. "Some fool of a peasant felling a tree brought down another across the road. No one hurt, just bad luck that we were there at the time. We were all

only afraid for you. Did you fall?"

"No, she ran off with me, but she didn't throw me. She's a good horse; she only ran because she was afraid, and then she stopped."

He hesitates. "She led me to you," he says. "It is quite a miracle. I saw her in the woods, and she brought me to you."

I hold up the reins I had tied to my wrist. "I didn't let her go."

"You had her tethered?"

He gazes around the little clearing, at the silver moonlight on the water, at the shadowy darkness of the trees, as if he is looking for something.

"Yes, of course. But I took her saddle off as you showed me."

"I saw her," he says flatly. "She was loose in the woods."

"She has been here all the time. I held her reins."

He shakes his head as if to clear his bewilderment. "That was well done. I will put her saddle on her, and I can lead you to the road." He picks up the beautifully worked saddle and slides it on Merry's back. He tightens the girth; then he turns to lift me up. For a moment he hesitates, with his hands on my waist. It is as if our bodies have come together, almost without our volition: my head to his shoulder, his hands on my waist. It is as if we are drawn, one to another, like the planets on their wires in my lord's library. Slowly, I realize that I am filled with an emotion I have never felt before; slowly I realize that this is a longing. I turn my face up towards him, and his darkened eyes look down at me, his hands warm, his face almost puzzled as he feels the desire that is slowly pulsing in me. We stand like that together, for a long time. Then, without a word, he lifts me up into the saddle, brushes down my gown, hands me my hat, and leads Merry through the wood towards the road.

Castle of Calais, France, June 1433

We are housed once more in the great castle of the garrison town of Calais; Woodville is greeted as its captain, but my lord says he cannot spare him from his side yet to take up residence. I am standing on the battlement at the top of the castle, looking anxiously up at the standard on the tower above my head, which cracks and ripples in the strengthening wind.

"Is it going to be rough?" I ask my husband.

He glances at me. "You are not afraid? But water is your element."

I bite my lip on a retort. Personally, I don't think that having a water goddess for an ancestress is a guarantee of freedom against seasickness, nor, come to that, shipwreck. "I am a little afraid. The waves look very high, are they always that big? Do they always break so high on the harbor wall? I don't remember them being like that before."

He glances out to sea as if to measure them for the first time. "It's a little rough, perhaps.

But we will leave on the next tide. It is too important for us to delay. I have to get to England. I am going to address the Parliament; they have to realize that there must be funds released to pay for the campaign season in France. And I have to find some way to get my brother Humphrey to work with our uncle, Cardinal Beaufort. The young king —" He breaks off. "Ah well, at any rate, we have to go, and I don't think the journey will be too uncomfortable for you, and there should be no danger. Can you not calm the waters? It's Midsummer Eve; surely you should be able to do a little magic on this of all evenings?"

I try to smile at the weak joke. "No, I wish that I could."

He turns and goes into the inner rooms. I hear him shouting for his clerks, and to tell the captain that he must complete loading, for we will leave on the next tide, whatever the weather. Woodville comes up with a warm cape and puts it around my shoulders. "My lord is worried by events in England. His brother Humphrey, Duke of Gloucester, does not give good advice; his nephew the king is young and inexperienced, and his other uncle, Cardinal Beaufort, has his own plans for the kingdom. The two of them, the Duke of Gloucester and the cardinal, try to turn the young king each to their own way of thinking, and he is torn between them."

"Is it safe to sail?"

"Oh yes. It may be a little rough, but I shall see you are comfortable in your cabin, my lady. And Merry safe in her stall. We will sail through the night, and in the morning you will wake up in your new country. And my lord will take you to see his new house."

"Spenhurst?" I ask, trying the odd name in my mouth.

"Penshurst," he corrects me. "You will like it. I promise you, it is a most beautiful house in one of the loveliest parts of England, in Kent, which is famous for its apple orchards and fruit gardens. Near to London, but far enough distant that you will not be troubled by too many people. A jewel of a house for a diamond of a duchess."

"And will we stay there all the time?" I let Woodville lead me from the roof of the tower into the warmth inside the castle. A fire burns in the center of the round room, and he sets a chair for me before it.

"I don't think my lord will be able to rest in the country," he says. "He will have to meet with the king and persuade him to give him men and arms to continue the campaigns in France. He will have to explain the campaign to Parliament to get their support. He will have to deal with his brother, Duke Humphrey, and their uncle, Cardinal Beaufort. He has much to do."

"And the king, Henry, will I see him? What

147

is he like?"

He smiles. "A very young man still, almost a boy; he is only twelve years old. You will have a state entry into London. The duke is a very great man in England as in France, and the young king will greet you." He smiles again. "I should think you will like him, he is a charming boy, and he . . ." He gives a little laugh, almost as if he is embarrassed. "I should think he will adore you. He will never have seen anyone quite like you. You will be the most beautiful woman in England, as well as the greatest."

WESTMINSTER PALACE, LONDON, SUMMER 1433

The young king is a disappointment to me. I have no experience of kings since my own county of Luxembourg is not a royal one, my father is a count, our overlords are the Dukes of Burgundy (though they are richer and more powerful than anyone in France), and the last French king, who was said to be most tragically mad, died when I was only a little girl, before I could see him. So I am counting on much from the English boy-king. I hope to see a youth who is the small mirror of his heroic father. After all, my husband's life is devoted to making this king safe in his lands in France. We are both sworn to his service. I am expecting a great being: something halfway between a boy and a god.

Not so. I first see him on our entry into London when we go through the city gates to the sound of singing choirs and the cheering of the citizens. My husband is an old friend to the people of London, and I am a novelty they delight to see. The men bellow approval of my youth and looks, and the women blow me kisses. The London merchants depend upon trade with the English lands in France, and my husband is well known for holding the lands in the keeping of England. The merchants and their wives and their households turn out to greet us and show our standards from their overhanging windows. The Mayor of London has prepared poems and pageants to greet us; in one tableau there is a beautiful mermaid who promises good health, fertility, and ever-flowing waters of happiness. My lord duke holds my hand and bows to the crowd and looks proud of me as they call my name and shout blessings on me.

"The Londoners love a pretty girl," he says to me. "I will have their favor forever while you keep your looks."

The king's servants greet us at the gate of the palace at Westminster and lead us through a maze of courts and gardens, rooms with inner rooms, galleries, and courtyards, until finally we come to the king's private rooms. One pair of double doors is flung open, another pair beyond them, then there is a room filled with people in the most beautiful clothes, and finally, like a tiny jack popping from a series of boxes, there is the young king, rising from his throne and coming forwards to greet his uncle.

He is slight and short — that is my first

impression — and he is pale, pale like a scholar, though I know that they make him take exercise, ride daily, and even joust with a safety cushion on the top of his opponent's lance. I wonder if he is ill, for there is something about the transparency of his skin and the slow pace of his walk towards us that gives me a feeling of his weariness, and suddenly, I see to my horror that in this light, for a moment, he looks to me like a being made of glass, so thin and translucent that he looks as if he might break if he were to topple on a stone floor.

I give a little gasp, and my husband glances down at me, distracted for a moment, and turns to the king his nephew and bows and embraces him in one movement. "Oh! Take care!" I whisper as if he might crush him, and then Woodville steps smartly across and takes my right hand on his arm, as if he is bringing me forwards to be presented.

"What is it?" he demands urgently in a low whisper. "Are you ill, my lady?"

My husband has both hands on the boy's shoulders; he is looking into the pale face, into the light gray eyes. I can almost feel the weight of his grip; I feel that it is too much. "He's so frail," I whisper, then I find the true word: "He is fragile, like a prince of ice, of glass."

"Not now!" Woodville commands, and pinches my hand hard. I am so surprised at his tone and the sudden sharp pain that I flinch and look at him, and am returned to myself to see that the men and women of the court are all around us, staring at me and my lord and the king, and that Woodville is marching me forwards to make my curtsey, with such determined briskness that I know I must not say another word.

I sink down into a deep curtsey, and the king raises me up with a light touch on my arms. He is respectful since I am his aunt, for all that I am only seventeen years old to his twelve: we are both young innocents in this court of hard-faced adults. He bids me welcome to England in a thin little voice that has not yet broken into a man's tone. He kisses my cheeks right and left; the touch of his lips is cold, like the brittle ice that I imagined when I first saw him, and his hands holding mine are thin; I can almost feel the bones of his fingers, like little icicles.

He bids us come in to dinner and turns and leads me in, at the head of all the court. A beautifully dressed woman steps back with a heavy tread, as if to make way for me, begrudgingly. I glance at the young king.

"My other aunt, Eleanor, Duchess of Gloucester," he flutes in his little-boy treble. "Wife of my much beloved uncle, Humphrey, Duke of Gloucester."

I curtsey to her and she to me, and behind her I see the handsome face of my husband's brother, the Duke of Gloucester. He and my husband embrace, arms on each other's shoulders, a great hug, but when my husband turns to his sister-in-law Eleanor, I see that he looks sternly at her.

"I hope we shall all live merrily together," the king says in his tentative piping voice. "I think a family should be as one. A royal family should always be as one, don't you think? We should all love one another and live in harmony."

"Of course," I say, though if ever I saw rivalry and envy in a woman, I am seeing it now on the beautiful spoiled face of the Duchess of Gloucester. She is wearing a towering headdress that makes her seem like a giantess, the tallest woman in the court. She is wearing a gown of deep blue trimmed with ermine: the most prestigious fur in the world. Around her neck are blue sapphires, and her eyes are bluer than they are. She smiles at me, and her white teeth are bared, but there is no warmth in her face.

The king seats me on his right-hand side and my lord duke to his left. Next to me comes the Duke of Gloucester, and his wife goes on the other side of my husband. We face the great dining room as if we were their tapestry, their entertainment: bright with the colors of our gowns and capes, sparkling with jewels. They gaze up at us as if we were a masque for their education. We look down at them as the gods might look down on mortals, and as the dishes go round the room we send out the best plates to our favorites as if to remind them that they eat at our behest.

After dinner there is dancing, and the Duke of Gloucester is quick to lead me out into a dance. We take our part and then stand as the other couples dance their steps. "You are so charming," the duke says to me. "They told me that John had married a heart stealer, but I didn't believe it. How is it that I have served my country in France over and over and yet never saw you?"

I smile and say nothing. The true answer would be that while my husband was engaged in endless warfare to keep the English lands safe in France, this worthless brother of his ran away with the Countess of Hainault, Jacqueline, and took on a war all of his own to try to win her lands for himself. He wasted his fortune and might have lost his life there, if his vagrant fancy had not wandered to her lady-in-waiting, this Eleanor; and then he ran away with her. In short, a man driven by his desires and not by duty. A man so unlike my husband that I can hardly believe they are both sons of King Henry IV of England.

"If I had seen you, I would never have come home to England," he whispers as a turn in the dance puts us together.

I don't know what to reply to this, and I don't like how he looks at me.

154

"If I had seen you, I would never have left your side," he says.

I glance over to my husband, but he is talking to the king and not looking at me.

"And would you have smiled on me?" my brother-in-law asks me. "Would you smile on me now? Or are you afraid of stealing my heart from me even now?"

I don't smile, I look very grave and wonder that he should speak like this to me, his sister-in-law, with such assurance, as if he believes that I will not be able to resist him. There is something repellent and fascinating about the way that he takes me by the waist, which is part of the movement of the dance, and presses me close to him, his hand warm on my back, his thigh brushing against me, which is not.

"And does my brother please you as a husband?" he whispers, his breath warm on my bare neck. I lean slightly away, but he tightens his grip and holds me close. "Does he touch you as a young girl loves to be touched — gently, but quickly?" He laughs. "Am I right, Jacquetta? Is that how you love to be touched? Gently, but quickly?"

I pull away from him, and there is a swirl of color and music, and Richard Woodville has my hand and has pulled me into the center of the dancers and has me turning one way and then another. "Forgive me!" he calls over his shoulder to the duke. "I am quite mistaken — I have been too long in France; I thought this was the moment that we changed partners."

"No, you are too soon, but no matter," the duke says, taking Woodville's abruptly abandoned partner by her hand and forming the chain of the dance as Woodville and I take the little steps in the center of the circle and then form an arch so everyone dances through, all the partners change again, and I move away, in the movement of the dance, away from Duke Humphrey.

"What did you think of the king?" my husband asks me, coming to my bedroom that night. The sheets have been turned down for him, the pillows piled high. He gets in with a sigh of exhaustion, and I notice his lined face is gray with fatigue.

"Very young."

He laughs shortly. "You are yourself such an old married lady."

"Young even for his age," I say. "And somehow, a little frail?" I don't tell my husband of the sense I had of a boy as fragile as glass, as cold as thin ice.

He frowns. "I believe he is strong enough, though I agree, he is slight for his age. His father —" He breaks off. "Well, it means nothing now what his father was, or how he was as a boy. But God knows my brother Henry was a strong powerful boy. At any rate,

156

this is no time for regrets, this boy will have to follow him. He will just have to grow into greatness. What did you make of my brother?"

I bite my tongue on my first response. "I don't think I have ever met anyone like him in my life before," I say honestly.

He laughs shortly. "I hope he didn't speak to you in a way you did not like?"

"No, he was perfectly courteous."

"He thinks he can have any woman in the world. He nearly ruined us in France when he courted Jacqueline of Hainault. It was the saving of my life when he seduced her lady-in-waiting and ran off to England with her."

"Was that the Duchess Eleanor?"

"It was. Dear God, what a scandal! Everyone said she had seduced him with love potions and witchcraft! And Jacqueline left all alone, declaring they were married, abandoned in Hainault! Typical of Humphrey, but thank God he left her and came back to England, where he can do no damage, or at any rate less damage."

"And Eleanor?" I ask. "His wife now?"

"She was his wife's lady-in-waiting, then his whore; now she is his wife, so who knows what she is in her heart?" my husband remarks. "But she is no friend of mine. I am the oldest brother and so I am heir to the throne. If anything happens to King Henry (which God forbid), then I inherit the crowns of England and France. Humphrey comes after me, second to me. She looks at me sometimes as if she would wish me away. She will be praying that you don't have a son who would put her another step from the throne. Can you see with the Sight and tell me, does she cast spells? Is she skilled? Would she ill-wish me?"

I think of the woman with the dazzling sapphires and the dazzling smile and the hard eyes. "I can see nothing for sure but pride and vanity and ambition."

"That's bad enough," my lord says cheerfully. "She can always hire someone to do the actual spells. Should I have her watched, d'you think?"

I consider the brilliant woman and her handsome whispering husband. "Yes," I say, thinking that this is a court very far from my girlhood in the sunny castles of France. "Yes, I think if I were you, I would have her watched. I would have them both watched."

PENSHURST,
AUTUMN 1433

All the summer my lord speaks with one great man and then another; then when the seasonal fear of the plague recedes and the Parliament returns to London, he meets with the men of the shires and the counties and begs them for funds to wage the war in France. He invokes the support of his uncle the cardinal; he prevails upon his brother to advise the young king. Slowly, they realize the service he has done for his country, and they tell him that they are so grateful that he can leave his office, retire from his work, abandon his regency in France and return to England, where we can live in his new beautiful house.

"He won't come," Woodville predicts to me. We are riding in the green lanes around the fields of Penshurst, in Kent. We have been waiting for my lord to leave London and come to his new home for days. "He won't come now, and he won't stay in England, even though they say he has earned his rest."

"Is he so very tired? I have not seen him for weeks."

He shakes his head in despair. "I would say he was working himself to death. But he won't stop."

"Why not? If they say that he can?"

"Because he would not leave men like your uncle Louis without his leadership in Paris. He would not leave France without its regent. He would not allow the Armagnacs to come to the peace meetings and make their demands without him there to answer them. A peace has to come; Burgundy is ready for it and probably talking with the Armagnacs behind our backs. The Armagnacs are exhausted and out of men and funds, and you see how my lord struggles to raise an army in England. We are all of us ready for peace, and my lord will see the peace talks through. He will get peace in France before he leaves his post."

"So we will have to go back to Paris?" I am reluctant to go. I have been using this time in England like a clerk at his lessons. I have been studying English; I have been reading the books in my lord's library; I have employed a scholar to read the alchemy texts with me and explain them. I have been looking for a herbalist to teach me the skills. I don't want to leave all this and go back to the grand palace in the starving city.

"We will. But if you were free to choose,

would you rather stay?"

I take a moment to answer; there is something in his voice that warns me that this is an important question. I look from the hedgerows, where the red pebbles of the hips gleam among the fading leaves, to the distant hills of the downs, where the beech trees are turning bronze. "It is a beautiful country," I say. "And, actually, I prefer London to Paris."

He beams with pride. "I knew you would," he says triumphantly. "I knew you would. You are an English duchess; you were born to be an Englishwoman. You should live in England."

"It does feel very like home," I concede. "Even more than France, even more than Luxembourg. The countryside is so pretty and the hills so green. And Paris is so poor and the people so angry, I can't help but like it better here."

"I said to my father that you were an Englishwoman in your heart."

I smile. "And what did your father say?"

"He said that so pretty a duchess should be kept in England where she can flourish."

"Where does your father live?"

"He has a small manor at Grafton; our family has been there for many years. He served the duke your husband, and the king before him. I think he will go to war again, and muster his own troop to support us when we go back to France."

"Is Grafton like here?"

"Just as beautiful," he says proudly. "You know, I wish I could take you to Grafton. I so want to take you there. I wish you could see my home."

Slowly, I glance sideways at him. "I wish it too," I say, and then we are both silent.

My lord stays in London and summons Richard to attend him, but every week or so the wagon comes with tapestries, furniture, or books that he has bought for the new house. Waiting in the stable yard as they unpack one of these treasure wagons, I am surprised by a dainty woman, wearing the gown of a townswoman and a modest white cap, who is handed down from the back of the wagon and makes her curtsey to me.

"I am Mrs. Jourdemayne," she says. "His Grace sent me to you with these as a gift."

She nods her head, and a lad jumps out of the wagon behind her with a wooden tray of tiny clay pots, each one holding a nodding head of a green plant. He sets the tray down at my feet and jumps back into the wagon to fetch another and another until I am surrounded by a little lawn of green, and Mrs. Jourdemayne laughs at my delighted face. "He said you would be glad," she observes. "I am a gardener and a herbalist. He said that I should bring you these, and he has paid me for a week's work. I am to stay with you and help you plant a garden of herbs, if you wish it."

"I do wish it!" I say. "There is a herb garden here by the kitchen, but it is very overgrown, and I don't know what half the things are."

"Tell the lad where to take the seedling trays, and we will start whenever you want," she says briskly.

I call my page boy, and he leads the way for the two of them while I go inside to fetch a broad hat to shield my face, and gloves for my first lesson as a gardener.

She is an odd gardener. She orders the Penshurst senior man to make twelve beds in the old kitchen garden, and while he is digging over the soil she lifts the little herbs, shows me their leaves and their flowers, and tells me of their properties. Each new bed is to be named for a house of the planets.

"This was the comfrey bed," Ralph says stubbornly. "Where are we going to put the comfrey now?"

"In the Aquarius bed," she says smoothly. "Comfrey is a plant that flourishes under the water sign. And this bed here is going to be the place we grow the plants under the sign of Taurus."

He puzzles over this all night, and in the morning he has a joke ready. "What will you plant there? In the Taurus bed? Bull rushes? Bull rushes?" he asks, and doubles up at his own humor. That jest keeps him laughing all day, but Mrs. Jourdemayne is not disturbed. She picks out seedlings from her tray of plants and puts them before me. "Taurus is an earth sign," she says. "When the moon is in Taurus, it favors the growth of crops that live below the soil. Root crops like white and purple carrots, onions, and turnips. It favors the herbs of Taurus, like mint and primrose, tansy, wormwood, and yarrow. We'll plant these in our Taurus bed."

I am enchanted. "You have all these?"

She smiles. "We can plant some of them now; some of them will have to wait until the moon is in a different phase. But I have brought them all, in the green or in seed. Your lord commanded that you should have all the herbs of England in your garden. He said that you have a gift. Do you?"

I dip my head. "I don't know. Sometimes I think I know things; sometimes I know nothing. I am studying his books, and I shall be glad to learn how to grow herbs and how to use them. But I have no certainty; all that I learn just teaches me that I know nothing."

She smiles. "That is the very path of learning," she says.

All afternoon we spend in the garden on our knees like peasant women, planting the herbs in the beds that she has prepared for them, and as the evening grows cool and the sun starts to set, I get to my feet and look around the garden that we have made. Twelve regular beds fan out from the circular seat at the heart of the garden. All of them are dug over and weeded, some of them are already planted. Mrs. Jourdemayne has labeled the seedlings with their names and their properties. "Tomorrow I shall show you how to make tinctures and dry herbs," she says. "I will give you my recipes."

I am so tired from our work that I sleep well, but in the night, as if the rising moon is calling to me as well as to the rising sap of the plants, I wake and see the cool light lying along my bedroom floor. My maid is heavily asleep in the bed beside me. I turn back the covers and go to the window. I can hear something, like the chiming of a bell, and I put a gown around my shoulders and push open my bedroom door, and then go out into the gallery.

In the shadows I can just see the outline of a woman: Mrs. Jourdemayne. For a moment I step back, fearful of what she is doing in the darkness. She is standing beside one of the windows, and she has thrown it open; the singing is louder as if the clear sweet noise is pouring into the gallery with the moonlight. As she hears my footstep she glances around, her face alert, as if she expects anyone, anything; but she fears nothing.

"Oh, it's you," she says, though she should curtsey. "Can you hear it?"

I nod. "I hear it."

"I've never heard such a thing before; I thought it was the music of the spheres."

"I know it," I say sadly. I reach forwards and close the window — at once the music is muffled — and then I draw the heavy curtain to shut out both music and moonlight.

She puts out her hand to stop me. "What is it?" she asks. "Why do you shut it out? What does it mean?"

"It's nothing to do with you," I say. "It is for me. Let me close it out."

"Why, what is it?"

"I have heard it twice in my life before," I say, thinking of my little sister, who died almost as she drew her first breath, and then the sighing choir that whispered good-bye to my great-aunt. "I am afraid it is the death of one of my family," I say quietly. "It is the singing of Melusina," and I turn from her and go down the darkened gallery to my bedroom.

In the morning she shows me how to dry herbs, how to make a tisane, how to make a tincture, and how to draw the essence from flowers using a bed of wax. We are alone in the still room, the pleasant smell of crushed leaves around us, the coolness of the stone floor beneath our feet, the marble sink filled with cold water.

"And does the singing tell you of a death?" she asks simply.

"Yes," I say. "I pray that my mother and

father are well. This seems to be the only gift I have: foreknowledge of loss."

"Hard," she says shortly, and passes me a pestle and mortar with some seeds for crushing.

We work together in silence for a while; then she speaks. "There are herbs especially for a young woman, newly married," she observes, as if to the leaves that she is washing in the sink. "Herbs that can prevent a baby, herbs that can cause one. They are in my recipe book."

"You can prevent a baby?" I ask.

"I can even stop one coming when a woman is already with child," she says with a nasty little smile. "Pennyroyal, mugwort, and parsley will do it. I have planted the herbs in your garden for you to use when you need. If you ever need." She glances at the flatness of my belly. "And if you want to make a baby, you have those herbs too, to your hand. Raspberry leaves from your orchard, and weeds, easy enough to find: nettle leaves, and clover flowers from the field."

I dust off my hands and pick up my slate and chalk. "Tell me how to prepare them," I say.

Margery stays for more than the week that she has promised, and when she leaves, my herb garden is planted with everything but those plants that need to wait for the descending moon, and the still room already has a few jars of herbs in wine, and a few bunches of herbs hung up to dry. She will go back to London in one of my lord's wagons, her servant boy with her, and I go to the stable yard to say good-bye. As I watch her clamber nimbly into the cart, a guard of half a dozen, with a messenger in my lord's livery of red and white, clatter into the yard, and Richard Woodville swings down from his horse.

"My lady, I bring a message from my lord," he says. "He has marked it for you, only."

I put out my hand, though I can feel my face is trembling and my eyes are filling with tears. I take the letter and break the seal, but I cannot see what he has written for my sight is blurred. "You read it," I say, handing it to him. "You tell me."

"I am sure there is no cause for you to be distressed . . ." he starts, then reads the few lines and looks at me aghast. "I am sorry, Your Grace. I am so sorry. My lord writes to tell you that your father has died. There is plague in Luxembourg, but your mother is well. She sent the news to my lord." He hesitates; he looks at me. "You knew already?"

I nod. "Well, I thought it was so. Though I closed the curtain on the moonlight, and I tried not to hear the music."

Mrs. Jourdemayne, seated beside the wagoner, looks down at me with shrewd sympathy in her face. "Sometimes you cannot help what you hear; you cannot help what you see," she says. "May the Lord who gave you the gift give you the courage to bear it."

PARIS, FRANCE,
DECEMBER 1434–
JANUARY 1435

Woodville does not get his wish that I should
see Grafton, though we stay in England for a
year, and my lord never gets his wish for an
adequate army to serve in France, nor —
though he takes power and rules England —
can he bring the king's Council or Parliament into proper order. We cannot stay in
England, for the city of Paris sends for my
lord duke and says that the people there are
besieged by robbers, mutinous soldiers, and
beggars, and starving for lack of supplies.

"He won't refuse them," Woodville warns
me. "We will have to go back to Paris."

The seas are rough for the crossing, and
when we arrive in Calais, the garrison is so
dispirited that my lord commands Woodville
to stay there, raise their spirits, and prepare
the soldiers for an attack on the French as
soon as the weather allows. Then my lord and
I prepare to press on down the muddy roads
for Paris.

Woodville stands in the archway of the great

gate to bid us farewell. He comes beside me and, without thinking, checks the tightness of the girth on my horse, as he always does. "How shall I manage without you?" I ask.

His face is grim. "I shall think of you," he says. His voice is low, and he does not meet my eyes. "God knows, I shall think of you every day."

He turns from me and goes to my lord duke. They clasp hands and then my lord leans down from his horse and hugs his squire. "God bless, lad, hold this for me and come when I send for you."

"Always," Woodville says briefly, and then my lord raises his hand, and we clatter out over the drawbridge, and I realize I don't know when I will see him again, and that I have not said good-bye, nor thanked him for his care of me, nor told him . . . nor told him . . . I shake my head. There is nothing that the Duchess of Bedford should tell her husband's squire, and there is no reason for me to have tears blurring my sight of the flat road in the flat lands ahead.

This time we ride in the center of the guard. The countryside is lawless, and no one knows whether a French troop might be riding through, destroying everything they find. We ride at a steady canter, my lord grim-faced, exhausted by the journey, bracing himself for trouble.

It is miserable in the city. We try to keep

Christmas in the Hôtel de Bourbon, but the cooks are in despair of getting good meat and vegetables. Every day messengers come in from the English lands in France reporting uprisings in distant villages, where the people have sworn that they will not endure the rule of the English for another moment. It is little comfort that we hear also that the Armagnac king is also troubled with rebellions. In truth, the whole land of France is sick of war and soldiers and is crying a plague on both our houses.

In the new year my lord duke tells me shortly that we are leaving Paris, and I know him well enough now not to question his plans when he looks so angry and so weary at the same time.

"Can you tell me if our luck will turn?" he asks sourly. "Just that?"

I shake my head. In truth, I think he has bad luck at his heels and sorrow at his shoulder.

"You look like a widow," he says sharply. "Smile, Jacquetta."

I smile at him, and I don't say that sometimes I feel like a widow too.

GISORS, FRANCE, FEBRUARY 1435

My lord sends for Woodville to escort us from Paris to Rouen. He tells me nothing, but I fear that he thinks that the city of Paris would not hold if we were to come under attack, and that we can be safe only in Rouen. He hopes to get there and negotiate for peace with the French court from the heartland of the English-held lands. Woodville comes with extra guards — his face grave — musters the guard in the stable yard, commands the order for greater safety, and helps my lord into the saddle for the first day of riding.

It is a cold damp ride, and we break the journey at the well-fortified castle of Gisors, when I wake in the night hearing a terribly rasping noise. It is my husband, flailing in bed as if someone has him by the throat, choking and gasping for breath. I jump up and light a candle from the fire — he is tearing at his nightgown; he cannot breathe. I fling open the bedroom door and call for my maid and send her running for Woodville and for my lord's groom of the stool.

In moments my room is filled with men, and they have lifted my husband up in bed, and flung open the window to give him air. His physician comes with one of the tinctures from the alchemists, and my lord sips, catches his breath, and sips again.

"I am well, I am well," he croaks, waving his hand at the household who are in the room, or gathered at the door. "Go, go, all of you, to your beds; there is nothing wrong." I see the doctor glance at Woodville as if they two know this is a reassuring lie, but Woodville ushers everyone from the room, telling only one man to wait at the door in case of need. Finally the doctor, my lord, Woodville, and I are alone.

"I shall send for the physician from Paris," Woodville says to my husband. "Fear not, I will send for him now."

"Yes," he says heavily. "There is a weight in my chest, a weight like lead. I can't breathe."

"Do you think you could sleep?"

"If you raised me up in the bed, but I can't lie flat. I'm tired, Richard, I am as tired as a beaten dog."

"I will sleep outside your door," Woodville says. "The duchess can call me if you wake."

"She had better go to another room," my husband says. "This is no place for her."

They all look at me as if I am a child who should be spared any distress. "I shall stay with you," I say. "And in the morning I will get some lemon and parsley, and make you a drink that will restore your breath."

My lord looks at me. "You are my greatest treasure," he says again. "But go to your lady's room for this night. I don't want to wake you again."

I wrap my night cloak around me and put some slippers on my feet. "Call me if my lord is taken ill again," I say to Woodville.

He bows. "I will, my lady. And I will sleep on the pallet bed on the floor beside him so I can watch over his sleep."

I move to the door, but my lord delays me with his hand raised. "Stand there," he says.

I stand as he bids me, before the open window, and the frosty air comes into the room. "Put out the lights," my lord says. The men snuff the candles, and the moonlight shines a clear white light into the room, falling on my head and shoulders and illuminating the white of my nightgown. I see Woodville steal a glance at me, a longing glance, and then he quickly looks away.

"Melusina and the moon," my lord says quietly.

"Jacquetta," I remind him. "I am Jacquetta."

He closes his eyes, he is asleep.

Two days later he is a little better. They bring him news of the Calais garrison, and he opens the letter and reads it in silence while we are seated at breakfast in the great hall. He looks around for Woodville.

"Trouble at Calais," he says. "You had better get back there, lick the men into order, then come back to me."

"Are they under attack?" Sir Richard asks coolly, as if he were not being ordered to ride into unknown dangers.

"Their wages haven't been paid again," my lord says. "I'll give you a draft on my own treasury. Try to satisfy them. I will write to England for funds."

Woodville does not look at me at all. "Will you be able to continue on to Rouen?" he asks.

"I'll manage," my lord says.

"I will help him," I say. It is as if I have not spoken. Neither man pays me any attention.

"Go then," my lord says shortly.

Woodville grips my lord's hand as if he would hold him, and then turns to me for the briefest of moments. I notice once more how very blue his eyes are, and then he has bowed and gone away. He hardly said good-bye.

We go on by gentle stages to Rouen. My lord is not well enough to ride, he travels in a litter, and his big warhorse is led beside it. It goes uneasily, unhappy with an empty saddle, its head drooping as if it fears the loss of its master. My lord lies in the grand litter that he commissioned for me, drawn by white mules, but he can get no rest in the jolting of the long journey. It is like watching a great plow horse coming wearily to the end of a field, at the end of a long day. My lord is drained of energy, and, looking at him, I can almost feel his deathly fatigue in my own young bones.

Rouen, France, September 1435

All through the long summer at Rouen my lord summons his lawyer, and the councillors who have served him and helped him to rule France for the thirteen hard years of his regency. Each day the envoys come and go from the peace conference that they are holding at Arras, each day my lord has them come to him and tell him of the progress they have made. He offers the young King of England in marriage to a French princess to resolve the conflict over the crown of France; he offers to leave the whole of the south of France under the rule of the Armagnacs. He cannot yield more. But they demand that the English leave all of France, deny our right to the throne — as if we have not spent nearly a hundred years fighting for it! Each day my lord suggests new concessions, or a new way of writing the treaty, and each day his messengers take the high road to Arras as he watches the sunset through the windows of the castle at Rouen. Then one evening I see the messenger gallop from our stable yard and take the road to Calais. My lord has sent for Richard Woodville, and then he sends for me.

His lawyer brings his will to him, and he commands that they make alterations. His entailed property will go to his male heir, his nephew, the young King of England. He smiles ruefully. "I don't doubt he needs it badly," he says. "There is not a penny left in the royal Treasury. And I don't doubt he will waste it. He will give it away too readily; he is a generous boy. But it is his by rights, and his council will advise him. God help him between the advice of my brother and my uncle." To me he leaves my dower share: a third of his fortune.

"My lord . . ." I stammer.

"It is yours; you have been my wife, and you have served me as a good wife. You deserve no less. Everything will be yours, while you carry my name."

"I did not expect . . ."

"No, nor I. Truly, I did not expect to be making my will so soon. But it is your right and my wish that you should have your share. But more than this, I will leave you my books, Jacquetta, my beautiful books. They will be yours now."

These are treasures indeed. I kneel at his bedside and put my cheek to his cold hand. "Thank you. You know I will study them and keep them safe."

He nods. "In the books, Jacquetta, in one of them — somewhere — is the answer that all men seek. The recipe for eternal life, for the pure water, for the gold that comes from soot, from dark matter. Perhaps you will read and find it when I am long gone."

There are tears in my eyes. "Don't say it, my lord."

"Go away now, child, I need to sign this and then sleep."

I curtsey and slip from the room, and leave him with the lawyers.

He does not allow me to come to him till the afternoon of the next day, and even in that short time I see that he has lost a little more ground. His dark eyes are duller, the great beak of his nose seems bigger in his thinner face; I can see he is failing.

He sits in his great chair, a chair as big as a throne, facing the window so that he can see the road to Arras, where the peace talks are still bickering on. The evening sunlight shines in the window, making everything glow. I think this may be his last evening, that he may be setting with the sun.

"This is where I first saw you, in this very castle, d'you remember?" he asks, watching the sun go down into clouds of gold, and a pale ghost of a moon rise in the sky. "We were in this castle, in the entry hall of this very castle, for the trial of the maid?"

"I remember." I remember only too well, but I have never reproached him with the death of Joan, though I do reproach myself for not speaking out for her.

"Odd that I should be here to burn one Maid, and then find another," he says. "I burned her as a witch, but I wanted you for your skills. Odd, that. I wanted you the moment I saw you. Not as a wife, for I was married to Anne then. I wanted you as a treasure. I believed you had the Sight; I knew you were descended from Melusina, and I thought you might bring the Stone to me."

"I am sorry," I say. "I am sorry I was not more skilled . . ."

"Oh . . ." He makes a dismissive gesture with his hand. "It was not to be. Perhaps if we had more time . . . but you did see a crown, didn't you? And a battle? And a queen with horseshoes on backwards? The victory of my house, and the inheritance of my nephew and his line going on forever?"

"Yes," I say to reassure him, though none of this was ever clear to me. "I saw your nephew on the throne, and I am sure that he will hold France. It won't be him who loses Calais."

"You are sure of that?"

At least I can promise him this. "I am sure it won't be him who loses Calais."

He nods and sits in silence for a moment.

Then he says very quietly: "Jacquetta, would you take off your gown?"

I am so surprised that I flinch a little and step back. "My gown?"

"Yes, and your linen, everything."

I feel myself glow with embarrassment. "You want to see me naked?"

He nods.

"Now?"

"Yes."

"I mean in this daylight?"

"In the sunset, yes."

I have no choice. "If you command it, my lord." I rise up from my chair and I untie the lacing on my top gown and let it drop to my feet. I step out of it and shyly put it to one side. I take off my ornate headdress and shake the plaits out of my hair. My hair falls over my face as a sort of veil to shield me, and then I slip off my linen petticoats and the fine underpetticoat of silk, and I stand before him, naked.

"Raise your hands," he commands. His voice is calm; he is looking at me without desire but with a sort of thoughtful pleasure. I realize that I have seen him look at pictures, at tapestries, at statues like this. I am, at this moment, what I have always been to him: an object of beauty. He has never loved me as a woman.

Obediently, I raise my hands over my head, like a swimmer about to dive into deep water.

The tears in my eyes are now running down my cheeks at the thought that I have been his wife and his bedfellow, his companion and his duchess, and even now, though he is near to death, still he does not love me. He has never loved me. He never will love me. He gestures that I should turn a little to one side so the last rays of golden sunlight shall fall on my bare skin, turning my flanks and belly and breasts to gold too.

"A girl of flame," he says quietly. "A golden maid. I am glad to have seen such a thing before I died."

I stand obediently still, though I can feel sobs shaking my slight body. At this moment of his death he sees me as an object transmuted into gold; he does not see me, he does not love me, he does not even want me for myself. His eyes go over every inch of me, thoughtfully, dreamily; but he does not notice my tears, and when I get dressed again, I wipe them away in silence.

"I'll rest now," he says. "I am glad to have seen such a thing. Tell them to get me into bed, and I will sleep."

His servants come in; they make him comfortable in his bed, and then I kiss his forehead and leave him for the night. As it happens, that is the last time I see him, for he dies in his sleep that night, and so that was the last he saw of me: not a loving wife but a statue gilded by the setting sun.

They call me at about seven in the morning, and I go to his room and see him, almost as I left him. He seems peacefully asleep, only the slow low tolling of the single bell in the tower of Rouen Cathedral tells the household and the city that the great Lord John is dead. Then the women come to wash and lay out his body; the master of the household starts to make the plans for his lying-in at the cathedral; the joiner orders wood and starts to make his coffin; and only Richard Woodville thinks to draw me aside, stunned and silent as I am, from all the bustle and work, and takes me back to my own rooms.

He orders breakfast for me and hands me over to the ladies of my chamber, telling them to see that I eat and then rest. The sempstress and the tailors will come at once to measure us up for our mourning clothes; the shoemaker will come to make black slippers for me. The glovemaker will produce dozens of pairs of black gloves for me to distribute to my household. They will order black cloth to swathe the way to the cathedral, and black capes for the one hundred poor men who will be hired to follow the coffin. My lord will be buried in Rouen Cathedral, and there will be a procession of lords and a great service to bid him farewell, and everything must be done exactly as he would have wished it, with dignity, in the English style.

I spend the day writing to everyone to announce the death of my husband. I write to my mother to tell her that I am a widow like her: my lord has died. I write to the King of England, to the Duke of Burgundy, to the Holy Roman emperor, to the other kings, to Yolande of Aragon. The rest of the time I pray; I attend every service of the day in our private chapel, and in the meantime the monks at the Rouen Cathedral will watch and pray all the hours of the day and night over my husband's body, which is guarded with four knights at every point of the compass: a vigil that will only end with his funeral.

I wait in case God has some guidance for me; I wait on my knees in case I can come to some understanding that my husband has been called to his reward, that at last he has come to lands that he does not have to defend. But I hear and see nothing. Not even Melusina whispers a lament for him. I wonder if I have lost my Sight and whether the brief glimpses I had in the mirror were the last views of another world that I will not see again.

In the evening, about the hour of sunset, Richard Woodville comes to my rooms and asks me will I dine in the great hall of the castle among the men and women of our household, or will I be served alone, in my rooms?

I hesitate.

"If you feel you can come to the hall, it

185

would cheer them to see you," he says. "There are many in deep grief for my lord, and they would like to see you among them, and of course your household will have to be broken up, and they would like to see you before they have to leave."

"The household broken up?" I ask foolishly.

He nods. "Of course, my lady. A new regent for France will be appointed by the English court, and you will be sent to the court at England, for them to arrange a new marriage for you."

I look at him quite aghast. "I cannot think of marrying again."

I am not likely to find another husband who asks me for nothing more than that he can see me naked. Another husband is likely to be far more demanding, another husband will force himself on me, and another husband is almost certain to be wealthy and powerful and old. But the next old man will not let me study; he will not leave me alone; he is certain to want a son and heir from me. He will buy me like a heifer to be put to the bull. I can squeal like a heifer in the meadow, but he will mount me. "Truly, I cannot bear to be married again!"

His smile is bitter. "Both you and I will have to learn to serve a new master," he says. "Alas for us."

I am silent, and then I say, "I will go to the

hall for dinner if you think everyone would like it?"

"They would," he says. "Can you walk in on your own?"

I nod. My ladies arrange themselves behind me, and Richard walks before me to the double doors of the great hall. The noisy chatter behind the doors is quieter than usual; this is a house of mourning. The guards throw the doors open, and I go in. At once, all the talk stops, and there is a sudden hush, then there is a rumble and a clatter as every man rises to his feet, pushing back benches and stools, and every man pulls off his hat and stands bareheaded as I go by, the hundreds and hundreds of them, showing respect to me as the duke's young widow, showing their love to him who has gone, and their sorrow at their loss and mine. I walk through them, and I hear them whispering, "God bless you, my lady" in a low mutter as I go by, all the way to the dais at the top of the hall, and I stand behind the high table, alone.

"I thank you for your kind wishes," I say to them, my voice ringing like a flute in the big-raftered hall. "My lord duke is dead, and we all feel the loss of him. You will all be paid your wages for another month, and I will recommend you to the new regent of France as good and trustworthy servants. God bless my lord the duke, and God save the king."

"God bless my lord the duke, and God save the king!"

"That was well done," Woodville says to me as we walk back to my private rooms. "Especially the wages. And you will be able to pay them. My lord was a good master, there is enough in the treasury to pay the wages and even some pensions for the older men. You yourself will be a very wealthy woman."

I pause in a little window bay and look out over the darkened town. An oval three-quarter moon is rising, warm yellow in color in the deep indigo sky. I should be planting herbs that need a waxing moon at Penshurst, but then I realize that I will never see Penshurst again. "And what will happen to you?" I ask.

He shrugs. "I will go back to Calais and then, when the new captain is appointed, I will go home to England. I will find a master whom I can respect, offer him my service. Perhaps I will come back to France in an expedition, or if the king does make peace with the Armagnacs, then perhaps I will serve the king at the English court. Perhaps I will go to the Holy Land and become a crusader."

"But I won't see you," I say, as the thought suddenly strikes me. "You won't be in my household. I don't even know where I will live, and you could go anywhere. We won't be together anymore." I look at him as the thought comes home to me. "We won't see each other anymore."

"No," he says. "This will be where we part. Perhaps we will never see each other again."

I gasp. The thought that I will never see him again is so momentous that I cannot grasp it. I give a shaky laugh. "It doesn't seem possible. I see you every day, I am so accustomed . . . You are always here, I have walked with you, or ridden with you, or been with you, every day for — what — more than two years? — ever since my wedding day. I am used to you . . ." I break off for fear of sounding too weak. "What I am really thinking is: Who will look after Merry? Who will keep her safe?"

"Your new husband?" he suggests.

"I don't know; I can't imagine that. I can't imagine you not being here. And Merry . . ."

"What about Merry?"

"She doesn't like strange men," I say foolishly. "She only likes you."

"My lady . . ."

I fall silent at the intensity of his tone. "Yes?"

He takes my hand and tucks it under his elbow and walks me down the gallery. To any of my ladies, seated at the far end by the fire, it looks as if we are walking together, planning the next few days, as we have always walked together, as we have always talked together, constant companions: the duchess and her faithful knight. But this time he keeps his hand on mine and his fingers are burning as if he has a fever. This time his head is turned so close to me that if I looked up at him our lips would brush. I walk with my head averted. I must not look up at him so that our lips brush.

"I cannot know what the future will bring us," he says in a rapid undertone. "I cannot know where you will be given in marriage, nor what life might hold for me. But I can't let you go without telling you — without telling you at least once — that I love you."

I snatch a breath at the words. "Woodville —"

"I can offer you nothing; I am next to nothing, and you are the greatest lady in France. But I wanted you to know, I love you and I want you, and I have done since the day I first saw you."

"I should —"

"I have to tell you, you have to know: I have loved you honorably as a knight should do his lady, and I have loved you passionately as a man might a woman; and now, before I leave you, I want to tell you that I love you, I love you —" He breaks off and looks at me desperately. "I had to tell you," he repeats.

I feel as if I am becoming as golden and as warm as alchemy could make me. I can feel myself smiling, glowing at these words. At once I know that he is telling the truth: that he is in love with me; and at once I recognize the truth: that I am in love with him. And he has told me, he has said the words: I have captured his heart, he loves me, he loves me, dear God, he loves me. And God knows — though Richard does not — that I love him.

Without another word we turn into a little room at the end of the gallery, and he closes the door behind us and takes me in his arms in one swift irresistible movement. I raise my head to him, and he kisses me. My hands stroke from his cropped handsome head to his broad shoulders, and I hold him to me, closer and still closer. I feel the muscle of his shoulders under his jerkin, the prickle of his short hair at the back of his neck.

"I want you," he says in my ear. "Not as a duchess, and not as a scryer. I want you just as a woman, as my woman."

He drops his head and kisses my shoulder, where the neck of the gown leaves my shoulder bare for his touch. He kisses my collarbone, my neck, up to my jaw line. I bury my face in his hair, in the crook of his neck, and he gives a little groan of desire and thrusts his fingers in my headdress, pulling the gold net off so that my hair comes tumbling down, and he rubs his face in it.

"I want you as a woman, an ordinary woman," he repeats breathlessly, pulling at the laces of my gown. "I don't want the Sight; I don't want your ancestry. I don't know anything about alchemy or the mysteries or the water goddess. I am a man of the earth, of ordinary things, an Englishman. I don't want mysteries — I just want you, as an ordinary woman. I have to have you."

"You would bring me down to earth," I say slowly, raising my head.

He hesitates, looks down into my face. "Not to diminish you," he says. "Never that. I want you to be whatever you are. But this is who I am. I don't know about the other world, and I don't care about it. I don't care about saints or spirits or goddesses or the Stone. All I want is to lie with you, Jacquetta" — we both register this, his first ever use of my name — "Jacquetta, I just desire you, as if you were an ordinary woman and I an ordinary man."

"Yes," I say. I can feel a sudden pulse of desire. "Yes, I don't care about anything else."

His mouth is on mine again, his hands are pulling at the neck of my gown, unfastening my belt. "Lock the door," I say as he shrugs out of his jerkin and draws me towards him. The moment when he enters me I feel a searing pain, which melts into a pleasure that I have never felt before, and so I don't care about the pain. But I do know, even as we move towards ecstasy, that it is a woman's pain and that I have become a woman of earth and fire, and I am no longer a girl of water and air.

■ ■ ■ ■

"We have to prevent a child," Woodville says
to me. We have had a week of secret meetings, and we are dizzy with desire and delight
in each other. My lord's funeral has come
and gone, and I am waiting to hear from my
mother as to what she will command me to
do. We are beginning, only slowly, to see
beyond the blindness of desire and to wonder
what the future will hold for us.

"I take herbs," I say. "After that first night I
took some herbs. There will be no child. I
have made sure of it."

"I wish you could foresee what will become
of us," he says. "For I really cannot let you
go."

"Hush," I caution him. My women are
nearby, sewing and talking among themselves,
but they are accustomed to Richard Woodville coming to my rooms every day. There
has been much to plan and arrange, and
Richard has always been in constant attendance.

"It's true," he says, his voice lower. "It is
true, Jacquetta. I cannot let you go."

"Then you will have to hold me," I reply,
smiling down at my work.

"The king will command that you go to
England," he says. "I can't just kidnap you."

I steal a quick glance at his frowning face.

"Really, you should just kidnap me," I prompt.

"I'll think of something," he swears.

That night I take the bracelet that my great-aunt gave me, the charm bracelet for foretelling the future. I take a charm shaped like a little ring, a wedding ring, and I take a charm shaped like a ship to represent my voyage to England, and I take a charm in the shape of the castle of St. Pol, in case I am summoned back home. I think that I will tie each of them to a thread, put them in the deepest water of the River Seine, and see which thread comes to my hand after the moon has changed. I am about to start tying the threads on the little charms when I stop and laugh at myself. I am not going to do this. There is no need for me to do this.

I am a woman of earth now, not a girl of water. I am not a maid, I am a lover. I am not interested in foreseeing; I will make my own future, not predict it. I don't need a charm to tell me what I hope will happen. I throw the gold charm which is like a wedding ring up in the air and catch it before it falls. This is my choice. I don't need magic to reveal my desire. The enchantment is already done: I am in love; I am sworn to a man of earth; I am not going to give this man up. All I have to do is consider how we can stay together.

I put the bracelet aside and draw a piece of paper to me and start to write to the King of England.

From the Dowager Duchess of Bedford to His Grace the King of England and France:

Your Grace and dear nephew, I greet you well. As you know, my late lord has left me dower lands and funds in England, and with your permission I will come home and set my affairs in order. My lord's master of horse, Sir Richard Woodville, will accompany me and my household. I await your royal permission.

I put the charm bracelet away in the purse and return it to my jewel case. I don't need a spell to foresee the future; I am going to make it happen.

England,
Summer 1436

The English court is at its summer pursuit of hunting, traveling, and flirtation. The young King of England starts and ends his day in prayer but rides out like a carefree boy for the rest of his day. Richard and I attend the young king as companions and friends; we hunt, dance, play at the summer sports, and join with the court. Nobody knows that every night Richard comes secretly to my room, and the best part of the day — the only part of the day when we are alone together — begins.

My dower lands are transferred into my name, the bulk of my lord's great fortune has been paid to his nephew the king. Our house in Paris is gone, lost to the Armagnac king whose star has risen since the death of my lord. My lord's beloved house of Penshurst has gone to his brother Humphrey, Duke of Gloucester; and Eleanor Cobham, the lady-in-waiting who betrayed the trust of her mistress, now walks down the beautiful allées and admires the roses in the garden as if she were worthy. She will cut the herbs that I planted; she will hang them to dry in my still room; she will take my place in the hall. I resent the loss of nothing from my married life but this.

The two of them, the handsome duke and his beautiful wife, are burning up with pride, and this is their summer of glory. Now that my husband is dead, the two of them are next in line to the throne, and every time the young king coughs at dinner, or mounts a horse that looks too strong for him, I see the duchess's head come up, like a hound hearing the horn. Their desire for the throne locks them in conflict with their uncle, Cardinal Beaufort, and the whole court mourns the loss of my husband, who was the only man who could hold these rivals together. The young king is advised by the duke in the morning and by the cardinal in the afternoon, and by evening he has no idea what he thinks about anything.

I am lulled like a fool by my happiness. I observe Eleanor Cobham, but I bear her no malice. I include her in the dazed pity I feel for everyone who is not me, who is not loved by Richard Woodville. She does not sleep next to a man she loves; she does not know his touch as the early summer dawn turns the windows to pearl; she does not know the whisper in the cool morning, "Oh, stay. Stay.

Just once more." I think nobody in the whole world knows what it is to be in love, to be so beloved. The summer days go by in a haze of desire. But the summer must come to an end. When September comes, I will have been widowed for a year, and the king's advisors will be considering a new marriage for me. They will want to employ me to bind a difficult English lord more closely to the throne; they will want to put my dower lands into the pocket of a favorite. Perhaps they will find a foreign prince who would take me as a wife to enforce an alliance. They will put me where it suits them, and unless we awake and rise up from our enchantment, then I predict that I will be married off by Christmas.

Richard is well aware of this danger, but he cannot think how we can prevent it. Richard says that he will go to the king and his council and tell them that he loves me and wants to marry me; but he cannot bring himself to do it, the disgrace would fall on me and I would be no longer a duchess but a commoner's wife, no longer the first lady in the kingdom but a woman of earth, indeed. At best, the fortune that my husband left me would be confiscated, and we would be left with nothing; at the worst they could arrest Richard for assaulting one of the royal family, send me to a convent, and then marry me off to a man commanded to control me, warning him that his wife is a whore and had better be taught submission.

As each dreamy warm summer day goes by, we know that we are closer to the moment when we will have to part, or face the danger of confessing. Richard torments himself with his fear that he will be the ruin of me; I am only afraid that he will leave me in a fit of self-sacrifice. He says I will be ruined if he declares his love, and he will be destroyed if he does not.

The wise woman Margery Jourdemayne visits the court, selling love potions, telling fortunes, scrying, and divining for lost things. Half of what she does is nonsense, but I have faith in her skills as a herbalist. I summon her to my rooms, and she comes discreetly late one evening, a hood drawn over her head, a scarf over her mouth. "And what does the *beautiful* duchess want?" she asks me.

I can't help but giggle at the emphasis. "What d'you call the other duchess?" I ask.

"I call her the royal duchess," she says. "And so I please you both. She prefers the thought of the crown to anything. All I can do for her is put her closer to the throne; but what can I do for you?"

I shake my head. I don't want to speculate about the succession: it is treason even to suggest that the young king is not strong and healthy, and he is both. "I'll tell you what I want," I say. "I want an herbal drink to make a baby."

She slides a sideways look at me. "You want a baby though you have no husband?"

"It's not for me," I lie quickly. "It's for a friend."

"And is the friend the same age and build as you?" she asks impertinently. "I have to know, for the herbs."

"You can make it as if you were making it for me, and give me the recipe."

She nods. "It will be ready tomorrow. You — your friend — should drink it every evening."

I nod. "Thank you. That will be all."

She hesitates at the doorway. "Any woman who dares to make her own destiny will always put herself in danger," she remarks, almost at random. "And you, of all people, might foresee this."

I smile at her warning, and then on impulse I put out my hand to her and make the gesture, the circle drawn in the air with the forefinger: fortune's wheel. She understands; she smiles in reply and goes.

I wait a month, two months, then quietly, at midnight, at the end of summer, Richard lets himself into my room, and I slip into his arms.

"I have news for you," I say. I pour him a glass of the best wine from Gascony. There is a bubble of laughter inside me at the words. I could laugh aloud at my sudden sense of daring, at my joy, at the intensity of my happiness.

"Good news?" he asks.

"Good news," I say. "My love, I have to tell you; but now I come to it, I hardly know how to tell you — I am with child."

The glass falls from his hands and cracks on the stone floor. He does not even turn his head to see the damage; he is deaf to the noise and oblivious to the cost. "What?"

"I am with child," I say steadily. "A good month into my time."

"What?"

"Actually, I think she will be a girl," I say. "I think she will be born early next summer."

"What?" he says again.

The giggle in my heart threatens to burst out, but his appalled expression does not frighten me. "Beloved," I say patiently. "Be happy. I am carrying your child. Nothing in the world could make me more happy than I am tonight. This is the start of everything for me. I am a woman of earth at last; I am fertile ground, and a seed is growing inside me."

He drops his head into his hands. "I have been your ruin," he says. "God forgive me. I will never forgive myself. I love you more than anything in the world, and I have been the road to your ruin."

"No," I say. "Don't speak of ruin. This is wonderful. This is the solution to everything. We will get married."

"We will have to get married!" he exclaims. "Or you will be shamed. But if we marry, you are disgraced. God, what a trap I have put myself in, and what a trap I have put you in!"

"This is the way out of the trap," I say. "For nobody will make us deny our marriage if we have exchanged our vows and have a child on the way. The council, my mother, the king — everyone will have to accept it. And though they won't like it — they will come to bear it. They say that the king's own mother married Owen Tudor without permission —"

"And was disgraced! She slept with the keeper of her wardrobe and never came back to court. Her own son changed the law of the land to prevent a royal widow ever doing such a thing again! That law applies to you!"

"She survived," I say steadily. "And she has two handsome boys, half brothers to the king. Richard, I cannot live without you. I cannot marry another man. We were driven by desire to become lovers, and now we are driven on to marry."

"I don't want to be your ruin," he says. "God forgive me, though I desire you, I won't desire that. I despised Owen Tudor for conceiving a child on the queen he should have served, a man who ruined a woman he should have laid down his life to protect — and now I have been as selfish as him! I should leave right now. I should go on crusade. I should be hanged for treason."

I take a long pause, and then I raise my eyes and give him a look as limpid as a forest pool. "Oh, have I been mistaken in you? Have I been long mistaken? Do you not love me? Don't you want to marry me? Shall you cast me aside?"

He drops to his knees. "Before God, I love you and cherish you more than anything in the world. Of course I want to marry you. I love you heart and soul."

"Then I accept," I say gleefully. "I shall be happy to be your wife."

He shakes his head. "I should be honored to marry you, my love, you are far, far above my deserts — but I so fear for you." The thought strikes him. "And for our child!" Gently he puts his hand on my belly. "My God, a child. I shall have to keep the two of you safe. I shall have two to care for now."

"I shall be Jacquetta Woodville," I say dreamily, turning the name over. "Jacquetta Woodville. And she will be Elizabeth Woodville."

"Elizabeth? You are sure it is a girl?"

"I am sure. She will be Elizabeth, the first of many children."

"If they don't behead me for treason."

"They won't behead you. I shall speak to the king, and I shall speak to Queen Catherine, his mother, if I have to. And we will be happy."

■ ■ ■ ■

When he leaves me that night, he is still torn between delight that we are to marry and remorse that he has led me into trouble. I sit up at my window, my hand on my belly, and I look at the moon. Tonight there is a new moon, in the first quarter, a good moon for new beginnings, new hopes, and for the start of a new life. On a whim, I take out the cards that my great-aunt gave me, and I spread them out facedown before me. My hand hovers over one card and then another, before I choose one. It is my favorite card of all: the Queen of Cups, the queen of water and of love, Melusina's own card, a card of insight and tenderness. A girl whose card this is will be a queen herself, a beloved queen.

"I shall marry your father," I say to the little spark of life inside me. "And I shall bring you into the world. I know you will be beautiful for your father is the most handsome man in England, but I wonder what you will do with your life, and how far you will go when it all becomes clear to you — when you too see the man whom you love, and know the life that you want?"

GRAFTON, NORTHAMPTONSHIRE, AUTUMN 1436

We wait till the court is on its slow way back to London, staying overnight at Northampton. Early one morning, before my ladies are stirring, I slip out of my rooms and meet Richard at the stables. He has Merry saddled and bridled, and his own warhorse ready to go, and we ride down the little road to his home village of Grafton. A priest lives here alone, in his retreat, and there is a little chapel near to the manor house. Richard's father is waiting there, his face stern and anxious, and he has brought three witnesses. Richard goes to find the priest as his father steps forwards.

"I hope you know what you are doing, Your Grace," he says bluntly, as he helps me down from my horse.

"I am marrying the finest man I have ever known."

"It will cost you dear," he warns.

"It would be worse to lose him."

He nods as if he is not so sure, but he offers me his arm and walks me into the chapel.

205

At the eastern end there is a little stone altar, a cross, and a candle burning. Before it stands the priest in the brown gown of the Franciscan order, and beside him, Richard, turning and smiling shyly at me as if we were before a crowd of hundreds and wearing cloth of gold.

I walk to the altar, and just as I start to respond to the priest's gentle prompting of our vows, the sun comes out and shines through the circular stained-glass window above the altar. For a moment, I forget what I am to say. There is a veil of colors at our feet on the stone floor of the chapel, and I think dizzily that I am here now, marrying the man that I love, and that one day I will stand here when my daughter marries the man of her choice, rainbows beneath her feet, and a crown before her. The sudden vision makes me hesitate, and Richard looks at me. "If you have any doubts, a moment's doubt, we need not marry," he says quickly. "I will think of something; I will make you safe, my love."

I smile up at him, the tears in my eyes making a rainbow around him too. "I have no doubts." I turn to the priest. "Go on."

He leads us through our vows and then declares us man and wife. Richard's father kisses my cheeks and gives his son a powerful hug. Richard turns and pays the three clerks he has hired as witnesses and tells them that if he calls on them they must remember the day and the time and that we were truly married in the sight of God, and he puts his family ring on my finger, and gives me a purse of gold before them all, to prove that I am his wife, that he trusts me with his honor and his fortune.

"What now?" his father asks grimly as we come out of the chapel into the sunshine.

"Back to court," Richard says. "And when the moment serves us, we will have to tell the king."

"He will forgive you," his father predicts. "He is a young man quick to forgive anything. It is his advisors who will cause your difficulties. They will call you a mountebank, my son. They will say you are pretending to a lady too far above you."

Richard shrugs. "They can say what they like as long as they leave her with her fortune and her reputation," he says.

His father shakes his head as if he is not sure of that either, and then helps me onto my horse. "Send for me if you need me," he says gruffly. "I am yours to command, Your Grace, and your honor is in my keeping too."

"You can call me Jacquetta," I say.

He pauses. "I was your late husband's chamberlain," he says. "It is not right that I should call you by your given name."

"You were his chamberlain, and I was his duchess, but now, God bless him, he has gone from us and the world is different, and I am your daughter-in-law," I say. "And at first they will say that Richard has leaped up, but then they will see that we are going to rise together."

"How high?" he asks dryly. "The higher you rise, the greater the fall."

"I don't know how high we will rise," I say stoutly. "And I have no fear of falling."

He looks at me. "You are ambitious to rise?"

"We are all on fortune's wheel," I say. "Without a doubt we will rise. We may fall. But still I have no fear of it."

The baby is not yet showing through the graceful sweep of my gowns, though I know that she is growing. My breasts are bigger and tender to the touch, and more than anything else I have a sense of being in company, everywhere I go, even when I am asleep. I decide to take the news of the baby and the marriage to the king's council before the anniversary of my husband's death, before anyone proposes another marriage for me, and so forces me to defy them. I try to choose a good time, but the council is torn between Cardinal Beaufort and his ally the Earl of Suffolk, William de la Pole, and their great rival Humphrey, Duke of Gloucester, and his court. There is never a time when they are not fretting about safety in the country and empty chests in the Treasury. There is never a moment when they can agree what should be done. I wait for a week after our wedding, and then I visit the great favorite William de la Pole in his rooms in

Westminster Palace, in the quiet hour before dinner.

"I am honored," he says, putting a chair before his table for me. "And what can I do for you, Your Grace?"

"I have to ask for your help in a matter of some delicacy," I say. This is not easy, but I press on. "A personal matter."

"A personal matter for a beautiful duchess?" he says. "I take it this is a matter of the heart?"

He makes it sound like a girl's folly. I retain my smile. "Indeed," I say. "To be blunt, sir, I have married without permission, and I am hoping that you will take the news to the king and speak for me."

There is a painful silence. Then he says: "Married?"

"Yes."

His gaze is sharp. "And who have you married?"

"A gentleman . . ."

"Not a nobleman?"

"No. A gentleman."

"And he is?"

"Richard Woodville, of my household."

His gleam of amusement is instantly hidden as he drops his eyes to the papers on the table before him. I know he will be thinking how he can take advantage of my folly. "And this is a love match, I take it?"

"Yes."

"You were not prevailed upon nor forced? It was done legally with your consent? There are no grounds for an annulment or a denial? If he seduced you or even persuaded you, then he can be arrested and hanged."

"There are no grounds for denial, and I want no grounds. This is the husband of my choice, this is a marriage I desired."

"Desire?" he asks coldly, as if he has never felt it.

He forces me to be shameless. "Desire," I confirm.

"The gentleman is to be congratulated; there are many men who would have been glad of your desire. Any man would be glad of your consent. Indeed, the council has been considering your next husband. Several names were proposed."

I hide a smile at this. There is almost no council but him, Cardinal Beaufort, and the Duke of Gloucester. If names were proposed, then it will be this man who was proposing them.

"The matter is already settled," I say stoutly. "And we are wedded and bedded — there is nothing that can be done. Whoever they have chosen for me is proposed too late. I am married to a good man. He has been very kind to me since the death of my lord John."

"And I see you have been very kind to him," he says with a little snigger. "Exception-

211

ally kind. Well, I will tell His Grace, the king, and you can ask him for forgiveness."

I nod. It would help me if William de la Pole would recommend this to the king. The king is always given to the opinion of the last man who spoke to him, and the three councillors compete to be the last out of the door. "Do you think he will be very angry?" The king is a boy of fifteen. It is ridiculous that I should fear his anger.

"No. But I am sure that his council will advise that you must be exiled from court, and they will fine you."

I nod. "But you could persuade them to be kind."

"They will fine you heavily," he warns. "The king's Treasury is short of money, and they all know you have the Bedford fortune. And it is a serious offense to marry without the king's permission. They will say that you don't deserve the money."

"I have only my dower," I say. "Most of the fortune has already gone to the king, and he has given it to his favorites." I don't say, "You among them," but we know that is what I mean. "My lord's brother, the Duke Humphrey, had the rest; I didn't keep Penshurst."

"You have the dower of a royal duchess, but you have chosen to be the woman of a squire. I think you will find they will want your dower. You may find you have to live as the wife of a squire. I only hope that in a few years' time you still think you have made a good bargain."

"I hope you will help me," I say. "I am counting on you."

He just sighs.

He is right. One thousand pounds in gold they demand from us, and they order Richard to return to his post at Calais.

Richard is aghast. "My God! A fortune! We will never raise it! It is the price of a house and an estate; it is greater than my father's entire fortune. Greater than any inheritance I could hope for. Greater than anything I could win. They mean to ruin us. They are forcing us to part."

I nod. "They are punishing us."

"They are destroying us!"

"We can find the money," I say. "And we are banished from court, but we don't care, do we? We can go together to Calais?"

He shakes his head. "I'm not taking you there. I'm not taking you into danger. The Earl of Suffolk has offered me a property where you can live. He has taken most of your wealth as a fine, and he is prepared to take the rest as a rent. He has said he will lease his manor at Grafton to us. It's not much of a favor since we cannot afford to pay him. But he knows I want it. It is near my home, I have had my eye on it since I was a boy."

"I will sell my jewels," I say. "And books, if we have to. I have lands that we can borrow on, some things that we can sell to raise the rent. This is the price of our life together."

"I have reduced you to the position of a squire's wife with a nobleman's debt," he says furiously. "You should hate me. I have betrayed you."

"How much do you love me?" I counter. I take his hands in mine, and I hold them to my heart. I can feel him catch his breath at my touch. He pauses and looks at me.

"More than life itself — you know that."

"If you had to put a price on it?"

"A king's ransom. A fortune."

"Then consider, husband mine, that we have a bargain, for our marriage has cost us only a thousand pounds."

His face lightens. "Jacquetta, you are my joy. You are worth tens of thousands."

"Then pack your things, for we can leave court this afternoon," I say.

"This afternoon? Do you want us to flee from disgrace?"

"I want us to be at your home tonight."

He hesitates for a moment, and then his smile breaks out, as he realizes what I am saying. "We will spend our first night together as a married couple? We will go to our bedroom as husband and wife? And tomorrow we will go to breakfast together openly? Ah, Jacquetta, this is the start of everything."

He bows his head and kisses my hands. "I love you," he says again. "And please God, you will always think that you have a good bargain for our thousand pounds."

GRAFTON, NORTHAMPTONSHIRE, AUTUMN 1436–1439

I do think it a good bargain. We raise the money for the fine by borrowing against my dower lands, and then we borrow more to buy the manor house at Grafton from the Earl of Suffolk. For all his sly smiles he does not refuse to sell to the disgraced duchess and her squire. He wants our friendship so that we can be his allies in the country as he gains power at court. Richard goes to Calais and prepares the garrison for a siege, as my kinsman, the faithless Duke of Burgundy, marches against his former allies. The great lords of England, the Earl of Mortmain and the Duke of York, turn out for their country, and Richard holds Calais for them. Finally, Humphrey, the Duke of Gloucester, sets sail for Calais and earns much credit for the saving of the town, though, as my husband points out, the siege was already defeated before the king's uncle came in with his standard flying.

I don't care. Richard's courage has been

demonstrated to all of England, and nobody can doubt his honor. He has come through a siege and several raids without a scratch and returns to England a hero. My first child, the daughter whom I had foretold, is born without difficulty when the hedge is bobbing white with May and the blackbirds are singing in the dusk, that first spring in the country. The next year comes our son and heir.

We call him Lewis, and I find I am entranced to have a boy of my making. He has very fair hair, almost silvery, but his eyes are as dark as the sky at night. The midwife who helps me for this, my second time, tells me that all babies' eyes are blue and that both his hair color and his eyes may change; but he seems to me a boy who is half fairy, with this angelic coloring. His sister is still sleeping in the Woodville cherrywood crib, and so at night I put them in together, side by side on their swaddling boards like pretty little dolls.

Richard says with satisfaction that I am a woman who has forgotten all about being a wife and a lover and that he is a miserably neglected man. He is joking though, and he revels in the beauty of our little daughter and in the growth and strength of our son. The next year I give birth to his sister, my Anne, and while I am confined with her, my father-in-law takes a fever and dies. It was a comfort to him that he lived long enough to learn that we had been forgiven by the king and summoned back to court. Only with a daughter of just two, a boy of one year, and a new baby in the carved cradle, I am not very eager to go.

"We will never earn enough to pay our debts, living in the country," my husband advises me. "I have the fattest cows in Northamptonshire, and the best sheep, but I do swear, Jacquetta, we will live and die in debt. You have married a poor man and should be glad that I don't make you beg in your petticoat."

I brandish the letter at him with the royal seal. "No, for see, we are commanded to court for the Easter feast, and I have another letter here from the king's groom of the household asking if we have enough rooms for the king to stay with us on his summer progress."

Richard all but blenches. "Good God, no, we cannot house the court. And we certainly cannot feed the court. Is the groom of the household run mad? What sort of house do they think we have?"

"I will write and tell them we have nothing but a modest house, and when we go to court at Easter we must make sure they know it."

"But won't you be glad to go to London?" he asks me. "You can buy new clothes and shoes and all sorts of pretty things. Have you not missed the court and all of that world?"

I come around the table to stand behind his chair, lean over, and put my cheek to his. "I shall be glad to be at court again, for the king is the source of all wealth and all patronage, and I have two pretty daughters who will one day need to marry well. You are too good a knight to spend your time raising cattle, the king could have no more loyal advisor, and I know they will want you to go to Calais again. But no, I have been happy here with you, and we will only go for a little while and come home again, won't we? We won't be courtiers, spending all our time there?"

"We are the squire and his lady of Grafton," my husband declares. "Ruined by lust, up to our eyes in debt, and living in the country. This is where we belong, among rutting animals with no money. They are our peers. This is where we should be."

LONDON,
SUMMER 1441

I told the truth when I said that I was happy at Grafton, but my heart leaps with the most frivolous joy when the king sends the royal barge to take us down the river and I see the high towers of Greenwich Castle and the new Bella Court that the Duke of Gloucester has built. It is so pretty and so rich, I cannot help but delight in coming to it as a favorite of the court and one of the greatest ladies in the land once more. The barge sweeps along as the drummers keep the oarsmen in time, and then they shoulder their oars and the liveried boatmen on the pier catch the ropes and draw the barge alongside.

I am stepping down the drawbridge when I look up and see that the royal party has been walking beside the river and is now strolling to greet us. In front of them all is the king, a boy-king no longer; he is a young man of nearly twenty, and he comes confidently forwards and kisses me, as a kinsman, on both cheeks, and gives his hand to my husband. I see the company behind him surprised at the warmth of his welcome, and then they have to come forwards too. First the Duke Humphrey of Gloucester, my former brother-in-law, whom my first husband said would bear watching, and behind him comes the Duchess Eleanor. She walks slowly towards the pier, a woman exulting in her own beauty, and at first I see only the dazzle of vanity, but then I look again. At her heels is a big black dog, a huge creature, a mastiff or some sort of fighting dog. The moment I see it I could almost hiss, like a cat will hiss, setting its fur on end and darkening its eyes. I am so distracted by the ugly dog that I let the duke take my hand and kiss my cheek and whisper in my ear, without hearing a word he says. As his lady, the Duchess Eleanor, comes close, I find I am staring at her, and when she steps forwards to kiss me, I flinch from her touch as if she smells of the spittle of an old fighting dog. I have to force myself to step into her cold embrace, and smile as she smiles, without affection. Only when she releases me and I step back do I see that there is no black dog at her heels, and never was. I have had a flicker of a vision from the other world, and I know, with a hidden shudder, that one day there will be a black dog that runs up stone stairs in a cold castle and howls at her door.

■ ■ ■ ■

As the months go on, I see that I am right to fear the duchess. She is everywhere at court; she is the first lady of the land, the queen in all but name. When the court is at Westminster Palace, she lives in the queen's apartments and wears the royal jewels. In procession she is hard on the heels of the king. She treats him with a treacly intimacy, forever laying her hand on his arm and whispering in his ear. Only his radiant innocence saves them from the appearance of conspiracy, or worse. Inevitably, as a dowager duchess of England, I am constantly in her company, and I know she does not like it when people compare us. When we go into dinner, I walk behind her; during the day I sit with her ladies, and she treats me with effortless disdain, for she believes I am a woman who wasted the currency of her youth and beauty by throwing it away for love.

"Can you imagine being a royal duchess and lowering yourself to marry a squire of your household?" I catch the hiss of her whisper to one of her ladies as I sew in her rooms. "What woman would do such a thing?"

I look up. "A woman who saw the finest of men, Your Grace," I reply. "And I have no regrets, and I have no doubts about my husband, who returns love with love and loyalty with faithfulness."

This is a hit at her, for as a mistress turned wife, she is always fearfully on the lookout for another mistress who might try to repeat the trick she played on the countess, who was her friend.

"It's not a choice I would make," she says more mildly. "Not a choice that a noble-woman, thinking of the good of her family, would ever make."

I bow my head. "I know it," I remark. "But I was not thinking of my family at the time. I was thinking of myself."

On Midsummer Eve she makes an entry into London, accompanied by the lords and nobles of her special favor, as grand as if she were a visiting princess. As a lady of the court I follow in her train and so hear, as the procession winds through the streets, the less flattering remarks from the citizens of London. I have loved the Londoners since my own state entry into the City and I know them to be people easily charmed by a smile, and easily offended by any sign of vanity. The duchess's great train makes them laugh at her, though they doff their caps as she goes by and then hide their smiling faces with them. But once she has gone by, they raise a cheer for me. They like the fact that I married an Englishman for love; the women at the windows blow kisses at my husband, who is famous for his good looks, and the men at the crossroads call out bawdy remarks to me, the pretty duchess, and say that if I like an Englishman so much I might try a Londoner if I fancy a change.

The citizens of London are not the only people to dislike Duchess Eleanor. Cardinal Beaufort is no great friend, and he is a dangerous man to have as an enemy. She does not care that she offends him; she is married to the heir to the throne and he can do nothing to change that. Indeed, I think she is courting trouble with him, wanting to force a challenge to decide once and for all who rules the king. The kingdom is dividing into those who favor the duke and those who favor the cardinal; matters are going to come to a head. In this triumphal progress into London the duchess is staking her claim.

The cardinal's reply comes swiftly. That very next night, when Richard and I are dining at her table in the King's Head in Cheap, her chamberlain comes in and whispers in her ear. I see her go pale; she looks at me as if she would say something, and then she waves away her dinner, rises to her feet without a word to anyone, and goes out. The rest of us look from one to another, her lady-in-waiting stands up to follow her and then hesitates. Richard, seated among the gentlemen, nods at me to stay seated and quietly leaves the room. He is gone only a few moments, and the shocked silence has turned into a buzz of speculation by the time he comes back in, smiles at each of my neighbors as if to excuse us, takes my hand, and leads me from the room.

Outside he throws his cloak over my shoulders. "We're going back to Westminster," he says. "We don't want to be seen with the duchess anymore."

"What's happened?" I ask, clutching at the laces of the cloak as he hurries me down the streets. We jump over the foul ditch in the center of the lane, and he helps me down the slippery stairs to the river. A waiting wherry boat comes to his whistle, and he helps me into the prow. "Cast off," he says over his shoulder. "Westminster Stairs."

"What is happening?" I whisper.

He leans towards me so that not even the boatman, pulling on his oars, can hear. "The duchess's clerk and her chaplain have been arrested."

"What for?"

"Conjuring, or astronomy, divining or something. I could only get a rumor, enough to tell me that I want you right out of this."

"Me?"

"She's a reader of alchemy books; her husband employs physicians; she's said to have seduced him with love potions; she mixes with men of learning, scholarship, and magic, and she's a royal duchess. Does this

225

sound like anyone you know?"

"Me?" I shiver as the oars dip quietly in the cold waters and the boatman pulls towards the stairs.

"You," Richard says quietly. "Have you ever met Roger Bolingbroke, a scholar of Oxford? Serves in her household."

I think for a moment. "My lord knew him, didn't he? Didn't he come to Penshurst one time? Didn't he bring a shield chart and show my lord the art of geomancy?"

The boat nudges against the Westminster Palace stairs, and my husband takes my hand and helps me up the wooden steps to the pier. A servant comes forwards with a torch and lights our way through the gardens to the river entrance.

"He's been arrested," Richard says.

"What for?"

"I don't know. I'll leave you in our rooms, and then I'll go and see what I can find out."

I pause under the archway of the entrance, and I take his cold hands in mine. "What do you fear?"

"Nothing yet," he says unconvincingly, then he takes my arm and guides me into the palace.

Richard comes in at night and tells me that nobody seems to know what is happening. Three of the duchess's household have been arrested: men whom I know, men whom I

226

greet daily. The scholar Roger Bolingbroke, who came to visit us at Penshurst; and the duchess's chaplain, who has served the Mass before me a dozen times; and one of the canons at St. Stephen's Chapel in this very palace. They are accused of drawing up a horoscope chart for Eleanor. The chart has been found, and they say that it foretells the death of the young king and her inheritance of the throne.

"Ever seen a chart for the king?" my husband asks me tersely. "He has left the palace for Sheen, with nobody but the closest men of his council. We are ordered to stay here. We are all under suspicion. He hates this sort of thing; it terrifies him. His council will come here, and there will be questions. They might call on us. My lord Bedford never showed you a chart for the king, did he?"

"You know he drew up charts for everyone," I say quietly. "You remember the machine that hung above the plan of France which showed the positions of stars? He used it to show the stars at someone's birth. He drew up a chart for me. He drew up his own. Probably one for you. Certainly, he will have drawn up a chart for the king."

"And where are all the charts?" my husband asks tightly. "Where are they now?"

"I gave them to the Duke of Gloucester." Quietly, the horror of this dawns on me. "Oh, Richard! All the charts and the maps I gave to Duke Humphrey. He said he had an interest. I only kept the books, the ones we have at home. My lord left the books to me, the equipment and the machines I gave to the duke." I can taste blood in my mouth, and I realize that I have peeled the skin from my lip. I put my finger to where the raw skin is stinging. "Are you thinking that the duchess might have taken the king's chart? Might she have used it? Will they link me to the charges since I gave her husband the king's chart?"

"Perhaps," is all he says.

We wait. The summer sun burns down on the city and there are reports of plague in the poor areas, near the stinking river. It is unbearably hot. I want to go home to Grafton and my children, but the king has commanded that everyone must stay at court. No one can leave London, it is like bringing a stewpot to the boil. As the hot air presses on the city like a lid on a cauldron, the king waits, trembling with distress, for his council to unravel the plot against him. He is a young man who cannot tolerate opposition, it strikes at his very sense of himself. He has been brought up by courtiers and flatterers; he cannot bear the thought that someone does not love him. To think that someone might use the dark arts against him fills him with a terror that he cannot admit. The people around him are afraid for him, and for themselves. Nobody knows what a scholar like Roger Bolingbroke could do if he was minded to cause harm. And if the duchess has put him in league with other skilled men, they may have forged a conspiracy against the king to do him deadly harm. What if even now some secret horror is working its way through his veins? What if he shatters like a glass or melts like wax?

The duchess appears at the high table in the Palace of Westminster, seated alone, her face bright and smiling, her air of confidence unshaken. In the airless hall, where the smell of the meat from the kitchens wafts in like a hot breath, she is cool and untroubled. Her husband is at the king's side in Sheen, trying to reassure the young man, trying to counter anything that his uncle the cardinal says, swearing that the young king is beloved, beloved of everyone, vowing on his life that he has never seen a horoscope for the king, his interest in alchemy is merely in the king's service, the herb bed at Penshurst was already planted under the signs of the stars when they got there. He does not know who planted it, perhaps the former owner? I sit with the ladies in the duchess's rooms and sew shirts for the poor and say nothing, not even when the duchess suddenly laughs at random and declares that she does not know why the king delays so long at Sheen Palace, surely he should come to London, and then we could all go on progress to the country and get out of this heat.

"I believe he is coming tonight," I volunteer.

She glances out of the window. "He should have come earlier," she says. "Now he'll be caught in the rain. There's going to be such a storm!"

A scud of sudden rain makes the women cry out; the sky is black as a crow over London, and there is a rumble of thunder. The window rattles in the rising wind, and then it is flung open by a gust of icy wind. Someone screams as the frame bangs, and I rise up and go to the window, catch the flying latch, and draw it shut. I flinch back from the crack of lightning over the city. A storm is rumbling in, over the king's route, and within moments there is the rattle of hail against the window, like someone flinging pebbles, and a woman turns her pale face to the duchess and cries, "A storm over the king! You said that there would be a storm over the king."

The duchess is hardly listening; she is watching me fighting with the wind at the window, and then the words — the accusation — sinks into her awareness, and she looks at the woman — Elizabeth Flyte — and says, "Oh, don't be so ridiculous. I was looking at the sky. Anyone could see there was going to be a storm."

Elizabeth gets up from her stool, dips a curtsey, and says, "Excuse me, my lady . . ."

"Where are you going?"

"Excuse me, my lady . . ."

"You can't leave without permission," the duchess says harshly. But the woman has tipped over her stool in her hurry to get to the door. Two other women rise too, uncertain whether to run or stay.

"Sit down! Sit down!" the duchess shrieks. "I order it!"

Elizabeth tears open the door and flings herself out of the room, while the other women sink to their stools, and one quickly crosses herself. A flash of lightning suddenly makes the scene look bleak and cold. Eleanor the duchess turns to me, her face haggard and white. "For God's sake, I just looked at the sky and saw that there was going to be a storm. There is no need for all this. I just saw the rain coming, that's all."

"I know," I say. "I know that's all."

Within half an hour the palace is barring its doors and windows and calling it a witch's wind that blows death down with rain. Within a day the young king has announced that his aunt the duchess may not come into his presence. The Oxford scholar, the friend of my first husband who came to visit us at Penshurst, is questioned by the council and confesses to heresy and magic. They put him on show, like a bear to be baited. Poor Roger Bolingbroke, a scholar for all his life, a man of learning, with a great love for the mysteries of the world and the stars, is put on a stage, like a scaffold, at St. Paul's Cross in London, while a sermon is preached against him and against all witches and warlocks, necromancers and heretics who threaten the king's life and his peace, who crowd into his festering city, who seek to enter his ports, who hide themselves in the country villages and do acts of malice, small and great. It is declared that there are thousands of evil men and women, conjuring with black arts to harm the king: herbalists, wise women, liars, heretics, murderers. The king knows they are out there, plotting against him in their malevolent thousands. Now he believes he has found a plot at the heart of his court, at the heart of his dangerously ambitious family.

We all parade around Bolingbroke, circling him and staring at his shame as if he were an animal brought back from the coast of Africa, some new sort of beast. He keeps his eyes down so that he cannot see the avid faces and need not recognize his former friends. The man who had spent his life in study, thinking about the harmonious nature of the world, sits on a painted chair wearing a paper crown, surrounded by his equipment and his books as if he were a Fool. They have his geomancy board laid on the ground before his feet, and a set of candles specially carved.

They have some charts showing the positions of the planets, and the horoscope that they say he drew up for the duchess, at her request. They have a little model of the earth and the planets moving around it. They have brass molds for casting figures, a still for making liquids, and the wax trays used for drawing the perfume of flowers. Worst of all, at his feet is a horrible little creature of wax, like a miscarried rabbit.

I shrink back when I see it, and Richard puts a strong arm around my waist. "Don't look at it," he advises me.

I look away. "What was it?"

"It was a wax image of the king. It is supposed to have a little crown on its head, and that golden thread is the scepter and the little bead is the orb."

The face is distorted, the feet are formless. I can see the outline of the cape and the dots to show the markings of ermine, but the head is almost melted away. "What have they done to it?"

"They heated it before a fire so that it would melt and run away. It would make the king's strength flow from him, too. They meant to destroy him as the image melted away."

I shudder. "Can't we go now?"

"No," he says. "We have to be here to show our revulsion at these crimes."

"I am revolted. I am so revolted I want to go."

"Keep your head up. Keep walking. You, of all people, have to be seen to be an enemy of this sort of work."

"Me of all people?" I fire up. "This is so disgusting it makes me sick."

"They are saying that the Duchess Eleanor got her husband the duke to marry her with a love potion so that he could not resist her. They are saying you did the same when you were a girl and my lord duke was a man brokenhearted at the loss of his wife, Anne."

I shudder, averting my eyes from the melted wax poppet. "Richard . . ."

"I shall keep you safe," he swears. "You are my lady and my love. I shall keep you safe, Jacquetta. You will never look for me and find me gone."

We come back from the shaming of Bolingbroke to find the duchess's rooms empty, the door thrown open to her privy chamber, her clothes chests overturned, her cupboards ransacked, her jewelry boxes missing, and the woman vanished.

"Where is the duchess?" my husband demands of her maid-in-waiting.

She shakes her head; she is crying unstoppably. "Gone."

"Gone where?"

"Gone," is all she can say.

"God save us, the child is an idiot," Richard snaps. "You ask her."

I take her by the shoulders. "Ellie, tell me, did they arrest Her Grace?"

She dips a curtsey. "She ran, Your Grace. She's run into sanctuary. She says they will kill her to punish her husband; she says they will destroy him through her. She says it is a wicked plot against him that is going to be the ruin of her. She says Cardinal Beaufort will tear them both down."

I turn to my husband. "Sanctuary?"

His face is grim. "Yes, but she is mistaken. That won't save her."

"They can't say she is a witch if she is hiding on holy ground and claiming the safety of the church."

"Then they'll accuse her of being a heretic," he says. "A heretic can't be protected by the church. So if she's claimed sanctuary, they'll charge her with heresy; it's the only way to get her out. Before this they might have charged her with forecasting. Now they'll accuse her of heresy. And heresy is a worse crime than forecasting. She's put herself in a worse place."

"The law of men always puts women in a bad place!" I flare up in anger.

Richard says nothing.

"Should we go away?" I ask him very quietly. "Can we go home to Grafton?" I look around the wreckage of the room. "I don't feel safe here. Can we go?"

He grimaces. "We can't go now. It looks like guilt if we go, just as she looks as if she admits guilt by hiding in sanctuary. I think we are better off staying here. At least we can get a ship to Flanders from here, if we need to."

"I can't leave the children!"

He pays no attention. "I wish to God your father was still alive; you could have gone on a visit to him." He squeezes my hand. "You stay here. I shall go and see William de la Pole, the Earl of Suffolk. He'll tell me what's going on in the council."

"And what shall I do?"

"Wait here," he says grimly. "Open these rooms and treat them like your own. Behave as if nothing were wrong. You are the first lady of the kingdom now, the only royal duchess left. Order the ladies to tidy the place up, and then have them sew with you; get someone to read from the Bible. Go to chapel this evening. Parade your innocence."

"But I am innocent," I say.

His face is dark. "I don't doubt that she will say the same."

She does not say the same. They bring Roger Bolingbroke before her with the horoscope that she commanded he cast for her, with the magical instruments that were the tools of his trade as an explorer of the unknown

236

realms, with the misshapen wax that they say is a melted image of the king, and she confesses to witchcraft and offenses against the Church. She admits that she has "long used witchcraft with the Witch of Eye" and then they tell her that the Witch of Eye has been under arrest since the night of the witch's wind.

"Who is the Witch of Eye?" I ask Richard in a hushed whisper, late at night with the curtains of the bed drawn around us.

"Margery Jourdemayne," he says, his brow knitted with worry. "Some practicing witch who was taken up for her crimes once before now. Comes from the village of Eye. She is known to the church as a witch, known to everyone as a witch."

I gasp in horror.

He looks at me. "For the love of God, tell me that you don't know her."

"Not as a witch."

He closes his eyes briefly in horror. "What do you know of her?"

"I never did anything with her but study the use of herbs, as my lord commanded: I swear to you, and I would swear to the court. I never did anything with her but study the use of herbs, and she did nothing at Penshurst but plan the herb garden with me, and tell me when the herbs should be cut and when they should be sown. I didn't know she was a witch."

"Did my lord command you to see her?"

"Yes, yes."

"Do you have that under his seal? Did he write the order?"

I shake my head. "He just sent her to me. And you saw her. That time in the stable yard when you came with the message from Luxembourg, and she was leaving with the wagon."

Richard clenches his hands into fists. "I can swear that my lord commanded that she serve you . . . but this isn't good, it's not good. But perhaps we can glide over this. Perhaps nobody will bring it up, if it was just making a herb bed. At least you never consulted her. You have never ordered her to attend you . . ."

I glance away.

He groans. "No. Oh no. Tell me, Jacquetta."

"I took a tincture to prevent a child. You knew about that."

"The herbs? That was her recipe?"

I nod.

"You told nobody?"

"No one but you."

"Then nobody will know. Anything else she made for you?"

"Later . . . a drink to get a child."

He checks as he realizes that this was the conception of our daughter, Elizabeth, the baby who forced him into marriage. "Good God, Jacquetta . . ." He throws back the covers and gets out of bed, pulls back the curtain, and strides to the fireside. It is the first time he has ever been angry with me. He thumps the post of the bed with his fist, as if he wishes he could fight the world. I sit up, gather the covers to my shoulders, and feel my heart hammer with dread at his rage.

"I wanted a child, and I wanted you," I say unsteadily. "I loved you, and I wanted us to be married. But I would not have cast a spell for it. I used herbs, not witchcraft."

He rubs his head, making his hair stand on end, as if these distinctions are beyond him. "You made our child with a witch's potion? Our daughter Elizabeth?"

"Herbs," I say steadily. "Herbs from a herbalist. Why not?"

He casts a furious look at me. "Because I don't want a child brought to life by a handful of herbs from some old witch!"

"She is not some old witch, she is a good woman, and we have a beautiful child. You are as bad as this witch hunt with your fears. I took herbs to help me to be fertile. We made a beautiful child. Don't you ill-wish us now!"

"For God's sake." He raises his voice. "I am afraid of nothing but you being mixed up with the most notorious witch in England, who has been trying to kill our king!"

"She is not! She would not!" I shout back at him. "She would not!"

"She is accused."

"Not by me!"

"By the lord chief justice! And if they look for her associates, they will find you, another royal duchess, another woman who dabbles in the unknown, another woman who can call up a storm or capture a unicorn."

"I am not! I am not!" I burst into tears. "You know I am not. You know I do nothing. Don't say such things, Richard. Don't you accuse me. You of all people!"

He loses his anger at my tears and comes quickly across the room, sits beside me, and gathers me against his shoulder. "I don't accuse you, my love. I know. I know you would never do anything to harm anyone. Hush, I am sorry. And you are not to blame."

"I can't help it that I foresee."

"I know you can't help it."

"And you of all people know that my lord put me before the scrying mirror day after day and all I could see was a battle in snow and a queen . . . a queen . . . with horseshoes reversed. He said it was useless. He said I could not foresee for him. I failed him. I failed him."

"I know. I know you don't conjure. Be still, my love."

"I did take herbs to get Elizabeth, but that was all. I would never conjure a child. Never."

"I know, my love. Be still."

I am silent, and as I dry my eyes on the sheet, he asks me, "Jacquetta, does anyone know of this recipe that she gave you but you and her? Did anyone see her with you at Penshurst? Any of the court know that she was there?"

"No. Just servants, and her boy."

"Then we will have to pray that she keeps her mouth shut about you, even if they take her to the stake."

"The stake?" I ask stupidly.

He nods in silence and then gets back into bed beside me. Together, we watch the fire burning down in the grate. "They will burn her for a witch," he says flatly. "And the duchess too."

WESTMINSTER PALACE, LONDON, OCTOBER 1441

The duchess and the witch come before the court charged together with both witchcraft and treason. The duchess claims that she only visited Mrs. Jourdemayne for herbs for fertility, and the herbalist gave her a drink and said that it would make her conceive a child. I sit at the back of the room behind the avid spectators and know that I did exactly the same.

Margery has been charged with witchcraft before, and so they ask her why she continued to practice her arts: the herbs, the incantations, the foreseeing. She looks at the Archbishop of Canterbury, Henry Chichele, as if he might understand her. "If you have eyes, you can't help but see," she says. "The herbs grow for me, the veil sometimes parts for me. It is a gift, I thought it was given by God."

He gestures at the wax doll that sits before him on the desk. "This is a most unholy curse, an attempted murder of an anointed king. How could it come from God?"

"It was a poppet to make a child," she says wearily. "It was a poppet in the shape of a great lord. See his ermine and his sword. It was a little doll to make a beautiful and talented child who would be an ornament to his country and a treasure to his family."

Without thinking, my hand steals to my belly, where a new baby is being made who I hope will be an ornament and a treasure.

Mrs. Jourdemayne looks at the archbishop. "You are frightening yourselves with a poppet," she says rudely. "Do you great men have nothing better to do?"

The archbishop shakes his head. "Silence," he orders.

They have all decided already that this was an image of the king, made for melting. They have all decided that she is a witch, a brand for the burning. Once more, I am watching the most powerful men in the kingdom bring their power to bear on a woman who has done nothing worse than live to the beat of her own heart, see with her own eyes; but this is not their tempo nor their vision, and they cannot tolerate any other.

They kill her for it. They take her to Smithfield, the meat market where the innocent cattle of the counties around London walk in to be butchered, and like an obedient lamb, trustingly herded into the bloodstained pen, she goes speechless to the stake; they light

243

the fire beneath her bare feet, and she dies in agony. Roger Bolingbroke, who confessed and recanted, finds no mercy either. They hang him on the public gallows, and as he is kicking in the air, whooping for breath, the executioner catches his feet and cuts the rope — restoring him to croaking life, lays him on a hurdle to revive him; but then slices open his belly, pulls out his entrails so that he can see his pulsing heart, his quivering stomach spilling out with his blood, and then they hack him into quarters, his legs from his spine, his arms from his chest, and they send his head with its horrified glare to be set on a spike on London Bridge for the ravens to peck out his weeping eyes. Thomas Southwell, my one-time confessor, the canon of St. Stephen's Chapel, dies of sorrow in the Tower of London. Richard says that his friends smuggled poison to him, to spare him the agony that Bolingbroke endured. The duchess's clerk, John Home, is sent to prison, awaiting pardon. And the proud duchess is forced to do public penance.

The woman who paraded into London in cloth of gold with the nobility of the kingdom in her train is stripped to her linen shift and sent out shoeless with a lighted taper to walk around Westminster as the people jeer and point at her as someone who was the first lady of the kingdom and is now humbled to dirt. I watch from the steps of the great gate of Westminster Palace as she walks by, her gaze fixed on the cold stones beneath her flinching bare feet. She does not look up to see me, or the women who once scrambled to serve her, but are now laughing and pointing; she does not raise her head, and her beautiful dark hair tumbles over her face like a veil to hide her shame. The most powerful men of the kingdom have dragged a duchess down and sent her out to be a marvel to the common people of London. They are so deeply afraid of her that they took the risk to dishonor their own. They are so anxious to save themselves that they thought they should throw her aside. Her husband, who is now generally known as the "good" Duke Humphrey, declares that he was seduced into marriage by her witchcraft; the marriage is instantly declared void. She, a royal duchess, the wife of the heir to the throne, is now a convicted witch in her petticoat; no man will give her his name, and they will keep her in prison for the rest of her life.

I think of the illusion that I saw as we came off the barge at Greenwich, that she was followed by a black dog, a fighting dog, a black mastiff, and the smell that lingered around her despite the perfume and the perfectly washed linen, and I think that the black dog will follow her and will run up and down the stairs of Peel Castle on the Isle of Man, as

she waits, long, long years, for her release
into death.

GRAFTON, NORTHAMPTONSHIRE, WINTER 1441–1444

As soon as we can be excused from court, Richard and I go back home, to Grafton. The terror of the court is only stoked by the death of the witch, the disgrace of the duchess, and the mood of witch taking. Apprehension of the unknown and fear of the hours of darkness infects all of London. Everyone who has been studying the stars for years, reading books, or testing metal finds a reason to leave for the country, and Richard thinks it is safer for us if I — with my perilous ancestry — am far away from court.

At Grafton there is much work to do. The death of Richard's father means that Richard inherits the land and the responsibilities of being the lord of the small village and the keeper of the peace. I too have work to do. The cradle is polished again and the swaddling bands laundered and aired. "I think this will be another son," I say to my husband.

"I don't mind," he says. "As long as the baby is well and strong and you rise up from childbed as joyfully as you lie down in it."

"I shall rise up with a son," I say certainly. "And he will be an ornament to his country and a treasure to his family."

He smiles and taps me on the nose. "You are a funny little thing. What d'you mean?"

"And we shall call him Anthony," I continue.

"For the saint?" my husband asks. "Why him?"

"Oh, because he went to the river to preach," I say. "I like the thought of honoring a saint who preached to the fishes, and they put their little heads out of the water to hear him, and the mermaids said 'Amen.' "

The next year after Anthony comes another girl, whom we name Mary, and after her, another girl. "Jacquetta," my husband declares. "She's to be named Jacquetta, the most beautiful name for the most beautiful woman." We are hanging over the little wooden cradle while the baby sleeps, her face turned to one side, her perfect eyelashes closed on her rosy cheek. Her eyelids flicker, she is dreaming. I wonder what a baby dreams. Do they know that they are to come to the parents that we are? Are they prepared for the world we are making? Richard slides his arm around my waist. "And though we love her, we have to leave her for just a little while."

"Hmm?" I am absorbed in the clenching of

her tiny fist.

"We have to leave her, for only a little while."

Now he has my attention. I turn towards him in his grip. "How so?"

"We are to go to France with a great party to fetch home the king's bride."

"It has been decided?" The marriage of Henry has been a long time coming. My own first husband, Lord John, was picking out French princesses for him when I was a new bride. "At last?"

"You have missed all the gossip while you were in confinement, but yes, it is decided at last. And she is a kinswoman to you."

"Margaret!" I guess at once. "Margaret of Anjou."

He kisses me as a reward. "Very clever, and since your sister is married to her uncle, you and I are to go and fetch her from France."

At once I look towards my sleeping baby.

"I know you don't want to leave her," he says tenderly. "But we will do our duty for Henry, fetch the bride, bring her home, and then we will come back here. I am summoned by the king to serve him. I have to go."

"You are asking me to leave a nursery with six babies," I say. "How can I go?"

"I know," he says gently. "But you have to do your duty too. You are an English duchess and my wife; and the head of our house is asking you to fetch his bride. When they marry, it will bring peace to England and France — the one thing my lord wanted when he died. We have to go, my love. You know that. It is a service to the king and to him — your first husband and my good lord — it is a service to him too."

Nancy, France, Spring 1445

I am not the only unenthusiastic member of the marriage party. Our leader, William de la Pole, the Earl of Suffolk, is said to be so mistrustful of the French, and so unimpressed with the fortune that Margaret of Anjou brings, that, before he left England to start the negotiations last year, he had the king swear that nobody should ever blame him for bringing the French princess to England. Cardinal Beaufort, who now rules everything, may see this as the way to lasting peace; but Duke Humphrey of Gloucester swears that the Valois king will just buy time with this marriage and then come against our lands in France. I know my late husband would have feared above everything else that this is a new ruse by the French to make us hand over Anjou and Maine to René of Anjou: the new queen's father. Almost everyone left behind in England, while we spend a fortune on a progress to France, regards the deal that we are making as utterly uncertain

251

to bring peace, costly to make, and most likely to be to our disadvantage.

The bride is brought by her mother from Anjou, and they say that she too is far from enthusiastic for a marriage that will put her in the bed of the king who has been an enemy of France ever since she was a baby.

"You're to go and see her first, before everyone," my husband tells me. I am standing by the window of the castle, looking down into the stable yard. The horses of the Anjou party, a sorry herd of hacks, are being brushed down and watered and led into their stables.

"Me? Why me?"

"Her mother knows your mother; they think that you can be her friend. You made much the same journey that she faces, from a Luxembourg castle to the royalty of England. They want you to meet her ahead of the rest of us so that you can introduce her to her new court."

"I don't know that I'll be any help," I say, turning to follow him.

"You'll speak the same language, and that will be something," he says. "She's even younger than you were when the duke married you. She's only fifteen. She'll need a friend at court."

He takes me to the double doors of the best apartment and steps to one side. The guards swing open the doors and bellow, "The

Dowager Duchess of Bedford!" as I go in.

The first thing that strikes me is that she is tiny, like a pretty doll. Her hair is a real bronze, a red-gold, and her eyes are gray-blue. She wears a gown of slate blue and a headdress perched far back on her head to show her exquisitely pretty face and her perfectly pale complexion. Her gown is scattered with embroidered marguerites — the daisies that are her emblem. The pout of her mouth suggests a spoiled child, but as she hears my name, she turns quickly, and the brightness of her smile is endearing.

"Ah! *Madame la duchesse!*" she exclaims in French, and runs forwards and kisses me as if we are old friends. "I am so glad you have come to see me."

I curtsey. "I am glad to meet you, Your Grace."

"And this is my mama. I was so happy when they told me you would come with the Earl of Suffolk to fetch me, for I thought you would tell me how I am to behave and everything. For you were married to the duke when you were only a little older than I am now? And fifteen is very young to marry, is it not?"

I smile at this nervous ripple of talk.

"Hush," her mother says. "The duchess will think you are a chatterbox."

"It is just that there are so many English people come to see me, and I find it so hard

253

to remember names. And their names are so hard to say!"

I laugh. "I could not even say the name of my house at first," I said. "It is a hard language to learn. But I am sure you will learn it. And everyone speaks French, and everyone is eager to meet you and to be your friend. We all want you to be happy."

Her lower lip quivers, but she speaks bravely enough. "Oh, I have started already, and I can say the Earl of Suffolk, and Cardinal Bouffé."

"Bouffé?" I query.

"Is that not right?"

"Beaufort!" I identify. "They say it Bowfutt."

She laughs and spreads out her hands. "You see! You will teach me how to say these words, and you will teach me how the English ladies dress. Will I have to wear great boots all the time?"

"Boots, Your Grace?"

"For the mud?"

I laugh. "Ah, they have been teasing you. England does get very muddy, especially in the winter, but the weather is no worse than — say — Paris. I prefer London to Paris, and I am very happy in England now."

She slips her hand in mine. "And you will stand by me and tell me everyone's name, won't you? And how to say everything?"

"I will," I promise her, and I feel the grip of

her little hand tighten as she turns to her mother and says: "You had better tell them they can come in. I had better meet them all now."

She is a delightful little princess, perfect in every detail, except that her father, though called a king, cannot conquer his many kingdoms, and never will. She has no dowry, and though she says she brings us the islands of Minorca and Majorca, we all know she will inherit nothing. Everything she requires for the wedding and the journey has been paid for by the Treasury of England — and there is nothing left in the Treasury of England. She is exquisitely beautiful, but so are many girls of fifteen. She is dearly loved by the French court, the declared favorite of her uncle, the Valois king Charles VII; yet she is not a princess of the House of Valois but only of Anjou. He is not offering one of his own daughters in marriage to the English, but only a niece. In short, most of the English who are sent to fetch her think that we have been cheated: in the peace treaty, in the dower, and in the little princess herself. This is not a good start to a marriage.

She is to be married in the chapel of St. George in the palace at Tours, where the Earl of Suffolk will represent the king and stand beside her before the altar, and take her little hand from her father and the French king. Her sister Yolande is to be married at the same time. I know she is nervous, but I am surprised to be summoned to her rooms two hours before the wedding and find myself shown alone into her bedroom; no other attendants are present. She is dressed in her wedding gown of white satin embroidered with marguerite daisies of silver and gold thread, but her hair is still plaited, and she is barefoot.

"My mother says you have a gift," she says, speaking rapidly in French without any preamble. "She says all the ladies of your house have the gift of foresight."

I curtsey, but I am apprehensive. "They say so, Your Grace, but I take all my hopes and fears to my priest and to God. I don't believe it is given to mortal men to know the future and certainly not to women."

She makes a quick exclamation and jumps onto the bed, careless of the priceless gown. "I want you to draw my cards for me; I want to know what the future holds." She pats the bed beside her, inviting me to sit.

I do not respond to the invitation. "Surely your mother did not suggest this?"

"No, she knows nothing of it — it is quite my own idea. Come, sit beside me."

"I cannot," I say, not moving. "The court of England does not like prophesying or casting horoscopes. They certainly won't like the cards."

"The court of England will never know," she says. "It will be just you and me."

I shake my head. "I dare not."

She looks stubborn. "If I command it, you will have to. You are my lady-in-waiting; you have to do what I say."

I hesitate. If William de la Pole, the Earl of Suffolk, hears that I have upset the princess, there will be serious trouble. "Of course, my only wish is to obey you, Your Grace. But what if you ask me to do something that your husband, our king, would not like? You must see that puts me in a difficult position. What am I to do then?"

"Oh then, you must do as I ask," she says simply. "Because the king will never know; nobody will ever know. But I will have my way in this. I can insist. I do insist."

I kneel and bow my head, privately cursing her for a spoiled child. "Your Grace, excuse me, I cannot."

She pauses. "All right, then I won't get married," she declares. "You can go out and tell them that you have refused to prepare me for my wedding, and so I will not marry. The wedding is off."

I look up, smiling, but she is perfectly serious.

"I mean it," she says. "You show me the cards, or I won't marry the king. I insist on seeing my future; I have to know that this is the right thing to do. I won't go ahead without seeing what the future holds for me."

"I don't have any cards," I say.

With a smile she lifts her pillow and puts a pack of beautifully colored cards in my hand. "Do it," she says simply. "It is my order."

I shuffle the pictures gently. I wonder what will happen if she draws a bad card. Is she such a stubborn fool as to call off the wedding? I run through the arcana in my mind and wonder if I can hide those that show bad prospects. "What if the cards are not good?" I ask. "What happens then?"

She puts her hand on mine. "The wedding will go ahead, and I will never tell anyone that you drew the cards for me," she promises. "But I will know in advance that I am going into danger, and what sort of danger it is. I will know to be on my guard. I want to know what is ahead of me. If I am going to die in childbirth within the year, I want to know. If my father and my husband are going to go to war against each other, I want to know. If the English lords who seem to agree on nothing are going to tear each other apart, I want to know."

"All right," I say. I can see no way of getting out of it. "But I am not doing a full spread." This at least cuts down the possibility of a series of pessimistic prophecies. "I will do just one card. You take the cards and shuffle them."

Her little hands stretch around the thick cards, she interleaves them, and then puts them down.

"And cut."

She cuts them and then puts the deck together. I spread them out before her in a fan, their faces down, their beautifully painted backs gleaming on the woolen covers of the bed. "Choose one," I say. "One will tell you enough."

Margaret's red-gold hair falls forwards, and she leans across, her pretty face very grave, trailing her finger along the pack, and then takes a card and holds it, without looking at it, to her heart.

"Now what?"

I sweep the untouched cards into a pile and then say to Margaret, "Show it."

She puts it faceup.

It could have been an awful lot worse.

It is the card Joan the maid saw in my hands, all those years ago: the Wheel of Fortune.

La Roue de Fortune," she reads. "Is that good? Is that very good?"

The card shows a wheel with two beasts balanced on either side of it, one climbing up, the other tumbling down as the wheel turns. The handle for the wheel is extended beyond the card so one cannot see who is turning it; perhaps it is spinning at random.

Seated at the very top of the card is a funny little blue animal, crowned and holding a sword. My great-aunt told me this little animal shows that it is possible to watch the wheel turn, and feel neither pride nor regret. One can stand above it and see one's own life both rise and fall with the real indifference that comes from true greatness of spirit. One can look at one's own ambition as if it were all a masque of vanities, a dance for fools. It could not be a more unlikely card for Margaret: she is not at all a girl of indifference.

"It's good and bad," I say. "It's a kind of warning that you can rise very high and fall very low. It says that fortune's wheel can take you, by no merit of your own, by no grace of yours, very high indeed. And then it can throw you down very low."

"So how do I rise again?" she asks me, as if I am some old hedgerow witch who tells fortunes for a groat.

"The whole point is that you can't," I say impatiently. "The whole point is that you can't make it happen. The whole point is that you cannot make your own fate. You are on fortune's wheel just like this poor monkey animal in the smart livery who is going to fall down; he can't help himself. You can't help yourself."

She makes a sulky little face. "That's not much of a foretelling," she says. "And anyway, doesn't the other animal rise up? This little cat thing? Maybe I am the cat thing and I am going to rise and rise."

"Maybe," I say. "But then you go over the top of the wheel and are falling down again. You are supposed to learn to bear it, whichever happens, as if they were both the same."

She looks blank. "But they are not the same. Victory and defeat are not the same. I only want victory."

I think of Joan and the sign she made with her forefinger, the circle in the air that meant that everything was dust. I make the sign to Margaret. "The Wheel of Fortune," I say. "It is your card: you drew it. You insisted on a reading, and this is the card that you got. It tells us that we all only want victory. We all want to triumph. But we all have to learn to endure what comes. We have to learn to treat misfortune and great fortune with indifference. That is wisdom." I look at her pretty, downcast face, and see she has little interest in wisdom. "But perhaps you will be lucky."

TITCHFIELD ABBEY, HAMPSHIRE, SUMMER 1445

At first she is lucky. She meets the king, and they like each other on sight — why would they not? He is a handsome boyish man of twenty-three, still somehow fragile, with a delicacy inherited from his French mother, and she is a strong-willed beauty eight years his junior. The Earl of Suffolk, William de la Pole, escorting her to her new country and enchanted with her, predicts that they will make a good match: her fire and passion will be softened by his sweetness; he will learn determination and courage from her.

They are married at the abbey at Titchfield in a service that reflects the young king's quiet seriousness. I suspect that Margaret would have preferred something more showy and more grand, but there is no money for a great wedding, and anyway, the king said that the wedding should be between him, his bride, and God.

Disastrously, his fool of a confessor, Bishop Ayscough, performs the wedding and warns the serious young king that he should not succumb to lust. He warns him that he should go to the bride's bed only for the purpose of getting heirs to the throne, and not for their pleasure. The boy, who has been cautiously raised by men anxious to protect his innocence, takes the advice like a novice monk and stays away from her bed for a full week. Margaret is not a young woman to deal patiently with such a husband. She summons me to her room the morning after her wedding and drags me into a window bay. "He does not like me," she whispers urgently. "He got up from my bed as soon as everyone had left the room and spent half the night in prayer, and then he crept in beside me like a mouse and slept all the night without so much as touching me. I am as much a maid as ever I was; the wedding was for nothing."

I take her hands. "It will happen," I say. "You must be patient."

"How is the marriage to be binding if it is not consummated?" she demands.

"It will be consummated, he will do the act, Your Grace, and we should be glad that he is not forceful."

"Is he even a man?" she hisses scornfully, not glad at all.

"He is a man, he is your husband, and he is your king," I say. "It will happen. He will do it within the week." As long as it is not a saint's day, or a holy day, I think to myself, if he can confess straight after the deed. Not in the morning before Mass, never in daylight. He is indeed extremely pious. "And Your Grace, when he approaches you, you must accept him without comment, without complaint."

She tosses her head. "But I want to be loved. I have always been loved. I want my husband to love me with passion, like in a troubadour tale, like a knight."

"He does love you, he will love you. But he is not a lustful man."

The anger goes from her as quickly as it came, and the face she turns to me is puzzled. "Why would he not desire me on the first night, on our wedding night?"

I shrug. "Your Grace, he is a thoughtful young man, and very spiritual. He will come to you when he thinks the time is right, and then you must be kind to him."

"But who will be kind to me?" she asks pitifully.

I smile and pat her cheek as if she were my younger sister and not my queen. "We will all be kind to you," I promise. "And you will be happy."

LONDON,
SUMMER 1445–1448

Margaret is lucky in that she is young and beautiful, and the Londoners take to her on sight and cheer her coronation. She is lucky in that she is endearing — I am not the only one who comes to love her and watch for her safety. Around her little court she gathers a collection of people who adore her. Me, she keeps close, her dearest friend and confidante. She loves Alice, William de la Pole's wife, too, and the three of us are inseparable in these early years of her marriage, except for when I go to Grafton for my confinements, a new baby, John, and one who comes early and is especially small and precious on that account: Richard.

But she makes some mistakes, and they are grave ones. Her liking for William de la Pole leads her to insist that he be consulted in the king's councils, and he — already a great man — rises to even higher importance through her favor. The two of them speak against the king's uncle, Duke Humphrey of Gloucester, and they whip up suspicion against him so powerfully that he is accused of trying for the throne on his own account, treason against his own nephew. The shock is too great for the duke, and he dies before they can bring him to trial. At once there is a storm of gossip which declares that the good duke was murdered, and people point the finger of blame at William de la Pole. After the loss of this, his last uncle, the king leans yet more on his other advisors and consults the opinion of his young wife. This is a terrible choice. She is little more than a girl, she knows nothing about England, and in truth she knows nothing about anything.

The king's other favorite is Edmund Beaufort, the Duke of Somerset, and Margaret is dazzled by the dashing penniless duke who calls her cousin and kisses her on the mouth in greeting. He is the most handsome man at court, always beautifully dressed in velvet studded with jewels, always riding a big black horse, though they say he has not a penny in the world and is sworn up and down from his handsome dark head to his best leather soles to the moneylenders of London and Antwerp. He brings the queen little gifts, fairings that he picks up in the market, and they delight her, as he pins a little brooch to the hem of her dress, or offers her a piece of candied peel, popping it in her mouth as if she were a child. He speaks to her in rapid intimate French and tucks a blossom behind her ear. He teases her as if she were a pretty maid and not a queen, he brings musicians in, and dancers — the court is always merry when Edmund Beaufort is in attendance, and the king and queen command him to stay at court all the time.

Perhaps it would have been better if they had not done so. But the handsome young duke is ambitious, and he asks and gets the command of the English forces in Normandy, as if they were toy soldiers for his amusement. The young king and queen can refuse him nothing. They load all their favorites with offices and money, and the court becomes a henhouse of strutting jealousy.

We all do well out of this. They are prodigal with titles and posts, they give away their own lands, the places at court for free, the opportunities for trade and bribery, licenses to import, licenses to export. Crown lands, which are supposed to pay for the king's living throughout his reign, get thrust into greedy hands, in a helter-skelter of generosity. William de la Pole finds himself ennobled beyond his dreams, made into a duke, the first man without royal blood ever to take such a title. Edmund Beaufort gets a dukedom, too; it is a hiring fair of honors. The king and queen take it into their heads that Edmund Beaufort should be given a fortune to match his title, he should be given a

fortune to match the famously wealthy Richard, Duke of York, a royal kinsman. No —
better still — he should overmatch the great
Duke of York, and the young king and queen
say they will give him whatever it takes to do
so.

Even Richard and I are swept along on this
torrent of gifts. They give us a great London
house, and then my husband comes to me
and says, smiling, "Tell me, my darling, what
name d'you think I should have?"

"Name?" I ask, and then I realize what he
is saying. "Oh! Richard! Is the king to give
you a title as well?"

"I think it is more the favor of the queen to
you," he says. "But at any rate I am to be a
baron. I am to be awarded an order of nobility for great service to my country — or at
least, because the queen likes my wife. What
d'you think of that?"

I gasp. "Oh, I am so pleased. I am so very
pleased for you. And for our children, too!
We will be so very grand." I pause uncertainly.
"Can the king just make up titles like this?"

"The two of them think they can, and, what
is more dangerous: they do. Never was a
young couple with so little power and money
in more of a hurry to give it all away. And
they will drive the rest of the court mad.
Anyone whom she likes, or whom he trusts,
gets loaded with favors; but good men are
excluded. Richard, Duke of York, gets noth-

ing, not even a civil hearing. They say they won't have him in the council now, though he is known as a good man and the best advisor they could have. But he is ignored, and worse men than he are praised to the skies. I shall be made a baron for no better reason than you keep her company."

"And what name shall we have, my lord? You will be Sir Richard Woodville, Baron . . . what?"

He pauses for a moment. "Baron Grafton?" he asks.

"Baron Grafton," I repeat, listening to the sounds. Even after all these years in England I still have a strong accent. "I really can't say it."

"But I wondered if you would like a title which came from your family. One of your family names?"

I think for a moment. "I don't really want to remind everyone that I am a daughter of Luxembourg, that I am French," I say cautiously. "The mood is more and more against the French. I was telling the queen, only the other day, that she should speak English in public. I am an English dowager duchess, and I am a good Englishwoman now. Give me an English name and let our children have English titles."

"Water!" he exclaims. "For your ancestor."

I laugh. "You can't be Baron Water. But what about Baron Rivers?"

"Rivers . . ." He rolls the word over in his mouth. "That's fine. Rivers. It's a good English name, and yet it is a tribute to your family. Baron Rivers I shall be, and, please God, one day I shall be an earl."

"No, really, would they ever make you an earl? Would they give away so much?"

"My dear, I am afraid they would give away the kingdom itself. They are not careful monarchs, and they are advised by rogues."

I mention my husband's anxiety about their extravagance as tactfully as I can to the queen, but she tosses her head. "We have to keep our friends satisfied," she says to me. "We cannot rule the country without William de la Pole; he is the greatest man in the land. And Edmund Beaufort is in such debt! We have to help him."

"Richard, Duke of York?" I suggest as a man they should reward.

"We cannot hold France without Edmund Beaufort. He is the only man we could trust to hold our French lands, and to restore those lands that we should return to their true owner."

"Your Grace?" I am dumbfounded at the suggestion that we should restore our lands to the French, and she flushes, as guilty as a child. "To hold our lands," she corrects herself. "Edmund Beaufort is the only man we can trust."

"I think that Richard, Duke of York, is the only man to successfully hold French lands since my first husband, the Duke of Bedford," I observe.

She throws her hands in the air. "Perhaps, perhaps, but I can trust no one but Edmund Beaufort and William de la Pole. The king himself can neither take decisions nor lead an army. These men are everything to me. They are the father and" — she breaks off and blushes — "friend that I need. They both deserve the highest of honors, and we will give honors where they are due."

WESTMINSTER PALACE, LONDON, SUMMER 1449

I can tell at once that something terrible has happened. Richard comes into our private rooms and takes my hands, his face grim. "Jacquetta, you must be brave."

"Is it the children?" My first thought is always for them, and my hand goes to my belly, where another life is growing.

"No, thank God. It is my lord's legacy, the lands of Normandy."

I don't really have to ask him — I guess at once. "Have they been lost?"

He grimaces. "All but. Edmund Beaufort has offered the French almost all of Normandy, including Rouen, in return for his safety in Caen."

"Rouen," I say quietly. The grave of my first husband, John, Duke of Bedford, is there. I have property there.

"This is a bitter blow," Richard says. "And all of us who fought to keep the English lands in France, nearly a hundred years of long warfare, and so many lives lost — good

comrades and brothers —" He breaks off.
"Well, we will find it hard to forgive the loss."

Westminster Palace, London, Spring 1450

Richard was right. Nobody can forgive the loss. The Parliament turns on William de la Pole, and his new titles and his new honors cannot save him from the rage of the English as the men who had farmed and the soldiers who had fought in Normandy come home defeated and homeless, and complain bitterly, bitterly, at every market cross and crossroads, that they have been betrayed by their commanders who should have stood by them, as they had stood to arms for more than a hundred years.

In the streets the London traders call out to me as I ride by, "What would Lord John have thought of it, eh? What would your lord have said?" and I can do nothing more but shake my head. I feel with them — what did we fight for, what did we die for, if the lands we won are to be handed back as part of a treaty, as part of a marriage, on the whim of a king who never fought for them as we fought for them?

They blame it all on William de la Pole, since it is treason to speak against the king. And they call him to Parliament and accuse him of treason, extortion, and murder. They say that he has been planning to seize the throne and set up his little son John and his ward Margaret Beaufort as king and queen, claiming the throne in her right.

"What is going to happen?" I ask the queen, who is striding back and forth in her rooms, the long train of her gown swishing like the tail of an angry cat.

"I will not allow him to face the charges. He will not be demeaned by such charges. His Grace, the king, has saved him. He has ruled that he, the king, shall be judge and jury of his friend William."

I hesitate. After all, this is not my country, but I really don't think the king can just step in like this. "Your Grace, I think he cannot. A nobleman has to be tried by his peers. The House of Lords will have to examine him. The king may not intervene."

"I say that no good friend of mine will be questioned in public like that. It is an insult to him, it is an insult to me. I have demanded that we protect our friends, and the king agrees with me. William will not go before Parliament. He is coming to my rooms tonight, in secret."

"Your Grace, this is not the English way. You should not meet any man alone, and certainly not in secret."

"You will be there," she says. "So they can say nothing vile about our meeting. Though, God knows, they say enough vile things already. But we have to meet in secret. The Parliament has become mad with jealousy, and now they are calling for his death. I cannot rule this kingdom without William de la Pole. I have to see him and decide what we should do."

"The king —"

"The king cannot rule without him. The king cannot choose a course and hold to it on his own. You know what the king is like. I have to have William de la Pole at the side of the king, he cannot be steady without William to hold him to a course. We have to have William at our side. We have to have his advice."

At midnight, the queen orders me to let William de la Pole in through the little door that connects the two royal apartments. The duke strides through, ducking his head under the stone lintel, and then, to my amazement, the king comes in quietly behind him, like his page boy. "Your Grace," I whisper, and sink down.

He does not even see me, for he is shaking with distress. "I am forced! I am abused!" he says at once to Margaret. "They dare to insult me. They want to rule me! William — tell her!"

She looks at once to de la Pole as if only he can explain. "The lords are refusing to accept that the king can examine me alone, as you wanted," he explains. "They are demanding that I am tried by my peers for treason. They deny the king's right to judge on his own. I am accused of betraying our interests in France. Of course, I have only ever done what you commanded. And the peace treaty demanded the return of Maine and Anjou. This is an attack on you, Your Grace, on you, and on me, and on the king's authority."

"You will never stand trial," she promises him. "I swear it. They shall withdraw."

"Your Grace . . ." I whisper, taking hold of her sleeve, "you cannot promise this."

"I have found him innocent of all charges," the king says. "But still they are calling for him to be tried and executed. They have to obey me! They must be made to listen to me!"

"If they want you, they will have to come and get you!" she swears passionately to William de la Pole. "They will have to get past me if they want to get you. They will have to take you from my chambers, if they dare!"

I slide my hand into hers and give her a little tug. But the king looks at her with admiration; he is fired up by her anger. "We will defy them! I will be king. I will rule how I choose: with you as my wife and William as my advisor. Does anyone dare say I cannot do this? Am I king or not?"

Of the three of them, only the newly minted duke does not bluster. "Yes, but we can't resist them," he says quietly. "What if they come for me? What if the lords turn out their forces? Despite all you have said? You have allowed every lord in London to keep his own small army. Every enemy of mine can command hundreds of men. What if their armies come for me?"

"Could you go to France?" I ask him very softly. "To Flanders? You have friends there. Till it all blows over?"

The king looks up, suddenly flushed. "Yes, yes, go now!" he commands. "While they are planning their next move. Go now. They will come for you and find the bird flown! I will give you gold."

"My jewels!" the queen commands me. "Fetch them for him."

I go as she orders and pick out a few of her smallest pieces — marguerites made of pearls, some inferior emeralds. I put them in a purse, and when I come back to the shadowy room, the queen is weeping in the duke's arms and he has the king's own cloak around his shoulders and is slipping a fat purse into his pocket. Begrudgingly, I give him the queen's pearls, and he takes them without a word of thanks.

"I will write to you," he says to them both. "I will not be far, just Flanders. And I will come home as soon as my name is cleared.

We will not be parted for long."

"We will visit you," she promises. "This is not good-bye. And we will send for you, and write. You shall send messages with your advice. And you will come home soon."

He kisses her hand and pulls his hood over his head. He bows to the king and nods to me and slides through the little door and is gone. We hear his footsteps going quietly down the stair, and then the muffled closing of the outer door as the king's chief advisor goes out into the night like a thief.

The king and queen are cock-a-hoop like children who have defied a stern governor. They do not go to bed at all that night, but stay up by the fireside in her rooms whispering and giggling, celebrating their victory over the Parliament of their own country, praising themselves for defending a man named as a traitor. At dawn the king goes to Mass and orders the priest to say a prayer of thankfulness for danger passed. While he is on his knees, praising the mercy of Jesus and exulting in his own cleverness, the City of London wakes to the astounding news that the man it blamed for the loss of France and the arrival of a penniless French princess, for rewarding himself from the royal Treasury, for the destruction of the peace of England, has been released by the king and is sailing away, merrily away, for a brief exile, gold in his pocket, the queen's jewels in his hat, and will return as soon as he can be certain that his head is safe on his shoulders.

The queen cannot hide her delight, nor her contempt for those who say that she is utterly misguided. She will heed no warning, neither from my husband nor the other men who serve the king, who say the people are whispering that the king has forgotten his loyalty to his own lords and commons, that a friend of a traitor is a traitor himself — and what can be done with a treacherous king? She remains stubbornly delighted, thrilled with their defiance of Parliament, and nothing I can say warns her to take care, not to blazon her triumph in the face of people who were, after all, only calling for good government of a country that is flung about like a toy of spoiled children.

I think that nothing will dampen their joyous high spirits. The news comes that William de la Pole has had to flee from the mob out of London, that he is hiding for as long as he dares at his own house in the country, and then finally that he has set sail. All over the country there are uprisings against men who are blamed for giving the king bad advice, who are blamed for associating with William de la Pole. Then, a few days later, one of the queen's maids-in-waiting comes running to find me and says I must go at once! at once! to the queen, who is gravely ill. I do not even stop to find Richard; I run to the royal apartments, bustling past the guards on the door, shooing pages out of my way, and find the rooms in an uproar and the queen nowhere to be seen.

"Where is she?" I demand, and someone points to the bedroom door.

"She swore we could not go in."

"Why?" I ask. They shake their heads.

"Is she alone?"

"The Duchess of Suffolk, William de la Pole's wife, is in with her."

At that name, my heart sinks. What has he done now? Slowly, I go to the door, tap on the panel, and then try the handle. It opens, and I step inside.

At once I remember what a young woman she is, just twenty years old. She looks very small in the big royal bed, lying hunched up as if wounded in the belly, her back to the room, her face to the wall. Alice de la Pole is seated on a stool by the fire, her face buried in her hands.

"*C'est moi,*" I whisper. "It's me. What's wrong?"

The little queen shakes her head. Her head-dress has fallen off, her hair tumbled all around her, her shoulders shaking with silent sobs. "He's dead," is all she says, as if her world has ended. "Dead. What will I do?"

I stagger and put my hand out to steady myself. "My God, the king?"

Violently, she bangs her head into her pillow. "No! No!"

"Your father?"

"William. William . . . my God, William."

I look at Alice, his widow. "I am sorry for your loss, my lady."

She nods.

"But how?"

Margaret raises herself on her elbow and looks over her shoulder at me. Her hair is a mass of gold, her eyes red. "Murdered," she spits.

At once, I glance at the door behind me, as if a killer might come in for us. "By who, Your Grace?"

"I don't know. That wicked Duke of York? Other lords? Anyone who is cowardly and vile and wants to pull us down and destroy us. Anyone who denies our right to govern as we wish, with the help of whomever we choose. Anyone who sails in secret and attacks an innocent man."

"They caught him at sea?"

"They took him on board their ship and beheaded him on the deck," she says, her voice nearly muffled by sobs. "Goddamn them to hell for cowards. They left his body on the beach at Dover. Jacquetta!" Blindly, she reaches out to me and clings to me as she wails. "They put his head on a pole. They left his head like a traitor's head. How shall I bear this? How shall Alice bear this?"

I hardly dare to glance over to William de la Pole's widow, who sits in silence while William de la Pole's queen is breaking her heart over him.

"Do we know who?" I repeat. My first fear is if someone dares to attack the king's favorite advisor, who will they come for next? The queen? Me?

She is crying so hard she cannot speak, her slender body shaking in my arms. "I must go to the king," she says finally, pulling herself up and wiping her eyes. "This will have broken his heart. How will we manage without him? Who will advise us?"

Dumbly, I shake my head. I don't know how they will manage without William de la Pole, nor what sort of world is opening before us when a noble lord on his own ship can be kidnapped and beheaded with a rusty sword on a rocking boat and his head left on a pike on the beach.

GRAFTON, NORTHAMPTONSHIRE, SUMMER 1450

As the warmer months come, the king and queen agree to travel north. They give out that they want to be away from London during the hot weather when plague often comes to the city; they say that they want to see the good people of Leicester. But those of us who live in the palace know that the guards have been doubled at the gates, and that they are employing tasters for their food. They are afraid of the people of London; they are afraid of the men of Kent; they are afraid that whoever murdered William de la Pole blames them for the loss of France, for the continual stream of defeated soldiers and settlers who come every day into every English port. There is no money to pay the London suppliers; the queen mistrusts the people of the city. The court is going to Leicester; in truth, it is running away to hide in Leicester.

Richard and I are granted leave to go and see our children at Grafton, as the court goes north, and we ride quickly out of London, which has become a surly city of secretive people whispering on street corners. There is a rumor that the king and queen will take a great revenge on the county of Kent. They blame the very seashore where William de la Pole's dishonored body was dumped. Lord Say of Knole and his heavy-handed son-in-law who is Sheriff of Kent say that together they will hunt down the guilty men and execute them and every one of their family; they say they will empty Kent of people, will make it a wasteland.

Once we are out of the city, away from city walls, Richard and I ride side by side, holding hands like young lovers, while our small armed guard falls back and rides behind us. The roads are clear and dry, the grass verges dotted with flowers, the birds singing in the greening hedgerows, ducklings on the village ponds, and roses in blossom.

"What if we never went back to court?" I ask him. "What if we were just to be the squire of Grafton and his lady?"

"And our nursery of children?" He smiles.

"Many, many children," I say. "I am not satisfied with eight, and one on the way; I am hoping for a round dozen."

He smiles at me. "I should still be summoned," he says. "Even if I were the smallest quietest squire of Grafton, with the largest family in England, I should still be mustered and sent to war."

"But you would come home again." I pursue the thought. "And we could make a living from our fields and farms."

He smiles. "Not much of a living, my lady. Not the sort of living you want. And your children would marry tenant farmers, and their children would run wild. Do you want a dirty-faced little peasant for a grandchild?"

I make a face at him. He knows how much I prize our books and our musical instruments, and how determined I am that all my children shall read and write in three languages, and master all the courtly skills.

"My children have to take their place in the world."

"You are ambitious," he says.

"I am not! I was the first lady in France. I have been as high as any woman could dream. And I gave it up for love."

"You're ambitious for your family and for your children. And you're ambitious for me — you like my being a baron."

"Oh well, a baron," I say, laughing. "Anyone would want their husband to be a baron. I don't count that as being ambitious. That is just . . . understandable."

"And I understand it," he says agreeably. "But would you really want to live always in the country and not go back to court?"

I think for a moment of the nervous king and the young queen. "We couldn't leave them, could we?" I ask wistfully.

He shakes his head. "It is our duty to serve the House of Lancaster, and — something else — I don't know how they would manage without us. I don't think we could just walk away and leave them. What would they do?"

We stay at Grafton for a week. It is the best time of the year, the orchards are rose-pink with the bobbing blossoms, and the cows are calving. The lambs are with their mothers in the higher meadows, running and frisking with their tails like woolly ribbons dancing behind them. The hay in the meadows is growing tall and starting to ripple in the wind, and the crops are green and rich, ankle-deep. My older children, Elizabeth, Lewis, Anne, and Anthony, have been staying with our cousins, to learn their manners and how to behave in a great household, but they come home to be with us for the summer. The four little ones, Mary, Jacquetta, John, and Richard, are beside themselves with excitement at having their big sisters and brothers home. Mary, the seven-year-old, is the leader of the little battalion, the others her sworn liege-men.

I am weary with this new pregnancy, and in the warm afternoons I take the four-year-old, little Diccon, in my arms for his afternoon nap; we lie down together, drowsy in the warmth of the day. When he is asleep and it is very quiet, I sometimes take the painted cards and turn them over, one after another, and look at them. I don't shuffle them or deal them out; I don't attempt to read them. I just look at the familiar pictures and wonder what life will bring me, and these my beloved children.

In the day Richard listens to the unending complaints of the people around us: the moving of a fence line, of cattle being allowed to stray and spoiling a crop. As lord of the manor it is his job to ensure that the rule of law and justice runs throughout our lands, whether or not our neighbors take bribes and order jurors what sentence they should bring in. Richard visits the local gentry to remind them of their duty to turn out for him in case of need, and tries to reassure them that the king is a strong lord, that the court is trustworthy, that the Treasury is secure, and that we will keep the remaining lands in France.

I work in my still room, Elizabeth my earnest apprentice, steeping herbs in oil, checking the cut and dried herbs, pounding them down into powder and conserving them in jars. I do this by the order of the stars, and I consult my lord's books for how it should be done. Now and then I find a book I had overlooked that talks of making the aqua vitae, the water of life itself, or of burning off impurities by the touch of distilled waters; but I remember Eleanor Cobham behind the cold walls of Peel Castle, and I take the book from Elizabeth and put it on a high shelf. I never grow or dry any but the herbs that would be known to a good cook. Knowledge is just another thing to conceal, these days.

I am hoping that we will stay at home for another month; I am tired by this pregnancy and daring to hope that I might spend the whole summer in the country, that the king and queen will prolong their travels and leave us in peace. We have been riding out to visit some neighbors and come home in the sunset to see a royal messenger waiting by the water pump. He gets to his feet when he sees us and hands Richard a letter sealed with the royal crest.

Richard tears it open and scans it. "I have to go," he says. "This is urgent. I shall have to muster a troop as I ride."

"What has happened?" I ask as I slip down from my saddle.

"There's a rising in Kent, as any fool could have foreseen. The king commands me to ride at his side and carry the royal standard."

"The king?" I can hardly believe that our king is going to ride out at the head of his men. His father was a remarkable commander of men at a far younger age, but our king has never worn his armor except for jousting. "The king is going himself?"

"He was very angry about de la Pole — God rest his soul," he reminds me. "He swore vengeance, and the queen swore she would see the murderers dead. Now he has his chance."

"You will be careful." I take his arm to look up into his face. Between us is the unspoken thought that his commander will be a young man who has never seen any sort of warfare, not even a distant siege. "You will have to advise him."

"I'll keep safe," my husband says wryly. "And I'll keep him safe too, if I can. They have ordered the Sheriff of Kent to turn the county into a deer park, to drive out every man, woman, and child: there will be hell to pay. I have to get back and see if I can advise them into some sense. I have to find a way to persuade them to rule the country with some sort of harmony. They make enemies every time they address Parliament. The queen rides through the streets of London as if she hates the very cobbles. We have to serve them, Jacquetta. We have to guide them to follow their best interests; we have to get this royal couple back into the hearts of their people. It is our duty. It is our task. It is what our lord the Duke of Bedford would have wanted us to do."

I hold him in my arms in bed that night, and in the cool morning I find I am filled with unease. "You will just ride out with the king to show his standard? You won't go into Kent, Richard?"

"I hope that nobody will be going into Kent," he says grimly.

He finishes his breakfast, and I trail out into the stable yard after him, pursuing my fears. "But if there is some kind of guard put together to punish the people of Kent, you won't join it?"

"Burning thatch? Spit roasting a poor man's cow?" he asks. "I have seen it done in France, and I never thought it a way to win loyalty. The Duke of Bedford himself said to me that the way to win a man's heart was to treat him fairly and make him safe. That will be my advice, if anyone asks me. But if anyone orders me out in the king's name, I will have to go."

"I will follow you as soon as you send for me." I try to sound confident, but my voice is thin and anxious.

"I will be waiting for you," he vows, suddenly warm, as he realizes I am afraid. "You take care of yourself and the baby that you are carrying. I will be waiting for you. I will always be there waiting for you. Remember I have promised you — you will never look for me in vain."

I tidy the house and command the servants to prepare them for my departure. I hear gossip that the king and queen have gone back to London and that the king himself has ridden out against the people of Kent. Then a message comes from Richard, written in his own hand.

Beloved,

I am sorry to trouble you. The king has been persuaded by the queen not to march into Kent himself, but he has ordered me to pursue the outlaws at the head of his guard and I am doing so. Trust me that I will be safe and come home to you when this is over. Your Richard.

I put the scrap of paper inside my gown, against my heart, and I go to the stable. "Saddle up," I say to the household guard. "And tell them to get my mare ready for a journey. We are going back to London."

London,
Summer 1450

All the way I ride with a heavy heart. I have such a strong sense that Richard is in danger, that he is outnumbered, that the thickly forested county of Kent will hide ambushes, traps, armies of the people who will take him, as they took William de la Pole, and behead him without clergy, with a rusty sword.

We take the London road in silence, but as we pass through the vegetable gardens and little dairy farms, the captain of my guard orders the men to close up and starts to look around him, as if he fears we are unsafe.

"What is it?" I ask.

He shakes his head. "I don't know, my lady. Something . . ." He pauses. "Too quiet," he says, speaking to himself. "Hens shut up before sunset, shutters closed on the cottages. Something's not right."

I don't need to be told twice. Something is wrong. My first husband, the duke, used to say that if you ride into a town and feel that something is wrong, it is usually because something is wrong. "Close up," I say. "We'll get inside the City before the gates close, and we'll go to our London house. Tell your men to be alert and look about them. We'll go on at a canter."

He beckons the men to close up, and we ride towards the city gates. But almost as soon as we are through Moorgate and in the narrow streets, I can hear the swell of noise, people cheering, people laughing, trumpets tooting, and the banging of a drum.

It sounds like a May Day procession, like joy unleashed, but there must be hundreds of people on the streets. I glance at my men, who draw their horses closer to mine in a defensive square.

"This way," the captain says, and leads us at a swift trot through the winding streets till we find our way to the great wall that runs around my London house. The torches, which are always kept burning either side of the gateway, are missing from the sconces. The gates themselves, which should be either barred for night or flung hospitably wide, are half open. The sweep of the cobbles approaching the house is empty, but there is a scattering of litter and the front door is ajar. I glance at George Cutler, the captain, and see my unease in his eyes.

"Your ladyship . . ." he says uncertainly. "Better that I go in and see what's amiss here. Something has gone wrong, perhaps . . ."

As he speaks a drunken man, no servant of mine, weaves out through the half-open gates and shambles past us, disappearing down the lane. Cutler and I exchange glances again. I kick my feet out of the stirrups, and swing down from my horse, and throw her reins to one of the guard.

"We'll go in," I say to Cutler. "Draw your sword and have two men behind us."

They follow me as I walk across the cobbles to the house, my London home, that I was so proud to receive and so pleased to furnish. One of the front doors is thrown off the hinges, there is the smell of smoke. As I push the other door open and go inside, I can see that a mob of people has run through the rooms and taken whatever they thought was of value. There are pale squares on the walls where my tapestries, the Duke of Bedford's tapestries, once hung. A huge wooden sideboard, too heavy to carry off, has been stripped of the pewter ware that it held, carved doors left banging. I go to the great hall. All the trenchers and wine jugs and drinking vessels are gone, but, absurdly, the huge beautiful tapestry that was behind the great table is still there, untouched.

"My books," I say, and jump up to the dais and through the door behind the great table and up the short flight of stairs into the upstairs solar. From there it is two steps through a wreckage of precious broken glass, into the gallery, and there I pause and look around me.

They have taken the brass grilles off the shelves, they have taken the brass chains that fettered the books to the reading desks. They have even taken the quills and the pots of ink. But the books are safe, the books are untouched. They have stolen everything made of metal but damaged nothing of paper. I snatch up a slim volume and hold it to my cheek.

"Get these safe," I say to Cutler. "Get your men in to put them in the cellar and board it up and mount a guard. These are worth more than the brass grilles, more than the tapestries. If we can salvage these, then I can meet my first husband at the Last Day of Judgment. They were his treasures, and he trusted them to me."

He nods. "I am sorry about the rest of it . . ." He gestures at the wrecked house, where the wooden staircase is scarred by sword cuts. Someone has hacked off the carved newel post and taken it away, as if to behead me by proxy. In the painted beams above, there is smoke blackening the ceiling. Someone tried to burn us to the ground. I shudder at the smell of the scorched plaster.

"If the books are safe, and my lord is safe, then I can start again," I say. "Board the books up for me, Cutler. And take down the big tapestry, too, and anything else you find of value. Thank God we took the best stuff with us to Grafton."

"What will you do?" he asks. "My lord will want you to find a safe haven. I should go with you."

"I'll go to the palace," I say. "I'll go to Westminster. Meet me there."

"Take two men with you," he advises. "I will make all safe here. And then we'll follow you." He hesitates. "I have seen worse done," he volunteers. "It looks as if they came through on a whim and took anything that was of great value. It was not an assault. You need not fear them. It was not directed at you. They are people driven to despair by poverty and fear of the lords. They are not bad people. It's just they cannot bear it anymore."

I look around the smoke-blackened hall, at the spaces where the missing tapestries used to be and the hacked banister. "No, it was an assault," I say slowly. "They did all that they wanted to do. It was not directed at me — but it was directed at the lords, at the wealthy, at the court. They no longer think that they have to wait at the gates; they no longer think they have no choice but to beg. They no longer think that we command them by right. When I was a girl in Paris and married to the Duke of Bedford, we were hated by the people of the city, by the people of France. We knew it, and they knew it. But nobody even dreamed that they could breach the gates and come inside and destroy our things. They think this now in London. They no longer obey their masters. Who knows where they will stop?"

I walk out. The guard outside is holding my horse, but already a crowd has gathered and is murmuring against them. "You two, come with me," I say. "You two, go in and set it to rights."

I snap my fingers, and one of the guard helps me into the saddle. "Go quickly," I urge him, under my breath. "Into the saddle and onwards."

He does as I bid him, and we are away from the courtyard and some distance from my house before anyone knows we are gone. I don't look back. But I remember, as I ride down the road, the dark smear of the smoke stain in the hall of my house, and my realization that the people had come into my house and taken what they wanted, and done just what they wished.

"To Westminster Palace," I say. I want to be with the court, behind the walls of the palace, guarded by the royal guard. London no longer feels safe for me. I have become like the queen — a woman uneasy in the heart of her own home.

We round a corner, and suddenly we are swirled into a mob of people, dancing laughing cheering people, a great joyous May Day crowd. Someone gets hold of my bridle, and I clench my hand on my whip, but the face that turns up towards me is beaming. "Easy!" I say quickly to the guard at my side who is spurring forwards, his hand on his sword.

"God be praised, we have our champion!" the woman says, sharing her happiness with me. "He is coming, God bless him! He is coming, and he will petition for our rights, and the good times will come again!"

"Hurrah!" shout half a dozen people in earshot, and I smile as if I know what is happening.

"Good woman," I say. "I have to get through. Let me go, I have to meet my husband. Let me go."

Someone laughs. "You'll get nowhere till he has come! The streets are packed with people like pilchards in a barrel. There is no going through nor going round."

"But won't you come and see him? He is coming over the bridge."

"Oh, come," somebody else says. "You will never see the like of this again; this is the greatest thing to ever happen in our lifetime, in any lifetime."

I look around for my two men, but they cannot keep their place at my side. They are separated from me by a dozen merrymakers, we are totally outnumbered. I wave to one. "Go your ways," I call. "I am safe enough. You know where we will meet." Clearly, there is no point trying to resist this crowd, and our safest way is to join with them. One of my men jumps from his horse and pushes his way through to come alongside me.

"Steady on!" someone says. "No shoving. Whose livery are you wearing?"

"Leave me," I whisper. "Meet me later. You know where. Don't upset them."

It is the safest way, but I see him struggle to obey the order.

"High and mighty!" someone complains. "The sort that should be brought down."

"Are you a king's man?" someone demands. "Think you should have everything and care nothing for the poor man?"

At last, he takes his cue. "Not I!" he says cheerfully. "I am with you all!"

I nod at him, and the movement of the crowd takes him from me, almost at once. I let my horse walk with them. Familiarly, a woman rests her hand on my horse's neck. "So where are we going?" I ask her.

"To the bridge, to see him come across the bridge!" she says exultantly. "I see you are a lady, but you will not be ashamed of the company he keeps. He has gentry and squires with him, knights and lords. He is a man for all the people, of all degree."

"And what will he do for us when he comes?"

"You don't know? Where have you been?"

Smiling, I shake my head. "I have been in

the country; all this is a surprise to me."

"Then you have come back to the City at the very hour of its joy. He will speak for us at last. He will tell the king that we cannot bear the taxation, that the fat lords will ruin us all. He will order the king to ignore the French slut, his wife, and take good advice from the good duke."

"The good duke?" I query. "Who do you call the good duke now?"

"Richard, Duke of York, of course. He will tell the king to lie with his worthless wife and get us a son and heir, to take our lands in France back again, to send away the wicked men who steal the wealth of the country and do nothing but make their own fortunes and fight among themselves. He will make this king as great as the king before, and we will be happy again."

"Can one man do all this?" I ask.

"He has raised an army and defeated the king's men already," she says delightedly. "They chased after him to Sevenoaks, and he struck them down. This is our champion. He has defeated the royal army, and now he takes the City."

I can feel a pain hammering in my head. "He destroyed the king's army?"

"Led them on, turned on them, and struck them down," she says. "Half of them ran away; half of them joined him. He is our hero!"

"And what of the lords who led the men?"

"Dead! All dead!"

Richard, I think to myself in silence. Surely the two of us did not come so far, and risk so much, for Richard to be ambushed by a hedge-sparrow commander at the head of patchwork rebels, and killed outside Seven-oaks? Surely I would know if he were injured or dead? Surely I would have heard Melusina sing or felt the very spheres dance sorrow-fully one with another, to mourn him? Surely the man whom I have loved for all my adult life, loved with a passion that I did not even know was possible, could not, cannot be dead in a Kentish ditch, and I not know?

"Are you ill, mistress?" she asks. "You've gone white as my washing."

"Who commanded the royal army?" I ask; though I know it was him. Who else would they send but Richard? Who has more experi-ence? Who is more reliable? Who is more loyal and honorable than my husband? Who would they choose if not my beloved?

"Ah, now that I don't know," she says cheerfully. "All I know is that he is dead now, for sure. Are you taken ill?"

"No, no," I say. My lips are numb. All I can say is the one word. "No. No."

We crowd together through the narrow streets. I cannot get away now, even if I could get the horse out of the crowd, I don't think I could ride. I am limp with fear, quite unable to take up the reins, even if the crowd would let me. And then, at last, we are at Bridgegate and the crowd thickens and pushes. My horse becomes anxious at being so crowded — her ears flicker, and she shifts from one leg to another — but we are hemmed in so fast that she cannot move and I cannot dismount. I can see the lord mayor of the city as he leaps up on a milestone, balancing with a hand on the broad shoulder of one of the City's guard, and shouts to the crowd, "I take it it is your will that Captain Mortimer and his men enter the city?"

"Yea!" comes the roar. "Open the gates!"

I can see that one of the aldermen is arguing, and the lord mayor gestures that he shall be roughly taken away. The guards throw open the gate, and we look out through the gateway beyond the drawbridge. On the south side, there is a small army waiting, standards furled. As I watch, they see the gate flung open, hear the encouraging bellow of the crowd, see the red of the mayor's robe, and they unfurl their banners, fall into ranks, and march briskly along the road. People are throwing flowers from the upper storys of the buildings, waving flags and cheering: this is the procession of a hero. The drawbridge is dropped before them, and the clang as it goes down is like the clash of cymbals for a conqueror. The captain at the head of the men turns and, using a great sword, slices through the ropes of the bridge so that it cannot ever be raised against him. Everyone around me is shouting a welcome; the women are blowing kisses and screaming. The captain marches before his army, his helmet under his arm, his golden spurs sparkling at his boots, a beautiful cape of deep blue velvet rippling from his shoulders, his armor shining. Before him comes his squire, holding a great sword before him, as if he is leading a king, entering into his kingdom.

I cannot tell if it is Richard's sword, I don't know if this man is wearing my husband's hard-won spurs. I close my eyes and feel the coldness of the sweat under my hat. Could he be dead without my knowing it? When I get to the palace, will the queen herself comfort me, another widow at court, like Alice de la Pole?

The lord mayor steps forwards, the keys to the city on a scarlet cushion, and bows his head to the conqueror, and hands him the keys. From all around, crowds of men are spilling out of the city gate to fall in with the soldiers behind the captain, and they are greeted by his army with slaps on the back and settled into rough ranks that march past us, waving at the girls and grinning at the cheers, like an army of liberation, come at last.

The crowd follows him. I swear if he marches on Westminster at the head of such a crowd, he can seat himself on the king's marble throne; this is a man with the city in his hand. But he leads the way to Candlewick Street, where the London stone stands proudly in the street to mark the very heart of the city. He strikes the stone with his sword, and at the ringing sound the crowd bellows in exultation. "Now is Mortimer the lord of this city!" he shouts, and stands by the stone, holding his shield in one hand and his sword over his head, while the men cheer him.

"To dine!" he declares, and they all move with him to Guildhall, where the lord mayor will spread a dinner for him and his officers. As the crowd goes with him, eager for the offcuts of beef and the broken baskets of bread, I slip from my horse, take hold of her reins, and lead her carefully out of the crowd, hoping to creep away unnoticed.

I edge down a side road and then into a smaller alley. I am almost lost, but I climb on a step and struggle up into the saddle and turn east, letting the slope of the street take me towards the river. I remember when I was a girl on my way to England, I was lost in the forest and Richard found me. I cannot believe that he will not come looking for me again. It does not seem possible that I should have touched him for the last time, kissed him for the last time; and now I cannot remember the last words I said to him. At least we parted lovingly, I know that. I cannot remember the words that we said nor how we looked; but I know that we parted tenderly, because we always parted tenderly. We used to kiss each other good night; we would kiss each other at breakfast. He was always loving to me, even when he should not have thought of me as anything but his lady. Even when I trapped him into giving me our child and insisted on a secret marriage. For fourteen years he has been lover and husband, and now I am afraid that he is lost to me.

I give my horse her head and let her pick her way through the maze of dirty streets. She knows well enough where the Westminster stables are, and I do not care. When I think of Richard dead in a ditch in Kent, I want to lie down in the gutter and die myself. I put my hand on my belly and think of the child who will never know her father. How can it be that I shall not show Richard his new baby?

It is growing dark as we come to one of the many back gates to the rambling palace. I am surprised to find no one on sentry duty. I would have expected the gates to be closed and manned with a double guard; but it is like the king to be careless, and without my husband who would command the guard?

"Hi!" I shout as I come close. "Holla! Open the gate!"

Silence. Silence, where there are usually

scores of people coming and going. Silence where I would have expected a shouted challenge. I rein the horse in, remembering that when you feel that something is wrong, it is because something is wrong. "Open the lantern gate!" I shout, readying myself to turn the horse and spur her away if we are attacked. "Open the lantern gate for the Duchess of Bedford!" Slowly, the small door in the great gate creaks open, and a stable lad peers nervously out.

"The Duchess of Bedford?"

I pull down my hood so he can see my face. "Myself. Where is everybody?"

His pinched white face looks up at me. "Run away," he says. "Everyone but me, and I couldn't go because my dog is sick and I didn't want to leave him. Had I better come with you?"

"Run where?"

He shrugs. "Run away from Captain Mortimer and his army. Some of them ran to join him; some of them ran away."

I shake my head. I cannot understand this. "Where is the king and the queen?"

"Run away too," he says.

"For God's sake! Where are they, boy?"

"Run away to Kenilworth," he whispers. "But I was told to tell no one."

I grip onto my horse's mane with cold hands as my heart thuds. "What? They have abandoned the city?"

"They sent out an army to chase Mortimer back to Kent, but Mortimer turned on them and beat them good. The royal commanders were all killed, the army ran back to London except for those that joined Mortimer. Half of them joined Mortimer. I wish I had gone."

"Who were the commanders that were killed?" I ask quietly. My voice is steady, and I am pleased at that.

He shrugs. "All the king's lords, I don't know: Lord Northumberland, Baron Rivers . . ."

"They are dead? All of them?"

"They didn't come back, at any rate."

"The king?"

"The king wouldn't go to war," he says contemptuously. "He went out with his standard, but he wouldn't go to war. He kept half his army back and sent out the lords with the other half. And when what was left of them came running back and said they had lost, he and the queen ran off to Kenilworth, the Duke of Somerset, Edmund Beaufort, with them, and Lord Scales went to the Tower."

"Is Scales there now? Has he fortified the Tower?"

He shrugs. "I dunno. What's going to happen to me?" he asks.

I look at him, my face as blank as his own. "I don't know. You'd better look out for yourself."

I turn my horse from the stable gate of Westminster, since there is no safety there for either of us. I think I had better get to the Tower before nightfall. She steps out bravely enough, but we are both weary, on every street corner there is a brazier and someone roasting meat, and men drinking ale and swearing that the good times have come and that Mortimer will advise the king and there will be no more taxation and no more cheating of the poor and the bad advisors will be driven away. They call me to join them, and they curse me when I shake my head. In the end I have to throw a coin and wish them well, and for the last few streets I pull my hood over my face and sit low in the saddle and hope to sidle by, like a thief in my own city.

I get to the gate of the Tower at last. There are sentries on every wall, and they shout down at me as soon as they see me: "Halt! Who's there? Stand where you are!"

"The Duchess of Bedford!" I call back, showing them my face. "Let me in."

"Your husband the baron has been searching for you all evening," the young guardsman says as he throws open the gate, comes out to take my bridle, and helps me down from the horse. "Your men came in and said they had lost you. He was afraid you had been captured by the mob. He said he would see them swing for treason if so much of a

309

hair of your head was hurt. He told them! I have never heard such language."

"My husband?" I ask, suddenly dizzy with hope. "Did you say my husband was looking for me?"

"Like a madman . . ." he starts, then he turns to listen, as we both hear the clatter of hooves on the cobbles. He shouts, "Horses! Close the gate!" and we rush inside as the gates creak behind us. Then I hear Richard shout, "Rivers! Open up!" and they fling open the double gates, and his little band of men rides in like thunder, and he sees me in a moment and jumps down from his horse and catches me up in his arms and kisses me as if we were a squire and his lady once more, and could not bear to part.

"Dear God, I have ridden all round London looking for you," he gasps. "I was so afraid they had taken you. Cutler at the house said you were going to Westminster, and the boy at Westminster knew nothing."

I shake my head, tears running down my face, laughing at the sight of him. "I'm safe! I'm safe! I got caught up in the crowd and separated from our men. Richard, I thought you were dead. I thought you had been killed in an ambush in Kent."

"Not I. Poor Stafford was killed, and his brother, but not I. Are you safe? Do you feel well? How did you get here?"

"I got swept up in the crowd. I saw him

310

enter London."

"Jack Cade?"

"The captain? He is John Mortimer."

"Jack Cade is his name, but he's calling himself Mortimer, and John Amend-All, and all sorts of names. The name Mortimer brings out the supporters of Richard of York for him; it's York's family name. Cade is borrowing it, or worse, the duke is lending it. Either way it means more trouble. Where did you see him?"

"Crossing the bridge, and getting the keys of the city."

"Getting the keys?" my husband demands, dumbfounded.

"They greeted him as a hero, all the common people and the mayor and the aldermen, too. He was dressed like a nobleman coming to rule."

He lets out a whistle. "God save the king. You'd better tell Lord Scales; he's in command here."

He tucks his hand under my elbow and leads me to the White Tower. "Are you tired, beloved?"

"A little."

"And you feel well? The baby?"

"All right, I think. All well."

"Were you frightened?"

"A little. My love, I thought you were dead."

"Not I."

I hesitate. "You have seen our house?"

"Nothing that we can't repair when this is over."

I glance at him. "They walked in through the door and took what they wanted. It will be hard to repair that."

He nods. "I know. But we will do it. Now, I'll get you some wine and some meat as soon as we find Scales. He'll need to know where Cade is tonight."

"Dining with the lord mayor, I think."

Richard pauses and looks at me. "A man who has brought an army out of Kent and defeated the king's men has the keys to the city of London and is dining with the lord mayor?"

I nod. "They greeted him like he was freeing them from a tyrant. The lord mayor and all the aldermen welcomed him to the city like a hero."

Richard scowls. "You'd better tell Scales," is all he says.

Lord Scales is in a state of ill-concealed terror. He is using the constable of the Tower's house, and he has double guards on the front and back doors and at the windows. Clearly, he fears that his king has abandoned him and the city together to the men from Kent. His men may be of the royal guard and have taken the king's shilling, but what is to say that they are not Kentishmen, or that they do not have a family making a poor living at

Dover? Half of them have come from Normandy and feel betrayed; why should they defend us now, who let them be driven from their own homes? When I tell him that Cade was welcomed as a hero, he tells me that I must have been mistaken. "He is a scoundrel and a villain," he rules.

"There were many in his train who were gentlemen," I say. "I could see they had good horses and good saddles. Cade himself rode like a man accustomed to command. And there was only one alderman in the whole of the city who did not welcome him."

"He's a villain," he says rudely.

I raise an eyebrow at Richard. He shrugs as if to say that I have done my best to give this most nervous commander an idea of the enemy, and if he is too afraid to listen, then I need do no more. "I'll take my wife to my rooms and get her something to eat," he says to Lord Scales. "Then shall I come back and we can plan an attack? Perhaps tonight when they have wined and dined? While they are celebrating? Or as they march back to Southwark? We could catch them in the narrow streets before the bridge and push them over?"

"Not tonight! Not tonight!" Scales says quickly. "Besides, I am expecting reinforcements from the king. He will send us men from the Midlands."

"They can't come for days, if they come at

all," my husband says. "Surely we should attack them now, before they expect it, while they are drinking."

"Not tonight," Scales repeats. "These are not Frenchmen, Rivers. Our experience is no use here. These are treasonous peasants, they fight around back streets and in hiding. We should wait till we have a great force to overwhelm them. I will send another message to the king and ask for his command."

I see my husband hesitate, and then he decides not to argue. He throws his cape around my shoulders and takes me to his lodgings. We have our usual rooms near the royal apartments in the Tower, but it feels strange, with the king and queen so far away, and the drawbridge up and the portcullis down and us besieged among the people who are our countrymen.

"It's damnable," my husband says shortly, snapping his fingers for the serving man to leave the tray of food. "Damnable. And the very men who should be putting down this unrest are either too halfhearted or too afraid to act. Get you to bed, sweetheart, and I will join you after I have posted a watch. That we should be all but besieged in the Tower of London? At war in England with Englishmen? It beggars belief."

We live under siege in the Tower, at war in our own country, besieged in our own capital city. Every day my husband sends out men and even the kitchen girls to get news in the marketplace and at the city gates. They come back saying that Cade's army is camped south of the river, with more joining them every day. Richard's great fear is that the uprising will spread and the men of Hampshire and Sussex will join the men of Kent. "What about our home?" I ask him, thinking of the children in their nursery. "Should I go back to them?"

"The roads aren't safe," he says, scowling with worry. "I'll send you with a guard as soon as I know what is happening. But I don't even know if the king is safely at Kenilworth. We have sent messages but have heard nothing back yet. If he's besieged —" He breaks off.

It feels like the end of the world. If the common people rise against the king, if they are armed with weapons they have won from us, if they are commanded by a man who has been trained by us and embittered by losses in France, then there is no hope that the world we know can continue. Only a heroic king who could capture the love of the people could save us — and we have only King Henry, hiding at Kenilworth, his beautiful armor laid aside after its one and only outing.

A message comes from the rebel army. They want Lord Say, the man who was Lord of

Kent, sent out for trial. "We cannot release him to them," my husband says to the commander, Lord Scales. "They will kill him."

"We are holding him here under arrest for treason," the lord says reasonably enough. "He could well have been tried and found guilty, and then he would have been executed anyway."

"The king sent him here for his safety, not to charge him with treason, as we both know, my lord. The king would have released him. You know the king would have forgiven him anything he has done."

"I shall release him to them, and if he is innocent of all they say, then he can tell them so," Lord Scales says.

My husband swears under his breath and then speaks clearly. "My lord, if we send Lord Say out to them, guilty or innocent, they will kill him. This is not a release, it is to push him out of safety to his death. If this doesn't matter to you now, then I ask you what you will do if the rebels ask for me to be sent out to them? What would you like us to do when they ask for you?"

His lordship glowers. "I wasn't the man who said I would make a deer park out of Kent. I didn't say they were too good for hanging and should be pushed into the sea."

"You are advisor to the king, as are we all. They could name any one of us and ask for us to be sent out. Are we going to obey the servants? Are they our new masters?"

Lord Scales rises from his seat behind the great dark wooden table and goes to the arrow-slit window that looks towards the city. "Woodville, my old friend, I know you are right; but if they attack us with the numbers they have now, they are likely to take the Tower, and then we will all be at their mercy, your wife as well as us."

"We can hold out," my husband says.

"They have a full-size army at Southwark, and every day more men come from Essex and camp out there. There are hundreds now. Who knows how strong they may become? If they come from Essex, what's to stop them coming from Hertfordshire? From Nottinghamshire? What if they can raise the whole country against us?"

"Better strike now then, before they grow any stronger."

"What if they have the king and we don't yet know it?"

"Then we will have to fight them."

"But if we negotiate with them, promise them a pardon, say that their grievances will be resolved, promise them an inquiry, they will go back to their little farms and get the hay in."

"If we pardon them, we will have taught them that they can take up arms against the King of England," my husband objects. "And that is a lesson we may regret one day."

"I cannot risk the safety of the Tower," Lord Scales says firmly. "We cannot attack; we must prepare to defend. At the worst, Lord Say buys us time."

There is a silence as my husband absorbs the fact that they are going to send one of the peers of England out to face a mob that wants him dead. "You are the commander," he says stiffly. "I am here under your command. But my advice is that we defy them."

That afternoon they send Lord Say out to Guildhall, where those aldermen who have the stomach for it, and the rebels who are eager for it, create a little court for the day. They persuade his lordship to confess, find him a priest, and take him to Cheapside for execution. His son-in-law, the Sheriff of Kent, William Crowmer, thinks himself lucky to be released from the Fleet Prison, and steps out of the stone doorway cheerfully, thinking a rescue party has come for him, only to find a scaffold waiting for him outside the gates. They don't even bother to try him but string him up without ceremony.

"God forgive them," my husband says as we stand on the walls of the Tower, hidden by the parapet, looking down into the streets below. A dancing, singing, chanting mob is weaving its unsteady way through the narrow lanes towards the Tower. My husband interposes his broad shoulder before me, but I peep around his arm and see what is leading the procession. They have the head of Lord Say on a pike, bobbing along at the front of the crowd. Behind on another pike is the stabbed head of William Crowmer, the sheriff who promised to lay waste to his county of Kent. As they come within range of the Tower gates, they pause and bawl defiance, and then dance the two heads together. The dead faces bump, the pike bearers jiggle the pikes so the mouths knock one against another. "They're kissing! They're kissing!" they howl and roar with laughter at the spectacle. "Send us out Lord Scales!" they bellow. "He can have a kiss, too!"

Richard draws me back into the shadow of the wall. "My God," I say quietly. "This is the end, isn't it? This is the end of the England we have known. This is the end of everything."

Next night, at dinner, I see Richard put his head down over his plate and eat steadily, hardly pausing for breath, but drinking no wine at all. Throughout the meal his servants come and whisper brief messages in his ear. After dinner there is never dancing or singing, not even playing at cards, but tonight it is even more hushed and nervous. The remnants of this beleaguered court stand around in groups and exchange fearful whispers. Then Richard stands up on the steps of the dais and raises his voice. "My lords, gentle-

men: a number of the gentlemen and merchants of London tell me that they are weary
of Cade and his men running riot through
the city. Also, matters are getting worse, and
no man can be sure that his home and his
goods are safe. Cade has lost control of his
men, and they are looting the city. The
London men tell me that they are determined
to push the soldiers out of the city, back to
their camp at Southwark tonight, and I have
agreed that we will join with them to drive
the rebels back, raise the drawbridge, and
close the gate. They are not going to enter
London again."

He raises his hand at the buzz of noise.
"Lord Scales will command," he says. "We
will muster in the courtyard at nine of the
clock; weapons will be distributed now. I
expect all able-bodied men to arm and come
with me."

He steps down, and men crowd around him
at once. I hear him explaining the plan and
sending men to get their weapons. I stand a
little closer and wait for him to turn to me.

"I'll leave a guard on the Tower," he says.
"Enough to hold it. The king is sending
reinforcements from the Midlands; they will
be here tomorrow or the next day. You'll be
safe here until I come back."

He sees the unspoken question in my face.
"If I don't come back, you should put on
your plainest clothes and make your way on

foot, out of the city," he says. "Cutler will go with you, or any of our men. Once you are out of the city you can buy or borrow horses to get home. I can't tell what will happen then. But if you can get home to the children, you can live off our lands, and you should be safe there until it all comes right again. Our tenants would stand by you. Jacquetta, I am sorry. I never thought it would come to this. I didn't mean to bring you out of France to danger in England."

"Because if the rebels take London, then nowhere is safe?" I ask him. "If you cannot drive them out of the city, then they will take England in time?"

"I don't know how this will end," he says. "A king who leaves London to the peasants and a half-pay captain? A penniless crowd who say that they own the city? I don't know what might happen next."

"Come back," is all I can manage.

"It is my intention," he says tightly. "You are the love of my life. I will come back to you if I possibly can. I have sworn it. I am going to be there at the baptism of our new baby, my love. And God willing, make another."

A vision of the dancing head of Lord Say comes to my mind, and I blink to try to rid myself of it. "Richard, God send you back safely to me," I whisper.

I watch them muster in the great central

yard of the Tower and then leave quietly by the sally port, into the silent streets. I climb to the walkway at the top of the walls that run around the Tower and stand by a soldier on guard to watch them make their way quietly to the city. Richard has them in squares, four men by four men, all of them with pikes, many with swords, most of them with muffled feet. I see all this, but I am trying to see more. I am trying to see if there is a shadow over them, if they are marching out to their death. Especially, I am looking for the tall figure of my husband, at the head of his division, his sword drawn, his hooded head looking this way and the other, every sense alert, vibrantly alive, angry to have been brought to this.

I glimpse him only briefly before they slip between the crowded buildings, but I have no sense of premonition. Richard seems, as he always has been, so passionately alive, so vital, that there could never be a shadow over him. For a moment I think that perhaps this proves that he will come home in the morning in triumph, and then I think that if he were going out to certain death, he would still go out to it with his head up, his shoulders squared, and his footstep light.

Then we wait. We can hear some shouting from the street, and we have the cannon trained on the raggle-taggle army camped in the marshes below the Tower, and pointed north to the streets, but no one comes within range. The fighting is going on hand to hand, in one street after another as the rebels surge forwards and the apprentices and merchants, well armed and defending their homes, push them back. My husband commanding one wing of our forces and Lord Scales commanding another fight their way through the treacherous streets, always heading for the river. The rebels make a stand before Bridge-gate, where the lanes grow close and narrow, but the soldiers from the Tower push forwards and push on and gradually they yield, falling back over the bridge, a yard at a time. This time the doors of the houses on the bridge are barred and the shutters are over the windows, the tradesmen and merchants on the bridge are battened inside their homes, sick of the disorder and fearing worse as the slow battle grinds across the river, a yard at a time. The grinning heads of Lord Say and William Crowmer look down from the spikes of the bridge as their murderers are pressed back, one slow pace after another, and the royal army doggedly pushes on.

Forewarned by me, my husband has thick coils of rope and craftsmen in the vanguard of the men, and as soon as they force their way past the anchor points, he has the work-men ringed with a guard as they feverishly replace the ropes that I saw Jack Cade slash with his stolen sword. Desperately the men work, fearing arrows and missiles from the rebel army, as my husband, at the head of his men, fights with his sword in one hand and an axe in the other, going forwards and forwards until Cade's army is thrust to the far side of the bridge, then at a shouted command from my husband and a blast of trumpets, loud above the noise, the royal army breaks off, runs back to its own side, and with a rumble and a roar the drawbridge is raised, and my husband leans on his bloody sword, grins at Lord Scales, and then looks back along the long twenty-span bridge at the English dead who are being rolled carelessly into the river, and the wounded who are groaning and calling for help.

That night he sits in a deep hot bath in our rooms, and I soap the nape of his neck and his strong muscled back as if we were a peasant and his doxy taking their annual bath on Shrove Tuesday. "Good," he says. "Pray God the worst of this is over."

"Will they beg for forgiveness?"

"The king has sent pardons already," he says, his eyes closed as I pour a jug of hot water over his head. "Hundreds of them, blank forms of pardons. Hundreds of them, without a thought. And a bishop to fill in the names. They are all to be forgiven and told to go home."

"Just like that?" I ask.

"Just like that," he says.

"Do you think they will each take a pardon and go home and forget all about it?"

"No," he says. "But the king hopes that they were misled and mistaken and that they have learned their lesson and will accept his rule. He wants to think that it is all the fault of a bad leader and the rest of them were just mistaken."

"Queen Margaret won't think that," I predict, knowing the power of her temper, and that she learned how to rule over a peasantry who were held down by force and deference.

"No, she won't. But the king has decided on pardons, whatever she thinks."

Jack Cade's army, which was so brave and so filled with hope for a better world, lines up to take the pardons, and seems to be glad to do so. Each man says his name, and Bishop William Waynflete's clerk, in the rebel camp with a little writing desk, writes each name down and tells each man to go home, that the king has forgiven his offense. The bishop blesses them, signing the cross over each bowed head, and tells them to go in peace. Jack Cade himself lines up for his piece of paper and is publicly forgiven for leading an army against the king, killing a noble lord, and invading London. Some men see this as the king's weakness, but the greatest number of them think themselves lucky to get off scot-free, and they go back to their poor homes, where they cannot pay their taxes, where they cannot get justice, where the great lords ride roughshod over them — and hope for better times. They are just as they were before, but more bitter — and still the good times have not come.

But not Cade. I find my husband in the stables, his face dark with temper, ordering our horses in a bellowing voice. It seems that we are going back to Grafton; we are going back to Grafton "at once!" The roads are safe enough if we take a good guard.

"What's the matter?" I ask. "Why are we going now? Isn't the king coming? Should we not stay in London?"

"I can't stand to see him, nor her," he says flatly. "I want to go home for a while. We'll come back, of course we will, we will come back the moment they send for us; but before God, Jacquetta, I cannot stomach the court a moment longer."

"Why? What has happened?"

He is tying his traveling cape on the back of his saddle, and his back is to me. I go behind him and put my hand on his shoulder. Slowly he turns to face me. "I see you're angry," I say. "But speak to me: tell me what has happened."

"The pardons," he says, through his clenched teeth. "Those damned pardons.

Those hundreds of pardons."

"Yes?"

"Jack Cade took his pardon in the name of John Mortimer. The name he used in battle."

"So?"

"So they chased after him, despite his pardon, and they have captured him, despite his pardon. He showed them his pardon, signed by the king, blessed by the bishop, written fair in the name of John Mortimer. But they are going to hang him in the name of Jack Cade."

I pause, struggling to understand. "The king gave him a pardon; he can't be hanged. He just has to show his pardon — they cannot hang him."

"The king's pardon is in one name, which they know him by. They will hang him under another."

I hesitate. "Richard, he should never have been pardoned in the first place."

"No. But here we show everyone that his very cause was just. He said that there was no rule of law, but that the lords and the king do as they please. Here we prove it is so. We make a peace on the battlefield while he is in arms, while he is strong and we are weak; when he is near to victory and we are trapped in the Tower. We give him a pardon — that is our word of honor — but we break it as soon as he is a fugitive. The king's name is on the pardon, the king gave his word. Turns out that means nothing. The pardon is worth no more than the paper, the king's own signature nothing more than ink. There is no agreement, there is no justice, we betray our own cause, we are forsworn."

"Richard, he is still our king. Right or wrong, he is still the king."

"I know, and that is why I say that we will come back to court and serve him again. He is our king; we are his people. He gave us our name and our fortune. We will come back to court in the autumn. But I swear to you, Jacquetta, I just can't stomach it this summer."

GRAFTON, NORTHAMPTONSHIRE, SUMMER 1450

We arrive at our home at the height of the year, with the harvest coming in and the calves weaned from the cows. In the loft the apples are laid in rows, strict as soldiers, and one of the tasks for Lewis, now twelve, is to go up every day with a basket and bring down eight apples for the children to eat after their dinners. I am feeling weary with this baby, and as the evenings are cool and quiet I am happy to sit by the fire in my small chamber and listen while Richard's cousin Louise, who serves as governess to the older ones and nurse to the babies, hears them read from the family Bible. Anthony, at eight, has a passion for books and will come to me to look at the pictures in the volumes of Latin and old French that I inherited from my husband, and puzzle out the words in the difficult script. I know that this autumn he and his brothers and sisters can no longer be taught by the priest and I must find a scholar to come and teach them. Lewis especially must learn to read and write in Latin and Greek if he is to attend the king's college.

The baby comes in the middle of August, and we fetch down the family crib, polish it up, launder the little sheets, and I go into my confinement. She is born easily; she comes early, without great trouble, and I call her Martha. Within a few weeks Richard has taken her into the small chapel where we were married, and she is christened, and soon I am churched and up and about again.

It is her, the new baby, whom I think of when I start up out of bed one night, as alert as if I had heard someone suddenly call my name. "What is it?" I demand into the darkness.

Richard, groggy from sleep, sits up in the bed. "Beloved?"

"Someone called my name! There is something wrong!"

"Did you have a bad dream?"

"I thought . . ." Our lovely old house is silent in the darkness; a beam creaks as the old timbers settle. Richard gets out of bed and lights a taper at the dying fire and then lights a candle so that he can see me. "Jacquetta, you are as white as a ghost."

"I thought someone woke me."

"I'll take a look round," he decides, and pulls on his boots and drags his sword out from under the bed.

"I'll go to the nursery," I say.

He lights me a candle, and the two of us go out together into the dark gallery above the hall. And then I hear it. The strong sweet singing of Melusina, so high and so pure that you would think it was the sound of the stars moving in their spheres. I put my hand on Richard's arm. "Do you hear that?"

"No, what?"

"Music," I say. I don't want to say her name. "I thought I heard music." It is so clear and so powerful that I cannot believe he cannot hear it, like silver church bells, like the truest choir.

"Who would be playing music at this time of night?" he starts to ask, but already I have turned to run down the corridor to the nursery. I stop at the door and make myself open it quietly. Martha, the new baby, is asleep in her crib, the nursemaid in the truckle bed nearest to the fire. I put my hand on the child's rosy cheek. She is warm but not in fever. Her breath comes slowly and steadily, like a little bird breathing in a safe nest. In the high-sided bed beside her sleeps Diccon, humped up with his face buried into the down mattress. Gently, I lift him and turn him on his back so I can see the curve of his sleeping eyelids, and his rosebud mouth. He stirs a little at my touch, but he does not wake.

The music grows louder, stronger.

I turn to the next bed. John, the five-year-

331

old, is sprawled out in sleep as if he is too hot, the covers kicked sideways, and at once I fear that he is ill, but when I touch his forehead, he is cool. Jacquetta, next to him, sleeps quietly, like the neat little six-year-old girl she is; Mary in bed beside her stirs at the light from my candle but still sleeps. Their eleven-year-old sister Anne is in a truckle bed beside them, fast asleep.

Anthony, eight years old in the bigger bed, sits up. "What is it, Mama?"

"Nothing, nothing," I say. "Go to sleep."

"I heard singing," he says.

"There is no singing," I say firmly. "Lie down and close your eyes."

"Lewis is really hot," he remarks, but does as he is told.

I go quickly to their bed. The two boys sleep together, and as Anthony turns on his side I see that Lewis, my darling son, is flushed and burning up. It is his fever that has made their shared bed so hot. As I see him, and hear the insistent ringing music, I know that it is Lewis, my darling twelve-year-old son, who is dying.

The door behind me opens, and Richard, my husband, says quietly, "It's all secure in the house. Are the children well?"

"Lewis," is all I can say. I bend to the bed, and I lift him. He is limp in my arms, it is like lifting a dead body. Richard takes him from me and leads the way to our bedroom.

"What is it?" he asks, laying the boy on our bed. "What is wrong with him? He was well during the day."

"A fever, I don't know," I say helplessly. "Watch him while I get something for him."

"I'll sponge him," he suggests. "He's burning up. I'll try to cool him down."

I nod and go quickly to my still room. I have a jar of dried yarrow leaves, and a bunch of the white blossom hangs from one of the beams. I set a pot on to boil and make a tea from the blossom and then steep the leaves in a bowl of the boiled water. I am fumbling in my haste, and all the time the music is ringing in my head, as if to tell me that there is no time, that this is the song of mourning, that all this brewing of tea that smells of summer harvests is too late for Lewis, all I need for him is rosemary.

I take the drink in a cup and the soaking leaves in the jar and run back up to the bedroom. On the way I tap on the door of my lady-in-waiting and call, "Anne, get up, Lewis is sick," and hear her scramble inside.

Then I go into our bedroom.

Richard has stirred the fire and lit more candles, but he has drawn the bed curtains so Lewis's face is shaded from the light. Lewis has turned away, I can see the rapid breaths as his thin little chest rises and falls. I put the mug and the jar on the table and go to the bedside.

"Lewis?" I whisper.

His eyelids flutter open at the sound of my voice.

"I want to go in the water," he says, quite clearly.

"No, stay with me." I hardly know what I am saying. I raise him so his head is against my shoulder, and Richard presses the mug of yarrow tea into my hand. "Take a little sip," I say gently. "Come along. Take a little sip."

He turns his head away. "I want to go in the water," he repeats.

Richard looks desperately at me. "What does he mean?"

"It is a vision from the fever," I say. "It means nothing." I am afraid of what it means.

Lewis smiles, and his eyelids flicker open, and he sees his father. He smiles at him. "I shall swim, Father," he says firmly. "I shall swim," and he turns his head and takes a little breath like someone preparing to dive in deep cool waters, and I feel his body quiver as if with joy, and then go still and quiet, and I realize that my son has gone from me.

"Open the window," I say to Richard.

Without a word he turns and opens the window, as if to let the little soul out and up to heaven. Then he comes back and puts the sign of the cross on Lewis's forehead. He is still warm, but he is slowly cooling. I think the sweet waters of his dream are washing him down.

Anne taps on the door, opens it, and sees me lay Lewis gently down on the bed.

"He's gone," I say to her. "Lewis has gone from us."

Hardly knowing what I am doing, I step towards Richard and he puts his arm around me and holds me close to him. "God bless him," he says quietly.

"Amen," I say. "Oh Richard, I could do nothing. I could do nothing!"

"I know," he says.

"I'll go and see the other children," Anne says into the silence. "And then I'll get Mrs. Westbury to come and wash the body."

"I'll wash him," I say at once. "And I'll dress him. I don't want anyone else to touch him. I'll put him . . ." I find that I can't say the word *coffin.*

"I'll help you," Richard says quietly. "And we'll bury him in the churchyard and know that he has just gone ahead of us, Jacquetta, and that one day we will swim in the water too, and find him on the other side."

We bury my son in the churchyard near to his grandfather, and Richard orders a grand stone monument with room for our names too. The rest of the children do not take the fever; even the new baby, Martha, is well and strong. I watch them, filled with a terror, for a week after we bury Lewis, but none of them so much as sneezes.

335

I think that I will dream of Lewis, but I sleep deeply every night and dream of nothing at all. Until one night, a month after his death, I dream of a river, a deep cool river studded with yellow water lilies, flowing over a bed of gold and bronze stones, and golden kingcups growing on the green reedy banks; I see my boy Lewis on the far side of the river, pulling on his linen shirt and his breeches, and he is smiling at me and waving to show that he is going to run on ahead, just a little way ahead. And in my dream, though I want to hold him back, I wave at him and call to him that I will see him later, that I will see him soon, that I will see him in the morning.

Our retreat to Grafton lasts only for a little while. In September the king's messenger rides down the green lanes and up to our front gates. The wide wooden doors swing open, and he comes across the courtyard, the royal standard before him, a guard of six riding with him. I am walking back from chapel in the morning, and I pause as I see the gate admit him, and I wait, my back to the door of our house, with a sense of danger coming our way. Behind my back I cross my fingers, as if a childish sign can prevent trouble.

"A message for Baron Rivers," he says, dismounting and bowing.

"I am the Dowager Duchess, Lady Rivers,"

I say, holding out my hand. "You can give it to me."

He hesitates. "My husband is hunting," I continue. "He will be back tomorrow. In his absence I rule here. You had better give the message to me."

"I beg your pardon, Your Grace," he says, and hands it over. The royal seal is shiny and hard. I break it, and look up to nod to him.

"You will find ale and bread and meat for you and your men in the hall," I tell him. "And someone will show you where to wash. I will read this and send a reply when you have eaten and rested."

He bows again, and the guards give their horses to the stable boys and go into the house. I wait and then walk slowly to a stone bench let into the wall at the side of the garden and sit in the warm sunshine to read the letter.

It is a letter of appointment, another great honor for us. It is an acknowledgment of Richard's service in the late troubles; it shows that the lords of the Privy Council were watching to see who was quick of mind and brave of heart and ready to serve them — even if the king and queen had run away to Kenilworth and saw nothing. It says that Richard is appointed as Seneschal of Gascony, the rich land around Bordeaux that the English have held for three hundred years and hope to hold forever. Once again, Richard and I are to be an occupying force in France. Reading through the lines I guess that the king, shocked by the loss of English lands in Normandy by Edmund Beaufort, Duke of Somerset, is inspired to fortify the lands in Gascony with a more experienced commander. This appointment is an honor; it will bring with it the danger and difficulty of strengthening the forces around Bordeaux, holding the lands against French incursions, keeping the people loyal to England, and reversing their sense that they are all but abandoned by a homeland that cannot rule itself, let alone maintain lands overseas.

I look up from the letter. It is grief which makes me feel that nothing matters. I know this is a great honor, to rule Gascony is a great command. The Rivers are rising, even if one of us is missing. And there is no point in letting my heart ache for the one who is missing.

I look at the letter again. In the margin, like a monk illustrating a manuscript, the king has written in his own clerkish hand.

Dear Rivers,

Oblige me by going at once to Plymouth and mustering and organizing a force to take to Gascony and a fleet to carry them. You should set sail on September 21, no later.

Below this the queen has written to me: "Jacquetta — Lucky you! Going back to France!"

"Lucky" is not how I feel. I look around the yard, at the warm red-brick walls capped with white coping stones that lean against the old chapel, the apple tree bowing low with the weight of the last of the fat fruit, ready for picking, the barn which abuts the granary, filled with hay, and our house set plumb in the middle of it all, warm in the sunshine, peaceful this morning, my children at their lessons. I think that the king is setting my husband a task that will likely be impossible, and that once again I have to go to a new country, a new city, and hope to survive among people who begrudge our very presence.

I try to encourage myself by thinking that Gascony will be beautiful in autumn, that perhaps I will be able to see my brothers and sisters, that winter in Bordeaux will be crisp and bright and clear, and that spring will be glorious. But I know that the people of the country will be surly and resentful, the French a constant threat, and we will wait for money from England to pay the soldiers, and end up paying out of our own pocket, while at home there will be endless accusations of failure and even treason. I will have to leave my children behind in England. I don't want to go, and I don't want Richard to go either.

I wait for a long time until the royal messenger comes out into the yard, wiping his mouth on his sleeve, then sees me, sketches a bow, and waits. "You can tell His Grace that my husband and I will leave for Plymouth at once," I say. "Tell him that we are honored to serve."

He smiles ruefully, as if he knows that the service of this king may be an honor, but is only a sinecure for the very few favorites who can get away with doing nothing or even fail outright, like Edmund Beaufort, Duke of Somerset, who is now constable of all England, as a reward for running to Kenilworth when there was dangerous work to do in Kent. "God save the king," he says, and goes off to the stable to find his horses.

"Amen," I respond, thinking that perhaps we should pray that the king is saved from himself.

Plymouth,
Autumn 1450–1451

One long year while we struggle with the burghers of Plymouth, trying to persuade them to house and equip an invasion fleet. One whole year while my husband assembles a fleet from the privately owned ships of merchants, traders, and the few great lords who keep their own vessels. By midwinter, months after we were supposed to sail, he has more than eighty boats tied up at the quaysides of Plymouth, Dartmouth, and Kingsbridge, and more than three thousand men housed in inns and rooms, cottages and farms, all round Devon and Cornwall: waiting.

That's all we do; from autumn, through winter to spring, we wait. First we wait for the men who have been promised by their lords to march to Plymouth, ready to embark. Richard rides out to meet them and bring them in, finds them quarters, finds them food, promises them wages. Then we wait for the ships that have been requisitioned to come in; Richard rides all around the West Country, buying up little sailing ships in their home ports, demanding that the greater merchants make their contribution. Then we wait for the stores to arrive; Richard rides to Somerset, even into Dorset, to get grain, then we wait for the lords who will sail with the invasion to finish the merry days of Christmas and come to Plymouth, then we wait for the king's command that we should finally set sail, then we wait for the spring northerlies to die down, and always, always, always, we wait for the ship that will bring the money from London so that we can pay the harborside merchants, the ship owners, the sailors, the men themselves. Always we wait, and the money never comes when it should.

Sometimes it comes late, and Richard and I have to send to Grafton and our friends at court to lend us money so that we can at least feed the army before they march out into the farms around the port and steal to feed themselves. Sometimes it comes, but in such small amounts that we can only pay the outstanding debts and offer the men just a quarter of their pay. Sometimes it comes as tally sticks that we take to the king's custom houses and they say, regretfully, "Yes, it's good, my lord; I grant your right to be paid. But I have no money to pay you with. Come again next month." Sometimes it is promised and never comes at all. I watch Richard, riding to the little towns of Devon, trying to appease the local landlords, who are furious at having this hungry horde quartered upon them. I watch him pursue roving bands of the men who were supposed to be his army and are becoming brigands. I watch Richard begging the shipmasters to keep their vessels ready to sail in case the order for the invasion comes tomorrow, the next day, or the day after. And I watch Richard when the news comes from France that the French king has advanced on Bergerac and Bazas and taken them. In spring we hear his forces are advancing on English lands on either side of the Gironde; he sets siege to Fronsac on the Dordogne, and the townspeople wait behind its great walls, swearing they will not give up, certain that our army is coming to relieve them. Our army is on the quayside, where the ships are bobbing, when we hear that Fronsac has surrendered. The English settlers are appealing for help; they vow that they will fight, that they will resist, that they are Englishmen and count themselves as Englishmen born and bred. They stake their lives on their faith in us; they swear that their countrymen will come to their aid. I watch Richard trying to hold his army together, trying to hold his fleet together, sending message after message to London, pleading with the court to send him the order to sail. Nothing comes.

Richard starts to say that when he gets the order to sail, he will leave me behind, he dare not take me to Bordeaux if the place is going to come under siege. I walk along the protective wall of the harbor and look south to the lands of France that my first husband used to command, and wish that we were both safely home in Grafton. I write to the queen myself. I tell her that we are ready to go to the rescue of Gascony, but we can do nothing without money to pay the soldiers, and that while they kick their heels in the farms and villages they complain of their treatment by us, their masters and lords, and the workingmen and -women of Devon see how badly the soldiers and sailors are treated and say that this is a kingdom where a man is not rewarded for doing his duty. They mutter that the men of Kent had it right — that this is a king who cannot hold his own lands here or abroad, that he is badly advised. They whisper that Jack Cade called for Richard, Duke of York, to be admitted to the king's councils, and that Jack Cade was right and died for his belief. They even say — though I never tell her this — that she is a French woman squandering the money that should go to the army so that her own country can seize the land of Gascony, and England be left with nothing in France at all. I beg her to tell her husband to send the order for his fleet to set sail.

Nothing comes.

In July we hear that Bordeaux has fallen to the French. In September the first refugees from Bayonne start to arrive in tattered craft and say that the whole of the duchy of Gascony has been captured by the French while the expedition to save them, commanded by my unhappy husband, waited in the dock at Plymouth, eating the stores and waiting for orders.

We have been living in a little house overlooking the harbor for all of this long year. Richard uses the first-floor room as his headquarters. I go up the narrow stairs, to find him at the small-paned window, looking out at the blue sea, where the wind is blowing briskly towards the coast of France, good sailing weather; but all his fleet is tied up at the quayside.

"It's over," he says bluntly to me as I quietly stand beside him. I put my hand on his shoulder; there is nothing I can say to comfort him in this, his moment of shame and failure. "It is all over, and I did nothing. I am seneschal of nothing. You have been the wife firstly of John, Duke of Bedford, a mighty lord, the regent of all of France, and secondly to the seneschal of nothing."

"You did all that you were commanded to do," I say softly. "You held the fleet and the army together, and you were ready to sail. If they had sent the money and the order, you would have gone. If they had sent the order alone, you would have gone without the money to pay them. I know that. Everyone knows that. You would have fought unpaid, and the men would have followed you. I don't doubt that you would have saved Gascony. You had to wait for your orders; that was all. It was not your fault."

"Oh." He laughs bitterly. "But I have my orders now."

I wait, my heart sinking.

"I am to take a force to defend Calais."

"Calais?" I stumble. "But surely the King of France is at Bordeaux?"

"They think that the Duke of Burgundy is massing to attack Calais."

"My kinsman."

"I know, I am sorry, Jacquetta."

"Who will go with you?"

"The king has appointed Edmund Beaufort, Duke of Somerset, as Captain of Calais. I am to go and support him as soon as I have dismissed the ships and sailors and the army from here."

"Edmund Beaufort, Duke of Somerset?" I repeat, disbelievingly. This is the man who lost us Normandy. Why would he be trusted with Calais, but for the king's unswerving belief in his kinsman and the queen's misplaced affection?

"Please God, he has learned how to soldier through defeat," my husband says grimly.

I lean my cheek against his arm. "At least you can save Calais for the English," I say. "They will call you a hero if you can hold the castle and the town."

"I will be commanded by the man who gave away Normandy," he says gloomily. "I will be in service to a man that Richard, Duke of York, has named as a traitor. If they don't send us men and money there either then I don't know that we can hold it."

GRAFTON, NORTHAMPTONSHIRE, AUTUMN 1451

Richard's mood does not lift as he prepares to leave for Calais. I send for Elizabeth, my oldest girl, to come home to see her father before he leaves. I have placed her at the house of the Grey family at Groby Hall, near Leicester, just fifty miles away. They are a wealthy family, with kinsmen all around the country, ruling thousands of acres. She is supervised by the lady of the house: Lady Elizabeth, heiress to the wealthy Ferrers family. I could not have chosen anyone better to teach my girl how a great woman runs her household. There is a son and heir at home, young John Grey, who rode out against Jack Cade, a handsome young man. He will inherit the estate, which is substantial, and the title, which is noble.

It takes her a day to ride home, and she comes with an armed escort. The roads are so dangerous with wandering bands of men, thrown out of France without a home to go to, or wages. Elizabeth is fourteen now, nearly as tall as me. I watch her, and have to stop myself smiling: she is such a beauty, and she has such grace. At her age I was probably her match for looks, but she has a calmness and a sweetness that I never had. She has my clear pale skin and my fair hair, she has gray eyes and a perfectly regular face like the sculpted marble face of a beautiful statue. When she laughs, she is a child; but sometimes she looks at me, and I think, dear God, what a girl this is: she has the Sight from Melusina; she is a woman of my line, and she has a future before her that I can neither imagine nor foresee.

Elizabeth's sister Anne is her little shadow; at just twelve she copies every gesture of Elizabeth's and follows her around like a devoted puppy. Richard laughs at me for my adoration of my children, and my favorite of them all is Elizabeth's brother: Anthony. He is nine, and a brighter scholar never lost count of the hours in a library. But he is not just a boy for his books; he plays with the village lads and can run as fast and fight as hard as they, with fists or in wrestling. His father is teaching him to joust, and he sits on a horse as if he were born in the saddle; they move together. You never see him shift to the leap of the horse: they are as one. He plays tennis with his sisters and is kind enough to let them win, he plays chess with me and makes me pause and puzzle over his moves, and sweetest, warmest of all, he goes down on one knee for his mother's blessing night and morning, and when I have put my hand on his head, he jumps up for a hug and will stand at my side, leaning lightly against me, like a foal at foot. Mary is eight this year, growing out of her dresses every season, and devoted to her father. She follows him everywhere, riding all day on her fat little pony so that she can be at his side, learning the names of the fields and the tracks to the villages so she can go out to meet him. He calls her his princess and swears he will make a marriage for her to a king who will have no kingdom but will come and live with us so no one will ever take her away. Our next child, just a year younger, Jacquetta, is named for me, but she could not be less like me. She is Richard's daughter through and through, she has his quiet humor and his calmness. She keeps a distance from her brothers' and sisters' tumblings and quarrels, and she laughs when they appeal to her to serve as judge and jury from the pinnacle of the wisdom of a seven-year-old. In the nursery, unruly as puppies, are my two boys John and Richard, six and five years old, and in the well-polished cradle is the new baby, the sweetest best-tempered baby of them all: Martha.

As Richard assembles the men he will take to Calais and starts to teach them how to use the lances, how to stand against a charge, how to march in an attack, I have to keep telling myself that this is the right thing to do — to send him off with the blessings of all his children; but there is something about gathering them together to say good-bye that fills me with dread.

"Jacquetta, are you fearful for me?" he asks me one evening.

I nod, almost ashamed to say yes.

"Have you seen anything?" he asks.

"Oh no! Thank God! No, it is not that. I don't know anything at all, nothing more than that I fear for you," I assure him. "I have not tried to scry or foretell since you told me to put it aside, after the trial of Eleanor Cobham."

He takes my hands and kisses them, first one and then the other. "My love, you must not fear for me. Do I not always tell you I will come home to you?"

"Yes."

"Have I ever failed you?"

"Never."

"I lost you once and swore I would never lose you again," he says.

"You found me by moonlight." I am smiling.

"By luck," he says, a man of earth as always. "But I swore then that I would never lose you again. You have nothing to fear."

"Nothing," I repeat. "But I should tell you — I am with child again, and you will have a

351

new baby next summer."

"Dear God, I can't leave you," he says at once. "This changes everything. I can't leave you here, not alone with the children, to face another childbed."

I had hoped he would be pleased; I am determined to hide my own fears. "Beloved, I have been brought to bed nine times; I think I know how to do it by now."

His face is creased with worry. "The danger is always the same," he says. "The danger of childbirth is the same the first time as the last. And you have lost one child, and I thought then your heart would break. Besides, the news from London is bad. The queen is certain to want you at her side, and I will be stuck in Calais with Edmund Beaufort."

"If you even get there."

He falls silent, and I know he is thinking of the idle ships and the army that wore out their time with a year of waiting, while their countrymen died outside Bordeaux.

"Don't look like that, I should not have said it. I am sure you will get there and then you will hold Calais for us," I say quickly.

"Yes, but I don't like to leave you here while the king is clinging to Somerset and York is building an affinity of more and more men who think as he does that the king is badly advised."

I shrug. "There is no way out, my love. The

baby is coming and I had better have her here, rather than come with you to Calais and give birth in a garrison."

"You think it will be another girl?" he asks.

"The girls will be the making of this family," I predict. "You wait and see."

"Queens militant?"

"One of these girls is going to make a marriage that will make our fortunes," I say. "Why else would God make them so beautiful?"

I speak bravely enough to Richard, but when he musters his men and marches out of the courtyard and down the road to London, where they will take ship to Calais, I am very low. My daughter Elizabeth finds me walking with my thick cape around my shoulders, my hands in a fur muff, beside the river, as the frosty banks and the icy reeds match my mood. She comes forwards and links her arm in mine and matches her steps to mine. I am only a head taller than her now, she keeps pace with me easily.

"Are you missing Father already?" she asks gently.

"Yes," I say. "I know I am a soldier's wife and I should be ready to let him go, but each time it is hard, and I think that it gets harder, not easier."

"Can you foretell his future?" she asks quietly. "Can't you see that he will come home safely? I am certain this time he will be safe. I just know it."

I turn and look at her. "Elizabeth, can you foresee things at will?"

She gives a little shrug of the shoulders. "I'm not sure," she says. "I don't know."

For a moment I am back in that hot summer, in the chamber of my great-aunt Jehanne as she showed me the cards and gave me the bracelet of charms, and told me the story of the women of our family.

"It's not something that I would press on you," I say. "It is a burden as well as a gift. And these are not the times for it."

"I don't think you can press it on me," she replies thoughtfully. "I don't think it is a gift you can give — is it? I just sometimes have a sense of things. At Groby, there is a corner, a cloister by the chapel, and when I walk there, I can see someone, a woman, almost a ghost of a woman. She stands there and she has her head on one side as if she is listening for me; she waits almost as if she is looking for me. But there is no one there really."

"You know the stories of our family," I say.

She gives a gurgle of laughter. "It is me who tells the story of Melusina every night to the little ones," she reminds me. "They love it, and I love it."

"You know that some of the women of our family have inherited gifts from Melusina. Gifts of the Sight."

She nods.

"My great-aunt Jehanne taught me some ways to use the gift, and then my lord the Duke of Bedford had me work with his alchemists, and sent a woman to teach me about herbs."

"What did you do with alchemists?" Like any child, she is fascinated by forbidden magic. The skill with herbs is too ordinary for her; she has learned it in my still room. She wants to know about dark arts.

"I read the books with them, sometimes I stirred a mixture or poured it out to cool." I am remembering the forge in the inner courtyard and the great room like a vast kitchen in the wing of the house, where they heated and cooled the liquor and stones. "And my lord had a great mirror where he wanted me to scry — to see the future. He wanted to see the future of the English lands in France." I make a little gesture. "I am glad now that I could not see clearly. It would have broken his heart, I think. I thought I failed him at the time, but now I think I served him best by not seeing."

"But you could see?"

"Sometimes," I say. "And sometimes, like with the cards or with the charms, you get a glimpse of what might be. And sometimes you show yourself only your own desires. And sometimes — though very rarely — you can put your heart in your own desires and bring them about. Take the dream and make it come into being."

"By magic?" she breathes. She is quite entranced at the thought of it.

"I don't know," I tell her honestly. "When I knew that your father was in love with me and I was in love with him, I wanted him to marry me and make me his wife and bring me to England, but I knew that he would not dare. He thought I was too far above him and he would not be my ruin."

"Did you make a spell?"

I smile, thinking back to the night when I brought out the charms but realized that I needed nothing but my own determination. "A spell and a prayer and knowing your desire are all the same thing," I say. "When you lose something precious, and you go to the chapel and you kneel before the little glass window of St. Anthony and pray to him to find the thing you need, what are you doing but reminding yourself that you have lost something and you want it back? What are you doing but showing yourself that you want it? And what is that but calling it back to you? And so often, when I pray, I remember then where I left it, and go back to find it. Is that an answer to prayer or is it magic? Or is it simply letting myself know what I want and seeking it? The prayer is just the same as a spell, which is just the same as knowing your desire that calls the thing back to your mind, and so back to your hand. Isn't it?"

"A spell would bring it back to you; you wouldn't just find it!"

"I believe that a desire and a prayer and a spell are all the same thing," I say. "When you pray, you know that you want something, that's always the first step. To let yourself know that you want something, that you yearn for it. Sometimes that's the hardest thing to do. Because you have to have courage to know what you desire. You have to have courage to acknowledge that you are unhappy without it. And sometimes you have to find courage to know that it was your folly or your wrongdoing which lost it; before you make a spell to bring it back, you have to change yourself. That's one of the deepest transformations that can be."

"How?"

"Say one day, when you are married, you want a baby, a child?"

She nods.

"First you have to know the emptiness of your womb, of your arms, of your heart. That can hurt. You have to have the courage to look at yourself and know the loss that you feel. Then you have to change your life to make a space for the child who will not come. You have to open your heart; you have to make a safe place for the baby. And then you have to sit with your longing and your desire, and that can be the most painful. You have to sit with your longing and know that you may not get what you want; you have to encounter the danger of longing for something without the expectation of getting your desire."

"But this never happened to you," she suggests.

"In my first marriage," I say quietly, "I knew that my husband would not have a child. But I had to let myself know that I was different from him. I longed for a baby, and I wanted to be loved."

"Did you wish for it?" she asks. "Did you make a spell to make him change?"

"I didn't try to change him, but I had to know the sorrow of what was missing in my life. I had to find the courage to know that I had made the mistake of marrying a man who would not love me for myself, and who would not give me a child; and once I knew that, truly knew that I was an unloved maid — though a married woman — then I could wish that someone loved me."

"And you wished for Father."

I smile at her. "And for you."

She blushes in pleasure. "Is this magic?"

"In a way. Magic is the act of making a wish come about. Like praying, like plotting, like herbs, like exerting your will on the world, making something happen."

"Will you teach me?" she asks.

I look at her consideringly. She is a daughter of our house and perhaps the most beautiful girl we have ever had. She has the inheritance of Melusina and the gift of Sight. One of my children must inherit the cards my great-aunt gave me and the bracelet of charms — I think I always knew that it would be Elizabeth, the child born of desire, of the herbs, and my wish. And as my great-aunt Jehanne said: it should be the oldest girl.

"Yes," I say. "These are not the times, and these are forbidden skills; but I will teach you, Elizabeth."

Over the next few weeks I show her the bracelet of charms and the cards, and I teach her about herbs that she will not find in Lady Elizabeth Grey's still room. I take all the older children out on one frosty day and teach them how to find water in underground springs by holding a peeled wand in their hands and feeling it turn in their palms. They laugh with delight as we find a spring in the water meadow, and a dirty old drain from the stable yard.

I show Elizabeth how to open a page of her Bible and then think and pray over the text that comes to her. I give her a freshwater pearl on a little cord and teach her how to watch it swing in answer to a question. And more importantly than anything else, I start to teach her how to clear her mind, how to know her desires, how to judge herself, putting aside favor and indulgence. "The alchemists always say you have to be pure. You are the first ingredient," I tell her. "You have to be clean."

When the time comes for her to go back to Groby Hall, she tells me that the young man of the house, John Grey, is a most handsome young man, kind and beautifully mannered, and that she wishes he would see her for herself, and not just as a girl being educated by his mother, one of three or four young women whom Lady Grey has in her keeping.

"He does," I assure her. "He sees you already. You just have to be patient."

"I like him so much," she confesses, her eyes down and her cheeks warm. "And when he speaks to me, I say nothing of any sense. I speak like a fool. He must think me a fool."

"He doesn't."

"Shall I use a love potion on him? Dare I?"

"Wait for spring," I advise her. "And pick some flowers from an apple tree in his orchard. Choose the prettiest tree . . ."

She nods.

"Put the petals in your pocket. And when the tree fruits, take one apple and give him half to eat with honey, and keep the other."

"Will that make him love me?"

I smile. "He will love you. And the petals and honeyed apple will give you something to do while you wait."

She giggles. "You're not much of a spell maker, Lady Mother."

"When a beautiful young woman wants to

enchant a man, she doesn't need much of a spell," I assure her. "A girl like you needs to do nothing much more than stand under an oak tree and wait for him to ride by. But do you remember about wishing?"

"Pure in heart," she says.

Together, we go out to the stable yard. The guard to take her back to Groby is mounted and ready. "One last thing," I say, and take her hand before she climbs on the mounting block. She turns to listen. "Don't curse," I say to her. "No ill-wishing."

She shakes her head. "I wouldn't. Not even Mary Sears. Not even when she smiles at him and curls her hair around her finger, and is so quick to sit beside him."

"Ill-wishing is a curse on the woman who does it, as well as the one who receives it. When you put such words out in the world, they can overshoot — like an arrow — that's what my great-aunt Jehanne told me. A curse can go beyond your target and harm another. A wise woman curses very sparingly. I would hope that you never curse at all." Even as I speak I feel the shadow of the future on her. "I pray that you never have cause to curse," I say.

She kneels for my blessing. I put my hand on the pretty velvet bonnet and her warm fair head. "Bless you, my daughter, and may you remain pure in heart and get your desires."

She peeps up at me, her gray eyes bright. "I think I will!"

"I think you will," I say.

LONDON,
SPRING 1452

With my husband serving in Calais, I return to court in the cold weather of January and find everyone talking about the treason of Richard, Duke of York, who is said to be preparing a complete rebellion against the king, his cousin, because of his hatred of the Duke of Somerset.

The queen is determined that the threat shall be faced and defeated. "If he is against the Duke of Somerset, he is against me," she says. "I have no better or more trustworthy friend. And this Richard of York wants him tried for treason! I know who the traitor is! But he shows his hand at last and confesses that he is against the king."

"He asks only for the great lords to intercede for him with the king," I remark calmly. "He wants them to put his case to the king. And in the meantime, he swears his loyalty."

She throws the manifesto that York has sent around the main towns of the kingdom on the table before me. "Who do you think this means? York says that the king is surrounded by enemies, adversaries, and evil willers. He is attacking the king's advisors. That's you, he means, and your husband, as well as Somerset and me."

"Me?"

"Jacquetta, he accuses me of being William de la Pole's lover; do you think he would blink at calling you a witch?"

I feel the room grow very still and cold. I put my hand to my belly as if to shield the new life within. The ladies-in-waiting in earshot look up at me, their eyes wide, but say nothing.

"He has no cause for such an accusation," I say quietly, though I can hear my heart hammering. "You yourself know that I would never play with such toys. I don't use herbs except for my family's health; I don't even consult with wise women. I read nothing but permitted books, I speak to no one . . ."

"He has no cause to say anything," she declares. "What cause does he have to speak against Edmund Beaufort, Duke of Somerset? Against me? But remember that he is my enemy and your enemy too. And that if he can destroy you he will do so, just to hurt me."

She takes her seat at the fireside, and I read the manifesto more carefully. The Duke of York demands that Edmund Beaufort be charged with treason and arrested. He warns against bad advisors who have gathered around the queen, foreign-born advisors, ill-wishers. In truth, he says nothing against me by name. But I cannot rid myself of the familiar pulse of fear.

The king is inspired to warlike behavior by the threat to his friend Edmund Beaufort, the Duke of Somerset. Nothing else would waken him but a threat to his beloved cousin. Suddenly, he is active, courageous, determined. He declares his absolute faith in Edmund Beaufort and his other advisors. He declares that Richard, Duke of York, is a rebel, and he demands forces to be mustered from all the towns, counties, and shires. The king's army pours in from all around the kingdom. Nobody wants to support the Duke of York, only the men of his affinity and those who share his hatred of Edmund Beaufort for their own reasons go to his standard and start to create an army.

Henry calls for his armor once more, again has his warhorse saddled up. The lads in the yard tease his standard-bearer that he will have another nice ride out for a day, and assure him that they will keep his dinner warm for him, for he will be back before sunset; but the lords of council and the commanders of the army are not laughing.

The queen and the ladies of her court go down to the frosty jousting green at Westminster to see the parade of the lords ride by on their way out to do battle with the Duke of York.

"I wish your husband were here to support him," she says to me as the king mounts his great gray warhorse, his standard before him and his crown on his helmet. He looks much younger than his thirty years, his eyes bright and eager; his smile, as he waves to Margaret, is excited.

"God save him," I say, thinking of the battle-hardened forty-year-old Duke of York mustering his own men.

The trumpets blow, the drummers sound the pace of the march, the cavalry go out first, their standards bright in the icy sunlight, their armor glinting, their horseshoes thunderous on the cobbles, and then after them come the archers, and after them the pikemen. This is only a small part of the royal army; tens of thousands of men are waiting for the king's orders at Blackheath. His councillors have mustered a mighty army for him. From there he will march north to confront the rebel duke.

The march does not happen. Richard, Duke of York, comes into the royal tent and kneels before his king, praying earnestly that the king dismiss the favored Duke of Somerset and citing old injuries: the loss of the lands in France, the shameful surrender of Rouen, and finally the likely destruction of the garrison of Calais by his selfish seizing of command, which is certain to fail.

He can do no more; he can say no more.

"We don't care," Margaret says to me, as I brush her hair before bed that evening. "We don't care what he thinks of Edmund Beaufort; we don't care what he says about Calais, or about me, or about you. He knew he was defeated when we raised an army three times the size of his. He knew he would have to withdraw everything he said. He knew he would have to beg our pardon. He is a broken man. His rebellion is ended. We have broken him."

I say nothing. The duke does indeed kneel to the king in public and swear never to assemble his men again. The country sees that the king is beloved and the duke is not. The country sees that Edmund Beaufort is unassailable and the Duke of York is defeated.

"I don't doubt the duke is outwardly penitent, but I doubt that the duke's complaints are over," Richard writes to me from Calais.

The royal couple at any rate are united in their joy. Margaret treats her young husband as if he had returned victorious from a mighty war. "He rode out," she justifies herself to me. "And if there had been fighting, I believe he would have led it. He was at the head of his army and he didn't run for Kenilworth."

The king takes to riding out every day in his beautifully engraved armor, as if to be

367

ready for anything. Edmund Beaufort comes back from Calais and rides beside him, his dark handsome face turned attentively to the king, agreeing with everything he says. The court moves to Windsor, and in an excess of happiness, the king offers a pardon to everybody, for anything.

"Why does he not arrest them all and behead them?" Margaret demands. "Why pardon?"

It seems to be his way. After he has issued pardons to all the rebels, his new enthusiasm for warfare spills over into a proposal for an expedition — to go to Calais and use the garrison as a base to reconquer the English lands in France. For the king this would be to step in the footsteps of his more heroic father; for Edmund Beaufort it would be to redeem his reputation. I expected the queen to be thrilled at the thought of Beaufort and the king on campaign, but I find her in her room picking over some embroidery, her head down. When she sees me, she shifts up in her seat and beckons me beside her. "I cannot bear for him to take such a risk," she says to me quietly. "I cannot bear to think of him in battle."

I am surprised and pleased at her emotion. "Are you so tender to His Grace, the king?" I ask hopefully. "I know I cannot bear it when Richard goes to war."

She turns her pretty head from me as if I

have said something too foolish to answer. "No. Not him. Edmund, Edmund Beaufort. What would become of us if he were to be hurt?"

I take a breath. "These are the fortunes of war," I say. "Your Grace should perhaps hold a special intercessory Mass for the safety of the king."

She brightens at the thought of it. "Yes. We could do that. It would be terrible if anything were to happen to him. He would leave no heir but Richard, Duke of York, and I would rather die myself than see York inherit the throne after all he has said and done. And if I were to be widowed, I would never be married again, as everyone will think I am barren." She looks askance at my broadening body. "You don't know what it is like," she says. "To wait and to hope and to pray but never, never to have a sign of a child coming."

"There is still no sign?" I ask. I had hoped that she might be with child, that the king militant might have been more of a husband than before.

She shakes her head. "No. None. And if the king goes to war, he will face my uncle the King of France on the battlefield. If Henry withdraws or retreats, then everyone will laugh at us."

"He will have good commanders in the field," I say. "Once he gets to Calais, Richard

369

will put a strong standard-bearer beside him, to keep him safe."

"Richard was beside him before, when all he had to face was Jack Cade and a rabble," she says. "A half-pay captain and a band of workingmen with pitchforks. You didn't see the king then, Jacquetta; he was terrified. He was frightened like a girl. I've never seen him ride as fast as when we left London." She puts her hand over her mouth as if to stop disloyal words. "If he runs from the French king, I will be shamed to the ground," she says very quietly. "Everyone will know. All my family will know."

"He will have his friends beside him," I say. "Men who are accustomed to warfare. My husband, and Edmund Beaufort, the Duke of Somerset."

"Edmund has sworn to save Calais," she says. "And he is absolutely a man of his word. He swore to me, he went down on his knees and swore to me that nobody would blame me for the loss of Calais, that he would keep it for England and for me. He said it would be his gift to me, like the little fairings he used to give me. He said he would have a golden key made and I can wear it in my hair. They will sail in April."

"So soon?"

"The king has told the Calais garrison to send all their ships to ferry him across the narrow seas. He is taking a great army and a thousand sailors to sail his ships. He is going in April without fail, he says."

I hesitate. "You know, once he gets the fleet assembled, he must go," I say carefully. "It is very hard to keep a force together, waiting."

The queen has no idea that I am talking of a year of our lives that Richard and I wasted on the quayside at Plymouth, waiting for her husband to do what he had promised. She has no idea of what that cost us.

"Of course," she says. "Edmund Beaufort will get the ships without fail, and then the king will go. Edmund will keep him safe, I know it."

I see that Edmund Beaufort has completely filled the place of William de la Pole in the affections of the young couple. The king has always needed a man to command him; he is afraid without someone at his side. And the queen is lonely. It is as simple as that.

"My lord Beaufort will take the king to Calais; thank God that we can rely on him."

THE WEST OF ENGLAND, SUMMER 1452

He does not go. Edmund Beaufort, Duke of Somerset, commands my husband to muster a fleet in Calais and sail with it across the narrow seas to escort the king to France to start his campaign. Richard in Calais recruits the fleet and waits for the order to send the ships to bring the English army to Calais, but spring comes and goes and the order never comes.

I enter my confinement in Grafton, glad to know that Richard is not campaigning this year, and, as it happens, I am right about the baby; I am always right about my babies. I hold my wedding ring on a thread over my curved belly, and when it swings clockwise it is a boy, and if it is a girl, it circles counterclockwise. This is hedge magic, superstition, and nonsense that the midwives believe, that the physicians deny. I smile and call it nonsense, but it has never been wrong. I call the new little mite Eleanor and put her in the wooden cradle that has now rocked nine of

Richard's children, and write to tell him that he has a little girl, that she has his dark curling hair and blue eyes, and that he is to take leave from Calais, come home, and see his new daughter.

He does not come. The garrison is under pressure from the Duke of Burgundy, whose forces are mustered nearby, they fear he may set a siege. Although Richard is just across the narrow seas and Calais is only a day's sail away, it feels as if we have been parted for a long time, and that he is far away.

In the nursery, one night, while the wet nurse is having her dinner in the hall below, I sit with my new baby and look at her sleeping in the cradle, and I take my great-aunt's cards from the hanging pocket at my belt, and shuffle them, cut them, and take the one card and put it on the little embroidered blanket in the baby's crib. I want to know when I will see Richard again; I want to know what the future holds for me.

It is the Fool, a peasant man with a stick over his shoulder, a gaping bag at the end of it, without a fortune now but with hopes. In his other hand he carries a stick to help him stride out on the road ahead. A dog pulls at his breeches, his lowly nature which draws him back from his destiny; but he goes onwards. He keeps trying. It is a card that tells the reader to set off in hope, that great things can be achieved, that one should walk out filled with courage, even if one is a fool to hope. But what catches my eye is the white rose he wears in his cap. I sit for a long time, the card in my hand, wondering what it means to be an adventurer with a white rose in your cap.

When I return to court, I ask the queen if Richard may come home, but she and the king are distracted by news of trouble, petty uprisings, and discontents in all the counties around London. They are the old complaints, stated all over again. Jack Cade was hunted down to his death, but his questions were never answered, and his demands — for justice, for the law, for fair taxation and an end to the court favorites — go on and on. The men of Kent turn out for another un-named captain, saying that the king must dismiss his favorites who steal the royal fortune and give him bad advice; the men of Warwickshire take up arms, saying that Jack Cade is still alive and will lead them. The king, deaf to all complaints against him, sets out on a summer progress determined to try men for treason and, wherever he goes, Ed-mund Beaufort, the Duke of Somerset, rides alongside, a companion and confidant, and sits beside the king when they go south and west to Exeter. Together, they pass the death sentence on men who have done nothing more than complain of the duke's influence.

The men here in the dock are the very ones

who complained of having troops quartered on them for a year, the very ones who said that we should go to Gascony and reclaim it, who raged against the waste and the shame of the army on the quayside of Plymouth. They saw, as none of this court will ever see, the spendthrift folly of creating an army and then leaving it with nothing to do. Now they will die for saying that. They said nothing more than Richard and I said to each other when the sailors wore out their patience and the soldiers ate up all the stores. But these men said it aloud when spies were listening, and now they will die, for the king's forgiving nature spins on its axis and suddenly turns to reveal its dark side and is sour.

"It is sorry work," Edmund Beaufort, Duke of Somerset, remarks to me, as he sees me walk slowly back from chapel to the queen's rooms at Exeter. "But you must not let yourself be saddened by the sins of the country people, my lady."

I glance at him; he seems genuinely concerned. "I saw the cost to them of the expedition that never sailed," I say briefly. "It was my husband who quartered the soldiers on them. We knew at the time that it was hard. And this is another price that they have to pay."

He takes my hand and tucks it into his arm. "And there was a heavy cost to you," he says sympathetically. "It was hard on you, I know, and on your husband, Lord Rivers. There is no better commander in England, and no safer man to hold Calais. There was no doubt in my mind he did everything he could to keep the army ready."

"He did," I say. "And he will do everything in Calais, but if the king sends no wages to pay the troops, then the garrison will turn against us. Just as Kent turned against us, just as Devon is turning against us now."

He nods. "I am trying, my lady," he says, as if he is answerable to me. "You can tell your husband that he is never far from my thoughts. I am captain of Calais, I never forget my duty to your husband and the garrison. There is no money in the Treasury and the court eats gold; every time we move it is a small fortune; and the king, God bless him, will have all the money for the colleges he is building to the glory of God, and for his friends who strive for their own glory. But I am trying; I will satisfy the king, and I will not see your husband and his comrade Lord Welles left short of funds in Calais."

"I am glad of it," I reply quietly. "I thank you for him."

"And now we are sending an expedition to Bordeaux, as we promised," he says brightly.

"Bordeaux?" I say blankly. "Bordeaux again?"

He nods. "We have to support the English in France," he says. "They are overrun by the

French, but they swear they will defy them and open the gates of Bordeaux to us if we can only get an army out to them. We can recapture the lands we lost. I am going to send John Talbot, Earl of Shrewsbury. You will remember him well, of course."

John Talbot was one of my first husband's most loyal and trusted commanders, famous for lightning raids and his utter bloody determination to win. But he is old now, and after he was captured and released by the French, he made a sacred promise never again to arm against the French king. "Surely he is too old to go to war," I say. "He must be sixty if he is a day."

"Sixty-five." The duke smiles. "And as ready and brave as he ever was."

"But he was paroled by the French. He promised not to fight again. How can we send him? He is a man of such honor — surely he won't go?"

"His presence alone will put the heart in them," he predicts. "He will ride at the head. He will not carry his sword, but he will ride before them. It's a glorious thing he does, and I will see him supported with a good army. I am doing my best, Lady Rivers. I am doing my very best." He raises his arm so that he can kiss my fingers, resting in the crook of his elbow, a graceful unusual gesture. "It is my pleasure to serve you, Lady Rivers. I would have you think of me as your friend."

I hesitate. He is a charming man, a handsome man, and there is something about his intimate whisper that would make any woman's heart beat a little faster. I cannot help but return his smile. "I do," I say.

We go west, through surly countryside where the people cannot earn enough to pay their taxes and who see the coming of our spendthrift court as an added burden, and we hear that Eleanor Cobham, who was once the Duchess of Gloucester, has died in her prison at Peel Castle on the Isle of Man. She died in silence of heartbreak and loneliness; they would not let her take her own life quickly and cleanly by a plunge from the battlements or a dagger in the veins of her wrist. They would not allow her to live any life at all, but they would not allow her death either. Now they are saying that her spirit haunts the castle in the shape of a big black dog that runs up and down the stairs as if looking for a way out.

I tell the queen that Eleanor Cobham is dead, but I do not say that I think Eleanor was a woman like Margaret herself, a woman like me: one who expects to take a great place in the world, who can see the world and wants to make it bend to her will, who cannot walk easily in the small steps of a demure woman, nor bow her head to the authority of men. I do not say that I saw the black dog when I first met the duchess and smelled its fetid breath beneath her perfume. I am sorry for the duchess and the black dog that followed her, and I give a little shudder when I think that they took her into imprisonment for studying as I have studied, for seeking the knowledge that I have learned, and for being a woman in her power: just like me.

This summer progress is not a merry tour to celebrate a king joyously passing through his kingdom in the best days of the year; it is a sour visitation into each town when the citizens and the clergy turn out to welcome the king and then find he has come to hold a court in their guildhall, and summon their friends to answer charges. A man can be accused of treason for a word spoken out of turn; an alehouse brawl is defined as rebellion. When accused and in the dock, he is invited to name others and a spiral of spite, gossip, and then charges follows. We go into the very heartlands of Richard, Duke of York, the wild beautiful country on the way to Wales, and put his tenants, his liegemen, and his vassals on trial. The queen is triumphant at this gauntlet that they are throwing down before the Duke of York. Edmund, Duke of Somerset, is gleeful that though York accused him of treason, the court is now on his very doorstep, arraigning the tenants of York for the exact same crime.

"He will be beside himself!" he declares to

the queen, and they laugh together like children who rattle sticks against the cage of a traveling bear to make him growl. "I have found an old peasant who claims that he heard the duke declare that Cade was only saying what most men think. That's treason. I have an alehouse keeper who says that Edward March, his son and heir, thinks the king is simple. I shall call him into court, and the king shall hear what the duke's own boy dares to say against him."

"I shall forbid the king from staying at York's home, Ludlow Castle," the queen says. "I shall refuse to go there. I shall snub Duchess Cecily. And you must support me."

Edmund Beaufort nods. "We can stay with the Carmelite Friars," he says. "The king always likes staying in a monastery."

She laughs, throwing back her head so that the lace from her high headdress brushes his cheek. Her face is flushed; her eyes are bright. "He does love a monastery," she agrees.

"I do hope they have good singers," he says. "I so love plainsong. I could listen to it all day."

She gives a little scream of laughter and slaps his arm. "Enough, enough!"

I wait till he has left, though I think he would have stayed longer if someone had not come from the king's rooms and said that the king was asking for him. He leaves then, kissing her hand, lingering over it. "I shall see you at dinner," he whispers — though of course he will see us all at dinner — and then he leaves, throwing a smiling wink at me as if we are special friends.

I take a seat beside her, and I glance around to see that none of her other ladies are in earshot. We are staying at Caldwell Castle, Kidderminster, and the best rooms are small; half the queen's ladies are sewing in another gallery.

"Your Grace," I begin carefully. "The duke is a handsome man, and a good companion, but you should take care that you are not seen to enjoy his company too much."

Her sideways look is gleeful. "Do you think he pays much attention to me?"

"I do," I say.

"I am a queen," she observes. "It is natural that men are going to gather round me, hoping for a smile."

"He doesn't have to hope," I say bluntly. "He is getting your smiles."

"And did you not smile on Sir Richard?" she asks sharply. "When he was nothing more than a knight in your husband's household?"

"You know I did," I say. "But I was a widow then, and I was the widow of a royal duke. I was not a married woman and a queen."

She gets to her feet so quickly that I am afraid that I have offended her, but she takes me by the hand and pulls me with her, into her bedchamber, closing the door behind her and putting her back to it, so that no one can come in.

"Jacquetta, you see my life," she says passionately. "You see my husband. You hear what they say of him; you know what he is. You see him giving out pardons like the Pope to the duke but trying poor men for treason. You know he didn't come to my bedroom in the first week of our marriage because his confessor said that our marriage had to be holy. You know that he is a man of melancholic humor: cool and moist."

I nod. It is undeniable.

"And Somerset is a man of fire," she breathes. "He rides out with an army, he is a commander of men, he has seen battles, he is a man of passion. He hates his enemies, loves his friends, and to women . . ." She gives a little shiver. "To women he is irresistible — they all say it."

I put my hands to my mouth. I would rather be putting them over my ears.

"I wouldn't be the first woman in the world to have a handsome admirer," she says. "I am queen; half the court is in love with me. It is how the world is. I can have a handsome chevalier."

"No, you cannot," I contradict her. "You cannot smile on him. You cannot allow him any favors, nothing at all, not even permission to adore you from a distance, not until you have a son and heir by the king."

"And when is that going to happen?" she demands. "And how is it going to happen? I have been married seven years, Jacquetta. When is he going to get me with child? I know my duty as well as any woman. Every night I go to bed and lie in the cold sheets, waiting for him to come. Some nights he does not come at all; some nights he comes and spends the night kneeling in prayer at the foot of the bed. The whole night, Jacquetta! What do you expect me to do?"

"I didn't know it was so bad," I say. "I am sorry. I had no idea."

"You must know," she says bitterly. "You are lying. You know, all my ladies know. You come to wake us in the morning, and we are lying side by side, as if we were dead and made of stone on our tombs. Have you ever caught us wrapped in each other's arms? Have you ever heard us call through the door, 'Not now! Come back later'? You have only to look at him and you would know. You cannot imagine that he is a lusty, passionate man who is going to father a strong son on me? We don't even rumple the sheets."

"Oh, Margaret, I am so sorry," I say tenderly. "Of course I didn't think he was lusty. But I did think that he came to your bed and did his duty."

She shrugs her shoulders. "Sometimes he does," she says bitterly. "Sometimes he rises up from his prayers, crosses himself, and makes a feeble effort. Can you think how that feels? But he doesn't have his heart in it; it is almost worse than nothing at all — an act of duty. It chills my skin; it makes me shudder. I look at you, Jacquetta, and I see you with a baby in your belly every year, and I see how Richard looks at you, and how you steal away early from dinner to be together, even now, and I know it is not the same for me. It is never going to be the same for me."

"I'm sorry," I say.

She turns her face away and rubs her eyes. "It is not the same for me. It will never be the same for me. I will never be loved like you are loved. And I think I am dying inside, Jacquetta."

GRAFTON,
NORTHAMPTONSHIRE,
AUTUMN 1452

I withdraw from court in the autumn to spend some time with my children and to make sure that my lands are in good heart at Grafton Manor, and my tenants paying their rents and not whispering behind their hands against the king and court. I am glad to be away. Without the company of Richard I find I am impatient with the flirtations and excitement of the ladies-in-waiting, and I cannot like the new vindictiveness that I see developing in the king. The Duke of Somerset says that the king is showing his power, growing into majesty; but I cannot admire it. They are calling his progress a "harvest of heads" and saying that every summer he will work his way around the counties where men have risen against him, or even spoken against him, and judge like a modern Solomon. He seems to take equal pleasure in tenderly pardoning as in harsh sentencing; and no man can know, when he is called before this king, whether he is going to meet a saint or a tyrant. Some men are paraded before him naked with a halter round their necks, and he sees their shame and their weakness and forgives them with tears, letting them kiss his hands and praying with them. Another old lady defies him with a curse, refuses to confess to anything, and she is hanged. The king weeps then too, in sorrow for a sinner.

And I am glad to be away from the queen's rooms, where I see that she grows closer and closer to Edmund Beaufort. They are thrown together all the time by the king's need of him, and it means that Margaret, still only a young woman of twenty-two, is in the constant company of the man who commands England, who advises her husband and counsels her. Of course she admires him; her husband holds him up as the very model of a perfect lord. He is the most handsome man at court; he is regarded as the champion of England, and he is clearly in love with her. He looks after her as she goes by; he whispers in her ear; he takes her hand on the least pretext and places himself beside her, her partner in games, her companion in walks, his horse rides next to hers. Of course she knows that she may not feel anything for him but respect and cousinly affection. But she is a young and passionate woman, and he is a seductive man. I think that no power in the world could stop her looking for him, smiling when she sees him, and simply glowing with joy when he comes to sit beside her and whispers in her ear.

And as for the king — he rests on the duke, as if Edmund is his only comfort and his peace of mind. Ever since the rise of Jack Cade, when the king fled from London, he cannot feel safe in his own capital city, nor in any of the counties of the south. He may go through them every summer, dispensing his spiteful justice with the gallows, but he knows he is not beloved. He only feels safe in the middle lands of England, at Leicester, Kenilworth, and Coventry. He relies on Edmund Beaufort to assure him that — despite all appearances — everything is well. Edmund reports that he is beloved, the people faithful, the court and the men of the household honest, Calais secure, and Bordeaux certain to be restored. It is a comforting list, and Beaufort is persuasive. His warm, honeyed tongue seduces the king and the queen together. The king praises Edmund to the skies as his only reliable advisor; he lauds him as the man whose military skill and courage will save us from rebels great and small. He thinks that Edmund can manage the Parliament, that Edmund understands the commons, and all the time the queen smiles and says that Edmund is a very great friend to them both, and she will go riding with him the next morning, while the king prays in his chapel.

She has learned to be cautious — she knows well enough that she is watched all the time and that people judge her harshly. But her pleasure in his company and his hidden desire for her is apparent to me, and this is enough to make me glad to leave a court with this dangerous secret at the very heart of it.

Richard is to come home to me at last, and sends to tell me he is on his way. We are to celebrate the marriage of Elizabeth. She is fifteen, ready for marriage, and the boy whom I had picked out in my mind and whose name I whispered to the new moon has found the courage to speak to his mother about her.

Lady Grey herself wrote to me with the proposal that her son John might marry our daughter. I knew that if Elizabeth stayed in their house for any length of time, John Grey would fall in love with her, and his parents would see the benefit of the match. And she picked the apple blossom and gave him the fruit to eat. She is more than pretty, she has real beauty; and Lady Grey cannot bear to refuse her beloved son anything. Besides, as I foresaw, Lady Grey is a woman of her own mind, a commander of her own acres, a queen in her county, and once she had the training of my daughter, she soon believed that no better-mannered girl could exist. She taught her how to keep the still room; she taught her how the linen room should be. She preached to her the value of well-trained maids; she took her into the dairy to watch as they churned the famous Groby butter and skimmed the fat cream. She taught her how to keep the account books and to write a civil letter to the Grey kinsmen all around the country. Together, they climbed the little hill that they call Tower Hill, and looked over the Ferrers acres, and Lady Grey remarked that all this had come to her on the death of her father; she had brought it to Sir Edward on their marriage; and now her beloved son John will inherit it all.

Elizabeth, who knew well enough how to run a household, who knew how to prepare herbs for the still room, indeed knows how they should be grown and when harvested, who knows the properties of a hundred plants and how to call the venom out of them — she is my daughter, after all — had the good sense and the good manners never to correct the lady of the house; but simply learned how it was done at Groby. Of course, she already knew how linen should be folded, or cream skimmed; she knew how a county lady should command her maids. Actually she knows far more than Lady Grey will ever dream: for she has learned from me how a royal court is run and how things were done in the courts of France and of Luxembourg. But she accepted the orders of the woman who would be her mother-in-law as a polite young woman should, and gave every appearance of a girl eager to learn the right way that things should be done: the Groby way. In short, as she picked and dried the herbs for the Groby still room, prepared the oils, polished the silver, and watched the cutting of the strewing rushes; my daughter enchanted the hardhearted lady of Groby, just as she enchanted the son of the house.

It is a good match for her. I had it in mind for years. She has my name and her father's position in our country, but next to no dowry. Service to this king has not brought us a fortune. It seems to be profitable only for those lords who take their fees and do nothing. Those courtiers who do nothing but sympathize with the king and conspire with his wife can take a great profit, as we see from the rich lands that were given to William de la Pole and the extraordinary wealth that Edmund Beaufort now enjoys. But my husband took sixty lancers and nearly six hundred archers with him to Calais, all trained under his command, all wearing our livery, and all paid by us. The Treasury has promised to reimburse us, but they might as well date the tally sticks the day of judgment; for the dead will rise from their graves before we can take the sticks into the Treasury and get a full repayment. We have a new name and a beautiful house; we have influence and a reputation; we are trusted by both the king and the queen, but money — no, we never have any money.

With this marriage my Elizabeth will become Lady Grey of Groby, mistress of a good part of Leicestershire, owner of Groby Hall and the other great properties in the Grey family, kinswoman to all the Greys. It is a good family, with good prospects for her, and they are solidly for the king and fiercely opposed to Richard, Duke of York, so we will never find her on the wrong side if the dispute between the Duke of York and his rival, the Duke of Somerset, grows worse.

Elizabeth is to go to her wedding from our house with her father and me, and all the children except the two babies. But Richard is not yet home.

"Where is Father?" she asks me the day before we are due to leave. "You said he would be here yesterday."

"He will come," I say steadily.

"What if he has been delayed? What if he could not get a ship? What if the seas were too rough to sail? I cannot be married without him to give me away. What if he does not get here?"

I put my hand on my wedding ring, as if to touch his fingers that placed it there. "He will be here," I say. "Elizabeth, in all the years that I have loved him, he has never failed me. He will be here."

She frets all the day, and I send her to bed that night with a tisane of valerian, and when

I peep into her room, she is fast asleep in her bed, her hair plaited under her nightcap, seeming as young as her sister Anne, who shares the bed with her. Then I hear the noise of horses in the stable yard and look from her window, and there is the Rivers standard, and there is my husband, heaving himself wearily from his horse, and in a moment I am down the stairs and out through the stable door and in his arms.

He holds me so tightly that I can hardly breathe, and then he turns my face up to his and kisses me.

"I daresay I stink," is the first thing he says when he gets his breath. "You must forgive me. The tide was against us, and so I have ridden hard to get here tonight. You knew I would not fail you, didn't you?"

I smile up at his handsome well-worn, well-loved face: the man I have adored for so many years. "I knew you would not fail me."

The Greys have a small chapel at their house, opposite the great hall, where the young couple exchange the vows that are solemnly witnessed by both sets of parents and the brothers and sisters. Our family fills up the chapel. I can see Lady Grey look at the ranks of my children and think that her son is marrying fertile stock. After the wedding we walk through the cloister to the hall, and there is a feast and singing and dancing, and then we prepare them for bed.

Elizabeth and I are alone in the bedroom that is going to be hers. It is a beautiful room, looking north over the pleasure grounds, towards the meadows and the river. I am feeling tenderhearted: this is my girl, the first child of mine to marry and leave her home. "What do you foresee for me, Lady Mother?" she asks.

This is a question I have been dreading. "You know I don't foresee anymore," I say. "That was something in my girlhood. They don't like such things in England, and I have put it aside. If it comes to me or to you, it is without our bidding. Your father does not like it."

She gives a little giggle. "Oh, Lady Mother!" she says reproachfully. "That you should stoop so low, and on my wedding day."

I cannot help but smile. "Stoop so low as to what?"

"As to lie," she whispers. "And to me! On my wedding day! I understand now that you foresaw that John would love me, and I him. I picked the apple blossom and I gave him the apple, just as you said. But long before that, the moment I first saw him, I knew exactly what you intended when you sent me here. I was standing before his mother when she was at her table in the rents room, and he came in the door behind her — I had not even known he was at home — and the moment I saw him, I knew why you had sent me to Groby and what you thought would happen."

"And were you glad? Was I right to send you?"

Her joy shines out of her bright gray eyes. "Very glad. I thought, if he were to like me, I should be the happiest girl in England."

"That was not foreseeing; that was nothing more than knowing that you are beautiful and lovable. I could have sent you to any handsome young man's household, and he would have fallen in love with you. There was no magic in that but a girl and a boy in springtime."

She is glowing. "I am glad. I wasn't sure. I am so glad that he is in love but not enchanted. But surely you have looked to see my future? Did you put the charms in the river? What did you draw from the waters? Did you look for us in the cards? What will my future be?"

"I didn't read the cards." I lie to her, my little daughter; I lie barefaced like a hardhearted old witch, denying the truth on her wedding night, and I lie to her with my face completely serene. I am going to tell her a lie that is utterly convincing. I will not have my foresight overshadowing her present happiness. I will deny my gift, deny what it has shown me. "You are mistaken, my dear. I didn't read the cards, and I didn't look in a mirror. I didn't put any charms in the river because I didn't have to. I can predict your happiness without any craft. Just as I knew he would love you. I can tell you that I know you will be happy, and I think there will be children, and the first one quite soon."

"Girl or boy?"

"You will be able to tell that yourself." I smile. "Now you have your own wedding ring."

"And I will be Lady Grey of Groby," she says, with quiet satisfaction.

I feel a shiver, like a cold hand on the nape of my neck. I know that she will never inherit here. "Yes," I say, defying my better knowledge. "You will be Lady Grey of Groby and the mother of many fine children." This is what she must hear as she goes into her wedding bed on her wedding night. "God bless you, my darling, and give you joy."

The girls tap on the door and come into the room in a flurry, with rose petals for the bed and the jug of wedding ale and a bowl of scented water for her to wash with and her linen gown, and I help her get ready, and when the men come in, boisterous and drunk, she is lying in her bed like a chaste little angel. My husband and Lord Grey help John in beside her, and he blushes furiously, like a boy, though he is twenty-one; and I smile as if I am wholly happy; and I wonder what it is that stops my heart in fear for the two of them.

In two days we go back to our own house at Grafton, and I never tell Elizabeth, or anyone, that I did indeed read the cards for her, the very day that Lady Grey wrote to me to ask what dowry Elizabeth might bring to the marriage. I sat at the table looking out over the water meadow and the dairy, certain of her happiness, and took the cards in my hand. I turned over three, chosen at random, and all three were blank.

The card maker had put three spare cards in the pack when he first painted the pictures, three cards just like the others with brightly colored backs but nothing on the front, spares for use in another game. And it was the three cards with nothing to say that came to my hand when I went to foresee Elizabeth's future with John Grey. I had hoped to see prosperity and children, grandchildren and a rise in the world, but the cards were empty of anything. There was no future that I could see, for Elizabeth and John Grey: no future for them at all.

Palace of Placentia, Greenwich, London, Christmas 1452

Richard and I attend the court at Greenwich for Christmas and find the festivities and the hunts and the music and the dancing all under the command of Edmund Beaufort, who is such a center of the happiness of the court that he is almost a king himself. He makes much of Richard, recommending him to the king as the man certain to hold Calais for us, and often takes him aside to discuss how an English expedition might force its way out of the Calais lands into Normandy once more. Richard follows his usual rule of fealty and loyalty to his commander, and I say nothing about the way that the queen's eyes follow them when they talk together. But I know I have to speak to her again.

I am forced to speak to her, driven to it, by a sense of duty. I almost smile to feel so bound; for I know this is the influence of my first husband, John, Duke of Bedford. He never avoided a difficult duty in his life, and I feel as if he has laid on me the obligation to serve England's queen even if it means challenging her behavior and calling her to account.

I choose a moment when we are preparing for a masque of Edmund Beaufort's planning. He has ordered that the queen should have a gown of white, fastened high at the waist with a plaited gold cord, and that her hair should be loose. She is supposed to represent a goddess, but she looks like a bride. He has designed new sleeves for the white gown, cut so short and so wide that you can see her arms almost to the elbow. "You will have to wear another set of sleeves," I say frankly. "These are quite indecent."

She strokes the inside of her arm. "It feels so lovely," she says. "My skin feels like silk. It feels so wonderful to be this —"

"Naked," I finish for her, and without another word I find another pair of sleeves in her chest of clothes and start to lace them on. She lets me exchange the sleeves without a word of complaint and then sits before her mirror. I wave away her maid and take the hairbrush to stroke out the tangles from the long red-gold ringlets that fall almost to her waist. "The noble duke Edmund Beaufort pays you much attention," I say. "It is noticeable, Your Grace."

She gleams with pleasure. "Ah, you said before, Jacquetta. This is an old song. But he looks at me as a good courtier, a chevalier."

"He looks like a man in love," I say bluntly, expecting to shock her. But I am horrified to see the color flame in her cheeks.

"Oh, does he?" she asks. "Does he really?"

"Your Grace — what is happening? You know you should not be speaking of real love. A little poetry, a little flirtation is one thing. But you cannot think of him with desire."

"When he speaks to me, I come alive." She addresses my reflected image in the mirror, and I see her face gleaming and silvery through the looking glass. It is as if we are in another world, the world of the scrying mirror, and such things can be said. "With the king it is as if I am caring for a child. I have to tell him that he is in the right, that he should ride out like a man, that he should rule like a king. I have to praise him for his wisdom and coax him when he is upset. I am more a mother to him than a lover. But Edmund . . ." She gives a little shuddering breath, lowers her eyes, and then looks up at the mirror and shrugs, as if there is nothing she can do.

"You must stop seeing him," I say hastily. "Or only see him when others are present. You must keep your distance."

She takes the brush from my hand. "Don't you like him?" she asks. "He says he likes and admires you. He says he is your friend. And he trusts Richard above all others. He praises him to the king."

"Nobody could help but like him," I say. "He is handsome, charming, and one of the greatest men in England. But that doesn't mean that the queen should feel anything for him but cousinly affection."

"You're too late to tell me," she says, her voice silky and warm. "It is too late for me. It's not cousinly affection. It is far beyond that. Jacquetta, for the first time in my life I feel as if I am alive. For the first time in my life I feel as if I am a woman. I feel beautiful. I feel desired. I cannot resist this."

"I told you before," I remind her. "I warned you."

Again, she lifts her beautiful shoulders. "Ah, Jacquetta. You know as well as I do what it is to be in love. Would you have stopped if someone had warned you?"

I don't answer her. "You will have to send him away from court," I say flatly. "You will have to avoid him, perhaps for months. This is a disaster."

"I can't," she says. "The king would never allow him to go. He won't let him out of his sight. And I would just die if I did not see him, Jacquetta. You don't know. He is my only companion; he is my chevalier; he is my champion: the queen's champion."

"This is not Camelot," I warn her grimly. "These are not the times of the troubadours. People will think badly of you if they see you so much as smile at him; they will accuse him of being your favorite, or worse. What you are saying here is enough to have you put aside and sent to a nunnery. And if anyone heard you say it, it would be the end of him. Already he is hated and envied for being the favorite of the king. If one word gets out to the people that you favor him, they will say the most terrible things. You are the queen, and your reputation is like Venetian glass: precious and fragile and rare. You have to take care. You are not a private lady; you cannot have private feelings."

"I will take care," she says breathlessly. "I swear I will take care." It is as if she is bartering for the right to be with him, and that she would offer anything for that right. "If I take care, if I don't smile on him or ride too close to him, or dance with him too often, I can still see him. Can't I? Everyone will think he is with us all the time at the king's command; nobody need know that he makes me so happy, that it makes my life worth living, just to be with him."

I know I should tell her that she should never be alone with him at all, but her face is too imploring. She is lonely, and she is young, and it is miserable to be a young woman in a great court when nobody really cares for you. I know that. I know what it is like to have a husband who hardly sees you, but that there is one young man who can't take his eyes from you. I know what it is like to burn up in a cold bed.

"Just take care," I say, though I know I should tell her to send him away. "You will have to be careful all the time, every day of your life. And you cannot see him alone. You must never be alone with him. This cannot go beyond the chevalier and his honorable love for his lady. It cannot go beyond your secret joy. It has to stop here."

She shakes her head. "I have to talk with him," she says. "I have to be with him."

"You cannot. There can be no future for the two of you but shame and disgrace."

She leaves her mirror and moves to the great bed with the rich golden hangings. She pats it invitingly, and slowly I come towards her. "Will you draw a card for him?" she asks. "Then we would know the answers. Then we would know what future there might be."

I shake my head. "You know that the king doesn't like the cards," I say. "It is forbidden."

"Just one card. Just once. So that we might know what is to come. So that I will take care?"

I hesitate, and in a moment she is at the bedroom door and calling for a pack of playing cards. One of the ladies offers to bring them through, but the queen takes them at the bedroom door and hands them to me. "Go on!" she says.

Slowly, I take the cards and shuffle them.

Of course, we play cards all the time at court; but the feeling of them in my hand as I seek only one, seek to divine the future, is quite different. I hand them to her.

"Shuffle them. Then cut the cards," I say very quietly. "And cut them again."

Her face is entranced. "We will foretell his future?"

I shake my head. "We cannot foretell his future — he would have to ask for the card; he would have to choose. We can't do it without him. But we can tell how his life will touch yours. We can see which card shows his feeling for you, and yours for him."

She nods. "I want to know that," she whispers longingly. "Do you think he loves me, Jacquetta? You have seen him with me. Do you think he loves me?"

"Spread the cards," I say.

She makes a fan of the cards, their bright faces downwards.

"Now choose."

Slowly, one finger moving across the painted backs, she muses on her choice, and then she points. "This one."

I turn it over. It is the Falling Tower. The tower of a castle, struck perhaps by lightning, a jagged streak of light flaming into the roof of the tower — the walls going one way, the roof the other. Two little figures fall from the tower to the grass below.

"What does it mean?" she whispers. "Will

he take the tower? Does it mean he will take the kingdom?"

For a moment I cannot understand her meaning. "Take the kingdom?" I repeat in horror. "Take the kingdom!"

She shakes her head, denying the very thought, hand over her mouth. "Nothing, nothing. But what does it mean? This card — what does it mean?"

"It means an overturning of all things," I say. "Disruption of the times. Perhaps a fall of a castle . . ." Of course, I think of Richard, who is sworn to hold the castle of Calais for this very commander. "A fall from on high, look — here are two people falling down from the tower, a rising of those who are low, and in the end, everything different. A new heir takes the throne, the old order is changed, everything is new."

Her eyes are shining. "Everything is new," she whispers. "Who do you think is the king's true heir?"

I look at her in something close to horror. "Richard, Duke of York," I say flatly. "Like him or not. Richard, Duke of York, is the king's heir."

She shakes her head. "Edmund Beaufort is the king's cousin," she whispers. "He could be the true heir. Perhaps this is what the card means."

"It never comes out quite how I think it will be," I warn her. "This is not a prediction: it is always more like a warning. D'you remember the Wheel of Fortune card? The card you drew on your wedding day that promises what rises will fall, that nothing is certain?"

Nothing I can say can dull her joy, her face is shining. She thinks I have foreseen the change of everything, and she is longing for something to change. She thinks that the tower shown in the card is her prison; she wants it broken down. She thinks the people who are clearly falling are breaking free. She thinks the lightning shaft that destroys and burns will break down the old and make new. There is nothing I can say that she will hear as a warning.

She makes the gesture that I showed her on her wedding day, the circling forefinger that shows the rise and the fall of life. "Everything new," she whispers again.

In bed, that night, I confide my worries to Richard, skirting over the queen's infatuation for the duke, but telling him only that she is lonely and that the duke is her closest friend. Richard is sitting up, beside the warmth of the fire, his gown thrown over his naked shoulders. "No harm in friendship," he says stoutly. "And she is a pretty girl and deserves some companionship."

"People will talk."

"People always talk."

"I am afraid that she may become too fond of the duke."

He narrows his eyes as if he would scrutinize my thoughts. "Are you saying she might fall in love with him?"

"I wouldn't be surprised if she did. She is young, he is handsome; she has nobody else in the world who shows any sign of caring for her. The king is kind to her and considerate, but he has no passion in him."

"Can the king give her a child?" Richard asks bluntly, going to the very core of the matter.

"I think he can," I say. "But he does not come often to her room."

"The man's a fool," my husband says. "A woman like Margaret cannot be neglected. D'you think the duke has eyes for her?"

I nod.

Richard scowls. "I think you could trust him to do nothing that would endanger her or the throne. It would be a selfish villain who would seduce her. She has everything to lose, and it would cost the throne of England as well. He's no fool. They are close — they are bound to be close — they are both in attendance on the king for most of every day. But Edmund Beaufort is running this kingdom through the king, he would not jeopardize his own future — never mind hers. The most important thing is for her to get an heir."

"She can hardly do it alone," I say crossly.

He laughs at me. "No need to defend her to me. But while there is no child, then Richard, Duke of York, is the rightful heir, but the king keeps favoring others of his family: Humphrey, Duke of Buckingham, who takes precedence, and Edmund Beaufort. Now I hear he is bringing his half brothers, the Tudor boys, to court as well. It makes everyone uneasy. Who does he think is his heir? Would he dare to put Richard, Duke of York, aside for one of these favorites?"

"He's young," I say. "She's young. They could get a child."

"Well, he's not likely to die on campaign like his father," my husband the soldier says cruelly. "He keeps himself safe enough."

At the end of the twelve days of Christmas Richard has to go back to his post at Calais. I go down to the river to see him set sail. He is wearing his thick traveling cloak against the cold wintry mist, and he wraps it around us both as we stand on the quayside. Inside the warmth, my head against his shoulder, my arms tight around his broad back, I hold him as if I cannot bear to let him go. "I'll come to Calais," I promise.

"Sweetheart, there is nothing for you there at all. I will come home again at Easter, or earlier."

"I can't wait till Easter."

"Then I will come sooner. Whenever you bid me. You know that. When you want me I will come."

"Can't you just go and inspect the garrison and come back?"

"Perhaps . . . if there is no expedition into Normandy this spring. The duke hopes to mount one. Does the queen say anything?"

"She says whatever the duke says."

"If we don't have an expedition by spring, there won't be one this year, and I can come home to you," he promises.

"You had better come home in the summer," I warn him. "Whatever happens. I will have something I will want you to see."

In the warm shelter of the cloak his hand goes to my belly.

"You are a ruby, my Jacquetta. A wife of noble character worth more than rubies. Are you with child again?"

"Yes, again," I say.

"A summer baby," he says with pleasure. "Another for the House of Rivers. We are making a nation, my love. The Rivers are becoming an estuary, a lake, an inland sea."

I giggle.

"Will you stay at court with the queen for now?"

"Yes, I will. I'll go down to Grafton for a few days to see the children, and then I'll come back to court. At the very least, I can guard her from slander."

Concealed by his cloak, he squeezes me. "I like the thought of you as a model of respectability, my love."

"I am a very respectable mother of nine," I remind him. "Soon ten, God willing."

"Good God, that I should feel like this for a mother of ten," he remarks, taking my hand and holding it against his breeches.

"God forgive me that I should feel like this for a married man and a father of ten," I say, pressing against him.

There is a shout from the deck of the ship above us. "I have to go," he says reluctantly. "We have to catch the tide. I love you, Jacquetta, and I will come home soon."

He kisses me hard and quickly, and then he steps back and runs up the gangplank to the ship. Without his cloak, without his warmth, without his smile, I feel very cold and alone. I let him go.

THE TOWER OF LONDON, SPRING 1453

I come back to court after a week at Grafton in time for the great celebration in the Tower of London where the king's half brothers Edmund and Jasper Tudor are made earls. I stand beside the queen as the two young men kneel before the king for their investiture. They are the sons of Queen Catherine of Valois, the king's mother, who made a second marriage as imprudent as my own. After her husband Henry V died, leaving her a widow with a baby, she did not, as everyone hoped, retire to a nunnery and spend the rest of her life in respectable grief. She stooped even lower than I did and fell in love with the keeper of her wardrobe, Owen Tudor, and married him in secret. She left an awkward situation when she died, with Tudor as her surviving widower or abductor — depending on your judgment — and his two sons as half brothers to the King of England or two bastards to a madly incontinent queen mother — depending on your charity.

King Henry has decided to acknowledge his half brothers, deny his mother's shame, and count them as royal kinsmen. What this will do to the expectations of the several men who are in line to inherit the throne is beyond understanding. These Tudors will just add to the confusion around the throne. The king honors the Duke of Buckingham, who counts himself as the greatest duke of England, but favors Edmund Beaufort, the Duke of Somerset, above anyone else. And all the while his true heir is the only man not here and never welcomed at court: Richard Plantagenet, Duke of York.

I glance at the queen, who must be shamed by her failure to solve all this by producing a son and heir, but she is looking down at her folded hands, her eyelashes veiling her expression. I see Edmund Beaufort look quickly away from her.

"His Grace is generous to the Tudor boys," I remark.

She gives a little start at my words. "Oh, yes. Well, you know what he is like. He can forgive anyone, anything. And now he is so afraid of the common people and of the York affinity that he wants to gather his family around him. He is giving the boys a fortune in lands and recognizing them as his half brothers."

"It is good for a man to have his family around him," I say cheerfully.

"Oh, he can make brothers," she says, and the unspoken words *but not a son* remain unsaid.

As the winter nights become lighter and the mornings become golden rather than gray, we receive great news from Bordeaux where John Talbot, Earl of Shrewsbury, four times the age of his page boy, sweeps through the rich cities of Gascony, wins back Bordeaux, and looks set to reclaim all the English lands. This sends the court into an ecstasy of confidence. They declare that first we will win back all of Gascony, and then we will win back all of Normandy, and Calais will be secure and Richard will be able to come home. Margaret and I are on the river walk in the gardens at Westminster, wrapped in our winter furs but feeling the spring sunshine on our faces, and looking at the first daffodils of the season.

"Jacquetta, you are like a lovesick girl," she says suddenly.

I jump. I had been looking at the river and thinking of Richard, over the sea in Calais; furious — I am sure — that he is not leading the campaign in Bordeaux. "I am sorry," I say with a little laugh. "I do miss him. And the children."

"He will be home soon," she assures me. "Once Talbot has won back our lands in Gascony, we can make peace again."

She takes my arm and walks beside me. "It is hard to be parted from people whom you love," she says. "I missed my mother so much when I first came to England, I feared that I would never see her again, and now she writes to me that she is ill and I wish I could go to her. I wonder if she would have sent me away if she had known what my life would be like, if she had known that she would never see me again, not even for a visit."

"She knows at least that the king is kind to you, and a gentle husband," I say. "When the Greys asked me for Elizabeth, my first thought was would he be kind to her. I think every mother would want that for her daughter."

"I so want to be able to tell her I am with child," she says. "That would make her happy; that is the one thing she wants — that everyone wants. But maybe this year. Perhaps one will come for me this year." Her eyelids sweep down and she smiles, almost to herself.

"Oh, dear Margaret, I hope so."

"I am more contented," she says quietly. "I am even hopeful. You need not fear for me, Jacquetta. It is true that I was very unhappy this summer, and even at Christmastime; but I am more contented now. You were a good friend to warn me to take care. I listened to you; I thought about what you said. I know I must not be indiscreet; I have put the duke at a distance and I think everything is going to be all right."

There is something going on here — I don't need the Sight to see it. There is a secret here, and a hidden joy. But I cannot complain of her behavior. She may smile on the duke, but she is always at the side of the king. She does not linger with the duke in the gallery nor let him whisper in her ear anymore. He comes to her rooms, as he always has done; but they talk of matters of state and there are always companions with him, and ladies with her. It is when she is alone or quiet among the crowd that I look at her and wonder what she is thinking, when she folds her hands so demurely in her lap and gazes down, her eyes veiled, smiling to herself.

"And how is your little girl?" she asks a little wistfully. "Is she well and fat and pretty like all your babies always seem to be?"

"Thank God she is strong and growing well," I say. "I called her Eleanor, you know. I sent them all Christmas fairings, and we had a couple of days of such fine weather when I was down with them. I took the older ones hunting and the younger ones sledging. I will go back to see them at Easter."

That night the queen dresses in her new gown of darkest red, a color no one has seen before, especially bought for her from the London merchants, and we go into the king's presence chamber with the ladies behind us. She takes her seat beside the king, and the little Beaufort heiress, Margaret, comes into the room, dressed far too ornately, paraded by her shameless mother. The child is wearing a gown of angelic white trimmed with red silk roses, as if to remind everyone that she is the daughter of John Beaufort, first Duke of Somerset, a great name but, God forgive him, not a great man. He was Edmund Beaufort's older brother, but he made a fool of himself in France and came home and died, so promptly and conveniently — just ahead of a charge of treason — that Richard says it was by his own hand and was the only good thing he ever did for his family. This scrap of a girl with the great name and greater fortune is his daughter, and the niece of Edmund Beaufort.

I see her staring at me, and I smile at her. At once she flushes scarlet and beams. She whispers to her mother, obviously asking who I am, and her mother very rightly gives her a pinch to make her stand straight and silent, as a girl at court should do.

"I am giving your daughter in wardship to my dearly loved half brothers, Edmund and Jasper Tudor," the king says to the girl's mother, the dowager duchess. "She can live with you, until it is time for her to marry."

Amusingly, the child looks up as if she has an opinion about this. When no one so much as glances at her, she whispers to her mother again. She is a dear little thing and so anxious to be consulted. It seems hard to me that she will be married off to Edmund Tudor and sent away to Wales.

The queen turns to me, and I lean forwards. "What do you think?" Margaret asks.

Margaret Beaufort is of the House of Lancaster; Edmund Tudor is the son of a Queen of England. Any child they conceive will have an impressive lineage: English royal blood on one side, French royal blood on the other, both of them kin to the King of England.

"Is the king making his brother over-mighty?" the queen whispers.

"Oh, look at her," I say gently. "She is a tiny little thing, and a long way from marriageable age. Her mother will keep her home for another ten years, surely. You will have half a dozen babies in the cradle before Edmund Tudor can wed or bed her."

We both look down the room at the girl whose little head is still bobbing up and down as if she wishes someone would speak to her. The queen laughs. "Well, I hope so; surely a little shrimp like that will never make a royal heir."

The next night I wait for a quiet moment in the hour before dinner when the queen is dressed and the duke and king have not yet come to our rooms. We are seated before the fire, listening to the musicians. I glance at her for her nod of permission, and then draw my stool a little closer.

"If you are waiting for a chance to tell me that you are with child again, you need not choose your time," she says mischievously. "I can see it."

I blush. "I'm certain it will be a boy, I am eating enough to make a man, God knows. I have had to let my belt out."

"Have you told Richard?"

"He guessed, before he left."

"I shall ask the duke to let him come home. You will want him at home with you, won't you?"

I glance at her. Sometimes the almost annual evidence of my reliable fertility makes her wistful; but this time she is smiling, her joy for me is without shadow. "Yes. I would want him home, if the duke can spare him."

"I shall command it." She smiles. "The duke tells me he will do anything for me. It is a little request for a man who has promised me the moon."

"I will stay at court until May," I say. "And then after my confinement, I will join you on the summer progress."

"Perhaps we won't go very far this year," she says.

"No?" I am slow to grasp her meaning.

"Perhaps I too will want an easy summer."

At last I understand her. "Oh, Margaret, is it possible?"

"I thought you had the Sight!" she crows. "And here I am, sitting before you, and I think . . . I am almost certain . . ."

I clasp her hands. "I think so too. I see it now; I really do." There is something about her luminous skin and the curves of her body. "How long?"

"I have missed two courses, I think," she says. "So I haven't told anyone yet. What d'you think?"

"And the king lay with you before Christmas? And gave you pleasure?"

She keeps her eyes down, but her color deepens. "Oh, Jacquetta — I did not know it could be like that."

I smile. "Sometimes it can." Something in her smile tells me that she knows, at last, after eight years of marriage, of the joy that a man can give his wife — if he cares to do so, if he loves her enough to want to make her cling to him and yearn for his touch.

"When would I be sure?" she asks.

"Next month," I say. "We will get a midwife I know and trust, to talk with you and see if you have the signs, and then you can tell His Grace yourself next month."

She does not want to write to her mother until she is quite certain, and this is a little tragedy, for while she is waiting for the signs that she is with child, a message comes from Anjou to say that Margaret's mother, Isabella

418

of Lorraine, has died. It is eight years since Margaret said good-bye to her mother and came to England for her wedding, and they were never especially close. But it is a blow to the young queen. I see her in the gallery with tears in her eyes and Edmund Beaufort holding both her hands in his own. Her head is turned towards him as if she would put her face to his broad shoulder and weep. When they hear my footsteps, they turn to me, still handclasped.

"Her Grace is distressed about the news from Anjou," the duke says simply. He leads Margaret to me. "Go with Jacquetta," he says tenderly. "Go and let her give you a tisane, something for grief. It is hard for a young woman to lose her mother and such a shame that you never told her —" He breaks off his words and puts the queen's hands in mine.

"You have something you can give her? Don't you? She should not cry and cry."

"I have some well-known herbs," I say carefully. "Will you come and lie down for a little while, Your Grace?"

"Yes," Margaret says, and lets me lead her away from the duke to the seclusion of her rooms.

I make her a tisane of Tipton's weed, and she hesitates before she drinks it. "It will not hurt a baby?"

"No," I reply. "It is very mild. You shall have a draft of it every morning for a week. Grief would be worse for a baby; you have to try to be calm and cheerful."

She nods.

"And you are sure?" I ask her quietly. "The midwives told me that they were almost certain?"

"I am certain," she says. "I will tell the king next week, when I miss my course again."

But she does not tell him herself. Oddly, she summons his chamberlain.

"I have a message for you to take to the king," she says. She is somber in her dark blue mourning clothes, and I am sorry that the loss of her mother has taken the brightness from her joy. Still, when she tells the king, they will both be elated. I assume she is going to invite the king to come to her rooms. But she goes on: "Pray give my compliments to the king and my good wishes, and inform him that I am with child."

Richard Tunstall simply goggles at her: he has never been asked to take such a message in his life. No royal chamberlain ever has. He looks at me, as if for advice, but I can do nothing but show, by a little shrug, that he had better take the message that this queen wishes to send to her husband.

He bows and steps backwards out of the room, and the guards close the door quietly behind him.

"I'll change my gown; the king is certain to

come to me," she says.

We hurry to her room and change her from her dark blue gown to one of pale green, a good color for spring. As her maid holds the dress out for her to step into, I can see that she has a rounded belly where she was once so spare, and her breasts fill the fine linen shift. I smile at the sight of her.

We wait for the king to come bursting in, his face alight with joy, his hands held out to her; we wait for an hour. We hear the watchman giving the time, and then finally we hear the footsteps outside and the guards throw open the doors to the queen's apartments. We all rise to our feet, expecting to see the king rush in, his boyish face beaming. But it is Richard Tunstall again, the king's chamberlain, with a reply to the queen's message.

"His Grace bid me tell you this: that the news is to our most singular consolation and to all true liege people's great joy and comfort," he says. He gulps and looks at me.

"Is that all?" I ask.

He nods.

The queen looks blankly at him. "Is he coming to me?"

"I don't think so, Your Grace." He clears his throat. "He was so happy that he rewarded me for bringing the news," he volunteers.

"Is he coming to visit Her Grace before dinner?"

"He has called his jeweler to see him. He is

having a special jewel made for the queen," he says.

"But what is he doing now?" she asks. "Right now? As you left him?"

Richard Tunstall gives another bow. "He has gone to give thanks in his private chapel," he says. "The king has gone to pray."

"Good," she says dismally. "Oh, good."

We don't see the king until that evening, when he comes to visit the queen in her rooms before dinner as usual. He kisses her hand before us all and tells her that he is most pleased. I glance round the room and see that all her ladies-in-waiting are looking, like me, bewildered. This is a couple who have conceived their first child — after nearly eight years of waiting. This child makes their marriage complete and their throne secure. Why do they behave as if they are barely acquainted?

Margaret is queenly; she gives no sign of expecting more warmth or enthusiasm from him. She bows her head, and she smiles at the king. "I am very happy," she says. "I pray that we have a son, and if not, a beautiful daughter and a son the next time."

"A blessing either way," he says kindly, and gives her his arm and leads her into dinner, seats her most carefully at his side, and then tenderly chooses for her the very choicest pieces of meat and the softest pieces of bread.

On his other side, Edmund Beaufort, Duke of Somerset, smiles on them both.

After dinner she says that she will retire early. The court rises as we withdraw, and when we get to the queen's rooms, she leaves her ladies and, beckoning me, goes into her bedroom.

"Take off my headdress," she says. "I am so tired, and it makes my head ache."

I untie the ribbons and lay the tall cone to one side. Underneath is the pad that keeps the heavy weight balanced upright on her head. I untie that too and then let down her hair. I take up a brush and gently start to free the tightly braided plaits, and she closes her eyes.

"That's better," she says. "Plait it up loosely, Jacquetta, and they can send in a glass of warm ale." I twist the thick red-gold hair into a plait, and help her take off her surcoat and gown. She pulls on a linen gown for the night and climbs into the big bed, looking like a little child among the rich hangings and thick covers.

"You are bound to feel weary," I say. "You can just rest. Everyone will want you to rest."

"I wonder what it will be," she says idly. "Do you think a boy?"

"Shall I get the cards?" I ask, ready to indulge her.

She turns her head away. "No," she says, surprising me. "And don't you think about it,

423

Jacquetta."

I laugh. "I am bound to think about it. This is your first baby; if it is a boy, he will be the next King of England. I am honor bound to think of him, and I would think of him anyway for love of you."

Gently, she puts a finger over my lips, to silence me. "Don't think too much then."

"Too much?"

"Don't think about him with the Sight," she says. "I want him to bloom like a flower, unobserved."

For a moment I think that she is afraid of some old horrible hedge witchery, casting the evil eye or ill-wishing. "You cannot think that I would do anything to harm him. Just thinking about him would not harm —"

"Oh, no." She shakes her golden head. "No, dear Jacquetta, I don't think that. It's just that . . . I don't want you to know everything . . . not everything. Some things are private." She blushes and turns her face away from me. "I don't want you to know everything."

I think I understand. Who knows what she had to do to gain the interest of such a cool husband? Who knows how seductive she must have been to get him off his knees and into her bed? Did she have to try sluts' tricks that left her feeling ashamed of herself? "Whatever you did to conceive this child, it is worth it," I say stoutly. "You had to conceive a child, and if you have made a son, it is all the better. Don't think badly of yourself, Margaret, and I will think of nothing at all."

She looks up. "Do you think that nothing would be a sin that gave England an heir?"

"It was a sin for love," I say. "And hurt no one. Then it's forgivable."

"I don't need to confess it?"

I think of Bishop Ayscough who told the young king not to bed his wife in the first week for fear that the young couple would experience the sin of lust. "You needn't confess anything you did to get this child. It had to be done, and it was an act of love, and men don't understand such things. Priests the least of all."

She gives a little sigh. "All right. And don't you think about it."

I wave my hand like a veil over my face. "I won't think. I have not a thought in my head."

She laughs. "I know you can't stop yourself thinking — I know that. And I know you have the Sight sometimes. But don't look for this baby: promise me you will not look for him? And think of him as a wildflower that grows and is a thing of beauty, but nobody knows how it was planted nor how it came to be there."

"He's the son of Marguerite the Daisy," I say. "He can be the flower that we rejoice to see in springtime, whose coming means spring."

"Yes," she says. "A wildflower that comes from who knows where."

GRAFTON, NORTHAMPTONSHIRE, SUMMER 1453

I keep my word to the queen and don't puzzle over this long-delayed conception, and she keeps her word to me and speaks to Edmund, the Duke of Somerset, and he sends my husband home to me, as I go into confinement at Grafton. I have a boy and we call him Lionel. My daughter Elizabeth, a married lady, comes and attends me in my confinement, very serious and very helpful, and I find her hanging over the cradle and cooing to the baby.

"You will have your own soon," I promise her.

"I hope so. He is so perfect; he is so beautiful."

"He is," I say with quiet pride. "Another son for the House of Rivers."

As soon as I am strong enough to return to court I get a message from the queen asking me to join them on progress. Richard has to return to the garrison of Calais, and it is painfully hard for us to part again.

"Let me come to Calais," I beg him. "I can't bear to be without you."

"All right," he says. "Next month. You can come and bring all the younger children, I can't bear to be without you and them either."

He kisses my mouth, he kisses both of my hands, and then he mounts his horse and rides away.

CLARENDON PALACE, WILTSHIRE, SUMMER 1453

The court itself is merry, traveling around the western counties and seeking out traitors and rabble-rousers. The Duke of Somerset has chosen the route and says that gradually the people are coming to learn that they cannot speak evil of the king, that there is no future in their demands and — more important than anything else — that Richard, Duke of York, will never be a power in the kingdom and so allying with him, or calling on his name, is a waste of time.

Edmund Beaufort is especially attentive to the king this summer, urging him on to be more and more severe in his judgments and rigorous in his sentencing. He strengthens his mind by applauding his decisions, and encourages him to speak out. The duke accompanies the king to chapel and brings him to the queen's rooms before dinner, where the three of them sit and talk, and the duke makes them laugh with his account of the day, sometimes mocking the ignorant people who have been before him.

The queen cannot ride in her condition, and Edmund Beaufort has trained a beautiful set of matched mules to carry her litter. He himself rides beside her, keeping his great horse reined back to the slow speed of the mules, watching her for any sign of fatigue. He consults me almost every day to make sure that I am happy with the queen's health, with her diet, with her exercise. Every day I assure him that she is well, that her belly is growing as it should, that I am certain that the baby is strong.

Almost every day he brings her a little gift, a posy of flowers, a poem, a little lad to dance for her, a kitten. The king and queen and the duke travel around the green lanes of Dorset in absolute accord, and whenever the queen steps down from her litter or turns to go up a stair, the duke's hand is out to support her, his arm to hold her steady.

I had seen him before as a charmer, a seducer, a rogue; but now I see something better in him, a man of great tenderness. He treats her as if he would spare her any fatigue, as if he has dedicated his life to her happiness. He serves the king as a most loyal friend, and he serves her as a knight of chivalry. More than this, I don't want to see; I won't let myself see.

In August we reach Wiltshire, and stay at the old royal palace at Clarendon, in the lush water meadows near Salisbury. I love this chalk meadowland and the broad watery valleys. The runs after the deer go on for hours through the woodland of the valley floors, and then we burst out onto the high downland and gallop across the even-cropped grass. When we halt to eat, we can see half of England spread before us. The palace is set among flowering meads, flooded into lakes for half the year, but a network of clean streams and pools and rivers in this high summer. The duke takes the queen fishing and swears that they will catch a salmon for her dinner, but they spend most of the day with her resting in the shade while he casts a line and gives her the rod to hold, and then casts the line again as the dragonflies dance over the kingcups and the swallows fly low over the water, skimming their little beaks into their own darting reflections.

We come home late in the evening as the clouds in the sky are like peach and lemon ribbons, swirled above the horizon. "It will be another beautiful day tomorrow," the duke predicts.

"And the next day?" she asks him.

"Why not? Why should you not have a beautiful day every day of your life?"

She laughs. "You would spoil me."

"I would," he says sweetly. "I would like you to have a beautiful day every day."

She takes his arm to help her up the stone

431

steps to the great front door of the hunting lodge. "Where is the king?" he asks one of the gentlemen of the bedchamber.

"In the chapel, Your Grace," the man replies. "With his confessor."

"I'll come to your rooms then," Edmund Beaufort says to the queen. "Shall I sit with you before dinner?"

"Yes, come," she says.

The ladies arrange themselves on stools and the window seats; the queen and the duke sit in a window embrasure, talking quietly together, their heads close, and then there is a knock and the doors are thrown open for a messenger from France, who comes hastily in, dirty from the road, and with his face grave. Nobody could doubt for a moment that he brings bad news.

The duke leaps swiftly to his feet. "Not now," he says sharply. "Where is the king?"

"He has given orders not to be disturbed," the man says. "But my orders are to come at all speed and give my message at once. So I've come to you. It's Lord Talbot, God bless him, and Bordeaux."

The duke grabs the man by the arm and marches him out of the door, without a word to the queen. She is already on her feet; I go to her side. "Be calm, Your Grace," I say quickly. "You must be calm for the baby."

"What's the news?" she asks. "What's the news from France? Edmund!"

"A moment," he throws over his shoulder, turning his back on her as if she were an ordinary woman. "Wait a moment."

There is a little gasp of shock from her ladies at how he speaks to her, but I put my arm around her waist and say, "Come and lie down, Your Grace. The duke will bring you the news when he has it. Come now."

"No," she says, pulling away from me. "I must know. Edmund! Tell me!"

For a moment he is in rapid conversation with the messenger, but when he turns he looks as if someone has struck him in the heart. "It's John Talbot," he says quietly.

I feel the queen stagger as her knees go weak, and she drops down in a faint. "Help me," I say quickly to one of the ladies-in-waiting, but it is the duke who brushes past us all and picks the queen up into his arms and carries her through her private rooms into her very bedroom, and lays her on the bed.

"Fetch the physicians," I snap at one of the ladies, and run in after them. He has half lain her on the bed; he is kneeling on the royal bed, his arms are around her, he is bending over her, holding her like a lover, whispering in her ear: "Margaret," he says urgently. "Margaret!"

"No!" I say. "Your Grace, Lord Edmund, let her go. I'll take care of her, leave her."

She holds him by his jacket, her two hands

grasping him tightly. "Tell me it all," she whispers desperately to him. "Tell me the worst, quickly."

I slam the bedroom door and put my back to it, before anyone can see that he has his hands either side of her face, that she is holding his wrists, that they are scanning each other's eyes.

"My love, I can hardly bear to tell you. Lord Talbot is dead and his son too. We have lost Castillon that he was defending; we have lost Bordeaux again; we have lost everything."

She quivers. "Dear God, the English will never forgive me. We have lost all of Gascony?"

"All," he says. "And John Talbot himself, God bless his soul."

The tears spill over from her eyes and pour down her cheeks, and Edmund Beaufort drops his head and kisses them away, kisses her like a lover trying to comfort his mistress.

"No!" I cry again, utterly horrified. I come to the bed and put my hand on his arm, pulling him away from her; but they are blind and deaf to me, clinging together, her arms around his neck. He is half lying on her, as he covers her face with kisses and whispers promises that he cannot keep, and at that moment, at that terrible, terrible moment, the door behind us opens and Henry, King of England, comes into the room and sees the two of them, wrapped in each other's arms:

434

his pregnant wife and his dearest friend.

For a long moment he takes in the scene. Slowly, the duke lifts his head and, gritting his jaw, gently releases Margaret, laying her back on the bed, pressing her shoulders to make her stay on the pillows, lifting her feet and straightening her gown around her ankles. Slowly, he turns to face her husband. He makes a little gesture with his hands to Henry, but he says nothing. There is nothing he can say. The king looks from his wife, raised on one elbow, white as a ghost on her bed, to the duke standing beside her, and then he looks at me. He looks puzzled, like a hurt child.

I reach out to him, as if he were one of my own children, cruelly struck. "Don't look," I say foolishly. "Don't see."

He puts his head on one side, like a whipped dog, as if he is trying to hear me.

"Don't look," I repeat. "Don't see."

Strangely, he steps towards me and lowers his pale face to me. Without knowing what I am doing, I lift my hands to him, and he takes one and then the other and cups my palms over his eyes, as if to blindfold himself. For a moment we are all quite frozen: my hands over his eyes, the duke waiting to speak, Margaret leaning back on her pillows, her hand over her curving belly. Then the king presses my hands hard against his closed eyelids and repeats my words: "Don't look.

Don't see."

Then he turns away. Without another word, he turns his back on all three of us and walks from the room, quietly closing the door behind him.

He does not come to dinner that night. The queen's dinner is served in her privy rooms; a dozen ladies and I sit down to eat with her and send half the courses back untouched. Edmund, Duke of Somerset, takes the head of the table in the great hall and tells the hushed diners that he has bad news for them: we have lost the last of our lands in France, except for the pale, town and garrison of Calais, and that John Talbot, the Earl of Shrewsbury, has died riding out for a forlorn cause that his gallantry and courage would not allow him to refuse. The town of Castillon begged him to come and relieve the French siege, and John Talbot could not turn a deaf ear when his countrymen asked for help. He held to his vow that he would not put on armor against the French king who had released him on that condition. So he rode out without armor, at the head of our troops, into battle without a weapon or a shield. It was an act of the most perfect chivalry and folly. An act worthy of the great man that he was. An archer felled his horse and an axe-man hacked him to death as he was pinned down underneath it. Our hopes of holding our lands in France are over; we have lost Gascony for the second, and almost certainly the last, time. Everything that was won by this king's father has been lost by his son, and we have been humiliated by France that once was our vassal.

The duke bows his head to the silent great hall. "We will pray for the soul of John Talbot and his noble son, Lord Lisle," he says. "He was a most gentle and perfect knight. And we will pray for the king, for England, and St. George."

Nobody cheers. Nobody repeats the prayer. Men say "Amen, Amen" quietly and pull out their benches and sit down and eat their dinner in silence.

The king goes to bed very early, the gentlemen of his chamber tell me, when I go to inquire. They say he seemed very tired. He did not speak to them. He did not say one word. I tell the queen, and she bites her lip and looks at me, white-faced. "What d'you think?" she asks. She seems as frightened as a little maid.

I shake my head. I don't know what to think.

"What should I do?"

I don't know what she should do.

In the morning, the queen is heavy-eyed from a sleepless night. Again, she sends me to the king's rooms to ask how is His Grace this morning? Again, the groom of the bedchamber tells me that the king is weary; this morning he is sleeping late. When they told him that it was time for Lauds, he just nodded and went back to sleep. They are surprised because he never misses chapel. They tried to wake him again for Prime, but he did not stir. I go back and tell the queen that he has slept through the morning and is still asleep.

She nods and says she will take breakfast in her rooms. In the great hall the Duke of Somerset breaks his fast with the court. Nobody speaks very much; we are all waiting for more news from France. We are all dreading more news from France.

The king sleeps on till midday.

"Is he ill?" I ask the groom of the wardrobe. "He never sleeps like this usually, does he?"

"He was shocked," the groom says. "I know that. He came into his rooms as white as a dove and lay down on the bed without a word to anyone."

"He said nothing?" I am ashamed of myself for this question.

"Nothing. He said not one word."

"Send for me as soon as he wakes," I say. "The queen is concerned about him."

The man nods, and I go back to the queen's rooms and tell her that the king lay down to sleep and said nothing to anyone.

"He said nothing?" she repeats, as I did.

"Nothing."

"He must have seen," she says.

"He saw," I say grimly.

"Jacquetta, what do you think he will do?"

I shake my head. I don't know.

All day he sleeps. Every hour I go to the door of the king's rooms and ask if he has woken. Every hour the groom of the chamber comes out, his face more and more worried, and shakes his head: "Still sleeping." Then, when the sun is setting and they are lighting the candles for dinner, the queen sends for Edmund Beaufort.

"I'll see him in my presence chamber," she says. "So that everyone can see we are not meeting in secret. But you stand before us so we can talk privately."

He comes in looking grave and handsome and kneels before her till she tells him that he can sit. I stand absentmindedly between them and the rest of the ladies and his entourage, so that nobody can hear their quiet-voiced conversation above the ripple of the harp.

They exchange three urgent sentences, and then she rises to her feet and the court rises too. She grits her teeth and leads the way into dinner, like the queen she is, to the great hall, where the men greet her in silence and the king's chair is empty.

After dinner she calls me to her side.

"They can't wake him," she says tightly. "The grooms tried to wake him for dinner but he would not stir. The duke has sent for the physicians to see if he is sick."

I nod.

"We'll sit in my rooms," she decides, and leads the way from the hall. As we go out there is a whisper like a breeze, men saying one to another that the king is mortally weary.

We wait for them to report in the queen's presence chamber, half the court gathered around, waiting to hear what is wrong with the king. The door opens, and the physicians come in; the queen beckons them to enter her private rooms, with the duke, and me, and half a dozen others.

"The king seems to be in good health, but he is sleeping," one of the doctors, John Arundel, says.

"Can you wake him up?"

"We judged it best to let him sleep," Dr. Faceby replies, bowing. "It might be best to let him sleep and wake when he is ready. Grief and a shock will sometimes be healed with a sleep, a long sleep."

"A shock?" the duke asks sharply. "What shock has the king had? What did he say?"

"The news from France," the doctor stumbles. "I believe the messenger blurted it out."

"Yes, he did," I say. "The queen fainted, and I took her into her rooms."

440

Margaret nips her lip. "Does he speak?"

"Not a word, not a word, since last night."

She nods as if it is of no matter to her whether he speaks or not; she is concerned only for his health. "Very well. Do you think he will wake in the morning?"

"Oh, almost certainly," Dr. Faceby answers. "Often someone will sleep deeply after distressing news. It is the body's way to heal itself."

"And wake remembering nothing?" she asks. The duke looks down at the floor as if indifferent.

"You may have to tell him of the loss of Gascony all over again, when he wakes," the doctor agrees.

She turns to the duke. "My lord, please give the king's grooms the order that they should wake him, as usual, in the morning, and prepare his rooms and his clothes as usual."

He bows. "Of course, Your Grace."

The physicians take their leave. One of them will sit in the king's bedroom to watch over his sleep. The duke's entourage and the queen's ladies leave behind the doctors. The couple takes one stolen moment when the duke is at her side, and everyone is leaving, and no one observing them.

"It'll be all right," he whispers. "We'll say nothing. Nothing. Trust me. It will be all right."

Mutely she nods, and he bows and goes out of the room.

The next day they go to wake the king, but he does not wake. One of the grooms of the bedchamber comes to the door and tells me that they had to lift the king to the close stool, clean him, and change his nightgown, which he had soiled. If one of them holds him on the close stool, he will pass water, and they can wash his face and hands. They can sit him in a chair though his head lolls, and if one of them holds his face up, the other can pour a little warm ale down his throat. He cannot stand, he cannot hear them; he does not respond to a touch. He shows no hunger, and he would lie in his filth.

"This isn't sleep," the groom says bluntly. "The doctors are fooling themselves. Nobody sleeps like this."

"D'you think he is dying?" I ask.

The man shakes his head. "I've never seen anything like it in my life before. It's like he's enchanted. Like he's cursed."

"Don't say such a thing," I reply at once. "Never say such a thing. He's just sleeping."

"Oh, aye," he repeats. "Sleeping, as the doctors say."

I walk slowly back to the queen's rooms, wishing that Richard were with me, wishing that I was at home in Grafton. I have a terrible fear that I have done something very wrong. I am filled with fear, superstitious fear, as if I have done something terrible. I wonder if it was my command to the king to see nothing that has blinded him. I wonder if he is the victim of my accidental power. My great-aunt Jehanne cautioned me to always be careful what I wished for, to consider very carefully the words of blessings or of curses. And now I have told the King of England: "Don't look! Don't see!" and he has closed his eyes and neither looks nor sees.

I shake my head, trying to dispel my own fears. Surely I must have said words like this a dozen times and nothing happened? Why would I have the powers to blind the King of England now? Perhaps he is just very tired? Perhaps he is, as the doctors think, shocked by the news from France? Perhaps he is like one of my mother's aunts, who froze up and lay still, lay quite like the king, neither speaking nor moving until she died years later. Perhaps I am frightening myself to think that it was my command that has made him blind.

In her rooms the queen is lying in her bed, I am so afraid of what I may have done that I recoil on the threshold of her darkened room, and whisper: "Margaret." She raises her hand: she can move; she is not enchanted. One of her younger ladies is at her side, while the rest of them are in the room outside, whispering about the danger to the baby, and the shock to the queen, and the likelihood of everything going terribly wrong, as women always do when one is near to childbirth.

"Enough," I say irritably, as I close the door on the queen's chamber so she cannot hear these fearful predictions. "If you can't say anything cheerful, then don't speak at all. And you, Bessie, I don't want to hear another word about your mother's travails in childbed. I have been brought to bed eleven times, raised ten, and never endured one quarter of the pains you report. Indeed, no woman could have borne what you describe. The queen may well be as lucky as me."

I stamp past them to the queen's rooms and send away my little maid with one wave of my hand. She goes in silence, and for a moment I think the queen is asleep; but she turns her head and looks at me, her eyes dark and hollowed with fatigue and fear.

"Has the king woken this morning?" Her lips are chapped where she has been biting them; she looks haggard with worry.

"No," I say. "Not yet. But they have washed him, and he has taken a little breakfast."

"He is sitting up?"

"No," I say uncomfortably. "They had to serve him."

"Serve him?"

"Feed him."

She is silent. "It's a blessing in a way," she says. "It means he says nothing rashly, in temper, at first thought. It gives us time to

444

consider. I keep thinking that it is a blessing in a way. It gives us time to . . . prepare."

"In a way," I agree.

"What do the doctors say?"

"They say they think he will wake, perhaps tomorrow."

"And then he will be himself again? And remember everything?"

"Perhaps. I don't believe that they really know."

"What shall we do?"

"I don't know."

She sits on the side of the bed, her hand cupped on her belly, and rises to her feet to look out of the window. Below her are the beautiful gardens running down to the river, where a punt bobs invitingly at a landing stage and a heron stands still and quiet in the water. She sighs.

"Do you have any pain?" I ask anxiously.

"No, no, I can just feel the baby moving."

"It is most important that you remain calm."

She laughs shortly. "We have lost Gascony; next the French are certain to attack Calais; the king has gone to sleep and cannot be wakened, and —" She breaks off. Neither of us has mentioned the duke taking her into his arms as an accustomed lover, kissing her face, promising to keep her safe. "And you tell me to remain calm."

"I do," I say stoutly. "For all this is nothing

to losing the child. You have to eat, and you have to sleep, Margaret. This is your duty to the child. You might be carrying a boy; it might be a prince for England. When all this has been forgotten, we will remember that you kept the prince safe."

She pauses, she nods. "Yes. Jacquetta, you are right. See? I will sit. I will be calm. You can bring me some bread and some meat and some ale. I will be calm. And fetch the duke."

"You cannot see him alone," I specify.

"No. I know that. But I have to see him. Until the king wakes, he and I will have to decide everything together. He is my only advisor and help."

I find the duke in his rooms, gazing blankly out of the window. He whirls around when his men hammer on the door, and as they throw it open I see the whiteness of his face and the fear in his eyes.

"Jacquetta," he says, and then corrects himself: "Your Grace."

I wait till they have closed the door behind me. "The queen commands your presence," I say shortly.

He takes up his cape and his hat. "How is she?"

"Anxious."

He offers me his arm, and childishly I pretend not to see the gesture but precede him to the door. He follows me out, and we

446

walk down the sunny gallery towards the royal rooms. Outside the leaded windows I can see swallows swooping low over the water meadows and hear the birds singing.

He strides faster to come alongside me. "You blame me," he says shortly.

"I don't know anything."

"You blame me, but Jacquetta, I assure you, the first move was —"

"I don't know anything, and if I know nothing, then I cannot be questioned, and I cannot confess," I say, cutting him off. "All I want to do is to see Her Grace at peace and strong enough to carry her child to full term and bring him into the world. All I pray is that His Grace, the king, wakes up with a calm mind and we can tell him the sad news from Gascony. And I hope, of course, all the time, ceaselessly, that my husband is safe in Calais. Other than these thoughts, I don't venture, Your Grace."

He nods his head, and we walk in silence.

In the queen's rooms I see that the three ladies-in-waiting are sitting in the window seats pretending to sew while craning their necks to eavesdrop. They rise up and curtsey and make a bustle as the duke and I enter; I tell them to sit again, and I nod to a couple of musicians to play. This covers the whispers between the queen and the duke. She allows him to sit on a stool at her side, and she beckons me to join them.

"His Grace says that if the king does not waken within a few days, we cannot stay here."

I look at him.

"People will start to wonder, and then there will be gossip. We can say that the king is weary, and he can ride in a litter back to London."

"We can draw the curtains of the litter," I agree. "But what then?"

"The queen has to go into her confinement at Westminster Palace. That's been planned for months; it can't be changed. I suggest the king stays quietly in his rooms."

"People will talk."

"We can say he is praying for her health. We can say he is keeping monastic hours."

I nod. It is possible that the king's illness can be kept from everyone but a small court circle.

"What about meeting with the lords? What about the king's council?" I ask.

"I can handle them," the duke says. "I will take decisions in the name of the king."

I look sharply at him, and then I lower my eyes so he cannot see my shock. This is to make himself all but King of England. The queen will be in confinement, the king asleep, and Edmund Beaufort will step up from being Constable of England to King of England.

"Richard, Duke of York, is likely to object,"

I remark to the floor beneath my feet.

"I can handle him," he says dismissively.

"And when the king wakes?"

"When the king wakes, we will all go back to normal," the queen says. Her voice is strained, her hand on her belly. "And we will have to explain to him that when he was taken so suddenly ill, we had to decide what to do without consulting him."

"He is likely to be confused when he wakes," the duke says. "I asked the physicians. They say that he may have troubling dreams, fantasies. He will be surprised at waking. He will not be able to tell what is real and what is a bad dream. Best that it should be in his own bedroom at Westminster, with the country well ruled."

"He may remember nothing," the queen says. "We may have to tell him again all about the loss of Gascony."

"We must make sure that he hears the news first from us, that we tell him the truth gently," the duke supplements.

They look like conspirators, their heads close together, whispering. I glance around at the queen's rooms; no one else seems to see anything out of the ordinary. I realize that I am the only one who suddenly sees a sickening intimacy.

The queen rises to her feet and gives a little moan at a twinge of pain. I see the duke's hand fly out, and then he checks the gesture:

he does not touch her. She pauses and smiles at him. "I am all right."

He glances at me like a young husband prompting a nurse. "Perhaps you should rest, Your Grace," I respond. "If we are to travel to London."

"We will go the day after tomorrow," the duke rules. "I will order them to get everything ready at once."

WESTMINSTER PALACE, LONDON, AUTUMN 1453

The rooms for the royal confinement are prepared, according to the traditions of the royal household. The tapestries are taken down; the windows shuttered tight and hung with thick material to keep out the disturbing light and drafts of air. The fires are banked up: the rooms must be kept warm; every day the fire boys haul logs up as far as the firmly barred doors. No man, not even the working boys, can come into the queen's rooms.

Fresh rushes are scattered on the floor, especially herbs that are helpful in childbirth: shepherd's purse and motherwort. A low birthing bed is brought into the room and dressed with special sheets. They bring in the royal cradle: an heirloom sent over from Anjou, of beautiful carved wood inlaid with gold. They make it up with the finest linen trimmed with lace. They prepare the swaddling board for the baby; his bands and his cap are all washed and pressed and made ready. An altar is set up in what is usually the privy chamber, and a screen placed between the bedroom and the chamber so the priest can come in and serve the Mass and the queen observe him without being seen. She will make her confession from behind a veiled screen. Not even an ordained priest can come into these rooms for six weeks before the birth and for six weeks after.

In practice, in most households, a loving husband will break the rules and come in to see his wife during her confinement, as soon as the baby is born, washed, swaddled, and laid in the cradle. Many husbands will not touch her until she has been churched, believing that she is unclean after the travail of childbed, and might contaminate him with female sin — but a husband like Richard disregards such fears as superstitions. He is always tender and affectionate and loving at these times and brings me fruit and sweetmeats that the older women say are not allowed, and has to be chased from the room by the midwives who protest that he will disturb me, or wake the baby, or make work for them.

No man will come near the poor little queen, of course. No man is allowed in the royal confinement chamber, and her husband, the only one who might trespass, is in his own shadowy room washed daily as if he were a big overgrown baby, fed as if he were in his dotage, limp as a new corpse.

We are holding the terrible news of the king's health tightly within the walls of the palace. The grooms of his chamber know; but they are so appalled at the work they have to do, and the collapse of the man they knew, that it has not been hard for Edmund Beaufort to take each one aside, swear him to secrecy, and threaten him with the most terrible punishments if he so much as whispers a word outside the walls. The king's household — his companions and his grooms, his page boys, his master of horse and the grooms in the stable — know only that the king is stricken with an illness that makes him very tired and very weak, incapable of riding. They wonder what can be wrong with him, but they are not troubled very much. It is not as if he was ever a lusty man who called for four hunters in the morning and would ride one after another, as each foundered. The quiet life of the king's stables remains quiet, and only the men who see him inert in his bed in his peaceful bedroom realize how gravely ill the king has become.

We are helped in our rule of silence by the fact that most of the lords and gentry had left London for the summer and are slow to return. The duke does not summon Parliament, so the country gentry have no reason to come into the city, and everything that has to be decided in the kingdom is done with a handful of men in the king's council in the name of the king but under the signature of the duke. He tells them that the king is unwell, too fatigued to come to council, and he, Edmund Beaufort, as his most trusted kinsman, will hold the king's seal and use it to ratify any decision. Almost no one suspects that the king is quite incapable of coming to the council. Most of them think he is in his private chapel, praying for the health of the queen, studying in silence, and that he has given the seal and the authority to Edmund Beaufort, who has always commanded so much anyway.

But the rumors start, as they are bound to do. The cooks remark that they never send good joints of meat into the king's rooms but only soups, and then some fool of a groom says that the king cannot chew his food, and then hushes himself and says "God save him!" and takes himself off. Of course the physicians come and go in and out of the king's rooms, and anyone seeing them is bound to notice that there are strange doctors and physicians, herbalists, and practitioners of all sorts coming at the bidding of the duke and going into the king's rooms. The physicians would not dare to speak, but they are attended by servants and have messengers bringing them herbs and physic. After a week of this, the duke invites me to his rooms and asks me to tell the queen that it is his advice that the king be taken to Windsor, where they can more easily nurse him without the news getting out.

"She won't like it," I tell him frankly. "She won't like him being kept there, and her trapped here in confinement."

"If he stays here, then people will start to talk," he says. "We cannot keep it secret. And she will want to avoid gossip more than anything else."

I curtsey and go to the door.

"What do you think?" he asks me as my hand is on the latch. "What do you think, Your Grace? You're a woman of gifts. What do you think will become of the king? And what of the queen if he never recovers?"

I say nothing. I am too old a hand at court to be led into speculation about the future of a king by the man who is standing in his shoes.

"You must have thoughts," he says impatiently.

"I may have thoughts, but I have no words," I say, and leave him. But that night I dream of the Fisher King of the legend: a country commanded by a king too frail and too weak to do anything but go fishing, while a young woman has to rule the land alone, and longs for a man who can stand at her side.

The queen finds her confinement tedious, and the daily reports from Windsor Castle make the days only worse. They are torturing the king with one remedy after another. The reports speak of draining him of cool fluids, and heating of his vital parts, and I know that they mean cupping him to draw off his blood and then burning him where he lies, silent as a crucified Christ, waiting to rise again. Some nights I get up from the little bed that I have in the queen's room and pull up the corner of the tapestry over the window so that I can see the moon, a big warm harvest moon, so near to earth that I can see every wrinkle and pockmark on her face, and I ask her: "Did I bewitch the king? Did I ill-wish him? In that moment of fright when I bade him see nothing, did I, in truth, make him blind? Could such a thing be? Could I be so powerful? And if it was me — how can I take the words back and restore him?"

I feel very alone with this worry. Of course I cannot share it with the queen, who has her own guilt and fear. I dare write nothing to Richard; such thoughts should not be in my mind, never on paper. I am sick and tired of being trapped in these shadowy rooms: the queen's confinement is long and anxious for us all. This should be the happiest autumn of her life, with a baby on the way at last; but instead we are all filled with fear about the king, and now some of the ladies are whispering that the baby will be born asleep too.

When I hear this, I go down to the river and sit on the pier as the sun is setting and look over the swiftly moving water that flows towards the sea, and I whisper to Melusina that if I ever said a word that wished the king blinded, I take back that word now. If I ever had a thought that he should see nothing, then I deny that thought now, and I wish with all my heart that the baby born to the queen will be well and healthy and live long and happy. I go slowly back to the palace, not knowing if the river has heard my wishes, or if the river can do anything anyway, or if the moon can understand how desolate a mere woman can feel, far from her husband and in a world that is filled with danger.

I walk in to a hushed bustle. "Her waters have broken," a maid hisses, running past me with some clean linen.

I hurry into the bedroom. The midwives are here already; the rockers are making up the cradle with clean sheets and the softest blanket, the mistress of the bedchamber is heating a poker to mull the special birthing ale, and the queen herself is standing at the foot of the best bed, bent over, holding the bedpost, sweat on her white face, gripping her lower lip in her teeth. I go straight to her. "The pain passes," I say. "Moment by moment, it comes and it goes away again. You have to be brave."

"I am brave," she says furiously. "No one shall ever say otherwise."

I see the irritability of childbirth, and I take a damp cloth soaked in lavender water and gently wipe her face. She sighs as the pain recedes and then braces herself for the next wave. It takes a long time to come. I glance at the midwife. "Going to take a while," she says wisely. "We'd all better have a mug of ale and a sit down."

It does take a while — all night — but next day, on the day of St. Edward, she gives birth to a boy, a precious Lancaster boy, and the safety and the inheritance of England is assured.

I go outside to the presence chamber, and there are the lords of England, waiting for news. Edmund Beaufort is among them, not standing forwards, as he usually does, commanding the room, but away from the bedchamber door, a little aside, making himself one of the crowd. For once in his life he is not claiming pride of place, and this makes me hesitate, not knowing if I should go directly and tell him. He is the Constable of England; he is the most favored lord in the land. He commands the Privy Council, and they are his nominated men in Parliament. He is the favorite of king and queen, and we are all accustomed to giving way to him. I would normally speak to him before any other.

Of course, the first man to have the news should be the baby's father: the king. But he, God bless him, is far, far away. There is no protocol for today, and I don't know what I am supposed to do. I hesitate for a moment, and then as all the talk dies down and the men turn to look at me in expectant silence, I say simply, "My lords, I give you joy. The queen has been brought to bed of a handsome boy and has named him Edward. God save the king."

A few days later, as the baby thrives and the queen rests, I am coming back to the queen's chambers after a walk in the gardens of the palace when I hesitate. At the closed door of her rooms is a young boy and a couple of guards wearing the white rose of the House of York on their livery. I know at once that this will mean trouble, as I open the door and go inside.

The queen is seated on her chair by the window, the wife of Richard, Duke of York, standing before her. Margaret has not invited her to sit, and the flush of color in Cecily Neville's cheeks tells me that she is well aware of the snub. She turns as I come in and says, "Her Grace, the Dowager Duchess, will confirm all that I say, I am sure."

I sweep her a small curtsey. "Good day to you, Your Grace," I say politely, and I go and stand beside the queen, my hand resting on the back of her chair, so that Cecily can be in no doubt which side I am on, whatever she is here for, whatever she hopes I will confirm.

"Her Grace has come to ask me to make sure that her husband is invited to all meetings of the royal council," the queen says wearily.

Cecily nods and says: "As he should be. As his family always has been. As the king promised he would be."

I wait.

"I have been explaining to Her Grace that since I am in confinement I can play no part in the business of ruling," the queen says.

"Really, you should not be seeing visitors at all," I remark.

"I am sorry to come, but how else is my husband's position to be considered?" the duchess says, looking remarkably impenitent. "The king will see no one, and is not even attended by a court. And the Duke of Somerset is no friend to my husband." She turns to the queen again. "You do the country a great disservice when you do not let my husband serve," she says. "He is the greatest magnate in the kingdom, and his loyalty to the king is unquestioned. He is the king's closest cousin and his heir. Why is he not invited to attend the king's council? How can business be agreed without considering his opinion? You call on him quickly enough when you want arms and money; he should be there when the decisions are taken."

The queen shrugs. "I will send the Duke of Somerset a note," she offers. "But I understand that not much is being undertaken. The king has withdrawn into prayer, and I am still confined. I imagine the duke is managing day-to-day affairs as best he can with a few advisors."

"My husband should be one of the advisors," the duchess insists.

I step forwards and make a little gesture towards the door. "I am sure the queen is glad that you brought it to her attention," I say. Unwillingly, the duchess allows herself to be guided away. "And since Her Grace has said that she will write a note to the duke, I am sure your husband will receive his invitation to the council."

"And he must be there when they present the baby to the king."

I freeze at this and exchange a quick aghast look with the queen. "Forgive me," I say when Margaret is silent. "You know I was not brought up in an English court. And this is the first time I have been present at the birth of a prince." I smile, but she — a born-and-bred Englishwoman — does not. "Please tell me. How is the baby presented to the king?"

"He has to be presented by the Privy Council," Cecily Neville says with just a hint of glee at my discomfort. I think she knows that we had not planned for this. "In order for the baby to be accepted as the heir to the throne and the prince of the realm, he has to be presented by the Privy Council to the king, and the king has to formally accept him as his son and heir. Without that, he is not the heir to the throne. If he is not recognized by his father, he cannot be recognized as heir to England. He cannot take his titles. But there can be no difficulty, can there?"

Margaret says nothing but leans back in the chair as if she is exhausted.

"Can there?" the duchess asks again.

"Of course not," I say smoothly. "I am sure the Duke of Somerset has all the arrangements in hand."

"And you will make sure that my husband is invited to attend," Cecily insists. "As is his right."

"I will take the queen's note to the duke myself," I assure her.

"And of course we will all be so happy to attend the baptism," she adds.

"Of course." I wait to see if she has the gall to ask if she can be godmother, but she contents herself with curtseying to the queen and stepping backwards for a few paces before letting me escort her to the door. We go out together. Outside in the presence chamber is the handsome boy whom I noticed earlier, who jumps to his feet. It is her oldest boy, Edward, and as he sees me, he makes a bow. He is the most bonny child, golden-brown hair, dark gray eyes, a merry smile, and tall, perhaps up to my shoulder, though he is only eleven.

"Ah, you have your boy with you," I exclaim. "I saw him as I came in, but I did not recognize him."

"This is my Edward," she says, her voice warm with pride. "Edward, you know Lady Rivers, the Dowager Duchess of Bedford."

I extend my hand, and he bows and kisses it.

"What a heartbreaker," I say to her with a smile. "He is just the same age as my boy Anthony, isn't he?"

"Only months apart," she says. "Is Anthony at Grafton?"

"Staying with his sister at Groby," I say. "Learning his manners. I think your boy is taller than mine."

"They shoot up like weeds," she says, disguising her pride. "And the shoes they get through! And the boots! Of course I have two other boys and Richard in the cradle."

"I have four boys now," I reply. "I lost my first, Lewis."

At once she crosses herself. "God keep them safe," she says. "And Our Lady comfort you."

This talk of children has united us. She steps closer to me and nods towards the queen's chamber. "Did it go well? Is she well?"

"Very well," I say. "It took all night; she was brave, and the baby came out quite perfect."

"Healthy and strong?"

"Giving suck, giving tongue," I tell her in

the old country saying. "A bonny boy."

"And the king? Is he well? Why is he not here? I would have thought he would have come to see his son?"

My smile is guileless. "He is serving God and his people in the best way that he can," I say. "On his knees for the safe delivery of his son and the security of an heir for England."

"Oh yes," she says. "But I had heard he was taken ill at Clarendon Palace, and came home in a litter?"

"He was tired," I say. "He had spent most of the summer pursuing and sentencing rebels. Both this year and last he spent all the days of summer making sure that justice runs through the lands. Sometimes your lands, as it happens."

She flings up her head at the implied rebuke. "If the king favors one man over his closest kin, his true friends and best advisors, there is always going to be trouble," she says hotly.

I raise my hand. "Forgive me," I say. "I did not mean to suggest that your tenants are exceptionally unruly, or your father's family, the Nevilles, make exceptionally irritable neighbors in the north of England. I meant only that the king has worked hard to see that his rule runs through all England. When the duke your husband comes to council, I am sure he will be able to reassure his peers that there is no hint of rebellion anywhere on his lands, and that his kinsmen, your family, can learn to live in peace with the Percys in the North."

She folds her lips on an angry reply. "Of course," she says. "We all want only to serve and support the king. And the North cannot be divided."

I smile at her boy. "And what do you hope to do when you are grown, Edward?" I ask. "Will you be a great general like your father? Or is it the church for you?"

He ducks his head. "One day I shall be head of the House of York," he says shyly to his shoes. "It is my duty to be ready to serve my house and my country however I am needed, when my time comes."

We have an impressive christening for the royal baby. The queen herself orders a cloth-of-gold train for his gown, which is brought from France and costs more than the gown of his godmother, Anne, the Duchess of Buckingham. The other godparents are the Archbishop of Canterbury and Edmund Beaufort, the Duke of Somerset.

"Is that wise?" I ask her quietly as she tells her confessor the names of the godparents she has chosen. She is on her knees before the little altar in her privy chamber, I am kneeling beside her, the priest behind the screen. Nobody can hear my urgent murmur.

She does not turn her head from her

clasped hands. "I would have no one else," she whispers. "The duke shall care for him and protect him as if he was his own."

I shake my head in silence, but I can see what she has done. She has surrounded her boy with the court party: people she trusts, people that Somerset has appointed, and Somerset's kin. If the king were to never speak again, she would have put a small army around her boy who should protect him.

Anne, the Duchess of Buckingham, carries the precious child to the font in Westminster Chapel. Cecily Neville glares at me from among the ladies as if I am responsible for yet another snub to her husband, Richard, Duke of York, who should have been a godfather. Nobody remarks on the king's absence, for a christening is the business of the godparents, and of course the queen is still in her confinement. But the secret cannot be kept forever, and the king surely cannot be ill forever? Surely he must get better soon?

At the christening feast Edmund Beaufort takes me to one side. "Tell the queen that I will call the great council, including the Duke of York, and take the baby prince to visit the king at Windsor."

I hesitate. "But, Your Grace, what if he does not wake at the sight of his child?"

"Then I will insist that they acknowledge the baby without the king's recognition."

"Could you do that without them seeing

him?" I say. "They all know that he is ill, but if they see him all but lifeless . . ."

He makes a little grimace. "I can't. Tell the queen I have tried, but the council insists that the child be presented to the king. Anything else would look too odd: they would think he is dead and we are concealing it. We have been blessed with a longer time than I dreamed possible. But it has come to an end now. They have to see the king, and the child has to be presented to him. There is nothing we can do to avoid this any longer." He hesitates. "There is one thing I had better tell you, and you had better forewarn the queen: they are saying that the child is not the true-born son of the king."

I stiffen, alert to danger. "They are?"

He nods. "I am doing what I can to quash the rumors. These allegations are treason, of course, and I will see anyone who gossips ends up on the gallows. But with the king hidden away from court, people are bound to talk."

"Do they name another man?" I ask him.

He looks at me, his dark eyes quite without guile. "I don't know," he says, though he does know. "I don't think it matters," he says, though it does matter. "And anyway, there is no evidence." This at least is true. Please God there is no evidence of any wrongdoing. "But the Duke of York has stirred up the council, and so the baby has to be seen and at least held by the king."

A council of twelve lords comes to the palace to take the baby upriver to be presented to his father, Somerset at their head. I am to go with them, along with the baby's nurses and rockers. Anne, the Duchess of Buckingham, his godmother, will come too. It is a cold autumn day, but the barge is well curtained and the baby is swaddled on his board and then wrapped in furs. The nurse holds him in her lap at the back of the boat, the baby's rockers seated near her and the wet nurse close by. Two barges follow us: the Duke of Somerset and his friends in one, the Duke of York and his allies in another. It is a fleet of undeclared enmity. I stand in the bow of the boat looking at the water, listening to the soothing swish of the river against the barge and the dip and pull of the oars in the current.

We sent ahead to say that the lords would visit the king, but I am shocked when we land at Windsor and go through the quiet castle to the upper ward. When the king and court leave one castle for another, then the servants take the chance to clean and shut down the state rooms. When we sent the king to Windsor without the court, they did not open all the bedrooms, nor the kitchens that cook for hundreds, the state rooms, nor the echoing stables. Instead the king's tiny entourage is camped in his own private rooms, and the rest of the castle is empty, quite desolate. The king's beautiful presence chamber, which is usually the heart of the court, has a shabby, neglected air; the servants have not cleaned the hearth, and the flickering flames show that they have only just lit the fire. It feels cold and deserted. There are no tapestries on the walls, and some of the shutters are closed so the room is shadowy and cool. There are old rushes on the floor, musty and dry; and half-burned rushlights in the sconces. I crook my finger to the groom of the household to call him to my side. "Why was the fire not lit earlier? Where are the king's tapestries? This room is a disgrace."

He ducks his head. "Forgive me, Your Grace. But I have so few servants here. They are all at Westminster with the queen and the Duke of Somerset. And the king never comes out here anyway. Would you want me to light the fire for the physicians and their servants? Nobody else visits, and our orders are to admit no one who does not come from the duke."

"I would want you to light the fire so the king's rooms are bright and clean and cheerful," I tell him. "And if you haven't enough servants to keep the rooms clean, then you should have told us. His Grace should be better served than this. This is the King of England; he should be served in state."

He bows at the reproof, but I doubt that he agrees with me. If the king can see nothing, what is the point of tapestries on the walls? If no one comes, then why sweep the state rooms? If there are no visitors, then why light a fire in the presence chamber? The Duke of Somerset beckons me to join him at the double doors of the privy chamber. There is only one man on duty. "No need to announce us," the duke says. The guard opens the door for us, and we slip in.

The room is transformed. Usually, it is a pretty chamber with two bay windows overlooking the water meadows and the river, the windows on the other side overlooking the upper ward, where there is always the sound of people coming and going, horses clip-clopping on the cobbles, sometimes music. The rooms are always busy with the courtiers and the advisors to the king. Usually, there are tapestries on the walls and tables laid with little objects of gold and silver, little painted boxes and curios. Today the room is empty, horribly bare but for a great table laid with the tools of the physicians' trade: bowls for cupping, lances, a big jar of wriggling leeches, some bandages, some ointments, a big box of herbs, a record book with daily entries of painful treatments, and some boxes holding spices and shavings of metals. There is a heavy chair with thick leather straps on the arms and legs where they bind the king to keep him still while they force drinks down his throat, or lance his thin arms. There is no seat to the chair but underneath there is a bowl to catch his urine and feces. The room is warm enough. There is a fire in the grate, and it is clean; but it is more like one of the best rooms in the Bethlem Hospital for the mad than a royal privy chamber. It is like a room for a well-nursed madman, not for a king. The duke exchanges one horrified glance with me. Nobody coming in here is going to imagine that the king has been on retreat from the world, quietly praying.

The king's chief three physicians, solemn in their dark gowns, are standing behind the table; they bow but say nothing.

"Where is His Grace the king?" the duke asks.

"He is being dressed," Dr. Arundel says. "They will bring him through now."

The duke takes a step forwards towards the bedchamber and then checks, as if he does not want to see inside. "Bring him out," he says shortly.

The doctor goes to the king's bedchamber door and opens it wide. "Bring him," he says. From inside we can hear furniture shift, and I find I am clutching my hands together, hidden in my sleeves. I am afraid. I am afraid of what is going to come out. Then a brawny man, dressed in royal livery, comes through the door carrying a heavy chair like a royal throne, set on a base with handles, like a litter. Behind him, holding the rear handles, comes another porter, and on the chair, head lolling, eyes closed, is all that is left of our king.

He is well dressed in a gown of blue with a surcoat of red, and his thin dark hair has been combed to his shoulders. He has been shaved, but they have nicked him, and there is a drop of blood on his throat. With his head lolling it looks as if they are bringing out a murdered man, his wounds bleeding in the presence of his killers. He is held steady in the chair by a band around his waist and another strap around his chest; but his head sags to one side, and when they put the chair down, it falls to his chest and he nods like a doll. Gently, the doctor raises him up and positions his head erect, but he does not stir at the touch. His eyes are closed; his breathing is heavy, like a man in drunken sleep.

"The Fisher King," I whisper to myself. He looks exactly like a man under an enchantment. This is not an illness of this world: this has to be a curse laid on him. He looks like the wax image of a king whom they lay on the coffin at a royal funeral, not a living man. Only the rise and fall of his chest, and the little noise that he makes from time to time, a little snuffling snore, tells us that he is alive. Alive but not a living man. I glance at the duke; he is looking at his king with an expression of horror. "This is worse than I thought," he says quietly to me. "Far worse."

The doctor steps forwards. "He is in good health . . . otherwise," he says.

I look at him blankly. This state cannot be described as good health. He is like a dead man. "Does nothing make him stir?"

He shakes his head, gestures at the table behind. "We have tried everything," he says. "We go on trying. At about noon every day, after he has broken his fast, we spend an hour trying to wake him, and every evening before dinner for another hour. But he seems to hear nothing, and he feels no pain. Every day we tell him that he must wake; sometimes we send for a priest to call on him to do his duty, to reproach him for failing us. But he shows no signs of hearing or understanding."

"Is he getting any worse?"

"No worse, but no better." He hesitates. "I think his sleep is a little deeper than when it first came on him." He gestures politely to the other doctors. One of them shakes his head. "Opinions vary."

"Do you think he might speak when we bring his son in to him?" the duke asks the doctors. "Does he ever say anything? Does he even dream?"

"He never says anything," Dr. Faceby volunteers. "But I think he dreams. Sometimes you can see his eyelids moving; sometimes he twitches in his sleep." He glances at me. "Once he wept."

I put my hand to my mouth at the thought of the king weeping in his sleep. I wonder if he is seeing in another world; I wonder what he has been watching. He has been asleep for nearly four months: it is a long dream. What can a four-month dream show a sleeping man?

"Could we prompt him to move at all?" The duke is thinking of the shock to the council, seeing the king like this for the first time. "Could he hold the baby if we put it in his arms?"

"He is quite limp," Dr. Arundel says. "I am afraid he would drop the baby. You could not trust him with anything of value. He is, himself, quite incapable."

There is an appalled silence.

"This has to be done," the duke decides.

"At least move that terrible chair," I say, and the two porters lift the chair with the straps and the close stool and carry it out.

The duke looks blankly at me. Neither of us can think of anything that will make this better. "Fetch them in," he says to me.

I go out to the waiting lords. "His Grace, the king, is in his privy chamber," I say, and stand to one side as they go in, the rockers and the nurse following with the duchess. I am foolishly relieved to see that the baby's dark blue eyes are open, blinking at the ceiling; there would have been something very horrible if the baby had been sleeping like his father.

In the privy chamber the lords have made an embarrassed half circle around the king. Not a word is spoken; I see one man cross himself. Richard, Duke of York, looks grim at the sight of the sleeping king. One man is shielding his eyes from the sight, one is weeping. They are all deeply shocked. Anne, Duchess of Buckingham, was forewarned of the state of the king by her kinsman Edmund Beaufort, but she is pale. She plays her part in this grotesque tableau, as if she presents a baby to his half-dead father every day of her life. She takes the child and walks towards the motionless king, strapped in his chair.

"Your Grace," she says quietly. "This is your son." She steps forwards, but the king does not lift his arms to receive the child. He is completely still. Awkwardly, the duchess holds the baby against his chest, but the king does not move. She looks to the Duke of Somerset, who takes the baby from her and lays it in the king's lap. He does not stir.

"Your Grace," the duke says loudly. "This is your son. Raise your hand to acknowledge him."

Nothing.

"Your Grace!" the duke says again, a little louder. "Just nod your head to acknowledge your son."

Nothing.

"Just blink, sire. Just blink to say that you know this is your son."

Now it is as if we are all enchanted. The physicians are still, looking at their patient, hoping for a miracle; the duchess waiting; the duke with one hand holding the baby on the king's unmoving knees, the other on the king's shoulder, squeezing him, hard and then harder, so his strong fingers are digging into the king's bony shoulder, pinching him cruelly. I am silent, standing still. For a moment I feel as if the king has a plague of stillness and we are all going to freeze and sleep with him, an enchanted court around a sleeping king. Then the baby lets out a little cry, and I step forwards and catch him up as if I fear that he might be infected with sleep.

"This is hopeless," the Duke of York says abruptly. "He sees and hears nothing. My God, Somerset: how long has he been like this? He can do nothing. You should have told us."

"He is still king," the duke says sharply.

"Nobody is denying that," Richard, Duke of York, snaps. "But he has not recognized his son, and he cannot transact the business of the kingdom. He is a king like a babe himself. We should have been told."

Edmund Beaufort looks around for support, but even the lords who are sworn to his house and hate and fear the Duke of York cannot deny that the king has not recognized his son, does nothing, sees nothing, hears nothing, is far, far from us — who knows where?

"We will return to Westminster," Edmund Beaufort announces. "And we will wait for His Grace to recover from this illness." He throws a furious look at the doctors. "The good physicians will waken him, I know."

That night as I start to doze in my bedchamber at Westminster Palace I wonder at a sleep that is unbroken, a sleep like death; except that in this sleep one would dream and stir and then sleep again. What would it be like to stir a little and glimpse the physicians and that terrible room with the chair and the knives and the leeches, and then slide back into sleep, unable to protest? What would it be like to open one's mouth in the silent scream of a dream and fall asleep mute? When I fall asleep, I dream again of the Fisher King, of a king who can do nothing as his kingdom falls into chaos and darkness, and leaves a young woman without her husband, alone. The Fisher King is wounded in his groin; he can neither father a child nor hold his lands. The cradle is empty, the fields are bare. I wake in the night and thank God that I have done so, that the enchantment that is lying like a blanket of darkness on the king has not smothered me, and I wonder; I shake my head on my pillow and wonder if it is my fault, if I commanded the king to be blind, if it was my incautious words that blinded him?

When I wake in the dawn light, I am clearheaded and alert at once, as if someone is calling my name, and I get up and go to the jewelry box that my great-aunt Jehanne gave me. There, untouched, is the purse of charms, and this time I choose a crown, to symbolize the king's return. I tie four different thin ribbons to this one charm. I choose a white ribbon to symbolize winter, if he will come back to us in the winter; a green ribbon if he will not come back till spring; a yellow ribbon if he will come back for haymaking; and a red ribbon if he will come back a year from now, when the berries are in the hedges. Then I tie each of these ribbons to four black strings, and take them to the riverside walk, where the Thames is flowing high and fast as the tide is coming in.

There is nobody about as I walk down to the little wooden pier where the wherry boatmen pick up their passengers, and so I tie the four dark threads to one of the stanchions of the pier, and I throw the little crown with the colored ribbons as far out as it will go, out into the river, and then I go back to the queen's confinement room, where she waits for her time of cleansing to be over and her release into the light.

■ ■ ■ ■

I leave the crown in the water for a week, while the queen comes out of her confinement and is churched in a magnificent service where all the duchesses of the kingdom walk behind her, to honor her, as if their husbands are not locked in a struggle to decide how the prince shall be recognized and how the kingdom shall be commanded while the king sees nothing and commands nothing. Now that the queen is returned to the world, the duke can come to her rooms and he tells her that the Earl of Salisbury, brother-in-law to the Duke of York, is saying publicly that the baby was not got by the king, and that there are many, dangerously many, who believe him. The queen lets it be known that anyone who listens to such slander need never come again to court; she tells her friends that no one should even speak to the Earl of Salisbury or to his spiteful son, the Earl of Warwick. She tells me that Richard, Duke of York, their kinsman, and even his duchess, Cecily, are her enemies, her enemies to death, and that I must never speak to any of them, ever again. What she does not do is comment on what they are saying, what many people are saying: that the king is not man enough to make a son, and that the baby is not a prince.

The queen and Edmund Beaufort decide that they must redouble the efforts to waken the king, and they hire new physicians and experts. They change the laws against alchemy, and men of learning are allowed to study once again and asked to consider the causes and cures of unknown illnesses of the mind. Everyone reopens their forges, refires their ovens, starts to send for foreign herbs and spices; herbalism, even magic is permitted if it can cure the king. They command the doctors to treat him more powerfully, but since nobody knows what is wrong with him, nobody knows what should be done. He has always been known to be melancholic, so they try to change his humor. They feed him burning-hot drinks and spicy soups to make him hotter; they make him sleep under thick furs heaped up on the bed, with a hot brick at his feet and a warming pan on either side of him until he sweats and weeps in his sleep; but still he never wakens. They lance his arms and bleed him to try to drain the watery humors; they poultice his back with paste of mustard seed till it is red and raw; they force boluses down his throat and purge him with enemas so that he vomits and voids in his sleep, burning waste that leaves his skin red and sore.

They try to make him angry by beating his feet, by shouting at him, by threatening him. They think it is their duty to taunt him with cowardice, with being a lesser man than his father. They abuse him terribly, God forgive them; they shout things in his face that would have broken his heart if he had heard them. But he hears nothing. They hurt him when they slap him — they can see his cheeks redden under the blows. But he does not rise up and leave them; he lies inert as they do what they want to him. I fear this is not treatment but torture.

In Westminster I wait for my week, and then I know that the morning has come when I wake again at dawn, wake as if I am alert in every part of my body and my mind is clear as the cold water washing round the pier. The four threads are there, safely tied to the leg of the pier, and I hope with all my heart that when I choose a black thread it will pull out the white ribbon on the crown so that I can see that the king will return to us this winter.

The sun is coming up as I put my hand on the threads, and I look east towards it, as it rises over the heart of England. There is a dazzle on the water from the rising sun, a wintry sun, a white and gold and silver wintry sun, in a cold blue sky, and as it rises and the mist swirls off the river, I see the most extraordinary sight: not one sun but three. I see three suns: one in the sky and two just above the water, reflections of mist and water, but clearly three suns. I blink and then rub my eyes, but the three suns blaze at me as I pull on the thread and I find it comes lightly, too lightly, into my hand. I don't have the thread with the white ribbon that would mean the king would come back to us in winter, nor even the green, which would mean the king would come back to us in spring. I pull on one thread after another and find all four ribbons empty with no crown; there is no crown at all. The king will never come back to us; instead, there will be the rise of a new dawn, and three suns in splendor.

I walk slowly back to the palace, a bunch of wet ribbons in my hand, and I wonder what three suns over England can mean. As I near the queen's rooms I can hear noise: soldiers grounding their weapons, and shouting. I pick up my long gown and hurry forwards. Outside her presence chamber there are men in the livery of Richard, Duke of York, his white rose on their collar. The doors are flung open to reveal the queen's personal guards standing irresolute as the queen shouts at them in French. Her women are screaming and running inwards to the privy chamber, and two or three of the lords of the council are trying to command quiet, as York's guard get hold of Edmund Beaufort, the Duke of Somerset, and march him out of the chamber and past me. He casts one furious look at me, but they take him past too fast for me to say anything, not even to ask where he is going. The queen comes flying out after him, and I catch her, and hold her, as she bursts into a flood of tears.

"Traitors! Treason!"

"What? What is happening?"

"The Duke of Somerset has been accused of treason," one of the lords tells me, as he rapidly withdraws from the queen's chamber. "They are taking him to the Tower. He will have a fair trial; the queen need not be distressed."

"Treason!" she screams. "You are the traitor, you, to stand by as that devil of York takes him!"

I help her back through the presence chamber, through the privy chamber, and into her bedroom. She flings herself on her bed and bursts into tears. "It's Richard, Duke of York," she says. "He has turned the council against Edmund. He wants to destroy him; he has always been his enemy. Then he will turn on me. Then he will rule the kingdom. I know it. I know it."

She raises herself up, her hair spilling from the plaits on either side of her face, her eyes red with tears and temper. "You hear this, Jacquetta. He is my enemy; he is my enemy, and I will destroy him. I will get Edmund out of the Tower, and I will put my son on the throne of England. And neither Richard, Duke of York, nor anyone else will stop me."

Westminster Palace, London, Spring 1454

Christmas comes and goes. Richard takes a ship from Calais and spends only the twelve days of the festival with me at the quiet court, and then says he has to return. The garrison is on the verge of mutiny and could come under attack at any time. The men do not know who is in command, and they are afraid of the French. Richard has to hold the garrison for Edmund Beaufort, and for England, against enemies within and without. Once again we are on the quayside, once again I am clinging to him. "I'll come with you," I say desperately. "We said I should come with you. I should come now."

"Beloved, you know I would never take you into a siege, and God alone knows what is going to happen."

"When will you come home again?"

He gives a resigned little shrug. "I have to hold my command until someone relieves me of it, and neither the king nor the duke is going to do that. If Richard, Duke of York, seizes power, then I will have to hold Calais against him, as well as against the French. I will have to hold it for Edmund Beaufort. He gave me the command, I can only return it to him. I have to go back, beloved. But you know I will return to you."

"I wish we were just squires at Grafton," I say miserably.

"I wish it too," he says. "Kiss the children for me, and tell them to be good. Tell them to do their duty and that I am doing mine."

"I wish you were not so dutiful," I say disagreeably.

He kisses me into silence. "I wish I could have another night," he says in my ear, and then he breaks away from me and runs up the gangplank to his ship.

I wait on the quayside until I see him at the rail, and I kiss my cold hand to him. "Come back soon," I call. "Be safe. Come back soon."

"I always come back to you," he calls back. "You know that. I will come back soon."

The dark nights grow shorter, but the king does not recover. Some alchemists predict that the sunshine will bring him to life as if he were a seed in the darkness of the earth, and they wheel him to an eastern window every morning and make him face the gray disc of the wintry sun. But nothing wakes him.

Edmund Beaufort, Duke of Somerset, is not released from his rooms in the Tower of

485

London; but neither is he accused. Richard, Duke of York, has enough power over the council of lords to make them arrest the duke, but not enough to persuade them to try him for treason.

"I am going to see him," the queen announces.

"Your Grace, people will talk," I warn her. "They are already saying things about you that don't bear repeating."

She raises an eyebrow.

"So I won't repeat them," I say.

"I know what they are saying," she declares boldly. "They are saying that he is my lover and that the prince is his son, and this is why my husband the king has not acknowledged him."

"Reason enough not to visit him," I caution.

"I have to see him."

"Your Grace —"

"Jacquetta, I have to."

I go with her and take two of her other ladies. They wait outside while the queen and I go into his rooms. He has a privy chamber with a bedroom beside it. The rooms, stone-walled with arrow-slit windows, are pleasant enough, close to the royal apartments in the White Tower; he is not by any means in a dungeon. He has a table and a chair and some books, but he is pale from being kept indoors, and he is looking thinner. His face lights up when he sees her, and he drops to his knee. She hurries towards him, and he passionately kisses her hands. The constable of the Tower stands at the door, his back turned tactfully to the room. I wait at the window looking out over the gray tide of the cold river. Behind me, I can hear the duke rise to his feet, and I can sense him mastering himself so that he does not reach for her.

"Will you sit, Your Grace?" he asks quietly, and puts the chair near the little fire for her.

"You can sit beside me," she says. I turn and see him pull up a small stool so they are close enough to whisper.

They are handclasped, his mouth to her ear, her turning to murmur to him, for half an hour, but when I hear the clock strike three, I go forwards and curtsey before her. "Your Grace, we have to go," I say.

For a moment I am afraid that she is going to cling to him, but she tucks her hands inside her sweeping sleeves, strokes the border of ermine as if for comfort, and rises to her feet. "I will come again," she says to him. "And I will do as you suggest. We have no choice."

He nods. "You know the names of the men who will serve you. It has to be done."

She nods and looks at him once, longingly, as if she wants his touch more than anything in the world, as if she cannot bear to leave;

then she ducks her head and goes quickly out of the room.

"What has to be done?" I ask as soon as we are outside, walking down the stone stairs towards the watergate. We came in a barge without flags and standards; I was anxious that as few people as possible knew that she was meeting the man accused of treason and named as her lover.

She is alight with excitement. "I am going to tell the Parliament to appoint me as regent," she says. "Edmund says the lords will support me."

"Regent? Can a woman be a regent in England? Your Grace, this is not Anjou. I don't think a woman can be a regent here. I don't think a woman can reign in England."

She hurries ahead of me, down the steps and onto the barge. "There's no law against it," she replies. "Edmund says. It is nothing but tradition. If the lords will support me, we will call a Parliament and tell the Parliament that I will serve as regent until the king is well again or — if he never wakes — until my son is old enough to be king."

"Never wakes?" I repeat in horror. "The duke is planning for the king to sleep forever?"

"How can we know?" she asks. "We can do nothing! You can be sure that Richard, Duke of York, is not doing nothing."

"Never wakes?"

She sits herself at the rear of the barge, her hand impatiently on the curtain. "Come on, Jacquetta. I want to get back and write to the lords and tell them my terms."

I hurry to take a seat beside her, and the oarsmen cast off and take the barge out into the river. All the way back to the palace I find I am squinting at the sky and trying to see three suns, and wondering what three suns might mean.

The queen's demand to be regent of England and rule the country with all the rights and wealth of the king during the illness of her husband does not resolve the whole problem as she and Edmund Beaufort confidently predicted. Instead, there is uproar. The people now know that the king is sick, mysteriously sick, and utterly disabled. The rumors of what ails him range from the black arts of his enemies, to poison given to him by his wife and her lover. Every great lord arms his men, and when he comes to London marches them into his house, for his own protection, so the city is filled with private armies, and the lord mayor himself imposes a curfew and tries to insist that weapons are left at the city gates. Every guild, almost every household, starts to plan their own defense in case fighting breaks out. There is an air of constant tension and anger, but no battle cries. As yet, nobody could name the sides, nobody knows the causes; but everybody knows that the Queen of England says that she will be king, that the Duke of York will save the people from this virago, that the Duke of Somerset has been locked up in the Tower of London to save the city from ruin, and that the King of England is sleeping, sleeping like Arthur under the lake, and perhaps he will waken only when ruin walks the land.

People ask me where my husband is, and what is his view? I say grimly that he is overseas, serving his king in Calais. I do not proffer his view, which I don't know; nor my own, which is that the world has run mad and there will be three suns in the sky before all this is over. I write to him, and send messages by the trading ships that go between here and Calais, but I think the messages do not always get through. In early March I write shortly: "I am with child again"; but he does not reply, and then I know for sure that either they are not delivering my messages, or that he is unable to write.

He was appointed as Commander in Calais under the captaincy of the Duke of Somerset. Now the Duke of Somerset is in the Tower, charged with treason. What should a loyal commander do? What will the garrison do?

The lords and Parliament go again to Windsor to see the king.

"Why do they keep going?" the queen demands, seeing the barges come back to the steps at the palace, and the great men in their furred robes helped ashore by their liveried servants. They trudge up the steps like men whose hopes have failed. "They must know he won't wake. I went myself and shouted at him, and he didn't wake. Why would he wake for them? Why don't they see that they have to make me regent and then I can hold down the Duke of York and his allies and restore peace to England?"

"They keep hoping," I say. I stand beside her at the window and we watch the doleful procession of the lords wind their way to the great hall. "Now they will have to nominate a regent. They can't go on without any king at all."

"They will have to nominate me," she says. She sets her jaw and stands a little taller. She is queenly; she believes she is called by God to rise into a yet greater role. "I am ready to serve," she says. "I will keep this country safe, and hand it to my son when he is a man. I will do my duty as Queen of England. If they make me regent, I will bring peace to England."

They make the Duke of York regent and they call him "protector of the realm."

"What?" Margaret is beside herself, striding up and down the privy chamber. She

491

kicks a footstool and sends it flying, a maid-in-waiting lets out a sob and cowers in the window; the rest of the ladies are frozen with terror. "They called him what?"

The hapless knight who brought the message from the council of the lords trembles before her. "They named him as protector of the realm."

"And what am I to do?" she demands of him. She means the question to be rhetorical. "What do they suggest that I do, while this duke, this mere kinsman, this paltry cousin of mine, thinks to rule my kingdom? What do they think that I, a Princess of France, a Queen of England, am going to do, when a jumped-up duke from nowhere thinks to pass laws in my land?"

"You are to go to Windsor Castle and care for your husband," he says. The poor fool thinks he is answering her question. He realizes swiftly that he would have done better to keep his mouth shut.

She goes from fire to ice. She freezes and turns to him, her eyes blazing with rage. "I did not hear you exactly. What did you say? What did you dare to say to me?"

He gulps. "Your Grace, I was trying to tell you that the lord protector —"

"The what?"

"The lord protector commands —"

"What?"

"Commands —"

She crosses the floor in two swift paces and stands before him, her tall headdress overtopping him, her eyes boring into his face. "Commands me?" she asks.

He shakes his head; he drops to his knees. "Commands that your household go to Windsor Castle," he says to the rushes beneath his knees. "And that you stay there, with your husband and your baby, and play no part in the ruling of the country, which will be done by him as lord protector, and the lords and the Parliament."

WINDSOR CASTLE,
SUMMER 1454

She goes to Windsor. There is a tantrum like a thunderstorm up and down the royal apartments, in and out of the chambers; but she goes. Really, she can do nothing but go. The Duke of York, whose own wife Cecily once came to the queen to eat humble pie and request a place on the council for him, rises high on the wheel of fortune. The council believes he is the only man who can restore order to the kingdom, who can prevent the dozens of small battles breaking out at every county quarrel, thinks that he is the only man who can save Calais, trusts that he will take the kingdom and hold it until our king, our sleeping king, comes back to us. It is as if they think the country is cursed and the Duke of York is the only man who can unsheathe his sword and stand in the doorway against an invisible enemy, and hold the post until the king awakes.

The queen — who had thought to be king herself — is cut down to wife, is pushed aside to be a mother. She goes as she is bidden, and they pay her the expenses of her household, reduce the numbers of horses in the stable, and ban her from returning to London without invitation. They treat her as if she is an ordinary woman, a woman of no importance; they reduce her to the care of her husband and the guardian of her son.

Edmund Beaufort is still in the Tower; he cannot help her. Indeed, she cannot defend him; her protection means nothing. Who can doubt that he will be tried and beheaded? Those lords who have loved her as a queen dare not imagine her as a regent. Though their own wives may run their lands when they are away, their own wives are given no title and draw no fees. They don't like to think of women in power, women as leaders. The ability of women is not acknowledged; indeed, it is concealed. Wise women pretend that all they are doing is running a household when they command a great estate; they write for their husband's advice while he is away, and they hand back the keys on his return. The queen's mistake is to claim the power and the title. The lords cannot bear the thought of a woman's rule; they cannot bear to even think that a woman can rule. It is as if they want to put her back into the confinement chamber. It is as if the king, her husband, by falling asleep, has set her free, free to command the kingdom; and that the duty of all the other great men is to return her to him. If they could put her to sleep like him, I think they would.

The queen is confined to Windsor. Richard is trapped in Calais. I live as her lady-in-waiting, as an estranged wife; but in truth we all wait. Every day Margaret goes to see the king, and every day he neither sees her nor hears her. She commands the doctors to be gentle with him, but sometimes her own temper snaps and she goes in and rails at him, cursing into his deaf ears.

I live with the queen and I long for Richard, and I am aware all the time of the rise of trouble on the streets of London, the danger on the country roads, the rumors that the North is up against the Duke of York, or up for their own ambitions — who knows with these wild lands on the border? The queen is plotting, I am sure of it. She asks me one day if I write to Richard, and I tell her that I write often, and send my letters with the wool merchants taking the fleeces to Calais. She asks if the ships come back empty; if they were to carry men, how many could be landed; if they could sail laden up the river to the Tower?

"You are thinking that they could come from Calais and rescue the Duke of Somerset from the Tower," I say flatly. "That would be to ask my husband to lead an invasion against the regent and protector of England."

"But in defense of the king," she says. "How could anyone call that treason?"

"I don't know," I say miserably. "I don't know what treason is anymore."

The plan comes to nothing, for we get news of an uprising in Calais. The soldiers have not been paid, and they lock up their officers in the barracks and raid the town and seize the trade goods, and sell them and keep the money for their wages. There are reports of looting and rioting. The queen finds me, in the stable yard of Windsor Castle, ordering my horse to be saddled and a guard to come with me to London. "I have to know what is happening," I say to her. "He could be in terrible danger; I have to know."

"He won't be in danger," she assures me. "His men love him. They may have locked him in his quarters so that they can raid the wool stores, but they won't hurt him. You know how beloved he is. Both he and Lord Welles. The men will release him when they have stolen their wages and drunk the town dry."

They bring my horse to me, and I climb up on the mounting block and into the saddle, awkward with my big belly. "I am sorry, Your Grace, but I need to know that for myself. I'll come back to you as soon as I know he is safe."

She raises a hand to me. "Yes, come back without fail," she says. "It is a lonely, lonely place here. I wish I could sleep the days away like my husband. I wish I could close my eyes and sleep forever, too."

I hardly know where to go in London to get news. My house has been closed down, there is no one there but a few guards for safety; the Parliament is not sitting; the Duke of York is no friend of mine. In the end I go to the wife of Lord Welles, who is commanding in Calais with Richard. My manservant announces me, and I walk into her solar chamber.

"I can guess why you have come," she says, rising and kissing me formally on the cheek. "How is Her Grace the queen?"

"She is well in her health, thank God."

"And the king?"

"God bless him, he is no better."

She nods and sits down and gestures me to take a stool near hers. Her two daughters come forwards with a glass of wine and biscuits, and then step back, as well-behaved girls should do, so that the adults can talk in private.

"Charming girls," I remark.

She nods. She knows I have sons who will have to marry well.

"The oldest one is betrothed," she says delicately.

I smile. "I hope she will be happy. I have come to you for news of my husband. I have

heard nothing. Have you any news of Calais?"
I ask.

She shakes her head. "I am sorry. There is
no news to be had. The last ship to get out of
the port said that there was an uprising, the
soldiers insisting on their pay. They had
captured the wool store and were selling the
goods for their own profit. They were holding
the ships in the harbor. Since then the
merchants will not send their cargoes to
Calais for fear that their own stocks are
captured. So I don't know anything, and I
can't get any news."

"Did they say what your husband or mine
was doing?" I ask. I have a great feeling of
dread that Richard would not sit idly by while
his men took the law into their own hands.

"I know they are both alive," she says. "Or
at any rate they were three weeks ago. I know
your husband cautioned the men and said
that what they were doing was common theft,
and they threw him into a cell." She sees the
terror on my face and puts her hand on mine.
"Really, they did not hurt him but locked
him up. You will have to be brave, my dear."

I swallow down the tears. "It has been so
long since we have been at home together," I
say. "And he has had one hard service after
another."

"We are all lost under the rule of a sleeping
king," she says gently. "The tenants on my
lands say that nothing will grow; nothing will

ever grow in a kingdom where the king himself lies like a fallow field. Will you go back to court?"

I give a little sigh. "I have to," I say simply. "The queen commands it, and the king says nothing."

In August I go to Grafton to see my children, and I try to explain to the older ones, Anne, Anthony, and Mary, that the king is well, but sleeping; that the queen has done nothing wrong but is confined with him; that their father's commander Edmund Beaufort, Duke of Somerset, is in the Tower, accused but not on trial; and that their father — and it is at this point that I have to grit my teeth and try to appear calm — their father is commanding the castle of Calais but is imprisoned by his own soldiers; the Constable of Calais is now Richard, Duke of York, and sooner or later their father will have to answer to him.

"Surely, the Duke of York will hold Calais, just as the Duke of Somerset would have done?" Anthony suggests. "Father won't like a new commander being put over him, but nobody can doubt that the Duke of York will send money to pay the soldiers and arms for the castle, won't he?"

I don't know. I think of the terrible year when I saw Richard wear himself out trying to hold soldiers to a cause when they had neither weapons nor wages. "He should do,"

I say carefully. "But we none of us can be sure what the duke will do, even what he can do. He has to govern as if he is king, but he is not king. He is only a lord among many lords, and some of them don't even like him. I just hope he does not blame your father for holding Calais for England; I just hope he lets him come home."

I go into my confinement in Grafton, sending a message to Richard when the baby is safely born. She is a girl, a beautiful girl, and I call her Margaret, for the queen, who is beating against the times we live in, like a bird against a window. I come out of confinement and see my little girl in the arms of my wet nurse and then kiss my other children. "I have to go back to court," I say. "The queen needs me."

The autumn is long and quiet for us in Windsor. Slowly, the trees start to grow yellow and then golden. The king gets no better; he does not change at all. The baby prince starts to pull himself to his feet, so that he can stand, and tries to take his first steps. This is the most interesting thing that happens in the whole year. Our world shrinks to the castle, and our lives to watching over a small baby and a sick man. The queen is a doting mother; she comes to the little prince's nursery morning and night, and she visits her husband every afternoon. It is like living under a spell, and we watch the baby grow as if we feared he might do nothing but sleep. Half a dozen of us always go to the nursery in the morning, as if we have to see for sure that the little prince has woken after another night. Apart from this we go through the motions of a court, attending on the king. But all we can do is sit with him as he sleeps. Every afternoon we sit with him and watch the slow rise and fall of his chest.

Richard sends me a letter as soon as he can get his reports into the hands of a ship's captain. He writes to the king's council — pointedly he does not address the lord protector — to say that the men cannot be commanded without wages. Without money from the Treasury the merchants of Calais are forced to pay for their own defense: the garrison there regards itself almost independent of England. Richard asks the council for orders, though he points out that it is only he and Lord Welles who are waiting for orders. All the rest — the great garrison, the soldiers, the sailors in the port, the merchants and the citizens — are taking the law into their own hands. To me, he writes to say that no one in the town accepts the lordship of the Duke of York; no one knows what to believe about the king; and do I think Edmund Beaufort is likely to get out of the Tower and reclaim his power? At the very end of the letter he writes to me that he loves and misses me. *I count the days,* he writes.

I am heart sore without you, my beloved. As soon as I can hand over this garrison to a new commander I will come home to you, but I do believe that if I were not here now, the town would fall to the French, who know full well the straits we are in. I am doing my duty as best I can to the poor king and to our poor country, as I know you are too. But when I come home this time, I swear I will never be parted from you again.

Windsor Castle, Winter 1454

The Duke of York, determined to show his mastery over Calais, and to prevent a French attack, musters a small fleet and takes ship to the garrison, saying he will enter it, pay the soldiers, make peace with the Calais merchants, hang any traitors, and be recognized as the Constable of Calais.

Calais is formidably fortified. It has been England's outpost in Normandy for generations, and now the soldiers have control of the fort; when they see the sails of York's fleet, they place the chain across the mouth of the harbor and turn the guns of the castle to the seaward side. York finds himself staring down the barrel of his own cannon, refused entry to his own city.

They bring the news to us as we are sitting with the king, one cold afternoon in November. Margaret is exultant. "I will see your husband honored for this!" she exclaims. "How York must be humbled! How shamed he must be! Out at sea, with a great fleet, and the city of Calais refusing him entry! Surely now the lords will put him out of office? Surely they will fetch Edmund from the Tower?"

I say nothing. Of course, all I am wondering is whether my husband will have stood by while his men mutinied, disobeying his order to admit their new captain. Or whether — and far worse, far more dangerous for us — he himself led them to defy the Duke of York, commanding them from the high tower to turn the guns on the lord regent, the legally appointed protector of England. Either way, he will be in danger; either way, the duke is his enemy from this hour.

The king, strapped in his chair, makes a little noise in his sleep; the queen does not even glance at him.

"Think of York, bobbing about in his ship and the guns trained down on him," she gloats. "I wish to God they had shot him. Think how it would be for us if they had only sunk his ship and he had drowned? Think if your Richard had sunk him!"

I cannot stop myself from shuddering. Surely, Richard would never have allowed his garrison to open fire on a royal duke appointed by the king's council? I am sure of that; I have to be sure of that.

"It's treason," I say simply. "Whether we like York or not, he is appointed by Privy Council and Parliament to rule in the king's place with his authority. It would be treason to attack him. And to have Calais open fire on English ships is a terrible thing to show to the French."

She shrugs. "Oh! Who cares? To be appointed by his own place men is no appointment," she says. "*I* did not appoint him; the king did not appoint him. As far as I am concerned he has just seized power. He is a usurper, and your husband should have shot him as soon as he was in range. Your husband failed to shoot him. He should have killed him when he could."

Again the king makes a little noise. I go to his side. "Did you speak, Your Grace?" I ask him. "Do you hear us talking? Can you hear me?"

The queen is at his side; she touches his hand. "Wake up," she says. It is all she ever says to him. "Wake up."

Amazingly, for a moment, he stirs. Truly, he does. For the first time in more than a year, he turns his head, opens his eyes, and sees. I know he does: he sees our absolutely amazed faces, and then he gives a little sigh, closes his eyes, and sleeps again.

"Physicians!" the queen screams, and runs to the door, tears it open, and shouts for the doctors who are dining and drinking and resting in the presence room outside. "The king is awake! The king is awake!"

They come tumbling into the room, wiping

their mouths on their sleeves, putting down their glasses of wine, leaving their games of chess. They surround him, listen to his chest, raise his eyelids, and peer into his eyes. They tap his temples and prick his hands with pins. But he has slid away into sleep again.

One of them turns to me. "Did he speak?"

"No, he just opened his eyes and gave a little sigh and then went back to sleep."

He glances towards the queen and lowers his voice. "And his face: was it the look of a madman, when he woke? Was there any understanding in his eyes or was he blank, like an idiot?"

I think for a moment. "No. He looked just like himself, only coming from a deep sleep. Do you think he will wake now?"

The excitement in the room is dying down very fast as everyone realizes that the king is quite inert, though they go on pulling him and patting him and speaking loudly in his ears.

"No," the man says. "He is gone again."

The queen turns, her face dark with anger. "Can't you wake him? Slap him!"

"No."

The little court at Windsor has been settled for so long to a routine that revolves around the queen and her little boy, who is now learning to speak and can now stagger from one waiting hand to another. But things are changing. In the king's rooms I think he is beginning to stir. They have been watching over him, and feeding him and washing him, but they had given up trying to cure him, as nothing that they did seemed to make any difference. Now we are starting to hope again that in his own time and without any physic, he is coming out of his sleep. I have taken to sitting with him for the morning, and another lady waits with him till evening. The queen visits briefly every afternoon. I have been watching him, and I think his sleep is lifting, I think it is getting lighter, and sometimes I am almost certain that he can hear what we say.

Of course, I start to wonder what he will know, when he comes out of his sleep. More than a year ago he saw a sight so shocking that he closed his eyes and went to sleep so that he should see it no more. The last words he heard were mine, when I said: "Don't look! Don't see!" If he is opening his eyes again, ready to look, ready to see, I cannot help but wonder what he will remember, what he will think of me, and if he will think that I am to blame for his long vigil in darkness and silence.

I grow so concerned that I dare to ask the queen if she thinks the king will blame us for the shock of his illness.

She looks at me limpidly. "You mean the terrible news from France?" she says.

"The way he learned it," I reply. "You were

so distressed, and the duke was there. I was there too. Do you think the king might feel that we should have told him the bad news with more care?"

"Yes," she says. "If he ever gets well enough to hear us, we will say that we were sorry that we did not prepare him for the shock. It was so terrible for us all. I myself cannot remember anything about that evening. I think I fainted and the duke tried to revive me. But I don't remember."

"No," I agree with her, understanding that this is the safest course for us all. "Neither do I."

We celebrate Christmas in the hall of Windsor Castle. It is a little feast for a sadly diminished household, but we have gifts and fairings for each other and little toys for the baby prince; and then, just a few days after Christmas Day, the king wakes, and this time, he stays awake.

It is a miracle. He just opens his eyes and yawns, and looks around him, surprised to be seated in a chair in his privy chamber in Windsor, surrounded by strangers. The doctors rush for us, and the queen and I go in alone.

"Better not frighten him with a great crowd," she says.

We go in quietly, almost as if we are approaching some wounded animal that might take fright. The king is rising to his feet, a doctor on either side to help him support himself. He is unsteady, but he lifts his head when he sees the queen, and he says, uncertainly — "Ah." I can almost see him seeking her name in the confusion in his mind. "Margaret," he says at last. "Margaret of Anjou."

I find there are tears in my eyes, and I am holding back sobs at the wreck of this man who was born to be King of England and who I first knew when he was a boy as handsome as little Edward March, the York boy. Now this hollowed-out man takes one tottering step, and the queen makes a deep curtsey to him. She does not reach out to touch him; she does not go into his arms. It is like the young woman and the Fisher King in the legend: she lives with him, but they never touch. "Your Grace, I am glad to see you well again," she says quietly.

"Have I been ill?"

One deeply secret glance passes between her and me.

"You fell asleep, into a deep sleep, and no one could wake you."

"Really?" He passes his hand over his head, and he sees for the first time the scar from a burning poultice on his arm. "Gracious me. Did I bump myself? How long was I asleep?"

She hesitates.

"A long time," I say. "And though you were asleep for a long time, the country is safe."

"That's good," he says. "Heigh-ho." He nods at the men who are holding him up. "Help me to the window."

He shuffles like an old man to the window and looks out at the water meadows and the river that still flows through the frosty white banks, just as it always did. He narrows his eyes against the glare. "It's very bright," he complains. He turns and goes back to his chair. "I'm very tired."

"Don't!" An involuntary cry escapes from the queen.

They ease him back into his chair, and I see him observe the straps on the arms and on the seat. I see him consider them, owlishly blinking, and then he looks around the stark bareness of the room. He looks at the table of physic. He looks at me. "How long was it, Jacquetta?"

I press my lips together to hold back an outburst. "It was a long time. But we are so pleased you are better now. If you sleep now, you will wake up again, won't you, Your Grace? You will try to wake up again?"

I really fear he is going back to sleep. His head is nodding, and his eyes are closing.

"I am so tired," he says like a little child, and in a moment he is asleep again.

We sit up through the night in case he wakes again, but he does not. In the morning the queen is pale and strained with anxiety. The doctors go in to him at seven in the morning and gently touch his shoulder, whisper in his ear that it is morning; and to their amazement he opens his eyes and sits up in his bed, and orders that the shutters be open.

He lasts till dinnertime, just after midday, and then sleeps again, but he wakes for his supper and asks for the queen, and when she enters the privy chamber, he orders a chair to be set for her and asks her how she does.

I am standing behind her chair as she answers him that she is well, and then she asks, gently, if he remembers that she was with child when he fell asleep.

His surprise is unfeigned. "No!" he exclaims. "I remember nothing. With child, did you say? Gracious, no."

She nods. "Indeed, yes. We were very happy about it." She shows him the jewel he had made for her; she had it in its case, ready to remind him. "You gave me this to celebrate the news."

"Did I?" He is quite delighted with it. He takes it in his hand and looks at it. "Very good workmanship. I must have been pleased."

She swallows. "You were. We were. The whole country was pleased."

We are waiting for him to ask after the baby, but clearly, he is not going to ask after the baby. His head nods as if he is drowsy. He gives a tiny little snore. Margaret glances at me.

"Do you not want to know about the child?" I prompt. "You see the jewel that you gave the queen when she told you she was with child? That was nearly two years ago. The baby has been born."

He blinks and turns to me. His look is quite without understanding. "What child?"

I go to the door and take Edward from his waiting nurse. Luckily, he is sleepy and quiet. I would not have dared to bring him lustily bawling into this hushed chamber. "This is the queen's baby," I say. "Your baby. The Prince of Wales, God bless him."

Edward stirs in his sleep, his sturdy little leg kicks out. He is a toddler, handsome and strong, so unlike a newborn baby, that my confidence wavers even as I carry him towards the king. He is so heavy in my arms, a healthy child of fifteen months. It seems nonsensical to be presenting him to his father like a newborn. The king looks at him with as much detachment as if I am bringing a fat little lamb into the royal rooms.

"I had no idea of it!" he says. "And is it a girl or a boy?"

The queen rises up, takes Edward from me, and proffers the sleeping child to the king. He shrinks away. "No, no. I don't want to hold it. Just tell me. Is this a girl or a boy?"

"A boy," the queen says, her voice quavering with disappointment at his response. "A boy, thank God. An heir to your throne, the

513

son we prayed for."

He inspects the rosy face. "A child of the Holy Spirit," he says wonderingly.

"No, your own true-born son," the queen corrects him sharply. I look and see that the doctors and their servants and two or three ladies-in-waiting will have heard this damning pronouncement from the king. "He is the prince, Your Grace. A son and heir for you, and a prince for England. The Prince of Wales; we christened him Edmund."

"Edward," I snap. "Edward."

She recovers herself. "Edward. He is Prince Edward of Lancaster."

The king smiles radiantly. "Oh, a boy! That's a bit of luck."

"You have a boy," I say. "A son and heir. *Your* son and heir, God bless him."

"Amen," he says. I take the little boy from the queen, and she sinks down again into her chair. The boy stirs, and I hold him against my shoulder and rock gently. He smells of soap and warm skin.

"And is he baptized?" the king asks conversationally.

I can see Margaret grit her teeth with irritation at this slow questioning of those terrible days. "Yes," she says pleasantly enough. "Yes, he is baptized, of course."

"And who are the godparents? Did I choose them?"

"No, you were asleep. We — I — chose

Archbishop Kemp, Edmund Beaufort, Duke of Somerset; and Anne, Duchess of Buckingham."

"Just who I would have chosen," the king declares, smiling. "My particular friends. Anne who?"

"Buckingham," the queen enunciates carefully. "The Duchess of Buckingham. But I am grieved to tell you that the archbishop is dead."

The king throws up his hands in wonder. "No! Why, how long have I been asleep?"

"Eighteen months, Your Grace," I say quietly. "A year and a half. It has been a long time; we were all of us very afraid for your health. It is very good to see you well again."

He looks at me with his childlike trusting gaze. "It is a long time, but I remember nothing of the sleep. Not even my dreams."

"Do you remember falling asleep?" I ask him quietly, hating myself.

"Not at all!" he chuckles. "Only last night. I can only remember falling asleep last night. I hope when I sleep tonight that I wake up again in the morning."

"Amen," I say. The queen has her face in her hands.

"I don't want to sleep another year away!" he jokes.

Margaret shudders, and then straightens up and folds her hands in her lap. Her face is like stone.

515

"It must have been very inconvenient for you all," he says benevolently, looking round the privy chamber. He does not seem to understand that he has been abandoned by his court, that the only people here are his doctors and nurses and us, his fellow prisoners. "I shall try not to do it again."

"We will leave you now," I say quietly. "This has been a great day for us all."

"I am very tired," he says confidingly. "But I do hope to wake tomorrow."

"Amen," I say again.

He beams like a child. "It will be as God wills; we are all of us in His hands."

THE PALACE OF PLACENTIA, GREENWICH, LONDON, SPRING 1455

With the king awake, it is not to be how God wills, but how the queen wills. She sends a message at once to the council of lords, so explosive in tone and so dangerous in temper that they release the Duke of Somerset at once from the Tower, laying on him the embargo that he may not go within twenty miles of the king, nor engage in any form of political life. The duke, setting his London house in order and speedily arming his retinue, sends at once to his friends and allies and tells them that no one will keep him from the king and that the Duke of York will be the first to realize that he has seized power.

As if to celebrate their return to the center of England, the queen and the king open the palace at Greenwich and summon the lords. The Duke of York obeys the summons and resigns his position as Protector of the Realm, and finds his other title, that of Constable of Calais, is to be lost too. It is given back once more to Edmund Beaufort, Duke of Somerset, out of jail and gloriously returned to greatness.

He walks into the queen's rooms in the palace as handsome and richly dressed as if he had been to the court of Burgundy for new clothes, not waiting for his trial for treason in the Tower. The wheel of fortune has thrown him high again, and there is no greater man at the court. All the ladies flutter as he comes into the room; nobody can take their eyes off him. He kneels in the center of the room to Margaret, who flies across the room, her hands outstretched, the moment she sees him. He bows his dark head and takes both of her hands to his lips, inhaling the perfume on her fingers. The maid-in-waiting beside me lets out a little envious sigh. Margaret stands completely still, quivering at his touch, then she very quietly says: "Please rise, my lord, we are glad to see you at liberty again."

He gets to his feet in one graceful movement, and offers her his arm. "Shall we walk?" he suggests, and the two of them lead the way into the great gallery. I follow with a lady-in-waiting, and I nod to the rest of them to stay where they are. Carefully, I dawdle behind, so that my companion cannot overhear their whispered speech.

He bows and leaves her at the end of the gallery and Margaret turns to me, her face alight. "He is going to advise the king that the Duke of York need not be admitted to the council," she says delightedly. "We are only going to have those of the House of Lancaster around us. Anything that York gained while he was protector will be taken away from him, and his brother-in-law, the Earl of Salisbury, and that overgrown cub, Richard Neville, the Earl of Warwick, will not be invited either. Edmund says that he will turn the king against our enemies, and that they will be banned from all positions of power." She laughs. "Edmund says that they will be sorry for the day that they put him in the Tower and confined me to Windsor. He says they will go on their knees to me. He says the king hardly knows where he is, or what he is doing, and that between us, the two of us can command him. And we will throw down our enemies, perhaps into jail, perhaps to the gallows."

I put out my hand to her. "Your Grace . . ." But she is too delighted with the thought of revenge to hear a word of caution.

"Edmund says that we have everything to play for now. We have the king returned to health and willing to do whatever we say; we have a son and heir that nobody can deny; and we can teach York a lesson that he will never forget. Edmund says that if we can prove York was planning to usurp the throne, then he is a dead man."

Now I do interrupt. "Your Grace, surely

this is going to send the Duke of York into outright rebellion? He is bound to defend himself against such charges. He will demand that the council renew the charges against the Duke of Somerset, and then it will be the two of you and yours, against him and his."

"No!" she replies. "For the king himself has declared before the lords that Somerset is a true friend and loyal kinsman, and nobody will dare say anything against him. We are going to hold a council at Westminster, and York is not to be invited, and then we are going to hold a hearing against him in Leicester, where he will be accused in his absence. And the Midlands are loyal to us, though London is sometimes uncertain. This is the end of the duke in his pride, and the beginning of my revenge on him."

I shake my head; there is nothing I can say to make her see that the Duke of York is too powerful to force into enmity.

"You, of all people, should be pleased!" she exclaims. "Edmund promises me that he will bring your husband, Richard, home."

Everyone has their price. Richard is mine. At once I forget to urge caution. I grasp her hands. "He will?"

"He promised me. The king is going to give Edmund the keys to Calais, in front of everyone. Richard will be commended as a loyal commander and come home to you; York will be arrested; the kingdom will be ruled rightly by Edmund Beaufort and me, and we will all be happy again."

I am happy; I am in his arms, my face crushed against his padded jacket, his arms around me as tight as a bear, so that I cannot breathe. When I look up into his beloved weary face, he kisses me so hard that I close my eyes and think myself a besotted girl again. I catch a breath, and he kisses me some more. Dockyard workers and sailors shout encouragement and bawdy comments, but Richard does not even hear them. Beneath my cloak his hands stray from my waist and clutch at my hips.

"Stop right there," I whisper.

"Where can we go?" he asks, as if we were young again.

"Come to the palace," I say. "Come on. Are your things packed?"

"Damn my things," he says cheerfully.

We walk handfast from the dockyard at Greenwich towards the palace, creep in by the backstairs like a lad and a slut from the stables, bolt my door, and stay bolted in all day and all night.

At midnight I send for some food, and we eat wrapped in sheets beside the warm fire.

"When shall we go to Grafton?"

"Tomorrow," he says. "I want to see my children, and my new daughter. Then I shall come straight back, and I shall have to take ship, Jacquetta."

"Ship?" I ask.

He grimaces. "I have to take Beaufort's orders myself," he says. "The fort has been torn apart from the inside out. I cannot leave them without a captain. I shall stay until the duke replaces me, and then I shall come straight home to you."

"I thought you were home now!" I cry out.

"Forgive me," he says. "I would fear for the garrison if I did not go back. Truly, my love, these have been terrible days."

"And then will you come home?"

"The queen has promised, the duke has promised, and I promise it," he says. He leans forwards and pulls a lock of my hair. "It is hard to serve a country such as ours, Jacquetta. But the king is well now and taking his power; our house is in the ascendancy again."

I put my hand over his. "My love, I wish it were so, but it is not as easy as this. When you see the court tomorrow, you will see."

"Tomorrow," he says, puts his jug of ale aside, and takes me back to bed.

We snatch a few days together, long enough for Richard to understand that the queen and the duke plan to turn the tables entirely, and accuse Richard of York of treason and throw him and his allies down. We ride to Grafton in thoughtful silence; Richard greets his children, admires the new baby, and tells them that he has to return to Calais to keep order at the garrison but that he will come home again.

"Do you think that they will persuade the Duke of York to beg pardon?" I ask him as he is saddling his horse in the stable yard. "And if he confesses and obeys the king, will you be able to come straight home?"

"He did so before," my husband says steadily. "And the king — sick or well — is still the king. The queen and the duke believe that they have to attack Richard of York to defend themselves, and if they defeat him, then they will be proved right. I have to keep Calais for England and for my own honor, and then I will come home. I love you, my wife. I will be home soon."

At first the plan goes beautifully. Richard returns to Calais, pays the soldiers, and tells the garrison the king is in his power again, advised by the Duke of Somerset, and the House of Lancaster is in the ascendancy. The Privy Council turn against the man they called on as their savior and agree to meet without the Duke of York. They choose the safe haven of Leicester for this meeting, the heartlands of the queen's influence, her favorite county, and the traditional base for the House of Lancaster. Their choosing Leicester makes them feel safe; but it tells me, and anyone else who cares to consider, that they are afraid of what the citizens will think in London, of what they will say in the villages of Sussex, of what they will do in Jack Cade's home of Kent.

It is hard to get everyone to act: the lords and the gentry have to be summoned, the plan has to be explained, so that everyone understands the Duke of York is to be ill-paid for loyal service to the country, his achievements traduced, and he and his allies are to be excluded from the council and the country turned against them.

The king is so slow to leave for Leicester that he comes to bid farewell to the queen, Edmund Beaufort on his right, Henry Stafford, the Duke of Buckingham, on his left, on the very day that he had said he would arrive in Leicester. His nobility behind him are dressed for the road, some wearing light armor, most of them dressed as if riding out for pleasure. I look from one familiar face to another. There is not a man here who is not either kin to the House of Lancaster, or paid by the House of Lancaster. This is no longer the court of England, drawing on the support of many families, of many houses; this is the court of the House of Lancaster, and anyone who is not part of it is an outsider. And anyone who is an outsider is an enemy. The king bows low to Margaret, and she formally wishes him a safe journey and prosperous return.

"I am sure it will be easily done and peacefully concluded," he says vaguely. "My cousin, the Duke of York, cannot be allowed to defy my authority — my authority, you know. I have told the Yorkist lords that they are to disband their armies. They can keep two hundred men each. Two hundred should be enough, shouldn't it?" He looks at the Duke of Somerset. "Two hundred is fair, isn't it?"

"More than fair," replies Edmund, who has about five hundred men in livery, and another thousand tenants whom he can call up at a moment's notice.

"So I shall bid you farewell, and see you at Windsor when this work is done," the king says. He smiles at Beaufort and the Duke of Buckingham. "My good kinsmen will take care of me, I know. You can be sure that they will be at my side."

We go down to the great doorway to wave as they ride by. The king's standard goes in front, then the royal guard, and the king comes next. He is wearing riding clothes for the journey; he looks thin and pale compared to the two most favored dukes on either side of him. As they go by, the Duke of Somerset pulls off his hat to Margaret and holds it to his heart. Hidden by her veil, she puts her fingers to her lips. The lesser noblemen, then the gentry, then the men-at-arms follow. There must be about two thousand men riding out with the king, and they rumble past us, the great warhorses with their mighty hooves, the smaller horses carrying goods and gear, and then the booted tramp of the foot soldiers who march in disciplined ranks, and the stragglers who follow.

The queen is restless at the Palace of Placentia, though the household is confident and busy, waiting for news of the king's success with his hand-picked council. The gardens that run down to the river are beautiful with the white and pale pink of dancing cherry blossom; when we walk to the river in a wind, the petals whirl about us like snow and make the little prince laugh, and he chases after them, his nursemaid bowed over him as he wobbles on his fat little legs. In the fields at the riverside the late daffodils are still bobbing their butter-yellow heads, and the hedges of the meadows are burnished white with flowers, the blackthorn thickly blooming on black spikes, the hawthorn a budding green of promise. At the riverside the willows rustle their boughs together and lean over the clear water, green water below reflecting the green leaves above.

In the chapel we are still saying prayers for the health of the king and giving thanks for his recovery. But nothing cheers the queen. She cannot forget that she was imprisoned by the lords of her own country, forced to wait on a sleeping husband, fearful that she would never be free again. She cannot forgive Richard, Duke of York, for the humiliation. She cannot be happy when the only man who stood by her in those hard months, enduring captivity as she did, has marched away again, to meet their enemy. She does not doubt that he will be victorious, but she cannot be happy without him.

Margaret shudders as she comes into her apartments, though there is a good fire in the grate and bright tapestries on the walls, and the last rays of the sun are warming the pretty rooms. "I wish they had not gone," she says. "I wish they had summoned the Duke of York to London to answer us there."

I don't remind her that York is a great favorite in London; the guilds and the merchants trust his calm common sense, and flourished when he established peace and good order in the city and country. While the duke was lord protector, the tradesmen could send their goods out along the safe roads, and taxes were reduced with the profligate royal household under his control. "They'll be back soon," I say. "Perhaps York will plead for forgiveness as he did before, and they will all come back soon."

Her uneasiness affects everyone. We dine in the queen's rooms, not in the great hall, where the men-at-arms and the men of the household grumble that there is no cheer, even though the king has recovered. They say that the court is not how it should be. It is too silent; it is like an enchanted castle under a spell of quietness. The queen ignores the criticism. She summons musicians to play only to her, in her rooms, and the younger ladies dance, but they only go through the paces without the handsome young men of the king's retinue to watch them. Finally, she commands one of the ladies-in-waiting to read to us from a romance, and we sit and sew and listen to a story about a queen who longed for a child in midwinter, and gave birth to a baby who was made entirely of snow. When the child grew to manhood, her husband took him on crusade, and he melted away into the hot sand, poor boy; and then they had no son, not even one made of ice.

This miserable story makes me ridiculously sentimental, and I feel disposed to sit and weep and brood over my boys at Grafton; Lewis whom I will never see again; and my oldest, Anthony, thirteen this year, who must soon have his own armor and go and serve as a squire to his father or another great man. He has grown up in no time, and I wish he were a baby again and I could carry him on my hip. It makes me long to be with Richard again; we have never been so long apart in our lives before. When the Duke of York is thrown down by the king, then Edmund Beaufort will take up his command in Calais and order Richard home, and our lives can get back to normal once more.

Margaret summons me to her bedroom, and I go to sit with her as they lift the tight headdress that fits like a cap, low over her ears, uncoil the plaits, and brush out her hair. "When do you think they will come home?" she asks.

"Within the week?" I guess. "If all goes well."

"Why should it not all go well?"

I shake my head. I don't know why she should not be happy and excited, as she was when this plan was first explained to her by the Duke of Somerset. I don't know why the palace, which is always such a pretty home for the court, should seem so cold and lonely tonight. I don't know why the girl should have picked a story about a son and heir who melts away before he can inherit.

"I don't know," I say. I shiver. "I expect it will all be well."

"I am going to bed," she says crossly. "And in the morning we can go hunting and be merry. You are poor company, Jacquetta. Go to bed yourself."

I don't go to bed as she bids me, though I know I am poor company. I go to my window and I swing open the wooden shutter and I look down over the water meadows in the moonlight and the long silver curve of the river, and I wonder why I feel so very low in my spirits on a warm May night in England, the prettiest month of the year, when my husband is coming home to me after grave danger, and the King of England is riding out in his power and his enemy is to be brought down.

Then, the next day, in the late afternoon, we get news, terrible news, unbelievable news. Nothing is clear to us, as we order messengers to be brought before the queen, as we demand that men scrambling away from some sort of battle are captured and brought to the royal chambers to say what they saw, as we send men speeding out towards St. Albans on the road going north, where it seems that the Duke of York, far from riding peaceably to his ordeal, and waiting patiently to be arraigned as a traitor, instead mustered an army and came to plead with the king that his enemies be set aside and that the king be a good lord for all England and not just for Lancaster.

One man tells us that there was some sort of riot in the narrow streets, but that he could not see who had the advantage as he was wounded and was left where he fell. Nobody helped him; a thing most discouraging for a common soldier, he said, one eye on the queen. "Makes you wonder whether your lord cares for you at all," he grumbles. "It's not good lordship to leave a man down."

Another man, riding back to us with news,

says that it is a war: the king raised his standard, and the Duke of York attacked, and the Duke of York was cut down. The queen is out of her chair, her hand to her heart at this report; but later in the evening, the messenger we sent to London comes back and says that, from what he can gather in the streets, the greatest fighting was between the Duke of Somerset and the Earl of Warwick's men, and that the Earl of Warwick's men fought through the gardens and over the little walls, climbed over henhouses and waded through pigsties to get to the heart of the town, avoiding the barricades and coming from a direction that no one could have predicted, surprising the Duke of Somerset's men and throwing them into confusion.

Margaret strides about her room, furious with waiting, mad with impatience. Her ladies shrink back against the walls and say nothing. I stop the nursemaid in the doorway with the little prince. There will be no playtime for him this afternoon. We have to know what is happening, but we cannot discover what is happening. The queen sends out more messengers to London, and three men are commanded to ride on to St. Albans with a private note from her to the Duke of Somerset, and then all we can do is wait. Wait and pray for the king.

Finally, as it grows dark and the servants come in with the lights and go quietly round lighting sconces and branches of candles, the guards swing open the doors and announce: "King's messenger."

The queen rises to her feet, I go to stand beside her. She is trembling slightly, but the face she shows to the world is calm and determined.

"You may come in and tell me your message," she says.

He strides in and drops to his knee, his hat in his hand. "From His Grace the king," he says, and shows in his clasped fist a ring. Margaret nods to me, and I go forwards and take it.

"What is your message?"

"His Grace the king wishes you well, and sends his blessing to the prince."

Margaret nods.

"He says he is in good company with his fair kinsman the Duke of York this night, and will come in the company of His Grace to London tomorrow."

Margaret's long-held breath comes out as a little hiss.

"The king bids you be of good cheer and says that God will arrange all things and all things will be well."

"And what of the battle?"

The messenger looks up at her. "He sent no message about the battle."

She bites her lower lip. "Anything else?"

"He asks you and the court to give thanks

for his escape from danger this very day."

"We will do so," Margaret says. I am so proud of her restraint and dignity that I put my hand gently on her back, in a hidden caress. She turns her head and whispers, "Get hold of him as he leaves and find out what in the name of God is happening," and then she turns to her ladies and says, "I will go straightaway and give thanks for the safety of the king, and the court will come with me."

She leads the way out of the rooms to the chapel, and the court has no choice but to follow her. The messenger starts to fall into line at the back; but I touch his sleeve, take his arm, back him into a convenient corner as if he were a skittish horse, and forestall anyone else getting hold of him.

"What happened?" I demand tersely. "The queen wants to know."

"I delivered the message as I was told," he says.

"Not the message, fool. What happened during the day? What did you see?"

He shakes his head. "I saw only a little fighting; it was in and out of the streets and the yards and the alehouses. More like a brawl than a battle."

"You saw the king?"

He glances around, as if he fears that people might overhear his words. "He was struck in the neck by an arrow," he says.

I gasp.

The messenger nods, his eyes as round with shock as my own. "I know."

"How ever was he within range?" I demand furiously.

"Because the Earl of Warwick brought his archers through the streets, up the gardens, and in and out of the alleys. He didn't come up the main street like everyone expected. Nobody was ready for him to advance like that. I don't think anyone has ever led an attack like that before."

I put my hand to my heart and know with a pulse of pure joy that Richard was stationed in Calais and not in the king's guard when Warwick's men came like murderers in and out of the little alleys. "Where was the royal guard?" I demand. "Why did they not shield him?"

"Cut down around him, most ran off," he says succinctly. "Saw the way it was going. After the duke died —"

"The duke?"

"Cut down as he came out of a tavern."

"Which duke?" I insist. I can feel my knees are shaking. "Which duke died as he came out of the tavern?"

"Somerset," he says.

I grit my teeth and straighten up, fighting a wave of sickness. "The Duke of Somerset is dead?"

"Aye, and the Duke of Buckingham surrendered."

I shake my head to clear it. "The Duke of Somerset is dead? You are sure? You are certain sure?"

"Saw him go down myself, outside a tavern. He had been hiding in it; he wouldn't surrender. He broke out with his men, thought he would fight himself out — but they cut him down on the threshold."

"Who? Who cut him down?"

"The Earl of Warwick," he says shortly.

I nod, recognizing a death feud. "And where is the king now?"

"Held by the Duke of York. They will rest tonight and pick up the wounded, they are looting St. Albans, of course, the town will be all but destroyed. And then tomorrow they will all come to London."

"The king is fit to travel?" I am so afraid for him; this is his first battle, and it sounds like a massacre.

"He is going in state," the messenger says mirthlessly. "With his good friend the Duke of York on one side, the Earl of Salisbury, Richard Neville, on the other, and the earl's son, the young Earl of Warwick, hero of the battle, leading the way holding the king's sword."

"A procession?"

"A triumphant procession, for some of them."

"The House of York has the king, they are carrying his sword before them, and they are coming to London?"

"He is going to show himself wearing the crown so that everyone knows he is well, and in his right mind at the moment. In St. Paul's. And the Duke of York is going to set the crown on his head."

"A crown wearing?" It is hard not to shiver. It is one of the sacred moments of a reign, when a king shows himself to his people in his coronation crown again. It is done to tell the world that the king has returned to them, that he is in his power. But this is going to be different. This will show the world that he has lost his power. He is going to show the world that the Duke of York holds the crown but lets him wear it. "He is going to allow the duke to crown him?"

"And we are all to know that their differences have been resolved."

I glance towards the door. I know that Margaret will be waiting for me, and I will have to tell her that the Duke of Somerset is dead and her husband in the hands of her enemy.

"Nobody can think that this is a lasting peace," I say quietly. "Nobody can think that the differences are resolved. It is the start of bloodshed, not the end of it."

"They had better think it, for it is going to be treason even to talk about the battle," he says grimly. "They say we must forget about it. As I came away, they passed a law that we were all to say nothing. It is to be as if it never was. What d'you think of that, eh? They passed a law to say we must be silent."

"They expect people to behave as if it didn't happen!" I exclaim.

His smile is grim. "Why not? It wasn't a very big battle, my lady. It wasn't very glorious. The greatest duke hid in a tavern and came out to his death. It was all over in half an hour, and the king never even drew his sword. They found him hiding in a tanner's shop amid the flayed hides, and they chased his army through the pigsties and gardens. It isn't one that any of us are going to be proud to remember. Nobody will be telling this at the fireside ten years from now. No one will tell his grandson about it. All of us who were there will be glad to forget it. It's not as if we were a happy few, a band of brothers."

I wait in Margaret's rooms as she leads the court back from their thanksgiving for the king's safekeeping. When she sees my grave face, she announces that she is tired and will sit with me alone. When the door closes behind the last of the ladies-in-waiting, I start to take the pins out of her hair.

She grips my hand. "Don't, Jacquetta. I can't bear to be touched. Just tell me. It's bad, isn't it?"

I know that in her place I would rather know the worst thing first. "Margaret, it breaks my heart to tell you — His Grace the Duke of Somerset is dead."

For a moment she does not hear me. "His Grace?"

"The Duke of Somerset."

"Did you say dead?"

"Dead."

"Do you mean Edmund?"

"Edmund Beaufort, yes."

Slowly, her gray-blue eyes fill with tears, her mouth trembles, and she puts her hands to her temples as if her head is ringing with pain. "He can't be."

"He is."

"You're sure? The man was sure? Battles can be so confusing; it could be a false report?"

"It might be. But he was very sure."

"How could it be?"

I shrug. I am not going to tell her the details now. "Hand-to-hand fighting, in the streets . . ."

"And the king sent me a message ordering me to lead a service of thanksgiving? Is he completely insane now? He wants a service of thanksgiving when Edmund is dead? Does he care for nothing? Nothing?"

There is a silence, then she gives a shuddering sigh as she realizes the extent of her loss.

"The king perhaps did not send the message for thanksgiving," I say. "It will have been ordered by the Duke of York."

"What do I care for that? Jacquetta — how

538

shall I ever manage without him?"

I take her hands to prevent her from pulling at her hair. "Margaret, you will have to bear it. You will have to be brave."

She shakes her head, a low moan starting in her throat. "Jacquetta, how shall I manage without him? How shall I live without him?"

I put my arms around her, and she rocks with me, the low cry of pain going on and on. "How shall I live without him? How am I going to survive here without him?"

I move her to the big bed and press her gently down. When her head is on the pillow, her tears run back from her face and wet the fine embroidered linen. She does not scream or sob; she just moans behind her gritted teeth, as if she is trying to muffle the sound, but it is unstoppable, like her grief.

I take her hand and sit beside her in silence. "And my son," she says. "Dear God, my little son. Who will teach him what a man should be? Who will keep him safe?"

"Hush," I say hopelessly. "Hush."

She closes her eyes, but still the tears spill down her cheeks and still she makes the quiet low noise, like an animal in deathly pain.

She opens her eyes and sits up a little. "And the king?" she asks as an afterthought. "I suppose he is well as he said? Safe? I suppose he has escaped scot-free? As he always does, praise God?"

"He was slightly injured," I say. "But he is

safe in the care of the Duke of York. He is bringing him to London with all honor."

"How shall I manage without Edmund?" she whispers. "Who is going to protect me now? Who is going to guard my son? Who is going to keep the king safe, and what if he goes to sleep again?"

I shake my head. There is nothing I can say to comfort her; she will have to suffer the pain of his loss and wake in the morning to know that she has to rule this kingdom, and face the Duke of York, without the support of the man she loved. She will be alone. She will have to be mother and father to her son. She will have to be king and queen to England. And nobody may ever know, nobody can even guess, that her heart is broken.

In the next few days she is not like Margaret of Anjou; she is like her ghost. She loses her voice; she is struck like a mute. I tell her ladies-in-waiting that the shock has given her a pain in the throat, like a cold, and that she must rest. But in her shadowy room, where she sits with her hand to her heart in silence, I see that in holding back the sobs, she is choking on her own grief. She dares make no sound, for if she spoke she would scream.

In London there is a terrible tableau enacted. The king, forgetful of himself, forgetful of his position, of his sacred trust from God, goes to the cathedral of St. Paul's for a renewed coronation. No archbishop crowns him; in a mockery of the coronation itself it is Richard of York who puts the crown on the king's head. To the hundreds of people who crowd into the cathedral and the thousands who hear of the ceremony, one royal cousin gives the crown to another, as if they were equals, as if obedience was a matter of choice.

I take this news to the queen as she sits in darkness, and she stands up, unsteadily, as if she is remembering how to walk. "I must go to the king," she says, her voice weak and croaky. "He is giving away everything we have. He must have lost his mind again, and now he is losing the crown and his son's inheritance."

"Wait," I say. "We can't undo this act. Let us wait and see what we can do. And while we wait you can come out of your rooms, and eat properly, and speak to your people."

She nods. She knows she has to lead the royal party, and now she has to lead it alone. "How will I do anything without him?" she whispers to me.

I take her hands, her fingers are icy. "You will, Margaret. You will."

I send an urgent note to Richard by a wool merchant that I have trusted before. I tell him that the Yorks are in command again, that he must prepare himself for them to try to take the garrison, that the king is in their keeping, and that I love and miss him. I don't beg him to come home, for in these troubled times I don't know if he would be safe at home. I begin to realize the court, the country, and we ourselves are sliding from a squabble between cousins into a war between cousins.

Richard, Duke of York, acts quickly, as I thought he would. He suggests to the palace officials that the queen should meet her husband at Hertford Castle, a day's ride north of London. When her steward tells her, she rounds on him. "He's going to arrest me."

The man steps back from her fury. "No, Your Grace. Just to give you and the king somewhere to rest until Parliament opens in London."

"Why can't we stay here?"

The man shoots a despairing look at me. I raise my eyebrows; I'm not disposed to help him, for I don't know why they want to send us to Henry's childhood home either, and the castle is completely walled, moated, and gated, like a prison. If the Duke of York wants to lock away the king, queen, and the young prince, he could hardly choose a better place.

"The king is not well, Your Grace," the steward finally admits. "They think he should not be seen by the people of London."

This is the news we have been dreading. She takes it calmly. "Not well?" she asks.

"What do you mean by 'not well'? Is he sleeping?"

"He certainly seems very weary. He is not asleep as he was before, but he took a wound to his neck and was very frightened. The duke believes he should not be exposed to the noise and bustle of London. The duke believes he should be quiet at the castle; it was his nursery, and he will be comforted there."

She looks at me, as if for advice. I know she is wondering what Edmund Beaufort would have told her to do. "You may tell His Grace the duke that we will journey to Hertford tomorrow," I say to the messenger, and as he turns away I whisper to the queen: "What else can we do? If the king is sick, we had better get him out of London. If the duke commands us to go to Hertford, we cannot refuse. When we have the king in our keeping, we can decide what to do. We have to get him away from the duke and his men. If we hold the king in our keeping, at least we know he is safe. We have to have possession of the king."

HERTFORD CASTLE, SUMMER 1455

He does not look like the king who rode out to reprimand the great lord with his two friends at his side, dressed for a day of pleasure. He looks as if he has collapsed in on himself, a pillow king with the stuffing gone, a bubble king deflated. His head is down; an ill-tied bandage round his throat shows where the Warwick archers nearly ended the reign altogether; his robe is trailing from his shoulders because he has not tightened his belt, and he stumbles over it, like an idiot, as he walks into the poky presence chamber of Hertford Castle.

The queen is waiting for him, surrounded by a few of her household and his, but the great lords of the land and their men have stayed in London, preparing for the Parliament that is going to do the bidding of the Duke of York. She rises up when she sees him and goes forwards to greet him, stately and dignified, but I can see her hands shaking until she tucks them inside the shelter of her

544

long sleeves. She can see, as I can see, that we have lost him again. At this crucial moment, when we so badly need a king to command us, he has slipped away.

He smiles at her. "Ah," he says, and again there is that betraying pause as he searches for her name. "Ah, Margaret."

She curtseys and rises up and kisses him. He puckers his lips like a child.

"Your Grace," she says. "I thank God that you are safe."

His eyes widen. "It was a terrible thing," he says, his voice thin and slight. "It was a terrible thing, Margaret. You have never seen such a terrible thing in your life. I was lucky that the Duke of York was there to take me safely away. The way that men behave! It was a terrible thing, Margaret. I was glad the duke was there. He was the only one who was kind to me; he is the only one who understands how I feel . . ."

Moving as one, Margaret and I go towards him. She takes his arm and leads him into the private rooms, and I stand blocking the way after them, so that no one can follow them. The door closes behind them, and her chief maid looks at me. "And what happens now?" she asks wryly. "Do we all fall asleep again?"

"We serve the queen," I say, with more certainty than I feel. "And you, in particular, mind your tongue."

■ ■ ■ ■

I have no letter from Richard, but a stonemason who went over to supervise some building work takes the trouble to ride out to Hertford Castle with news for me. "He is alive," is the first thing he says. "God bless him, alive and well and drilling the men and maintaining the guard and doing all that he can to keep Calais for England . . ." He drops his voice. "And for Lancaster."

"You have seen him?"

"Before I came away. I couldn't speak to him — I had to take ship — but I knew you would want news of him, and if you have a letter for him, Your Grace, I will carry it back for you. I go back next month unless there are new orders."

"I will write at once; I will write before you leave," I promise. "And the garrison?"

"Loyal to Edmund Beaufort," he says. "They had your husband locked up while they broke into the warehouses and sold the wool, but once they had taken their wages, they let him out again and released the ships from port. That's how I left on the day of his release. Of course, nobody knew then that the duke was dead. They will know now."

"What d'you think they will do?"

He shrugs. "Your husband will wait for his orders from the king. He is the king's man through and through. Will the king command him to hold Calais against the new captain — the Earl of Warwick?"

I shake my head.

"Drifted off again?" the merchant asks with cruel accuracy.

"I am afraid so."

The king sleeps during the day; he eats lightly and without appetite; he prays at every service. Sometimes he rises in the night and wanders in his nightgown around the castle and the guards have to call the groom of his bedchamber to take him back to his bed. He is not melancholy, for when there is music, he will tap his hand to the beat and sometimes nod his head; once he lifts up his chin and sings a song in a wavering piping voice, a pretty song about nymphs and shepherds, and I see a page boy cram his knuckles in his mouth to stop the laughter. But most of the time, he is once again a lost king, a watery king, a moon king. He has lost his print upon the earth; he has lost any fire. His words are written on the water, and I think of the little crown charm which I lost in the river and which told me so clearly that there was no season when the king would come back to us: the gleam of his gold would be drowned in the deep water.

GROBY HALL, LEICESTERSHIRE, AUTUMN 1455

I take permission from the queen to leave court and go to my daughter's home at Groby Hall. The queen laughingly remarks that she could stop a cavalry charge more easily than she could deny me permission to go. My Elizabeth is with child, her first baby, and it is due in November. I too am expecting a baby, a child made from our day and night of lovemaking when Richard came home and went again. I expect to see Elizabeth safely out of childbed and then I will go to my own home and confinement.

Richard will not be here to see this, his first grandchild, of course. He won't be at my side at Groby Hall, while I wait for Elizabeth's firstborn, nor at our home at Grafton when I go into my birthing chamber, nor when I return to Hertford Castle, nor in London. His lord the Duke of Somerset is dead, and his command, that Richard should return to me, will not be obeyed. Richard cannot keep his promise to come home to me while the future of Calais is so uncertain. The Earl of Warwick is the new Constable of Calais, and Richard will have to decide whether or not to admit the new commander or defy him. Once again Richard is far from me, having to decide which side to join, his loyalty on one side, his greater safety on another, and we cannot even write to each other, as Calais has barricaded itself in again.

Elizabeth's mother-in-law, Lady Grey, greets me at the door, resplendent in a gown of deep blue velvet, her hair arranged in two great plaits on either side of her head, which makes her round face look like a baker's stall with three great buns. She sweeps me a dignified curtsey. "I am so glad you have come to keep your daughter company during her confinement," she says. "The birth of my grandchild is a most important event for me."

"And mine for me," I say, staking my claim with relish, there being no doubt in my mind that this will be my daughter's son, my grandson, and Melusina's descendant. All that he will have of the Grey family will be the name, and I have paid for that already with Elizabeth's dowry.

"I will show you to her room," she says. "I have given her the best bedroom for her confinement. I have spared neither trouble nor expense for the birth of my first grandchild."

The house is large and beautiful, I grant

them that. Elizabeth's three rooms look east towards Tower Hill, and south to the old chapel. The shutters are all closed, but there is a gleam of autumn sunshine through the slats. The room is warm, with a good fire of thick logs, and furnished well, with a big bed for sleeping, a smaller day bed, a stool for visitors, and a bench along the wall for her companions. As I enter, my daughter rises up from the day bed, and I see in her the little girl whom I loved first of all my children and the beautiful woman she has become.

She is broad as a beam, laughing at my expression as I take in her size. "I know! I know!" she says, and comes into my arms. I hold her gently, her big belly between us. "Tell me it's not twins."

"I tell her it's a girl if she carries her so low and broad," Lady Grey says, coming in behind me.

I don't correct her; we will have time enough to see what this baby is, and what it will do. I hold Elizabeth's broad body in my arms, and then I cup her beautiful face in my hands. "You are more lovely than ever."

It is true. Her face is rounded, and her golden hair has darkened a little, after a summer spent indoors, but the exquisite beauty of her features, the fine-drawn nose and eyebrows, the perfect curve of her mouth, are as lovely as when she was a girl.

She makes a little pout. "Only you would

think so, Lady Mother. I cannot get through doorways, and John left my bed three months ago because the baby kicks me so much when I lie down that I move about all night and he cannot sleep."

"That will soon be over," I say. "And it's good that he has strong legs." I draw her back to the day bed and lift up her feet. "Rest," I say. "You will have enough to do within a few days."

"Do you think days?" Lady Grey asks.

I look at Elizabeth. "I can't tell yet," I say. "And a first child often takes his time."

Lady Grey leaves us, promising to send up a good dinner as soon as it grows dark. Elizabeth waits for the door to close behind her, and says: "You said 'his'; you said 'his' time."

"Did I?" I smile at her. "What d'you think?"

"I did the wedding ring spell," she says eagerly. "Shall I tell you what it said?"

"Let me try," I say, as excited as a girl. "Let me try with my ring."

I slip my wedding ring from my finger and take a thin gold chain from my neck. I put the ring on the chain, wondering a little that I should be so blessed as to be dowsing for my daughter, to see what her baby will be. I hold the chain over her belly and wait for it to hang still. "Clockwise for a boy, widdershins for a girl," I say. Without my moving it, the ring begins to stir, slowly at first as if in a breeze, and then more positively, round and round in a circle. Clockwise. "A boy," I say, catching it up and restoring the ring to my finger and the chain to my neck. "What did you think?"

"I thought a boy," she confirms. "And what are you going to have?"

"A boy too, I think," I say proudly. "What a family we are making; I swear they should all be dukes. What will you name him?"

"I am going to call him Thomas."

"Thomas the survivor," I say.

She is instantly curious. "Why d'you call him that? What is he going to survive?"

I look at her beautiful face, and for a moment it is as if I am seeing her in a stained-glass window, in a shadowy hall, and she is years away from me. "I don't know," I say. "I just think he will have a long journey and survive many dangers."

"So when do you think he will come?" she asks impatiently.

I smile. "On a Thursday, of course," I reply, and quote the old saying: "Thursday's child has far to go."

She is diverted at once. "What was I?"

"Monday. Monday's child is fair of face."

She laughs. "Oh, Lady Mother, I look like a pumpkin!"

"You do," I say. "But only till Thursday."

It turns out that I am right on both counts, though I don't crow over Lady Grey, who would make a bad enemy. The baby is a boy, he is born on a Thursday, and my Elizabeth insists he shall be called Thomas. I wait until she is up and about; I take her to be churched myself, and when she is well and the baby feeding, and her husband has stopped coming to me ten times each day to ask if I am sure that everything is well, then I go to Grafton to see my other children and promise them that their father is bravely serving his king, as he always does, that he will come home to us, as soon as he can, as he always does, that their father has sworn to be faithful to us over and over, that he will always come home to me.

I go into my confinement in December, and the night before the baby is born I dream of a knight as brave and as bold as my husband, Sir Richard, and a country dry and hot and brown, a flickering standard against a blazing sun, and a man who is afraid of nothing. When he is born, he is just a tiny crying baby, and I hold him in my arms and wonder what he will be. I call him Edward, thinking of the little prince, and I feel certain that he will be lucky.

HERTFORD CASTLE, SPRING 1456

Richard does not come home, though I write to him from the hushed and fearful court to tell him he is a father again and now a grandfather too. I remind him that Anthony must be sent to serve some great lord; but how am I to judge which one, in this new world that is ruled by York once again? I don't even know if he gets the letter; certainly I don't get a reply.

The garrison and town of Calais are at war with themselves, and are no more welcoming to the newly nominated commander, the victorious young Earl of Warwick, than they were to the former Constable, his ally, the Duke of York. I imagine, and I fear it, that Richard is keeping the York allies out of the castle and holding the town for Lancaster. A forlorn hope, and a lonely posting. I imagine that he is keeping faith with Lancaster and thinks that to hold Calais for the silent king is the best service he can offer. But through the Christmas feast and the winter months, I cannot get any news of him, except to know that he is alive, and that the garrison has sent word that they will never admit the Earl of Warwick to the castle that is loyal to the man he killed: the dead Lord Somerset.

It is not until spring that things start to improve. "The king is better," Margaret announces to me.

I look at her doubtfully. "He speaks better than he did," I agree. "But he is not himself yet."

She grits her teeth. "Jacquetta — perhaps he will never be as he was. His wound has healed; he can speak clearly; he can walk without stumbling. He can pass as a king. From a distance he can look commanding. That has to be enough for me."

"For you to do what?"

"For me to take him back to London, show him to the council, and take the power from the Duke of York once more."

"He is the shell of a king," I warn her. "A puppet king."

"Then it will be me who pulls the strings," she promises, "and not the Duke of York. While we are here and allow the protectorate to reign, the Duke of York takes all the posts, all the fees, all the taxes, and all the favors. He will strip the country bare, and we will end up with nothing. I have to put the king back on his throne and York back in his place. I have to save my son's inheritance for when he can come of age and fight his own battles."

I hesitate, thinking of the king's nervous tremor of the head, of the way he flinches at sudden noise. He will be unhappy in London; he will be frightened in Westminster. The lords will appeal to his judgment and demand that he rule. He cannot do it. "There will be continual quarrels in the council and shouting. He will break down, Margaret."

"I will order your husband home," she tempts me. "I will tell the king to pardon the garrison and allow the guard home. Richard can come home and see his grandson and meet his son. He has not even seen your new baby."

"A bribe," I remark.

"A brilliant bribe," she replies. "Because it's irresistible, isn't it? So do you agree? Shall we set the king to claim his throne again?"

"Would you stop on this course if I disagree with you?"

She shakes her head. "I am determined. Whether you are with me or not, Jacquetta, I will take command through my husband; I will save England for my son."

"Then bring Richard home, and we will support you. I want him in my life again, in my sight, and in my bed."

Westminster Palace, London, Spring 1456

Richard's recall from Calais is one of the first acts of the restored king. We go in state to Westminster and announce the king's recovery to the council. It goes better than I had dared to hope. The king is gracious, and the council openly relieved at his return; the king is now to govern with the advice of the Duke of York. The king pardons the garrison of Calais for refusing to admit both York and Warwick, and he signs a pardon especially for Richard, to forgive him for his part in the rebellion against the lord protector.

"Your husband is a loyal servant to me and my house," he remarks to me, when he comes to the queen's rooms before dinner. "I will not forget it, Lady Rivers."

"And may he come home?" I ask. "He has been away such a long time, Your Grace."

"Soon," he promises me. "I have written to him and to Lord Welles that I myself appoint the Earl of Warwick as Captain of Calais, and so they can take it as my command that they are to admit him. When they admit the earl, and he takes up his post, your husband can come home." He sighs. "If only they would live together in loving kindness," he says. "If only they would be as birds in the trees, as little birds in the nest."

I curtsey. The king is drifting into one of his dreams. He has a vision of a kinder world, a better world, which nobody could deny. But it is no help for those of us who have to live in this one.

The king's pain at his unexpected wound, his shock at the brutality of battle and the cruelty of death in the streets of St. Albans seems to have gone very deep. He says that he is well now; we have given thanks in a special Mass, and everyone has seen him walk without stumbling, talk to petitioners, and sit on his throne; but neither the queen nor I can feel confident that he won't drift away again. He especially dislikes noise or disagreement, and the court, the Parliament, and the king's council is riven with faction; there are daily quarrels between the followers of the York lords and our people. Any trouble, any discord, any unhappiness, and his gaze drifts away; he looks out of the window and he falls silent, slipping away in a daydream. The queen has learned never to disagree with him, and the little prince is whisked from the room whenever he raises his voice or runs about. The whole court tiptoes about its business so as not to disturb the king, and so far we have managed to keep him in at least the appearance of kingship.

The queen has learned to control her temper, and it has been very sweet to see her discipline herself so that she never startles or alarms her husband. Margaret has a quick temper and a powerful desire to rule, and to see her bite her tongue and hear her lower her voice so as not to confront the king with the usurpation of his powers is to see a young woman growing into wisdom. She is kind to him in a way that I thought she could never be. She sees him as a wounded animal, and when his eyes grow vague or he looks about him, trying to remember a word or a name, she puts her hand gently on his and prompts him, as sweetly as a daughter with a father in his dotage. It is a sorry end for the marriage that started in such hopes, and the king's hidden weakness is her hidden grief. She is a woman sobered by loss: she has lost the man she loved, and she has lost her husband; but she does not complain of her life to anyone but me.

To me, her temper is not muted, and often she blazes out when we are alone. "He does whatever the Duke of York tells him," she spits. "He is his puppet, his dog."

"He is obliged to govern with the agreement of the duke, and with the Earls of Salisbury and Warwick," I say. "He has to answer the objection that the Privy Council made against him: that he was only for Lancaster. Now there is a Parliament that is influenced by all the great men, York as well as Lancaster. In England, this is how they like it, Your Grace. They like to share power. They like many advisors."

"And what about what I like?" she demands. "And what about the Duke of Somerset, who lies dead, thanks to them? The dearest truest —" She breaks off and turns away so that I cannot see the grief in her face. "And what about the interest of the prince, my son? Who will serve me and the prince? Who will satisfy our likes, never mind those of the council?"

I say nothing. There is no arguing with her when she rages against the Duke of York. "I won't stand for it," she says. "I am taking the prince and going to Tutbury Castle for the summer, and then on to Kenilworth. I won't stay in London; I won't be imprisoned in Windsor again."

"Nobody is going to imprison you —"

"You can go and see your children," she rules. "And then you can meet me. I won't stay in London to be ordered about by the duke and insulted by the citizens. I know what they say about me. They think I am a virago married to a fool. I won't be so abused. I shall go and I shall take the court with me, far from London and far from the duke, and he can give what orders he likes; but I won't have to see them. And the people of London can see how they like their city when there is no court here, and no council and no Parliament. I will see them go bankrupt; they will be sorry when I take the court away and give our presence and our wealth to the people of the Midlands."

"What about the king?" I ask carefully. "You can't just leave him in London on his own. It is to throw him into the keeping of the Duke of York."

"He will join me when I order it," she says. "No one will dare to tell me that my husband shall not be with me, when I command it. The duke will not dare to keep us apart, and I am damned if he will have me locked up in Windsor again."

GRAFTON, NORTHAMPTONSHIRE, SUMMER 1456

I wait for Richard to come home to us at Grafton, enjoying my summer with our children. Elizabeth is at Groby with her new baby, and her sister Anne is visiting her. I have placed Anthony with Lord Scales, serving as his squire, learning the ways of a noble house, and Lord Scales as it happens has a daughter, an only daughter, his heiress, Elizabeth. My Mary is thirteen now, and I must look around for a husband for her; she and her sister Jacquetta are staying with the Duchess of Buckingham, learning the ways of that house. My boy John is at home; he and Richard are set to their studies with a new tutor; Martha will join them in the schoolroom this year. Eleanor and Lionel are still in the nursery, with their two-year-old sister Margaret, and their little brother Edward.

I don't have to wait long for my husband's return. First I get a message that Richard has been released from his duty at Calais, and then — hard on the heels of the messenger — I see the dust on the road from Grafton coming up the drive to the house, and I pick up Edward out of the cradle and hold him to me, shading my eyes with my hand and looking down the road. I plan that Richard shall ride up and see me here, my newest baby in my arms, our house behind me, our lands safe around us, and he will know that I have kept faith with him, raised his children, guarded his lands, as he has kept faith with me.

I can see, I think I can see, the colors of his standard, and then I am certain it is his flag, and then I know for sure that the man on the big horse at the head of the company is him, and I forget all about how I want him to see me, thrust Edward into the arms of his wet nurse, pick up my skirts, and start to run down the terrace of the house, down the steps to the road. And I hear Richard shout, "Holloa! My duchess! My little duchess!" and see him pull his horse to a standstill and fling himself down, and in a moment I am in his arms and he is kissing me so hard that I have to push him away, and then I pull him close again to hold him to me, my face to his warm neck, his kisses on my hair, as if we were sweethearts who have been parted for a lifetime.

"Beloved," he says to me, breathless himself. "It has been forever. I was afraid you would forget all about me."

"I have missed you so," I whisper.

My tears are wet on my cheeks, and he kisses them, murmuring, "I missed you too; dear God there were times when I thought I would never get home."

"And you are released? You don't have to go back again?"

"I am released. Warwick will put in his own men, I hope to God I never see the town again. It was a misery, Jacquetta. It was like being in a cage for all that long time. The countryside outside is unsafe, the Duke of Burgundy raids and the King of France threatens, we were constantly alert for an invasion from England and the York lords, and the town was on the brink of bankruptcy. The men were mutinous, and nobody could blame them, and worst of all I was never sure what I should do for the best. I could not tell what was happening in England. And then, I could get no news of you. I didn't even know if you were safely up from childbirth . . ."

"I kept writing," I say. "I kept writing, but I guessed you didn't get the letters. And sometimes I couldn't find anyone to take a message. But I sent you fruits and a barrel of salted pork?"

He shakes his head. "I never got a thing. And I was desperate for a kind word from you. And you had to manage all alone — and with a new baby!"

"This is Edward," I say proudly, and beckon to the wet nurse to come up and hand our son to his father. Edward opens his dark blue eyes and regards his father gravely.

"He is thriving?"

"Oh yes, and all the others too."

Richard looks around at his other children, tumbling out of the front door, the boys pulling off their caps, the girls running towards him, and he goes down on his knees to them, spreading his arms wide so they can all run at him and hug him. "Thank God I am home," he says with tears in his eyes. "Thank God for bringing me safe to this my home, and my wife and my children."

That night in bed, I find I am shy, fearing that he will see a difference in me — another year gone by, and another birth to broaden my hips and thicken my waist — but he is gentle and tender with me, loving as if he was still my squire and I was the young duchess. "Like playing a lute," he says with a roll of laughter under the whisper. "You always remember the way, when it is in your hand again. The mind can play tricks, but the body remembers."

"And is there many a good tune played on an old fiddle?" I demand with pretend offense.

"If you find a perfect match, then you keep it," he says gently. "And I knew when I first saw you that you were the woman I would want for all my life." Then he gathers me into his warm shoulder and falls asleep, holding me tightly.

I fall asleep in his arms like a mermaid diving into dark water, but in the night something wakes me. At first I think it may be one of the children, so I struggle awake and slide from under the covers to sit on the side of the bed to listen. But there is no sound in our quiet house, just the creak of a floorboard and the sigh of wind through an open window. The house is at peace; the master is safely home at last. I go into the chamber outside our bedroom and open the window and swing wide the wooden shutter. The summer sky is dark, dark blue, as dark as a silk ribbon, and the moon is on the wax, like a round silver seal, low on the horizon, sinking down. But in the sky, towards the east, is a great light — low over the earth, a blaze of light, shaped like a saber, pointing to the heart of England, pointing to the Midlands, where I know Margaret is arming her castle and preparing her attack on the Yorks. I gaze up at the comet, yellow in color, not white and pale like the moon, but golden, a gilt saber pointed at the heart of my country. There is no doubt in my mind that it foretells war and fighting and that Richard will be in the forefront as ever, and that now I have new men to worry about as well: Elizabeth's husband, John, and Anthony, my own son, and all the other sons who will be raised in a country at war. For a moment I even think of the young son of the Duke of York whom I saw with his mother that day at Westminster: young Edward, a handsome boy, no doubt his father will take him to war, and his life will be at risk too. The saber hangs in the sky above us all, like a sword waiting to fall. I look at it for a long time, and think that this star should be called the widow maker; and then I close the shutter and go back to my bed to sleep.

KENILWORTH CASTLE, WARWICKSHIRE, SUMMER 1457

Richard and I join the court at the very heart of Margaret's lands, in the castle she loves best in England: Kenilworth. As my guard and I ride up, I see to my horror that she has prepared it for a siege, just as the night sky foretold. The guns are mounted and looking over the newly repaired walls. The drawbridge is down for now, bridging the moat, but the chains are oiled and taut, ready to raise it in a moment. The portcullis is glinting at the top of the arch, ready to fall at the moment the command is given, and the number and the smartness of the household show that she has manned a castle here, not staffed a home.

"She is ready for a war," my husband says grimly. "Does she think Richard of York would dare to attack the king?"

We come into her presence as soon as we have washed off the dust from the road and find her sitting with the king. I can see at once that he is worse again; his hands are trembling slightly, and he is shaking his head, as if denying his thoughts, as if wanting to look away. He shivers a little, like a frightened leveret that only wants to lie down in the springing corn and be ignored. I cannot look at him without wanting to hold him still.

Margaret looks up as I come in and beams her happiness to see me. She declares, "See, my lord, we have many friends: here is Jacquetta, Lady Rivers, the Dowager Duchess of Bedford. You remember what a good friend she is to us? You remember her first husband who was your uncle John, Duke of Bedford? And here is her second husband, the good Lord Rivers, who held Calais for us, when the bad Duke of York wanted to take it away."

He looks at me, but there is no recognition in his face, just the blank gaze of a lost boy. He seems younger than ever; all his knowledge of the world has been forgotten, and his innocence shines out of him. I hear Richard behind me make a small muffled exclamation. He is shocked at the sight of his king. I had warned him several times, but he had not realized that the king had become a prince, a boy, a babe.

"Your Grace," I say, curtseying to him.

"Jacquetta will tell you that the Duke of York is our enemy, and we must prepare to fight him," the queen says. "Jacquetta will tell you that I have everything prepared; we are certain to win. Jacquetta will tell you that when I say the word, our troubles are over and he is destroyed. He has to be destroyed; he is our enemy."

"Oh, is he French?" the king asks in his little-boy voice.

"Dear God," Richard mutters quietly.

I see her bite her lip to curb her irritation. "No," she says. "He is a traitor."

This satisfies the king for only a moment. "What is his name?"

"The Duke of York, Richard. Richard, Duke of York."

"Because I am sure someone told me that it was the Duke of Somerset who was a traitor, and he is in the Tower."

This sudden reference to Edmund Beaufort, and from the king himself, is shockingly painful to her, and I see her suddenly go pale and look away. She takes a moment, and when she turns back to us, she has herself utterly under control. I see that she has grown in determination and courage this summer; she is forging herself into a powerful woman. She has always been strong-willed; but now she has a sick husband and a rebellious country, and she is turning herself into a woman who can protect her husband and dominate her country.

"No, not at all. Edmund Beaufort, the Duke of Somerset, was never a traitor, and anyway, now he is dead," she says very quietly and steadily. "He was killed at the battle of St. Albans by the Duke of York's ally, the wicked Earl of Warwick. He died a hero, fighting for us. We will never forgive them for his death. D'you remember we said that? We said that we would never forgive him."

"Oh no . . . er . . . Margaret." He shakes his head. "We must forgive our enemies. We forgive our enemies as we hope to be forgiven. Is he French?"

She glances at me, and I know my horror is plain on my face. She pats his hand gently and rises up from her throne and falls into my arms, as easily as if she were my little sister, weeping for some hurt. We turn together to the window, leaving Richard to approach the throne and speak quietly to the king. My arm is around her waist, as she leans against me; together we look, unseeing, over the beautiful sunny gardens inside the thick castle walls, laid out below us like a piece of embroidery in a frame. "I have to command everything now," she says quietly. "Edmund is dead, and the king is lost to himself. I am so alone, Jacquetta; I am like a widow with no friends."

"The council?" I ask. I am guessing that they would put York back in as lord protector if they knew how frail the king truly is.

"I appoint the council," she says. "They do as I say."

"But they will talk —"

"What they say in London doesn't matter to us here, at Kenilworth."

"But when you have to call a Parliament?"

"I will summon them to Coventry, where they love me and honor the king. We won't go back to London. And I will only summon the men who honor me. No one who follows York."

I look at her, quite appalled. "You will have to go to London, Your Grace. Summer is all very well, but you cannot move the court and the Parliament from the city forever. And you cannot exclude the men of York from government."

She shakes her head. "I hate the people there, and they hate me. London is diseased and rebellious. They take the side of Parliament and York against me. They call me a foreign queen. I shall rule them from a distance. I am Queen of London, but they shall never see me, nor have a penny of my money, nor a glimpse of my patronage nor a word of my blessing. Kent, Essex, Sussex, Hampshire, London — they are all my enemies. They are all traitors, and I will never forgive them."

"But the king —"

"He will get better," she says determinedly. "This is a bad day for him. Today is a bad day. Just today. Some days he is quite well. And I will find a way of curing him, I have doctors working on new cures all the time, I have licensed alchemists to distill waters for him."

"The king doesn't like alchemy, or anything like that."

"We have to find a cure. I am issuing licenses to alchemists to pursue their studies. I have to consult them. It is allowed now."

"And what do they say?" I ask her. "The alchemists?"

"They say that he has to be weak as the kingdom is weak; but that they will see him reborn, he will be as new again, and the kingdom will be as new again. They say he will go through fire and be made as pure as a white rose."

"A white rose?" I am shocked.

She shakes her head. "They don't mean York. They mean as pure as a white moon, as pure as white water, driven snow — it doesn't matter."

I bow my head, but I think it probably does matter. I glance back at Richard. He is kneeling beside the throne, and the king is leaning forwards to speak earnestly to him. Richard is nodding, gentle as when he is talking to one of our little boys. I see the king, his head shaking, stammering over a sentence, and I see my husband take his hand and say the words slowly, carefully, as a kind man will speak slowly to an idiot.

"Oh, Margaret, oh my Margaret, I am so sorry for you," I blurt out.

Her gray-blue eyes are filled with tears. "I am all alone now," she says. "I have never been so alone in all my life before. But I will not be turned on the wheel of fortune, I will not fall down. I will rule this country, and make the king well, and see my son inherit."

Richard thought that she could not rule the country from the Midlands; but summer comes and goes, the swallows swirl every evening around the roofs of Kenilworth, and every evening there are fewer and fewer as they are flying south, slipping away from us, and still the queen refuses to go back to London. She rules by command; there is no pretense of discussion. She simply orders a royal council who are picked to do her bidding and never argue with her. She does not call a Parliament of the commons who would have demanded to see the king in his capital city. Londoners are quick to complain that the foreigners who steal their trade and overcharge decent Englishmen are the result of a foreign queen who hates London and will not defend honest merchants. Then a French fleet raids the coast and goes farther than any has dared to go before. They enter right into the port of Sandwich and loot the town, tearing the place apart, taking away everything of value, and firing the market-place. Everyone blames the queen.

"Are they really saying that I ordered them to come?" she exclaims to Richard. "Are they mad? Why would I order the French to attack Sandwich?"

"The attack was led by a friend of yours, Pierre de Brézé," my husband points out dryly. "And he had maps of the shoals and the riverbed: English maps. People ask how did he get them if not from you? They are saying that you helped him because you may need him to help you. And you swore that you would see Kent punished for their support of Warwick. You know, de Brézé played a merry jest on us. He brought balls and racquets and played a game of tennis in the town square. It was an insult. The people of Sandwich think that you set him on to insult them. That this is French humor. We don't find it funny."

She narrows her eyes at him. "I hope you are not turning Yorkist," she says quietly. "I should be sorry to think that you turned against me, and it would break Jacquetta's heart. I should be sorry to see you executed. You have avoided death a hundred times, Richard Woodville. I should be sorry to be the one who ordered it."

Richard faces her, without flinching. "You asked me why people blame you. I am telling you, Your Grace. It does not mean that I think such things, except I am puzzled by de Brézé holding the charts. I am only making a fair report. And I will tell you more: if you do not control the pirates and the French ships in the narrow seas, then the Earl of Warwick will sail out of Calais and do it for you, and everyone will hail him as a hero. You do not damage his reputation by letting pirates rule the narrow seas, by letting de Brézé raid Sandwich: you damage your own. The southern towns have to be protected. The king has to be seen to respond to this challenge. You have to make the narrow seas safe for English ships. Even if you don't like Kent, it is the beachhead of your kingdom, and you have to defend it."

She nods, her anger dissipated at once. "Yes, I see. I do see, Richard. I just hadn't thought of the south coast. Would you draw up a plan for me? How we should protect the south coast?"

He bows, steady as always. "It would be my honor, Your Grace."

ROCHESTER CASTLE, KENT, NOVEMBER 1457

"Well, I for one don't think much of your plan," I say to him sarcastically. We are in an old damp castle on the wide wet estuary of the Medway in November: one of the grayest coldest darkest months of the English year. The castle was built by the Normans for defense, not for comfort; and it is so cold and so miserable here that I have commanded the children to stay at home at Grafton rather than join us. Richard's piecemeal map of the southern coast of England is spread before us on his worktable, the towns that he knows are vulnerable ringed in red, as he considers how to fortify and defend them with no armaments and no men. "I would have hoped that your plan would have had you posted to garrison the Tower and we could have been in London for Christmas," I say. "For sure, that would have suited me better."

He smiles; he is too absorbed to reply properly. "I know. I am sorry for it, beloved."

I look a little closer at his work. He does not even have a complete map of the coast-line; no one has ever drawn such a thing. This is pieced together from his own knowledge and from the reports of sailors and pilots. Even fishermen have sent him little sketches of their own bay, their own dock, the reefs and shoals outside their harbor. "Is the queen sending you enough weapons?"

He shakes his head. "She has a huge grant from Parliament to raise archers and buy cannon to use against the French, but there is nothing issued to me. And how can I fortify the towns with no men to serve and no cannon to fire?"

"How can you?" I ask.

"I shall have to train the townsmen," he says. "And these are all towns on the coast, so at least I have ships' captains and sailors, if I can persuade them to enlist. I shall have to get them trained up into some kind of defense."

"So what is she doing with the money?" I ask.

Now I have his full attention; he looks up at me, his face grave. "She is not protecting us against France; she is arming her men in London," he says. "I think she plans to charge the Earl of Warwick, the Earl of Salisbury, and the Duke of York with treason and bring them to London to stand trial."

I gasp. "They will never come?"

"She is certainly preparing for them to come. If they come at all, they will bring their own forces and their own retinue, and she will need her thirteen hundred archers," my husband says grimly. "I think she is preparing for war with them."

WESTMINSTER PALACE, LONDON, WINTER–SPRING 1458

We are summoned, along with the rest of the lords, in the cold days after Christmas, to a London more dark and suspicious than ever before, to find that far from accusation and punishment, the king has overruled the queen and plans a reconciliation. He has risen up, fired by a vision. He is suddenly well again and strong and burning with an idea to resolve the conflict between the two great houses by demanding that the York lords shall pay for their cruelties at St. Albans by being fined, building a chantry for the honored dead, and then swearing to end the blood feud with the heirs of their enemies. The queen is calling for the Earl of Warwick to be impeached for treason, but the king wants him forgiven as a repentant sinner. The whole of London is like a keg of dynamite with a dozen boys striking sparks around it, and the king quietly saying the Pater Noster, uplifted by his new idea. The vengeful heirs of Somerset and Northumberland go everywhere with their swords at the ready and the promise of a feud that will last for ten generations; the York lords are impenitent — the Earl of Warwick's men richly turned out in their liveries, Warwick a byword for generosity and gifts to Londoners, boasting that already they hold Calais and the narrow seas and who dare gainsay them? And the lord mayor has armed every good man in London and commanded him to patrol to keep the peace, which just introduces another army for everyone to fear.

The queen summons me in the twilight of a winter afternoon. "I want you to come out with me," she says. "There is a man I want you to meet."

Together we don our capes, pull up our hoods to shield our faces. "Who is it?"

"I want you to come with me to an alchemist."

I freeze, like a deer scenting danger. "Your Grace, Eleanor Cobham consulted alchemists, and Eleanor Cobham was imprisoned for eleven years and died in Peel Castle."

She looks at me blankly. "And so?"

"One of the fixed plans of my life is not to end as Eleanor Cobham."

I wait. For a moment her heart lifts, her face smiles, she dissolves into laughter. "Ah Jacquetta, are you telling me that you are not some mad ugly bad old witch?"

"Your Grace, every woman is a mad ugly

bad old witch, somewhere in her heart. The task of my life is to conceal this. The task of every woman is to deny this."

"What do you mean?"

"The world does not allow women like Eleanor, women like me, to thrive. The world cannot tolerate women who think and feel. Women like me. When we weaken, or when we get old, the world falls on us with the weight of a waterfall. We cannot bring our gifts to the world. The world we live in will not tolerate things that cannot be understood, things that cannot be easily explained. In this world, a wise woman hides her gifts. Eleanor Cobham was an inquiring woman. She met with others who sought the truth. She educated herself, and she sought masters with whom to study. She paid a terrible price for this. She was an ambitious woman. She paid the price for this too." I wait to see if she has understood, but her round pretty face is puzzled. "Your Grace, you will put me in danger if you ask me to use my gifts."

She faces me; she knows what she is doing. "Jacquetta, I have to ask you to do this, even if it is dangerous for you."

"It is a great demand, Your Grace."

"Your husband, the Duke of Bedford, asked for nothing less. He married you so that you would serve England in this way."

"I had to obey him: he was my husband. And he could protect me."

"He was right to ask you to use your gifts to save England. And now I ask it too, and I will protect you."

I shake my head. I have a very real sense that there will come a time when she will not be there, and I will face a court like Joan of Arc, like Eleanor Cobham, a court of men, and there will be documents written against me and evidence produced against me and witnesses who will swear against me, and no one will protect me.

"Why now?"

"Because I think the king is under a spell, and has been for years. The Duke of York, or Duchess Cecily, or the French king or somebody — how should I know who? — but someone has put him under a spell that makes him like a sleeping baby, or makes him like a trusting child. I have to make sure he never slips away from us again. Only alchemy or magic can protect him."

"He is awake now."

"He's like a wakeful child now. He has a dream of harmony and peace, and then he will fall asleep again, smiling at his lovely dream."

I pause. I know she is right. The king has slipped through to another world, and we need him in this one. "I will come with you. But if I think your alchemist is a charlatan, I will have no truck with him."

"That's the very reason I want you to

583

come," she says. "To see what you think of him. But come now."

We go on foot, through the darkened streets of Westminster, hand in hand. We have no ladies-in-waiting, not even a guard. For one moment only, I close my eyes in horror at what Richard, my husband, would say if he knew that I was taking such a risk and with the queen herself. But she knows where she is going. Sure-footed on the muck of the streets, imperious to the crossing sweepers, with a little lad going ahead of us with a flaming torch, she guides us down the narrow lanes and turns into an alley. At the end of it is a great door set in the wall.

I take the iron ring set beside it, and pull. A great carillon answers us, and the sound of dogs barking somewhere at the back. The porter opens the grille. "Who calls?" he asks.

Margaret steps up. "Tell your master that she of Anjou has come," she says.

At once the door swings open. She beckons to me, and we go inside. We step into a forest, not a garden. It is like a plantation of fir trees inside the tall walls, in the very heart of London, a secret woodland like a London garden under an enchantment to grow wild. I glance at Margaret, and she smiles at me as if she knows how this place will strike me: as a hidden world within the real one, perhaps it is even the doorway to another world inside this.

We walk down a twisting path that takes us through the green shadow of towering trees and then to a small house, overburdened with dark trees around it, sweet-scented boughs leaning on every roof, chimneys poking through foliage and singeing the needles of the pine trees. I sniff the air; there is the smell of a forge, thin smoke from hot coals, and the familiar, never-forgotten scent of sulfur. "He lives here," I say.

She nods. "You will see him. You can judge for yourself."

We wait, beside a stone bench before the house, and then a little door swings open and the alchemist comes out, a dark cloak around him, wiping his hands on his sleeves. He bows to the queen and directs a piercing look at me.

"You are of the House of Melusina?" he asks me.

"I am Lady Rivers now," I say.

"I have long wanted to meet you. I knew Master Forte, who worked for your husband the duke. He told me that you had the gift of scrying."

"I never saw anything that made much sense to me," I say.

He nods. "Will you scry for me?"

I hesitate. "What if I see something that is against the law?"

He looks at the queen.

"I say it is allowed," she rules. "Anything."

His smile is gentle. "Only you and I will see the looking glass, and I will keep it secret. It shall be as a confessional. I am an ordained priest; I am Father Jefferies. No one will know what you see, but you and I. I will tell Her Grace only the interpretation."

"Is it to find the spell that will heal the king? It is to do good for him?"

"That is my intention. I am already preparing some waters for him, I think that your presence at the moment of distilling will make the difference. He is well now, he can stay awake now, but I think he has some deep wound inside. He has never grown away from his mother; he has never truly become a man. He needs to transform. He needs that change from a child to a man; it is an alchemy of the person." He looks at me. "You have lived at his court — you have known him for many years. Do you think this?"

I nod. "He is of the moon," I tell him unwillingly. "And cold, and damp. My lord Bedford used to say he needed fire." I nod towards Margaret. "He thought Her Grace would bring fire and power to him."

The queen's face works as if she is about to cry. "No," she says sadly. "He has all but put me out. He is too much for me. I am chilled, and I have all but lost my spirit. I have no one who can make me warm any more."

"If the king is cold and wet, the kingdom will sink beneath floods of tears," the alchemist says.

"Please do it, Jacquetta," the queen whispers. "We will all three swear never to tell anyone about this."

I sigh. "I will."

Father Jefferies bows to the queen. "Will you wait here, Your Grace?"

She glances to the half-open door of his house. I know she is longing to see inside. But she submits to his rules. "Very well." She wraps her cloak around herself and sits on the stone bench.

He gestures to me to go inside, and I step over the threshold. In the room on the right there is a great fireplace in the center with a fire of charcoal warming a big-bellied cauldron. In the cauldron, in warm water, is a great vessel with a silver tube that passes through a cold bath; at the end of the tube is the steady drip of an elixir made from the steam. The heat in the room is stifling, and he guides me to the room on the left where there is a table and a great book — and beyond it: the scrying mirror. It is all so familiar, from the sweet smell of the elixir to the scent of the forge outside, that I pause for a moment and am back in the Hôtel de Bourbon at Paris, a maid and yet a bride, the new wife of the Duke of Bedford.

"Do you see something?" he asks eagerly.

"Only the past."

He puts a chair before me and takes the

curtain from the mirror. I see myself reflected back, so much older than the girl who was commanded to look in the mirror at Paris.

"I have some salts for you to sniff," he says. "I think it will help you to see."

He takes a little purse from the drawer in the table and opens the drawstring. "Here," he says.

I take the purse in my hand; inside is some white powder. I hold it to my face and cautiously breathe in. There is a moment when my head seems to swim, and then I look up, and there is the scrying mirror, but I cannot see my own reflection. My image has disappeared, and in my place there is a swirl of snow, and white flakes falling like the petals of white roses. It is the battle I saw once before, the men fighting uphill, a swaying bridge that falls, throwing them into the water, the snow on the ground turning red with blood, and always the swirling petals of the white snow. I see the iron gray of wide, wide skies; it is the north of England, bitterly cold, and out of the snow comes a young man like a lion.

"Look again." I can hear his voice, but I cannot see him. "What is going to become of the king? What would heal his wound?"

I see a small room, a dark room, a hidden room. It is hot and stuffy, and there is a sense of terrible menace in the warm silent darkness. There is only one arrow slit of a window in the thick stone walls. The only light comes from the window; the only brightness in the darkness of the room is that single thread of light. I look towards it, drawn by the only sign of life in the black. Then it is blocked as if by a man standing before it, and there is nothing but darkness.

I hear the alchemist sigh behind me, as if I have whispered my vision to him and he has seen it all. "God bless," he says quietly. "God bless him and keep him." Then he speaks a little more clearly: "Anything else?"

I see the charm that I threw into the deep water of the Thames tied to the ribbons, a different ribbon for each season, the charm shaped like a crown that washed away and told me that the king would never come back to us. I see it deep in the water, dangling on a thread; then I see it being pulled to the surface, up and up, and then it breaks from the water like a little fish popping on the surface of a summer stream, and it is my daughter Elizabeth who smilingly pulls it from the water, and laughs with joy, and puts it on her finger like a ring.

"Elizabeth?" I say wonderingly. "My girl?"

He steps forwards and gives me a glass of small ale. "Who is Elizabeth?" he asks.

"My daughter. I don't know why I was thinking of her."

"She has a ring shaped like a crown?"

"In my vision she had the ring that signified the king. She put it on her own finger."

He smiles gently. "These are mysteries."

"There is no mystery about the vision: she had the ring that was the crown of England, and she smiled and put it on her finger."

He drops the curtain across the mirror. "Do you know what this means?" he asks.

"My daughter is to be close to the crown," I say. I am puzzling through the scrying. "How could such a thing be? She is married to Sir John Grey; they have a son and another baby on the way. How can she put the crown of England on her finger?"

"It is not clear to me," he says. "I will think on it, and perhaps I will ask you to come again."

"How could Elizabeth have a ring like a crown on her finger?"

"Sometimes our visions come darkly. We don't know what we see. This one is very unclear. It is a mystery. I will pray on it."

I nod. When a man wants a mystery, it is generally better to leave him mystified. Nobody loves a clever woman.

"Will you come here and pour this liquid into a mold?" he asks me.

I follow him into the first room, and he takes a flask from the wall, shakes it gently, and then hands it to me. "Hold it." I cup the bowl in my hands, and at once I feel it grow warm under the heat of my fingers.

"Now pour it," he says, and gestures to the

molds that are on his table.

Carefully, I fill each one with the silvery liquid and then pass the flask back to him.

"Some processes call for the touch of a woman," he says quietly. "Some of the greatest alchemy has been done by a husband and wife, working together." He gestures to the bowl of warm water that is over the charcoal stove. "This method was invented by a woman and named for her."

"I have no skills," I say, denying my own abilities. "And when I have visions, they are sent by God and are unclear to me."

He takes my hand and tucks it under his arm as he leads the way to the door. "I understand. I will send for you only if I cannot manage to work for the queen without you. And you are right to hide your light. This is a world that does not understand a skilled woman; it is a world that fears the craft. We all have to do our work in secret, even now, when the kingdom needs our guidance so much."

"The king will not get better," I say suddenly, as if the truth is forced out of me.

"No," he agrees sadly. "We must do what we can."

"And the vision I had of him in the Tower . . ."

"Yes?"

"I saw him, and then someone stood before the window, and it was all dark . . ."

"You think he will meet his death in the Tower?"

"Not just him." I am filled with a sudden urgency. "I feel — I don't know why — it is as if one of my own children were in there. A boy of mine, perhaps two of my boys. I see it, but I'm not there, I can't prevent it. I can't save the king, and I can't save them either. They will go into the Tower and not come out."

Gently, he takes my hand. "We can make our own destiny," he says. "You can protect your children; we can perhaps help the king. Take your visions to church and pray, and I will hope for understanding too. Will you tell the queen what you have seen?"

"No," I say. "She has enough sorrows for a young woman already. And besides, I know nothing for certain."

"What did you see?" Margaret demands of me as we walk home, anonymous in our cloaks through the crowded dark streets. We link arms in case we are jostled, and Margaret's bright hair is covered by her hood. "He would tell me nothing."

"I had three visions: none of them very helpful," I say.

"What were they?"

"One of a battle, uphill in snow, and a bridge that gave way and threw the soldiers into the stream."

"You think it will come to a battle?" she demands.

"You think it won't?" I say dryly.

She nods at my common-sense appraisal. "I want a battle," she declares. "I'm not afraid of it. I am not afraid of anything. And the other vision?"

"Of a small room in the Tower, and the light going out."

She hesitates for a moment. "There are many small rooms in the Tower, and the light gets blocked for many young men."

A cold finger is laid on the nape of my neck. I wonder if a child of mine will ever be housed in the Tower and one dawn see the light blocked as a big man moves across the arrow slit. "That's all I saw," I say.

"And your last vision, you said there were three?"

"A ring shaped like a crown, which signified the crown of England, and it was in deep water and was drawn out of the water."

"By who?" she demands. "Was it me?"

It is very rare that I lie to Margaret of Anjou. I love her, and besides, I am sworn to follow her and her house. But I would not name my beautiful daughter to her as the girl who holds the ring of England in her hand.

"A swan," I say at random. "A swan took the ring of the crown of England in its beak."

"A swan?" she asks me breathlessly. "Are you sure?" She pauses in the middle of the street, and a carter shouts at us and we step aside.

"Just so."

"What can it mean? Do you see what it means?"

I shake my head. I had only conjured the swan because I didn't want to mention my daughter's name in this vision. Now, as so often, I find that the lie needs another lie.

"A swan is the badge of heir to the House of Lancaster," she reminds me. "Your vision means that my son Edward will take the throne."

"Visions are never certain . . ."

Her smile is radiant. "Don't you see? This is the solution for us? The king can step aside for his son," she says. "This is my way forwards. The swan is my boy. I will put Prince Edward on the throne of England."

Although he has launched one of the most controversial and dangerous meetings that Parliament has ever had to endure, although he has summoned three magnates who have brought their own armies, the king is joyously at peace with himself and with the world. He has every faith that these great matters will be best agreed in loving-kindness without him, he plans to arrive after everything has been decided, to give it all his blessing. He absents himself from London to pray for peace, while they argue and calculate the price of agreement, threaten each other, come near to blows, and finally forge a settlement.

It drives Margaret beside herself to see her husband step back from his work of ruling his lords to become the king who will intercede only with heaven for his country's safety — but leaves it to others to make it safe. "How can he summon them to London and just abandon us?" she demands of me. "How can he be such a fool to make half a peace?"

It is indeed only half a peace. Everyone agrees that the York lords should pay for attacking the king's own standard, and they promise to pay great fines to the Lancaster heirs, to compensate them for the deaths of their fathers. But they pay in tally sticks that were given to them from the king's exchequer — worthless promises of royal wealth that the king will never honor, but that Lancaster can never refuse, because to do so would be to admit that the kingdom is penniless. It is a brilliant joke and a powerful insult to the king. They promise to build a chantry at St. Albans for Masses for the souls of the fallen, and they all vow to keep a future peace. Only the king thinks that a blood feud that is set to go down the generations can be thus halted with sweet words, a bouquet of sticks, and a promise. The rest of us see lies laid upon deaths, dishonor on murder.

Then the king returns to London from his retreat and declares a love day — a day when we shall all walk together, hand in hand, and all will be forgiven. "The lion shall lie down with the lamb," he says to me. "Do you see?"

I do see — I see a city riven with faction and ready to make war. I see Edmund Beaufort's son, who lost his father at St. Albans, is ordered to walk hand in hand with the Earl of Salisbury, and they stand at arm's length, fingers touching, as if they could feel wet blood on their fingertips. Behind them comes his father's killer, the Earl of Warwick, and he walks handfast with the Duke of Exeter, who has sworn secretly that there shall be no forgiveness. Next comes the king, looking well, glowing with happiness at this procession that he thinks shows to the people that the peers are united under his rule once more, and behind him comes the queen.

She should have walked alone. As soon as I saw her, I knew that she should have walked alone, like a queen. Instead, the king has placed her hand in hand with the Duke of York. He thinks it shows their friendship. It does not. It says to the whole world that they were enemies once, and that they could be enemies again. It says nothing of goodwill and forgiveness, but it exposes Margaret as a player in this deadly game — not a queen above faction, but a queen militant, and York as her enemy. Of all the follies on this day when we all went hand in hand — Richard and I among the others — this is the worst of them.

WESTMINSTER PALACE, LONDON, WINTER 1458

The love day peace lasts only for eight months. I leave court in the summer for my confinement and give birth to another baby, a daughter whom we call Katherine, and when she is well and strong and thriving at the breast of the wet nurse, we leave home and stay with my daughter Elizabeth at Groby Hall. She is brought to bed with a child, and she has another boy.

"What a blessing you are to the Greys," I say to her as I am leaning over the cradle. "Another baby: and a boy."

"You would think they would thank me for it," she says. "John is as dear to me as ever, but his mother does nothing but complain."

I shrug. "Perhaps it is time for the two of you to move to one of the other Grey houses," I suggest. "Perhaps there is not room for two mistresses in Groby Hall."

"Perhaps I should come to court," Elizabeth says. "I could serve Queen Margaret and stay with you."

I shake my head. "It is no pleasant place at the moment," I say. "Not even for the lady-in-waiting whom you would be. Your father and I have to go back, and I dread what I will find."

I return to a court busy with rumor. The queen requires that the Earl of Warwick take the almost impossible task of keeping the narrow seas safe for English shipping; but at the same time hand over the fortress of Calais to Edmund Beaufort's son, the new young Duke of Somerset, an inveterate enemy of all the York lords.

This is to ask a man to do difficult and dangerous work and to give the reward to his rival. Warwick of course refuses. And just as Richard predicted, the queen hopes to entrap him with an accusation of treason. In November she publicly blames him for piracy — using his ships out of Calais — and a Parliament packed with her supporters commands him to come to London and stand trial. Proudly, he arrives to defend himself and confronts them all, a courageous young man alone before his enemies. Richard comes out of the royal council room to find me waiting outside and tells me that Warwick shouted down the accusations and claimed in turn that the love day agreement had been betrayed by the queen herself. "He is raging," he says. "And it's so heated it could come to blows."

Just at that moment there is a crash against the council chamber door, and at once Richard jumps forwards, drawing his sword, his other arm outstretched to shield me. "Jacquetta, go to the queen!" he shouts.

I am about to turn and run when my way is barred by men in the livery of the Duke of Buckingham, storming down the hall with their swords drawn. "Behind you!" I say quickly to Richard and step back against the wall as the men come towards us. Richard is on guard, sword drawn to defend us, but the men run past us without a glance, and I see from the other direction Somerset's guard are ready, blocking the hall. It is an ambush. The council doors are flung open, and Warwick and his men, in tight formation, come out fighting. They have been attacked in the very council chamber, and outside the men are waiting to finish them off. Richard steps abruptly back and crushes me against the wall. "Stay quiet!" he commands me.

Warwick, sword like a flail, goes straight at his enemies, stabbing and striking, his men tight behind him. One loses his sword, and I see him punch out in rage. One falls, and they step over him to hold the defensive box around their commander: clearly they would die for him. The hall is too narrow for a fight; the soldiers jostle one another and then Warwick puts down his bare head, shouts "À Warwick!," his battle cry, and makes a run for it.

Moving as one, his men charge at their attackers; they break out and are free, the men of Somerset and Buckingham running after them like hounds after deer, and they are gone. We hear a bellow of rage as the royal guard catches the Buckingham men and holds them, and then the noise of running feet as Warwick gets away.

Richard steps back and pulls me to his side, sheathing his sword. "Did I hurt you, love? I am sorry."

"No, no . . ." I am breathless with shock. "What was that? What is happening?"

"That, I think, was the queen sending the two dukes to finish what their fathers started. The end of the truce. And that, I think, was Warwick drawing his sword in the demesne of a royal palace and getting away to Calais. Betrayal and treason. We'd better go to the queen and see what she knows about this."

By the time we get to her rooms the privy chamber door is closed and her women are outside in her presence chamber, gossiping furiously. They rush towards us as we come in, but I brush them aside and tap on the door, and she calls me and Richard in together. The young Duke of Somerset is there already, whispering to her.

She glances at my shocked face and hurries to me. "Jacquetta, were you there? Not hurt?"

"Your Grace, the Earl of Warwick was attacked in the council chamber itself," I say bluntly. "By men in the livery of Buckingham and Somerset."

"But not by me," the twenty-two-year-old duke says, as pert as a child.

"Your men," my husband observes, his tone level. "And it is illegal to draw a sword in the royal court." He turns to the queen. "Your Grace, everyone will think this is ordered by you, and it is most treacherous. It was in the council chamber, in the demesne of the court. You are supposed to be reconciled. You gave your royal word. It is dishonorable. Warwick will complain, and he will be right to do so."

She flushes at that and glances to the duke, who shrugs his shoulders. "Warwick doesn't deserve an honorable death," he says pettishly. "He did not give my father an honorable death."

"Your father died in battle," Richard points out. "A fair fight. And Warwick has begged and been given your forgiveness, and paid for a chantry in your father's name. That grievance is over, and you have been paid for the loss of your father. This was an attack inside the safety of the court. How will the council do its business if a man risks his life attending? How will any of the York lords dare to come again? How can men of goodwill come to a council that attacks its own members? How can a man of honor serve such a rule?"

"He got away?" the queen ignores Richard to ask me, as if this is all that matters.

"He got away," I say.

"I should think he will get away all the way to Calais, and you will have a powerful enemy in a fortified castle off your shores," Richard says bitterly. "And I can tell you that not one town in a hundred can be defended against attack on the south coast. He could sail up the Thames and bombard the Tower, and now he will think himself free to do so. You have broken his alliance for nothing and put us all in danger."

"He was our enemy at any time," young Somerset remarks. "He was our enemy before this."

"He was bound by a truce," Richard insists. "And by his oath of allegiance to the king. He honored it. Attacking him in the council chamber releases him from both."

"We shall leave London," the queen rules.

"That's not the solution!" Richard explodes. "You can't make an enemy like this and think that all you need do is flee. Where will be safe? Tutbury? Kenilworth? Coventry? Do you think to abandon the southern counties of England altogether? Shall Warwick just march in? Is it your plan to give him Sandwich, as you have given him Calais? Shall you give him London?"

"I shall take my son and go." She rounds on him. "And I shall raise troops, loyal men, and arm. When Warwick lands, he will find my army waiting for him. And this time we will beat him, and he will pay for his crime."

On Campaign, Summer — Autumn 1459

The queen is like a woman possessed by a vision. She takes the court with her to Coventry, the king in her train. He has no say in what happens now, he is startled by the failure of his truce and the sudden rush into war. She defies advice to be careful; she can smell victory, and she is eager for it. She enters Coventry with all the ceremony of a reigning king, and they bow to her as if she were the acknowledged ruler of the country.

No one has seen a Queen of England like this before. She is served on one knee, like a king. She sits under the royal canopy. She musters men; she demands a levy of every man from every county in England, ignoring the traditional way of raising an army which is that each lord calls out his own men. From Cheshire she recruits her own army; she calls it the prince's army, and she distributes his own badge, the new livery of the swan. She calls his captains the Knights of the Swan and promises them a special place in the battle that is certain to come.

"The swan children wore collars of gold and were hidden by their mother to appear like swans, and they all came back but one," I say, uneasy at her sudden love of this badge, at her invoking this old myth. "This is nothing to do with Prince Edward."

The prince looks up at me and beams one of his sudden radiant smiles. "Swan," he repeats. She has taught him the word. She has sewn two swan badges of silver on his collar.

"You said you had seen the crown of England taken by a swan," she reminds me.

I flush, thinking of the lie I told to hide the real vision, of my daughter Elizabeth laughing with a ring shaped like a crown on her finger. "It came to me like a daydream, Your Grace, and I warned you that it might mean nothing."

"I will take England, if I have to turn into a swan myself to do it."

We move to Eccleshall Castle fifty miles north of Coventry in September, and we are less and less like a court, more like an army. Many of the ladies-in-waiting have gone back to their homes as their husbands have been summoned to march with the queen militant. Some of them stay away. The few ladies who travel with the queen and me all have husbands in her rapidly growing army; we are like a baggage train on the march, not a court. The king is with us, and the prince; both of them go out daily to attend the musters of men as Margaret brings in more and more recruits that she houses in the buildings inside the castle walls and in tents in the fields around. She calls on the loyal lords to come to her support, she parades the young prince before them. He is only six years old; he rides his little white pony around the ranks of the men, straight-backed and obedient to his mother's commands. His father comes to the castle gate and holds up his hand as if blessing the thousands of men who are under his standard.

"Is it the French?" he asks me wonderingly. "Are we going to take Bordeaux?"

"There is no war yet," I reassure him. "Perhaps we can avoid war."

Old James Touchet, Lord Audley, is to command the army, and Lord Thomas Stanley is to support him. Lord Audley comes to the queen with the news that the York lords are assembling their forces in England and mustering their men. They are planning to meet at York's castle at Ludlow; and so the Earl of Salisbury will have to march south from his castle of Middleham, in the North of England, to Ludlow, on the borders of Wales. Lord Audley swears that we will catch him as he marches nearby, and take him by surprise as he hurries to join the other treasonous lords. Our forces will be about ten thousand men; thousands more will come with Lord Stanley. Salisbury has a force of less than half that number — he is marching to his death, hopelessly undermanned, and he does not know it.

I find it a grim process, watching the men arm, check their weapons and their equipment, and form up in ranks. Elizabeth's husband, Sir John Grey, on his beautiful horse, leads an armed band of his tenants on the two-day march from his home. He tells me that Elizabeth cried unstoppably as he left and seemed filled with foreboding. She asked him not to go, and his mother ordered her to her room, like a naughty child.

"Should I have stayed with her?" he asks me. "I thought it my duty to come."

"You are right to do your duty." I repeat the worn phrase, which allows wives to release their husbands and women to send their sons to war. "I am sure you are right to do your duty, John."

The queen appoints him as head of cavalry. Anthony, my most precious son, comes from our home at Grafton and will fight alongside his father. They will ride to the battle and then dismount and fight on foot. The thought of my son in battle makes me so sick that I cannot eat for fear.

"I am lucky," Richard says stoutly to me. "You know I am lucky; you have seen me ride out to a dozen battles, and I always come safe home to you. I will keep him at my side, he will be lucky too."

"Don't say it! Don't say it!" I put my hand over his mouth. "It's to tempt fate. Dear God, do you have to go out this time?"

"This time, and every time, until the country is at peace," my husband says simply.

"But the king himself has not commanded it!"

"Jacquetta, are you asking me to turn traitor? Do you want me to wear a white rose for York?"

"Of course not! Of course not. It's just . . ."

Gently, he takes me in his arms. "It's just what? Just that you cannot bear to see Anthony in danger?"

Ashamed, I nod. "My son . . ." I whisper, anguished.

"He is a man now; danger comes to him like snow in winter, like flowers in springtime. He is a brave young man — I have taught him courage. Don't you teach him to be a coward."

My head comes up at that, and my husband chuckles. "So you don't want him to go to war, but you don't want him to be a coward? Where's the sense in it? Now you be brave, and come and see us march out, and wave your hand and smile and give us your blessing."

We go to the door together, his hand warm

on my waist. The queen has ordered the army to troop before the drawbridge of the castle, and the little prince is there on his white pony. Anthony comes from the ranks and kneels swiftly before me, and I put my hand down on the warm soft hair of his precious head.

"God bless you, my son." I can hardly speak for the tightness in my throat. I can feel the tears hot in my eyes. He rises up and stands before me, excited and ready to go. I want to add, "And do what your father tells you, and keep your horse near you so that you can get away, and stay out of danger, and there is no need to get too close to the fighting . . ." but Richard draws me close and kisses me quickly on the mouth to silence me.

"God bless you, my husband," I say. "Come home safely to me, both of you."

"I always do," Richard replies. "And I will bring Anthony safe home too."

The queen and I, her ladies-in-waiting, and the prince and his household stand and wave as they march past us, the standards flapping in the breeze and the men looking eager and confident. They are well equipped, the queen has used the money granted her by Parliament, which was supposed to improve defense against the French to pay for weapons and boots for this army. When they are gone and the dust has settled on the lane, the queen orders the prince to go with his nurse and turns to me.

"And now we wait," she says. "But when they find Salisbury and join battle, I want to see it. I'm going out to watch it."

I almost think she is joking, but the next day we get a message sent from James Touchet to say that his scouts have found the Earl of Salisbury's men and he is lying in wait for them near a little village called Blore Heath. At once the queen orders her horse as if we are going out on a ride for pleasure. "Are you coming with me?" she asks.

"The king would not like you to put yourself in danger," I say, already knowing that the king's opinions mean nothing to her.

"He won't even know that I have gone and come back again," she says. "And I have told my ladies we are going out hawking."

"Just you and me?" I ask skeptically.

"Why not?"

"No hawks?"

"Oh, come on!" she says, as impatient as a girl. "Don't you want to watch over Richard? And your son Anthony?"

"We'll never be able to see them," I say.

"We'll climb a tree," she replies, and then steps up on the mounting block, swings her leg over her horse, and nods to the groom to pull down her gown over her boots. "Are you coming? For I will go without you if I have to."

"I'm coming," I say, and I mount and ride beside her as we go towards Blore Heath.

We are greeted with a messenger from James Touchet, who suggests that we might like to go to the church at nearby Mucklestone, where we will be able to see the battlefield from the belfry. The noble lord is arranging a viewing tower as if for a day's jousting. We clatter into the little village, sending chickens fluttering away from our horses' hooves, and leave the horses at the village forge.

"You can shoe my horse while he is waiting here," the queen says to the blacksmith, throwing him a penny, then she turns and leads the way to the church.

Inside it is quiet and dim, and we take the winding stone stair upwards and upwards to where the bell is hung in the tower. It is like a great watchtower — the great bell behind us, a stone parapet before us — and clearly across the fields we can see the road from the north, and in the distance the trail of dust that is the marching army of the Earl of Salisbury.

The queen touches my arm, her face alight with excitement, and points ahead. We can see a great hedge and behind it the standards of our army. I put my hand over my eyes and scowl, trying to identify the Rivers flag in case I can make out Anthony or my husband nearby, but it is too far to see. Our forces are perfectly positioned; Salisbury will not know they are there, nor in what numbers, until he comes out of the little wood either side of his road, and then they will face him. There is something very dreadful about looking down on the battlefield, as if we were stone gargoyles on the tower, watching the deaths of mortals for sport. I look at the queen. She does not feel this; she is alight with excitement, her hands clasped tight together as the outriders at the front of the York army come briskly out from the wood, and fall back when they see the mighty force before them arranged in battle order on the little hill with a small river between them.

"What are they doing?" the queen demands irritably, as we see a herald ride out from each side and meet in the middle ground between the two armies.

"Parlaying?" I ask.

"There is nothing to talk about," she says. "He is named a traitor. Lord Audley's instructions are to take him, or kill him, not to talk to him."

As if to confirm the instructions, the heralds break off and ride back to their own ranks, and almost at once there is a storm of arrows from the Lancaster side, shooting downhill and finding targets. A sigh, a defeated sigh, comes from the York side, and we can see the men going down on their knees in a swift prayer, before rising to their feet and pulling on their helmets.

"What are they doing?" the queen asks avidly.

"They are kissing the ground," I say. There is something terrible about the doomed men putting their lips to the earth that they think will be their deathbed. "They are kissing the ground where they will be buried. They know they will be defeated, and yet they are not running away."

"Too late to run," the queen says harshly. "We would chase them and kill them."

From our vantage point we can see that the Yorks are outnumbered by almost two to one, perhaps even more. This is not going to be a battle, it is going to be a massacre.

"Where is Lord Stanley?" the queen demands. "He wanted to lead the attack, but I ordered him to be in support. Where is he?"

I look around. "Could he be hiding in ambush?"

"Look!" she says.

The very center of the York army, where they should be at their strongest, is giving way before the arrows. "They're retreating!" the queen cries. "We're winning! So quickly!"

They are. The men at the very center of the line are turning, dropping their weapons, and running away. At once I see our cavalry come forwards and start the charge downhill, towards the stream. I clasp my hands together as I see Elizabeth's husband, out in front, thundering into the shallow water and riding across, struggling up the steep banks of the far side, just as the York forces inexplicably swing round and run back into the very heart of the battle, picking up their weapons and returning to the fight.

"What's happening?" Margaret is as bewildered as I am. "What are they doing?"

"They've come back," I say. "They've turned. It was a trick, and now our cavalry is bogged down in the river and the Yorks are able to fight them from the bank. They have tricked us off our good position, into the river, and our men can't get out."

It is a terrible sight. Our men in battle armor on their metal-plated horses go plunging into the water, and then struggle to get up the other side of the stream, where they are battered by the York men-at-arms, wielding great swords, war axes, and pikes. The knights fall from their horses, but cannot get to their feet to defend themselves, the horses' hooves crash down through the water to crush them as they struggle to rise, or weighed down by their flooded breastplates they drown, scrambling in the churning waters of the stream. Those who can grab a stirrup leather try to pull themselves up but the Yorks are dancing up and down the dry banks, quick to thrust a knife in an unguarded armpit or lean towards the stream to slash at a throat, or one of the strong soldiers steps into the stream, swinging a great battle axe, and down goes the Lancaster knight into the water, which blooms red. It is a savage muddle of men and horses. There is nothing beautiful about it, or noble, or even orderly; nothing like the battles that are made into ballads or celebrated in the romances. It is a savage mess of brutish men killing each other for blood lust. A few of the Lancaster lords scramble up the bank on their great war-horses and tear through the York lines and disappear — they simply run away. Worse, even more of them, hundreds of them, drop their swords point down to indicate they are not fighting, pull up their horses into a walk, and go slowly, humbly, towards the enemy lines.

"What are they doing?" Margaret is aghast. "What is my cavalry doing? Is it a trick?"

"They are changing sides," I say. My hand is on the base of my throat as if to hold my thudding heart. I am so afraid that John Grey may be turning traitor as the queen and I watch. Hundreds of cavalrymen have turned from our side to the Yorks: surely, he must be among them.

"My cavalry?" she asks disbelievingly.

Her hand creeps into mine, and we stand in silence, watching the slow progress of the horsemen across the battlefield, towards the Yorks, with their standards drooped down low in surrender. Stray horses plunge and kick and pull themselves out of the stream and trot away. But many, many men are left struggling in the stream until they do not struggle anymore.

"John," I say quietly, thinking of my son-in-law at the head of the cavalry charge. For all I know he is drowned in his armor, and not turned traitor at all. From this distance I can see neither his standard nor his horse. He will leave my daughter a widow and two little boys fatherless, if he is choking in that red water this afternoon.

The armies break off from engagement, retreating to their own lines. From the banks of the river, even in the water, the wounded men stir and call for help.

"Why don't they attack?" Margaret demands, her teeth bared, her hands gripped tight together. "Why don't they attack again?"

"They're regrouping," I say. "God spare them, they are regrouping to charge again."

As we watch, the horsemen who are left of the Lancaster force charge once more, down the hill at a brave pace; but still they have to get through the stream. This time, knowing the danger, they force the horses into the water and then in a great bound, up the steep banks, spurring them on to the York lines, and battle is joined. They are followed by the men who are fighting on foot; I know that my son and my husband will be among them. I cannot see them, but I can see the movement of the Lancaster forces as they come forwards like a wave, struggle through the stream, and break on the rock of the York line, which holds, and fights, and they slug at each other, until we can see our line fall back, and the men on the wings start to slip away.

"What are they doing?" the queen demands incredulously. "What are they doing?"

"We are losing," I say. I hear the words in my own voice, but I cannot believe it, not for a moment. I cannot believe that I am here, high as an eagle, remote as a soaring gull, watching my husband's defeat, perhaps watching my son's death. "We are losing. Our men are running away; it is a rout. We thought we were unbeatable, but we are losing."

It is getting darker — we can see less and less. Suddenly, I realize that we are in terrible danger, and we have put ourselves here by our own folly. When the battle is lost and the York soldiers chase the Lancaster lords to their deaths, hunting them down through the lanes, they will come to this village and they will scale this tower and they will find the greatest prize of the battle: the queen. Our cause will be lost forever if they can take the queen and win control of the prince and the king. Our cause will be lost, and I will have lost it, letting her persuade me to come to this church and climb up to watch a life-or-death battle as if it was a pretty day of jousting.

"We have to go," I say suddenly.

She does not move, staring into the grayness of the twilight. "I think we're winning," she says. "I think that was another charge and we broke through their line."

"We're not winning, and we didn't break through, we are running away, and they are chasing us," I say harshly. "Margaret, come on."

She turns to me, surprised by my use of her name, and I grab her by the hand and pull her towards the stone stairs. "What d'you think they'll do with you if they catch you?" I demand. "They'll hold you in the Tower forever. Or worse, they'll break your neck and say you fell from your horse. Come on!"

Suddenly she realizes her danger, and she races down the stone steps of the tower, her feet pattering on the stone treads. "I'll go alone," she says tersely. "I'll go back to Eccleshall. You must stop them coming after me."

She is ahead of me as we run to the forge where the blacksmith is just about to put the shoes on her horse.

"Put them on backwards," she snaps.

"Eh?" he says.

She gives him a silver coin from her pocket. "Backwards," she says. "Put them on backwards. Hurry. A couple of nails to each shoe." To me she says: "If they want to follow me, they will have no tracks. They will see only the horses coming here, they won't realize I was going away."

I realize I am staring at her, the queen of my vision, who had her horseshoes on backwards. "Where are we going?"

"I'm going," she says. "Back to Eccleshall to fetch the prince and the king and to raise the main army to chase the Earl of Salisbury all the way to Ludlow if we have to."

"And what am I to do?"

She looks at the blacksmith. "Hurry. Hurry."

"What am I to do?"

"Will you stay here? And if they come through, you are to tell them that I was going to meet my army at Nottingham."

"You're leaving me here?"

"They won't hurt you, Jacquetta. They like you. Everyone likes you."

"They are an army hot from the battlefield; they have probably just killed my son-in-law, my husband, and my son."

"Yes, but they won't hurt you. They won't make war on women. But I have to get away, and get the prince and the king safe. You will save me if you tell them I have gone to Nottingham."

I hesitate for a moment. "I am afraid."

She holds out her hand to me and she makes the gesture that I taught her myself. The pointing finger gesture that draws the circle in the air, which shows the wheel of fortune. "I am afraid too," she says.

"Go on then." I release her.

The smith hammers in the last nail; the horse walks a little awkwardly, but he is sound enough. The smith drops to his hands and knees in the dirt, and Margaret steps on his back to get into the saddle. She raises her hand to me. *"À tout à l'heure,"* she says as if she is just going out for a little ride for pleasure, and then she digs her heels in her horse's sides and she goes flying off. I look down at the ground; the marks in the soft earth clearly show a horse coming into the forge, but there is no sign of one leaving.

Slowly, I walk to where the track goes through the little village of Mucklestone, and wait for the first York lords to ride in.

It grows dark. In the distance at Blore Heath I hear a cannon shot, and then another; slowly through the night. I wonder that they can see anything to fire upon. Groups of men come by, some of them supporting their wounded companions, some of them with their heads down, running as if from fear itself. I shrink back inside the forge, and they don't see me as they go by. They don't even stop to ask for drink or food; all the windows and doors in the village are barred to all soldiers — whatever badge they wear. When I see a Lancaster badge, I step out into the lane: "Lord Rivers? Sir Anthony Woodville? Sir John Grey?" I ask.

The man shakes his head. "Were they on horses? They'll be dead, missus."

I make myself stand, though my knees are weak beneath me. I lean against the door of the forge and wonder what I should do, alone at a battlefield, and if Richard is dead out there, and my son, and my son-in-law? I wonder if I should go out to the heath and look for Richard's body. I cannot believe I would not know of his death. I would surely sense it, when I was so close to the battle that I could even see the churning of the stream where he might have drowned?

"Here," the blacksmith says kindly, coming out of his little cottage to put a dirty mug in my hand. "What are you going to do, lady?"

I shake my head. There is no pursuing force to misdirect; the York men are not coming through this way, just the broken remnants of our army. I fear that my husband is dead, but I don't know where to look for him. I am weak with fear and with a sense of my own lack of heroism. "I don't know," I say. I feel utterly lost. The last time I was lost and alone was in the forest when I was a girl in France, and Richard came for me then. I cannot believe that Richard will not come for me now.

"Better come in with us," the blacksmith says. "Can't stay out here all night. And you can't go to the battlefield, my lady; there are thieves working the place, and they'd stab you as soon as look at you. You'd better come in with us."

I shrug. I don't know what I should do. There is no point standing in the street if no one is going to come past me to ask where the queen has gone. I have done my duty by hurrying her away; I don't need to stand out till dawn. I duck my head under the narrow doorway of the cottage and step into the small dark earth-floored room and the stench of five people sleeping, cooking, eating, and pissing in the same space.

They are kind to me. What they have, they share. They have a corner of black bread made with rye; they have never tasted white bread. They have a thin gruel made with vegetables and a rind of cheese. They have small ale to drink, which the goodwife brews herself, and they give me the first gulp from an earthenware cup, which tastes of mud. I think that these are the people we should be fighting for; these are the people who live in a rich country, where land is fertile and water is clean, where there are more acres to grow than farmers to harvest. This is a country where wages should be high and markets should be rich and busy. And yet it is not. It is a land where no one can sleep safely in their bed at night for fear of raids or brigands or thieves, where the king's justice is bought and paid for by the king's friends, where an honest workingman is tried for treason and hanged if he asks for his rights, and where we cannot seem to stop a French courtier landing in our own ports and laying them waste.

We say that we are the rulers of this country, but we do not make a rule of law. We say that we command these people, but we do not lead them to peace or prosperity. We, their own lords, quarrel among ourselves and bring death to their door, as if our opinions and thoughts and dreams are worth far more than their safety and health and children.

I think of the queen, riding through the night with her horseshoes on backwards so that no one can know where she has gone, and her army lying facedown in Hempmill Brook, perhaps my husband and my son among them. The blacksmith's wife, Goody Skelhorn, sees me grow pale and asks me if the gruel has turned my stomach.

"No," I say. "But my husband was fighting today, and I am afraid for him." I can't even bear to tell her of my fears for my boy.

She shakes her head and says something about terrible times. Her accent is so broad that I can hardly make out what she says. Then she spreads a flea-filled rug on a straw mattress that is their best bed, beside the dying fire, and shows me that I can lie down. I thank her. I lie down; she joins me on one side and her daughter on the other. The men sleep on the other side of the fire. I lie on my back and wait for the long sleepless night to wear away.

Through the night we hear the clatter of hooves down the village street, and occasional shouts. The girl, the woman, and I cower like frightened children together: this is what it is like to live in a country at war. There is nothing of the grace of the joust or even the inspiration of great principles — it is about being a poor woman hearing a detachment of horse thunder down your street and praying that they do not stop to hammer on your frail door.

When dawn comes, the goodwife gets up and cautiously opens the door and peers outside. When it seems safe, she goes out and I hear her clucking to her hens and releasing the pig to roam around the village and eat the rubbish. I get up from the bed and scratch the swelling insect bites on my arms and neck and face. My hair is falling down from the careful coiled plait on the top of my head. I feel filthy, and I am afraid that I smell; but I am alive. I did not stand and misdirect the invading lords as the queen asked me to do; I hid like a serf in a peasant's cottage and was glad of their kindness. I ducked out of sight when I heard the horses in the night, and I lay down on dirty straw. In truth, I would have given anything to stay alive last night, and I would give anything to know my husband and sons are alive this dawn. I am fearful and low. I don't feel much of a duchess this morning.

The girl gets up, shakes out her petticoat, which serves as both underwear and nightgown, pulls on a dress of coarse fustian over the top, rubs her face on the corner of a dirty apron, and she is ready for the day. I look at her and think of the scented bath that is waiting for me at Eccleshall Castle and the clean linen that I will put on. Then, before I grow too confident of my own future comforts, I remember that I can't be sure that the court will be at Eccleshall Castle, nor that my son and husband will come home to me.

"I must leave," I say abruptly.

I go outside, and the smith is tacking up my horse. His wife has a mug of small ale for me, and a heel of stale bread. I drink the ale and dip the bread in it to make it soft enough to eat, then I give them my purse. There is silver in it, and some copper coins, a fortune for them, though it was next to nothing for me. "Thank you," I say, and I wish I could say more: that I am sorry for the ruin that this king and queen have brought upon them; I am sorry that they work hard and yet cannot rise from the poverty of their home; I am sorry that I have slept on linen all my life and seldom thought of those who sleep on straw.

They smile. The girl is missing a rotting tooth at the front of her face, and it gives her a gap-toothed grin like a little child. "D'ye know the way?" the woman worries. It is all of nine miles; she has never been so far from her home.

"You go to Loggerheads, and they will set you on the road there," the smith volunteers. "But take care, the soldiers will be making their way home too. Shall I send the lad with you?"

"No," I say. "You will be busy in the forge today, I should think."

He hefts my purse and grins up at me. "It's a good day already," he says. "The best we've had in all our lives. God bless you, my lady."

"God bless you," I say, and turn my horse to the south.

I have been riding for about half an hour when I hear a blast of trumpets and see the dust of a great army on the move. I look around me for somewhere to hide, but this is wide empty country, the fields are broad and bare and the hedges are low. I pull my horse over to an open gateway by a field and think that if they are the York army or York reinforcements, then I can rein in, sit tight, look like a duchess, and let them go by. Perhaps they will have news of my husband and my boy.

When they are half a mile from me, I can make out the king's standard, and I know that I am safe for the moment, as the army

627

comes up, the queen and the king himself at the head.

"Jacquetta!" she cries out with genuine joy. "God bless you! Well met!"

She pulls her horse over to the side of the road to let the army keep on marching past us. Thousands of men are following her. "You are safe!" she says. "And well! And the king here is so angry at the death of Lord Audley that he is marching himself to bring the York lords to account." She lowers her voice. "He has suddenly come to his senses and said he will lead the army himself. I'm so happy. He says he will never again forgive them, and he is going to avenge the death of our true friend."

"Lord Audley is dead?" I ask. I can feel myself starting to tremble at the thought of what her next words might be. "And do you have news . . ."

A man from the center of the knights thrusts his horse forwards and pushes up his visor to show his face. "It's me!" my husband yells. "Jacquetta! Beloved! It's me!"

I gasp, he is unrecognizable, as they all are, weighed down in their armor and with helmets on. But he comes forwards, jumps down from his horse with a clatter, throws his helmet aside, and pulls me into his arms. His breastplate is hard against me; the greaves on his arms cut into my back, but I cling to him and kiss him and swear to him that I love him.

"And Anthony is safe," he says. "And Elizabeth's husband. We all came through scot-free. I told you I was lucky."

"Don't look at me, I must smell," I say, suddenly remembering my clothes and my hair and the raised welts of flea bites on my skin. "I am ashamed of myself."

"You should never have stayed there," he says, glancing at the queen. "You should never have been there. You should never have been left there."

Margaret gives me a merry smile. "He has been most angry with me," she says. "He is not speaking to me for rage. But see, here you are, safe now."

"I am safe now," I agree.

"Now come! Come!" she urges. "We are on the trail of the traitor Salisbury. And we are not far behind him."

We have a wild couple of days, riding at the head of the royal army. The king is restored to health by action; he is once again the young man who we thought might rule the kingdom. He rides at the head of his army, and Margaret rides beside him, as if they were true husband and wife: friends and comrades in deed as well as by contract. The weather is warm, a golden end of summer, and the harvest is in from the fields, leaving golden stubble, crisscrossed by hundreds of loping hare. There is a big harvest moon in the evenings, so bright that we can march late into the night. One night we set up tents and camp, just as if we were on an evening hunting party. We have news of the York lords; they have met together at Worcester and swore a solemn oath of loyalty in the cathedral, and sent a message to the king.

"Send it back to them," the queen snaps. "We have seen what their loyalty is worth. They killed Lord Audley and Lord Dudley; they killed Edmund Beaufort. We won't parlay with them."

"I think I might send a public pardon," the king says mildly. He beckons the Bishop of Salisbury to his side. "A public pardon so that they know they can be forgiven," he says.

The queen compresses her lips and shakes her head. "No message," she says to the bishop. "No pardon," she says to the king.

Like a rat outside its hole, Richard, Duke of York, takes his stand outside his own town of Ludlow. He and the two lords, Warwick and Salisbury, take up position just outside the town, on the far side of the Ludford Bridge. On our side of the river the king flies the royal standard and sends one last offer of pardon to any soldier who abandons his loyalty to the Duke of York and comes over to us.

That night, my husband comes into the

royal chambers, where the queen and I and a couple of ladies are sitting with the king. "I have a comrade who served with me in Calais, who wants to leave the Earl of Salisbury and come to our side," Richard says. "I have promised him full pardon and a welcome. I have to know that he can trust this."

We all look to the king who smiles mildly. "Of course," he says. "Everyone can be forgiven if they truly repent."

"I have your word, Your Grace?" Richard asks.

"Oh yes. Everyone can be forgiven."

Richard turns to the queen. "And I have yours?"

The queen rises from her chair. "Who is it?" she asks eagerly.

"I cannot advise my friend to come to you unless you, yourself, guarantee his safety," Richard says tightly. "Do you promise him your pardon for serving against you, Your Grace? Can I trust to your word of pardon?"

"Yes! Yes!" the queen exclaims. "Who will join us?"

"Andrew Trollope, and the six hundred trained and loyal men under his command," Richard announces, and steps aside to allow the slim hard-faced man into the royal presence. "And that," Richard says to me, as he comes to stand beside me, "has just decided the battle."

■ ■ ■ ■

Richard is right. As soon as they know that Trollope has turned his coat and come over to us with his men, the three York lords disappear, like mist in the morning. They slip away, overnight, abandoning their men, abandoning their town, even abandoning Cecily Neville, the Duchess of York, the wife of Richard the duke. When our army pours into the town of Ludlow and starts to strip away everything they can carry, she is standing there, with the keys of the castle in her hand, waiting for the queen. She, who has always been a proud woman, married to a royal lord, is most terribly afraid. I can see it on her white face; and I, who had to wait in Mucklestone for their victorious army to sweep by, take no pleasure in seeing such a proud woman brought down so low.

"You have the keys of the castle for me," the queen sings out, looking down on the duchess from high on her great horse.

"Yes, Your Grace," Cecily says steadily. "And I plead for my own safety, and for the safety of these my children."

"Of course," the king says at once. "Sir Richard — take the keys and escort the duchess to a safe place, her children with her. She is under my protection."

"Hold a minute," Margaret says. "What

children are these?"

"This is my daughter, Margaret," Duchess Cecily says. A tall girl of thirteen blushes painfully red and curtseys low to the queen, recovers from her mistake, and curtseys again to the king. "This is my son George, and my youngest boy, Richard."

I would judge George to be about eleven years of age and Richard about seven. They both look stunned with shock, as well they might; for they are boys who yesterday thought their father was heir to the throne of England, likely to fight his way through to the throne, and today find themselves facing the king's army and their father run away. A crash from a house behind us and a piercing scream from a woman, begging for help as she is pulled down and raped, reminds us all that we are in the middle of a war, talking in a battlefield.

"Take them away," the king says quickly.

"And your husband has left you here?" the queen torments the defeated duchess. "Do you remember how you insisted that you be admitted to my chamber when I had just given birth to my baby, and you told me that your husband must visit my husband when he was ill, in the time of our travail? He forced his way into the Privy Council once, but now we see he just ups and goes. He is present where he is not wanted; but when he is needed, he just abandons you. He declares war and then disappears from the battlefield."

The duchess sways on her feet, her face as white as skimmed milk. Smoke drifts across the market square; someone somewhere has fired a thatch. The woman who screamed for help is sobbing in rhythmic pain. I see the little boy Richard look around at the sound of someone smashing an axe into a locked door and the babble of an old voice praying to be spared, calling for mercy to someone who is not listening.

"Your Grace," I say to the queen. "This is no place for any of us. Let us leave the lords to regain control of the men and get out of this town."

To my surprise, she smiles at me, a gleam of malice that shows clearly before she drops her eyes to her horse's mane and hides her expression. "It's a very blunt weapon: an army of uncontrolled men," she says. "When York raised an army against me, he cannot have imagined that I would bring my army against him and that it would be like this. He has taught me a lesson that I have learned well. An army of poor men is a terror indeed. He nearly frightened me. He must be sorry now, now that there is an army of poor men tearing apart his hometown."

The little dark-haired boy Richard flushes in temper, looks up, opens his mouth as if to shout his defiance. "Let's go," I say swiftly, and my husband calls a couple of horses forwards, lifts the duchess into the saddle without ceremony, settles her children in the saddle before three cavalrymen, and we leave the town. As we clatter over the bridge I can hear another woman scream and the noise of running feet. Ludlow is paying the price for the flight of their lord, the Duke of York.

"Yes, but not his death," my son Anthony observes. The three of us are riding home to Grafton together, our men straggling down the road behind us. I observe, but try to make it clear that I have not seen, that they are weighed down with loot; every one of them has some cloth bound tight in his pack, or a piece of plate, or a cup of pewter. They were our tenants, but we put them in the queen's army and they fought by her rules. They were told that they might loot Ludlow to punish the treasonous York lords, and we will never muster them to ride out for us again if we spoil their sport and demand that they hand back the goods they have thieved. "While York lives, while Warwick lives, while Salisbury lives, the wars are not over; they are only put off for a little while longer."

Richard nods. "Warwick is back in Calais, Richard, Duke of York, back in Ireland. The kingdom's greatest enemies have returned to refuge, safe in their castles overseas. We will have to prepare for an invasion again."

"The queen is confident," I say.

The queen is tremendously confident. November comes, and still she does not return to London, hating London and blaming the London ballad makers and chap-book sellers for her unpopularity in the kingdom. Their tales and songs describe her as a wolf, a she-wolf who commands a Fisher King — a man reduced to a shell of what he should be. The most bawdy rhymes say she cuckolded him with a bold duke and popped their bastard in the royal cradle. There is a drawing of a swan with the face of Edmund Beaufort, waddling towards the throne. There are songs and alehouse jokes about her. She hates London and the apprentices who laugh at her.

Instead, she orders the Parliament to come to Coventry — as if Parliaments can be ordered by a woman like outriders — and they obediently come as if they were her messengers, bound to do her bidding when she orders new oaths of loyalty to the king but also to her by name, and to the prince. Nobody has ever sworn loyalty to a queen before — but they do now. She cites the three York lords for treason, takes their lands and fortunes, and hands them out as if it were all the twelve days of Christmas come early. She orders the Duchess Cecily to attend so that she can hear her husband named as a traitor, and listen to the death sentence passed on him. Everything the York lords owned, every rood of land, every banner, every honor and title, every purse of gold, is stripped from them. The poor Duchess of York, now a royal pensioner and a pauper, goes to live with her sister, the queen's loyal lady, Anne, the Duchess of Buckingham, in something between house arrest and torment; a half-life for a woman who was once called "Proud Cis" and now finds herself a married woman with a husband in exile, a mother missing her oldest son, Edward, the daughter of a great house who has lost all her lands and her inheritance.

Sandwich, Kent, and Calais, Winter 1460

Richard is ill-paid for warning the queen that the Warwick ownership of Calais has put an enemy on our shoreline, for as soon as the fighting is done and the peace won, she asks him to go to Sandwich and reinforce the town against attack.

"I'll come too," I say at once. "I can't bear you to be in danger and me far away. I can't bear for us to be parted again."

"I'm not going to be in danger," he lies to reassure me, and then, catching my skeptical expression, he giggles like a boy caught out in a blatant falsehood. "All right, Jacquetta, don't look at me like that. But if there is any danger of an invasion from Calais, you will have to go home to Grafton. I'll take Anthony with me."

I nod. It's useless to suggest that Anthony is too precious to be exposed to danger. He is a young man born into a country constantly at war with itself. Another young man, of just his age, is Edward March, the Duke of York's son, across the narrow seas, serving his apprenticeship in soldiering with the Earls of Warwick and Salisbury. His mother, the Duchess of York, held in England, will not be able to get a word to him. She will have to wait and worry, as I wait and worry. This is not a time when mothers can hope to keep their sons safe at home.

Richard and I take a house in the port of Sandwich, while Anthony commands the men at Richborough Fort nearby. The town has still not recovered from the French raid of only a few years ago, and the burned-out shells of houses are a vivid statement of the danger from our enemies, and the narrowness of the seas between us. The town defenses were destroyed in the raid; the French fired cannon at the sea walls and captured the town's own armament. They mocked the citizens, playing tennis in the market square as if to say that they cared nothing for Englishmen, that they thought us powerless. Richard sets builders to work, begs the armorer at the Tower of London to cast new cannon for the town, and starts to train the townsmen to form a guard. Meanwhile, just a mile away, Anthony drills our men and rebuilds the defenses of the old Roman castle that guard the river entrance.

We have been in the town little more than a week when I am suddenly frightened from sleep by the loud clanging of the tocsin bell.

For a moment I think it is the goose bell that rings in the darkness of five o'clock every morning, to wake the goose girls, but then I realize that the loud constant clanging of the bell means a raid.

Richard is out of bed already, pulling on his leather jerkin and snatching up his helmet and his sword.

"What is it? What is happening?" I shout at him.

"God knows," he says. "You stay safe in here. Go to the kitchen and wait for news. If Warwick has landed from Calais, get down into the cellar and bolt yourself in."

He is out of the door before he can say more, and then I hear the front door bang and a yelling from the street, and the clash of sword on sword. "Richard!" I shout, and swing open the little window to look down into the cobbled street below.

My husband is unconscious, a man has hold of him and is in the act of dropping his body to the cobblestones. He looks up and sees me. "Come down, Lady Rivers," he says. "You cannot hide or run."

I close the casement window. My maid appears in the doorway, shaking with fear. "They have the master; he looks as if he is dead. I think they have killed him."

"I know," I say. "I saw. Get my gown."

She holds the gown for me, and I step into it, let her tie the laces, and then put on my slippers and go downstairs, my hair in its nighttime plait. I pull up the hood of my cape as I step out into the icy-cold January street. I look around, but all I can see, as if engraved on my eyelids, is the man lowering Richard to the ground, and the fall of Richard's limp hand. At the end of the street I can make out half a dozen guardsmen struggling with a man. A glimpse of his face, as he looks desperately towards me, shows me Anthony. They are taking him on board ship.

"What are you doing with my son? That is my son — release him."

The man does not even bother to answer me, and I run across the slippery cobbles to where they have left Richard on the ground, like a dead man. As I reach him he stirs and opens his dark blue eyes; he looks dazed. "Jacquetta," he says.

"My love. Are you hurt?" I am dreading him saying that he has been stabbed.

"A cracked head. I'll live."

A man roughly takes him under the shoulders. "Carry him into our house," I order.

"I'm taking him on board," the man says simply. "You're to come too."

"Where d'you think you are taking us? On whose authority? This is not an act of war; it is a crime!"

He ignores me. One man takes Richard's boots, another his shoulders; they lug him like a carcass. "You may not take him," I

641

insist. "He is a lord of the realm, under the command of the king. This is rebellion."

I put my hand on the man's arm, but he simply ignores me and lugs Richard down to the quayside. Behind me, all around me, I can hear men shouting and women screaming as the soldiers go through the town, taking what they want, throwing open doors and banging the precious glass out of windows.

"Where do you think you are taking my husband?"

"Calais," he says shortly.

It's a quick voyage. Richard recovers his senses; they give us clean water and something to eat. Anthony is unhurt. We are locked in a little cabin at first and then, once the ship is at sea and the great sail unfurled and creaking, they let us out on deck. For a little while we cannot see any land; England is lost behind us, but then we see a dark line ahead of us on the horizon, and as we watch we can see the squat mound of the city and, on its crest, the round walls of the castle. I realize I am returning to Calais under guard, as a hostage, to the town that I once entered as a duchess.

I glance at Richard and see that he remembers this too. This is an outpost that was under his command. He was the Captain of Calais; now he is a prisoner. This is the turn of fortune's wheel indeed.

"Take care," he says quietly to me and to our son. "They shouldn't harm you, Jacquetta; they know you, and they like you. And they don't make war on women. But the queen's treatment of the Duchess of York will have angered them, and we are quite in their power. No one is going to rescue us. We will have to get out of this alive, by our own wits. We are quite alone."

"The Duke of Somerset holds Guisnes Castle; he might come for us," Anthony suggests.

"Won't get within half a mile," my husband says. "I have fortified this town, son, I know its strengths. Nobody will take it by force this century. So we are hostages in enemy hands. They have every reason to spare you, Jacquetta, and many a good reason to kill me."

"They can't kill you," I say. "You have done nothing wrong but be loyal to the king from the day you were born."

"That's why I'm the very man they should kill," he says. "It will fill the others with fear. So I am going to mind my manners and speak gently, and if I have to swear to give up my sword to save my life, I will do that. And" — he addresses Anthony, who flings himself aside with an impatient word — "so will you. If they ask for our parole and for our promise that we never take arms against them, we will give that too. We have no choice. We are defeated. And I don't plan to be beheaded on the gallows that I built here. I don't plan to be buried in the cemetery that I tidied and cleared. Do you understand?"

"I do," Anthony says shortly. "But how could we have let ourselves be taken!"

"What's done is done," Richard says sternly. "These are the fortunes of war. All we have to think about now is how to get out of this alive. And we are going to do this by speaking sweetly, biding our time, and keeping out of a rage. More than anything, my son, I want you to be polite, surrender if you have to, and come out of this alive."

They keep us on the ship till nightfall; they do not want Richard paraded through the town and seen by the people. The influential merchants of Calais love him for defending them when the castle was claimed by York. The men of the town remember him as a loyal and brave captain of the castle, whose word was law and could be trusted like gold. The troop of Calais love him as a firm and just commander. It was the experience of serving under Richard that persuaded the six hundred men to change sides at Ludlow, and support the king. Any troop that has been commanded by him will follow him to hell and back. Warwick does not want this most popular captain to appeal to the people as he goes through the town.

So they wait till late at night and bring us

like secret captives into the great hall of the castle under cover of darkness, and the sudden blaze of torches is blindingly bright after the black streets outside. They bring us through the gateway, under the stone arch and then into the great hall with blazing fires at either end and the men of the garrison at the trestle tables, uneasy at the sight of us.

The three of us stand, like penniless runaways from a war, and look around the great hall, the vaulted ceiling with the smoke-blackened beams, the torches ablaze in the sconces all round, some men standing, drinking ale, some seated at dining trestle tables, and some rising to their feet at the sight of my husband and pulling off their caps. At the top of the hall, the Earl of Salisbury, his son the Earl of Warwick, and the young Edward, Earl of March, son of Richard, Duke of York, sit at the head table, raised on the dais, the white rose of York on a banner behind them.

"We have taken you as prisoners of war and will consider your parole," the Earl of Warwick starts, solemn as a judge from his seat at the head table.

"It was not an act of war, since I am under the command of the King of England; an act against me is an act of rebellion and treason against my king," Richard says, his deep voice very strong and loud in the hall. The men stiffen at the note of absolute defiance. "And I warn you that anyone who lays a hand on me, on my son, or on my wife, is guilty of rebellion and treason and illegal assault. Anyone who harms my wife is, of course, not worthy of his spurs nor of his name. If you make war on a woman, you are no better than a savage and should be thrown down like one. Your name will be defamed forever. I would pity a man who insulted my wife, a royal duchess and an heiress of the House of Luxembourg. Her name and her reputation must protect her wherever she goes. My son is under my protection and under hers, a loyal subject of an ordained king. We three are all loyal subjects of the king and should be free to go our own ways. I demand safe passage to England for the three of us. In the name of the King of England, I demand it."

"So much for the soft answer that turneth away wrath," Anthony says quietly to me. "So much for surrender and parole. My God, look at Salisbury's face!"

The old earl looks likely to explode. "You!" he bellows. "You dare to speak to me like this?"

The York lords are seated high on the dais and Richard has to look up at them. They rise from their chairs and glower down at him. He is utterly unrepentant. He walks towards the stage, and stands, his hands on his hips. "Aye. Of course. Why not?"

"You don't even deserve to be in our company! You have no right even to speak without being spoken to. We are of the blood royal, and you are a nobody."

"I am a peer of England, and I have served under my king in France and Calais and England, and never disobeyed him or betrayed him," Richard says very loudly and clearly.

"Unlike them," Anthony supplements gleefully to me.

"You are an upstart nobody, the son of a groom of the household," Warwick shouts. "A nothing. You wouldn't even be here if it was not for your marriage."

"The duchess demeaned herself," young Edward of March says. I see Anthony stiffen at the insult from a youth of his own age. "She lowered herself to you, and you raised yourself only by her. They say she is a witch who inspired you to the sin of lust."

"Before God, this is unbearable," Anthony swears. He plunges forwards, and I snatch at his arm.

"Don't you dare move, or I will stab you myself!" I say furiously. "Don't you dare say a thing or do a thing. Stand still, boy!"

"What?"

"You are not fit to come among us," Salisbury says. "You are not fit to keep company."

"I see what they are doing; they're hoping you will lose your temper," I tell him. "They are hoping you will attack them and then they can cut you down. Remember what your father said. Stay calm."

"They insult you!" Anthony is sweating with rage.

"Look at me!" I demand.

He darts a fierce glance at me and then hesitates. Despite my hasty words to him, my face is utterly calm. I am smiling. "I was not the woman left in Ludlow marketplace when my husband ran away," I say to him in a rapid whisper. "I was the daughter of the Count of Luxembourg when Cecily Neville was nothing more than a pretty girl in a northern castle. I am the descendant of the goddess Melusina. You are my son. We come from a line of nobles who trace their line back to a goddess. They can say what they like behind my back; they can say it to my face. I know who I am. I know what you were born to be. And it is more, far more, than they."

Anthony hesitates. "Smile," I command him.

"What?"

"Smile at them."

He raises his head; he can hardly twist his face into a smile, but he does it.

"You have no pride!" Edward of March spits at him. "There is nothing here to smile at!"

Anthony inclines his head slightly, as if accepting a great compliment.

"You let me speak like this of your own mother? Before her very face?" Edward demands, his voice cracking with rage. "Do you have no pride?"

"My mother does not need your good opinion," Anthony says icily. "None of us care what you think."

"*Your* own mother is well," I say to Edward gently. "She was very distressed at Ludlow, to be left on her own in such danger, but my husband, Lord Rivers, took her and your sister Margaret and your brothers George and Richard to safety. My husband, Lord Rivers, protected them when the army was running through the town. He made sure that no one insulted them. The king is paying her a pension, and she is in no hardship. I saw her myself a little while ago, and she told me she prays for you and for your father."

It shocks him into silence. "You have my husband to thank for her safety," I repeat.

"He is baseborn," Edward says, as someone repeating a lesson by rote.

I shrug my shoulders, as if it is nothing to me. Indeed, it is nothing to me. "We are in your keeping," I say simply. "Base or noble. And you have no cause to complain of us. Will you give us safe passage to England?"

"Take them away," the Earl of Salisbury snaps.

"I would like my usual rooms," Richard says. "I was captain of this castle for more than four years, and I kept it safe for England. I usually have the rooms that look over the harbor."

The Earl of Warwick curses like a tavern owner.

"Take them away," Salisbury repeats.

We don't have the rooms of the Captain of the Castle, of course, but we have good ones looking over the inner courtyard. They keep us only for a couple of nights, and then a guard comes to the door and says that I am to be taken by ship to London.

"What about us?" my husband demands.

"You're hostages," the soldier says. "You're to wait here."

"They are to be held with honor? They are safe?" I insist.

He nods to Richard. "I served under you, sir. I'm Abel Stride."

"I remember you, Stride," my husband says. "What's the plan?"

"My orders are to hold you here until we move out, and then to release you, unhurt," he says. "And I'll obey them, and no others." He hesitates. "There's not a man in the garrison would harm you, sir, nor your son. My word on it."

"Thank you," my husband says. To me, he whispers: "Go to the queen; tell her they are preparing to invade. Try to see how many ships you can count in the pool. Tell her I don't think they have many men, perhaps only two thousand or so."

"And you?"

"You heard him. I'll get home when I can. God bless you, beloved."

I kiss him. I turn to my son, who goes down on his knee for my blessing and then comes up to hug me. I know he is broad and strong and a good fighter, but to leave him in danger is almost unbearable.

"Your Grace, you have to come now," the guard says.

I have to leave them both. I don't know how I get up the gangplank of the merchant ship or into the little cabin. But I have to leave them both.

Coventry,
Spring 1460

The court is in Coventry, readying for war, when I arrive in England and take the queen the news that our enemies in Calais are holding my husband and son, and that they are certain to invade this year.

"Jacquetta, I am so sorry," Margaret says to me. "I had no idea. I would never have put you in danger like that . . . when they told me that you had been captured, I was beside myself." She glances around and whispers to me. "I wrote to Pierre de Brézé, the Seneschal of Normandy, and asked him to take Calais and rescue you. You know what would happen to me if anyone found out I am writing to him. But you are this important to me."

"I was never in any great danger," I say. "But the rebel lords taunted Richard and Anthony, and I think if they could have killed them in a brawl they would have done so."

"I hate them," she says simply. "Warwick and his father, York and his son. They are my enemies till death. You know the rumors they are spreading now?"

I nod. They have spoken slander against this queen from the moment she arrived in England.

"They are openly saying that my son is a bastard, that the king knew nothing about his birth and christening and also — nothing about his conception. They think to disinherit him with slander, since they cannot hurt him by war."

"Do you have news of the Yorkist lords?"

"They have met," she says shortly. "I have spies at York's little court in Ireland, and they tell me. Warwick went to meet the Duke of York in his castle in Ireland. We know that they met; we can guess they plan to invade. We cannot know when for sure."

"And are you ready for an invasion?"

She nods grimly. "The king has been ill again — oh, not very ill — but he has lost interest in everything but praying. He has been at prayer for all of this week and sleeping, sometimes as much as sixteen hours a day." She breaks off. "I never know if he is here or if he has gone. But, at any rate, I am ready; I am ready for anything. I have the troops, I have the lords, I have the country on my side — all but the perfidious people of Kent and the guttersnipes of London."

"When, do you think?" I do not really need to ask. All campaigns start in the summer season. It cannot be long before they bring the news that York is on the march from Ireland, and Warwick has set sail from Calais.

"I'll go and see my children," I say. "They will be anxious about their father and their brother."

"And then come back," she says. "I need you with me, Jacquetta."

NORTHAMPTON, SUMMER 1460

In June, in the richest greenest easiest month of the year, the York lords make their move from Calais, and Richard, the Duke of York, bides his time in Ireland, letting them do his dirty work for him. They land, as my husband predicted, with only a small force of about two thousand, but as they march, their ranks are swelled with men who run out of the fields and from the stable yards to join them. Kent has not forgotten Jack Cade or the harvest of heads, and there are many who march out for Warwick now, who remember the queen swearing that she would make a deer park of their home. London throws the city gates open to Warwick and poor Lord Scales finds himself once again alone in the Tower, with orders to hold it for the king, whatever the cost. The York lords do not even trouble themselves to starve him out; they leave Lord Cobham in charge of the city and march north, to Kenilworth, looking for their enemy: us.

Every day they add recruits; everywhere they go men flock to join them. Their army swells, and they grow stronger; they pay wages with money voted to them by the towns that they march by. The mood of the country has swung against the queen and her puppet king. The people want a leader they can trust to hold the country to peace and justice. They have come to think that Richard, Duke of York, will be their protector, and they fear the queen for the danger and uncertainty that comes in her train.

The queen makes the Duke of Buckingham the commander of the king's armies, and the king is taken out of his monastic retreat to fly the royal standard, which flaps miserably in the wet weather. But this time, nobody deserts before a blow is struck because they cannot bear to attack the king's personal flag. No powerful troop abandons the cause of the York lords. Everyone is becoming hardened. The king sits quietly in his tent below his standard, and the peacemakers — among them the Bishop of Salisbury — go to and fro all morning, hoping to broker a settlement. It cannot be done. The York lords send personal messages to the king, but the Duke of Buckingham intercepts them. They will settle for nothing less than the queen and her advisors banned from their influential place beside the king; they will trust nothing else. And the queen will not compromise. She wants to see them dead: it is as simple as that. There are really no grounds for parlay at all.

The royal army is before Delapre Abbey at Northampton, dug in before the River Nene with sharp staves set in the ground in front of them. No cavalry charge can take them here, no head-on attack can possibly succeed. The queen, the prince, and I are waiting at Eccleshall Castle again.

"I almost want to ride out and watch," she says to me.

I try to laugh. "Not again."

It is raining now, and it has been raining for the last two days. We stand together at the window looking out at the lowering gray skies with the dark clouds on the horizon. Below us, in the courtyard, we can see the bustle of messengers arriving from the battlefield. "Let's go down," says Margaret, suddenly nervous.

We meet them in the great hall as they are coming in, dripping wet.

"It's over," the man says to the queen. "You told me to come the moment that I could see which way it was going, and so I waited for a while and then I came."

"Have we won?" she asks urgently.

He makes a grimace. "We are destroyed," he says bluntly. "Betrayed."

She hisses like a cat. "Who betrayed us? Who was it? Stanley?"

"Grey of Ruthin."

She rounds on me. "Your daughter's kinsman! Your daughter's family are unfaithful?"

"A distant relation," I say at once. "What did he do?"

"He waited till York's son, the young Edward of March, charged him. Our line was well protected; we had the river behind us and a ditch before us fortified with sharp staves, but when the York boy came up at the head of his men, Lord Grey put down his sword and just helped him over the barricades with all his troop, and then they fought their way down our own lines. They were inside our lines; our men couldn't get away from them. We were perfectly placed when we started, then we found we were perfectly trapped."

She goes white and staggers. I hold her by the waist, and she leans against me. "The king?"

"I went as they were fighting their way towards his tent. His lords were outside, covering his retreat; they were shouting to him to get away."

"Did he go?"

The darkness of his face tells us that he did not, and perhaps the lords gave their lives for nothing. "I didn't see. I came to warn you. The battle is lost. You had better get yourself away. I think they may have the king."

She turns to me. "Get the prince," she says.

Without a word I hurry to the royal nurseries and find the boy in his traveling cape and riding breeches, his toys and books packed. His governor stands beside him. "Her Grace, the queen, commands that her son shall come at once," I say.

The man turns gravely to the six-year-old boy. "You are ready, Your Grace?"

"I am ready. I am ready now," the little prince says bravely.

I hold out my hand, but he does not take it. Instead, he walks ahead of me and stands before the door, waiting for me to open it for him. At another time this would be amusing. Not today: "Oh, go on!" I say impatiently, and open the door and bustle him through.

In the great hall the queen's jewel boxes and chests of clothes are being rushed through the door to the stables. The queen is outside; her guard is mounting up. She pulls her hood over her head and nods at her son as he comes out with me.

"Get on your horse; we have to hurry," she says. "The bad York lords have won and perhaps captured your father. We have to get you to safety. You are our only hope."

"I know," he says gravely, and steps up on the mounting block as they bring his horse to him.

To me, she says: "Jacquetta, I will send for you as soon as I am safe."

My head is whirling at the speed of this rout. "Where are you going?"

"To Jasper Tudor in Wales to start with. If we can invade from there, I will, if not France, or Scotland. I will win back my son's inheritance, this is just a setback."

She leans down from her saddle, and I kiss her and smooth her hair under the hood. "Godspeed," I say. I try to blink the tears from my eyes, but I can hardly bear to see her fleeing, with her baggage and her guard and her little son, from the country that I brought her to with such hopes. "Godspeed."

I stand in the courtyard as the small train walks to the road and then sets off, at a steady canter, due west. She will be safe if she can get to Jasper Tudor; he is a faithful man, and he has been fighting for his lands in Wales ever since she gave them to him. But if they catch her on the way? I shudder. If they catch her on the way, then she and the House of Lancaster are lost.

I turn to the stable yard. The grooms are carrying away everything they can take; the looting of the royal goods is beginning. I shout for one of my men and tell him to pack up everything that is mine and guard it. We are leaving at once. We will go home to Grafton, and all I can do is hope that Richard and Anthony come there.

GRAFTON, NORTHAMPTONSHIRE, SUMMER 1460

It is a weary ride to Grafton, a long journey of nearly a hundred miles, through country-side that is loyal to Warwick the invader. At every stop there is a panic-stricken exchange of news: What do we know? What have we seen? And always — is the queen bringing her army this way? I order my men to give out that I am a widow traveling privately on a pilgrimage, and we stay at an abbey for one night, and a church house the second, and on the third we bed down in a barn, always avoiding the inns. Even so, the gossip that is swirling around the country comes to me every evening. They say that the king has been taken to London and that Richard, Duke of York, has landed from Ireland and is proceeding in royal state to the capital city. Some say that when he gets there, he will become protector and regent once more; some say that he will rule the king from behind the throne, the king will be his little doll, his moppet. I say nothing. I wonder if the queen has got safely to Wales, and I wonder if I will ever see my husband or my son again.

It takes us four days to get home, and as we turn up the familiar track to the house I feel my heart lift. At least I shall see my children and stay with them safely and quietly here while the great changes in the country take place without me. At least I can find a refuge here. As we ride up, I hear someone start tolling the bell in the stable yard, to warn the household of the arrival of an armed troop, ourselves. The front door opens, and the men-at-arms spill out of the house. At their head — I could not mistake him, for I would know him anywhere — is my husband, Richard.

He sees me in the same moment and comes bounding down the steps at the front of the house, so fast that my horse shies and I have to hold her still as he pulls me from the saddle and into his arms. He kisses my face, and I cling to him. "You're alive!" I say. "You're alive!"

"They let us go as soon as they had made landfall themselves," he says. "Didn't even take a ransom. They just released us from the castle at Calais, and then I had to find a ship to bring us home. Took us into Greenwich."

"Anthony is with you?"

"Of course. Safe and sound."

I twist in his arms to see my son, smiling at

me from the doorway. Richard releases me, and I run to Anthony as he kneels for my blessing. To feel his warm head under my hand is to know that the greatest joy of my life is restored to me. I turn back to my husband and wrap my arms around Richard once more.

"Have you news?"

"The York lords win all," Richard says shortly. "London greeted them like heroes, Lord Scales tried to get away from the Tower and was killed, and the Duke of York is making his way to London. I think they'll appoint him protector. The king is safe in the Palace of Westminster, completely under the rule of Warwick. They say his wits are gone again. What of the queen?"

I glance around, even on the terrace of my own manor house I am afraid that someone will hear where she is, and betray her. "Gone to Jasper Tudor," I whisper. "And from there to France or Scotland, I should think."

Richard nods. "Come in," he says gently to me. "You must be weary. You weren't near the battle, were you? You had no danger on the roads?"

I lean against him and feel the familiar sense of relief that he is by my side. "I feel safe now, at any rate," I say.

GRAFTON, NORTHAMPTONSHIRE, WINTER 1460–61

We live, as we did when we were first married, as if we had no work to do but to keep the lands around Grafton, as if we were nothing but a squire and his wife. We don't want the attention of the York lords as they make the country their own, impose massive fines on the lords they now call traitors, take posts and fees from the men they have defeated. There is a greed here, and a thirst for revenge, and all I want is for it to pass us by. We live quietly and hope to escape notice. We hear, in snatches of gossip from travelers who ask for a bed for the night, and occasional visitors, that the king is living quietly at Westminster Palace in the queen's rooms while his conquering cousin, Richard, Duke of York, has taken up residence in the king's own apartments. I think of my king in the rooms that I knew so well, and I pray that he does not slide into sleep again to escape a waking world that is so hard on him.

The duke forges an extraordinary agreement with the Privy Council and the Parliament: he will be regent and protector of the realm until the death of the king, and then he will become king himself. A pedlar, who comes by with York ribbons of white and white roses of silk in his pack, says that the king has agreed to this and is going to take vows and become a monk.

"He's not in the Tower?" I ask urgently. I have a horror of the king being sent to the Tower.

"No, he is living freely as a fool at the court," he says. "And York will be the next king."

"The queen will never consent to it," I say incautiously.

"She's in Scotland, so they say," he replies, spreading his goods before me. "Good riddance. Let her stay there, I say. D'you want some pepper? I have some pepper and a nutmeg so fresh that you could eat it whole."

"In Scotland?"

"They say she is meeting with the Scottish queen, and they are going to bring an army of harpies down on us," he says cheerfully. "An army of women — think of that as a horror! A nice little polished mirror here? Or look, some hairnets of gold thread. That's real gold, that is."

We celebrate Christmas at Grafton. Elizabeth comes to stay with her husband, Sir John, and their two boys: Thomas is five years old now, and Richard just two. All my children come home for the twelve days of the feast, and the house is alive with their singing and dancing and chasing each other up and down the wooden staircase. For the six youngest children, from Katherine, who at two, can only toddle after her bigger siblings, imploring them not to leave her behind, through Edward, Margaret, Lionel, Eleanor, and Martha, the oldest of the nursery at ten years, the return of their older brothers and sisters is like an explosion of noise and excitement. Richard and John are inseparable, young men of fourteen and fifteen years, Jacquetta and Mary are thoughtful young women, placed in the houses of neighbors in these difficult times. Anthony and Anne are the oldest of course. Anne should be married by now, but what can I do when the whole country is turned upside down and there is not even a court for her to join as a maid-in-waiting? And how am I to find Anthony the bride he should have when I cannot tell who will be wealthy and in the favor of the king next month — let alone ten years from now? There is a promise between him and the daughter of Lord Scales, but Lord Scales is dead and his family disgraced like us. And finally, and most puzzling for me, who should be planning matches for my children and looking around for the great houses where they should be placed to learn the skills they need: How can I know which will stay loyal to Lancaster, when the House of Lancaster is a king living in the queen's rooms, an absent queen, and a boy of seven? And I cannot yet bring myself to consider an alliance with anyone who serves the traitorous House of York.

I think I will keep all the children at home with us at Grafton till the spring, perhaps longer. There can be no positions for us at the new royal household, which will be the York court — since there are now York placemen and lords and members of Parliament I assume that soon there will be York courtiers and ladies-in-waiting. Cecily Neville, the Duchess of York, riding high on fortune's wheel, is sleeping in the king's apartments under a canopy of cloth of gold like a queen herself; she must think that every day is Christmas. Clearly, we can never attend a York court: I doubt that any of us will ever forgive or forget the humiliation in the great hall at Calais Castle. Perhaps we will learn to be exiles in our own lands. Perhaps I shall now, at the age of forty-five, with my last child learning to talk, live in a country that is like that of my childhood: with one king in the north of the kingdom and one in the south, and everyone forced to choose which they think is the true one, and everyone knowing their enemy, and everyone waiting for revenge.

I really despair of organizing the future of our family in such a world, at such a time, and instead I take comfort in the future of our lands. I start to plan to enlarge our orchard and go to a farm near Northampton where I can buy some whips of trees. Richard tells me that the seas are safe for shipping, and he will get better prices for the wool from his sheep this year in the market at Calais. The roads are safe to and from London, the Duke of York is restoring the powers of the sheriffs and commanding them to see that justice is done in every county. Slowly, the counties are starting to rid themselves of bandits and thieves on the highway. We never admit it, not even to each other, but these are great improvements. We start to think, never saying it out loud, that perhaps we can live like this, as country landowners in a country at peace. Perhaps we can grow an orchard, farm our sheep, watch our children come to adulthood without the fear of treachery and war. Perhaps Richard, Duke of York, has thrown us down from the court but given us peace in the country.

Then, at the end of January, I see three riders come splashing down the lane, their horses' hooves cracking the ice in the puddles. I see them from the nursery window, where I am watching Katherine as she sleeps, and I know at once that they are bringing us bad news, and that these cold winter months of stillness are over. It was not a peace at all; it was just the usual winter break in a war that goes on and on forever. A war that will go on and on forever until everyone is dead. For a brief moment I even think that I will close the shutters on the windows and sit in the nursery and pretend that I am not here. I will not have to respond to a call that I don't hear. But it is only a moment. I know that if I am summoned, I have to go. I have served Lancaster for all my life; I cannot fail now.

I bend over the little crib and kiss Katherine on her warm smooth baby forehead, and then I leave the nursery and close the door quietly behind me. I walk slowly down the stairs, looking over the wooden banister as down below Richard throws a cape around his shoulders, picks up his sword, and goes out to see the visitors. I wait inside the great hall, listening.

"Sir Richard Woodville, Lord Rivers?" says the first man.

"Who wants him?"

The man lowers his voice. "The Queen of England. Do you answer to her? Are you faithful still?"

"Aye," Richard says shortly.

"I have this for you," the man says, and proffers a letter.

Through the crack in the doorway I see Richard take it. "Go round the back to the stables," he says. "They'll see you have food and ale. It's a cold day. Go into the hall and warm yourselves. This is a loyal house, but there is no need to tell anyone where you come from."

The men salute in thanks, and Richard comes into the entrance hall, breaking the seal.

"Greetings, well beloved . . ." he starts to read, and then breaks off. "It's a standard letter; she has probably sent out hundreds. It's a summons."

"To arms?" I can taste my own fear.

"Anthony and me. We're to go to York, she's mustering there."

"Will you go?" Almost, I want to ask him to refuse.

"I have to. This may be the last chance for her." He is reading down the letter, and he gives a long low whistle. "Good God! Her men have taken Richard, Duke of York, and killed him." He looks up at me, clenches the letter in his fist. "My God! Who would have thought it? The protector dead! She has won!"

"How?" I cannot believe this sudden leap to victory. "What are you saying?"

"She just writes he rode out from his castle, that must be Sandal — why would he ever do that? You could hold that place for a month! And that they cut him down. Good God, I can't believe it. Jacquetta, this is the end of the York campaign. This is the end of the Yorks. Richard of York dead! And his son alongside him."

I gasp as if his death is a loss to me. "Not young Edward! Not Edward of March!"

"No, his other son, Edmund. Edward of March is in Wales somewhere, but he can do nothing now his father is dead. They are finished. The Yorks are defeated." He turns the letter over. "Oh, look, she's written a note at the end of the letter. She says: 'Dear Sir Richard, come at once, the tide is turning for me. We have crowned Richard of York with a paper crown and set his head on a spike at the Micklegate. Soon we will put Warwick's face up beside him, and everything will be as it should be again.' " He puts the letter into my hand. "This changes everything. Would you believe it? Our queen has won; our king is restored."

"Richard of York is dead?" I read the letter for myself.

"Now she can beat Warwick," he says. "Without the alliance with York he's a dead man. He's lost the regent and lord protector; it's all over for them. They have no one who can pretend to be heir to the throne. Nobody would ever have Warwick as lord protector; he has no claim to the throne at all. The king is the only man who can be king, once more. The House of York is finished; we have only the House of Lancaster. They have made a mistake that has cost them everything." He gives a whistle and takes the letter back. "Talk about fortune's wheel, they are thrown down to nothing."

I go to his side and look over his shoulder at the queen's familiar scrawl on the clerk's letter. In one corner she has written: *Jacquetta, come to me at once.*

"When do we leave?" I ask. I am ashamed at my own reluctance to hear this call to arms.

"We'll have to go now," he says.

We take the great north road to York, certain that the queen's army will be marching down to London, and we will meet them on the way. At every stop during the cold days, at every night in inns or abbeys, or the great houses, people are talking about the queen's army as if it were an invading force of foreigners, as if it were a source of terror. They say that she has soldiers from Scotland and that they march barefoot over stones, their chests naked even in the worst of weather. They are afraid of nothing and they eat their meat raw; they will run down the cattle in the fields and gouge flesh from their flanks with their bare hands. She has no money to pay them, and she has promised them that they can have anything they can carry if they will take her to London and rip out the heart of the Earl of Warwick.

They say that she has given the country to the King of France in return for his support.

He will sail his fleet up the Thames and lay waste to London; he will claim every port on the south coast. She has already signed over Calais to him; she has sold Berwick and Carlisle to the Scots queen. Newcastle will be the new line of the frontier, the North is lost to us forever, and Cecily Neville, the York widow, will be a Scots peasant.

There is no point trying to argue with this mixture of terror and truth. The queen, a woman in armor, leading her own army, with a son conceived by a sleeping husband, a woman who uses alchemy and possibly the dark arts, a French princess in alliance with our enemies has become an object of utter horror to the people of her country. With the Scots behind her, she has become a winter queen, one who comes out of the darkness of the North like a wolf.

We stop for two nights at Groby Hall to see Elizabeth and meet with her husband, Sir John Grey, who has mustered his men and will march north with us. Elizabeth is strained and unhappy.

"I can't bear waiting for news," she says. "Send to me as soon as you can. I can't bear the waiting. I wish you didn't have to go out again."

"I wish it too," I say softly to her. "I've never ridden out with such a heavy heart. I am tired of war."

"Can't you refuse to go?"

I shake my head. "She is my queen, and she is my friend. If I did not go for duty, I would go for love of her. But what about you, Elizabeth? Do you want to go and stay with the children at Grafton while we are away?"

She makes a little grimace. "My place is here," she says. "And Lady Grey would not like me to be away. I am just so fearful for John."

I put my hand on her restless fingers. "You have to be calm. I know it is difficult, but you have to be calm and hope for the best. Your father has been out to battle a dozen times, and each time it is as bad as the first — but each time he has come home to me."

She catches my hand. "What do you see?" she asks me very quietly. "What do you see for John? It is him I fear for, much more even than Anthony or Father."

I shake my head. "I can't foretell," I say. "I feel as if I am waiting for a sign, as if we all are. Who would have thought that we brought Margaret of Anjou, that pretty girl, to England for this?"

On the March,
Spring 1461

We ride as a small troop, my son-in-law John, Richard, Anthony, and me at the head of our tenants and household men. We can go no faster than their marching pace, and the road is flooded in some parts. As we get farther and farther north it starts to snow. I think of the signs that my lord John, Duke of Bedford, asked me to see; I remember a vision of a battle in snow, which ended in blood, and I wonder if we are riding towards it.

Finally, on the third day, the scout that Richard has sent ahead comes cantering back and says that all the country people have bolted their doors and shutters because they believe that the queen's army is a day's march away. Richard calls a halt, and we go to a manor farm to ask for a bed for the night and a barn where our men can sleep. The place is deserted, they have locked the door and abandoned the house. They would rather take to the hills than welcome the true Queen of England. We break in and forage for food, light the fire, and order the men to stay in the barn and the yard and to steal nothing. But everything valuable has been taken away and hidden already. Whoever lived here feared the queen as a thief in the night. They left nothing for the queen and her army; they would certainly never fight for her. She has become an enemy to her own people.

At dawn the next day, we understand why. There is a great hammering on the front door, and as I get out of bed there is a wild face glowering at the window, and in a moment the little pane of glass is smashed and a man is in the room, another coming through the window behind him, a knife in his teeth. I scream "Richard!" and snatch up my knife and face them. "I am the Duchess of Bedford, friend to the queen," I shout.

The man says something in reply; I cannot understand a word of it. "I am of the House of Lancaster!" I say again. I try in French: *"Je suis la duchesse de Bedford."*

"Get ready to stand aside," Richard says quietly behind me. "Jump to your right when I say . . . Now."

I fling myself to the right as he lunges forwards, and the man folds over Richard's sword with a terrible gurgle. Blood gushes from his mouth; he staggers, hands out towards me, as he falls to the floor, groaning terribly. Richard puts his booted foot on the man's belly and pulls out his sword; there is a flood of scarlet blood, and the man screams in pain. His comrade disappears out through the window as Richard bends down with his dagger and quickly cuts the man's throat as he would slaughter a pig.

There is a silence.

"Are you all right?" Richard asks, wiping his sword and dagger on the curtains of the bed.

I feel the vomit rising in my throat. I gag, and I put my hand over my mouth and run to the door.

"Do it there," Richard says, pointing to the fireplace. "I don't know if the house is safe."

I retch into the fireplace, the smell of my vomit mingling with the smell of hot blood, and Richard pats my back. "I've got to see what's happening outside. Lock yourself in here and bolt the shutters. I'll send a man to guard the door."

He is gone before I can protest. I go to the window to swing the shutter closed. Outside in the winter darkness I can see a couple of torches around the barn, but I cannot tell if they are our men or the Scots. I bolt the shutters. The room is pitch-black now, but I can smell the dead man's blood oozing slowly from his wounds, and I feel for the bed and step around him. I am so afraid that he will reach out from hell and grasp my ankle that I can hardly get to the door, and then I bolt it as Richard ordered, and, horribly, the fresh corpse and I are locked in together.

There is shouting outside and the sudden terrifying blast of a trumpet, and then I hear Richard outside the door. "You can come out now. The queen is arriving, and they have the men back in ranks. Those were her scouts, apparently. They were on our side."

My hands are shaking as I unbolt the door and throw it open. Richard has a torch, and in its flickering light his face is grim. "Get your cape and your gloves," he says. "We're falling in."

I have to go back into the room past the dead man to get my cape, which was spread over the bed for warmth. I don't look at him, and we leave him there, unshriven, dead in his own blood with his throat cut.

"Jacquetta!" she says.

"Margaret." We hold each other, arms wrapped around each other, cheeks warm one to the other. I feel the energy of her joy and optimism coursing through her slight body. I smell the perfume in her hair, and her fur collar tickles my chin.

"I have had such adventures! You will never believe the journeys I have made. Are you safe?"

I can feel myself still trembling with shock from the violence in the bedroom. "Richard had to kill one of your men," I say. "He came in my bedroom window."

She shakes her head disapprovingly, as at a

678

minor foible. "Oh! They are hopeless! Good for nothing but killing people. But you must see our prince," she says. "He is a young man born to be king. He has been so brave. We had to ride to Wales and then take ship to Scotland. We were robbed and wrecked! You'll never believe it."

"Margaret, the people are terrified of your army."

"Yes, I know. They are tremendous. You will see; we have such plans!"

She is radiant — she is a woman in her power, free at last to take her power. "I have the lords of Somerset, Exeter, and Northumberland," she says. "The north of England is ours. We will march south, and when Warwick comes out to defend London, we will crush him."

"He will be able to raise London against you," I warn her. "And the country is terrified of your army, not welcoming at all."

She laughs aloud. "I have raised the Scots and the North against him," she says. "They will be too afraid even to lift a weapon. I am coming like a wolf into England, Jacquetta, with an army of wolves. I am at the very height of the wheel of fortune; this is an unbeatable army because nobody will dare to take the field against them. People run from us before we even arrive. I have become a bad queen to my people, a scourge in the land, and they will be sorry that they ever raised a sword or a pitchfork against me."

We ride south with the queen's army, the royal party at the head of the marching men, the pillaging, looting, and terror going on behind us in a broad swathe that we know about, but ignore. Some of the men ride off from the main column to forage for food, breaking into barns, raiding shops and isolated little farms, demanding a levy from villages; but others are madmen, men from the North like Vikings going berserk, killing for the sake of it, stealing from churches, raping women. We bring terror to England; we are like a plague on our own people. Richard and some of the lords are deeply shamed and do what they can to impose some order on the army, controlling their own levies, demanding that the Scots fall in and march. But some of the other lords, the queen herself, and even her little boy seem to revel in punishing the country that rejected them. Margaret is like a woman released from the bonds of honor; she is free to be anything she likes for the first time in her life, free of her husband, free of the constraints of the court, free of the careful manners of a French princess; she is free, at last, to be wicked.

On the second day of our march, the four of us riding at the head of the army see a lone horseman, standing by the roadside, waiting for us to come up. Richard nods to

Anthony and John. "Go and see who that is," he says. "Take care. I don't want to find that he's a scout and Warwick is the other side of the hill."

My two boys canter slowly towards the man, holding the reins in their left hands, their right hands held down, outspread, to show they are holding no weapon. The man trots towards them, making the same gesture. They halt to speak briefly, then all three turn and ride towards us.

The stranger is filthy from the mud of the road, and his horse's coat is matted with sweat. He is unarmed; he has a scabbard at his side, but he has lost his sword.

"A messenger," Anthony says with a nod to the queen, who has pulled up her horse and is waiting. "Bad news, I am afraid, Your Grace."

She waits, impassively, as a queen should wait for bad news.

"Edward of March has come out of Wales like a sun in winter," the man says. "I was there. Jasper Tudor sent me to tell you to beware the sun in splendor."

"He never did," my husband interrupts. "Jasper Tudor never sent such a message in his life. Tell us what you were ordered to say, fool, and don't embroider."

Corrected, the man straightens in his saddle. "Tudor told me to say this: that his army is defeated and that he is in hiding. We

681

met the York force, and we lost. Sir William Herbert led the Yorks against us; Edward of March was at his side. They broke the Welsh line and rode right through us; Jasper sent me to you to warn you. He was on his way to join you when Edward blocked our path."

The queen nods. "Will Jasper Tudor come on to join us?"

"Half his army is dead. The Yorks are everywhere. I doubt he'll get through. He might be dead now."

She takes a breath but says nothing.

"There was a vision," the man offers, one eye on Richard.

"Who else saw it?" he demands irritably. "Anyone? Or just you? Or you just think you did?"

"Everyone saw it. That's why we lost. Everyone saw it."

"No matter," my husband says.

"What was it?" the queen asks.

My husband sighs and rolls his eyes.

"In the sky, over Edward, Earl of March, when he raised his standard: the morning sun came up, and then there were three suns. Three suns in the sky above him, the middle one shining down on him. It was like a miracle. We didn't know what it meant, but we could see he was blessed. We didn't know why."

"Three suns," the queen repeats. She turns to me. "What does it mean?"

I turn away as if she might see, reflected in my eyes, the three suns I saw, dazzling on the water of the Thames. These are three suns I know; these three suns I have seen. But I did not know then what they meant, and I still don't know now.

"Some said it was the blessed Trinity honoring Edward March. But why would Father, Son, and Holy Ghost bless a rebel? Some said it was him and his two living brothers, born to rise high."

The queen looks at me. I shake my head and stay silent. I was hoping that I would see the season when the king would recover when I went out in that cold dawn and looked at the shine on the waters of the river. I was looking for the rising of my king, but instead I saw three suns rising out of the mist and burning brightly.

"What does it mean?" The man asks the question in my direction, as if he expects me to know.

"Nothing," my husband says stoutly. "It means that there was a bright dawn and you were all dazzled by fear." He turns back to the man. "I don't want to know about visions, I want to know about a day's march. If Edward brings his troop due west and marches as quick as he can, when d'you think they will get to London?"

The man thinks; he is so weary he cannot calculate the days. "A week? Three, four days?" he asks. "He's fast. He's the fastest commander in battle I have ever seen. Could he be here tomorrow?"

That night my husband disappears from our camp, and comes back late, as the queen is about to retire. "Your Grace, I ask permission to bring a friend to join us."

She rises. "Ah Richard, you are a good man in my service. You brought me a great commander in Sir Andrew Trollope, who won Ludford for us without raising his sword. Who do you have now?"

"I have to have your oath that you will forgive him for former error," he says.

"I forgive him," she says easily.

"He is pardoned?" Richard confirms.

"He has a royal pardon. You have my word."

"Then, may I present Sir Henry Lovelace, who is proud to come to serve you," he says.

She extends her hand, and Richard's friend steps forwards, bows, and kisses it. "You have not always been my friend, Sir Henry," she observes coolly.

"I didn't know then that York would try to take the crown," he says. "I joined him only to see the council well run. And now York is dead. I have joined you late: before your last battle and your final victory, I know. But I am proud to join you now."

She smiles on him; she can still invoke that irresistible charm. "I am glad to have you in my service," she says. "And you will be well rewarded."

"Sir Henry says that Warwick is dug in around St. Albans," my husband tells her. "We must defeat him before Edward March can come up and reinforce him."

"We're not afraid of a boy of nineteen, are we? Andrew Trollope will command my army, with you, Lord Rivers. And we will attack at once, as you suggest."

"We'll draw up a plan," Richard says. "And Sir Henry will go back to Warwick and serve alongside him until we join in battle. We'll march tonight, in darkness. With good luck we will come upon them when they think we are still a day away."

The queen smiles on him. "I'll get ready," she says.

We wait. The royal army with the Scots forces goes almost silently down the lane in the darkness. The Scots are barefoot, they have no horses, they can disappear into the night with no sound. They like coming unexpectedly out of the darkness to kill. Richard is at the head, our son Anthony commanding a troop, and John is leading the cavalry. The queen and I doze in our chairs, either side of a banked-in fire in the hall of the Dominican friary at Dunstable, dressed in riding clothes, ready to get to our horses and ride forwards or away, depending on the luck of the battle.

She keeps the prince beside her, though he is restless, playing with his badge of the swan. He says he wants to ride with the men; he may only be seven years, but he is old enough to kill his enemies. She laughs at him but never checks him.

St. Albans,
Spring 1461

We have to wait all day. As darkness falls, one of the queen's household comes riding back to us and says that the town is taken, St. Albans is ours, and the terrible shame of our earlier defeat there is wiped out. The prince drops his livery badge and runs for his sword, and the queen gives the order to her household that we can proceed. As we ride south, filled with excitement at our triumph, the guards around us, their swords drawn, we can hear the noise of battle, the erratic firing of guns with damp powder. It starts to snow, cold wet flakes that melt on our shoulders and heads. Occasionally, we see men, running from the battle, coming up the road towards us, but when they catch sight of our troops, swords out at the ready, they vault over a gate and get into a field, or melt through the hedge and disappear. We can't tell if they are Warwick's men or our own.

We halt outside the town, and the queen orders two scouts to go forwards. They are jubilant when they return.

"Warwick grouped his men on Nomansland Common, and was firing on our men. But then Sir Henry Lovelace led his men out of Warwick's army, leaving a gap in his line, and our cavalry charged straight at it."

The queen makes a fist of her hand and holds it to her throat. "And?"

"We broke the line!" the man shouts.

"Huzzah!" the prince calls. "Huzzah!"

"We broke Warwick?"

"He's sounded the retreat; he's off like a scalded cat. His men are running away or surrendering. We've won, Your Grace. We've won!"

The queen is laughing and crying at once, the prince is beside himself. He draws his little sword and whirls it round his head.

"And the king?" she says. "My husband, the king?"

"Lord Warwick brought him to the battle; but left him and all the baggage, as he fled. He's here, Your Grace."

She looks suddenly stunned. They have been apart for seven months, and she has been on the road, in hiding, or marching, for every day of their separation, living like a brigand, living like a thief, while he has been in the queen's rooms in Westminster Palace or praying in a monastery, weak as a girl. Of course she is afraid that he has lost his wits again. Of course she fears that she will be a stranger to him. "Take me to him." She glances back at me. "Come with me, Jacquetta. Ride with me."

As we ride along the road the wounded and defeated soldiers clear out of our way, heads down, their hands outspread, fearing a blow. As we get closer to the town we see the dead lying in the fields. In the High Street Warwick's crack archers are fallen among their bows, their heads cleaved open by battle axes, their bellies ripped with swords. The queen rides through it all, blind to the misery of it, and the prince rides beside her, beaming at our victory, his little sword held up before him.

They have made a camp for the queen away from the horrors of the town. The royal standard is flying over her tent, a brazier is burning inside; there are carpets down against the mud. We go into the big tent that serves as her presence chamber, a little tent behind will be her bedroom. She seats herself on her chair, I stand beside her, the prince between the two of us. For the first time in days she looks uncertain. She glances at me. "I don't know how he will be," is all she says. She puts her hand on the prince's shoulder. "Take him out if his father is unwell," she says quietly to me. "I don't want him to see . . ."

The flap of the door opens, and they bring the king inside. He is warmly dressed in a long gown and riding boots and a thick cape around his shoulders, the hood pulled up over his head. Behind him, standing in the doorway, I recognize Lord Bonville and Sir Thomas Kyriell, men who served with my first husband in France, loyal men, good men, who joined the cause of York in the early days and stayed with the king throughout the battle to keep him safe.

"Oh," the king says vaguely, taking in the queen and his son. "Ah . . . Margaret."

A shiver goes through her as she sees — we all see — that he is not well again. He can barely remember her name, he smiles distantly at the prince, who kneels to his father for his blessing. Henry puts an absentminded hand on the young boy's head. "Ah . . ." he says. This time he cannot find the name in his muddled mind at all. "Ah . . . yes."

The prince rises. He looks up at his father.

"This is Sir Thomas, and Lord Bonville," the king says to his wife. "They have been very good . . . very good."

"How?" she spits.

"They kept me amused," he says, smiling. "While it was all going on, you know. While the noise was going on. We played marbles. I won. I liked playing when the noise was going on."

The queen looks past him at Lord Bonville. He goes down on one knee. "Your Grace, he is very weak," he says quietly. "Sometimes he doesn't know himself. We stayed with him to stop him wandering off and getting hurt. He gets lost if he's not watched. And then he gets distressed."

She leaps to her feet. "How dare you? This is the King of England," she says. "He is perfectly well."

Bonville is silenced by the look on her face, but Sir Thomas Kyriell hardly hears her, he is watching the king. He steps forwards to steady Henry, who is swaying and looks as if he might fall. He guides the king into the queen's vacated chair. "No, I am afraid he is not well," he says gently, helping Henry to sit. "He can't tell a hawk from a handsaw, Your Grace. He is far from us all, God bless him."

The queen whirls around to her son in a white-faced fury. "These lords have held your father the king prisoner," she says flatly. "What death would you have them die?"

"Death?" Bonville looks up, shocked.

Sir Thomas, still holding the king's hand in a comforting grip, says: "Your Grace! We have kept him safe. We were promised safe conduct. He gave us his own word!"

"What death would you have these rebels die?" she repeats, staring at her son. "These men, who kept your father prisoner, and now dare tell me that he is ill?"

The little boy puts his hand on the hilt of his sword as if he would like to kill them himself. "If they were common men, I would

691

put them on the gallows," he says in his little-boy piping voice, each word beautifully spoken as his tutor has taught him to do. "But since they are lords and peers of the realm, I say they should be beheaded."

The queen nods at her guards. "Do as the prince says."

"Your Grace!" Sir Thomas does not raise his voice so as not to frighten the king, who is clinging to his hand.

"Don't go, Sir Thomas," the king says. "Don't leave me here with . . ." He glances at the queen, but he cannot find her name again in his addled brain. "We can play again," he says, as if to tempt his friend to stay with him. "You like to play."

"Your Grace." Sir Thomas holds his hand and gently closes his other one over it in a warm clasp. "I need you to tell Her Grace, the queen, that I have cared for you. You said that we should stay with you and we would be safe. You gave us your word! Do you remember? Don't let the queen behead us."

The king looks confused. "I did?" he asks. "Oh yes, I did. I promised them they would be safe. Er— Margaret, you won't hurt these men, will you?"

She has a face of ice. "Not at all," she says to him. "You have nothing to worry about." And to the guard she says: "Take them out."

I whisper urgently. "Margaret — they have his word."

"Three fools together," she hisses. To the guards, she nods again. "Take them out."

We have lodgings in the dorter house of the abbey of St. Albans, overlooking the frozen orchard. The fighting was in the streets around the abbey, and many of the wounded are coming in to the chapter house and the barns, where the nuns are caring for them and the monks carrying them out for burial when they die. I have managed to get a tub for Richard, and he is washing himself with jugs of water. He has taken a wound to his sword arm, and I have sponged it with thyme water from home and bandaged it tightly. Anthony, thank God, is unhurt.

"Where's John?" I ask. "Is he with the cavalry?"

Richard has his back to me, as he gets out of the tub, dripping water all over the floor. I cannot see his face. "No."

"Where is he?"

His silence alerts me. "Richard, is he hurt? Richard? Is he here in the abbey?"

"No."

I'm afraid now. "Where is he? He's not hurt? I must go to him. I should send to Elizabeth; I promised her I would."

Richard ties a sheet around his waist and steps out of the tub, wincing slightly. He sits down by the little fire. "I am sorry, Jacquetta. He's dead."

"Dead?" I say stupidly.

"Yes."

"John?" I repeat.

He nods.

"But the cavalry broke Warwick's line; they won the battle for us. The cavalry won this battle."

"John was in the lead. He took a spear in the belly. He's dead."

I sink down onto the stool. "This will break Elizabeth's heart," I say. "Dear God. He is nothing but a boy. And you have come through unscathed so many times!"

"It's luck," he says. "He wasn't lucky, that's all. He was unlucky, God save him. Did you foresee it at all?"

"I never foresaw a future for them," I say bitterly. "But I said nothing, and I let her marry him, though I could see nothing ahead for the two of them. But it was a good match, and I wanted her well married and rich. I should have warned her; I should have warned him. I have the Sight sometimes, but I might as well be blind."

He leans forwards and takes my hand. "It's just fortune," he says. "A cruel goddess. Will you write to Elizabeth? I can send a man with a message."

"I'll go to her," I say. "I can't bear that she should hear this from anyone but me. I'll go and tell her myself."

694

■ ■ ■ ■

I leave St. Albans at dawn and ride through the fields. I sleep one night in an abbey and one in an inn. It is a weary journey, but the gray skies and the muddy lanes match my mood. I am part of a victorious army on a winning campaign, but I have never before felt so defeated. I think of the two lords on their knees before Margaret and the enmity in her face. I think of her son, our little prince, and his boyish treble when he ordered two good men to be killed. I ride blindly, hardly seeing the way. I know myself to be losing my faith.

It takes me two days to get to the little village of Groby, and as I ride in through the great gates of the hall, I wish I was not there. Elizabeth herself opens the door, and as soon as she sees me, she knows why I have come.

"Is he wounded?" she asks; but I see that she knows he is dead. "Have you come to fetch me?"

"No, I am sorry, Elizabeth."

"Not wounded?"

"He is dead."

I had thought she would collapse, but she takes the blow and then straightens herself and stands very tall. "And have we lost again?" she asks impatiently, as if it means nothing either way.

I get down from my horse and throw the reins at a groom. "Feed him and water him and rub him down," I say. "I have to leave the day after tomorrow." To Elizabeth, I say: "No, dearest. We won. Your husband led the charge that broke Warwick's line. He was very brave."

She looks at me, her gray eyes blank with misery. "Brave? D'you think it was worth it? This victory in this little battle, another battle, another little victory in exchange for him?"

"No," I say honestly. "For there will be another battle, and your father and Anthony will have to fight in it again. It goes on and on."

She nods. "Will you come and tell his mother?"

I step over the threshold into the warm shadows of Groby Hall and know that I will have to do the worst, the very worst thing that one woman can do to another: tell her that her son is dead.

When I get back to St. Albans, I find most of the town empty, the shops gutted, and the houses barred. The townspeople are terrified of the queen's army, which has looted all the valuables and foraged all the food for an area of ten miles all around the town. "Thank God you're back," Richard says to me, helping me from my horse in the front yard of the abbey.

"It is like trying to command the enemy. The monks have left the abbey; the townspeople have fled from the town. And the lord mayor of London has sent for you."

"For me?"

"He wants you and the Duchess of Buckingham to meet him and agree whether the king and the queen can enter London."

I look at him blankly. "Richard, London has to admit the King and Queen of England."

"They won't," he says flatly. "They have heard what it is like here. The merchants won't have this army anywhere near their warehouses, shops, and daughters, if they can possibly prevent it. It's as simple as that. What you have to do is to see if you can get an agreement that they let the king and queen into Westminster Palace with their household, and feed and quarter the army outside."

"Why me? Why not the master of the queen's household? Or the king's confessor?"

His smile is bitter. "It is an honor for you, actually. The Londoners don't trust anyone. Not anyone of her army or of the king's advisors. They trust you because they remember you coming into London as the pretty duchess, all that long time ago. They remember you in the Tower when Jack Cade came in. They remember you at Sandwich when Warwick took you. They think they can trust you. And you can meet the Duchess of Buckingham there."

He puts his arm around my waist and his mouth to my ear. "Can you do this, Jacquetta? If you can't, say the word and we go back to Grafton."

I lean against him for a moment. "I am sick of it," I say quietly. "I am sick of the fighting, and I am sick of the death, and I don't think she can be trusted with the throne of England. I don't know what to do. I thought of it all the way to Groby and all the way back again, and I don't know what I think or where my duty lies. I can't foresee the future, and I can't even say what we should do tomorrow."

His face is grim. "This is my house," he says simply. "My father served the House of Lancaster, and I have too. My son follows me. But this is hard on you, my love. If you want to go home, you should go. The queen will have to release you. If London bars the gates on her, it is her own doing."

"Would they really lock her out of her own city?"

He nods. "She's not loved, and her army is a terror."

"Did they ask for no one else to speak for her?"

He smiles wryly. "Only the pretty duchess will do."

"Then I must do it," I decide reluctantly. "London has to admit the King and Queen of England. What will become of the country if they close the gates to their own king? We have won the battle; she is Queen of England, and we have to be able to enter London."

"Can you go now?" he asks. "For I imagine that Warwick has met up with his friend Edward March, and they will be coming towards us. We should get the king and queen into the Tower of London and in possession of the city at once. Then they can parlay or they can fight. But we have to hold the kingdom."

I look at the stable yard, where the cavalry horses nod their heads over the stalls. One of them will be John Grey's horse, without his rider, now and forever.

"I can go now," I say.

He nods. They bring me out a fresh horse; Richard helps me into the saddle. The door behind us opens from the abbey, and the queen comes out.

"I knew you'd go for me," she says to me with her sweetest smile. "Agree to anything for me. We have to get into London before Edward gets here."

"I'll do what I can," I say. "How is His Grace today?"

She nods to the abbey. "Praying," she says. "If wars were won by prayers, we would have won a hundred times over. And see if you can get them to send us some food. I can't keep my army from raiding." She looks at Richard. "I've issued orders, but the officers cannot command them."

"The devil from hell couldn't command them," Richard says grimly. He puts his hand on my knee and looks up at me. "I'll be waiting for you," he promises. "Anthony will lead your guard. You'll be safe."

I glance over to where Anthony is mounting into his saddle. He throws me a smiling salute. "Come on then," I say. Anthony shouts a command to our guard, and we ride out of the abbey courtyard, south down the road to London.

We meet Anne, the Duchess of Buckingham, and her little train a few miles from the city. I smile at the duchess, and she nods at me, a little toss of her head that shows me that she can hardly believe we are suing for the royal family to enter their capital. She has lost a son in this war; her lined face is weary. She leads the way to Bishopsgate, where the lord mayor and the aldermen come out to meet us. They don't want to admit us, not even over the threshold. The duchess sits up high on her horse with a face like thunder; but I get down, and the lord mayor kisses my hand and the aldermen pull off their bonnets and bow their heads as I smile around at them. Behind them I see the London merchants and the great men of the city; these are the men I have to persuade.

I tell them that the king and queen, the

700

royal family of England with their son the prince, require entry to their own house, in their own city. Are these men going to deny their own anointed king the right to sit on his own throne or sleep in his own bed?

I see them mutter among themselves. The sense of ownership of property is a powerful argument to these men, who have worked so hard to earn their beautiful houses. Is the prince to be denied the right to walk in his father's garden?

"His own father denied him!" someone calls out from the back. "King Henry hasn't slept in his own bed or sat on his own chair since he handed it all over to the Duke of York! And the queen took to her heels. They gave away their palace, not us. It's their own fault they are not at home."

I start again, addressing the lord mayor but speaking clearly enough so that they can hear me beyond the stone arch of the gate, in the streets beyond. I say that the women of the city know the queen should be admitted to raise the prince in her own palace; a woman has a right to her own home. That the king should be master in his own house.

Someone laughs at the mention of the king, and shouts a bawdy joke that he has never been master in his own house and probably not master in his own bed. I see that the months of York's rule have left them certain that the king has no powers, that he is unfit to rule as the York lords said.

"I would send the queen's army the food they need," the lord mayor says to me in an undertone. "Please assure Her Grace of that. I had the wagons ready to leave, but the citizens stopped me. They're very afraid of the Scots in her army. What we hear is terrifying. In short, they won't let them in, and they won't allow me to send supplies."

"People are leaving the city," an alderman steps forwards to tell me. "Closing up their houses and going to France, and she's only at St. Albans. Nobody will stay in London if she comes any closer. The Duchess of York has sent her boys George and Richard to Flanders for their safekeeping, and this is the duchess who surrendered to her once before! Now she swears that she won't again. Nobody trusts her; everyone fears her army."

"There is nothing to fear," I insist. "Let me make you an offer: How would this be? How would it be if the queen agrees to leave the army outside? Then you could let the royal family in, and their household with them. The king and queen have to be safe in the Tower of London. You cannot deny them that."

He turns to the senior aldermen, and they mutter together. "I am asking this in the name of the King of England," I say. "You all swore to be loyal to him. Now he asks that you admit him into your city."

"If the king will guarantee our safety" — the lord mayor turns to me — "we will admit the king and the royal family and their household. But not the Scots. And the king and the queen have to promise that the Scots will be kept outside the walls, and that the city will not be sacked. Four of us will come with you, to tell the queen this."

Anthony, who has been standing behind me, rigid as any commander, silent while I do my work, cups his hands for my foot and helps me into the saddle. He holds my horse as the lord mayor comes close for a quiet word. I lean down to hear him.

"Has the poor king stopped weeping?" he asks. "When he was living here under the command of the Duke of York, he wept all the time. He went to Westminster Abbey and measured out the space for his own tomb. They say he never smiled but cried all the time like a sorrowful child."

"He is happy with the queen and with his son," I say steadily, hiding my embarrassment at this report. "And he is strong, and issuing orders." I do not say that the order was to end the looting of the abbey and town of St. Albans, and that it had no effect at all.

"Thank you for coming here today, Your Grace," he says, stepping back.

"God bless the pretty duchess!" someone shouts from the crowd.

I laugh and raise my hand.

"I remember when you were the most beautiful woman in England," a woman says from the shadow of the gate.

I shrug. "Truly, I think my daughter is now," I say.

"Well, God bless her pretty face; bring her to London so we can all see her," somebody jokes.

Anthony swings into his saddle and gives the command; the four aldermen fall in behind me and the duchess, and together we head north to tell the queen that the city will let them in, but will never admit her army.

We find the queen with the royal household, now advanced to Barnet — just eleven miles north of London, dangerously close, as the aldermen riding with us remark. She has handpicked the troops who are advancing with her; the worst of the northern raiders are kept at some distance, at Dunstable, where they are amusing themselves by tearing the town apart.

"Half of them have simply deserted," Richard says to me gloomily as we go to the queen's presence chamber. "You can't blame them. We couldn't feed them, and she had said outright that she would never pay them. They got sick of waiting to get into London and have gone home. God help the villages that lie in their path."

The queen commands that the aldermen

and the duchess and I go back to London and demand entrance for the royal family and a household of four hundred men. "That's all!" she says irritably to me. "Surely you can make them admit me with an entourage that Richard, Duke of York, would have considered a nothing!"

We ride at the head of the household troops, and we get to Aldgate, where the lord mayor meets us again.

"Your Grace, I cannot let you in," he says, nervously eyeing the troops who are standing in ranks behind me, Richard at their head. "I would do so if it were left to me, but the citizens of London won't have the queen's men in their streets."

"These are not the northern men," I say reasonably. "Look, they wear the livery of the Lancaster lords, men who have come and gone through the city for all time. See, they are commanded by my husband, a lord you know well. You can trust them; you can trust the queen when she has given her word. And there are only four hundred."

He looks down at the cobbles below his feet, up at the sky above us, at the men behind me, he looks anywhere but into my eyes. "Truth is," he says finally, "the city doesn't want the queen here, nor the king, nor the prince. They don't want any of them. Sworn to peace or not."

For a moment I can hardly argue. I too have

thought that I wanted neither queen nor king nor prince in my life. But who is there, if not them? "She is the Queen of England," I say flatly.

"She is our ruin," he replies bitterly. "And he is a holy fool. And the prince is none of his begetting. I am sorry, Lady Rivers, I am sorry indeed. But I cannot open the gates to the queen nor to any of her court."

There is a shout and a noise of running feet coming to the gate. The troops behind me grasp their weapons, and I hear Richard order "Steady!" as Anthony takes one swift step to stand beside me, his hand on the hilt of his sword.

A man runs to the lord mayor and whispers urgently in his ear. He rounds on me, his face suddenly flushed red with rage. "Did you know of this?"

I shake my head. "No. Whatever it is. I know of nothing. What's happening?"

"While we are standing here, talking to you, the queen has sent a party to raid Westminster."

There's a roar of anger from the crowd. "Hold ranks, steady," Richard shouts at our guard. "Close up."

"I did not know," I say quickly to the lord mayor. "I swear on my honor I did not know. I would not so have betrayed you."

He shakes his head at me. "She is faithless and a danger, and we want no more of her," he says. "She used you to divert us and try to take us by force. She is faithless. Tell her to go away and take her soldiers with her. We will never admit her. Make her go away, Duchess, help us. Get rid of her. Save London. You take the queen from our door." He bows to me and turns on his heel. "Duchess, we are counting on you to deliver us from that she-wolf," he shouts as he runs under the great gateway. We stand in our ranks as the big doors of Aldgate are pushed shut, slammed tight in our faces, and then we hear the bolts shooting home.

We march north. It seems that though we won the last battle, we are losing England. Behind us, the city of London throws open the gates to the young Edward, the Duke of York's oldest son and heir, and they take him to the throne and proclaim him King of England.

"It means nothing," the queen says as I ride beside her up the north road. "I am not troubled by it."

"He's crowned king," Richard says quietly to me that night. "It means that London closed its doors to us but admitted him and crowned him king. It means something."

"I feel that I failed her. I should have been able to persuade them to let her in."

"When she had sent her soldiers around to Westminster? You were lucky to get us out without a riot. You failed her, perhaps, but you saved London, Jacquetta. No other woman could have done it."

YORK,
SPRING 1461

The king, the queen, the prince, and the members of their household are housed in York, the royal family at the abbey, the rest of us wherever in the city that we can find rooms. Richard and Anthony ride out almost straightaway with the army commanded by the Duke of Somerset, to block the road north and prepare the stand against Warwick and the boy who now calls himself king: Cecily Neville's handsome son, Edward.

The king rises to the danger he is in, his wits sharpened on the ride, and writes a letter to Edward's army reproaching them for rebellion and commanding them to come over to our side. The queen rides out every day with the prince, calling on men to leave their villages and their occupations and join the army and defend the country against the rebels and their rebel leader, the false king.

Andrew Trollope, the royals' best general, advises that the army should make its stand on a ridge, some fourteen miles south of

York. He puts Lord Clifford as an advance guard to prevent the Yorks crossing the River Aire, and Clifford tears the bridge down so that when the young Edward marches up the road from London, there is no way across. Boldly, Edward orders his men into the water, and as the snow falls on them in the swirling current in the evening light, they work on the bridge, up to their waists in freezing water with the winter floods running strong. It is easy work for Lord Clifford to ride down on them, kill Lord Fitzwalter, and wipe out the troop. Richard sends me a note: *Edward's inexperience has cost him dear. We have sprung the first trap; he can come on to Towton and see what we have for him here.*

Then I wait for more news. The queen comes to York Castle, and we both put on our capes and go up Clifford's Tower. The armies are too far away for us to see anything, and the light is failing, but we both look south.

"Can't you wish him dead?" she asks. "Can't you strike him down?"

"Warwick?" I ask.

She shakes her head. "Warwick would change his coat, I know it. No, curse that boy Edward, who dares to call himself king."

"I don't know how to do such things, and I never wanted to know. I'm not a witch, Margaret, I'm not even much of a wise woman. If I could do anything right now, I would make

710

my son and husband invulnerable."

"I would curse Edward," she says. "I would throw him down."

I think of the boy the same age as my son, the handsome golden-haired boy, the pride of Duchess Cecily's proud heart. I think of him losing his temper in Calais, but his quick flush of shame when I told him that we had guarded his mother. I think of him bowing over my hand outside the queen's rooms in Westminster. "I have a liking for him," I say. "I wouldn't ill-wish him. Besides, someone else will kill him for you, before the day is out. There has been enough killing, God knows."

She shivers and pulls up her hood. "It's going to snow," she says. "It's late in the year for snow."

We go to the abbey for dinner, and the king leads her in through the great hall filled with his household. "I have written to Edward, Earl of March," he says in his fluting voice. "I have asked for a truce for tomorrow. It is Palm Sunday; he cannot think of fighting a battle on Palm Sunday. It is the day of Our Lord's entry into Jerusalem. He must want to be at prayer. We will all be at prayer on such a holy day; it is God's will."

The queen exchanges a quick look with me.

"Has he replied?" I ask.

He casts his eyes down. "I am sorry to say that he refused a truce," he says. "He will

711

risk the fortunes of war, on the very day that Our Lord went into Jerusalem. Edward thinks to ride out on the very morning that Our Lord rode to His holy city. He must be a very hardened young man."

"He's very bad," Margaret says, biting down on her irritation. "But it must be to our advantage."

"I shall order the Duke of Somerset not to give battle," the king tells us. "Our men should not make war on a Sunday, not on Palm Sunday? They must just stand in their ranks to show our faith in God. If Edward charges, they must turn the other cheek."

"We have to defend ourselves," the queen says quickly. "And God will bless us all the more for defending ourselves against such a faithless act."

The king considers. "Perhaps Somerset should withdraw until Monday?"

"He has a good position, Your Grace," I say gently. "Perhaps we should wait and see what is the outcome. You have offered a holy truce — that must be enough."

"I shall ask the bishop for his view," the king says. "And I shall pray tonight for guidance. I shall pray all night."

The king performs his vigil in the minster, the monks from the abbey coming and going in the great church as he prays. I go to bed, but I am wakeful too; I cannot sleep for thinking of Richard and Anthony, out all night in the cold, a north wind blowing snow, with a battle coming tomorrow on a holy day.

In the morning the sky is heavy and white, as if the clouds are pressing down on the very walls of the city. At about nine o'clock it starts to snow, great white flakes swirling round in dizzy circles and lying on the frozen ground. The city seems to huddle down under the snowflakes, which come thicker and thicker.

I go to the queen's rooms and find her prowling around, her hands tucked in her sleeves for warmth. The king is praying at the abbey; she is giving orders for their goods to be packed up again. "If we win, we will advance on London, and this time they will open the gates to me. Otherwise . . ." She does not finish the sentence, and both of us cross ourselves.

I go to the window. I can hardly see the city walls, for the snow is blinding; it is a blizzard blowing round and round. I put my hand over my eyes, I have a memory of a vision of a battle uphill in snow, but I cannot see the standards, and I do not know, when the snow turns red, whose blood is staining the slush.

We wait, all day we wait for news. One or two men come limping into York with wounds to be dressed, and they say that we had a good position on the hillside, but the snow made it hard for the archers and impossible

713

for the cannon. "He always has bad weather," the queen remarks. "The boy Edward always fights in bad weather. He always has a storm behind him. You would think he was born of bad weather."

They serve dinner in the hall, but there is almost no one there to eat — just the household staff, who are too old or too frail to be pressed into service or are maimed from earlier battles in the queen's service. I look at one serving man who is deft with his one remaining arm, and I shudder as I think of my whole-limbed son, somewhere out in the snow, facing a cavalry charge.

The queen sits proudly at the center of the high table, her son at her side, and makes a tableau of eating. I am at the head of the table of her ladies, and I push some ragout around my plate for the entire meal. Anyone who does not have a husband or a son or a brother in the field called North Acres eats with a good appetite. The rest of us are sick to our bellies with fear.

In the afternoon a steady stream of men start to come in from the battle, the ones who can still walk. They tell of hundreds dying on the road to York, thousands dead on the battlefield. The abbey hospital, the poor men's hospital, the leper hospital — all the sanctuaries and hostels throw open their doors and start to strap on rough bandages, pack wounds, and amputate. Mostly, they start to stack dead bodies for burial. It is like a charnel house in York; the south gate sees a constant flow of men staggering like drunkards, bleeding like stuck calves. I want to go down to look in every face, for fear that I will see Richard or Anthony glaring sightlessly back, his face blown away by one of the new handguns or smashed to a pulp by an axe. But I make myself sit by the window in the queen's apartments, some sewing in my hands, always listening for the roar and rumble of an approaching army.

It gets dark; surely the day is over? Nobody can fight in the dark, but the bells toll for Compline, and still nobody comes to tell us that we have won. The king is on his knees in the abbey; he has been there since nine this morning, and it is now nine o'clock at night. The queen sends his grooms of the bedchamber to fetch him from his prayers, feed him, and put him to bed. She and I wait up, by a dying fire, her feet up on her traveling box of jewels, her traveling cape laid over the chair beside her.

We sit up all night, and at dawn, in the cold light of the earliest spring morning, there is a bang on the door of the abbey and Margaret starts up. We hear the porter slowly opening the door and a voice asking for the queen. Margaret snatches up her cloak and goes down. "Wake the king," she says to me as she goes.

I run to the king's apartments and shake his grooms of the bedchamber awake. "News from the battle; get His Grace ready to leave," I say shortly. "Now."

Then I hurry down to the great entrance hall, and there is a man in Clifford livery on his knees before the queen.

She turns her white face to me, and for a moment I see the frightened girl who would not marry on her wedding day unless someone told her future. I did not foresee this, then. I wish I had been able to warn her. "We have lost," she says bleakly.

I step forwards. "My husband?" I ask. "My son?"

The man shakes his head. "I don't know, Your Grace. There were too many to see. The field was covered in dead it was as if everyone in England was dead. I have never seen . . ." He puts his hands over his eyes. "Some of them were getting away over a little bridge," he said. "The Yorks came after them and there was fighting on the bridge, and then it broke and they all went into the waters: Lancaster, Yorks, all in together, and they drowned in their heavy armor. The meadow is covered in corpses; the river, filled with men, is running red. The snow is falling on everything like tears."

"Your lord," Margaret whispers. "Lord Clifford."

"Dead."

"My commander, Sir Andrew Trollope."

"Dead. And Lord Welles, and Lord Scrope. Hundreds of lords, thousands of soldiers. It looks like the final day when the dead come from the ground but are not moving. They are not rising up. Every man in England is down. The wars must be over now, for every man in England is dead."

I go to her and take her icy hand. The king comes down the stairs and looks at the two of us, handclasped, horrified.

"We have to go," Margaret says. "We have lost a battle."

He nods. "I did warn him," he says irritably. "I did not want fighting on a holy day, but he would not be warned."

Behind him, down the stairs, come the grooms of the household carrying his Bible and his crucifix, his prayer stool and his altar. Margaret's clothes and her crate of furs follow.

We go out into the yard. "Come with me?" she asks, like a girl again. "I don't want to go alone."

Not for a moment do I think I will go with her. I will leave her now, even if I never see her again in all my life. "I have to look for Richard, and Anthony," I say, I can hardly speak. "I will have to go out and find their bodies. I may have to see them buried. Then I will go to my children."

She nods. The horses are saddled and

ready; they put the goods into a wagon, her jewels strapped behind her on her horse. The prince is in the saddle already, dressed warmly in his riding cape with his bonnet on his head, his swan badge pinned at the front. "We will be avenged for this," he says cheerfully to me. "I will see the traitors dead. I swear it."

I shake my head. I am sick of vengeance.

They lift Margaret into the saddle, and I go to stand near her. "Where will you go?"

"We'll regroup," she says. "They can't all be dead. We'll raise more men. I'll get more money from Scotland, from France. I have the king, I have the prince; we will come back, and I will put Edward March's head on the spike at Micklegate Bar beside his father's rotting face. I'll never stop," she says. "Not while I have my son. He was conceived to be king, he was born to be king, I have raised him to be king."

"I know," I say. I step back, and she holds up her hand to give the signal for them to ride out. She waves them out, and then she tightens her grip on the reins and looks down at me, her face warm with love. She holds out her hand, extends her finger; in the air she makes the sign for the wheel of fortune, then she clicks to her horse and digs in her heels, and she is gone.

All day more and more men come hobbling

into the city, looking for food, looking for someone to strap their wounds. I wrap myself in my cape and get my horse from the stables and ride, in the opposite direction to all the others of the royal court: I ride south down the road to Towton, looking in the faces of all the hundreds and hundreds of men whom I pass, for someone I recognize. I am hoping to see Richard or Anthony, I am afraid when I see a man hopping with a makeshift crutch, I freeze when I see a brown curly head facedown in a ditch, a congealing patch of blood in the hair. I ride down the road with one man to go before me, and every time we meet a man on horseback, head down, slumped in the saddle, I ask him if he has seen Lord Rivers, or if he knows what happened to his company. Nobody knows.

I start to see that it was a long, long battle, fought in snow so thick that nobody could see farther than the end of his sword. Enemies loomed up out of a white blindness and thrust blindly and were blindly cut down. The Lancastrian archers were firing against the wind into driving snow and missed their mark. The Yorks, with the wind behind them, fired uphill and scythed down the Lancaster men, waiting to charge. When the lines met, they barged and stabbed and hacked at each other, not knowing what they were doing nor who was winning. One man tells me that when night fell, half of the survivors dropped down on the battlefield and slept among the dead, covered with snow as if they were all to be buried together.

The road is crowded with men, so many men, so bedraggled in their livery or working clothes that I cannot tell one from another, and their sheer numbers and misery forces me off the road. I stand in a gateway and gaze at them as they go by. It seems as if it will never end, this procession of men who have escaped death but are still bloodstained, and bruised, and wet with snow.

"Lady Mother? Lady Mother?"

I can hear his voice, and for a moment I think I am imagining it. "Anthony?" I say disbelievingly. I slide down from my horse and stumble forwards until I am almost submerged in the sea of wounded men who barge towards me and jostle me. I pull at their arms and look into their shocked gray faces. "Anthony? Anthony!"

From a group of men he steps out. My gaze rakes him from head to foot in an instant, taking in his weary eyes, his grim smile, his unharmed body. He is holding his arms out to me, and his hands, his precious hands, are whole, he is not missing a finger, his arms are not slashed to the bone. He is standing upright. His helmet is off, and his face, though gray with weariness, is unmarked. "Are you all right?" I ask incredulously. "My son? Are you all right? Have you got through this unhurt?"

His smile has lost its joyous light. "I'm safe," he says. "I thank God who guarded me the whole long night and day. What are you doing here? It's like hell, here."

"Looking for you," I say. "And . . . Anthony, where is your father?"

"Oh!" he exclaims, realizing what I am thinking. "Oh no, don't, Mother. He is fine. He's not injured. He's just . . ." He looks around. "Here he is."

I turn, and there is Richard. I would hardly have recognized him. His breastplate is dented across his heart, his face blackened with smoke and blood, but he walks towards me, as he always walks towards me, as if nothing could ever separate us.

"Richard," I whisper.

"Beloved," he says hoarsely.

"You're safe?"

"I always come home to you."

We go west, to get away from the road to York, which is choked with men falling to their knees and crying for water, and lined with those who have fallen out to die. We ride cross-country across the broad plain of York until we can find a farmhouse where they will allow us to sleep in the barn, wash in the stream, and sell us food. We eat farmer's broth: a speck of overstewed mutton with gruel and carrots, and we drink their small ale.

When he has eaten and is looking less drained, I ask, tentatively, for I fear his reply: "Richard, the queen is going north to regroup, and then on to Scotland to raise more recruits, and then she says she will come back. What are we going to do?"

There is a silence. Anthony and my husband exchange a long look, as if they have been dreading what they are about to say.

"What is it?" I look from one to the other. "What has happened?"

"We're finished," Anthony volunteers. "I am sorry, Lady Mother. I have handed in my sword. I have sworn loyalty to York."

I am stunned. I turn to Richard.

"I too," he says. "I would not serve the queen again, not in such an army, not under such a command. But anyway, we lost on the battlefield; we handed in our swords and surrendered. I thought Edward would have us executed but —" He has a ghost of a smile. "He was merciful to us. He took our swords from us. I am dishonored. I am no longer a knight. I am sorry. We swore fealty to him, and it is over for us. I cannot take arms against him. I was defeated, and I surrendered my sword. I am sworn to the House of York. I cannot serve Henry or Margaret; they are outlaws now to me."

It is his use of their names that shakes me as much as anything, that tells me that everything is over, and everything is changed.

"Henry," I repeat, as if saying the name for the very first time. "You call the king Henry."

"The king's name is Edward," my husband says, as if repeating a lesson. "King Edward."

I shake my head. Even though I had ridden all day against the tide of wounded men, I had not thought of our cause as lost. I have been with Margaret for so long that I can think only in terms of battles. I thought that we had lost another battle, but that there will be yet another battle after this. Now, as I look at my husband's weary face and the hollow eyes of my son, I say: "You think that Henry and Margaret will never win back the throne?"

He shows me his empty scabbard, where his beautifully embossed sword used to be. "I cannot help them to it, at any rate," he says. "I have surrendered my sword to the new king. I am sworn."

"We are no longer of the House of Lancaster?" I am still incredulous.

Anthony nods. "It's over," he says. "And we are lucky to have escaped with our heads on our necks."

"That's all that matters," I say, grasping at a truth. "That must be all that matters, at the very end. You are alive, and your father. At any rate, that's what matters most to me."

We lie, that night, like a poor family, in the straw together under our heaped capes for warmth, our small troop of men in the stable with our horses. Richard's arm is around me, all the night long. "We'll go to Grafton," I whisper as I fall asleep. "And we will be squires again, and we will think of all of this as a romance, a story that someone might write one day."

GRAFTON, NORTHAMPTONSHIRE, SPRING 1464

I gather my children about me, and Elizabeth comes home with her two boys from Groby Hall. She is all but penniless; her mother-in-law will not pay her dower, and in these troubled times we have neither power nor influence to make her keep her side of the marriage contract, which gave me such pride and pleasure only a few years ago and now means nothing.

Richard and Anthony are given official pardons and appointed to the Privy Council. The new king turns out to be an astute commander of men, a king for all parties. He rules with the advice of the Earl of Warwick, who put him on the throne, but he calls as many of the lords into government as will come. He does not favor York lords; he truly seems to want to be a king for all the people of the country. A few lords go into exile, a few are with the queen — sometimes in Scotland, sometimes in France, forever raising forces, threatening England, planning a return. I think I will never see her again, the pretty French girl who would not marry until I had told her what her destiny would be. It has been the wheel of fortune indeed. She was the greatest woman in England, and now she cannot have so much as a roof over her head in her own country; but she is hunted down like the last wolf.

I hardly ever hear of her, my news is all of the parish and the gossip is all from the neighboring town. I see my son Anthony married to Elizabeth, Lady Scales, I start to consider suitable partners for my other children; but we do not command the wealth and the power that we had when Margaret of Anjou was on the throne and I was her dearest friend and lady-in-waiting, and my husband one of the great men of court. Now we are only squires of Grafton, and though I find I am interested in my growing orchard, and even more in my children and grandsons, it is hard for me to look at other small country squires and think that my children should be married among them. I expect more for them. I want more for them.

Especially for my Elizabeth.

One day in spring, I go to the great chest in my bedroom and I take out the purse that my great-aunt Jehanne gave me, all those years ago. I look at the charms, and at all the choices that there might be in the world for Elizabeth: a young woman — but not in the first blush of her youth; a beauty — but not a maiden; a clever scholarly girl — but not with the faith to make an abbess. I choose the charm of a ship to signify that she might travel, I choose the charm of a little house to signify that she might win her dower lands and get a house for herself; and I am about to choose a third charm, when one of them breaks from the bracelet and falls into my lap. It is a ring for a small finger curiously wrought in the shape of a crown. I hold it up to the light and look at it. I start to try it on my own finger and then I hesitate. I don't want it on my finger; I don't know what it means. I tie it on a long black thread, and tie the other two on their own long black threads, and I go out of the house as the early silver moon starts to rise in the pale sky.

"Can we come with you, Lady Grandmother?" Her boys appear from nowhere, mud on their faces as usual. "Where are you going with that basket?"

"You can't come with me," I say. "I am looking for plover eggs. But I will take you tomorrow if I find a nest."

"Can't we come now?" asks Thomas, Elizabeth's oldest boy.

I put my hand on his head, his warm silky curls remind me of Anthony when he was a loving little boy like this one. "No. You must find your mother and eat your supper and go to bed when she orders you. But I will take you with me tomorrow."

I leave them and go across the gravel garden at the front of the house, through the wicket gate and down to the river. There is a little bridge across the river, a couple of small wooden planks where the children like to come to fish, and I go across, ducking my head under the upturned branches of the ash tree, and scramble down the little bank to the trunk of the tree.

I put my arms around the tree to tie the three strings around it, and my cheek lies against the rippled gray bark. For a moment I listen. Almost I can hear the heart of the tree beating. "What will become of Elizabeth?" I whisper, and it is almost as if the leaves can whisper back to me. "What will become of my Elizabeth?"

I have never been able to foresee her future, even though of all my children she has always been the one who promised so much. I have always thought she might be especially blessed. I wait; the leaves rustle. "Well, I don't know," I say to myself. "Perhaps the stream will tell us."

Each charm is now tied to the tree by its own long dark string, and when I throw them out into the water, as far as they can go, I hear three splashes like a salmon snapping a fly, and they are gone and the threads are invisible.

I stand for a moment and look into the

moving water. "Elizabeth," I say quietly to the stream. "Tell me what will become of Elizabeth, my daughter."

At dinner that night my husband says that the king is recruiting soldiers for a new battle. He will be marching north. "You won't have to go?" I ask in sudden alarm. "Nor Anthony?"

"We'll have to send men, but to be honest, my dear, I don't think they would especially want us in the line."

Anthony gives a rueful chuckle. "Like Lovelace," he says, and his father laughs.

"Like Trollope."

"I should ask King Edward to inquire into my dower," Elizabeth remarks. "For sure my boys will have nothing unless I can find someone who will make Lady Grey keep her promise to me."

"Kidnap him as he rides by," Anthony suggests. "Fall on your knees to him."

"My daughter will do no such thing," my husband rules. "And we can provide for you here, until you reach agreement with Lady Grey."

Elizabeth sensibly holds her tongue, but the next day, I see her wash her boys' hair and dress them in their Sunday suits, and I say nothing. I splash a little perfume of my own brewing on the veil of her headdress, but I give her neither apple blossom nor apple. I

729

believe there is not a man in the world who could ride past my daughter and not stop and ask her name. She puts on her plain gray gown and sets off from the house holding her boys firmly by their hands, walking down the track to the road from London, where the king is certain to ride by with his troop.

I watch her go, a pretty young woman on a warm spring day, and it is like a dream to see her, stepping lightly down the lane between the hedges where the white roses are coming into flower. She is walking out to her future, to claim her own, though I still don't know what her future will be.

I go to the still room and take down a small jar, sealed tight with a waxed cork. It is a love philter I made for Anthony's wedding night. I take it to the brew house and put three drops in a jug of our best ale, and take it to the great hall, with our best glasses, and then I wait, quietly, with the spring sunshine coming through the mullioned windows and a blackbird singing in the tree outside.

I don't have to wait very long. I look down the road, and there is Elizabeth, smiling and laughing, and walking beside her is the handsome boy whom I first saw outside the queen's rooms when he bowed over my hand so politely. Now he is a grown man and the King of England. He is leading his great warhorse, and high up on its back, clinging to the saddle, their faces bright with joy, are my two grandsons.

I leave the window and open the great hall door to them myself. I see Elizabeth's flush and the young king's bright smile, and I think to myself this is fortune's wheel indeed — can it be? Can such a thing be?

AUTHOR'S NOTE

I discovered the character of Jacquetta when I was working on the history of her daughter, Elizabeth Woodville, who made her extraordinary secret marriage to Edward IV under her mother's supervision. Jacquetta was one of the named witnesses at the wedding, along with the priest, perhaps two others, and a boy to sing the psalms. She then arranged the secret honeymoon nights for the young couple.

Indeed, she may have done more. She was later accused of enchanting the young king into marriage with her daughter; and figures of lead said to represent Edward and Elizabeth, bound together with gold wire, were produced at her trial for witchcraft.

Enough here to intrigue me! I have spent my life as an historian of women, their place in society, and their struggle for power. The more I read about Jacquetta, the more she seemed to me to be the sort of character I particularly love: one who is overlooked or denied by the traditional histories, but who can be discovered by piecing together the evidence.

She lived an extraordinary life, and one that is nowhere coherently recorded. In the absence of any biography of Jacquetta, I wrote my own essay and published it with two other historians: David Baldwin, writing on Elizabeth Woodville; and Mike Jones, writing on Margaret Beaufort in *The Women of the Cousins' War: The Duchess, the Queen, and the King's Mother* (Simon & Schuster, 2011). Readers who want to trace the history behind my novels may be interested in this collection.

Jacquetta married the Duke of Bedford and lived as the first woman of English-ruled France. Her second marriage was for love: she married Sir Richard Woodville, experienced disapproval, and had to pay a fine for stepping outside the rules of marriage for royal kinswomen. She served Margaret of Anjou as one of her most favored ladies-in-waiting, and was at her side through most of the troubled years of the Wars of the Roses — then known as the Cousins' War. On the defeat of the Lancastrians at the terrible battle of Towton, her son Anthony and her husband Richard surrendered to the victorious Edward IV. The family would probably have lived quietly at peace under the new York regime, if it had not been for the beauty of their widowed daughter, the passionate nature of the young king, and — who knows — the magic of Jacquetta.

The family became kin to the king, and Jacquetta took full advantage of her rise, becoming once again the leading lady at the royal court. She lived long enough to endure the murder of her beloved husband and son, to support her daughter through defeat and flight into sanctuary, and to witness her son-in-law's triumphant return to the throne. For most of her life Jacquetta was at the very center of the great events. Often she was a player.

Why she has not been studied is a mystery to me. But she belongs to that large population of women whose lives have been ignored by historians in favor of the lives of prominent men. Also this period is relatively neglected compared to — say — more recent times, or even the Tudor period. I expect more historians will work on the fifteenth century, and I hope there will be more research into its women, including Jacquetta.

I suggest that she was inspired by her family legend of Melusina, the water goddess, whose story is beautifully described in Luxembourg Museum as part of the history of the county. To this day, the city guides point out the rocks through which Melusina's bath sank, when her husband broke his promise and spied on her. Certainly, the legend of

Melusina was used in the art and alchemy of the period, and Jacquetta owned a book that told the story of her goddess ancestor. I think it very important that we as modern readers understand that religion, spiritualism, and magic played a central part in the imaginative life of medieval people.

There is a thread running through the historical record associating Jacquetta and even Elizabeth with witchcraft, and I have based some fictional scenes on this. The use of playing cards to predict the future was a medieval practice; we would call the cards "tarot." Alchemy was regarded as a spiritual and scientific practice, and Margaret of Anjou licensed alchemists when she was looking for a cure for her husband's illness, which was indeed blamed by some on witchcraft. The practice of herbalism and planting by the phases of the moon was well known in most households, and the rise of anxiety about witchcraft occurs throughout Europe around 1450 onwards. The trial and punishment of Eleanor Cobham is based on the historical records, and she was one of the witch-hunt victims.

There follows a bibliography listing the books that I have read for this novel, and readers may also like to visit my Web site, www.PhilippaGregory.com, for new essays, historical debates, and responses to questions about this and other novels in the series. The next novel will be about the daughters of Richard Neville, the Earl of Warwick, and I am already enjoying the research and excited about writing the story.

BIBLIOGRAPHY

Amt, Emilie. *Women's Lives in Medieval Europe.* New York: Routledge, 1993.

Baldwin, David. *Elizabeth Woodville: Mother of the Princes in the Tower.* Stroud: Sutton Publishing, 2002.

Barnhouse, Rebecca. *The Book of the Knight of the Tower: Manners for Young Medieval Women.* Basingstoke: Palgrave Macmillan, 2006.

Bramley, Peter. *The Wars of the Roses: A Field Guide & Companion.* Stroud: Sutton Publishing, 2007.

Castor, Helen. *Blood & Roses: The Paston Family and the Wars of the Roses.* London: Faber and Faber, 2004.

Cheetham, Anthony. *The Life and Times of Richard III.* London: Weidenfeld & Nicolson, 1972.

Chrimes, S. B. *Lancastrians, Yorkists, and Henry VII.* London: Macmillan, 1964.

Cooper, Charles Henry. *Memoir of Margaret: Countess of Richmond and Derby.* Cambridge: Cambridge University Press, 1874.

Duggan, Anne J. *Queens and Queenship in Medieval Europe.* Woodbridge: Boydell Press, 1997.

Field, P. J. C. *The Life and Times of Sir Thomas Malory.* Cambridge: D. S. Brewer, 1993.

Freeman, J. "Sorcery at Court and Manor: Margery Jourdemayne the Witch of Eye Next Westminster," *Journal of Medieval History* 30 (2004), 343–57.

Godwin, William. *Lives of the Necromancers: or, An Account of the Most Eminent Persons in Successive Ages, Who Have Claimed for Themselves, or to Whom Has Been Imputed by Others, the Exercise of Magical Power.* London: F. J. Mason, 1834.

Goodman, Anthony. *The Wars of the Roses: Military Activity and English Society, 1452–97.* London: Routledge & Kegan Paul, 1981.

Goodman, Anthony. *The Wars of the Roses: The Soldiers' Experience.* Stroud: Tempus, 2006.

Griffiths, Ralph A. *The Reign of King Henry VI.* Stroud: Sutton Publishing, 1998.

Grummitt, David. *The Calais Garrison, War and Military Service in England, 1436–1558.* Woodbridge: Boydell & Brewer, 2008.

Haswell, Jock. *The Ardent Queen: Margaret of Anjou and the Lancastrian Heritage.* London: Peter Davies, 1976.

Hicks, Michael. *Warwick the Kingmaker.* London: Blackwell Publishing, 1998.

Hipshon, David. *Richard III and the Death of Chivalry.* Stroud: The History Press, 2009.

Hughes, Jonathan. *Arthurian Myths and Alchemy: The Kingship of Edward IV.* Stroud: Sutton Publishing, 2002.

Jones, Michael. K., and Underwood, Malcolm G. *The King's Mother: Lady Margaret Beaufort, Countess of Richmond and Derby.* Cambridge: Cambridge University Press, 1992.

Karras, Ruth Mazo. *Sexuality in Medieval Europe: Doing unto Others.* New York: Routledge, 2005.

Laynesmith, J. L. *The Last Medieval Queens: English Queenship, 1445–1503.* Oxford: Oxford University Press, 2004.

Levine, Nina. "The Case of Eleanor Cobham: Authorizing History' in *2 Henry VI*", *Shakespeare Studies* 22 (1994), 104–121.

Lewis, Katherine J., Menuge, Noel James, Phillips, Kim. M. (eds). *Young Medieval Women.* Basingstoke: Palgrave Macmillan, 1999.

MacGibbon, David. *Elizabeth Woodville (1437–1492): Her Life and Times.* London: Arthur Barker, 1938.

Martin, Sean. *Alchemy & Alchemists.* London: Pocket Essentials, 2006.

Maurer, Helen E. *Margaret of Anjou: Queen-*

ship and Power in Late Medieval England. Woodbridge: The Boydell Press, 2003.

Neillands, Robin. *The Wars of the Roses.* London: Cassell, 1992.

Newcomer, James. *The Grand Duchy of Luxembourg: The Evolution of Nationhood.* Luxembourg: Editions Emile Borschette, 1995.

Péporté, Pit. *Constructing the Middle Ages: Historiography, Collective Memory and Nation Building in Luxembourg.* Leiden and Boston: Brill, 2011.

Phillips, Kim M. *Medieval Maidens: Young Women and Gender in England, 1270–1540.* Manchester: Manchester University Press, 2003.

Prestwich, Michael. *Plantagenet England, 1225–1360.* Oxford: Clarendon Press, 2005.

Ross, Charles Derek. *Edward IV.* London: Eyre Methuen, 1974.

Rubin, Miri. *The Hollow Crown: A History of Britain in the Late Middle Ages.* London: Allen Lane, 2005.

Seward, Desmond. *A Brief History of The Hundred Years War.* London: Constable, 1973.

Simon, Linda. *Of Virtue Rare: Margaret Beaufort: Matriarch of the House of Tudor.* Boston: Houghton Mifflin Company, 1982.

Storey, R. L. *The End of the House of Lancaster.* Stroud: Sutton Publishing, 1999.

Thomas, Keith. *Religion and the Decline of*

Magic. New York: Weidenfeld & Nicolson, 1971.

Vergil, Polydore, and Ellis, Henry. *Three Books of Polydore Vergil's English History: Comprising the Reigns of Henry VI, Edward IV and Richard III.* Kessinger Publishing Legacy Reprint, 1971.

Ward, Jennifer. *Women in Medieval Europe, 1200–1500.* Essex: Pearson Education, 2002.

Warner, Marina. *Joan of Arc: The Image of Female Heroism.* London: Weidenfeld & Nicolson, 1981.

Weinberg, S. Carole. "Caxton, Anthony Woodville and the Prologue to the 'Morte Darthur.' " *Studies in Philology,* 102: no I (2005), 45–65.

Weir, Alison. *Lancaster and York: The Wars of the Roses.* London: Cape, 1995.

Williams, E. Carleton. *My Lord of Bedford, 1389–1435: Being a Life of John of Lancaster, First Duke of Bedford, Brother of Henry V and Regent of France.* London: Longmans, 1963.

Wilson-Smith, Timothy. *Joan of Arc: Maid, Myth and History.* Stroud: Sutton Publishing, 2006.

Wolffe, Bertram. *Henry VI.* London: Eyre Methuen, 1981.

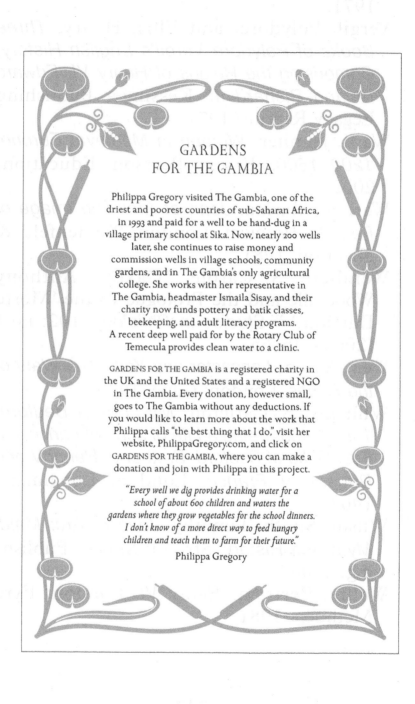

GARDENS
FOR THE GAMBIA

Philippa Gregory visited The Gambia, one of the
driest and poorest countries of sub-Saharan Africa,
in 1993 and paid for a well to be hand-dug in a
village primary school at Sika. Now, nearly 200 wells
later, she continues to raise money and
commission wells in village schools, community
gardens, and in The Gambia's only agricultural
college. She works with her representative in
The Gambia, headmaster Ismaila Sisay, and their
charity now funds pottery and batik classes,
beekeeping, and adult literacy programs.
A recent deep well paid for by the Rotary Club of
Temecula provides clean water to a clinic.

GARDENS FOR THE GAMBIA is a registered charity in
the UK and the United States and a registered NGO
in The Gambia. Every donation, however small,
goes to The Gambia without any deductions. If
you would like to learn more about the work that
Philippa calls "the best thing that I do," visit her
website, PhilippaGregory.com, and click on
GARDENS FOR THE GAMBIA, where you can make a
donation and join with Philippa in this project.

*"Every well we dig provides drinking water for a
school of about 600 children and waters the
gardens where they grow vegetables for the school dinners.
I don't know of a more direct way to feed hungry
children and teach them to farm for their future."*

Philippa Gregory

ABOUT THE AUTHOR

Philippa Gregory is the author of several bestselling novels, including *The Other Boleyn Girl*, and is a recognized authority on women's history. She studied history at the University of Sussex and received a Ph.D. at the University of Edinburgh. She welcomes visitors to her website, www.philippagregory.com.

We hope you have enjoyed this Large Print book. Other Thorndike, Wheeler, Kennebec, and Chivers Press Large Print books are available at your library or directly from the publishers.

For information about current and upcoming titles, please call or write, without obligation, to:

Publisher
Thorndike Press
10 Water St., Suite 310
Waterville, ME 04901
Tel. (800) 223-1244

or visit our Web site at:

http://gale.cengage.com/thorndike

OR

Chivers Large Print
published by AudioGO Ltd
St James House, The Square
Lower Bristol Road
Bath BA2 3SB
England
Tel. +44(0) 800 136919
email: info@audiogo.co.uk
www.audiogo.co.uk

All our Large Print titles are designed for easy reading, and all our books are made to last.